GARY JENNINGS

THE JOURNEYER

"SUPERB"
*New York Times
Book Review*

"A CLASSIC"
Newsweek

"PERFECT ENTERTAINMENT"
Philadelphia Inquirer

"A first-rate narrative…spiced with bawdy tales and bizarre customs…Sensual delights… Jennings is a *superb* storyteller.
Houston Post

"Wild adventure…endlessly intriguing…constantly surprising."
Atlantic Monthly

"Relentlessly gripping"
Publishers Weekly

"Remarkable…Extraordinary…Recreates a whole lost civilization."
Miami Herald

Other Avon Books by
Gary Jennings

AZTEC
SOW THE SEEDS OF HEMP
THE TERRIBLE TEAGUE BUNCH

Avon Books are available at special quantity discounts for bulk purchases for sales promotions, premiums, fund raising or educational use. Special books, or book excerpts, can also be created to fit specific needs.

For details write or telephone the office of the Director of Special Markets, Avon Books, Dept. FP, 1790 Broadway, New York, New York 10019, 212-399-1357. *IN CANADA:* Director of Special Sales, Avon Books of Canada, Suite 210, 2061 McCowan Rd., Scarborough, Ontario M1S 3Y6, 416-293-9404.

THE JOURNEYER

GARY JENNINGS

AVON
PUBLISHERS OF BARD, CAMELOT, DISCUS AND FLARE BOOKS

AVON BOOKS
A division of
The Hearst Corporation
1790 Broadway
New York, New York 10019

The Atheneum edition contains the following Library of Congress
Cataloging in Publication Data:

Jennings, Gary.
    The journeyer.

    I. Title.
PS3560.E518J6   1984   813'.54   83-45077

First Avon Printing, January, 1985

FOR GLENDA

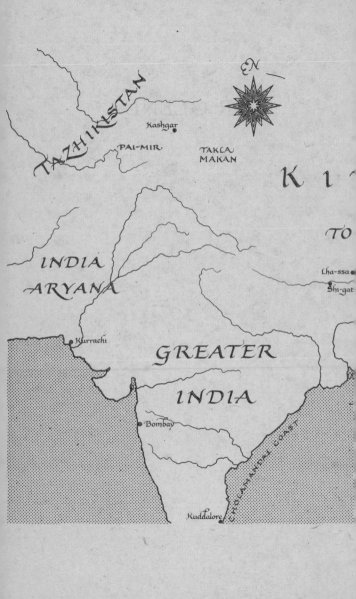

Dun-huang

GOBI

Xan-du

Khanbalik

HAI

Lan-zhou

Huang-ho R.
(Yellow R.)

Sea of
Kithai

Xian

OT

Jin-sha R.

Lan-tsang R.

Cheng-du

Yang-tze R. (Tremendous R.)

Hang-zho

Ba-tang

Nu R.

Sea of
Kithai

MANZI
(SUNG)

AVA

Yun-nan-fu

YUN-NAN

Quan-zho

Salween R.

Pagan

to
JIHPEN-
KWE

Chiang Rai

Irrawaddy R.

CHAMPA
(INDO-CHINA)

Me-kong R.

ENGLAND

Bruges

Cherbourg

FRANCE

VENETO
Venice

Genoa
Pisa

Rome

SICILY

Adriatic Sea

GREECE

THESSALY

CRETE

Constantinople

Sea of
Marmara

Euxine or Black S.

ANATOLIA

GREATER ARMENI.

LESSER ARMENI.

Aleppo

KURDIST

Antioch

CYPRUS

Baghe

Kingdor
Acre OF
JERUSALE

Mediterranean Sea

Alexandria

EGYPT

AFRICA

The WORLD
AS DRAWN BY
AL-IDRISI
ca. A.D. 1154

NUBIA

ETHIOPIA

TERRA BOREALIS INCOGNITA

SIBIR

KOREA

Xan-du

Khanbalik

Ghelan or
Caspian
Sea

KITHAI

Kashgar

GOBI

Lake
Karakul

PERSIA

KARAKUM

TAZHIKISTAN

Kashan

DASHT-
E-KAVIR

Mashhad

Balkh

PAI-MIR

Hang-zho

Buzai Gumbad

PAROPAMISUS
MTS.

TO-BHOT

MANZI
(SUNG)

ra

INDIA
ARYANA

KARAKORAM
MTS.

YUN-NAN

BALUCHISTAN

Hormuz

GREATER
INDIA

BURMA

CHAMPA
(INDO-CHINA)

Kurrachi

Indian
Ocean

SRIHALAM
(SRI LANKA)

SUMATRA

JAVA

TERRA AUSTRALIS INCOGNITA

When Marco Polo lay on his deathbed,
his priest, his friends and relations
clustered around him to plead that he
at last renounce the countless lies he
had related as his true adventures, so his
soul would go cleansed to Heaven. The
old man raised up, roundly damned them
all and declared, "I have not told
the half of what I saw and did!"

ACCORDING TO
FRA JACOPO D'ACQUI,
MARCO POLO'S CONTEMPORARY
AND HIS FIRST BIOGRAPHER

CY APRES COMMENCE
LE LIURE DE
MESSIRE MARC PAULE
DES DIUERSES
ET GRANDISMES
MERUEILLES DU MONDE

Come hither, great princes! Come hither,
emperors and kings, dukes and marquises,
knights and burgesses! Come hither, you people of
all degrees, who wish to see the many faces of mankind
and to know the diversities of the whole world!
Take up this book and read it, or have it read to you.
For herein you will find all the greatest wonders
and most marvelous curiosities. . . .

Aн, Luigi, Luigi! In the worn and wrinkled fustian of those old pages I hear your very voice again.

It had been many years since I last looked into our book, but when your letter came I fetched it out once more. I can still smile at it and admire it simultaneously. The admiration is for its having made me famous, however little I may deserve that fame, and the smile is for its having made me notorious. Now you say that you wish to write another work, an epic poem this time, again incorporating the adventures of Marco Polo—if I will grant that liberty—but attributing them to an invented protagonist.

I cast back in my memory to our first meeting, in the cellars of that Genoa palazzo where we prisoners of war were

1

lodged. I remember how diffidently you approached me, and with what reticence you spoke:

"Messer Marco, I am Luigi Rustichello, late of Pisa, and I have been a captive here since long before you arrived. I have listened to you telling that hilariously ribald story of the Hindu with his *ahem* caught in the holy rock hole. I have heard you tell it three times now. Once to your fellow prisoners, again to the warder, and yet again to the visiting almoner of the Brotherhood of Justice."

I inquired, "Are you weary of hearing it, Messere?"

And you said, "Not at all, Messere, but you will soon be weary of the telling. Many more persons will want to hear that tale, and all the other tales you have told, and any others which perhaps you have not told yet. Before you tire of the telling, or of the stories themselves, why do you not simply tell to *me* all your recollections of your travels and adventures? Tell them only the once and let me set them down on paper. I am a writer of some facility and much experience. Your tales could make a considerable book, Messer Marco, and multitudes of people then can read it for themselves."

And so I did, and so you did, and so the multitudes have done. Though many other journeyers before me had written of their travels, none of those works ever enjoyed the immediate and continuing popularity of our *Description of the World*. Perhaps, Luigi, it was because you chose to transcribe my words in French, the most widely known Western language. Or perhaps you made my stories better in the writing than I could do in the telling. At any rate, somewhat to my surprise, our book became much read and talked of and sought after. It was copied and recopied, and by now has been translated into every other language of Christendom, and of those versions, too, countless copies have been taken and circulated.

But none of them tells the singular story of the anguished Hindu and his rape of a rock.

When I sat in that clammy Genoa prison, recounting my reminiscences, and you sat putting them into proper words, we decided that they would be told in *only* the most proper words. You had your reputation to consider, and I had my family name. You were the Rustichello of Pisa, and I was a Polo of Venice. You were the romancier courtois, already known for your retellings of the classic tales of chivalry—of

Tristan and Isolde, of Lancelot and Ginevra, of Amys and Amyllion. I was, as you described me in the book, representative of the "sajes et nobles citaiens de Venece." So we agreed that our pages would contain only those of my adventures and observations which we could publish without a blush or a qualm, and which could be read without offending the Christian sensibilities even of maiden ladies or nuns.

Further, we determined to leave out of the book anything which might strain the credence of any stay-at-home reader. I recall that we even debated before we included my encounters with the stone that burns and the fabric that will not. Thus many of the most marvelous incidents of my travels were, so to speak, abandoned by the wayside of my wanderings. We left out the unbelievable and the bawdy and the scandalous. But now, you tell me, you want to mend those gaps—though still without hazarding my good name.

So your new protagonist will be called Monsieur Bauduin, not Messer Marco, and he will hail from Cherbourg, not Venice. But in all else he will be me. He will experience, enjoy, endure all that I did—*and* all that I left untold heretofore—if I will refresh your memory by telling those many stories to you again.

It is a great temptation, certainly. It would be like living those days anew—and those nights—and that is a thing I have long yearned to do. I always intended, you know, to journey again to the far eastward. But no, you could not have known. I have not spoken of that even in my family circle. It has been a dream I treasured too much to share. . . .

Yes, I meant to go again sometime. But when I was freed from Genoa and returned to Venice, the family business demanded my attention, and so I hesitated to depart. And then I met Donata, and she became my wife. So I hesitated again a while, and then there was a daughter. Naturally that gave me cause to hesitate, and there came a second daughter, and then there were three. So, for one reason and another, I kept on hesitating, and suddenly one day I was old.

Old! It is inconceivable! When I look into our book, Luigi, I see myself there a boy, and then a youth, and then in my manhood, and even at the book's very end I am still a stalwart. But when I look into a glass, I see there an aged stranger, sapped and sagged and blemished and enfeebled by the corroding rusts of five and sixty years. I murmur, "*That* old man cannot go again a-journeying," and then I realize: that old man is Marco Polo.

So your letter came to me at a vulnerable moment. And your suggestion that I contribute to a new book is an opportunity I will not let pass. If I cannot do again the things I once did, at least I can remember them and take relish in them while I relate them, since I can now do that with the impunity of your Bauduin disguise. You may wonder at my so welcoming that disguise, as you may also have wondered at my remark that the earlier book earned me both undeserved renown and undeserved notoriety. I shall explain.

I never claimed to have been the first man to travel from the West into the far East, and you did not put any such boast into our book. Nevertheless, that seems to have been the impression produced upon most of its readers—or those readers living elsewhere than Venice, where no such illusion obtains. After all, my own Venetian father and uncle had gone to and returned from the East before they retraced their journey and that time took me with them. Also, in the East itself I met many other Westerners, all of nations from England to Hungary, who had arrived there before me, and some of whom stayed there longer than I did.

But long previous to them, many other Europeans had traversed the same Silk Road I trod. There was the Spanish rabbi Benjamin of Tudela, and the Franciscan friar Zuàne of Carpini, and the Flemish friar Guillaume of Rubrouck—and, like me, all those men published accounts of their travels. As far back as seven or eight hundred years ago, there were missionaries of the Nestorian Christian Church penetrating into Kithai, and there are many laboring there today. Even before Christian times, there must have been Western traders wandering to and from the East. It is known that the Pharaones of ancient Egypt wore the silk of the Orient, and silk is thrice mentioned in the Old Testament.

Numerous other things and the words describing them were, long before my time, made part of our Venetian language. Several of our city's buildings are decorated, inside or out, with that sort of filigree fancywork we adopted from the Arabs and have long called arabesco. The murderous sassìn gets his name from the hashishiyin of Persia, men who kill at the instigation of a religious fervor induced by the drug hashish. The making of that cheap glazed fabric called indiana was learned in India, where that cloth is called chint, and where the inhabitants also inspired our Venetian expression "far l'Indiàn," meaning to behave utterly stupidly.

No, I was not the first to go East or to return from there. Insofar as my fame rests on the misapprehension that I was, it is indeed unmerited. But my notoriety is even less deserved, for it depends on the widespread assumption of my dishonesty and untruthfulness. You and I, Luigi, put into our book only those observations and experiences we judged believable, but even so I am disbelieved. Here in Venice I am jeeringly called Marco Millions—an epithet implying not any wealth of ducats, but my supposed store of lies and exaggerations. That amuses me more than it annoys me, but my wife and daughters are exceedingly vexed at being known as the Dona and Damìne Milioni.

Hence my willingness to put on the mask of your fictional Bauduin as I commence to tell everything that has not until now been told. Let the world, if the world chooses, think it *all* a fiction. It is better to be disbelieved in such matters than to remain forever mute about them.

But first, Luigi:

From the sample of manuscript you sent with your letter, to show me how you propose to open Bauduin's story, I gather that your command of French has considerably improved since you set down our *Description of the World.* I am emboldened to make another small comment on that earlier book. A reader of those pages might think that Marco Polo had been a man of sober age and judgment through all his traveling days—and that he had somehow done that traveling through the sky, so high aloft that he could see all at once the entire breadth of our earth, and point to one and then another land and say with certainty, "Herein this one differs from that." True, I was forty when I came home from my journeying. I hope I came back a little more wise and discerning than when I went, for I was then only a wide-eyed adolescent—ignorant, inexperienced, foolish. Also, like any journeyer, I had to see all lands and the contents of them, not from the hindsight vantage of some twenty-five years later, but in the order in which I came upon them in my travels. It was kind and flattering of you, Luigi, to portray me in that earlier book as having been always a man all-seeing and all-knowing, but your new work might benefit if you made its narrator somewhat more true to life.

I would further suggest, Luigi, if you truly intend to cut your Monsieur Bauduin to the pattern of Marco Polo, that you commence his career by giving him a misspent youth of reckless abandon and misbehavior. That is one thing which I am here telling for the first time. I did not depart from Venice merely because I was eager for new horizons. I left Venice because I had to—or, at any rate, because Venice decreed that I had to.

Of course I cannot know, Luigi, *how* closely you wish to make your Bauduin's history parallel my own. But you did say "tell all," so I will begin even before the beginning.

VENICE

1

ALTHOUGH the Polo family has been Venetian, and proud of it, for perhaps three hundred years now, it did not originate on this Italian peninsula, but on the other side of the Adriatic Sea. Yes, we were originally from Dalmatia, and the family name would then have been something like Pavlo. The first of my forebears to sail to Venice, and stay here, did so sometime after the year 1000. He and his descendants must have risen rather quickly to prominence in Venice, for already in the year 1094 a Domènico Polo was a member of the Grand Council of the Republic, and in the following century so was a Piero Polo

The most remote ancestor of whom I have even a dim recollection was my grandfather Andrea. By his time, every man of our house of Polo was officially designated an Ene Aca (meaning N.H., which in Venice means Nobilis Homo or gentleman), and was addressed as Messere, and we had acquired the family arms: a field argent bearing three birds sable with beaks gules. This is actually a visual play on words, for that emblematic bird of ours is the bold and industrious jackdaw, which is called in the Venetian tongue the pola.

Nono Andrea had three sons: my uncle Marco, for whom I was named, my father Nicolò and my uncle Mafìo. What they did when they were boys I do not know, but when they grew up, the eldest son, Marco, became the Polo trading company's agent in Constantinople in the Latin Empire, while his brothers remained in Venice to manage the company's headquarters and keep up the family palazzo. Not

until after Nono Andrea's death did Nicolò and Mafìo
scratch the itch to go traveling themselves, but when they
did they went farther than any Polo before them had gone.

In the year 1259, when they sailed away from Venice, I
was five years old. My father had told my mother that they
intended to go only as far as Constantinople, to visit their
long-absent elder brother. But, as that brother eventually
reported to my mother, after they had stayed with him
there for a time, they took a notion to go on eastward. She
never heard another report of them, and, after a twelvemonth, she decided they must be dead. That was not just
the vaporings of an abandoned and grieving woman; it was
the most likely possible surmise. For it was in that year of
1259 that the barbarian Mongols, having conquered all
the rest of the Eastern world, pushed their implacable advance to the very gates of Constantinople. While every
other white man was fleeing or quailing before "the
Golden Horde," Mafìo and Nicolò Polo had gone marching
foolhardily right into their front line—or, considering how
the Mongols were then regarded, better say: into their
slavering and champing jaws.

We had reason to regard the Mongols as monsters, did
we not? The Mongols were something more and something
less than human, were they not? More than human, in
their fighting ability and physical endurance. Less than
human, in their savagery and lust for blood. Even their
everyday food was known to be reeking raw meat and the
rancid milk of mares. And it was known that, when a Mongol army ran out of those rations, it would unhesitatingly
cast lots to choose every tenth man of its ranks to be
slaughtered for food for the others. It was known that
every Mongol warrior wore leather armor only on his
breast, not his back; so that, if he ever *did* feel cowardice,
he could not turn and run from an opponent. It was known
that the Mongols polished their leather armor with grease,
and they procured that grease by boiling down their human victims. All those things were known in Venice, and
were repeated and retold, in hushed voices of horror, and
some of those things were even true.

I was just five years old when my father went away, but I
could share the universal dread of those savages from the
East, for I was already familiar with the spoken threat:
"The Mongols will get you! The orda will get you!" I had

heard that all through my childhood, and so had every other little boy whenever he required admonishment. "The orda will get you if you do not eat up all your supper. If you do not go straight to bed. If you do not cease your noise." The orda was wielded by mothers and governesses, in those times, as they had earlier threatened their misbehaving children with "The orco will get you!"

The orco is the demon giant that mothers and nursemaids have forever kept on call, so it was no strain for them to substitute the word orda: the horde. And the Mongol horde was assuredly the more real and believable monster; the women invoking it did not have to feign the fright in their voices. The fact that they even knew that word is evidence that they had reason to fear the orda as much as any child did. For it was the Mongols' own word, yurtu, originally meaning the great pavilioned tent of the chieftain of a Mongol encampment, and it was adopted, only slightly changed, into all the European languages, to mean what Europeans thought of when they thought of Mongols—a marching mob, a teeming mass, an irresistible swarm, a horde.

But I did not much longer hear that threat from my mother. As soon as she decided that my father was dead and gone, she commenced to languish and dwindle and weaken. When I was seven years old, she died. I have only one recollection of her, from a few months before that. The last time she ventured outside our Casa Polo, before she took to her bed and never got up again, was to accompany me on the day I was enrolled in school. Indeed, although that day was in another century, nearly sixty years ago, I recall it quite clearly.

At that time, our Ca' Polo was a small palazzo in the city's confino of San Felice. In the bright morning hour of mezza-terza, my mother and I came out the house door onto the cobbled street alongside the canal. Our old boatman, the black Nubian slave Michièl, was waiting with our batèlo moored to its striped pole, and the boat was freshly waxed for the occasion, gleaming in all its colors. My mother and I got into it and seated ourselves under the canopy. Also for the occasion, I was dressed in new and fine raiment: a tunic of brown Lucca silk, I remember, and hose soled with leather. So, as old Michièl rowed us down the narrow Rio San Felice, he kept exclaiming things like

"Che zentilòmo!" and "Dassèno, xestu, Messer Marco?"—
meaning "Quite the gentleman!" and "Truly, is that you,
Master Marco?"—which unaccustomed admiration made
me feel proud and uncomfortable. He did not desist until
he turned the batèlo into the Grand Canal, where the
heavy boat traffic required all his attention.

That day was one of Venice's best sort of days. The sun
was shining, but its light lay on the city in a manner
more diffused than sharp-edged. There was no sea mist or
land haze, for the sunlight was by no means diminished.
Rather, the sun seemed to shine not in direct beams, but
with a more subtle luminosity, the way candles glow when
they are set in a many-crystaled chandelier. Anyone who
knows Venice has known that light: as if pearls had been
crushed and powdered—pearl-colored pearls and the pale
pink ones and the pale blue—and that powder ground so
fine that its particles hung in the air, not dimming the
light but making it more lustrous yet soft at the same
time. And the light came from other places than the sky
alone. It was reflected from the canals' dancing waters, so
it put dapples and spangles and roundels of that pearl-
powder light bouncing about on all the walls of old wood
and brick and stone, and softened their rough textures as
well. That day had a gentling bloom on it like the bloom on
a peach.

Our boat slid under the Grand Canal's bridge, the Ponte
Rialto—the old, low, pontoon bridge with the swing-away
center section; it had not been rebuilt as the arched draw-
bridge it is now. Then we passed the Erbarìa, the market
where young men, after a night of wine, go strolling in the
early morning to clear their heads with the fragrance of its
flowers and herbs and fruits. Then we turned off the canal
again into another narrow one. A little way up that, my
mother and I debarked at the Campo San Todaro. Around
that square are situated all the lower-grade schools of the
city, and at that hour the open space seethed with boys of
all ages, playing, running, chattering, wrestling, while
they waited for the school day to begin.

My mother presented me to the school maistro, presenting him also with the documents pertaining to my birth
and to my registry in the Libro d'Oro. ("The Golden Book"
is the popular name for the Register of Protocol in which
the Republic keeps the records of all its Ene Aca families.)

Fra Varisto, a very stout and forbidding man in voluminous robes, appeared less than impressed by the documents. He looked at them and snorted, "Brate!" which is a
not very polite word meaning a Slav or Dalmatian. My
mother countered with a ladylike sniff, and murmured,
"Veneziàn nato e spuà."

"Venetian spawned and born, perhaps," rumbled the
friar. "But Venetian *bred*, not yet. Not until he has endured proper schooling and the stiffening of school discipline."

He took up a quill and rubbed the point of it on the shiny
skin of his tonsure, I suppose to lubricate its nib, then
dipped it in an inkwell and opened a tremendous book.
"Date of Confirmation?" he inquired. "Of First Communion?"

My mother told him and added, with some hauteur, that
I had not, like most children, been allowed to forget my
Catechism as soon as I had been confirmed, but could still
say it and the Creed and the Commandments on demand,
as facilely as I could say the Our Father. The maistro
grunted, but made no additional notation in his big book.
My mother then went on to ask some questions of her own:
about the school's curriculum and its examinations and its
rewards for achievement and its punishments for failure
and . . .

All mothers take their sons to school for the first time
with a considerable pride, I suppose, but also, I think, with
an equal measure of wariness and even sadness, for they
are relinquishing those sons to a mysterious realm they
never can enter. Almost no female, unless she is destined
for holy orders, ever gets the least bit of formal schooling.
So her son, as soon as he learns just so much as to write his
own name, has vaulted somewhere beyond her reach forever after.

Fra Varisto patiently told my mother that I would be
taught the proper use of my own language and of Trade
French as well, that I would be taught to read and to write
and to figure in numbers, that I would learn at least the ru-
diment of Latin from the *Timen* of Donadello, and the rudiments of history and cosmography from Callisthenes' *Book
of Alexander,* and religion from Bible stories. But my
mother persisted with so many other anxious questions
that the friar finally said, in a voice mingling compassion

and exasperation, "Dona e Madona, the boy is merely being enrolled in school. He is not taking the veil. We will immure him merely during the daylight hours. You will still have him the rest of the time."

She had me for the rest of her life, but that was not long. So thereafter I heard the threat that "the Mongols will get you if" only from Fra Varisto at school, and at home from old Zulià. This was a woman who really was a Slav, born in some back corner of Bohemia, and clearly of peasant stock, for she always walked like a washerwoman waddling with a full wash bucket dangling from either hand. She had been my mother's personal maid since before I was born. After my mother's death, Zulià took her place as my nurse and monitor, and took the courtesy title of Aunt. In assuming the task of raising me up to be a decent and responsible young man, Zia Zulià did not exert much strictness—apart from frequently invoking the orda—nor did she, I must confess, have much success in her self-appointed task.

In part, this was because my namesake Uncle Marco had not come back to Venice after the disappearance of his two brothers. He had for too long made his home in Constantinople, and was comfortable there, although by this time the Latin Empire had succumbed to the Byzantine. Since my other uncle and my father had left the family business in the keeping of expert and trustworthy clerks, and the family palazzo in the keeping of similarly efficient domestics, Zio Marco left them so. Only the most weighty but least urgent matters were referred to him, by courier vessel, for his consideration and decision. Managed in that manner, both the Compagnia Polo and the Ca' Polo went on functioning as well as ever.

The one Polo property that misfunctioned was myself. Being the last and sole male scion of the Polo line—the only one in Venice, anyway—I had to be tenderly preserved, and I knew it. Though I was not of an age to have any say in the management of either the business or the house (fortunately), neither was I answerable to any adult authority for my own actions. At home I demanded my own way, and I got it. Not Zia Zulià, nor the maggiordomo, old Attilio, nor any of the lesser servants dared to raise a hand against me, and seldom a voice. My Catechism I never again recited, and soon forgot all the responses. At school I began to shirk my lessons. When Fra Varisto despaired of wielding the Mongols and resorted to wielding a ferrule, I simply stayed away from school.

It is a small wonder that I got as much formal education as I did. But I remained in school long enough to learn to read and write and do arithmetic and speak the Trade French of commerce, mainly because I knew I should need those abilities when I grew old enough to take over the family business. And I learned what history of the wrold, and what description of it, is supplied by *The Book of Alexander.* I absorbed all of that, mainly because the great Alexander's journeys of conquest had taken him eastward, and I could imagine my father and uncle having followed some of the same trails. But I saw little likelihood of my ever needing a knowledge of Latin, and it was when my school class had its collective nose forced into the boring rules and precepts of the *Timen* that I pointed my nose elsewhere.

Though my seniors loudly lamented and predicted dire ends for me, I really do not think that my willfulness signified that I was an evil child. My chief besetting sin was curiosity, but of course that *is* a sin by our Western standards. Tradition insists that we behave in conformity with our neighbors and peers. The Holy Church demands that we believe and have faith, that we stifle any questions or opinions derived from our own reasoning. The Venetian mercantile philosophy decrees that the only palpable truths are those numerated on the bottommost ledger line where debits and credits are balanced.

But something in my nature rebelled against the constraints accepted by all others of my age and class and situation. I wished to live a life beyond the rules and the ruled ledger lines and the lines written in the Missal. I was impatient and perhaps distrustful of received wisdom, those morsels of information and exhortations so neatly selected and prepared and served up like courses of a meal, for consumption and assimilation. I much preferred to make my own hunt for knowledge, even if I found it raw and unpalatable to chew and nauseating to swallow, as often I would do. My guardians and preceptors accused me of lazy avoidance of the hard work required to gain an education. They never realized that I had chosen to follow a far harder path, and would follow it—wherever it led—from that childhood time through all the years of my manhood.

On the days when I stayed away from the school and could not go home, I had to idle the days away somewhere, so sometimes I loitered about the establishment of the Compagnia Polo. It was situated then, as now, on the Riva Ca' de Dio, the waterfront esplanade which looks directly out onto the lagoon. On the water side, that esplanade is fringed with wooden quays, between which are ships and boats moored stem to stern and side by side. There are vessels of small and medium size: the shallow-draft batèli and gòndole of private houses, the bragozi fishing boats, the floating saloons called burchielli. And there are the much grander seagoing galleys and galeazze of Venice, interspersed with English and Flemish cogs, Slavic trabacoli and Levantine caïques. Many of those ocean vessels are so large that their stems and bowsprits overhang the street, and cast a latticed shadow on its cobbles, almost all the way to the variegated building fronts that line the esplanade's landward side. One of those buildings was (and still is) ours: a cavernous warehouse, with one little interior space of it partitioned off for a counting room.

I liked the warehouse. It was aromatic of all the smells of all the countries of the world, for it was heaped and piled with sacks and boxes and bales and barrels of all the world's produce—everything from Barbary wax and English wool to Alexandria sugar and Marseilles sardines. The warehouse workers were heavily muscled men, hung about with hammers, fist-hooks, coils of rope and other implements. They were forever busy, one man perhaps wrapping in burlap a consignment of Cornish tinware, another hammering the lid on a barrel of Catalonia olive oil, yet another shouldering a crate of Valencia soap out to the docks, and every man seeming always to be shouting some command like "logo!" or "a corando!" at the others.

But I liked the counting room, too. In that cramped coop sat the director of all that business and busy-ness, the old clerk Isidoro Priuli. With no apparent exertion of muscle, no rushing about or bellowing, no tools but his abaco, his quill and his ledger books, Maistro Doro controlled that crossroads of all the world's goods. With a little clicking of the abaco's colored counters and a scribble of ink in a ledger column, he could send to Bruges an ànfora of Corsican red wine and to Corsica, in exchange, a skein of Flanders lace, and, as the two items passed each other in our warehouse, dip off a metadella measure of the wine and snip off a braccio length of the lace to pay the Polos' profit on the transaction.

Because so many of the warehouse's contents were flammable, Isidoro did not allow himself the aid of a lamp or even a single candle to light his working space. Instead, he had arranged on the wall above and behind his head a large concave mirror made of real glass, which scooped in what light it could from the day outside and directed it down onto his high table. Seated there at his books, Maistro Doro looked like a very small and shriveled saint with an oversized halo. I would stand peering over the edge of that table, marveling that just the twitch of the maistro's fingers could exercise so much authority, and he would tell me things about the work in which he took such pride.

"It was the heathen Arabs, my boy, who gave the world these curlicue marks representing numbers, and this abaco for counting them with. But it was Venice that gave the world this system of *keeping* account—the books with facing pages for double entry. On the left, the debits. On the right, the credits."

I pointed to an entry on the left: "to the account of Messer Domeneddio," and asked, just for instance, who that Messere might be.

"Mefè!" the maistro exclaimed. "You do not recognize the name under which our Lord God does business?"

He flipped over the pages of that ledger to show me the flyleaf in the front, with its inked inscription: "In the name of God and of Profit."

"We mere mortals can take care of our own goods when they are secure here in this warehouse," he explained. "But when they go out in flimsy ships upon the hazardous seas, they are at the mercy of—who else but God? So we count Him a partner in our every enterprise. In our books He is allotted two full shares of every transaction at venture. And if that venture succeeds, if our cargo safely reaches its destination and pays us the expected profit, why then those two shares are entered to il conto di Messer Domeneddio, and at the end of each year, when our dividends are apportioned, they are paid to Him. Or rather, to His factor and agent, in the person of Mother Church. Every Christian merchant does the same."

If all my days stolen from school had been passed in such improving conversations, no one could have complained. I probably would have had a better education than I could ever have got from Fra Varisto. But inevitably my loitering about the waterfront brought me into contact with persons less admirable than the clerk Isidoro.

I do not mean to say that the Riva is in any sense a low-class street. While it teems with workmen, seamen and fishermen at all hours of the day, there are just as many well-dressed merchants and brokers and other businessmen, often accompanied by their genteel wives. The Riva is also the promenade, even after dark on fine nights, of fashionable men and women come merely to stroll and enjoy the lagoon breeze. Nevertheless, among those people, day or night, there lurk the louts and cutpurses and prostitutes and other specimens of the rabble we call the popolàzo. There were, for example, the urchins I met one afternoon on that Riva dockside, when one of them introduced himself by throwing a fish at me.

2

IT was not a very large fish, and he was not a very large boy. He was of about my own size and age, and I was not hurt when the fish hit me between my shoulder blades. But it left a smelly slime on my Lucca silk tunic, which was clearly what the boy had intended, for he was clad in rags already redolent of fish. He danced about, gleefully pointing at me and singing a taunt:

> Un ducato, un ducatòn!
> Bùtelo . . . bùtelo . . . zo per el cavròn!

That is merely a fragment of a children's chant, meaning to be sung during a throwing game, but he had changed the last word of it into a word which, though I could not then have told you its meaning, I knew to be the worst insult one man can fling at another. I was not a man and neither was he, but my honor was obviously in dispute. I interrupted his dance of mockery by stepping up to him and striking him in the face with my fist. His nose gushed bright red blood.

In the next moment, I was flattened under the weight of four other rascals. My assailant had not been alone on that dockside, and he was not alone in resenting the fine clothes Zia Zulià made me don on schooldays. For a while, our struggles made the dock planks rattle. Numerous of the passersby stopped to watch us, and some of the rougher sorts shouted things like "Gouge him!" and "Kick the beggar in his baggage!" I fought valiantly, but I could strike back at only one boy at a time, while they all five were pummeling me. Before long, I had the wind knocked out of me and my arms pinned down. I simply lay there being beaten and kneaded like pasta dough.

"Let him up!" said a voice from outside our entangled heap.

It was only a piping falsetto of a voice, but it was loud and commanding. The five boys stopped pounding on me, and one after another, although reluctantly, peeled off me. Even when I was unencumbered, I still had to lie there for a bit and get my breath back before I could stand.

The other boys were shuffling their bare feet and sullenly regarding the owner of the voice. I was surprised to see that they had obeyed a mere girl. She was as ragged and aromatic as they were, but smaller and younger than any of them. She wore the short, tight, tubelike dress worn by all Venetian girl children until about the age of twelve—or I should say she wore the remains of one. Hers was so tattered that she would have been quite indecently exposed, except that what showed of her body was the same dingy gray color as her frock. Perhaps she derived some authority from the fact that she, alone of the urchins, wore shoes—the cloglike wooden tofi of the poor.

The girl came close to me and maternally brushed at my clothes, which were now not very disparate from her own. She also informed me that she was the sister of the boy whose nose I had bloodied.

"Mama told Boldo never to fight," she said, and added, "Papà told him always to fight his own fights without help."

I said, panting, "I wish he had listened to one of them."

"My sister is a liar! We do not have a mama or a papà!"

"Well, if we did, that is what they would tell you. Now

pick up that fish, Boldo. It was hard enough to steal." To me she said, "What is your name? He is Ubaldo Tagiabue and I am Doris."

Tagiabue means "built like an ox," and I had learned in school that Doris was the daughter of the pagan god Oceanus. This Doris was too pitifully skinny to merit the surname, and far too dirty to resemble any water goddess. But she stood staunch as the ox, imperious as the goddess, as we watched her brother obediently go to pick up the discarded fish. He could not exactly pick it up; it had several times been stepped on during the brawl; he had more or less to gather it up.

"You must have done something terrible," Doris said to me, "to have made him throw our supper at you."

"I did nothing at all," I said truthfully. "Until I hit him. And that was because he called me a cavròn."

She looked amused and asked, "Do you know what that means?"

"Yes, it means one must fight."

She looked even more amused and said, "A cavròn is a man who lets his wife be used by other men."

I wondered why, if that was all it meant, the word should be such a deadly insult. I knew of several men whose wives were washerwomen or seamstresses, and those women's services were used by many other men, and that excited no public commotion or private vendèta. I made some remark to that effect, and Doris burst out laughing.

"Marcolfo!" she jeered at me. "It means the men put their candles into the woman's scabbard and together they do the dance of San Vito!"

No doubt you can divine the street meaning of her words, so I will not tell you the bizarre picture they brought to my ignorant mind. But some respectably merchant-looking gentlemen were strolling nearby at that moment, and they recoiled from Doris, their various mustaches and beards bristling like quills, when they heard those obscenities shouted by so small a female child.

Bringing the mangled corpse of his fish cradled in his grimy hands, Ubaldo said to me, "Will you share our supper?" I did not, but in the course of that afternoon he and I forgot our quarrel and became friends.

He and I were perhaps eleven or twelve years old then,

and Doris about two years younger, and during the next
few years I spent most of my days with them and their
somewhat fluid following of other dockside brats. I could
easily have been consorting in those years with the well-
fed and well-dressed, prim and priggish offspring of the
lustrìsimi families, such as the Balbi and the Cornari—
and Zia Zulià used every effort and persuasion to make me
do so—but I preferred my vile and more vivacious friends. I
admired their pungent language, and I adopted it. I admired their independence and their fichèvelo attitude to
life, and I did my best to imitate it. As could be expected,
since I did not slough off those attitudes when I went home
or elsewhere, they did not make me any better beloved by
the other people in my life.

During my infrequent attendances at school, I began
calling Fra Varisto by a couple of nicknames I had learned
from Boldo—"il bel de Roma" and "il Culiseo"—and soon
had all the other schoolboys doing the same. The friar-
maistro put up with that informality, even seemed flattered by it, until gradually it dawned on him that we were
not likening him to the grand old Beauty of Rome, the Col-
osseum, but were making a play on the word culo, and in
effect were calling him the "landmark of buttocks." At
home, I scandalized the servants almost daily. On one occasion, after I had done a thing reprehensible, I overheard
a conversation between Zia Zulià and Maistro Attilio, the
maggiordomo of the household.

"Crispo!" I heard the old man exclaim. That was his fastidious way of uttering a profanity without actually saying
the words "per Cristo!" but he managed, anyway, to sound
outraged and disgusted. "Do you know what the whelp has
done now? He called the boatman a black turd of merda,
and now poor Michièl is dissolving in tears. It is an unfor-
givable cruelty to speak so to a slave, and remind him that
he is a slave."

"But Attilio, what can I do?" whimpered Zulià. "I cannot beat the boy and risk injuring his precious self."

The chief servant said sternly, "Better he be beaten
young, and here in the privacy of his home, than that he
grow up to earn a public scourging at the pillars."

"If I could keep him always under my eye . . ." sniffled
my nena. "But I cannot chase him throughout the city.

And since he took to running with those popolàzo boat children . . ."

"He will be running with the bravi next," growled Attilio, "if he lives long enough. I warn you, woman: you are letting that boy become a real bimbo viziato."

A bimbo viziato is a child spoiled to rottenness, which is what I was, and I would have been delighted with a promotion from bimbo to bravo. In my childishness, I thought the bravi were what their name implies, but of course they are anything but brave.

The skulking bravi are the modern Vandals of Venice. They are young men, sometimes of good family, who have no morals and no useful employment, and no ability except low cunning and perhaps some swordsmanship, and no ambition except to earn an occasional ducat for committing a sneak murder. They are sometimes hired for that purpose by politicians seeking a short road to preferment, or merchants seeking to eliminate competition by the easiest means. But, ironically, the bravi are more often utilized by *lovers*—to dispose of an impediment to their love, like an inconvenient husband or a jealous wife. If, in daytime, you should see a young man swaggering about with the air of a cavaliere errante, he is either a bravo or wishes to be mistaken for one. But if you should meet a bravo by night, he will be masked and cloaked, and wearing modern chain mail under his cloak, and lurking furtively far from any lamplight, and when he stabs you with sword or stilèto, it will be in the back.

This is no digression from my history, for I did live to become a bravo. Of sorts.

However, I was speaking of the time when I was still a bimbo viziato, when Zia Zulià complained of my being so often in the company of those boat children. Of course, considering the foul mouth and abominable manners I acquired from them, she had good reason to disapprove. But only a Slav, not Venice-born, would have thought it unnatural that I should loiter about the docks. I was a Venetian, so the salt of the sea was in my blood, and it urged me seaward. I was a boy, so I did not resist the urge, and to consort with the boat children was as close as I could then get to the sea.

I have, since then, known many seaside cities, but I have known none that is so nearly a part of the sea as is this

Venice. The sea is not just our means of livelihood—as it is also for Genoa and Constantinople and the Cherbourg of the fictional Bauduin—here it is indissoluble from our lives. It washes about the verge of every island and islet composing Venice, and through the city's canals, and sometimes—when the wind and the tide come in from the same quarter—it laps at the very steps of the Basilica of San Marco, and a gondolier can row his boat among the portal arches of Samarco's great piazza.

Only Venice, of all the world's port cities, claims the sea for its bride, and annually affirms that espousal with priests and panoply. I watched the ceremony again just last Thursday. That was Ascension Day, and I was one of the honored guests aboard the gold-encrusted bark of our Doge Zuàne Soranzo. His splendid buzino d'oro, rowed by forty oarsmen, was but one of a great fleet of vessels, crowded with seamen and fishermen and priests and min-strels and lustrìsimi citizens, going in stately procession out upon the lagoon. At the Lido, the most seaward of our islands, Doge Soranzo made the ages-old proclamation, "Ti sposiamo, O mare nostro, in cigno di vero e perpetuo dominio," and threw into the water a gold wedding ring, while the priests led our waterborne congregation in a prayer that the sea might, in the coming twelvemonth, prove as generous and submissive as a human bride. If the tradition is true—that same ceremony has been performed on every Ascension Day since the year 1000—then there is a considerable fortune of more than three hundred gold rings lying on the sea bottom off the beaches of the Lido.

The sea does not merely surround and pervade Venice: it is within every Venetian; it salts the sweat of his laboring arms, and the weeping or laughing tears of his eyes, and even the speech of his tongue. Nowhere else in the world have I heard men meet and greet each other with the glad cry of *"Che bon vento?"* That phrase means "What good wind?" and to a Venetian it means "What good wind has wafted you across the sea to this happy destination of Ven-ice?"

Ubaldo Tagiabue and his sister Doris and the other deni-zens of the docks had an even more terse greeting, but the salt was in that one, too. They said simply, "Sana capàna," which is short for a salute "to the health of our company," and assumes the understanding that what is meant is the company of boat people. When, after we had been acquainted for some time, they began to salute me with that phrase, I felt included, and proud to be so.

Those children lived, like a swarm of dock rats, in a rotting hulk of a tow barge mired in a mud flat off the side of the city that faces the Dead Lagoon and, beyond that, the little cemetery isle of San Michièl, or Isle of the Dead. They really spent only their sleeping hours inside that dark and clammy hull, for their waking hours had to be mainly devoted to scavenging bits of food and clothing. They lived almost entirely on fish because, when they could steal no other nutriment, they could always descend on the Fish Market at the close of each day, when, by Venetian law—to prevent any stale fish from ever being vended—the fishmongers have to scatter on the ground whatever stock is left unsold. There was always a crowd of poor people to scramble and fight for those leavings, which seldom consisted of anything tastier than molefish.

I did bring to my new friends what scraps I could save from the table at home, or pilfer from the kitchen. At least that put some vegetables in the children's diet when I fetched something like kale ravioli or turnip jam, and some eggs and cheese when I brought them a maccherone, and even good meat when I could sneak a bit of mortadella or pork jelly. Once in a while I provided some viand they found most marvelous. I had always thought that, on Christmas Eve, Father Baba brought to all Venetian children the traditional torta di lasagna of the season. But when, one Christmas Day, I carried a portion of that confection to Ubaldo and Doris, their eyes widened in wonder, and they exclaimed with delight at every raisin and pine-nut and preserved onion and candied orange peel they found among the pasta.

I also brought what clothing I could—outgrown or worn-out garb of my own for the boys and, for the girls, articles that had belonged to my late mother. Not everything fit everybody, but they did not mind. Doris and the other three or four girls paraded about, most proudly, in shawls and gowns so much too big for them that they tripped on the dragging ends. I even brought along—for my own wear when I was with the boat children—various of my old tunics and hose so derelict that Zia Zulià had consigned them to the household bin of dust rags. I would remove

whatever fine attire I had left my house in, and leave that
wedged among the barge's timbers, and dress in the rags
and look just like another boat urchin, until it was time to
change again and go home.

You might wonder why I did not give the children
money instead of my meager gifts. But you must remember that I was as much of an orphan as any of them were,
and under strict guardianship, and too young to make any
dispensation from the Polo family coffers. Our household's
money was doled out by the company, meaning by the
clerk Isidoro Priuli. Whenever Zulià or the maggiordomo
or any other servant had to buy any sort of supplies or
provender for the Ca' Polo, he or she went to the markets
accompanied by a page from the company. That page boy
carried the purse and counted out the ducats or sequins or
soldi as they were spent, and made a memorandum of
every one. If there was anything I personally needed or
wanted, and if I could put up a good argument, that thing
would be bought for me. If I contracted a debt, it would be
paid for me. But I never possessed, at any one time, more
than a few copper bagatini of my own, for jingling money.

I did manage to improve the boat children's existence at
least to the extent of improving the scope of their thievery.
They had always filched from the mongers and hucksters
of their own squalid neighborhood; in other words, from
petty merchants who were not much less poor than they
were, and whose goods were hardly worth the stealing. I
led the children to my own higher-class confino, where the
wares displayed for sale were of better quality. And there
we devised a better mode of theft than mere snatch-and-
run.

The Mercerìa is the widest, straightest and longest
street in Venice, meaning that it is practically the *only*
street that can be called wide or straight or long. Open-
fronted shops line both sides of it and, between them, long
ranks of stalls and carts do an even brisker business, selling everything from mercery to hourglasses, and all kinds
of groceries from staples to delicacies.

Suppose we saw, on a meat man's cart, a tray of veal
chops that made the children's mouths water. A boy
named Daniele was our swiftest runner. So he it was who
elbowed his way to the cart, seized up a handful of the
chops and ran, nearly knocking down a small girl who had

blundered into his path. Daniele continued running, stupidly it seemed, along the broad, straight, open Mercerìa where he was visible and easily pursued. So the meat man's assistant and a couple of outraged customers took out after him, shouting "alto!" and "salva!" and "al ladro!"

But the girl who had been shoved was our Doris, and Daniele had in that scuffling moment, unobserved, handed to her the stolen veal chops. Doris, still unnoticed in the commotion, quickly and safely disappeared down one of the narrow, twisty side alleys leading off the open area. Meanwhile, his flight being somewhat impeded by the crowds on the Mercerìa, Daniele was in peril of capture. His pursuers were closing in on him, and other passersby were clutching at him, and all were bellowing for a "sbiro!" The sbiri are Venice's apelike policemen, and one of them, heeding the call, was angling through the crowd to intercept the thief. But I was nearby, as I always contrived to be on those occasions. Daniele stopped running and I started, which made me seem the quarry, and I ran deliberately into the sbiro's ape arms.

After being soundly buffeted about the ears, I was recognized, as I always was and expected to be. The sbiro and the angry citizens hauled me to my house not far from the Mercerìa. When the street door was hammered on, the unhappy maggiordomo Attilio opened it. He heard out the people's babble of accusation and condemnation and then wearily put his thumbprint on a pagherò, which is a paper promising to pay, and thereby committed the Compagnia Polo to reimburse the meat man for his loss. The sbiro, after giving me a stern lecture and a vigorous shaking, let go of my collar, and he and the crowd departed.

Though I did not have to interpose myself every time the boat children stole something—more often it was deftly managed, with both the grabber and the receiver getting clean away—nevertheless I was dragged to the Ca' Polo more times than I can remember. That did not much lessen Maistro Attilio's opinion that Zia Zulià had raised the first black sheep in the Polo line.

It might be supposed that the boat children would have resented the participation of a "rich boy" in their pranks, and that they would have resented the "condescension" implicit in my gifts to them. Not so. The popolàzo may ad-

mire or envy or even revile the lustrìsimi, but they keep
their active resentment and loathing for their fellow poor,
who are, after all, their chief competitors in this world. It
is not the rich who wrestle with the poor for the discarded
molefish at the Fish Market. So when I came along, giving
what I could and taking nothing, the boat people tolerated
my presence rather better than if I had been another hungry beggar.

3

JUST to remind myself now and again that I was *not* of the
popolàzo, I would drop in at the Compagnia Polo to luxuriate in its rich aromas and industrious activity and prosperous ambience. On one of those visits, I found on the clerk
Isidoro's table an object like a brick, but of a more glowing
red color, and lighter in weight, and soft and vaguely moist
to the touch, and I asked him what it was.

Again he exclaimed, "My faith!" and shook his gray
head and said, "Do you not recognize the very foundation
of your family's fortune? It was built on those bricks of
zafràn."

"Oh," I said, respectfully regarding the brick. "And
what is zafràn?"

"Mefè! You have been eating it and smelling it and
wearing it all your life! Zafràn is what gives that special
flavor and yellow color to rice and polenta and pasta. What
gives that unique yellow color to fabrics. What gives the
women's favorite scent to their salves and pomades. A
mèdego uses it, too, in his medicines, but what it does
there I do not know."

"Oh," I said again, my respect somewhat less for such an
everyday article. "Is that all?"

"All!" he blurted. "Hear me, marcolfo." That word is not
an affectionate play on my name; it is addressed to any exceedingly stupid boy. "Zafràn has a history more ancient
and more noble even than the history of Venice. Long before Venice existed, zafràn was used by the Greeks and Romans to perfume their baths. They scattered it on their
floors to perfume whole rooms. When the Emperor Nero

made his entry into Rome, the streets of *the entire city* were strewn with zafràn and made fragrant."

"Well," I said, "if it has always been so commonly available . . ."

"It may have been common then," said Isidoro, "in the days when slaves were numerous and cost nothing. Zafràn is not common today. It is a scarce commodity, and therefore of much value. That one brick you see there is worth an ingot of gold of almost equal weight."

"Is it indeed?" I said, perhaps sounding unconvinced. "But why?"

"Because that brick was made by the labor of many hands and immeasurable zonte of land and a countless multitude of flowers."

"Flowers!"

Maistro Doro sighed and said patiently, "There is a purple flower called the crocus. When it blooms, it extends from that blossom three delicate stigmi of an orange-red color. Those stigmi are ever so carefully detached by human hands. When some millions of those dainty and almost impalpable stigmi are collected, they are either dried to make loose zafràn, what is called hay zafràn, or they are what is called 'sweated' and compressed together to make brick zafràn like this one. The arable land must be devoted to nothing but that crop, and the crocus blooms only once a year. That blooming season is brief, so many gatherers must work at the same time, and they must work diligently. I do not know how many zonte of land and how many hands are required to produce just one brick of zafràn in a year, but you will understand why it is of such extravagant value."

I was by now convinced. "And where do we buy the zafràn?"

"We do not. We grow it." He put on the table beside the brick another object; I would have said it was a bulb of ordinary garlic. "That is a culm of the crocus flower. The Compagnia Polo plants them and harvests from the blossoms."

I was astonished. "Not in Venice, surely!"

"Of course not. On the teraferma of the mainland southwest of here. I told you it requires innumerable zonte of terrain."

"I never knew," I said.

He laughed. "Probably half the people of Venice do not even know that the milk and eggs of their daily meals are extracted from animals, and that those animals must have dry land to live on. We Venetians are inclined to pay little attention to anything but our lagoon and sea and ocean."

"How long have we been doing this, Doro? Growing crocuses and zafràn?"

He shrugged. "How long have there been Poles in Venice? That was the genius of some one of your long-ago ancestors. After the time of the Romans, zafràn became too much of a luxury to cultivate. No one farmer could grow enough of it to make it worth his while. And even a landowner of great estates could not afford all the paid laborers that crop would require. So zafràn was pretty well forgotten. Until some early Polo remembered it, and also realized that modern Venice has almost as big a supply of slaves as Rome had. Of course, we now have to buy our slaves, not just capture them. But the gathering of crocus stigmi is not an arduous labor. It does not require strong and expensive male slaves. The puniest women and children can do it; weaklings and cripples can do it. So that was the cheap sort of slaves your ancestor bought; the sort the Compagnia Polo has been acquiring ever since. They are a motley sort, of all nations and colors—Moors, Lezghians, Circassians, Russniaks, Armeniyans—but their colors blend, so to speak, to make that red-gold zafràn."

"The foundation of our fortune," I repeated.

"It buys everything else we sell," said Isidoro. "Oh, we sell the zafràn too, for a price, when the price is right—to be used as a foodstuff, a dye, a perfume, a medicament. But basically it is our company's capital, with which we barter for all our other articles of merchandise. Everything from Ibiza's salt to Còrdoba's leather to Sardinia's wheat. Just as the house of Spinola in Genoa has the monopoly of trading in raisins, our Venetian house of Polo has the zafràn."

The only son of the Venetian house of Polo thanked the old clerk for that edifying lesson in high commerce and bold endeavor—and, as usual, sauntered off again to partake of the easy indolence of the boat children.

As I have said, those children tended to come and go; there was seldom the same lot living in the derelict barge from one week to the next. Like all the grown-up popolàzo, the children dreamed of somewhere finding a Land of

Cockaigne, where they could shirk work in luxury instead
of squalor. So they might hear of some place offering better
prospects than the Venice waterfront, and they might stow
away aboard an outbound vessel to get there. Some of
them would come back after a while, either because they
could not reach their destination or because they had and
were disillusioned. Some never came back at all, because—we never knew—the vessel sank and they drowned,
or because they were apprehended and thrown into an or-
phanage, or maybe because they did find "il paese di
Cuccagna" and stayed there.

But Ubaldo and Doris Tagiabue were the constants, and
it was from them that I got most of my education in the
ways and the language of the lower classes. That education was not force-fed to me in the way Fra Varisto stuffed
Latin conjugations into his schoolboys; rather, the brother
and sister parceled it out to me in fragments, as I required
it. Whenever Ubaldo would jeer at some backwardness or
bewilderment of mine, I would realize that I lacked some
bit of knowledge, and Doris would supply it.

One day, I remember, Ubaldo said he was going to the
western side of the city, and going by way of the Dogs'
Ferry. I had never heard of that, so I went along, to see
what strange kind of boat he meant. But we crossed the
Grand Canal by the quite ordinary agency of the Rialto
Bridge, and I must have looked either disappointed or
mystified, for he scoffed at me, "You are as ignorant as a
cornerstone!" and Doris explained:

"There is only one way to get from the eastern to the
western side of the city, no? That is to cross the Grand Canal. Cats are allowed in boats, to catch the rats, but dogs
are not. So the dogs can cross the canal only on the Ponte
Rialto. So that is the Dogs' Ferry, no xe vero?"

Some of their street jargon I could translate without assistance. They spoke of every priest and monk as le rigioso,
which could mean "the stiff one," but it did not take me
long to realize that they were merely twisting the word re-
ligioso. When, in fine summer weather, they announced
that they were moving from the barge hulk to La Locanda
de la Stela, I knew that they were not going to reside in
any Starlight Inn; they meant that they would be sleeping
outdoors for a season. When they spoke of a female person
as una largazza, they were playing on the proper term for a

girl, la ragazza, but coarsely suggesting that she was ample, even cavernous, in her genital aperture. As a matter of fact, the greater part of the boat people's language—and the greater part of their conversations, and their interests—dealt with such indelicate topics. I absorbed a lot of information, but it sometimes did more to confuse than to enlighten me.

Zia Zulià and Fra Varisto had taught me to refer to those parts between my legs—if I had to refer to them at all—as le vergogne, "the shames." On the docks I heard many other terms. The word baggage for a man's genital equipment was clear enough; and candelòto was an apt word for his erect organ, which is like a stout candle; and so was fava for the bulbous end of that organ, since it does somewhat resemble a broad bean; and so was capèla for the foreskin, which does enclose the fava like a little cloak or a little chapel. But it was a mystery to me why the word lumaghèta was sometimes spoken in reference to a woman's parts. I understood that a woman had nothing but an opening down there, and the word lumaghèta can mean either a small snail or the tiny peg with which a minstrel tunes each string of his lute.

Ubaldo and Doris and I were playing on a dock one day when a greengrocer came pushing his cart along the esplanade, and the boat wives ambled over to paw through his produce. One of the women fondled a large yellowish cucumber, and grinned and said, "Il mescolòto," and all the women cackled lasciviously. "The stirrer"—I could make out the implications of that. But then two lissome young men came strolling along the esplanade, arm in arm, walking with a sort of springiness in their step, and one of the boat women growled, "Don Meta and Sior Mona." Another woman glanced scornfully at the more delicate of the two young men and muttered, "That one wears a split seat in his hose." I had no notion of what they were talking about, and Doris's explanation did not tell me much:

"Those are the sorts of men who do with each other what a real man does only with a woman."

Well, *there* was the main flaw in my comprehension: I had no very clear idea of *what* a man did with a woman.

Mind you, I was not entirely benighted in the matter of sex, any more than other upper-class Venetian children are—or, I daresay, upper-class children of any other European nationality. We may not consciously remember it, but we have all had an early introduction to sex, from our mothers or our nursemaids, or both.

It seems that mothers and nurses have known, from the beginning of time, that the best way to quiet a restless baby or put it easily to sleep is to do for it the act of manustupraziòn. I have watched many a mother do that to an infant boy whose bimbìn was so tiny that she could only just manipulate it with her finger and thumb. Yet the wee organ lifted and grew, though not in proportion as a man's does, of course. As the woman stroked, the baby quivered, then smiled, then squirmed voluptuously. He did not ejaculate any spruzzo, but there was no doubt that he enjoyed a climax of release. Then his little bimbìn shrank again to its littlest, and he lay quiet and soon he slept.

Assuredly my own mother often did that for me, and I think it is good that mothers do so. That early manipulation, besides being an excellent pacifier of the infant, clearly stimulates development in that part of him. The mothers in the Eastern countries do not engage in that practice, and the omission is sadly evident when their babies grow up. I have seen many Eastern men undressed, and almost all had organs pitifully minute in comparison to mine.

Although our mothers and nursemaids gradually leave off doing that, when their children are about two years old—that is, at the age when they are weaned from the breast milk and introduced to wine—nevertheless, every child retains some dim recollection of it. Therefore a boy is not puzzled or frightened when he grows to adolescence and that organ seeks attention of its own accord. When a boy wakes in the night with it coming erect under his hand, he knows what it wants.

"A cold sponge bath," Fra Varisto used to tell us boys at school. "That will quell the upstart, and avert the risk of its shaming you with the midnight stain."

We listened respectfully, but on our way home we laughed at him. Perhaps friars and priests do endure involuntary and surprising spruzzi, and feel embarrassed or somehow guilty on that account. But no healthy boy of my acquaintance ever did. And none would choose a cold douche in place of the warm pleasure of doing for his candelòto what his mother had done for it when it was just

a bimbìn. However, Ubaldo was contemptuous when he
heard that those night games were the total extent of my
sexual experience to date.

"What? You are still waging the war of the priests?" he
jeered. "You have never had a girl?"

Once again uncomprehending, I inquired, "The war of
the priests?"

"Five against one," Doris said, without a blush. She
added, "You must get yourself a smanza. A compliant girl
friend."

I thought about that and said, "I do not know any girls I
could ask. Except you, and you are too young."

She bridled and said angrily, "I may not have hair on
my artichoke yet, but I am twelve, and that is of marrying
age!"

"I do not wish to marry anybody," I protested. "Only
to—"

"Oh, no!" Ubaldo interrupted me. "My sister is a *good*
girl."

You might smile at the assertion that a girl who could
talk as she did could be a "good" girl. But there you have
evidence of one thing our upper and lower classes have in
common: their reverent regard for a maiden's virginity. To
the lustrìsimi and the popolàzo alike, that counts for more
than all other feminine qualities: beauty, charm, sweetness, demureness, whatever. Their women may be plain
and malicious and ill-spoken and ungracious and slovenly,
but they must retain unbroken that little tuck of maidenhead tissue. In that respect at least, the most primitive
and barbarous savages of the East are superior to us: they
value a female for attributes other than the bung in her
hole.

To our upper classes, virginity is not so much a matter of
virtue as of good business, and they regard a daughter
with the same cool calculation as they would a slave girl in
the market. A daughter or a slave, like a cask of wine, commands a better price if it is sealed and demonstrably
untampered with. Thus they barter their daughters for
commercial advantage or social enhancement. But the
lower classes foolishly think that their betters have a high
moral regard for virginity, and they try to imitate that.
Also, they are more easily frightened by the thunders of
the Church, and the Church demands the preservation of

virginity as a sort of negative show of virtue, in the same
way that good Christians show virtue by abstaining from
meat during Lent.

But even in those days when I was still a boy, I found
reason to wonder just how many girls, of any class, really
were kept "good" by the prevailing social precepts and attitudes. From the time I was old enough to sprout the first
fuzz of "hair on my artichoke," I had to listen to lectures
from Fra Varisto and Zia Zulià on the moral and physical
dangers of consorting with bad girls. I listened with close
attention to their descriptions of such vile creatures, and
their warnings about them, and their inveighings against
them. I wanted to make sure I would recognize any bad
girl at first sight, because I hoped with all my heart that I
would soon get to meet one. That seemed quite likely, because the main impression I got from those lectures was
that the bad girls must considerably outnumber the good
ones.

There is other evidence for that impression. Venice is
not a very tidy city, because it does not have to be. All of
its discards go straight into the canals. Street garbage,
kitchen trash, the wastes from our chamber pots and licet
closets, all gets dumped into the nearest canal and is soon
flushed away. The tide comes in twice daily, and surges
through every least waterway, roiling up whatever matter
lies on the bottom or is crusted on the canal walls. Then
the tide departs and takes all those substances with it,
through the lagoon, out past the Lido and off to sea. That
keeps the city clean and sweet-smelling, but it frequently
afflicts fishermen with unwelcome catches. There is not
one of them who has not many times found on his hook or
in his net the glistening pale blue and purple cadaver of a
newborn infant. Granted, Venice is one of the three most
populous cities of Europe. Still, only half of its citizens are
female, and of those perhaps only half are of childbearing
age. So the fishermen's annual catch of discarded infants
would seem to indicate a scarcity of "good" Venetian girls.

"There is always Daniele's sister Malgarita," said Ubaldo. He was not enumerating good girls, but quite the contrary. He was counting those females of our acquaintance
who might serve to wean me from the war of the priests to
a more manly diversion. "She will do it with anybody who
will give her a bagatìn."

"Malgarita is a fat pig," said Doris.

"She is a fat pig," I concurred.

"Who are you to sneer at pigs?" said Ubaldo. "Pigs have a patron saint. San Tonio was very fond of pigs."

"He would not have been fond of Malgarita," Doris said firmly.

Ubaldo went on, "Also there is Daniele's mother. She will do it and not even ask a bagatìn."

Doris and I made noises of revulsion. Then she said, "There is someone down there waving at us."

We three were idling the afternoon away on a rooftop. That is a favorite occupation of the lower classes. Because all the common houses of Venice are one story high, and all have flat roofs, their people like to stroll or loll upon them and enjoy the view. From that vantage, they can behold the streets and canals below, the lagoon and its ships beyond, and Venice's more elegant buildings that stand above the mass: the domes and spires of churches, the bell towers, the carved facades of palazzi.

"He is waving at me," I said. "That is our boatman, taking our batèlo home from somewhere. I might as well ride with him."

There was no necessity for me to go home before the bells began ringing the nighttime coprifuoco, when all honest citizens who do not retire indoors are supposed to carry lanterns to show that they are abroad on honest errands. But, to be truthful, I was at that moment feeling a bit apprehensive that Ubaldo might insist on my immediately coupling with some boat woman or girl. I did not so much fear the adventure, even with a slattern like Daniele's mother; I feared making a fool of myself, not knowing what to *do* with her.

From time to time, I tried to atone for my being so often rude to poor old Michièl, so that day I took the oars from him and myself rowed us homeward, while he took his ease under the boat canopy. We conversed as we went, and he told me that he was going to boil an onion when he got to the house.

"What?" I said, unsure I had heard him right.

The black slave explained that he suffered from the bane of boatmen. Because his profession required him to spend most of his time with his backside on a hard and damp boat thwart, he was often troubled by bleeding piles. Our family mèdego, he said, had prescribed a simple allevement for that malady. "You boil an onion until it is soft, and you wad it well up in there, and you wind a cloth around your loins to hold it there. Truly, it does help. If you ever have piles, Messer Marco, you try that."

I said I would indeed, and forgot about it. I arrived home to be accosted by Zia Zulià.

"The good friar Varisto was here today, and he was so angry that his dear face was bright red, clear to his tonsure."

I remarked that that was not unusual.

She said warningly, "A marcolfo with no schooling should speak with a smaller mouth. Fra Varisto said you have been shirking your classes again. For more than a week this time. And tomorrow your class must be heard in recitation, whatever that is, by the Censori de Scole, whoever they are. It is required that you participate. The friar told me—and I am telling you, young man—you *will* be in school tomorrow."

I said a word that made her gasp, and stalked off to my room to sulk. I refused to come out even when called to supper. But by the time the coprifuoco was rung, my better instincts had begun to overcome my worse ones. I thought to myself: today when I behaved with kindness to old Michièl it gratified him; I ought to say a kindly word of apology to old Zulià.

(I realize that I have characterized as "old" almost all the people I knew in my youth. That is because they seemed so to my young eyes, though only a few of them really were. The company's clerk Isidoro and the chief servant Attilio were perhaps as old as I am now. But the friar Varisto and the black slave Michièl were no more than middle-aged. Zulià of course seemed old because she was about the same age as my mother, and my mother was dead; but I suppose Zulià was a year or two younger than Michièl.)

That night, when I determined to make amends to her, I did not wait for Zia Zulià to do her customary before-bedtime rounds of the house. I went to her little room and rapped on the door and opened it without waiting for an avanti. I probably had always assumed that servants did nothing at night except sleep to restore their energies for service the next day. But what was happening in that room that night was not sleep. It was something appalling and ludicrous and astounding to me—and educational.

Immediately before me on the bed was a pair of immense buttocks bouncing up and down. They were distinctive buttocks, being as purple-black as aubergines, and even more distinctive because they had a strip of cloth binding a large, pale-yellow onion in the cleft between them. At my sudden entrance, there was a squawk of dismay and the buttocks bounded out of the candlelight into a darker corner of the room. This revealed on the bed a contrastingly fish-white body—the naked Zulià, sprawled supine and splayed wide open. Her eyes were shut, so she had not noticed my arrival.

At the buttocks' abrupt withdrawal, she gave a wail of deprivation, but continued to move as if she were still being bounced upon. I had never seen my nena except in gowns of many layers and floor length, and of atrociously garish Slavic colors. And the woman's broad Slavic face was so very plain that I had never even tried to imagine her similarly broad body as it might look undressed. But now I took avid notice of everything so wantonly displayed before me, and one detail was so eminently noticeable that I could not restrain a blurted comment:

"Zia Zulià," I said wonderingly, "you have a bright red mole down there on your—"

Her meaty legs closed together with a slap, and her eyes flew open almost as audibly. She grabbed for the bed covers, but Michièl had taken those along in his leap, so she seized at the bed curtains. There was a moment of consternation and contortion, as she and the slave fumbled to swaddle themselves. Then there was a much longer moment of petrified embarrassment, during which I was stared at by four eyeballs almost as big and luminous as the onion had been. I congratulate myself that I was the first to regain composure. I smiled sweetly upon my nena and spoke, not the words of apology I had come to say, but the words of an arrant extortioner.

With smug assurance I said, "I will *not* go to school tomorrow, Zia Zulià," and I backed out of the room and closed the door.

4

BECAUSE I knew what I *would* be doing the next day, I was too restless with anticipation to sleep very well. I was up and dressed before any of the servants awoke, and I broke my fast with a bun and a gulp of wine as I went through the kitchen on my way out into the pearly morning. I hurried along the empty alleys and over the many bridges to that northside mud flat where some of the barge children were just emerging from their quarters. Considering what I had come to ask, I probably should have sought out Daniele, but I went instead to Ubaldo and put my request to him.

"At this hour?" he said, mildly scandalized. "Malgarita is likely still asleep, the pig. But I will see."

He ducked back inside the barge, and Doris, who had overheard us, said to me, "I do not think you ought to, Marco."

I was accustomed to her always commenting on everything that everybody did or said, and I did not always appreciate it, but I asked, "Why ought I not?"

"I do not want you to."

"That is no reason."

"Malgarita is a fat pig." I could not deny that, and I did not, so she added, "Even I am better looking than Malgarita."

Impolitely I laughed, but I was polite enough not to say that there was small choice between a fat pig and a scrawny kitten.

Doris kicked moodily at the mud where she stood, and then said in a rush of words, "Malgarita will do it with you because she does not care what man or boy she does it with you. But I would do it with you because I do care."

I looked at her with amused surprise, and perhaps I also looked at her for the first time with appraisal. Her maidenly blush was perceptible even through the dirt on her face, and so was her earnestness, and so was a dim prefiguring of prettiness. At any rate, her undirtied eyes were of a nice blue, and seemed extraordinarily large, though that was probably because her face was somewhat pinched by lifelong hunger.

"You will be a comely woman someday, Doris," I said, to

36

make her feel better. "If you ever get washed—or at least scraped. And if you grow more of a figure than a broomstick. Malgarita already is grown as ample as her mother."

Doris said acidly, "Actually she looks more like her father, since she also grew a mustache."

A head with frowzy hair and gummy eyelids poked out through one of the splintery holes in the barge hull, and Malgarita called, "Well, come on then, before I put on my frock, so I do not have to take it off!"

I turned to go and Doris said, "Marco!" but when I turned back impatiently, she said, "No matter. Go and play the pig."

I clambered inside the dark, dank hull and crept along its rotting plank decking until I came to the hold partition where Malgarita squatted on a pallet of reeds and rags. My groping hands encountered her before I saw her, and her bare body felt sweaty and spongy as the barge's timbers. She immediately said, "Not even a feel until I get my bagatìn."

I gave her the copper, and she lay back on the pallet. I got over her, in a position in which I had seen Michièl. Then I flinched, as there came a loud *wham!* from the outside of the barge hull, but just beside my ear, and then a *screech!* The boat boys were playing one of their favorite games. One of them had caught a cat—and that is no easy feat, although Venice does teem with cats—and had tied it to the barge side, and the boys were taking turns running and butting it with their heads, competing to see who would first mash it to death.

As my eyes adapted to the darkness, I noted that Malgarita was indeed hairy. Her palely shining breasts seemed the only hairless part of her. In addition to the frowze on her head and the fuzz on her upper lip, she was shaggy of legs and arms, and a large plume of hair hung from either armpit. What with the darkness in the hold and the veritable bush on her artichoke, I could see considerably less of her female apparatus than I had seen of Zia Zulià's. (I could smell it, however, Malgarita being no more given to bathing than were any of the boat people.) I knew that I was expected to insert myself somewhere down there, but . . .

Wham! from the hull, and a yowl from the cat, further

confounding me. In some perplexity, I began to feel about Malgarita's nether regions.

"Why are you playing with my pota?" she demanded, using the most vulgar word for that orifice.

I laughed, no doubt shakily, and said, "I am trying to find the—er—your lumaghèta."

"Whatever for? That is of no use to you. Here is what you want." She reached down one hand to spread herself and the other to guide me in. It was easily done, she was so well reamed.

Wham! Squawl!

"Clumsy, you jerked it out again!" she said peevishly, and did some brisk rearranging.

I lay there for a moment, trying to ignore her piggishness and her aroma and the dismal surroundings, trying to enjoy the unfamiliar, warm, moist cavity in which I was loosely clasped.

"Well, get on with it," she whined. "I have not yet peed this morning."

I commenced to bounce as I had seen Michièl do, but, before I could get fairly started, the barge hold seemed to darken still more before my eyes. Though I tried to restrain and savor it, my spruzzo gushed unbidden and without any sensation of pleasure whatever.

Wham! Yee-oww!

"Oh, che braga! What a lot of it!" Malgarita said disgustedly. "My legs will be sticking together all day. All right, get off, you fool, so I can jump!"

"What?" I said groggily.

She wriggled out from under me, stood up, and took a jump backward. She jumped forward, then backward again, and the whole barge rocked. "Make me laugh!" she commanded, between jumps.

"What?" I said.

"Tell me a funny story! There, that was seven jumps. I said make me laugh, marcolfo! O would you rather make a baby?"

"What?"

"Oh, never mind. I will sneeze instead." She grabbed a lock of her hair, stuck the frowzy ends of it up one of her nostrils, and sneezed explosively.

Wham! Rowr-rr-rrr . . . The cat's complaint died off as, evidently, the cat died, too. I could hear the boys squab-

bling about what to do with the carcass. Ubaldo wanted to
throw it in onto me and Malgarita, Daniele wanted to
throw it in some Jew's shop door.

"I hope I have jarred it all out," said Malgarita, wiping
at her thighs with one of her bed rags. She dropped the rag
back on her pallet, moved to the opposite side of the hold,
squatted down and began copiously to urinate. I waited,
thinking that one of us ought to say something more. But
finally I decided that her morning bladder was inexhausti-
ble, and so crept out of the barge the way I had come in.

"Sana capàna!" shouted Ubaldo, as if I had just then
joined the company. "How was it?"

I gave him the jaded smile of a man of the world. All the
boys whooped and hooted good-naturedly, and Daniele
called, "My sister is good, yes, but my mother is better!"

Doris was nowhere about, and I was glad I did not have
to meet her eyes. I had made my first journey of discovery—a short foray toward manhood—but I was not disposed to preen myself on that accomplishment. I felt dirty
and I was sure I smelled of Malgarita. I wished I had listened to Doris and not done it. If that was all there was to
being a man, and doing it with a woman, well, I had done
it. From now on, I was entitled to swagger as brashly as
any of the other boys, and swagger I would. But I was privately determining, all over again, to be kind to Zia Zulià.
I would not tease her about what I had found in her room,
or despise her, or tell on her, or wrest concessions with the
threat of telling. I was sorry for her. If I felt soiled and
wretched after my experience with a mere boat girl, how
much more miserable my nena must feel, having no one
willing to do it with her but a contemptible black man.

However, I was to have no opportunity to demonstrate
my noblemindedness. I got home again to find all the other
servants in a turmoil, because Zulià and Michièl had disappeared during the night.

The sbiri had already been called in by Maistro Attilio,
and those police apes were making conjectures typical of
them: that Michièl had forcibly abducted Zulià in his
batèlo, or that the two of them had for some reason gone
out in the boat in the night, overturned it, and drowned. So
the sbiri were going to ask the fishermen on the seaward
side of Venice to keep a close eye on their hooks and nets,
and the peasants on the Vèneto mainland to keep a look-

out for a black boatman conveying a captive white damsel.
But then they thought to investigate the canal right outside the Ca' Polo, and there lay the batèlo innocently
moored to its post, so the sbiri scratched their heads for
new theories. In any event, if they could have caught
Michièl even without the woman, they would have had the
pleasure of executing him. A runaway slave is ipso facto a
thief, in that he steals his master's property: his own living self.

I kept silent about what I knew. I was convinced that
Michièl and Zulià, alarmed by my discovery of their sordid
connection, had eloped together. Anyway, they were never
apprehended and never heard from again. So they must
have made their way to some back corner of the world, like
his native Nubia or her native Bohemia, where they could
live squalidly ever after.

5

I WAS feeling so guilty, for so many different reasons, that
I did something unprecedented for me. Of my own accord,
not impelled by any authority, I betook myself to church to
make my confession. I did not go to our confino's San
Felice, for its old Pare Nunziata knew me as well as the
local sbiri did, and I desired a more disinterested auditor.
So I went all the way to the Basilica of San Marco. None of
the priests there knew me, but the bones of my namesake
saint lay there, and I hoped they would be sympathetic.

In that great vaulted nave, I felt like a bug, diminished
by all the glowing gold and marble and the holy notables
aloft and aloof in the ceiling mosaics. Everything in that
most beautiful building is bigger than real life, including
the sonorous music, which brays and bleats from a riga-
bèlo that seems too small to contain so much noise. San
Marco's is always thronged, so I had to stand in line before
one of the confessionals. Finally, I got in and got launched
on my purgation: "Father, I have too freely followed where
my curiosity has led me, and it has led me astray from the
paths of virtue. . . ." I went on in that vein for some time,
until the priest impatiently requested that I not regale

him with *all* the circumstances preliminary to my misde-
meanors. So, albeit reluctantly, I fell back on formula—
"have sinned in thought and word and deed"—and the
pare decreed some number of Paternosters and Avemar-
ias, and I left the box to begin on them, and I got hit by
lightning.

I mean that almost literally, so vivid was the shock I felt
when I first laid eyes on the Dona Ilaria. I did not then
know her name, of course; I knew only that I was looking
at the most beautiful woman I had yet seen in my life, and
that my heart was hers. She was just then coming out of a
confessional herself, so her veil was up. I could not believe
that a lady of such radiant loveliness could have had anything more than trivial to confess, but, before she lowered
her veil, I saw a sparkle as of tears in her glorious eyes. I
heard a creak as the priest shut the slide in the box she had
just quitted, and he too came out. He said something to the
other supplicants waiting in line there, and they all mumbled grouchily and dispersed to other lines. He joined the
Dona Ilaria and both of them knelt in an empty pew.

In a sort of trance, I moved closer and slid into the pew
across the aisle from them, and fixed my gaze sideways on
them. Though they both kept their heads bent, I could see
that the priest was a young man and handsome in an austere kind of way. You may not credit this, but I felt a
twinge of jealousy that my lady—*my lady*—had not chosen
a drier old stick to tell her troubles to. Both he and she, as I
could tell even through her veil, were moving their lips
prayerfully, but they were doing so alternately. I supposed
he must be leading her in some litany. I might have been
consumed with curiosity to know what she could have said
in the confessional to require such intimate attention from
her confessor, but I was too much occupied with devouring
her beauty.

How do I describe her? When we view a monument or an
edifice, any such work of art or architecture, we remark on
this and that element of it. Either the combination of details makes it handsome, or some particular detail is so
noteworthy as to redeem the whole from mediocrity. But
the human face is never viewed as an accretion of details.
It either strikes us immediately as beautiful in its entirety, or it does not. If we can say of a woman only that
"she has nicely arched eyebrows," then clearly we had to

look hard to see that, and the rest of her features are little worth remarking.

I can say that Ilaria had a fine and fair complexion and hair of a glowing auburn color, but many other Venetian women do, too. I can say that she had eyes so alive that they seemed to be lighted from within instead of reflecting the light without. That she had a chin one would want to cup in the palm of a hand. That she had what I have always thought of as "the Verona nose," because it is seen most often there—thin and pronounced, but shapely, like a sleek boat's fine prow, with the eyes deepset on either side.

I could praise her mouth especially. It was exquisitely shaped and gave promise of being soft if ever other lips should press upon it. But more than that. When Ilaria and the priest rose together after their orisons and genuflected, she curtsied again to him and said some few words in a soft voice. I do not recall what they were, but let me suppose that they were these: "I will join you behind the chantry, Father, after the compline." I do recall that she concluded by saying "Ciao," because that is the languid Venetian way of saying *schiavo,* "your slave," and I thought it an oddly familiar way of saying goodbye to a priest. But all that mattered then was the manner in which she spoke: "I will j-join you behind the ch-chantry, Father, after the compline. Ci-ciao." Each time she pouted her lips to form the *ch* or *j* sound, she stammered ever so slightly and thus prolonged the pout. It made her lips look ready and waiting for a kiss. It was delicious.

I instantly forgot that I was supposed to be petitioning for absolution of other misdeeds, and tried to follow her when she left the church. She could not possibly have been aware of my existence, but she departed from San Marco's in a way that almost seemed intended to discourage pursuit. Moving more swiftly and adroitly than I could have done even if chased by a sbiro, she flickered through the crowd in the atrium and vanished from my sight. Marveling, I went all the long way around the basilica's outside, then up and down all the arcades surrounding the vast piazza. Mystified, I several times crisscrossed the piazza itself, through clouds of pigeons—then the smaller piazzetta, from the bell tower down to the two pillars at the waterfront. Despairing, I returned to the great church and looked in every last chapel and the sanctuary and the

baptistery. Desolated, I even went up the stairs to the loggia where the golden horses stand. At last, heartbroken, I
went home.

After a tormented night, I went again the next day to
comb the church and its environs. I must have looked like
a wandering soul seeking solace. And the woman might
have been a wandering angel who had alighted only the
once; she was not to be found. So I made my mournful way
to the neighborhood of the boat people. The boys gave me a
cheery salute, and Doris gave me a glance of disdain.
When I responded with a forlorn sigh, Ubaldo was solicitous and asked what ailed me. I told him—I had lost my
heart to a lady and then lost my lady—and all the children
laughed, except Doris, who looked suddenly stricken.

"You have largazze on your mind these days," Ubaldo
said. "Do you intend to be the cock of every hen in the
world?"

"This is a full-grown woman, not a girl," I said. "And
she is too sublime even to be thought of as . . ."

"As a pota!" several of the boys chorused.

"Anyway," I said, in a bored drawl, "as regards the pota,
all women are alike." Man of the world, I had now seen a
grand total of two females in the nude.

"I do not know about that," one boy said ruminatively.
"I once heard a much-traveled mariner tell how to recognize a woman of the most utterly desirable bedworthiness."

"Tell us! Tell!" came the chorus.

"When she stands upright, with her legs pressed together, there should be a little, a tiny little triangle of daylight between her thighs and her artichoke."

"Does your lady show daylight?" someone asked me.

"I have seen her the once, and that was in church! Do
you suppose she was undressed in church?"

"Well, then, does Malgarita show daylight?"

I said, and so did several other boys, "I did not think to
look."

Malgarita giggled, and giggled again when her brother
said, "You could not have seen, anyway. Her bottom hangs
down too far behind, and her belly in front."

"Let us look at Doris!" someone shouted. "Olà, Doris!
Stand with your legs together and raise your skirt."

"Ask a real woman!" Malgarita sneered. "That one would not know whether to lay eggs or give milk."

Instead of lashing back with some retort, as I would have expected of her, Doris sobbed and ran away.

All the chaffering was amusing enough, and maybe even educational, but my concern was elsewhere. I said, "If I can find my lady again, and point her out to you fellows, perhaps you could manage to follow her better than I did, and tell me where she lives."

"No, grazie!" Ubaldo said firmly. "To molest a highborn lady is to gamble between the pillars."

Daniele snapped his fingers. "That reminds me. I heard that there is to be a frusta at the pillars this very afternoon. Some poor bastard who gambled and lost. Let us go and see it."

And so we did. A frusta is a public scourging and the pillars are those two I have mentioned, near the waterfront in Samarco's piazzetta. One of the columns is dedicated to my namesake saint and the other to Venice's earlier patron saint Teodoro, called Todaro here. All public punishments and executions of malefactors are carried out there—"between Marco and Todaro," as we say.

The centerpiece that day was a man we boys all knew, though we did not know his name. He was universally called only Il Zudìo, which means either the Jew or the usurer, or more commonly both. He resided in the burghèto set aside for his race, but the narrow shop in which he changed money and lent money was on the Mercerìa, where we boys lately did most of our thieving, and we had often seen him huddled at his counting table. He had hair and beard like a sort of curly red fungus going gray; he wore on his long coat the round yellow patch proclaiming him a Jew and the red hat that proclaimed him a Western Jew.

There were numerous others of his race in the crowd that afternoon, most in red hats, but some in the yellow head-wrappings signifying their Levantine origin. They would probably not have come of their own will to see a fellow Jew whipped and humiliated, for which reason Venetian law makes it mandatory for all adult male Jews to attend on such occasions. Of course, the crowd consisted mostly of non-Jews, gathered just for the sport, and an unusually high proportion were female.

The zudìo had been convicted of a fairly common offense—the gouging of excessive interest on some loan—but gossip had him guilty of more spicy intrigues. There was a widespread rumor that he, unlike any sensible Christian pawnbroker who dealt only in jewels and plate and other valuables, would take in pawn and lend good money for letters of mere paper, though they had to be letters of an indiscreet or compromising nature. Since so many Venetian women employed scribes to write for them letters of just that nature, or to read to them the letters of that nature which they received, perhaps the women wanted to look at the zudìo and speculate on whether he held incriminating copies of their correspondence. Or maybe, as so many women so often do, they simply wished to see a man flogged.

The usurer was accompanied to the flogging post by several uniformed gastaldi guards and his assigned comforter, a member of the lay Brotherhood of Justice. The brother, to remain anonymous in that degrading capacity of comforter to a Jew, wore a full gown and a hood over his head with eyeholes cut in it. A preco of the Quarantia stood where I had stood on the day before—high above the crowd on San Marco's loggia of the four horses—and read in a ringing voice:

"Inasmuch as the convict Mordecai Cartafilo has behaved very cruelly, against the peace of the State and the honor of the Republic and the virtue of its citizens . . . he is sentenced to endure thirteen vigorous strokes of the frusta, and thereafter to be confined in a pozzo of the Palace Prison while the Signori della Notte make inquiry of him into further particulars of his crimes. . . ."

The zudìo, when by custom he was asked if he had any complaint to make of the judgment, merely growled uncaringly, "Nè tibi nè catabi." The wretch may have shrugged coolly enough before he felt the scourge, but he did other things during the next several minutes. First he grunted, then he cried out, and then he howled. I glanced around at the crowd—the Christians were all nodding approvingly and the Jews were trying to look elsewhere—and my glance stopped at a certain face, and locked there, and I began sidling through the pack of people to get nearer to my lost lady found.

There came a shriek from behind me, and Ubaldo's voice

calling, "Olà, Marco, you are not listening to the music of the sinagòga!"

But I did not turn around. I was taking no chance of letting the woman slip from my sight this time. She was again unveiled, the better to watch the frusta, and again I feasted my eyes on her beauty. As I got closer I saw that she stood next to a tall man who wore a cloak with a hood closely drawn about his face; he was nearly as anonymous as the Brother of Justice at the flogging post. And when I stood very close I heard that man murmur to my lady, "Then it was you who spoke to the snout."

"The J-Jew deserved it," she said, the delicious pout lingering briefly on her lips.

He murmured, "A chicken before a tribunal of foxes."

She laughed lightly but without humor. "Would you have preferred that I let the ch-chicken go to the confessional, Father?"

I wondered if the lady was younger than she looked, that she addressed every man as father. But then I sneaked a look up into the man's hood, I being shorter than he was, and saw that it was the San Marco priest of the day before. Wondering why he should be going about with his vestments hidden, I listened some more, but their disjointed conversation gave me no hint.

He said, still in a murmurous voice, "You fixed on the wrong victim. The one who might talk, not the someone who might listen."

She laughed again and said archly, "You never speak the name of that someone."

"Then you speak it," he murmured. "To the snout. Give the foxes a goat instead of a chicken."

She shook her head. "That someone—that old goat—has friends among the foxes. I require a means even more secret than the snout."

He was silent for a time. Then he murmured, "Bravo."

I assumed that he was murmurously applauding the performance of the frusta, which, after one last loud and piercing screech, was just then ending. The crowd began to mill about in preparation for dispersal.

My lady said, "Yes, I will inquire into that possibility. But now"—she touched his cloaked arm—"that someone approaches."

He clasped the hood still closer about his face and moved

off with the crowd, away from her. She was joined by another man, this one gray-haired, red-faced, dressed in
clothes as fine as hers—perhaps her real father, I
thought—who said, "Ah, there you are, Ilaria. How did we
get separated?"

That was the first time I heard her name. She and the
older man strolled off together, she chattering brightly
about "how well the frusta was done, what a nice day for
it," and other such typically feminine remarks. I hung far
enough behind them not to be noticeable, but I followed as
if I were being tugged on a string. I feared that they would
walk only as far as the waterfront and there step into the
man's batèlo or gòndola. In that case I should have had a
hard time following them. Everyone in the crowd who did
not have a private craft was competing for the boats for
hire. But Ilaria and her companion turned the other way
and walked up the piazzetta toward the main piazza,
skirting the crowd by staying close to the wall of the
Doge's Palace.

Ilaria's rich robe flicked the very muzzles of the lionlike
marble masks which protrude from the palace wall at
waist level. Those are what we Venetians call the musi da
denonzie secrete, and there is one of them for each of several sorts of crime: smuggling, tax evasion, usury, conspiracy against the State, and so on. The snouts have slits for
mouths and on the other side of them, inside the palace,
the agents of the Quarantia squat like spiders waiting for
a web to twitch. They do not have to wait long between
alarms. Those marble slits have been worn ever wider and
smoother over the years, by the countless hands slipping
into them unsigned messages imputing crimes to enemies,
creditors, lovers, neighbors, blood relations and even total
strangers. Because the accusers remain unknown and can
accuse without proof, and because the law makes little al-
lowance for malice, slander, frustration and spite, it is the
accused who must disprove the accusations. That is not
easy, and it is seldom done.

The man and woman circled around two sides of the ar-
caded square, with me close enough behind to overhear
their desultory talk. Then they entered one of the houses
there on the piazza itself, and, from the demeanor of the
servant who opened the door, it was evident that they lived
there. Those houses of the innermost heart of the city are

not elaborately decorated on the outside, and so are not called palazzi. They are known as the "mute houses" because their outward simplicity says nothing about the wealth of their occupants, who comprise the oldest and noblest families of Venice. So I will be likewise mute about which house I followed Ilaria to, and not risk casting shame on that family name.

I learned two other things during that brief surveillance. From the bits of conversation, it became apparent even to my besotted self that the gray-haired man was not Ilaria's father but her husband. That caused me some hurt, but I salved it with the thought that a young woman with an old husband ought to be readily susceptible to the attentions of a younger man, like myself.

The other thing I overheard was their talk of the festa to be celebrated the next week, the Samarco dei Bòcoli. (I should have mentioned that the month was April, of which the twenty-fifth is the day of San Marco, and in Venice that day is always a feast of flowers and gaiety and masquerade dedicated to "San Marco of the Buds." This city loves feste, and it welcomes that day because it comes around each year when there has been no festa since Carnevale, perhaps two months agone.)

The man and woman spoke of the costumes they were having made, and the several balls to which they had been invited, and I felt another heart pang because those festivities would be held behind doors closed to me. But then Ilaria declared that she was also going to mingle in the outdoor torchlight promenades of that night. Her husband made some remonstrance, grumbling about the crowds and the crush to be endured "among the common herd," but Ilaria laughingly insisted, and my heart beat with hope and resolve again.

Directly they disappeared inside their casa muta, I ran to a shop I knew near the Rialto. Its front was hung with masks of cloth and wood and cartapesta, red and black and white and face-colored, in forms grotesque and comic and demonic and lifelike. I burst into the shop, shouting to the maskmaker, "Make me a mask for the Samarco festa! Make me a mask that will make me look handsome but old! Make me look more than twenty! But make me look well preserved and manly and gallant!"

6

So it was that, on the morning of that late-April festa day, I dressed in my best without having to be bidden to do so by any of the servants. I put on a cerise velvet doublet and lavender silk hose and my seldom worn red Còrdoba shoes, and over all a heavy wool cloak intended to disguise the slenderness of my figure. I hid my mask beneath the cloak, and left the house, and went to try my masquerade on the boat children. As I approached their barge, I took out and put on the mask. It had eyebrows and a dashing mustache made of real hair, and its face was the craggy, sun-browned visage of a mariner who had sailed far seas.

"Olà, Marco," said the boys. "Sana capàna."

"You *recognize* me? I look like *Marco?*"

"Hm. Now that you mention it . . .," said Daniele. "No, not much like the Marco we know. Who do you think he looks like, Boldo?"

Impatient, I said, "I do not look like a seafarer more than twenty years old?"

"Well . . .," said Ubaldo. "Sort of a *short* seafarer . . ."

"Ship's food is sometimes scanty," Daniele said helpfully. "It could have stunted your growth."

I was much annoyed. When Doris emerged from the barge and immediately said, "Olà, Marco," I wheeled to snarl at her. But what I saw gave me pause.

She too appeared to be in masquerade in honor of the day, She had washed her formerly nondescript hair, revealing it to be of a nice strawgold color. She had washed her face clean and powdered it attractively pale, as grown-up Venetian women do. She was also wearing womanly garb, a gown of brocade cut down and remade from one that had been my mother's. Doris spun around to make the skirts whirl, and said shyly, "Am I not as fine and beautiful as your lustrìsima lady love, Marco?"

Ubaldo muttered something about "all these dwarf ladies and gentlemen," but I only stared through the eyes of my mask.

Doris persisted, "Will you not walk out with me, Marco, on this day of festa?. . . What are you laughing at?"

"Your shoes."

"What?" she whispered, and her face fell.

49

"I laugh because no *lady* ever wore those awful wooden tofi."

She looked inexpressibly hurt, and retired again inside the barge. I loitered long enough for the boys to assure me—and make me half believe—that nobody would recognize me as a mere boy except those who already knew me to be a mere boy. Then I left them, and went to the piazza San Marco. It was far too early for any ordinary celebrants to be yet abroad, but the Dona Ilaria had not described her costume while I was eavesdropping. She might be as heavily disguised as I was, so to recognize her I had to be lurking outside her door when she departed for the first of her balls.

I might have attracted some unwelcome attention, idling about that one end of one arcade like a novice cutpurse of extreme stupidity, but fortunately I was not the only person in the piazza already strikingly attired. Under almost every arch, a costumed matacìn or a montimbanco was setting up his platform and, long before there was really enough of a crowd to play to, they were displaying their talents. I was glad, for they gave me something to look at besides the doorway of the casa muta.

The montimbanchi, swathed in robes like those of physicians or astrologers, but more extravagantly spangled with stars and moons and suns, did various conjuring tricks or cranked music from an ordegnogorgia to attract attention, and, when they had caught the eye of any passerby, began vociferously to hawk their simples—dried herbs and colored liquids and moon-milk mushrooms and the like. The matacìni, even more resplendent in gaudy face paint and costumes of checks and diamonds and patches, had nothing to peddle but their agility. So they bounded up and down on their platforms, and onto and off them, doing energetic acrobatics and sword dances, and they contorted themselves into fantastic convolutions, and they juggled balls and oranges and each other, and then, when they paused to take breath, they passed their hats around for coins.

As the day went on, more entertainers came and took up stands in the piazza, also the sellers of confèti and sweets and refreshing drinks, and more commonfolk strolled through, too, though not yet wearing their own festa finery. Those would congregate about a platform and watch

the tricks of a montimbanco or listen to a castròn singing
barcarole to lute accompaniment, and then, as soon as the
artist began passing his hat or peddling his wares, would
move on to another platform. Many of those people ambled
from one performer to another until they came to where I
lurked in my mask and cloak, and they would stand stol-
idly and ogle me and expect me to do something entertaining. It was slightly distressing, as I could do nothing but
sweat at them—the spring day had become most unseasonably warm—and try to look as if I were a servant posted
there, waiting patiently for my master.

The day wore on and on interminably, and I wished fervently that I had worn a lighter cloak, and I wished I could
kill every one of the million nasty pigeons in the piazza,
and I was grateful for every new diversion that came
along. The first citizens arriving in anything but everyday
raiment were the arti guilds wearing their ceremonial
clothes. The arte of physicans, barber-surgeons and apothecaries wore high conical hats and billowing robes. The
guild of painters and illuminators wore garments that
may have been of mere canvas, but were most fancifully
gold-leafed and colored over. The arte of tanners, curriers
and leatherworkers wore hide aprons with decorative designs not painted or sewn but branded onto them. . . .

When all the many guilds were assembled in the piazza,
there came from his palace the Doge Ranieri Zeno, and,
though his public costume was familiar enough to me and
everybody else, it was sufficiently lavish for any festive
day. He had the white scufieta on his head and the ermine
cape over his golden gown, the train of which was carried
by three servants clad in the ducal livery. Behind them
emerged the retinue of Council and Quarantia and other
nobles and officials, all likewise richly attired. And behind
them came a band of musicians, but they held their lutes
and pipes and rebecs silent while they moved with measured pace down to the waterfront. The Doge's forty-oared
buzino d'oro was just gliding up against the mole, and the
procession marched aboard. Not until the gleaming bark
was well out upon the water did the musicians begin to
play. They always wait like that, because they know how
the music gains a special sweetness when it skips across
the wavelets to us listeners on the land.

About the hour of compieta the twilight came down, and

the lampaderi moved about the piazza, setting alight the torch baskets bracketed above the arches, and I was still hovering within sight of the Lady Ilaria's door. I felt as if I had been there all my life, and I was getting faint with hunger—for I had not even gone as far from it as a fruit peddler's stand—but I was prepared to wait all the rest of my life if that should be necessary. At least by that hour I was not so conspicuous, for the square was well populated, and almost all the promenaders were in some kind of costume.

Some of them danced to the distant music of the Doge's band, some sang along with the warbling castròni, but most simply paraded about to show off their own regalia and admire that of others. The young people pelted each other with confèti, which are the little sprinkles of sweets and the eggshells filled with perfumed waters. The older girls carried oranges and waited to catch a glimpse of some favorite gallant at whom they could throw one. That custom is supposed to commemorate the wedding-gift orange of Jupiter and Juno, and a young man can boast himself an especially favored Jupiter if his Juno throws the orange hard enough to give him a black eye or knock out a tooth.

Then, as the twilight deepened, there came in from the sea the caligo, the briny mist that so often envelops Venice by night, and I began to be glad for my woolen cloak. In that fog, the hanging torches changed from iron baskets of curly flames into soft-edged globes of light magically suspended in space. The people in the piazza became merely darker and more coherent blobs of mist moving through the mist, except when they passed between me and one of the blurs of torchlight. Then they radiated extravagant spokes and wedges of shadow that flickered like black swordblades slashing at the gray fog. Only when some stroller passed quite near me did he or she briefly become solid, then in the next moment dissolve again. Like something out of a dream, an angel would take substance: a girl of tinsel and gauze and laughing eyes, and she would melt into something out of a nightmare: a Satan with varnished red face and horns.

Suddenly the door behind me opened and the gray fog was gashed by bright lamplight. I turned and saw two shadows against the dazzle, and they resolved themselves into my lady and her husband. Truly, if I had not been posted at the door, I could not have recognized either of them. He was totally transformed into one of the standard characters of masquerade, the comic physician, Dotòr Balanzòn. But Ilaria was so much changed that I could not immediately determine into what she was changed. A white and gold miter concealed her bronze hair, a brief dòmino mask hid her eyes, and layers of alb, chasuble, cope and stole made a dumpy dome shape of her fine figure. Then I realized that she was adórned as the long-ago female Pope Zuàna. Her costume must have cost a fortune, and I feared that it would cost her a heavy penance if any real cleric caught her dressed as that legendary lady Pope.

They crossed the square through the porridge of people, and themselves immediately entered into the festa spirit: she scattering confèti in the manner of a priest aspersing holy water, and he tossing them in the manner of a mèdego dispensing dosages. Their gòndola was waiting at the lagoon-side, and they stepped into it, and it pushed off toward the Grand Canal. After a moment's thought, I did not bother to hail a boat in which to follow them. The caligo was by then so thick that all the vessels on the water were moving with extreme caution, close to the banks. It was easier for me to keep my quarry in sight, and to pursue it, by trotting along the canalside streets and occasionally waiting on a bridge to see which canal it would take when the waterways diverged. I did a good deal of trotting that night, as Ilaria and her consort went from one grand palazzo and casa muta to another. But I did a lot more of waiting outside those places, in the company of only prowling cats, while my lady enjoyed the feste within.

I lurked in the salt-smelling fog, which was now so heavy that it collected and dripped from eaves and arches and the end of my mask's nose, and I listened to the muffled music from indoors and I imagined Ilaria dancing the furlàna. I leaned against slippery, streaming stone walls and I enviously eyed the windowpanes where the candlelight glowed through the murk. I sat on cold, wet bridge balustrades and heard my stomach growling and envisioned Ilaria daintily nibbling at scalete pastries and bignè buns. I stood and stamped my gradually numbing feet, and I again cursed my cloak as it weighed ever more heavy and dank and cold and dragged at my ankles. Notwithstanding my sodden misery, I perked up and tried to

look like an innocent merrymaker whenever other mas-
queraders loomed out of the caligo and shouted tipsy greetings at me—a cackling bufòn, a swaggering corsàro, three
boys capering in company as the three Ms: mèdego, musician and madman.

The city does not sound the coprifuoco on feste nights,
but, when we had arrived at the third or fourth palazzo of
that night and I was waiting soggily outside it, I heard all
the church bells ringing the compline. As if that had been
a signal, Ilaria slipped away from the ballroom and came
outdoors and came straight to where I crouched in an al-
cove of the house wall, my hood and cloak clasped close
about me. She was still in her papal vestments, but she
had taken off the dòmino.

She said softly, "Caro là," the greeting used only between lovers, and I was struck stiff as a statue. Her breath
smelled sweetly of bevarìn hazelnut liqueur when she
whispered to the folds of my hood, "The old goat is drunk
at last, and will not be ch-chasing after—*Dio me varda!
Who are you?*" And she shrank back from me.

"My name is Marco Polo," I said. "I have been following—"

"I am discovered!" she cried, so shrilly that I feared a
sbiro might hear. "You are his bravo!"

"No, no, my lady!" I stood up and threw back my hood.
Since my seafarer mask had so affrighted her, I slipped
that off, too. "I am nobody's but yours only!"

She backed farther away, her eyes wide in disbelief.
"You are a boy!"

I could not deny that, but I could qualify it. "Of a man's
experience," I said quickly. "I have loved you and sought
you since first I saw you."

Her eyes narrowed to examine me more closely. "What
are you doing here?"

"I was waiting," I babbled, "to put my heart at your feet
and my arm in your service and my destiny in your keeping."

She looked nervously about her. "I have page boys
enough. I do not wish to hire—"

"Not for hire!" I declared. "For love of my lady I shall
serve her forever!"

I may have hoped for a look of melting surrender. The
look she gave me conveyed more of exasperation. "But it is

the hour of compline," she said. "Where is—? I mean, have you seen no one else hereabout? Are you alone?"

"No, he is not," said another voice, a very quiet one.

I turned about and realized that a sword's point had been very near the back of my neck. It was just then withdrawing into the fog, and it glinted a gleam of cold, bedewed steel as it vanished beneath the cloak of its wielder. I had thought the voice was that of Ilaria's priest acquaintance, but priests do not carry swords. Before I or she could speak, the hooded figure murmured again:

"I see by your raiment tonight, my lady, that you are a mocker. So be it. Now is the mocker mocked. This young intruder desires to be a lady's bravo, and will serve for no hire but love. Let him, then, and let that be your penance for mockery."

Ilaria gasped and started to say, "Are you suggesting—?"

"I am absolving. You are already forgiven whatever must be done. And when the greater obstacle has been removed, a smaller one will be more easily dismissed."

With that, the shape in the fog moved farther back in the fog and blended into the fog and was gone. I had no idea what the stranger's words had meant, but I did perceive that he had spoken in my behalf, and I was grateful. I turned again to Ilaria, who was regarding me with a sort of rueful appraisal. She put one slim hand inside her robe and brought out the dòmino and raised it before her eyes as if to mask something there.

"Your name is . . . Marco?" I bowed my head and mumbled that it was. "You said you followed me. You know my house?" I mumbled yes. "Come there tomorrow, Marco. To the servants' door. At the hour of mezza-vespro. Do not fail me."

7

I DID not fail her, at least in the matter of promptness. The next afternoon, I presented myself as commanded, and the servants' door was opened by an ancient hag. The hag's little eyes were as mistrustful as if she knew every shameful thing about Venice, and she admitted me to the house as distastefully as if I had been one of the worst. She led me upstairs, along a hall, pointed a withered finger at the door, and left me. I knocked at the panel and the Dona Ilaria opened it. I stepped inside and she secured the latch behind me.

She bade me be seated, and then she walked up and down before my chair, regarding me speculatively. She wore a dress covered with gold-colored flakes that shimmered like a serpent's scales. It was a close-fitting dress and her walk was sinuous. The lady would have looked rather repitilian and dangerous, except that she kept wringing her hands the while, and thus betrayed her own uncertainty at our being alone together.

"I have been thinking about you ever since last night," she said. I started to echo that, wholeheartedly, but I could not make my voice work, and she went on. "You say you ch-choose to serve me, and there is indeed a service you could do. You say you would do it for love, and I confess that arouses my . . . my curiosity. But I think you are aware that I have a husband."

I swallowed loudly and said yes, I was aware.

"He is much older than I, and he is embittered by age. He is j-jealous of my youth and envious of all things youthful. He also has a violent temper. Clearly I cannot enlist the service of a—of a young man—not to mention enjoy the love of one. You understand? I might wish to, even yearn to, but I cannot, being a married woman."

I gave that some thought, then cleared my throat and said what seemed to be obvious, "An old husband will die and you will still be young."

"You do understand!" She stopped wringing her hands and clapped them, applauding. "You are quick of intellect for such a—such a young man." She cocked her head, the better to look admiringly at me. "So he must die. Yes?"

Dejectedly I stood up to go, supposing that we had

56

agreed that any yearned-for connection between us must simply wait until her bad-natured old husband was dead. I was not happy at that postponement, but, as Ilaria said, we both were young. We could restrain ourselves for a while.

Before I could turn to the door, though, she came and stood very close to me. She pressed herself against me, in fact, and looked down into my eyes and very softly inquired, "How will you do it?"

I gulped and said hoarsely, "How will I do what, my lady?"

She laughed a conspiratorial laugh. "You are discreet besides! But I think I will have to know, because it will require some prior planning to ensure that I am not. . . . However, that can wait. For now, pretend that I asked how you will—love me."

"With all my heart!" I said in a croak.

"Oh, with that, too, let us hope. But surely—do I shock you, Marco?—with some other part of you as well?" She laughed merrily at what must have been the expression on my face.

I made a strangled noise and coughed and said, "I have been taught by an experienced teacher. When you are free and we can make love, I will know how to do that. I assure you, my lady, I will not make a fool of myself."

She lifted her eyebrows and said, "Well! I have been wooed with promises of many different delights, but never quite that one." She studied me again, through eyelashes that were like talons reaching for my heart. "Show me, then, how you do not make a fool of yourself. I owe you at least an earnest payment for your service."

Ilaria raised her hands to her shoulders and somehow unfastened the top of her gold-serpent gown. It slipped down to her waist, and she undid the bustenca underneath, and let that drop to the floor, and I was gazing upon her breasts of milk and roses. I think I must have tried simultaneously to grab for her and to peel off my own clothes, for she gave a small shriek.

"Who was it taught you, boy? A goat? Come to the bed."

I tried to temper my boyish eagerness with manly decorum, but that was even more difficult when we were on the bed and both of us were totally unclad. Ilaria's body was mine to savor in every inviting detail, and even a stronger man than myself might have wished to abandon all re-

straint. Tinted of milk and roses, fragrant of milk and
roses, soft as milk and roses, her flesh was so beautifully
different from the gross meat of Malgarita and Zulià that
she might have been a woman of a new and superior race.
It was all I could do to keep from nibbling her to see if she
tasted as delectable as she looked and smelled and felt to
the touch.

I told her that, and she smiled and stretched languor-
ously and closed her eyes and suggested, "Nibble, then,
but g-gently. Do to me *all* the interesting things you have
learned."

I ran one tremulous finger along the length of her—from
the fringe of closed eyelashes down her shapely Verona
nose, across the pouted lips, down her chin and her satin
throat, over the mound of one-firm breast and its pert nipple, down her smoothly rounded belly to the feathering of
fine hair below—and she squirmed and mewed with pleasure. I remembered something that made me halt my tracing finger there. To demonstrate that I knew very well
how to do things, I told her with suave assurance, "I will
not play with your pota, in case you have to pee."

Her whole body jerked and her eyes flew open and she
exploded, *"Amoredèi!"* and she flailed angrily out from under my hand and well away from me.

She knelt at the far edge of the bed and stared as if I
were something that had just emerged from a crack in the
floor. After vibrating at me for a moment, she demanded,
"Who *was* it taught you, asenazzo?"

I, the ass, mumbled, "A girl of the boat people."

"Dio v'agiuta," she sighed. "Better a goat."

She lay down again, but on her side, with her head
propped on a hand so she could go on staring at me. "Now I
really am curious," she said. "Since I do not have to—
excuse myself—what do you do next?"

"Well," I said, disconcerted. "I put my. You know, my
candle. Into your uh. And move it. Back and forth. And,
well, that is it." A wondering and terrible silence ensued,
until I said uncomfortably, "Is it not?"

"Do you truly believe that is all there is to it? A melody
on one string?" She shook her head in slow marveling. I
began miserably to collect myself. "No, do not go away. Do
not move. Stay where you are and let me teach your properly. Now, to begin with . . ."

I was surprised, but pleasantly so, to learn that making
love should be rather like making music, and that "to begin with," both players should commence the playing so
far away from their main instruments—instead, using lips
and eyelashes and earlobes—and that the music could be
so enjoyable even in its pianìsimo beginning. The music
swelled to vivace when Ilaria introduced for instruments
her full breasts and softly rigid nipples, and teased and
coaxed me into using my tongue instead of fingers to pluck
the notes from them. At that pizzicato, she literally gave
voice and sang in accompaniment to the music.

In a brief interval between those choruses, she informed
me, in a voice gone whispery, "You have now heard the
hymn of the convent."

I also learned that a woman really does possess such a
thing as the lumaghèta of which I had heard, and that the
word is correct in both its meanings. The lumaghèta is indeed a thing somewhat resembling a small snail, but in
function it is more like the tuning key that a lutist employs. When Ilaria showed me, by doing it first herself,
how to manipulate the lumaghèta delicately and adroitly,
I could make her, like a veritable lute herself, hum and
twang and ring delightfully. She taught me how to do
other things, too, which she could not do to herself, and
which would never have occurred to my imagination. So at
one moment I would be twiddling my fingers as on the
frets of a viella, and the next I would be using my lips in
the manner of playing a dulzaina, and the next I would be
flutter-tonguing in the way a flutist blows his flute.

It was not until well along in that afternoon's diverti-
mento that Ilaria gave the cue for us to join our main instruments, and we played all'unisono, and the music rose
in crescendo to an unbelievable climax of tuti fortìsimi.
Then we kept on bringing it back up to that peak, again
and again, during most of the rest of the afternoon. Then
we played several codas, each a little more diminuendo,
until we were both fairly drained of music. Then we lay
quietly side by side, enjoying the waning tremolo after-
echoes . . . dolce, dolce . . . dolce . . .

When some time had passed, I thought to make gallant
inquiry: "Do you not want to jump around and sneeze?"

She gave a slight start, looked sideways at me, and muttered something I could not hear. Then she said, "No, grazie, I do not, Marco. I wish now to talk of my husband."

"Why darken the day?" I objected. "Let us rest a little longer and then see if we can play another tune."

"Oh, no! As long as I remain a married woman, I shall remain a ch-chaste one. We do not do this again until my husband is dead."

I had acquiesced when she earlier set that condition. But now I had sampled the ecstasy that awaited, and the thought of waiting was insupportable. I said, "Even though he is old, that might take years."

She gave me a look and said sharply, "Why should it? What means do you propose using?"

Bewildered, I said, "I?"

"Did you intend j-just to go on following him, as you did last night? Until perhaps you *annoy* him to death?"

The truth finally began to filter through my density. I said in awe, "Do you seriously mean he is to be killed?"

"I mean he is to be killed seriously," she said, with flat sarcasm. "What did you think we have been talking about, asenazzo, when we talked of your doing me a service?"

"I thought you meant . . . this." And I shyly touched her there.

"No more of that." She wriggled a little away from me. "And by the way, if you must use vulgar language, try at least to call that my mona. It sounds a *little* less awful than that other word."

"But am I never to touch your mona again?" I said wretchedly. "Not until I do that other service for you?"

"To the victor the spoils. I have enjoyed polishing your stilèto, Marco, but another bravo might offer me a sword."

"A bravo," I reflected. "Yes, such a deed would make me a real bravo, would it not?"

She said persuasively, "And I would much rather love a dashing bravo than a furtive despoiler of other men's wives."

"There is a sword in a closet at home," I muttered to myself. "It must have belonged to my father or one of his brothers. It is old, but it is kept honed and bright."

"You will never be blamed or even suspected. My husband must have many enemies, for what important man has not? And they will be of his own age and standing. No one would think to suspect a mere—I mean a younger man who has no discernible motive for taking his life. You have only to accost him in the dark, when he is alone, and make sure of your strike so he does not linger long enough to give any description—"

"No," I interrupted her. "Better if I could find him among a gathering of his peers, those who include his actual enemies. If in those circumstances I could do it unobserved . . . But no." I suddenly realized that I was contemplating murder. I concluded lamely, "That would probably be impossible."

"Not for a g-genuine bravo," Ilaria said, in the voice of a dove. "Not for one who will be rewarded so bounteously."

She moved against me again, and continued to move, tantalizing with the promise of that reward. This aroused in me several conflicting emotions, but my body recognized only one of them and raised a baton to play a fanfare of salute.

"No," said Ilaria, fending me off and becoming very businesslike. "A music maistra may give the first lesson free, to indicate what can be learned. But if you wish further lessons in more advanced execution, you must earn them."

She was clever, to send me away not completely satiated. As it was, I left the house—again by the servants' door—throbbing almost painfully and lusting as if I had not been satisfied at all. I was being led and directed, so to speak, by that baton of mine, and its inclination was to lead me back to Ilaria's bower, whatever that might require of me. Other events seemed also to be conspiring toward that end. When I came around from the back of the block of houses, I found the Samarco piazza full of people in a buzzing commotion, and a uniformed banditore was crying the news:

The Doge Ranieri Zeno had been stricken by a sudden seizure that afternoon in his palace chambers. The Doge was dead. The Council was being summoned to start voting for a successor to the ducal crown. The whole of Venice was bidden to observe a three-day period of mourning before the funeral of the Doge Zeno.

Well, I thought as I went on my way, if a great Doge can die, why cannot a lesser noble? And, it occurred to me, the funeral ceremonies would entail more than one assemblage of those lesser nobles all together. Among them

would be my lady's husband and undoubtedly, as she had
suggested, some of his enviers and enemies.

8

FOR the next three days, the late Doge Zeno lay in state in
his palace, being visited by respectful citizens during the
days and being watched over by the professional vigil-
keeper during the nights. I spent most of that time in my
room, practicing with the old but still worthy sword until I
became quite adept at slashing and stabbing phantom husbands. What I had the most trouble with was simply carrying the sword about, because it was nearly as long as my
leg. I could not just slip it naked under my belt or else,
when I walked, I might impale my own foot. To carry the
thing anywhere, I should have to carry it in its scabbard,
and that made it even more unwieldy. Also, for conceal-
ment of it, I should have to wear my all-enveloping long
cloak, which would not permit any quick draw-and-lunge.

Meanwhile, I made cunning plans. On the second day of
vigil, I wrote a note, most carefully drawing the characters
in my schoolboy hand: "Will he be at both the Funeral and
the Installation?" I regarded that critically, then under-
scored the *he* so that there should be no mistaking whom I
meant. I painstakingly drew my name underneath, so that
there should be no mistaking the note's author. Then I did
not entrust it to any servant, but carried it myself to the
casa muta, and waited for another interminable time until
I saw the *he* leave the house, dressed in dark mourning
clothes. I went around to the back door, gave the note to
the old hag doorkeeper, and told her I would wait for a reply.

After another while, she returned. She bore no reply but
beckoned me with a gnarled finger. Again I followed her to
Ilaria's suite of rooms, and found my lady studying the paper. She looked flustered, somehow, and neglected to give
me any fond greeting, saying only, "I can read, of course,
but I cannot make out your wretched writing. Read this to
me."

I did, and she said yes, her husband, like every other

member of the Venetian Grand Council, would be attending both the funeral rites for the late Doge and the installation ceremonies of the new one when he had been selected. "Why do you ask?"

"It gives me two opportunities," I said. "I shall try to—accomplish my service—on the funeral day. If that proves impossible, I will at least have a better idea of how to go about it at the next gathering of nobles."

She took the paper from me and looked at it. "I do not see my name on this."

"Naturally not," I said, the experienced conspirator. "I would not compromise a lustrìsima."

"Is your name on it?"

"Yes." I pointed with pride. "There. That is my name, my lady."

"I have learned that it is not always wise to commit things to paper." She folded and tucked the paper into her bodice. "I will keep this safe." I started to tell her just to tear it up, but she went on, sounding peevish, "I hope you realize that you were very foolish to come here unbidden."

"I waited to make certain *he* left."

"But if someone else—if one of his relatives or friends was here? Listen to me now. You are never to come here again until I summon you."

I smiled. "Until we are free of—"

"*Until I summon you.* Now go, and go quickly. I am expecting—I mean, *he* may come back any minute."

So I went home and practiced some more. And the next day, when at sundown the pompe funebri began, I was among the spectators. Even the least commoner's burial in Venice is always dignified by as much pageantry as his or her family can afford, so the Doge's was splendid indeed. The dead man lay not in a coffin but on an open litter, dressed in his finest robes of state, his stiff hands clasping his mace of office, his face fixed by the pomp-masters in an expression of serene sanctimony. The widowed Dogaressa stayed always beside it, so draped in veils that only her white hand was visible where it rested on her late husband's shoulder.

The litter was first laid on the roof of the Doge's great buzino d'oro, at the prow of which the gold-and-scarlet ducal flag hung at half staff. The bark was rowed with sol-

emn slowness—the forty oars seeming scarcely to move—
up and down the main canals of the city. Behind it and
around it were grouped black funeral gòndole and crape-
hung batèli and burchielli, bearing the members of the
Council and the Signoria and the Quarantia and the city's
chief priests and the confratèli of the arti guilds, the whole
retinue alternately singing hymns and chanting prayers.

When the dead man had been sufficiently paraded on
the waterways, his litter was lifted off the bark and onto
the shoulders of eight of his nobles. Because the corteggio
then had to wind up and down all the main streets of the
central city, and because so many of the pallbearers were
elderly, they changed places frequently with new men.
And the litter was again followed by the Dogaressa and all
the other court mourners, now on foot, and by bands of musicians playing doleful slow music, and contingents from
the flagellant brotherhoods lethargically pretending to
whip themselves, and finally by every other Venetian not
too young or old or crippled to walk.

I could do nothing during the water-borne procession except watch it from the banks with the rest of the citizens.
But by the time it came ashore, I decided that good fortune
was attending my scheme. For there also came in from the
water the twilight caligo again, and the obsequies became
even more melancholy and mysterious, shrouded by fog,
the music muffled and the chants lugubriously hollow.

Bracket torches were lighted along the route, and most
of the marchers took out and lighted candles. For a while I
walked among the common herd—or limped, rather, since
the sword along my left leg forced me to swing it stiffly—
and gradually eased myself to the forefront of that throng.
From there I could verify that almost every official
mourner was cloaked and hooded, except the priests. So
was I well covered, and in the thick mist I could be taken
for one of the guilds' artists or artisans. Even my size was
not conspicuous; the procession included numerous veiled
women no bigger than I was, and a few cowled dwarfs and
hunchbacks smaller than I was. So I edged my way imperceptibly among the court mourners, and ever farther forward, being challenged by nobody at all, until I was
separated from the litter and its pallbearers only by a rank
of priests yammering their ritual pimpirimpàra and
swinging censers to add smoke to the fog.

I was not the only inconspicuous marcher in the procession. What with everybody being so shrouded in cloth and in the almost equally woolly mist, I had a hard time picking out my quarry. But the street march was long enough that, by moving cautiously from side to side and peering sharply at the little of each man's profile that protruded beyond his cowl, I at last was able to perceive which was Ilaria's husband, and thereafter I kept my eye on him.

My chance came when the corteggio finally debouched from a narrow street onto the cobbled embankment of the city's north shore—on the Dead Lagoon, not far from where the boat children's barge lay, though that was invisible in the fog and the now near-dark. Alongside the embankment was the Doge's bark, which had circled the city to get ahead of us, waiting to ferry him on his last voyage—to the Isle of the Dead, also invisible far offshore. There was a milling of the mourners, as all the men nearest the litter tried to help its bearers hoist it aboard the bark, and that gave me the opportunity to mingle in with them. I elbowed until I was right beside my quarry, and in all the shoving and bustling no one remarked the struggle I had to make to unsheathe my sword. Fortunately, Ilaria's husband did not manage to get his shoulder under the litter—or the dispatching of him might have meant the Doge's getting dropped into the Dead Lagoon.

What did get dropped was my heavy scabbard; somehow my fumbling had unhooked it from my tunic belt. It clattered heavily onto the cobblestones and kept on noisily proclaiming itself as the many shuffling feet kicked it about. My heart bounded into my throat and then almost popped out of my mouth as Ilaria's husband bent down to pick up the scabbard. But he made no outcry; he handed it back to me with the kindly comment, "Here, young fellow, you dropped this." I was still right next to the man, and both of us were still being buffeted by the movement of the crowd around us, and my sword was in my hand beneath my cloak, and that was the moment to strike, but how could I? He had saved me from immediate discovery; could I stab him in return for the favor?

But then another voice spoke, hissing beside my ear, "You stupid asenazzo!" and something else made a rasping noise, and something metallic glinted in the torchlight. It happened at the edge of my vision, so my impressions were fragmentary and confused. But it appeared to me that one of the priests who had been swinging a golden censer had abruptly swung something silvery instead. And then Ilaria's husband leaned into my view, and opened his mouth and belched a substance that looked black in that light. I had done nothing to him, but *something* had happened to him. He tottered and jostled against the other men in the bunched group, and he and at least two others fell down. Then a heavy hand clutched at my shoulder, but I yanked away from it, and the recoil took me out of the center of the tumult. As I struggled through the outer fringe of people, and caromed off a couple of them, I again dropped my scabbard and then the sword as well, but I did not pause. I was in panic and I could think of nothing but to run fast and far. Behind me I heard exclamations of astonishment and outrage, but by then I was well away from the massed torch and candlelight and well away into the blessed darkness and fog.

I kept on running along the embankment until I saw two new figures taking form before me in the misty night. I might have shied away, but I saw they were children's figures and, after a moment, they resolved themselves into Ubaldo and Doris Tagiabue. I was ever so relieved to see someone familiar—and small. I tried to put on a glad face and probably put on a ghastly one, but I hailed them jollily:

"Doris, you are still scrubbed and clean!"

"You are not," she said, and pointed.

I looked down at myself. The front of my cloak was wet with more than a soaking of caligo. It was splotched and spattered with glistening red.

"And your face is as pale as a tombstone," said Ubaldo. "What happened, Marco?"

"I was . . . I was almost a bravo," I said, my voice gone suddenly unsteady. They stared at me, and I explained. It felt good to tell it to somebody unconcerned in the matter. "My lady sent me to slay a man. But I think he died before I could do it. Some other enemy must have intervened, or hired a bravo to do it."

Ubaldo exclaimed, "You *think* he died?"

"Everything happened all at once. I had to flee. I suppose I will not know what really happened until the banditori of the night watch cry the news."

"Where was this?"

"Back yonder, where the dead Doge is being put aboard his bark. Or maybe he is not yet. All is turmoil."

"I could go and see. I can tell you sooner than a banditore."

"Yes," I said. "But be careful, Boldo. They will be suspecting every stranger."

He ran off the way I had come, and Doris and I sat down on a waterside bollard. She regarded me gravely, and after a while said, "The man was the lady's husband." She did not frame it as a question, but I nodded numbly. "And you hope to take his place."

"I already have," I said, with as much of boastfulness as I could muster. Doris seemed to wince, so I added truthfully, "Once, anyway."

That one afternoon now seemed long in the past, and at the moment I felt no arousal of the urge to repeat it. Curious, I thought to myself, how anxiety can so diminish a man's ardor. Why, if I were in Ilaria's room right now, and she was naked and smiling and beckoning, I could not . . . .

"You may be in terrible trouble," said Doris, as if to shrivel my ardor utterly.

"I think not," I said, to convince myself rather than the girl. "I did nothing more criminal than to be where I did not belong. And I got away without being caught or recognized, so no one knows I did even that much. Except you, now."

"And what happens next?"

"If the man is dead, my lady will soon summon me to her grateful embrace. I will go slightly shamefaced, for I had hoped to go to her as a gallant bravo, the slayer of her oppressor." A thought came to me. "But now at least I can go to her with a clear conscience." The thought brought a little cheer with it.

"And if he is not dead?"

The cheer evaporated. I had not yet considered that eventuality. I said nothing, and sat trying to think what I might do—or might have to do.

"Perhaps then," Doris ventured in a very small voice, "you might take me instead of her for your smanza?"

I ground my teeth. "Why do you keep on making that ridiculous proposal? Especially now, when I have so many other problems to think about?"

"If you had accepted when I first offered, you would not now have so many problems."

That was either female or juvenile illogic, and palpably absurd, but there was just enough truth in it to make me respond with cruelty, "The Dona Ilaria is beautiful; you are not. She is a woman; you are a child. She merits the Dona to her name, and I also am of the Ene Aca. I could never take for my lady anyone not nobly born and—"

"She has not behaved very nobly. Neither have you."

But I careered on, "She is always clean and fragrant; you have only just discovered washing. She knows how to make love sublimely; you will never know more than the pig Malgarita—"

"If your lady knows how to fottere so well, then you must have learned, too, and you could teach me—"

"There you are! No lady would use a word like fottere! Ilaria calls it musicare."

"Then teach me to talk like a lady. Teach me to musicare like a lady."

"This is insupportable! With everything else on my mind, why am I sitting here arguing with an imbecile?" I stood up and said sternly, "Doris, you are supposed to be a good girl. Why do you keep offering not to be?"

"Because . . ." She bowed her head so that her fair hair fell like a casque around her face and hid her expression. "Because that is all I can offer."

"Olà, Marco!" called Ubaldo, solidifying out of the fog and coming up to us, panting from his run.

"What did you find out?"

"Let me tell you one thing, zenso. Be glad you are not the bravo who did that."

"Who did what, exactly?" I asked apprehensively.

"Killed the man. The man you spoke of. Yes, he is dead. They have the sword that did it."

"They do not!" I protested. "The sword they have must be mine, and there is no blood on it."

Ubaldo shrugged. "They found a weapon. They will assuredly find a sassìn. They will have to find somebody to blame, because of who it was he assassinated."

"Only Ilaria's husband—"

"The next Doge."

"*What?*"

"The same man. But for this, the banditori would have been proclaiming him Doge of Venice tomorrow. Sacro! That is what I overheard, and I heard it several times repeated. The Council had elected him to succeed the Serenità Zeno, and were only waiting until after the pompe funebri to make the announcement."

"Oh, Dio mio!" I would have said, but Doris said it for me.

"Now they must start the voting all over again. But not before they find the bravo who is guilty. This is not just another back-alley knifing. From the way they were talking, this is something that has never before occurred in the history of the Republic."

"Dio mio," Doris breathed again, then asked me, "What will you do now?"

After some thought, if my mind's perturbation could be called thinking, I said, "Perhaps I ought not go to my house. Can I sleep in a corner of your barge?"

9

So that is where I passed the night, on a pallet of smelly rags—but not in sleep; in staring, glaring wakefulness. When, at some small hour, Doris heard my restless tossing and came creeping to ask if I would like to be held and soothed, I simply snarled, and she crept away again. She and Ubaldo and all the other boat children were asleep when the dawn began to poke its fingers through the many cracks in the old barge hull, and I got up, leaving my blood-stained cloak, and slipped out into the morning.

The city was all fresh pink and amber in color, and every stone sparkled with dew left by the caligo. By contrast, I felt anything but sparkly, and an over-all drab brown in color, even to the inside of my mouth. I wandered aim-

lessly through the awakening streets, the turnings of my
path determined by my veering away from every other person out walking that early. But gradually the streets began to fill with people, too many for me to avoid them all,
and I heard the bells ringing the terza, the start of the
working day. So I let myself drift lagoonward, to the Riva
Ca' de Dio and into the warehouse of the Compagnia Polo.
I think I had some dim notion of asking the clerk Isidoro
Priuli if he could quickly and quietly arrange for me the
berth of cabin boy on some outbound vessel.

I trudged into his little counting room, so sunk in my
morosity that it took me a moment to notice that the room
was more than usually cramped and that Maistro Doro
was saying to a crowd of visitors, "I can only tell you that
he has not set foot in Venice in more than twenty years. I
repeat, the Messer Marco Polo has long lived in Constantinople and still lives there. If you refuse to believe me, here
is his nephew of the same name, who can vouch—"

I spun on my heel to go out again, having recognized the
crowd in the room as no more than two, but extremely
burly, uniformed gastaldi of the Quarantia. Before I could
escape, one of them growled, "Same name, eh? And look at
the guilty face on him!" and the other reached out to clamp
a massive hand around my upper arm.

Well, I was marched away, while the clerk and the warehouse men goggled. We had no great distance to go, but it
seemed the longest of all the journeys I have ever made. I
struggled feebly in the iron grip of the gastaldi and, more
like a bimbo than a bravo, pleaded tearfully to know of
what I was accused, but the stolid bailiffs never replied. As
we tramped along the Riva, through crowds of passersby
also goggling, my mind was a tumult of questions: Was
there a reward? Who turned me in? Did Doris or Ubaldo
somehow send word? We crossed over the Bridge of the
Straw, but did not continue as far as the piazzetta entrance
to the Doge's Palace. At the Gate of the Wheat, we turned
in to the Torresella, which stands adjacent to the palace
and is the last remainder of what was in ancient times a
fortified castle. It is now officially the State Prison of Venice, but its inmates have another name for it. The prison is
called by the name our ancestors called the fiery pit before
Christianity taught them to call it Hell. The prison is
called Vulcano.

From the bright pink and amber morning outside, I found myself suddenly thrust into an orbà, which might not sound like much unless you know that it means "blinded." An orbà is a cell just big enough to contain one man. It is a stone box, totally unfurnished and absolutely without any opening for light or air. I stood in a darkness unrelieved, suffocatingly close, foul with stench. The floor was thick with some gluey mess that sucked at my feet when I moved them, so I did not even try to sit down, and the walls were spongy with some slime that seemed to crawl when I touched it, so I did not even lean; when I tired of standing, I squatted. And I shook with an ague as I slowly comprehended the full horror of where I was and what had become of me. I, Marco Polo, son of the Ene Aca house of Polo, bearer of a name inscribed in the Libro d'Oro—so recently a free man, a carefree youth, free to wander where I would in the whole wide world—I was in *prison*, disgraced, despised, shut up in a box that no rat would willingly inhabit. Oh, how I wept!

I do not know how long I stayed in that blind cell. It was at least the remainder of that day, and it may have been two or three days, for, although I tried hard to control my fright-churned bowels, I several times contributed to the mess on the floor. When finally a guard came to let me out, I assumed I had been freed as innocent, and I exulted. Even had I been guilty of killing the Doge-elect, I was sure I had suffered punishment enough for it, and had felt enough remorse and sworn enough repentance. But of course my exultation was dashed when the guard told me that I had endured only the first and probably least of my punishments—that the orbà is only the temporary cell where a prisoner is held until time for his preliminary examination.

So I was brought before the tribunal called the Gentlemen of the Night. In an upstairs room of the Vulcano, I was stood in front of a long table behind which sat eight grave and elderly men in black gowns. I was not positioned too close to their table, and the guard on either side of me did not stand too close to me, for I must have smelled as terrible as I felt. If I also looked as terrible, I must have appeared the very portrait of a low and brutish criminal.

The Signori della Notte began by taking turns at asking me some innocuous questions: my name, my age, my resi-

dence, particulars of my family history and the like. Then
one of them, referring to a paper before him, told me,
"Many other questions must be asked before we can determine on a bill of indictment. But that interrogation will be
postponed until you have been assigned a Brother of Justice to act as your advocate, for you have been denounced
as the perpetrator of a crime which is capitally punishable. . . ."

Denounced! I was so stunned that I missed most of the
man's subsequent words. The denouncer had to be either
Doris or Ubaldo, for only they knew that I had even been
near the murdered man. But how could either of them
have done it so quickly? And who did they get to write for
them the denunciation to be slid into one of the snouts?

The gentleman concluded his speech by asking, "Have
you any comment to make on these most serious charges?"

I cleared my throat and said hesitantly, "Who—who denounced me, Messere?" It was an inane thing to ask, since
I could not reasonably expect an answer, but it was the
question uppermost in my mind. And much to my surprise,
the examiner did answer:

"You denounced yourself, young Messere." I must have
blinked at him stupidly, for he added, "Did you not write
this?" and read from a piece of paper: "Will *he* be at both
the Funeral and the Installation?" I am sure I blinked at
him stupidly, for he added, "It is signed Marco Polo."

Walking like a sleepwalker, I was taken by my guards
down the stairs again, and then down another flight of
stairs into what they called the wells, the deepest part of
the Vulcano. Even that, they told me, was not the real dungeon of the prison; I could look forward, when I had been
properly convicted, to being shifted into the Dark Gardens
reserved for the keeping of condemned men until their execution. Laughing coarsely, they opened a thick but only
knee-high wooden door in the stone wall, pushed me down
and shoved me through it, and gave the door a slam like
the knell of Doomsday.

This cell was at least considerably larger than the orbà
and had at least a hole in the low door. The hole was too
small to permit me to shake a fist through it at the departing jailers, but it did admit a trace of air and enough
light to keep the cell from being utterly dark. When my
eyes had adjusted to the murk, I could see that the cell was

furnished with a lidded pail for a pissòta and two bare
plank shelves for beds. I could see nothing else except what
looked like a tumbled heap of bedclothes in one corner.
However, when I approached it, the heap heaved and stood
up and was a man.

"Salamelèch," he said hoarsely. The greeting sounded
foreign. I squinted at him and recognized the red-gray,
fungoid hair and beard. It was the zudìo whose public
scourging I had witnessed on a day memorable for much
else.

10

"MORDECAI," he introduced himself. "Mordecai Cartafilo." And he asked the question that all prisoners ask
each other at first meeting: "What are you in for?"

"Murder," I said with a sniffle. "And I think treason and
lesa-maestà and a few other things."

"Murder will suffice," he said drily. "Not to worry lad.
They will overlook those trifling other things. You cannot
be punished for them once you have been punished for
murder. That would be what is called double jeopardy, and
that is forbidden by the law of the land."

I gave him a sour look. "You are jesting, old man."

He shrugged. "One lightens the dark as best one can."

We sat gloomy in the gloom for a while. Then I said,
"You are in here for usury, are you not?"

"I am not. I am in here because a certain lady *accused*
me of usury."

"That is a coincidence. I am also in here—at least indirectly—because of a lady."

"Well, I only said lady to indicate the gender. She is
really"—he spat on the floor—"a shèquesa kàrove."

"I do not understand your foreign words."

"A gentile putana cagna," he said, as if still spitting.
"She begged a loan from me and pledged some love letters
as security. When she could not pay, and I would not return the letters, she made sure I would not deliver them to
anyone else."

I shook my head sympathetically. "Yours is a sad case,

but mine is more ironic. My lady begged a service from me and pledged herself as reward. The deed was done, but not by me. Nevertheless here I am, rather differently rewarded, but my lady probably does not even know of it yet. Is that not ironic?"

"Hilarious."

"Yes, Ilaria! Do you know the lady?"

"What?" He glared at me. "Your kàrove is named Ilaria, too?"

I glared at him. "How dare you call my lady a putana cagna?"

Then we ceased glaring at each other, and we sat down on the bed shelves and began comparing experiences, and alas, it became evident that we had both known the same Dona Ilaria. I told old Cartafilo my whole adventure, concluding:

"But you mentioned love letters. I never sent her any."

He said, "I am sorry to be the one to tell you. They were not signed with your name."

"Then she was in love with someone else all the time?"

"So it would seem."

I muttered, "She seduced me only so I would play the bravo for her. I have been nothing but a dupe. I have been exceptionally stupid."

"So it would seem."

"And the one message that I did sign—the one the Signori now have—*she* must have slipped it into the snout. But why should she do that to me?"

"She has no further use for her bravo. Her husband is dead, her lover is available, you are but an encumbrance to be shed."

"But I did not kill her husband!"

"So who did? Probably the lover. Do you expect her to denounce him, when she can offer you up instead and thereby keep him safe?" I had no answer to that. After a moment he asked, "Did you ever hear of the lamia?"

"Lamia? It means a witch."

"Not exactly. The lamia can take the form of a very *young* witch, and very beautiful. She does that to entice young men to fall in love with her. When she has snared one, she makes love to him so voluptuously and industriously that he gets quite exhausted. And when he is limp and helpless, she eats him alive. It is only a myth, of course, but a curiously pervasive and persistent myth. I have encountered it in every country I have visited around the Mediterranean Sea. And I have traveled much. It is strange, how so many different peoples believe in the bloodthirstiness of beauty."

I considered that, and said, "She did smile while she watched you flogged, old man."

"I am not surprised. She will probably reach the very height of venereal excitement when she watches you go to the Meatmaker."

"To the what?"

"That is what we old prison veterans call the executioner—the Meatmaker."

I cried, distraught, "But I cannot be executed! I am innocent! I am of the Ene Aca! I should not even be shut up with a Jew!"

"Oh, excuse me, your lordship. It is that the bad light in here has dimmed my eyesight. I took you for a common prisoner in the pozzi of the Vulcano."

"I am not *common!*"

"Excuse me again," he said, and reached a hand across the space between our bed shelves. He plucked something off my tunic and regarded it closely. "Only a flea. A common flea." He popped it between his fingernails. "It appeared as common as my own."

I grumbled, "There is nothing wrong with your eyesight."

"If you really are a noble, young Marco, you must do what all the noble prisoners do. Agitate for a better cell, a private one, with a window over the street or the water. Then you can let down a string, and send messages, or haul of delicacies of food. That is not supposed to be allowed, but in the case of nobility the rules are winked at."

"You make it sound as if I will be here for a long time."

"No." He sighed. "Probably not long."

The import of that remark made my hair prickle. "I keep telling you, old fool. *I am innocent!*"

And that made him reply, just as loudly and indignantly, "Why tell me, unhappy mamzar? Tell it to the Signori della Notte! I am innocent, too, but here I sit and here I will rot!"

"Wait! I have an idea," I said. "We are both here because of the Lady Ilaria's wiles and lies. If together we tell

that to the Signori, they ought to wonder about her verac-
ity."

Mordecai shook his head doubtfully. "Whom would they
believe? She is the widow of an almost Doge. You are an accused murderer and I am a convicted usurer."

"You may be right," I said, dispirited. "It is unfortunate
that you are a Jew."

He fixed me with a not at all dim eye and said, "People
are forever telling me that. Why do you?"

"Oh . . . only that the testimony of a Jew is naturally
suspect."

"So I have frequently noticed. I wonder why."

"Well . . . you did kill our Lord Jesus. . . ."

He snorted and said, "I, indeed!" As if disgusted with
me, he turned his back and stretched out on his shelf and
drew his voluminous robe about him. He muttered to the
wall, "I only spoke to the man . . . only two words . . ." and
then apparently went to sleep.

When a long and dismal time had passed, and the door
hole had darkened, the door was noisily unlocked and two
guards crawled in dragging a large vat. Old Cartafilo
stopped snoring and sat up eagerly. The guards gave him
and me each a wooden shingle, onto which they spooned
from the vat a lukewarm, glutinous glob. Then they left for
us a feeble lamp, a bowl of fish oil in which a scrap of rag
burned with much smoke and little light, and they went
away and slammed the door. I looked dubiously at the food.

"Polenta gruel," Mordecai told me, avidly scooping his
up with two fingers. "A holòsh, but you had better eat it.
Only meal of the day. You will get nothing else."

"I am not hungry," I said. "You may have mine."

He almost snatched it, and ate both portions with much
lip smacking. When he had done, he sat and sucked his
teeth as if unwilling to miss a particle, and peered at me
from under his fungus eyebrows, and finally said:

"What would you ordinarily be eating for supper?"

"Oh . . . perhaps a platter of tagiadèle with persuto . . .
and a zabagiòn to drink . . ."

"Bongusto," he said sardonically. "I cannot pretend to
tempt such a refined taste, but perhaps you would like
some of these." He rummaged inside his robe. "The tolerant Venetian laws allow me some religious observance,
even in prison." I could not see how that accounted for the

square white crackers he brought out and handed to me. But I ate them gratefully, though they were almost tasteless, and I thanked him.

By the next day's suppertime, I was hungry enough not to be fastidious. I would probably have eaten the prison gruel just because it meant a break in the monotony of doing nothing but sitting, and sleeping on the coverless hard bench, and walking the two or three steps the cell permitted, and occasionally making conversation with Cartafilo. But that is how the days went on, each of them marked off only by the lightening and darkening of the door hole, and the old zudìo's praying three times a day, and the evening arrival of the horrid food.

Perhaps it was not such a dreadful experience for Mordecai since, to the best of my knowledge, he had spent all of his prior days huddled in his cell-like money shop on the Mercerìa, and this could not be a much different confinement. But I had been free and untrammeled and convivial; being immured in the Vulcano was like being buried alive. I realized that I ought to be grateful for having some company in my untimely grave, even if it was only a Jew, and even if his conversation was not always buoyant. One day I mentioned to him that I had seen several sorts of punishment administered at the pillars of Marco and Todaro, but never an execution.

He said, "That is because most of them are done here inside the walls, so that not even the other prisoners are aware of them until they are over. The condemned man is put into one of the cells of the Giardini Foschi, so called, and those cells have barred windows. The Meatmaker waits outside the cell, and waits patiently, until the man inside, moving about, moves before that window and with his back to it. Then the Meatmaker whips a garrotta through the bars and around the man's throat, so that either his neck snaps or he strangles to death. The Dark Gardens are on the canal side of this building, and there is a removable stone slab in the corridor there. In the night, the victim's body is slid through that secret hole and into a waiting boat, and it is conveyed to the Sepoltùra Pùblica. Not until it is all finished is the execution announced. Far less fuss that way. Venice does not care to have it widely known that the old Roman lege de tagiòn is still so often exercised here. So the *public* executions are few. They are inflicted only on those convicted of really heinous crimes."

"Crimes like what?" I asked.

"In my time, one man has died so for having raped a nun, and another for having told a foreigner some of the secrets of the Murano art of glassworking. I daresay the murder of a Doge-elect will rank with those, if that is what you are wondering."

I swallowed. "What is—how is it done—in public?"

"The culprit kneels between the pillars and is beheaded by the Meatmaker. But before that, the Meatmaker has cut off whatever part of him was guilty of crime. The nun raper, of course, had his gid amputated. The glassworker had his tongue cut out. And the condemned man marches to the pillars with the guilty piece of him suspended from a string around his neck. In your case, I suppose it will be only your hand."

"And only my head," I said thickly.

"Try not to laugh," said Mordecai.

"Laugh?!" I cried in anguish—and then I did laugh, his words were so preposterous. "You are jesting again, old man."

He shrugged. "One does what one can."

One day, the monotony of my confinement was interrupted. The door was unlocked to let a stranger come stooping in. He was a fairly young man who wore not a uniform but the gown of the Brotherhood of Justice, and he introduced himself to me as Fratello Ugo.

"Already," he said briskly, "you owe a considerable casermagio of room and board in this State Prison. If you are poor, you are entitled to the assistance of the Brotherhood. It will pay your casermagio for as long as you are incarcerated. I am a licensed advocate, and I will represent you to the best of my ability. I will also carry messages to and from the outside, and procure some few small comforts—salt for your meals, oil for your lamp, things like that. I can also arrange for you"—he glanced over at old Cartafilo and sniffed slightly—"a private cell."

I said, "I doubt that I would be any less unhappy elsewhere, Fra Ugo. I will stay in this one."

"As you wish," he said. "Now I have been in communication with the house of Polo, of which it seems you are the titular head, albeit still a minor. If you prefer, you can well afford to pay the prison casermagio, and also to hire an advocate of your own choice. You have only to write out the necessary pagherì and authorize the company to pay them."

I said uncertainly, "That would be a public humiliation to the company. And I do not know if I have any right to squander the company's funds. . . ."

"On a lost cause," he finished for me, nodding in agreement. "I quite understand."

Alarmed, I started to remonstrate, "I did not mean—that is, I would hope. . . ."

"The alternative is to accept the help of the Brotherhood of Justice. For its reimbursement, the Brotherhood is then allowed to send upon the streets two beggars, asking alms of the citizens for pity of the wretched Marco P—"

"Amoredèi!" I exclaimed. "That would be infinitely more humiliating!"

"You do not have to decide your choice this instant. Let us discuss your case instead. How do you intend to plead?"

"Plead?" I said, indignant. "I shall not plead, I shall protest! I am innocent!"

Brother Ugo looked over at the Jew again, and distastefully, as if he suspected that I had already been receiving counsel. Mordecai only pulled a face of skeptical amusement.

I went on, "For my first witness I shall call the Dona Ilaria. When she is compelled to tell of our—"

"She will not be called," the Brother interrupted. "The Signori della Notte would not allow it. That lady has been recently bereaved and is still prostrate with grief."

I scoffed, "Are you trying to tell me that she grieves for her husband?"

"Well. . .," he said, with deliberation. "If not that, you can be sure that she exhibits some extreme emotion because she is not now the Dogaressa of Venice."

Old Cartafilo made a noise like a smothered snicker. Maybe I made a noise, too—of dismay—for that aspect of the situation had not before occurred to me. Ilaria must be seething with disappointment and frustration and anger. When she sought her husband's removal, she had not dreamed of the honor he was about to be accorded, and she with him. So now she would be inclined to forget her own involvement; she would be consumed with a desire to exact revenge for her forfeited title. It would not matter on *whom* she vented her rage, and who was an easier target than myself?"

"If you are innocent, young Messer Marco," said Ugo, "who did murder the man?"

I said, "I think it was a priest."

Brother Ugo gave me a long look, then rapped on the cell door for a guard to let him out. As the door creaked open at his knee level, he said to me, "I suggest that you do choose to hire some other advocate. If you intend to accuse a reverend father, and your prime witness is a woman bent on vendèta, you will need the best legal talent there is in the Republic. Ciao."

When he had gone, I said to Mordecai, "Everyone takes it for granted that I am doomed, whether I am guilty *or not.* Surely there must be some law to safeguard the innocent against unjust conviction."

"Oh, almost surely. But there is an old saying: the laws of Venice are supremely fair and they are sedulously obeyed . . . for a week. Do not let your hopes get too high."

"I would have more hope if I had more help," I said. "And you could help us both. Let the Brother Ugo have those letters you hold, and let him show them in evidence. They would at least cast a shadow of suspicion on the lady and her lover."

He gazed at me with his blackberry eyes and scratched reflectively in his fungus beard, and said, "You think that would be the Christian thing to do?"

"Why . . . yes. To save my life, to set you free. I see nothing *un*Christian about it."

"Then I am sorry that I adhere to a different morality, for I cannot do it. I did not do that to save myself from the frusta, and I will not do it for both of us."

I stared, unbelieving. "Why in the world not?"

"My trade is founded on trust. I am the only moneylender who takes such documents in pawn. I can do that only if I trust my clients to repay their loans and the accrued interest. The clients pledge such papers only because they can trust me to keep their contents inviolable. Do you think women would otherwise hand over *love letters?*"

"But I told you, old man, no human being trusts a Jew. Look how the Lady Ilaria repaid you with treachery. Is

that not proof enough that she thought you untrust-
worthy?"

"It is proof of something, yes," he said wryly. "But if
even once I should fail my trust, even on the most dire
provocation, I must abandon my chosen trade. Not because
others would think me contemptible, but because *I*
would."

"What trade, you old fool? You may be in here the rest of
your life! You said so yourself. You cannot conduct any—"

"I can conduct myself according to my conscience. It may
be small comfort, but it is my only comfort. To sit here and
scratch my flea and bedbug bites, and see my once prosperously fat flesh shrinking gaunt, and feel myself superior to
the Christian morality that put me here."

I snarled, "You could preen yourself just as well *outside*—"

"Zito! Enough! The instruction of fools is folly. We will
not speak of it further. Look here on the floor, my boy, here
are two large spiders. Let us race them against each other
and wager incalculable fortunes on the outcome. You may
choose which spider will be yours. . . ."

11

MORE time passed, in dismalness, and then Brother Ugo
came again, stooping in through the low door. I waited
glumly for him to say something as disheartening as he
had the other time, but what he said was astounding:

"Your father and his brother have returned to Venice!"

"What?" I gasped, unable to comprehend. "You mean
their bodies have been returned? For burial in their native
land?"

"I mean they are here! Alive and well!"

"Alive? After almost ten years of silence?"

"Yes! All their acquaintances are as amazed as you are.
The entire community of merchants is talking of nothing
else. It is said that they bear an embassy from Far Tartary
to the Pope at Rome. But by good fortune—*your* good fortune, young Messer Marco—they came home to Venice before going to Rome."

"Why my good fortune?" I said shakily.

"Could they have come at a more opportune time? They are even now petitioning the Quarantia for permission to visit you, which is not normally allowed to anyone but a prisoner's advocate. It may just be that your father and uncle can influence some lenity in your case. If nothing else, their presence at your trial ought to give you some moral support. And some stiffness to your spine when you walk to the pillars."

On that equivocal note, he departed again. Mordecai and I sat talking with animated speculation far into the night, even after the coprifuoco had rung and a guard growled through the door hole for us to extinguish the dim light of our rag lamp.

Another four or five days had to pass, fretful ones for me, but then the door creaked open and a man came in, a man so burly he had to struggle through it. Inside the cell he stood up, and he seemed to keep on standing up, so tall was he. I had no least recollection of being related to a man so immense. He was as hairy as he was big, with tousled black locks and a bristling blue-black beard. He looked down at me from his intimidating great height, and his voice was disdainful when he boomed loudly:

"Well! If this is not pure merda with a piecrust on it!"

I said meekly, "Benvegnùo, caro pare."

"I am not your dear father, young toad! I am your uncle Mafìo."

"Benvegnùo, caro zio. Is not my father coming?"

"No. We could get permission for only one visitor. And he should rightly be secluded in mourning for your mother."

"Oh. Yes."

"In truth, however, he is busy courting his next wife."

That rocked me on my heels. "What? How could he do such a thing?"

"Who are you to sound disapproving, you disreputable scagaròn? The poor man comes back from abroad to find his wife long buried, her maid-servant disappeared, a valuable slave lost, his friend the Doge dead—and his son, the hope of the family, in prison charged with the foulest murder in Venetian history!" So loudly that everybody in the Vulcano must have heard, he bellowed, "Tell me the truth! Did you do the deed?"

"No, my lord uncle," I said, quailing. "But what has all that to do with a new wife?"

My uncle said more quietly, with a snort of deprecation, "Your father is an uxorious man. For some reason, he likes being married."

"He chose an odd way to demonstrate it to my mother," I said. "Going away and staying as he did."

"And he will be going away again," said Uncle Mafìo. "That is why he must have someone with good sense to leave in charge of the family interests. He has not time to wait for another son. Another wife will have to do."

"Why another anything?" I said hotly. "He *has* a son!"

My uncle did not reply to that with words. He merely looked me up and down, with scathing eyes, and then let his gaze roam around the constricted, dim, fetid cell.

Again abashed, I said, "I had hoped he could get me out of here."

"No, you must get yourself out," said my uncle, and my heart sank. But he continued to look about the room and said, as if thinking aloud, "Of all the kinds of disaster that can befall a city, Venice has always most feared the risk of a great fire. It would be especially fearsome if it threatened the Doge's Palace and the civic treasures contained in it, or the Basilica of San Marco and its even more irreplaceable treasures. Since that palace is next door to this prison on one side, and that church adjoining on the other side, the guards here in the Vulcano used to take particular precautions—I imagine they do still—that any smallest lamp flame in these cells is carefully monitored."

"Why, yes, they—"

"Shut up. They do that because if in the nighttime such a lamp were to set fire to, say, these wooden bed planks there would be urgent outcry and much running about with pails of water. A prisoner would have to be let out of his burning cell so the fire could be extinguished. And then, if, in the smoke and turmoil, that prisoner could get as far as the corridor of the Giardini Foschi on the canal side of the prison, he might think to slide away the moveable stone panel in the wall there, which leads to the outside. And if he contrived to do that, say, tomorrow night, he would probably find a batèlo idling about on the water immediately below."

Mafìo finally brought his eyes around to me again. I was

too busy contemplating the possibilities to say anything, but old Mordecai spoke up unbidden:

"That has been done before. And because of that, there is now a law that any prisoner attempting such an arson—no matter how trivial his original offense—will be himself condemned to burn. And from that sentence there is no appeal."

Uncle Mafio said sardonically, "Thank you, Matùsalem." To me he said, "Well, you have just heard one more good reason to make not a try but a success of it." He kicked at the door to summon the guard. "Until tomorrow night, nephew."

I lay awake most of that night. It was not that the escape required much planning; I simply lay awake to enjoy the prospect of being free again. And old Cartafilo roused up suddenly out of an apparently sound sleep to say:

"I hope your family know what they are doing. Another law is that a prisoner's closest relation is responsible for his behavior. A father for a son—khas vesholem—a husband for a female prisoner, a master for a slave. If a prisoner does escape by arson, that one responsible for him will be burned instead."

"My uncle does not appear to be a man much concerned about laws," I said, rather proudly, "or even much afraid of burning. But Mordecai, I cannot do it without your participation. We must make the break together. What say you?"

He was silent for a while, then he mumbled, "I daresay burning is preferable to a slow death from the pettechie, the prison disease. And I long ago outlived every last one of my relations."

So the next night came, and when the coprifuoco tolled and the guards commanded us to put out our lamp, we only shaded its light with the pissòta pail. When the guards had gone by, I spilled most of the fish oil from the lamp onto my bed planks. Mordecai contributed his outer robe—it was quite green with mold and mildew and would make the blaze smokier—and we bundled that under my bed and lighted it from the lamp's rag wick. In just moments the cell was clouded black and the wood had begun to flicker with flames. Mordecai and I fanned our arms to help the smoke out through the door hole, and clamored loudly, "Fuoco! Al fuoco!" and heard running feet in the corridor.

Then, as my uncle had predicted, there was commotion and confusion, and Mordecai and I were ordered out of the cell so the men with water buckets could crawl in. Smoke billowed out with us, and the guards shoved us out of their way. There was quite a number of them in the passage, but they paid us little heed. So, aided by the concealing smoke and darkness, we sneaked farther down the corridor and around a bend in it. "Now this way!" said Mordecai, and he set off at a speed remarkable for a man of his age. He had been in the prison long enough to have learned its passages, and he led me this way and that, until we glimpsed light at the end of one long hall. He stopped there at a corner, peered around it and waved me on. We turned into a shorter corridor furnished with two or three wall lamps, but otherwise empty.

Mordecai knelt, motioned for me to help, and I saw that one large square stone in the bottom of the wall had iron grips bolted to it. Mordecai seized one, I the other, and we heaved and the stone came away, revealing itself to be shallower than the others around it. Wonderfully fresh air, damp and smelling of salt, swept in through the opening. I stood up straight to take a gratefully deep inhalation, and in the next instant I was knocked down. A guard had sprung from somewhere and was shouting for help.

There was a moment of even more confusion than before. The guard threw himself upon me and we thrashed about on the stone floor, while Mordecai crouched by the hole and regarded us with open mouth and wide eyes. I found myself briefly on top of the guard, and took advantage of it. I knelt so that he had my full weight on his chest and my knees pinned his arms to the floor. I clamped both hands over his loudly flapping mouth, turned to Mordecai and gasped, "I cannot hold—for long."

"Here, lad," he said. "Let me do that."

"No. One can escape. You go." I heard more running feet somewhere in the corridors. "Hurry!"

Mordecai stuck his feet out through the hole, then turned to ask, "Why me?"

Between grapplings and thrashings, I got out a few last words in spurts, "You gave—my choice—of spiders. Get out!"

Mordecai gave me a wondering look, and he said slowly, "The reward of a mitzva is another mitzva," and he slid

out through the opening and vanished. I heard a distant
splash out there beyond the dark hole, and then I was overwhelmed.

I was roughly manhandled along the passages and literally thrown into a new cell. I mean another very ancient
cell, of course, but a different one. It had only a bed shelf
for furniture, and no door hole and not so much as a candle
stub for light. I sat there in the darkness, my bruises aching, and reviewed my situation. In attempting the escape,
I had forfeited all hope of ever proving my innocence of the
earlier charge. In failing to escape, I had doomed myself to
burn. I had just one reason to be thankful: I now had a private cell. I had no cellmate to watch me weep.

Since the guards, for a considerable while thereafter,
spitefully refrained from feeding me even the awful prison
gruel, and the darkness and monotony were unrelieved, I
have no idea how long I was alone in the cell before a visitor was admitted. It was the Brother of Justice again.

I said, "I assume that my uncle's permission to visit has
been revoked."

"I doubt that he would willingly come," said Brother
Ugo. "I understand he became quite irate and profane
when he saw that the nephew he hauled from the water
had turned into an elderly Jew."

"And, since there is no further need for your advocacy,"
I said resignedly, "I assume you have come only in the
guise of prisoner's comforter."

"At any rate, I bring news you should find comforting.
The Council this morning elected a new Doge."

"Ah, yes. They were postponing the election until they
had the sassìn of Doge Zeno. And they have me. Why
should you think I find that comforting?"

"Perhaps you forget that your father and uncle are
members of that Council. And since their miraculous return from their long absence, they are quite the most popular members of the community of merchants. Therefore, in
the election, they could exert noticeable influence on the
votes of all the merchant nobles. A man named Lorenzo
Tiepolo was eager to become Doge, and in return for the
merchants' bloc of votes, he was prepared to make certain
commitments to your father and uncle."

"Such as what?" I asked, not daring to hope.

"It is traditional that a new Doge, on his accession, proclaims some amnesties. The Serenità Tiepolo is going to forgive your felonious commission of arson, which permitted the escape of one Mordecai Cartafilo from this prison."

"So I do not burn as an arsonist," I said. "I merely lose my hand and my head as a murderer."

"No, you do not. You are right that the sassìn has been captured, but you are wrong about its being you. Another man has confessed to the sassinàda."

Fortunately the cell was small or I should have fallen down. But I only reeled and slumped against the wall.

The Brother went on, at an infuriatingly slow pace. "I told you I brought news of comfort. You have more advocates than you know, and they have all been busy in your behalf. That zudìo you freed, he did not just keep on running, or take ship to some distant land. He did not even hide in the warrens of the Jews' burghèto. Instead, he went to visit a priest—not a rabìno, a real Christian priest—one of the under-priests of the San Marco Basilica itself."

I said, "I tried to tell you about that priest."

"Well, it seems the priest had been the Lady Ilaria's secret lover, but she turned bitter toward him when she so nearly became our Dogaressa and then did not. When she put away the priest from her affections, he became remorseful of having done such a vile deed as murder, and to no profitable end. Of course, he might still have kept silent, and kept the matter between himself and God. But then Mordecai Cartafilo called on him. It seems the Jew spoke of some papers he holds in pawn. He did not even show them, he had only to mention them, and that was enough to turn the priest's secret remorse into open repentance. He went to his superiors and made full confession, waiving the privilege of the confessional. So he is now under house arrest in his canònica chambers. The Dona Ilaria is also confined to her house, as an accomplice in the crime."

"What happens next?"

"All must await the new Doge's taking office. Lorenzo Tiepolo will not wish the very start of his Dogato made notorious, for this case now involves rather more prominent persons than just a boy playing bravo. The lady widow of the murdered Doge-elect, a priest of San Marco . . . well, the Doge Tiepolo will do everything possible to minify the scandal. He will probably allow the priest to be tried in camera by an ecclesiastical court, instead of the Quarantia. My guess is that the priest will be exiled to some remote parish in the Vèneto mainland. And the Doge will probably command the Lady Ilaria to take the veil in some remote nunnery. There is precedent for such procedure. A hundred or so years ago, in France, there was a similar situation involving a priest and a lady."

"And what happens to me?"

"As soon as the Doge dons the white scufieta, he proclaims his amnesties, and yours will be among them. You will be pardoned of the arson, and you have already been acquitted of the sassinàda. You will be released from prison."

"Free!" I breathed.

"Well, perhaps a trifle more free than you might wish."

"What?"

"I said the Doge will arrange that this whole sordid affair be soon forgotten. If he simply turned you loose in Venice, you would be an ever present reminder of it. Your amnesty is conditional upon your banishment. You are outcast. You are to leave Venice forever."

During the subsequent days that I remained in the cell, I reflected on all that had come to pass. It was hurtful to think of leaving Venice, la serenìsima, la clarìsima. But that was better than dying in the piazzetta or staying in the Vulcano, which provided neither serenity nor brightness. I could even feel sorry for the priest who had struck the bravo's blow in my stead. As a young curate in the Basilica, he had doubtless looked forward to high advancement in the Church, which he could never hope for in backwoods exile. And Ilaria would endure an even more pitiable exile, her beauty and talents to be forever useless to her now. But maybe not; she had managed to lavish them rather prodigally when she was a married woman; she might also manage to enjoy them as a bride of Christ. She would at least have ample opportunity to sing the hymn of the nuns, as she had called it. All in all, compared to our victim's irrevocable fate, we three had got off lightly.

I was released from the prison even less ceremoniously than I had been bundled into it. The guards unlocked my

cell door, led me along the corridors and down stairs and
through other doors, unlocking the final one to let me out
into the courtyard. There I had only to walk through the
Gate of the Wheat onto the sunlit lagoonside Riva, and I
was as free as the countless wheeling sea gulls. It was a
good feeling, but I would have felt even better if I had been
able to clean myself and don fresh raiment before emerging. I had been unwashed and clad in the same clothes all
this time, and I stank of fish oil, smoke and pissòta efflu-
vium. My garments were torn, from my struggle on the
night of the aborted escape, and what was left of them was
dirty and rumpled. Also, in those days I was just sprouting
my first down of beard; it may not have been very visible,
but it added to my feeling of scruffiness. I could have
wished for better circumstances in which to meet my father for the first time in my memory. He and my uncle
Mafìo were waiting on the Riva, both dressed in the elegant robes they had probably worn, as members of the
Council, at the new Doge's accession.

"Behold your son!" bellowed my uncle. "Your arcistupendonazzìsimo son! Behold the namesake of our brother
and our patron saint! Is this not a wretched and puny
meschìn, to have caused so much ado?"

"Father?" I said timorously to the other man.

"My boy?" he said, almost as hesitantly, but opening his
arms.

I had expected someone even more overwhelming than
my uncle, since my father was the elder of the two. But he
was actually pale alongside his brother; not nearly so big
and burly, and much softer of voice. Like my uncle, he
wore a journeyer's beard, but his was neatly trimmed. His
beard and hair were not of a fearsome raven black, but a
decorous mouse color, like my own hair.

"My son. My poor orphan boy," said my father. He embraced me, but quickly put me away at arm's length, and
said worriedly, "Do you always smell like that?"

"No, Father. I have been locked up for—"

"You forget, Nico, that this is a bravo and a bonvivàn
and a gambler between the pillars," boomed my uncle. "A
champion of ill-married matrons, a lurker in the night, a
wielder of the sword, a liberator of Jews!"

"Ah, well," said my father indulgently. "A chick must

stretch his wings farther than the nest. Come, let us go home."

12

THE house servants were all moving with more alacrity and more cheerful demeanor than they had shown since my mother died. They even seemed glad to see me home again. The maid hastened to heat water when I asked, and Maistro Attilio, at my polite request, lent me his razor. I bathed several times over, inexpertly scraped the fuzz off my face, dressed in clean tunic and hose, and joined my father and uncle in the main room, where the tile stove was.

"Now," I said, "I want to hear about your travels. All about everywhere you have been."

"Dear God, not again," Uncle Mafìo groaned. "We have been let talk of nothing else."

"Time enough for that later, Marco," said my father. "All things in their time. Let us speak now of your own adventures."

"They are over now," I said hastily. "I would rather hear of new things."

But they would not relent. So I told them, fully and frankly, everything that had happened since my first glimpse of Ilaria in San Marco's—only omitting the amatory afternoon she and I had spent together. Thus I made it seem that mere mooncalf chivalry had impelled me to make my calamitous try at bravura.

When I was done, my father sighed. "Any woman could give pointers to the devil. Ah, well, you did what seemed best to you. And he who does all he can, does much. But the consequences have been tragic indeed. I had to agree to the Doge's stipulation that you leave Venice, my son. He could, however, have been much harder on you."

"I know," I said contritely. "Where shall I go, Father? Should I go seeking a Land of Cockaigne?"

"Mafìo and I have business in Rome. You will go with us."

"Do I spend the rest of my life in Rome, then? The sentence was banishment forever."

My uncle said what old Mordecai had said, "The laws of Venice are obeyed . . . for a week. A Doge's forever is a Doge's lifetime. When Tiepolo dies, his successor will hardly prevent your returning. Still, that could be a good while from now."

My father said, "Your uncle and I are bearing to Rome a letter from the Khakhan of Kithai—"

I had never heard either of those harsh-sounding words before, and I interrupted to say so.

"The Khan of All Khans of the Mongols," my father explained. "You may have heard him titled the Great Khan of what is here miscalled Cathay."

I stared at him. "You met the Mongols? And you survived?"

"Met and made friends among them. The most powerful friend possible—the Khan Kubilai, who rules the world's widest empire. He asked us to carry a request to Pope Clement. . . ."

He went on explaining, but I was not hearing. I was still staring at him in awe and admiration, and thinking—this was my father, whom I had believed long dead, and this very ordinary-looking man claimed to be a confidant of barbarian Khans and holy Popes!

He concluded, ". . . And then, if the Pope lends us the hundred priests requested by Kubilai, we will lead them east. We will go again to Kithai."

"When do we depart for Rome?" I asked.

My father said bashfully, "Well . . ."

"After your father marries your new mother," said my uncle. "And that must wait for the proclamation of the bandi."

"Oh, I think not, Mafìo," said my father. "Since Fiordelisa and I are hardly youngsters, both of us widowed, Pare Nunziata will probably dispense with all three cryings of the bandi."

"Who is Fiordelisa?" I asked. "And is this not rather abrupt, Father?"

"You know her," he said. "Fiordelisa Trevan, mistress of the house three doors down the canal."

"Yes. She is a nice woman. She was Mother's best friend among all our neighbors."

"If you are implying what I think you are, Marco, I remind you that your mother is in her grave, where there is no jealousy or envy or recrimination."

"Yes," I said. And I added impertinently, "But you are not wearing the luto vedovile."

"Your mother has been *eight years* in her grave. I should wear black now, and for another twelvemonth? I am not young enough to sequester myself in mourning for a year. Neither is the Dona Lisa any bambina."

"Have you proposed to her yet, Father?"

"Yes, and she has accepted. We go tomorrow for our pastoral interview with Pare Nunziata."

"Is she aware that you are going away immediately after you marry her?"

My uncle burst out, "What is this inquisition, you saputèlo?"

My father said patiently, "I am marrying her, Marco, *because* I am going away. Needs must when the devil drives. I came home expecting to find your mother still alive and head of the house of Polo. She is not. And now—through your own fault—I cannot leave you entrusted with the business. Old Doro is a good man, and needs no one peering over his shoulder. Nevertheless, I prefer to have someone of the name of Polo standing as the figurehead of the company, if nothing more. Dona Fiordelisa will serve in that capacity, and willingly. Also, she has no children to compete for your inheritance, if that is what concerns you."

"It does not," I said. And again I spoke impertinently, "I am only concerned for the seeming disrespect to my own mother—and to the Dona Trevan as well—in your haste to marry solely for mercenary reasons. She must know that all Venice will be whispering and snickering."

My father said mildly, but with finality, "I am a merchant and she is the widow of a merchant and Venice is a merchant city, where all know that there is no better reason for doing *anything* than a mercenary reason. To a Venetian, money is the second blood, and you are a Venetian. Now, I have heard your objections, Marco, and I have dismissed them. I wish to hear no more. Remember, a closed mouth says nothing wrong."

So I kept my mouth closed and said nothing more on the subject, wrong or otherwise, and on the day my father married the Dona Lisa I stood in the confino church of San

Felice with my uncle and all the free servants of both households and numerous neighbors and merchant nobles and their families, while the ancient Pare Nunziata tremblingly conducted the nuptial mass. But when the ceremony was over and the Pare pronounced them Messere e Madona and it was time for my father to lead his bride to her new dwelling, together with all the reception guests, I slipped away from the happy procession.

Although I was dressed in my best, I let my feet take me to the neighborhood of the boat people. I had only infrequently and briefly visited the children since my release from prison. Now that I was an ex-convict, the boys all seemed to regard me as a grown man, or maybe even a person of celebrity; anyway, there had come a sort of distance between us that had not existed before. However, on that day I found no one at the barge except Doris. She was kneeling on the planking inside its hull, wearing only a skimpy shift, and lifting wet wads of cloth from one pail to another.

"Boldo and the others begged a ride on a garbage scow going out to Torcello," she told me. "They will be gone all day, so I am taking the opportunity to wash everything not being worn by somebody."

"May I keep you company?" I asked. "And sleep here again in the barge tonight?"

"Your clothes will also need laundering, if you do," she said, eyeing them critically.

"I have had worse accommodations," I said. "And I own other clothes."

"What are you running away from this time, Marco?"

"This is my father's wedding day. He is bringing home a marègna for me, and I do not particularly want one. I have already had a real mother."

"I must have had one, too, but I would not mind having a marègna." She added, sighing like an exasperated grown woman, "Sometimes I feel I *am* one, to all this crowd of orphans."

"This Dona Fiordelisa is a nice enough woman," I said, sitting down with my back against the hull. "But I somehow do not wish to be under the same roof on my father's wedding night."

Doris looked at me with evident surmise, dropped what she was doing, and came to sit beside me.

"Very well," she whispered into my ear. "Stay here. And pretend that it is your own wedding night."

"Oh, Doris, are you starting that again?"

"I do not know why you should refuse. I am accustomed now to keeping myself clean, as you told me a lady ought to do. I keep myself clean all over. Look."

Before I could protest, she stripped off her one garment in one lithe movement. She was certainly clean, even to being totally hairless of body. The Lady Ilaria had not been quite so smooth and glossy all over. Of course, Doris was also lacking in feminine curves and rotundities. Her breasts were only just beginning to be distinct from her chest, and their nipples were only a faintly darker pink than her skin, and her flanks and buttocks were but lightly padded with womanly flesh.

"You are still a zuzzurullona," I said, trying to sound bored and uninterested. "You have a long way to go to become a woman."

That was true, but her very youth and smallness and immaturity had their own sort of appeal. Though all boys are lecherous, they usually lust for real women. Any girl of their own age, they tend to regard as only another playmate, a tomboy among the boys, a zuzzurullona. However, I was somewhat more advanced in that respect than most boys; I had already had the experience of a real woman. It had given me a taste for musical duets—and I had for some time been without that music—and here was a pretty novice pleading to be introduced to it.

"It would be dishonorable of me," I said, "even to pretend a wedding night." I was arguing with myself more than with her. "I have told you that I am going far away to Rome in a few days."

"So is your father. But it has not prevented his getting *really* married."

"True, and we quarreled about that. I did not think it right. But his new wife seems perfectly content."

"And so would I be. For now, let us pretend, Marco, and afterward I will wait, and you will come back. You said so—when there is another change of Doge."

"You look ridiculous, little Doris. Sitting here naked and talking of Doges and such." But she did not look ridiculous; she looked like one of the pert nymphs of old legend.

I truly tried to argue. "Your brother always talks of what a good girl his sister—"

"Boldo will not be back until tonight, and he will know nothing of what happens between now and then."

"He would be furious," I went on, as if she had not interrupted. "We should have to fight again, the way we fought after he threw that fish so long ago."

Doris pouted. "You do not appreciate my generosity. It is a pleasure I offer you at the cost of pain to myself."

"Pain? How so?"

"The first time is always painful for a virgin. And unsatisfying. Every girl knows that. Every woman tells us so."

I said reflectively, "I do not know why it should be painful. Not if it is done the way my—" I decided it would be maladroit of me to mention my Lady Ilaria at this moment. "I mean, the way I have learned to do it."

"If that is true," said Doris, "you could earn the adoration of many virgins in your lifetime. Do show me this way you have learned."

"One begins by doing—certain preliminary things. Like this." I touched one of her diminutive nipples.

"The zizza? That only tickles."

"I believe the tickling changes to another sensation very soon."

Very soon she said, "Yes. You are right."

"The zizza likes it, too. See, it lifts to ask for more."

"Yes. Yes, it does." She slowly lay back, supine on the deck, and I followed her down.

I said, "A zizza likes even more to be kissed."

"Yes." Like a lazing cat, she stretched her whole little body, voluptuously.

"Then there is this," I said.

"That tickles, too."

"It also gets better than tickling."

"Yes. Truly it does. I feel . . ."

"Not pained, surely."

She shook her head, her eyes now closed.

"These things do not even require the presence of a man. It is called the hymn of the convent, because girls can do this for themselves." I was being scrupulously fair, giving her the opportunity to send me away.

But she said only, and breathlessly, "I had no idea . . . I do not even know what I *look* like down there."

"You could easily see your mona with a looking glass."

She said faintly, "I do not know anyone who owns a looking glass."

"Then look at—no, she is all hairy down there. Yours is still bare and visible and soft. And pretty. It looks like . . ." I reached for a poetic comparison. "You know that kind of pasta shaped like a folded little shell? The kind called ladylips?"

"You make it feel like lips being kissed," she said, as if talking in her sleep. Her eyes were closed again and her small body was moving in a slow squirm.

"Kissed, yes," I said.

From the slow squirm, her body seemed to clench briefly, then to relax, and she made a whimpering noise of delight. As I continued to play musically upon her, she made that slight convulsion again and again, each time lasting longer, as if she was learning through practice to prolong the enjoyment. Not ceasing my attentions to her, but using only my mouth, I had my hands free to strip off my own clothes. When I was naked against her, she appeared to enjoy her gentle spasms all the more, and her hands fluttered eagerly over my body. So I went on for quite a while, making the music of the convent, as Ilaria had taught me. When finally Doris was shiny with perspiration, I stopped and let her rest.

Her breathing slowed from its rapid pace, and she opened her eyes, looking dazed. Then she frowned, because she felt me hard against her, and she shamelessly moved a hand to take hold of me, and she said with surprise, "You did all that . . . or you made me do all that . . . and you never . . ."

"No, not yet."

"I did not know." She laughed in great good humor. "I could not have known. I was far away. In the clouds somewhere." Still holding me in one hand, she felt herself with the other. "All that . . . and I am still a virgin. It is miraculous. Do you suppose, Marco, that is how Our Blessed Virgin Lady—?"

"We are already sinning, Doris," I said quickly. "Let us not add blasphemy."

"No. Let us sin some more."

And we did, and I soon had Doris cooing and quivering again—in the clouds somewhere, as she had said—enjoying the hymn of the nuns. And finally I did what no nun can do, and that happened not roughly or forcibly, but easily and naturally. Doris, sleek with perspiration, moved without friction in my arms, and that part of her was even more moist. So she felt no violation, but only a more intense sensation among the many new ones she had been experiencing. She opened her eyes when that happened, and her eyes were brimming with pleasure, and the whimper she gave was merely in a different musical register from the previous ones.

It was a new sensatio for me, too. Inside Doris, I was held as tightly as in a tender fist, far more tightly than I had been in either of the other two females with whom I had lain. Even in that moment of high excitement, I realized that I was disproving my onetime ignorant assertion that all women are alike in their private parts.

For the next while, both Doris and I made many different noises. And the final sound, when we stopped moving to rest, was her sigh of commingled wonder and satisfaction: "Oh, my!"

"I think it was not painful," I said, and smiled at her.

She shook her head vehemently, and returned the smile. "I have dreamt of it many times. But I never dreamed it would be so . . . And I never heard any woman recall her first time as so . . . Thank you, Marco."

"I thank you, Doris," I said politely. "And now that you know how—"

"Hush. I do not wish to do anything like that with anyone but you."

"I will soon be gone."

"I know. But I know you will be back. And I will not do that again until you come back from Rome."

However, I did not get to Rome. I have never been there yet. Doris and I went on disporting ourselves until nightfall, and we were dressed again and behaving most properly when Ubaldo and Daniele and Malgarita and the others returned from their day's excursion. When we retired into the barge to sleep, I slept alone, on the same pallet of rags I had used once before. And we were all awakened in the morning by the bawling of a banditore, making unusually early rounds because he had unusual

news to cry. Pope Clement IV had died in Viterbo. The
Doge of Venice was proclaiming a period of mourning and
of prayer for the Holy Father's soul.

"Damnation!" bellowed my uncle, slapping the table
and making the books on it jump. "Did we bring bad luck
home with us, Nico?"

"First a Doge dies, and now the Pope," my father said
sadly. "Ah, well, all psalms end in glory."

"And the word from Viterbo," said the clerk Isidoro, in
whose counting room we were gathered, "is that there may
be a long deadlock in the Conclave. It seems there are
many feet twitching with eagerness to step into the Fisherman's shoes."

"We cannot wait for the election, soon or late," my uncle
muttered, and he glowered at me. "We must get this
galeotto out of Venice, or we may all go to prison."

"We need not wait," my father said, unperturbed. "Doro
has most capably purchased and collected all the travel
gear we will need. We only lack the hundred priests, and
Kubilai will not care if they are not chosen by a Pope. Any
high prelate can provide them."

"To what prelate do we apply?" demanded Mafìo. "If we
asked the Patriarch of Venice, he would tell us—and with
reason—that to lend us one hundred priests would empty
every church in the city."

"And we would have to take them the extra distance,"
my father mused. "Better we seek them closer to our destination."

"Forgive my ignorance," said my new marègna, Fiordelisa. "But why on earth are you recruiting priests—and so
many priests—for a savage Mongol warlord? Surely he
cannot be a Christian."

My father said, "He is of no discernible religion, Lisa."

"I would have thought not."

"But he has that virtue peculiar to the ungodly: he is tolerant of what other people choose to believe. Indeed, he
wishes his subjects to have an ample array of beliefs from
which to choose. There are in his lands many preachers of
many pagan religions, but of the Christian faith there are
only the deluded and debased Nestorian priests. Kubilai
desires that we provide adequate representation for the
true Christian Church of Rome. Naturally, Mafìo and I are
eager to comply—and not alone for the propagation of the

Holy Faith. If we can accomplish this mission, we can ask the Khan's permission to engage in missions more profitable."

"Nico means to say," my uncle said, "that we hope to arrange to trade between Venice and the Eastern lands—to start again the flow of commerce along the Silk Road."

Lisa said wonderingly, "There is a road laid of silk?"

"Would that it were!" said my uncle, rolling his eyes. "It is more tortuous and terrible and punishing than any pathway to Heaven. Even to call it a road is an extravagance."

Isidoro begged leave to explain to the lady: "The route from the Levantine shores across the interior of Asia has been called the Silk Road since ancient times, because the silk of Cathay was the most costly merchandise carried along it. In those days, silk was worth its weight in gold. And perhaps the road itself, being so precious, was better maintained and easier to travel. But in more recent times it fell into disuse—partly because the secret of silkmaking was stolen from Cathay, and today silk is cultivated even in Sicily. But also those Eastern lands became impossible to traverse, what with the depredations of Huns, Tartars, Mongols, marauding back and forth across Asia. So our Western traders abandoned the overland route in favor of the sea routes known to the Arab seafarers."

"If you can get there by sea," Lisa said to my father, "why suffer all the rigors and dangers of going by land?"

He said, "Those sea routes are forbidden to our ships. The once pacific Arabs, long content to live meekly in the peace of their Prophet, rose up to become the warrior Saracens, who now seek to impose that religion of Islam on the entire world. And they are as jealous of their sea lanes as they are of their current possession of the Holy Land."

Mafìo said, "The Saracens are willing to trade with us Venetians, and with any other Christians from whom they can make a profit. But we would deprive them of that profit if we sent fleets of our own ships to trade in the East. So the Saracen corsairs are on constant patrol in the seas between, to make sure we do not."

Lisa looked primly shocked, and said, "They are our enemies, but we trade with them?"

Isidoro shrugged, "Business is business."

"Even the Popes," said Uncle Mafìo, "have never been

unwilling to deal with the heathen, when it has been profitable. And a Pope or any other pragmatist ought to be
eager to institute trade with the even farther East. There
are fortunes to be made. We know; we have seen the richness of those lands. Our former journey was mere explora-
tion, but this time we will take along something to trade.
The Silk Road is awful, but it is not impossible. We have
now traversed those lands twice, going and coming. We
can do it again."

"Whoever is the new Pope," said my father, "he should
give his blessing to this venture. Rome was much affrighted when it looked as if the Mongols would overrun
Europe. But the several Mongol Khans seem to have extended their Khanates as far westward as they intend to
encroach. That means the Saracens are the chief threat to
Christianity. So Rome ought to welcome this chance for an
alliance with the Mongols against Islam. Our mission on
behalf of the Khan of All Khans could be of supreme
importance—to the aims of Mother Church as well as the
prosperity of Venice."

"And the house of Polo," said Fiordelisa, who was now of
our house.

"That above all," said Mafìo. "So let us stop beating our
beaks, Nico, and get on with it. Shall we go again by way of
Constantinople and collect our priests there?"

My father thought it over and said, "No. The priests
there are too comfortable—all gone soft as eunuchs. The
gloved cat catches no mice. However, in the ranks of the
Crusaders are many chaplain priests, and they will be
hard men accustomed to hard living. Let us go to the Holy
Land, to San Zuàne de Acre, where the Crusaders are presently encamped. Doro, is there a ship sailing eastward that
can put us in Acre?"

The clerk turned to consult his registers, and I left the
warehouse to go and tell Doris of my new destination and
to say, to her and to Venice, goodbye.

It was to be a quarter of a century before I saw either of
them again. Much would have changed and aged in that
time, not least myself. But Venice would still be Venice,
and—strangely—so would Doris somehow still be the Doris
I had left. What she had said: that she would not love again
until I came back—those words could have been a magic
charm that preserved her unchanged by the years. For she

would still, that long time later, be so young and so pretty and so vibrantly still Doris that I would recognize her on sight and fall instantly enamored of her. Or so it would seem to me.

But that story I will tell in its place.

THE LEVANT

1

At the hour of vespro on a day of blue and gold, we departed from the basin of Malamoco on the Lido, the only paying passengers in a great freight galeazza, the *Doge Anafesto*. She was carrying arms and supplies to the Crusaders; after unloading those things and us in Acre, she would go on to Alexandria for a cargo of grain to bring back to Venice. When the ship was outside the basin, on the open Adriatic, the rowers shipped their oars while the seamen stepped the two masts and unfurled their graceful lateen sails. The spreads of canvas fluttered and snapped and then bellied full in the afternoon breeze , as white and billowy as the clouds above.

"A sublime day!" I exclaimed. "A superb ship!"

My father, never inclined to rhapsodize, replied with one of his ever ready adages: "Praise not the day until night has brought its close; praise not the inn until the next day's awakening."

But even on the next day, and on succeeding days, he could not deny that the ship was as decent in its accommodations as any inn on the land. In earlier years, a vessel that touched at the Holy Land would have been crowded with Christian pilgrims from every country of Europe, sleeping in rows and layers on the deck and in the hold, like sardines in a butt. However, by that time of which I am telling, the port of San Zuàne de Acre was the last and only spot in the Holy Land not yet overwhelmed by the Saracens, so all Christians except Crusaders were staying at home.

103

We three Polos had a cabin all to ourselves, right under the captain's quarters in the sterncastle. The ship's galley was provided with a livestock pen, so we and the seamen had meals of fresh meat and fowl, not salted. There was pasta of all varieties, and olive oil and onions, and good Corsican wine kept cool in the damp sand the ship carried for ballast at the bottom of the hold. All we missed was fresh-baked bread; in its place we were served hard agiàda biscuits, which cannot be bitten or chewed but have to be sucked, and that was the only fare of which we might have complained. There was a medegòto on board, to treat any ailments or injuries, and a chaplain, to hear confessions and hold masses. On the first Sunday, he preached on a text from Ecclesiasticus: "The wise man shall pass into strange countries, and good and evil shall he try in all things."

"Tell me, please, about the strange countries yonder," I said to my father after that mass, for he and I had really not had much time in Venice to talk just between ourselves. His reply told me more about him, however, than about any lands beyond the horizon.

"Ah, they brim with opportunities for an ambitious merchant!" he said exultantly, rubbing his hands. "Silks, jewels, spices—even the dullest tradesman dreams of those obvious things—but there are many more possibilities for a clever man. Yes, Marco. Even in coming with us only as far as the Levant, you can, if you keep your eyes open and your wits about you, perhaps begin the making of a fortune of your very own. Yes, indeed, all the lands yonder are lands of opportunity."

"I look forward to them," I said dutifully. "But I could learn of commerce without leaving Venice. I was thinking more of . . . well, adventure . . ."

"Adventure? Why, my boy, could there ever be any more satisfying adventure than the descrying of a commercial opportunity not yet glimpsed by others? And the seizing advantage of it? And the taking of a profit from it?"

"Of course, most satisfying, those things," I said, not to dampen his ebullience. "But what of excitement? Exotic things seen and done? Surely in all your travels there have been many such."

"Oh, yes. Exotic things." He scratched meditatively in his beard. "Yes, on our way back to Venice, through Cappadocia, we came upon one instance. There grows in that land a poppy, very like our common red field poppy, but of a silvery-blue color, and from the milk of its pod can be decocted a soporific oil that is a most potent medicine. I knew it would be a useful addition to the simples employed by our Western physicians, and I foresaw a good profit to our Compagnia from that. I sought to collect some of the seeds of that poppy, intending to sow them among the crocuses in our Vèneto plantations. Now, that was an exotic thing, no xe vero? And a grand opportunity. Unfortunately, there was a war going on in Cappadocia at that time. The poppy fields were all devastated, and the populace in such disarray that I could find no one who could provide me with the seeds. Gramo de mi, an opportunity lost."

I said, with some amazement, "You were in the middle of a war, and all that concerned you was poppy seeds?"

"Ah, war is a terrible thing. A disruption of commerce."

"But, Father, you saw in it no opportunity for adventure?"

"You keep on about *adventure*," he said tartly. "Adventure is no more than discomfort and annoyance recollected in the safety of reminiscence. Believe me, an experienced traveler makes plans and takes pains *not* to have such adventures. The most successful journey is a dull journey."

"Oh," I said. "I was rather looking forward to—well, hazards overcome . . . hidden things discovered . . . enemies bested . . . maidens rescued . . ."

"There speaks the bravo!" boomed Uncle Mafìo, joining us just then. "I hope you are disabusing him of such notions, Nico."

"I am trying," said my father. "Adventure, Marco, never put a bagatìn in anybody's purse."

"But is the purse the only thing a man is to fill?" I cried. "Should not he seek something else in life? What of his appetite for wonders and marvels?"

"No one ever found marvels by seeking them," my uncle grunted. "They are like true love—or happiness—which, in fact are marvels themselves. You cannot say: I will go out and have an adventure. The best you can do is put yourself in a place where it may occur."

"Well, then," I said. "We are bound for Acre, the city of the Crusaders, fabled for daring deeds and dark secrets and silken damsels and the life voluptuous. What better place?"

"The Crusaders!" snorted Uncle Mafìo. "Fables, indeed! The Crusaders who survived to come home had to pretend to themselves that their futile missions had been worthwhile. So they bragged of the wonders they had seen, the marvels of the far lands. About the only thing they brought back was a case of the scolamento so painful they could hardly sit a saddle."

I said wistfully, "Acre is not a city of beauty and temptation and mystery and luxury and—?"

My father said, "Crusaders and Saracens have been fighting over San Zuàne de Acre for more than a century and a half. Imagine for yourself what it must be like. But, no, you need not. You will see it soon enough."

So I left them, feeling rather dashed in my expectations, but not demolished. I was privately coming to the conclusion that my father had the soul of a line-ruled ledger, and my uncle was too blunt and gruff to contain any finer feelings. They would not recognize adventure if it was thrust upon them. But I would. I went and stood on the foredeck, not to miss seeing any mermaids or sea monsters that might swim by.

A sea voyage, after the first exhilarating day or so, becomes mere monotony—unless a storm enlivens it with terror, but the Mediterranean is stormy only in winter—so I occupied myself with learning all I could about the workings of a ship. In the absence of bad weather, the crew had nothing but routine work to do, so everyone from the captain to the cook willingly let me watch and ask questions and even occasionally lend a hand with the work. The men were of many different nationalities, but all spoke the Trade French—which they called Sabir—so we were able to converse.

"Do you know anything at all about sailing, boy?" one of the seamen asked me. "Do you know, for instance, which are the liveworks of a ship, and which are the deadworks?"

I thought about that, and looked up at the sails, spread out on either side of the ship like a living bird's wings, and guessed that they must be the liveworks.

"Wrong," said the mariner. "The liveworks are every part of a ship that is in the water. The deadworks are everything above the water."

I thought about that, and said, "But if the deadworks were to plunge under water, they could hardly then be called live. We should all be dead."

The seaman said quickly, "Do not speak of such things!" and crossed himself.

Another said, "If you would be a seafarer, boy, you must learn the seventeen names of the seventeen winds that blow over the Mediterranean." He began ticking them off on his fingers. "At this moment, we are sailing before the etesia, which blows from the northwest. In winter, the ostralada blows fiercely from the south, and makes storms. The gregalada is the wind that blows out of Greece, and makes the sea turbulent. From the west blows the maistràl. The levante blows out of the east, out of Armeniya—"

Another seaman interrupted, "When the levante blows, you can smell the Cyclopedes."

"Islands?" I asked.

"No. Strange people who live in Armeniya. Each of them has only one arm and one leg. It takes two of those people to use a bow and arrow. Since they cannot walk, they hop on the one leg. But if they are in a hurry, they go spinning sideways, wheeling on that hand and foot. That is why they are called the Cyclopedes, the wheel-feet."

Besides telling me of many other marvels, the seamen also taught me to play the guessing and gambling game called venturina, which was devised by mariners to while away long and boring voyages. They must endure many such voyages, for venturina is an exceedingly long and boring game, and no player can win or lose more than a few soldi in the course of it.

When I later asked my uncle if, in his travels, he had ever encountered curiosities like the wheel-feet Armeniyans, he laughed and sneered. "Bah! No seaman ever ventures farther into a foreign port than the nearest dockside wineshop or whorehouse. So when he is asked what sights he saw abroad, he must invent things. Only a marcolfo who would believe a woman would believe a seaman!"

So from then on I listened only tolerantly, with half an ear, when the mariners told of landward wonders, but I still gave full attention when they spoke of things to do with the sea and sailing. I learned their special names for common objects—the small sooty bird called in Venice a stormbird is at sea called petrelo, "little Pietro," because, like the saint, it seems to walk on the water—and I learned the rhymes which seamen use when talking of the weather—

> Sera rosa e bianco matino:
> Alegro il pelegrino

—which is to say that a red sky in the evening or a white sky in the morning foretells good weather in the offing, hence the pilgrim is pleased. And I learned how to toss the scandàgio line, with its little ribbons of red and white at intervals along its length, to measure the depth of water under our keel. And I learned how to speak to other vessels we passed—wwhich I was allowed to do two or three times, for there were many ships asea upon the Mediterranean—shouting in Sabir through the trumpet:

"A good voyage! What ship?"

And the reply would come hollowly back: "A good voyage! The *Saint Sang,* out of Bruges, homeward bound from Famagusta! And you, what ship are you?"

"The *Anafesto,* of Venice, outward bound for Acre and Alexandria! A good voyage!"

The ship's steerer showed me how, through an ingenious arrangement of ropes, he single-handedly controlled both the immense steering oars, one raked down either side of the ship to the stern. "But in heavy weather," he said, "a steerer is required on each, and they must be masters of dexterity, to swing the tillers separately and variously, but always in perfect concert, at the captain's calls."

The ship's striker let me practice pounding his mallets when none of the rowers was at the oars. They seldom were. The etesia wind was so nearly constant that the oars were not often needed to help the ship make way, so the rowers had their only sustained work on that voyage in taking us out of the Malamoco basin and into the harbor of Acre. At those times they took their places—"in the mode called *a zenzile,*" the striker told me—three men to each of the twenty benches along each side of the vessel.

Each rower worked an oar that was separately pivoted to the ship's outriggers, so that the shortest oars rowed inboard, the longest outboard and the medium-length oars between them. And the men did not sit, as oarsmen do, for example, in the Doge's buzino d'oro. They stood, each with his left foot on the bench before him, while they swept the oars forward. Then they all fell back supine on the benches when they made their powerful strokes, propelling the ship in a sort of series of rushing leaps. This was done in time to the striker's striking, a tempo that began slow, but got faster as the ship did, and the two mallets made different sounds so the rowers on one side would know when they had to pull harder than the others.

I was never let to row, for that is a job requiring such skill that apprentices are made to practice first in mock galleys set up on dry land. Because the word galeotto is so often used in Venice to mean a convict, I had always assumed that galleys and galeazze and galeotte were rowed by criminals caught and condemned to drudgery. But the striker pointed out that freight ships compete for trade on the basis of their speed and efficiency, for which they would hardly depend on reluctant forced labor. "So the merchant fleet hires only professional and experienced oarsmen," he said. "And war ships are rowed by citizens who choose to do that service as their military obligation, instead of taking up the sword."

The ship's cook told me why he baked no bread. "I keep no flour in my galley," he said. "Fine ground flour is impossible to preserve from contamination at sea. Either it breeds weevils or it gets wet. That is why the Romans first thought of making the pasta we enjoy today—because it is well-nigh imperishable. Indeed, it is said that a Roman ship's cook invented that foodstuff, volente o nolente, when his stock of flour got soaked by an errant wave. He kneaded the mess into pasta to save it, and he rolled it thin and he cut it into strips so it would more quickly dry solid. From that beginning have come all the numerous sizes and shapes of vermicelli and maccheroni. They were a godsend to us mariner cooks, and to the landbound as well."

The ship's captain showed me how the needle of his bussola pointed always to the North Star, even when that star is invisible. The bussola, in those times, was just beginning to be regarded as a fixture almost as necessary for sea voyages as a ship's San Cristoforo medal, but the instrument was yet a novelty to me. So was the periplus, which the captain also showed me, a sheaf of charts on which were drawn the curly coastlines of the whole Mediterranean, from the Levant to the Pillars of Hercules, and all its subsidiary seas: the Adriatic, the Aegean and so on. Along those inked coastlines, the captain—and other captains of his acquaintance—had marked the land features visible from the sea: lighthouses, headlands, standing rocks and other such objects which would help a mariner to determine where he was. On the water areas of the charts, the captain had scribbled notations of their various depths and currents and hidden reefs. He told me that he kept changing those notations according as he found, or heard from other captains, that those depths had changed through silting up, as often happens off Egypt, or through the activity of undersea volcanoes, as often happens around Greece.

When I told my father about the periplus, he smiled and said, "Almost is better than nothing. But we have something much better than a periplus." He brought out from our cabin an even thicker sheaf of papers. "We have the Kitab."

My uncle said proudly, "If the captain possessed the Kitab, and if his ship could sail overland, he could go clear across Asia, to the eastern Ocean of Kithai."

"I had this made at great expense," said my father, handing it to me. "It was copied for us from the original, which was done by the Arab mapmaker al-Idrisi for King Ruggiero of Sicily."

Kitab, I later discovered, means in Arabic only "a book," but then so does our word Bible. And al-Idrisi's Kitab, like the Holy Bible, is much more than just a book. The first page was inscribed with its full title, which I could read, for it was rendered in French: *The going out of a Curious Man to explore the Regions of the Globe, its Provinces, Islands, Cities and their Dimensions and Situation; for the Instruction and Assistance of him who desires to Traverse the Earth.* But all the many other words on the pages were done in the execrable worm-writing of the infidel Arab countries. Only here and there had my father or uncle penned in a legible translation of this or that place-name. Turning the pages so I could read those words, I realized something and I laughed.

"Every chart is upside down. Look, he has the foot of the Italian peninsula kicking Sicily *up* toward Africa."

"In the East, everything is upside down or backward or contrary," said my uncle. "The Arab maps are all made with south at the top. The people of Kithai call thé bussola the *south*-pointing needle. You will get accustomed to such customs."

"Aside from that peculiarity," said my father, "al-Idrisi has been amazingly accurate in representing the lands of the Levant, and beyond them as far as Middle Asia. Presumably he himself once traveled those regions."

The Kitab comprised seventy-three separate pages which, laid side by side (and upside down), showed the entire extent of the world from west to east, and a goodly part of it north and south, the whole divided by curving parallels according to climatic zones. The salt sea waters were painted in blue with choppy white lines for the waves; inland lakes were green with white waves; rivers were squiggly green ribbons. The land areas were painted dun yellow, with dots of gold leaf applied to show cities and towns. Wherever the land rose in hills and mountains, those were represented by shapes rather like caterpillars, which were colored purple, pink, and orange.

I asked, "Are the highlands of the East really so vividly colored? Purple mountaintops and—?"

As if in reply, the lookout shouted down from his basket atop the ship's taller mast, "Terra là! Terre là!"

"You can look and see for yourself, Marco," said my father. "The shore is in sight. Behold the Holy Land."

2

OF course, I eventually discovered that the coloring on al-Idrisi's maps was to indicate the height of the land, with purple representing the highest mountains, pink those of moderate altitude, and orange the lowest, and yellow land of no particular elevation. But there was nothing in the vicinity of Acre to prove this discovery by, that part of the Holy Land being an almost colorless country of low sand dunes and even lower sand flats. What color there was to the land was a dirty gray-yellow, not even a vestige of green growing there, and the city was a dirty gray-brown.

The oarsmen swept the *Anafesto* around the base of a lighthouse and into the meager harbor. It was awash with

every sort of garbage and offal, its waters slimy and
greasy, stinking of fish, fish guts and decayed fish. Beyond
the docks were buildings that appeared to be made of dried
mud—they were all inns and hostels, the captain told us,
there being nothing in Acre that could be termed a private
residence—and above those low buildings, here and there,
stood the taller stone edifices of churches, monasteries, a
hospital and the city's castle. Farther landward beyond
that castle was a high stone wall, stretching in a semicircle from the harbor to the sea side of the city, with a dozen
towers upjutting from it. To me it looked like a dead man's
jawbone sparsely studded with teeth. On the other side of
that wall, said the captain, was the encampment of the
Crusader knights, and beyond that yet another and even
stouter wall, fencing Acre's point of land off from the mainland where the Saracens held sway.

"This is the last Christian holding in the Holy Land,"
the ship's priest said sadly. "And it will fall, too, whenever
the infidels choose to overrun it. This eighth Crusade has
been so futile that the Christians of Europe have lost their
fervor for crusading. The newly arriving knights are fewer
and fewer. You notice that we brought none on this passage. So Acre's force is too small to do anything but make
occasional skirmishes outside the walls."

"Humph," said the captain. "The knights seldom even
bother to do that any more. They are all of different
orders—Templars and Hospitalers and whatnot—so they
much prefer to fight among themselves . . . when they are
not scandalously disporting themselves with the Carmelitas and Clarissas."

The chaplain winced, for no reason I could see, and said
petulantly, "Sir, have a regard for my cloth."

The captain shrugged. "Deplore it if you will, Pare, but
you cannot refute it." He turned to speak to my father.
"Not only the troops are in disarray. The civilian population, what there is of it, consists entirely of suppliers and
servitors to the knights. Acre's native Arabs are too venal
to be inimical to us Christians, but they are forever at odds
with Acre's native Jews. The remainder of the population
is a shifting motley of Pisans and Genoese and your fellow
Venetians—all rivals and all quarrelsome. If you wish to
conduct your business here in peace, I suggest that you go
straight to the Venetian quarter when we debark, and

take lodgings there, and try not to get involved in the local discords."

So we three gathered our belongings from the cabin and prepared to debark. The quay was crowded with ragged and dirty men, pressing close around the ship's gangplank and waving their arms and jostling each other, crying their services in Trade French and any number of other languages:

"Carry your bags, monsieur! Lord merchant! Messere! Mirza! Sheikh khaja!. . ."

"Lead you to the auberge! The inn! Locanda! Karwan-sarai! Khane!. . ."

"Provide for you horses! Asses! Camels! Porters!. . ."

"A guide! A guide speaking Sabir! A guide speaking Farsi!. . ."

"A woman! A beautiful fat woman! A nun! My sister! My little brother!. . ."

My uncle demanded only porters, and selected four or five of the least scabrous of the men. The rest drifted away, shaking their fists and shouting imprecations:

"May Allah look upon you sideways!"

"May you choke while eating pig meat!"

". . . Eating your lover's zab!"

". . . Your mother's nether parts!"

The seamen unloaded our portion of the ship's cargo, and our new porters slung our bundles on their backs or shoulders or perched them atop their heads. Uncle Mafio commanded them, first in French, then in Farsi, to take us to the part of the city reserved for Venetians, and to the best inn there, and we all moved off along the quay.

I was not much impressed by Acre—or Akko, as its native inhabitants call it. The city was no cleaner than the harbor, being mostly of squalid buildings with the widest streets between them no wider than the narrowest alleys of Venice. In its most open areas, the city stank of old urine. Where walls closed it in, it smelled even worse, for the alleys were sinks of sewage and swill, in which gaunt dogs competed for the pickings with monster rats, abroad even in full daylight.

More overpowering than Acre's stink was its noise. In every alley wide enough for a sitting rug to be spread, there were vendors, shoulder to shoulder, squatting be-hind little heaps of trashy merchandise—scarves and ribbons, shriveled oranges, overripe figs, pilgrims' shells and palm leaves—every man of them bellowing to be heard above the others. Beggars, legless or blind or leprous, whined and sniveled and clawed at our sleeves as we passed. Asses, horses and mangy-furred camels—the first camels I had ever seen—shouldered us out of their way as they shuffled through the garbage of the narrow lanes. They all looked weary and miserable under their heavy loads, but they were driven by the drumming sticks and bawled curses of their herders. Groups of men of all nations stood about conversing at the top of their lungs. I suppose some of their talk dealt with mundane matters of trade, or the war, or maybe just the weather, but their conversations were so clamorous as to be indistinguishable from raging quarrels.

I said to my father, when we were in a street wide enough for us to walk abreast, "You said that you were bringing trade goods on this journey. I did not see any merchandise put aboard the *Anafesto* in Venice, and I do not see anything of that nature now. Is it still on the ship?"

He shook his head. "To have brought a pack train's load of goods would have been to tempt the innumerable bandits and thieves between us and our destination." He hefted the one small pack he was carrying at that moment, having refused to relinquish it to any of the porters. "Instead, we are carrying something light and inconspicuous, but of great trading value."

"Zafràn!" I exclaimed.

"Just so. Some in pressed bricks, some in loose hay. And also a good number of the culms."

I laughed. "Surely you will not stop to plant them, and wait a whole year for the harvest."

"If circumstances require, yes. One must try to be prepared against all contingencies, my boy. Who has, God helps. And other journeyers have traveled on the three-bean march."

"What?"

My uncle spoke. "The famed and feared Chinghiz Khan, grandfather of our Kubilai, conquered most of the world in exactly that slow-marching manner. His armies and all their families had to cross the entire vast extent of Asia, and they were far too numerous to have lived off the land, whether by pillaging or scavenging. No, they carried seeds for planting, and animals fit for breeding. Whenever they had marched to the limit of their rations, and beyond the reach of their supply trains, they simply stopped and settled. They planted their grains and beans, bred their horses and cattle, and waited for the harvest and the calving. Then, again well fed and well provisioned, they moved on toward the next objective."

I said, "I heard that they ate every tenth man of their own men."

"Nonsense!" said my uncle. "Would any commander decimate his fighting men? He might as sensibly command them to eat their swords and spears. And the weapons would be about equally edible. I doubt that even a Mongol has teeth capable of chewing another warrior Mongol. No, they stopped and planted and harvested, and moved again, and stopped again."

My father said, "They called that the three-bean march. And it inspired one of their war cries. Whenever the Mongols fought their way into an enemy city, Chinghiz would shout, 'The hay is cut! Give your horses fodder!' And that was the signal for the horde to go wild, to plunder and rape and ravage and slaughter. Thus they laid waste Tashkent and Bukhara and Kiev and many another great city. It is said that when the Mongols took Herat, in India Aryana, they butchered every last one of its inhabitants, to the number of nearly *two million*. Ten times the population of Venice! Of course, of Indians such a diminution is hardly worth remark."

"The three-bean march sounds efficient enough," I conceded, "but intolerably slow."

"He who endures, wins," said my father. "That slow march took the Mongols all the way to the borders of Poland and Romania."

"And all the way to here," added my uncle. We were just then passing two swarthy men in clothing that appeared to be made of hides, much too heavy and hot for the climate. To them Uncle Mafìo said, "Sain bina."

They both looked slightly startled, but one of them responded, "Mendu, sain bina!"

"What language was that?" I asked.

"Mongol," said my uncle. "Those two are Mongols."

I stared at him, then turned to stare at the men. They were also walking with their heads turned, looking won-

deringly back at us. The streets of Acre teemed with so
many people of exotic features and complexions and raiment that I could not yet distinguish one kind of foreigner
from another. But those were *Mongols?* The orda, the orco,
the bogle, the terror of my childhood? The bane of Christianity and menace to all Western civilization? Why, they
might have been merchants of Venice, exchanging a "bon
zorno" with us as we all promenaded on the Riva Ca' de
Dio. Of course, they did not *look* like merchants of Venice.
Those two men had eyes like slits in faces like well-tanned
leather. . . .

"Those are Mongols?" I said, thinking of the miles and
the millions of corpses they must have tramped across to
get to the Holy Land. "What are they doing here?"

"I have no idea," said my father. "I daresay we will find
out in good time."

"Here in Acre," said my uncle, "as in Constantinople,
there seem to be at least a few persons of every nationality
on earth. Yonder goes a black man, a Nubian or an
Ethiope. And that woman there is certainly an Armeniyan: each of her breasts is exactly as large as her head. The
man with her I would say is a Persian. Now, the Jews and
Arabs I can never tell apart, except by their garb. That one
yonder has on his head a white tulband, which Islam forbids to Jews and Christians, so he has to be a Muslim. . . ."

His speculations were interrupted because we were almost run down by a war horse ridden at an uncaring canter through the tangled streets. The eight-pointed cross on
the rider's surcoat identified him as a Knight of the Order
of the Hospital of San Zuàne of Jerusalem. He went past
with a noise of jingling chain mail and creaking leather,
but with no apology for his rudeness and not even a nod to
us brother Christians.

We came to the square of buildings set aside for Venetians, and the porters led us to one of the several inns
there. Its landlord met us at the entrance, and he and my
father exchanged some deep bows and flowery greetings.
Though the landlord was an Arab, he spoke in Venetian:
"Peace be unto you, my lords."

My father said, "And on you, peace."

"May Allah give you strength."

"Strong have we become."

"The day is blessed which brings you to my door, my lords. But Allah has led you to choose well. My khane has clean beds, and a hammam for your refreshment, and the best food in Akko. Even now, a lamb is being stuffed with pistachios for the evening meal. I have the honor to be your servant, and my miserable name is Ishaq, may you speak it with not too much contempt."

We introduced ourselves, and each of us thereafter was addressed by the landlord and servants as Sheikh Folo, because the Arabs have no *p* in their own language, and find it difficult to make the sound when speaking any other. As we Folos were disposing our belongings about our room, I asked my father and uncle, "Why is a Saracen so hospitable to us, his enemies?"

My uncle sid, "Not all Arabs are engaged in this jihad—which is their name for a holy war against Christianity. The ones here in Acre are profiting too much from it to take sides, even with their fellow Muslims."

"There are good Arabs and there are bad," said my father. "The ones now fighting to oust all Christians from the Holy Land—from the entire eastern Mediterranean—are actually the Mamluks of Egypt, and they are very bad Arabs indeed."

When we had unpacked the things necessary for our stay in Acre, we went to the inn's hammam. And the hammam, I think, must rank with those other great Arabian inventions: arithmetic and its numbers and the abaco for counting. Essentially a hammam is only a room full of steam, generated by throwing water on fire-hot stones. But after we had sat for a time on benches in that room, sweating copiously, half a dozen menservants came in and said, "Health and delight to you, lords, from this bath!" and directed us to lie prostrate on the benches. Then, two men to each of us, their four hands wearing gloves made of coarse hemp, they rubbed us all over, briskly and for a long time. As they rubbed, the accumulated salt and dirt of our voyage was scraped off our skin in long gray rolls. We might have deemed that sufficient for cleanliness, but they kept on rubbing, and more dirt came out of our pores, like thin gray worms.

When we were exuding no more grayness, and were steamed and rubbed to redness, the men offered to depilate us of our body hair. My father declined that treatment, and so did I. I had already that day shaved off what skimpy whiskers I had, and I wished to keep what other hair I possessed. Uncle Mafìo, after a moment's consideration, told the servants to remove his artichoke escutcheon, but not to tamper with his beard or chest hair. So two of the men, the two youngest and most handsome, hastened to the task. They applied a dun-colored ointment to his crotch area, and the thick thatch of hair there began to disappear like smoke. Almost immediately, he was as bald in that place as was Doris Tagiabue.

"That salve is magical," he said admiringly, looking down at himself.

"In truth it is, Sheikh Folo," said one of the young men, smiling so that he leered. "The removal of the hair makes your zab more visible, as prominent and as pretty as a war lance. A veritable torch to guide your lover to you in the night. It is a pity that the Sheikh is not circumcised, so that his zab's bright plum might be more readily observed and admired and—"

"Enough of that! Tell me, can this ointment be purchased?"

"Certainly. You have but to order me, Sheikh, and I will run to the apothecary for a fresh jar of the mumum. Or many jars."

My father said, "You see it as a commodity, Mafìo? But there would be scant market for it in Venice. A Venetian treasures every least bloom on the peach."

"But we are going eastward, Nico. Remember, many of those Eastern peoples regard body hair as a blemish on either sex. If this mumum is not too costly here, we could turn a considerable profit there." He said to his rubber, "Please stop fondling me, boy, and get on with the bathing."

So the men washed us all over, using a creamy sort of soap, and washed our hair and beards in fragrant rose water, and dried us with great fleecy, musk-scented towels. When we were dressed again, they gave us cool drinks of sweetened lemon-juice sharbat, to restore our internal moisture, which by then had been depleted by all the heat. I left the hammam feeling cleaner than I had ever felt before, and I was grateful for the Arabs' invention of that facility. I made frequent use of that one, and others thereafter, and the only complaint I might ever have had was that so many of the Arab people themselves preferred filth and fetor to the cleanness available in the hammam.

The landlord Ishaq had spoken the truth about the khane's food being good, though of course we were paying enough that he could profitably have fed us on ambrosia and nectar. That first night's meal was the lamb stuffed with pistachios, also rice and a dish of cucumbers sliced and dripped with lemon juice, and afterwards a confection of sugared pomegranate pulp mixed with grated almonds and delicately perfumed. It was all delicious, but I was most taken by the accompanying beverage. Ishaq told me it is an infusion from ripe berries in hot water, and is called Qahwah. That Arabic word means "wine," which qahwah is not, for the Arabs' religion forbids them wine. Only in color is the qahwah winelike, a deep garnet-brown, rather resembling a Barolo of the Piedmont, but it does not have Barolo's strong flavor or its faint aftertaste of violets. Neither is it sweet or sour, like some other wines. Neither does it intoxicate like wine, or make the head to ache the next day. But it does gladden the heart and enliven the senses and—so said Ishaq—a few glasses of qahwah enable a traveler or a warrior to march or fight untiringly for hours on end.

The meal was served upon a cloth around which we sat on the floor, and it was served without any table implements. So we used our belt knives for cutting and slicing, as we would have employed table knives at home, and used the knife points to spear our bits of meat, in place of the little metal skewers we would have had at home. Lacking skewers or spoons, we ate the lamb's stuffing and the rice and the sweet with our fingers.

"Only the thumb and first two fingers of the right hand," my father cautioned me in a low voice. "The left hand's fingers are considered by the Arabs nasty, for they are reserved to the wiping of one's behind. Also, sit only upon your left haunch, take only small portions of the food with your fingers, chew well each mouthful, and look not at your fellow diners while they eat, lest you embarrass them and make them lose their appetite."

There is much to be read in an Arab's use of his hands, as I gradually learned. If, while he is speaking, he strokes his beard, his most precious possession, then he is swearing by his beard that his words are truthful. If he puts his in-

dex finger to his eye, it is his sign of assent to your words or
consent to your command. If he puts his hand to his head,
he is vowing that his head will answer for any disobedience. If, however, he makes any of those gestures with his
left hand, he is merely mocking you, and if he touches you
with that left hand, it is the direst insult.

3

SOME days later, when we had ascertained that the commander of the Crusaders was in the city's castle, we went
to pay our courtesy call upon him. The forecourt of the castle was full of knights of the various orders, some merely
lounging about, others gambling with dice, others chatting or quarreling, still others quite visibly drunk for that
early in the day. None seemed to be about to dash out and
do battle with the Saracens, or eager to do so, or sorry that
he was not doing so. When my father had explained our
mission to the two drowsy-looking knights guarding the
castle door, they said nothing, but only jerked their heads
for us to enter. Inside, my father explained our business to
one lackey and squire after another, in one hall after another, until we were ushered into a room hung with battle
flags and told to wait. After a time, a lady entered. She was
about thirty years of age, not pretty but gracious of demeanor, and wearing a gold coronet. She said, in Castilian-
accented French, "I am Princess Eleanor."

"Nicolò Polo," said my father, bowing. "And my brother
Mafìo and my son Marco." And for the sixth or seventh
time, he told why we were seeking audience.

The lady said, with admiration and a little apprehension, "Going all the way to Cathay? Dear me, I hope my
husband will not volunteer to go with you. He does love to
travel, and he does abhor this dismal Acre." The room door
opened again, admitting a man of about her age. "Here he
is now. Prince Edward. My love, these are—"

"The Polo family," he said brusquely, with an Anglo ac-
cent. "You came in on the supply ship." He too wore a coronet, and a surcoat emblazoned with the cross of San Zorzi.

"What can I do for *you?*" He stressed the last word as if we were only the latest in a long procession of appellants.

For the seventh or eighth time, my father explained, concluding, "We merely ask Your Royal Highness to introduce us to the chief prelate among your Crusader chaplains. We would ask him for the loan of some of his priests."

"You may have all of them, as far as I am concerned. And all the Crusaders as well. Eleanor, my dear, would you ask the Archdeacon to join us?"

As the Princess left the room, my uncle said boldly, "Your Royal Highness appears less than pleased with this crusade."

Edward grimaced. "It has been one disaster after another. Our latest best hope was the leadership of the pious French Louis, since he was so successful with the previous Crusade, but he sickened and died on his way here. His brother took his place, but Charles is only a politician, and spends all his time negotiating. For his own advantage, I might add. Every Christian monarch embroiled in this mess is seeking only to advance his own interests, not those of Christianity. Small wonder the knights are disillusioned and lackadaisical."

My father remarked, "Those outside do not look particularly enterprising."

"What few have not gone home in disgust, I can only seldom pry from their wenches' beds, to make a sally among the foe. And even in the field, they prefer bed to battle. One night not long ago, they slept while a Saracen hashishi slipped through the pickets and into my tent, can you imagine that? And I do not wear a sword under my nightshirt. I had to snatch up a pricket candlestick and stab him with that." The Prince sighed profoundly. "As the situation stands, I must resort to politicking myself. I am presently treating with an embassy of Mongols, hoping to enlist their alliance against our common enemy of Islam."

"So that is it," said my uncle. "We had marveled to see a couple of Mongols in the city."

My father began hopefully, "Then our mission closely accords with the aims of Your Royal—"

The door opened again and the Princess Eleanor returned, bringing with her a tall and quite old man wearing a splendidly embroidered dalmatic. Prince Edward made the introductions:

"The Venerable Tebaldo Visconti, Archdeacon of Liège. This good man despaired of the impiety of his fellow churchmen in Flanders, and applied for a papal legacy to accompany me hither. Teo, these are some near countrymen of your own Piacenza. The Polos of Venice."

"Yes, indeed, i Pantaleoni," said the old man, calling us by the sneering nickname with which the citizens of rival cities refer to Venetians. "Are you here to further your vile republic's trade with the enemy infidels?"

"Come now, Teo," said the Prince, looking amused.

"Really, Teo," said the Princess, looking embarrassed. "I told you: the gentlemen are not here to trade at all."

"To do what wickedness, then?" said the Archdeacon. "I will believe anything but good of Venice. Liège was evil enough, but Venice is notorious as the Babylon of Europe. A city of avaricious men and salacious women."

He seemed to be glaring straight at me, as if he knew of my recent adventures in that Babylon. I started to protest in my defense that I was not avaricious, but my father spoke first, and placatively:

"Perhaps our city is rightly so known, Your Reverence. Tuti semo fati de carne. But we are not traveling on behalf of Venice. We bear a request from the Khan of All Khans of the Mongols, and it can only redound to the good of all Europe and Mother Church." He went on to explain why Kubilai had asked for missionary priests. Visconti heard him out, but then asked haughtily:

"Why do you apply to me, Polo? I am only in deacon's orders, an appointed administrator, not even an ordained priest."

He was not even polite, moreover, and I hoped my father would tell him so. But he said only, "You are the highest ranking Christian churchman in the Holy Land. The Pope's legate."

"There is no Pope," Visconti retorted. "And until an apostolic authority is chosen, who am I to delegate a hundred priests to go into the far unknown, at the whim of a heathen barbarian?"

"Come now, Teo," said the Prince again. "I think we have in our entourage more chaplains than we have fighting men. Surely we can spare some of them, for a good purpose."

"If it *is* a good purpose, Your Grace," said the Archdeacon, scowling. "Remember, these are Venetians proposing it. And this is not the first such proposal. Some twenty-five years ago, the Mongols made a similar overture, and directly to Rome. One of their Khans, one named Kuyuk, a cousin to this Kubilai, sent a letter to Pope Innocent asking—no, demanding—that His Holiness and all the monarchs of the West come to him, in a body, to render homage and submission. Naturally he was ignored. But *that* is the kind of invitation the Mongols proffer, and when it comes by the agency of a Venetian . . . ."

"Despise our provenance, if you will," said my father, still equably. "If there were no fault in the world, there could be no pardon. But please, Your Reverence, do not despise this opportunity. The Khakhan Kubilai asks nothing but that your priests come and preach their religion. I have here the missive written by the Khan's scribe at the Khan's dictation. Does Your Reverence read Farsi?"

"No," said Visconti, adding a snort of expasperation. "It will require an interpreter." He shrugged his narrow shoulders. "Very well. Let us retire to another room while it is read to me. No need to waste the time of Their Graces."

So he and my father adjourned for their conference. Prince Edward and Princess Eleanor, as if to make up for the Archdeacon's bad manners, stayed long enough to make some conversation with me and Uncle Mafìo. The Princess asked me:

"Do *you* read Farsi, young Marco?"

"No, my Lady—Your Royal Highness. That language is written in the Arabic alphabet, the fish-worm writing, and I cannot make sense of it."

"Whether you read it or not," said the Prince, "you had better learn to speak Farsi, if you are going eastward with your father. Farsi is the common trade tongue of all of Asia, just as French is in the Mediterranean lands."

The Princess asked my uncle, "Where do you go from here, Monsieur Polo?"

"If we get the priests we want, Your Royal Highness, we will lead them to the court of the Khakhan Kubilai. Which means we must somehow make our way past the Saracens inland."

"Oh, you should get the priests," said Prince Edward. "You could probably have nuns, too, if you want them. Teo will be glad to rid himself of all of them, for they are the cause of his ill humor. You must not let his behavior dismay you. Teo is from Piacenza, so you can hardly be surprised by his attitude toward Venice. He is also a godly and pious old gentleman, staunch in his disapproval of sin. So, even in the best of humors, he is a trial to us mere mortals."

I said impertinently, "I was hoping that my father would talk back to him, just as ill-humoredly."

"Your father may be wiser than you are," said Princess Eleanor. "The rumor is that Teobaldo may be the next Pope."

"What?" I blurted, so surprised that I forgot to use her due address. "But he just said that he is not even a priest!"

"Also he is a very old man," she said. "But that seems to be his chief qualification. The Conclave is at a standstill because, as usual, every faction has its own favorite candidate. The laity are growing clamorous; they demand a Pope. Visconti would be at least acceptable to them, and to the cardinals as well. So, if the Conclave remains much longer at impasse, it is expected to choose Teo because he *is* old. Thus there will be a Pope at Rome, but not for too long. Just long enough for the various factions to do their secret maneuvers and machinations and settle which favorite will don the beehive tiara when our Visconti dies under it."

Prince Edward said mischievously, "Teo will die in a hurry, of an apoplexy, if he finds Rome to be anything like Liège or Acre—or Venice."

My uncle said, smiling, "Babylonian, you mean?"

"Yes. That is why I think you will get the priests you want. Visconti may make a show of grumbling, but he will not grieve at seeing these Acre priests go far, far away from him. All the monastic orders are in residence here to serve the needs of the fighting men, of course, but they have taken a rather liberal view of that duty. In addition to their hospital ministrations and spiritual solacements, they are providing some services that would dismay the saintly founders of their orders. You can imagine which of the men's needs the Carmelitas and Clarissas are taking care of, and most lucratively, too. Meanwhile, the monks and friars are getting rich by trading illicitly with the natives, even peddling the provisions and medical supplies donated to their monasteries by the good-hearted Christians back in Europe. Meanwhile, also, the priests are selling indulgences and trafficking in absurd superstitions. Have you seen one of these?"

He took out a slip of scarlet paper and handed it to Uncle Mafìo, who unfolded it and read aloud:

" 'Bless, O God, sanctify this paper that it may frustrate the work of the Devil. He who upon his person carries this paper writ with Holy Word shall be free from the visitation of Satan.' "

"There is a ready market for such daubs, among men going into battle," the Prince said drily. "Men of both sides, since Satan is the adversary of Muslims as well as Christians. The priests will also, for a price—for an English groat or an Arabian dinar—treat a wound with holy water. Any man's wound, and no matter if it is the gash of a sword or a sore of the venereal pox. The latter is the more frequent."

"Be glad you will soon get out of Acre," sighed the Princess. "Would that we could."

Uncle Mafìo thanked them for our audience, and he and I took our leave. He told me he was going back to the khane, for he wished to learn more about the availability of the mumum ointment. I set out merely to wander about the city, in hope of hearing some Farsi words and memorizing them, as Prince Edward had recommended. As it happened, I learned some that the Prince might not have approved of.

I fell in with three native boys of about my own age, whose names were Ibrahim, Daud and Naser. They did not have much grasp of French, but we managed to communicate—boys always will—in this case with gestures and facial expressions. We roamed together through the streets, and I would point to this or that object and speak the name by which I knew it, in French or Venetian, and then ask, "Farsi?" and they would tell me its name in that language, sometimes having to consult among themselves as to what that name was. Thus I learned that a merchant or a trader or a vendor is called a khaja, and all young boys are ashbal or "lion cubs," and all young girls are zaharat or "little flowers," and a pistachio nut is a fistuk, and a camel is a shutur, and so on: Farsi words that would be

useful anywhere in my Eastern journeying. It was later
that I learned the others.

We passed a shop where an Arab khaja offered writing
materials for sale, including fine parchments and even
finer vellums, and also papers of various qualities, from
the flimsy Indian rice-made to the Khorasan flax-made to
the expensive Moorish kind called cloth parchment because it is so smooth and elegant. I chose what I could afford, a medium grade but sturdy, and had the khaja cut it
into small pieces that I could easily carry or pack. I also
bought some rubric chalks to write with when I had no
time to prepare pen and ink. And I began then to set down
my first lexicon of unfamiliar words. Later, I would begin
to make note of the names of places I passed through and
people I met, and then incidents which occurred, and in
time my papers came to constitute a log of all my travels
and adventures.

It was by then past midday, and I was bareheaded in the
hot sun, and I began to perspire. The boys noticed and,
giggling, suggested by gesture that I was warm because of
my comical clothing. They seemed to find particularly
funny the fact that my spindly legs were exposed to public
view but tightly enclosed in my Venetian hose. So I indicated that I found equally risible their baggy and
voluminous robes, and suggested that they must be more
uncomfortably warm than I was. They argued back that
theirs was the only practical dress for that climate. Finally, to test our arguments, we went into a secluded alley
cul-de-sac and Daud and I exchanged clothes.

Naturally, when we stripped down to the skin, another
disparity between Christian and Muslim became evident,
and there was much mutual examination and many exclamations in our different languages. I had not known before
exactly what mutilation was involved in circumcision, and
they had never before seen a male over the age of thirteen
with his fava still wearing its capèla. We all minutely
scrutinized the difference between me and Daud—how his
fava, because it was always exposed, was dry and shiny
and almost scaly, and stuck with bits of lint and fluff;
while mine, enclosable or exposable at my whim, was more
pliant and velvety to the touch, even when, because of all
the attention it was getting, my organ rose erect and firm.

The three Arab boys made excited remarks which

seemed to mean "Let us try this new thing," and that
made no sense to me. So the naked Daud sought to demonstrate, reaching behind him to take my candelòto in his
hand, then directing it toward his scrawny backside
which, bending over, he wiggled at me, meanwhile saying
in a seductive voice, "Kus! Baghlah! Kus!" Ibrahim and
Naser laughed at that and made poking gestures with
their middle fingers and shouted, "Ghunj! Ghunj!" I still
comprehended nothing of the words or byplay, but I resented Daud's taking liberties with my person. I loosed his
hand and shoved it away, then hurried to cover myself
by getting into my clothes he had doffed. The boys all
shrugged good-naturedly at my Christian prudery, and
Daud put on my clothes.

The nether garment of an Arab is, like the hose of a Venetian, a forked pair of leg-envelopers. They go from the
waist, where they tie with a cord, down to the ankles,
where they are snug, but in between they are vastly capacious instead of tight. The boys told me that the Farsi word
for that garment is pai-jamah, but the best they could do
by way of a French translation was troussés. The Arab upper garment is a long-sleeved shirt, not much different
from ours except in its loose and blousy fit. And over that
goes an aba, a sort of light surcoat with slits for the arms to
go through, and the rest of it hanging loose around the
body, almost to the ground. The Arab shoes are like ours,
except that they are made to fit any foot, being of considerable length, the unoccupied portion of which curls up and
backward over the foot. On the head goes a kaffiyah, a
square of cloth large enough to hang well below the shoulders at the sides and back, and it is held on with a cord
loosely bound around the head.

To my surprise, I did feel cooler in that ensemble. I wore
it for some while before Daud and I exchanged again, and I
continued to feel cooler than in my Venetian garb. The
many layers of clothing, instead of being stifling to the
skin as I would have expected, seem somehow to entrap
what cool air there is and to be a barrier against the sun's
warming it. The clothes, being loose, are quite comfortable
and not constrictive.

Because those clothes are so loose, and so easily made
looser yet, I could not understand why the Arab boys—and
all Arab males of every age—urinate as they do. They

squat when they make water, in the same way women do.
And furthermore they do it just anywhere, as blandly re-
gardless of the people passing as those passersby are of
them. When I expressed curiosity and distaste, the boys
wanted to know how a Christian makes water. I indicated
that we do it standing up, and preferably invisible inside a
licet closet. They made me understand that such a vertical
position is called unclean by their holy book, the Quran—
and further, that an Arab dislikes to go inside a privy, or
mustarah, except when he has to do the more substantial
evacuation of his bowels, because privies are dangerous
places. On learning that, I expressed still more curiosity,
so the boys explained. Muslims, like Christians, believe in
devils and demons that emanate from the underworld—
beings called jinn and afarit—and those beings can most
easily climb up from the underworld by way of the pit dug
under a mustarah. It sounded reasonable. For a long time
afterward, I could not crouch comfortably over a licet hole
for dread of feeling the clutch of talons from underneath.

The street clothes of an Arab man may be ugly to our
eyes, but they are less so than the street clothes of an Arab
woman. And hers are uglier because they are so unfemin-
inely indistinguishable from his. She wears identically voluminous troussés and shirt and aba, but instead of a
kaffiyah headcloth she wears a chador, or veil, which
hangs from the crown of her head almost to her feet, before
and behind and all around her. Some women wear a black
chador thin enough so that they can see dimly through it
without being seen themselves; others wear a heavier
chador with a narrow slit opening in front of their eyes.
Swathed in all those layers of clothes and veil, a woman's
form is only a sort of walking heap. Indeed, unless she *is*
walking, a non-Arab can hardly tell which is her front and
which her back.

With grimaces and gestures, I managed to convey a
question to my companions. Suppose that, in the manner
of Venetian young men, they should go strolling about the
streets to ogle the beautiful young women—how would
they know if a woman *was* beautiful?

They gave me to understand that the prime mark of
beauty in a Muslim woman is not the comeliness of her
face or her eyes or her figure in general. It is the massive
amplitude of her hips and her behind. To the experienced

eye, the boys assured me, those great quivery rotundities are discernible even in a woman's street garb. But they warned me not to be misled by appearances; many women, they indicated, falsely padded out their haunches and buttocks to a counterfeit immensity.

I put another question. Suppose that, in the manner of Venetian young men, Ibrahim and Naser and Daud wished to strike up an acquaintance with a beautiful stranger—how would they go about it?

That inquiry seemed to puzzle them slightly. They asked me to elaborate. Did I mean a beautiful strange *woman?*

Yes. Certainly. What else should I mean?

Not, perchance, a beautiful strange man or boy?

I had earlier suspected, and now I was becoming sure, that I had fallen in with a troop of fledgling Don Metas and Sior Monas. I was not unduly surprised, for I knew that the site of the erstwhile city of Sodom was not far distant to the east of Acre.

The boys were again giggling at my Christian naïveté. From their pantomime and their rudimentary French, I gathered that—in the view of Islam and its holy Quran—women had been created solely so that men could beget male children upon them. Except for the occasional wealthy ruling sheikh, who could afford to collect and keep a whole hive of certified virgins, to be used one time apiece and then discarded, few Muslim men utilized women for their sexual enjoyment. Why should they? There were so many men and boys to be had, more plump and beautiful than any woman. Other considerations aside, a male lover was preferable to a female simply because he *was* male.

There, for an example of the worth intrinsic in the male—they pointed out to me a walking heap of clothing that was a woman, carrying a baby in an extra looped swath of cloth—they could ascertain that the child was a boy baby, because its face was entirely obscured by a crawling swarm of flies. Did I not wonder, they inquired, why the mother did not shoo away the flies? I might have suggested "sheer sloth," but the boys went on to explain. The mother *liked* having the flies cover the baby's face *because* it was a male infant. Any malicious jinn or afarit hovering about would not easily see that the baby was a valuable male child, hence would be less likely to attack it

with a disease or a curse or some other affliction. If the
baby had been a girl child, the mother would uncaringly
flick the flies away, and let the evil beings see it un-
obscured, because no demons would bother to molest a female, and the mother would not greatly care even if they
did.

Well, fortunately being a male myself, I supposed I had
to concur in the prevailing opinion that males were vastly
superior to females, and infinitely more to be treasured.
Nevertheless, I had had some small sexual experience,
which had led me to conclude that a woman or girl was useful and desirable and functional in that respect. If she was
or could be nothing else in the world, as a *receptacle* she
was incomparable, even necessary, even indispensable.

Not a bit of it, the boys indicated, laughing yet again at
my simplemindedness. Even as a receptacle, any Muslim
male was far more sexually responsive and delightful than
any Muslim female, whose parts had been properly dead-
ened by circumcision.

"Wait a moment," I conveyed to the boys. "You mean
the males' circumcision somehow causes. . . ?"

No, no, no. They shook their heads firmly. They meant
the circumcision of the females. I shook my own head. I
could not imagine how such an operation could be performed on a creature that possesses no Christian candelòto
or Muslim zab or even an infantile bimbìn. I was thoroughly mystified, and I told them so.

With an air of amused indulgence, they pointed out—
pointing toward their own truncated organs—that the
trimming of a boy's foreskin was done merely to mark him
as a Muslim. But, in every Muslim family of better than
beggar or slave status, every female infant was subjected
to an equivalent trimming in the cause of feminine de-
cency. To illustrate: it was a terrible revilement to call another man the "son of an uncircumcised mother." I was
still mystified.

"Toutes les bonnes femmes—tabzir de leurs zambur,"
they repeated over and over. They said that the tabzir,
whatever that was, was done to divest a baby girl of her
zambur, whatever that was, so that when she was grown to
womanhood she would be devoid of unseemly yearnings,
hence disinclined to adultery. She would be forever chaste
and above suspicion, as every bonne femme of Islam

should be: a passive pulp with no function but to dribble out as many male children as possible in her bleak lifetime. No doubt that was a commendable end result, but I still did not understand the boys' attempted explication of the tabzir means that effected it.

So I changed the subject and put another question. Suppose that, in the manner of Venetian young men, Ibrahim or Daud or Naser *did* want a woman, not a man or boy— and a woman not condemned to numbness and torpor— how would they go about finding one?

Naser and Daud snickered contemptuously. Ibrahim raised his eyebrows in disdainful inquiry, and at the same time raised his middle finger and moved it up and down.

"Yes," I said, nodding. "That sort of woman, if that is the only sort with any life left in her."

Though limited in their means of communication, the boys made it all too plain that, to find such a shameful woman, I should have to seek among the Christian women resident in Acre. Not that I should have to seek very strenuously, for there were many of those sluts. I had only to go—they pointed—to that building directly across the market square we stood in at that moment.

I said angrily, "That is a convent! A house of Christian nuns!"

They shrugged and stroked imaginary beards, asserting that they had spoken truly. And just then the door of the convent opened and a man and a woman came out into the square. He was a Crusader knight, wearing the surcoat insigne of the Order of San Làzaro. She was unveiled, obviously not an Arab woman, and she wore the white mantle and brown habit of the Order of Our Lady of Mount Carmel. Both of them were flushed of face and reeling with wine.

Then, of course, but only then, did I recall having heard two previous mentions of the "scandalous" Carmelitas and Clarissas. I had ignorantly assumed that the references were to the names of particular women. But now it was clear that what had been meant were the Carmelite sisters and those other nuns, the Minoresses of the Order of San Francesco, affectionately nicknamed Clarissas.

Feeling as if I had been personally disgraced in the eyes of the three infidel boys, I abruptly said goodbye to them. At that, they clamored and gestured insistently for me to join them soon again, indicating that then they would show me something *really* marvelous. I gave them a non-committal reply, and made my way through the streets and alleys back to the khane.

4

I arrived there at the same time my father was returning from his conference with the Archdeacon at the castle. As we approached our chamber, a young man came out of it, the hammam rubber who had attended Uncle Mafìo on our first day at the khane. He gave us a radiant smile and said, "Salaam aleikum," and my father properly responded, "Wa aleikum es-salaam."

Uncle Mafìo was in the room, apparently just in the process of putting on fresh clothes for the evening meal. In his hearty way, he began talking as soon as we entered:

"I had the boy bring me a new jar of the depilatory mumum, for determination of its constituents. It consists only of orpiment and quicklime, pounded together in a little olive oil, with a touch of musk added to make its aroma more pleasant. We could easily compound it ourselves, but its price here is so cheap that that is hardly worth our while. I told the boy to fetch me four dozen of the little jars. What of our priests, Nico?"

My father sighed. "Visconti seems ready enough to delegate every priest in Acre to go away with us. But he feels that, in fairness, they themselves should have something to say about making such a long and arduous journey. So he will only exert himself to the extent of asking for volunteers. He will let us know how many or how few they will be."

On one of the subsequent days, it happened that we were the only guests in residence at the khane, so my father genially asked the proprietor if he would do us the honor of joining us at our supper cloth.

"Your words are before my eyes, Sheikh Folo," said Ishaq, arranging his vast troussés so he could fold his legs to sit.

"And perhaps the Sheikha, your good wife, would join

us?" said my uncle. "That is your wife, is it not, in the kitchen?"

"She is indeed, Sheikh Folo. But she would not offend the decencies by presuming to eat in the company of men."

"Of course," said my uncle. "Forgive me. I was forgetting the decencies."

"As the Prophet has said (may blessing and peace be upon him): 'I stood at the gate of Heaven and saw that most of its inhabitants were paupers. I stood at the gate of Hell and saw that most of its inhabitants were women.' "

"Um, yes. Well, perhaps your children might join us, then, as company for Marco here. If you have children."

"Alas, I have none," Ishaq said dolefully. "I have only three daughters. My wife is a baghlah, and barren. Gentlemen, will you permit me humbly to petition grace upon this supper?" We all bowed our heads, and he muttered, "Allah ekber rakmet," adding in Venetian, "Allah is great, we thank Him."

We began helping ourselves to the mutton slices cooked with tomatoes and pearl onions, and to the baked cucumbers stuffed with rice and nuts. As we did so, I said to the landlord, "Excuse me, Sheikh Ishaq. May I ask you a question?"

He nodded affably. "Pleasure me with some command, young Sheikh."

"That word you used in speaking of your lady wife. Baghlah. I have heard it before. What does it mean?"

He looked a trifle discomfited. "A baghlah is a female mule. The word is also used to speak of a woman likewise infertile. Ah, I perceive that you think it a harsh word for me to use of my wife. And you are right. She is, after all, an excellent woman in other respects. You gentlemen may have noticed how magnificently moonlike is her behind. Wonderfully big and ponderously heavy. It forces her to sit down when she would stand up, and to sit up when she would lie down. Yes, an excellent woman. She also has beautiful hair, though you cannot have seen that. Longer and more luxuriant than my beard. No doubt you are aware that Allah appointed one of His angels to do nothing but stand by His throne and praise Him on that account. The angel has no other employment. He simply and constantly praises Allah for His having dispensed beards to men and long tresses to women."

When he paused for a moment in his prattle, I said, "I have heard another word. Kus. What is that?"

The servant who was waiting upon us made a strangled noise and Ishaq looked even more discomfited. "That is a very low word for—this is hardly a topic fit for mealtime discussion. I will not repeat the word, but it is a low term for the even lower parts of a woman."

"And ghunj?" I asked. "What is ghunj?"

The waiter gasped and hurriedly left the room, and Ishaq looked discomfited to the point of distress. "Where have you been spending your time, young Sheikh? That is also a low word. It means—it means the movement a woman makes. A woman or a—that is to say, the passive partner. The word refers to the movement made during— Allah forgive me—during the act of sexual congress."

Uncle Mafìo snorted and said, "My saputèlo nephew is eager to acquire new words, that he may be more useful when he travels with us into far regions."

Ishaq murmured, "As the Prophet has said (peace be upon him): 'A companion is the best provision for the road.'"

"There are a couple of other words—" I began.

"And, as the saying goes on," Ishaq growled, "'Even bad company is better than none.' But really, young Sheikh Folo, I must decline to translate any more of your acquisitions."

My father spoke then, and changed the subject to something innocuous, and our meal progressed to the sweet, a conserve of crystallized apricots, dates and citron rind, perfumed with amber. So I did not find out the meaning of those mysterious words tabzir and zambur until a long time afterward. When the meal ended, with qahwah and sharbat to drink, Ishaq again said the grace—unlike us Christians, the infidels do that at the close of a meal as well as at the beginning—"Allah ekber rakmet" and, with an air of relief, left our company.

When, some days later, my father, my uncle and I went again to Acre castle at the summons of the Archdeacon, he met us in assemblage with the Prince and Princess, and also two men wearing the white habits and black mantles of the Order of Friars Preachers of San Domènico. When we had all exchanged greetings, the Archdeacon Visconti introduced the newcomers:

"Fra Nicolò of Vicenza and Fra Guglielmo of Tripoli. They have volunteered to accompany you, Messeri Polo."

Whatever disappointment he may have felt, my father dissembled, saying only, "I am grateful to you, Brothers, and I welcome you to our party. But may I inquire why you have volunteered to join our mission?"

One of them said, in rather a petulant voice, "Because we are disgusted with the behavior of our Christian fellows here in Acre."

The other said, in the same tone, "We look forward to the cleaner and purer air of Far Tartary."

"Thank you, Brothers," my father said, still politely. "Now, would you excuse our having a private word with His Reverence and Their Royal Highnesses?"

The two friars sniffed as if offended, but left the room. To the Archdeacon, my father then quoted the Bible, "The harvest indeed is great, but the laborers are few."

Visconti countered with the quotation, "Where there are two or three gathered together in My name, there am I in the midst of them."

"But, Your Reverence, I asked for priests."

"And no priest volunteered. These two, however, are Preaching Friars. As such, they are empowered to undertake practically any ecclesiastical task—from founding a church to settling a matrimonial dispute. Their powers of consecration and absolution are somewhat limited, of course, and they cannot confer ordination, but you would have to take along a bishop for that. I am sorry for the fewness of the volunteers, but I cannot in conscience conscript or compel any others. Have you any further complaint?"

My father hesitated, but my uncle boldly spoke up, "Yes, Your Reverence. The friars admit they are not going for any positive purpose. They wish simply to get away from this dissolute city."

"Just like Saint Paul," the Archdeacon said drily. "I refer you to the Book of Acts of the Apostles. This city was in those times called Ptolemais, and Paul once set foot here, and evidently he could stand the place for only a single day."

Princess Eleanor said fervently, "Amen!" and Prince Edward chuckled in sympathy.

"You have your choice," Visconti said to us. "You can apply elsewhere, or you can await the election of a Pope and apply to him. Or you can accept the services of the two Dominican brothers. They declare that they will be ready and eager to leave on the morrow."

"We accept them, of course, Your Reverence," said my father. "And we thank you for your good offices."

"Now," said Prince Edward. "You must get beyond the Saracen lands in order to go eastward. There is one best route."

"We would be gratified to know it," said Uncle Mafìo. He had brought with him the Kitab of al-Idrisi, and he opened it to the pages showing Acre and its environs.

"A good map," the Prince said approvingly. "Look you, then. To go east from here, you must first go north, to skirt around the Mamluks inland." Like every other Christian, the Prince held the pages upside down to put north at the top. "But the major ports nearest to the northward: Beirut, Tripoli, Latakia . . ."—he tapped the gilded dots on the map which represented those seaports—"if they have not already fallen to the Saracens, they are heavily under siege. You must go—let me calculate: more than two hundred English miles—north along the coast. To this place in Lesser Armeniya." He tapped a spot on the map which apparently did not merit a gilded dot. "There, where the Orontes River debouches into the sea, is the old port of Suvediye. It is inhabited by Christian Armeniyans and peaceable Avedi Arabs, and the Mamluks have not yet got near it."

"That was once a major port of the Roman Empire, called Selucia," said the Archdeacon. "It has since been called Ayas and Ajazzo and many other names. Of course, you will go to Suvediye by sea, not along the coast itself."

"Yes," said the Prince. "There is an English ship leaving here for Cyprus on tomorrow's evening tide. I will instruct the captain to go by way of Suvediye, and to take you and your friars along. I will give you a letter to the Ostikan, the governor of Suvediye, bidding him see to your safe conduct." He directed our attention again to the Kitab. "When you have procured pack animals in Suvediye, you will go inland through the river pass—here—then east to the Euphrates River. You should have an easy journey down the Euphrates valley to Baghdad. And from Baghdad, there are diverse routes to the farther eastward."

My father and uncle stayed on at the castle while the Prince wrote the letter of safe conduct. But they let me make my farewells to His Reverence and Their Royal Highnesses, so that I might take my leave and spend that last day in Acre as I pleased. I did not see the Archdeacon or the Prince and Princess again, but I did hear news of them. My father, my uncle and I had not been long gone from the Levant when we got word that the Archdeacon Visconti had been elected Pope of the Church of Rome, and had taken the papal name of Gregory X. About the same time, Prince Edward gave up the Crusade as a lost cause, and sailed for home. He had got as far as Sicily when he too received some news: that his father had died and that he was King of England. So, all unknowing, I had been acquainted with two of the men of highest eminence in Europe. But I have never much preened in that brief acquaintance. After all, I was later to meet men in the East whose eminence made midgets of Popes and kings.

When I left the castle that day, it was at one of the five hours when Arabs pray to their god Allah, and the beadles whom they call muedhdhin were perched on every tower and high rooftop, loudly but monotonously intoning the chants that announce those hours. Everywhere—in shops and doorways and in the dusty street—men of the Islamic faith were unfolding tatty little rugs and kneeling on them. Turning their faces to the southeast, they pressed those faces to the ground between their hands, while they elevated their rear ends in the air. At those hours, any man you could look in the face instead of the rump had to be a Christian or a Jew.

As soon as everyone in Acre was vertical again, I spotted my three acquaintances of a week or so before. Ibrahim, Naser and Daud had seen me go into the castle and had waited near its entrance for me to emerge. They were all shiny-eyed with eagerness to show me the great marvel they had promised. First, they conveyed to me, I must eat something they had brought. Naser was carrying a little leather bag, which proved to contain a quantity of figs preserved in sesame oil. I liked figs well enough, but these were so oil-soaked that they were pulpy and slimy and disagreeable in the mouth. Nevertheless, the boys insisted that I must ingest them as preparation for the revelation

to come, so I forced myself to swallow four or five of the
dreadful things.

Then the boys led me on a roundabout way through the
streets and alleys. It began to seem a very long way, and I
began to feel very weary in my limbs and addled in my
mind. I wondered if the hot sun was affecting my bare head
or if the figs had been somehow tainted. My vision was dis-
turbed; the people and buildings about me seemed to sway
and distort themselves in odd ways. My ears sang as if I
were beset by swarms of flies. My feet stumbled on every
least irregularity in our path, and I pleaded with the boys
to let me stop and rest for a bit. But they, still insistent and
excited, took my arms and helped me plod along. I understood from them that my muzziness was indeed an effect of
the specially pickled figs, and that it was necessary to
what was to come next.

I found myself dragged to an open but very dark doorway, and I started obediently to enter. But the boys set up
an angry uproar, and I interpreted it to mean something
like "You stupid infidel, you must take off your shoes and
enter barefooted"—from which I assumed the building
must be one of the houses of worship the Muslims call a
masjid. Since I was not wearing shoes, but soled hose, I had
to strip myself naked from the waist down. I clutched my
tunic and stretched it as far down over my exposed self as I
could, meanwhile wondering woozily why it should be
more acceptable to enter a masjid with one's privates bare
than with one's feet shod. Anyway, the boys did not hesitate, but propelled me through the doorway and inside the
place.

Never having been in a masjid, I did not know what to
expect, but I was vaguely surprised to find it absolutely
unlighted and empty of worshipers or anybody else. All I
could see in the dim interior was a row of immense stoneware jars, nearly as tall as I was, standing against one
wall. The boys led me to the jar at the end of the row and
bade me get into it.

I had been slightly apprehensive—being outnumbered
and half nude and not in full command of myself—that the
juvenile Sodomites perhaps had designs upon my body,
and I was prepared to fight. But what they proposed struck
me as more hilarious than outrageous. When I asked for
an explanation, they simply continued to motion at the

massive jar, and I was too fuddled to balk. Instead, even while laughing at the preposterousness of what I was doing, I let the boys boost me up to a sitting position on the lip of the jar, and swung my feet over and let myself down into it.

Not until I was inside it did I perceive that the jar contained a fluid, because there was no splash or sudden feeling of coldness or wetness. But the jar was at least half filled with oil, so nearly at body warmth that I hardly felt it until my immersion raised its level to my throat. It really felt rather pleasant: emollient and enveloping and smooth and soothing, especially around my tired legs and my sensitively exposed private parts. That realization roused me a little. Was this a prelude peculiar to some strange and exotic sexual rite? Well, thus far at least, it felt good and I did not complain.

Only my head protruded from the collar of the jar, and my fingers still rested on its rim. The boys laughingly pushed my hands inside with me, and then produced something they must have found nearby: a large disk of wood and hinges, rather like a portable pillory. Before I could protest or dodge, they fitted the thing around my neck and closed it shut. It made a lid for the jar I stood in, and, though it was not uncomfortably constrictive around my neck, it somehow had clamped onto the jar so securely that I could not dislodge or lift it.

"What is this?" I demanded, as I sloshed my arms around inside the jar and vainly shoved upward against the wooden lid. I could slosh and shove only slowly, as sometimes one moves in a dream, because of the warm oil's viscosity. My confused senses finally registered the sesame smell of that oil. Like the figs I had earlier been made to eat, I had apparently been put to steep in sesame oil. "What is this?" I shouted again.

"Va istadan! Attendez!" commanded the boys, making gestures for me to stand patient in my jar and wait.

"Wait?" I bellowed. "Wait for what?"

"Attendez le sorcier," said Naser with a giggle. Then he and Daud ran out through the gray oblong that was the door to the outside.

"Wait for the wizard?" I repeated in mystification. "Wait for how long?"

Ibrahim lingered long enough to hold up some fingers

for me to count. I peered through the gloom and saw that
he had splayed the fingers of both hands.

"Ten?" I said . "Ten what?" He too edged backward toward the door, meanwhile closing his fingers and flicking
them open again—four times. "Forty?" I said desperately.
"Forty what? Quarante à propos de quoi?"

"Chihil ruz," he said. "Quarante jours." And he disappeared out the door.

"Wait for forty *days?*" I wailed, but got no answer.

All three boys were gone and, it seemed evident, not just
to hide from me for a while. I was left alone in my pickling
jar in the dark room, with the smell of the sesame oil in my
nose, and the loathsome taste of figs and sesame in my
mouth, and still a whirl of confusion in my mind. I tried
hard to think what all this meant. Wait for the wizard? No
doubt it was a boyish prank, something to do with Arab
custom. The khane landlord Ishaq would probably explain
it to me, with many a laugh at my gullibility. But what
kind of prank could keep me immured for forty days? I
would miss tomorrow's ship and be marooned in Acre, and
Ishaq would have ample time to explain Arab customs to
me at leisure. Or would I have vanished in the clutches of
the wizard? Did the infidel Muslim religion, unlike the
rectitudinous Christian, allow wizards to practice their
evil arts unmolested? I tried to imagine what a Muslim
wizard would want with a bottled Christian. I hoped I
would not find out. Would my father and uncle come looking for me before they sailed? Would they find me before
the wizard did? Would anybody?

Just then somebody did. A shadowy shape, larger than
any of the boys, loomed in the gray doorway. It paused
there, as if waiting for its eyes to adjust to the darkness,
and then moved slowly toward my jar. It was tall and
bulky—and ominous. I felt as if I were contracting, or
shriveling, inside the jar, and wished I could retract my
head below the lid.

When the man got close enough, I saw that he wore
clothes of the Arab style, except that he had no cords binding his headcloth. He had a curly red-gray beard like a sort
of fungus, and he stared at me with bright blackberry eyes.
When he spoke the traditional greeting of peace-be-with-
you, I noticed even in my befuddlement that he pro-

nounced it slightly differently from the Arab manner: "Shalom aleichem."

"Are you the wizard?" I whispered, so frightened that I said it in Venetian. I cleared my throat and repeated it in French.

"Do I look like a wizard?" he demanded in a rasping voice.

"No," I whispered, though I had no idea what a wizard ought to look like. I cleared my throat again and said, "You look more like someone I used to know."

"And you," he said scornfully, "seem to seek out smaller and ever smaller prison cells."

"How did you know—?"

"I saw those three little mamzarim manhandle you in here. This place is well and infamously known."

"I meant—"

"And I saw them leave again without you, just the three of them. You would not be the first fair-haired and blue-eyed lad to come in here and never come out again."

"Surely there are not many hereabouts with eyes and hair not black."

"Precisely. You are a rarity in these parts, and the oracle must speak through a rarity."

I was already confused enough. I think I just blinked at him. He bent down out of my sight for a moment, and then reappeared, holding the leather bag that Naser must have dropped when he departed. The man reached into it and took out an oil-dripping fig. I nearly retched at sight of it.

"They find such a boy," he said. "They bring him here and soak him in sesame oil, and they feed him only these oil-soaked figs. At the end of forty days and nights, he has become macerated as soft as a fig. So soft that his head can be easily lifted off his body." He demonstrated, twisting the fig in his fingers to that, with a squishy noise just barely audible, it came in two.

"Whatever for?" I said breathlessly. I seemed to feel my body softening below the wooden lid, becoming waxy and malleable like the fig, already sagging, preparing to part from my neck stump with a squishy noise and sink slowly to rest on the bottom of the jar. "I mean, why kill a perfect stranger, and in such a way?"

"It does not kill him, so they say. It is an affair of black sorcery." He dropped the bag and the pieces of fig and wiped his fingers on the hem of his gown. "At any rate, the head part of him goes on living."

"What?"

"The wizard props the severed head in that niche in the wall yonder, on a comfortable bed of olivewood ashes. He burns incense before it, and chants magic words, and after a while the head speaks. On command, it will foretell famines or bounteous harvests, forthcoming wars or times of peace, all manner of useful prophecies like that."

I began to laugh, at least realizing that he was merely joining in the prank that had been played on me, and prolonging it.

"Very well," I said between laughs. "You have paralyzed me with terror, old cellmate. I am uncontrollably pissing and adulterating this fine oil. But now, enough. When I last saw you, Mordecai, I did not know you would flee this far from Venice. But you are here, and I am glad to see you, and you have had your joke. Now release me, and we will go and drink a qahwah together and talk of our adventures since last we met." He did not move; he simply stood and looked sorrowfully at me. "Mordecai, enough!"

"My name is Levi," he said. "Poor lad, you are already ensorceled to the point of derangement."

"Mordecai, Levi, whoever you are!" I ranted, beginning to feel a touch of panic. "Lift this accursed lid and let me out!"

"I? I will not touch that terephah uncleanness," he said, fastidiously taking a step backward. "I am not a filthy Arab. I am a Jew."

My disquiet and anger and exasperation were beginning to clear my head, but they were not influencing me to be tactful. I said, "Did you come here, then, only to entertain me in my confinement? Are you going to leave me here for the idiot Arabs? Is a Jew as idiotically superstitious as they are?"

He grunted, "Al tidàg," and left me. He trudged across the chamber and out through the gray doorway opening. I looked after him, appalled. Did al tidàg mean something like be-damned-to-you? He was probably my only hope of rescue, and I had insulted him.

But he came back almost immediately, and he was carrying a heavy bar of metal. "Al tidàg," he said again, and then thought to translate: "Do not worry. I will get you out, as I am bidden, but I must do it without touching the uncleanness. Happily for you, I am a blacksmith, and my smithy is just across the way. This bar will do it. Stand firm, now, young Marco, so you do not fall when it breaks."

He swung the bar and, at the moment it crashed against the jar, he leapt well to one side, so that his garments would not be defiled by the resultant cascade of oil. The jar shattered with a great noise, and I swayed unsteadily, as the pieces and all the oil fell away from me. The wooden lid suddenly weighed heavily on my neck. But, since I could now reach my hands to the upper surface of it, I quickly found and undid the catches that held it closed, and I dropped the wooden disk in the spreading pool of oil at my feet.

"Will you not get into trouble over this?" I asked, indicating the mess all about us. Very elaborately, Levi shrugged his shoulders, his hands and his fungoid eyebrows. I went on, "You called me by name, and you said something about having been bidden to rescue me from this danger."

"Not from this danger specifically," he said. "The word was merely to try to keep Marco Polo out of trouble. There were also some words of description—that you could easily be recognized by your proximity to the nearest available trouble."

"That is interesting. The word from whom?"

"I have no idea. I gather that you once helped some Jew get out of a bad spot. And the proverb says that the reward of a mitzva is another mitzva."

"Ah, as I suspected: old Mordecai Cartafilo."

Levi said, almost peevishly, "That could be no Jew. Mordecai is a name from ancient Babylon. And Cartafilo is a gentile name."

"He said he was a Jew, and so he seemed to be, and that was the name he used."

"Next you will say that he wandered, as well."

Puzzled, I said, "Well, he did tell me that he had traveled extensively."

"Khakma," he said, which rasping noise I took to be a word of derision. "That is a fable concocted by fabulists of the goyim. There is not one immortal wandering Jew. The Lamed-vav are mortal, but there are always thirty-six of them going secretly and helpfully about the world."

I was disinclined to linger in that dark place while Levi argued about fables. I said, "You are a fine one to sneer at fabulists, after your ludicrous tale of wizards and talking heads."

He gave me a long look, and scratched thoughtfully in his curly beard. "Ludicrous?" He held out to me his metal bar. "Here. I do not wish to put my feet in the oil. You break the next jar in the row."

I hesitated for a moment. Even if this place was just an ordinary masjid house of worship, we had already considerably desecrated it. But then I thought: one jar, two jars, what matter? And I swung the bar as hard as I could, and the second jar broke with a brittle smash, and loosed its surge of sesame oil with a splash, and something else hit the ground with a thick, moist thud. I bent over to see it better, and then hastily recoiled, and said to Levi, "Come, let us go away."

On the threshold I found my hose where I had discarded them, and I gratefully put them on again. I did not mind that they got instantly soaked with the oil clinging to me; the rest of my garb already was sopping and clammy. I thanked Levi for his having rescued me, and for his explication of Arabian sorcery. He bade me "lechàim and boy voyage," and cautioned me not to depend on the relayed word of a nonexistent Jew to keep me forever out of *every* trouble. Then he went off to his forge and I hastened back toward the inn, looking repeatedly over my shoulder in case I should be seen and pursued by the three Arab boys or the wizard for whom they had captured me. I no longer believed the adventure to have been a prank, and I no longer contemned the sorcery as a fable.

When Levi watched me break that second jar, he did not ask me what it was I bent to peer at among its shards, and I did not try to tell him, and I cannot tell it clearly even yet. The place was very dark, as I have said. But the object that fell onto the ground with that sickening wet plop was a human body. What I was and can tell about it is that the corpse was naked, and had been a male, not full grown to manhood. Also it lay oddly on the ground, like a sack made of skin, a sack that had been emptied of its contents. I mean it looked more than soft, it looked flaccid, as if somehow all its bones had been extracted, or dissolved. The only other thing I could see was that the body had no head. I have never since that time been able to eat figs or anything flavored with sesame.

5

THE next afternoon, my father paid our bill to landlord Ishaq, who accepted the money with the words, "May Allah smother you with gifts, Sheikh Folo, and repay every generous act of yours." And my uncle distributed to the khane servants the gratuities of smaller money, which are in all the East called by the Farsi word bakhshish. He gave the largest amount to the hammam rubber who had introduced him to the mumum ointment, and that young man thanked him with the words, "May Allah conduct you through every hazard and keep you ever smiling." And all the staff, Ishaq and the servants together, stood in the inn door to wave after us with many other cries:

"May Allah flatten the road before you!"

"May you travel as upon a silken carpet!" and the like.

So our expedition proceeded northward up the Levantine coast, and I congratulated myself on having got out of Acre intact, and I trusted that I had had my one and last encounter with sorcery.

That short sea voyage was unremarkable, as we stayed in sight of the shore the whole way, and that shore is everywhere much the same to look at: dun-colored dunes with dun-colored hills behind them, the occasional dun-colored mud hut or village of mud huts almost imperceptible against the landscape. The cities we sailed past were slightly more distinguishable, since each was marked by a Crusaders' castle. The most noticeable from the sea was the city of Beirut, it being sizable and set upon an outjutting point of land, but I judged it to be inferior, as a city, even to Acre.

My father and uncle occupied themselves on shipboard with making lists of the equipment and supplies they should have to procure in Suvediye. I occupied myself mainly in chatting with the crew; although most of them were Englishmen, they of course spoke the Sabir of travelers and traders. The Brothers Guglielmo and Nicolò occu-

pied themselves in talking to each other, and talking
endlessly, about the iniquities of Acre and how thankful
they were to God for His having let them decamp from
there. Of all the complaints they might have aired in regard to Acre, they seemed most exercised about the
unchaste and licentious behavior of the resident Clarissas
and Carmelitas. But, from what I overheard of their lam-
entations, they sounded more like hurt husbands or rejected suitors of those nuns than like their brothers in
Christ. Lest I sound disrespectful of a noble calling, I will
say no more about my impressions of the two friars. For
they deserted our expedition before we got any farther
than Suvediye.

That city was a poor and small place. To judge from the
ruins and remains of a much larger city standing around
it, Suvediye had gradually been reduced from what grandeur it may have had in Roman times, or perhaps earlier,
when Alexander had come its way. The reason for its diminishment was not far to seek. Our own ship, not a large
one, had to anchor well out of the little bay, and we passengers had to be brought ashore in a skiff, because the harbor
was so badly silted and shallowed by the outflow of the
Orontes River there. I do not know if Suvediye still is a
functioning seaport, but at that time it clearly did not have
very many more years in which to be so.

For all the city's puniness and poor prospects, Suvediye's inhabitant Armeniyans seemed to regard it as the
equal of a Venice or a Bruges. Though only one other ship
was anchored there when ours arrived, the port officials
behaved as if their harbor roads were thronged with vessels, and all requiring the most scrupulous attention. A fat
and greasy Armeniyan inspector came bustling aboard,
his arms laden with papers, while we five passengers were
in the process of debarking. He insisted on counting us—
five—and all our packs and bundles, and entered the numbers in a ledger. Then he let us go, and began to pester the
English captain for the information with which to fill out
innumerable other manifests of cargo, origin, destination
and so forth.

There was no Crusaders' castle in Suvediye, so we five—
pushing our way through the city's throngs of beggars—
went directly to the palace of the Ostikan, or governor, to
present our letters from Prince Edward. I charitably call

the Ostikan's residence a palace; it was in fact a rather shabby building, but it was respectable in extent and two stories in height. After numerous entry guards and reception clerks and under-officials had severally demonstrated their importance, each of them delaying us with an officious show of fuss, we were finally conducted into the palace throne room. I charitably call it a throne room, for the Ostikan sat on no imposing throne, but lolled on what is called a daiwan, which is only a heap of cushions. In spite of the day's warmth, he repeatedly rubbed his hands over a brazier of coals before him. In a corner, a young man sat on the floor, using a large knife to cut his toenails. Those nails must have been exceedingly horny; each gave a loud thwack as it was cut off, and then went *whiz* and fell elsewhere in the room with an audible click.

The Ostikan's name was Hampig Bagratunian, but his name was the only wonderful thing about him. He was small and wizened, and like all Armeniyans, he had no back to his head. It was flat there, as if his head had been designed to hang on a wall. He did not look at all like a governor of anything, and he was as clerkly as his clerks in tongue-clucking fussiness. Unlike an Arab or a Jew, who obey their religions' injunctions to entertain strangers with a good grace, the Christian Armeniyan received us with unconcealed annoyance.

When he had read the letter, he said in Sabir, "Just because I am a fellow monarch"—casually inflating his rank to regality—"any other prince seems to think he can rid himself of a bother by shunting it on to me."

We politely said nothing. A toenail went *thwack,* whiz, *click.*

Ostikan Hampig continued, "Here you arrive on the very eve of my son's wedding"—he indicated the toenail cutter—"when I have countless other things to attend to, and guests coming from all over the Levant, trying not to get themselves slaughtered by the Mamluks on their way, and all the festivities to arrange, and . . ." He went on listing the botherations to which our arrival had added another.

His son carved off a final clamorous toenail, then looked up and said, "Wait, Father."

The Ostikan, interrupted in his recital, said, "Yes, Kagig?"

Kagig got up from where he sat, but did not quite rise eréct. Instead, he began to roam about the room, bent over, as if to give us a good view of the flat back of his head. He picked up something, and I realized that he was for some reason retrieving his pared bits of toenail. While he worked, he said over his shoulder to the Ostikan, "These strangers brought two churchmen with them."

"Yes, so they did," his father said impatiently. "What of it?"

One of the toenail crescents had landed near my own foot; I picked it up and gave it to Kagig. He nodded and, seeming satisfied that he had all the bits, he sat down beside his father on the daiwan, brushing the horny scraps from his hand into the brazier. "There," he said. "No sorcerer will use those to conjure against me." The toenails seemed still determined not to die quietly: they sizzled and popped among the coals.

"What about these churchmen, my boy?" Hampig inquired again, paternally stroking his son's backless head.

"Well, we have old Dimirjian to conduct my nuptial mass," Kagig said languidly. "But every common peasant has *one* priest to do the marrying of him. Suppose I had three . . ."

"Hm," said his father, turning his eyes to the Brothers Nicolò and Guglielmo; they stared haughtily back at him. "Yes, that would add to the pomp of the occasion." To my father and uncle he said, "You may not be unwelcome, after all. Are these clerics empowered to confer the sacrament of matrimony?"

"Yes, Your Excellency," said my father. "These are Friars Preachers."

"They could serve the mass as acolytes suffragan to the Metropolitan Dimirjian. And they should feel honored to participate. My son is marrying a pshi—a Princess—of the Adighei. What you call the Circassians."

"A people famous for their beauty," said Uncle Mafìo. "But . . . Christian?"

"My son's betrothed has taken instruction from the Metropolitan Dimirjian himself, and Confirmation and First Communion. The Princess Seosseres is now a Christian."

"And a beautiful Christian indeed," said Kagig, smacking his liverlike lips. "People stop in their footsteps when they see her—even Muslims and other infidels—and bow their heads and thank the Creator for having created the Pshi Seosseres."

"Well?" Hampig said to us. "The wedding is tomorrow."

My father said, "I am sure the frati will be honored to participate. Your Excellency has only to bid me, and I will bid them serve."

The two frati looked somewhat indignant at not having been personally consulted during the conversation, but they raised no objection.

"Good," said the Ostikan. "We shall have three ecclesiastics at the nuptials, and two of them foreigners from afar. Yes, that will impress my guests and my subjects. On that condition, then, messieurs, you will—"

"We will remain here in Suvediye for the royal wedding," said Uncle Mafìo, smoothly dropping in the adjective. "Of course, we will desire to continue our journey immediately afterward. And so, of course, Your Excellency will meantime have helped to expedite our procurement of mounts and supplies."

"Er . . . yes . . . of course," said Hampig, looking fussed at having been given some conditions in return. He rang a bell by his hand, and one of the under-officials entered. "This is my palace steward, messieurs. Arpad, you will show these gentlemen to quarters here in the palace, then introduce the friars to the Metropolitan, then accompany the gentlemen to the market and render whatever assistance they may require." He turned again to us. "Very well, then. I welcome you to Suvediye, messieurs, and I formally invite you to the royal wedding and all the attendant festivities."

So Arpad led us to two chambers on the upper floor, one for us and one for the friars. As soon as we had unpacked enough of our belongings for a brief stay, we went downstairs again and handed the Brothers over to the Metropolitan Dimirjian. He was a large old man, the backlessness of whose head was less remarkable than what could be seen on the forward side of it: a massive nose, a weighty underslung jaw, overslung eyebrows and long fleshy ears. When he had taken the friars off to rehearse them in the morrow's ritual, my father, my uncle and I went with Steward Arpad to the Suvediye marketplace.

"You might as well get used to calling it the bazàr," he said helpfully. "That is the Farsi word used from here to the eastward. You are buying at a good time, for the wedding has attracted vendors from everywhere, hawking every conceivable thing, so you will have ample choice of goods. But I beg that you will let me assist you in the bargaining for your selections. God knows the Arab merchants are tricksters and swindlers, but the Armeniyans are so much shiftier that only a fellow Armeniyan dares deal with them. The Arabs would merely cheat you naked. The Armeniyans would flay you of your very skins."

"The chief thing we need is riding animals," said my uncle. "They can carry us and what goods we have, as well."

"I suggest horses," said Arapd. "You may wish to change them later for camels, when you have much desert to cross. But for now, since your next destination is Baghdad, no hard journey, horses will be more speedy, and much more easy to handle than camels. Mules would be even better, but I doubt that you wish to spend what they would cost."

In much of the East, as in civilized Europe, the mule, because it is so gentle and amenable and intelligent, is the preferred mount of men and ladies of high degree—meaning the very rich—so a mule breeder unblushingly asks exorbitant prices for his animals. My father and uncle agreed that they did not care to pay such prices, that horses would have to do for us.

So we visited the several rope corrals set up around the outskirts of the bazàr, where could be bought all sorts of riding and pack animals: mules, asses, horses of every breed from the exquisite Arabian to the heftiest drafter, and also camels and their cousins, the sleek racing dromedaries. After examining many horses, my father and uncle and the steward settled on five—two geldings and three mares—of good appearance and conformation, not so heavy as the draft animals but nowhere near so elegant as the fine-boned Arabians.

Buying five horses meant five separate dickerings. So there in the Suvediye bazàr, for the first time, I witnessed a procedure that I was eventually to become weary of, for I had to endure it in every bazàr of the East. I mean the curious Eastern manner of transacting a purchase. Although the steward Arpad kindly did it for us that time, it was a prolonged and tedious affair.

Arpad and the horse trader each extended a hand to the

other, letting their long sleeves drape over the meeting
hands to make them invisible to anyone looking on—and
in any bazàr there are always countless loiterers with
nothing better to do than to watch other people's business
dealings. Then Arpad and the trader each wiggled and
tapped his hidden fingers against the other's hidden hand,
the trader signaling the price he wanted, Arpad the price
he would give. Although I learned the signals and remember them well, I will not set them out in all their intricacy.
Suffice it to say that one man first taps to indicate either
single digits or tens or hundreds, and thus, by subsequently tapping thrice, say, indicates either three or thirty
or three hundred. And so on. The system allows the signaling even of fractions, and even of the different values
when buyer and merchant must deal in different currencies, say dinars and ducats.

By exchanging the taps, the horse trader gradually reduced his demand, and the steward gradually increased
his offer. In this way, they worked their way through all
the reasonable prices and unreasonable extortions conceivable. In the East, the various sorts of prices even have
names: the great price, the small price, the city price, the
beautiful price, the fixed price, the good price—and an in-
finity of others. When they reached a mutually acceptable
deal for the first horse, they had to repeat the process for
each of the four others, and in each case the steward had to
consult at intervals with us, not to exceed his authority or
our purse.

Any of those sessions could easily have been conducted
in spoken words, but that is never done, for the secrecy
of the hand-and-sleeve method benefits both buyer and
seller, since no one else ever knows the original asking
price or the final price agreed on. Thus a buyer sometimes
can drive a merchant down to a figure the merchant would
be ashamed to speak aloud, but he may finally sell at that
price, knowing that any next prospective buyer will not
know of it and cannot take advantage of it. Or a buyer, so
eager to acquire some item that he will not haggle much
over the price, can pay it knowing that he will not be jeered
by the bystanders for a spendthrift fool.

Our five transactions were not completed until the sun
was almost down, leaving us not time enough that day
even to buy saddles for the horses, not to mention the

many other necessities on our lists. We had to return to the palace, to visit its hammam and get thoroughly clean before donning our best clothes for the evening meal. For it was to be a banquet, Arpad told us, the traditional all-male celebration on the eve of a wedding. While we were being rubbed and pummeled in the hammam, my father said anxiously to my uncle:

"Mafìo, we must present some sort of celebratory gift to the Ostikan or his son or his son's bride, if not a gift to each of them. I cannot think what might be suitable. Worse, I cannot think what we might afford. Our budget was much depleted by the purchase of those mounts, and we have many other things yet to buy."

"No fear. I had already given that some thought," said my uncle, sounding confident as usual. "I looked into the kitchen where the banquet is being prepared. For color and condiment, the cooks are using what they told me was safflower. I tasted it and—can you imagine?—it is nothing but common càrtamo, bastard zafràn. They have none of the real thing. So we will give the Ostikan a brick of our good golden zafràn, and it should delight him more than the golden trinkets everyone else will be giving."

For all its decrepitude, the palace had a commendably large dining hall, and that night it needed it, because just the males among the Ostikan's guests made a tremendous crowd. They were mostly Armeniyans and Arabs—the former including the "royal" Bagratunian family and its relations, from close to remote; plus the palace and government officials; plus what I suppose passed for the nobility of Suvediye; plus legions of visitors from elsewhere in Lesser Armeniya and the rest of the Levant. The Arabs seemed all to be of the Avendi tribe, which must have been a huge tribe, for all the Arabs claimed to be sheikhs of high or lower degree. My father, my uncle, the two Dominicans and myself were not the only foreigners, for all of the bride's Circassian family had come south from the Caucasus Mountains for the occasion. I might say that they were—as is reputed of all Circassians—a strikingly handsome people, and by far the best looking men in the company that night.

The banquet actually consisted of two separate meals, served simultaneously, each meal comprising numberless courses. Those courses served to us and the Armeniyan

Christians were the most various, because they were not
limited by any infidel superstitions. The courses set before
the Muslim guests had to exclude the many foods their Quran forbids them to eat—pork, of course, and shellfish, and
every meat from every sort of creature that lives in a hole,
whether a hole in the ground, a hole in a tree or a hole in
the underwater mud.

I paid no particular attention to what the Arab guests
were given to eat, but I recall that our Christian main
course was a young camel calf stuffed with a lamb which
was stuffed with a goose which was stuffed with minced
pork, pistachios, raisins, pine seeds and spices. There were
also stuffed aubergines and stuffed marrows and stuffed
vine leaves. For drink, there were sharbats made with
still-frozen *snow,* brought from God knows where and by
God knows what swift means and at God knows what cost.
The sharbats were of different flavors—lemon, rose, quince,
peach—and all perfumed with nard and frankincense. For
sweets, there were pastries rich with butter and honey and
as crisp as honeycombs, and a paste called halwah, made of
powdered almonds, and lime tarts, and little cakes unbelievably made of rose petals and orange blossoms, and a
conserve of dates stuffed with almonds and cloves. There
was also the uniquely wonderful qahwah. There were
wines of many different colors, and other intoxicating liquors.

The Christians speedily got drunk on those drinks, and
the Arabs and Circassians were not far behind them. It is
well known that the Muslims' Quran forbids them to drink
wine, but it is not so well known that many Muslims observe that stricture *precisely* to the letter of the law. I will
explain. Since wine must have been the only intoxicant in
the world at the time the Prophet Muhammad wrote the
Quran, it did not occur to him to proscribe every inebriat-
ing substance that might subsequently be discovered or invented. Thus many Muslims, even the most rigidly
religious in other respects, feel at liberty—especially on
festive occasions—to drink any intoxicant not, like wine,
made from grapes, and also to chew the herb they variously call hashish, banj, bhang and ghanja, which is quite
as potently deranging as any wine.

Since that night's banquet was well provided with vivacious drinks never dreamed of by the Prophet—a sparkling

urine-colored liquid called abijau, which is brewed from grain, and araq, which is wrung from dates, and something called medhu, which is an essence of honey, and also gummy wads of hashish for chewing—the Arabs and Circassians, except for a few elderly holy men among them, became just as addled and jolly and argumentative and lachrymose as did all the Christians. Well, not all the Christians; my uncle got notably bleary and inclined to sing, but my father and I and the friars abstained.

There was a band of musicians—or acrobats, it was hard to say which, for they did the most astonishing capers and tricks and contortions *while they played*. Their instruments were bagpipes and drums and long-necked lutes, and I would have called their music a dreadful caterwauling, except that I suppose it was admirable that they could play at all while they were doing somersaults and walking on their hands and bounding on and off each other's shoulders.

The guests knelt or squatted or half-reclined on daiwan pillows around the dining cloths which covered every square inch of the floor, except in the narrow aisles where the servers and servants moved about in a sort of crouch. The guests got up, one or a group of them after another, to carry to the Ostikan and his son, who sat on a dais raised a little above the rest of the company, the gifts they had brought for the occasion. They knelt and bowed their heads and raised up in their hands ewers and platters and dishes of gold and silver, and jeweled brooches and tiaras and tulband medallions, and fabrics of silk threaded with gold, and many other fine things.

I discovered that night that, in the lands of the East, the recipient of a gift must give in return not just thanks but a gift at least as rich as that which he is given. I was to see that exchange take place often and often thereafter, and to see many a donor walk away with something incalculably more valuable than what he gave. But that night I was more amused than impressed by the practice. For the Ostikan Hampig, having the soul of a clerk, complied with the custom simply by giving to each new donor some object from the pile of valuables he had been given by earlier givers. It amounted to nothing more than a brisk shuffle of the gifts, so that, in effect, the guests would all go home with the same goods they had brought—only each would go home with someone else's.

Hampig made only one departure from that routine, when it came our turn to get up and advance to the dais. As my uncle had predicted, the Ostikan was so overjoyed to receive our brick of zafràn that he bade his son Kagig get up and run to fetch something extraordinary to give in return. Kagig came back with three objects that looked—as a brick of zafràn does at first glance—rather commonplace. They appeared to be merely three small leather purses. But when Hampig handed them reverently to my father, we saw that they were the cods of musk deer, tightly packed with the precious grains of musk obtained from those deer. The three deer scrota were provided with long rawhide strings, for a reason which Hampig explained:

"If you know the value of these cods, messieurs, you will tie them behind your own testicles, and wear them there, hidden for safekeeping during your journey."

My father gave sincere thanks for the gift, and my uncle made a drunkenly fulsome speech of gratitude that might have gone on endlessly, except that he got to coughing. I did not realize how really precious that gift was, and how untypical of the clerkly Hampig, until my father told me later that the value of the three cods full of musk was easily equal to what we had spent that day in the bazàr.

When we made our last bows to the Ostikan and left the dais, his son came lurching along, to join us at our cloth. It was of course quite far from the dais of honor, down among some barbarous-looking lesser guests, perhaps some poor country relations. Kagig, who was by then as drunk as anyone else in the hall, told us he wished to sit with us for a while, because his soon-to-be bride resembled us more than she did him or any of his people. Being a Circassian, Seosseres was fair of skin, he said, with chestnut hair and features of incomparable beauty. He went on at great length about her beauty: "More beautiful than the moon!" and her gentleness: "Gentler than the west wind!" and her sweetness: "Sweeter than the fragrance of the rose!" and her various other virtues:

"She is fourteen years of age, which may be somewhat overripe for marriage, but she is as virgin as any un-pierced and unstrung pearl. She is educated and can talk well on a number of subjects about which I, even I, know nothing. Philosophy and logic, the canons of the great physician ibn Sina, the poems of Majnun and Laila, the mathematics called geometry and al-jebr . . ."

I think we listeners were rightly doubtful that the Pshi Seosseres could be so sublime. If so, why would she be willing to marry an uncouth Armeniyan with liver lips and no back to his head and a dedication to keeping his toenails safe from sorcerers? And I think our dubiety must have shown in our faces, and Kagig must have seen it, for he finally got up, staggered from the hall and clumped upstairs to fetch the Princess from her sequestered chamber. When he dragged her down, hauling on one of her wrists, she was trying maidenly to hold back, yet trying also not to put up an unwifely show of fight. He brought her into the hall and stood her in front of the company, and stripped off the chador that covered her face.

If all the guests had not been occupied with the viands before them, and most of them sodden with drink, probably someone would have prevented Kagig's act of boorishness. The girl's forced entry certainly caused a muttering in the hall, loudest and angriest among her male relations. Several Muslim holy men covered their faces, and several Christian elders averted theirs. But the rest of us, while we might deplore Kagig's breach of good behavior, were able to be pleasured by the result of it. For the Pshi Seosseres was indeed an outstanding representative of her famously handsome people.

Her face was long and wavy, her figure breathtakingly superb, her face so lovely that its light adornments of al-kohl around the eyes and red berry juice on the lips were quite unnecessary. The girl's fair skin blushed pink in her embarrassment, and she only briefly let us see her qahwah-brown eyes before she lowered them and kept them lowered. Still we could gaze upon her unblemished brow and long lashes and perfect nose and winsome mouth and delicate chin. Kagig held her standing there for at least a full minute, while he made clownish bows and gestures of presentation. Then, as soon as he let go her wrist, she fled the hall and disappeared from our sight.

The Armeniyans, it is said, were once good men and valiant, and did dauntless deeds of arms. But in our time they are but poor simulacra of men, and good at nothing, unless it be drinking and bazàr-cheating. So I had heard, and so the Ostikan's son demonstrated. I do not mean his exposure to the male banqueters of his bride-to-be; I mean what happened afterward.

When Seosseres had gone, Kagig flopped down again at our cloth, between me and my father, and looked around with a self-satisfied smirk, and asked of all within hearing, "What did you think of her, eh?" The girl's male relations sitting nearby responded only with black looks; other men in our vicinity merely murmured respectful remarks of praise. Kagig preened as if they had been complimenting *him,* and proceeded to get even more drunk and even more vile. His continued eulogies on his Princess began to dwell less on the beauty of her face than on the attractiveness of some other parts of her, and his smirks became open leers, and his liver lips drooled. Before long, he was so besotted with wine and lust that he was muttering, "Why wait? Why should I wait for old Dimirjian to croak words over us? I am her husband in all but title. Tonight, tomorrow night, what difference. . . ?"

And suddenly he unfolded himself from the pillows and staggered again out of the hall and lumbered loudly up the stairs. As I have said, the palace was of no very sturdy construction. So anyone in the hall who bothered to direct an ear—as I did—could hear what happened next. However, none of the other guests, not even the Ostikan or the Circassians who might have been most interested, seemed to notice Kagig's abrupt departure or the subsequent sounds. I did, and so did my still sober father and our two frati. Listening carefully, I heard distant thumps and little cries and indistinct commands and thin protests and then some more thumps that became a regular and insistent pulse of thumps. My father and the friars rose up from the cloth, and so did I, and we all helped Uncle Mafìo get up, and the five of us made our salutations to the host Hampig—who was drunk and quite uncaring if we left or stayed—and we departed to our own quarters.

We Polos spent the next morning in the bazàr again, and again accompanied by the steward Arpad. It was heroic of him to be still assisting us, for he clearly was suffering from the bibulous night before. But, headache notwithstanding, her performed capably as our hand-and-sleeve bargainer in another tedious series of interminable transactions. We bought saddles and saddle panniers and bridles and blankets, and had them and our horses delivered by bazàr boys to the palace stables, to be ready for our de-camping. We bought leather water bags, and many sacks of dried fruits and raisins, and large goat cheeses sheathed against spoilage by heavy wax coatings. At Arpad's sug-gestion, we bought a thing called a kamàl. It was only a palm-sized rectangle of wood strips, like a small and empty picture frame, with a long string depending from it.

"Any journeyer," said Arpad, "can determine from the sun or the stars the directions of north, east, west and south. You are going eastward, and you will be able to judge each day's progress eastward by your traveling pace. But it will sometimes be difficult to judge how far north or south of due east you have gone, and that is what the kamàl can tell you."

My father and uncle made noises of surprise and inter-est. Arpad tenderly held his head in both hands, for it evi-dently hurt him when noises were made.

"The Arabs are infidels," he said, "and unworthy of re-spect or admiration, but they did invent this useful device. Here, you will have the use of it, young Monsieur Marco, and I will show you how. Tonight, when the stars come out, you face north and hold the kamàl up at arm's length. Move it back and forth from your face until the lower edge of the frame rests on the northern horizon and the North Star sits just on top of the frame. Then tie a knot in the string so that when you hold the knot in your teeth the string is at such a length that you always hold the rectan-gle out at that same distance from your eye."

"Very well, Steward Arpad," I said obediently. "Then what?"

"As you travel eastward from here, the land is almost all flat, so you will always have a more or less level horizon. Each night, hold the kamàl out to the length of the string's knot and position the rectangle's lower bar on the north-ern horizon. If the North Star is still on the upper bar, you are due east of Suvediye here. If the star is perceptibly above the wooden bar, you have veered to the north of east. If the star is below that bar, you have wandered to the south."

"Cazza beta!" my uncle exclaimed in admiration.

"The kamàl can do even more," said the steward. "Put a tag marked Suvediye on that first knot you make, young

Marco. Then, when you reach Baghdad, do the same positioning of the rectangle away from or closer to your face, so
that it just fits between the northern horizon and the
North Star, and tie another knot in the string at that distance, and mark the knot Baghdad. If you continue to do
that, making and marking a new horizon-knot for each
destination as you reach it, you will always know—as you
go on eastward—whether you are north or south of your
last stopping place, or any of your previous stopping
places."

Deeming the kamàl a most useful addition to our equipment, we gladly paid for it—after Arpad and the merchant
had done their long bargaining and set the price at a
laughably few copper shahis. We went on to buy numerous
other things we thought we would need on the road. And,
thanks to the Ostikan's musk-cod replenishment of our
budget, we even bought a few extra comforts and small
luxuries that we might otherwise have done without.

Not until that afternoon did we see again any of the
other participants in the previous night's banquet. That
was when we all gathered in Suvediye's Church of San
Gregorio for the nuptial mass. To judge from the haggard
faces in the congregation, and an occasional subdued
groan, most of the men were, like Arpad, still feeling the
effects of their indulgence at that banquet. The bride-
groom-to-be looked worst of all. I might have expected him
to look satisfied or smug or guilty, but he merely looked
more lumpish than usual. The bride-to-be was so heavily
veiled that I could not see her expression, but her handsome mother and the various other female relations all exhibited extremely angry eyes glaring through the slits of
their chador veils.

The wedding went off without incident, and our two
frati, almost unrecognizable in the garish vestments of the
Armeniyan Church, ably supported the Metropolitan in
his conduct of the service. Afterwards, the wedding party
and the whole congregation trooped from the church to the
palace again for another banquet. This time, of course, the
female guests—all of them except the female Muslims—
also were allowed to partake. Again there were entertainments: the tumblers with their music, and conjurers and
singers and dancers. While the evening was yet young, the
newly married couple—he looking pained and she looking

more woebegone than even a bride of that lout should have looked—had their hands joined by the Metropolitan and, after he said an Armeniyan prayer over them, trudged away upstairs to their bridal chamber, trailed by some halfhearted rude jesting and cheering from the guests.

This time there was enough noise in the hall—the musicians and dancers making most of it—that not even my inquisitive ear could catch any sounds identifiable as denoting the consummation of the marriage. But after a while there came a number of heavy thuds and something suspiciously like a distant scream, audible even above the music. And suddenly, there came Kagig again, his clothes disheveled, as if they had been once doffed and then thrown on again just anyhow. He came stamping angrily down the stairs and into the hall. He strode straight to the nearest jar of wine and, disdaining a cup, drained it to the vertical.

I was not the only one who watched his entrance. But I think the other guests, astounded at seeing a husband deserting his bride on their wedding night, at first tried to pretend he was not there among them. However, he began loudly to curse and swear—or that is what the Armeniyan words sounded like to me—and none could ignore his presence. The Circassians again began to growl, and the Ostikan Hampig cried anxiously something like, "What on earth is wrong, Kagig?"

"Wrong!" the young man exclaimed—or so I was told later; he was too distraught to speak anything but Armeniyan. "My new wife is revealed to be a harlot, that is what is wrong!"

Several people ejaculated protests and refutations, and the Circassians exclaimed what was probably "Liar!" and "How dare you?"

"Do you think I could not tell?" Kagig raged, as I was later told. "She wept all during the ceremony, behind her veil, for she knew what I was soon to discover! She wept when we went together to our chamber, for the moment of revelation was at hand! She wept as she and I undressed, for she was at the brink of her perfidy's disclosure! She wept even more loudly when I embraced her. And at the crucial moment, *she did not give the cry that must be cried!* So I investigated, and I could feel no maidenhead in her, and I saw no spot of blood upon the bed, and—"

One of the Seosseres' male relatives interrupted him, shouting, "Oh, mongrel dog of an Armeniyan, do you not *remember?*"

"I remember that I was promised a virgin! Not your shouting nor her weeping can change the fact that she had been had by some man before me!"

"You accursed defamer! You nothing!" shouted the Circassians, frothing from the lips. "Our sister Seosseres has never been near a man before!" They were all trying to get at Kagig, but other guests were holding them back.

"Then she has made love to a phallocrypt!" Kagig shouted wildly. "A tent peg or a cucumber or one of those haramlik carvings! But that is the only kind of thing that will ever love her again!"

"Oh, putridity! Oh, spew!" the Circassians bellowed, struggling against the holders-back. "Have you harmed our sister?"

"I should have!" he grumbled. "I should have cut out her duplicious tongue and thrust it up between her legs. I should have boiled oil and poured it into the defiled hole. I should have nailed her alive to the palace gate."

At that, several of his own relatives seized him and shook him roughly, demanding, "Never mind that! What *did* you do?"

He fought loose of them, and petulantly shrugged his clothes back into an approximation of place. "I did only what a cuckolded husband is entitled to do, and I shall sue for annulment of this mock marriage!"

Not just the Circassians, but also the Arabs and Armeniyans shouted at him every kind of filthy name and revilement. There was so much commotion and tearing of hair and beards and rending of garments that it was several minutes before anyone could collect himself to speak coherently and tell the detestable husband what, in his drunkenness, he had done and then forgotten. It was his father, the Ostikan Hampig, who, weeping, told him:

"Oh, unfortunate Kagig, it was *you* who deflowered the maiden! Last night, on your wedding eve. You thought it would be clever and amusing to anticipate your husbandly rights. You went upstairs and forced her to bed, and you boasted of it afterward in this very room. It cost me dearly to persuade these her people not to slay you and anticipate her widowhood. The Princess is guiltless of any sin. It was you! You yourself!"

The cries in the hall redoubled:

"Pig!"

"Carrion!"

"Putrescence!"

And Kagig turned pale and his thick lips twitched, and for the first time in my knowledge of him he acted like a man. He showed genuine chagrin and he called for retribution as if he meant it, crying, "May the coals of Hell lie hot upon my head! I truly loved the beautiful Seossères, and I have cut off her nose and her lips!"

6

My father plucked at my sleeve, and he and I and my uncle slipped discreetly through the roiling crowd and out of the dining hall.

"This is not bread to my teeth," said my father, frowning. "The Ostikan is in bad trouble, and any sovereign in trouble can make things trebly troublous for everyone around him."

I said, "Surely he cannot blame us for anything."

"When the head hurts, the whole body may suffer. I think it best that we get our horses loaded for a departure at first light. Let us go to our chamber and start packing."

There we were joined by the two Dominicans, who spoke loudly of their nausea and disgust at what Kagig had done, as if only they of us all had sensibilities to be offended.

"Ho ho," said Uncle Mafìo without humor. "These are fellow Christians. You have yet to meet some real barbarians."

"That is what most disturbs us," said Brother Guglielmo. "We understand that such horrendous cruelties are common practices in farther Tartary."

My father remarked placidly that he had known of atrocities having been committed in the West, as well.

"Nevertheless," said Brother Nicolò, "we fear that we could not competently minister to such monsters as you would have us go among. We wish to be excused from our preaching mission."

"Would you now?" My uncle coughed and hawked and spat. "You wish to desert before we are even underway? Well, wish all you like. We have committed ourselves, and so have you."

Brother Guglielmo said frostily, "Perhaps Fra Nico did not put it strongly enough. We are not asking your permission, Messeri, we are telling you our decision. The conversion of such raw savages would require more—more authority than we possess. And the Scriptures say: Turn away thy foot from evil. He that touches pitch shall be defiled with it. We decline to accompany you any farther."

"You could not have supposed that this would be an easy or enjoyable mission," said my father. "As the old saying has it, nobody goes to Heaven on a cushion."

"A cushion? Fichèvelo!" boomed my uncle, thereby suggesting a unique use for a cushion. "We have paid good money to buy horses for these two manfroditi!"

"Calling us filthy names is not likely to persuade us," said Brother Nicolò with hauteur. "In the manner of the Apostle Paolo, we do shun profane and vain babblings. The ship which brought us here is now preparing to sail on to Cyprus, and we will be aboard."

My uncle would have blustered on, probably using still more words that sacerdoti seldom get to hear, but my father gestured him to silence, saying:

"We wanted emissaries of the Church to prove to Kubilai Khan the worth and superiority of Christianity over other religions. These sheep in priestly clothing would hardly be the best examples to show him. Go to your ship, Brothers, and God go with you."

"And God and you go *quickly!*" snarled my uncle. When they had gathered up their belongings and left the chambers, he grumbled, "Those two merely seized upon our venture as an excuse to get away from the wicked women of Acre. Now they welcome this ugly incident here as an excuse to get away from us. We were bidden to bring a hundred priests, and we got two spineless old zitelle. Now we do not even have them."

"Well, it is less hurtful losing the two than a hundred," said my father. "The proverb says it is better to fall from a window than from the roof."

"I can bear losing those two," said Uncle Mafìo. "But now what? Do *we* go on? Without *any* clerics for the Khan?"

"We promised him we would return," said my father. "And we have already been long away. If we do not go back, the Khan will lose faith in any Westerner's word. He may bar the gates against all traveling merchants, including us, and we are merchants before anything else. We have no priests to take, but we do have enough capital—our zafràn and Hampig's musk—that we can multiply it yonder into an estimable fortune. I say yes, let us go on. We shall simply tell Kubilai that our Church was in disarray during this papal interregnum. It is true enough."

"I concur," said Uncle Mafìo. "We go on. But what about this sprout?"

They both looked at me.

"He cannot return yet to Venice," my father mused. "And the English ship is sailing on to England. But he could change at Cyprus to some vessel headed for Constantinople. . . ."

I said quickly, "I will not sail even to Cyprus with those two poltroon Dominicans. I might be tempted to do them some injury, and that would be a sacrilege, and that would imperil my hope of Heaven."

Uncle Mafìo laughed and said, "But if we leave him here, and those Circassians start a blood feud with the Armeniyans, Marco may get to Heaven sooner than one might have hoped."

My father sighed and said to me, "You will come with us as far as Baghdad. There we will seek out a merchant train headed westward by way of Constantinople. You will go to visit your Uncle Marco. You can either stay with him until we return or, if you hear that a new Doge has succeeded Tiepolo, you can take ship for Venice."

I think only we, of all the people then inhabiting Hampig's palace, even tried to sleep that night. And we slept but little, for the whole building kept shaking to the tread of heavy feet and the shouting of angry voices. The Circassian guests had all put on clothes of the sky-blue color they affect for mourning, but evidently they were unmournfully storming about the building, threatening to wreak some vengeance for the mutilation of their Seosseres, and the Armeniyans were as loudly trying to placate them, or

at least shout them down. The turmoil was still undimin-
ished when we rode out of the palace stable yard, eastward
into the dawn. I do not know what finally became of the
people we left behind there: whether the two craven friars
got safely away to Cyprus, or whether the wretched
Bagratunians ever did suffer any retaliation from the
Princess's people. I have never heard of any of them since
that day. And on that day I truthfully was not worrying
about them, but about staying in my saddle.

I had never in my life been transported by any conveyance other than water craft. So my father bridled and saddled my mare for me, and made me watch the procedure,
telling me that I should have to do that job myself thereafter. Then he showed me how to mount, and the proper
side of the animal from which to do it. I imitated his demonstration. I put my left foot into the stirrup, bounced
briefly on my right foot, bounded high with enthusiasm,
swung my right leg over, came down with a smack astride
the hard seat, and gave a wild ululation of pain. Each of us
was, as instructed by the Ostikan, wearing one of the
leather cods of musk tied so that it hung under our crotch,
and it was *that* that I thumped down on—and I thought for
an agonized and writhing few minutes that it had cost me
my own personal cod.

My father and uncle abruptly turned away, their shoulders shaking, to attend to their own mounts. I gradually
recovered, and rearranged the musk pouch so it would not
again endanger my vitals. Realizing that I was for the first
time perched atop an animal, I rather wished that I had
commenced with one not so tall, an ass perhaps, for I
seemed to be teetering very high and insecurely far above
the ground away down there. But I stayed in the saddle
while my father and uncle also mounted, and each of them
took the lead rope of one of the two extra horses, on which
we had loaded all our packs and traveling gear. We rode
out of the yard and toward the river, just as the day was
breaking.

At the bank, we turned upriver toward the cleft in the
hills where it came from inland. Very soon the troubled
city of Suvediye was behind us, and then so were the ruins
of earlier Suvediyes, and we were in the Orontes valley. It
was a lovely warm morning, and the valley was lush with
vegetation—green orchards of fruit trees separating exten-

sive fields of spring-sown barley, now golden ripe for harvesting. Even that early in the day, the women workers
were out and cutting the grain. We could see only a few of
them, bent over their knives, but we knew that many were
working there, from the multitudinous clicking noise. Because in Armeniya all the field hands are female, and because barley stalks are coarse and rough and injurious to
their skin, the women wore wooden tubes on their fingers
while they worked. In their numbers and their busyness,
those fingers made a pervasive rattle that could have been
mistaken for a fire crackling through the grain.

When we got beyond the cultivated lands, the valley was
still verdant and colorful and full of life. There were the
vast, spreading, dark-green plane trees, called hereabouts
chinar trees, of welcome deep shade; and vividly green
tiger-thistles; and the bountiful, silver-leaved, thorny
trees called zizafun, from which a traveler can pluck the
plumlike golden jujube fruit, good to eat whether fresh or
dried. There were herds of goats munching the tiger-
thistles; and on every goatherd's mud hut there was the
scraggly rooftop nest of a stork; and there were whole nations of pigeons, in every flock as many of them as in all of
Venice; and there were the golden eagles, almost always
on the wing, because they are so clumsy and vulnerable
when they light, having to run and struggle and beat their
pinions for a long way before they can get aloft again.

In the East, an overland journey is called by the Farsi
word karwan. We were on one of the principal east-west
karwan routes, so at easy intervals of about every sixth
farsakh—which is to say about every fifteen miles—there
stood one of the stopping places called a karwansarai. Although we rode leisurely, not pushing ourselves on our
horses, we could always depend on finding, about sundown, one of those places on the Orontes riverside.

I do not remember the first of them very well, for that
night I was mainly occupied with my own discomfort. During our first day on the trail we had not made our horses
move faster than a walking gait, and I had thought I was
enjoying a comfortable ride, and I several times dismounted and mounted again without noticing that the
ride was affecting me in the least. However, at the karwansarai, when I finally got down from the saddle for the
night, I found that I was sore and suffering. My backside

hurt as if it had been thrashed, the inner sides of my legs were chafed and burning, the thews inside my thighs were so stretched and aching that I felt as if I would forever after walk bowlegged. But the discomfort gradually ebbed, and in a few days I could ride my horse at a walk and at intermittent canters and gallops—or even at the trot, which is the roughest gait—all day long, if necessary, without feeling any ill effect. That was a pleasing development, except that, no longer being intent on my own misery, I could take more notice of the miseries of putting up each night at a karwansarai.

It is a sort of combination inn for traveling people and stable or corral for their animals, though the accommodations for men and animals are not, in their comfort and cleanliness, easily distinguishable. No doubt that is because each such establishment must be of a size and readiness to receive and provide for a hundred times more people and beasts than we comprised. On several nights, indeed, we shared a karwansarai with a veritable throng of merchants, Arabs or Persians, traveling in karwan with countless horses, mules, asses, camels and dromedaries, all heavy laden, hungry, thirsty and sleepy. Nevertheless, I would as soon eat the dry fodder stocked for the animals as the meals set before the humans, and rather sleep in the stable straw than on one of the webbed-rope affairs called a bed.

The first two or three places we came to had signboards identifying each as a "Christian rest house." They were run by Armeniyan monks, and were filthy and verminous and smelly, but the meals at least had the virtue of variety in their composition. Farther eastward, each karwansarai was run by Arabs and bore a signboard announcing, "Here, the true and pure religion." Those establishments were a trifle cleaner and better kept, but the Muslim meals were monotonously unvarying—mutton, rice, a bread the exact size and shape and texture and taste of a wicker chair seat, and weak, warm, much-watered sharbats for drink.

Only a few days out of Suvediye, we came to the riverside town of Antakya. When one is making a journey across country, any community appearing on the horizon ahead is a welcome sight, and even a beautiful one from a distance. But that beauty lent by distance is all too often dispelled by closer approach. Antakya was, like every other town in those regions, ugly and dirty and dull and swarming with beggars. But it had the one distinction of having given its name to the surrounding land: Antioch, as it is called in the Bible. In other times, when the region was a part of Alexander's empire, that land was called Syria. At the time of our passing through, it was an adjunct of the Kingdom of Jerusalem, or what still remained of that kingdom, which has since fallen entirely under the rule of the Mamluk Saracens. Anyway, I tried to look at Antakya and all of Antioch, or Syria, as Alexander might have regarded it, for I was mightily excited to be traveling one of the karwan trails that Alexander the Great once had trodden.

There at Antakya, the Orontes River bends due south. So we left it at that point and kept on bearing east, to another and much larger town, but also a dreary one—Haleb, called Aleppo by Westerners. We stayed the night in a karwansarai there and, because the landlord strongly advised that we would ride more comfortably if we changed our traveling costume, we bought from him Arab garments for each of us. When we left Aleppo, and for a long time afterward, we wore the full garb, from kaffiyah headcloth to the baggy leg coverings. That costume really is more comfortable for a man riding horseback than a tight Venetian tunic and hose. And from a distance at least, we looked like three of the nomad Arabs who call themselves the empty-landers, or bedawin.

Since most of the karwansarai keepers in those regions are Arabs, I of course learned many Arab words. But those landlords also spoke the universal trade language of Asia, which is Farsi, and we were getting nearer every day to the land of Persia, where Farsi is the native tongue. So, to help me more quickly pick up that language, my father and uncle did their best to converse always in what they knew of Farsi, instead of our own Venetian or the other jargon of Sabir French. And I did learn. In truth, I found Farsi considerably less difficult than some of the other tongues I had to contend with later on. Also, it must be supposed that young people acquire new languages more easily than do their elders, for it was not long before I was speaking Farsi far more fluently than either my father or my uncle did.

Somewhere east of Aleppo, we came to the next river, the Furat, which is better known as the Euphrates, named in the Book of Genesis as one of the four rivers of the Garden of Eden. I do not dispute the Bible, but I saw little that was gardenlike along the entire great length of the Furat. Where we joined it, to follow it downstream to the southeastward, that river does not, like the Orontes, flow through a pleasant valley; it merely wanders vagrantly through a flat country which is one immense pasture of grass for herds of goats and sheep. That is a useful enough function for a country, but it makes an extremely uninteresting terrain to travel across. One rejoices to see the occasional grove of olive trees or date palms, and one can see even a single isolated tree from a great distance before reaching it.

Over that level land a breeze blows almost constantly from the east, and, there being deserts far to the eastward, even that light breeze comes heavily freighted with a fine gray dust. Since only the far-apart trees and the infrequent travelers stick up above the low grass, it is on those things that the drifting dust collects. Our horses put their muzzles down and drooped their ears and closed their eyes and kept their direction by keeping the breeze on their left shoulders as they ambled along. We riders wrapped our abas tightly about our bodies and our kaffiyahs across our faces, and still we had dust making our eyelids gritty and our skins scratchy, clogging our nostrils and crunching between our teeth. I realized why my father and uncle and most other journeyers let their beards grow, for to shave each day in such conditions is a painful drudgery. But my own beard was yet too scanty to grow out handsomely. So I tried Uncle Mafìo's depilatory mumum, and it worked well, and I continued to use the salve in preference to a razor.

But I think my most enduring recollection of that dust-laden Eden was the sight of a pigeon one day lighting in a tree there: when the bird touched the branch it puffed up a cloud of dust as if it had lighted in a flour barrel.

I will set down here two other things that came into my mind during that long ride down the River Furat:

One is that the world is large. That may seem no very original observation, but it had just then begun to dawn upon me with the awesomeness of revelation. I had heretofore lived in the constricted city of Venice, which in all of history has never sprawled beyond its seawalls and never can—so it gives us Venetians a sense of being enclosed in safety and snugness; in coziness, if you will. Although Venice fronts upon the Adriatic, the sea's horizon seems not impossibly far away. Even aboard ship, I saw that horizon staying fixed on every side; there was no sense of progression toward it or away from it. But traveling overland is different. The contour of the horizon changes constantly, and one is always moving toward or away from some landmark. In just the early weeks of our riding, we approached and arrived at and traversed and left again several different towns or villages, several contrasting kinds of countryside, several separate rivers. And always we realized that there was more beyond: more countries, more cities, more rivers. The world's land is *visibly* bigger than any empty ocean. It is vast and diverse, and always promising yet more vastness and diversity to come, and then producing them and promising more. The overland journeyer knows the same sensation that a man feels when he is stark naked—a fine sense of unfettered freedom, but also a sense of being vulnerable, unprotected and, compared to the world about him, very small.

The other thing I wish to say here is that maps lie. Even the best of maps, those in the Kitab of al-Idrisi, are liars, and they cannot help being liars. That is because everything shown on a map appears measurable by the same standards, and that is a delusion. For one instance, suppose your journey must take you over a mountain. The map can warn you of that mountain before you get to it, and even indicate more or less how high and wide and long it is, but the map cannot tell you what will be the conditions of terrain and weather when you get there, or what condition *you* will be in. A mountain that can be easily scaled on a good day in high summer by a young man in prime health may be a mountain considerably more forbidding in the cold and gales of winter, to a man enfeebled by age or illness and wearied by all the country he has already traversed. Because the limited representations of a map are thus deceptive, it may take a journeyer longer to travel the last little fingerbreadth of distance across a map than it took him to travel all the many handspans previous.

Of course, we had no such difficulties on that journey to Baghdad, since we had only to follow the River Furat downstream through the flat grassland. We did get out the Kitab at intervals, but just to see how its maps conformed to the actuality about us—and they did, with commendable accuracy—and sometimes my father or uncle would add markings to them to indicate useful landmarks which the maps omitted: bends of the river, islands in it, things like that. And every few nights, though it was not then needed, I would get out the kamàl we had bought. Extending it toward the North Star at the length of the knot I had tied in the string at Suvediye, and laying the lower bar of the wooden rectangle on the flat horizon, I saw each time that the star was farther down below the upper bar of the frame. It indicated what we knew: that we were moving south of east.

Everywhere in that country, we were continually crossing the invisible borders of one little nation after another, the nations being likewise invisible except in name. It is the same in all the Levant lands: the larger expanses are labeled on maps as Armeniya, Antioch, the Holy Land and so on, but within those areas the local folk recognize innumerable smaller expanses, and give them names and call them nations and dignify their paltry chieftains with resounding titles. In my childhood Bible classes, I had heard of such Levantine kingdoms as Samaria and Tyre and Israel, and I had envisioned them as mighty lands of awesome extent, and their kings Ahab and Hiram and Saul as monarchs over vast populations. And now I was learning, from the natives we met along our way, that I was traversing such self-proclaimed nations as Nabaj and Bishri and Khubbaz, ruled by various kings and sultans and atabegs and sheikhs.

But any of those nations could be crossed in a ride of a day or two, and they were drab and featureless and poor and full of beggars and otherwise scantily populated, and the one "king" we encountered there was merely the oldest goatherd in a bedawi tribe of goatherding Arabs. Not a single one of all those crammed-together fragment kingdoms and sheikhdoms in that part of the world is larger than the Republic of Venice. And Venice, though thriving and important, occupies but a handful of islands and a meager portion of the Adriatic coast. I gradually came to

realize that all those biblical kings, too—even the great
ones like Solomon and David—had ruled domains that in
the Western world would be called only confini or counties
or parishes. The great migrations recorded in the Bible
must really have been negligible wanderings like those of
the modern goatherding tribes I had seen. The great wars
of which the Bible tells must really have been trifling skirmishes between puny armies to settle insignificant dis-
putes between those petty kings. It made me wonder why
the Lord God had bothered, in those olden times, to send
fires and tempests and prophets and plagues to influence
the destinies of such fence-corner nations.

7

O N two nights in that country, we deliberately skirted the
nearest karwansarai and camped outdoors on our own. It
was something we would later have to do, when we got into
even less populous regions, so my father and uncle thought
I should start having the experience in an easy terrain and
clement weather. Also, all three of us were by then getting
extremely tired of filth and mutton. So, on each of those
nights, we made pallets of our blankets, with our saddles
for pillows, and laid a fire for cooking, and turned our
horses free to graze, hobbling their front legs together so
they could not wander far.

I had already learned from my much-traveled father and
uncle some of the tricks of traveling. For example, they
had taught me always to carry my bedding in one saddle
pannier and my clothing in another, and always to keep
the two apart. Since a traveler has to use his own blankets
at every karwansarai, they inevitably get full of fleas and
lice and bedbugs. Those vermin are a torment even when
one sleeps the usual deep sleep of exhaustion, but they
would be intolerable when one is dressed and awake and
about. So, getting naked out of bed each morning, I
would pick myself clean of the accumulated bugs, and
then, having carefully kept my clothing apart from the
bedding, I could put on either used or clean garments without their having been contaminated. When we did not stay

at a karwansarai, but made our own camp, I learned other things. I remember, the first night we camped, I started to tilt one of the water bags for a good long drink, but my father stopped me.

"Why?" I said. "We have one of the blessed rivers of Eden with which to refill it."

"Better get used to thirst when it is not necessary," he said, "for you will have to when it is. Just wait and I will show you something."

He built a fire of branches hacked with his belt knife from a convenient zizafun tree, the thorny wood of which burns hot and quickly, and he let it burn until the wood was all charcoal but not yet ashes. Then he scraped most of the charcoal to one side, and laid new branches on what was left, to make up the fire again. He let the removed charcoal cool, then crushed it to powder and heaped that onto a cloth and put the cloth like a sieve over the mouth of one of the pottery bowls we had brought. He handed me another bowl and bade me go and fill it from the river.

"Taste that Eden water," he said, when I fetched it.

I did and said, "Muddy. Some insects. But not bad water."

"Watch. I will make it better." He poured it slowly through the charcoal and cloth into the other bowl.

When it had finished its slow trickling, I tasted it again from that bowl. "Yes. Clear and good. It even tastes cooler."

"Remember that trick," he said. "Many times your only source of water will be putrid or vile with salts or even suspect of poison. That trick will render it potable at least, and harmless, if not delicious. However, in the deserts where the water is worst, there is usually no wood to burn. Therefore, try always to carry a supply of charcoal with you. It can be used over and over again before it gets saturated and ineffectual."

The reason we made our outdoor camp only twice during the journey down the Furat was that, while my father could strain insects and impurities out of the water, he could not remove the birds from the air, and I have mentioned that that country abounds in golden eagles.

On that day of which I speak, my uncle had, by good luck, come upon a large hare in the grass, and it stood immobile and trembling in that moment of surprise, and he

whipped out and threw his belt knife, and killed the creature. It was on that account—having our own provender for
a non-mutton meal—that we decided to make the first
camp. But when Uncle Mafìo skewered the skinned hare
on a zizafun stick and hung it over the fire, and it began to
sizzle and its aroma rose with the smoke into the air, we
got as much of a surprise as the hare had got.

There came a loud, rustling, swooshing noise from out of
the night sky above us. Before we could even look up, a
blur of brown flashed in an arc down between us, through
the firelight and upward into the darkness again. At the
same instant, there was a sound like *klop!* and the fire flew
all apart in a spray of sparks and ashes, and the hare was
gone, complete with its stick, and we heard a triumphant
barking yell, *"Kya!"*

"Malevolenza!" exclaimed my uncle, picking up a large
feather from the remains of the fire. "A damned thieving
eagle! Acrimonia!" And that night we had to make our
meal on some hard salt pork from our packs.

The same thing, or very near it, happened the second
time we stayed outdoors. That camping was occasioned by
our having bought, from a passing family of bedawin
Arabs, a haunch of fresh-killed camel calf. When we put
that on the fire, and the eagles espied it, another of them
came in a rush. The moment my uncle heard the first
rustle of its pinions in the air, he made a dive to throw himself protectively over the cooking meat. That saved our
meal for us, but nearly lost us Uncle Mafìo.

A golden eagle has wings that spread wider than a
man's outstretched arms, and it weighs about as much as a
fair-sized dog, so when it comes plummeting down—when
it stoops, as the hawkers say—it is a formidable projectile.
That one hit the back of my uncle's head, fortunately only
with its wing and not with its talons, but that was a blow
heavy enough to knock him sprawling across the fire. My
father and I dragged him out, and beat the sparks out of
his smoldering aba, and he had to shake his head for a time
to get his senses back, and then he cursed magnificently,
until he went into a fit of coughing. Meanwhile, I stood
over the spitted meat, ostentatiously swinging a heavy
branch, and the eagles stayed away, so we did manage to
cook and eat the meal. But we decided that, as long as we

were in eagle country, we would stifle our revulsions and
spend each night in a karwansarai from then on.

"You are wise to do so," said the next night's landlord to
us, as we ate yet another nasty meal of mutton and rice.
We were the only guests that night, so he conversed while
he swept the day's collected dust out the door. His name
was Hasan Badr-al-Din, which did not suit him at all, for it
means Beauty of Faith's Moon. He was wizened and
gnarled, like an old olive tree. He had a face as leathery
and wrinkled as a cobbler's apron, and a wispy beard like a
nimbus of wrinkles that could not find room on his face. He
went on, "It is not good to be out of doors and unprotected
at night in the lands of the Mulahidat, the Misguided
Ones."

"What are the Misguided Ones?" I asked, sipping a
sharbat so bitter that it must have been made of green
fruit.

Beauty of Faith's Moon was now going about the room,
sprinkling water to lay the remaining dust. "You perhaps
have heard them called hashishiyin. The killers who kill
for the Old Man of the Mountain."

"What mountain?" growled my uncle. "This land is flatter than a halycon sea."

"He has always been called that—the Sheikh ul-Jibal—
though no one knows really where he lives. Whether his
castle is really on a mountain or not."

"He does not live," said my father. "That old nuisance
was slain by the Ilkhan Hulagu when the Mongols came
this way fifteen years ago."

"True," said the aged Beauty. "Yet not true. That was
the Old Man Rokn-ed-Din Kurshah. But there is always
another Old Man, you know."

"I did not know."

"Oh, yes, indeed. And an Old Man still commands the
Mulahidat, though some of the Misguided must be old men
themselves by now. He hires them out to the faithful who
have need of their services. I hear that the Mamluks of
Egypt paid high to have a hashishi slay that English
Prince who leads the Christian Crusaders."

"Then they wasted their money," said Uncle Mafìo.
"The Englishman slew the sassìn."

Beauty shrugged and said, "Another will try, and another, until it is done. The Old Man will command, and they will obey."

"Why?" I asked, and swallowed a wad of rice that tasted of taint. "Why should any man risk his own life to kill at the behest of another man?"

"Ah. To understand that, young Sheikh, you must know something of the Holy Quran." He came and sat down at our . cloth, as if pleased to explain. "In that Book, the Prophet (blessing and peace be upon him) makes a promise to the men of the Faith. He promises to every man that, if he is unswervingly devout, then once in his life he will enjoy one miraculous night, the Night of the Possible, in which he will be granted his every desire." The old man arranged his wrinkles in a smile, a smile that was half happy and half melancholy. "A night replete with ease and luxury, with marvelous food and drink and banj, with beautiful and compliant haura women and boys, with renewed youth and virility for the zina enjoyment of them. Thus, every man who believes will live his life in fierce devoutness, and hope for that Night of the Possible."

He stopped, and seemed to lose himself in contemplation. After a moment, Uncle Mafìo said, "It is an appealing dream."

Beauty said distantly, "Dreams are the painted pictures in the book of sleep."

Again we waited, then I said, "But I do not see what that has to do with—"

'The Old Man of the Mountain," he said, as if coming abruptly awake. "The Old Man *gives* that Night of the Possible. Then he holds out promise of still other such nights."

My father, my uncle and I exchanged glances of amusement.

"Do not doubt it!" the landlord said testily. "The Old Man, or one of his Mulahidat recruiters, will find a qualified man—a strong and bold man—and will slip a potent bit of banj into his food or drink. When the man swoons to sleep, he is spirited away to the Castle ul-Jibal. He wakes to find himself in the most lovely garden imaginable, surrounded by comely lads and ladies. Those haura feed him rich viands and more of the hashish and even forbidden wines. They sing and dance enchantingly, and reveal their nippled breasts, their smooth bellies, their inviting bottoms. They seduce him to such raptures of lovemaking that at last he swoons again. And again he is spirited away—back to his former place and life, which is humdrum at best, and more probably dismal. Like the life of a karwansarai keeper."

My father yawned and said, "I begin to comprehend. As the saying goes, he has been given cake and a kick."

"Yes. He has now partaken of the Night of the Possible, and he yearns to do so again. He wishes and begs and prays for that, and the recruiters come and tantalize him until he promises to do *anything*. He is set a task—to slay some enemy of the Faith, to steal or rob for the enrichment of the Old Man's coffers, to waylay infidels intruding on the lands of the Mulahidat. If he successfully performs that task, he is rewarded with another Night of the Possible. And after each subsequent deed of devotion, another night and another."

"Each of which," said my skeptical uncle, "is really nothing but a hashish dream. Misguided, indeed."

"Oh, unbeliever!" Beauty chided him. "Tell me, by your beard, can *you* distinguish between the memory of a delightful dream and the memory of a delightful occurrence? Each exists only in your memory. Telling of them to another, how could you prove which happened when you were awake and which when you were asleep?"

Uncle Mafìo said affably, "I will let you know tomorrow, for I am sleepy now." He stood up, with a massive stretch and a gaping yawn.

It was rather earlier in the night than we were accustomed to go to bed, but I and my father also were yawning, so we all followed Beauty of Faith's Moon as he led us down a long hall and—because we were the only guests—allotted us each a separate room, and quite clean, with clean straw on the floor. "Rooms deliberately well apart from each other," he said, "so that your snores will not disturb each other, and your dreams will not get intertangled."

Nevertheless, my own dream was tangled enough. I slept and dreamed that I awoke from my sleep, to find myself, like a recruit of the Misguided Ones, in a dreamlike garden, for it was full of flowers I had never seen when awake. Among the sunlit flower beds danced dancers so dreamily beautiful that one could not say, or care, whether they were girls or boys. In a dreamy languor, I joined the

dance and found, as often happens in dreams, that my
every step and prance and movement was dreamily slow,
as if the air were sesame oil.

That thought was so repugnant—even in my dream I remembered my experience with sesame oil—that the sunlit
garden instantly became a bosky palace corridor, down
which I was dancing in pursuit of a dancing girl whose face
was the face of the Lady Ilaria. But when she pirouetted
into a room and I followed through the only door and
caught her there, her face got old and warty and sprouted a
red-gray beard like a fungus. She said, "Salamelèch" in a
man's deep voice, and I was not in a palace chamber, or
even a bedroom of a karwansarai, but in the dark, cramped
cell of the Venice Vulcano. Old Mordecai Cartafilo said,
"Misguided One, will you never learn the bloodthirstiness
of beauty?" and gave me a square white cracker to eat.

Its dryness was choking and its taste was nauseous. I
retched so convulsively that I woke myself up—really
awoke this time, in the karwansarai room, to find that I
was not dreaming the nausea. Evidently our meal's mutton or something *had* been tainted, for I was about to be violently sick. I scrambled out of my blankets and ran naked
and barefoot down the midnight hall to the little back
room with the hole in the ground. I hung my head over it,
too wretched to recoil from the stink or to fear that a demon jinni might reach up out of the depths and snatch at
me. As quietly as I could, I vomited up a vile green mess
and, after wiping the tears from my eyes and getting my
breath back, I padded quietly toward my room again. The
hall took me past the door of the chamber my uncle had
been given, and I heard a muttering behind it.

Giddy anyway, I leaned against the wall there and gave
ear to the noise. It was partly my uncle's snoring and
partly a sibilant low speaking of words. I wondered how he
could snore and talk at the same time, so I listened more
intently. The words were Farsi, so I could not make out all
of them. But when the voice, sounding astonished, spoke
louder, I clearly heard:

"Garlic? The infidels pretend to be merchants, but they
carry only worthless *garlic?*"

I touched the door of the room, and it was unlatched. It
swung easily and silently open. Inside, there was a small
light moving, and when I peered I could see that it was a

wick lamp in the hand of Beauty of Faith's Moon, and he was bending over my uncle's saddle panniers, piled in a corner of the room. The landlord was obviously seeking to steal from us, and he had opened the packs and found the precious culms of zafràn and had mistaken them for garlic.

I was more amused than angry, and I held my tongue, so as to see what he would do next. Still muttering, telling himself that the unbeliever probably had taken his purse and true valuables to bed with him, the old man sidled over beside the bed and, with his free hand, began cautiously groping about beneath Uncle Mafìo's blankets. He encountered something, for he gave a start, and again spoke aloud in astonishment:

"By the ninety-nine attributes of Allah, but this infidel is hung like a horse!"

Sick though I still felt, I very nearly giggled at that, and my uncle smiled in his sleep as if he enjoyed the fondling.

"Not only an untrimmed long zab," the thief continued to marvel, "but also—praise Allah in His munificence even to the unworthy—*two* sacks of balls!"

I might really have giggled then, but in the next moment the situation ceased to be amusing. I saw in the lamplight the glint of metal, as old Beauty drew a knife from his robes and lifted it. I did not know whether he intended to trim my uncle's zab or to amputate his supernumerary scrotum or to cut his throat, and I did not wait to find out. I stepped forward and swung my fist and hit the thief hard in the back of his neck. I might have expected the blow to incapacitate such a fragile old specimen, but he was not so delicate as he looked. He fell sideways, but rolled like an acrobat and came up from the floor slashing the blade at me. It was more by happenstance than by deftness that I caught his wrist. I twisted it, and wrenched at his hand, and found the knife in my own hand, and used it. At that, he did fall down and stay down, groaning and burbling.

The scuffle had been brief, but not silent, yet my uncle had slept through it, and he still slept, still smiling in his sleep. Appalled by what I had just done, as well as by what had almost been done, I felt very alone in the room and badly needed a supporting ally. Though my hands were trembling, I shook Uncle Mafìo, and had to shake him violently to bring him to consciousness. I realized now that

the more than ordinarily nasty evening meal had been
heavily laced with banj. We would all three have been
dead but for the dream that had wakened me to the danger
and made me disgorge the drug.

My uncle finally, unwillingly, began to come awake,
smiling and murmuring, "The flowers . . . the dancers . . .
the fingers and lips playing on my flute . . ." Then he
blinked and exclaimed, "Dio me varda! Marco, that was
not *you?*"

"No, Zio Mafìo," I said, in my agitation speaking Venetian. "You were in peril. We are still in peril. Please wake
up!"

"Adrìo de vu!" he said crossly. "Why have you snatched
me from that wondrous garden?"

"I believe it was the garden of the hashishiyin. And I
have just stabbed a Misguided One."

"Our host!" cried my uncle, sitting up and seeing the
crumpled form on the floor. "Oh, scagaròn, what have you
done? Are you playing bravo again?"

"No, Zio, look. That is his own knife sticking in him. He
was about to kill you for your cod of musk." As I related
the circumstances, I began to weep.

Uncle Mafìo bent over the old man and examined him,
growling, "Right in the belly. Not dead, but dying." Then
he turned to me and said kindly, "There, there, boy. Stop
slobbering. Go and wake your father."

Beauty of Faith's Moon was nothing to weep over, alive
or dead or dying. But he was the first man I ever slew with
my own hand, and the killing of another human being is
no trivial milestone in a man's career. As I went to fetch
my father out of the hashish garden, I was thinking how
more than ever I was glad that, back in Venice, another
hand had thrust the sword into my guiltless earlier prey.
For I had just learned one thing about killing a man, or at
least about killing him with a blade. It slides into the victim's belly easily enough, almost eagerly, almost of its own
accord. But there it is instantly seized by the violated
muscles, held as tightly as another tool of mine had once
been clasped in the virgin flesh of the girl Doris. I had
pushed the knife into old Beauty with no effort whatever,
but I could not withdraw it again when I had done so. And
in that instant I had known a sickening realization: that a
deed so ugly and so easily done cannot thereafter be un-

done. It made killing seem rather less gallant and dashing and bravìsimo than I had imagined it to be.

When I had, with difficulty, roused my father, I took him to the scene of the crime. Uncle Mafìo had laid the landlord on his own pallet of blankets, despite the flow of blood, and had composed Beauty's limbs for death, and the two of them were conversing, it seemed companionably. The old man was the only one of us who had any clothes on. He looked up at me, his murderer, and he must have seen the traces of tears on my face, for he said:

"Do not feel bad, young infidel. You have slain the most Misguided One of all. I have done a terrible wrong. The Prophet (peace and blessing be upon him) enjoins us to treat a guest with the most reverent care and respect. Though he be the lowliest darwish, or even an unbeliever, and though there be only one crumb in the house, and though the host's family and children go hungry, the guest must be given that crumb. Be he a sworn enemy, he must be accorded every hospitality and safeguard while he is under one's roof. My disobedience to that holy law would have deprived me of my Night of the Possible, even did I live. In my avarice, I acted hastily, and I have sinned, and for that sin I beg forgiveness."

I tried to say that I gave the forgiveness, but I choked on a sob, and in the next moment I was glad of that, for he continued:

"I could as easily have drugged your breakfast meal in the morning, and let you get some way upon the road before you fell. Then I could have robbed and murdered you under the open sky instead of under my roof, and it would have been a deed of virtue, and pleasing to Allah. But I did not. Though in all my lifetime before now I have lived devoutly in the Faith and have slain many other infidels to the greater glory of Islam, this one impiety will cost me my eternity in the Paradise of Djennet, with its haura beauties and perpetual happiness and unfettered indulgence. And for that loss, I grieve sincerely. I should have killed you in fitter fashion."

Well, those words at any rate stopped my weeping. We all stared stonily at the landlord as again he went on:

"But you have yourselves a chance at virtue. When I am dead, do me the kindness of wrapping me in a winding sheet. Take me to the main room and lay me in the middle of it, in the prescribed position. Wind my tulband over my face, and place me so my feet are turned to the south, toward the Holy Kaaba in Mecca."

My father and uncle looked at each other, and they shrugged, but we were all glad they made no promise, for the old fiend now spoke his last words:

"Having done that, vile dogs, you will die virtuous, when my brothers of the Mulahidat come and find me here dead with a knife wound in my gut, and they follow the tracks of your horses and hunt you down and do to you what I failed to do. Salaam aleikum."

His voice had not at all weakened, but, after perversely calling peace upon us, Beauty of Faith's Moon closed his eyes and died. And, that being the first deathbed I had ever stood close to, I first learned then that most deaths are as ugly as most killings. For in dying, Beauty unbeautifully and copiously evacuated both his bladder and his bowels, befouling his garments and the blankets and filling the room with a ghastly stench.

A disgusting indignity is not what any person would wish to be last remembered for. But I have since attended many dyings and—except in the rare case when there has been opportunity of a purge aforetime—that is how all human beings make their farewell to life; even the strongest and bravest of men, the fairest and purest of women, whether they die a violent death or go serenely in their sleep.

We stepped outside the room to breathe clean air, and my father sighed. "Well. Now what?"

"First of all," said my uncle, untying the thongs of his musk cod, "let us relieve ourselves of these uncomfortable danglers. It is clear that they will be as safe inside our packs—or no less safe—and anyway I would rather lose the musk than again imperil my own dear cod."

My father muttered, "Worry about balls when we may be about to lose our heads?"

I said, "I am sorry, Father, Uncle. If we are to be hunted by the surviving Misguided Ones, then I did wrong to kill that one."

"Nonsense," said my father. "Had you not awakened and acted with celerity, we would not even have lived to be hunted."

"It is true that you are impetuous, Marco," said Uncle

Mafìo. "But if a man stopped to consider all the consequences of his every action before he acted, he would be a
very old man before he ever did any damned thing at all.
Nico, I think that we might keep this fortunately impetuous young man as our companion. Let him not be tucked
safe away in Constantinople or Venice, but let him come
with us clear to Kithai. However, you are his father. It is
for you to say."

"I am inclined to concur, Mafìo," said my father. And to
me, "If you wish to come along, Marco . . ." I grinned
broadly at him. "Then you come. You deserve to come. You
did well this night."

"Perhaps better than well," said my uncle thoughtfully.
"That bricòn vechio called himself the most Misguided
One of all. Is it not possible he meant also the chief one of
them all? The latest and reigning Sheikh ul-Jibal? An old
man he certainly was."

"The Old Man of the Mountain?" I exclaimed. "I slew
him?"

"We cannot know," said my father. "Not unless the
other hashishiyin tell us when they catch up to us. I am not
that eager to know."

"They must not catch us," said Uncle Mafìo. "We have
already been remiss, coming this far into alien country
with no weapons but our work knives."

My father said, "They will not catch us if they have no
reason to chase after us. We have only to remove the reason. Let the next comers find the karwansarai deserted.
Let them presume that the landlord is afield on an errand
—killing a sheep for the larder, perhaps. It could be days
before those next guests come, and days more before they
begin to wonder where the landlord is. By the time any of
the Misguided Ones get involved in the search for him, and
by the time they give up looking for him and start to suspect foul play, we shall be long gone and far away and beyond their tracing."

"Take the old Beauty with us?" asked my uncle.

"And risk an embarrassing encounter before we have
gone far at all?" My father shook his head. "Nor can we
just drop him down the well here, or hide him or bury him.
Any arriving guest will go first to the water. And any Arab
has a nose like a staghound, to sniff out a hiding place or
fresh-turned earth."

"Not on land, not in water," said my uncle. "There is
only one alternative. I had better do it before I put any
clothes on."

"Yes," said my father, and he turned to me. "Marco, go
through this whole establishment and search out some
blankets to replace those of your uncle. While you are at it,
see if you can find any sort of weapons we can carry when
we go."

The command was obviously given just to get me out of
the way while they did what they did next. And it took me
quite a while to comply, for the karwansarai was old, and
must have had a long succession of owners, each of whom
had built and added on new portions. The main building
was a warren of hallways and rooms and closets and nooks,
and there were also stables and sheds and sheep pens and
other outbuildings. But the old man, evidently having felt
secure in his drugs and deceits, had not taken much trouble to hide his possessions. To judge from the armory of
weapons and provisions, he *had* been, if not the veritable
Old Man, at least a main supplier of the Mulahidat.

I first selected the best two woolen blankets from the
considerable stock of traveling gear. Then I searched
among the weapons and, though I could not find any
straight swords of the type we Venetians were accustomed
to, I picked out the shiniest and sharpest of the local sort.
This was a broad and curved blade—more of a saber, since
it was sharp only on the outcurved edge—called the shimshir, which means "silent lion." I took three of them, one
for each of us, and belts with loops from which to hang
them. I could have further enriched our purses, for Beauty
had secreted a small fortune in the form of bags of dried
banj, bricks of compacted banj, and flagons of oil of banj.
But I left all that where it was.

The dawn was breaking outdoors when I brought my acquisitions to the main room, where we had dined the night
before. My father was preparing a breakfast meal at the
brazier, and being most carefully selective of the ingredients. Just as I entered the room, I heard a series of noises
from the yard outside: a long, rustling whistle, a loud *klop!*
and a screeching yell of *kya!* Then my uncle came in from
that yard, still naked, his skin spattered with blood spots,
his beard smelling of smoke, and he saying with satisfaction:

"That was the last of the old devil, and it went as he wished. I have burned his garments and the blankets, and dispersed the ashes. We can depart as soon as we have dressed and eaten."

I realized, of course, that Beauty of Faith's Moon had been given no laying-out, but an extremely un-Muslim obsequy, and that made me curious as to what Uncle Mafìo meant by "went as he wished." I asked him, and he chuckled and said:

"The last of him went flying southward. Toward Mecca."

BAGHDAD

1

W E kept on downstream along The Furat, still southeastward, now traversing a particularly unappealing stretch of country where the river had cut its channel through solid basalt rock—a land bleak and black and barren even of grass, pigeons and eagles—but we were not pursued by the Misguided Ones or anyone else. And gradually, as if in celebration of our deliverance from danger, the countryside became more pleasant and hospitable. The terrain began perceptibly to rise up on either side of the river, until it was flowing through a wide and verdant valley. There were orchards and forests, pastures and farms, flowers and fruits. But the orchards were as shaggy and untended as the native forests, the farms as overgrown and weedy as the fields of wild flowers. The land's owners had all gone away, and the only people we met in that valley were nomad families of bedawin shepherds, the landless and rootless roamers, roaming in that valley as they roamed in the grasslands. There were nowhere any settled folk, nobody working to keep the once domesticated land from reverting to wilderness.

"It is the doing of the Mongols," said my father. "When the Ilkhan Hulagu—that is to say, the lesser Khan Hulagu, brother to our friend Kubilai—when he swept through this land and overthrew the Persian Empire, most of the Persians fled or fell before him, and the survivors have not yet returned to rework their lands. But the nomad Arabs and Kurdi are like the grass on which they live and in search of which they wander. The bedawin bend

uncaringly before any wind that blows—whether it be a
gentle breeze or the fierce simùn—but they rebound as
does the grass. To the nomads it matters not who rules the
land, and it never will matter to them until the end of
time, as long as the land itself remains."

I turned in my saddle, looking at the land all about us,
the richest, most fertile, most promising land we had yet
seen in our journey, and I asked, "Who does rule Persia
now?"

"When Hulagu died, his son Abagha succeeded as Ilkhan, and he has established a new capital in the northern
city of Maragheh instead of in Baghdad. Although the Persian Empire is now a part of the Mongol Khanate, it is still
divided into Shahnates, as before, for convenience of administration. But each Shah is subordinate to the Ilkhan
Abagha, just as Abagha is subordinate to the Khakhan
Kubilai."

I was impressed. I knew we were yet many months of
hard travel distant from the court city of that Khakhan
Kubilai. But already, here in the western reaches of Persia, *already* we were within the borders of the domain of
that far distant Khan. In school, I had bent my most
admiring and enthusiastic study on *The Book of Alexander,* so I knew that Persia was once a part of that conquer-
or's empire, and his empire was so extensive as to earn
him the sobriquet of "the Great." But the lands won and
held by that Macedonian comprised a mere fragment of the
world, compared to the immensities conquered by
Chinghiz Khan, and further enlarged by his conqueror
sons, and still further enlarged by his conqueror grandsons, into the unimaginably immense Mongol Empire over
which the grandson Kubilai now reigned as Khan of All
Khans.

I believe that not the ancient Pharaones nor the ambitious Alexander nor the avaricious Caesars could have
dreamed that so much world existed, so they could hardly
have dreamed of acquiring it. As for all the later Western
rulers, their ambitions and acquisitions have been even
more paltry. Alongside the Mongol Empire, the entire continent called Europe seems merely a small and crowded
peninsula, and all its nations, like those of the Levant,
only so many peevishly self-important little provinces.
From the eminence on which the Khakhan sits enthroned,

my native Republic of Venice, proud of its glory and grandeur, must appear as trivial as the Suvediye cranny of the
Ostikan Hampig. If the history keepers will continue to
dignify Alexander as the Great, surely they ought to acknowledge Kubilai as the immeasurably Greater. That is
not for me to say. But what I can say is that, on my entrance into Persia, I was thrilled to realize that I, mere
Marco Polo, was setting foot in the most far-flung empire
ever ruled by one man in all the years in which the world
of men has existed.

"When we get to Baghdad," my father went on, "we will
show to the current Shah, whoever he may be, the letter
we carry from Kubilai. And the Shah will have to make us
welcome, as accredited ambassadors of his overlord."

So we processed on down the Furat, watching the valley
get ever more marked with the traces of civilization, for
hereabouts it was criss-crossed by many irrigation canals
branching off the river. However, the towering wooden
wheels in the canals were not being turned by men or animals or any other agency; they stood still, the clay jugs
around their rims not lifting and pouring any water. In the
widest and most verdant part of that valley, the Furat
makes its nearest approach to the other great south-
running river of that country, the Dijlah, sometimes called
Tigris, which is supposedly one of the other rivers of the
Garden of Eden. If that is so, then the land between the
two rivers would presumably be the site of that biblical
garden. And if *that* is so, then the garden, when we saw it,
was as empty of resident men and women as it was immediately after the expulsion of Adam and Eve.

In that vicinity, we turned our horses eastward from the
Furat and rode the intervening ten farsakhs to the Dijlah,
and crossed that river on the bridge there—made of empty
boat hulls supporting a plank roadway—to Baghdad on the
eastern bank.

The city's population, like that of the surrounding countryside, had been grievously diminished during Hulagu's
siege and capture of it. But in the fifteen or so ensuing
years, much of its populace had returned and repaired
what damage it had suffered. City merchants, it seems, are
more resilient than country farmers. Like the primitive
bedawin, civilized tradesmen seem to recover quickly from
the prostrations of disaster. In the case of Baghdad, that

may have been because so many of its merchants were not passive and fatalistic Muslims, but irrepressibly energetic Jews and Christians—some of them having come originally from Venice and even more of them from Genoa.

Or perhaps Baghdad recovered because it is such a *necessary* city, at an important crossroads of trade. Besides being a western terminus of the Silk Road which comes overland, it is a northern terminus of the sea route from the Indies. The city is not itself on the seaside, of course, but its Dijlah River bears a heavy traffic of large river boats, sailing downstream with the current or being poled upriver against it, going to and coming from Basra in the south, on the Persian Gulf, where the seagoing Arab ships make Landfall. Anyway, whatever the beneficent reason, Baghdad was, when we arrived there, what it had been before the Mongols came: a rich and vital and busy trading center.

It was as beautiful as it was busy. Of the Eastern cities I had seen so far, Baghdad was the most reminiscent of my native Venice. Its Dijlah waterfront was as thronged and tumultous and littered and odorous as the Riva of Venice, though the vessels to be seen here—all of them built and manned by Arabs—were nowise comparable to ours. They were alarmingly shoddy craft to be entrusted to the water, built entirely without pegs or nails or iron fastenings of any fashion, their hull planking instead *stitched* together by ropes of some coarse fiber. Their seams and interstices were not plugged watertight with pitch, but with a sort of lard made from fish oil. Even the biggest of those boats had only a single steering oar, and it was not very manipulable since it was firmly hinged at mid-stern. Another deplorable thing about those Arab boats was the unfastidious way their cargoes were stored. After filling the hold with a load of, as it may be, all foodstuffs—dates and fruits and grains and such—the Arab boatmen might then crowd the deck above the hold with a herd of livestock. That frequently consisted of fine Arabian horses, and they are beauteous beasts, but they evacuate themselves as often and as hugely as any other horses, and their droppings would dribble and seep between the planks onto the cargo of edibles belowdecks.

Baghdad is not, like Venice, interlaced with canals, but its streets are constantly sprinkled with water to lay the dust, so they have a humid fragrance reminiscent to me of canals. And the city has a great many open squares equivalent to Venice's piazze. Some are bazàr marketplaces, but most are public gardens, for the Persians are passionately fond of gardens. (I learned there that the Farsi word meaning garden, pairi-daeza, became our Bible's word Paradise.) Those public gardens have benches for passersby to rest on, and streamlets running through, and many birds in residence, and trees and shrubs and perfumed plants and luminous flowers—roses especially, for the Persians are passionately fond of roses. (They call any and every flower a gul, though that Farsi word means specifically a rose.) Likewise, the palaces of noble families and the larger houses of rich merchant families are built around private gardens as big as the public ones, and as full of roses and birds, and as nearly like earthly Paradises.

I suppose I had got it into my head that the words Muslim and Arab were interchangeable, and therefore that any Muslim community must be indistinguishable—in matters of filth and vermin and beggars and stench—from the Arab cities, towns and villages I had passed through. I was agreeably surprised to find that the Persians, although their religion is Islam, are more inclined to keep their buildings and streets and garments and persons clean. That, with the abundance of flowers everywhere, and a comparative fewness of beggars, made Baghdad a most pleasant and even nice-smelling city—except, of necessity, around the waterfront and the bazàr markets.

Although much of Baghdad's architecture was of course peculiarly Eastern, even that was not entirely exotic to my Western eyes. I saw a great deal of that lacy filigree "arabesco" stonework which Venice has also adopted for some of its building fronts. Baghdad being still a Muslim city, even after its absorption into the Khanate—for the Mongols, unlike most conquerors, do not anywhere impose any change of religion—it was studded with those great Muslim masjid temples of worship. But their immense domes were not much different from the domes of San Marco and the other churches of Venice. Their slender manarat towers were not too dissimilar to the campanili of Venice, only being generally round instead of square in cross-section, and having little balconies at their tops,

from which the muedhdhin beadles shouted at intervals to
announce the hours of prayer.

Those muedhdhin in Baghdad, incidentally, were all
blind men. I inquired whether that was a necessary qualification for the post, something demanded by Islam, and
was told it was not. Blind men were engaged as the prayer-
calling beadles for two pragmatic reasons. Being unfit for
most other employments, they could not demand much pay
for the work. And they could not take sinful advantage of
their literally high position: they could not look down to
ogle any decent woman who ascended to her rooftop to doff
her veil—or more of her coverings—for a private sunbath.

In their interiors, the masjid temples differ notably from
our Christian churches. In none of them, anywhere, is
there ever to be found any statue or painting or other recognizable image. Though Islam recognizes, I think, as
many angels and saints and prophets as Christianity does,
it will allow no representation of them, or of any other
creature alive or which ever has lived. Muslims believe
that their Allah, like our Lord God, created all things living. But, unlike us Christians, they maintain that all creation, even in paint or wood or stone imitation of life, must
be forever reserved to Allah. Their Quran warns them that
on Judgment Day any maker of any such image will be
commanded to bring that image to life; if the maker cannot
do that, and of course he cannot, he will be damned to Hell
for his presumption in having made it. Therefore, although a Muslim masjid—or palace or home—is always
rich in decoration, those decorations are never pictures of
anything; they consist only of patterns and colors and intricate arabeschi. Sometimes, though, the patterns are discernible as being woven of the Arabic fish-worm letters
and spelling out some phrase or verse from the Quran.

(I learned these several uncommonly odd things about
Islam—and I learned many other uncommonly odd things
besides —because, during my stay in Baghdad, I acquired
first one and then another uncommonly odd teacher, and I
will tell of them in their turn.)

I was particularly taken with one form of decoration I
saw in the interior rooms of every public and private building in Baghdad. I should say that I first saw it there, but
afterward I saw it in other palaces, homes and temples
throughout Persia and throughout much of the rest of the

East. I should think it might be advantageously adopted
by any people anywhere which loves a garden, and what
people does not love a garden?

What it is, is a way to bring a garden *indoors*, though
never having to tend or weed or water it. Called in Persia a
qali, it is a sort of carpet or tapicierie made to lie on a floor
or hang on a wall, but it is unlike any such work we know
in the West. The qali is colored in all the colors of a bounteous garden, and its figures form the shapes of multitudes
of flowers, vines, trellises, leaves—everything to be found
in a garden—all disposed in pleasing designs and arrangements. (In keeping with the Quran's ban on images, however, a Persian qali is made so that the flowers are not
recognizable as any known existing flowers.) At first sight
of a qali, I thought the garden must be painted or embroidered upon it. But, on examination, I found that all that intricacy was *woven into it.* I marveled that any tapicier
could contrive such a fanciful thing with mere warp and
weft of dyed yarns, and it was some while before I learned
the marvelous manner in which it is done.

But I have already got ahead of my chronicle.

We three led our five horses across the wobbling and
undulating boat bridge which spanned the Dijlah River.
At the Baghdad waterfront, teeming with men of all complexions and costumes and languages, we accosted the
first one we saw wearing Western clothes. He was a Genoan, but I should remark that, out East, all Westerners get
along convivially enough—even Genoans and Venetians,
albeit they are rivals in trade and even though their home
republics may be embroiled in one of their frequent sea
wars. The Genoan merchant amiably told us the name of
the incumbent Shah—he gave it as "Shahinshah Zaman
Mirza"—and directed us to the palace "in the Karkh quarter, which is the exclusively royal quarter of the city."

We rode thither, and found the palace in a gated garden,
and made ourselves known to the guards at the gate.
Those guards wore helmets that seemed to be of solid
gold—but could not have been, or their weight would have
been intolerable—and, even if only of plated wood or
leather, were objects of great value. They were also objects
of interest, being fashioned to give their wearers a wealth
of curly golden hair and side whiskers. One of the guards
went inside the gate and through the garden to the palace.

When he returned and beckoned to us, another guard took charge of our horses, and we entered.

We were led to a chamber richly hung and carpeted with brilliant qali, where the Shahinshah half-sat and half-reclined on a heap of daiwan cushions of equally vivid colors and fine fabrics. He himself was not gaudily garbed; from tulband to slippers, his dress was a uniform pale brown. That is the Persian color of mourning, and the Shah always wore pale brown now in mourning for his lost empire. We were somewhat surprised—this being a Muslim household—to see that a woman occupied another heap of pillows beside him, and there were also two other females in the room. We made the proper bows of salaam and, still bowed down, my father greeted the Shahinshah in the Farsi tongue, then raised up upon his two hands the letter of Kubilai Khan. The Shah took it and read aloud its salutation:

" 'Most Serene, most Puissant, most High, Noble, Illustrious, Honorable, Wise and Prudent Emperors, Ilkhani, Shahi, Kings, Lords, Princes, Dukes, Earls, Barons and Knights, as also Magistrates, Officers, Justicians and Regents of all good cities and places, whether ecclesiastic or secular, who shall see these patents or hear them read . . .' "

When he had perused the whole thing, the Shahinshah bade us welcome, addressing each of us as "Mirza Polo." That was a little confusing, as I had understood Mirza to be one of *his* names. But I gradually gathered that he was using the word as a respectful honorific, as the Arabs use Sheikh. And eventually I realized that Mirza before a name means only what Messer does in Venice; when it is appended after the name, it signifies royalty. The Shah's name was actually and simply Zaman, and his full title of Shahinshah meant Shah of All Shahs, and he introduced the lady beside him as his Royal First Wife, or Shahryar, by the name of Zahd.

That was very nearly all he got to say that day, because, once she was introduced into the conversation, the Shahryar Zahd proved to be effusively and endlessly talkative. First interrupting, then overriding her husband, she gave us her own welcome to Persia and to Baghdad and to the palace, and she sent our accompanying guard back to the gate, and she hammered a little gong at her side to sum-

mon a palace maggiordomo whom she told us was called a
wazir, and she instructed the wazir to prepare quarters for
us in the palace and assign palace servants to us, and she
introduced us to the other two females in the room: one her
mother, the other the eldest daughter of herself and the
Shah Zaman, and she informed us that she herself, Zahd
Mirza, was a direct descendant of the fabled Balkis, Queen
of Sabaea—and, of course, so were her mother and
daughter—and she reminded us that the famous encounter
of Queen Balkis with the Padshah Solaiman was recorded
in the annals of Islam as well as those of Judaism and
Christianity (which remark enabled me to recognize the
biblical Queen of Sheba and King Solomon), and she further informed us that the Sebaean Queen Balkis herself
was a jinniyeh, descended from a demon named Eblis, who
was chief jinni of all the demon jinn, and furthermore . . .

"Tell us, Mirza Polo," the Shah said, almost desperately, to my father, "something of your journey thus far."

My father obligingly began an account of our travels,
but he had not even got us out of the Venice lagoon when
the Shahryar Zahd pounced in with a lyrical description of
some pieces of Murano glass she had recently bought from
a Venetian merchant in downtown Baghdad, and that reminded her of an old but little-known Persian tale of a
glassblower who, once upon a time, fashioned a horse of
blown glass and persuaded a jinni to make some magic by
which the horse was enabled to fly like a bird, and . . .

The tale was interesting enough, but unbelievable, so I
let my attention wander to the other two females in the
room. The women's very presence in a meeting of men—
not to mention the Shahryar's unquenchable garrulity—
was evidence that the Persians did not shield and
sequester and stifle their womenfolk as most other Muslims do. Each woman's eyes were visible above a mere
half-veil of chador, which was diaphanous anyway and did
not conceal her nose and mouth and chin. On their upper
bodies they wore blouse and waistcoat, and on their lower
limbs the voluminous pai-jamah. However, those garments were not thick and many-layered as on Arab
women, but gossamer light and translucent, so the shapes
of their bodies could be easily discerned and appreciated.

I gave only one look at the aged grandmother: wrinkled,
bony, hunched, almost bald, toothlessly champing her

granulated lips, her eyes red and gummy, her withered paps flapping against slatted ribs. One look at the crone was enough for me. But her daughter, the Shahryar Zahd Mirza, was an exceptionally handsome woman, anyway when she was not talking, and *her* daughter was a superbly beautiful and shapely girl about my own age. She was the Crown Princess or Shahzrad, and named Magas, which means Moth, and subtitled with the royal Mirza. I have neglected to say that the Persians are not, like Arabs, of dark and muddy complexion. Though they all have blue-black hair, and the men wear blue-black beards like Uncle Mafìo's, their skin is as fair as any Venetian's, and many have eyes of lighter color than brown. The Shahzrad Magas Mirza was at that moment taking my measure with eyes of emerald green.

"Speaking of horses," said the Shah, seizing on the tail of the flying-horse tale, before his wife could be reminded of some other story. "You gentlemen should consider trading your horses for camels before you leave Baghdad. Eastward of here you must cross the Dasht-e-Kavir, a vast and terrible desert. Horses cannot endure the—"

"The Mongols' horses did," his wife sharply contradicted him. "A Mongol goes everywhere on a horse, and no Mongol would ever bestride a camel. I will tell you how they despise and mistreat camels. While they were besieging this city, the Mongols captured a herd of camels somewhere, and they loaded them with bales of dry grass, and set that hay afire, and stampeded the poor beasts into our streets. The camels, their own fur and humps of fat burning as well, ran mad in agony and could not be caught. So they careered up and down our streets, setting fire to much of Baghdad, before the flames ate into them and reached their vitals, and they collapsed and died."

"Or," said the Shah to us, when the Shahryar paused to take a breath, "your journey could be much shortened if you went part way by sea. You might wish to go southeast from here, to Basra—or even farther down the Gulf, to Hormuz—and take passage on some ship sailing to India."

"In Hormuz," said the Shahryar Zahd, "every man has only a thumb and the two outer fingers on his right hand. I will tell you why. That seaport city has for ages treasured its importance and its independence, so its every adult male citizen has always been trained as an archer to de-

fend it. When the Mongols under the Ilkhan Hulagu laid
seige to Hormuz, the Ilkhan made an offer to the city fathers. Hulagu said he would let Hormuz stand, and retain
its independence, and keep its citizen archers, if only the
city fathers would *lend* him those bowmen for long enough
to help him conquer Baghdad. Then, he promised, he
would let the men come home to Hormuz and be its
staunch defense again. The city fathers agreed to that proposal, and all its men—however reluctantly—joined Hulagu in his siege of this city, and fought well for him, and
eventually our beloved Baghdad fell."

She and the Shah both sighed deeply.

"Well," she went on, "Hulagu had been so impressed by
the valor and prowess of the Hormuz men that he then
sent them to bed with all the young Mongol women who always accompany the Mongol armies. Hulagu wished to
add the potency of the Hormuz seed to the Mongol birth-
lines, you see. After a few nights of that enforced cohabita-
tion, when Hulagu presumed his females had been
sufficiently impregnated, he kept his promise and freed
the archers to go home to Hormuz. But before he let them
depart, he had every man's two bowstring fingers amputated. In effect, Hulagu took the fruit from the trees and
then felled the trees. Those mutilated men could make no
defense of Hormuz at all, and of course that city soon became, like our dear defeated Baghdad, a possession of the
Mongol Khanate."

"My dear," said the Shah, looking flustered. "These
gentlemen are emissaries of that Khanate. The letter they
showed me is a ferman from the Khakhan Kubilai himself.
I very much doubt that they are amused to hear tales of the
Mongols'—er—misbehavior."

"Oh, you can freely say *atrocities,* Shah Zaman," my uncle boomed heartily. "We are still Venetians, not adoptive
Mongols nor apologists for them."

"Then I should tell you," said the Shahryar, again lean-
ing eagerly forward, "the ghastly way Hulagu treated our
Qalif al-Mustasim Billah, the holiest man of Islam." The
Shah breathed another sigh, and fixed his gaze on a re-
mote corner of the room. "As perhaps you know, Mirza
Polo, Baghdad was to Islam what Rome is to Christianity.
And the Qalif of Baghdad was to Muslims what your Pope
is to you Christians. So, when Hulagu laid siege here, it

was to the Qalif Mustasim that he proposed surrender
terms, not to the Shah Zaman." She flicked a disparaging
glance at her husband. "Hulagu offered to lift the siege if
the Qalif acceded to certain demands, among them the
handing over of much gold. The Qalif refused, saying, 'Our
gold sustains our Holy Islam.' And the reigning Shah did
not overrule that decision."

"How could I?" that Shah said weakly, as if it was an
argument much argued previously. "The spiritual leader
outranks the temporal."

His wife went implacably on. "Baghdad might have
withstood the Mongols and their Hormuz allies, but it
could not withstand the hunger imposed by a siege. Our
people ate everything edible, even the city rats, but the
people got weaker and weaker, and many died and the
rest could fight no longer. When the city inevitably fell,
Hulagu imprisoned the Qalif Mustasim in solitary confinement, and let him get even hungrier. At last the holy old
man had to beg for food. Hulagu with his own hands gave
him a plate full of gold coins, and the Qalif whimpered, 'No
man can eat gold.' And Hylagu said, 'You called it sustenance when I asked for it. Did it sustain your holy city?
Pray, then, that it will sustain you.' And he had the gold
melted, and he poured that glowing-hot liquid metal down
the old man's throat, killing him horribly. Mustasim was
the last of the Qalifate, which had endured for more than
five hundred years, and Baghdad is no longer the capital
either of Persia or of Islam."

We dutifully shook our heads in commiseration, which
encouraged the Shahryar to add:

"As an illustration of how low the Shahnate has been
brought: this my husband, Shah Zaman, who was once
Shahinshah of all the Empire of Persia, is now a pigeon
keeper and cherry picker!"

"My dear . . . ," said the Shah.

"It is true. One of the lesser Khans—somewhere to the
eastward; we have never even met this Ilkhan—has a taste
for ripe cherries. He is also a fancier of pigeons, and his
pigeons are trained always to fly home to him from wherever they may be transported. So there are now some hundred of those feathered rats in a dovecote behind the palace
stables, and for each there is a tiny silken bag. My Emperor husband has instructions. Next summer when our

orchards ripen, we are to pick the cherries, put one or two of them into each of those little bags, fasten the bags to the legs of the pigeons and let the birds free. Like the rukh bird carrying off men and lions and princesses, the pigeons will carry our cherries to the waiting Ilkhan. If we do not pay that humiliating tribute, he will doubtless come rampaging from out of the east and lay our city waste again."

"My dear, I am sure the gentlemen are now weary of—of traveling hither," said the Shah, sounding weary himself. He struck the gong to summon the wazir once more, and said to us, "You will wish to rest and refresh yourselves. Then, if you will do me the honor, we will foregather again at the evening meal."

The wazir, a middle-aged and melancholy man named Jamshid, showed us to our chambers, a suite of three rooms with doors between. They were well furnished, with many qali on the floors and walls, and windows of stone tracery inset with glass, and soft beds of quilts and pillows. Our packs had already been removed from our horses and brought there.

"And here is a manservant for each of you," said the Wazir Jamshid, producing three lissome, beardless young men. "They are all expert in the Indian art of champna, which they will perform for you after you have been to the hammam."

"Ah, yes," said Uncle Mafìo, sounding pleased. "We have not enjoyed a shampoo, Nico, since we came through Tazhikistan."

So again we had the thorough cleansing and refreshment of a hammam, an elegantly appointed one this time, in which our three young men served as our rubbers. And afterward we lay nude on our separate beds in our separate rooms for what was called the champna—or shampoo, as my uncle had pronounced it. I had no idea what to expect; it had sounded like a dance performance. But it proved to be a vigorous rubbing and pummeling and kneading of my entire body, more energetically done than the hammam rubbing, and with the intent not of extruding dirt from the skin, but of exercising every part in a manner to make one feel even healthier and more invigorated than a hammam bath can do.

My young servant, Karim, pounded and pinched and
tweaked me, and at first it was painful. But after a while,
my muscles and joints and sinews, stiffened by long riding,
began to uncoil and unknot under that assault, and gradually I lay at ease and enjoyed it, and felt myself beginning
to tingle with vitality. As a matter of fact, one impertinent
part of me became obtrusively alive, and I was embarrassed. Then I was startled, for Karim with an evidently
practiced hand started to exercise that also.

"I can do that for myself," I snapped, "if I deem it necessary."

He shrugged delicately and said, "As the Mirza commands. When the Mirza commands," and concentrated on
less intimate parts of me.

He finished the mauling at last, and I lay half wanting
to doze, half wanting to leap up and do athletic feats, and
he asked to be excused.

"To attend the Mirza your uncle," he explained. "For
such a massive man, it will require all three of us to give
him an adequate champna."

I graciously gave him leave, and abandoned myself to
my drowsiness. I think my father also slept the afternoon
away, but Uncle Mafìo must have had a most thorough
working-over, for the three young men were just leaving
his room when Jamshid came to see us dressed for the
evening meal. He brought for us new and myrrh-scented
clothing of the Persian style: the lightweight pai-jamah,
and loose shirts with tight cuffs, and, to wear over the
shirts, beautifully embroidered short waistcoats, and kamarbands to go tightly about our waists, and silk shoes
with upturned, curly, pointed toes, and tulbands instead of
hanging kaffiyah headcloths. My father and uncle each
proficiently and neatly wound his tulband around his
head, but young Karim had to instruct me in the winding
and tucking of mine. When we were dressed, we all looked
exceptionally handsome and nobly Mirza and genuinely
Persian.

WAZIR Jamshid led us to a large but not overpowering dining hall, lighted with torches and ringed about with servants and attendants. They were all males, and only the
Shah Zaman joined us at the sumptuously laid dining
cloth. I was rather relieved to see that the palace household was not so unorthodox that females were allowed to
violate Muslim custom and routinely sit down to eat with
men. We and the Shah had a meal uninterrupted by the
facundities of the Shahryar, and he only once referred to
her:

"The First Wife, being of royal Sabaean blood, has never
reconciled herself to the fact that this Shahnate was heretofore subordinate to the Qalif and now is subordinate to
the Khanate. Like a fine-bred Arabian mare, the Shahryar
Zahd bucks at being harnessed. But otherwise she is an excellent consort, and more tender than the tail of a fat-
tailed sheep."

His barnyard similes perhaps explained, but to my mind
did not excuse, her seeming to be the cock of that yard, and
he the much-pecked hen. Nevertheless, the Shah was a
congenial fellow, and he drank with us like a Christian,
and he was a knowledgeable conversationalist when he
was unencumbered of his wife. At my remark that I was
thrilled to be following the trails which Alexander the
Great had trodden, the Shah said:

"Those trails of his ended not far from here, you know,
after Alexander had returned from his conquest of India's
Kashmir and Sind and the Panjab. Only fourteen farsakhs
south of here are the ruins of Babylon, where he died. Of a
fever brought on, it is said, by his having drunk too much
of our wine of Shiraz."

I thanked the Shah for the information, but I privately
wondered how anyone could drink a killing amount of that
sticky liquid. Even in Venice I had heard travelers extol
their remembrance of the wine of Shiraz, and it is much
praised in song and fable, but we were drinking it at that
very meal, and I thought it fell far short of its reputation.
That wine is an unappetizing orange in color, and cloyingly sweet, and thick as treacle. A man would have to be

determined on drunkenness, I decided, to drink very much
of it.

The other elements of the meal, though, were unquali-
fiedly superb. There was chicken cooked in pomegranate
juice, and lamb cubed and marinated and broiled in a manner called kabab, and a rose-flavored sharbat cold with
snow, and a billowy, trembling confection like a fluffed-up
nougat, made of fine white flour, cream, honey, daintily
flavored with oil of pistachio, and called a balesh. After the
meal, we lolled among our cushions and sipped an exquisite liqueur expressed from rose petals, while we watched
two court wrestlers, naked and shiny and slippery with almond oil, try to bend each other double or break each other
in half. Then, when they had escaped the performance
unharmed, we listened to a court minstrel play on a
stringed instrument called al-ud, very like a lute, while he
recited Persian poems, of which I can recall only that their
every line ended in a mouselike squeak or a mournful sob.

When that torment was concluded, I was given leave by
the elder men to go and amuse myself, if I wished, I did so,
leaving my father and uncle discussing with the Shah the
various land and water routes they might take after Baghdad. I left the room and walked down a long corridor,
where were many closed doors guarded by giant men holding spears or shimshir sabers. They all wore the sort of helmet I had seen at the palace gates, but some of the guards
had faces of African black or Arab brown, ill according
with the helmets' gold-sculptured tresses.

At the end of the corridor was an unguarded archway
giving onto the outdoor garden, and I went there. The
smooth gravel pathways and lush flower beds were softly
illuminated by a full moon that was like a great pearl displayed on the black velvet of the night. I wandered idly
about, admiring the unfamiliar blooms made even more
new to me by the pearl light shining on them. Then I came
to something so novel as to be astonishing: a flower bed
that was visibly and all on its own *doing* something. I
stopped to watch and ponder what appeared to be an
unvegetably deliberate behavior. The flower bed was a tremendous circular area, divided piewise into twelve slices,
each segment planted densely with a different variety of
flowers. All of them were at the blooming stage, but in ten
of the slices the flowers had closed their blossoms, as many

flowers do at night. However, in one segment, some pale
pink flowers were just then folding their petals, and in the
adjoining segment some large white flowers were at
the same time just opening their blossoms and loosing on
the night a heady perfume.

"It is the gulsa'at," said a voice that might also have
been perfumed. I turned to see the young and comely
Shahzrad and, standing some way behind her, the aged
grandmother. Princess Moth went on, "Gulsa'at means
the flower dial. In your country, you have sand glasses and
water glasses to tell the hours, do you not?"

"Yes, Shahzrad Magas Mirza," I said, taking care to use
her whole regalia of address.

"You may call me Moth," she said, with a sweet smile
visible through her sheer chador. She indicated the gulsa'at. "This flower dial also tells the hours, but it never
has to be turned or refilled. Each kind of flower in that
round bed naturally opens at a certain hour of the day or
night, and closes at another. They are selected for their
regularity of habit, and planted here in proper sequence
and—lo! They silently announce each of the twelve hours
we count from sunset to sunset."

I said daringly, "It is a thing as beautiful as you are,
Princess Moth."

"My father the Shah takes a delight in measuring
time," she said. "Yonder is the palace masjid in which we
worship, but it is also a calendar. In one wall it has openings so the sun in its rounds shines its light each dawn
through one after another to tell the day and the month."

Somewhat similarly, I was sidling around the girl, to put
her between me and the moon, so its light shone through
her filmy garments and outlined her delectable body. The
old grandmother evidently perceived my intention, for she
grinned her gums evilly at me.

"And yonder, beyond," the Princess continued, "is the
anderun where reside all my father's other wives and concubines. He has more than three hundred, so he can have a
different one almost every night of the year if he chooses.
However, he prefers my mother, the First Wife, except
that she talks all night. So he only takes one of the others
to bed when he wishes to have a good night's sleep."

Looking at the Shahzrad's moon-revealed body, I felt my
own body again stirring as vivaciously as it had done dur-

ing the champna. I was glad I was not wearing tight Venetian hose, or I would have bulged them most disgracefully. Dressed as I was in ample pai-jamah, I did not think my arousal could have been visible. But the Princess Moth must have sensed it anyway, for to my shocked amazement she said:

"You would like to take *me* to bed and make zina, would you not?"

I stammered and stuttered, and managed to say, "Surely you should not speak so, Princess, in the presence of your royal grandmother! I assume she is your"—I did not know the Farsi word, so I said it in French—"your chaperon?"

The Shahzrad made an airy gesture. "The old woman is as deaf as that gulsa'at. Be not concerned, but answer me. You would like to put your zab into my mihrab, no?"

I swallowed and gulped. "I could hardly be so presumptuous . . . I mean, a Royal Highness . . ."

She nodded and said briskly, "I believe we can arrange something of the sort. No, do not grab at me. The grandmother can see, if she cannot hear. We must be discreet. I will ask my father's permission to be your guide while you are here, to show you the delights of Baghdad. I can be a very good guide to those delights. You will see."

And with that, she drifted away down the moonlit garden, leaving me shaken and shaking. I might say vibrant. When I tottered to my room, Karim was waiting to help me doff the unfamiliar Persian clothes, and he laughed and made noises of admiration and said:

"Surely now the young Mirza will allow me to complete the relaxing champna!" and he poured almond oil into his hand, and he did so with expertness, and I fell languidly into sleep.

The next day I slept late, and so did my father and uncle, for their consultation with Shah Zaman had lasted well into the night. As we ate our breakfast meal, brought by the servants to our suite, they told me that they were contemplating the Shah's suggestion that we go by sea as far as the Indies. But they would first have to find out if it was practicable. They would each go to one of the Gulf ports— my father to Hormuz, my uncle to Basra—and see if, as the Shah believed, an Arab trader-captain could be persuaded to allow passage to us rival Venetian traders.

"When we have investigated," said my father, "we will regather here in Baghdad, because the Shah will be wanting us to carry many gifts from him to the Khakhan. So you, Marco, can come along with either one of us to the Gulf, or you can await our return here."

Thinking of the Shahzrad Magas, but having the good sense not to mention her, I said I thought I would stay. I would take the opportunity to get better acquainted with Baghdad.

Uncle Mafìo snorted. "In the way that you got so well acquainted with Venice when we were last away? Truly, not so very many Venetians get to know the interior of the Vulcano." To my father he said, "Is it prudent, Nico, to leave this malanòso alone in an alien city?"

"Alone?" I protested. "I have the servant Karim and"—I again refrained from mentioning the Princess Moth—"and the whole palace guard."

"They are responsible to the Shah, not to you or us," said my father. "If you should get into trouble again . . ."

I indignantly reminded him that my most recent trouble had involved my saving them from being slaughtered in their sleep, and they had praised me for it, and that was why I was still in their company, and—

My father sternly interrupted with a proverb, "One sees better backwards than forwards. We are not going to set a warden over you, my boy. But I think it would be a good idea to buy a slave to be your personal servant and see to your best interests. We will go to the bazàr."

The melancholy Wazir Jamshid walked with us, to interpret for us if our command of Farsi should prove inadequate. Along the way he explained several curious things I was seeing for the first time. For example, in eyeing the other men on the streets, I observed that they did not allow their blue-black beards to go gray or white as they aged. Every elderly man I saw had a beard of a violent pink-orange color, like Shiraz wine. Jamshid told me that it was done with a dye made from the leaves of a shrub called hinna, and he said the hinna was also much used by women as a cosmetic and by carters to adorn their horses. I should mention that the horses used in Baghdad for carriage and cartage are not the fine Arabians used for riding. They are tiny little ponies, not much bigger than mastiff

dogs, and they do look very pretty with their flowing manes and tails dyed that brilliant pink-orange color.

There were, on the Baghdad streets, men of many other
nations than Persia. Some wore Western clothes and had
faces, like ours, that would have been white had they not
been sun-darkened. Some had black faces, some brown,
some a sort of tan-yellow hue, and there were many whose
faces were like weathered leather. Those were the Mongols of the occupying garrison, all dressed in armor of varnished hides or metal chain mail, and striding
contemptuously through the street crowds, shoving aside
anybody who stepped in their way. Also on the streets
were many women, also of various complexions, the Persians only lightly veiled, and others not wearing chador at
all, a strange thing to see in a Muslim city. But, even in
liberal Baghdad, no woman walked alone; whatever her
race or nationality, she was attended either by one or several other women or by a male attendant of considerable
bulk and beardless face.

I was so bedazzled by the Baghdad bazàr that I could
hardly believe the city had been conquered and plundered
and held to tribute by the Mongols. It must have recovered
commendably from its recent impoverishment, for it was
the richest and most thriving center of commerce I had yet
seen, far surpassing every marketplace of Venice in the variety and abundance and value of the goods for sale.

The cloth merchants stood proudly among bales and
bolts of fabrics woven of silk and wool and Ankara-goat
hair and cotton and linen and fine camel hair and sturdier
camelot. There were more exotic Eastern fabrics like
mussoline from Mosul and dungri from India and bokhram
from Bukhara and demesq from Damascus. The book merchants displayed volumes of fine vellum and parchment
and paper, gorgeously engrossed in many colors and gold
leaf besides. Most of the books, being copies of the works of
Persian authors like Sadi and Nimazi, and of course written in Farsi and rendered in the convulsed-worm Arabic
lettering, were incomprehensible to me. But one of them,
titled *Iskandarnama*, I could recognize from its illuminations as being a Persian version of my favorite reading,
The Book of Alexander.

The bazàr's apothecaries stocked jars and phials of cosmetics for men and women: black al-kohl and green mala-

chite and brown summaq and red hinna and eye-
brightening collyrium washes, and perfumes of nard and
myrrh and frankincense and rose attar. There were tiny
bags of an almost impalpably fine grit which Jamshid said
was fern seed, to be employed by those who knew the
proper accompaniment of magical incantations, to make
their corporeal persons invisible. There was an oil called
teryak, expressed from the petals and pods of poppy flowers, which Jamshid said physicians prescribed for the relief of cramps and other pains, but which any person
depressed by age or misery could buy and drink as an easy
way out of an unbearable life.

The bazàr was also shiny and glittering and coruscating
with precious metals and gems and jewelry. But of all the
treasures for sale there, I was most taken with a particular
sort. There was a merchant who dealt exclusively in sets of
a certain board game. In Venice it is unimaginatively
called the Game of Squares, and it is played with cheap
pieces carved of ordinary woods. In Persia that game is
called the War of the Shahi, and the playing sets are works
of art, priced beyond the reach of all but a real Shah or
someone of equal wealth. A typical board offered for sale
by that Baghdad merchant was of alternate ebony and
ivory squares, expensive all by itself. The pieces on one
side of it—the Shah and his General, the two elephants,
the two horsemen, the two rukhi warriors and the eight
peyadeh foot soldiers—were made of gem-encrusted gold,
the sixteen facing pieces across the board being of gem-
encrusted silver. The price asked for that set I cannot remember, but it was staggering. He had other Shahi sets
variously fashioned of porcelain and jade and rare woods
and pure crystal, and all of those pieces were sculptured as
exquisitely as if they had been miniature statues of living
monarchs and generals and their men at arms.

There were merchants of livestock—of horses and ponies
and asses and camels, of course, but also of other beasts.
Some of them I had known only by repute and never seen
before that day, such as a big and shaggy bear, which I
thought resembled my Uncle Mafìo; a delicate kind of deer
called a qazèl, which people bought to grace their gardens;
and a yellow wild dog called a shaqàl, which a hunter
could tame and train to stop and kill a charging boar. (A
Persian hunter will go alone and with only a knife to chal-

lenge a savage lion, but he is timid of meeting a wild pig.
Since a Muslim recoils even from speaking of pig meat, he
would deem it a death horrific beyond imagination if he
should die at the tusks of a boar.) Also in the livestock market was the shuturmurq, which means "camel-bird," and
it certainly did look like a mongrel offspring of those two
different creatures. The camel-bird has the body and feathers and beak of a giant goose, but its neck is unfeathered
and long, like a camel's, and its two legs are ungainly long,
like a camel's four, and its splayed feet are as big as a camel's pads, and it can no more fly than a camel can. Jamshid
said the shuturmurq was caught and kept for the one
pretty thing it can supply: the billowy plumes it grows on
its rump. There were also apes for sale, of the sort which
uncouth seamen sometimes bring to Venice, where they
are called simiazze: those apes as big and ugly as Ethiope
children. Jamshid called that animal nedjis, which
means "unspeakably unclean," but he did not tell me why
it was so named or why anyone, even a seaman, would buy
such a thing.

In the bazàr were many fardarbab, or tomorrow-tellers.
They were shriveled, orange-bearded old men who squatted
behind trays of carefully smoothed sand. A client who paid
a coin would shake the tray and the sand would ripple into
patterns which the old man would read and interpret.
There were also many of the darwish holy beggars, as ragged, scabby, filthy and evil-looking as those in any other
Eastern city. Here in Baghdad they had an additional attribute: they danced and skipped and howled and whirled
and convulsed as violently as any epilept in a seizure. It
was, I suppose, at least some entertainment in return for
the bakhshish they beseeched.

Before we could even inspect any of the bazàr's wares,
we had to be interviewed by a market official called the
revenue-farmer, and satisfy him that we possessed both
the means to buy and also the means to pay the jizya,
which is a tax levied on non-Muslim sellers and buyers
alike. Wazir Jamshid, although he was himself a court official, privately confided to us that all such petty officials
and civil servants were despised by the people and were
called batlanim, which means "the idle ones." When my
father produced for that idle one a cod of musk, surely

wealth enough to pay for a Shahi set at least, the revenue-farmer grumbled suspiciously.

"Got it from an Armeniyan, you say? Then it probably contains not the deer's musk, but his chopped liver. It must be tested."

The idle one took out a needle and thread and a clove of garlic. He threaded the needle and ran it several times through and through the garlic, until the thread was reeking with the garlic odor. Then he took the musk cod and ran the needle and thread just once through it. He sniffed at the thread and looked surprised.

"The smell is all gone, totally absorbed. Verily, you have genuine musk. Where on this earth did you meet an honest Armeniyan?" And he gave us a ferman, a paper authorizing us to trade in the Baghdad bazàr.

Jamshid took us to the slave pen of a Persian dealer who he said was trustworthy, and we stood among the crowd of other prospective purchasers and mere lookers-on, while the dealer detailed the lineage, history, attributes and merits of each slave brought to the block by his burly assistants.

"Here is a standard eunuch," he said, presenting an obese and shiny black man, who looked quite cheerful for a slave. "Guaranteed placid and amenable to orders and never known to steal more than the allowable. He would make an excellent servant. However, if you seek a veritable Keeper of the Keys, here is a perfect eunuch." He presented a young white man, blond and muscular, who was quite handsome but who looked as melancholy as a slave might be expected to look. "You are invited to examine the merchandise."

My uncle said to the wazir, "I know, of course, what a eunuch is. We have castròni in our own country, sweet-singing boys neutered so they will always sing sweetly. But how can a totally sexless creature be differentiated as standard and perfect? Is it because one is an Ethiope and the other a Russniak?"

"No, Mirza Polo," said Jamshid, and he explained in French, so we would not be confounded by unfamiliar Farsi words. "The eunuque ordinaire is deprived of his testicles when he is yet a baby, to make him grow up docile and obedient and not contrary of nature. It is easily done. A thread is tied tightly around the roots of a boy infant's

scrotum, and in a matter of weeks that cod withers, turns
black and drops off. That is quite enough to make him become a good servant of general utility."

"What more could a master want?" said Uncle Mafìo,
perhaps sincerely, perhaps sarcastically.

"Well, to be a Keeper of the Keys, the eunuque extraordinaire is preferred. For he must live in and watch over the
anderun, the quarters in which reside his master's wives
and concubines. And those women, especially if they are
not often favored in the matter of the master's bed, can be
most enterprising and inventive, even with inert male
flesh. So that sort of slave must be shorn of *all* his
equipment—the rod as well as the stones. And that removal is a serious operation, not so easily done. Look
younder and observe. The merchandise is being examined."

We looked. The dealer had directed the two slaves to
drop their pai-jamah, and they stood with their crotches
exposed to the scrutiny of an elderly Persian Jew. The fat
black man was hairless down there, and bagless, but he
did have a member of respectable size, though of a repellent black and purple color. I supposed that a woman of the
anderun, if she was so desperate for a man and so depraved
as to want that thing inside her, might contrive some kind
of splint to stiffen it. But the far more presentable young
Russniak had not even a flaccid appendage. He showed
only a growth of blond artichoke hair, and something like
the tip of a small white stick grotesquely protruding from
the hair, and otherwise his groin was as featureless as a
woman's.

"Bruto barabào!" grunted Uncle Mafìo. "How *is* it done,
Jamshid?"

As expressionlessly as if he was reading from a medical
text, the wazir said, "The slave is taken into a room dense
with the smoke of smoldering banj leaves and he is set in a
hot bath and he is given teryak to sip, all that done to dull
his sense of pain. The hakim doing the operation takes a
long ribbon and winds it tightly about him, starting at the
tip of the slave's penis and wrapping inward to the roots,
bundling in with it the cod of testicles, so that the organs
make a single package. Then, using a keenly sharp blade,
the hakim removes that whole beribboned package with a
single slicing stroke. He immediately applies to the wound

a styptic of powdered raisins, puffball fungus and alum. When the bleeding stops, he inserts a clean quill, which will stay there during the slave's whole life. For the chief danger of the operation is that the urinary passage may close in the healing. If, by the third or fourth day afterward, the slave has not passed water through the quill, he is certain to die. And sad to say, that does occur in perhaps three out of five cases."

"Capòn mal caponà!" exclaimed my father. "It sounds gruesome. You have actually witnessed such a procedure?"

"Yes," said Jamshid. "I watched with some interest when it was done to me."

I should have realized that that accounted for his always melancholy aspect, and I should have kept silent. Instead I blurted, "But you are not fat, Wazir, and you have a full beard!"

He did not rebuke my impertinence. He replied, "Those who endure castration in infancy never grow a beard, and their bodies grow corpulent and feminine of contour, often even growing heavy breasts. But when the operation is done after a slave's passing puberty, he remains masculine, at least in outward appearance. I was a full-grown man, with a wife and son, when our farm was raided by Kurdi slave-takers. The Kurdi sought only robust worker slaves, so my wife and little boy were spared. They were merely raped several times apiece, and then slain."

An appalled silence ensued and might have got uncomfortable, but Jamshid added, almost offhandedly, "Ah, well, can I complain? I might have been a mere millet farmer to this day. But having been relieved of a man's natural desires—to sow and cultivate land and lineage—I was freed to cultivate my intellect instead. Now I have risen to become Wazir to the Shahinshah of Persia, and that is no small attainment."

Having so graciously dismissed the subject, he summoned the slave dealer to come and give ear to our requirements. The dealer left his assistants to oversee the inspection of the two slaves already on display, and came smiling and rubbing his hands together.

I had half hoped that my father would buy for me a comely girl slave, who could be more than a servant, or at least a young man of my own age, who would be a congenial companion. But of course he told the dealer not what I might want, but what he wanted for me:

"An older man, well versed in travel, but still agile enough to travel farther yet. Wise in the ways of the East, so that he can both safeguard and instruct my son. And I think"—he flicked a sympathetic glance at the wazir—"not a eunuch. I had rather not help to perpetuate that practice."

"I have the very man, messieurs," said the dealer, speaking good French. "Mature but not old, wily but not willful, experienced but not inflexible to command. Now, where has he got to? He was here just moments ago. . . ."

We followed him about through his herd—or herds, I should say, for there were a considerable number of slaves in the pen, and also a number of the tiny hinna'ed Persian horses which drew his wagons from town to town. The pen was partly fenced and partly enclosed by those canvas-hooped wagons, in which he and his assistants and his merchandise traveled by day and slept by night.

"The ideal slave for you, messieurs, this man," the dealer went on, as he kept looking around. "He has belonged to numerous master, hence has traveled widely and knows many lands. He speaks several tongues and has a vast repertoire of useful talents. But where *is* he?"

We continued circulating among the men and women slaves, who had lengths of light chain connecting their ankle rings, and among the midget horses, which were not fettered. The dealer began to look slightly embarrassed at having misplaced the very slave he was trying to peddle.

"I had loosed him from the skein," he muttered, "and shackled him to one of my mares, which he was currying for me—"

He was interrupted by a loud, piercing, prolonged equine whinny. With a ripple of orange mane and tail, a little horse came flying out through the front flaps of one of the covered wagons. Literally, it was in flight for a moment, like the magic glass horse of which the Shahryar Zahd had told us, for it had to bound from the interior of the wagon bed and clear the driver's bench and the dashboard to get to the ground below. As it made that high arcing bound, a chain attached to its rear leg came trailing in the same looping arc, and at the other end of the chain a man popped out legs-first through the canvas flaps, like a

stopper yanked from a bottle. The man also flew over the
front of the wagon and hit the ground in a thump of dust.
Because the horse tried to flee farther yet, the man got
dragged about and raised quite a cloud of dust before the
slave dealer could catch the frightened animal's bridle and
bring that brief entertainment to a halt.

The little horse's orange mane was silkily combed, but
its orange tail was disheveled. So were the man's nether
regions, for his pai-jamah were down around his feet. He
sat for a moment, too winded to do anything but make several faint exclamations in several languages. Then he
hastily rearranged his garments, as the slave dealer came
and stood over him and bellowed imprecations and kicked
him until he got upright. The slave was about my father's
age, but his scruffy beard appeared to be only about two
weeks' growth and did not adequately conceal a receding
chin. He had bright, shifty pig's eyes and a large fleshy
nose that drooped over fleshy lips. He was no taller than I,
but much thicker, with a paunch that drooped as did his
nose. All in all, he looked something like a camelbird.

"My newly acquired mare!" the dealer was raging, in
Farsi, still kicking the slave. "You indescribable wretch!"

"The mischievous horse was wandering, master," whined
the wretch, his arms raised protectively around his head.
"I had to follow—"

"The horse wandered *up*? And climbed into a *wagon*?
You lie to me as readily as you lie with innocent animals!
You execrable pervert!"

"But give me due credit, master," whimpered the pervert. "Your mare could have gone farther, and been lost.
Or I could have gone with her, and escaped."

"Bismillah, I wish you had! You are an insult to the noble institution of slavery!"

"Then sell me, master," sniveled the insult. "Foist me
onto some unsuspecting purchaser and get me out of your
sight."

"Estag farullah!" the dealer prayed toward Heaven at
the top of his voice. "Allah pardon me my sins, I thought I
had done just that. These gentlemen might have bought
you, abomination, but now they have seen you caught in
the act of raping my best mare!"

"Oh, I dispute that accusation, master," said the abomination, daring to speak with an air of righteous indignation. "I have known much better mares."

Speechless of words, the dealer clenched his fists and teeth and roared, "Arrrgh!"

Jamshid interrupted this singular colloquy, saying sternly, "Mirza Dealer, I assured the messieurs that you were a trustworthy seller of dependable merchandise."

"Before Allah, that I am, Wazir! I would not sell, I would not *give* them this walking pustule! I would not sell him to the harridan wife Awwa of the Devil Shaitan, I swear it, now that I know his true nature. I sincerely apologize to you, messieurs. And so will this creature apologize. You hear me? Apologize for that disgraceful exhibition. Abase yourself! Speak, Nostril!"

"Nostril?" we all exclaimed.

"It is my name, good masters," said the slave, unapologetically. "I have other names, but I am most often called Nostril, and for a reason."

He put a grimy finger to his blob of nose and pushed up the tip of it so we could see that instead of two nostrils he had only one large one. It would have been a sight repulsive enough, but was made more so by the profusion of snotty hair growing out of it.

"A minor punishment I once incurred for an even more minor misdemeanor. But be not prejudiced against me on that account, kind masters. As you can perceive, I am otherwise a distinguished figure of a man and I have countless virtues besides. I was by profession a seaman, before I fell into slavery, and I have traveled *everywhere*, from my native Sind to the farthermost shores of—"

"Gèsu Maria Isèpo," said Uncle Mafìo, marveling. "The man's tongue is as limber as his middle leg!"

We all stood fascinated and let Nostril babble on. "I would still be traveling, but for my misfortunate seizure by slavers. I was making love to a female shaqàl when the slave-raiders attacked, and you gentlemen doubtless know how a bitch's mihrab enclasps the loving zab and holds it trapped. So I could not run very fast, with the shaqàl bitch dangling from my front and bouncing and squawling. So I was caught, and my sea career ended and my slave career began. But I say in all modesty that I quickly became a nonpareil slave. You will have remarked that I am now speaking in Sabir, your trade language of the West—and now hearken, auspicious masters, I am speaking in Farsi, the trade language of the East. I am also fluent in my native Sindi, in Pashtun, in Hindi and Panjabi. I speak also a passable Arabic, and can get along in several of the Turki dialects and—"

"Do you never shut up in any of them?" asked my father.

Nostril went on, unheeding. "And I have many more qualities and talents of which I have not begun yet to speak. I am good with horses, as you must have noticed. I grew up with horses and—"

"You just said you were a seaman," my uncle pointed out.

"That was after I grew up, perspicacious master. I am also an expert with camels. I can cast and divine horoscopes in the Arab manner or the Persian or the Indian. I have refused offers from the most exclusive hammams to hire them my services as a rubber unsurpassed. I can dye gray beards with hinna, or remove wrinkles by applying quicksilver salve. With my single nostril I can play a flute more sweetly than any musician with his mouth. Also, employing that orifice in a certain other fashion—"

In unison, my father and uncle and the wazir severally exclaimed:

"Dio me varda!" and

"This man would disgust a maggot!" and

"Remove him, Mirza Dealer! He is a blot on Baghdad! Stake him out somewhere for the vultures!"

"I hear and obey, Wazir," said the dealer. "After I have shown you some other wares, perhaps?"

"It is late," said Jamshid, instead of what he might have said about the dealer and his wares. "We are expected back at the palace. Come, messieurs. There is always tomorrow."

"And tomorrow will be a cleaner day," said the dealer, glaring vengefully at the slave.

So we left the slave pen and the bazàr and wended our way through the streets and garden squares. We were nearly back at the palace before Uncle Mafìo thought to remark:

"You know? That despicable scoundrel Nostril never *did* apologize."

3

AGAIN we had our servants dress us in our best new raiment, and again we joined the Shah Zaman for the evening meal, and again it was a delicious repast, again excepting the Shiraz wine. I remember that the concluding course was a confection of sheriye, which are a sort of pasta ribbons like our fetucine, these cooked in cream with almonds and pistachios and tiny slivers of gold and silver foil so very thin and dainty that they were to be eaten along with the rest of the sweet.

While we dined, the Shah told us that his Royal First Daughter, the Shahzrad Magas, had asked his permission, and he had given it, to act as my companion and guide, to show me the sights of the city and its environs—with of course the additional company of a lady chaperon—as long as I should be in Baghdad. My father gave me a sidelong glance, but thanked the Shah for his and the Princess's kindness. My father further declared that, since I would obviously be in good hands, it would be unnecessary to buy a slave to look after me. So he would head southward the very next morning toward Hormuz, and Mafìo toward Basra.

I saw them off at dawn, each of them riding away in the company of a palace guard assigned by the Shah to be their servants and protectors on the journey. Then I went to the palace garden, where the Shahzrad Magas waited, again with her grandmother discreetly shadowing, to give me my first day of sightseeing under her tutelage. I made her a very formal greeting of salaam, and said nothing of what else she had hinted at giving me, and neither did she speak of it for a while.

"Dawn is a good time to see our palace masjid," she said, and escorted me to that temple of worship, where she bade me admire the exterior of it, which was admirable indeed. The immense dome was covered with a mosaic of blue and silver tiles and topped with a golden knob, all shining in the sunrise. The manaret spire was like an elaborate giant candlestick, richly chased and engraved and inlaid with glowing gemstones.

At that moment I formed a private surmise, and I would speak of it here.

216

I already knew that Muslim men are bidden to keep their women sequestered and useless and mute and veiled from all eyes—in pardah, as the Persians call that lifelong suppression of their females. I knew that, by decree of the Prophet Muhammad and the Quran he wrote, a woman is merely one of a man's chattels, like his sword or his goats or his wardrobe, and she differs only in being the one of his chattels with which he occasionally couples, and that with the sole purpose of siring children, and those valued only when they are male, like him. The majority of devout Muslims, men and women alike, must not speak of sexual relations between them, or even the relation of mutual companionship, though a man might be leeringly frank about his relations with other men.

But I decided, on that morning when I gazed at the palace masjid, that Islam's strictures against the normal expression of normal sexuality has not been able to stifle *all* expression of it. Look at any masjid and you will see each dome copied from the female human breast, its aroused nipple erect to the sky, and in each manaret a representation of the male organ, likewise joyously erect. I might be mistaken in discerning those similarities, but I do not think so. The Quran has decreed inequality between men and women. It has made indecent and unmentionable the natural relation between them, and distorted it most shamefully. But Islam's own temples bravely declare that the Prophet was wrong, and that Allah made man and woman to cleave to each other and to be of one flesh.

The Princess and I went inside the masjid's wonderfully high and broad central chamber, and it was beautifully decorated, though of course entirely with patterns, not pictures or statues. The walls were covered with mosaic designs made of blue lapis lazura alternating with white marble, so the chamber was a soft and restful pale-blue place.

Just as there are no images in Muslim temples, there also are no altars, no priests, no musicians or choristers, no apparatus of the ceremonial, like censers and fonts and candelabra. There are no masses or communions or other such rites, and a Muslim congregation observes only one ritual rule: in praying, they all prostrate themselves in the direction of the holy city Mecca, birthplace of their Prophet Muhammad. Since Mecca lies southwest of Baghdad, that masjid's farther wall was to the southwest, and in the center of it was a shallow niche, a little taller than a man, also tiled blue and white.

"That is the mihrab," said Princess Moth. "Though Islam has no priests, we are sometimes addressed by a visiting wise man. Perhaps an imam, one whose deep study of the Quran has made him an authority on its spiritual tenets. Or a mufti, who is similarly an expert on the temporal laws laid down by the Prophet (peace and blessing be upon him). Or a hajji, one who has made the long hajj pilgrimage to Holy Mecca. And to lead our devotions, the wise man takes position yonder in the mihrab."

I said, "I thought the word mihrab meant—" and then I stopped, and the Princess smiled naughtily at me.

I was about to say that I had thought the word mihrab meant a woman's most private part, what a Venetian girl had once vulgarly called her pota, and a Venetian lady had more fastidiously called her mona. But then I took notice of the shape of that mihrab niche in the masjid wall. It was shaped exactly like a woman's genital orifice, slightly oval in outline and narrowing at the top to close in a pointed arch. I have been inside many another masjid, and in every one that niche is so shaped. I believe it to be an additional corroboration of my theory that human sexuality has influenced Islamic architecture. Of course I do not know—and I doubt that any Muslim knows—which use of the word mihrab came first: the ecclesiastical or the bawdy.

"And there," said Princess Moth, pointing upward, "are the windows which make the sun tell the passing days."

Sure enough, there were openings carefully spaced about the upper periphery of the dome, and the new-risen sun was sending a beam across to the dome's opposite inner side, where there were inset slabs with Arabic writings entwined in their mosaics. The Princess read aloud the words where the beam rested. According to that evidence, the present day was, in the Muslim reckoning, the third day of the month Jumada Second in the 670th year of Muhammad's Hijra, or, in the Persian calendar, the 199th year of the Jalali Era. Then Princess Moth and I together, with much muttering and counting on our fingers, did the calculations necessary to convert the date to the Christian reckoning.

"Today is the twentieth of the month September!" I exclaimed. "It is my birthday!"

She congratulated me and said, "You Christians sometimes are given gifts on your birthdays, are you not, as we are?"

"Sometimes, yes."

"Then I will give you a gift this very night, if you are brave enough to run some risk in receiving it. I will give you a night of zina."

"What is zina?" I asked, though I suspected I knew.

"It is illicit intercourse between a man and a woman. It is haram, which means forbidden. If you are to receive the gift, I must sneak you into my chamber in the anderun of the palace women, which is also haram."

"I will brave any risk!" I cried wholeheartedly. Then I thought of something. "But . . . excuse me for asking, Princess Moth. But I have been informed that Muslim women are somehow deprived of—of their enthusiasm for zina. I have been told that they are, well, somehow circumcised, though I cannot imagine how."

"Oh, yes, tabzir," she said casually. "That is done to the general run of women, yes, when they are infants. But not to any infants of royal blood, or any who could in future become the wives or concubines of a royal court. It was certainly not done to me."

"I am happy for you," I said, and meant it. "But what *is* done to those unfortunate females? What *is* tabzir?"

"Let me show you," she said.

I was startled, expecting her to undress, right then and there, so I made a cautionary gesture at the lurking grandmother. But Moth only grinned at me and stepped to the preacher's niche in the masjid wall, saying, "Are you much acquainted with the anatomy of a female person? Then you know that here"—she pointed at the top of the arch—"toward the front of her mihrab opening, a woman has a tender buttonlike protrusion. It is called the zambur."

"Ah," I said, enlightened at last. "In Venice it is called the lumaghèta." I tried to sound as clinical as a physician, but I know I blushed as I spoke.

"The exact position of the zambur may vary slightly in different women," Moth went on, herself unblushingly clinical. "And the size of it may vary considerably. My own

zambur is commendably large, and in arousal it extends to
the length of my little finger's first joint."

Just the thought of it made *me* arouse and extend. Since
the grandmother was present, I was again grateful for my
voluminous nether garments.

The Princess blithely continued, "So I am much in demand by the other women of the anderun, because my
zambur can service them almost as well as a man's zab.
And women's play is halal, which means allowable, not
haram."

And if my face had been pink before, it must have been
maroon by now. But if Princess Moth noticed, it did not deter her.

"In every woman, that is her most sensitive place, the
very nub of her sexual excitability. Without the arousal of
her zambur, she is unresponsive in the sexual embrace.
And lacking any enjoyment of that act, she does not yearn
for it. That of course is the reason for the tabzir—the circumcision, as you called it. In a grown woman, until she is
very much aroused, the zambur is modestly hidden between the closed lips of her mihrab. But in an infant female, that zambur protrudes beyond the little baby lips.
An attending hakim can very easily snip it off with just a
scissors."

"Dear God!" I exclaimed, my own arousal going instantly limp from horror. "That is not circumcision. That
is the making of a female eunuch!"

"Very like it," she agreed, as if it were not horrible at
all. "The child grows up to be a woman virtuously cold and
devoid of sexual response, or even any desire for it. The
perfect Muslim wife."

"Perfect?! What husband would want such a wife?"

"A Muslim husband," she said simply. "That wife will
never commit adultery and make him a cuckold. She is incapable of contemplating an act of zina, or anything else
haram. She will not even tease her husband to anger by
flirting with another man. If she correctly keeps pardah,
she will never even *see* another man—until she gives birth
to a man-child. You understand, tabzir does not hamper
her function of maternity. She can become a mother, and
in that she is superior to a eunuch, who cannot become a
father."

"Even so, it is a ghastly fate for a woman."

"It is the fate decreed by the Prophet (may blessing and peace be upon him). Nevertheless, I am thankful that we upper classes are exempted from many such inconveniences visited upon the common folk. Now, about your birthday gift, young Mirza Marco . . ."

"I wish it was already night," I said, glancing up at the slow-creeping sunbeam. "This will be the longest birthday of my life, waiting for night and zina with you."

"Oh, not with *me!*"

"What?"

She giggled. "Well, not exactly with me."

Bewildered, I said again, "What?"

"You distracted me, Marco, asking about the tabzir, so I did not explain the gift I am giving you. Before I explain, you must bear in mind that I am a virgin."

I started pettishly to say, "You have not been talking like—" but she laid a finger across my lips.

"True, I am not tabzir and I am not cold and perhaps you would call me not entirely virtuous, since I am inviting you to do something haram. It is true, too, that I have a most charming zambur, and I dearly love to exercise it, but only in ways halal which will not diminish my virginity. In addition to my zambur, you see, I have *all* my parts, including my sangar. That maiden membrane has not been breached, and never will be until I wed some royal Prince. It must not be breached, or no Prince would have me. I should be lucky if I were not beheaded for letting myself be despoiled. No, Marco, do not even dream of consummating the zina with me."

"I am confused, Princess Moth. You distinctly said you would sneak me into your chamber. . . ."

"And so I shall. And I shall remain with you there to assist you in zina with my sister."

"With your *sister?!*"

"Hush! The old grandmother is deaf, but sometimes she can read simple words from the lips. Now keep silent and listen. My father has many wives, so I have many sisters. One of them is amenable to zina. In fact, she can never get enough of it. And it is she who will be your birthday gift."

"But if she is also a royal Princess, why is her virginity not equally—?"

"I said keep silent. Yes, she is as royal as I, but there is a reason why she does not treasure maidenhood as I do. You will know everything tonight. But until tonight I will say no more, and if you pester me with questions I will rescind the gift. Now, Marco, let us enjoy the day. Let me command a coachman to take us for a ride about the city."

The coach, when it came for us, was really only a dainty cart on two high wheels, drawn by a single midget Persian horse. Its driver helped me hoist the infirm old grandmother up to sit beside him at the front, and the Princess and I sat on the inside seat. As the cart rolled down the garden drive and out through the palace gates into Baghdad, Moth remarked that she had not yet had anything of breakfast to eat, opened a cloth bag, took from it some greenish-yellow fruits, and bit into one and offered another to me.

"Banyan," she called it. "A variety of fig."

I winced at the word fig, and politely declined, not bothering to mention my Acre misadventure that had made figs repulsive to me. Moth looked sulky when I refused, and I asked her why.

"Do you know," she said, leaning close and whispering so the coachman would not hear, "that this is the forbidden fruit with which Eve seduced Adam?"

I whispered back, "I prefer the seduction without the fruit. And speaking of which—"

"I told you not to speak of it. Not until tonight."

Several other times during the morning's ride, I tried to broach that subject, but every time she ignored me, speaking only to call my attention to this or that point of interest and to tell me informative things about it.

She said, "Here we are in the bazàr, which you have already visited, but perhaps you do not recognize it now, all empty and deserted and silent. That is because today is Jumè—Friday, as you call it—which Allah appointed to be the day of rest, and there is no doing of trade or business or labor."

And she said, "That grassy parkland which you see yonder is a graveyard, which we call a City of the Silent."

And she said, "That large building is the House of Delusion, a charitable institution founded by my father the Shah. In it are confined and cared for all the persons who go insane, as many persons do in the hot summertime. They are regularly examined by a hakim, and if they ever regain their reason, they are set free again."

In the outer skirts of the city, we crossed a bridge over a small stream, and I was struck by the color of that water, which was a most unusually deep blue for mere water. Then we crossed another stream, and it was a most unwaterly vivid green. But not until we had crossed yet another, and it was as red as blood, did I make any comment.

The Princess explained, "The waters of all the streams out here are colored by the dyes of the makers of qali. You have never seen a qali made? You must see." And she gave directions to the coachman.

I would have expected to be taken back into Baghdad, and to some city workshop, but the cart went farther still into the countryside, and came to a stop beside a hill that had a low cave entrance halfway up it. Moth and I got down from the cart, climbed the hill and ducked our heads to go into the hole.

We had to go crouching through a short, dark tunnel, but then we came out inside the hill, and into a vastly wide and high rock cavern, full of people, its floor cluttered with work tables and benches and dye vats. The cavern was dark until my eyes got accustomed to its half-light, cast by innumerable candles and lamps and torches. The lamps were set on the various pieces of furniture, the torches were ensconced at intervals around the rock walls, some of the candles were stuck to the rocks by their own drip, and other candles were carried about in the hands of the multitude of workers.

I said to the Princess, "I thought this was a day of rest."

"For Muslims," she said. "These are all slaves, Christian Russniaks and Lezghians and such. They are allowed their due sabbath on Sundays."

Only a few of the slaves were grown men and women, and they worked at various tasks, like the stirring of the dye vats, on the floor of the cavern. All the rest were children, and they worked while floating high in the air. That may sound like one of the Shahryar Zahd's stories of magic, but it was a fact. From the high dome of the cavern hung a giant comb of strings, hundreds of strings, parallel and close together, a vertical web as high and as wide as the entire cavern's height and width. It was obviously the weft for a qali which, when finished, would carpet some immense palace chamber or ballroom. High up against

that wall of weft, hung in loops of rope that depended from
somewhere even higher in the roof darkness, dangled a
crowd of children.

The little boys and girls were all naked—because of the
heat of the air up there, Princess Moth told me—and they
were suspended across the width of the work, but at various levels, some higher and some lower. Up there, the qali
was partially completed, from its hem at the top of the weft
down to those levels where the children worked, and I
could see that it was, even at that early stage of progress, a
qali of a most intricate and varicolored flower-garden design. Each of the dangling children had a candle stuck on
its head with the wax, and all were busily engaged, but at
what I could not discern; they seemed to be plucking with
their little fingers at the unfinished lower edge of the qali.

The Princess said, "They are weaving the warp threads
through the weft. Each slave holds a shuttle and a hank of
thread of a single color. He or she weaves it through and
makes it tight, in the order required by the design."

"How in the world," I asked, "can one child know when
and where to contribute his bit, among so many other
slaves and threads, and in such a complex work?"

"The qali master sings to them," she said. "Our arrival
interrupted him. There, he begins again."

It was a wonderful thing. The man called the qali master
sat before a table on which was spread a tremendous sheet
of paper. It was ruled in countless neat little squares, over
which was superimposed a drawing of the qali's entire intended design, with the innumerable different colors
indicated. The qali master read aloud from that design,
singing something on this order:

"One, red! . . . Thirteen, blue! . . . Forty-five, brown! . . ."

Except that what he chanted was far more complicated
than that. It had to be audible away up there near the cavern roof, and it had to be unmistakably understood by each
boy and girl it called upon, and it had to have a cadence
that kept them all working in rhythm. While the *words* addressed one slave child after another, out of the great
many of them, and told each one when to bring in his individual shuttle, the *singing* of the words either in a high
tone or a low tone told that slave how far across the weft to
warp his thread and when to knot it. In that marvelous
manner of working, the slaves would bring the qali, thread

by thread, line by line, all the way down to the cavern
floor, and when it was finished it would be as perfect in execution as if it had been painted by a single artist.

"Just that one qali can eventually cost many slaves,"
said the Princess, as we turned to leave the cavern. "The
weavers must be as young as possible, so they are light of
weight and have tiny, agile fingers. But it is not easy to
teach such demanding work to such young boys and girls.
Also, they frequently swoon from the heat up yonder, and
fall and break and die. Or, if they live long enough, they
are almost sure to go blind from the close work and poor
light. And for every one lost, another slave child must be
already trained and standing by."

"I can understand," I said, "why even the smallest qali
is so valuable."

"But just imagine what one would cost," she said, as we
emerged again into the sunlight, "if we had to employ real
people."

4

THE cart took us back to the city, and through it, and
again into the palace gardens. Once or twice more I tried to
pry from the Princess some hint of what would happen in
the nighttime, but she remained adamant against my curiosity. Not until we got down from the cart, and she and her
grandmother were leaving me to go to their anderun quarters, did she refer to our rendezvous.

"At moonrise," she said. "By the gulsa'at again."

I had a minor ordeal to go through before then. When I
got to my room, the servant Karim informed me that I was
to be accorded the honor of dining that evening with the
Shah Zaman and his Shahryar Zahd. It was no doubt a signal kindness on their part, considering my youth and my
insignificance in the absence of my ambassadorial father
and uncle. But I confess that I did not much esteem the
honor, and I sat wishing that the meal would hasten to its
conclusion. For one reason, I felt slightly uncomfortable in
the presence of the parents of the girl who had invited me
to zina later that night. (Of the other girl, who would some-

how share in the zina, I knew the Shah had to be the father, but I could not guess who might be her mother.) Also,
I was literally salivating at the prospect of that which was
to occur, even though I did not know exactly what *was* to
occur. With my tongue glands thus uncontrollably gushing, I could hardly eat of the fine meal, let alone make
sustained conversation. Fortunately, the Shahryar's lo-
quacity precluded my having to say more than an
occasional "Yes, Your Majesty" and "Is that a fact?" and
"Do tell." For she did tell; nothing could have stopped her
telling; but she told not many facts, I think.

"So," she said, "today you visited the makers of qali."

"Yes, Your Majesty."

"You know, in olden times there were magic qali which
were capable of carrying a man through the air."

"Is that a fact?"

"Yes, a man could step onto a qali and command it to
take him to some far, far distant part of the world. And off
it would fly, over mountains and seas and deserts, whisking him there in the twinkling of an eyelid."

"Do tell."

"Yes, I will tell you the story of a Prince. His Princess
lover was abducted by the giant rukh bird, and he was
desolate. So he procured from a jinni one of the magic
qali and . . ."

And finally the story was over, and finally so was the
meal, and finally so was my impatient waiting, and like
the story Prince, I hurried to my Princess lover. She was at
the flower dial, and for the first time she was unaccompanied by her crone chaperon. She took my hand and led me
along the garden paths and around the palace to a wing of
it I had not known existed. Its doors were guarded like all
the other palace entrances, but Princess Moth and I
merely had to wait in the concealment of a flower shrub
until both the guards turned their heads. They did so in
unison, and almost as if they were doing it on command,
and I wondered if Moth had bribed them. She and I flitted
inside unseen, or at least unchallenged, and she led me
along several corridors oddly empty of guards, and around
corners, and finally through an unguarded door.

We were in her chambers, a place hung with many
splendid qali and with filmy, transparent curtains and
draperies in the many colors of sharbats, looped and

swathed and swagged in a delicious confusion, but all carefully kept clear of the lamps burning among them. The
room was carpeted almost from wall to wall with sharbat-
colored cushions, so many that I could not tell which were
daiwan and which composed the Princess's bed.

"Welcome to my chambers, Mirza Marco," she said.
"And to this."

And somehow she undid what must have been a single
knot or clasp sustaining all her clothes, for they all
dropped away from her at once. She stood before me in the
warm lamplight, garbed only in her beauty and her provocative smile and her seeming surrender and one ornament, one only, a spray of three brilliant red cherries in
the elaborately arranged black hair of her head.

Against the pale sharbat colors of the room, the Princess
stood out vividly red and black and green and white: the
cherries red upon her black tresses, her eyes green and
their long lashes black and her lips red in her ivory face,
her nipples red and her nether curls black against the
ivory body. She smiled more broadly as she watched my
gaze wander down her naked body and up again, to rest on
the three living ornaments in her hair, and she murmured:

"As bright as rubies, are they not? But more precious
than rubies, for the cherries will wither. Or will they
instead"—she asked it seductively, running the red tip of
her tongue across her red upper lip—"will they be eaten?"
She was laughed then.

I was panting as if I had run all the way across Baghdad
to that enchanted chamber. Clumsily I moved toward her,
and she let me approach to her arm's length, for that was
where her hand stopped me, reaching out to touch my foremost approaching part.

"Good," she said, approving what she had touched.
"Quite ready and eager for zina. Take off your clothes,
Marco, while I attend to the lamps."

I obediently disrobed, though keeping my fascinated
eyes on her the while. She moved gracefully about the
room, snuffing one wick after another. When for a moment
Moth stood before one of the lamps, though she stood with
her legs neatly together, I could see a tiny triangle of lamplight shine like a beckoning beacon between her upper
thighs and her artichoke mount, and I remembered what a
Venetian boy had said long ago: that such was the mark of

"a woman of the most utterly desirable bedworthiness."
When all the lamps were extinguished, she came back
through the darkness to me.

"I wish you had left the lamps alight," I said. "You are
beautiful, Moth, and I delight in looking at you."

"Ah, but lamp flames are fatal to moths," she said, and
laughed. "There is enough moonlight coming through the
window for you to see me, and see nothing else, Now—"

"Now!" I echoed in total and joyful accord, and I lunged,
but she dodged adroitly.

"Wait, Marco! You forget, I am not your birthday gift."

"Yes," I mumbled. "I was forgetting. Your sister. I remember now. But why are you stripped naked, Moth, if it
is she who—?"

"I said I would explain tonight. And I will, if you will restrain your groping. Hear me now. This sister of mine,
being also a royal Princess, did not have to endure the mutilation of tabzir when she was a baby, because it was expected that she would someday marry royalty. Therefore,
she is a complete female, unimpaired in her organs, with
all of a female's needs and desires and capabilities. Unfortunately, the dear girl grew up to be ugly. Dreadfully ugly,
I cannot tell you how ugly."

I said wonderingly, "I have seen no one like that about
the palace."

"Of course not. She would not wish to be seen. She is excruciatingly ugly, but tender of heart. So she keeps forever
to her chambers here in the anderun, not to chance meeting even a child or a eunuch and frightening the wits out of
such a one."

"Mare mia," I muttered. "Just *how* is she ugly, Moth?
Only in the face? Or is she deformed? Hunchbacked?
What?"

"Hush! She waits just outside the door, and she might
hear."

I lowered my voice. "What is this thing's—what is this
girl's name?"

"The Princess Shams, and that is also a pity, for the
word means Sunlight. However, let us not dwell on her devastating ugliness. Suffice it to say that this poor sister
long ago gave up hope of making any sort of marriage, or
even of attracting a transient lover. No man could look at

her in the light, or feel her in the dark, and still keep his lance atilt for zina."

"Che braga!" I muttered, feeling a frisson of chill. If Moth had not been still visible to me, only dimly but alluringly, my own lance might have drooped then.

"Nevertheless, I assure you that her feminine parts are quite normal. And they quite normally wish to be filled and fulfilled. That is why she and I contrived a plan. And, because I love my sister Shams, I conspire with her in that plan. Whenever she espies from her hiding place a man who wakens her yearning, I invite him here and—"

"You have done this before!" I bleated in dismay.

"Imbecile infidel, of course we have! Many and many a time. That is why I can promise you will enjoy it. Because so many other men have."

"You said it was a birthday gift—"

"Do you disdain a gift because it comes from a generous giver of gifts? Be still and listen. What we do is this. You lie down, on your back. I lie across your waist, staying always in your view. While you and I fondle and frolic—and we will do everything but the ultimate thing—my sister creeps quietly in and contents herself with your lower half. You never see Shams or touch her, except with your zab, and it encounters nothing repugnant. Meanwhile, you see and feel only me. And you and I will excite each other to a delirium, so that when the zina is accomplished down there, you will never know it is *not* me you are having it with."

"This is grotesque."

"You may of course decline the gift," she said coldly. But she moved close, so that her breast touched me, and it was anything but cold. "Or you can give me and yourself a delight, and at the same time do a good deed for a poor creature doomed always to darkness and nonentity. Well . . . do you decline it?" Her hand reached for the answer. "Ah, I thought you would not. I knew you for a kindly man. Very well, Marco, let us lie down."

We did so. I lay on my back, as instructed, and Moth draped her upper body across my waist, so I could not see below it, and we commenced the preludes of music-making. She lightly stroked her fingertips over my face and through my hair and over my chest, and I did the same to her, and every time we touched, everywhere we touched, we felt the sort of tingling shock one can feel by briskly rubbing a cat's fur the wrong way. But there *was* no wrong way she could have fondled me—or I her, as I discovered. Her nipples got perkily swollen under my touch, and even in the dim light I could see the dilation of her eyes, and I could taste that her lips were engorged with passion.

"Why do you call it music-making?" she softly asked at one point. "It is far nicer than music."

"Well, yes," I said, after thinking about it. "I had forgotten the kind of music you have here in Persia. . . ."

Now and then, she would extend a hand behind her, to stroke the part of me she was shielding from my sight, and each time that gave me a deliciously urgent start, and each time she withdrew her hand just in time, or I should have made spruzzo into the air. She let me reach a hand down to her own parts, only whispering in a quaver, "Careful with the fingers. Only the zambur. Not inside, remember." And that fondling made her several times come to paroxysm.

And later she was straddling my chest, her body upright, her nether curls soft against my face, so that her mihrab was within reach of my tongue, and she whispered, "A tongue cannot break the sangar membrane. You may do with your tongue all you can do." Though the Princess wore no perfume, that part of her was coolly fragrant, like fresh fern or lettuce. And she had not exaggerated in speaking of her zambur; it was like having the tip of another tongue meet mine there, and lick and flick and probe in response to mine. And that sent Moth into a constant paroxysm, only waxing and waning slightly in intensity, like the wordless singing she did in accompaniment.

Delirium, Moth had said, and delirium it became. I truly believed, when I made spruzzo the first time, that I was somehow doing it inside her mihrab, even though the mihrab was still close and warm and wet against my mouth. Not until my wits began to collect again did I realize that another female person had to be astride my lower body, and it had to be the seclusive sister Shams. I could not see her, and I did not try to or want to, but from her light weight upon me I could deduce that the other Princess must be small and fragile. I turned my mouth from Moth's avidly thrusting mount to ask, "Is your sister much younger than you are?"

As if coming reluctantly back from far distances, she paused in her ecstasy just long enough to say, in a breathless small voice, "Not . . . very much . . ."

And then she dissolved into her distances again, and I resumed doing my best to send her ever farther and higher, and I repeatedly joined her in that soaring exultation, and I made my subsequent several spruzzi into the alien mihrab, not really caring whose it was, but retaining enough consciousness to hope vaguely that the younger and ugly Princess Sunlight was enjoying her employment of me as much as I was enjoying it.

The tripartite zina went on for a long time. After all, the Princess Moth and I were in the springtime of our youth, and we could keep on exciting each other to renewed flowerings, and the Princess Shams gleefully (I assumed) gathered in my every bouquet. But at last even the seemingly insatiable Moth seemed sated, and her tremors dwindled, and so did my zab finally dwindle and sink to weary rest. That member felt quite raw and chafed by then, and my tongue ached at its roots, and my whole body felt empty and expended. Moth and I lay still for a while of recuperation, she limp upon my chest, with her hair disposed across my face. The three ornamenting cherries had long before been shaken loose and lost. While we lay there, I was conscious of a smeary wet kiss being bestowed upon my belly skin, and then there was a brief rustling sound as Shams scuttled unseen out of the room.

I got up and dressed, and Princess Moth slipped into a scanty little tunic that did nothing really to cover her nakedness, and she led me again through the anderun corridors and out into the gardens. From a manaret somewhere, the day's first muedhdhin was warbling the call to the hour-before-sunrise prayer. Still unchallenged by any guards, I found my own way through the gardens to the palace wing where my chamber was. The servant Karim was conscientiously waiting awake for me. He helped me undress for bed, and he made some awed exclamations when he saw my extremely spent condition.

"So the young Mirza's lance found its target," he said, but he did not ask any audacious questions. He only sniffled a bit, seeming aggrieved that I would not be having further need for his small ministrations, and he went to his own bed.

My father and uncle were absent from Baghdad for three weeks or more. During that time, I spent almost every day being escorted about and shown interesting things by the Shahzrad Magas, with her grandmother trailing, and almost every night I spent indulging in zina with both of the royal sisters, Moth and Sunlight.

In the daytime, the Princess and I did such things as going to the House of Delusion, that building which combined a hospital and a prison. We went there on a Friday, the day of rest when the place was much frequented by citizens at leisure, and also by foreign visitors from elsewhere, as one of the chief amusements of Baghdad. People came in families and in groups shepherded by guides, and at the door everyone was given by the doorkeeper a large smock to cover his clothes. Then all would stroll through the building, being lectured by the guides on the several kinds of madness exhibited by the men and women inmates, all of us laughing at their antics or commenting on them. Some of those antics were truly risible, and some were pitiable, and others were entertainingly lewd, but other doings were merely dirty. For example, a number of the deranged men and women appeared to resent us visitors, and pelted us with anything that came to their hand. Since all those inmates were sensibly kept naked and empty-handed, their only available missiles were their own body wastes. That was the reason for the doorman's distribution of smocks, and we were glad to be wearing them.

Sometimes in the nights in the Princess's chamber, I felt like some kind of inmate myself, subjected to supervision and exhortation. On perhaps the third or fourth of those occasions, early in the night's proceedings, before the sister crept in, when Moth and I had just disrobed and were enjoying our preliminary play, she stopped her roving hands to hold my roving own, and said:

"My sister Shams would beg a favor of you, Marco."

"I was afraid of this," I said. "She wishes to dispense with you as intermediary, and take your place up front."

"No, no. She would never. She and I are both happy with the arrangement as it is. Except for one small detail."

I only grunted, being wary.

"I told you, Marco, that Sunlight has had zina often and often. So often and so vigorously that, well, the poor girl's mihrab opening has been quite enlarged by that indul-

gence. To speak frankly, she is as open down there as a
woman who has borne many children. Her pleasure in our
zina would be much increased if your zab were in a sense
enlarged by—"

"No!" I said firmly, and began to wriggle, trying to move
crabwise out from under Moth. "I will not submit to any
tampering—"

"Wait!" she protested. "Hold still. I suggest no such
thing."

"I do not know what you have in mind, or why," I said,
still wriggling. "I have seen the zab of numerous Eastern
men, and my own is already superior. I refuse any—"

"I said be still! You have an admirable zab, Marco. It
quite fills my hand. And I am sure that in length and girth
it satisfies Shams. She suggests only a refinement of performance."

Now that was vexatious. "No other woman ever complained of my performance!" I shouted. "If this one is as
ugly as you say she is, I suggest that she is hardly in a position to be critical of whatever she can get!"

"Hark to who is being critical!" Moth mocked me. "Have
you any notion how many men dream, and dream fruit-
lessly, of ever lying with a royal Princess? Ever even once
seeing a Princess with her *face* unveiled? And here you
have *two* of them lying with you absolutely naked and
compliant each night! You would presume to deny one of
them a small whim?"

"Well. . . .," I said, chastened. "What is the whim?"

"There is a way to heighten the pleasure of a woman
who has a large orifice. It enhances not the zab itself, but
the—what do you call the blunt head of it?"

"In Venetian it is the fava, the broad bean. I think in
Farsi that is the lubya."

"Very well. Now, I noticed of course that you are uncircumcised, and that is good, for this refinement cannot be
accomplished with a circumcised zab. All you do is this."
And she did it, tightening her hand around my zab and
pulling the capèla skin back as far as it would go, and then
a trifle farther. "See? It makes the broad bean bulge more
grandly broad."

"And it is uncomfortable, almost to hurting."

"Only briefly, Marco, and bearably. Just do that as you
first insert it. Shams says it gives to her mihrab lips that

fine first feeling of being spread apart. Sort of a welcome
violation, she says. Women enjoy that, I think, though of
course I cannot know until I am married."

"Dio me varda," I muttered.

"And of course *you* do not have to do it, and risk touching
Sunlight's ugly body. She will do that little stretching and
broadening for you, with her own hand. She merely wished
your permission."

"Would Shams wish anything further?" I asked acidly.
"For a monster, she seems uncommonly finicking."

"Hark at you!" Moth mocked me again. "Here you are,
in company that any other man would envy you. Being
taught by royalty a trick of sex that most men never learn.
You will be grateful, Marco, someday when you desire to
give pleasure to a woman of large or slack mihrab, you will
be grateful that you learned how. And so will she be grateful. Now, before Sunlight arrives, make *me* grateful a time
or two, in other ways. . . ."

5

ON some days, for entertainment and edification, Moth
and I attended the sittings of the royal court of justice. It
was called simply the Daiwan, from its profusion of daiwan pillows on which sat the Shah Zaman and the Wazir
Jamshid and various elderly muftis of Muslim law, and
sometimes some visiting Mongol emissaries of the Ilkhan
Abagha. Before them were brought criminals to be tried,
and citizens with complaints to be heard or boons to be
asked, and the Shah and his wazir and the other officials
would listen to the charges or pleas or supplications, and
then would confer, and then would render their judgments
or devisements or sentences.

I found the Daiwan instructive, as a mere onlooker. But
had I been a criminal, I would have dreaded being hauled
there. And had I been a citizen with a grievance, it would
have had to be a towering grievance before I should have
dared to take it to the Daiwan. For on the open terrace just
outside that room stood a tremendous burning brazier, and
on it was a giant cauldron of oil heated to bubbling, and be-

side it waited a number of robust palace guards and the
Shah's official executioner, ready to put it to use. Princess Moth confided to me that its use was sanctioned, not
only for convicted evildoers, but also for those citizens
who brought false charges or spiteful complaints or gave
untruthful testimony. The vat guards looked fearsome
enough, but the executioner was a figure calculated to inspire terror. He was hooded and masked and garbed all in
a red as red as Hell fire.

I saw only one malefactor actually sentenced to the vat. I
would have judged him less harshly, but then I am not a
Muslim. He was a wealthy Persian merchant whose household anderun consisted of the allowable four wives and the
usual numerous concubines besides. The offense with
which he was charged was read aloud: "Khalwat." That
means only "compromising proximity," but the details of
the indictment were more enlightening. The merchant
was accused of having made zina with two of his concubines at the same time, while his four wives and a third
concubine were let to watch, and all together those circumstances were haram under Muslim law.

Listening to the charges, I felt distinctly sympathetic to
the defendant, but distinctly uneasy in my own person,
since I was almost every night making zina with two
women not my wives. But I stole a look at my companion
Princess Moth, and saw in her face neither guilt nor apprehension. I gradually learned from the proceedings that
even the most vilely haram offense is not punishable by
Muslim law unless at least four eyewitnesses testify to its
having been committed. The merchant had willingly, or
pridefully, or stupidly, let five women observe his prowess
and later, out of pique or jealousy or some other feminine
reason, they had brought the khalwat complaint against
him. So the five women also got to observe his being taken,
kicking and screaming, out to the terrace and pitched alive
into the seething oil. I will not dwell on the subsequent few
minutes.

Not all the punishments decreed by the Daiwan were so
extraordinary. Some were nicely devised to fit the crimes
involved. One day a baker was hauled before the court and
convicted of having given his customers short weight of
bread, and he was sentenced to be crammed into his own
oven and baked to death. Another time, a man was

brought in for the singular offense of having stepped on a
scrap of paper as he walked along the street. His accuser
was a boy who, walking behind the man, had picked up
that paper and discovered that the name of Allah was
among the words written on it. The defendant pleaded that
he had only unwittingly committed that insult to almighty
Allah, but other witnesses testified that he was an incorri-
gible blasphemer. They said he had often been seen to lay
other books atop his copy of the Quran, and had sometimes
even held the Holy Book below his waist level, and once
had held it *with his left hand.* So he was sentenced to be
trodden, like the piece of paper, by the executioner and the
guards until he was dead.

But only during the Daiwan sittings was the Shah's palace a place df pious dread. On more frequent religious occasions, the palace was the scene of galas and gaiety. The
Persians recognize some seven thousand old-time prophets
of Islam, and accord to every one of them a day of celebration. On the dates honoring the more major prophets, the
Shah would give parties, usually inviting all the royalty
and nobility of Baghdad, but sometimes throwing open the
palace grounds to all comers.

Though I was not royal or noble, and not Muslim, I was a
palace resident, and I attended several of those feste. I recall one night's holiday celebration of some long-defunct
prophet, which celebration was held outdoors in the palace
gardens. Every guest was given not the usual pile of
daiwan cushions to sit or recline upon, but an individual,
high-heaped mound of fresh and fragrant rose petals.
Every branch of every tree was outlined in candles affixed
to the bark, and that candlelight shone through the leaves
in every shade and hue of green. Every flower bed was full
of candelabra, and their candles' light shone through the
multitudes of different blossoms in every shade and hue of
every color. All those candles were sufficient to make the
garden almost as bright and colorful as it was in daytime.
But, in addition, the Shah's servants had beforehand collected every little tortoise and turtle to be bought in the
bazàr or caught by children in the countryside, and had affixed a candle to the carapace of each one, and had let all
those thousands of creatures loose to crawl about the gardens as moving points of illumination.

As always, there was more and richer food and drink

provided than I had ever seen laid out at any Western
festa. Among the entertainments there were players of
musical instruments, many of which I had never seen or
heard before, and to their music dancers danced and singers sang. The male dancers re-created, with lances and sabers and much foot stamping, famous battles of famous
Persian warriors of the past, like Rustam and Sohrab. The
female dancers scarcely moved their feet at all, but convulsed their breasts and bellies in a manner to make a
watcher's eyeballs spin. The singers sang no song of a religious nature—Islam frowns on that—but quite the other
sort: I mean exceedingly bawdy songs. There were also
bear trainers with agile and acrobatic bears, and snake
charmers making the hooded snakes called najhaya to
dance in their baskets, and fardarbab telling the tomorrows in their trays of sand, and shaukhran clowns comically garbed and capering and reciting or acting out lewd
jests.

When I had got quite addled on the date liquor araq, I
dismissed my Christian scruples against divination, and
applied to one of the fardarbab, an old Arab or Jew with a
funguslike beard, and asked what he could see in my future. But he must have recognized me for a good Christian
unbeliever in his sorcerous art, for he only looked once into
the shaken sand and growled, "Beware the bloodthirstiness of the beautiful," which told me nothing of my future
at all, though I recalled having heard something like that
before, in the past. So I laughed jeeringly at the old fraud,
and stood up and twirled and pirouetted away from him,
and fell down, and Karim came and supported me to my
bedchamber.

That was one of the nights on which the Princess Moth
and Sunlight and I did not convene. On another occasion,
Moth told me to find something else to do with my next few
nights, because she was enduring her moon curse.

"Moon curse?" I echoed.

She said impatiently, "The female bleeding."

"And what is that?" I asked, truly never having heard of
it before then.

Her green eyes gave me a sidelong look of amused exasperation, and she said fondly, "Fool. Like all young men,
you perceive a beautiful woman as a pure and perfect
thing—like the race of little winged beings called the peri.

The delicate peri do not even eat, but live on the fragrance
they inhale from flowers, and therefore they never have to
urinate or defecate. Just so, you think a beautiful woman
can have none of the imperfections or nastinesses common
to the rest of humankind."

I shrugged. "Is it bad to think that way?"

"Oh, I would not say that, for we beautiful women often
take advantage of that masculine delusion. But a delusion
it is, Marco, and I will now betray my sex and disabuse you
of it. Hear me."

She explained what happens to a girl child at about the
age of ten, which turns her into a woman, and goes on happening to her thereafter, once in every moon of the year.

"Really?" I said. "I never knew. All women?"

"Yes, and they must bear that moon curse until they get
old and dry up in every respect. The curse is also accompanied by cramps and backaches and ill temper. A woman is
morose and hateful during that time, and a wise woman
keeps herself away from other people, or drugged to stupefaction with teryak or banj, until the curse passes."

"It sounds frightful."

Moth laughed, but without humor. "Far more frightful
for the woman if there comes a moon when she is not
cursed. For that means she is pregnant. And of the damps
and leaks and disgusts and embarrassments which then
ensue, I will not even begin to speak. I am feeling morose
and ill-tempered and hateful, and I will betake myself to
seclusion. You go away, Marco, and make merry and enjoy
your body's freedom, like all damned disencumbered men,
and leave me to my woman's misery."

Despite the Princess Moth's depiction of the weaknesses
of her sex, I could not then, or ever since then, think of a
beautiful woman as being inherently flawed or faulty—or
at least not until she proved herself to be so, as the Lady
Ilaria once had done, and thereby had lost all my esteem.
Out here in the East, I was still learning new ways to appreciate beautiful women, and still making new discoveries about them, and I was disinclined to disparage them.

To illustrate: when I was younger, I had believed that
the physical beauty of a woman resided only in such easily
observable features as her face and breasts and legs and
buttocks, and in less easily observable ones like a pretty
and inviting (and accessible) artichoke mound and medal-

lion and mihrab. But by this time, I had had enough
women to realize that there were more subtle points of
physical beauty. To mention just one: I am particularly
fond of the delicate sinews that extend from a woman's
groin along the inner sides of her thighs when she opens
them apart. I also had come to realize that, even in the features common to all beautiful women, there are differences which are discernible, and exciting for being so.
Every beautiful woman has beautiful breasts and nipples,
but there are innumerable variations in size and shape
and proportions and coloration, all beautiful. Every beautiful woman has a beautiful mihrab, but oh, how delectably different each is from another: in its placement
forward or underneath, in its tint and downiness of the
outer lips, in its purse-likeness and purge-tightness of closure, in its zambur's position and size and erectabil-
ity. . . .

Perhaps I make myself sound more lecherous than gallant. But I only wish to emphasize that I never could and
never did and never will disprize the beautiful women of
this world—not even then, in Baghdad, when the Princess
Moth, although herself one of them, did her best to show
me their worst. For instance, one day she arranged for me
to sneak into the palace anderun, not for our nighttime
frolic, but in the afternoon, because I had said to her:

"Moth, do you remember that merchant whom we saw
executed for his haram method of making zina? Is that the
sort of thing that usually goes on in an anderun?"

She gave me one of her green looks and said, "Come and
see for yourself."

On that occasion, indubitably, she had to have bribed
the guards and eunuchs to look the other way, for she did
not merely get me unseen into that wing of the palace, but
also put me into a corridor wall's closet which had two
peepholes drilled to look into either of two large and voluptuously furnished chambers. I peeped through one hole
and then the other; both rooms were empty at the moment.

Moth said, "Those are communal rooms, where the
women can congregate when they weary of being alone in
their separate quarters. And this closet is one of the many
watch places throughout the anderun where a eunuch
takes station at intervals. He watches for quarrels or
fights among the women, or other sorts of misbehavior,

and reports them to my mother, the Royal First Wife, who
is responsible for order being kept. The eunuch will not be
in here today, and I will now go and let the women know
that. Then we shall watch together and see what advantage they may take of the warder's absence."

She went away and then returned, and we stood back to
back in the close space, each with an eye to one of the
holes. For a long time nothing happened. Then four women
came into the room I was watching, and disposed themselves here and there on the daiwan cushions. They were
all about the age of the Shahryar Zahd, and about equally
as handsome. One woman was apparently a native Persian, for she had ivory skin and night-black hair, but eyes
as blue as lapis lazura. Another I took to be an Armeniyan,
for each of her breasts was exactly the size of her head. Another was a black woman, Ethiope or Nubian, and she of
course had paddle feet and spindly calves and a behind like
a balcony, but she was otherwise fairly comely: pretty face
with not too-everted lips, shapely bosom and fine long
hands. And the fourth woman was so dusky of skin and
dark of eyes that she must have been an Arab.

But the women's believing themselves to be not under
scrutiny, and free to do what they liked, did not provoke
any libertine throwing off of restraint or modesty. Except
that none wore the chador, they were all fully clothed, and
remained so, and they were not joined by any sneaked-in
lovers. The black woman and the Arab had brought with
them some kind of hand-held needlework, and occupied
themselves with that lethargic pastime. The Persian sat
with pots and brushes and little implements, and painstakingly manicured the finger and toe nails of the Armeniyan, and when that was done, both the women began
coloring the palms of their hands and soles of their feet
with hinna dye.

I was very soon bored to apathy, and so were the four
women—I could see them yawn and hear them belch and
smell them breaking wind—and I wondered why I had entertained any spicy suspicions of Babylonian orgies in a
house full of women, just because all the women belonged
to one man. Clearly, when so many women had nothing to
do but wait for a summons from their master, there literally *was* nothing else for them to do. They could only loll
about, no more enterprising or vivacious than vegetables,

until the infrequent calls for the exercise of their animal parts. I might as well have been watching a row of cabbages going to seed, and I turned in the closet to say something like that to the Princess.

But she was grinning lasciviously, and she put a cautionary finger to her lips, then pointed it at her peephole. I leaned over and looked through, and barely suppressed an exclamation of surprise. That room had two occupants, one of them female, a girl considerably younger than any of my room's four—and also much prettier, perhaps because more of her was visible. She had taken off her pai-jamah and anything else she wore under that garment, and was bare from the waist down. She was another dusky-skinned Arab, but her pretty face was now pink with exertion. The male occupant of the room was one of those child-sized simiazze apes, so hairy all over that I would not have known it for a male, except that the girl was fervently working with one hand to encourage the animal's maleness. She eventually accomplished that, but the ape only looked stupidly at the upright small evidence, and the girl had to work just as strenuously to show him what to do with it, and where. But eventually that too was accomplished, while Moth and I took turns observing through the peephole.

When the ridiculous performance was concluded, the Arab girl wiped herself with a cloth, and then wiped at some scratches her partner had inflicted on her. Then she pulled on her pai-jamah and led the ape shuffling and hopping out of the room. Moth and I struggled from our closet, which had got quite warm and humid, out into the corridor where we could talk unheard by the four women still in the other room.

I said, "No wonder the wazir told me that animal is called the unspeakably unclean."

"Oh, Jamshid is just envious," the Princess said lightly. "It can do what he cannot."

"But not very well. Its zab was·even smaller than an Arab's. Anyway, I should think a decent woman would rather employ the finger of a eunuch than the zab of an ape."

"Indeed, some do. And also you know now why my zambur is so much in demand. There are many women here who must wait a long and hungry time between summonses from the Shah. That is why the Prophet (peace and blessing be upon him) long ago instituted the tabzir. So that decent women should not be urged by their yearnings to unwifely resorts."

"I think, if I were Shah, I should much prefer my women's resorting to each other's zambur than to a random zab. Why, suppose that Arab girl gets pregnant by that ape! What revolting kind of offspring would she have?" The awful thought brought an even more awful one to my mind. "Per Cristo, suppose your gruesome sister Shams gets pregnant by me! Would I have to marry her?"

"Be not alarmed, Marco. Every woman here, of whatever nation, has her own native specific against such an occurrence."

I stared. "They know how to prevent conception?"

"With varying degrees of success, but all better than relying on chance. An Arab woman, for example, before making zina, pushes inside herself a plug of wool soaked in the juice of weeping willow. A Persian woman lines her inner self with the delicate white membrane from under the rind of a pomegranate."

"How abominably sinful," I said, as a Christian should. "Which works better?"

"Surely the Persian way is preferable, if only because it is more comfortable for both partners. Shams uses it, and I will wager that you never have felt it."

"No."

"But imagine ramming your tender lubya against that thick woolen plug inside an Arab woman. Anyway, I should distrust the efficacy of that method. What would an Arab woman know about preventing conception? Unless an Arab man *wants* to make a baby, he never does zina with his woman except through her rear entrance, as he is accustomed to using other men and boys, and they him."

I was relieved to learn that the Princess Shams was not going to be fruitful and multiply her ugliness, thanks to her pomegranate preventive, though by rights I should have been disquieted, because I was thereby participating in one of the most abhorrent and mortal sins a Christian can commit. At some time in my travels, or when I returned home to Venice, I should again be in the vicinity of a Christian priest, and I should be obliged to make confession. Of course the priest would belabor me with penances

for my having fornicated with two unmarried women at
one time, but that was only a venial sin in comparison to
the other. I could well foresee his horror when I confessed
that, through the wicked arts of the East, I had been enabled to copulate for the sheer enjoyment of the act, with
no Christian intention or expectation of progeny resulting
from it.

Needless to say, I went on sinfully enjoying it. If there
was any slight thing that hampered my total and complete
enjoyment, it was not any nagging sense of guilt. It was
my natural wish that each of my zina consummations
could take place inside the Princess Moth to whom I was
making love, and not in the unloved, unlovely Princess
Shams. However, when Moth sternly repulsed my few tentative hints in that regard, I had the good sense to stop
making them. I would not risk losing a happy situation out
of greed for an unattainable happier one. What I did instead, I invented for myself a story, of a kind that might
have been told by the story-telling Shahryar Zahd.

In my mind's story, I made Sunlight not what she was,
the ugliest female person in Persia, but *the most gloriously
beautiful.* I made her *so beautiful* that Allah in His wisdom
decreed: "It is unthinkable that the divine beauty and the
blessed love of the Princess Shams should be limited to the
enjoyment of any one man alone." And *that* was why
Shams was not married, and never would be. In obedience
to almighty Allah, she was constrained to dispense her
favors to all good and deserving suitors, and that was why
I was currently the favored one. For a while, I utilized that
story only when necessary. During most of each night's
zina, I had no need of anything more than the real loveliness and closeness of the Princess Moth to stir and sustain
my ardor. But then, when our mutual play had made the
delicious pressure mount inside me until it could no longer
be contained, and I had to let it go, then I brought to mind
my invented, alternate, imaginary, unreally sublime Princess Sunlight, and made her the receptacle of my surge
and my love.

As I say, that sufficed me for a while. But after that
while, I gradually fell prey to a sort of mild lunacy; I began
to wonder if my story might not be something near *the
truth.* Getting increasingly demented, I began to suspect a
deep secret here, and to suspect that, by the workings of

my subtle mind, I had been the first and only to uncover
that secret. Eventually, I had got so deranged that I began
making new hints to Moth: hinting that I really would like
to see her unseeable sister. Moth looked worried and agitated when I did that, and even more so when I daringly
began mentioning her sister's name on occasions when we
were in the presence of her parents and grandmother.

"I have had the honor of meeting most of your royal family, Your Majesty," I would say to the Shah Zaman or the
Shahryar Zahd, and then add in an offhand manner, "Except, I think, the estimable Princess Shams."

"Shams?" he or she would say guardedly, and would
look about in a shifty sort of way, and Moth would begin
talking volubly to distract us all, while she rudely and almost literally elbowed me out of whatever room we were
in.

God knows where that behavior might finally have got
me—perhaps committed to the House of Delusion—but
then my father and uncle returned to Baghdad, and it was
time for me to say farewell to all three of my zina partners:
to Moth and Shams and my story-made Shams.

6

MY father and uncle returned together, having met somewhere on the roads north from the Gulf. On first setting
eyes on me, before we even exchanged a greeting, my uncle
jovially roared out:

"Ecco Marco! For a wonder, still alive and still vertical
and still at liberty! Are you not in any trouble then,
scagaròn?"

I replied, "Not yet, I think," and went to make sure I
would not be. I sought out the Princess Moth and told her
that our liaisons were at an end. "I can no longer stay out
at night without causing suspicion."

"It is too bad," she pouted. "My sister has by no means
tired of our zina."

"Nor have I, Shahzrad Magas Mirza. But in truth I am
much weakened by it. And now I must regain my strength
for the rest of our journey."

"Yes, you do look somewhat strained and haggard. Very well, I give you leave to desist. We will say our formal farewells before you depart."

So my father and uncle and I sat down with the Shah, and they told him they had decided against taking the sea route to shorten our way eastward.

"We thank you sincerely, Shah Zaman, for having made the suggestion," my father said. "But there is an old Venetian proverb. Loda el mar e tiente a la tera."

"Which means—?" the Shah said affably.

"Laud the sea and attend to the land. In more general application it means: Praise the mighty and the dangerous, but cling to the small and secure. Now, Mafìo and I have done much sailing on mighty seas, but never aboard such ships as those of the Arab traders. No overland route could be less safe or more risky."

"The Arabs," said my uncle, "build their ocean-going ships in exactly the same slipshod way they build their ramshackle river boats, which Your Majesty sees here at Baghdad. All tied and fish-glued together, not a bit of metal in the construction. And deckloads of horses or goats dropping their merda into the passenger cabins below. Maybe an Arab is ignorant enough to venture to sea in such a squalid and rickety cockleshell, but we are not."

"You are perhaps wise not to do so," said the Shahryar Zahd, coming into the room at that moment, although we were a gathering of men. "I will tell you a tale. . . ."

She told several, and all of them concerned a certain Sindbad the Sailor, who had suffered a series of unlikely adventures—with a giant rukh bird, and with an Old Sheikh of the Sea, and with a fish as big as an island, and I do not remember what else. But the point of her recitation was that Sindbad's every adventure had proceeded from his repeatedly taking passage on Arab ships, and each of those craft getting wrecked at sea, and his surviving to drift alone onto some uncharted shore.

"Thank you, my dear," said the Shah, when she had concluded the sixth or seventh of the Sindbad tales. Before she might begin another, he said to my father and uncle, "Was your trip to the Gulf entirely unprofitable, then?"

"Oh, no," said my father. "There was much of interest to see and to learn and to procure. For example, I bought this fine and keen new shimshir saber in Neyriz, and its artificer told me it was made of steel from Your Majesty's iron mines nearby. His words bewildered me. I said to him, 'Surely you mean steel mines.' And he said, 'No, we take the iron from the mines and put it into an ingenious sort of furnace, and the iron becomes steel.' And I said, 'What? You would have me believe that if I put an ass into a furnace it will come out a horse?' And the artificer had to make much explanation to convince me. In solemn truth, Your Majesty, I and all of Europe have always believed that steel was a totally different and much superior metal to mere iron."

"No," said the Shah, smiling. "Steel is but iron much refined by a process which perhaps your Europe has not yet learned."

"So I improved my education there in Neyriz," said my father. "Also, my trip took me through Shiraz, of course, and its extensive vineyards, and I sampled all the famous wines in the very wineries where they are produced. I also sampled—" He paused, and glanced at the Shahryar Zahd. "Also, there are in Shiraz more comely women, and more of them, than in any city I have visited."

"Yes," said the lady. "I was born there myself. It is a proverb of Persia that if you seek a beautiful woman, look in Shiraz; if you seek a beautiful boy, look in Kashan. You will be passing through Kashan as you go on eastward."

"Ah," said Uncle Mafìo. "And for my part, I found a new thing in Basra. The oil called naft, which comes not from olives or nuts or fish or fat, but seeps from the very ground. It burns more brightly than other oils, and for a longer time, and with no suffocating odor. I filled several flasks with it, to light our journey's nights, and perhaps also to astonish others like myself who never saw such a substance before."

"Regarding your journey," said the Shah. "Now that you have decided to continue overland, remember my warning of the Dasht-e-Kavir, the Great Salt Desert to the eastward. This late autumn season is the best time of year in which to cross it, but truthfully there is no good time. I have suggested camels for your karwan, and I suggest five of them. One for each of you and your personal panniers, one for your puller, one for the burden of your main packs. The wazir will go with you tomorrow to the bazàr and help you choose them, and he will pay for them, and I will accept your horses in exchange for that payment."

"That is kind of Your Majesty," said my father. "Just one thing—we have no camel-puller."

"Unless you are well versed in the management of those beasts, you will need one. I probably can help you with that item, too. But first get the camels."

So the next day, we three went again to the bazàr in company with Jamshid. The camel market was an extensive square area set off by itself, and it had a raised skirting of stone laid around it. The camels for sale were all arrayed standing with their forefeet on that shelf of stone, to make them seem to stand taller and prouder. That market was vastly more noisy than any other part of the bazàr, for to the customary shouting and quarreling of buyers and sellers were added the angry bellowing and mournful groans of the camels, as their muzzles were repeatedly seized and twisted to make them demonstrate their agility in kneeling and rising. Jamshid made that test and many others. He tweaked the camels' humps and felt up and down their legs and peered into their nostrils. After examining almost every full-grown beast on sale that day, he had five of them led apart, a bull and four cows. To my father he said:

"See if you agree with my selection, Mirza Polo. You will note that all have much larger forefeet than rear feet, a sure sign of superior staying power. Also they are all clean of nose worms. Always keep a watch for that infestation, and if you ever see worms, dust the nostrils well with pepper."

Since my father and uncle owned to no expertness in camel trading, they were pleased to concur in the wazir's selections. The merchant sent an assistant to lead the camels, hitched together in single file, to the palace stables, and we followed at our leisure.

At the palace, the Shah Zaman and Shahryar Zahd were waiting for us, in a room well heaped with gifts they wished us to convey for them to the Khakhan Kubilai. There were tightly rolled qali of the highest quality, and caskets of jewels and platters and ewers of exquisitely worked gold, and shimshirs of Neyriz steel in gem-encrusted scabbards, and for the Khakhan's women polished looking glasses also of Neyriz steel, and cosmetics of al-kohl and hinna, and leather flasks of Shiraz wine, and ten-

derly wrapped cuttings of the palace garden's most prized
roses, and also cuttings of seedless banj plants and of the
poppies from which teryak is made. The most striking of
all the gifts was a board on which some court artist had
painted the portrait of a man, a man grim and ascetic of
mien, but blind, his eyeballs being all white. It was the
only delineation of any animate being I had ever seen in a
Muslim country.

The Shah said, "It is a likeness of the Prophet Muhammad (peace and blessing be upon him). There are many
Muslims in the Khakhan's realms, and many have no idea
what the Prophet (blessing and peace be his) looked like in
life. You will take this to show them."

"Excuse me," said Uncle Mafìo, with uncharacteristic
hesitancy. "I thought lifelike images were forbidden by Islam. And an image of the very Prophet himself . . . ?"

The Shahryar Zahd explained, "It does not live until the
eyes are painted in. You will engage some artist to do that
just before you present the picture to the Khan. It requires
only two brown dots painted onto the eyeballs."

The Shah added, "And the picture itself is painted in
magic tinctures which in a few months will begin to fade,
until the picture totally disappears. Thus it cannot become
an image of worship, like those you Christians revere,
which are forbidden because they are unnecessary to our
more civilized religion."

"The portrait," said my father, "will be a gift unique
among all the gifts the Khan is forever receiving. Your
Majesties have been more than generous in your tribute."

"I should have liked to send him also some virgin Shiraz
girls and Kashan boys," mused the Shah. "But I have tried
to do that before, and somehow they never arrive at his
court. Virgins must be difficult of transport."

"I just hope we can transport all *this,*" said my uncle,
gesturing.

"Oh, yes, with no trouble," said the Wazir Jamshid.
"Any one of your new camels will easily carry all that burden, and carry it at the pace of eight farsakhs in a day, and
for three days between drinks of water, if that be necessary. Assuming, of course, that you have a competent
camelpuller."

"Which now you do have," said the Shah. "Another gift
of mine, and this one is for you, gentlemen." He signaled to

the guard at the door and the guard went out. "A slave which I myself only recently acquired, bought for me by one of my court eunuchs."

My father murmured, "Your Majesty's generosity continues to abound, and to astound."

"Ah, well," said the Shah modestly. "What is one slave between friends? Even a slave which cost me five hundred dinars?"

The guard returned with that slave, who immediately fell to the floor in salaam, and cried shrilly, "Allah be praised! We meet again, good masters!"

"Sia budelà!" exclaimed Uncle Mafìo. "That is the reptile *we* recoiled from buying!"

"The creature Nostril!" exclaimed the wazir. "Really, my Lord Shah, how did you come to acquire this excrescence?"

"I think the eunuch fell enamored of him," the Shah said sourly. "But I have not. So he is yours, gentlemen."

"Well . . ." said my father and uncle, uncomfortable and unwilling to give offense.

"I have never known a slave more rebellious and odious," said the Shah, dropping any pretense of lauding his gift. "He curses and reviles me in half a dozen languages which I do not comprehend, except that the word pork occurs in all of them."

"He has also been insolent to me," said the Shahryar. "Fancy a slave criticizing the sweetness of his mistress's voice."

"The Prophet (on whom be all peace and blessing)," said the creature Nostril, as if ruminating aloud to himself. "The Prophet called that house accursed where a woman's voice could be heard outside its doors."

The Shahryar glared venomously at him, and the Shah said, "You hear? Well, the eunuch who bought him unbidden has been pulled asunder by four wild horses. The eunuch was expendable, having been born under this roof to one of my other slaves, and having cost nothing. But this son of a bitch shaqàl cost five hundred dinars, and should be more usefully disposed of. You gentlemen need a camel-puller, and he claims to be one."

"Verily!" cried the son of a bitch shaqàl. "Good masters, I grew up with camels, and I love them like my sisters—"

"That," said my uncle, "I believe."

"Answer me this, slave!" Jamshid barked at him. "A camel kneels to be loaded. It groans and complains mightily at each new weight of the loading. How do you know when to load it no further?"

"That is easy, Wazir Mirza. When it *ceases* to grumble, you have laid upon it the last straw it will bear."

Jamshid shrugged. "He knows camels."

"Well . . . ," mumbled my father and uncle.

The Shah said flatly, "You take him with you, gentlemen, or you stand by and watch while he goes to the vat."

"The vat?" inquired my father, who knew not what that was.

"Let us take him, Father," I said, speaking up for the first time. I did not say it with enthusiasm, but I could not have watched again an execution by boiling oil, even of this obnoxious vermin.

"Allah will reward you, young Master Mirza!" cried the vermin. "Oh, ornament upon perfection, you are as compassionate as the old-time darwish Bayazid, who while traveling found an ant caught in the lint of his navel, and went hundreds of farsakhs back to his starting place, to return that abducted ant to its home nest, and—"

"Be silent!" bellowed my uncle. "We will take you, for we would rid our friend the Shah Zaman of your reeking presence. But I warn you, putridity, you will enjoy precious little compassion!"

"I am content!" cried the putridity. "The words of vituperation and beatings bestowed by a sage are more to be valued than the flattery and flowers lavished by the ignorant. And furthermore—"

"Gèsu," my uncle said wearily. "You will be beaten not on your buttocks but on your clattering tongue. Your Majesty, we will depart at dawn tomorrow, and take this stench speedily out of your vicinity."

Early the next morning, Karim and our other two servants dressed us in good sturdy traveling garb in the Persian style, and helped us pack our personal belongings, and presented us with a large hamper of fine foods and wines and other delicacies, prepared by the palace cooks so that the viands would keep well and sustain us for a good part of our way. Then all three servants indulged in a performance of wild grief, as if we had been their lifelong beloved masters and were leaving them forever. They prostrated themselves in salaams and tore off their tulbands and beat their bare heads on the floor, and did not desist until my father distributed bakhshish among them, at which they saw us off with broad smiles and commendations to the protection of Allah.

At the palace stable, we found that Nostril had, without command or beating or supervision, got our riding camels saddled and the pack camel loaded. He had even carefully wrapped and arranged all the gifts being sent by the Shah, so they would not fall or jar against each other or be dirtied by the dust of the road, and, so far as we could determine, he had not stolen a single item from among them.

Instead of complimenting him, my uncle said sternly, "You scoundrel, you think to please us now and cozen us into leniency, so that we will be easygoing when you regress into your natural sloth. But I warn you, Nostril, we will *expect* this sort of efficiency, and—"

The slave interrupted, but obsequiously. "A good master makes a good servant, and gets from him service and obedience in direct proportion to the respect and trust accorded him."

"From all report," said my father, "you have not very well served your recent owners—the Shah, the slave dealer . . ."

"Ah, good Master Mirza Polo, I have been too long pent in cities and households, and my spirit gets crabbed by confinement. I was made by Allah to be a wanderer. Once I learned that you gentlemen are journeyers, I bent every effort to get myself expelled from this palace and attached to your karwan."

"Hm," said my father and uncle, skeptically.

"In so doing, I knew I risked an even more immediate release—like a dunking in the oil vat. But this young Mirza Marco saved me from that, and he will never regret it. To you elder masters, I will be the obedient servant, but to him I will be the devoted mentor. I will stand between him and harm, as he did for me, and I will sedulously instruct him in the wisdoms of the road."

So here was the second of the uncommon teachers I acquired in Baghdad. I heartily wished that it could have been another as comely and companionable and desirable as the Princess Moth. I was not much pleased at the prospect of being the ward of this scruffy slave, and possibly having some of his nasty attributes rub off on me. But I was disinclined to wound him by saying those things aloud, and I responded merely by making a face of tolerant acceptance.

"Mind, I do not claim to be a good man," said Nostril, as if he had overheard my thoughts. "I am a man of the world, and not all my tastes and habits are acceptable in polite society. Doubtless you will have frequent occasion to chide me or beat me. But a good traveler, *that* I am. And now that I shall be again upon the open road, you will appreciate my usefulness. You will see!"

So we three went to make our final and formal leavetakings of the Shah and the Shahryar and her old mother and the Shahzrad Magas. They had all risen early on purpose, and they said their farewells as feelingly as if we had been real guests instead of merely bearers of the Khakhan's ferman who had to be accommodated.

"These are the papers of ownership of that slave," said the Shah Zaman, giving them to my father. "You will cross many borders from here eastward, and the border guards may require to know the identities of all in your karwan. Now goodbye, good friends, and may you walk always in the shadow of Allah."

Princess Moth said to us all, but with a special smile for me, "May you never meet an afriti or an evil jinni on the way, but only the sweet and perfect peri."

The grandmother nodded a mute goodbye, but the Shahryar Zahd said a leavetaking almost as long as one of her stories, concluding fulsomely, "Your departure leaves all of us here bereft."

At that, I made bold to say to her, "There is one here in the palace to whom I would like my personal regards conveyed." I confess, I was still slightly bemazed by my own made-up story about the Princess Sunlight, and by my delusion that I had almost uncovered some long-kept secret regarding her. Anyway, whether or not she was as sublimely beautiful as I had made her in my mind, she *had* been my unflagging lover, and it was only politeness to make especial farewell to her. "Would you give her my fond goodbye, Your Lady Majesty? I do not think the Princess Shams is your own daughter, but—"

"Really," said the Shahryar, with a giggle. "My daughter indeed. You jest, young Mirza Marco, to leave us all laughing in good humor. I am sure you must be aware that the Shahrpiryar is the only Persian Princess named Shams."

I said uncertainly, "I have never heard that title before." I was puzzled, having noticed that the Princess Moth had retreated to a corner of the room and muffled her face in the qali draperies, only her green eyes visible and sparkling naughtily, as she tried to contain the laughter that was nearly doubling her over.

"The title Shahrpiryar," said her mother, "means the Dowager Princess Shams, the Venerable Royal Matriarch." She gestured. "My mother here."

Speechless with astonishment and horror and revulsion, I stared at the Shahrpiryar Shams, the wrinkled, balding, mottled, shrunken, moldy, decrepit, unspeakably old grandmother. She responded to my eye-extruding stare with a lascivious and gloating smile that bared her withered gray gums. Then, as if to make sure I did not fail of realization, she slowly ran the tip of her mossy tongue across her granulated upper lip.

I think I may have reeled where I stood, but somehow I followed my father and uncle out of the room without falling unconscious or vomiting on the alabaster floor. I only vaguely heard the cheery, laughing, mocking goodbyes Moth called after me, for I was hearing inside my head other mocking noises—my own fatuous query, "Is your sister much younger than you are?" and my imagined Allah's decree about "the divine beauty of the Princess Shams" and the fardarbab's sand reading, "Beware the bloodthirstiness of the beautiful . . ."

Well, this latest encounter with Beauty had cost me no blood, and I daresay no one ever died of disgust or humiliation. If anything, the experience served to keep my blood long astir and red and vigorous afterward, for my every recollection of those nights in the anderun of the palace of Baghdad made my blood suffuse me with a blazing red blush.

THE wazir, riding a horse, accompanied our little camel train for the isteqbal—the half a day's journey—which the Persians traditionally perform as a courteous escort for departing guests. During that morning's ride, Jamshid several times solicitously remarked on my mien of glazed eyes and slack jaw. My father and uncle and the slave Nostril also several times inquired if I was being made ill by the rolling gait of my camel. To each I made some evasive reply; I could not admit that I was simply stunned by the knowledge that for the past three weeks or so I had been blissfully coupling with a drooling hag some sixty years older than myself.

However, because I *was* young, I was resilient. After a while, I convinced myself that no real harm had been done—except perhaps to my self-esteem—and that neither of the Princesses was likely to gossip and make me a universal laughing stock. By the time Jamshid gave us his final "salaam aleikum" and turned his horse back for Baghdad, I was able again to look about me and see the country through which we were riding. We were then, and would be for some time, in a land of pleasantly green valleys winding among cool blue hills. That was good, for it enabled us to get used to our camels before we should reach the harder going in the desert.

I will mention that riding a camel is no more difficult than riding a horse, once one has acquired a head for the much higher altitude where one is perched. A camel walks with a mincing gait and wears a supercilious sneer, exactly like certain men of a certain sort. That gait is easy for even a new rider to adjust to, and the riding is easiest done with both legs on the same side, in the way a woman rides a horse sidesaddle, one's forward leg crooked around the saddle bow. The camel is reined, not with a bridle, but with a line tied to a wooden peg permanently fixed in its snout. The camel's sneer gives it a look of haughty intelligence, but that is entirely spurious. One must constantly be aware that a camel is among the most stupid of beasts. An intelligent horse may take a notion to play pranks, to vex or unseat its rider. A camel would never be capable of such an idea, but neither does it have a horse's good sense to watch its way and sidestep avoidable hazards. A camel's rider must stay alert and guide it even around obvious rocks and holes, lest it fall or snap a leg.

As we had been doing ever since Acre, we were still traveling through country that was as new to my father and uncle as it was to me, because they had earlier crossed Asia, both going eastward and returning home, by a much more northerly route. Therefore, with whatever misgivings, they left our direction to the slave Nostril, who claimed to have traversed this country many times in his life of wandering. And so he must have done, for he confidently led us along, and did not pause at the frequent branchings of the trail, but always seemed to know which fork to take. Precisely at that first day's sundown, he brought us to a comfortably appointed karwansarai. By way of rewarding Nostril's good conduct, we did not make him put up in the stable with the camels, but paid for him to eat and sleep in the main building of the establishment.

As we sat about the dining cloth that night, my father studied the papers the Shah had given us, and said:

"I remember your telling us, Nostril, that you have borne other names. It appears from these documents that you have served each of your previous masters under a different one. Sindbad. Ali Babar. Ali-ad-Din. They are all nicer sounding names than Nostril. By which would you prefer that we call you?"

"By none of them, if you please, Master Nicolò. They all belong to past and forgotten phases of my life. Sindbad, for example, refers only to the land of Sind where I was born. I long ago left that name behind."

I said, "The Shahryar Zahd told us some stories about the adventures of another habitual journeyer who called himself Sindbad the Sailor. Could that possibly have been you?"

"Someone very like me, perhaps, for the man was clearly a liar." He chuckled at his own self-deprecation. "You gentlemen are from the marine republic of Venice, so you must know that no seaman ever calls himself a sailor. Always seaman or mariner, sailor being a landsman's ignorant word. If that Sindbad could not get his own byname correct, then his stories must be suspect."

My father persisted, "I must inscribe on this paper some name for you under our ownership. . . ."

"Put down Nostril, good master," he said airily. "That has been my name ever since the contretemps which earned it for me. You gentlemen might not believe it, but I was a surpassingly handsome man before that multilation of my nose ruined my looks."

He went on at great length about how handsome he had been when he still had two nostrils, and how sought after by women enamored of his manly beauty. In his early days, as Sindbad, he said, he had so entranced a lovely girl that she had risked her life to save him from an island peopled by winged and wicked men. Later, as Ali Babar, he had been captured by a band of thieves and thrust into a jar of sesame oil and would have had his talking head pulled off his softened neck but that another lovely girl, beguiled by his charm, had rescued him from the jar and the thieves. As Ali-ad-Din, he with his handsome looks had emboldened yet another comely girl to save him from the clutches of an afriti commanded by an evil sorcerer. . . .

Well, the tales were as implausible as any told by the Shahryar Zahd, but no more implausible than his assertion that he had once been a good-looking man. No one could have believed that. Had he had the normal two nostrils, or three, or none, it would not have improved his resemblance to a large-beaked, chinless, pot-bellied shut-urmurq camel-bird, made even more comical by a stubble of beard under its beak. He went on even more incredibly, embellishing his claim of physical appeal by claiming to have done exploits of bravery and ingenuity and fortitude. We listened politely, but we knew all his rodomontata to be—as my father said later—"All vine and no grapes."

Some days afterward, when my uncle compared our eastward progress against the maps in the Kitab of al-Idrisi, he announced that we had arrived at a historic place. According to his calculations, we were somewhere very near the spot, recorded in *The Book of Alexander,* where, during the conqueror's march across Persia, the Amazon Queen Thalestris had come with her host of warrior women to greet and pay homage to him. We could only take Uncle Mafìo's word, for there was in that place no monument to commemorate the occasion.

In after years, I have often been asked whether I in my journeyings ever found the nation of Amazonia, or, as

some call it, the Land of Femynye. Not there in Persia, I
did not. Later, in the Mongol domains, I met many warrior
women, but they were all subservient to their menfolk. I
have also been often asked whether, out yonder in those
far lands, I ever met the Prete Zuàne, called in other languages Presbyter Johannes and Prester John, that reverend and mighty man so shrouded in myth and fable and
legend and enigma.

For more than a hundred years, the Western world has
been hearing rumor and report of him: a direct descendant
of the royal Magi who first worshiped the Christ child,
hence himself royal and devoutly Christian, and furthermore wealthy and powerful and wise. As the Christian
monarch of a reputedly immense Christian realm, he has
been a figure to tantalize Western imagination. Given our
fragmented West, of many and little nations, ruled by comparatively petty kings and dukes and such, forever
warring against each other—and a Christianity continually sprouting new and schismatic and antagonistic
sects—we needs must look with wistful admiration on a
vast congeries of peoples all peaceably united under one
ruler and one supreme pontiff, and both of those embodied
in one majestic man.

Also, whenever our West has been beleaguered by heathen savages swarming out of the East—Huns, Tàtars,
Mongols, the Muslim Saracens—we have fervently hoped
and prayed that the Prete Zuàne would emerge from his
still farther East and come up *behind* the invaders with his
legions of Christian warriors, so that those heathens
would be caught and crushed between his armies and ours.
But the Prete Zuàne never *has* ventured out of his mysterious fastnesses, neither to help the Christian West in its re-
current times of need nor even to make demonstration of
his existence in reality. Does he then exist, and if so, who is
he? Does he really hold sway over a far-off Christian empire, and if so, where is it?

I have already speculated, in my earlier published
chronicle of my travels, that the Prete Zuàne did exist, *in a
sense,* and in that sense may still exist, but he is not and
never was a Christian potentate.

Back when the Mongols were only separate and disor-
ganized tribes, they called each tribal chief a Khan. When
the many tribes united under the fearsome Chinghiz, he

became the only Eastern monarch ruling over an empire resembling the one rumored to belong to the Prete Zuàne. Since the time of Chinghiz, that Mongol Khanate was ruled in part or in whole by various of his descendants, before his grandson Kubilai became Khakhan and enlarged it even further and consolidated it more firmly. All of those Mongol rulers down the years had different names, but all were titled Khan or Khakhan.

Now, I invite you to notice how easily the spoken or written word Khan or Khakhan could be misread or misheard as Zuàne or John or Johannes. Suppose a long-ago Christian traveler in the East misheard it so. He naturally would be reminded of the sainted Apostle of that name. It would be no small wonder if he thereafter believed he had heard mention of a priest or bishop named for the Apostle. He had only to mingle the misapprehension with the reality—the extent and power and wealth of the Mongol Khanate—and by the time he went home to the West he would have been eager to tell of an imaginary Prete Zuàne ruling an imaginary Christian empire.

Well, if I am right, the Khans probably did inspire the legend, through no doing of their own, but they are not Christians. And they never have owned any of the fabulous possessions ascribed to that Prete Zuàne—the enchanted mirror in which he spies on the distant doings of his enemies, the magic medicaments with which he can cure any mortal ill, his man-eating warriors who are invincible because they can subsist only on the enemies they vanquish—all those other fanciful marvels so reminiscent of the Shahryar Zahd's stories.

This is not to say that there are no Christians in the East. There are, and many of them individuals and groups and entire communities of Christians, to be found everywhere from the Mediterranean Levant to the farther shores of Kithai, and they are of all colors, from white to dun and brown and black. Unfortunately, they are all communicants of the Eastern Church, which is to say followers of the doctrines of the fifth-century schismatic Abbot Nestorius, which is to say heretics in the eyes of us Christians of the Roman Church. For the Nestorians deny the Virgin Mary the title of Mother of God, they do not allow a crucifix in their churches, and they revere the despised Nestorius as a saint. They practice many other heresies be-

sides. Their priests are not celibate, many of them are
married, and all are simoniacs, for they will not administer any of the sacraments except for a fee of money paid.
The Nestorians' only tie with us real Christians is that
they worship the same Lord God, and recognize Christ as
His Son.

That at least made them seem more kin to me and my father and uncle than did the far more numerous surrounding worshipers of Allah or Buddha or even more alien
divinities. So we tried not to abhor the Nestorians too
much—even while we disputed their doctrines—and they
were usually hospitable and helpful to us.

If indeed the Prete Zuàne existed in actuality, not just in
the Western imagination—and if, as rumored, he were a
descendant of one of the Magi kings—then we ought to
have found him during our traverse of Persia, for that is
where the Magi lived, and it was from Persia that they followed the Nativity star to Bethlehem. However, that
would have made the Prete Zuàne a Nestorian, since those
are the only sorts of Christians existing in those parts.
And in fact we did find among the Persians a Christian
elder of that name, but he could hardly have been the
Prete Zuàne of the legend.

His name was Vizan, which is the Persian rendition of
the name rendered elsewhere Zuàne or Giovanni or Johannes or John. He had been born into the royalty of Persia—
had indeed been born a Shahzadè, or Prince—but in his
youth he had embraced the Eastern Church, which meant
renouncing not only Islam, but also his title and heritage
and wealth and privilege and right to succession in the
Shahnate. All of that he had forsworn, to join a roving
tribe of Nestorian bedawin. Now a very old man, he was
that tribe's elder and leader and acknowledged Presbyter.
We found him to be a good man and a wise man, and altogether an admirable man. In those particulars he well fit
the character of the fabled Prete Zuàne. But he reigned
over no broad and rich and populous domain, only a ragtag
tribe of some twenty impoverished and landless shepherd
families.

We encountered that bunch of sheep herders on a night
when there was no karwansarai nearby, and they invited
us to share their camping ground in the middle of their

herd, and so we spent that evening in the company of their
Presbyter Vizan.

While he and we made our simple meal around a small
fire, my father and uncle engaged him in a theological discussion, and they ably discredited and demolished many of
the old bedawi's most cherished heresies. But he seemed
not in the least dismayed or ready to discard the shreds
they left of his beliefs. Instead, he cheerfully turned the
conversation to the Baghdad court we had recently inhabited, and asked after all there, who were of course his royal
relatives. We told him that they were well and thriving
and happy, although understandably chafing under the
overlordship of the Khanate. Old Vizan seemed pleased
with the news, though no whit nostalgic for that life of
courtly ease he had long ago given up. Only when Uncle
Mafìo chanced to mention the Shahrpiryar Shams—making me inwardly flinch—did the ancient shepherd-bishop
leave a sigh that might have denoted regret.

"The Dowager Princess still lives, then?" he said. "Why,
she would be nearly eighty years of age by now, as I am."
And I flinched again.

He was silent for a time, and he took a stick and stirred
the fire, and stared thoughtfully into its heart, and then he
said, "Doubtless the Shahrpiryar Shams no longer shows
it—and you good brethren may not credit my telling of it—
but that Princess Sunlight in her youth was the most beautiful woman in Persia, perhaps the most beautiful of all
time."

My father and uncle murmured noncommittally. I was
still flinching at my all too vivid recollection of the
wrecked and ravaged crone.

"Ah, when she and I and the world were young," said old
Vizan, dreamily. "I was then still Shahzadè of Tabriz and
she was the Shahzrad, first daughter of the Shah of
Kerman. The report of her loveliness brought me from
Tabriz, and brought innumerable other princes from as far
away as Sabaea and the Kashmir, and none was disappointed when he saw her."

Under my breath, I made an impolite noise of scoffing
incredulity, not loud enough for him to hear.

"I could tell you of that maiden's radiant eyes and rose
lips and willow grace, but that would not begin to picture
her for you. Why, just to look at her could heat a man to fe-

ver and yet refresh him at the same time. She was like—
like a field of clover that has been warmed in the sun and
then washed by a gentle rain. Yes. That is the sweetest-
scented thing God ever put on this earth, and always when
I come upon that fragrance I remember the young and
beautiful Princess Shams."

Comparing a woman to clover: how like a rustic and
unimaginative shepherd, I thought. Surely the old man's
wits had been dulled if not scrambled by his decades of association with nothing but greasy sheep and greasier Nestorians.

"There was not a man in all Persia who would not have
risked a drubbing from the Kerman palace guards, just to
sneak near and steal a glimpse of Princess Sunlight walking in her garden. To have seen her uncovered of her
chador veil, a man would have given his very life. In the
remote hope of a smile from her, why, a man would have
relinquished his immortal soul. As for any further intimacy, that would have been an unthinkable thought, even
for the multitude of princes already hopelessly in love with
her."

I sat staring at Vizan, amazed and unbelieving. The old
hag I had spent so many nights naked with—a vision unattainable and inviolable? Impossible! Ludicrous!

"There were so many suitors, and all so anguished in
their yearning, that the tender-hearted Shams could not or
would not choose from among them, and thus blight the
lives of all the rest. Neither could her father the Shah, for a
long time, choose for her; he was so besieged by so many,
each imploring more eloquently, each pressing upon him
more precious gifts. That tumult of courtship went on literally for years. Any other maiden would have fretted at the
passing of her springtime, and she not yet wed. But Shams
only grew the more rose-beautiful and willow-graceful and
clover-sweet as the time went on."

I still sat and stared at him, but my skepticism was
slowly giving way to wonder. My lover had been all *that*?
So exquisitely desirable to this man and to other men in
that long-gone time, so exquisitely memorable that she
was not yet forgotten, by this one at least, even now at the
approaching end of his life?

Uncle Mafìo went to speak, and got to coughing, but at

last cleared his throat and asked, "What was the outcome of that crowded courtship?"

"Oh, it had to come to a conclusion at last. Her father the Shah—with her approval, I trust—finally chose for her the Shahzadè of Shiraz. He and Shams were wed, and the whole Persian Empire—all but the rejected suitors—celebrated with joyous holiday. However, for a long time the marriage had no issue. I strongly suspect that the bridegroom was so overwhelmed by his good fortune, and by the pure beauty of his bride, that it was a long time before he could perform the consummation. It was not until after his father died, and he had succeeded as Shah in Shiraz, and Shams was thirty or older, that she gave birth to their only child, and then only a daughter. She was also handsome, so I have heard, but nothing like her mother. That was Zahd, who is now Shahryar of Baghdad, and I think has a nearly grown daughter of her own."

"Yes," I said faintly.

Vizan went on, "Had it not been for those events I have recounted—had the Princess Shams chosen otherwise—I might still be . . ." He poked at the fire again, but it was now only embers fast fading. "Ah, well. I was inspired to go away into the wilderness, and to seek. And I sought, and I found the true religion, and these my wandering brethren, and with them a new life. I think I have lived it well, and have been a good Christian. I have some small hope of Heaven . . . and in Heaven, who knows . . . ?"

His voice seemed to fail him. He said no more, not even a goodnight, and got up from among us and walked away— wafting his smell of sheep wool and sheep dip and sheep manure—and disappeared into his much-weathered, many-patched little tent. No, I never did take him to be the Prete Zuàne of the legends.

When my father and uncle had also gone to roll into their blankets, I sat on by the darkening embers of the fire, thinking, trying to reconcile in my mind the derelict old grandmother and she who was the Princess Sunlight, unsurpassable in beauty. I was confused. If Vizan saw her now, would he see the aged and ugly crone, or the glorious maiden she once had been? And I, should I keep on feeling disgust because, in her old age, hardly even recognizable as female, she still felt feminine hungers? Or should I pity her for the deceit she had to employ now to slake them, when once she could have had any price for the beckoning?

To look at it another way, should I congratulate myself and delight in the knowledge that I had enjoyed the Princess Sunlight for whom a whole generation of men had yearned in vain? But, trying to think along that line, I found myself wrenching present time into past time, and past into present, and confronting even more insubstantial questions—I was led to wonder: does immortality reside in memory?—and with such deep metaphysic my mind was incapable of grappling.

My mind still is, as most minds are. But I know one thing now which I did not then. I know it from my own experience and knowledge of myself. A man stays always the same age, somewhere down inside himself. Only the outside of him grows older—his wrapping of body, and *its* integument, which is the whole world. Inwardly he attains to a certain age, and stays there throughout his whole remaining life. That perpetual inner age may vary, I suppose, with different individuals. But in general I suspect that it gets fixed at early maturity, when the mind has reached adult awareness and acuity, but has not yet been calloused by habit and disillusion: when the body is newly full-grown and feeling the fires of life, but not yet any of life's ashes. The calendar and his glass and the solicitude of his juniors may tell a man that he is old, and he can see for himself that the world and all around him have aged, but secretly he knows that *he* is still a youth of eighteen or twenty.

And what I have said of a man, I have said because a man is what I am. It must be even more true of a woman, to whom youth and beauty and vitality are so much more to be reasured and conserved. I am sure there is not anywhere a woman of advanced age who has not inside her a maiden of tender years. I believe that the Princess Shams, even when I knew her, could see in her glass the radiant eyes and rose lips and willow grace that her suitor Vizan still could see, more than half a century after parting from her, and could smell the fragrance of clover after rain, the sweetest-scented thing God ever put on this earth.

THE GREAT SALT

1

KASHAN was the last city we came to in the habitable green part of Persia; eastward beyond it lay the empty wasteland called the Dasht-e-Kavir, or Great Salt Desert. On the day before we arrived in that city, the slave Nostril said:

"Observe, my masters, the pack camel has begun to limp, I believe he has suffered a stone bruise. Unless it is relieved, that could cause us bad trouble when we get into the desert."

"You are the camel-puller," said my uncle. "What is your professional advice?"

"The cure is simple enough, Master Mafìo. A few days of rest for the animal. Three days should do it."

"Very well," said my father. "We will put up in Kashan, and we can make use of the delay. Replenish our traveling rations. Get our clothes cleaned, and so on."

During the journey from Baghdad to this point, Nostril had behaved so efficiently and submissively that we had quite forgotten his penchant for devilry. But soon I, at least, had reason to suspect that the slave had deliberately inflicted the camel's minor injury just to provide himself with a holiday.

Kashan's foremost industry (and the source of the city's name) has for centuries been the manufacture of kashi, or what we would call mosaic, those artfully glazed tiles which are used throughout Islam for the decoration of masjid temples, palaces and other fine buildings. The kashi manufacture is done inside enclosed workshops, but Kashan's second most valuable article of commerce was more immediately visible to us as we rode into the city: its beautiful boys and young men.

While the girls and women to be seen on the streets—as well as could be seen through their chador veils—were of the usual mix, ranging from plain to pretty, with here and there one really worth noticing, *all* the young males were of strikingly handsome face and physique and bearing. I do not know why that should have been so. Kashan's climate and foods and water did not differ from those we had encountered elsewhere in Persia, and I could see nothing extraordinary in those local folk who were of an age to be mothers and fathers. So I have no least idea why their male offspring should have been so superior to the boys and young men of other localities—but they undeniably were.

Of course, being a young male myself, I should have preferred to be riding into Kashan's counterpart city, Shiraz, reportedly just as full of beautiful females. Nevertheless, even my uncaring eye had to admire what it saw in Kashan. The boys and youths were not dirty or pimply or spotty; they were immaculately clean, with glossy hair, brilliant eyes, clear and almost translucent complexions. They were not sullen of demeanor or slouching of posture; they stood straight and proud, and their gaze was forthright. They were not mumbly and slovenly of speech; they spoke articulately and intelligently. One and all, and of whatever class, they were as comely and attractive as girls—and girls of high birth, well cared for, well brought up and well mannered. The smaller boys were like the exquisite little Cupids drawn by Alexandrian artists. The larger lads were like the angels pictured in the panels of the San Marco Basilica. Though I was honestly impressed, and even a little envious of them, I made no vocal acknowledgment of that. After all, I flattered myself that *I* was no inferior specimen of my sex and age. But my three companions did exclaim.

"Non persiani, ma prezioni," my uncle said admiringly.

"A precious sight, yes," said my father.

"Veritable jewels," said Nostril, casting a leer about.

"Are they all young eunuchs?" asked my uncle. "Or fated to be?"

"Oh, no, Master Mafìo," said Nostril. "They can give as

good as they get, if you take my meaning. Far from being impaired in their virile parts, they are *improved* in their other nether region. Made more accessible and hospitable, if you take my meaning. Do you comprehend the words fa'il and mafa'ul? Well, al-fa'il means 'the doer' and al-mafa'ul means 'the done-to.' These Kashan boys are bred to be beautiful and trained to be obedient and they are physically, er, modified—so that they perform equally delightfully as fa'il or mafa'ul."

"You make them sound far less angelic than they look," said my father, with distaste. "But the Shah Zaman said it was from Kashan that he procures virgin boys to distribute as gifts to other monarchs."

"Ah, the virgins, now, they are something else. You will not see the virgin boys on the streets, Master Nicolò. They are kept confined in pardah as strict as that of virgin Princesses. For they are reserved to become the concubines of those Princes and other rich men who maintain not just one anderun but two: one of women and one of boys. Until the virgin lads are ripe for presentation, their parents keep them in perpetual indolence. The boys do nothing but loll about on daiwan cushions, while they are force-fed on boiled chestnuts."

"Boiled chestnuts! Whatever for?"

"That diet makes their flesh get immensely plump and pale and so soft you can dent it with a fingertip. Boys of that maggot appearance are especially esteemed by the anderun procurers. There is no accounting for taste. I myself prefer a boy who is sinewy and sinuous and athletic in the act, not a sulky lump of suet that—"

"There is evidently lewdness enough here," my father said. "Spare us yours."

"As you command, master. I will only remark further that the virgin boys are vastly expensive to buy, and cannot be hired. On the other hand, observe! Even the street urchins here are beautiful. They can be cheaply bought for keeping, or even more cheaply hired for a quick—"

"I said be silent!" snapped my father. "Now, where shall we seek lodging?"

"Is there such a thing as a Jewish karwansarai?" said my uncle. "I should like to eat properly for a change."

I must explain that remark. During the past weeks, we had found most of the wayside inns run by Muslims, of

course, but several of them had been the property of Nestorian Christians. And the degenerate Eastern Church foolishly observes so many fast days and feast days that *every*
day is one or the other. So in those places we were either
piously starved or piously glutted. Also, we were now in
the month the Persian Muslims call Ramazan. That word
means "the hot month," but, because the Islamic calendar
follows the moon, its Hot Month occurs variously in each
year, and can fall in August or January or any other time,
and this year it came in late autumn. Whenever it comes,
it is the month ordained for Muslims to fast. On each of the
thirty days of Ramazan, from that morning hour when
there is light enough to distinguish a white thread from a
black one, a Muslim cannot partake of food or drink—or
sex between man and woman—until the fall of night. Neither can he serve any comestible to his guests, whatever
their religion. So in the daytimes we journeyers had not
been able to beg even a dipper of well water from any Muslim establishment, while in every one of them, every day
after sundown, we were absolutely gorged to stupefaction.
For some time, then, we had all been suffering miseries of
indigestion, and Uncle Mafìo's suggestion was no expression of idle whim.

I need hardly remark that Jews in the East seldom engage in such an occupation as renting bed and board to
passing strangers—any more than they do in the West—no
doubt because it is less profitable and more laborious than
moneylending and other such forms of usury. However,
our slave Nostril was a most resourceful person. After only
a little inquiry of passersby, he learned of an elderly Jewish widow whose house adjoined a stable which she no
longer used. Nostril led us there, and got himself admitted
to audience with the widow, and proved himself to be also
a most persuasive envoy. He came out of her house to report that she would let us house our camels in her stable
and ourselves in the hayloft above it.

"Furthermore," he said, as we towed the beasts in there
and began to unload them, "since all the household servants are Kashan Persians and therefore bound by the
strictures of Ramazan, the Almauna Esther has agreed to
prepare and serve you gentlemen your meals with her own
hands. So again you will be eating at your accustomed

hours, and she assures me she is a good cook. The payment she asks for our stay is also most reasonable."

My uncle frankly gaped at the slave, and said in awe, "You are a Muslim, the thing most despised by a Jew, and we are Christians, the next-most despised things. If that were not enough to make this Widow Esther spurn us from her door, you must be the most repulsive creature she has ever set eyes on. How in God's name did you accomplish all this?"

"I am only a Sindi and a slave, master, but I am not ignorant or lacking in initiative. Also I can read and I can observe."

"I congratulate you. But that does not answer my question or lessen your ugliness."

Nostril scratched thoughtfully in his meager beard. "Master Mafìo, in the holy books of your religion and of mine and of the Almauna Esther's religion, you will find the word beauty often mentioned, but never the word ugliness, not in any of those scriptures. Perhaps our several gods are not offended by the physical ugliness of mere mortals, and perhaps the Almauna Esther is a godly woman. Anyway, before those holy books were written, we were of one religion—my ancestors, the almauna's, perhaps yours as well—all were of the old Babylonian religion that is now abhorred as pagan and demonic."

"Impertinent upstart! How dare you suggest such a thing?" my father demanded.

"The almauna's name is Esther," said Nostril, "and there are Christian ladies also of that name, and it derives from the demon goddess Ishtar. The almauna's late husband, she tells me, was named Mordecai, which name comes from the demon god Marduk. But long before those gods existed in Babylon, there existed Noah and his son Shem, and the almauna and I are Shem's descendants. Only the later difference of our religions divides us Semites, and that should not have been too severely divisive. Muslims and Jews, we both eschew certain foods, we both seal our sons in the Faith with circumcision, we both believe in heavenly angels and loathe the same adversary, whether he is called Satan or Shaitan. We both revere the holy city of Jerusalem. Perhaps you did not know that the Prophet (may peace and blessing be upon him) originally bade us Muslims bow to Jerusalem, not to Mecca, when we

make our devotions. The language originally spoken by
the Jews and that spoken by the Prophet (all blessing and
peace be his) were not greatly dissimilar, and—"

"And Muslims and Jews alike," my father said drily,
"have tongues hinged in the middle, to wag at both ends.
Come, Mafìo, Marco. Let us go and pay our own respects to
our hostess. Nostril, you finish unloading the animals and
then procure feed for them."

The Widow Esther was a white-haired and sweet-faced
little woman, and she greeted us as graciously as if we had
not been Christians. She insisted that we sit down and
drink what she called her "restorative for travelers,"
which turned out to be hot milk flavored with cardamom.
The lady prepared it herself, since it was not yet sundown
and none of her Muslim servants could do so much as heat
the milk or pulverize the seeds.

It seemed that the Jew lady did have, as my father had
supposed, a tongue hinged in the middle, for she kept us in
conversation for some while. Rather, my father and uncle
conversed with her: I looked about me. The house clearly
had been a fine one, and richly appointed, but—after the
death of its Master Mordecai, I guessed—had got somewhat dilapidated and its furnishings threadbare. There
was still a full staff of servants, but I got the impression
that they remained not for wages but out of loyalty to their
Mistress Esther and, unbeknownst to her, took in washing
at the back door, or through some such genteel subterfuge
supported themselves and her as well.

Two or three of the servants were as old and unremarkable as the mistress, but three or four others were the
supernally handsome Kashan boys and young men. And
one servant, I was pleased to note, was a female as pretty
as any of the males, a young woman with dark-red hair
and a voluptuous body. To pass the time while the Widow
Esther prattled on, I made the cascamorto at that maidservant, giving her languishing looks and suggestive
winks. And she, when her mistress was not observing,
smiled encouragingly back at me.

The next day, while the lame camel rested, and so did
the other four, we travelers all went separately out into
the city. My father went seeking a kashi workshop, expressing a wish to learn something about the manufacture
of those tiles, for he deemed it a useful industry that he

might introduce to the artisans of Kithai. Our camel-
puller Nostril went out to buy some kine of salve for the
camel's bruised foot, and Uncle Mafìo went to get a new
supply of the mumum depilatory. As it turned out, none of
them found what he sought, because no one in Kashan was
working during Ramazan. Having no errands of my own, I
simply strolled and observed.

As I was to see in every city from there eastward, the sky
over Kashan was constantly awhirl with the big, dark,
fork-tailed scavenger kites circling and swooping. As also
in every city from there eastward, the other most prevalent bird seemed to spend all its time scavenging on the
ground. That was the mynah, which strutted aggressively
about with its lower beak puffed out like the pugnacious
underjaw of a little man looking for a quarrel. And of
course the next most visible denizens of Kashan were the
pretty boys at play in the streets. They chanted their ball-
bouncing songs and their hide-and-seek songs and their
whirling-dance songs, just as Venetian children do, except
that these songs were of the cat-screech variety. So was
the music played by the street entertainers soliciting
bakhshish. They seemed to own no instruments except the
changal, which is nothing but a guimbarde or Jew's harp,
and the chimta, which is nothing but iron kitchen tongs, so
their music was nothing but a horrid cacophony of twang
and clatter. I think the passerby who tossed them a coin or
two did so not out of thanks for the entertainment but to
interrupt it, however briefly.

I did not wander far that morning, for my stroll brought
me around through the streets in a circle, and I soon found
myself again approaching the widow's house. From a window the pretty maidservant beckoned, as if she had been
waiting there just to see me pass. She let me into the
house, into a room furnished with slightly shabby qali and
daiwan pillows, and confided to me that her mistress was
occupied elsewhere, and told me that her name was Sitarè,
which means Star.

We sat down together on a pile of pillows. Being no
longer a callow and inexperienced stripling, I did not set
upon her with clumsy juvenile avidity. I began with soft
words and sweet compliments, and only gradually moved
closer until my whispers tickled her dainty ear and made

her wriggle and giggle, and only then raised her chador
veil and moved my lips to hers and tenderly kissed her.

"That is nice, Mirza Marco," she said. "But you need not
waste time."

"I count it no waste," I said. "I enjoy the preliminaries
as much as the fulfillment. We can take the whole day
if—"

"I mean you need not do anything with me."

"You are a considerate girl, Sitarè, and kind. But I must
tell you that I am not a Muslim. I do not abstain during
Ramazan."

"Oh, your being an infidel does not matter."

"I rejoice to hear it. Then let us proceed."

"Very well. Loose your embrace of me and I will fetch
him."

"What?"

"I told you. There is no need to continue in pretense with
me. He is already waiting to come in."

"Who is waiting?"

"My brother Aziz."

"Why the devil would we want your brother in here with
us?"

"Not we. You. I will go away."

I loosed my hold on her, and sat up and looked at her.
"Excuse me, Sitarè," I said warily, not knowing any better
way to ask it than to ask it: "Are you perhaps, er, divanè?"
Divanè means crazy.

She looked genuinely puzzled. "I assumed you took notice of our resemblance when you were here last evening.
Aziz is the boy who looks like me, and has red hair like
mine, but is much prettier. His name means Beloved.
Surely that was why you winked and leered at me?"

Now I was the one puzzled. "Even if he were as pretty as
a peri, why would I wink at *you*—except that you were the
one I—?"

"I tell you no pretext is necessary. Aziz saw you also,
and was also instantly enthralled, and he already is waiting and eager."

"I do not care if Aziz is eternally adrift in Purgatory!" I
cried in exasperation. "Let me put this as plainly as I
know how. I am at this moment trying to seduce you into
letting me have my way with you."

"Me? You wish to make zina with me? Not with my brother Aziz?"

I briefly pounded my fists on an unoffending pillow, and then said, "Tell me something, Sitarè. Does every girl in all of Persia misspend her energies in acting as procurer for someone else?"

She thought about that. "All of Persia? I do not know. But here in Kashan, yes, that is often the case. It is the result of established custom. A man sees another man, or a boy, and is smitten with him. But he cannot pay court to him outright, for that is against the law laid down by the Prophet."

"Peace and blessing be upon him," I muttered.

"Yes. So the man pays court to the other man's nearest woman relative. He will even marry her, if necessary. So that then he has excuse to be near his true heart's desire— the woman's brother perhaps, or maybe her son if she is a widow, or even her father—and has every opportunity to make zina with him. That way, you see, the proprieties are not openly flouted."

"Gèsu."

"That is why I supposed you were paying court to me. But of course, if you do not want my brother, you cannot have me."

"Whyever not? You seemed pleased to learn that I wanted you and not him."

"Yes, I am. Both surprised and pleased. That is an unusual preference; a Christian eccentricity, I daresay. But I am a virgin, and I must remain so, for my brother's sake. You have by now crossed many Muslim lands; surely you have comprehended. That is why a family keeps its maiden daughters and sisters in strict pardah, and jealously guards their virtue. Only if a maiden remains intact or a widow chaste can she hope to make a good marriage. At least, so it is here in Kashan."

"Well, it is the same where I come from. . . ," I had to admit.

"Yes, I shall seek to make a good marriage to a good man who will be a good provider and a good lover to us both, for my brother Aziz is all the family I have."

"Wait a moment," I said, scandalized. "A Venetian female's chastity is often an item of barter, yes, and often traded for a good marriage, yes. But only for the commer-

cial or social advancement of her whole family. Do you
mean the woman here willingly endorse and connive in
the lust of one man for another? You would deliberately
become the wife of a man just so you could share him with
your brother?"

"Oh, not just any man who comes along," she said airily.
"You should feel flattered that both Aziz and I found you
to our liking."

"Gèsu."

"To couple with Aziz commits you to nothing, you see,
since a male has no sangar membrane. But if you wish to
be the breaker of mine, you must wed me and take us
both."

"Gèsu." I got up from the daiwan.

"You are going? Then you do not want me? But what of
Aziz? You will not have him even once?"

"I think not, thank you, Sitarè." I slouched toward the
door. "I simply was ignorant of local custom."

"He will be desolated. Especially if I have to tell him it
was me you desired."

"Then do not," I mumbled. "Just tell him I was ignorant
of local custom." And I went on out the door.

2

BETWEEN the house and the stable was a little garden plot
planted with kitchen herbs, and the Widow Esther was out
there. She was wearing only one slipper, her other foot was
bare, and she had the removed slipper in her hand, beating
with it at the ground. Curious, I approached her, and saw
that she was pounding at a large black scorpion. When it
was pulped, she moved on and turned over a rock; another
scorpion sluggishly crawled into view and she squashed
that one, too.

"Only way to get the nasty things," she said to me.
"They do their prowling at night, when they are impossible to see. You have to turn them up in daylight. This city
is infested with them. I do not know why. My late dear husband Mordecai (alav ha-sholom) used to grumble that the
Lord erred miserably in sending mere locusts upon Egypt,

when He could have sent these venomous Kashan scorpions."

"Your husband must have been a brave man, Mirza Esther, to criticize the Lord God Himself."

She laughed. "Read your scriptures, young man. The Jews have been giving censure and advice to God ever since Abraham. You can read in the Book of Genesis how Abraham first argued with the Lord and then proceeded to haggle Him into a bargain. My Mordecai was no less hesitant to cavil at God's doings."

I said, "I once had a friend—a Jew named Mordecai."

"A Jew was your friend?" She sounded skeptical, but I could not tell whether she doubted that a Christian would befriend a Jew, or a Jew a Christian.

"Well," I said, "he was a Jew when I first met him, when he called himself Mordecai. But I seem to keep on meeting him under other names or in other guises. I even saw him once in one of my dreams."

And I told her of those various encounters and manifestations, each of them evidently intended to impress upon me "the bloodthirstiness of beauty." The widow stared at me as I talked, and her eyes widened, and when I was done she said:

"Bar mazel, and you a gentile! Whatever he is trying to tell you, I suggest that you take it to heart. Do you know who that is you keep meeting? That must be one of the Lamed-vav. The thirty-six."

"The thirty-six what?"

"Tzaddikim. Let me see—saints, I suppose a Christian would call them. It is an old Jewish belief. That there are always in the world just thirty-six men of perfect righteousness. No one ever knows who they are, and they themselves do not realize they are tzaddikim—or else, you see, that self-consciousness would impair their perfection. But they go constantly about the world, doing good deeds, for no reward or recognition. Some say the tzaddikim never die. Others say that whenever one tzaddik dies, another good man is appointed by God to that office, without his knowing he has been so honored. Still others say that there is really only one tzaddik, who can be in thirty-six places simultaneously, if he chooses. But all who believe in the legend agree that God will end this world if ever the Lamed-vav should cease doing their good works. I must say, though, that I never heard of one of them extending his good offices to a gentile."

I said, "The one I met in Baghdad may not even have been a Jew. He was a fardarbab tomorrow-teller. He could have been an Arab."

She shrugged. "The Arabs have an identical legend. They call the righteous man an abdal. The true identity of each of them is known only to Allah, and it is only on their account that Allah lets the world go on existing. I do not know if the Arabs borrowed the legend of our Lamed-vav, or if it is a belief which they and we have shared ever since the long-ago time when we were mutually the children of Shem. But whichever yours is, young man—an abdal bestowing his favor on an infidel or a tzaddik on a gentile— you are highly favored and you should pay heed."

I said, "They seem never to speak to me of anything but beauty and bloodthirstiness. I already seek the one and shun the other, insofar as I can. I hardly need further counsel in either of those respects."

"Those sound to me like the two sides of a single coin," said the widow, as she slapped with her slipper at another scorpion. "If there is danger in beauty, is there not also beauty in danger? Or why else does a man so gladly go a-journeying?"

"Me? Oh, I journey just out of curiosity, Mirza Esther."

"*Just* curiosity! Listen to him! Young man, do not ever deprecate the passion called curiosity. Where would danger be without it, or beauty either?"

I failed to see much connection among the three things, and again began to wonder if I was talking to someone slightly divanè. I knew that old people could sometimes get wonderfully disjointed in their conversations, and so this one seemed when she said next:

"Shall I tell you the saddest words I ever heard?"

In the manner of all old people, she did not wait for me to say yes or no, but went right on:

"They were the last words spoken by my husband Mordecai (alav ha-sholom). It was when he lay dying. The darshan was in attendance, and other members of our little congregation, and of course I was there, weeping and trying to weep with quiet dignity. Mordecai had made all his farewells, and he had said the Shema Yisrael, and he was composed for death. His eyes were closed, his hands folded, and we all thought he was peacefully slipping away. But then, without opening his eyes or addressing anybody in particular, he spoke again, quite clearly and distinctly. And what he said was this . . ."

The widow pantomimed the deathbed occasion. She closed her eyes and crossed her hands on her bosom, one of them still holding her dirty slipper, and she leaned her head back a little, and she said in a sepulchral voice, "I always wanted to go there . . . and do that . . . but I never did."

Then she stayed in that pose; evidently I was expected to say something. I repeated the dying man's words, "I always wanted to go there . . . and do that . . ." and I asked, "What did he mean? Go where? Do what?"

The widow opened her eyes and shook her slipper at me. "That was what the darshan said, after we had waited for some moments to hear more. He leaned over the bed and said, 'Go to what place, Mordecai? To do what thing?' But Mordecai said no more. He was dead."

I made the only comment I could think to make. "I am sorry, Mirza Esther."

"So am I. But so was he. Here was a man in the very last flicker of his life, lamenting something that had once piqued his curiosity, but he had neglected to go and see it or do it or have it—and now he never could."

"Was Mordecai a journeyer?"

"No. He was a cloth merchant, and a very successful one. He never traveled farther from here than to Baghdad and Basra. But who knows what he would have liked to be and do?"

"You think he died unhappy, then?"

"Unfulfilled, at least. I do not know what it was he spoke of, but oh! how I wish he *had* gone there while he was alive, wherever it was, and done whatever it was."

I tried tactfully to suggest that it could not matter to him now.

She said firmly, "It mattered to him when it mattered most. When he knew the chance was gone forever."

Hoping to make her feel better, I said, "But if he had seized the chance, you might be sorrier now. It may have been something—something less than approvable. I have noticed that sinful temptations abound in these lands. In all lands, I suppose. I myself once had to confess to a priest for having too freely followed where my curiosity led me, and—"

"Confess it, if you must, but do not ever abjure it or ignore it. That is what I am trying to tell you. If a man is to have a fault, it should be a passionate one, like insatiable curiosity. It would be a pity to be damned for something paltry."

"I hope not to be damned, Mirza Esther," I said piously, "as I trust the Mirza Mordecai was not. It may well have been out of virtue that he let that chance go by, whatever it was. Since you cannot know, you need not weep for—"

"I am not weeping. I did not broach the matter to sniffle over it."

I wondered why, then, she had bothered to broach it. And, as if in reply to my silent question, she went on:

"I wanted you to know this. When you come at last to die, you may be devoid of all other urges and senses and faculties, but you will still possess your passion of curiosity. It is something that even cloth merchants have, perhaps even clerks and other such drudges. Certainly a journeyer has it. And in those last moments it will make you grieve—as Mordecai did—not for anything you have done in your lifetime, but for the things you never got to do."

"Mirza Esther," I protested. "A man cannot live always in dread of missing something. I fully expect never to be Pope, for instance, or Shah of Persia, but I hope that lack will not blight my life. Or my deathbed either."

"I do not mean things unattainable. Mordecai died lamenting something that had been within his reach, within his capability, within his having, and he let it go by. Imagine yourself pining for the sights and delights and experiences you could have had, but missed—or even just one single small such experience—and pining too late, when it is forever unattainable."

Obediently, I did try to imagine that. And young though I was, remote though I assumed that prospect to be, I felt a faint chill.

"Imagine going into death," she went on implacably, "without having tasted everything in this world. The good, the bad, the indifferent even. And to know, at that final movement, that it was no one but you who deprived yourself, through your own careful caution or careless choice or failure to follow where your curiosity led. Tell me, young man, could there be any more hurtful pang on the *other* side of death? Even damnation itself?"

After the moment it took me to shake off the chill, I said, as cheerfully as I could, "Well, with the help of those thirty-six you spoke of, maybe I can avoid both deprivation in my lifetime and damnation after it."

"Aleichem sholem," she said. But, as she was swatting with her slipper at another scorpion at that moment, I was not sure if she was wishing peace to me or to it.

She moved on down the garden, turning over rocks, and I idly ambled into the stable to see if any of our party had returned from wandering about town. One of them had, but not alone, and the sight brought me up short, with a gasp.

Our slave Nostril was there, with a stranger, one of the gorgeous young Kashan men. Perhaps my conversation with the maidservant Sitarè had made me temporarily impervious to disgust, for I did not make violent outcry or retreat from the scene. I looked on as indifferently as did the camels, which only shuffled and mumbled and munched. Both of the men were naked, and the stranger was on his hands and knees in the straw, and our slave was hunched over his backside, bucking like a camel in rut. The lewdly coupling Sodomites turned their heads when I entered, but only grinned at me and kept on with their indecency.

The young man had a body that was as handsome to look upon as his face was. But Nostril, even when fully clothed, was of a repellent appearance, as I have already described. I can only say further that his paunchy torso and pimply buttocks and spindly limbs, when totally exposed, were a sight to make most onlookers retch up their most recent meal. I was amazed that such a revolting creature could have persuaded anyone the least bit less revolting to play al-mafa'ul to his al-fa'il.

Nostril's fa'il implement was invisible to me, being inserted where it was, but the young man's organ was visible below his belly, and stiffened into its candelòto aspect. I thought that somewhat odd, since neither he nor Nostril was manipulating it in any way. And it seemed even more odd, when he and Nostril finally groaned and writhed together, to see his candelòto—still without benefit of touch or fondling—squirt spruzzo into the straw on the floor.

After they had briefly rested and panted, Nostril heaved his sweat-shiny bulk off the young man's back. Without dipping a wash of water from the camel trough, without even wadding some straw to wipe his extremely wee little organ, he began putting his clothes back on, and humming a merry tune as he did so. The young stranger more indolently and slowly began to get dressed, as if he frankly enjoyed displaying his nude body even under such disgraceful circumstances.

Leaning against a stall partition, I said to our slave, as if we had all the while been chatting companionably, "You know something, Nostril? There are many rascals and scamps portrayed in song and story—characters like Encolpios and Renart the Fox. They live a gay vagabond life, and they live by their foxy wits, but somehow they are never guilty of crime or sin. They commit only pranks and jests. They steal from none but thieves, their amatory exploits are never sordid, they drink and carouse without ever getting drunk or foolish, their swordplay never causes more than a flesh wound. They have winning ways and twinkling eyes and a ready laugh, even on the scaffold, for they never hang. Whatever the adventure, those adventurous scoundrels are always charming and dashing, clever and amusing. Such stories make one want to *meet* such a brave, bold, lovable rascal."

"And now you have," said Nostril. He twinkled his piggy eyes and smiled to show his stubble teeth and struck a pose that he probably thought was dashing.

"Now I have," I said. "And there is nothing lovable or admirable about you. If you are the typical rascal, then all the stories are lies, and a rascal is a swine. You are filthy of person and of habit, loathsome in appearance and character, cloacal in your proclivities. You are altogether deserving of that seething oil vat from which I too indulgently argued for your rescue."

The handsome stranger laughed coarsely at that. Nostril sniffled and muttered, "Master Marco, as a devout Muslim I must object to being likened to a swine."

"I hope you would also balk at coupling with a sow," I said. "But I doubt it."

"Please, young master. I am devoutly keeping Ramazan, which prohibits intercourse between Muslim men and women. I must also admit that, even in the permissible months, women are sometimes hard for me to come by, ever since my pretty face was disfigured by my nose's misfortune."

"Oh, do not exaggerate," I said. "There is always somewhere a woman desperate enough for anything. In my lifetime, I have seen a Slavic woman couple with a black man and an Arab woman couple with an actual ape."

Nostril said loftily, "I hope you do not suppose that I would condescend to a woman as ugly as I am. Ah, but Jafar here—Jafar is as comely as the comeliest woman."

I growled, "Tell your comely wretch to hurry with his dressing and get out of here, or I will feed him to the camels."

The comely wretch glared at me, then gave a melting look of entreaty to Nostril, who immediately insulted me with an impertinent question: "You would not like to try him yourself, Master Marco? The experience might broaden your mind."

"I will broaden your one nose-hole!" I snarled, taking the dagger from my belt. "I will open it all the way around your ugly head! How dare you speak so to a master? What do you take me for?"

"For a young man with much yet to learn," he said. "You are a journeyer now, Master Marco, and before you get home again you will have traveled much farther yet, and seen and experienced much more. When you do arrive home at last, you will be rightfully scornful of men there who call mountains high and swamps deep, without their ever having scaled a mountain or plumbed a swamp—men who have never ventured beyond their narrow streets and their commonplace routines and their cautious pastimes and their pinched little lives."

"Perhaps so. But what has that to do with your galineta whore?"

"There are other journeys that can take a man beyond the ordinary, Master Marco, not in distance of travel but in breadth of understanding. Consider. You have reviled this young man as a whore, when he is only what he was bred and developed and trained and expected to be."

"A Sodomite, then, if you prefer. To a Christian, that is a sinful thing to be—a sinner and a sin to be abhorred."

"I ask you, Master Marco, to make only a short journey

into the world of this young man." Before I could object, he said, "Jafar, tell the foreigner of your upbringing."

Still clutching his lower garment in his hand, and glancing uneasily at me, Jafar began. "Oh, young Mirza, reflection of the light of Allah—"

"Never mind that," said Nostril. "Just tell of your body's preparation for sexual commerce."

"Oh, blessing of the world," Jafar began again. "From the earliest years I can remember, always while I slept I wore inserted into my nether aperture a golulè, which is an implement made of kashi ceramic, a sort of small tapered cone. Every time my bedtime toilet was completed, the golulè was put into me, well greased with some drug to stimulate the development of my badàm. My mother or nurse would at intervals ease it farther inside me, and when I could accommodate it all, a larger golulè was substituted. Thus my opening gradually grew more ample, but without impairing the muscle of closure which surrounds it."

"Thank you for the story," I said to him, but coldly, and to Nostril I said, "Born so or made so, a Sodomite is still an abomination."

"I think his story is not finished," said Nostril. "Bear with the journey only a little farther."

"When I was perhaps five or six years old," Jafar went on, "I was relieved of having to wear the golulè, and instead my next older brother was encouraged to use me whenever he had an urge and an erected organ."

"Adrìo de vu!" I gasped, compassion getting the better of my revulsion. "What a horrible childhood!"

"It could have been worse," said Nostril. "When a bandit or slavetaker captures a boy, and that boy has not been thus carefully prepared, the captor brutally impales him there with a tent peg, to make the opening fit for subsequent use. But that tears the encircling muscle, and the boy can never thereafter contain himself, but excretes incontinently. Also, he cannot thereafter utilize that muscle to give pleasurable contractions during the act. Go on, Jafar."

"When I had got accustomed to that brother's usage, my next older and better-equipped brother helped my further development. And when my badàm was mature enough to let me begin to *enjoy* the act, then my father . . ."

"Adrìo de vu!" I exclaimed again. But now curiosity had got the better of both my revulsion and my compassion. "What do you mean about the badàm?" I could not comprehend that detail, for the word badàm means an almond.

"You did not know of it?" said Nostril with surprise. "Why, you have one yourself. Every male does. We call it the almond because of its shape and size, but physicians sometimes refer to it as the third testicle. It is situated behind the other two, not in the bag, but hidden up inside your groin. A finger or, ahem, any other object inserted far enough into your anus rubs against that almond and stimulates it to a pleasurable excitement."

"Ah," I said, enlightened. "So that is why, just now, Jafar made spruzzo seemingly without any caress or provocation."

"We call that spurt the almond milk," Nostril said primly. He added, "Some women of talent and experience know of that invisible male gland. In one way or another, they tickle it while they are coupling with a man, so that when he ejaculates the almond milk his enjoyment is blissfully heightened."

I wagged my head wonderingly, and said, "You are right, Nostril. A man can learn new things from journeying." I slid my dagger back into its sheath. "This time at least, I forgive the brash way you spoke to me."

He replied smugly, "A good slave puts utility before humility. And now, Master Marco, perhaps you would like to slip your other weapon into another sheath? Observe Jafar's splendid scabbard—"

"Scagaròn!" I snapped. "I may tolerate such customs of others while I am in these regions, but I will not partake of them. Even if Sodomy were not a vile sin, I should still prefer the love of women."

"Love, master?" echoed Nostril, and Jafar laughed in his coarse way, and one of the camels belched. "No one spoke of love. The love between a man and a man is another thing entirely and I believe that only we warmhearted warrior Muslims can know that most sublime of all emotions. I doubt that any cold-blooded and peacepreaching Christian could be capable of that love. No, master, I was suggesting merely a matter of convenient release and relief and satisfaction. For that, what difference what sex?"

I snorted like a supercilious camel. "Easy for you to say, slave, since to you it makes no difference what *animal.* As for me, I am happy to say that as long as there are women in the world I shall have no yearning for men to couple with. I am a man myself, and I am too familiar with my own body to have the least interest in that of any other male. But women—ah, women! They are so magnificently different from me, and each so exquisitely different from another—I can never value them enough!"

"Value them, master?" He sounded amused.

"Yes." I paused, then said with due solemnity, "I once killed a man, Nostril, but I could never bring myself to kill a woman."

"You are young yet."

"Now, Jafar," I said to the young man, "put on the rest of your clothes and go, before my father and uncle get back here."

"I saw them arrive just now, Master Marco," said Nostril. "They went with the Almauna Esther into her house."

So I went over there, too, and was again waylaid by the maidservant Sitarè, as she let me in the door. I would have gone on by her unheeding, but she took me by the arm and whispered, "Do not speak loudly."

I said, not whispering, "I have nothing to speak to you about."

"Hush. The mistress is inside, and your father and uncle are with her. So do not let them hear, but answer me. My brother Aziz and I have discussed the matter of you and—"

"I am not a matter!" I said testily. "I do not much like my being discussed."

"Oh, do please hush. Are you aware that the day after tomorrow is the Eid-al-Fitr?"

"No. I do not even know what that is."

"Tomorrow at sundown Ramazan ends. At that moment begins the month of Shawal, and its first day is the Feast of Fast-Broken, when we Muslims are released from abstinence and restriction. Any time after sundown tomorrow, you and I can licitly make zina."

"Except that you are a virgin," I reminded her. "And must stay that way, for your brother's sake."

"That is what Aziz and I discussed. We have a small favor to ask of you, Mirza Marco. If you will consent to it, I will consent—and I have my brother's consent—to make zina with you. Of course, you can have him too, if you like."

I said suspiciously, "Your offer sounds like a considerable return for a small favor. And your beloved brother sounds brotherly indeed. I can hardly wait to meet this pimping and simpering lout."

"You have met him. He is the kitchen scullion, with hair dark red like mine, and—"

"I do not remember." But I could imagine him: the twin to Nostril's stable mate Jafar, a muscular and handsome hulk of a man, with the orifice of a woman, the wits of a camel and the morals of a jack weasel.

"When I say a small favor," Sitarè went on, "I mean a small one for me and Aziz. For yourself it will be a greater favor, since you will profit by it. Actually earn money from it."

Here was a beautiful chestnut-haired maiden, offering me herself and her maidenhead and a monetary return as well—plus, if I wanted him, her reputedly even more beautiful brother into the bargain. Naturally this brought to my recollection the phrase I had several times heard, "the bloodthirstiness of beauty." And naturally that made me cautious, but not so cautious that I would flatly refuse the offer without hearing more.

"Tell me more," I said.

"Not now. Here comes your uncle. Hush."

"Well, well!" boomed Uncle Mafìo, approaching us from the darker interior of the house. "Collecting *fiame*, are we?" And his black beard split in a bright white grin, as he shouldered past us and went out the door toward the stable.

The remark was a ply on the word fiame, since in Venice "flames" can mean—in addition to fire—either red-headed persons or secret lovers. So I assumed that my uncle was jocosely twitting what he took to be a boy-and-girl flirtation.

As soon as he was out of hearing, Sitarè said to me, "Tomorrow. At the kitchen door, where I let you in before. At this same hour." And then she too was gone, somewhere into the back parts of the house.

I strolled on along the front passage, into the room from which I heard the voices of my father and the Widow Esther. As I entered, he was saying, in a muted and serious tone, "I know it was your good heart that proposed it. I only wish you had asked me first, and me alone."

"I never would have suspected," she said, also in a hushed tone. "And if, as you say, he has nobly exerted himself to reform, I would not wish to be the provocation of a relapse."

"No, no," said my father. "No blame can be laid to you, even if the good deed should turn out ill. We will talk it over, and I will ask flatly whether this would be an irresistible temptation, and on that basis we will decide."

Then they noticed my presence, and abruptly dropped whatever it was they were privily discussing, and my father said, "Yes, it was as well that we stopped these few days. There are several items we need which are unobtainable in the bazàr during this holy month. When the month ends tomorrow, they will be purchasable, and by then the lame camel will be healed, and we will aim at departure the day after. We cannot thank you enough for the hospitality you have shown us during our stay."

"Which reminds me," she said. "I have your evening meal almost done. I will bring it out to your quarters as soon as it is."

My father and I went together to the hayloft, where we found Uncle Mafìo perusing the pages of our Kitab. He looked up from it and said, "Our next destination, Mashhad, is no easy one to get to. Desert all the way, and the very widest extent of that desert. We will be dried and shriveled like a bacalà." He broke off to scratch vigorously at the inside of his left elbow. "Some damned bug has bitten me, and I itch."

I said, "The widow told me that this city is infested with scorpions."

My uncle gave me a scornful look. "If you ever get stung by one, asenazzo, you will learn that scorpions do not *bite*. No, this was a tiny fly, perfectly triangular in shape. It was so tiny that I cannot believe this tormenting itch it left."

The Widow Esther made several crossings of the yard, bringing out the dishes of our meal, and we three ate while bent together over the Kitab. Nòstril ate apart, in the stable below, among the camels, but he ate almost as audibly as a camel eats. I tried to disregard his noises and concentrate on the maps.

"You are right, Mafìo," said my father. "The broadest part of the desert to cross. God send us good."

"Still, an easy route to keep to. Mashhad is just a little north of east from here. At this season, we will only have to take aim at the sunrise each morning."

"And I," I put in, "will frequently verify our course with our kamàl."

"I notice," said my father, "that al-Idrisi shows not a single well or oasis or karwansarai in that desert."

"But some such things must exist. It is a trade route, after all. Mashhad, like Baghdad, is a major stop on the Silk Road."

"And as big a city as Kashan, the widow told me. Also, thank God, it is in the cool mountains."

"But beyond it, we will come to genuinely cold ones. We shall probably have to lay up for the winter somewhere."

"Well, we cannot expect to go through the world with the wind always astern."

"And we will not be on territory familiar to you and me, Nico, until we get all the way to Kashgar, in Kithai itself."

"Distant from the eye, Mafìo, is distant from the heart. Sufficient the evils of the day, and all that. For the time being, let us not plan or worry beyond Mashhad."

3

THE next day, the last day of Ramazan, we spent mostly in just lazing about the widow's property. I think I have neglected to mention that, in Muslim countries, a day's beginning is not counted from dawn, as one might expect, or from the midnight hour, as it is in civilized countries, but from the moment of the sun's setting. Anyway, there was no point in our haunting the Kashan bazàr, as my father had remarked, until it should be again fully stocked with goods for purchase. We had no other tasks except to feed and water the camels and shovel their manure out of the stable. Of course, Nostril attended to that—and at the widow's request he spread the manure on her herb garden.

Now and again, I or my father or uncle would go out for a stroll in the streets. And so did Nostril, in the intervals between his chores, and in the process, I have no doubt, managed to consummate some more of his nasty liaisons.

When I went walking out into the city in the late afternoon, I found a crowd of people standing at a corner where two streets intersected. Most of them were young—good-looking males and nondescript females. I would have assumed that they were merely engaged in the favorite occupation of the East, which is standing and staring—or, in the case of Eastern men, standing and staring and scratching their crotches—except that I heard a droning voice proceeding from the center of the group. So I stopped and joined the audience, and gradually worked my way through them until I could see the object of their attention.

It was an old man seated cross-legged on the ground: a sha'ir, or poet, and he was entertaining the people by telling a story. From time to time, evidently whenever he spoke an especially poetic and felicitous phrase, one of the bystanders would drop a coin into the begging bowl on the ground beside the old man. My grasp of Farsi was not good enough to enable me to appreciate anything of that sort, but it was good enough at least to follow the thread of the tale, and it was an interesting tale, so I stood and listened. The sha'ir was telling how dreams came to be.

In the Beginning, he said, among all the kinds of spirits which exist—the jinn and the afarit and the peri and so on—there was a spirit named Sleep. He had charge then, as he has now, of that dormant condition in all living creatures. Now, Sleep had a whole swarm of children, who were called Dreams, but in that far-off time neither Sleep nor his children had ever thought of the Dreams getting inside people's heads. But one day, it being a nice day, and Sleep not having much to do during the daytime, that good spirit decided to take all his boys and girls for a holiday at the seashore. And there he let them get into a little boat they found, and fondly watched as they paddled out upon the water a short way.

Unfortunately, said the old poet, the spirit Sleep had earlier done something to offend the mighty spirit called Storm, and Storm had been waiting an opportunity for revenge. So when Sleep's little Dreams ventured upon the sea, the malevolent Storm whipped the sea into a frothing

fury, and blew a driving wind, and washed the frail boat
far out into the ocean and wrecked it on the rocky reefs of a
desert island called Boredom.

Ever since that time, said the sha'ir, all the Dream boys
and girls have been marooned on that bleak island. (And
you know, he said, how restless children become when subjected to idleness in Boredom.) During the days, the poor
Dreams must endure that monotonous exile from the living world. But every night—al-hamdo-lillah!—the spirit
Storm must wane in power, because the kindlier spirit
Moon has charge of the night. So that is when the Dream
children can most easily escape for a while from their
Boredom. And they do. That is when they leave the island
and go about the world and occupy themselves by entering
the heads of sleeping men and women. That is why, said
the sha'ir, on any night, any sleeper may be entertained or
instructed or warned or frightened by a Dream, depending
on whether that particular Dream on that particular night
is a beneficent little-girl Dream or a mischievous little-boy
Dream, and depending on his or her mood that night.

The listeners all made gratified noises at the tale's conclusion, and fairly showered coins into the old man's bowl.
I tossed in a copper shahi myself, having found the story
amusing—and not incredible, like so many of the more
foolish Eastern myths. I found quite logical the poet's notion of innumerable Dream children of both sexes and mer-
curial temperaments and meddlesome ways. That notion
could even suggest an acceptable explanation of certain
phenomena frequently occurring in the West, and well attested but never before explicable. I mean the dreaded
nighttime visitations of the incubo which seduces otherwise chaste women and the succubo which seduces otherwise chaste priests.

When sundown marked the close of Ramazan, I was at
the back door of the Widow Esther's house, and Sitarè let
me into the kitchen. She and I were its only occupants, and
she seemed in a state of barely suppressed excitement: her
eyes sparkled and her hands fluttered. She was dressed in
what must have been her very best garments, and she had
put al-kohl around her eyelids and berry juice on her lips,
but the pink flush on her cheeks had not come out of a cosmetic jar.

"You are attired for the feast day," I said.

"Yes, but to please you, too. I will not dissemble, Mirza Marco. I said I was glad to be the object of your ardor, and I truly am. Look, I have spread a pallet for us yonder in the corner. And I have made sure that the mistress and the other servants are all occupied elsewhere, so we will not be interrupted. I am frankly eager for our—"

"Now wait," I said, but feebly. "I have acceded to no bargain. You are a beauty to make a man's mouth water, and mine does, but I must know first. What is this favor for which you wish to trade yourself?"

"Indulge me only for a moment, then I will tell you. I should like to set you a riddle beforehand."

"Is this another local custom?"

"Just sit on this bench here. Keep your hands at your sides—hold onto the bench—so you are not tempted to touch me. Now close your eyes. Tight. And keep them closed until I tell you."

I shrugged, and did as I was bidden, and heard her briefly moving about. Then she kissed me on my lips, in a shy and inexpert and maidenly way, but most deliciously, and for a long time. It so stimulated me that I was made quite dizzy. If I had not been holding onto the bench, I might actually have rocked from side to side. I waited for her to speak. Instead, she kissed me again, and as if practice was making her enjoy it more, and for even a longer time. There was another pause, and I waited for another kiss, but now she said, "Open your eyes."

I did, and smiled at her. She was standing directly before me, and the flush of her cheeks had suffused her whole face, and her eyes were bright, and her rosebud lips were merry, and she asked, "Could you tell the kisses apart?"

"Apart? Why, no," I said gallantly. I added, in what I imagined might be the style of a Persian poet, "How can a man say, of equally sweet perfumes or equally intoxicating flavors, that one is better than another? He simply wants more. And I do, I do!"

"And more you shall have. But of me? It was I who kissed you first. Or of Aziz, who kissed you next?"

At that, I did rock upon my bench. Then she reached a hand around behind her and drew him into my view, and I wobbled even more unsteadily.

"He is only a child!"

"He is my little brother Aziz."

No wonder I had failed to notice him among the household servants. He could have been no older than eight or
nine, and was small even for his age. But, once noticed,
Aziz would have been hard to overlook again. Like all the
local boy-children I had seen, he was an Alexandrian Cu-
pid, but even more beautiful than the Kashan standard,
just as his sister was superior to all the other Kashan girls
I had seen. Ìncubo and sùccubo, I thought wildly.

I being still seated on the low bench, my eyes and his
were at the same level. And his blue eyes were clear and
solemn, seeming, in his small face, even bigger and more
luminous than his sister's. His mouth was a rosebud identical to hers. His body was perfectly formed, right down to
his tapering tiny fingers. His hair was the same deep
chestnut-red as his sister's, and his skin the same ivory.
The boy's beauty was further adorned by an application of
al-kohl around the eyelids and berry juice on his lips. I
thought them unnecessary additions, but, before I could
say so, Sitarè spoke.

"Whenever, in my hours off from attendance on the mistress, I am allowed to wear cosmetics"—she talked rapidly,
as if to ward off my saying anything—"I like to do the same
decoration of Aziz." Again forestalling my comment, she
said, "Here, let me show you something, Mirza Marco."
With hurried and fumbling fingers, she undid and took off
the blouse her brother wore. "Being a boy, of course he has
no breasts, but regard his delicately shaped and prominent
nipples." I stared at them, for they were tinted bright red
with hinna. Sitarè said, "Are they not very similar to my
own?" My eyes widened further, for she had whipped off
her own upper garment, and was presenting her hinna-
nippled bosom for my comparison. "See? His get aroused
and erect, just like my own."

Still she chattered on, though I was already incapable of
interrupting. "Also, being a boy, Aziz of course has something I do not have." She undid the string of his pai-jamah,
and let the garment fall to the floor, and knelt beside him.
"Is it not a perfect zab in miniature? And watch, when I
stroke. Just like a little man's. Now look at this." She
turned the boy around, and with her hands spread his dim-
pled pink buttocks apart. "Our mother always was punctilious about using the golulè, and after she died so was I,
and you see the superb result." In another quick move-

ment, and without any maidenly coyness, she let drop her
own pai-jamah. She turned and bent far over, so that I
could observe the under part of her that was not veiled by
dark-red fluff. "Mine is two or three fingers' breadth farther forward, but could you truly distinguish between my
mihrab and his—?"

"Stop this!" I managed at last to say. "You are trying to
importune me into sin with this boy-child!"

She did not deny it, but the boy-child did. Aziz turned to
face me again and spoke for the first time. His voice was
the musical small voice of a songbird, but firm. "No, Mirza
Marco. My sister does not importune, nor do I. Do you
really think I would ever have to?"

Taken aback by the direct question, I had to say, "No."
But then I rallied my Christian principles and said accusingly, "Flaunting is as reprehensible as importuning.
When I was your age, child, I barely knew the *normal* purposes that my parts were for. God forbid I should have
exposed them so consciously and wickedly and—and vul-
nerably. Just standing there like that, you are a sin!"

Aziz looked as hurt as if I had slapped him, and knit his
feathery brows in seeming perplexity. "I am still very
young, Mirza Marco, and perhaps ignorant, for no one has
yet taught me how to be a sin. Only how to be al-fa'il or al-
mafa'ul, as the occasion requires."

I sighed, "Alas, I was again forgetting the local customs." So I momentarily dismissed my principles in favor
of honesty, and said, "As the doer or the done-to, you probably could make a man forget it *is* a sin. And if to you it is
not, then I apologize for castigating you unjustly."

He gave me such a radiant smile that his whole naked
little body seemed to glow in the darkening room.

I added, "I apologize also for having thought other unjust things about you, Aziz, without knowing you. Beyond
a doubt, you are the most bewitchingly beautiful child I
have ever seen, of either sex, and more tantalizing than
many grown women I have seen. You are like one of the
Dream children of whom I have recently heard. You would
be a temptation even to a Christian, in the absence of your
sister here. Alongside *her* desirability, you understand,
you must take only second place."

"I understand," the boy said, still smiling. "And I
agree."

Sitarè, also a figure of glowing alabaster in the twilight, regarded me with some amazement. She breathed almost unbelievingly, "You still want *me?*"

"Very much. So much, indeed, that I am now praying that the favor you desire is something within my power to grant."

"Oh, it is." She picked up her discarded clothes and held them bunched in front of her, that I should not be distracted by her nudity. "We ask only that you take Aziz along in your karwan, and only as far as Mashhad."

I blinked. "Why?"

"You said yourself that you have never seen a more beautiful or more winning child. And Mashhad is a convergence of many trade routes, a place of many opportunities."

"I myself do not much want to go," said Aziz. His nudity was also a distraction, so I picked up his clothes and gave them to him to hold. "I do not wish to leave my sister, who is all the family I have. But she has convinced me that it is for the best."

"Here in Kashan," Sitarè went on, "Aziz is but one of countless pretty boys, all competing for the notice of any anderun purveyor who passes through. At best, Aziz can hope to be chosen by one of those, to become the concubine of some nobleman, who may turn out to be an evil and vicious person. But in Mashhad he could be presented to and appreciated by and acquired by some rich traveling merchant. He may start his life as that man's concubine, but he will have the opportunity to travel, and in time he can hope to learn his master's profession, and he can go on to make something much better of himself than a mere anderun plaything."

Playing was much on my own mind at that moment. I would have been happy to conclude the talking and start doing other things. Nevertheless, I was also at that moment realizing a truth that I think not many journeyers ever do.

We who wander about the world, we pause briefly in this community or that, and to us each is but one flash of vague impression in a long series of such forgettable flashes. The people there are only dim figures looming momentarily out of the dust clouds of the trail. We travelers usually have a destination and a purpose in aiming for it, and

every stop along the way is merely one more milestone in
our progress. But in actuality the people living there had
an existence before we came, and will have after we leave,
and they have their own concerns—hopes and worries and
ambitions and plans—which, being of great moment to
them, might sometimes be worth remarking also by us
passersby. We might learn something worth knowing, or
enjoy a laugh of amusement, or garner a sweet memory
worth treasuring, or sometimes even improve our own
selves, by taking notice of such things. So I paid sympathetic attention to the wistful words and glowing faces of
Sitarè and Aziz, as they spoke of their plans and their ambitions and their hopes. And ever since that time, in all my
journeyings, I have tried always to see in its entirety every
least place I have passed through, and to see its humblest
inhabitants with an unhurried eye.

"So we ask only," said the girl, "that you take Aziz with
you to Mashhad, and that in Mashhad you seek out a
karwan merchant of wealth and kindly nature and other
good qualities. . . ."

"Someone like yourself, Mirza Marco," suggested the
boy.

". . . And sell Aziz to him."

"Sell your brother?" I exclaimed.

"You cannot just take him there and abandon him, a
little boy in a strange city. We would wish you to place him
in the keeping of the best possible master. And, as I said,
you will realize a profit on the transaction. For your trouble of transporting him, and your taking pains to find the
right sort of buyer for him, you may keep the entire
amount you get for him. It ought to be a handsome price for
such a fine boy. Is that not fair enough?"

"More than fair," I said. "It may sway my father and uncle, but I cannot promise. After all, I am just one of three in
our party. I must put the proposition to them."

"That should suffice," said Sitarè. "Our mistress has already spoken to them. The Mirza Esther also wishes to see
young Aziz set upon a better road in life. I understand that
your father and uncle are considering the matter. So, if
you are agreeable to taking Aziz, yours should be the persuading voice."

I said truthfully, "The widow's word probably carries
more weight than mine does. That being so, Sitarè, why

were you prepared to"—I gestured, indicating her state of undress—"to go to such lengths to cajole me?"

"Well . . . ," she said, smiling. She moved aside the clothes she held to give me another unimpeded look at her body. "I hoped you would be *very* agreeable . . ."

Still being truthful, I said, "I would be, anyway. But there are some other aspects you ought to consider. For one thing, we must cross a perilous and uncomfortable desert. It is no fit place for any human being, not to mention a small boy. As is well known, the Devil Satan is most evident and most powerful in the desert wastes. It is into deserts that saintly Christians go, simply to test their strength of faith—and I mean the most sublimely devout Christians, like San Antonio. Unsaintly mortals go there only at great hazard."

"Perhaps so, but they do go," said young Aziz, sounding unperturbed by the prospect. "And since I am not a Christian, I may be in less danger. I may even be some protection for the rest of you."

"We have another non-Christian in the party, " I said sourly. "And that is a thing I would have you also consider. Our camel-puller is a beast, who habitually consorts and couples with the vilest of other beasts. To tempt his bestial nature with a desirable and accessible little boy . . ."

"Ah," said Sitarè. "That must be the objection your father raised. I knew the mistress was concerned about something. Then Aziz must promise to avoid the beast, and you must promise to watch over Aziz."

"I will stay always by your side, Mirza Marco," declared the boy. "By day and by night."

"Aziz may not be chaste, by your standards," his sister went on. "But neither is he promiscuous. As long as he is with you, he will be yours only, not lifting his zab or his buttocks or even his eyes to any other man."

"I will be yours only, Mirza Marco," he affirmed, with what might have been charming innocence, except that he held aside the garments in his hands, as Sitarè had done, to let me look my fill.

"No, no, no," I said, in some agitation. "Aziz, you are to promise not to tempt *any* of us. Our slave is only a beast, but we other three are Christians! You are to be *totally* chaste, from here to Mashhad."

"If that is what you wish," he said, though he appeared crestfallen. "Then I swear it. On the beard of the Prophet (peace and blessing be upon him)."

Skeptical, I asked Sitarè, "Is that oath binding on a beardless child?"

"Indeed it is," she said, regarding me askance. "Your dreary desert journey will not be at all enlivened. You Christians must take some morbid pleasure in the denial of pleasure. But so be it, Aziz, you may put on your clothes again."

"You too, Sitarè," I said, and if Aziz had looked crestfallen, she looked thunderstruck. "I assure you, dear girl, I say that unwillingly, but with the best of will."

"I do not understand. When you take responsibility for my brother, my virginity is worth nothing toward his advancement. So I give it to you, and thankfully."

"And with all thanks I decline it. For a reason I am sure you are aware of, Sitarè. Because, when your brother departs, what becomes of you?"

"What matter? I am only a female person."

"In a person most *beautifully* female. Therefore, once Aziz is provided for, you can offer yourself for your own advancement. A good marriage, or concubinage, or whatever you can attain to. But I know that a woman cannot attain to much unless she is virginally intact. So I will leave you that way."

She and Aziz both stared at me, and the boy murmured, "Verily, Christians are divanè."

"Some, no doubt. Some try to behave as Christians should."

Sitarè's stare turned to a softer look, and she said in a soft voice, "Perhaps some few succeed." But again, provocatively, she moved the screening clothes aside from her fair body. "You are sure you decline? You are steadfast in your kindly resolve?"

I laughed shakily. "Not at all steadfast. For that reason, let me go quickly from here. I will consult with my father and uncle about taking Aziz with us."

The consultation did not take long, for they were in the stable talking it over at that very time.

"So there," said Uncle Mafìo to my father. "Marco is also in favor of letting the boy come along. That makes two of us voting yes, against one vote wavering."

My father frowned and tangled his fingers into his beard.

"We will be doing a good deed," I said.

"How can we refuse to do a good deed?" demanded my uncle.

My father growled an old saying, "Saint Charity is dead and her daughter Clemency is ailing."

My uncle retorted with another, "Cease believing in the saints and they will cease doing miracles."

They then looked at each other in a silence of impasse, until I ventured to break it.

"I have already warned the lad about the likelihood of his being molested." They both swiveled their gaze to me, looking astonished. "You know," I mumbled uncomfortably, "Nostril's propensities for, er, making mischief."

"Oh, that," said my father. "Yes, there is that."

I was glad that he seemed not unduly concerned about it, for I did not wish to be the one to tell of Nostril's most recent indecency, and probably earn the slave a belated beating.

"I made Aziz promise," I said, "to be wary of any suspicious advances. And I have promised to watch over him. As for his transportation, the pack camel is not at all heavily laden, and the boy weighs very little. His sister offered to let us pocket whatever money we can sell him for, which should be a substantial amount. But I rather think we ought merely to subtract from it the cost of his keep, and let the boy have the rest. As a sort of legacy, to start his new life with."

"So there!" said Uncle Mafìo again, scratching at his elbow. "The lad has a mount to ride and a guardian to protect him. He is paying his own way to Mashhad, and earning himself a dowry as well. There can be no further possible objection."

My father said solemnly, "If we take him, Marco, he will be your responsibility. You guarantee to keep the child from harm?"

"Yes, Father," I said, and put my hand significantly on my belt knife. "Any harm must take me before it takes him."

"You hear, Mafìo."

I perceived that I must be making a weighty vow indeed,

since my father was commanding my uncle to bear witness.

"I hear, Nico."

My father sighed, looked from one to the other of us, clawed in his beard some more, and finally said, "Then he comes with us. Go, Marco, and tell him so. Tell his sister and the Widow Esther to pack whatever belongings Aziz is to take."

So Sitarè and I took the opportunity for a flurry of kisses and caresses, and the last thing she said to me was, "I will not forget, Mirza Marco. I will not forget you, or your kindness to us both, or your consideration of my fortunes hereafter. I should very much like to reward you—and with that which you have so gallantly forgone. If ever you should journey this way again . . ."

4

WE had been told that we were crossing the Dasht-e-Kavir at the best time of the year. I should hate to have to cross it at the worst. We did it in the late autumn, when the sun was not infernally hot, but, even without incident, that would by no means have been a pleasant trip. I had hitherto supposed that a long sea voyage was the most unvarying and boring and interminable and monotonous sort of travel possible, at least when not made terrible by storm. But a desert crossing is all of that, and besides is thirsty, itchy, scratchy, rasping, scraping, parching—the list of hateful adjectives could go on and on. And the list does go on, like a chant of curses, through the morose mind of the desert journeyer, as he endlessly trudges from one featureless horizon across a featureless flat surface toward the featureless skyline ever receding ahead of him.

When we left Kashan, we were again dressed for hard traveling. No longer did we wear the neat Persian tulbands on our heads and the gorgeously embroidered body garments. We were again loosely enwrapped in the Arabs' hanging kaffiyah headcloths and ample aba cloaks, that less handsome but more practical attire which does not cling about a person but billows free, so it allows the dissi-

pation of body heat and sweat, and affords no folds in
which the drifting sand can accumulate. Our camels were
hung all about with leather bags of good Kashan water
and sacks of dried mutton and fruits and the brittle local
bread. (It was to procure these foodstuffs that we had had
to wait for the bazàr to restock after Ramazan.) We had
also acquired in Kashan some new items to carry with us:
smooth round sticks and lengths of light fabric with their
hems sewn to form sheaths. By inserting the sticks into
those sheaths, we could quickly shape the cloths into tents,
each just of a size to shelter one man comfortably, or if necessary, to accommodate two persons in rather less comfortable intimacy.

Before we even got out of Kashan, I warned Aziz never
to let our slave Nostril tempt him inside a tent or anywhere else out of sight of the rest of us, and to report to me
any other sorts of advances the camel-puller might make
to him. For Nostril, on first seeing the boy among us, had
widened his piggy eyes almost to human size and dilated
his single nostril as if he scented prey. That first day, also,
Aziz had been briefly naked in our company—and Nostril
had hung about, ogling—while I helped the boy doff the
Persian garb his sister had dressed him in, and showed
him how to put on the Arab kaffiyah and aba. So I gave
Nostril some stern warnings, too, and toyed significantly
with my belt knife while I was haranguing him, and he
made insincere promises of obedience and good behavior.

I would hardly have trusted Nostril's promises, but, as
things turned out, he never did molest the little boy, or
even try to. We were not many days into the desert when
Nostril began noticeably to suffer from some painful ailment in his under parts. If, as I suspected, the slave had deliberately made one of the camels lame to make us stop in
Kashan, then another of the beasts was now exacting revenge. Every time Nostril's camel made a misstep and
jounced him, he would cry out sharply. Soon he had his
saddle pillowed with everything soft he could find among
our packs. But then, every time he went away from our
camp fire to make water, we could hear him groaning and
thrashing about and cursing vehemently.

"One of the Kashan boys must have clapped him with
the scolamento," said Uncle Mafìo derisively. "Serves him
right, for being unvirtuous—and indiscriminate."

I had not then and indeed never have been similarly afflicted myself, for which I give more thanks to my good fortune than to my virtue or my discrimination. Nevertheless, I might have shown more comradely sympathy to Nostril, and laughed less at his predicament, if I had not been thankful that his zab was giving him other concerns than trying to put it into my young ward. The slave's ailment gradually abated and finally went away, leaving him apparently no worse for the experience, but by that time other events had occurred to put Aziz beyond threat of his lechery.

A tent, or some shelter like a tent, is an absolute necessity in the Dasht-e-Kavir, for a man cannot just lie down in his blankets to sleep, or he would be covered by sand before he woke. Most of that desert can be likened to the giant tray of a giant fardarbab tomorrow-teller. It is a flat expanse of smooth, dun-colored sand, a sand so fine that it flows through one's fingers like water. In the intervals between winds, that sand lies as virginally unmarked as the sand in the tomorrow-teller's tray. So fine and so smooth is it that the least passing insect—a centipede, a grasshopper, a scorpion—leaves a trail visible from afar. A man could, if he got bored enough by the tedium of desert traveling, find distraction by following the meandering track of a single ant.

However, in the daytime, it was seldom that a wind was not blowing, stirring that sand and picking it up and carrying it and throwing it. Since the winds of the Dasht-e-Kavir blow always from the same direction, from the southwest, it is easy to tell in which direction a stranger is traveling—even if you meet him camped and immobile— simply by seeing which flank of his mount is the most heavily coated with blown sand. In the nighttime, the desert wind drops, and lets drop from the air the heavier particles of sand. But the finer particles hang in the air like dust, and hang there so densely as to constitute a dry fog. It blots out whatever stars there may be in the sky, sometimes obscures even a full moon. In the combined darkness and fogginess, one's vision may be limited to just a few arm-lengths. Nostril told us that there were creatures called Karauna which took advantage of that dark fog—according to Persian folk legend the Karauna create it, said Nostril, by some dark magic—in which to do dark deeds. More usually, the chief danger of that fog is that the suspended dust sifts imperceptibly down from the air during the stillness of night, and a traveler not sheltered under a tent could be quietly, stealthily buried and smothered to death in his sleep.

We had still the greater part of Persia to cross, but it was the empty part—perhaps the emptiest part of the entire world—and we did not meet a single Persian along our way, or much of anything else, or see in the sand the tracks of anything larger than insects. In other regions of Persia, similarly unoccupied and uncultivated by man, we journeyers might have had to be on our guard against predatory prides of lions, or scavenging packs of shaqàl dogs, or even flocks of the big flightless shuturmurq camel-birds, which, we had been told, can disembowel a man with a kick. But none of those hazards had to be feared in the desert, for no wild thing lives in it. We saw an occasional vulture or kite, but they stayed high in the windy sky above and did not tarry in their passing. Even vegetable plants seem to shun that desert. The only green thing I saw growing there was a low shrub with thick and fleshy-looking leaves.

"Euphorbia," Nostril said it was. "And it grows here only because Allah put it here to be a help to the journeyer. In the hot season, the euphorbia's seed pods grow ripe and burst and fling out their seeds. They begin to pop when the desert air gets exactly as hot as a human's blood. Then the pods burst with increasing frequency as the air gets even hotter. So a desert wanderer can tell, by listening to the loudness of the popping of the euphorbia, when the air is getting so perilously hot that he *must* stop and put up a shelter for shade, or he will die."

That slave, for all his squalid person and sexual erethism and detestable character, was an experienced traveler, and told us or showed us many things of use or interest. For example, on our very first night in that wasteland, when we stopped to camp, he got down from his camel and stuck his prodding pole into the sand, pointed in the direction we were going.

"It may be needful in the morning," he explained. "We have determined to go always toward the spot where the sun rises. But if the sand is blowing at that hour, we may not be able otherwise to fix on the spot."

The treacherous sands of the Dasht-e-Kavir are not its only menace to man. That name, as I have said, means the Great Salt Desert, and for a reason. Vast extents of it are not of sand at all; they are immense reaches of a salty paste, not quite wet enough to be called mud or marsh, and the wind and sun have dried the paste to a surface of caked solid salt. Often a traveler must cross one of those glittering, crunching, quivering, blindingly white salt crusts, and he must do it gingerly. The salt crystals are more abrasive than sand; even a camel's callused pads can quickly be worn to bleeding rawness, and, if the rider has to dismount, his boots can be likewise shredded, and then his feet. Also, the salt surfaces are of uneven thickness, making of those areas what Nostril called "the trembling lands." Sometimes the weight of a camel or a man will break through the crust. If that happens, the animal or the man falls into the pasty muck beneath. From that salt quicksand it is impossible to climb out unaided, or even to stay put and wait for help to come. It slowly but ineluctably draws down whatever falls into it, and sucks the fallen creature under the surface, and closes over it. Unless a rescuer is nearby, and on firmer ground, the unfortunate fallen one is doomed. According to Nostril, entire karwan trains of men and animals have thus disappeared and left no trace.

So, when we came to the first of those salt flats, though it looked as innocuous as a layer of hoarfrost unseasonably on the ground, we halted and studied it with respect. The white crust gleamed out before us, clear to the skyline, and away as far as we could see to either side.

"We could try going around," said my father.

"The maps of the Kitab show no such details as this," said my uncle, scratching meditatively at his elbow. "We have no way of knowing its extent, or of guessing whether a north or a south detour would be shorter."

"And if we are going to skirt every one of these," said Nostril, "we will be in this desert forever."

I said nothing, being totally ignorant of desert travel, and not ashamed to leave the decisions to the more expert. So we four sat our camels and looked out over the sparkling waste. But the boy Aziz, behind us, prodded his pack camel and made it kneel, and he dismounted. We did not notice what he was doing until he walked out from among us and walked onto the salt crust. He turned and looked up at us, and smiled prettily, and said in his little bird voice:

"Now I can repay your kindness in bringing me along. I shall walk ahead, and I can tell from the trembling underfoot how strong is the surface. I will keep to the firmest ground, and you have only to follow."

"You will cut your feet!" I protested.

"No, Mirza Marco, for I am of light weight. Also, I took the liberty of extracting these plates from the packs." He held up two of the golden dishes the Shah Zaman had sent. "I shall strap them under my boots as an extra protection."

"It is dangerous nonetheless," said my uncle. "You are brave to volunteer, lad, but we have sworn that no harm must come to you. Better one of us—"

"No, Mirza Mafìo," said Aziz, still staunchly. "If by chance I should fall through, it would be easier for you to pluck me out than any larger person."

"He is right, masters," said Nostril. "The child has good sense. And, as you remark, a good heart for courage and initiative."

So we let Aziz precede us, and we followed at a discreet distance. It was slow going, keeping to his shuffle pace, but that made the walking less painful for the camels. And we did cross that trembling land in safety, and before nightfall had come to an area of more trustworthy sand on which to camp.

Only once that day did Aziz misjudge the crust. With a sharp crackle, it broke like a sheet of glass, and he plummeted waist-deep into the muck under it. He did not exclaim in fright when it happened, nor did he make so much as a whimper during the time it took for Uncle Mafìo to get down from his camel and make a loop in his saddle rope and cast it over the boy and draw him gently back above ground and onto a firmer place. But Aziz had known very well that he was, for that while, precariously suspended over a bottomless abyss, for his face was very pale and his blue eyes very big when we all clustered solicitously around him. Uncle Mafìo embraced the boy and held him, murmuring inspiriting words, while my father and I brushed the fast-drying salt mud from his garments. By the time that was done, the boy's courage had returned, and he insisted on going ahead again, to the admiration of us all.

In the days thereafter, each time we again came upon a salt flat, we could do no more than make guesses or take a vote to determine whether we should venture upon it at once, or camp there at its near edge and wait to start upon it early the next morning. We were always apprehensive that we might find ourselves still in the middle of a trembling land at nightfall, and therefore have to take one of two equally unappealing alternatives: try to press on, braving the night's dark and its dry fog, which could be much more nerve-racking than making such a crossing by day; or camp upon the salt flat and have to do without a fire, for we feared that laying a fire upon such a surface might melt it, and drop ourselves, our animals and all our packs into the quicksand. Surely it was only through good fortune—or Allah's blessing, as our two Muslims would have put it—certainly not through any wisdom informing our guesses, but each time we guessed right, and each time got across the salt to safe sand by nightfall.

So we never had to make a cold camp on the dreaded trembling lands, but making camp anywhere in that desert, even on the sand which we could trust not to dissolve from under us, was no holiday treat. Sand, if you look closely enough at it, is nothing but an infinite multitude of little tiny rocks. Rocks do not hold heat, and no more does sand. The desert days were comfortable enough, even warm, but when the sun went down the nights were cold, and the sand under us even colder. We always needed a fire just to keep us warm until we crawled into our blankets inside our tents. But many nights were so very cold that we would rake the fire into five separate fires, well apart, and let them burn a while to warm those separate plots of sand, and only then spread our blankets and raise our tents on top of the warmed places. Even so, the sand did not for long hold that heat either, and by morning we would be chilled and stiff, in which unjoyous condition we would have to rise and face another day of the joyless desert.

The nightly camp fires served for warmth, and for some illusion of homelikeness in the middle of that empty, lonely, silent, dark wasteland, but they were not much use for cookery. Wood being nonexistent in the Dasht-e-Kavir, we used dried animal dung for fuel. The animals of countless generations of earlier desert crossers had dropped easily found supplies of it, and our own camels contributed their deposits for the benefit of future wayfarers. Our only comestibles, however, were several varieties of dried meats and fruits. A hunk of cold dry mutton might be rendered more palatable by soaking it and then broiling it over a fire, but *not* over a fire built of camel dung. Though we ourselves already reeked of the smoke of those fires, we could not bring ourselves to eat something similarly impregnated. When we felt we could spare the water, we sometimes heated it and steeped our meat in it, but that did not make a very tasty dish either. When water has been carried for a long time in a hide bag, it begins to look and smell and taste rather like the water a man carries in his bladder. We had to drink it to survive, but we less and less desired to cook our foods in it, preferring to gnaw them dry and cold.

Each night we also fed the camels—a double handful of dried peas apiece, and then a fair drink of water to make the peas swell inside their bellies and simulate a hearty meal. I will not say the beasts enjoyed those scant rations, but then camels have never been known to enjoy anything. They would not have muttered and grumbled less if we had been feeding them banquets of delicacies, and they would not, out of gratitude, have performed any better at their labors the next day.

If I sound unloving of camels, it is because I am. I think I have straddled or perched upon every sort of transport animal there is in the world, and I would prefer any other to a camel. I grant that the two-humped camel of the colder lands of the East is somewhat more intelligent and tractable than the single-humped camel of the warm lands. And that lends some credibility to the belief of some people that the camel's brains are in its hump, if it has any anywhere. A camel whose hump has diminished from thirst and starvation is even more sullen, irritable and unmanageable than a well-fed camel, but not much more.

The camels had to be unloaded each night, as would any other karwan animals, but no other animals would have been so maddeningly difficult to reload in the morning. The camels would bawl and back away and roar and prance about and, when those tricks only exasperated but did not dissuade us, they would spit on us. Also, once on the trail, no other animals are so devoid of a sense of direction, or self-preservation. Our camels would have walked indifferently, and one after another, into every quicksand hole in those salt flats if we riders or our puller had not taken pains to steer them around. Camels are also, more than any other animals, devoid of a sense of balance. A camel, like a man, can lift and carry about one-third of its own weight for a whole day and a goodly distance. But a man, with only two legs, is not so teetery as a camel with four. One or another of ours would frequently slip in the sand, even more often on the salt, and grotesquely collapse sideways, and be impossible to raise again until it was entirely unloaded and loudly encouraged and powerfully assisted by our combined strength. At which it would give thanks by spitting on us.

I have used the word "spit" because, even back home in Venice, I had heard far-travelers speak of camels doing that, but in fact they do not. I wish they did. What they actually do is to hawk up from their nethermost cud an awfulness of regurgitated matter to spew. In the case of our camels, that was a substance compounded of peas first dried, then eaten, then soaked and swollen and made gaseous, then half-digested and half-fermented, then—at that substance's peak of noxiousness—churned together with stomach juices, vomited up, collected in the camel's mouth, aimed through pouted lips and ejected with all possible force at some one of us, and preferably into his eye.

There is of course no such thing as a karwansarai anywhere in the Dasht-e-Kavir, but on two occasions in the month or more that it took us to cross it, we had the blessedly good fortune to come upon an oasis. This is a spring which wells up from underground, only God or Allah knows why. Its waters are fresh, not salt, and around it has sprung up an area of vegetation, several zonte in extent. I never could discover anything edible growing there, but the very greenness of the scrub trees and stunted bushes and sparse grass was a refreshment as welcome as fresh fruit or vegetables. On both those occasions, we were pleased to halt our journey for a while before moving on. During that time, we dipped up water from the spring to bathe our dust-coated and salt-encrusted and dung-smoke-smelling bodies, and water to fill the camels' bowel tanks, and water to be boiled—and sieved through the charcoal my father always carried—to flush out and refill our water bags. Those labors done, we just lay about to enjoy the novel sensation of resting in a green shade.

I noticed, at the first oasis halt, how we all soon separated and drew apart and found separate shade trees under which to loll, and later put up our individual tents at a considerable distance from each other. None of us had recently quarreled, and we had no definable reason for shunning each other's company—except that for so long we *had been* in each other's company, and now it was pleasant to have some privacy for a change. I might have kept Aziz protectively close to me, but the slave Nostril was at that time all too plainly preoccupied with his shameful private affliction, and I deemed him incapable of molesting the little boy. So I let Aziz also go off to be by himself.

Or so I thought. But, after we had been luxuriating in the oasis for a day and a night, I took a notion on the succeeding night to go for a stroll through the surrounding grove. I pretended that I was in a less constricted garden, perhaps the environs of the Baghdad palace, where I had walked so often with the Princess Moth. It was easy enough to pretend, for that night had brought the dry fog, making it impossible for me to see anything but the trees closest about me. Even sounds were muffled by that fog, so I must have been almost stepping on Aziz when I heard him laugh his musical laugh and say:

"Harm? But *that* is no harm to me. Or to anybody. Let us do it."

A deeper voice responded, but in a murmur, so its words were indistinguishable. I was about to shout in outrage, and seize Nostril and drag him off the boy, but Aziz spoke again, and in a voice of marveling:

"I never saw one like that before. With a sheath of skin that encloses it . . ."

I stood where I was, unmoving, stupefied.

". . . Or can be pulled back at will." Aziz still sounded awed. "Why, it is like having your own private mihrab always tenderly enveloping your zab."

Nostril possessed no such apparatus. He was a Muslim, and circumcised, like the boy. I began to back away from that place, being careful to make no noise.

"It must make for a blissful sensation, even without a

partner," the little bird voice went on, "when you move
the sheath back and forth like that. May I do it for
you . . . ?"

The fog closed around his voice, as I got farther away.
But I was waiting, awake and watchful outside his tent,
when he eventually returned to it. He came like a stray
moonbeam out of the darkness, radiant, for he was entirely
naked and carrying his clothes.

"Look at you!" I said sternly, but keeping my voice low.
"I swore a binding oath that no harm would come to you—"

"None has, Mirza Marco," he said, blinking, all innocence.

"And you swore on the Prophet's beard not to tempt any
of us—"

"I have not, Mirza Marco," he said, looking hurt. "I was
fully dressed when he and I chanced to meet in the grove
yonder."

"And to be totally chaste!"

"And I have been, Mirza Marco, all the way from Kashan. No one has penetrated me, and I no one. All we did
was kiss." He came close and sweetly kissed me. "And
this . . ." He demonstrated, and after a moment insinuated his little self into my hand, and breathed, "To each
other we did it . . ."

"Enough!" I said hoarsely. I let go of him and put his
hand away from me. "Go to sleep now, Aziz. We ride again
at sunrise."

I myself did not get to sleep that night until I acknowledged the excitement Aziz had raised in me, and manually
relieved myself of it. But my sleeplessness was also partly
on account of my new view of my uncle, and the disillusionment it caused me, and the tinge of disdain that now
colored my feelings toward him. It was no trivial disappointment, to have learned that Uncle Mafio's bold, bluff,
black-bearded and hearty aspect was a mask he wore, and
that behind it he was only a simpering and sly and despicable Sodomite.

I knew I was no saint, and I tried hard not to be a hypo-
crite. I could frankly admit that I, too, was susceptible to
the charms of the boy Aziz. But that was because he was
here, near at hand, and no woman was, and he was as
comely and seductive as a woman, and he was freely amenable to being used as a substitute for a woman. But Uncle

Mafìo, I now realized, must see him differently; he must see Aziz as an available and beautiful and beddable *boy*.

I recalled previous events involving other males: hammam rubbers, for instance—and previous words spoken: that furtive exchange between my father and the Widow Esther, for instance. The inference was unavoidable: Uncle Mafìo was a lover of persons of his own sex. A man of that bent was no curiosity here in the Muslim lands, where almost every male seemed similarly warped. But I knew very well that, in our more civilized West, his kind was laughed at and sneered at and cursed at. I suspected that the same situation must obtain in the totally uncivilized nations farther east. At any rate, it appeared that *somewhere* my uncle's depravity had caused problems in the past. I gathered that my father had already had reason to try breaking his brother of his perversion, and Mafìo himself had apparently made some attempt to suppress the urges. If that was so, I reflected, then he was not entirely detestable, and perhaps there was hope for him.

Very well. I would lend my own best efforts to help his reformation and redemption. When we rode on, I would not ride reproachfully far apart from him, or avoid his eye, or refuse to speak to him. I would say nothing of what had occurred. I would give no hint that I was privy to his shameful secret. What I *would* do was resume keeping a close watch on Aziz, and not again let the child run at liberty under cover of night. Especially would I be paternally careful and strict if we should come upon another green oasis. In such a place, there was a tendency to let discipline lapse, and self-restraints, just as we let our weary muscles relax. If we again found ourselves in that ambience of comparative ease and abandon, my uncle might find the temptation irresistible: to enjoy more of Aziz than he had already sampled.

The next day, as we proceeded once more northeastward into the ungreen wasteland, I was as affable as usual to all in the party, Uncle Mafìo included, and I think no one could have discerned my inner feelings. Nevertheless, I was glad that the burden of conversation that day was taken by the slave Nostril. Possibly to get his own mind off his own problems, he began expatiating on one subject, then veered onto others, and I, at least, was content to ride silent and listen and let him ramble.

What started him off was that, during our loading of the
camels, he had found a small snake coiled asleep in one of
our pack hampers. He had let out a screech at first, but
then he said, "We must have brought the poor thing all the
way from Kashan," and, instead of killing the thing, he
had tipped it out onto the sand and let it slither away. As
we rode, he told us why.

"We Muslims do not abhor and loathe serpents as you
Christians do. Oh, we are not particularly fond of them,
but neither do we fear and hate them as you do. According
to your Holy Bible, the snake is the incarnation of the
Devil Satan. And in your legends, you have inflated the
snake to the monster called a dragon. All our Muslim monsters take the form of human beings—the jinn and afarit
—or a bird, in the case of the giant rukh, or combinations
like the mardkhora. That is a monster comprising the
head of a man, the body of a lion, the quills of a procupine
and the tail of a scorpion. Notice, there is no snake included."

My father said mildly, "The serpent has been accursed
ever since that unfortunate affair in the Garden of Eden. It
is understandable that Christians should fear it, and right
that they should hate it and kill it at every opportunity."

"We Muslims," said Nostril, "give credit where credit is
due. It was the serpent of Eden who bequeathed to Arabs
the Arabic language, for he contrived that language in
which to speak to Eve and seduce her, because Arabic, as
every man knows, is the most subtle and suasive of languages. Of course, Adam and Eve spoke Farsi when they
were alone together, for the Persian Farsi is the loveliest
of all languages. And the avenging angel Gabriel always
speaks Turki, for that is the most menacing of all languages. However, that is by the way. I was speaking of serpents, and it must be obvious that it was the snake's
sinuosity and convolutions which inspired the writing of
characters, the Arabic alphabet which is also employed for
the transcription of Farsi, Turki, Sindi and all other civilized languages."

My father spoke again. "We Westerners have always
called it the fish-worm writing, and never knew how
nearly right we were."

"And the serpent gave us more than that, Master Nicolò. His mode of progression along the ground, by bending and straightening himself—that inspired some ingenious one of our ancestors to invent the bow and arrow. The bow is thin and sinuous, like a snake. The arrow is thin and straight, like a snake, and it has a killing head. We have good reason to honor the serpent, and we do. For example, we call the rainbow the celestial snake, and that is a compliment to them both."

"Interesting," my father murmured, with a tolerant smile.

"By contrast," Nostril went on, "you Christians liken the snake to your own zab, and assert that the serpent of Eden introduced sexual pleasure into the world, and that therefore sexual pleasure is wrong and ugly and abominable. We Muslims put the blame where it belongs. Not on the inoffensive snake, but on Eve and all her female descendants. As the Quran says in the fourth sura, 'Woman is the source of all evil on the earth, and Allah only made this monster that the man should be repelled, and turn away from earthly—'"

"Ciacche-ciacche!" said my uncle.

"Pardon, master?"

"I said *nonsense!* Sciocchezze! Sottise! Bifam ishtibah!"

Looking shocked, Nostril exclaimed, "Master Mafìo, you call the Holy Book a bifam ishtibah?"

"Your Quran was written by a man, you cannot deny it. So were the Talmud and the Bible written by men."

"Come now, Mafìo," my pious father put in. "They only transcribed the words of God. And the Savior."

"But they were men, indisputably men, with the minds of men. All the prophets and apostles and sages have been men. And what sort of men did the writing of the holy books? Circumcised men!"

"I beg to suggest, master," said Nostril, "that they did not write with their—"

"In a sense, they did exactly that. All those men were religiously mutilated in their infant organs. When they grew to manhood, they found themselves diminished in their sexual pleasure, to the degree they had been diminished in their parts. *That* is why they made their holy books decree that sex should be not for delight, but solely for procreation, and in all other respects a matter for shame and guilt."

"Good master," Nostril persisted. "We are only divested of foreskin, we are not pruned to eunuchs."

"Any mutilation is a deprivation," Uncle Mafìo retorted. He dropped his camel's rein to scratch his elbow. "The sages of ancient days, realizing that the trimming of their members had blunted their sensations and their enjoyment, were envious and fearful that others might find more pleasure in sex. Misery loves company, so they wrote their scriptures in a way to ensure that they had company. First the Jews, then the Christians—for the Evangelists and the other early Christians were only converted Jews—and then Muhammad and the subsequent Muslim sages. All of those having been circumcised men, their disquisitions on the subject of sex are akin to the singing of the deaf."

My father looked as shocked as Nostril did. "Mafìo," he cautioned, "on this open desert we are terribly exposed to thunderbolts. Your criticism is a novel one in my experience, perhaps even original, but I suggest you temper it with discretion."

Unheeding, my uncle went on, "Their putting fetters on human sexuality was like cripples writing the rules for an athletic contest."

"Cripples, master?" Nostril inquired. "But how could they have known they were cripples? You contend that my sensations have been blunted. Since I myself have no exterior standard alongside which to measure my own enjoyments, I wonder how anyone else could possibly do so. I can think of only one sort who might qualify to judge even himself. That would be a man who has had experience, so to speak, before and after. Excuse my impertinence, Master Mafìo, but were you perhaps not circumcised until midway in your adult life?"

"Insolent infidel! I never have been!"

"Ah. Then, excepting such a man, it seems to me that no one could adjudicate the matter but a *woman*. A woman who has given joy to both sorts of men, the circumcised and the uncircumcised, and paid close heed to their comparative heights of enjoyment."

I winced at that. Whether Nostril spoke in snide malice or sheer ingenuousness, his words hit very close to Uncle Mafìo's true nature and probable experience. I glanced at my uncle, fearing he would blush or bluster or maybe knock Nostril's head off, and thereby confess what he had so far kept concealed. But he bore the seeming insinuation as if he had not noticed it, and only continued to muse aloud:

"If the choice were mine, I should seek out a religion whose scriptures were not written by men already ritually maimed in their manhood."

"Where we are going," my father remarked, "there are several such religions."

"As I well know," said my uncle. "That is what makes me wonder how we Christians and Jews and Muslims dare to speak of the more Eastern peoples as barbarians."

My father said, "The traveled man can look with a pitying smile at the crude pebbles still treasured by his home folk, yes, for he has seen real rubies and pearls in far places. Whether that also holds true for the home-kept religions, I cannot say, not being a theologian." He added, rather sharply for him, "But this I do know: we are at present still under the Heaven of those religions you so openly disprize, and vulnerable to heavenly rebuke. If your blasphemies provoke a whirlwind, we may not get any farther. I strongly recommend a change of subject."

Nostril obliged. He reverted to his earlier topic and told us, at stupefying length, how each letter of the Arabic fishworm writing is permeated by a certain specific emanation from Allah, and therefore, as the letters squirm into the shape of words and the words into reptilian sentences, any piece of Arabic writing—even something as mundane as a signpost or a landlord's bill—contains a beneficent power which is greater than the sum of the individual characters, and therefore is efficacious as a talisman against evil and jinn and afarit and the Devil Shaitan . . . and so on and on. To which the only rejoinder was made by one of our bull camels. He unfurled his underworks as he strode along, and copiously made water.

5

WELL, we did not get annihilated by any thunderbolt or whirlwind, and I cannot recall that anything else of significance happened on that journey until, as I have remarked, we did come to a second green oasis in that dun dreariness, and again made camp, intending to luxuriate there for two or even three days. In keeping with my resolve, I did not this time let Aziz out of my arm's reach while we drank our fill of the good water and watered the camels and topped up our water bags and—especially—while we bathed our bodies and laundered our clothes, during which time he and all the rest of us were necessarily naked. And when again we were disposed to pitch our tents privily apart from each other, I made sure that his and mine were side by side.

We did, however, all cluster together around the camp fire for our evening meal. And I recollect, as if it were yesterday, every trivial incident of that night. Aziz took his seat across the fire from me and Nostril, and first my uncle sat companionably close beside him, and then my father plumped down on his other side. While we gnawed gristly mutton and munched moldy cheese and dipped shriveled jujubes into our water cups to soften them, my uncle gave arch sidewise looks at the boy, and I and my father cast wary looks at both of them. Apparently unaware of any tension in the group, Nostril casually remarked to me:

"You are beginning to look like a real journeyer, Master Marco."

He was referring to my new-grown beard. In the desert, no man would be fool enough to waste water on shaving, or vain enough to endure a lather that must get mixed with abrasive sand and salt. My own beard was by then of a manly density, and I had ceased even to use the easy depilatory of the mumum salve, letting the beard grow as a protection for the skin of my face. I took only the trouble to keep it clipped to a tidy and comfortable shortness, and I have worn it so ever since.

"Now you may realize," Nostril chatted on, "how merciful it was of Allah to give whiskers to men, but not to women."

I thought about that. "It is clearly good that men have beards, for they may have to go into the scouring desert sands. But why is it a mercy that women have them not?"

The camel-puller raised up his hands and his eyes, as if in consternation at my ignorance. But before he could reply, little Aziz laughed and said:

"Oh, let me tell him! Think, Mirza Marco! Was it not considerate of the Creator? He did not put a beard upon that creature who could never keep it shaven clean or even trimmed to neatness, because *her jaw waggles so!*"

I laughed, too, and so did my father and uncle, and I remarked, "If that is the reason, then I am glad for it. I would recoil from a whiskered woman. But would it not have been wiser of the Creator to create females less inclined to wag the jaw?"

"Ah," said my father, the proverbialist. "Wherever there are pots, they will rattle."

"Mirza Marco, here is another riddle for you, Mirza Marco!" chirruped Aziz, merrily bouncing where he sat. The boy was admittedly a soiled angel, and in many respects more worldly-wise than any adult Christian, but he was, after all, still a child. His words almost tumbled over each other, he was so eager to get them out. "There are few animals in this desert. But there is one to be found here which unites in itself the natures of *seven different beasts.* What is it, then, Marco?"

I knit my brow and pretended to think ponderously, and then said, "I give it up."

Aziz crowed with triumphant laughter, and opened his mouth to speak. But then his mouth opened wider, and his big eyes got bigger. So did the eyes and mouths of my father and uncle. Nostril and I had to spin about to see what they were staring at.

Three shaggy brown men had materialized out of the night's dry fog, and were regarding us with slit eyes in expressionless faces. They wore skins and leathers, not Arab garments, and they must have ridden far and fast, for they were coated with dust caked by perspiration, and they stank even from the distance where they stood.

"Sain bina," said my uncle, the first to recover from his surprise, and he slowly got to his feet.

"Mendu, sain bina," said one of the strangers, looking faintly surprised himself.

My father also stood up, and he and Uncle Mafìo made gestures of welcome, and they went on speaking to the intruders in a language I did not comprehend. The shaggy men drew three horses by their reins out of the fog behind them, and led the animals to the spring. Not until the horses had been watered did the men take a drink.

Nostril, Aziz and I got up from the fire, and let the strangers take our places. My father and uncle sat down with them, and got out food from our packs and offered it, and continued sitting and talking while the visitors ate voraciously. I scrutinized the newcome three as well as I could while standing discreetly apart from the confabulation. They were of short but sturdy stature. Their faces were the color and texture of tanned kid leather, and two of them had long but wispy mustaches; none wore a beard. Their coarse black hair was womanly long, and plaited into numerous braids. Their eyes, I repeat, were mere slits, so very narrowly slitted that I wondered how they could see out of them. Each man carried a short and sharply curved-and-recurved bow slung on his back, with its bowstring across his chest, and a quiver of short arrows for it, and at his waist what was either a short sword or a long knife.

I recognized, now, that the men were Mongols, for I had seen the occasional Mongol by this time, and this land was, although nominally Persia, a province of the Mongol Khanate. But why were three Mongols prowling out here in the wilderness? They did not seem to be bandits or to mean us any harm—or at least my father and uncle had quickly talked them out of any such notìon. And why were they in such an apparent hurry? In the everlasting desert, no man hurries.

But these men stayed in the oasis only long enough to eat to repletion. And they might not have halted for even that long, except that our foodstuffs, unappealing though they were, must have seemed real viands and delicacies to the Mongols, for these men carried no traveling rations at all except strips of jerked horsemeat like rawhide bootlaces. My father and uncle, to judge from their gesturings, were cordially and almost insistently inviting the newcomers to rest for a while, but the Mongols only shook their shaggy heads and grunted as they devoured mutton and cheese and fruits. Then they rose, belched appreciatively, gathered up the reins of their horses and remounted.

The horses rather resembled the men, being exceptionally shaggy and wild-looking and almost as small as the hinna'ed horses of Baghdad, but much more stocky and muscular. They were crusted with dried foam and dust, from having been hard ridden, but they acted as eager as their riders to be off and going again. One of the Mongols, from his saddle, jabbered to my father a lengthy speech that sounded monitory. Then they all tugged their mounts' heads around, and cantered off southwestward, and almost instantly they were gone from our sight into the foggy dark, and the creak and jingle of their arms and harness was as instantly gone from our hearing.

"That was a military patrol," my father made haste to tell us, perceiving that Nostril and Aziz looked quite frightened. "It seems that some bandits have lately been, er, active in this desert, and the Ilkhan Abagha desires to have them brought quickly to justice. Mafìo and I, being naturally concerned for the safety of us all, tried to persuade them to stay and guard us, or even to travel for a time in our company. But they prefer to keep on the trail of the bandits, and press them hard, hoping to wear them down by thirst and hunger."

Nostril cleared his throat and said, "Excuse me, Master Nicolò. I would of course never eavesdrop on a master, but I heard some of the conversation. Turki is one of the languages known to me, and the Mongols speak a variant of the Turki tongue. May I ask—when those Mongols mentioned bandits, did they actually say *bandits?*"

"No, they used a name. A tribal name, I assume. Karauna. But I take them to be—"

"Ayee, that is what I thought I heard!" Nostril keened. "And that is what I feared I heard! May Allah preserve us! *The Karauna!*"

Let me say here that almost all the languages I heard spoken from the Levant eastward, no matter how disparate they were in other respects, contained a word or word-element that was the same in all, and that was *kara.* It was variously pronounced: Kara, khara, qara or k'ra, and in some languages kala, and it could have various meanings.

Kara could mean black or it could mean cold or it could mean iron or it could mean evil or it could mean death—or kara could mean all those things at the same time. It might be spoken in admiration or deprecation or revilement, as for instance the Mongols were pleased to call their onetime capital city Karakoren, meaning Black Palisade, while they called a certain large and venomous spider the karakurt, meaning evil or deadly insect.

"Karauna!" Nostril repeated, almost gagging on the word. "The Black Ones, the Cold Hearts, the Iron Men, the Evil Fiends, the Death Bringers! The name is of no tribe, Master Nicolò. It was bestowed on them as a curse. The Karauna are the outcasts of other tribes—of the Turki and Kipchak of the north, the Baluchi of the south. And *those* peoples are bandits born, so imagine how terrible a man has to be, that he is expelled from such a tribe. Some of the Karauna are even former Mongols, and you *know* they must be loathly indeed, to be outcast by the Mongols. The Karauna are the soulless men, the most cruel and bloodthirsty and feared of all predators in these lands. Oh, my lords and masters, we are in awful danger!"

"Then let us extinguish the fire," said Uncle Mafìo. "In truth, Nico, we have been sauntering rather blithely through this desert. I will break out swords from the packs, and I suggest we begin tonight to take turns at guard."

I volunteered to take the first watch awake, and asked Nostril how I should recognize the Karauna if they came.

Somewhat sarcastically he said, "You may have noticed that the Mongols fastened their coats on their right side. The Turki and Baluchi and such, they lap their coats to the left." Then his sarcasm dissolved in his dread, and he cried, "Oh, Master Marco, if you even have a chance to see them before they strike, you will have no doubt whatever. Ayee, bismillah, kheli zahmat dadam . . ." and, praying at the top of his lungs, he made an astonishing number of deep salaam prostrations before crawling into his tent.

When all my companions were abed, I walked, with my shimshir sword in hand, twice or thrice around the entire perimeter of the oasis, peering out as far as I could into the surrounding thick, black, foggy night. Since that darkness was so impenetrable, and since I could not possibly stand athwart all the approaches to our camp, I decided to post myself at my own tent, beside that of Aziz. The night being one of the more chilly nights of the journey, I lay prone inside my tent, under the blankets, and let just my head protrude beyond the flaps. Either Aziz was lying sleepless or I waked him with the noise of my getting settled, for he also stuck his head out, and whispered, "I am frightened, Marco, and I am cold. May I sleep next to you?"

"Yes, it is cold," I agreed. "I am shivering even with all my clothes on. I would go and fetch more blankets, but I dislike to rouse the camels. Here, you bring your covers, Aziz, and I will take down your tent as well, to use for an extra cover. If you lie close to me, and we pile all the fabrics on us, we ought to be snug enough."

This is what we did. Aziz wriggled out of his tent, like a little naked newt, and into mine. Working quickly in the cold, I shook the supporting rods out of his tent's hems, and bundled the cloth in on top of him. I burrowed in beside him, leaving only my head still out, and my hands and the shimshir. Very soon I had stopped shivering, but inwardly I felt quivery in a different way, not from the chill, but from the warmth and nearness and softness of the little boy's body. He was pressed against me in a most intimate embrace, and I suspected he had done that deliberately. In a moment I was sure of it, for he loosed the cord of my paijamah, and nestled his bare body against my bare bottom, and then he did something even more intimate. It made me gasp, and I heard him whisper, "Does this not warm you even more?"

Warm was not the word for it. His sister Sitarè had boasted that Aziz was expert at his art, and he clearly knew how to excite the thing that Nostril had called "the almond inside," for my member came erect as quickly and as stiffly as a tent cloth does when the rod is slid inside its hem sheath. What would have occurred next, I do not know. It might be asserted that I was grievously neglecting my guard watch, but I think the Karauna would have approached and struck unseen, even if I had been more attentive. Something struck the back of my head, so hard that the black night around me went even blacker, and when I was next conscious of anything, it was of being painfully dragged by my hair across the grass and sand.

I was dragged to where the camp fire was being rekindled, but not by any of us. The intruders were men to make

the earlier visiting Mongols look like elegant and polished
court gentlemen by comparison. There were seven of
these, and they were filthy and ragged and ugly and somehow, though they never smiled, they kept their snaggle
teeth always bared. They each had a horse, a small one
like a Mongol horse, but bony and ribby and pustular with
sores. One other thing I noticed about those horses, even in
my dazed condition: they had no ears.

One of the marauders was making up the fire, the others
were dragging my companions to it, and all of them were
babbling in a high voice another language new to me. Nostril alone seemed to understand it, and he, though also
having been knocked about and yanked from his bed and
consumed with terror, took the pains to translate and
shout to us all:

"These are the Karauna! They are mortally hungry!
They say they will not kill us if we feed them! Please, my
masters, in the name of Allah, get busy and show them
food!"

The Karauna dumped us all beside the fire and then began frantically scooping up water from the spring with
their hands and dashing it down their throats. My father
and uncle obediently hurried to get out the food stores. I
still lay on the ground, shaking my head, striving to get
the pain and darkness and buzzing out of it. Nostril, trying
to look properly and obsequiously busy, and doubtless half
scared to death, nevertheless kept shouting:

"They say they will not rob or kill *the four of us!* Of
course they are lying, and they will, but not until after *the
four of us* have fed them. So, please Allah, let us keep on
feeding them as long as there is food to feed! *All four of us!*"

Mainly concerned with the havoc inside my head, I
dimly supposed that he was urging me, too, to show some
life and activity. So I struggled upright and bestirred myself to pour some dried apricots into a pot of water to
soften. I heard Uncle Mafìo also shouting:

"We must comply, *the four of us!* But then, while they
are gorging themselves, *the four of us* may see a chance to
retrieve our swords and to fight."

I finally caught the message he and Nostril were trying
to impart. Aziz was not among us. When the Karauna
swooped down, they had seen four tents, had dragged four
men out of them, and now had four captives dutifully scur-

rying at their command. It was because I had taken down
Aziz's tent. When they plucked me from mine, Aziz might
have come along, attached, but he had not. And he must
have realized what was happening, so he would stay hidden, unless. . . . The boy was brave. He might try some
desperate expedient. . . .

One of the Karauna roared at us. His thirst quenched,
he seemed delighted to see us slaving for him. Like a victorious conqueror, he thumped his chest with his fists, and
bellowed quite a long narrative, which Nostril translated
in a quaver:

"They have been so hotly pursued that they were near
dead of thirst and starvation. They several times opened
the veins of their horses to drink their blood for sustenance. But the horses got so weak that they desisted from
that, but at last cut off and ate the horses' ears. Ayee,
mashallah, che arz konam? . . ." and he tailed off into another spate of praying.

The confusion also diminished, as the seven Karauna
ceased to mill about the spring, and let their mistreated
horses get to it, and came to where we had laid all our food
around the fire. With bared teeth and guttural growls,
they indicated that we should all stand aside, well out of
range to interfere. The four of us backed away, and the Karauna fell slavering upon the provender, and in the next
moment there was confusion confounded. Three more
horses came plunging suddenly out of the darkness, bearing three howling riders swinging swords.

The Mongol patrol had returned! I might better say, the
Mongols had all the while been lurking somewhere nearby, and not even I, the camp guard, had suspected it. They
had known that we would be an irresistible bait to the Karauna, and simply had waited for the bandits to walk into
the trap.

But the Karauna, although taken unawares and un-
mounted and with their attention fixed upon the food before them, neither surrendered on the instant nor fell
before the flashing swords. Two or three of the dirty brown
men magically turned bright red before our eyes, as blood
spurted from the cuts given them by the Mongols. But
they, like the not immediately wounded others, whipped
out swords of their own.

The Mongols, having leapt in on horseback, could make

only that one flailing slash before their mounts carried
them a little way past the fray. Not turning their horses,
they slid from their saddles to continue the fight on foot.
But the Karauna, in their avidness to feed, had not tethered or hobbled or unsaddled their own mounts. They must
have been mightily tempted to stand and fight, with the
food all laid out for them, and they being seven against
three. Probably only because they *were* weak with hunger—and knowing that three well-fed Mongols were their
fighting equal—they bounded astride their pitiful horses
and, beating their blades down on the swords of the Mongols now afoot, put spurs to their horses and surged out of
the firelight in the direction from which they had dragged
me.

The Mongols considerately hesitated long enough to
glance around at us, and ascertain that we were not visibly
injured, before they caught their own horses, vaulted to
their saddles, and were off in hot pursuit. Everything had
happened in such a furious tumult—from the moment I
had been clouted to this sudden quiet fallen on the oasis—
that it might have been a simùm desert storm that had
swept down and embroiled us and swept on past.

"Gèsu . . . ," my father breathed.

"Al-hamdo-lillah . . . ," prayed Nostril.

"Where is the boy Aziz?" Uncle Mafìo asked me.

"He is safe," I said loudly, to be heard above the ringing
still going on in my head. "He is in my tent." And I gestured toward where the dust of the horses' departure was
hanging in the air.

As soon as he could get some clothes on, my uncle went
running off in that direction. My father saw me rubbing
my head, and came and felt of it. He remarked that I had a
palpable knot there, and told Nostril to put a cup of water
to heat.

Then my uncle came running back, out of the darkness,
shouting, "Aziz is not there! His clothes are, but he is not!"

Leaving Nostril to bathe my head and bind a poultice of
salve about it, my father and uncle went to beat the bushes
for the boy. They did not find him. Nor did any of us, when
Nostril and I joined them, and we did a methodical back-
and-forth pacing of the entire oasis. Consulting together,
we tried to reconstruct what must have happened.

"He would have left the tent. Even undressed and in this cold."

"Yes, he would have known they would loot it soon or later."

"So he sought a safer place to hide."

"More likely he was creeping close, to see if he could aid us."

"Anyway, he was in the open when the Karauna suddenly fled."

"And they saw him and snatched him up and took him with them."

"At the first opportunity, they will kill him." It was Uncle Mafìo who said that, and he said it in the voice of one bereaved. "They will kill him in some bestial manner, for they must be furious, thinking we arranged that ambuscade."

"They may have no opportunity. The Mongols are close behind."

"The Karauna will not kill the boy, but hold him hostage. A shield to ward off the Mongols."

"And *if* the Mongols hold off, which they may not," said my uncle, *"think* what the Karauna will be doing to that little boy."

"Let us not weep until someone is hurt," said my father. "But whatever the outcome, we must be there. Nostril, you stay. Mafìo, Marco, mount up!"

We laid the sticks to our camels. Since we had never pressed them before, the beasts were so startled that they did not think to complain or balk, but went at a stretch-out gallop, and maintained it. The movement made my head seem to pound upon the neck-top of my spine with an excruciating beat, but I said nothing.

On sand, camels run faster than horses can, so we caught up to the Mongols well before dawn. We would eventually have met them in any case, as they were leisurely returning toward the oasis. The dry fog having settled to the ground by then, we saw them at some distance in the starlight. Two of them were walking and leading the horses, and supporting the third in his saddle, where he sagged and wobbled, being evidently badly hurt. The two called something to us as we approached, and waved their hands to indicate where they had come from.

"A miracle! The boy lives!" said my father, and lashed his camel harder.

We did not pause to speak to the Mongols, but kept on going, until we saw far off a scattering of dark, motionless shapes on the sand. They were the seven Karauna and their horses, all dead and much hacked and arrow-punctured, and some of the men lay separate from their severed sword hands. But we paid them no mind. Aziz was sitting on the sand, in a large puddle of blood from one of the fallen horses, his back propped against its saddle. He had covered his bare body with a blanket he must have pulled from the saddle pannier, and it was drenched with gore. We jumped off our camels before they had entirely knelt, and ran to him. Uncle Mafìo, with tears pouring down his face, fondly rumpled the child's hair, and my father patted him on the shoulder, and we all exclaimed in wonder and relief:

"You are all right!"

"Praise the good San Zudo of the Impossible!"

"What happened, dear Aziz?"

He said, his little bird voice even quieter than usual. "They passed me from one to another as we rode, so each could take a turn, and so they did not have to slow their pace."

"And you are unhurt?" my uncle asked.

"I am cold," Aziz said listlessly. Indeed, he was shivering violently under the threadbare old blanket.

Uncle Mafìo persisted anxiously. "They did not—abuse you? Here?" He laid a hand on the blanket between the boy's thighs.

"No, they did nothing like that. There was no time. And I think they were too hungry. And then the Mongols caught us up." He puckered his pale face as if to cry. "I am so *cold* . . ."

"Yes, yes, lad," said my father. "We will set you soon to rights. Marco, you stay by him and comfort him. Mafìo, help me look about for dung to make a fire."

I took off my aba and spread it over the boy for an extra cover, uncaring about the blood that soaked into it. But he did not hug the covers about him. He only sat where he was, against the sideways saddle, his little legs stuck out in front of him and his hands lying limp alongside. Hoping to cheer and enliven him, I said:

"All this time, Aziz, I have been wondering about the curious animal you challenged me to guess."

A faint smile came briefly to his lips. "I did riddle you to puzzlement, Marco, did I not?"

"Yes, you did. How does it go again?"

"A desert creature . . . that unites in itself . . . the natures of seven different beasts." His voice was fading again to listlessness. "Can you still not divine it?"

"No," I said, frowning as before, and pretending to delve deep in my mind. "No, I confess I cannot."

"It has the head of a horse . . ." he said slowly, as if he were having trouble remembering, or having trouble speaking. "And the neck of a bull . . . the wings of a rukh . . . belly of a scorpion . . . feet of a camel . . . horns of a qazèl . . . and the . . . and the hindquarters . . . of a serpent . . ."

I was worried by his uncharacteristic lack of vivacity, but I could discern no cause for it. As his voice dwindled, his eyelids drooped. I squeezed his shoulder encouragingly, and said:

"That must be a most marvelous beast. But what is it? Aziz, unriddle the riddle. What is it?"

He opened his beautiful eyes and gazed at me, and he smiled and he said, "It is only a common grasshopper." Then he fell abruptly forward, his face hitting the sand between his knees, as if he had been loosely hinged at the waist. There was a sudden, noticeable increase in the prevailing stench of blood and body odors and horse manure and human excrement. Aghast, I leaped up and called for my father and uncle. They came running, and stared down at the boy, unbelieving.

"No living human being ever bent over flat like that!" my uncle exclaimed in horror.

My father knelt and took one of the boy's wrists and held it for a moment, then looked up at us and somberly shook his head.

"The child has died! But of what? Did he not say he was unhurt? That they only handed him back and forth as they rode?"

I helplessly raised my hands. "We spoke for a little. Then he fell over like that. Like a sawdust doll from which all the sawdust is gone."

My uncle turned away, sobbing and coughing. My father

gently took the boy's shoulders and lifted him, and laid the
lolling head back against the saddle, and with one hand
held him sitting up while with the other he pulled down
the gory covers. Then my father made a retching noise
and, repeating what the boy had told us, he muttered,
"The Karauna were hungry," and he backed away in sick
revulsion, letting the body topple forward flat again, but
not before I also saw. What had happened to Aziz—I could
liken it to nothing except an ancient Greek tale I had once
been told in school, about a stalwart boy of Sparta and a voracious fox cub he hid beneath his tunic.

6

WE left the dead Karauna where they lay, carrion for the
beaks of any scavenger vultures that might find them. But
we took with us the already bitten and gouged and partially devoured little corpse of Aziz, as we headed back for
the oasis. We would not leave him on the surface of the
sand, or even bury him under it, for nothing can be so
deeply buried in the sand but the wind will continually
cover and uncover it again, as indifferently as it does the
karwan leaving of camel dung.

On our way forth from the oasis, we had passed the
white fringe of a minor salt flat, so we stopped there on our
return. We carried Aziz out upon the trembling land,
wrapped in my aba for a shroud, and we found a place
where we could break through the glittering crust, and we
laid Aziz on the quaggy quicksand under it. We said our
farewells and some prayers during the time it took the
small bundle to sink from our sight.

"The salt slab will soon re-form over him," mused my father. "He will rest under it undisturbed, even by corruption, for the salts will permeate his body and preserve
him."

My uncle, scratching absentmindedly at his elbow, said
with resignation. "It may even be that this land, like
others I have seen, will in time heave and break and rearrange its topography. Some future journeyer may find
him, centuries hence, and gaze upon his sweet face, and

wonder how it came to pass that an angel fell from Heaven
to be interred here."

That was as fine a valedictory as could be pronounced
over any departed one, so we left Aziz then and remounted
and rode on. When we arrived again at the oasis, Nostril
came running, all worry and concern, and then all lamentation when he saw there were still only the three of us.
We told him, in as few words as possible, how we had been
deprived of the smallest member of our party. Looking
properly grieved and woebegone, he muttered some Muslim prayers, and then he spoke to us a typically fatalistic
Muslim condolence:

"May your own spans be lengthened, good masters, by
the days which the boy has lost. Inshallah."

The day was at its noon by then, and anyway we were
weary and my head was near to splitting with pain and we
had no heart for hastening to resume our journey, so we
prepared to spend another night in the oasis, even though
it was no longer any happy place for us. The three Mongols
had preceded us there, and Nostril went on with what he
had been doing when we came: helping those men clean
and anoint and bind up their wounds.

Those wounds were many, but none very serious. The
man we had thought worst hurt had only had his brains
temporarily scrambled when he was kicked in the head by
a horse during the final affray with the Karauna; he had
considerably recovered. Even so, all three of the men bore
numerous sword cuts and had lost much blood and must
have been much weakened, and we would have expected
them to remain in the oasis for some days while they recu-
perated. But no, they said, they were Mongols, indestructi-
ble, unstoppable, and they would ride on.

My father asked where they would go. They said they
had no assigned destination, only a mandate to go and
seek and chase and destroy the Karauna of the Dasht-e-
Kavir, and they wanted to get on with that job. So my father showed them our passepartout signed by the Khakhan
Kubilai. For certain, none of those men could read, but
they easily recognized the distinctive seal of the Khan of
All Khans. They were agog at our possession of it, as they
had earlier been impressed to hear my father and uncle
speaking their tongue, and they inquired if we wished to
give them any orders in the name of the Khakhan. My fa-

ther suggested that, since we were carrying rich gifts for
their great lord, the men might help ensure the delivery of
them by riding as our escort as far as Mashhad, and they
readily agreed to do so.

The next day, we were seven when we moved on northeastward. Since the Mongols disdained conversing with a
lowly camel-puller, and since Uncle Mafìo seemed indisposed to speak to anybody, and since my head still hurt
whenever I jarred it by talking, only my father and our
three new companions talked as we rode, and I was satisfied to ride close to them and listen, and thereby begin
learning yet another new language.

The first thing I learned was that the name Mongol does
not connote a race or a nation of people—the name derives
from the word *mong,* meaning brave—and similar though
our three escorting Mongols appeared to my unaccustomed
eye, they were in fact as disparate as if they had been Venetian, Genoan and Pisan. One was of the Khalkas tribe,
one was of the Merkit and one was of the Buriat—which
tribes, I gathered, originally hailed from widely separated
parts of those lands that the mighty Chinghiz (himself a
Khalkas) long ago first united and so began building the
Mongol Khanate. Also, one of the men was of the Buddhist
faith, another of the Taoist—religions of which I then knew
nothing—and the third was, of all things, a Nestorian
Christian. But I learned at the same time that, whatever a
Mongol's tribal origin or his religious affiliation or his soldierly occupation, he is never to be referred to as a
Khalkas or a Christian or even as a bowman or an armorer
or any other such applicable appellation. He calls himself
only a Mongol—and proudly, thus: *"Mongol!"*—and he
must be spoken of only as a Mongol, for his being a Mongol
supersedes anything else he may be, and that name of
Mongol takes precedence over all other names.

However, long before I could make the least conversation with our three escorts, I had discerned from their behavior some of the Mongols' curious ways and customs
—or, I might better say, their barbaric superstitions.
While we were still in the oasis, Nostril had suggested to
them that they might like to wash the blood and sweat and
long-accumulated dirt out of their clothes, and so have
them fresh and clean for the next stage of traveling. The
men declined, giving as a reason that it was unwise to

launder any article of apparel when abroad from one's home camp, because that would raise a thunderstorm. *How* it would do that, they could not say, and would not demonstrate. Now, any man of ordinary good sense, in the middle of a parched and bleached desert, would scarcely object to any kind of wet storm, however mysteriously produced. But the Mongols, who fear nothing else under heaven, are as terrified of thunder and lightning as is the most timid child or woman.

Also, while still in that abundantly watered oasis, the three Mongols never once treated themselves to a thorough and refreshing bath, though God knows they needed one. They were so crusty they almost creaked, and their aroma would have gagged a shaqàl. But they washed no more of themselves than their heads and hands, and did that little washing most miserly. One of them would dip a gourd in the spring, but use not even the dipper's amount of water. He would slurp from the gourd only a single mouthful, and hold it in his mouth, then spit the water into his cupped hands, a little at a time, and with one spurt wet his hair, with the next his ears, and so on. Granted, that may not have been a matter of superstition, but of conservation, a custom decreed by a people who spend so much of their time in arid lands. But I did think they would have been a more socially acceptable people if they had relaxed that stringency when it was not needful.

Another thing. Those three men had been traveling from out of the northeast when they first came upon us. Now that we were proceeding in that direction, and perforce so were they, the men insisted that we ride a farsakh or so to one side of their prior trail, because, they assured us, it was unlucky to return over the exact same route by which one has gone out.

It was also extremely unlucky, they remarked, during the first night we all camped together on the trail, for any member of a party to sit with his head hanging as in sorrow, or to lean his cheek or chin on his hand as an aid to cogitation. That, they said, could bring sadness on the entire company. And they said it while glancing uneasily at Uncle Mafìo, who was sitting just that way, and looking mournful indeed. My father or I might jolly him into sociability for a while, but he soon would lapse into gloom again.

For a very long time after the death of Aziz, my uncle spoke seldom and sighed often and looked miserably bereft. Where earlier I had tried to take a tolerant attitude toward his unmanly nature, I was now more inclined to an amused and exasperated contempt. No doubt a man who can find sensual pleasure only with one of his own sex can also find a deep and lasting love for one of them, and such a true ardor—like the more conventional instances of true love—can be esteemed and admired and commended. However, Uncle Mafìo had had only a single and insignificant sexual encounter with Aziz, and otherwise he had been no closer to the boy than any of the rest of us. We all grieved for Aziz, and felt sorrow at his loss. But for Uncle Mafìo to carry on, in the way that another man might grieve for a wife lost after many years of happy marriage—that was lugubrious and farcical and unworthy. He was still my uncle, and I would continue to treat him with all due respect, but I had come privately to conclude that his big and burly and strong outer semblance had not much inside it.

No one could have been sorrier for the death of Aziz than I was, but I realized that my reasons were mainly selfish, and gave me no right to make loud lamentation. One reason was that I had promised both Sitarè and my father that I would keep the boy from harm, and I had not. So I could not be sure whether I was feeling more sorry for his death or for my failure as a guardian. Another of my selfish reasons was that I was grieving because someone worth keeping had been snatched out of my world. Oh, I know that all people grieve so, on the occasion of a death, but that makes it no less a selfish reason. We survivors are deprived of that one person newly dead. But he or she is deprived of everything—of all other persons, of all things worth keeping, of the entire world and every least thing in it, all in an instant—and such a loss deserves a lamentation so loud and vast and lasting that we who stay are incapable of expressing it.

I had yet another selfish reason for lamenting the death of Aziz. I could not help recalling the Widow Esther's admonition: that a man should avail himself of everything life offers, lest he die repining for those opportunities he neglected to seize. It was perhaps virtuous of me, and laudable, that I had declined what Aziz offered me, and so left his chastity unsmirched. It would perhaps have been

sinful of me, and reprehensible, if I had accepted, and so
despoiled his chastity. But, I asked myself now, since Aziz
would have gone so soon to his grave in either case, what
difference could it have made? If we had embraced, it
might have meant one last pleasure for him, and a unique
one for me: what Nostril had called "a journey beyond the
ordinary"—and whether it had been innocuous or iniqui-
tous, it would have left no trace on the all-covering quicksand. But I had refused, and in all the rest of my life, if any
such chance ever came again, it could not come from the
beautiful Aziz. He was gone, and that opportunity was
lost, and now—not on some putative future deathbed—*now*
I was sorry.

But I was alive. And I and my uncle and my father and
our companions journeyed on, for that is all that the living
can do to forget death, or defy it.

We were not accosted by any more Karauna, or any
other sorts of lurkers, and we did not even meet any other
fellow travelers during the rest of our desert crossing.
Either our Mongol escort had been unnecessary or its presence had discouraged any further molestation. We came finally out of the lowland sands at the Binalud Mountains,
and up through that range to Mashhad. It was a fair and
pleasant city, somewhat larger than Kashan, and its
streets were lined with chinar and mulberry trees.

Mashhad is one of the very holy cities of Persian Islam,
because a highly revered martyr of olden time, the Imam
Riza, is entombed in an ornate masjid there. A Muslim's
worshipful visit to Mashhad earns him the prefix of Mes-
hadi to his name, as a pilgrimage to Mecca earns him the
right to be addressed as Hajji. So the greater part of the
city's population consisted of transient pilgrims and, because of that, Mashhad had very good and clean and comfortable karwansarai inns. Our three Mongols led us to
one of the best, and themselves spent a night there before
turning back to resume their patrol of the Dasht-e-Kavir.

There at the karwansarai, the Mongols demonstrated
yet another of their customs. While my father, my uncle,
and I gratefully took lodging inside the inn, and our camel-
puller Nostril gratefully took lodging in the stable with his
animals, the Mongols insisted on laying their bedrolls outside in the center of the courtyard, and staked their horses
to the ground about them. The Mashhad landlord indulged

them in that eccentricity, but some landlords will not. As I later discovered, when a Mongol party is commanded by the innkeeper to lodge indoors like civilized folk, the Mongols will grudgingly comply, but they still will not depend on the karwansarai kitchen. They will lay a fire in the middle of their chamber floor, put a tripod over it and do their own cooking. Come night, they will not repose on the beds provided, but will unroll their own carpets and blankets and sleep on the floor.

Well, I could now sympathize in some measure with the Mongols' reluctance to reside under a fixed roof. Myself, my father and my uncle, after our long crossing of the Great Salt, had also developed a taste for unconfined spaces and unrestricted elbow room, and the limitless silence and clean air of the outdoors. Though at first we exulted in the refreshment of a hammam bath and rubbing, and were pleased to have our meals cooked and presented to us by servants, we soon found ourselves vexed by the noise and agitation and turmoil of indoor living. The air seemed close and the walls even closer and the other karwansarai guests a terribly talkative crowd. The all-pervading smoke especially tormented Uncle Mafìo, who was troubled by intermittent coughing spells. So, for all that the inn was well appointed and Mashhad an estimable city, we stayed only long enough to exchange our camels again for horses, and to replenish our traveling gear and rations, and we moved on.

BALKH

1

WE went now a little south of east, to skirt the Karakum, or Black Sands, which is another desert lying due eastward of Mashhad. We chose a route across the Karabil, or Cold Plateau, which is a long shelf of more solid and verdant land extending like a coastline between the bleak dry ocean of Black Sands to the north and the bleak escarpment of the treeless Paropamisus Mountains to the south.

It would have made a shorter journey to go straight across the Karakum desert, but we were weary of desert. And it would have been a more easeful journey if we had gone farther to the southward, through the valleys of the Paropamisus, for there we would have found accommodation in a succession of villages and towns and even cities of respectable size, such as Herat and Maimana. But we preferred to take the middle course. We were well accustomed to camping out of doors, and that high Karabil plateau must have got its name only by comparison to lower and warmer lands, for it was not terribly cold even then in early wintertime. We simply added layers of shirts and pai-jamah and abas as we needed them, and found the weather tolerable enough.

The Karabil consisted mostly of monotonous grassland, but there were also stands of trees—pistachio, zizafun, willow and conifers. We had seen many greener and more pleasant lands, and would see many others, but, after having endured the Great Salt, we found even the dull gray grass and scanty foliage of the Karabil a delight to our

eyes, and our horses found it adequate for forage. After the
lifeless desert, that plateau seemed to us to teem with
wildlife. There were conveys of quail, and flocks of a red-
legged partridge, and everywhere marmots peeking from
their burrows and whistling peevishly at our passing.
There were migrant geese and ducks wintering there, or at
least passing through: a kind of goose with a barred head-
feathering, and a duck of lovely russet and gold plumage.
There were multitudes of brown lizards, some of them so
immense—longer than my leg—that they frequently startled our horses.

There were herds of several different sorts of delicate
qazèl, and of a large and handsome wild ass, called in that
region the kulan. When we first saw it, my father said that
he almost wished we could stop and capture some, and
tame them, and take them back to the West for sale, as
they would fetch a far better price than the mules which
noblemen and ladies buy for their mounts. The kulan is
veritably as big as a mule, and has the same jug head and
short tail, but it is of an extraordinarily rich dark-brown
coat with a pale belly, and it is beautiful. A man can never
tire of watching the herds of them swiftly running and
frisking and wheeling in unison. But the Karabil natives
told us the kulan cannot be tamed and ridden; they value
it only for its edible flesh.

We ourselves, and Uncle Mafìo especially, did much
hunting on that stage of our journey, to supplement our
travel rations. In Mashhad we had each procured a com-
pact Mongol-style bow and the short arrows for it, and my
uncle had practiced until he was expert with that weapon.
As a rule, we tried to shy clear of the herds of qazèl and kulan, for we feared they might be attended by other hunters:
wolves or lions, which also abound in the Karabil. But we
did occasionally risk stalking a herd, and several times
brought down a qazèl, and once a kulan. Almost every day
we could count on getting a goose or duck or quail or partridge. That fresh meat would have been eminently enjoyable, except for one thing.

I forget what was the first creature we brought down
with an arrow, or which of us it was who got it. But when
we started to carve it for spitting over our fire, we discovered that it was riddled with some kind of small blind
insects, dozens of them, alive and wriggling, snugged be-

tween the skin and flesh. Disgusted, we flung it aside and
made do that night with a desert-type dried-food meal. But
the very next day, we brought down some other sort of
game, and found it identically infested. I do not know what
demon afflicts every living wild creature of the Karabil.
The natives we asked could not tell us, and seemed not to
care, and even expressed disdain of our queasiness. So,
since all our subsequently bagged game was similarly
crawly, we forced ourselves to pick out the vermin and
cook and eat the meat, and it did not make us ill, and eventually we came to regard the matter as commonplace.

Another thing we might have thought bothersome—but
which, after the desert, we found rather exhilarating—was
that three times during our traverse of the Karabil we had
to cross a river. As I recall, their names were the Tedzhen,
the Kushka and the Takhta. They were not wide waters,
but they were cold and deep and fast-running, tumbling
down from the Paropamisus heights to the Karakum flats,
where eventually they would seep into the Black Sands
and disappear. At each riverside we found a karwansarai,
and each provided a ferry service, of a sort I found amusing. Our horses we simply unsaddled and unloaded and let
swim across the rivers, which they did with aplomb. But
we travelers were taken across, one at time, with our
packs, by a ferryman plying a peculiar kind of raft called a
masak. Each of those craft was not much bigger than a tub
and consisted of a light framework of wood, supported by a
score or so of inflated goatskins.

A masak was ludicrous looking, with all the tied-off
stumps of goat legs poking up among its framing poles, but
I learned that there was a reason for that. Those rivers ran
briskly, and the men paddling had little control over something as awkward as a masak, so it yawed and rocked and
revolved and pitched wildly as it went careening on a long
diagonal from one shore to the other. Each crossing took
quite a while, during which time the inflated goatskins
leaked and bubbled and whistled. When the masak began
to get alarmingly low in the water, the ferryman would
stop paddling, untie the goat legs and vigorously blow into
the hide bags, one after another, until they were buoyant
again, and then deftly retie them. I should amend my
earlier remark and say I found that an amusing mode of
ferriage *after* I was on each occasion put safely aground on

the other side. During the turbulent crossings, I had other
feelings—compounded of giddiness, wetness, coldness, sea-
sickness and expectation of imminent drowning.

At the Kushka ferry, I remember, another karwan party
was preparing to cross, and we watched and wondered how
it would manage, for it was traveling in a number of horse-
drawn carts. But that did not deter the ferrymen. They un-
hitched the horses and sent them swimming for the far
bank, and made several raft trips to transport the occupants and contents of the wagons. Then, as each cart was
emptied, they eased it down the riverbank until its four
wheels rested one apiece in four of the tubby little masaks,
and they rowed it across in quaternion. That made a sight
to see: each wagon dipping and dancing and whirling down
the river, and its raftmen at each of its corners alternately
paddling like Charon to make headway and puffing like
Aeolus to keep the goatskins inflated.

I must remark that the riverside inns in the Karabil provided better ferriage than forage for their guests. At only
one karwansarai did we have a decent meal, in fact something unique in our experience thus far: huge and tasty
steaks carved from a fish caught in the river outside the
door. The steaks were so tremendous that we marveled
and asked permission to go into the kitchen for a look at
the fish they had been cut from. It was called an ashyotr,
and it was bigger than a big man, bigger than Uncle
Mafìo, and instead of scales it had a shell of bony plates,
and beneath its long snout it had barbels like whiskers. In
addition to giving edible flesh, the ashyotr yielded a black
roe, each egg of seed-pearly size, and we ate some of that
too, salted and pressed to make a relish called khavyah.

But at the other inns the food was awful, and there was
no reason for it to be, given the abundance of game in that
country. Every landlord of a karwansarai seemed to think
that he must serve his guests something they had not
lately been eating. Since we had been dining on such delicacies as game birds and wild qazèl does, the innkeepers
fed us the mutton of domestic sheep. The Karabil is not
sheep country, meaning that the meat had probably traveled as far from its point of origin as we had, to get to the
karwansarai. Mutton had long since ceased to delight me,
and this was dried and salted and tough, and there was no
oil or vinegar or anything else to season it with, only pun-

gent red meleghèta pepper, and it was invariably accompanied by beans boiled in sugar water. After enough such gaseous meals, we could probably have served instead of the goatskins to support the masak rafts. But, to say one good thing about the inns in the Karabil, they charged only for their human patrons, not for the karwan animals. That was because wood was hard to come by, and the beasts paid their own way by leaving their dung to be dried for fuel.

The next city of any consequence to which we came was Balkh, and in times past that had been a city of truly great consequence: the site of one of Alexander's main encampments, a major station for karwan traders and luxurious karwansarais. But it had stood in the path of the first waves of Mongols rampaging out of the fastnesses to the east—meaning that earliest Mongol Horde commanded by the invincible Chinghiz Khan—and in the year 1220 the Horde had stamped upon Balkh as a booted foot might stamp upon an ant nest.

It was more than half a century later that my father, my uncle, our slave and I arrived in Balkh, but the city had not even yet recovered from that disaster. Balkh was a grand and noble ruin, but it was still a ruin. It was perhaps as busy and thriving as of old, but its inns and granaries and warehouses were only slatternly buildings thrown together of the broken bricks and planks left after the ruination. They looked even more dingy and pathetic, standing as they did among the stumps of once towering columns, the tumbled remains of once mighty walls and the jagged shells of once perfect domes.

Of course, few of Balkh's current inhabitants were old enough to have been there when Chinghiz sacked the city, or before, when it had been far-famed as Balkh Umn-al-Bulud, the "Mother of Cities." But their sons and grandsons, who were now the proprietors of the inns and counting houses and other establishments, appeared as dazed and miserable as if the devastation had occurred only yesterday, and in their own seeing. When they spoke of the Mongols, they recited what must have been a litany committed to memory by every Balkhite: "Amdand u khandand u sokhtand u kushtand u burdand u raftand," which means, "They came and they slew and they burned and they plundered and they seized their spoils and they went on."

They had gone on, yes, but this whole land, like so many others, was still under tribute and allegiance to the Mongol Khanate. The glum demeanor of the Balkhites was understandable, since a Mongol garrison was still encamped nearby. Armed Mongol warriors strode through the bazàr crowds, remindful that the grandson of Chinghiz, the Khakhan Kubilai, still held his heavy boot poised over the city. And his appointed magistrates and tax collectors still peered watchfully over the shoulders of the Balkhites in their market stalls and money-changing booths.

I could say, as I have said before, and say it truthfully, that everywhere east of the Furat River basin away back at the far western beginning of Persia, we journeyers had been traversing the lands of the Mongol Khanate. But if we had thus simplistically marked our maps—writing nothing but "Mongol Khanate" over that whole vast area of the world—we might as well not have kept up our maps at all. They would have been of little use to us or anyone else without more detail than that. We did expect to retrace our trail someday, when we returned home again, and we also hoped that the maps would be of use even after that, for the guidance of whole streams of commerce flowing back and forth between Venice and Kithai. So, every day or so, my father and uncle would get out our copy of the Kitab and, only after deliberation and consultation and final agreement, they would inscribe upon it the symbols for mountains and rivers and towns and deserts and other such landmarks.

That had now become a more necessary task than before. From the shores of the Levant all the way across Asia, to Balkh or hereabouts, the Arab mapmaker al-Idrisi had proved a dependable guide for us. As my father had long ago remarked, al-Idrisi himself must at some time have traveled through all those regions and seen them with his own eyes. But, from the vicinity of Balkh on eastward, al-Idrisi seemed to have relied on hearsay information from other travelers, and not very observant travelers at that. The Kitab's more easterly map pages were notably empty of landmarks, and what major things it did show —things like rivers and mountain ranges—frequently turned out to be incorrectly located.

"Also, the maps from here on seem exceedingly *small,*" said my father, frowning at those pages.

"Yes, by God," said my uncle, scratching and coughing. "There is an almighty lot more land than he indicates, between here and the eastern ocean."

"Well," said my father. "We must be that much more assiduous in our own mapping."

He and Uncle Mafìo could usually agree, without long debate, on the penning-in of mountains and waters and towns and deserts, because those were things we could see and judge the measure of. What required deliberation and discussion, and sometimes sheer guesswork, was the drawing-in of invisible things, which is to say the borders of nations. That was maddeningly difficult, and only partly because the spread of the Mongol Khanate had engulfed so many once-independent states and nations and even whole races as to render immaterial—except to a mapmaker—the question of where they had been, and where they had abutted, and where the lines between them had lain. It would have been difficult even if some native of each nation had come with us to pace off the bounds of it for us. I daresay that would be a troublesome job on our own Italian peninsula, where no two city-states can yet agree on each other's limits of ownership and authority. But in central Asia the extents of the nations and their frontiers and even their names have been in flux since long before the Mongols made those matters moot.

I shall illustrate. Somewhere during our long traverse from Mashhad to Balkh, we had crossed the invisible line which, in Alexander's time marked the division between two lands known as Arya and Bactria. Now it marks—or at least it did until the Mongols came—the division between the lands of Greater Persia and Greater India. But let me pretend for a moment that the Mongol Khanate does not exist, and try to give some idea of the confusion attendant throughout history on that imprecise border.

India may once have been inhabited in all its vastness by the small, dark people we now know as the Indians. But long ago the incursions of more vigorous and courageous peoples pushed those original Indians into a smaller and smaller compass of land, so that nowadays the Hindu India lies far distant to the South and east of here. This northern India Aryana is the habitat of the descendants of those

long-ago invaders, and they are not of the Hindu but of the
Muslim religion. Every least tribe calls itself a nation and
gives its nation a name and asserts that its nation has
mappable borders. Most of the names hereabout end in
-stan, which signifies "land of"—Khaljistan, meaning
Land of the Khalji, and Pakhtunistan and Kohistan and
Afghanistan and Nuristan and I disremember how many
others.

In olden time, it was somewhere in this area, in either
the then-Arya or the then-Bactria, that Alexander the
Great, during his eastward march of conquest, met and fell
enamored of and took to wife the Princess Roxana. Nobody
can say exactly where that happened, or of what tribe's
"royal family" Roxana was a member. But nowadays and
hereabout, every one of the local tribes—Pakhtuni, Khalji,
Afghani, Kirghiz and every other—claims descent from,
first, the royal line which produced Roxana and, also, the
Macedonians of Alexander's army. There may even be
some cause for those claims. Although the greater number
of people one sees in Balkh and its environs possess dark
hair and skin and eyes, which presumably Roxana also
had, there are among them many persons of fair complexion and blue or gray eyes and reddish or even yellow hair.

However, each tribe purports to be the *only* true descendants, and on that basis claims sole sovereignty over
all these lands now constituting India Aryana. To me, that
seemed a devious sort of reasoning, since even Alexander
was a latecomer here, and an unwelcome marauder, so all
the natives here—except perhaps the Princess Roxana—
should have felt about the Macedonians as they now feel
about the Mongols.

The one thing we found common to all the peoples in
these regions was the still later-come religion of Islam. In
accord with Muslim custom, then, we never got to converse
with any but the *male* persons, and that made Uncle Mafìo
skeptical of their boasts of their lineage. He quoted an old
Venetian couplet:

La mare xe segura
E'l pare de ventura.

Which is to say that, while a father may claim to know, only
a mother can know for certain who sired each of her children.

I have recounted this tangled and disjointed bit of history merely to indicate how it added to the other frustrations of us would-be mapmakers. Whenever my father and uncle sat down together to decide the designations to ink onto our map pages, hoping to do that tidily, the discussions might go untidily thus:

"To begin with, Mafìo, this land is in the portion of the Khanate governed by the Ilkhan Kaidu. But we must be more specific."

"How specific, Nico? We do not know what Kaidu or Kubilai or any other Mongol officially calls this region. All the Western cosmographers call it merely the India Aryana of Greater India."

"They have never set foot upon it. The Westerner Alexander did, and he called it Bactria."

"But most of the local folk call it Pakhtunistan."

"On the other hand, al-Idrisi has it marked as Mazar-i-Sharif."

"Gèsu! It occupies only a thumb span of the map. Is it worth this fuss?"

"The Ilkhan Kaidu would not maintain a garrison here if the land were worthless. And the Khakhan Kubilai will wish to see how accurately we have done our maps."

"All right." Sigh of exasperation. "Let us give it a good thinking over. . . ."

2

WE dawdled in Balkh for a time, not because it was an attractive city, but because there were high mountains to the eastward, on the way we had yet to go. And now there was snow thick on the ground even here in the lower lands, so we knew the mountains would be impassable until perhaps late in the spring. Since we had to wait out the winter somewhere, we decided that our Balkh karwansarai was a comfortable enough place to spend at least part of it.

The food was good and ample and fairly various, as it should have been, at such a crossroads of commerce. There were excellent breads, and several sorts of fish, and the meat, though it was mutton, was broiled in a tasty bro-

chette manner called shashlik. There were savory winter
melons and well-kept pomegranates, besides all the usual
dried fruits. There was no qahwah in those parts, but there
was another hot beverage called cha, made of steeped
leaves, almost as vivifying as qahwah and equally fragrant, though in a different way, and much thinner in consistency. The staple vegetable was still beans and the only
other accompaniment to the meals was the everlasting
rice, but we contributed a fragment of a brick of zafràn to
the kitchen, and so made the rice palatable and won those
cooks the praise of every other patron of that karwansarai.

Since zafràn was as much of a novelty and a nonesuch in
Balkh as it had been in other places, our budgets were ample for buying anything we needed or wanted. My father
traded bits of the brick and hay zafràn for coin of the realm
and, when an occasional merchant pleaded eloquently
enough, would even deign to sell him a culm or two or
three, so the khaja could start growing his own crocus crop.
For each culm, my father demanded and got a number of
gems of beryl or lapis lazura, of which stones this land is
the chief source in all the world, and those were worth a
great deal of coin indeed. So we were nicely well-to-do, and
had not yet so much as opened our cods of musk.

We bought for ourselves heavy winter clothing, wools
and furs, made in the local style. In that locality, the main
garment was the chapon, which, as need required, could
serve either for an overcoat or for a blanket or for a tent.
When worn as a coat, it hung to the ground all around and
its capacious sleeves hung a good foot-length beyond the
fingertips. It looked ungainly and comical, but what people really looked at was not the fit but the color of one's
chapon, for that told one's wealth. The lighter the color of
the chapon, the harder it was to keep clean, and the more
frequently it had to be cleaned, and the more it cost for
that cleaning, and so it signified that the man wearing it
cared little for that cost, and a chapon of pure snow-white
color meant that its wearer was a man so rich he could be
criminally spendthrift. My father and uncle and I each settled for a chapon of a medium tan color, indicating something modestly between opulence and the dark-brown of
the chapon we bought for our slave Nostril. We also
donned the local style of boot, called the chamus, which
had a tough but flexible leather sole, bound to a soft

leather upper which reached to the knee, and was held on
by thongs wrapped around the calf. We also traded our
flatland saddles, and paid a goodly sum of coin besides, to
buy new saddles with high pommels and cantles that
would seat us more securely during upland riding.

What time we were not buying or trading in the bazàr,
we put to other uses. The slave Nostril fed and curried and
combed our horses to prime condition, and we Polos made
conversation with other karwan journeyers. We gave them
our observations on the routes to the westward of Balkh,
and those of them who had come from the east told us news
of the routes and travel conditions out there. My father
painstakingly wrote a letter of several pages to the Dona
Fiordelisa, recounting our travels and progress and assuring her of our wellbeing, and gave it to the leader of a
westbound train, to start it on the long way back to Venice.
I remarked that a letter might have had a better prospect
of getting there if he had posted one on the other side of the
Great Salt.

"I did," he said. "I gave one to a train going west from
Kashan."

I also remarked, without rancor, that he might have apprised my mother in the same way.

"I did," he said again. "I wrote a letter every year, to her
or to Isidoro. I had no way of knowing that they never arrived. But in those days the Mongols were still actively
conquering new territories, not just occupying them, and
the Silk Road was an even less reliable post route than it is
now."

In the evenings, he and my uncle put much devoted
labor, as I have said, into bringing our maps up to date and
place, and I did the same with my log papers of notes taken
so far.

While doing that, I came upon the names of the Princesses Moth and Sunlight, away back in Baghdad, and I
was made acutely aware that I had not lain with a woman
since that long ago. Not that I really needed reminding; I
had got quite tired of the only substitute: waging a war of
the priests in the middle of every other night or so. But I
have mentioned that the Mongols, having no perceptible
organized religion of their own, do not interfere with the
religions practiced by their tributary peoples; neither do
they interfere with the laws observed by those peoples. So

Balkh was still of Islam, and still abided by the sharaiyah, the law of Islam, and all of Balkh's resident females either stayed at home in close pardah or walked abroad only in chador-muffled invisibility. For me to have brashly approached one would have meant, first, chancing the possibility that she was an aged crone like Sunlight, and worse, chancing the likely wrath of her menfolk or the imams and muftis of Islamic law.

Nostril, of course, had found one of his usual perverse (but lawful) outlets for his animal urges. In every karwan train that stopped at Balkh, each Muslim man who did not have an accompanying wife or concubine, or two or three of each, had his kuch-i-safari. That term also signifies "traveling wives," but those really were boys, carried along to be used for wifely purposes, and there was no sharaiyah prohibition against strangers paying for a share of their favors. I knew that Nostril had hastened to do just that, for he had wheedled from me the money for it. But I was not tempted to emulate him. I had seen the kuch-i-safari, and had seen none among them to compare even remotely with the late Aziz.

So I went on wanting and wishing and lusting, and finding nothing to lust *for*. I could only stare hard at every walking heap I passed on the streets, and try in vain to descry what sort of female was inside that bale of clothing. Even doing no more than that, I was risking the outrage of the Balkhites. They call that idle ogling "Eve-baiting," and condemn it as vicious.

Meanwhile, Uncle Mafìo was also being celibate, almost ostentatiously so. For a while, I assumed it was because he was still grieving for Aziz. But it was soon evident that he was simply becoming too physically weak to engage in any dalliance. His persistent cough had been for some time past getting insistent. Now it would come upon him in such racking spells as to leave him feeble afterwards, and compel him to take bed rest. He looked hale enough, and he seemed still as robust as ever, and his color was good. But now, when he began to find it intolerably tiring just to walk from our karwansarai to the bazàr and back, my father and I overrode his protestations and called in a hakim.

Now, that word hakim merely means "wise," not necessarily educated in medicine or professionally qualified or

experienced, and it may be given as a title to one who deserves it—say, the trusted physician to a palace court—or
to one who may not, like a bazàr tomorrow-teller or an old
beggar who gathers and sells herbs. So we were a trifle apprehensive about finding in these parts a person of real
mèdego skill. We had seen many Balkhites with all too obvious afflictions—the most numerous being men with
dangling goiters, like scrotums or melons, under their
jawline—and that did not much inspire us with confidence
in the local medicinal arts. But our karwansarai keeper
fetched for us a certain Hakim Khosro, and we put Uncle
Mafìo in his hands.

He *seemed* to know what he was doing. He had to make
only a brief examination diagnostic to tell my father,
"Your brother is suffering from the hasht nafri. That
means one-of-eight, and we call it that because one of eight
will die of it. But even those mortally stricken do not often
die until after a long time. The jinni of that disease is in no
hurry. Your brother tells me he has had this condition for
some while, and it has worsened only gradually."

"The tisichezza it is, then," said my father, nodding solemnly. "Where we come from, it is sometimes also called
the subtle sickness. Can it be cured?"

"Seven times out of eight, yes," said Hakim Khosro
cheerfully enough. "To begin, I will need certain things
from the kitchen."

He called on the landlord to bring him eggs and millet
seed and barley flour. Then he wrote some words on a number of bits of paper—"powerful verses from the Quran," he
said—and stuck those papers onto Uncle Mafìo's bare chest
with dabs of egg yolk into which he had mixed the millet
seed—"the jinni of this ailment seems to have some affin-
ity to millet seeds." Then he had the innkeeper help him
sprinkle and rub flour all over my uncle's torso, and rolled
a number of goatskins tightly around him, explaining that
this was "to promote the active sweating-out of the jinni's
poisons."

"Malevolenza," growled my uncle. "I cannot even
scratch my itching elbow."

Then he began coughing. Either the flour dust or the excessive heat inside the goatskins sent him into a fit of
coughing that was worse than ever. His arms being pin-
ioned by the wrapping, he could not pummel his chest for

relief, or even cover his mouth, so the coughing went on until it seemed he would strangle, and his ruddy face got more red, and he sprayed little flecks of blood onto the hakim's white aba. After some time of that agony, he turned pale and swooned dead away, and I thought he *had* strangled.

"No, be not alarmed, young man," said Hakim Khosro. "This is nature's means of cure. The jinni of this disease will not trouble a victim when he is not conscious of being troubled. You notice, when your uncle is in the faint, he does not cough."

"He has only to die, then," I said skeptically, "and he is permanently cured of coughing."

The hakim laughed, unoffended, and said, "Be not suspicious either. The hasht nafri can only be arrested in nature's good time, and I can but lend assistance to nature. See, he wakes now, and the fit has passed."

"Gèsu," Uncle Mafìo muttered weakly.

"For now," the hakim went on, "the best prescriptive is rest and perspiration. He is to stay in bed except when he must go to the mustarah, and that he will do frequently, for I am also giving him a strong purgative. There are always jinn hiding in the bowels, and it does no harm to get rid of them. So, each time the patient returns from the mustarah to bed, one of you—since I will not always be here—must dust him with a new coating of barley flour and rewrap the skins about him. I will look in from time to time, to write new verses to be pasted on his chest."

So my father and I and the slave Nostril took turns tending Uncle Mafìo. But that was no onerous duty—except for having to listen to his continuous grumbling about his enforced prostration—and after a while my father decided he might as well make another use of our stay in Balkh. He would leave Mafìo in my keeping, and he and Nostril would travel to the capital city of these regions, to pay our respects to the local ruler (whose title was Sultan) and make us known to him as emissaries of the Khakhan Kubilai. Of course, that city was only nominally a capital, and its sovereign Sultan was, like the Shah Zaman of Persia, only a token ruler, subordinate to the Mongol Khanate. But the journey would also enable my father to embellish our maps with further details and modern designations. For example, our Kitab gave the name of that city as

Kophes, and it was Nikaia in Alexander's time, but nowadays and hereabout we heard it always called Kabul. So my father and Nostril saddled two of our horses and prepared to ride there.

The evening before they departed, Nostril sidled up to me. He had apparently taken notice of my lovelorn and forlorn condition, and perhaps he hoped to keep me out of trouble while I was left on my own in Balkh. He said:

"Master Marco, there is a certain house here in this city. It is the house of a Gebr, and I would have you look at it."

"A Gebr?" I said. "Is that some sort of rare beast?"

"Not all that rare, but bestial, yes. A Gebr is one of the unregenerate Persians who never accepted the enlightenment of the Prophet (blessing and peace be upon him). Those people still worship Ormuzd, the discredited old-time god of fire, and engage in many wicked practices."

"Oh," I said, losing interest. "Why should I look at the house of yet another misbegotten heathen religion?"

"Because this Gebr, not being bound by Muslim law, expectably flouts all decencies. In front, his building is a shop vending articles made of amianthus, but in the rear it is a house of assignation, let by the Gebr to illicit lovers for their clandestine meetings. By the beard, it is an abomination!"

"What would you have me do about it? Go yourself and report it to a mufti."

"No doubt I should, being a devout Muslim, but I will not yet. Not until you have verified the Gebr's abomination, Master Marco."

"I? What the devil do I care about it?"

"Are not you Christians even more scrupulous about other people's decencies?"

"I do not abominate lovers," I said, with a self-pitying sniffle. "I envy them. Would that I had one of my own to take to the Gebr's back door."

"Well, he also perpetrates another offense against morality. For those who do not have a convenient lover, the Gebr keeps two or three young girls in residence and available for hire."

"Hm. This does begin to sound like a matter for reprobation. You did right to bring it to my attention, Nostril. Now, if you could point out that house, I would suitably reward your almost Christian vigilance. . . ."

And so the next day, a day when snow was falling, after
he and my father had ridden off to the southeastward, and
after I had made sure Uncle Mafìo was well snugged in his
goatskins, I walked into the shop Nostril had shown me.
There was a counter piled with bolts and swatches of some
heavy cloth, and also on it was a stone bowl of naft oil feeding a wick burning with a bright yellow flame, and behind
the counter stood añ elderly Persian with a red-hinna'ed
beard.

"Show me your softest goods," I said, as Nostril had instructed me to say.

"Room on the left," said the Gebr, jerking his beard at a
beaded curtain at the back of the shop. "One dirham."

"I should like," I specified, "a beautiful piece of goods."

He sneered. "You show me a beautiful one among these
country rustics, I will pay *you*. Be glad the goods are clean.
One dirham."

"Oh, well, any water to put out a fire," I said. The man
glowered as if I had spat at him, and I realized that was not
the most tactful thing to say to a person who allegedly
worshiped fire. I hastily laid my coin on the counter and
pushed through the rattling curtain.

The little room was hung all about with locust twigs, for
their sweet scent, and was furnished only with a charcoal
brazier and a charpai, which is a crude bed made of a
wooden frame laced crisscross with ropes. The girl was no
prettier of face than the only other female I had paid to
use, that boat girl Malgarita. This one was plainly of some
local tribe, for she spoke the prevailing Pashtun tongue,
and had a woefully scant vocabulary of Trade Farsi. If she
told me her name, I did not catch it, because anybody
speaking Pashtun sounds as if he or she is rapidly and repeatedly and simultaneously clearing the throat, spitting
and sneezing.

But the girl was, as the Gebr had claimed, rather more
cleanly of person than Malgarita had been. In fact, she
made unmistakable complaint that I was *not*, and with
some reason. In coming here, I had not worn my new-
bought clothes; they were too bulky and difficult to get out
of and into. I was wearing the garments I had worn while
crossing the Great Salt and the Karabil, and I daresay
they were markedly odoriferous. They were certainly so

caked with dust and sweat and dirt and salt that they
could almost stand upright even when I got out of them.

The girl held them at arm's length, by her fingertips,
and said, "dirty-dirty!" and "dahb!" and "bohut purana!"
and several other gargled Pashtun noises indicative of revulsion. "I send yours, mine together, be clean."

She swiftly took off her own clothes, bundled them with
mine, bawled what was evidently a call for a servant, and
handed the bundle out the door. I confess that my attention was mainly on the first naked female body I had seen
since Kashan; nevertheless, I noticed that the girl's clothing was made of a material so coarse and thick that,
though cleaner than mine, it also could almost have stood
alone.

The girl's body was more fetching than her face, it being
slim but bearing amazingly large, round, firm breasts for
such a slender figure. I assumed that that was one reason
why the girl had chosen a career in which she would cater
mainly to transient infidels. Muslim men are better attracted by a big fundament, and do not much admire wom-
en's breasts, regarding them only as milk spouts. Anyway,
I hoped the girl would make her fortune in her chosen career while she was still young and shapely. Every woman
of those "Alexandrine" tribes, well before middle age,
grows so gross in the rest of her physique that her once-
splendid bosom becomes just one of a series of fleshy
shelves descending from her several chins to her several
rolls of abdomen.

Another reason why I hoped the girl would make a fortune was that her chosen career was clearly no pleasure to
her. When I attempted to share with her the enjoyment of
the sexual act, by arousing her with fondling of her
zambur, I found she had none. At the arch tip of her
mihrab, where the tiny tuning key should have been, there
was no slightest protrusion. For a moment I thought she
was pathetically deformed, but then I realized that she
was tabzir, as Islam demands. She had nothing there but a
fissure of soft scar tissue. That lack may have diminished
my own delight in my several ejaculations, because every
time I approached spruzzo and she cried, "Ghi, ghi, ghi-
ghi!"—meaning "Yes, yes, yes-yes!"—I was aware that she
was only feigning an ecstasy of her own, and I thought it
sad. But who am I to call criminal other people's religious

observances? Besides, I soon discovered that I had a lack of my own to worry about.

The Gebr came and banged on the outside of the door, shouting, "What do you want for a single dirham, eh?"

I had to concede that I had had my money's worth, so I let the girl get up. She went, still naked, out the door to fetch a pan of water and a towel, meanwhile calling down the corridor for the return of our laundered clothes. She set the pan of tamarind-scented water on the room's brazier to warm, and was using it to wash my parts when the next knock came on the door. But the servant handed in only the girl's garments, with a long spate of Pashtun that must have been an explanation. The girl came back to me, an unreadable expression on her face, and said tentatively, as if asking a question, "Your clothes burn?"

"Yes, I suppose they would. Where are they?"

"No got," she said, showing me that she had only her own.

"Ah, you do not mean burn. You mean dry. Is that it? Mine are not dry yet?"

"No. Gone. Your clothes all burn."

"What does that mean? You said they would be washed."

"No wash. Clean. Not in water. In fire."

"You put my clothes in a *fire?* They have *burned?*"

"Ghi."

"Are you a fire worshiper too, or are you just divanè? You sent them to be washed in fire instead of water? Olà. Gebr! Persian! Olà, whore-master!"

"No make trouble!" the girl pleaded, looking scared. "I give you dirham back."

"I cannot wear a dirham across the city! What kind of lunatic place is this? Why did you people burn my clothes?"

"Wait. Look." She snatched up a piece of unburned charcoal from the brazier and gave it a swipe across a sleeve of her own tunic to make a black mark. Then she held the sleeve over the burning coals.

"You are divanè!" I exclaimed. But the cloth did not take fire. There was only a single flash as the black mark burned away. The girl took the sleeve from the fire to show me how it was suddenly spotless, and babbled a mixture of Pashtun and Farsi, of which I gradually got the import. That heavy and mysterious fabric was always cleaned in

that manner, and my clothes had been so crusty that she
had taken them to be of the same material.

"All right," I said. "I forgive you. It was a well-
intentioned mistake. But I am still without anything to
wear. Now what?"

She indicated that I could choose which of two things I
would do. I could lodge a complaint with the Gebr master,
and demand that he procure new raiment for men, which
would cost the girl her day's wages and probably a beating
besides. Or I could put on what clothes were available—
meaning some of hers—and go across the city of Balkh in
feminine masquerade. Well, that meant no choice at all: I
must be a gentleman; therefore I must play the lady.

I scuttled out through the shop as fast as I could, but I
was still adjusting my cador veil, and the old Gebr behind
the counter raised his eyebrow, exclaiming, "You took me
seriously! You are showing me a beautiful one among
these country rustics!"

I snarled at him one of the few Pashtun expressions I
knew: "Bahi chut!" which is a directive to do something to
one's own sister.

He guffawed and called after me, "I would, if she were as
pretty as you!" while I scurried out into the still falling
snow.

Except for stumbling now and then, because I could see
the ground only dimly through the obscuring snow and my
chador, and also because I frequently stepped on my own
hems, I got back to the karwansarai without incident.
That disappointed me a little, for I had gone the whole way
with my teeth and fists clenched and my temper seething,
hoping to be rudely addressed or winked at by some Eve-
baiting oaf, so I could kill him. I slipped into the inn by a
rear door, unobserved, and hurried to put on clothes of my
own, and started to throw away the girl's. But then I recon-
sidered, and cut from her gown a square of the cloth to
keep for a curiosity, and with it I have since astonished
many persons disinclined to believe that any cloth could be
proof against fire.

Now, I had *heard* of such a substance long before I left
Venice. I had heard priests tell that the Pope at Rome kept
among the treasured relics of the Church a sudarium, a
cloth which had been used to wipe the Holy Brow of Jesus
Christ. The cloth had been so sanctified by that use they

said, that it could nevermore be destroyed. It could be thrown into a fire, and left there for a long time, and taken out again miraculously entire and unscorched. I also had heard a distinguished physician contest the priestly claim that it was the Holy Sweat which made the sudarium impervious to destruction. He insisted that the cloth must be woven of the wool of the salamander, that creature which Aristotle averred lives comfortably in fire.

I will respectfully contradict both the reverent believers and the pragmatic Aristotelian. For I took the trouble to inquire about that unburnable fabric woven by the Gebr fire worshipers, and eventually I was shown how it is made, and the truth of the matter is this. In the mountains in the regions of Balkh is found a certain rock of palpable softness. When that rock is crushed, it comes apart not in grains, as of sand, but in fibers, as of raw flax. And those fibers, after repeated mashing and drying and washing and drying again and carding and spindling, are spun together into thread. It is clear that of any thread a cloth can be woven, and it is equally clear that a cloth made of earth's rock ought not burn. The curious rock and the coarse fiber and the magical material woven of it, all are regarded by the Gebr as sacred to their fire god Ahura Mazda, and they call that substance by a word meaning "unsoilable stone," which I take the liberty of rendering in a more civilized tongue as amianthus.

3

My father and Nostril were gone for some five or six weeks, and, because Uncle Mafìo required my attendance only intermittently, I had a good deal of spare time on my hands. So I went back several times to the house of the Gebr Persian—each time taking care to wear clothes that would not need "laundering." And every time I spoke the password, "Show me your softest goods," the old man would convulse with amusement and roar, "Why, *you* were the softest and most appealing piece that ever passed through this shop!" and I would have to stand and endure his guffaws until he finally subsided into giggles and took my dirham and told me which room was available.

At one time or another, I sampled all three of his back-room wares. But all the girls were Pakhtuni Muslims and tabzir, meaning that I found only release with them, not any satisfaction worth mentioning. I could have done that with the kuch-i-safari, and more cheaply. I did not even learn more than a few words of Pashtun from the girls, deeming it too slovenly a language to be worth learning. Just for example, the sound *gau*, when spoken normally on an exhaled breath, means "cow," but the same gau, spoken while breathing in, means "calf." So imagine what the simple sentence "The cow has a calf" sounds like in Pashtun, and then try to imagine conducting a conversation of any more complexity.

On my way out through the amianthus-cloth shop, though, I would pause to exchange some few words in Farsi with the Gebr proprietor. He would usually make some further mocking remarks about the day I had had to masquerade as a woman, but he would also condescend to answer my questions about this peculiar religion. I asked because he was the only devotee of that old-time Persian religion I had ever met. He admitted that there were few believers left in these days, but he maintained that the religion once had reigned supreme, not only in Persia but west and east of there as well, from Armeniya to Bactria. And the first thing he told me about it was that I should not call a Gebr a Gebr.

"The word means only 'non-Muslim' and it is used by the Muslims derisively. We prefer to be called Zarduchi, for we are the followers of the prophet Zaratushtra, the Golden Camel. It was he who taught us to worship the god Ahura Mazda, whose name is nowadays slurred to Ormuzd."

"And that means fire," I said knowledgably, for Nostril had told me that much. I nodded toward the bright lamp that always burned in the shop.

"*Not* fire," he said, sounding annoyed. "It is a stupid misbelief that we worship fire. Ahura Mazda is the God of Light, and we merely keep a flame burning as a reminder of His beneficent light which banishes the darkness of his adversary Ahriman."

"Ah," I said. "Not too different, then, from our own Lord God, Who contends against the adversary Satan."

"No, not different at all. Your Christian God and Satan you got from the Jews, as the Muslims derived their Allah and Shaitan. And the God and the Devil of the Jews were frankly patterned on our Ahura Mazda and Ahriman. So were your God's angels and your Satan's demons copied from our celestial malakhim messengers and their daeva counterparts. So were your Heaven and Hell copied from Zaratushtra's teachings about the nature of the afterlife."

"Oh, come now!" I protested. "I hold no brief for the Jews or the Muslims, but the True Religion cannot have been a mere imitation of somebody else's—"

He interrupted, "Look at any picture of a Christian deity or angel or saint. He or she is portrayed with a glowing halo, is that not so? It is a pretty fancy, but it was our fancy first. That halo imitates the light of our ever-burning flame, which in turn signifies the light of Ahura Mazda forever shining on His messengers and holy ones."

That sounded likely enough that I could not dispute it, but neither would I concede it, of course. He went on:

"That is why we Zardushi have for centuries been persecuted and derided and dispersed and driven into exile. By Muslims and Jews and Christians alike. A people who pride themselves on possessing the only true religion must pretend that it came to them through some exclusive revelation. They do not like to be reminded that it merely derives from some other people's original."

I went back to the karwansarai that day, thinking: the Church is perhaps wise to demand faith and forbid reason in Christians. The more questions I ask, and the more answers I get, the less I seem to know of anything for certain. As I walked along, I scooped up a handful of snow from a snowbank I was passing, and I wadded it to a snowball. It was round and solid, like a certainty. But if I looked at it closely enough, its roundness really was a dense multitude of points and corners. If I held it long enough, its solidity would melt to water. That is the hazard in curiosity, I thought: all the certainties fragment and dissolve. A man curious enough and persistent enough might find even the round and solid ball of earth to be not so. He might be less proud of his faculty of reasoning when it left him with nothing whereon to stand. But then again, was not the truth a more solid foundation than illusion?

I forget whether it was on that day or another that I got back to the karwansarai to find that my father and Nostril had returned from their journey. The Hakim Khosro was there, too, and they were gathered about the sickbed of Uncle Mafìo, all talking at once.

". . . Not in the city called Kabul. The Sultan Kutb-ud-Din now has a capital far to the southeast of there, a city called Delhi. . . ."

"No wonder you were gone so long," said my uncle.

". . . Had to cross the vasty mountains, through a pass called the Khaibar . . ."

". . . Then clear across the land called Panjab . . ."

"Or properly Panch Ab," the hakim put in, "meaning Five Rivers."

". . . But worth the effort. The Sultan, like the Shah of Persia, was eager to send gifts of tribute and fealty to the Khakhan. . . ."

". . . So we now have an extra horse, laden with objects of gold and Kashmir cloth and rubies and . . ."

"But more important," said my father, "how fares our patient Mafìo?"

"Empty," growled my uncle, scratching his elbow. "From one end I have coughed out all my sputum, from the other I have spewed out every last turd and fart, and in between I have sweated out every last bead of perspiration. I am also infernally tired of being stuck all over with paper charms and powdered all over like a bignè bun."

"Otherwise, his condition is unchanged," the Hakim Khosro said soberly. "My efforts to assist nature in a cure have not availed much. I am happy you are all together again, for I now wish you all to go from this place, and take the patient even closer to nature. Up, into the high mountains to the east, where the air is more clear and pure."

"But cold," my father objected. "As cold as charity. Can that be good for him?"

"Cold air is the cleanest air," said the hakim. "I have determined that, by close observation and professional study. Witness: people who live in always cold climates, like the Russniaks, are a clean white of skin color; in hot climates, like the Indian Hindus, dirty brown or black. We Pakhtuni, living midway, are a sort of tan color. I urge you to take the patient, and take him soon, to those cold, clean, white mountain heights."

When the hakim and we helped Uncle Mafìo get up and get out of the goatskin wrappings and get dressed for the first time in weeks, we were dismayed to see how thin he had become. He looked even taller in his suddenly over-sized clothes than he had seemed before, when his burli-ness had strained his clothes at the seams. He was also pale instead of ruddy, and his limbs were tremulous from disuse, but he proclaimed himself tremendously glad to be up and about. And later, in the hall of the karwansarai, when we dined that night, he bellowed to the other diners, in a voice as stentorian as ever, asking for the latest word on the mountain trails to the eastward.

Men from several other karwan trains responded, and told us of current conditions, and gave us much advice rele-vant to mountain travel. Or we hoped the advice was rele-vant, but we could not be sure, since no two of our informants seemed to agree on even the name of those mountains east of here.

One man said, "Those are the Himalaya, the Abode of the Snows. Before you go up into them, buy a phial of poppy juice to carry. In case of snowblindness, a few drops in the eyes will relieve the pain."

And another man said, "Those are the Karakoram, the Black Mountains, the Cold Mountains. And the snow-fed waters up there are cold at all seasons of the year. Do not let your horses drink, except from a pail in which you have warmed the water a little, or they will be convulsed by cramps."

And another said, "Those are the mountains called Hindu Kush, the Hindu Killers. In that hard terrain, a horse sometimes gets rebellious and unmanageable. Should that occur, simply tie the hair of the horse's tail to its tongue, and it will quieten on the instant."

And another said, "Those mountains are the Pai-Mir, meaning the Way to the Peaks. The only forage your horses will find yonder is the slate-colored, strong-smell-ing little shrub called burtsa. But your horses *will* always find it for you, and it is also good fuel for a fire, being natu-rally full of oil. Oddly enough, the greener it looks, the bet-ter the burtsa burns."

And another said, "Those mountains are the Khwaja,

the Masters. And up there the Masters make it impossible
for you to lose your direction, even in the thickest storm.
Just remember that every mountain is barren on its south
face. If you see any trees or shrubs or growth at all, it is on
the mountain's north face."

And another said, "Those mountains are the Muztagh,
the Keepers. Try to get completely through and out of
them before spring becomes summer, for then begins the
Bad-i-sad-o-bist, the terrible Wind of One Hundred and
Twenty Days."

And yet another man said, "Those mountains are Solomon's Throne, the Takht-i-Sulaiman. If you should encounter a whirlwind up there, you may be sure it issues
from some cavern nearby, the den of one of the demons
banished into that exile by the good King Solomon. Simply
find that cavern and stop it with boulders, and the wind
will die."

So we packed and we paid for our keep and we said some
goodbyes to those with whom we had got acquainted and
again we moved on, my father and uncle and Nostril and I,
riding our four mounts and leading a packhorse and two
extra packhorses loaded with a princely amount of valuables. We went straight east from Balkh, through villages
named Kholm and Qonduz and Taloqan, which seemed to
exist only as marketplaces for the horse breeders who inhabit that grassy region. Everybody thereabout raises
horses and is continually trading breed stallions and brood
mares with his neighbors at the markets. The horses are
fine ones, comparable to Arabians, though not so dainty in
the shape of the head. Every breeder claims that his stock
are descended from Alexander's steed Bucephalas. Every
breeder makes that claim for his stock only, which is ridiculous, with all the trading that goes on. Anyway, I never
saw any horses there that had the peacock tail worn by
Bucephalas in the illuminations to *The Book of Alexander*
that I had pored over in my youth.

At this season, the grazing lands were covered by snow,
so we could not see how the verdure thinned out as we
went eastward. But we knew it did so, because the ground
under the snow got pebbly, then rocky, and the villages
ceased to be, and there was only an infrequent and inadequate karwansarai along the trail. After we had passed
the last village, a cluster of piled-stone huts which called

itself Keshem, in the foothills preceding the mountains, we had to make our own stopping places perhaps three nights out of four. That was not an idyllic way to live, sleeping under tents and under our chapons in snow and chill and wind, and generally having to dine on dried or salted travel rations.

We had worried that the outdoor life would be especially hard on Uncle Mafìo. But he made no complaint even when we healthier ones did. He maintained that he *was* feeling better in that sharp, cold air, as the Hakim Khosro had predicted, and his cough had lessened and did not lately bring up any blood. He allowed the rest of us to take over what heavy work had to be done, but he would not let us shorten the marches on his account, and each day he sat his saddle or, on the rougher stretches, walked beside his horse, as indefatigably as any of us. We were not hurrying, anyway, for we knew we would have to halt for the rest of the winter as soon as we came up against the mountain ramparts. Also, after a while on that hard trail, living on hard rations, the rest of us were nearly as gaunt as Uncle Mafìo was, and not eager to exert ourselves. Only Nostril kept his paunch, but it looked now less integral to him, like a separate melon he was carrying under his clothes.

When we came to the Ab-e-Panj River, we followed its broad valley upstream to the eastward, and from then on we were going uphill, ever higher above the level of the rest of the world. To speak of a valley ordinarily brings to mind a depression in the earth, but that one is many farsakhs wide and is lower only in relation to the mountains that rise far off on either side of it. If it were anywhere else in the world, that valley would not be *on* the world, but immeasurably far above it, high among the clouds, unseeable by mortal eyes, unattainable, like Heaven. Not that the valley resembles Heaven in any way, I hasten to say, it being cold and hard and inhospitable, not balmy and soft and welcoming.

The landscape was unvarying: the wide valley of tumbled rocks and scrub growth, all humped under quilts of snow; the white-water river running through; and far away on both sides the tooth-white, tooth-sharp mountains. Nothing ever changed there but the light, which ranged from sunrises colored like gilded peaches to sunsets colored like roses on fire, and in between, skies so blue they were near to purple, except when the valley was roofed by clouds of wet gray wool wringing out snow or sleet.

The ground was nowhere level, being all a clutter of boulders and rocks and talus that we had to thread our way around or gingerly make our way across. But, apart from those ups and downs, our continuous climb was imperceptible to our sight, and we might almost have supposed that we were still on the plains. For, each night when we stopped to camp, the mountains on either horizon seemed identically high to those of the night before. But that was only because the mountains were getting higher, the farther we climbed that up-sloping valley. It was like going up a staircase where the banister always keeps pace with you and, if you do not look over, you do not realize that everything beyond is dropping down and away from you.

Nevertheless, we had various means of knowing that we were climbing all the time. One was the behavior of our horses. We two-legged creatures, when we occasionally dismounted to walk for a while, might not have been physically aware that each step forward was also a trifle higher, but the animals with legs fore and aft knew well that they always stood or moved at an incline. And, horses having good sense, they slyly exaggerated their trudging walk to make it seem a plodding labor, so that we would not press them to move faster.

Another indicator of the climb was the river running the length of the valley. The Ab-e-Panj, we had been told, is one of the headwater sources of the Oxus, that great river which Alexander crossed and recrossed, and in his *Book* it is described as immensely broad and slow-running and tranquil. However, that is far to the west and downhill of where we were now. The Ab-e-Panj alongside our trail was not wide nor deep, but it raced through that valley like an endless stampede of white horses, tossing white manes and tails. It even sounded sometimes more like a stampede than a river, the noise of its cascading water being often lost in the scrape and grate and rumble of the sizable boulders it rolled and jostled along its bed. A blind man could have told that the Ab-e-Panj was hurtling downhill and, for it to have such momemtum, the river's uphill end had to be somewhere far higher yet. In this winter season, cer-

tainly, the river could not for a moment have slowed its tumultuous pace, or it would have frozen solid, and there
might not have existed any Oxus downstream. This was
apparent, because every splash and spatter and lick of the
water on the rock banks instantly turned to blue-white ice.
Since that made the footing close to the river even more
treacherous than the snow-covered ground—and also because every splash of the water that reached us froze on
our horses' legs and flanks, or on ours—we kept our trail
well to one side of the river wherever we could.

Still another indicator of our continuous climb was the
noticeable thinning of the very air. Now, I have been often
disbelieved, and even jeered, when I have told of this to
non-journeyers. I know as well as they do that air is
weightless at all times, impalpable except when it moves
as wind. When the disbelievers demanded to know *how* an
element without the least weight can have less weight yet,
I cannot tell them how, or why; I only know it does. It gets
less and less substantial in those upland heights, and
there are evidences to show it.

For one, a man has to breathe deeper to fill his lungs.
This is not the panting occasioned by fast movement or
brisk exercise; a man standing still has to do it. When I exerted myself—loading a horse's packsaddle, say, or clambering over a boulder blocking the trail—I had to breathe
so fast and hard and deep that it seemed I never would get
enough air into me to sustain me. Some disbelievers have
dismissed that as a delusion fostered by tedium and hardship, of which God knows we had enough to contend with,
but I maintain that the insubstantial air was a very real
thing. I will additionally adduce the fact that Uncle Mafìo,
though he like all of us had to breathe deep, was not so frequently or painfully afflicted by the need to cough. Clearly, the thin air of the heights lay not so heavily in his lungs
and did not so often have to be forcibly expelled.

I have other evidence. Fire and air, both being weightless, are the closest-related of the four elements; everybody
will concede that. And in the high lands where the air is
feebler, so is fire. It burns more blue and dim than yellow
and bright. This was not just a result of our having to burn
the local burtsa shrub for fuel; I experimented with burning other and more familiar things, like paper, and the resultant flame was equally debile and languid. Even when

we had a well-fueled and well-laid camp fire, it took longer
to char a piece of meat or to boil a pot of water than it had
done in lower lands. Not only that, the boiling water also
took longer than customary to cook something put into it.

In that winter season, there were no great karwan
trains on the trail, but we did meet an occasional other
traveling party. Most of these were hunters and trappers
of furs, moving from place to place in the mountains. The
winter was their working season, and in the clement
springtime they would take their accumulated stores of
hides and pelts down to market in one of the lowland
towns. Their shaggy little packhorses were heaped with
the baled pelts of fox, wolf, pard, the urial, which is a wild
sheep, and the goral, which is something between a goat
and a qazèl. The hunter-trappers told us that this valley
which we were climbing was called the Wakhàn—or sometimes the Wakhàn Corridor, because many mountain
passes open off it on all sides, like doors off a corridor, and
the valley constitutes both the border between and the access to all the lands beyond. To the south, they said, were
passes leading out of the Corridor to lands called Chitral
and Hunza and Kashmir, in the east leading to a land
called To-Bhot, and in the north to the land of Tazhikistan.

"Ah, Tazhikistan is yonder?" said my father, turning to
gaze to the north. "Then we are not too far now, Mafìo,
from the route we took homeward."

"True," said my uncle, sounding tired and relieved. "We
have only to go through Tazhikistan, then a short way east
to the city of Kashgar, and we are again in Kubilai's Kithai."

On their packhorses, the hunter-trappers also carried
many horns which they had taken from a kind of wild
sheep called the artak, and I, having so far seen only the
lesser horn-racks of such animals as the qazèl and cows
and domestic sheep, was mightily impressed by those
horns. At their root end they were as big around as my
thigh, and from there they spiraled tightly to points. On
the animal's head, the points would be easily a man's
length apart; but if the spirals could have been unwound
and stretched out straight, *each* of the horns must have
measured a man's length. They were such magnificent
things that I supposed the hunters took them and sold
them for ornaments to be admired. No, they said, laugh-

ing; those great horns were to be cut and fashioned into all
manner of useful articles: eating bowls and drinking cups
and saddle stirrups and even horse shoes. They averred
that a horse shod with such horn shoes would never slip on
the most slippery road.

(Many months later, and higher in the mountains, when
I saw some of those artak sheep alive and at liberty in the
wild, I thought them so splendidly beautiful that I deplored the killing of them for merely utile purposes. My father and uncle, to whom utility meant commerce and
commerce meant everything, laughed as the hunters had
done, and chided my sentimentality, and from that time on
referred sarcastically to the artak as "Marco's sheep.")

As we went up on the Wakhàn, the mountains on either
side remained as awesomely high as ever, but now, each
time the snowfall let up enough for us to raise our eyes to
the mountains' immensity, they stood perceptibly closer to
us. And the banks of ice on either side of the Ab-e-Panj
River built up thicker and bluer, and constricted the
racing water to an ever narrower stream between them, as
if vividly to illustrate how the winter was closing its grip
on the land.

The mountains kept shouldering in on us day by day,
and finally others reared up in front of us as well, until we
had those Titans standing close all around us except at our
backs. We had come to the head end of that high valley,
and the snowfall ceased briefly and the clouds cleared, for
us to see the white mountain peaks and the cold blue sky
magnificently reflected in a tremendous frozen lake, the
Chaqmaqtin. From under the ice at its western end spilled
the Ab-e-Panj we had been following, so we took the lake to
be the river's source, hence also the ultimate headwater of
the fabled Oxus. My father and uncle marked it so, according to their practice, on the Kitab's otherwise imprecise
map of that region. I was not any help in locating our position, as the horizon was much too high and jagged for me to
make use of the kamàl. But, when the night sky was clear,
I could at least tell, from the height of the North Star, that
we were now a far way north of where we had begun our
overland march at Suvediye on the Levant shore.

At the northeastern end of Lake Chaqmaqtin stood a
community that called itself a town, Buzai Gumbad, but
it really comprised only a single extensive karwansarai of

many buildings, and roundabout it a tent city and the corrals of karwan trains encamped for the winter. It was evident that, come better weather, almost the entire population of Buzai Gumbad would get up and vacate the Wakhàn Corridor by way of its various passes. The landlord of the karwansarai was a jolly and expansive man named Iqbal, which means Good Fortune, and the name was apt for one who prospered richly by owning the only karwan stopping place on that stretch of the Silk Road. He was a native Wakhani, he said, born right there in the inn. But, as the son and grandson and great-grandson of previous generations of Buzai Gumbad's innkeepers, he of course spoke Trade Farsi, and had, if not experience, good hearsay knowledge of the world beyond the mountains.

Spreading his arms wide, Iqbal welcomed us most cordially to "the high Pai-Mir, the Way to the Peaks, the Roof of the World," and then confided that his extravagant words were no exaggeration. Here, he said, we were exactly one farsakh straight up—that is, two and a half miles—above the level of the earth's seas and such sea-level cities as Venice and Acre and Basra. Landlord Iqbal did not explain how he could know so *exactly* the local altitude. But, assuming he spoke true—and because the mountain peaks around us visibly stood as high again—I would not dispute his claim that we had come to the Roof of the World.

THE ROOF OF
THE WORLD

1

WE engaged a room for ourselves, including Nostril as one of us, in the main building of the inn, and corral space for our horses outside, and prepared to stay in Buzai Gumbad until the winter broke. The karwansarai was no very elegant place, and, because all its appurtenances and most of its supplies had to be imported from beyond the mountains, Iqbal charged his guests high for their keep. But the place was actually more comfortable than it had to be, considering the circumstance that it was all there was, and that neither Iqbal nor his forebears need ever have bothered to provide any more than the most rudimentary shelter and provender.

The main building was of two stories—the first karwansarai I had seen built so—the bottom half being a commodious stable for Iqbal's own cattle and sheep, which constituted both his life savings and his inn's larder. The upstairs was for people, and was encircled by an open portico which had, outside each sleeping chamber, a privy hole cut in its floor, so that the guests' droppings fell into the inn yard for the benefit of a flock of scrawny chickens. The lodgings being upstairs over the stable meant that we enjoyed the warmth wafting upward from the animals, but we did not much enjoy the smell of them. Still, that was not so bad as the smell of us and the other long-unwashed guests and our unwashed garments. The landlord would

not squander precious dried-dung fuel on anything like a
hammam or hot water for washing clothes.

He preferred, and so did we guests, to use the fuel to
keep our beds warm at night. All of Iqbal's beds were of the
style called in the East the kang, a hollow platform of
piled-up stones covered with boards supporting a heap of
camel-hair blankets. Before retiring, one lifted the planks,
spread some dry dung inside the kang and placed on that a
few burning coals. The newcome traveler usually did it
inexpertly at first, and either froze all night or set the
planks afire under him. But with practice one learned to
lay the fire so that it smoldered all night at an even
warmth, and did not make quite enough smoke to suffocate everybody in the room. Each guest chamber also had a
lamp, handmade by Iqbal himself, and the like of which I
never saw elsewhere. To make one, he would take a camel's bladder, blow it up to a sphere, then paint it with lacquer to make it hold that shape and to give it a bright
design of many colors. With a hole cut out of it so it could
be positioned over a candle or an oil lamp, that big globe
gave a varicolored and most radiant glow.

The inn's everyday meals were the usual Muslim monotony: mutton and rice, rice and mutton, boiled beans, big
rounds of a thin-rolled, chewy bread called nan, and, for
drink, a green-colored cha that always had an inexplicable
slight taste of fish. But good host Iqbal did his best to vary
the monotony whenever he had an excuse: on every Muslim Sabbath Friday and on the various Muslim feste days
which occurred during that winter. I do not know what the
days celebrated—they had names like Zu-l-Heggeh and
Yom Ashura—but on such occasions we were served beef
instead of mutton, and a rice called pilaf, colored red or yellow or blue. There were also sometimes fried meat tarts
called samosa, and a sort of sharbat confection of snow flavored with pistachio or sandalwood, and once—once only,
but I think I still can taste it—for a sweet, we were served a
pudding made of crushed ginger and garlic.

There was nothing to prevent our eating the various
foods of other nationalities and religions, and we frequently did. In the lesser outbuildings of the karwansarai,
and in tents all around it, were camped the people of many
karwan trains, and they were people of many different
countries and customs and languages. There were Persian

and Arab merchants and Pakhtuni horse traders who had
come, like us, from the west, and big blond Russniaks from
the far north, and shaggy, burly Tazhiks from the nearer
north, and flat-faced Bho from the easterly land called the
High Place of the Bho, or To-Bhot in their language, and
dark-skinned little Hindus and Tamil Cholas from southern India, and gray-eyed, sandy-haired people called
Hunzukut and Kalash from the nearer south, and some
Jews of indeterminate origin, and numerous others. This
was the commingled population which made of Buzai
Gumbad a town-sized community—in the wintertime,
anyway—and they all exerted themselves to make it a
well-run and livable town. Indeed, it was a much more
neighborly and friendly community than many settled and
permanent ones I have been in.

At any mealtime, anybody could sit down at any family's cook fire and be made welcome—even if he and they
could not speak a mutually comprehensible language—the
understanding being that his next cook fire would be
equally hospitable to any comer. By the end of that winter,
I think we Polos had sampled every kind of food that was
served in Buzai Gumbad, and, since we did there no cooking of our own, had treated as many strangers to meals in
Iqbal's dining hall. Besides offering a variety of eating
experiences—some memorable for their deliciousness, a
few memorable for their awfulness—the community provided other diversions. Almost every day was a festa day
for some group of people, and they were pleased to have
everybody else in the encampment come and watch or join
in their music making and singing and dancing and games
of sport. All the doings in Buzai Gumbad were not festive,
of course, but the diversity of people managed to unite in
more solemn matters, too. Because they observed among
them so many different codes of law, they had elected one
man of every color, tongue, and religion gathered there, to
sit together as a court for hearing complaints of pilferage
and trespass and other disturbances of the peace.

I have mentioned the law court and the festivities in the
same breath, as it were, because they figured together in
one incident I found amusing. The handsome people called
the Kalash were a quarrelsome sort, but only among themselves, and not ferociously so; their quarrels usually ended
in laughter all around. They were also a merry and mu-

sical and graceful sort; they had any number of different
Kalash dances, with names like the kikli and the dhamal,
and they danced them almost every day. But one of their
dances, called the luddi, remains unique in my experience
of dances.

I saw it performed first by a Kalash man who had been
hailed before the motley court of Buzai Gumbad, accused
of having stolen a set of camel bells from a Kalash neighbor. When the court acquitted him, for lack of evidence,
the entire contingent of Kalash folk—including his accuser—set up a squalling and clattering music of flutes and
chimta tongs and hand drums, and the man began to dance
the flailing, flinging luddi dance, and eventually his whole
family joined him in it. I saw the luddi performed next by
the other Kalash man, the one who had lost the camel
bells. When the court was unable to produce either the
bells or a punishable culprit, it ordered that a collection be
taken up from every head of household in the encampment
to recompense the victim. This meant only a few coppers
from every contributor, but the total was probably more
than the purloined bells had been worth. And when the
man was handed the money, the entire contingent of
Kalash folk—including the accused but acquitted thief—
again set up a screechy, rackety music of flutes and tongs
and hand drums, and *that* man began to dance the flailing,
flinging luddi dance, and eventually *his* whole family
joined him in it. The luddi, I learned, is a Kalash dance
which the happily quarrelsome Kalash dance only and
specifically to celebrate a victory in litigation. I wish I
could introduce to litigious Venice something of the sort.

I thought the composite court had judged wisely in that
case, as I thought they did in most cases, considering what
a touchy job they had. Of all the peoples gathered in Buzai
Gumbad, probably no two were accustomed to abiding by
(or disobeying) the same set of laws. Drunken rape seemed
to be a commonplace among the Nestorian Russniaks, as
Sodomite sex was among the Muslim Arabs, while both
those practices were regarded with horror by the pagan
and irreligious Kalash. Petty thievery was a way of life for
the Hindus, and that was tolerantly condoned by the Bho,
who regarded anything not tied down as ownerless, but
theft was condemned as criminal by the dirty but honest
Tazhiks. So the members of the court had to tread a nar-

row course, trying to dispense acceptable justice while not insulting any group's accepted customs. And not every case brought to trial was as trivial as the affair of the stolen camel bells.

One that had come to court before we Polos arrived was still being recounted and discussed and argued over. An elderly Arab merchant had charged the youngest and comliest of his four wives with having abandoned him and eloped to the tent of a young and good-looking Russniak. The outraged husband did not want her back; he wanted her and her lover condemned to death. The Russniak contended that under the law of his homeland a woman was as fair game as any forest animal, and belonged to the taker. Besides, he said, he truly loved her. The errant wife, a woman of the Kirghiz people, pleaded that she had found her lawful husband repugnant, in that he never entered her except in the foul Arab manner, by the rear entrance, and she felt entitled to a change of partners, if only to get a change of position. But besides that, she said, she truly loved the Russniak. I asked our landlord Iqbal how the trial had come out. (Iqbal, being one of the few permanent inhabitants of Buzai Gumbad, hence a leading citizen, was naturally elected to every winter's new court.)

He shrugged and said, "Marriage is marriage in any land, and a man's wife is his property. We had to find for the cuckolded husband in that aspect of the case. He was given permission to put his faithless wife to death. But we denied him any part in deciding the fate of her lover."

"What was his punishment?"

"He was only made to stop loving her."

"But she was dead. What use—?"

"We decreed that his love for her must die, too."

"I—I do not quite understand. How could that be done?"

"The woman's dead body was laid naked on a hillside. The convicted adulterer was chained and staked just out of reach of her. They were left that way."

"For him to starve to death beside her?"

"Oh, no. He was fed and watered and kept quite comfortable until he was released. He is free now, and he still lives, but he no longer loves her."

I shook my head. "Forgive me, Mirza Iqbal, but I really do not understand."

"A dead body, lying unburied, does not just lie there. It

changes, day by day. On the first day, only some discoloration, wherever there was last a pressure on the skin. In the
woman's case, some mottling about the throat, where her
husband's fingers had strangled her. The lover had to sit
and see those blotches appearing on her flesh. Perhaps
they were not too gruesome to look at. But a day or so later,
a cadaver's abdomen begins to swell. In another little
while, a dead body begins to belch and otherwise expel its
inner pressures in manners most unmannerly. Later,
there come flies—"

"Thank you. I begin to understand."

"Yes, and he had to watch it all. In the cold here, the process is slowed somewhat, but the decay is inexorable. And
as the corpse putrefies, the vultures and the kites descend,
and the shaqàl dogs come boldly closer, and—"

"Yes, yes."

"In ten days or thereabouts, when the remains were
deliquescing, the young man had lost all love for her. We
believe so, anyway. He was quite insane by then. He went
away with the Russniak train, but being led on a rope behind their wagons. He still lives, yes, but if Allah is merciful, perhaps he will not live long."

The karwan trains wintering there on the Roof of the
World were laden with all sorts of goods and, while I found
many of them worth admiring—silks and spices, jewels
and pearls, furs and hides—most of those were no great
novelty to me. But some of the trade items I had never
even heard of before. A train of Samoyeds, for instance,
was bringing down from the far north baled sheets of what
they called Muscovy glass. It looked like glass cut into rectangular panes, and each sheet measured about my arm's
length square, but its transparency was marred by crack-
lings and webbings and blemishes. I learned that it was
not real glass at all, but a product of another strange kind
of rock. Rather like amianthus, which comes apart in fibers, this rock peels apart like the pages of a book, yielding
the thin, brittle, blearily transparent sheets. The material
was far inferior to real glass, such as that made at Murano,
but the art of glassworking is unknown in most of the
East, so the Muscovy glass was a fairly adequate substitute and, said the Samoyeds, fetched a good price in the
markets.

From the other end of the earth, from the far south, a

train of Tamil Cholas was transporting out of India toward Balkh heavy bags of nothing but salt. I laughed at the dark-skinned little men. I had seen no lack of salt in Balkh, and I thought them stupid to be lugging such a common commodity across whole continents. The tiny, timid Cholas begged my indulgence of their obsequious explanation: it was "sea salt," they said. I tasted it—no different from any other salt—and I laughed again. So they explained further: there was some quality inherent to sea salt, they claimed, that is lacking in other sorts. The use of it as a seasoning for foods would prevent people's being beset by goiters, and for that reason they expected the sea salt to sell in these lands for a price worth their trouble of bringing it so far. "Magic salt?" I scoffed, for I had seen many of those ghastly goiters, and I knew they would require more than the eating of a sprinkling of salt to remove. I laughed again at the Cholas' credulity and folly, and they looked properly chastened, and I went on my way.

The riding and pack animals corraled about the lakeside were almost as various as their owners. There were whole herds of horses and asses, of course, and even a few fine mules. But the many camels there were not the same sort that we had formerly seen and used in the lowland deserts. These were not so tall or long-legged, but bulkier of build, and made to look even more ponderous by their long, thick hair. They also wore a mane, like a horse, except that the mane depended from the bottom, not the top, of their long necks. But the chief novelty of them was that they all had two humps instead of one; it made them easier to ride, since they had a natural saddle declivity between the two humps. I was told that these Bactrian camels were best adapted to wintry conditions and mountainous terrain, as the single-humped Arabian camels are to heat and thirst and desert sands.

Another animal new to me was the pack-carrier of the Bho people, called by them an yyag and by most other people a yak. This was a massive ends of a body resembling a haystack in shape and size and texture. The yak may stand as high as a man's shoulder, but its head is carried low, at about a man's knee level. Its shaggy, coarse hair—black or gray or mixed dark and white in patches—hangs all the way to the ground, obscuring hoofs that look too

dainty for its great bulk, but those hoofs are astonishingly
precise of step and placement on narrow mountain trails.
A yak grunts and grumbles like a pig, and continuously
gnashes its millstone teeth as it shambles along.

I learned later that yak meat is as good to eat as the best
beef, but no yak-herder in Buzai Gumbad had occasion to
slaughter one of the animals while we were there. The Bho
did, however, milk the cow yaks of their herds, a procedure
which takes some daring, given the immense size and
unpredictable irritability of those animals. That milk, of
which the Bho had so much that they gave it freely to
others, was delicious, and the butter which the Bho made
from it would have been a praiseworthy delicacy if only it
had not always had long yak hairs embedded in it. The yak
gives other useful products: its coarse hair can be woven
into tents so sturdy that they will stand against mountain
gales, and its much finer tail hairs make excellent fly
whisks.

Among the smaller animals at Buzai Gumbad, I saw
many of the red-legged partridges I had in other places
seen wild, these having their wings clipped so they could
not fly. Since the camp children were forever playing hide-
and-seek with the bird, I took them to be kept for either
pets or pest catchers—every tent and building being infested with insect vermin. But I soon learned that the partridges had another and peculiar utility for the Kalash and
Hunzukut women.

They would chop the red legs off those birds, keep the
flesh for the pot, and burn the legs to a fine ash, which
came out of the fire as a purple powder. That powder they
used, as other Eastern women use alkohl, as a cosmetic for
ringing and enhancing their eyes. The Kalash women also
painted their faces all over with a cream made from the
yellow seeds of flowers called bechu, and I can attest that a
woman with a face entirely bright yellow, except for the
great, purple-masked eyes, is a sight to see. No doubt the
women deemed that it made them sexually attractive, because their other favorite ornamentation was a cap or hood
and a cape made of innumerable little shells called kauri,
and a kauri shell is easily seen as a perfect human female
sex organ in miniature.

Speaking of which, I was pleased to hear that Buzai
Gumbad offered a sexual outlet other than drunken rape,

Sodomy and hideously punishable adultery. It was Nostril
who nosed it out, when we had been in the community only
a day or two, and again he sidled up to me as he had done
in Balkh, pretending disgust at the discovery:

"A foul Jew this time, Master Marco. He has taken the
small karwansarai building farthest from the lake. In
front, it pretends to be a grinding shop for the sharpening
of knives and swords and tools. But in the rear he keeps a
variety of females of varied race and color. As a good Muslim, I should denounce this carrion bird perched on the
Roof of the World, but I will not unless you bid me to, after
you have cast a Christian eye upon the establishment."

I told him I would, and I did, a few days later, after we
were unpacked and well settled in residence. In the shop at
the front of the building, a man sat hunched, holding a
scythe blade to a grinding wheel that he was turning with
a foot treadle. Except that he wore a skullcap, he would
have resembled a khers bear, for he was very hairy of face,
and those locks and whiskers seemed to merge into the
great furry coat he wore. I took note that the coat was of
costly karakul, an elegant garment for the mere knife
grinder he pretended to be. I waited for a pause in the
gritty whir of the spinning stone wheel and the rain of
sparks it was spraying all about.

Then I said, as Nostril had instructed, "I have a special
tool I wish pointed and greased."

The man raised his head, and I blinked. His hair and
eyebrows and beard were like a curly red fungus going
gray, and his eyes were like blackberries, and his nose like
a shimshir blade.

"One dirham," he said, "or twenty shahis or a hundred
kauri shells. Strangers coming for the first time pay in advance."

"I am no stranger," I said warmly. "Do you not know
me?"

Less than warmly, he said, "I know no one. That is how I
stay in business in a place rife with contradictory laws."

"But I am Marco!"

"Here, you drop your name when you drop your lower
garment. If I am questioned by some meddling mufti, I can
say truthfully that I know no names except my own, which
is Shimon."

"The Tzaddik Shimon?" I asked impudently. "One of the Lamed-vav? Or all thirty-six of them?"

He looked either alarmed or suspicious. "You speak the Ivrit? You are no Jew! What do you know of the Lamed-vav?"

"Only that I seem to keep meeting them." I sighed. "A woman named Esther told me what they are called and what they do."

He said disgustedly, "She could not have told you very accurately, if you can mistake a brothel keeper for a tzaddik."

"She said the tzaddikim do good for men. So does a brothel, in my opinion. Now—are you not going to warn me, as always before?"

"I just did. The kerwan muftis can often be meddlesome. Do not go braying your name around here."

"I mean about the bloodthirstiness of beauty."

He snorted. "If at your age, Nameless, you have not yet learned the danger of beauty, I will not attempt to instruct a fool. Now, one dirham or the equivalent, or begone."

I dropped the coin into his callused palm and said, "I should like a woman who is not Muslim. Or at least not tabzir in her parts. Also, if possible, I should like one I can talk to for a change."

"Take the Domm girl," he grunted. "She never stops talking. Through that door, second room on the right." He bent again to the scythe and the wheel, and the rasping noise and the flying sparks again filled the shop.

The brothel consisted, like the one in Balkh, of a number of rooms that would better have been called cubicles, opening off a corridor. The Domm girl's cubicle was sketchily furnished: a dung-fired brazier for warmth and light—and smoke and smell—and, for the business transaction, the sort of bed called a hindora. This is a pallet that does not stand on legs, but is hung from a ceiling beam by four ropes, and adds some movement of its own to the movements that go on in it.

Never having heard the word Domm before, I did not know what sort of girl to expect. The one sitting and swinging idly on the hindora turned out to be something new in my experience, a girl so dark-brown she was almost black. Apart from that, though, she was sufficiently pleasing of face and figure. Her features were finely shaped, not

Ethiope gross, and her body was small and slight but well
formed. She spoke several languages, among them Farsi,
so we were able to converse. Her name, she told me, was
Chiv, which in her native Romm tongue meant Blade.

"Romm? The Jew said you were Domm."

"Not the Domm!" she protested fiercely. "I am a Romni!
I am a juvel, a young woman, of the *Romm!*"

Since I had no idea what either a Domm or a Romm was,
I avoided argument by getting on with what I had come
for. And I soon discovered that, whatever else the juvel
Chiv might be—and she claimed to be of the Muslim
religion—she was anyhow a *complete* juvel, not Muslimly
deprived of any of her female parts. And those parts, once I
got past the dark-brown entryway, were as prettily pink as
those of any other female. Also, I could tell that Chiv was
not feigning delight, but truly did enjoy the frolic as much
as I did. When, afterward, I lazily inquired how she had
come to this brothel occupation, she did not spin me any
tale of having been brought low by woe, but said blithely:

"I would be doing zina anyway, what we call surata, because I like to. Getting paid for making surata is an extra
bounty, but I like that, too. Would you refuse a wage, if it
were offered, for every time you have the pleasure of making water?"

Well, I thought, Chiv might not be a girl of flowery sentiments, but she was honest. I even gave her a dirham that
she would not have to share with the Jew. And, on my way
out through the grinding shop, I was pleased to be able to
make a snide remark to that person:

"You were mistaken, old Shimon. As I have found you to
be on other occasions. The girl is of the Romm."

"Romm, Domm, those wretched people call themselves
anything they take a mind to," he said uncaringly. But he
went on, more amiably talkative than he had been when I
came in. "They were originally the Dhoma, one of the lowest classes of all the Hindu jati of India. The Dhoma are
among the untouchables, the loathed and detested. So they
are continually seeping out of India to seek better situations elsewhere. God knows how, since they have no trades
but dancing and whoring and tinkering and thieving. And
dissimulation. When they call themselves Romm, it is to
pretend descent from the Western Caesars. When they call
themselves Atzigàn, it is to pretend descent from the con-

queror Alexander. When they call themselves Egypsies, it is to pretend descent from the ancient Pharaones." He laughed. "They descended only from the swinish Dhoma, but they are descending on all the lands of the earth."

I said, "You Jews have also dispersed widely about the world. Who are you to look down on others for doing the same?"

He gave me a look, but he answered with deliberation, as if I had not spoken spitefully. "True, we Jews adapt to the circumstances in which our dispersal puts us. But one thing the Domm do which we never will. And that is to seek acceptance by cravenly adopting the prevailing local religion." He laughed again. "You see? Any despised people can always discern some more lowly people to look down on and despise."

I sniffed and said, "It follows, then, that the Domm also have someone to look down on."

"Oh, yes. Everyone else in creation. To them, you and I and all others are the Gazhi. Which means only 'the dupes, the victims,' those who are to be cheated and swindled and deceived."

"Surely a pretty girl, like your Chiv yonder, need not deceive—"

He gave an impatient shake of his head. "You walked in here yammering about beauty as a basis for suspicion. Were you carrying any valuables when you came?"

"Do you take me for an ass, to carry anything of worth into a whorehouse? I brought only a few coins and my belt knife. Where *is* my knife?"

Shimon smiled pityingly. I brushed past him, stormed into the back room and found Chiv happily counting a handful of coppers.

"Your knife? I already sold it, was that not quick of me?" she said, as I stood over her, fuming. "I did not expect you to miss it so soon. I sold it to a Tazhik herdsman just now passing at the back door, so it is gone. But do not be angry with me. I will steal a better blade from someone else, and keep it until you come again, and give it to you. This I will do—out of my great esteem for your handsomeness and your generosity and your exceptional prowess at surata."

Being so liberally praised, I of course stopped being angry, and said I would look forward to visiting her soon again. Nevertheless, in making my second departure from the place, I slunk past Shimon at his wheel, much as I had slunk from another brothel at another time in female raiment.

2

I think Nostril could have produced for us, if we had required it, a fish in a desert. When my father asked him to seek out a physician to give us an opinion on the seeming improvement of Uncle Mafìo's tisichezza, Nostril had no trouble in finding one, even on the Roof of the World. And the elderly, bald Hakim Mimdad impressed us as being a competent doctor. He was a Persian, and that alone certified him as a civilized man. He was traveling as karwan keeper-of-the-health in a train of Persian qali merchants. In just his general conversation, he gave evidence of having more than just routine knowledge of his profession. I remember his telling us:

"Myself, I prefer to prevent afflictions, rather than have to cure them, even though prevention puts no money in my purse. For example, I instruct all the mothers here in this encampment to boil the milk they give their children. Whether it be yak milk, camel milk, whatever, I urge that it first be boiled, and in a vessel of iron. As is known to all people, the nastier jinn and other sorts of demons are repelled by iron. And I have determined by experiment that the boiling of milk liberates from the vessel its iron juice, and mixes that into the milk, and thereby fends off any jinni that might lurk in readiness to inflict some childhood disease."

"It sounds reasonable," said my father.

"I am a strong advocate of experiment," the old hakim went on. "Medicine's accepted rules and recipes are all very well, but I have often found by experiment new cures which do not accord with the old rules. Sea salt, for one. Not even the greatest of all healers, the sage ibn Sina, seems ever to have noticed that there is some subtle difference between sea salt and that obtained from inland salt flats. From none of the ancient treatises can I divine any reason for there being such a difference. But *something* about sea salt prevents and cures goiters and other such tumorous swellings of the body. Experiment has proven it to me."

I made a private resolve to go and apologize to the little Chola salt merchants I had laughed at.

"Well, come then, Dotòr Balanzòn!" my uncle boomed, mischievously calling him by the name of that Venetian comic personage. "Let us get this over with, so you can tell me which you prescribe for my damned tisichezza—the sea salt or the boiled milk."

So the hakim proceeded to his examination diagnostic, probing here and there at Uncle Mafìo and asking him questions. After some while he said:

"I cannot know how bad was the coughing before. But, as you say, it is not very bad now, and I hear little crepitation inside the chest. Do you have any pain there?"

"Only now and then," said my uncle. "Understandable, I suppose, after all the hard coughing I have done."

"But allow me a guess," said Hakim Mimdad. "You feel it only in one place. Under your left breastbone."

"Why, yes. Yes, that is so."

"Also, your skin is quite warm. Is this fever constant?"

"It comes and goes. It comes, I sweat, it goes away."

"Open your mouth, please." He peered inside it, then lifted the lips away to look at the gums. "Now hold out your hands." He looked at them front and back. "Now, if I may pluck just one hair of your head?" He did, and Uncle Mafìo did not wince, and the physician scrutinized the hair, bending it in his fingers. Then he asked, "Do you feel a frequent need to make kut?"

My uncle laughed and rolled his eyes bawdily. "I feel many needs, and frequently. How does one make kut?"

The hakim, looking tolerant, as if he were dealing with a child, significantly patted a hand on his own backside.

"Ah, kut is *merda!*" roared my uncle, still laughing. "Yes, I have to make it frequently. Ever since that earlier hakim gave me his damned purgative, I have been afflicted with the cagasangue. It keeps me trotting. But what does all this have to do with a lung ailment?"

"I think you do not have the hasht nafri."

"Not the tisichezza?" my father spoke up, surprised. "But he was coughing blood at one time."

"Not from the lungs," said Hakim Mimdad. "It is his gums exuding blood."

"Well," said Uncle Mafìo, "a man can hardly be displeased to hear that his lungs are not failing. But I gather that you suspect some other ailment."

"I will ask you to make water into this little jar. I can tell you more after I have inspected the urine for signs diagnostic."

"Experiments," my uncle muttered.

"Exactly. In the meantime, if the innkeeper Iqbal will bring me some egg yolks, I would have you allow the application of more of the little Quran papers."

"Do they do any good?"

"They do no harm. Much of medicine consists of precisely that: not doing harm."

When the hakim departed, carrying the small jar of urine with his hand capping it to prevent any contamination, I also left the karwansarai. I went first to the tents of the Tamil Cholas and said words of apology and wished those men all prosperity—which seemed to make them even more nervous than they always were anyway—and then wended my way to the establishment of the Jew Shimon.

I asked again to have my tool greased, and asked to have Chiv do it again, and I got her, and as she had promised, she did present me with a fine new knife, and to show my gratitude, I tried to outdo my former prowess in the performance of surata. Afterward, on my way out, I paused to chide old Shimon yet again:

"You and your nasty mind. You said all those belittling things about the Romm people, but look what a splendid gift the girl just gave me in exchange for my old blade."

He humphed indifferently and said, "Be glad she has not yet given you one between your ribs."

I showed him the knife. "I never saw one like this before. It resembles any ordinary dagger, yes? A single wide blade. But watch. When I have stabbed it into some prey, I squeeze the handle: so. And that wide blade separates into two, and they spring apart, and this third, hidden, inner blade darts out from between them, to pierce the prey even more deeply. Is it not a marvelous contrivance?"

"Yes. I recognize it now. I gave it a good sharpening not long ago. And I suggest, if you keep it, that you keep it

handy. It formerly belonged to a very large Hunzuk mountain man who drops in here occasionally. I do not know his
name, for everyone calls him simply the Squeeze Knife
Man, because of his proficiency with it and his ready employment of it when his temper is . . . Must you dash off?"

"My uncle is ailing," I said, as I went out the door. "I
really should not stay away too long at a time."

I did not know if the Jew was just making a crude jest,
but I was not confronted by any large and ill-tempered
Hunzik man between Shimon's place and the karwansarai. To avoid any such confrontation, I stayed prudently
close to the inn's main building for the next few days, listening, in company with my father or uncle, to the various
bits of advice dispensed by the landlord Iqbal.

When we loudly praised the good milk given by the cow
yaks, and loudly marveled at the bravery of the Bho who
dared to milk those monsters, Iqbal told us, "There is a
simple trick to milking a cow yak without hazard. Only
give her a calf to lick and nuzzle, and she will stand still
and serene while it is being done."

But not all the information we got at that time was welcome. The Hakim Mimdad cane again to confer with Uncle
Mafìo, and began by suggesting gravely that it be done in
private. My father and Nostril and I were present, and we
got up to leave the chamber, but my uncle stopped us with
a peremptory flap of his hand.

"I do not keep secret any matters that may eventually
concern my karwan partners. Whatever you have to tell,
you may tell us all."

The hakim shrugged. "Then, if you will drop your pai-
jamah . . ."

My uncle did, and the hakim eyed his bare crotch and
big zab. "The hairlessness, is that natural or do you shave
yourself there?"

"I take it off with a salve called mumum. Why?"

"Without the hair, the discoloration is easy to see," said
the hakim, pointing. "Look down at your abdomen. You
see that metallic gray tinge to the skin there?"

My uncle looked, and so did all of us. He asked, "Caused
by the mumum?"

"No," said Hakim Mimdad. "I noticed the lividity also
on the skin of your hands. When next you remove your
chamus boots, you will see it on your feet as well. These

manifestations tend to confirm what I suspected from my earlier examination and from observation of your urine. Here, I have poured it into a white jar so you may observe for yourself. The smoky color of it."

"So?" said Uncle Mafìo, as he reclothed himself. "Perhaps I had been dining on the colored pilaf that day. I do not remember."

The hakim shook his head, slowly but positively. "I have seen too many other signs, as I said. Your fingernails are opaque. Your hair is brittle and breaks easily. There is only one other confirming sign I have not seen, but you must have it somewhere on your body. A gummatous small sore that refuses to heal."

Uncle Mafìo looked at him as if the hakim had been a sorcerer, and said in awe, "A fly bite, away back in Kashan. A mere fly bite, no more."

"Show me."

My uncle rolled up his left sleeve. Near his elbow was an angry and shiny red spot. The hakim leaned to peer at it, saying, "Tell me if I am wrong. Where the fly first bit, the bite healed and a small scar formed, in the natural manner. But then the sore erupted anew beyond the scar, and then healed again, and then erupted again, always beyond the old scar . . ."

"You are not wrong," my uncle said weakly. "What does it mean?"

"It confirms my conclusion diagnostic—that you are suffering from the kala-azar. The black sickness, the evil sickness. It does indeed proceed from the bite of a fly. But that fly is, of course, the incarnation of an evil jinni. A jinni who cunningly takes the form of a fly so small that it would hardly be suspected of bearing so much harm."

"Oh, not so much that I cannot bear it. Some mottled skin, some coughing, a little fever, a little sore . . ."

"But unhappily it will not for long be not so much. The manifestations will multiply, and worsen. Your brittle hair will break and you will go bald all over. The fever will bring emaciation and asthenia and lassitude, until you have no will to move at all. The pain below your breast bone proceeds from the organ called your spleen. That will hurt even more, and begin to bulge frighteningly outward, as it hardens and loses all function. Meanwhile, the lividity will spread over your skin, and it will darken to black, and it will pouch out into gummata and blebs and furuncles and squamations until your entire body—including your face—resembles one great bunch of black raisins. By then, you will be ardently wishing to die. And die you will, when your splenic functions fail. Without immediate and continuing treatment, you are sure to die."

"But there is a treatment?"

"Yes. This is it." Hakim Mimdad produced a small cloth sack. "This medicament consists principally of a fine-powdered metal, a trituration of the metal called stibium. It is a sure vanquisher of the jinni and a sure cure for the kala-azar. If you start now to take this, in exceedingly minute amounts, and go on taking it as I prescribe, you will soon start to improve. You will regain the weight you have lost. Your strength will return. You will be again in the best of health. But this stibium is the only cure."

"Well? Only one cure is needed, surely. I will gladly settle for the one."

"I regret to tell you that the stibium, while it arrests the kala-azar, is itself physically harmful in another particular." He paused. "Are you sure you would not prefer to continue this consultation in private?"

Uncle Mafìo hesitated, glancing about at us, but squared his shoulders and growled, "Whatever it is, tell it."

"Stibium is a heavy metal. When it is ingested, it settles downward from the stomach into the splanchnic area, working its beneficial effects as it goes, subduing the jinni of the kala-azar. But being heavy, it precipitates into the lower part of the body, which is to say the bag containing the virile stones."

"So my cod dangles heavier. I am strong enough to carry it."

"I assume that you are a man who enjoys, er, exercising it. Now that you are afflicted with the black sickness, there is no time to waste. If you do not yet have a lady friend in this locality, I recommend that you hire yourself to the local brothel maintained by the Jew Shimon."

Uncle Mafìo barked a laugh, which perhaps I or my father could better interpret than the Hakim Mimdad. "I fail to see the connection. Why should I do that?"

"To indulge your virile capability while you can. Were I you, Mirza Mafìo, I should hasten to make all the zina I could. You are doomed either to be horribly disfigured by

the kala-azar, and eventually to die of it—or, if you are to
be cured and kept alive, you must begin immediately taking the stibium."

"What do you mean, *if?* Of course I want to be cured."

"Think on it. Some would rather die of the black sickness."

"In the name of God, why? Speak plainly, man!"

"Because the stibium, settling in your scrotum, will instantly start exercising its other and deleterious effect—of
petrifying your testicles. Very soon, and for the rest of your
life, you will be totally impotent."

"Gèsu."

No one else said anything. There was a terrible silence
in the room, and it seemed that no one wished to brave the
breaking of it. Finally Uncle Mafìo spoke again himself,
saying ruefully:

"I called you Dotòr Balanzòn, little realizing how truly I
spoke. That you would indeed present me with a mordant
jest. Giving me such a comical choice: that I die miserably
or I live unmanned."

"That is the choice. And the decision cannot be long
postponed."

"I will be a eunuch?"

"In effect, yes."

"No capability?"

"None."

"But . . . perhaps . . . dar mafa'ul be-vasilè al-badàm?"

"Nakher. The badàm, the so-called third testicle, also
gets petrified."

"No way at all, then. Capòn mal caponà. But . . . desire?"

"Nakher. Not even that."

"Ah, well!" Uncle Mafìo surprised us all by sounding as
jovial as ever. "Why did you not say that at the first? What
matter if I cannot function, if I shall not even want to?
Why, think of it! No desire—therefore no need, therefore
no nuisance, therefore no complicated aftermath. I ought
to be the envy of every priest ever tempted by a woman or a
choirboy or a sùccubo." I decided that Uncle Mafìo was not
really so jovial as he was trying to sound. "And after all,
not many of my desires could ever have been realized, anyway. My most recent one dwindled away in a trembling
land. So it is fortunate that this jinni of castration assailed

only me and not someone of worthier desires." He barked
another laugh, with that horrid false joviality. "But listen
to me—raving and maundering. If I am not careful, I may
even become a moral philosopher, the last refuge of
eunuchdom. God forfend. A moralist is more to be shunned
than a sensualist, no xe vero? By all means, good hakim, I
shall choose to live. Let us commence the medication—but
not until tomorrow, eh?" He picked up and put on his voluminous chapon overcoat. "As you have also prescribed,
while I still have desires, I ought to squander them. While
I still have juices, wallow in them, yes? So excuse me, gentlemen, Ciao." And he left us, slamming vigorously out the
door.

"The patient puts a brave face on it," murmured the hakim.

"He may honestly mean it," my father said speculatively. "The most dauntless mariner, after having many
ships sink under him, may be thankful when he is finally
beached on a placid strand."

"I hope not!" blurted Nostril. He added hastily, "Only
my own opinion, good masters. But no mariner should be
grateful for being dismasted. Especially not one of Master
Mafìo's age—which is approximately the same as my own.
Excuse me, Hakim Mimdad, but is this grisly kala-azar
possibly . . . infectious?"

"Oh, no. Not unless you also should be bitten by the
jinni fly."

"Still and all," Nostril said uneasily, "one feels compelled to . . . to make sure. If you masters have no commands for me, I too will ask to be excused."

And off he went, and shortly so did I. Probably the fearful and superstitious slave had not believed the physician's assurance, I did, but even so. . . .

When one attends a dying, as I have said before, one of
course comes away grieving for the loss of the dead one,
but even more—even if only secretly, even if only uncon-
sciously—rejoicing at being oneself still alive. Having just
now attended what might be called a partial dying, or a dying by parts, I rejoiced in still possessing those parts, and,
like Nostril, I was anxious to verify that I did still possess
them. I went straight to Shimon's establishment.

I did not meet Nostril or my uncle there; most likely the
slave had gone in search of some accessible boy of the

kuch-i-safari, and possibly so had Uncle Mafìo. I again
asked the Jew for the dark-brown girl Chiv, and got her,
and had her, so energetically that she gasped Romm words
of astonished pleasure—"yilo!" and "friska!" and "alo! alo!
alo!"—and I felt sadness and compassion for all the eunuchs and Sodomites and castròni and every other sort of
cripple who would never know the delight of making a
woman sing that sweet song.

3

ON my every subsequent visit to Shimon's place of business—and they were fairly frequent, once or twice a
week—I asked for Chiv. I was quite satisfied with her performance of surata, and had almost ceased to notice her
skin's qahwah color, and was not at all disposed to try the
other colors and races of females the Jew kept in his stable,
for they were all inferior to Chiv in face and figure. But
surata was not my only diversion during that winter.
There was always something happening in Buzai Gumbad
that was of novelty and interest to me. Whenever I heard a
burst of noise that was either someone stepping on a cat or
someone starting to play the native music, I always assumed it was the latter, and went to see what kind of entertainment it promised. I might find just a mirasi or a
najhaya malang, but it would as often be something more
worth observing.

A mirasi was only a male singer, but of a special sort: he
sang nothing but family histories. On request, and on payment, he would squat before his sarangi—which was an instrument rather like a viella, played with a bow, but laid
flat on the ground—and he would saw at its strings, and to
that wailing accompaniment he would warble the names
of all the forebears of the Prophet Muhammad or Alexander the Great or any other historical personage. But not
many requested that sort of performance; it seemed that
everybody already knew by heart the genealogies of all the
accepted notables. A mirasi was oftenest hired by a family
to sing *its* history. Sometimes, I suppose, they indulged in
the expense just to enjoy hearing their family tree set to

music, and perhaps sometimes just to impress all their
neighbors within hearing. But usually they engaged a
mirasi when a matrimonial match was contemplated with
some other family, and so would set forth, at the top of the
mirasi's lungs, the estimable heritage of the boy or girl
about to be betrothed. The family's head would write down
or recite that entire genealogy to the mirasi, who would
then arrange all the names into rhyme and rhythm—or so
I was told; I never could perceive much other than monotonous noise—the singing and sarangi sawing of which could
occupy hours. I assume this took a considerable talent, but
after one stint of hearing how "Reza Feruz begat Lotf Ali
and Lotf Ali begat Rahim Yadollah" and so on, from Adam
to date, I did not exert myself to attend any other such performances.

The doings of a najhaya malang did not pall *quite* so
quickly. A malang is the same thing as a darwish, a holy
beggar, and even up on top of the Roof of the World there
were beggars, both native and transient. Some of these offered entertainment before demanding bakhshish. A malang would sit down cross-legged in front of a basket and
tweedle on a simple wood or clay pipe. A najhaya snake
would raise its head from the basket, spread its hood and
gracefully sway, seeming to dance in time to the raucous
tweedling. The najhaya is a fearsomely cross and venomous snake, and every malang maintained that none but he
had such power over the serpent—a power acquired in occult ways. For instance, the basket was a special sort
called a khajur, and could be woven only by a man; the
cheap pipe had to be mystically sanctified; the music was a
melody known only to the initiated. But I soon perceived
that every snake had had its fangs drawn and was harmless. It was also apparent, since snakes have no ears, that
the najhaya was simply swaying back and forth to keep its
impotent aim fixed on the wiggling pipe end. The malang
could have played a melodious Venetian furlàna and got
the same effect.

But sometimes I would hear a sudden burst of music and
follow it to its source and find a group of handsome Kalash
men chanting in baritone, "Dhama dham mast qalan-
dar . . ." as they put on their red shoes called utzar, which
they donned only when they were about to charge into the
stamping, kicking, pounding dance they called the dha-

mal. Or I might hear the rumbling drumbeat and wild piping that accompanied an even more frenzied, furious,
whirling dance called the attan, in which half the camp,
men and women alike, might join.

Once, when I heard music swelling forth in the darkness
of night, I followed it to a Sindi train's encampment of
wagons in a circle, and found the Sindi women doing a
dance for women only, and singing as they danced, "Sammi
meri warra, ma'in wa'ir. . . ." I found Nostril also looking
on, smiling and beating time with his fingers on his
paunch, for these were women of his own native land. They
were rather too brawny for my taste, and inclined to mustaches, but their dance was pretty, being done by the light
of the moon. I sat down beside Nostril, where he sat
propped against a wheel of one of the covered wagons, and
he interpreted the song and dance for me. The women were
recounting a tragic love story, he said—the story of a Princess Sammi, who was a girl much in love with a boy Prince
named Dhola, but when they grew up he went away and
forgot her and never came back. A sad story, but I could
sympathize with Prince Dhola, if his little Princess Sammi
had grown meaty and mustached as she matured.

Every woman in the train must have been recruited into
the dance, because, inside the wagon against which Nostril and I leaned, an unattended and restive baby was bellowing loud enough to drown out even the sonorous Sindi
music. I endured it for some time, hoping the child would
eventually doze—or strangle, I did not much care which.
When after a long time it did neither, I grumbled irascibly.

"Allow me to hush it, master," said Nostril, and he got
up and climbed inside the wagon.

The child's wails subsided to gurgles and then to silence.
I was grateful, and bent all my attention on the dance. The
infant remained blessedly quiet, but Nostril stayed in
there for some time. When at last he climbed down to sit
beside me again, I thanked him and said in jest, "What did
you do? Kill and bury it?"

He replied complacently, "No, master, I had an inspira-
tion of the moment. I delighted the child with a fine new
pacifier to suck, and a creamier milk than its mother's."

It took me a little while to realize what he had said.
Then I recoiled from him and exclaimed, "Good God! You
did not!" He looked not at all ashamed, only mildly sur-

prised at my outburst. "Gèsu! That miserable little thing
of yours has been foully diseased, and filthily inserted in
animals and backsides and—and now a baby! Of your own
people!"

He shrugged. "You wished the infant quieted, Master
Marco. Behold, it still sleeps the sleep of contentment. And
I do not feel half bad myself."

"Bad! Gèsu Marìa Isèpo, but you are the worst—the most
vile and loathsome excuse for a human being that I have
ever met!"

He deserved at least to be beaten bloody, and surely he
would have got worse than that from the baby's parents.
But, since I had in a way incited him, I did not strike the
slave. I merely scolded and reviled him and quoted to him
the words of Our Lord Jesus—or Nostril's Prophet Isa—
that we should always treat tenderly little children, "for of
such is the kingdom of God."

"But I *did* it tenderly, master. Now you have peace in
which to enjoy the rest of the dancing."

"I will not! Not in your comapny, creature! I could not
meet the eyes of the dancing women, knowing that one of
them is the mother of that wretched innocent." So I went
away before that performance was concluded.

But happily, most such occasions were not spoiled for me
by any such incident. Sometimes, when I heeded the call of
music, it led me not to a dance but to a game. There were
two kinds of outdoor sport popular at Buzai Gumbad, and
neither could have been played in a much smaller area, for
both involved a considerable number of men on horseback,
riding hard.

One game was played only by the Hunzukut men, because it had been originally invented in their home valley
of Hunza, somewhere to the south of these mountains. In
that game, the men swung heavy sticks, like mallets, bat-
ting at an object they called the puly, a rounded-off knot of
willow wood which rolled on the ground like a ball. Each
team comprised six mounted Hunzukut, who tried to
strike that pulu with their sticks—meanwhile often and
enthusiastically striking their opponents, their horses and
their own teammates—in order to drive the pulu past the
six opponents' flailing defense until it rolled or flew beyond a winning line at the far end of the field.

I often lost track of a game's progress because I had a

hard time telling the members of the two teams apart. They all wore heavy garments of fur and hide, plus the typical Hunzuk hat, which makes a man look as if he is balancing two thick pies atop his head. The hat actually consists of a long tube of coarse cloth rolled from both ends until the two rolls meet, and the whole then plopped onto the head. For a contest of the pulu, the six men on one team would don red pie-hats and the other six put on blue ones. But, after a very short time of play, the colors would be almost indistinguishable.

I also often lost sight of the wooden pulu itself, among the horses' forty-eight pounding hoofs and the thrown-about snow and mud and sweat, and the intermixed clashing mallets and, not infrequently, some unhorsed players being whacked and kicked about as well. But the more experienced game-watchers, meaning almost everybody else in Buzai Gumbad, were keener of eye. Everytime they saw the pulu bounce past the winning line at one or the other end of the field, the whole crowd would shout, "Gol! Go-o-o-ol!"—a Hunzuk word signifying that one team had tallied a point toward winning the game—and simultaneously a band of musicians would pound drums and blow flutes in a cacophony of celebration.

A game did not end until one team had nine times put the pulu past the opposing gol line. So that herd of twelve horses might spend a whole day thundering up and down the increasingly sloppy and treacherous field, with the players bellowing and cursing and the spectators roaring encouragement, and the sticks waving and crashing and often splintering, and the churned-up terrain plastering the players and horses and watchers and musicians, and the riders falling from their saddles and trying to scurry to safety and being cheerfully ridden down by their fellows, and, toward the end of the day, when the field was a mere swamp of mud and slime, the horses also slipping and slewing and falling down. It was a splendid kind of sport, and I never missed a chance to watch it.

The other game was similar, in that it was played by many men on horseback. But in that sport it did not matter how many, for there were no teams; each rider played for himself, against all the others. It was called bous-kashia, and I think that is a Tazhik term, but the game was not the specialty of any one people or tribe, and all the

men joined in it on one occasion or another. Instead of a
pulu, the central object in bous-kashia was the cadaver of a
goat from which the head had just been severed.

The newly dead thing was simply tossed onto the ground
among the horses' legs, and the many riders all spurred
close around it and wrestled and shoved and pummeled
one another, each striving to reach down and snatch up the
goat from the ground. He who finally succeeded in that,
next had to gallop and carry it across a line at the end of
the field. But of course he was pursued by all the others,
snatching at his trophy and trying to trip or swerve his
horse or knock him out of the saddle. And whoever did
seize the contested cadaver himself became the prey of all
the other riders. So the game really amounted to not much
more than a wrestling and grabbing match on horseback
and at the gallop. It was furious and exciting, and few
players emerged from it in good health, and many a spectator got trodden on by the herd of horses, or got knocked insensible by a flying goat, or a ripped-loose bloody haunch
of it.

During those long winter months on the Roof of the
World, besides the time I spent watching games and
dances, and in the hindora bed with Chiv, and in other diversions, I also spent some less frivolous whiles in conversation with the Hakim Mimdad.

Uncle Mafìo invited no comment on his ailment or the
other troubles it had brought upon him. He was taking the
powdered stibium as prescribed, and we could see that he
was putting on the weight he had lost, and getting stronger day by day, but we restrained any curiosity we might
have had as to exactly when the medicine turned him into
a eunuch, and he did not volunteer the information. Since I
never encountered him in company with a boy or any other
sort of partner while we stayed in Buzai Gumbad, I could
not say when he may finally have desisted from such part-
nerships. Anyway, the hakim still called on us at regular
intervals, to make a routine examination of Uncle Mafìo's
progress and to increase or decrease by minute amounts
the stibium he was taking. After the physician's sessions
with the patient, he and I would often sit and talk together, for I found him to be a most interesting old fellow.

Like every other mèdego I have ever known, Mimdad regarded his everyday medical practice only as a necessary

drudgery by which he had to earn his living, and preferred to concentrate most of his energies and devotions on his private studies. Like every other mèdego, he dreamed of discovering something new and medically miraculous, to astound the world and to enshrine his name forever alongside those of physician deities like Asklepios and Hippocrates and ibn Sina. However, most doctors of my acquaintance—in Venice, anyway—pursue studies sanctioned or at least tolerated by Mother Church, such as the seeking of new ways to expel or expunge the demons of disease. Mimdad's studies and experiments, I learned, were less in the realm of the healing arts than in the realm of Hermes Trismegistus, which arts verge on sorcery.

Because the Hermetic arts were originally and for so long practiced by pagans like Greeks and Arabs and Alexandrians, Christians are naturally forbidden to delve into them. But every Christian has heard of them. I, for one, knew that the Hermetics ancient and modern—the adepts, as they like to be called—have almost always and to a man been seeking to discover one of two arcane secrets: the Elixir of Life or the Universal Touchstone that will change base metals into gold. So I was surprised when the Hakim Mimdad scoffed at both of those aims as "unrealistic prospects."

He admitted that yes, he too was an adept of the age-old and occult art. He called it al-kimia, and claimed that Allah had first taught it to the prophets Musa and Haroun, meaning Moses and Aaron, whence it had been passed down through the years to such other famous experimenters as the great Arab sage Jabir. And Mimdad admitted that yes, like every other adept, he was chasing an elusive quarry, but one less grandiose than immortality or untold wealth. All he hoped to discover—or rediscover, rather—was what he called "the philter of Majnun and Laila." One day when the upland winter had begun to ease its clamp, and the karwan leaders were studying the sky to decide when they would start downhill from the Roof of the World, Mimdad told me the history of that remarkable philter.

"Majnun was a poet and Laila a poetess, and they lived long ago and far away. No one knows where or when. Except for the poems that have survived them, all that is known about Majnun and Laila is this: they had the power

of changing their forms at will. They could become younger or older, more handsome or more ugly, and of whichever sex they chose. Or they could change their persons
entirely, becoming giant rukh birds or mighty lions or
terrible mardkhora. Or, in a lighter mood, they could become gentle deer or beautiful horses or pretty
butterflies. . . ."

"A useful talent," I said. "Their poetry then could depict
those alien ways of life more accurately than any other
poet had done."

"No doubt," said Mimdad. "But they never sought to
make capital or renown of their peculiar power. They used
it only for sport—and their favorite sport was love. The
physical act of making love."

"Dio me varda! They liked making love to horses and
such? Why, our slave must have the blood of a poet in his
veins!"

"No, no, no. Majnun and Laila made love only to each
other. Consider, Marco. What need had they of anyone or
anything else?"

"Hm . . . yes," I mused.

"Imagine the variety of experiences available to them.
She could become the male and he the female. Or she could
be Laila and he could mount her as a lion. Or he could be
Majnun and she a delicate qazèl. Or they could both be
other people entirely. Or they could both be dewy children,
or both men, or both women, or one an adult and the other
a child. Or both of them freaks of grotesque configuration."

"Gèsu . . ."

"When they tired of making human love, however various or capricious, they could sample the even more different pleasures that must be known to beasts and serpents
and the demon jinn and the fair peri. They could be two
birds, doing it in midair, or two butterflies, doing it within
the embrace of a fragrant flower."

"What a pleasant thought."

"Or they could even take the form of hermaphrodite humans, and both Majnun and Laila could be simultaneously
al-fa'il and al-mafa'ul to each other. The possibilities
would have been infinite, and they must have tried every
one, for that was their lifelong occupation—except when

they were momentarily sated, and paused to write a poem or two."

"And you hope to emulate them."

"I? Oh, no, I am old, and long past all venereal yearning. Also, an adept must not do al-kimia for his own advantage. I hope to make the philter and its power accessible to all men and women."

"How do you know it was a philter they employed? Suppose it was a spell or a poem they recited before each change."

"In that case, I am confounded. I cannot write a poem, or even recite one with any eloquence. Please do not make discouraging suggestions, Marco. A philter I *can* concoct, with liquids and powders and incantations."

It sounded to me a slim hope, seeking the power in a philter because a philter was all he could make. But I asked, "Well? Have you had any success?"

"Some, yes. Back home in Masul. One of my wives died after trying one of my preparations, but she died with a blissful smile on her lips. A variant of that preparation gave another of my wives an eminently vivid dream. In her sleep she began fondling and pawing and even clawing at her private parts, and that was a good many years ago, and she has not left off yet, for she has never awakened from that dream. She lives now in a cloth-walled room at Mosul's House of Delusion, and every time I travel there to inquire of her condition, my hakim colleague there tells me she is still interminably performing her interminable self-arousal. I wish I could know what she is dreaming."

"Gèsu. You call that *success?*"

"Any experiment is a success when one learns something from it. So I have since deleted the heavy metallic salts from my recipe, having concluded that those are what cause the deep coma or death. Now I lean to the postulates of Anaxagoras, and employ only organic and homoeomeric ingredients. Yohimbinum, cantharis, the phalloid mushroom, things like that. Oysters pulv., Nux v., Onosm., Pip. nig., Squilla . . . There is no longer any danger of the subject's not awakening."

"I rejoice to hear it. And now?"

"Well, there was a childless couple, who had given up all hope of a family. They now have four or five fine boys, and I think they never counted the number of girl progeny."

"That does sound like success of a sort."

"Of a sort, yes. But all the children are human. And normal. They must have been conceived in the ordinary way."

"I see what you mean."

"And those were my last volunteers to try the philter. I think the hakim of that House of Delusion has perhaps been spreading gossip around Mosul, in violation of the physicians' oath. So my chief difficulty is not in making new variants of the philter, it is the finding of test subjects. I am too old for the purpose, and my two remaining wives would refuse, anyway, to join me in the experiments. As you must appreciate, it is best to try the philter on a man and a woman at the same time. Preferably a young and vital man and woman."

"Yes, clearly. A Majnun and a Laila, so to speak."

There was a long silence.

Then he quietly, shyly, tentatively, hopefully, "Marco, do you perchance have access to a complaisant Laila?"

The beauty of danger.

4

THE danger of beauty.

"I suggest you leave your knife out here," said Shimon, as I came through his shop. "That Domm female is in a vile humor today. But perhaps you would like one of the others this time? Now that the camp is starting to break up, I suppose your party too will soon be gone. Now at the last, perhaps you would like a change? A girl other than the Domm?"

No, I wanted Chiv for the playing of Laila to my Majnun. However, considering the unpredictable nature of that play, I did take the Jew's advice and left my squeeze knife on his counter. I also left there a small stack of dirhams, to pay for however long I might stay, and avert his interrupting us to say my time was up. Then I went on into Chiv's room, saying as I entered:

"I have something for you, my girl."

"I have something for you, too," she said. She was sitting naked on the hindora, and she was making the bed

sway slightly on its ropes as she rubbed oil onto her round
dark-brown breasts and her flat dark-brown belly to make
them shine. "Or I will have something, before too long."

"Another knife?" I asked idly, starting to undress.

"No. Have you lost the other already? It appears that
you have. No, this will be something you cannot disown so
easily. I am going to have a baby."

I stopped moving, standing stockstill and probably looking silly, for I was half out of my pai-jamah and standing
like a stork on one leg. "What do you mean, I cannot
disown? Why tell me?"

"Whom else should I tell?"

"Why not that Hunzuk mountain man? To mention just
one other."

"I would, if it were another's doing. It is not."

I had weathered the first astonishment by now and was
again in command of my faculties. I resumed my undressing, but not so eagerly as before, and I said reasonably, "I
have been coming here for only three months or so. How
could you possibly know?"

"I know. I am a Romni juvel. We of the Romm have ways
of knowing such things."

"Then you also ought to know how to prevent such
things."

"I do. I usually insert beforehand a plug made of sea salt
moistened with walnut oil. If I neglected the precaution, it
was because I was overwhelmed by your vyadhi, your impetuous desire."

"Do not blame me, or flatter me, whichever you think
will win me over. I do not want any dark-brown offspring."

"Oh?" was all she said to that, but she narrowed her
eyes as she regarded me.

"Anyway, I refuse to believe you, Chiv. I see absolutely
no change in your body. It is still very nice and trim."

"It is, yes, and my occupation depends on my keeping it
that way. Not deformed by pregnancy and useless for
surata. So why do you not believe me?"

"I think you are only pretending. To keep me by you. Or
to make me take you along when I leave Buzai Gumbad."

Quietly, "You are so desirable."

"I am at least not a simpleton. I am surprised that you
would think me gullible by such an old and common woman's trick."

Quietly, "Common woman, is it?"

"Anyway, if you are with child, surely an experienced—surely a clever Romni juvel knows how to get rid of it."

"Oh, yes. There are various ways. I only thought you ought to have some say in the matter of disowning it."

"Then what are we quarreling about? We are in complete accord. Now, in the meantime, I have something for you. For both of us."

As I dropped the last of my garments, I tossed onto the hindora a paper-wrapped packet and a small clay phial.

She opened the paper and said, "This is only common bhang. What is in the little bottle?"

"Chiv, have you ever heard of Majnun the poet and Laila the poetess?"

I sat down beside her and related to her what the Hakim Mimdad had told me about the long-ago lovers and their facility at being so many other kinds of lovers. I did not, however, repeat what the hakim had said when I volunteered myself and Chiv as test subjects for his latest version of the philter. He had looked dubious and he had muttered, "A girl of the Romm? Those people claim to know sorceries of their own. It could conflict with al-kimia." I concluded my account with the instructions he had given me. "We share the drink from the phial. Then, while we wait for it to take effect, we set the hashish burning. The bhang, as you call it. We inhale the smoke and that exhilarates us and suspends our wills, and makes us more receptive to the powers of the philter."

She smiled, as if quietly amused. "You would try a Gazho magic on a Romni? There is a saying, Marco. About a fool's taking the trouble to lay sticks on the devil's fire."

"This is not some foolish magic. This is al-kimia, carefully concocted by a sage and studious physician."

The smile stayed on her face, but it lost its amusement. "You said you saw no change in my body, but now you would change both our bodies. You scolded me for what you called pretending, but now you would have us both pretend."

"This is not a pretense, this is an *experiment.* Look, I do not expect a mere—I do not expect you to comprehend Hermetic philosophy. Just take my word that this is something much loftier and finer than any barbaric superstition."

She unstopped the phial and sniffed at it. "This smells sick-making."

"The hakim said that the hashish fumes will quell any nausea. And he told me all the ingredients of the philter. Fern seed, dodder leaves, the chob-i-kot root, powdered antler, goat wine—other innocuous things, none of them noxious. I certainly would not swallow the stuff myself, or ask you to, if it were otherwise."

"Very well," she said, her smile becoming a rather wicked grin, and she tilted the phial and took a sip. "I will spread the bhang on the brazier."

She had left most of the philter for me—"Your body is larger than mine, perhaps harder to change"—and I drank it down. The little room quickly filled with the thick, blue, cloyingly sweet smoke of the hashish, as Chiv stirred it into the brazier coals, meanwhile muttering to herself in what I took to be her native tongue. I lay back at full length on the hindora, and closed my eyes, the better to be surprised when I opened them to see what I had changed into.

Maybe I fell into a hashish-drugged sleep, but I do not think so. The last time I had done that, the dream occurrences had been mixed and swimmy and confused. This time, all the consequent events seemed very real and sharp-edged and *happening*.

I lay with my eyes closed, feeling all over my naked body the heat from the stirred brazier, and I vigorously inhaled its sweet smoke, and I waited to feel some difference in myself. I do not know what I expected: perhaps the unfolding at my shoulder blades of bird wings or butterfly wings or peri wings; or perhaps the unfurling of my virile member, which was already erect in anticipation, to the massive size of a bull's. But all I felt was a gradual and unpleasant increase of the room's thick heat, and then a definite need to void my bladder. It was like that common morning phenomenon, when you wake with your member in candelòto stiffness, but only gorged by vulgar urine, which makes it an embarrassment for employment in either of its normal functions. You do not then want to utilize it sexually, but you also dislike to disengorge it by urination, because in that erection it always pees upward and you usually make a mess.

This was not at all a promising beginning to my amatory

expectations, so I continued to lie still, with my eyes closed, and hoped the sensation would go away. It did not. It increased, and so did the room's heat, until I was annoyed and uncomfortable. Then a pain suddenly went through my groin, as it sometimes does when micturition is too long withheld, but so intensely hurtfully that, not meaning to, I let at least a brief spurt of urine. For another moment, I only lay there feeling ashamed of myself and hoping that Chiv had not noticed. But then I realized that I had felt no sprinkle on my bare belly, as I should have done if my erect organ had peed into the air. Instead, I felt the wetness down the inside of my legs. Unusual. A small puzzlement. I opened my eyes. All around me there was nothing but the blue smoke haze; the walls of the room, the brazier, the girl, all were invisible in it. I cast my glance downward, to see why my candelòto had behaved so oddly, but my view of it was impeded by my breasts.

Breasts! I had the breasts of a woman, and very fine ones they were, too: shapely, upthrusting, ivory-skinned, with nicely large, fawn-colored areole around tumescent nipples, the whole array shining with sweat and a trickle meandering down the cleft between. The philter was working! I was changing! I was embarked upon the most bizarre journey of discovery I had ever undertaken!

I raised my head to see how my candelòto accorded with these new additions. But I still could not see it, for I had an immense rounded belly, like a mountain to which my breasts were the foothills. I began to sweat in earnest. It should be a novel experience to be a woman for a while— but an obesely *fat* woman? Maybe I was even a deformed woman, for my navel, which had always before been nothing but an insignificant dimple depression, was now a protrusion, perched like a little lighthouse atop my mountain stomach.

Unable to see my member, I groped for it with a hand. All I encountered was the hair on my artichoke, but it was rather more luxuriant and kinky than I was accustomed to feeling. When I reached down past it, I discovered—no great surprise now—that my candelòto was gone, and so was my cod. In their place I had the organs of a woman.

I did not leap up screaming. After all, I had been inviting and expecting a change. To have changed into something like a rukh would probably have been more of a

shock and dismay to me. Anyway, I was confident that the
change was not going to be permanent. But I was not entirely happy, either. The organs of a woman should have
felt familiar enough to my inquiring hand, but they too
had a disturbing difference about them. To my fingers,
they felt tight and hard and hot, and nastily clammy from
my involuntary micturition. They did not, to my touch, resemble the soft and darling and hospitable purse—the
mihrab, the kus, the pota, the mona—into which I had so
often put fingers and other things.

Besides that, to my *self* they felt . . . how do I put this?

I would have expected, if I were a woman being fingered
in my private parts, even if by my own fingers, to feel some
pleasurable sensation or an intimate tickle or at least a
comfortable old acquaintance. But now I *was* a woman,
and I perceived only the prod of fingers, and it made me
feel only molested, and my only internal response was a
surge of irritability. I slowly slid a finger inside myself,
but it did not go far before it was blocked, and then the soft
sheathing around it rejected it—I could almost say *spat* it
out. There was something up there inside me. Perhaps a
precautionary plug of sea salt? But my probing aroused in
me more revulsion than curiosity, and I was disinclined to
probe again. Even when I deliberately let a finger lightly
flick my zambur, my lumaghèta—that tenderest part of
my new parts, as sensitive as an eyelash to any touch—I
felt nothing but an intensification of my peevishness and a
wish to be let alone.

I wondered: does a woman when fondled never experience anything nicer than this? Surely not, I told myself.
Then maybe a fat woman never experiences anything? I
had yet to fondle a really fat woman, but I doubted that.
Anyway, in my new womanly incarnation, *was* I a fat
woman? I sat up to see.

Well, I still had that grossly swollen abdomen, and now I
could see that it was made even uglier by a discoloration
marring the taut ivory skin, a brown line that extended
from my protuberant navel down to my artichoke. But the
belly seemed to be the only fat thing about me. My legs
were slim enough, and hairless, and would have been
pretty, except that the veins of them were all raised and
visible and squirmy-looking, like a net of worm burrows
just under the skin. My hands and arms also looked slim

enough, and girlishly soft. But they did not feel soft to me; they felt gnarled and painful. Even as I looked at them and flexed them, both of my hands crooked in a cramp that made me groan.

The groan was loud enough to have brought some response from Chiv, but she did not materialize out of the blue smoke around me, even when I several times called her name. What had the philter made of her? I would have supposed, just on the principle of turnabout, that if I had become female, Chiv would have become male. But the hakim had said that Majnun and Laila sometimes disported themselves as both of the same sex. And sometimes one or both of them had availed themselves of invisibility. Still, the philter's main purpose was to enhance the partners' lovemaking, and in that I judged this trial philter to be a failure. No kind of partner—male, female, invisible—was likely to want to couple with a creature as grotesque as what I had turned into. Nevertheless, what *had* become of Chiv? I called her again and again . . . and then I screamed.

I screamed because another sensation had shaken my body, a sensation more gruesome than mere pain. Something had *moved,* something that was not me, but it had moved *inside me,* inside the monstrous bloat that was my belly. I knew it was not just unsettled food in my stomach, for it happened somewhere below my stomach. And it was not ill-digested food making wind in my lower gut, for I had known that sensation before. That can be unpleasant enough, and sometimes startling, even when it is not noisy or noisome. But this was something different, something I had never experienced before. It felt as if I might have swallowed some small sleeping animal, and it had been digested well down into my bowels, and there it had suddenly awakened and stretched and yawned. My God, I thought, suppose it tries to fight its way out!

Just then it moved again, and I shrieked again, for it seemed about to do exactly that. But it did not. The movement quickly abated, making me ashamed of having shrieked. The animal might only have turned about a bit in its snuggery, as if to judge how inextricably it was held there. I felt renewed wetness between my legs, and thought I had once more soiled myself in my fright. But when I put a hand down there I felt something awfuller

than urine. I brought my hand up into my view, and my
fingers were webbed with a viscous substance that clung
in strings between hand and groin, moistly stretching and
sagging and soggily breaking. The substance was wet but
not liquid; it was a gray slime, like nose-blown mucus, and
it was streaked with blood. I began to curse the Hakim
Mimdad and his unholy philter. Not only had he and it
given me an ugly woman's body, and evidently one with
defective female parts, there was also something ailing
this body and causing a nauseous discharge from those
parts.

If my new integument was indeed ill or injured, I
thought, I had better not risk standing it up and taking it
to look for Chiv. I had better remain lying where I was. So I
called for her some more, still without result. I even began
calling for Shimon, though I could imagine how the Jew
would sneer and snicker, seeing me in a woman's form. He
did not come, either, and now I regretted having paid him
in advance for a long stay. Whatever noises or cries he
might hear from in here, he would probably take for boisterous lovemaking, and not intrude.

For a long time, I lay supine there, and nothing further
happened except that the room got more and more hot, and
I got sweatier, and my need to urinate became also a need
to defecate. It might have been that the imagined small
animal inside me was pressing its weight against my bladder and my bowels and squeezing them intolerably. I had
to make a determined effort not to let go, but I did resist,
not wanting to spew between my legs and all over the bed.
Then suddenly, as if a door had been opened to the thawing
snows outside, I was blasted by a chill. The film of sweat on
my body became icy, I shook in every limb, my teeth chattered, my skin turned all to gooseflesh, my already prominent nipples stood up like sentries. There was nothing for
me to cover myself with; if my discarded clothes were still
on the floor, they were out of my sight and reach, and I was
afraid to get up and look for them. But then the chill was
as suddenly gone again, and the room was as muggy as before and my sweat started out afresh and I panted for
breath.

Not having much else to meditate on, I tried to take
stock of my feelings. They were numerous and various. I
felt a measure of anticipation: the philter was bound to do

something more, and it might be interesting. But most of
my emotions were not at all pleasant. I felt discomfort: my
hands kept cramping, and my need to evacuate my bowels
was becoming extreme. I felt disgust: there was still a
seepage of that puslike stuff from my mihrab. I felt indignation: being put in this situation—and I felt self-pity:
being left all alone to endure this situation. I felt guilt: by
right, I should be at the karwansarai, helping my companions pack and prepare to take the trail again, not here
indulging my demon curiosity. I felt fear: Not really knowing what the philter might have yet in store for me—and I
felt apprehension: whatever happened next might be no
improvement on what already had.

Then, in one paralyzing instant, all other feelings went
away, abolished, demolished by the one feeling that takes
precedence over everything else, and that is pain. It was a
tearing pain that tore through my lower vitals, and I
might have thought I heard the sound of it, like the rip-
ping of sturdy cloth, except that I could hear only my agonized cry. I would have clawed at my betrayer belly, but I
was so shaken by the pain that I had to clutch the sides of
the swaying hindora to keep from pitching out of it.

In any access of agony, one instinctively tries to move,
hoping that some movement might alleviate it, and the
only movement I could make was to draw up my legs. That
abruptness broke my control of my more intimate muscles,
and my urine gushed out in a sudden wet warmth, down
and about my buttocks. Instead of quickly abating, the
pain made a leisurely departure, merging into an alternation of heat and chill. I jolted as each flush of fever gave
way to a clamp of cold and that to heat once more. When
those pulses finally, gradually subsided, leaving me awash
in sweat and urine, I lay weak and flaccid and gasping as if
I had been scourged, and now that I could make words I
cried aloud, *"What is happening to me?"*

And then I knew. Look: here on this pallet lies a woman,
flat on her back, and most of her body is flat, too, only
curved and shaped as a woman's body ought to be, except
for that horrendous bulge of distended abdomen. She lies
with her legs drawn up and apart, exposing a mihrab that
is tight and numb with tension. Something is up in there,
inside her. It is what makes the belly big, and it is alive,
and she has felt it move in there, and she has felt the first

pangs of its wanting to get out of there, and where shall it come out except through that mihrab canal between her legs? This is obviously a woman in advanced pregnancy and about to give birth.

All very well, that lofty and cool and detached view. But I was not any viewer looking on; I was *it*. The pitiful, slow-writhing object on the pallet, in the absurb posture and semblance of a frog flipped underside up, was *me*.

Gèsu Marìa Isèpo, I thought—and loosed one hand from gripping the bedside to cross myself—how could the philter have made two beings of me, and put one inside the other? Whatever that was inside me, must I go through the whole process of birthing it? How long does that take? What does one do to help it along? In addition to thinking those things, I was thinking some less repeatable things about the Hakim Mimdad, recommending him to eternity in Hell. That was perhaps unwise of me, for if ever I needed a hakim it was now. The nearest I had ever been to child-birth was the time or two I had seen a pale blue and purple, flayed-looking newborn infant dredged dead from the waters of Venice. I had never been present while even a street cat actually gave birth. The more knowledgeable Venetian boat children had occasionally discussed the sub-ject, but all I could remember was their mention of "labor pains," and in those I now required no instruction. I knew, too, that women often perished of their childbed travail. Suppose I died in this alien body! No one would even know who I was. I would be buried as a nameless, unclaimed, probably unwed wench who had been killed by her own bastard . . . .

But I had more immediate concerns than the disposition of my inglorious remains. The tearing pain came again, and it was as rippingly severe as before, but I gritted my teeth and did not cry out, and even tried to examine the pain. It seemed to start deep in my abdomen, somewhere back toward my spine, and to wrench its way around to my front. Then I had a respite in which to breathe again before the pain made a new onslaught. With each succeeding wave, though the pain did not lessen, I seemed a little bet-ter able to stand it. So I tried to take a measure of the pains and the intervals between them. Each seizure lasted while I could count slowly to thirty or forty, but when I tried to time the intervening lulls I counted so high that I became confused and lost count.

There were other afflictions contributing to my confusion. Either the room or myself was still alternating between fever and chill, and I was alternately roasted to limpness or frozen to a clench. My belly, somewhere among its other troubles, found room for nausea; I burped and belched repeatedly, and several times had to fight against vomiting. I was still incontinently urinating each time the pain struck, and only by determined muscular contraction not emptying my bowels as well. The spilled urine might have been a caustic; it made my thighs and my groin and my underneath feel raw and chafed and sore. I had developed a maddening thirst, probably because I had sweated and peed out so much of my internal moisture. My hands continued spasmodically to cramp, and now so did my legs, from the ungainly position I kept them in. The contact of the bed against my back was an irritation. In truth, I was hurting everywhere, even at the mouth; it was locked open in such a distorted rictus that my very lips hurt. I could almost be glad when the labor pains rasped through my gut; they were so terribly much worse that they took my mind off the lesser hurts.

I had resigned myself to the realization that my drinking of the philter was not going to bring me any enjoyment. Now, as the endless hours ground on and on, I tried to resign myself to enduring what the philter had brought instead—thirst and nausea and self-pollution and general misery, varied by intermittent jolting pain—either until its power wore off and I was restored to being myself again, or until it besieged me with some new and different miseries.

Which is what it did. When the pains were squeezing out of me no more spurts of urine, I thought my body had finally been emptied of all its fluids. But suddenly I felt my lower self washed by more wetness than I had yet ejected, a flood of wetness, as if someone had upended a pitcher between my legs. It was warm like urine, but when I raised up to look, I could see that the spreading puddle was colorless. I realized also that the water had not come from my bladder, by way of the little female peeing hole, but out of the mihrab canal. I had to suppose that this mess signaled

some new and messier stage in the exceedingly messy process of giving birth.

The abdominal pains were now coming at intervals
closer together barely giving me time to get my breath after each onslaught, and to stiffen my preparedness, before
the next was upon me. It made me think to myself: perhaps
it is your bracing yourself against each pain, and trying to
flinch away from it, that makes them hurt so much. Maybe
if you bravely met each pain and bore down against it . . .
So I tried that, but "bearing down" in this situation
meant exerting the same muscular push as is involved in
defecation, and it had the same result. When that particular grinding pain briefly let up again, I discovered that I
had extruded onto the bed between my legs a considerable
mess of stinking merda. But I was really beyond caring by
this time. I merely thought to myself: you already knew
that human life ends with merda; now you know that human life also begins in merda.

"Of such is the kingdom of God." I suddenly recollected
having preached that to the slave Nostril, not long ago.
"Suffer the little children to come unto me," I recited, and
laughed ruefully.

I did not laugh for long. Though it is hardly believable,
things now got even worse. The pains were coming not in
waves or pulses, but in fast succession, and each lasting
longer, until they became just one constant agony in my
belly, unremitting, rising in intensity until I was unashamedly sobbing and whimpering and moaning, and I
feared I could not stand it, and I wished mightily for a merciful faint. If someone had leaned over me then and said,
"This is nothing. You can hurt worse than this, and you
will," I might, even in that excruciation, have got out another laugh among my sobs. But the someone would have
been right.

I felt my mihrab begin to open and stretch, like a mouth
yawning, and the lips of it continued to gape wider, until
they must have made the orifice a full circle, like a mouth
screaming. And, as if that was not torment enough, the entire round of the circle seemed suddenly to have been
painted with liquid fire. I put a hand down there, to pat
desperately at the blaze. But it felt no burning, only a crumbly something. I brought the hand back to my streaming
eyes and saw through my tears that the fingers were

smeared with a cheesy, pale green substance. How could
that burn so?

And even then, besides the rampaging pain in my belly
and the searing fire at the bottom, I could sense other awful things. I could taste the sweat running from my face
into my mouth, and the blood from where I had by now
gnawed my lips raw. I could hear my grunts and moans
and racking gasps. I could smell the stench of my squalidly
spilled body wastes. I could feel the creature inside me
moving again, and apparently tumbling and kicking and
flailing, as it edged its ponderous way through the belly
pain toward the blaze below. As it moved, it pressed still
more intolerably upon my bladder and bowels in there,
and somehow they found more contents to void. And out,
through that last extrusion of urine and turds, the creature began to come. And *ah, God!* when God decreed, "In
sorrow shalt thou bring forth," God did make it so. I had
known trivial pains in earlier times, and I had known real
pain throughout these hours, and I have known other
pains since, but I think there must be no pain in all the
world like the pain I felt now. I have seen torture done, by
men expert in torture, but I think no man is so cruel and
inventive and accomplished in pain as God is.

The pain was compounded of two different sorts of pain.
One was that of my mihrab flesh tearing, front and back.
Take a piece of skin and rip it, ruthlessly but slowly, and
try to imagine how that feels to the skin, and then imagine
that it is the skin between your own legs, from artichoke to
anus. While that was happening to me, and making me
scream, the head of the creature inside me was butting its
way through the enclosing bones down there, and that
made me bellow between my screams. The bones of that
place are close together; they must be shoved apart and
aside, with a grinding and grating like that of a boulder
going implacably through a too narrow cleft of rocks. That
is what I felt, and what I felt all at the same time: the sickening movement and pain inside me, the crunching and
buckling of all the bones between my legs, the tearing and
burning of the outside flesh. And God allows, even in that
extremity, only screaming and bellowing; no swooning to
get away from the unbearable agony.

I did not faint until after the creature came out, with a
final brutal bulge and billow and rasp of pain like an audi-

ble screech—and the dark-brown head raised up between my thighs, slimy with blood and mucus, and said in Chiv's voice, maliciously, "Something you cannot disown so easily . . ." Then I seemed to die.

5

WHEN I came back to myself, I was myself. I was still naked and supine on the hindora bed, but I was a male again, and the body appeared to be my own. I was scummed with dried sweat and my mouth was terribly dry and thirsty and I had a pounding headache, but I felt no pains anywhere else. There was not any mess of my body wastes on the pallet; it looked as clean as it ever looked. The room was very nearly clear of the smoke, and I saw my discarded clothes on the floor. Chiv was also there, and fully dressed. She was hunkered down, wrapping a small something, pale blue and purple, in the paper I had brought the hashish in.

"Was it all a dream, Chiv?" I asked. She did not speak or look up, but went on with what she was doing. "What happened to you in the meantime, Chiv?" She did not reply. "I thought I had a baby," I said, with a dismissive laugh. No response. I added, "You were there. You were it."

At that, she raised her head, and her face wore much the same expression it had worn in the dream or whatever that had been. She asked, "I was dark brown?"

"Why, er, yes."

She shook her head. "Babies of the Romm do not get dark brown until later. They are the same color as white women's babies when they are born."

She stood up and carried her little package out of the room. When the door opened, I was surprised to see the brightness of daylight. Had I been here all through the night and into the next day? My companions would be much annoyed at my leaving them all the work to do. I began hurriedly putting on my clothes. When Chiv came back to the room, without her bundle, I said conversationally:

"For the life of me, I cannot believe that any sane

woman would ever *want* to go through that horror. Would you, Chiv?"

"No."

"Then I was right? You were only pretending before? You are really not with child?"

"I am not." For a normally talkative person, she was being very brusque.

"Have no fear. I am not angry with you. I am glad, for your sake. Now I must get back to the karwansarai. I am going."

"Yes. Go."

She said it in a way that implied "do not come back." I could not see any reason for her surliness. It was I who had done all the suffering, and I strongly suspected that she had contributed in some cunning way to the philter's miscarriage of purpose.

"She is in a vile humor, as you said, Shimon," I told the Jew, on my way out. "But I suppose I owe you more money, anyway, for all the time I spent."

"Why, no," he said. "You were not long. In conscience—here—I give you a dirham back. Here also is your squeeze knife. Shalom."

So it was still the same day, then, and not really far into the afternoon, at that, and my travail had only seemed much, much longer. I got back to the inn to find my father and uncle and Nostril still collecting and packing our possessions, but having no immediate need of my assistance. I went down to the lakeside, where the washerwomen of Buzai Gumbad kept always a patch of water cleared of ice. The water was so blue-cold that it seemed to bite, so my bath was perfunctory—my hands and face, and then I briefly took off my upper garments to dash some few drops at my chest and armpits. That wetting was the first I had had all winter; I would probably have been revolted by my own smell, except that everyone else smelled the same or worse. At least it made me feel a trifle cleaner of the sweat that had dried on me in Chiv's room. And, as the sweat got diluted, so did my worst recollections of my experience. Pain is like that; it is excruciating to endure, but easy to forget. I daresay that is the only reason why any woman, after having been agonized and riven by the extrusion of one child, can even contemplate chancing the ordeal of another.

On the eve of our departure from the Roof of the World, the Hakim Mimdad, whose own karwan train would also be leaving, but in a different direction, came to the karwansarai to say his goodbyes to us all, and to give Uncle Mafìo a traveling supply of his medicine. Then, while my father and uncle looked rather agog, I told the Hakim how his philter had failed—or else had succeeded widly far beyond his intent. I told him graphically what had happened, and I told it not at all enthusiastically, and not a little accusingly.

"The girl must have meddled," he said. "I was afraid of that. But no experiment is a total failure if something can be learned from it. Did you learn anything?"

"Only that human life begins and ends in merda, or kut. No, one other thing: to be careful when I love in future. I will never condemn any woman I love to such a hideous fate as motherhood."

"Well, there you are, then. You learned something. Perhaps you would like to try again? I have here another phial, another slight variant on the recipe. Take it along with you, and try it with some female who is not a Romni sorceress."

My uncle grumbled ruefully, "There is a Dotòr Balanzòn for you. Gives me a stunting potion and, to level the scales, gives an enhancer to one too young and brisk to need it."

I said, "I will take it, Mimdad, as a keepsake curiosity. The notion is appealing—to sample lovemaking in a multitude of shapes. But I have a long way to go before I exhaust all the possibilities of this body, and I will remain in it for now. Doubtless, when you have finally refined your philter to perfection, the word of it will be noised all about the world, and by then I may be jaded with my own possibilities, and I will seek you out and ask then to try your perfected potion. For now, I wish you success and salaam and farewell."

I did not get to say even that much to Chiv, when that same evening I went to Shimon's place.

"Earlier this afternoon," he told me indifferently, "the Domm girl asked for her share of her income to date, and resigned from this establishment, and joined an Uzbek karwan train departing for Balkh. The Domm do things like that. When they are not being shiftless, they are being

shifty. Ah, well. You still have the squeeze knife to remember her by."

"Yes. And to remind me of her name. Chiv means
blade."

"Does it now. And she never stuck one into you."

"I am not so sure of that."

"There are still the other females. Will you have one,
this last night?"

"I think not, Shimon. From the glances I have had of
them, they are exceedingly unbeautiful."

"By your reckoning as once expressed, then, they are
nicely undangerous."

"You know something? Old Mordecai never said so, but
that may be a count *against* unbeautiful people, not in
their favor. I think I will always prefer the beautiful, and
take my chances. Now I thank you for your good offices,
Tzaddik Shimon, and I bid you farewell."

"Sakanà aleichem, nosèyah."

"That sounded different from the usual peace-go-with-
you."

"I thought you would appreciate it." He repeated the
Ivrit words, then translated them into Farsi: "Danger go
with you, journeyer."

Although there was still plenty of snow about Buzai
Gumbad, the whole of Lake Chaqmaqtin had gradually exchanged its cover of bluewhite ice for a multicolored cover
of waterfowl—numberless flocks of ducks and geese and
swans that had flown in from the south, and continued to
come. The noise of their contented honks and quacks was a
continuous clamor, and they would make a rustling rumble like a windstorm in a forest whenever a thousand of
them suddenly vaulted from the water all at once for a joyous flight around the lake. They provided a welcome addition to our diet, and their arrival had been the signal for
the karwan trains to begin packing their gear, harnessing
and herding their animals, forming up their wagons in
line, and one after another plodding off for the horizon.

The first trains to leave had been those headed westward, to Balkh or farther, because the long decline of the
Wakhàn Corridor was the easiest route down from the
Roof of the World, and the earliest to become negotiable in
the spring. The journeyers bound for the north or east or
south prudently waited a while longer, because to go in

any of those directions meant first climbing the mountains surrounding this place on those three sides, and descending through their high passes only to climb the next mountains beyond, and the ones beyond them. To the north, east and south of here, we were informed, the high passes never completely shed their snow and ice even in midsummer.

So we Polos, having to go north and having no experience of travel in such terrain and conditions, had waited for the prudent others. We might really have hesitated longer than we needed to, but one day there had come to us a delegation of the little dark Tamil Chola men at whom I had once laughed and to whom I had later apologized. They told us, speaking the Trade Farsi very badly, that they had decided not to carry their cargo of sea salt to Balkh, for they had heard reliable report that it would fetch a much better price in a place called Murghab, which was a trading town in Tazhikistan, on the east-west route between Kithai and Samarkand.

"Samarkand is far to the northwest of here," Uncle Mafìo remarked.

"But Murghab is directly to the north," said one of the Cholas, a spindly little man named Talvar. "It is on your way, O twice-born, and you will have crossed the worst of the mountains when you get there, and the mountain journey from here to Murghab will be easier for you if you travel in karwan with us, and we wish only to say that you would be welcome to join us, for we have been much impressed by the good manners of this twice-born Saudara Marco, and we believe you will be congenial companions for the trail."

My father and uncle, and even Nostril, looked slightly bemazed at being called twice-born, and at my being praised by strangers for my good manners. But we all concurred in accepting the Cholas' invitation, expressing gratitude and thanks, and it was in their train that we rode our horses out of Buzai Gumbad and up into the forbidding mountains to the northward.

This was a small train compared to some we had seen in the encampment, trains comprising scores of people and hundreds of animals. The Cholas numbered only a dozen, all men, no women or children, with only half a dozen small and scrawny saddle horses, so they took turns riding and walking. For vehicles they had only three rickety, two-wheeled carts, each drawn by a small harness horse, in which carts they hauled their bedding, provender, animal feed, smithy and other traveling necessities. They had brought their sea salt as far as Buzai Gumbad on twenty or thirty pack asses, but had there effected a trade for a dozen yaks, which could carry the same load but were better suited to the more northerly terrain.

The yaks were good trailbreakers. They were uncaring of snow and cold and discomfort, and they were sure of foot, even when heavy laden. So, as they trudged at the head of our train, they not only picked the best trail, but also plowed it clean of snow and tramped it firm for us who followed. In the evenings, when we made camp and staked the animals roundabout, the yaks showed the horses how to paw down through the snow to find the dingy and shriveled but edible burtsa shrubs left from the last growing season.

I imagine the Cholas had invited us to accompany them only because we were big men—at least in comparison to them—and they must have supposed that we would be good fighters if the train should encounter bandits on the way to Murghab. We did not meet any, so our muscularity was not required for that contingency, but it did come in useful on the frequent occasions when a cart overturned on the rugged trail, or a horse fell into a crevice, or a yak scraped off one of its pack sacks when squeezing past a boulder. We also helped in preparing the meals at evening, but that we did more out of self-interest than affability.

The Cholas' way of preparing every meat dish was to drench it with a sauce of gray color and mucoid consistency, compounded of numerous different and pungent spices, a sauce called by them kàri. The effect was that, whatever one ate, one could taste only kàri. This was admittedly a blessing when the dish was a tasteless knob of dried or salted meat, or was high on its way toward green putrefaction. But we non-Cholas soon got tired of tasting only kàri and never knowing whether the substance underneath was mutton or fowl or, as it could have been, hay. We first asked permission to improve the sauce, and added to it some of our zafràn, a condiment hitherto unknown to the Cholas. They were much pleased by the new flavor and the new golden color it added to the kàri, and my father gave them a few culms of the zafràn to take back to India with them. When even the improved sauce began to weary us, I and Nostril and my father volunteered to alternate with the Cholas as cooks of the camp-time meals, and Uncle Mafìo got from our packs his bow and arrows and began to supply us with fresh-killed game. It was usually small things like snow hares and red-legged partridges, but once in a while something larger, like a goral or an urial, and we cooked plain and simple meals of boiled or broiled meat, served blessedly sauceless.

The Cholas' addiction to kàri excepted, those men were good traveling companions. In fact, they were so retiring, and so shy of speaking until they were spoken to, and so reticent of seeming obtrusive, that we others could have journeyed all the way to Murghab without much awareness of their presence. Their timidity was understandable. Although the Cholas spoke Tamil, not Hindi, they were of the Hindu religion and they came from India, so they had to endure the contempt and derision with which all other nations rightly regard the Hindus. Our slave Nostril was the only non-Hindu person I knew who had bothered to learn the lowly Hindi language, and not even he had ever learned the Tamil. So none of us could converse with these Cholas in their own tongue, and they were very imperfect in the Trade Farsi. However, when we made it clear to them that we were not going to shun and scorn them overtly, or laugh at their halting speech, they became almost fawningly friendly to us and exerted themselves to tell us things of interest about this part of the world and things of usefulness on our way through it.

This is the land which most Westerners call Far Tartary and think of as the uttermost eastern end of the earth. But the name is doubly mistaken. The world extends far eastward beyond this Far Tartary, and the word Tartary is even more of a misnomer. A Mongol is called a Tàtar in the Farsi language of Persia, which is where Westerners first heard mention of the Mongol people. Later, when the Mongols-called-Tàtars rampaged across the borders of Europe, and all Europe trembled with fear and hatred of them, it was perhaps natural that many Westerners confused the word Tàtar with the ancient classical name for the infernal regions, which was Tartarus. So the Westerners came to speak of "the Tartars from Tartary," much as they would speak of "the demons from Hell."

But even Eastern men who should have known the proper names hereabout, the veterans of many karwan journeys across this land, had told us several different names for the mountains we were now making our way through—the Hindu Kush, the Himalaya, the Karakoram and so on. I can attest that there are indeed enough individual mountains and entire ranges of mountains and whole nations of mountains to justify and support any number of appellations. However, for the sake of our mapmaking, we asked our Chola companions if they could clarify the matter. They listened as we repeated all the various names we had heard, and they did not deride the men who had told them to us—because no man, they affirmed, could possibly say precisely where one range and one name left off and another began.

But, to locate us as accurately as possible, they said we were currently forging northward through the ranges called the Pai-Mir, having left behind us the Hindu Kush range to the southwest, and the Karakoram range to the south, and the Himalaya range somewhere far off to the southeast. The other names which we had been told—the Keepers, the Masters, Solomon's Throne—the Cholas said were probably local and parochial names bestowed by and used only by the folk living among the various ranges. So my father and uncle marked the maps of our Kitab accordingly. To me, the mountains all looked very much alike: great high crags and sharp-edged boulders and sheer cliffs and the tumbled detritus of rock slides—all of rock that would have been gray and brown and black if it had not been so heavily quilted with snow and festooned with icicles. In my opinion, the name of Himalaya, Abode of the Snows, could have served for any and every range in Far Tartary.

For all its bleakness and the lack of lively color, however, this was the most magnificent landscape I have seen in all my travels. The Pai-Mir mountains, immense and massive and awesome, stood ranked and ranged and towering heedless above us few fidgety creatures, us insignificant insects twitching our way across their mighty flanks. But how can I portray in mere insect words the overwhelming majesty of these mountains? Let me say this: the fact of the highness and the grandeur of the Alps of Europe is known to every traveled or literate person in the

West. And let me add this: if there could be such a thing as a world made entirely of Alps, then the peaks of the Pai-Mir would be the Alps of that world.

One other thing I will say about these Pai-Mir mountains, a thing I have never heard remarked by any other journeyer returned from them. The karwan veterans who had told us so many different names for this region had also been free with advice about what we could expect to experience when we got here. But not one of those men spoke of the aspect of the mountains that I found most distinctive and memorable. They talked of the Pai-Mir's terrible trails and punishing weathers, and told us how best a traveler could survive those rigors. But the men never mentioned the one thing I remember most vividly: the unceasing *noise* these mountains make.

I do not mean the sound of wind or snowstorm or sandstorm raging through them, though God knows we heard those sounds often enough. We were frequently breasting a wind into which a man could literally let himself fall, and not hit the ground but hang atilt, held up by the blast. And to that wind's bawling noise would be added the seethe of windblown snow or the sizzle of windblown dust, according as we were in the heights where winter still held sway or in the deep gorges where it was now late springtime.

No, the noise I remember so well was the sound of the mountains' decay. It was a surprise to me, that mountains so titanic could be falling to pieces all the time, falling apart, falling down. When I first heard the sound, I thought it was thunder rolling among the crags, and I marveled, for there were no clouds anywhere in the pure blue sky that day, and anyway I could not imagine a thunderstorm occurring in such crystalline cold weather. I reined my mount to a halt, and sat still in the saddle, listening attentively.

The sound began as a deep-throated rumble somewhere out ahead of us, and it loudened to a distant roar, and then that sound was compounded by its echoes. Other mountains heard it and repeated it, like a choir of voices taking up, one after another, the theme from a solo singer singing bass. The voices enlarged on that theme and amplified it and added to it the resonances of tenors and baritones, until the sound was coming from over there and from over yonder and from behind me and from all around me. I remained transfixed by the thrumming reverberation, while it dwindled from a thunder to a mutter and a mumble and faded away diminuendo. The mountains' voices only lingeringly let go, one after another, so that my human ear could not discern the moment when the sound died into silence.

The Chola named Talvar rode up beside me on his scraggly little horse, and gave me a look and broke my enthrallment by saying in his Tamil tongue, "Batu jatuh," and in Farsi, "Khak uftadan," both of which said, "Avalanche." I nodded as if I had known it all the while, and kneed my horse to move on.

That was only the first of innumerable occasions; the noice could be heard almost any time of day or night. Sometimes it would come from so near our trail that we would hear it above the creak and clatter of our harness and cartwheels and the grumbling and tooth-gnashing of our yak herd. And if we looked up quickly, before the echoes confused the direction, we would see rising into the sky from behind some ridge a smokelike plume of dust or a glittering billow of snow particles, marking the place where the slide had occurred. But I could hear the noise of more distant rockfalls whenever I chose to listen for them. I had only to ride ahead of the train or dawdle behind its racket, and wait for not long. I would hear, from one direction or another, a mountain groaning in the agony of losing a part of itself, and then the echoes overlapping from every other direction: all the other mountains joining in a dirge.

The slides were sometimes of snow and ice, as can happen also in the Alps. But they more often marked the slow corruption of the mountains themselves, for these Pai-Mir, though infinitely bigger than the Alps, are notably less substantial. They appear steadfast and eternal from a distance, but I have seen them close. They are made of a rock much veined and cracked and flawed, and the mountains' very loftiness contributes to their instability. If the wind nudges a single pebble from a high place, its rolling can dislodge other fragments, and their movement shoves loose other stones until, all rolling together, their ever more rapid downhill progress can topple huge boulders, and those in falling can sheer the lip off a vast cliff, and that in coming down can cleave away the whole side of a mountain. And so on, until a mass of rocks, stones, pebbles, gravel, earth and dust, usually mushed with snow, slush and ice—a mass perhaps the size of a minor Alp—sluices down into the narrow gorges or even narrower ravines that separate the mountains.

Any living thing in the path of a Pai-Mir avalanche is doomed. We came upon much evidence—the bones and skulls and splendid horn racks of goral, urial and "Marco's sheep," and the bones and skulls and pathetically broken belongings of men—the relics of long-dead wild flocks and long-lost karwan trains. Those unfortunates had heard the mountains moan, then groan, then bellow, and they had never since heard anything at all. Only chance preserved us from the same fate, for there is no trail or camping spot or time of day that is exempt from avalanche. Happily, none fell on us, but on many occasions we found the trail absolutely obliterated, and had to seek a way around the interruption. This was trouble enough when the slide had left in our path an unclimbable barrier of rubble. It was much harder on the frequent trail that was nothing but a narrow shelf chiseled from the face of a cliff, and an avalanche had broken it with an unvaultable void. Then we would have to retrace our steps for many farsakhs backward, and trudge many, many weary farsakhs circuitously roundabout before we were headed north again.

So my father and uncle and Nostril all cursed bitterly and the Cholas whimpered miserably every time they heard the rumble of rockfall, from whatever direction. But I was always stirred by the sound, and I cannot understand why other travelers seem to think it not worth mentioning in their reminiscences, for what the noise means is that these great mountains will not last forever. The crumbling of them will of course take centuries and millennia and eons before the Pai-Mir crumble down even to the still-grand stature of the Alps—but crumble they will, and eventually to a featureless flat land. Realizing that, I wondered why, if God intended only to let them fall, He had piled them so extravagantly high as they are now. And I wondered too, and I wonder still, how immeasurably, stupendously, unutterably high these mountains must have been when God made them in the Beginning.

All the mountains being of unvarying colors, the only

changes we could see in their appearance were those made
by weather and time of day. On clear days, the high peaks
caught the brilliance of dawn while we were still benighted, and they held the glow of sunset long after we had
camped and suppèd and bedded down in darkness. On days
when there were clouds in the sky, we would see a white
cloud trail across a bare brown crag and hide it. Then,
when the cloud had passed, the pinnacle would reappear,
but now as white with snow as if it had shredded off rags of
the cloud in which to drape itself.

When we ourselves were high up, climbing an upward
trail, the high light up there played tricks with our eyesight. In most mountain country there is always a slight
haze which renders each farther object a little dimmer to
the eye, so one can judge which objects are near and which
far. But in the Pai-Mir there is no trace of haze, and it is
impossible to reckon the distance or even the size of the
most common and familiar objects. I would often fix my
gaze on a mountain peak on the far horizon, then be startled to see our pack yaks scrambling over it, a mere rock
pile and only a hundred paces distant from me. Or I would
glimpse a hulking surragoy—one of the wild mountain
yaks, like a fragment of mountain himself—lurking just to
one side of our trail, and I would worry that he might lure
our tame yaks to run away from us, but then realize that
he was actually standing a farsakh away, and there was a
whole valley between us.

The high air was as tricksome as the light. As it had
done in the Wakhàn (which we now regarded as a mere
lowland), the air refused to support the flames of our cook
fires more than meagerly, and they burned only pale and
blue and tepid, and our water pots took an eternity to come
to a boil. Up here, somehow, the thin air also affected the
heat of the very sunshine. The sunny side of a boulder
would be too uncomfortably hot to lean against, but its
shady side would be too uncomfortably cold. Sometimes we
would have to doff our heavy chapon overcoats because the
sun made them so swelteringly hot, but not a crystal of the
snow all about us would be melting. The sun would fire icicles into blindingly bright and iridescent rainbows, but
never make them drip.

However, that was only in clear and sunny weather on
the heights, when the winter briefly slept. I think these

heights are where the old man winter goes to mope and
sulk when the all the rest of the world spurns him and welcomes warmer seasons. And in here, perhaps in one or another of the many mountain caves and caverns, old winter
retired to doze from time to time. But he sleeps uneasily
and he continually reawakens, yawning great gusts of cold
and flailing long arms of wind and from his white beard
coming cascades of snow. Often and often, I watched the
snowy high peaks blend into a fresh fall of snow and van-
ish in its whiteness; then the nearer ridges would disappear, and then the yaks leading our train, and then the
rest of it, and finally everything beyond my horse's wind-
whipped mane would disappear in whiteness. In some of
those storms the snow was so thick and the gale so fierce
that we riders could progress best by turning and sitting
backward on our saddles, letting our mounts pick their onward way, tacking like boats against the blast.

Since we were constantly going uphill and down, that
iron weather would soften every few days, when we descended into the warm, dry, dusty gorges where young
lady spring had arrived, then would harden around us
again when we ascended once more into the domains still
held by old man winter. So we alternated: plodding
through snow above, slogging through mud below; half frozen by a sleet storm above, half suffocated by a whirling
dust-devil below. But as we progressed ever northward, we
began to see in the narrow valley bottoms bits of living
green—stunted bushes and sparse grasses, then small and
timid patches of meadow; an occasional greening-out tree,
then stands of them. Those fragmentary verdant areas
looked so new and alien, set among the snow-white and
harsh-black and arid-dun heights, that they might have
been snippets of faraway other countries cut out with scissors and inexplicably scattered through this wasteland.

Still farther north, the mountains were farther apart, allowing for wider and greener valleys, and the terrain was
even more remarkable for its contrasts. Against the mountains' cold white background shone a hundred different
greens, all warm with sunlight—voluminous dark-green
chinar trees, pale silver-green locust trees, poplars tall and
slender like green feathers, aspens twinkling their leaves
from the green side to the gray-pearl side. And under and
among the trees glowed a hundred different other colors—

the bright yellow cups of the flowers called tulbands, the bright reds and pinks of wild roses, the radiant purple of the flower called lilak. That is a tall-growing shrub, so the lilak's purple plumes looked even more vivacious for our seeing them always from below, against the stark white snowline, and its perfume—one of the most delicious of all flower fragrances—smelled the sweeter for being borne on the absolutely odorless and sterile wind from the snow-fields.

In one of those valleys we came to the first river we had encountered since leaving the Ab-e-Panj, this one the Murghab by name, and beside it was the town of the same name. We took the opportunity to rest for two nights in a karwansarai there, and to bathe ourselves and wash our clothes in the river. Then we bade goodbye to the Cholas and kept on northward. I hoped that Talvar and his comrades did get much coin for their sea salt, because Murghab had not much else to offer. It was a shabby town and its Tazhik inhabitants were distinctive only for their exceptional resemblance to their co-inhabitants, the yaks—men and women alike being hairy, smelly, broad of face and features and torso, bovine in their impassivity and incuriosity. Murghab was empty of enticements to linger there, but the Cholas would leave it having nothing better to look forward to, only the grueling journey back across the high Pai-Mir and all of India.

Our own journey, from Murghab on, was not too arduous, we having got well used to traveling in these highlands. Also, the farther-north ranges were not so high or wintry, their slopes were not so steep, the passes were not so far to climb up to and over and down from, and the intervening valleys were broad and green and flowery and pleasant. According to what calculations I could make with our kamàl, we were now much farther north than Alexander had ever penetrated into central Asia, and, according to our Kitab maps, we were now squarely in the center of that largest land mass on earth. So we were astonished and bewildered one day to find ourselves on the shore of a *sea*. From the shore where the wavelets lapped at our horses' fetlocks, the waters stretched away to the west as far as the eye could see. We knew, of course, that a mighty inland sea does exist in central Asia, the Ghelan or Caspian by name, but we had to be far, far east of that one.

I briefly felt sorry for our recent companions, the Cholas, thinking they had fetched all their sea salt to a land already provided with a more than ample salt sea.

But we tasted the water, and it was fresh and sweet and crystal clear. This was a lake, then, but that was not much less astounding—to encounter a vastly big and deep lake situated as high as an Alp above the bulk of the world. Our northward route took us up its eastern shore, and we were many days in passing it. On every one of those days, we made excuse to camp early in the evening, so we could bathe and wade and disport ourselves in those balmy, sparkling waters. We found no towns on the lake shore, but there were the mud-brick and driftwood huts of Tazhik shepherds and woodcutters and charcoal burners. They told us that the lake was called Karakul, which is to say Black Fleece, which is the name of that breed of domestic sheep raised by all the shepherds in the vicinity.

That was one more oddity about the lake: that it should have the name of an animal; but that animal is admittedly not a common one. In fact, looking at a herd of those sheep, one might wonder why they are called kara, since the adult rams and ewes are mostly of varying shades of gray and grayish-white, only a few of them being black. The explanation is in the much-prized fur for which the karakul is noted. That costly pelt, of tight and kinky black curls, is not just a shearing of the sheep's fleece. It is a lamb skin, and all the karakul lambs are born black, and the pelt is obtained by killing and flaying a lamb before it is three days old. A day older, and the pure black color loses some of its black intensity, and no fur trader will accept it as karakul.

A week's journey north of the lake, we came to a river flowing from west to east. It was called by the local Tazhiks the Kek-Su, or Passage River. The name was fitting, for its broad valley did constitute a clear passage through the mountains, and we gladly followed it eastward, down and down from the highlands we had been among for so long. Even our horses were grateful for that easier passage; the rocky mountains had been hard on both their bellies and their hoofs; down here was ample grass for feed and it was soft under their feet. Curiously, at every single village and even isolated hut we came to, my father or uncle asked again the name of the river, and

every time were told, "Kek-Su." Nostril and I wondered at
their insistent repeated question, but they only laughed at
our puzzlement and would not explain why they needed so
many reassurances that we were following the Passage
River. Then one day we came upon the sixth or seventh of
the valley villages and, when my father asked a man
there, "What do you call the river?" the man politely replied, "Ko-Tzu."

The river was the same as yesterday, the terrain was no
different from yesterday's, the man looked as yaklike as
any other Tazhik, but he had pronounced the name differently. My father turned in his saddle to shout back to Uncle Mafìo, riding a little way behind us—and he shouted it
triumphantly—"We have arrived!" Then he dismounted,
picked up a handful of the road's yellowish dirt and regarded it almost fondly.

"Arrived where?" I asked. "I do not understand."

"The river's name is the same: the Passage," said my father. "But this good fellow spoke it in the Han language.
We have crossed the border from Tazhikistan. This is the
stretch of the Silk Road by which your uncle and I went
westward home. The city of Kashgar is only two days or so
ahead of us."

"So we are now in the province of Sin-kiang," said Uncle
Mafìo, who had ridden up to us. "Formerly a province of
the Chin Empire. But now Sin-kiang, and everything east
of here, is a part of the Mongol Empire. Nephew Marco,
you are finally in the heartland of the Khanate."

"You are standing," said my father, "upon the yellow
earth of Kithai, which extends from here to the great eastern ocean. Marco, my son, you have come at last to the domain of the Khakhan Kubilai."

KITHAI

1

THE city of Kashgar I found to be of respectable size
and of sturdy-built inns and shops and residences, not the
mud-brick shacks we had been seeing in Tazhikistan.
Kashgar was built for permanence, because it is the western gateway of Kithai, through which all Silk Road trains
coming from or going to the West must pass. And we found
that no train could pass without challenge. Some farsakhs
before we got to the city walls, we were waved down by a
group of Mongol sentries at a guardpost on the road. Beyond their shelter we could see the countless round yurtu
tents of what appeared to be an entire army camped
around Kashgar's approaches.

"Mendu, Elder Brothers," said one of the sentries. He
was a typical Mongol warrior of forbidding brawn and ugliness, hung all about with weapons, but his salute was
friendly enough.

"Mendu, sain bina," said my father.

I could not then understand all the words which were
spoken, but my father later repeated the conversation to
me, in translation, and told me it was the standard sort of
exchange between parties meeting anywhere in Mongol
country. It was odd to hear such gracious formalities spoken by a seeming brute, for the sentry went on to inquire
politely, "From under what part of Heaven do you come?"

"We are from under the skies of the far West," my father
replied. "And you, Elder Brother, where do you erect your
yurtu?"

"Behold, my poor tent stands now among the bok of the

423

Ilkhan Kaidu, who is currently encamped in this place, while surveying his dominions. Elder Brother, across what lands have you cast your beneficent shadow on your way hither?"

"We come most recently from the high Pai-Mir, down this Passage River. We wintered in the estimable place called Buzai Gumbad, which is also among your master Kaidu's territories."

"Verily, his dominions are far-flung and many. Has peace accompanied your journey?"

"So far we have traveled safely. And you, Elder Brother, are you at peace? Are your mares fruitful, and your wives?"

"All is prosperous and peaceful in our pastures. Wither does your karwan party proceed, then, Elder Brother?"

"We plan to stop some days in Kashgar. Is the place wholesome?"

"You can there light your fire in comfort and tranquility, and the sheep are fat for eating. Before you proceed, however, this lowly minion of the Ilkhan would be pleased to know your ultimate destination."

"We are bound eastward, for the far capital Khanbalik, to pay our respects to your very highest lord, the Khakhan Kubilai." My father took out the letter we had carried for so long. "Has my Elder Brother stooped to learn the clerk's humble art of reading?"

"Alas, Elder Brother, I have not attained to that high learning," said the man, taking the document. "But even I can perceive and recognize the Great Seal of the Khakhan. I am desolated to realize that I have impeded the peaceful passage of such dignitaries as you must be."

"You are but doing your duty, Elder Brother. Now, if I may have the letter back, we will proceed."

But the sentry did not give it back. "My master Kaidu is but a miserable hut to a mighty pavilion alongside his Elder Cousin the high lord Kubilai. For that reason he will yearn for the privilege of seeing his cousin's written words, and reading them with reverence. No doubt my master will also wish to receive and greet his lordly cousin's distinguished emissaries from the West. So, if I may, Elder Brother, I will show him this paper."

"Really, Elder Brother," my father said, with some impatience, "we require no pomp or ceremony. We would be pleased just to go straight on through Kashgar without causing any fuss."

The sentry paid no heed. "Here in Kashgar, the various inns are reserved to various sorts of guests. There is a karwansarai for horse traders, another for grain merchants . . . ."

"We already knew that," growled Uncle Mafìo. "We have been here before."

"Then I recommend to you, Elder Brothers, the one that is reserved for passing travelers, the Inn of the Five Felicities. It is in the Lane of Perfumed Humanity. Anyone in Kashgar can direct—"

"We know where it is."

"Then you will be so kind as to lodge there until the Ilkhan Kaidu requests the honor of your presence in his pavilion yurtu." He stepped back, still holding the letter, and waved us on. "Now go in peace, Elder Brothers. A good journey to you."

When we had ridden out of the sentry's hearing, Uncle Mafìo grumbled, "Merda with a piecrust on it! Of all the Mongol armies, we ride into Kaidu's."

"Yes," said my father. "To have come all this way through his lands without incident, only to come up against the man himself."

My uncle nodded glumly and said, "This may be as far as we get."

To explain why my father and uncle voiced annoyance and concern, I must explain some things about this land of Kithai to which we had come. First, its name is universally pronounced in the West "Cathay," and there is nothing I can do to change that. I would not even try, because the rightly pronounced "Kithai" is itself rather an arbitrary name, bestowed by the Mongols, and only comparatively recently, only some fifty years before I was born. This land was the first the Mongols conquered in their rampage across the world, and it is where Kubilai chose to set his throne, and it is the hub of the many spokes of the Mongols' widespread empire—just as our Venice is the holding center of our Republic's many possessions: Thessaly and Crete and the Vèneto mainland and all the rest. However, just as the Vèneti people originally came to the Venetian lagoon from somewhere out of the north, so did the Mongols come to Kithai.

"They have a legend," said my father, when we all were comfortably settled in Kashgar's karwansarai of the Five Felicities, and were discussing our situation. "It is a laughable legend, but the Mongols believe it. They say that once upon a time, long ago, a widow woman lived alone and lonely in a yurtu on the snowy plains. And out of loneliness, she befriended a blue wolf of the wild, and eventually she mated with it, and from their coupling sprang the first ancestors of the Mongols."

That legendary start of their race occurred in a land far north of Kithai, a land called Sibir. I have never visited there, nor ever wanted to, for it is said to be a flat and uninteresting country of perpetual snow and frost. In such a harsh land, it was perhaps only natural that the various Mongol tribes (one of which called itself "the Kithai") should have found nothing better to do than to fight among themselves. But one man of them, Temuchin by name, rallied together several tribes and, one by one, subdued the others, until all the Mongols were his to command, and name, Chinghiz, meaning Perfect Warrior.

Under Chinghiz Khan, the Mongols left their northland and swept southward—to this immense country, which was then the Empire of Chin—and they conquered it, and called it Kithai. The other conquests made by the Mongols, in the rest of the world, I need not recount in series, since they are too well known to history. Suffice it to say that Chinghiz and his lesser Ilkhans and later his sons and grandsons extended the Mongol domains westward to the banks of the River Dnieper in the Polish Ukraine, and to the gates of Constantinople on the Sea of Marmara—which sea, incidentally, like the Adriatic, we Venetians regard as our private pond.

"We Venetians made the word 'horde' from the Mongol word yurtu," my father reminded me, "and we called the marauders collectively the Mongol Horde." Then he went on to tell me something I had not known. "In Constantinople I heard them called by a different name: the *Golden* Horde. That was because the Mongol armies invading that region had come originally from this region, and you have seen the yellowness of the soil hereabout. They always colored their tents yellow like the earth, for partial conceal-ment. So—yellow yurtu: Golden Horde. However, the Mongols who marched straight west out of their native

Sibir were accustomed to coloring their yurtus white, like the Sibir snows. So those armies, invading the Ukraine, were called by their victims the White Horde. I suppose there may yet be Other-Colored Hordes."

If the Mongols had never conquered more than Kithai, they would have had much to boast about. The tremendous land stretches from the mountains of Tazhikistan eastward to the shores of the great ocean called the Sea of Kithai, or by some people the Sea of Chin. To the north, Kithai abuts on the Sibir wasteland where the Mongols originated. In the south—in those days, when I had first arrived in the country—Kithai bordered on the Empire of Sung. However, as I shall tell in its place, the Mongols later conquered that empire, too, and called it Manzi, and absorbed it into Kubilai's Khanate.

But even in those days of my first arrival, the Mongol Empire was so immense that—as I have repeatedly indicated—it was divided into numerous provinces, each under the sovereignty of a different Ilkhan. Those provinces had been parceled out with no particular attention paid to any previous map-drawn borders observed by former rulers now overthrown. The Ilkhan Abagha, for example, was the lord of what had been the Empire of Persia, but his lands also included much of what had been Greater Armenia and Anatolia to the west of Persia and, on the east, India Aryana. There, Abagha's domain bordered on the lands apportioned to his distant cousin, the Ilkhan Kaidu, who reigned over the Balkh region, the Pai-Mir, all of Tazhikistan and this western Sin-kiang Province of Kithai where my father, my uncle and I now lodged.

The Mongols' accession to empire and power and wealth had not lessened their lamentable propensity for quarreling among themselves. They quite frequently fought each other, just as they had used to do when they were only ragged savages in the wastes of Sibir, before Chinghiz unified them and impelled them to greatness. The Khakhan Kubilai was a grandson of that Chinghiz, and all the Ilkhans of the outlying provinces were likewise direct descendants of that Perfect Warrior. It might be supposed that they should have constituted a close-knit royal family. But several were descended from different sons of Chinghiz, and had been distanced from each other by two or three generations of the family tree's branchings apart, and not all

were satisfied that they had inherited their fair share of
the empire bequeathed by their mutual progenitor.

This Ilkhan Kaidu, for instance, whose summons to audience we were now awaiting, was the grandson of Kubilai's uncle, Okkodai. That Okkodai, in his time, had
himself been the ruling Khakhan, the second after
Chinghiz, and evidently his grandson Kaidu resented the
fact that the title and throne had passed to a different
branch of the line. Evidently he felt, too, that he deserved
more of the Khanate than he presently held. Anyway,
Kaidu had several times made incursions on the lands
given to Abagha, which was tantamount to insubordina-
tion against the Khakhan, for Abagha was Kubilai's
nephew, son of his brother, and his close ally in the otherwise disputatious family.

"Kaidu has never yet rebelled openly against Kubilai,"
said my father. "But, besides harassing Kubilai's favorite
nephew, he has disregarded many court edicts, and
usurped privileges to which he is not entitled, and in other
ways has flouted the Khakhan's authority. If he deems us
friends of Kubilai, then he must regard us as enemies of
himself."

Nostril, sounding woeful, said, "I thought we were only
having a trivial delay, master. Are we instead in danger
again?"

Uncle Mafìo muttered, "As the rabbit said in the fable:
'If that is not a wolf, it is a damned big dog.'"

"He may snatch for himself all the gifts we are carrying
to Khanbalik," said my father. "Out of envy and spite, as
much as rapacity."

"Surely not," I said. "That would most certainly be flagrant lesamaestà, defying the Khakhan's letter of safe
conduct. And Kubilai would be furious, would he not, if we
arrived empty-handed at his court, and told him why?"

"Only if we did arrive there," my father said ominously.
"Kaidu is presently the gatekeeper of this stage of the Silk
Road. He holds the power of life and death here. We can
only wait and see."

We were kept waiting for some days before we were bidden to our confrontation with the Ilkhan, but no one hin-
dered our freedom of movement. So I spent some of that
time in wandering about within the walls of Kashgar. I
had long ago learned that crossing a border between two

nations is not like going through a gate between two different gardens. Even in the far countries, all so exotically different from Venice, to go from one land into the next usually brought no more surprise than one finds, say, in crossing from the Vèneto into the Duchy of Padua or Verona. The first commonfolk I had seen in Kithai looked just like those I had been seeing for months, and at first glimpse the city of Kashgar might have been only a much bigger and better-built version of the Tazhik trade town of Murghab. But on closer acquaintance I did find Kashgar different in many respects from anywhere I had visited before.

In addition to the Mongol occupiers and settlers in the vicinity, the population included Tazhiks from across the border, and people of various other origins, Uzbek and Turki and I know not how many others. All of those the Mongols lumped under the name of Uighur, a word which means only "ally," but signified more. The various Uighurs were not just allied to the Mongols, they were all in some measure related by racial heritage, language and customs. Anyway, except for some variation in their dress and adornments, they all *looked* like Mongols—berry-brown of complexion, slit-eyed, notably hairy, big-boned, burly and squat and rough-hewn. But the population also included persons who were totally distinct—from me as well as from the Mongoloid peoples—in appearance, language and comportment. Those were the Han people, I learned, the aboriginal inhabitants of these lands.

Most of them had faces paler than mine, of a delicate ivory tint, like the best grade of parchment, and bearing little or no facial hair. Their eyes were not narrowed by heavily pouched lids, like the Mongols', but were nevertheless so very slitlike as to appear slanted. Their bodies and limbs were fine-boned, slim and seeming almost fragile. If, when one looked at a shaggy Mongol or one of his Uighur relatives, one thought at once, "That man has lived always out of doors," then one was inclined to think, when looking at a Han, even a wretched farmer hard at work in his field, filthy with mud and manure, "That man was born and raised indoors." But one did not have to look; a blind man would perceive a Han to be unique, merely hearing him talk.

The Han language resembles no other on this earth.

While I had no trouble learning to speak Mongol, and to write its alphabet, I never learned more than a rudimentary comprehension of Han. The Mongol speech is gruff and harsh, like its speakers, but it at least employs sounds not too different from those heard in our Western languages. The Han, by contrast, is a speech of staccato syllables, and they are *sung* rather than spoken. Evidently the Han throat is incapable of forming more than a very few of the sounds that other people make. The sound of *r*, for one, is quite beyond them. My name in their speech was always Mah-ko. And, having so very few noises to work with, the Han must sound them on different tones—high, mid, low, rising, falling—to make a sufficient variety for compiling a vocabulary. It is like this: suppose our Ambrosian plainsong *Gloria in excelsis* had that meaning of "glory in the highest" *only* when sung to its traditional up and down neumes, and, if the syllables were sung in different ups and downs, were to change its meaning utterly—to "darkness in the lowest" or "dishonor to the basest" or even "fish for the frying."

But there were no fish to be had in Kashgar. Our Uighur innkeeper almost proudly explained why. Here in this place, he said, we were as far inland as a person could get from any sea on the earth—the temperate oceans to the east and west, the tropic seas to the south, the frozen white ones in the north. Nowhere else in the world, he said, as if it were a thing to boast about, was there any spot farther from the sea. Kashgar had no freshwater fish either, he said, for the Passage River was too much befouled by the city's effluxions to support any. I was already aware of the effluxions, having noticed one sort here that I had never seen before. Every city spews out sewage and garbage and smoke, but the smoke of Kashgar was peculiar. It came from the stone that burns, and this was the first place I saw it.

In a sense, the burnable rock is the exact opposite of that rock I earlier saw in Balkh, which produces the cloth that will not burn. Many of my untraveled fellow Venetians have derided both stones as unbelievable, when I have spoken of them. But other Venetians—mariners in the English trade—tell me that the burning rock is well known and commonly used for fuel in England, where it is called kohle. In the Mongol lands it was called simply "the black"—kara—for that is its color. It occurs in extensive strata just a little way under the yellow soil, so it is easily got at with simple picks and spades, and, being rather crumbly, the stone is easily broken into wieldy chunks. A hearth or brazier heaped with those chunks requires a kindling fire of wood, but once the kara is alight it burns much longer than wood and gives a greater heat, as does naft oil. It is abundant and free for the digging and its only fault is its dense smoke. Because every Kashgar household and workshop and karwansarai used it for fuel, a pall hung perpetually between the city and the sky.

At least the kara did not, like camel or yak dung, give a noxious flavor to the food cooked over it, and the food served us in Kashgar was already dismally familiar of flavor. There were flocks of goats as well as sheep, and herds of cows and domestic yaks all over the landscape, and pigs and chickens and ducks in every backyard, but the staple meat at the Five Felicities was still the everlasting mutton. The Uighur peoples, like the Mongol, have no national religion, and I could not then make out whether the Han did. But Kashgar, as a trade crossroads, represented in its permanent and transient population just about every religion that exists, and the sheep is the one animal edible by communicants of all of them. And the aromatic, weak, not intoxicating, hence not religiously objectionable cha was still the staple beverage.

Kithai did introduce one pleasing improvement to our meals. Instead of rice, we got a side dish called miàn. That was not exactly new to us, as it was only a pasta of the vermicelli string sort, but it was a welcome old acquaintance. Usually it was served boiled al dente, just as Venetian vermicelli is, but sometimes it was cut into small bits and fried to crunchy kinks. What *was* new about it—to me, anyway—was that it was served with two slender sticks for the eating of it. I stared at this curiosity, nonplussed, and my father and uncle laughed at the expression on my face.

"They are called kuài-zi," said my father. "The nimble tongs. And they are more practical than they look. Observe, Marco."

Holding both of his sticks in the fingers of one hand, he began most adroitly to pick up bits of meat and skeins of the miàn. It took me some fumbling minutes to learn the use of the nimble-tong sticks, but, when I had, I found them to be notably neater than the Mongol fashion of eating with the fingers, and indeed more efficacious for twirling up strings of pasta than our Venetian skewers and spoons.

The Uighur landlord smiled approvingly when he saw me begin to pick and peck and spool with the sticks, and informed me that the nimble tongs were a Han contribution to fine dining. He went on to assert that the miàn-vermicelli was a Han invention, too, but I contested that. I told him that pasta of every variety had been on every table of the Italian peninsula ever since a Roman ship's cook fortuitously conceived the making of it. Perhaps, I suggested, the Han had learned of it during some Caesarean era of trade between Rome and Kithai.

"No doubt it happened so," said the innkeeper, he being a man of impeccable politeness.

I must say that I found all the commonfolk of Kithai, of every race—when they were not bloodily engaged in feud, revenge, banditry, rebellion or warfare—to be exceptionally courteous of address and comportment. And that gentility, I believe, was a contribution of the Han.

The Han language, as if to make up for its many inherent deficiencies, is replete with flowery expressions and ornate turns of phrase and intricate formalities, and the Han's manners are also exquisitely refined. They are a people of a very ancient and high culture, but whether their elegant speech and graces impelled their civilization or simply grew out of it, I have no idea. However, I do believe that all the other nations in proximity to the Han, though woefully inferior in culture, acquired from them at least those outward trappings of advanced civilization. Even in Venice, I had seen how people ape their betters, in appearance if not in substance. No shopkeeper is ever anything loftier than a shopkeeper, but he who purveys to fine ladies will converse better than the one who sells only to boat wives. A Mongol warrior may be by nature an uncouth barbarian, but when he chooses—as witness the first sentry who had challenged us—he can speak as politely as any Han, and exhibit manners suitable for a court ballroom.

Even in this rough frontier trade town, the Han influence was evident. I walked through streets with names like Flowery Benevolence and Crystallized Fragrance and,

in a market square called Productive Endeavor and Fair
Exchange, I saw lumpish Mongol soldiers buying caged
bright songbirds and bowls of shiny tiny fish to adorn their
rude army quarters. Every stall in the market had a sign,
a long, narrow board hung vertically, and passersby helpfully translated for me the words inscribed in the Mongol
alphabet or the Han characters. Besides giving notice of
what the stall sold: "Pheasant Eggs for Making Hair Po-
made" or "Spicy-Ordered Indigo Dye," each board added a
few words of advice: "Loitering and Gossiping Are Not
Conducive to Good Business" or "Former Customers Have
Induced the Sad Necessity of Denying Credit" or something of the sort.

But if there was one aspect of Kashgar that first told me
Kithai was different from other places I had been, it was
the endless variety of smells. True, every other Eastern
community had been odorous, but chiefly and awfully of
old urine. Kashgar was not free of that stale smell, but it
had many and better others. Most noticable was the odor of
kara smoke, which is not unpleasant, and into that were
blended countless and fragrant incenses, which the people
burned in their houses and shops as well as in places of
worship. Also, at all hours of the day and night, one could
smell foodstuffs cooking. That was sometimes familiar: the
simple, good, mouth-watering aroma of pork chops frying
in some non-Muslim kitchen. But the scent was often otherwise: the smell of a pot of frogs being boiled or a dog
being stewed defies description. And sometimes it was an
exotically nice smell: that of burned sugar, for example,
when I watched a Han vendor of sweets melt bright-
colored sugars over a brazier and then, as magically as a
sorcerer, somehow blow and spin that fondant into delicate
shapes of floss—a flower with pink petals and green leaves,
a brown man on a white horse, a dragon with many wings
of different colors.

In baskets in the market were more kinds of cha leaves
than I had known existed, all aromatic and no two smelling alike; and jars of spices of pungencies new to me; and
baskets of flowers of shapes and colors and perfumes I had
never encountered before. Even our Inn of the Five Felicities smelled different from all the others we had inhabited,
and the landlord told me why. In the plaster of the walls
was mixed red meleghèta pepper. It discouraged insects,

he said, and I believed him, for the place was singularly clean of vermin. However, this being early summer, I could not verify his other claim: that the hot red pepper made the rooms warmer in winter.

I saw no other Venetian traders in the city, or Genoese or Pisan or any other of our commercial rivals, but we Polos were not the only white men. Or white men, so-called; I remember being asked by a Han scholar, many years later:

"Why are you people of Europe called white? You have more of a brick-red complexion."

Anyway, there were a few other whites in Kashgar, and their brick-redness was easily visible among the Eastern skin colors. During my first day's stroll through the streets, I saw two bearded white men deep in conversation, and one of them was Uncle Mafìo. The other wore the vestments of a Nestorian priest, and had a flat-backed head that identified him as an Armeniyan. I wondered what my uncle could have found to discuss with a heretic cleric, but I did not intrude, only waved a greeting as I went by.

2

ON one of the days of our enforced idleness, I went outside the city walls to view the camp of the Mongols—what they called their bok—and to exercise what Mongol words I knew, and to learn some new ones.

The first new words I learned were these: "Hui! Nohaigan hori!" and I learned them in a hurry, for they mean "Olà! Call off your dogs!" Packs of large and truculent mastiffs prowled freely through the whole bok, and every yurtu had two or three chained at its entrance. I learned also that I was wise to be carrying my riding quirt, as the Mongols always do, for beating off the curs. And I early learned to leave the quirt outside whenever I entered a yurtu, for to carry it inside would be unmannerly, would offend the human occupants, being an implication that they were no better than dogs.

There were other niceties of behavior to be observed. A stranger must approach a yurtu by walking first between

two of the camp fires outside, thus properly purifying himself. Also, one never steps upon the threshold of a yurtu
when entering or leaving it, and never whistles while inside it. I learned those things because the Mongols were
eager to receive me and to instruct me in their ways and to
query me about mine. Indeed, they were almost over-
whelmingly eager. If the Mongols have one trait exceeding
the ferocity they show to inimical outsiders, it is the inquisitiveness they show about peaceable ones. The single
most frequent sound in their speech is "uu," which is not a
word but a vocal question mark.

"Sain bina, sain urkek! Good meeting, good brother!" a
group of warriors greeted me, and then immediately inquired, "From under what skies do you come, uu?"

"From under the skies of the West," I said, and they widened their eyes as much as those slits would widen, and
they exclaimed:

"Hui! Those skies are immense, and they shelter many
lands. In your Western country, did you dwell beneath a
roof, uu, or a tent, uu?"

"In my native city, a roof. But I have been long upon the
road, and living under a tent, when not the open sky."

"Sain!" they cried, smiling broadly. "All men are brothers, is that not true, uu? But those men who dwell beneath
tents are even closer brothers, as close as twins. Welcome,
twin brother!"

And they bowed and gestured me into the yurtu belonging to one of them. Except for its being portable, it bore
little relation to my flimsy sleeping tent. Its interior was
only a single round room, but it was a commodious six
paces in diámeter and its top was well above a standing
man's head. The walls were of interlaced wooden laths,
vertical walls from ground level to shoulder height, then
curving inward to form a dome. At its top center was an
open roundel, whence the smoke from the room's heating
brazier escaped. The lath framework supported the yurtu's
outer covering: overlapping sheets of heavy felt, colored
yellow with clay, lashed to the frame by crisscrossed ropes.
The furnishings were few and simple, but of good quality:
floor carpets and couches of cushions, also all made of
brightly colored felt. The yurtu was as sturdy and warm
and weather-repellent as any house, but it could be dis-

mantled in an hour and compacted into bundles small and light enough to be carried on a single pack saddle.

My Mongol greeters and I entered the yurtu through the felt-flapped opening which, as in all Mongol edifices, was on its southern side. I was motioned to take a seat on the "man's bed" of the establishment, the one on the north side of the yurtu, where I could sit facing the good-omened south. (Beds for women and children were ranged around the less-auspicious other sides.) I sank down on the felt-covered cushions, and my host pressed into my hand a drinking vessel that was simply a ram's horn. Into it, he poured from a leather bag a rank-smelling and bluish-white thin liquid.

"Kumis," he said it was.

I waited politely until all the men held full horns. Then I did as they did, which was to dip fingers into the kumis and flick a few drops in each direction of the compass. They explained, well enough for me to comprehend, that we were saluting "the fire" to the south, "the air" to the east, "the water" to the west and "the dead" to the north. Then we all raised our horns and drank deeply, and I committed a bad breach of manners. Kumis, I would learn, is to the Mongols a drink as beloved and sacrosanct as qahwah is to the Arabs. I thought it was awful and, unpardonably, I let my face express my opinion. The men all looked distressed. One of them said hopefully that I would grow to like the taste in time, and another said I would like the exhilarating effect of it even more. But my host took my horn and drank it empty, then refilled it from a different leather bag and handed the vessel back to me, saying, "This is arkhi."

The arkhi had a better smell, but I sipped at it cautiously, for it looked just like the kumis. I was gratified that it tasted much better, rather like a wine of medium quality. I nodded and smiled and asked the source of their beverages, for I had seen no vineyards in the vicinity. I was astonished when my host said proudly:

"From the good milk of healthy mares."

Except for their weapons and armor, the Mongols manufacture two things, and only two, and those are made by the Mongol women, and I had just encountered both of them. I was seated on felt-covered pillows in a felt-covered tent, and I was drinking a beverage made from mare's milk. I think the Mongol females are not ignorant of the arts of spinning and weaving, but scorn them as basely effeminate, for these women are veritable Amazons. Anyway, the woven fabrics they wear they buy from other peoples. But they are most expert in beating and matting together the hairs of animals into felts of every weight, from the heavy yurtu coverings to a cloth that is as soft and fine as Welsh flannel.

The Mongol women also disdain every kind of milk except the equine. They do not even give their children to suck from their own breasts, but nourish them from infancy on mare's milk. They do some uncommon things with that fluid, and it did not take me long to overcome my repugnance and become an enthusiastic partaker of all the Mongol milk products. The most prevalent is the mildly intoxicating kumis. It is made by putting fresh mare's milk into a great leather sack, which the women beat with heavy clubs until butter forms. They scoop off the butter and leave the fluid residue to ferment. That kumis then is pungent and sharp to the tongue, with an aftertaste rather like almonds, and a man who drinks enough of it can get estimably drunk. If the sack of milk is beaten longer, until both butter and curds are separated, and the very thin remaining liquid left to ferment, it becomes the more agreeably sweet and wholesome and effervescent sort of kumis called arkhi. And a man can get drunk on that without drinking a very great deal of it.

Besides making use of the butter acquired from the milk, the Mongol women make an ingenious use of the curds. They spread them in the sun and let them dry to a hard cake. That substance, called grut, they crumble into pellets which can be kept indefinitely without spoiling. Some of it is set aside for the wintertime, when the herd mares give no milk, and some is put into pouches to be carried as emergency rations by men going on the march. The grut has only to be dissolved in water to make a quick and nourishing thick drink.

The actual milking of the herd mares is done by the Mongol men; it constitutes some kind of masculine prerogative and is forbidden to the women. But the subsequent making of kumis and arkhi and grut, like the making of felt, is women's work. In fact, *all* the work in a Mongol bok is done by the women.

"Because the only proper concern of men is the making

of war," said my host that day. "And the only proper concern of women is the tending of their men. Uu?"

It cannot be denied that, since a Mongol army goes
everywhere accompanied by all the warriors' wives, and
extra women for the unmarried men, and the offspring of
all those women, the men seldom have to give attention to
anything but the fighting. A woman unaided can take
down or put up a yurtu, and do all the necessary chores of
keeping it supplied and maintained and clean and in good
repair, and keeping her man fed and clothed and in fighting humor and cosseted when he is wounded, and keeping
his war gear in ready condition, and his horses as well. The
children also work, collecting dung or kara for the bok
fires, doing herdsman and guard duty. On the few occasions when a battle has gone against the Mongols, and
they have had to call up their encamped reserves, the
women have been known to seize up weapons and go themselves into the fray, and give good account of themselves.

I regret to say that the Mongol females do not resemble
the warrior Amazons of antiquity as portrayed by Western
artists. They could almost be mistaken for Mongol males,
because they have the same flat face, the broad cheek-
bones, the leathery complexion, the puffed eyelids making
slits of eyes that, when visible, are always redly inflamed.
The women may be less burly than the men, but they do
not appear so, because they wear equally bulky clothes.
Like the men, accustomed to riding for most of their lives,
and riding astride, they have the same shambling horseman's gait when afoot. The women do differ in not wearing
a wispy beard or mustache, which some of the men do. The
men also have their hair hanging long and braided behind,
and sometimes shaven on the crown like a priest's tonsure.
The women pile their hair up on top of their head in an
elaborate fashion—and perhaps they do this just once in a
lifetime, because they then varnish it in place with the sap
of the wutung tree. And on top of that, they fix a high head-
piece called a gugu, a thing made of bark, decorated with
bits of colored felt and ribbons. Her cemented hair and her
gugu together make a woman some two feet taller than a
man, so cumbrously tall that she can enter a yurtu only by
bowing her head.

While I sat conversing with my hosts, the woman of the
yurtu several times came in and went out, and she had to

bend like that every time. But the bending was not a genu-
flection, and she showed no other signs of servility. She
simply bustled about at her work, fetching fresh flagons of
kumis and arkhi for us, taking out the emptied ones, and
otherwise seeing to our comfort. The man who was her
husband addressed her as Nai, which just means Woman,
but the other men said courteously Sain Nai. I was interested to see that a Good Woman, although she works like a
slave, does not behave like a slave and is not treated as a
slave. A Mongol woman does not, like a Muslim woman,
have to hide her face behind a chador or hide her whole self
in pardah or endure any of the other female humiliations
of Islam. She is expected to be chaste, at least after marriage, but no one is appalled if she uses immodest language or laughs at a bawdy story—or tells one, as this Sain
Nai did.

She had, unbidden, laid a meal for us on the felt carpet
in the middle of the yurtu. And then, equally unbidden,
she squatted down to eat with us—and was not forbidden—
which surprised and delighted me almost as much as the
meal did. She had served a sort of Mongol version of the
Venetian scaldavivande: a bowl of boiling-hot broth, a
smaller bowl of red-brown sauce and a platter of strips of
raw lamb. We all took turns dipping pieces of meat into the
scalding broth, cooking it to our taste, dipping it into the
piquant sauce and then eating it. The Sain Nai, like the
men, dipped her bits of meat barely long enough to warm
them, and ate them nearly raw. Any doubts about Mongol
women being as robust as their men were dispelled by the
sight of that one tearing at the hunks of meat, her hands
and teeth and lips all bloodied. One difference: the men ate
without talking, giving all their attention to the food; the
woman, in the intervals between her devourings, was most
voluble.

I gathered that she was making fun of the newest wife
her husband had acquired. (There was no limit to the number of women a Mongol man could wed, so long as he could
afford to set up each one in a separate yurtu.) The woman
acidly remarked that he had been dead drunk when he
asked for the hand of this latest one. All the men chuckled,
the husband included. And they all snickered and giggled
as she listed the new wife's shortcomings, evidently in ribald terms. And they absolutely guffawed and fell about on

the carpet when she concluded by suggesting that the new wife probably urinated standing up, like a man.

That was not the most comical thing I had ever heard, but it was certain evidence that the Mongol women enjoy a freedom denied to almost all other females in the East. Except in comeliness, they are more like Venetian women: full of liveliness and good cheer, because they know they are the equals and comrades of their men, only having different functions and responsibilities in life.

The Mongol males do not simply sit idle while their women drudge, or at least do not all the time. After our meal, my hosts walked with me about the bok, showing me the work of men variously occupied at fletching, armoring, currying, cutling and other military crafts. The fletchers, having already laid up a good store of ordinary arrows, were that day forging special arrowheads pierced with holes in a way that, they told me, would make the arrows whistle and shriek in their flight, thereby putting fear in the heart of an enemy. Some of the armorers were thunderously hammering sheets of red-hot iron into the form of breastplatcs for men and horses, and others were more quietly doing the same with cuirbouilli, heavy leather boiled to softness, then shaped and let dry, when it gets almost as hard as iron. The curriers were making wide waist belts ornamented with colored stones—not to be worn for mere decoration, they told me, but to protect the wearers against thunder and lightning. The cutlers were making wicked shimshirs and daggers, and putting new edges onto old blades, and fitting helves to battle axes, and one of them was forging a lance that had a curious hook projecting from the blade—to yank an enemy from his saddle, the maker told me.

"A fallen foe can be more neatly skewered," added one of my guides. "The earth makes a firmer stop than the air, to pin him against."

"However, we disdain too easy a stroke," said another. "When the foe is unhorsed, we ride back a way from where he lies, and wait for him to cry defiance—or mercy."

"Yes, and then plunge the lance point through his open mouth," said another. "That is a fine feat of aim when done at the gallop."

Those remarks put my hosts in a mood of happy reminiscence, and they went on to recount for me various stories of their people's wars and campaigns and battles. None of those engagements seemed ever to have ended in a defeat for the Mongols, but always a victory and a conquest and a profitable pillage afterward. Of the many tales they told, I recall two with special clarity, for in them the Mongols contended, not just with other men, but with fire and ice.

They told how, once upon a time, during their siege of some city in India, the cowardly but cunning Hindu defenders had tried to rout them by sending against them a cavalry troop of unusual composition. The horses bore riders made of hammered copper in the shape of men, and each of those charging riders was in reality a mobile furnace, the copper shell being filled with burning coals and flaming oil-soaked cotton. Whether the Hindus intended to spread conflagration among the Mongol Horde, or merely consternation, never was known. For the furnace-warriors so singed their own mounts that the horses sensibly bucked them off, and the Mongols rode unimpeded into the city, and slaughtered all its less-incandescent defenders, and made the city their own.

Again, the Mongols waged a campaign against a savage tribe of Samoyeds in the cold far north. Before the battle began, the men of that tribe ran to a nearby river and plunged into it, and then, on emerging, rolled in the dust of the riverbank. They let that coating freeze upon their bodies, then repeated the process several more times, until they were armored all over with thick mud-ice, and judged themselves safe against the Mongols' arrows and blades. Perhaps they were, but the frozen armor made the Samoyeds so thick and clumsy that they could neither fight nor dodge, and the Mongols simply trampled them under the hoofs of their steeds.

So fire and ice had unsuccessfully been used against them, but the Mongols themselves had occasionally used water, and successfully. In the Kazhak country, for example, the Mongols once besieged a city called Kzyl-Orda, and it long held out against them. The word Kazhak means "man without a master," and the Kazhak warriors, whom we in the West call Cossacks, are very nearly as formidable as the Mongols. But the besiegers did not simply sit encircling the city and waiting for it to surrender. They made use of their wait by digging a new channel for the

nearby Syr-Daria River. They diverted its course and let it
flood Kzyl-Orda and drown every person in it.

"Flooding is a good way of taking a city," said one of the
men. "Better than pitching in big boulders or fire arrows.
Another good way is the catapulting into it of diseased
dead bodies. Kills all the defenders, you see, but leaves the
buildings intact for new occupants. The only bad thing
about those methods is that they cheat our leaders of their
favorite enjoyment—making their celebration banquet on
human tables."

"Human tables?" I said, thinking I must have misheard.
"Uu?"

They laughed as they explained. The tables were heavy
planks supported on the bent backs of kneeling men, the
vanquished officers of whatever army they defeated. And
they laughed right heartily as they imitated the moans
and sobs of those hungry men bowed under the weight of
planks laden with high-heaped trenchers of meat and
brimming jugs of kumis. And they positively guffawed as
they imitated the even more piteous cries of those table-
men when the feasting was done, when the Mongol celebrants vaulted onto the tables to do their furious,
stamping, leaping victory dances.

In telling their war stories, the men mentioned various
leaders under whom they had served, and the leaders all
seemed to have had a confusing variety of titles and ranks.
But I gradually divined that a Mongol army is really not a
shapeless horde, but a model of organization. Of every ten
warriors, the strongest and fiercest and most war-experi-
enced is made captain. Similarly, of every ten captains,
one is chief, thereby having command of a hundred men.
And the ordering continues to progress by tens. Of every
ten chief-captains, one is flag-captain, with fully a thousand men rallying to his pennant. Then, of every ten flag-
captains, one is the sardar, having command of ten
thousand men. The word for "ten thousand" is toman, and
that word also means "yak's tail," so the sardar's standard
is a plume of yak tail on a pole instead of a flag.

It is a superbly efficient system of command, since any
officer at any level from captain up to sardar need confer
with only nine other equals when making his plans and decisions and dispositions. There is only one rank higher
than sardar. That is orlok, meaning roughly a commander-

in-chief, who has under him at least ten sardars and their tomans, making a tuk of a hundred thousand warriors, sometimes more. His power is so awesome that the rank of orlok is seldom given to any man but an actual ruling Ilkhan of the Chinghiz family line. The army then camped in bok about Kashgar was a part of the forces commanded by the Orlok-and-Olkhan Kaidu.

Any Mongol officer, besides being a good leader in combat, must at other times be what Moses was to the Israelites on the move. Whether he is the captain of ten men or the sardar of ten thousand, he is responsible for the movement and the provisioning of them and their wives and their women and their children and many other camp followers—such as the aged veterans who have no usefulness whatever, but who have the right to refuse retirement into garrison inactivity. The officer is also responsible for the herds of livestock that go afield with his troops: the horses for riding, the beasts for butchering, the yaks or asses or mules or camels for pack carrying. To count just the horses, every Mongol man travels with a string of war steeds and humis-milk mares that number, on the average, eighteen all together.

Of the various leading officers mentioned by my hosts, the only name I recognized was that of the Ilkhan Kaidu. So I asked if they had ever been led in battle by the Khakhan Kubilai whom I hoped to meet in the not too distant future. They said they had never had the high honor to be directly under his command, but had been fortunate enough to glimpse him once or twice at some remove. They said he was of manly beauty and soldierly bearing and statesmanlike wisdom, but that the most impressive of his qualities was his much-feared temper.

"He can be more fierce even than our fierce Ilkhan Kaidu," said one of them. "No man is eager to raise the wrath of the Khakhan Kubilai. Not even Kaidu."

"Nor the very elements of the earth and sky," said another. "Why, people call out the name of the Khakhan when it thunders—'Kubilai!'—so the lightning will not strike them. I have heard even our fearless Kaidu do that."

"Truly," said another, "in the presence of the Khakhan Kubilai, the wind does not presume to blow too strongly, or the rain to fall harder than a drizzle, or to splash up any mud on his boots. Even the water in his pitcher shrinks fearfully from him."

I commented that that must be rather a nuisance when he was thirsty. That was a sacrilegious remark to make about the most powerful man in the world, but no one present raised an eyebrow, for we were all quite drunk by then. We were seated again in the yurtu, and my hosts had gone through several flagons of kumis, and I had imbibed a goodly amount of their arkhi. The Mongols will not ever constrain themselves to have just one drink, or let a guest have just one, for when the one is downed they exclaim: "A man cannot walk on one foot!" and they pour another. And *that* one foot requires another, and that another, and so on. The Mongols go even into death still drinking, so to speak. A slain warrior is always buried on the battlefield under a cairn of stones, and he is interred in a seated position, holding his drinking horn in his hand at waist level.

The day had given way to darkness when I decided that I had better stop drinking or risk qualifying for interment myself. I climbed to my feet and thanked my hosts for their hospitality and made my farewells and took my leave of them, while they cried cordially after me, "Mendu, sain urkek! A good horse and a wide plain to you, until we meet again!"

I was not on a horse, but afoot, and therefore staggered somewhat. But that excited no comment from anybody, as I weaved through the bok and back through the Kashgar gate and through the scented streets to the karwansarai of the Five Felicities. I lurched into our chamber, and stopped short, staring. A large, black-garbed, black-bearded priest stood there. It took me a moment to recognize him as my Uncle Mafìo and, in my fuddled condition, all I could think was, "Dear God, what depth of depravity has he sunk to now? Uu?"

3

I slumped onto a bench and sat grinning as my uncle preened piously in his cassock. My father, sounding peeved, quoted an old saying: "The clothes make the man, but a habit does not make a monk. Let alone a priest, Mafìo. Where did you get it?"

"I bought it from that Father Boyajian. You remember him, Nico, from when we were here last."

"Yes. An Armeniyan would probably peddle the Host. Why did you not make him an offer for that?"

"A sacramental wafer would mean nothing to the Ilkhan Kaidu, but this disguise will. His own chief wife, the Ilkhatun, is a converted Christian—at least a Nestorian. So I am trusting that Kaidu will respect this cloth."

"Why? You do not. I have heard you criticize the Church in utterances that verge on heresy. And now this. It is blasphemy!"

Uncle Mafìo protested, "The cassock is not in itself a liturgical garment. Anybody can wear one, as long as he does not pretend to its sanctity. I do not. I could not, if I wanted to. Deuteronomy, you know: 'An eunuch, whose testicles are broken, shall not enter into the Church of the Lord.' Capòn mal caponà."

"Mafìo! Do not try to justify your impiety with self-pity."

"I am only saying that if Kaidu mistakes me for a priest, I see no need to correct him. Boyajian gives it as his opinion that a Christian may employ any subterfuge in dealing with a heathen."

"I do not accept a Nestorian reprobate as an authority on Christian behavior."

"Had you rather accept Kaidu's decree? Confiscation, or worse? Look, Nico. He has Kubilai's letter; he knows that we were bidden to bring priests to Kithai. Without any priests, we are mere vagrants wandering through Kaidu's domain with a most tempting lot of valuables. I will not claim that I am a priest, but if Kaidu supposes it—"

"That white collar never protected anybody's neck from a headsman's ax."

"It is better than nothing. Kaidu can do as he pleases to ordinary travelers, but if he slays or detains a priest, the ripples will eventually reach Kubilai's court. And a priest whom Kubilai sent for? We know that Kaidu is temerarious, but I doubt that he is suicidally so." Uncle Mafìo turned to me. "What do you say, Marco? Observe your uncle as a reverend father. How do I look?"

"Magnissifent," I said thickly.

"Hm," he murmured, regarding me more closely. "It will help, yes, if Kaidu is as drunk as you are."

I started to say that he probably would be, but I fell suddenly asleep where I sat.

The next morning, my uncle was again wearing the cassock when he came to the karwansarai's dining table, and my father again began berating him. Nostril and I were present, but did not participate in the dispute. To the Muslim slave it was, I suppose, a matter of total unconcern. And I stayed silent because my head was hurting. But both the argument and our breaking of our fast were interrupted by the arrival of a Mongol messenger from the bok. The man, dressed in splendid war regalia, swaggered into the inn like a newcome conqueror, strode directly to our table and, without any courtesy of greeting, said to us—in Farsi to make sure we all understood:

"Arise and come with me, dead men, for the Ilkhan Kaidu would hear your last words!"

Nostril gasped so that he choked on whatever he was eating, and began to cough, meanwhile goggling his eyes with terror. My father pounded him on the back and said, "Be not alarmed, good slave. That is the usual wording of a summons from a Mongol lord. It portends no harm."

"Or it does not necessarily," my uncle amended. "I am still glad that I thought of this disguise."

"Too late to make you doff it now," muttered my father, for the messenger was pointing imperiously toward the outer door. "I just hope, Mafìo, that you will temper your profane performance with priestly decorum."

Uncle Mafìo raised his right hand to each of the three of us in the sign of benediction, smiled beatifically and said with utmost unction, "Si non caste, tamen caute."

The mock-pious gesture and the mock-solemn Latin play on words were so typical of my uncle's mischievously cheerful bravado that I—even feeling as sour as I did—had to laugh aloud. Granted, Mafìo Polo had some lamentable shortcomings as a Christian and as a man, but he was a good companion to have standing by in an uneasy situation. The Mongol messenger glowered at me when I laughed, and he barked his command at us again, and we all got up and followed him from the building at a quick march.

It was raining that day, which did not do much to

lighten my mal di capo, or to make more cheerful our trudge through the streets and beyond the city wall and through the packs of yapping and snarling dogs of the Mongol bok. We hardly raised our heads to look around until the messenger shouted, "Halt!" and directed us to pass between the two fires burning before the entrance to Kaidu's yurtu.

I had not been near it on my previous visit to the camp, and now I realized that *this* was the sort of yurtu which must have inspired the Western word "horde." It would indeed have encompassed a whole horde of the ordinary yurtu tents, for this was a grand pavilion. It was almost as high and as big around as the karwansarai in which we were residing; but that was a solidly built edifice, and this was entirely of yellow-clayed felt, supported by tent poles and stakes and braided horse-hair ropes. Several mastiffs roared and lunged against their chains at the south-facing entrance, and on either side of that flapped opening hung elaborately embroidered felt panels. The yurtu was no palace, but it certainly overshadowed the lesser ones of the bok. And next to it rested the wagon which transported it from place to place, for Kaidu's pavilion was usually moved intact, not dismantled and bundled. The wagon was the most huge I have ever seen anywhere: a flat bed of planks, as big as a meadow, balanced on an axle like a tree trunk and with wheels like mill wheels. The drawing of it, I learned later, required fully twenty-two yaks hitched in two wide spans of eleven abreast. (The drafters had to be placid yaks or oxen; no horses or camels would have worked in such close proximity.)

The messenger ducked under the yurtu's flap to announce us to his lord, emerged again and jerked his arm to order us inside. Then, as we passed him, he barred Nostril's way, growling, "No slaves!" and kept him outside. There was a reason for that. The Mongols regard themselves as naturally superior to all other freemen in the world, even kings and such, so any man who is held inferior by *their* inferiors is considered unworthy even of contempt.

The Ilkhan Kaidu regarded us in silence as we crossed the brilliantly carpeted and pillow-furnished interior, to where he sat sprawled on a heap of furs—all gorgeously striped and spotted: evidently the pelts of tigers and pards—on a dais that set him above us. He was dressed in battle armor of polished metals and leathers, and wore on his head an earflapped hat of karakul. He had eyebrows that looked like detached bits of the kinky black karakul, and not small bits either. Under them, his slit eyes were red-shot, seemingly inflamed by rage at the very sight of us. On his either side stood a warrior, as handsomely caparisoned as the man who had fetched us. One held a lance erect, the other held a sort of canopy on a pole over Kaidu's head, and both stood as rigid as statues.

We three made a slow approach. In front of the furry throne, we made a dignified slight bow, all together, as if we had rehearsed it, and looked up at Kaidu, waiting for him to make the first indication of the mood of this meeting. He continued for some moments to stare at us, as if we were vermin that had crawled out from under the yurtu's carpetings. Then he did something disgusting. He made a hawking noise from deep in his throat, bringing up a great wad of phlegm into his mouth. Then he languidly unsprawled himself from his couch and stood upright and turned to the guardsman at his right, and with his thumb pressed the man's chin so that his mouth opened. Then Kaidu spat his hawked-up gob of substance directly into the man's mouth and thumbed it shut again—the warrior's expression and rigidity never changing—and languidly resumed his seat, his eyes again on us and glittering evilly.

It had clearly been a gesture intended to awe us with his power and arrogance and uncordiality, and it would have served to cow me, I think. But at least one of us—Mafìo Polo—was not impressed. When Kaidu spoke his first words, in the Mongol language and in a harsh voice: "Now, interlopers—" he got no further, for my uncle daringly interrupted, in the same language:

"First, if it please the Ilkhan, we will sing a praise to God for having conducted us safely across so many lands into the Lord Kaidu's august presence." And, to the astonishment of myself—probably also of my father and the Mongols—he began bawling out the old Christmas hymn:

A solis orbu cardine
Et usque terre limitem . . .

"It does *not* please the Ilkhan," Kaidu said through his teeth, when my uncle drew breath at that point. But my father and I, emboldened, had joined in for the next two lines:

> Christum canamus principem
> Natum Maria virgine . . .

"Enough!" bellowed Kaidu, and our voices trailed off. Fixing his red eyes on Uncle Mafìo, the Ilkhan said, "You are a Christian priest." He said it flatly—loathingly, in fact—so my uncle did not have to take it as a question, which would have required him to deny it.

He said only, "I am here at the behest of the Khan of All Khans," and indicated the paper Kaidu was holding clenched in one hand.

"Hui, yes," said Kaidu, with an acid smile. He unfolded the document in a manner suggesting that it was filthy to the touch. "At the behest of my esteemed cousin. I notice that my cousin wrote this ukaz on yellow paper, as the Chin emperors used to do. Kubilai and I conquered that decadent empire, but he more and more imitates its effete customs. Vakh! He has become no better than a Kalmuk! And our old war god Tengri is no longer good enough for him, either, it seems. Now he must import womanish Ferenghi priests."

"Merely to enlarge his knowledge of the world, Lord Kaidu," said my father, in a conciliatory voice. "Not to propagate any new—"

"The only way to know the world," Kaidu said savagely, "is to seize it and wring it!" He flicked his lurid gaze from one to another of us. "Do you dispute that, uu?"

"To dispute the Lord Kaidu," murmured my father, "would be like eggs attacking stones, as the saying goes."

"Well, at least you manifest some good sense," the Ilkhan said grudgingly. "I trust you also have the sense to realize that this ukaz is dated some years ago and some seven thousand li distant from here. Even if cousin Kubilai has not totally forgotten it by now, I am in no way bound to honor it."

My uncle murmured, even more meekly than my father had done, "It is said: How can a tiger be subject to the law?"

"Exactly," grunted the Ilkhan. "If I choose, I can regard you as mere trespassers. Ferenghi interlopers with no good intent. And I can condemn you to summary execution."

"Some say," murmured my father, more meekly yet, "that tigers are really the agents of Heaven, appointed to chase down those who have somehow eluded their deserved date with death."

"Yes," said the Ilkhan, looking slightly exasperated by all this agreement and mollification. "On the other hand, even a tiger can sometimes be lenient. Much as I detest my cousin for abandoning his Mongol heritage—much as I despise the increasing degeneracy of his court—I would let you go there and join his retinue. I could, if I so choose."

My father clapped his hands, as if in admiration of the Ilkhan's wisdom, and said with delight, "Clearly the Lord Kaidu remembers, then, the old Han story of the clever . wife Ling."

"Of course," said the Ilkhan. "It was in my mind as I spoke." He unbent enough to smile frigidly at my father. My father smiled ~~warmly back~~. There was an interval of silence. "However," Kaidu resumed, "that story is told in many variations. In which version did you hear it, uu, trespasser?"

My father cleared his throat and declaimed, "Ling was wife to a rich man who was overfond of wine, and was forever sending her to the wine shop to fetch bottles for him. The lady Ling, fearing for his health, would deliberately prolong the errands, or water the wine, or hide it, to keep him from drinking so much. At which her husband would be wroth and would beat her. Finally, two things happened. The lady Ling fell out of love with her husband, although he was rich, and she noticed how handsome was the wine-shop clerk, although he was a humble tradesman. Thereafter, she willingly bought wine at her husband's command, and even poured it for him, and urged it on him. Eventually the husband died in a drunkard's convulsions, and she inherited all his wealth, and she married the wine-shop clerk, and they both were rich and happy ever after."

"Yes," said the Ilkhan. "That is the correct story." There was another silence, and a longer one. Then Kaidu said, more to himself than to us, "Yes, the drunkard caused his own rot, and others helped it along, until he rotted through and fell, and was supplanted by a better. It is legendary, and it is salutary."

Just as quietly, my uncle said, "Also legendary is the tiger's patience in the tracking of his prey."

Kaidu shook himself, as if awakening from a reverie, and said, "A tiger can be lenient as well as patient. I have already said so. I shall therefore let you all proceed in peace. I will even give you an escort against the hazards of the road. And you, priest, for all I care, you may convert cousin Kubilai and his entire court to your enfeebling religion. I hope you do. I wish you success."

"One nod of the head," my father exclaimed, "is heard farther than a thunderclap. You have done a good thing, Lord Kaidu, and its echoes will long resound."

"Just one thing," said the Ilkhan, again using a tone of severity. "I am told by my Lady Ilkhatun, who is a Christian and should know, that Christian priests maintain a vow of poverty, and possess nothing of material value. But I am also informed that you men travel with horses heavy-laden with treasure."

My father threw my uncle a look of annoyance, and said, "Some baubles, Lord Kaidu. They belong to no priest, but are destined for your cousin Kubilai. They are tokens of tribute from the Shah of Persia and the Sultan of India Aryana."

"The Sultan is my liege subject," said Kaidu. "He has no right to give away what belongs to me. And the Shah is a subject of my cousin the Ilkhan Abagha, who is no friend to me. Whatever he sends is contraband, subject to confiscation. Do you understand me, uu?"

"But, Lord Kaidu, we have promised to deliver—"

"A broken promise is no more than a broken pot. The potter can always make more. Have no concern for your promises, Ferenghi. Just bring your packhorses at this hour tomorrow, here to my yurtu, and let me see which of the baubles catch my fancy. I may let you keep some few of them. Do you understand, uu?"

"Lord Kaidu—"

"Uu! Do you understand?"

"Yes, Lord Kaidu."

"Since you understand, then obey!" He abruptly stood up, signaling the end of the audience.

We bowed our way out of the great yurtu, and collected Nostril from where he waited outside, and we started back through the rain and the mud underfoot, this time unaccompanied, and my uncle said to my father:

"I think we did rather well, Nico, in concert there. Especially adroit of you to remember that Ling story. I never heard it before."

"Neither did I," my father said drily. "But surely the Han have some such instructive tale, among the many they do have."

I opened my mouth for the first time. "Something else you said, Father, gave me an idea. I will meet you back at the inn."

I parted from them, to go and call on my Mongol hosts of the day before. I requested an introduction to one of their armorers, and got it, and asked the man at the forge if I might borrow for a day one of his yet-unhammered sheets of metal. He graciously found for me a piece of copper that was long and broad, but thin, so it wobbled and rippled and thrummed as I carried it to the karwansarai. My father and uncle paid no attention as I carried it into our room and leaned it against the wall, for they were again arguing.

"All the fault of that cassock," said my father. "Your being an impoverished priest gave Kaidu the notion of impoverishing us."

"Nonsense, Nico," said my uncle. "He would have found some other excuse, if that had not occurred to him. What we must do is offer him freely something from our hoard, and hope he will ignore the rest."

"Well . . .," said my father, thinking. "Suppose we give him our cods of musk. At least they are ours to give."

"Oh, come, Nico! To that sweaty barbarian? Musk is for making fine perfume. You might as well give Kaidu a powder puff, for all the use he would have of it."

They kept on like that, but I stopped listening, for I had my own idea, and I went to explain to Nostril the part he would play in it.

The next day, a day of only drizzling rain, Nostril loaded two of the three packhorses with our cargo of valuables —we of course always kept them safe inside our chambers whenever we lodged in a karwansarai—and also roped my sheet of metal onto one of the horses, and led them for us to the Mongol bok. There, when we entered the Ilkhan's yurtu, he stayed outside to unload the goods, and Kaidu's guardsmen began carrying them in and stripped off their protective wrappers.

"Hui!" Kaidu exclaimed, as he started to inspect the various objects. "These engraved golden platters are superb! A gift from the Shah Zaman, you said, uu?"

"Yes," my father said coldly, and my uncle added, in a melancholy voice, "A boy named Aziz once strapped them on his feet to cross a quicksand," and I took out a kerchief and loudly blew my nose.

There came from outside a low, mumbling, bumbling mutter of sound. The Ilkhan looked up, surprised, saying, "Was that thunder, uu? I thought there was only a sprinkle of rain . . ."

"I beg to inform the Great Lord Kaidu," said one of his guardsmen, bowing low, "that the day is gray and wet, but there are no thunderclouds to be seen."

"Curious," Kaidu muttered, and put down the golden dishes. He rummaged among the many other things accumulating in the tent and finding a particularly elegant ruby necklace, again exclaimed, "Hui!" He held it up to admire it. "The Ilkhatun will thank you personally for this."

"Thank the Sultan Kutb-ud-Din," said my father.

I blew my nose into my kerchief. The rippling rumble of thunder came again from outside, and somewhat louder now. The Ilkhan started so that he dropped the string of rubies, and his mouth closed and opened soundlessly—but framing a word I could read from his lips—and then said aloud, "There it is again! But thunder without thunderclouds . . . uu . . . ?"

When a third item caught his greedy eye, a bolt of fine Kashmir cloth, I barely gave him time to cry "Hui!" before I blew my nose, and the thunder gave a menacing grumble, and he jerked his hand away as if the cloth had burned him, and again he mouthed the word, and my father and uncle gave me an odd look.

"Pardon, Lord Kaidu," I said. "I think this thunder weather has given me a head cold."

"You are pardoned," he said offhandedly. "Aha! And this, is this one of those famous Persian qali carpets, uu?"

Nose blow. Veritable clamor of thunder. His hand again

jerked away and his lips convulsively made the word, and he glanced fearfully skyward. Then he looked around at us, his slit eyes almost opened to roundness, and he said:

"I was but toying with you!"

"My lord?" inquired Uncle Mafìo, whose own lips were twitching now.

"Toying! Jesting! Teasing you!" Kaidu said, almost pleadingly. "A tiger sometimes toys with his quarry, when he is not hungry. And I am not hungry! Not for tawdry acquisitions. I am Kaidu, and I own countless mou of land and innumerable li of the Silk Road and more cities than I have hairs and more subject people than a gobi has pebbles. Did you really think I lack for rubies and gold dishes and Persian qali, uu?" He feigned a hearty laugh, "Ah, ha, ha, ha!" even bending double to pound his meaty fists on his massive knees. "But I had you worried, did I not, uu? You took my toying in earnest."

"Yes, you truly fooled us, Lord Kaidu," said my uncle, managing to subdue his own incipient merriment.

"And now the thunder has ceased," said the Ilkhan, listening. "Guards! Wrap up all these things again and reload them on the horses of these elder brothers."

"Why, thank you, Lord Kaidu," said my father, but his twinkling eyes were on me.

"And here, here is my cousin's letter of ukaz," said the Ilkhan, pressing it into my uncle's hand. "I return it to you, priest. Take yourself and your religion and these paltry baubles to Kubilai. Perhaps he is a collector of such trinkets, but Kaidu is not. Kaidu does not take, he gives! Two of the best warriors of my personal pavilion guard will attend you to your karwansarai, and they will ride with you whenever you are ready to continue your journey eastward . . . ."

I slipped out of the yurtu as the guardsmen began to carry out the rejected goods, and slipped around to the back side of it, where Nostril stood holding the metal sheet by one edge and waiting to flap it again whenever he heard me blow my nose. I gave him the signal employed throughout the East to mean "purpose accomplished"—showing him my fist with upraised thumb—took the piece of copper from him and trotted across the bok to return it to the armorer, and got back to the Ilkhan's yurtu by the time the horses were reloaded.

Kaidu stood in the entrance of his pavilion, waving and shouting, "A good horse and a wide plain to you!" until we were out of earshot.

Then my uncle said, in Venetian, not to be overheard by the two Mongol escorts leading our horses and theirs, "Verily, we have all done well in concert. Nico, you only invented a good story. Marco invented a thunder god!" and he flung his arms about my shoulders and Nostril's, and gave us both a hearty squeeze.

4

WE had now come so far around the world, and into lands so very little known, that our Kitab was no longer of the slightest use to us. Clearly, the mapmaker al-Idrisi had never ventured into these regions, and apparently never had met anyone who had, from whom he could ask even hearsay information. His maps rounded off the eastern edge of Asia much too shortly and abruptly at the great ocean called the Sea of Kithai. Thus they gave the false impression that Kashgar was at no enormous distance from our destination, Kubilai's capital city of Khanbalik, which itself lies well inland of that ocean. But, as my father and uncle warned me, and as I wearily verified for myself, Kashgar and Khanbalik in fact are a whole half a continent apart—half of a continent immeasurably bigger than al-Idrisi had imagined it to be. We journeyers had almost exactly as far yet to go *as we had already come* from Suvediye away back on the Levant shore of the Mediterranean.

Distance is distance, no matter whether it is calculated in the number of human footsteps or the number of days on horseback required to get over it. Nevertheless, here in Kithai, any distance always *sounded* longer, because here it was counted not in farsakhs but in li. The farsakh, comprising about two and a half of our Western miles, was invented by Persians and Arabs who, having always been far travelers, are accustomed to think in expansive terms of measurement. But the li, which is only about one-third of a mile, was invented by the Han, and they are for the most part homebodies. The common Han peasant in his lifetime

probably never ventures more than a few li away from the
farm village where he was born. So I suppose, to his mind,
a third of a mile is a far distance. Anyway, when we Polos
left Kashgar, I was still accustomed to calculating in
farsakhs, so it did not much dismay me to say to myself
that we had only some eight or nine hundred of them to go
to Khanbalik. But when I gradually got used to calculating in li, the number of them was appalling: some six
thousand seven hundred from Kashgar to Khanbalik. If I
had not previously appreciated the vastness of the Mongol
Empire, I surely did now, as I contemplated the vastness of
just its central nation of Kithai.

There were two ceremonies attendant on our departure
from Kashgar. Our Mongol escorts insisted that our
horses—now numbering six mounts and three pack
animals—must be treated to a certain ritual for protection
against the "azghun" of the trail. Azghun means "desert
voices," and I gathered that those were some sort of goblins which infest the wilderness. So the warriors brought
from their bok a man called a shamàn—what they would
describe as a priest and we would describe as a sorcerer.
The wild-eyed and paint-daubed shamàn, who looked
rather like a goblin himself, mumbled some incantations
and poured some drops of blood on the heads of our horses
and pronounced them protected. He offered to do the same
for us unbelievers, but we politely declined on the ground
that we had our own accompanying priest.

The other ceremony was the settling of our bill with the
landlord of the karwansarai, and that involved more time
and fuss than the sorcery had. My father and uncle did not
simply accept and pay the innkeeper's account, but hag-
gled with him over every single item. And the bill did include every single item of our stay—the space we had
occupied in the inn and our beasts had occupied in the stable, the quantity of food eaten by ourselves and grain
eaten by our horses, the amounts of water we and they had
swallowed, and the cha leaves steeped in ours, the kara
fuel that had been burned for our comfort, the amount of
lamplight we had enjoyed and the measures of oil required
for that—everything but the air we had breathed. As the
discussion heated up, it was joined by the inn's cook, or
Governor of the Kettle, as he styled himself, and the man
who had served our meals, or the Steward of the Table, and

they two began vociferously adding up the number of paces they had walked and the weights they had carried and the amounts of efficiency and sweat and genius they had expended in our behalf. . . .

But I soon realized that this was not a contest of larceny on the landlord's part versus outrage on ours. It was merely an expected formality—another custom derived from the complicated comportment of the Han people—a ceremony that is so enjoyed by both creditor and debtor that they can string it out to hours of eloquent argument, mutual abuse and reconciliation, claim and denial, refusal and compromise, until eventually they agree to agree, and the account is paid, and they emerge better friends than they were before. When we finally rode away from the inn, the landlord, the Kettle Governor, the Table Steward and all the other servants stood at the door, waving and calling after us the Han farewell: "Man zou," which means, "Leave us only if you must."

The Silk Road forks into two as it goes eastward from Kashgar. This is because there is a desert directly to the east of the city, a dry, peeling, curling desert, like a plain of shattered yellow pottery, a desert as big as a nation, and just the name of it gives good reason to avoid it, for its name is Takla Makan, meaning "once in, never out." So a traveler on the Silk Road can choose the branch which loops northeasterly around that desert or the one looping southeast of it, which is the one we took. The road led us from one to the next of a chain of habitable oases and small farm villages, about a day's journey apart. Always off to our left were the lion-tawny sands of the Takla Makan and, to our right, the snow-topped Kun-lun mountain range, beyond which, to the south, lies the high land of To-Bhot.

Although we were skirting clear of the desert, along its pleasantly verdant and well-watered rimlands, this was high summertime, so we had to endure a lot of desert weather that edged over from it. The only really tolerable days were those on which a wind blew down from the snowy mountains. Most frequently the days were windless, but not still, for on those days the nearness of the smoldering desert made the air about us seem to tremble. The sun might have been a blunt instrument, a brass bludgeon, beating on the air so that it rang shrill with heat. And when occasionally there came a wind from the desert, it brought the desert with it. The Takla Makan then stood on end—making moving towers of pale-yellow dust, and those towers gradually turned brown, getting darker and heavier until they toppled over onto us, turning high noon to an oppressive dusk, seething viciously and stinging the skin like a beating with twig brooms.

That dun-colored dust of the lion-colored Takla Makan is known everywhere in Kithai, even by untraveled people who have no least suspicion of the desert's existence. The dust rustles through the streets of Khanbalik, thousands of li away, and powders the flowers in the gardens of Xan-du, farther yet, and scums the lake waters of Hang-zho, farther yet, and is cursed by the tidy housekeepers of every other Kithai city I ever was in. And once, when I sailed in a ship far upon the Sea of Kithai, not just out of touch but out of sight of the shore, I found that same dust sifting down upon the deck. A visitor to Kithai might later lose his memory of everything else he saw and experienced there, but he will forever feel the pale dun dust settling on him, never letting him forget that once he walked that lion-colored land.

The buran, as the Mongols call a dust storm of the Takla Makan, has a curious effect which I never encountered in any such storm in any other desert. While a buran was buffeting us, and for a long while after it had blown on past, it somehow made the hair of our heads stand fantastically on end, and the hairs of our beards bristle like quills, and our clothes crackle as if they had turned to stiff paper, and if we chanced to touch another person we saw a snapping spark and felt a small jolt like that from cat fur briskly rubbed.

Also, the buran's passing, like the passing of a celestial broom, would leave the night air immaculately clean and clear. The stars came out in multitudes untellable, infinitely more of them than I ever saw elsewhere, every tiniest one as bright as a gem and the familiar bigger stars so big that they looked globular, like little moons. Meanwhile, the actual moon up there, even if it was in the phase we would ordinarily call "new"—only a fragile fingernail crescent of it lighted—was nevertheless visible in its whole roundness, a bronze full moon cradled in the new moon's silver arms.

And on such a night, if we looked out over the Takla Makan from our camping or lodging place, we could see even stranger lights, blue ones, bobbing and dipping and twinkling over the surface of the desert, sometimes one or two, sometimes whole bevies of them. They might have been lamps or candles carried about by persons in a distant karwan camp out there, but we knew they were not. They were too blue to be flames of fire, and they winked on and off too abruptly to have been kindled by any human agency, and their presence, like that of the day's buran, made our hair and beards stir uneasily. Besides all that, it was well-known that no human beings ever traveled or camped in the Takla Makan. Not living human beings. Not willingly.

The first time we saw the lights, I inquired of our escorts what they might be. The Mongol named Ussu said, in a hushed voice, "The beads of Heaven, Ferenghi."

"But what makes them?"

The one named Donduk said curtly, "Be silent and listen, Ferenghi."

I did, and, even as far from the desert as we were standing, I heard faint sighs and sobs and soughings, as if small night winds were fitfully blowing. But there was no wind.

"The azghun, Ferenghi," Ussu explained. "The beads and the voices always come together."

"Many an inexperienced traveler," added Donduk, in a supercilious way, "has seen the lights and heard the cries, and thought them to be a fellow traveler in trouble, and gone seeking to help, and been lured by them away, not ever to be seen again. They are the azghun, the desert voices, and the mysterious beads of Heaven. Hence the desert's name—once in, never out."

I wish I could claim that I divined the cause of those manifestations, or at least a better explanation of them than wicked goblins, but I did not. I knew that the azghun and the lights occurred only after the passing of a buran, and a buran was only a mighty mass of dry sand blowing about. I wondered, did that friction have something in common with the rubbing of a cat's fur? But out there in the desert, the sand grains had nothing to rub against except each other. . . .

So, baffled by that mystery, I applied my mind to a smaller but more accessible one. Why did Ussu and

Donduk, though they knew all our names and had no trouble saying them, always address us Polos indiscriminately
as Ferenghi? Ussu spoke the word amiably enough; he
seemed to enjoy traveling with us, as a change from boring
garrison duty back at Kaidu's bok. But Donduk spoke the
word distastefully, seeming to regard this journey as a
nursemaid attention to us unworthy persons. I rather
liked Ussu, and did not like Donduk, but they always were
together, so I asked them both: why Ferenghi?

"Because you *are* Ferenghi," said Ussu, looking puzzled,
as if I had asked a witless question.

"But you also call my father Ferenghi. And my uncle."

"He and he is Ferenghi also," said Ussu.

"But you call Nostril Nostril. Is that because he is a
slave?"

"No," said Donduk scornfully. "Because he is not Ferenghi."

"Elder Brothers," I persisted. "I am trying to find out
what Ferenghi means."

"Ferenghi means only Ferenghi," snapped Donduk, and
threw up his hands in disgust, and so did I.

But that mystery I finally *did* figure out: Ferenghi was
only their pronunciation of Frank. Their people must first
have heard Westerners call themselves Franks eight centuries ago, in the time of the Frankish Empire, when some of
the Mongols' own ancestors, then called Bulgars and
Hiung-nu, or Huns, invaded the West and gave their
names to Bulgaria and Hungary. Ever since then, apparently, the Mongols have called any white Westerner a Ferenghi, no matter his real nationality. Well, it was no
more inaccurate than the calling of all Mongols Mongols,
though they were really of many different origins.

Usuu and Donduk told me, for instance, how their Mongol cousins the Kirghiz had come into existence. The name
derived from the Mongol words kirk kiz, they said, meaning "forty virgins," because sometime in the remote past
there had existed in some remote place that many virgin
females, unlikely though it might seem to us moderns, and
all forty of them had got impregnated by the foam blown
from an enchanted lake, and from the resultant miraculous mass birth had descended all the people now called
Kirghiz. That was interesting, but I found more interesting another thing Ussu and Donduk told me about the Kir-

ghiz. They lived in the perpetually frozen Sibir, far north of Kithai, and perforce had invented two ingenious methods of getting about those harsh lands. They would strap to the bottom of their boots bits of highly polished bone, on which they could glide far and fast upon the ice of frozen waters. Or they would similarly strap on long boards like barrel staves, to skim far and fast over the snowy wastes.

The very next farm village on our way was populated by yet another breed of Mongols. Some of the communities on that stretch of the Silk Road were peopled by Uighurs, those nationalities "allied" to the Mongols, and others were peopled by Han folk, and Ussu and Donduk had not made any comment about them. But when we came to this particular village, they told us the people were Kalmuk Mongols, and they spat the name, thus: "Kalmuk! Vakh!"—*vakh* being a Mongol noise to register sheer disgust, and the Kalmuk were disgusting, right enough. They were the filthiest human creatures I ever saw outside of India. To depict just one aspect of their filthiness, let me say this: not only did they never wash their bodies, they never even took off their clothes, day or night. When a Kalmuk's outer garment got too worn to be serviceable, he or she did not discard it, but simply donned a new one over it, and continued wearing layers upon layers of ragged clothes until the undermost gradually rotted and shredded away from underneath, like a sort of ghastly scurf of the crotch. I will not attempt to say how they smelled.

But the name Kalmuk, I learned, is not a national or tribal designation. It is only the Mongol word meaning one who stays, or one who settles down in any place. All normal Mongols being nomads, they have a deep disdain for any of their race who ceases roaming and takes up a fixed abode. In the majority opinion, any Mongol who becomes a Kalmuk is doomed to degeneracy and depravity, and if the Kalmuk people I saw and smelled were typical, then the majority have good reason to despise them. And now I recalled having heard the Ilkhan Kaidu speak slightingly of the Khakhan Kubilai as "no better than a Kalmuk." Vakh, I thought, if I find that he is, I shall turn around and go straight back to Venice.

However, despite my awareness that the word Mongol was a too general term for a multiplicity of peoples, I found it convenient to go on using the name. I soon realized also

that the other, the original, inhabitants of Kithai were not
all Han, either. There were nationalities called Yi and Hui
and Naxi and Hezhe and Miao and God knows how many
others of skin colors ranging from ivory to bronze. But, as
with the Mongols, I continued to think of all those other
nationalities as Han. For one reason, their languages all
sounded very much alike to me. For another, every one of
those races regarded every other as inferior, and so called
each other by their various words meaning Dog People.
For still another reason, they all called any foreigner, including me, a name even less deserved than Frank. In Han
and in every other of their singsong languages and dialects, any outlander is a Barbarian.

As we rode farther and farther along the Silk Road, it became increasingly crowded with traffic—groups and trains
of traveling traders like ourselves, individual farmers and
herders and artisans taking their wares to market towns,
Mongol families and clans and whole boks on the move. I
remembered how Isidoro Priuli, our clerk of the Compagnia Polo, had remarked, just before we left Venice, that the
Silk Road had been a busy thoroughfare from the most ancient times, and now I saw reason to believe him. Over the
years and centuries and maybe millennia, the traffic on
that road had worn it down far below the level of the surrounding terrain. In places it was a broad trench so deep
that a farmer in his nearby bean patch might see no more
of the passing processions than the flick of a cart driver's
upraised whip. And down inside that trench, the cartwheels' ruts had worn so deep that every cart now had to
go where the ruts went. A carter never had to worry about
his vehicle's overturning, but neither could he pull it to
one side when he needed to relieve himself. To change direction on the road—say, to turn off to some side-village
destination—a driver had to keep going until he came to a
junction where there were diverging ruts in which to set
his wheels.

The carts used in that region of Kithai were of a peculiar
type. They had immensely big wheels with knobbed rims,
standing so high that they often reached above the wooden
or canvas cart roof. Perhaps the wheels had had to be built
bigger and bigger over the years just so their axles would
clear the hump of ground between the road ruts. Each such
wagon also had an awning projecting from its top front, to

cover the driver from inclement weather, and that awning was considerately extended on poles far enough so that it also sheltered the team of horses, oxen or asses pulling the wagon.

I had heard much about the cleverness and inventiveness and ingenuity of the inhabitants of Kithai, but I now had cause to wonder if those qualities might be overrated. Very well, every cart had an awning to shelter its draft animals as well as its driver, and maybe that was a clever invention. But every wagon also had to carry several sets of spare axles for its wheels. That was because every separate province of Kithai has its own idea of how far apart a cart's wheels should be, and of course its local wagons have long ago put the roads' ruts that far apart. So the distance between the ruts is wide, for example, on the stretch of Silk Road that goes through Sin-kiang, but narrow on the road through the province of Tsing-hai, wide again but not quite so wide in Ho-nan, and so on. A carter traversing any considerable length of the Silk Road must stop every so often, laboriously take the wheels and axles off his wagon, put on axles of a different breadth and replace the wheels.

Every draft animal wore a bag slung under its tail by a webbing around its hindquarters, to collect its droppings while on the move. That was not to keep the road clean or to spare annoyance to people coming along behind. We were by now out of the region where the earth was full of burnable kara rock, free for the taking, so every carter carefully hoarded his animals' dung to fuel the camp fire on which he would prepare his mutton and miàn and cha.

We saw many herds of sheep being driven to market or to pasture, and the sheep too wore peculiar backside appendages. The sheep were of the fat-tailed breed, and that breed is to be seen all over the East, but I had never seen any so fat-tailed as these. A sheep's clublike tail might weigh ten or twelve pounds, nearly a tenth of its whole body weight. It was a genuine burden to the creature, and also that tail is considered the best part of the animal for eating. So each sheep had a light rope harness to drag a little plank behind it, and on that trailing shelf its tail rode safe from being bruised or unnecessarily dirtied. We saw also many herds of swine being driven, and it seemed to me that they could have used some expenditure of inventiveness, too. The pigs of Kithai are also a distinctive breed, being long in the body and ludicrously swaybacked, so that their bellies actually drag the ground, and I wondered why their herders had not considerately provided something like belly wheels.

Our escorts Ussu and Donduk were contemptuous of the wheeled vehicles and slow-plodding herds on the road. They were Mongols, and they thought all rights of way should be reserved to horseback riders. They grumbled that the Khakhan Kubilai had not yet kept a promise he had made some time ago: to level every least obstruction on every plain in Kithai, so that a horseman could canter across the entire country, even in darkest night, and never fear his horse's stumbling. They were naturally impatient of our having to lead packhorses and proceed at a sedate pace instead of galloping headlong. So they now and then found a way to enliven what to them was a boring journey.

At one of our night stops, when we camped by the road instead of pushing on to a karwansarai, Ussu and Donduk brought from a nearby camp of drovers one of their fat-tailed sheep and some doughy ewe cheese. (I should probably say they *procured* those things, for I doubt that they paid anything to the Han shepherds.) Donduk unslung his battle-ax, sliced away the sheep's tail-drag harness and in almost the same single motion cut off the animal's head. He and Ussu sprang onto their horses, and one of them reached down to catch up by the club tail the sheep's still-twitching and blood-spouting carcass, and the two riders began a gleefully galloping game of bous-kashia. They thundered back and forth between our camp and that of the sheepherders, wrenching the trophy animal from one another, slinging it about, dropping it frequently, trampling over it. Which of them won the game, or how they could tell, I do not know, but they tired at last and flung down at our feet the limp and gory thing, all covered with dust and dead leaves.

"Tonight's meal," said Ussu. "Good and tender now, uu?"

Somewhat to my surprise, he and Donduk volunteered to do the skinning and butchering and cooking themselves. It seems that Mongol men do not mind doing woman's work when there are no women about to do it. The meal they made was one to remember, but not with bon-gusto. They began by retrieving the sheep's lopped-off

head, and it was spitted with the rest of the animal over
our fire. A whole sheep should have sufficed to gorge several families of hearty eaters, but Ussu and Donduk and
Nostril, with not much help from us other three, consumed
that entire animal from nose to fat tail. The eating of the
head was the least appetizing to watch and listen to. One
of the gourmands would slice off a cheek from it, another
an ear, the other a lip, and they would dip those awful fragments in a bowl of peppered juice from the meat, and chew
and slurp and slobber and swallow and belch and fart.
Since Mongols consider it bad manners for men to talk
while they dine, that succession of good-mannered noises
was not varied until they got down to the body bones and
added the sound of sucking out the marrow.

We Polos ate only the meat sliced from the sheep's
lions—well-beaten by the bous-kashia and admittedly
most tender. Or we would have preferred to eat only that,
but Ussu and Donduk kept carving and pressing on us the
real delicacies: pieces of the tail, meaning blobs of yellow-
white fat. They quivered and trembled repulsively in our
fingers, but we could not in politeness refuse, so we somehow managed to gag them down, and I can still feel the
way those ghastly gobbets went slimily palpitating down
my gullet. After the first dreadful mouthful, I tried to
clean my palate with a hearty swig of cha—and nearly
strangled. Too late I discovered that Ussu, after brewing
the cha leaves with boiling water, had not stopped there as
civilized cooks do, but had melted into the drink chunks of
mutton fat and ewe cheese. That Mongol-style cha would
make a nourishing full meal all by itself, I suppose, but I
must say that it was downright revolting.

We ate other meals on the Silk Road that are more pleasant to recall. This far into the interior of Kithai, the Han
and Uighur karwansarai landlords did not limit their fare
to only the things a Muslim can eat, so we found a good diversity of meats—including that of the illik, which is a tiny
roe deer that barks like a dog, and of a lovelily golden-
feathered pheasant, and steaks cut from yaks, and even
the meat of black bears and brown bears, which abound
here. When we camped in the open, Uncle Mafìo and the
two Mongols vied at providing game for the pot: ducks and
geese and rabbits and once a desert qazèl, but more usually they sought ground squirrels to shoot, because those

little creatures thoughtfully provide the fuel for their own
cooking. A hunter knows that, when he has no kara or
wood or dried dung to make a fire with, he has only to look
for the ground squirrels and their holes; even in a desert
barren, they somehow contrive to put a weather-protective
dome over their holes, of laced twigs and grass, well dried
for the burning.

There were many other wild creatures in that region,
not for eating but interesting to observe. There were black
vultures with wings so broad that a man would have to
take three paces to walk from tip to tip; and a snake so
much resmbling yellow metal that I would have sworn it
was made of molten gold, but, having been informed that it
was deadly venomous, I never touched one to find out.
There was a little animal called a yerbò, like a mouse but
with extravagantly long hind legs and tail, upon which
three appendages it hopped about upright; and a magnificently beautiful wild cat called a palang, which I once saw
making a meal of a wild ass it had downed, and which was
like the heraldic pard, only not yellow of coat, but silvery
gray with black rosettes spotted all over it.

The Mongols taught me to pick various wild plants as
vegetable dishes for our meals—wild onions, for example,
which go so well with any vension meat. There was a
growth that they called the hair plant, and it did look exactly like a shock of black human hair. Neither its name
nor its appearance was very appetizing, but when boiled
and seasoned with a bit of vinegar, it made a delicate
pickle condiment. Another oddity was what they called the
vegetable lamb; they averred that it was indeed a mongrel
creature bred from a mating of animal and plant, and said
they preferred eating it to eating real lamb. It was tasty
enough, but it was really only the woolly rootstalk of a certain fern.

The one ravishingly delicious novelty I found on that
stage of the journey was the wonderful melon called the
hami. Even the method of its growing was a novelty. When
the vines started forming their fruit buds, the melon farmers paved over the whole field with slabs of slate for the
vines to lie on. Instead of the melons' getting sunshine
only on their upper sides, those slates reflected the sun's
heat so that the hami ripened evenly all the way around.
The hami had flesh of a pale greenish-white, so crisp that

it crackled when bitten, dripping with juice, of a cool and refreshing flavor, not cloying but *just* the right sweetness. The hami had a taste and a fragrance different from all other fruits, and was almost as good when dried into flakes for travel rations, and has never been surpassed in my experience by any other garden sweet.

When we had been traveling for two or three weeks, the Silk Road abruptly turned northward for a little way, the only time it touched the Takla Makan, making a very short traverse across that desert's easternmost edge, then turning directly east again toward a town named Dunhuang. That northward jink of the road took us through a pass that twined among some low mountains—really they were extremely high sand dunes—called the Flame Hills.

There is a legend to account for every place-name in Kithai, and according to legend these hills once were lushly forested and green, until they were set afire by some malicious kwei, or demons. A monkey god came along and kindly blew out the flames, but there was nothing left except these mountainous heaps of sand, still glowing like embers. That is the legend. I am more inclined to think that the Flame Hills are so called because their sands are a sort of burnt ocher color, and are wind-swept into flame-shaped furrows and wrinkles, and they perpetually shimmer behind a curtain of hot air, and—especially at sunset—they do glow a truly fiery red-orange color. But the most curious thing about them was a nest of four eggs which Ussu and Donduk uncovered from the sand at the base of one of the dunes. I would have thought the objects were only large stones, perfectly oval and smooth and about the size of hami melons, but Donduk insisted:

"These are the abandoned eggs of a giant rukh bird. Such nests can be found all along the Flame Hills here."

When I held one, I realized that it was indeed too light for a stone of that size. And when I examined it, I saw that it did have a porous surface, exactly as do the eggs of hens or ducks or any other bird. These were eggs, all right, and far bigger even than those of the camel-bird, which I had seen in Persian markets. I wondered what kind of a fortagiona these would make if I broke them and scrambled them and fried them for our evening meal.

"These Flame Hills," said Ussu, "must have been the

rukh's favored nesting place in times past, Ferenghi, do you not think so, uu?"

"Times *very* long past," I suggested, for I had just tried to crack one of the eggs. Although it was not of stonelike weight, it had long ago aged and petrified to stonelike solidity. So the things were both uneatable and unhatchable, and they were too unwieldy for me to carry one off for a memento. They were most certainly eggs, and of a size that could have been laid only by a monster bird, but whether in truth that bird had been a rukh, I cannot say.

5

DUN-HUANG was a thriving trade town, about as big and as populous as Kashgar, sitting in a sandy basin ringed by camel-colored rock cliffs. But where Kashgar's inns had catered to Muslim travelers, those of Dun-huang made special provision for the tastes and customs of Buddhists. This was because the town had been founded, some nine hundred years ago, when a traveling trader of the Buddhist faith was beset, somewhere on the Silk Road hereabout, by bandits or the azghun voices or a kwei demon or something, and was somehow miraculously saved from those malign clutches. So he paused here to give thanks to the Buddha, and he did that by making a statue of that deity and placing it in a niche in one of the cliffs. In the nine centuries since, every other Buddhist traveler on the Silk Road has added an adornment to another of those caves. And now the name of Dun-huang, though it really means only Yellow Cliffs, is sometimes translated as the Caves of the Thousand Buddhas.

The designation is too modest. I would call these the Caves of the Million Buddhas, at the very least. For there are now some hundreds of caves pocking the cliffs, some natural, some hewn out by hand, and in them are perhaps two thousand statues of the Buddha, large and small, but on the cave walls are painted frescoes displaying at least a thousand *times* that many images of the Buddha, not to mention lesser divinities and worthies of the Buddha's retinue. I could discern that most of the images were male, and some just as clearly female, but a goodly number were indistinct as to sex. However, all had one feature in common: they all had tremendously elongated ears with lobes dangling to their shoulders.

"It is a common belief," said the old Han caretaker, "that a person born with large ears and well-defined earlobes is destined for good fortune. Since the most fortunate of all humans were the Buddha and his disciples, we assume that they had such ears, and we depict them so."

That aged ubashi, or monk, was pleased to conduct me on a tour of the caves, and he spoke Farsi for the occasion. I followed him from niche to cavern to grotto, and in all of them were statues of the Buddha, standing or lying peacefully asleep or, most often, sitting cross-legged on a giant lotus blossom. The monk told me that Buddha is an ancient Indian word meaning the Enlightened One, and that the Buddha had been a Prince of India before his apotheosis. So I might have expected the statues to be all of a black and runty man, but they were not. Buddhism long ago spread from India to other nations, and evidently every devout traveler who paid to put up a statue or a painting had envisioned the Buddha as looking like *him*. Some of the older images were indeed dark and scrawny like Hindus, but others could have been Alexandrine Apollos or hawklike Persians or leathery Mongols, and the most recently done all had unlined faces with waxy complexions and placid expressions and slanted slit eyes; that is to say, they were pure Han.

It was also evident that, in the past, Muslim marauders had often swept through Dun-huang, for many of the statues were in ruins, hacked apart, revealing their simple construction of gesso molded onto cane and reed armatures, or at the least were cruelly disfigured. As I have told, the Muslims detest any portrayal of a living being. So here, when they had not had time to destroy a statue utterly, they had chopped the head off it (the head being the abode of life) or, in even more haste, they had been satisfied to gouge out the eyes from it (the eyes being the expression of life). The Muslims had taken the trouble to scratch out even the tiny eyes of many thousands of miniature painted images on the walls—even those of delicate and pretty female figures.

"And the females," said the old monk mournfully, "are not even divinities at all." He pointed to one lively little figure. "She is a Devatas, one of the celestial dancing girls who entertain the blessed souls in the Sukhavati, the Pure Land between lives. And this one"—he pointed to a girl who was painted in the act of flying, in a swallowlike swirl of skirts and veils—"she is an Apsaras, one of the celestial temptresses."

"There are temptresses in the Buddhist Heaven?" I asked, intrigued.

He sniffed and said, "Only to prevent an overcrowding of the Pure Land."

"Indeed? How?"

"The Apsarases have the duty of seducing holy men here on earth, so their souls get damned to the Awful Land of Naraka between lives, instead of the blissful Sukhavati."

"Ah," said I, to show that I comprehended. "An Apsaras is a sùccubo."

Buddhism has certain other parallels to our True Faith. Its devotees are adjured not to kill, not to tell untruths, not to take what is not given, not to indulge in sexual misbehavior. But in other respects, it is very different from Christianity. Buddhists are also adjured not to drink intoxicants, not to eat after the noon hour, not to attend entertainments, not to wear bodily adornments, not to sleep or even rest on a comfortable mattress. The religion does have the equivalents of our monks and nuns and priests, called ubashi and ubashanza and lamas, and Buddha enjoined them to live lives of poverty, as ours also are admonished, but few of them comply.

For example, Buddha told his followers to wear nothing but "yellowed garments"—by which he meant mere rags discolored by mold and decay. But the Buddhist monks and nuns obey that instruction only to the letter, not the spirit, for they are now arrayed in robes of the costliest fabrics, gaudily dyed in hues from brilliant yellow to fiery orange. They also have grand temples, called potkadas, and monasteries, called lamasarais, richly endowed and furnished. Also, I suspect that every Buddhist owns many more personal possessions than the few that Buddha specified: a sleeping mat, three rags for garments, a knife, a needle, a begging bowl with which to solicit one meager meal a day, and a water strainer with which to dip out from one's drinking water any incautious insects or fry or tadpoles, lest they get swallowed.

The water strainer illustrates Buddhism's foremost rule: that no creature alive, however humble or minute, shall ever be killed, deliberately or even accidentally. However, this has nothing in common with a Christian's wish to be good so as to go to Heaven after death. A Buddhist believes that a good man dies only to be reborn as a better man, further on his way to Enlightenment. And he believes that a bad man dies only to be reborn as a lesser grade of creature: an animal, bird, fish or insect. That is why a Buddhist must not kill anything. Since every least speck of life in Creation is presumably a soul trying to clamber up the ladder of enlightenment, a Buddhist dares not squash so much as a louse, for it could be his late grandfather, demoted after death, or his future grandson on the way to being born.

A Christian might admire a Buddhist's reverence for life, no matter the ludicrous illogic behind it, except for two inevitable results of it. One is that every Buddhist man, woman and child is a seething nest of lice and fleas, and I found those vermin all too ready to risk their Enlightenment by emigrating onto Christian unbelievers like me. Also, a Buddhist of course cannot eat animal flesh. The devout confine themselves to boiled rice and water, and the most liberal will not eat anything more daring than milk and fruit and vegetables. So that is what we journeyers got in the Dun-huang inn: at mealtime, boiled fronds and tendrils and weak cha and bland custards, and at bedtime, fleas and ticks and bedbugs and lice.

"There was formerly here in Dun-huang a very holy lama," said my Han monk, in a voice of reverence, "so holy that he ate only *raw* rice, uncooked. And to further his humility even more, he wore an iron chain clenched about his shrunken belly. The chafing of the rusty chain made a sore, and it became quite putrid, generating a quantity of maggots. And if one of those munching maggots chanced to fall to the ground, the lama would lovingly pick it up, saying, 'Why do you flee, beloved? Did you not find enough to eat?' and he would tenderly replace it in the juiciest part of the sore."

That instructive tale may not have furthered my own humility, but it did diminish my appetite so that, when I got back to the inn, I was easily able to forgo that night's meal of pallid pap. Meanwhile, the monk went on:

"That lama eventually became a walking sore, and was consumed by it, and died of it. We all admire and envy him, for he surely moved far along the way to Enlightenment."

"I sincerely hope so," I said. "But what happens at the end of that way? Does the Enlightened One finally get to Heaven then?"

"Nothing so crass," said the ubashi. "One hopes, by means of sequacious rebirths and lifetimes of striving upward, eventually to be freed of having to live at all. To be liberated from the bondage of human needs and desires and passions and griefs and miseries. One hopes to achieve Nirvana, which means 'the blowing-out.'"

He was not jesting. A Buddhist has not the aim, as we do, of meriting for his soul an eternity of glad existence in the mansions of Heaven. A Buddhist yearns only for absolute extinction, or, as the monk put it, "a merging with the Infinite." He did admit that his religion makes provision for several heavenly Pure Lands and hellish Awful Lands, but they are—something like our Purgatory or Limbo—only way stations between a soul's successive rebirths on the way to Nirvana. And at that ultimate destination a soul gets snuffed out, as a candle flame is snuffed, nevermore to enjoy or endure not earth nor Heaven nor Hell nor anything.

I had cause to reflect on those beliefs, as our company continued eastward from Dun-huang, on a day that was marvelously full of things to reflect on.

We departed the inn at sunrise, when all the just-waking birds were uttering their morning chirps and cheeps and twitters, so many so loud that they sounded like grease sizzling in a great pan. Then the later-rousing doves awoke, to murmur their discreet plaints and regrets, but in such numbers that their low warbling was near a roar. A considerable karwan train was also leaving the inn yard that morning, and in these regions the camels wore their bells not on a neckband, but on their front knees. So they strode out jingling and clanging and bonging as if they musically rejoiced in being on the move. I rode my horse alongside one of that train's wagons for a space, and one of its massive wheels had caught up somewhere a spray of jasmine in its spokes, and every time that high wheel revolved it brought the blossoms past my face and wafted their sweet scent to my nose.

The route out of the Dun-huang basin took us through a cleft in the cave-pocked cliffs, and that opened into a valley verdant with trees and fields and wildflowers, the last such oasis we would see for a while. As we rode through that valley I saw something so beautiful that I still can see it in my memory. Some way ahead of us, a plume of golden-yellow smoke rose up on the morning breeze, and we all re-marked on it and wondered at it. Perhaps it came from a fire in a karwan camp, but what could the campers be burning to make such a distinctively colored cloud? The smoke continued to rise and billow, and eventually we came up to it and saw that it was not smoke at all. On the left side of the valley there was a meadow totally covered with golden-yellow flowers, and all those numberless flow-ers were exultantly freeing their golden-yellow pollen to let the breeze carry it across the Silk Road and away to the other slopes of the valley. We rode through that cloud of seeming smoke, and we came out the other side of it, and we and our horses shimmered in the sunlight as if we had been freshly plated with pure gold.

Another thing. From the valley, we emerged into a land of undulant sand dunes, but the sand was no longer the color of camels or lions, it was a dark silvery gray, like a powdered metal. Nostril got down from his horse to relieve himself, and climbed over a dune of the gray sand, seeking privacy, and to his surprise—and mine—the sand *barked* like a peevish dog at each of his footsteps. It made no par-ticular noise when Nostril wetted on it, but, as he turned to descend the dune, his foot slipped and he slid the whole way down from the crest, and his slide was accompanied by a lovely loud musical note, vibrato, as if a string on the world's biggest lute had been thrummed.

"Mashallah!" Nostril blurted fearfully, as he picked himself up. He ran all the way from the sand to the firmer surface of the road before pausing to dust himself off.

My father and uncle and the two escorts were all laugh-

ing at him. One of the Mongols said, "These sands are
called the lui-ing."

"The thunder voices," Uncle Mafìo translated for me.
"Nico and I have heard them when we passed this way before. They will cry also if the wind blows hard, and they cry
loudest in winter, when the sands are cold."

Now, that was a thing most marvelous. But it was only a
thing of this earth, as were the sunrise birdsongs and the
common camel bells and the perfumed jasmine and the
golden wild flowers so determined to flourish that they
flung their seed haphazard to the wind.

This world is fair, I thought, and life is good, no matter
whether one is certain of Heaven or apprehensive of Hell
at the end of it. I could only pity such pathetic persons as
Buddhists, deeming the earth and their existence on it so
ugly and miserable and repugnant that their highest
yearning was to flee into sheer oblivion. Not I, not ever I. If
I might accept any of the Buddhist beliefs, it would be that
of rebirth over and over into this world, though it mean
coming back sometimes as a lowly dove or a sprig of jasmine between my human incarnations. Yes, I thought, if I
could I would go on living forever.

6

THE land continued gray, but that color got darker as we
went eastward, darkening to veritable black—black grit
and black gravel drifting over black bedrock—for we had
come now to another desert, one too broad and extensive
for the Silk Road to skirt around. It was called by the Mongols the Gobi, and by the Han the Sha-mo, both words
meaning a desert of that peculiar composition: one from
which all the sand had long ago blown away, leaving only
the heavier particles, and they all black. It made for an unearthly landscape, appearing to be not of pebbles and
stones and rocks, but of even harder metal. In the sun,
every black hill and boulder and ridge glittered with a
sharp bright rim as if it had been honed on a whetstone.
The only growing things were the colorless plumes of

camel-weed and some tufts of colorless grass like fine metal wires.

The Gobi is also called by travelers the Great Silence, because any conversation softer than a shout goes unheard there, and so does the clatter of black stones rolling and shifting underfoot, and so do the piteous whinnies of sore-footed horses, and so do the whines and grumbles of a com-plainer like Nostril, all such noises blotted out by the everlasting wail of the wind. Over the Gobi the wind blows ceaselessly through three hundred and sixty days of the year, and, in the late summer days of our crossing, it blew as hot as a blast from the opened doors of the fearsome ovens of the vasty kitchens of the nethermost levels of Satan's fiercest Inferno.

The next town we came to, Anxi, must be the most des-olately situated community in all Kithai. It was a mere cluster of shacky shops peddling karwan necessities, and some travelers' inns and stables, all of unpainted wood and mud-brick much pitted and eroded by wind-blown grit. The town had come into being there on the edge of the dreary Gobi only because at this point the two branches of the Silk Road came together again—the southerly one by which we arrived in town, and the other route that had circled around north of the Takla Makan—and at Anxi they merged into the single road that goes on, without again dividing, over the interminable more li to the Kithai capital of Khanbalik. At this conver-gence of roads, there was of course an even more bustling traffic of individual traders and groups and families and karwan trains. But one procession of mule-drawn wagons made me ask our escorts:

"What kind of train is that? It moves so slowly and so quietly."

All the wheels of the wagons had their rims tied about with bunched hay and rags, to muffle the sound of them, and the mules had their hoofs tied in bags of wadding for the same purpose. That did not make the train entirely noiseless, for the wheels and hoofs still made a rumbling and clumping sound, and there was much creaking of the wooden wagon beds and leather harness, but its progress was quieter than that of most trains. Besides the Han men driving the wagon mules, other Han were mounted on mules as outriders and, as they accompanied the train through Anxi, they rode like an honor guard, shouldering a path through the crowded streets, but never using their voices to demand clear passage.

The street folk moved obligingly aside and silenced their own chatter and averted their faces, as if the train were that of some **grand and** haughty personage. But there was no one in the procession *except* those drivers and escorts; no one rode in any of the several score wagons. They were occupied only by heaps of what might have been rolled tents or rugs, many hundreds of them, cloth-wrapped long bundles, piled like cordwood in the wagon beds. Whatever those objects were, they looked very old, and they gave off a dry, musty smell, and their cloth wrappings were all tattered and shredded and flapping. When the wagons jounced on the rutted streets, they shed bits and flakes of cloth.

"Like shrouds decaying," I remarked.

To my astonishment, Ussu said, "That is what they are." In a hushed voice, he added, "Show respect, Ferenghi. Turn away and do not stare as they go by."

He did not speak again until the muffled train had passed. Then he told me that all Han people have a great desire to be buried in the places where they were born, and their survivors bend every effort to have that done. Since most of the Han who keep inns and shops on the far western reaches of the Silk Road had come originally from the more populous eastern end of the country, that was where they wished their remains to rest. So any Han who died in the west was only shallowly buried, and when—after many years—a sufficiency of them had died, their families in the east would organize a train and send it west. All those bodies would be dug up and collected and transported together back to their native regions. It happened perhaps only once in a generation, said Ussu, so I could count myself unique among Ferenghi, to have glimpsed one of the karwans of the corpses.

All along the Silk Road from Kashgar, we had been fording the occasional minor river—meager streams trickling down from the mountain snows in the south and quickly soaking into the desert to the north. But some weeks eastward of Anxi we found a more considerable river going easterly with us. In its beginnings, it was a merrily tumbling clear water, but every time the road

brought us again alongside it, we saw that it was wider
and deeper and more turbulent and turning dun-yellow
with its accumulation of silt; hence the name given it,
Huang, the Yellow River. Swooping throughout the whole
breadth of Kithai, the Huang is one of the two great river
systems of these lands. The other is far to the south of this,
an even mightier water—called Yang-tze, meaning simply
Tremendous River—traversing the land of Kithai.

"That Yang-tze and this Huang," my father said instructively, "they are, after the historic Nile, the second
and third longest rivers in all the traveled world."

I might facetiously have remarked that the Huang must
be the *tallest* river on earth. What I mean—and I am seldom believed when I say this—is that through much of its
length the Huang River stands *above* the land surrounding it.

"But how can that be?" people protest. "A river is not independent of the earth. If a river should rise, it would
merely overflow onto the land about."

But the Yellow River does not, except at disastrous intervals. Over the years and generations and centuries, the
Han farmers along the river have built up earthen levees
to reinforce its banks. But, because the Huang carries such
quantities of silt, and continuously deposits that on its bed,
its surface level also continuously goes up. So the Han
farmers, over generations and centuries and eons, have
had to keep building the levees higher. Thus, between
those artificial banks, the Yellow River literally does
stand higher than the land. In some places, if I had wished
to jump into the river, I would have had to climb a bank
higher than a four-storied building.

"But big as they are, those levees are only of packed
earth," said my father. "In one very rainy year while we
were last here, we saw the Huang get so full and boisterous that it broke those banks."

" A river held up in the air and then let fall," I mused.
"It must have been something to see."

Uncle Mafìo said, "Like watching Venice and the whole
mainland Vèneto submerge beneath the lagoon, if you can
imagine such a thing. A flood of unbelievable extent. Entire villages and towns dissolved. Whole nations of people
drowned."

"It happens not every year, God be thanked," said my fa-

ther. "But often enough to have given the Yellow River its
other name—the Scourge of the Sons of Han."

However, as long as the river runs tame, the Han make
good use of it. Here and there along the banks, I saw the
biggest wheels in the world: waterwheels of wood and cane
as high as twenty men standing atop one another. Around
the wheels' rims were multitudes of buckets and scoops,
which the river considerately filled and lifted and spilled
into irrigation canals.

And in one place, I saw a boat beside the bank that had
immense, revolving paddlewheels on either side. On first
seeing it, I thought it was some kind of Han invention to
replace man-worked oars for propulsion. But again I was
disillusioned of the vaunted Han inventiveness, for I realized that the craft was only moored to the bank and the
paddlewheels were merely turned by the river current.
They in turn rotated axles and spokes inside the vessel to
make millstones grind grain. So the whole thing was nothing but a water mill, novel only in that it was not station-
ary, but could be moved up and down the river, to any
place where there was a harvest of grain to be ground into
flour.

There were innumerable other kinds of vessels, for the
Yellow River was more crowded with traffic than was
the Silk Road. The Han people, having such tremendous
distances over which to freight their goods and produce,
prefer to use their waterways rather than overland
methods of transport. It is really a sensible practice,
however much their Mongol masters ridicule the Han's
disregard for horses. A horse or any other pack animal,
over any distance, will eat more grain than it can carry,
but the river boatmen consume very little man-fueling
food to accomplish each li of travel. So the Han rightfully respect and revere their rivers; they even give the
name of River of Heaven to what we Westerners call the
Milky Way.

On the Yellow River there were many shallow scows,
called san-pan, and each scow's crew was a family, to
whom the boat was simultaneously home, transport and
livelihood. The males of the family did the san-pan's rowing or towing upstream, and the steering downstream, and
the loading and unloading of the cargo. The females did
what seemed to be perpetual cooking and laundering. And

among them played a multitude of smaller boys and girls, all blithely naked except for a large gourd tied at the waist, to help them float when they fell overboard, which they did with regularity.

There were many larger craft propelled by sails. When I asked our escorts what they were called, the Mongols indifferently said what sounded like "chunk." The correct Han word, I learned, is chuan, but that means only sailing vessels in general. I never did learn the thirty-eight different names of the thirty-eight different kinds of rivergoing and seagoing "chunks."

Anyway, the smallest of them was as big as a Flemish cog, but of shallow draft, and looked to me ridiculously cumbersome, like an immense floating wooden shoe. But I gradually perceived that the chuan's shape is not patterned on a fish, as most Western vessels are, for a fishlike celerity. It is patterned on a duck, for stability on the water, and I could see that it floated serenely over the Yellow River's most tumultuous whirlpools and whitecaps. Perhaps because the chuan is slow and sturdy, it has only a single rudder for steering, not two as on our vessels, and it is set amidship at the stern and requires no more than a single steersman. A chuan's sails are also odd, not being let to belly in the wind, but latticed by slats at intervals, so they look rather like ribbed bat wings. And when it is necessary to shorten sail, they are not reefed like ours, but are folded, slat by slat, like a griglia of persiana window blinds.

Of all the craft I saw on that river, though, the most striking was a small oared skiff called a hu-pan. It was ludicrously unsymmetrical, being bent in a sideways arc. Now, a Venetian gòndola is also built with a touch of camber to allow for the fact that the gondolier paddles always on the right side, but a gòndola's keel bend is so slight as to be unnoticeable. These hu-pan were as skewed as a shimshir sword laid on its side. Again, it was a matter of practicality. A hu-pan always travels close against the riverbank, and as its oarsman variously keeps its concave or convex side to the bending shore, it more easily slips around the river bends. Of course, the rower must keep switching stern for bow as the river twists this way and that, so his progress resembles that of an agitated water-strider insect.

Before long, however, I had something even more
strange to wonder at—on the land, not on the river. Near a
village called Zong-zhai, we came to a deserted and
tumbledown ruin that must once have been a substantial
stone edifice with two stout watchtowers. Our escort Ussu
told me that it had in olden time been a Han fortress of
some long-past dynasty, and was still called by its old
name: the Gates of Jade. The fortress was not actually a
gate, and certainly not made of jade, but it constituted the
western end of a massively thick and impressively high
wall stretching northeastward from this point.

The Great Wall, as foreigners call it, is more colorfully
called by the Han the "Mouth" of their land. In times past,
the Han spoke of themselves as the People Within the
Mouth, meaning this wall, and spoke of all other nations to
the north and westward as the People Outside the Mouth.
Whenever a Han criminal or traitor was condemned to exile, he was said to have been "spat beyond the Mouth."
The wall was built to *keep* all but the Han outside it, and it
is unquestionably the longest and strongest defensive barrier ever built by human hands. How many hands, or how
long they labored, no one can say. But the construction of
it must have consumed the entire lives of many generations of whole populations of men.

According to tradition, the wall follows the wandering
course laid out by a favorite white horse of a certain Emperor Chin, the Han ruler who commenced its construction
in some distantly ancient time. But I doubt that story, for
no horse would willingly have taken such a difficult route
along mountaintop ridges, as much of the wall does. Certainly we and our horses did not. Though the remaining
weeks of our seemingly never-to-end journey across Kithai
required us generally to follow the course of that seemingly never-to-end wall—and while we were seldom out of
sight of it from then on—we could usually find lower and
easier ground downhill of it.

The Great Wall winds sinuously across Kithai, sometimes uninterruptedly from horizon to horizon, but in
other places it takes advantage of natural ramparts like
peaks and cliffs, and incorporates them into its length,
then resumes again on more vulnerable ground beyond.
Also, it is not everywhere just a single wall. In one region
of eastern Kithai, we found that there were three parallel

walls, one behind another, at intervals some hundred li apart.

The wall is not everywhere of the same composition. Its more easterly stretches are built of great squared rocks, neatly and firmly mortared together—as if in those places it was built under the Emperor Chin's stern eye—and is to this day still staunch and unbroken: a great, high, thick, solid bulwark, its top wide enough for a troop of horsemen to ride abreast, and with embrasured battlements on either side of that walltop roadway, and with bulky watch-towers jutting up even higher at intervals. But in some of its western lengths—as if the Emperor's subjects and slaves did only perfunctory work, knowing he would never come to inspect—the wall was built only shoddily, of stones and mud slapped together in a structure not so high nor thick, and consequently has been much crumbled and interrupted by gaps over the centuries.

Nevertheless, in sum, the Great Wall is a majestic and awesome thing, and I am not easily able to describe it in terms comprehensible to a Westerner. But let me put it this way. If the wall could somehow be transported intact out of Kithai, and all its numerous segments laid end to end, starting from Venice, thence going northwestward over the continent of Europe, across the Alps, over the meadows and rivers and forests and everything else, clear to the North Sea at the Flemish port of Bruges, there would yet be enough of the wall to *double back again* that same tremendous distance to Venice, and *still* there would be enough of the wall left over to extend from Venice westward to the border of France.

Considering the undeniable grandeur of the Great Wall, why did my father and uncle, who had seen it before, not ever mention it to me, to excite my anticipation of seeing it? And why did I myself not tell of such a marvel in that earlier book recounting my journeys? It was not, in this case, an omission of something which I judged people would refuse to believe. I neglected to mention the wall because—for all its prodigiousness—I deemed it a trivial achievement of the Han, and I still do. It seemed to me one more disavowal of the reputed genius of the natives of Ki-thai, and it still does. For this reason:

As we rode along beside the Great Wall, I remarked to Ussu and Donduk, "You Mongols were People Outside the Mouth, but now you are inside it. Did your armies have no trouble breaching that barrier?"

Donduk sneered. "Since the wall was first built, in times before history, no invader has ever had any trouble getting over it. We Mongols and our ancestors have done it again and again over the centuries. Even a puny Ferenghi could do it."

"Why is that?" I asked. "Were all other armies always better warriors than the Han defenders?"

"What defenders, uu?" Ussu said contemptuously.

"Why, the sentries on the parapets. They must have been able to see any enemy approaching from afar. And surely they had legions to summon for the repelling of enemies."

"Oh, yes, that is true."

"Well, then? Were they so easy to defeat?"

"Defeat!" they said together, their voices still heavy with disdain. Ussu explained the reason for their scorn. "No one ever had to defeat them. Any outsider who ever wished to cross the wall had merely to bribe the sentries with a bit of silver. Vakh! No wall is any taller or stronger or more forbidding than the men behind it."

And I saw that it was so. The Great Wall, built with God knows what expenditure of money and time and labor and sweat and blood and lives, has never been any more a deterrent to invaders than has the merest boundary line casually drawn on a map. The Great Wall's only real claim to notability is in its being the world's most stupendous monument to futility.

As witness: we came at last, some weeks later, to the city which that wall enwraps most securely, where the wall is highest and thickest and best preserved. The city there behind the wall has been known through the ages by many different names: Ji-cheng and Ji and Yu-zho and Chung-tu and other names—and at one time or another it has been the capital of many different empires of the Han people: the Chin and the Chou and the Tang dynasties, and no doubt others. But what availed the enormous wall? Today that city into which we rode is named Khanbalik, "City of

the Khan"—commemorating the latest invader to cross
the Great Wall and conquer this land, and by my reckoning the grandest of them: the man who resoundingly but
justifiably titled himself Great Khan, Khan of All Khans,
Khan of the Nations, son of Tulei and brother of Mangu
Khan, grandson of Chinghiz Khan, Mightiest of the Mongols, the Khakhan Kubilai.

KHANBALIK

1

To my surprise, when we entered Khanbalik—that is to say, when we came in the twilight of a fading day to the place where the dusty road became a broad, paved, clean avenue leading into the city—our little train was met by a considerable reception party.

First there was waiting a band of Mongol foot soldiers wearing dress armor of highly polished metal and gleaming oiled leathers. They did not step out to impede our way, as Kaidu's road guards at Kashgar had done. With unanimous precision, they presented their glittering lances at a slant of salute, then formed a hollow square about our train and marched with us along the avenue, between crowds of the city's everyday inhabitants, who paused in their occupations to ogle us curiously.

The next waiting greeters were a number of distinguished-looking, elderly gentlemen—some Mongols, some Han, some evidently Arab and Persian—wearing long silk robes of various vivid colors, each man attended by a servant holding over him a fringed canopy on a tall pole. The elders strode out to march on our either flank, their servants scurrying to keep the canopies in place over them, and all smiled at us and made sedate gestures of welcome and called in their several languages: "Mendu! Ying-jie! Salaam!"—though those words were quickly drowned out by a troop of musicians joining the procession with an unearthly screech and clangor of horns and cymbals. My father and uncle smiled and nodded and bowed from their saddles, appearing to have expected this extravagant re-

ception, but Nostril and Ussu and Donduk looked as astonished as I was.

Ussu said to me, over the noise, "Of course, your party
has been watched all along the road, as is every traveler,
and post riders will have kept the Khanbalik authorities
informed of your approach. No one arrives at the City of
the Khan unobserved."

"But," said Donduk, in a newly respectful voice, "usually it is only the city's Wang who keeps account of visitors' comings and goings. You Ferenghi"—he pronounced
the word benignly for a change—"seem to be known to the
very palace, and warmly awaited, and exceptionally welcome. Those elders marching alongside, I believe they are
courtiers of the Khakhan himself."

I was looking from side to side of the avenue, eager to get
some idea of the city's appearance, but suddenly the view
was obscured and my attention diverted elsewhere. There
came a noise like a crack of thunder and a light like a
lightning flash, not high in the sky but frighteningly close
overhead. It made me start and made my horse shy, so violently that I lost my stirrups. I curbed the animal before he
could bolt, and held him to a skittish dance, while the ter-
rific noise banged again and again, each time with a flare
of light. I saw that all our other horses had also shied, and
all our party were occupied in keeping them under control.
I would have expected every one of the city folk in the avenue to be running for cover, but all seemed not only composed but actually to be enjoying the tumult and the
brightening of the dusk. My father and uncle and the two
Mongols were equally tranquil; they even grinned broadly
as they sawed on the reins of the plunging horses. It
seemed that the flicker and the racket were a bewilderment only to me and to Nostril—I could see his eyeballs
protruding whitely from his head as he looked wildly
about for the source of the commotion.

It came from the curly-eaved rooftops along both sides of
the avenue. Blobs of bright light, like great sparks—or
more like the desert's mysterious "beads of Heaven"—
went lofting upward from those roofs and arcing into the
air overhead. Directly above us, they burst asunder, making that ear-clapping thump of sound, and became whole
constellations of different-colored sprinkles and streaks
and splinters of light that drifted down and dwindled and

died before they reached the street pavement, leaving a trail of sharp-smelling blue smoke. So many were going up from the roofs and bursting at such close intervals that their flares made an almost constant glow, abolishing the natural twilight, and their bangs concerted in such a roar that our accompanying band was inaudible. The musicians, trudging unconcerned through the clouds of blue smoke, appeared to be only pantomiming the play of their instruments. Though also inaudible, the crowds of city folk along each side of our line of march seemed, from their jumpings and arm wavings and wagging mouths, to be cheering exuberantly at every new burst and blast.

It may be that my own eyes were bulging at sight of that strange and unaccountable flying fire. For, when we had proceeded farther along the avenue, and the smoke and the artificial lightning storm were behind us, Ussu again brought his horse close beside mine and spoke loudly to be heard above the again rambunctious band music:

"You never saw such a show before, Ferenghi? It is a toy devised by the childish Han people. They call it huo-shu yin-hua—fiery trees and sparkling flowers."

I shook my head and said, "Toy, indeed!" but managed to smile as if I too had enjoyed it. Then I resumed my glancing about to see what the fabled city of Khanbalik looked like.

I will speak later of that. For now, let me just say that the city, which I suppose had suffered much ruination in the Mongols' taking of it, sometime before I was born, had ever since been in the process of rebuilding from the ground up. These many years later, it was still being added to and refined and embellished and made as grand as the capital of the world's greatest empire rightly ought to be. The broad avenue led us and our procession of troops and elders and musicians straight on for quite a long way, between the fronts of handsome buildings, until it ended at a towering, south-facing gateway in a wall that was almost as high and thick and impressive as the best-built stretches of the Great Wall out in the countryside.

We went through the gateway and we were in one of the courtyards of the Khakhan's palace. But palace is a word not comprehensive enough. That was more than a palace; it was a fair-sized city within the city; and it also was still a-building. The courtyard was full of the wagons and carts

and draft animals of stonemasons and carpenters and plas-
terers and gilders and such, and the conveyances of farmers and tradesmen purveying provender and necessities to
the inhabitants of the palace city, and the mounts and carriages and porter-borne palanquins of other visitors come
on other business from near and far.

From the group of courtiers who had accompanied us
through the city, one stepped forward, a quite old and
fragile-appearing Han, saying in Farsi, "I shall summon
servants, my lords." He only gently clapped his pallid, pa-
pery hands, but somehow that imperceptible command
carried through the confusion of the courtyard and he was
instantly obeyed. Out of somewhere came half a dozen stable grooms, and he instructed them to take charge of our
mounts and packhorses, also to lead Ussu and Donduk and
Nostril to quarters in the palace guard barracks. He
clapped his hands almost soundlessly again, and three female servants just as magically appeared.

"These maids will attend you, my lords," he said to my
father and uncle and me. "You will lodge temporarily in
the pavilion of honored guests. I will come on the morrow
and conduct you to the Khakhan, who is most eager to
greet you, and at that time doubtless he will appoint more
permanent quarters for you."

The three women bowed four times before us in the abjectly humble Han salute called the ko-tou, which is a prostration so low that the bowing forehead actually is
supposed to knock the ground. Then the women smilingly
beckoned and, with curiously birdlike, tripping little
steps led us across the courtyard, and the crowd made way
before us. We went another considerable distance through
the twilit palace city—along galleries and through clois-
ters and across other open courtyards and down corridors
and over terraces—until the women again did the ko-tou at
the guest pavilion. It had a seemingly blank wall of translucent oiled paper in frames of wood filigree, but the
women easily opened it by sliding two panels apart and
aside, and bowed us in. Our chambers were three bedrooms and a sitting room, en suite, lavishly decorated and
ornamented, with an ornate brazier already alight—
burning clean charcoal, not animal dung or the smoky
kara coals. One of the women began turning down our
beds—real beds, high standing and piled higher with

downy quilts and pillows—while another set water to heat on the brazier for our baths and the third began bringing in trays of already hot food from some kitchen somewhere.

We fell first on the food, almost snatching and stabbing with our nimble-tong sticks, for we were hungry and it was fine fare: bits of steamed shoat in a garlic sauce, pickled mustard greens cooked with broad beans, the familiar miàn pasta, a porridge very like our Venetian chestnut-meal polenta, a cha flavored with almonds and, for the sweet, red-candied little crabapples impaled on twigs for ease of eating. Then, in our separate rooms, we bathed all over—or got bathed, I should say. My father and uncle seemed to accept those ministrations as indifferently as if the young women had been male rubbers in a hammam. But it was the first time I had been so served by a female since the long-ago days of Zia Zulià, and I felt both embarrassment and titillation.

To distract myself, I watched the maid instead of what she was doing to me. She was a young woman of the Han, perhaps a little older than I, but at that time I knew not how to gauge the age of such alien beings. She was far better dressed than any Western servant would have been, but also was much more meek and docile and solicitous than any Western servant.

She had face and hands of ivory tint, an upswept mass of blue-black hair, barely perceptible eyebrows, no apparent eyelashes, and eyes also invisible because their opening was so narrow and she kept them always downcast. She had rosebud lips, red and dewy-looking, but a nose almost nonexistent. (I was beginning to resign myself to never seeing a shapely Verona-style nose in these lands.) Her ivory face was at the moment marred by a smudge on her forehead, from her ko-tou in the courtyard. However, a small imperfection in a woman can sometimes be a most appealing feature. I began to wish very much that I could see what the rest of the young woman looked like, under her many layers of brocade—stole and robe and gown and sashes and ties and other furbelows.

I was tempted to suggest that, as soon as she had me clean all over, she might serve me in other ways. But I did not. I could not speak her language, and the necessary gestures of suggestion might have been taken as more offensive than inviting. Also, I did not know how liberal or how

strict the local conventions might be in regard to such
things. So I decided prudence was called for, and, when she
finished my bath and made the ko-tou, I let her depart. The
hour was still early, but the day had been a tiring one. My
combined fatigue of traveling, excitement at having finally arrived, and languor induced by the bath put me immediately to sleep. I dreamed that I was undressing the
Han maidservant like a toy doll, layer by layer, and when
the last garment was peeled away she suddenly became
the other toy: that bursting, blazing display called fiery
trees and sparkling flowers.

In the morning, the same three women brought trays of
food which they served upon our laps while we still lay in
bed, and, while we broke our fast, prepared hot water to
give us each another bath. I endured it without complaint,
though I did think that two all-over bathings in the course
of a single day was rather excessive. Then Nostril came,
leading some of the stable hands carrying our travel packs.
So, after the baths, we donned the finest and least worn
clothes we owned. Those were our dashing Persian costumes—tulbands on our heads, embroidered waistcoats
over loose shirts with tight cuffs, kamarbands around our
middles, and ample pai-jamah tucked into well-cut boots.
Our three maids giggled, and nervously put their hands
over their mouths, as Han women always do when they
laugh, but they hastened to indicate that they were tit-
tering in admiration of our handsomeness.

Then arrived our elderly Han guide of the evening
before—this time he introduced himself: Lin-ngan, the
Court Mathematician—and led us from the pavilion. Now,
in full morning light, I could better appreciate our surroundings, as we went along arcades and colonnades
and through vine-trellised bowers and along porticoes
overhung by curly-edged roof eaves and along terraces
that overlooked flower-filled gardens and over high-arched
bridges that spanned lotus ponds and little streams in
which golden fish swam. In every place and passage we
saw servants, most of them Han, male and female, richly
garbed but timorously hastening on their errands, and
many Mongol guardsmen in dress uniforms, standing
rigid as statues but holding weapons which they looked
ready to use, and we saw the occasional strolling noble or
elder or courtier, as dignified and sumptuously robed and

important-appearing as our guide Lin-ngan, with whom
they exchanged ceremonious nods in passing.

All the unwalled passages open to the air had intricately
carved and fretted balustrades and exquisitely sculptured
pillars and hanging, tinkling wind chimes and silk tassels
swishing like horses' tails. All the enclosed passages
where the sun did not enter were lighted by tinted
Muscovy-glass lanterns like soft-colored moons, and they
glowed with a lovely diffuse light, because every such passage was misted by the fragrant smoke of burning incense.
And all the passages, open or enclosed, were decorated
with standing objects of art: elegant marble sundials and
lacquered screens and figured gongs and images of lions
and horses and dragons and other animals which I could
not recognize, and great urns of bronze and vases of porcelain and jade, overflowing with cut flowers.

We crossed again the gateside courtyard by which we
had entered on the previous evening, and it was again or
still thronged with saddle horses and pack asses and camels and carts and wagons and palanquins and people.
Among that press, I happened to see two Han men just dismounting from mules and, though they were but two faces
in an innumerable crowd, I had a vague sense of having
seen those men before. After leading us some way farther,
old Lin-ngan brought us finally to a south-facing pair of
immense doors, chased and gilded and lacquered in many
colors, doors so massive in size and so weighty with metal
studs and bosses that they might have been intended to
keep giants out—or in. Pausing with his wisp of a hand on
one of the formidable wrought-dragon handles, Lin-ngan
said in his whisper of a voice:

"This is the Cheng, the Hall of Justice, and this is the
hour of the Khakhan's dispensing judgment to plaintiffs
and supplicants and miscreants. If you will but attend until that is concluded, my Lords Polo, he wishes to make his
greetings immediately afterward."

The frail old man, with no apparent effort, swung open
the ponderous doors—they must have been cleverly coun-
terpoised and on well-oiled hinges—and bowed us inside.
He followed us in and closed the door behind us, and remained standing with us to provide helpful interpretations of what was going on in the hall.

The Cheng was a tremendous and lofty chamber, fully as

big as an indoor courtyard, its ceiling held up by carved
and gilded columns, its walls paneled with red leather, but
its floor space empty of furniture. At the far end was a
raised platform and on that a substantial thronelike chair,
flanked by rows of lower and less elegantly upholstered
chairs. There were dignitaries occupying all those seats,
and in the shadows behind the dais were other figures
standing and moving about. Between us and the platform
knelt a great crowd of petitioners, enough to fill the chamber from wall to wall, most of them in coarse peasant dress
but others in noble raiment.

Even from the distance at which we stood, I knew the
man seated centrally on the dais. I would have known him
even if he had been shabbily clothed and crammed igno-
miniously among the ranks of commoners on the chamber
floor. The Khan Kubilai needed not his elevated throne
nor his gold-threaded, fur-trimmed silk robes to proclaim
himself; his sovereignty was implicit in the upright way he
sat, as if he still were astride a battle charger, and in the
strength of his craggy face and in the forcefulness of his
voice, though he spoke only infrequently and in low tones.
The men in the chairs to either side of him were almost as
well dressed, but their manner made evident that they
were subordinates. Our guide Lin-ngan, pointing discreetly and murmuring quietly, explained who they all
were.

"One is the official called Suo-ke, which means the
Tongue. Four are the Khakhan's secretary scribes who
record on scrolls the proceedings here. Eight are ministers
of the Khakhan, two each of four ascending degrees. Behind the dais, those running about are relays of clerks who
fetch documents from the Cheng archives, when any are
needed for reference."

The one called Tongue of the Cheng was continuously
occupied, leaning down from the platform to hear a peti-
tioner, then turning to converse with one or another of the
ministers. And those eight ministers also were continuously busy, consulting with the Tongue, bidding clerks
bring them documents, peering into those papers and
scrolls, consulting among themselves and occasionally
with the Khakhan. But the four secretaries seemed only
now and then to bestir themselves to write anything on
their papers. I commented that it seemed odd: the lordly

ministers of the Cheng working harder than the mere secretaries.

"Yes," said Master Lin-ngan. "The scribes do not trouble to write down anything of these proceedings except the words spoken by the Khan Kubilai himself. Everything else is but preliminary discussion, for the Khakhan's words sum up and distill and supersede all other words spoken."

Such a vast room with so many people in it might have been cacophonous and echoing, but the crowd was quiet and orderly, like a congregation in church. Only one person at a time went up to the dais, and he spoke only to the official called the Tongue, and in a murmur so respectful or fearful that we in the back of the room could hear nothing that passed until, after all the deliberations, the Tongue announced the judgment for all to know.

Lin-ngan said, "During the Cheng, no one but the Tongue ever addresses the Khan Kubilai directly, nor ever is directly addressed by him. A supplicant or prosecutor puts his case to the Tongue—who, incidentally, is so called because he is fluent in all the languages of the realm. The Tongue then puts the case to one of the two ministers of least degree. If that official deems it a subject of sufficient importance, he will refer it upward. At whatever level, and after whatever precedents are consulted, an adjudication is suggested and told to the Tongue, who then tells it to the Khakhan. He may give assent, or make some slight change in the ruling, or controvert it completely. Then the Tongue pronounces aloud that final decree to the persons concerned and to all within hearing—damages to be paid to a plaintiff, or to be exacted from a defendant, or a punishment laid on, or sometimes a dismissal of the whole affair—and the case is closed forever."

I preceived that this Cheng of Khanbalik was not like the Daiwan of Baghdad, where every case had been a matter for discussion and mutual agreement among the Shah and hìs wazir and an assortment of officious Muslim imams and muftis. Here, the cases might be argued first among the ministers, but every single verdict was finally at the sole discretion of the Khan Kubilai, and his pronouncement was not to be disputed or appealed. I also perceived that his verdicts were sometimes witty or

whimsical, but sometimes appalling in their cruel inventiveness.

Old Lin-ngan was at that moment saying, "The farmer
who just petitioned the Cheng is a delegate sent by a whole
district of farmers in the province of Ho-nan. He brings
word that the rice fields have been chewed clean by a
plague of locusts. A famine is on the land and the farm
families are starving. The delegate asks relief for the people of Ho-nan and inquires what might be done. Regard,
the ministers have discussed the problem and referred it to
the Khakhan, and now the Tongue will deliver the Khakhan's decree."

The Tongue did, in a bellow of Han that I could not understand, but Lin-ngan translated:

"The Khan Kubilai speaks thus. With all that rice in-
side them, the locusts should be delicious. The families of
Ho-nan have the Khakhan's permission to eat the locusts.
The Khan Kubilai has spoken."

"By God," muttered Uncle Mafìo, "the old tyrant is just
as flippantly imperious as I had remembered him."

"Honey in his mouth and a dagger at his belt," my father said admiringly.

The next case was that of a provincial notary named
Xen-ning, responsible for recording deeds of land transfer
and testaments of bequest and such things. He was accused, and found guilty, of having falsified his ledgers for
his own aggrandizement, and the Tongue proclaimed and
Lin-ngan translated the sentence accorded him:

"The Khan Kubilai speaks thus. You have lived all your
life by words, Notary Xen-ning. Henceforth you shall live
on them. You are to be imprisoned in a solitary cell, and at
every mealtime you will be served pieces of paper inscribed 'meat' and 'rice' and 'cha.' Those will be your food
and drink for as long as you can survive on them. The
Khan Kubilai has spoken."

"Truly," said my father, "he has a tongue of scissors."

The next and last case that morning was the matter of a
woman taken in adultery. It would have been a thing too
trivial for the Cheng's consideration, said old Lin-ngan,
except that she was a Mongol woman, and wife to a Mongol
functionary of the Khanate, a certain Lord Amursama;
therefore her crime was more heinous than if she had been
a mere Han. Her outraged husband had stabbed her lover

to death at the moment of discovery, said Lin-ngan, meaning that the miscreant had died too mercifully quickly and without the torment he deserved. So now the husband was petitioning the Cheng to decide a more salutary fate for his unfaithful wife. The cuckold's petition was duly granted, and I trust it satisfied him. Lin-ngan translated:

"The Khan Kubilai speaks thus. The guilty Lady Amursama will be delivered to the Fondler—"

"The Fondler?" I exclaimed, and I laughed. "I thought she had just been delivered *from* one of those."

"The Fondler," the old man said stiffly, "is our name for the Court Executioner."

"In Venice we more realistically call him the Meatmaker."

"It so happens that in the Han language the term for physical torture, dong-xing, and the term for sexual arousal, dong-qing, are, as you have just heard, very similar in pronunciation."

"Gèsu," I muttered.

"I resume," said Lin-ngan. "The wife will be delivered to the Fondler, accompanied by her betrayed husband. In the presence of the Fondler, and if necessary employing his assistance, the husband will with his teeth and fingernails tear out his wife's pudendal sphincter, and with that he will strangle her to death. The Khan Kubilai has spoken."

Neither my father nor my uncle saw fit to comment on that decree, but I did. I scoffed knowingly:

"Vakh! This is pure show. The Khakhan is well aware that we are present. He is only making such eccentric judgments to impress and confound us. Just as the Ilkhan Kaidu did when he spat in his guardsman's mouth."

My father and the Mathematician Lin-ngan gave me looks askance, and my uncle growled, "Brash upstart! Do you really think that the Khan of All Khans would exert himself to impress any human being alive? Least of all, some unimportant wretches from an inconsequential cranny of the world far beyond his domains?"

I made no reply, but neither did I put on a contrite look, being sure that my disparaging opinion would eventually be confirmed. But it never was. Uncle Mafìo was right, of course, and I was wrong, and I would soon know how foolishly I had misread the Khakhan's temperament.

But at that moment the Cheng was emptying. The hud-

dled ruck of petitioners humped to their feet and shuffled
out through the door by which we had entered, and the pre-
siding justices at the dais, all except the Khakhan, disappeared through some doorway at the end of the hall. When
there was no one left between him and us except his ring of
guards, Lin-ngan said, "The Khakhan beckons. Let us approach."

Following the Mathematician's example, we all knelt to
make the ko-tou obeisance to the Khakhan. But before we
had folded far enough to put our foreheads to the floor, he
said in a boomingly hearty voice:

"Rise! Stand! Old friends, welcome back to Kithai!"

He spoke in Mongol, and I never afterwards heard him
speak anything else, so I do not know if he was acquainted
with Trade Farsi or any others of the multifarious languages employed in his realm, and I never heard anyone
else address him in anything but his native Mongol. He
did not embrace my father or uncle in the fashion of Venetian friends meeting, but he did clap each of them on the
shoulder with a big, heavily beringed hand.

"It is good to see you again, Brothers Polo. How fared
you in the journeying, uu? Is this the first of my priests,
uu? How young he looks, for a sage cleric!"

"No, Sire," said my father. "This is my son Marco, also
now an experienced journeyer. He, like us, puts himself at
the service of the Khakhan."

"Then welcome is he, as well," said Kubilai, nodding
amiably to me. "But the priests, friend Nicolò, do they follow behind you, uu?"

My father and uncle explained apologetically, but not
abjectly, that we had failed to bring the requested one hundred missionary priests—or any priests at all—because
they had had the misfortune to return home during the papal interregnum and the consequent disarray of the
Church hierarchy. (They did not mention the two fainthearted Friars Preachers who had come no farther than
the Levant.) While they explained, I took the opportunity
to look closely at this most powerful monarch in the world.

The Khan of All Khans was then just short of his sixti-
eth birthday, an age which in the West would have
counted him an ancient, but he was still a hale and sturdy
specimen of mature manhood. For a crown, he wore a simple gold morion helmet, like an inverted soup bowl, with

nape and jugular lappets depending from its back and sides. His hair, what I could see of it under the morion, was gray but still thick. His full mustache and his beard, which was close-trimmed in the style worn by shipwrights, were more pepper than salt. His eyes were rather round, for a Mongol, and bright with intelligence. His ruddy complexion was weathered but not wrinkled, as if his face had been carved from well-seasoned walnut. His nose was his only unhandsome feature, it being short like those of all Mongols, but also bulbous and quite red. His garments were all of splendid silks, thickly brocaded with figures and patterns, and they covered a figure that was stout but nowise suety. On his feet were soft boots of a peculiar leather; I learned later that they were made from the skin of a certain fish, which is alleged to allay the pains of gout, the only affliction I ever heard the Khakhan complain of.

"Well," he said, when my father and uncle had finished, "perhaps your Church of Rome shows a cunning wisdom in keeping close its mysteries."

I was still holding my newly formed opinion that the Khan Kubilai was like any other mortal—as evidenced by his posturings for our benefit during the proceedings of the Cheng—and now he seemed to validate that opinion, for he went on talking, as chattily as any ordinary man making idle conversation with friends.

"Yes, your Church may be right *not* to send missionaries here. When it comes to religion, I often think that none is better than too much. We already have Nestorian Christians, and they are ubiquitous and vociferous, to the point of pestilence. Even my old mother, the Dowager Khatun Sorghaktani, who long ago converted to that faith, is still so besotted with it that she harangues me and every other pagan she meets. Our courtiers are lately desperate to avoid meeting her in the corridors. Such fanaticism defeats its own aims. So, yes, I believe your Roman Christian Church may well attract more converts if it pretends to stand aloof from the herd. That is the of the Jews, you know. Thus the few pagans who do get accepted into Judaism can feel flattered and honored by the fact."

"Oh, please, Sire," my father said anxiously. "Do not compare the True Faith with the heretic Nestorian sect. And do not equate it with the despised Judaism. Blame me and Mafìo, if you will, for our error of timing. But at any

and all other times, I sincerely assure you, the Church of
Rome holds open its warm embrace to enfold all who desire
salvation."

The Khakhan said sharply, "Why, uu?"

That was my first experience of that particular one of
Kubilai's attributes, but I was often to remark it thereafter. The Khakhan could be as congenial and discursive
and loquacious as an old woman, when it suited his mood
and purpose. But when he wanted to know something,
when he wanted an answer, when he sought a particle of
information, he could suddenly emerge from the clouds of
garrulity—his own or a whole roomful of other people's—
and swoop like a falcon to strike to the meat of a matter.

"Why?" echoed Uncle Mafìo, taken aback. "Why does
Christianity seek to save all mankind?"

"But we told you years ago, Sire," said my father. "The
faith which preaches love and which was founded on Jesus,
the Christ and Savior, is the only hope of bringing about
perpetual peace on earth, and plenty, and ease of body and
mind and soul, and good will among men. And after life, an
eternity of bliss in the Bosom of Our Lord."

I thought my father had put the case for Christianity as
well as any ordained cleric could have done. But the Khakhan only smiled sadly and sighed.

"I had hoped you would bring learned men of persuasive
arguments, good Brothers Polo. Fond as I am of you, and
much as I respect your own convictions, I fear that you—
like my dowager mother and like every missionary I have
ever met—offer only unsupported asseveration."

Before my father or uncle could profess further, Kubilai
launched into another of his periphrases:

"I do indeed remember your telling me how your Jesus
came to earth, with His message and His promise. That
was more than one thousand and two hundred years ago,
you said. Well, I myself have lived long, and I have studied
the histories of times before my own. In all ages, it seems,
all sorts of religions have held out promises of worldwide
peace and bounty and good health and brotherly love and
pervading happiness—and some kind of Heaven hereafter.
About the hereafter I know nothing. But of my own knowledge, most of the people on this earth, including those who
pray and worship with sincerest faith and devotion, remain poor and sickly and unhappy and unfulfilled and in

utter detestation of each other—even when they are not actively at war, which is seldom."

My father opened his mouth, perhaps to comment on the incongruity of a Mongol deploring war, but the Khakhan went on:

"The Han people tell a legend about a bird called the jing-wei. Since the beginning of time, the jing-wei has been carrying pebbles in its beak, to fill in the limitless, bottomless Sea of Kithai and make solid land of it, and the jing-wei will continue that futile endeavor until the other end of time. So it must be, I think, with faiths and religions and devotions. You can hardly deny that your own Christian Church has been playing the jing-wei bird for twelve whole centuries now—forever futile, forever fatuously promising what it can never provide."

"Never, Sire?" said my father. "Enough pebbles *will* fill a sea. Even the Sea of Kithai, in time."

"Never, friend Nicolò," the Khakhan said flatly. "Our learned cosmographers have proved that the world is more sea than land. There do not exist enough pebbles."

"Facts cannot prevail against faith, Sire."

"Nor against adamant folly, I fear. Well, well, enough of this. You are men in whom we placed our trust, and you have failed that trust in not fetching the priests requested. However, it is a custom here: never to dispraise men of good breeding in the presence of others." He turned to the Mathematician, who had been listening to those exchanges with an expression of polite boredom. "Master Lin-ngan, will you kindly retire, uu? Leave me alone with these Masters Polo while I chastise them for their nonfeasance."

I was startled and angry and a little uneasy. So that was why he had had us present in the Cheng to observe his capricious judgments—to have us already fearful and trembling even before we heard his judgment on us. Had we come all this weary way only for some frightful punishment? But he surprised me again. When Lin-ngan had gone, he chuckled and said:

"There. All the Han are notorious for their swift conveyance of gossip, and Lin-ngan is a true Han. The whole court already knew of your priestly mission, and now it will be told that our conversation concerned nothing else. Therefore, let us proceed to the nothing-else."

Uncle Mafìo said, smiling, "There are numerous nothing-elses to speak of, Sire. Which first?"

"I am told that your road brought you right into the hand of my cousin Kaidu, and that he closed his fist on you for a time."

"A brief delay only, Sire," said my father, and waved toward me. "Marco yonder most ingeniously aided us to elude him, but we will tell you of that another time. Kaidu wished to plunder the gifts we have brought you from your liege subjects the Shah of Persia and the Sultan of India Aryana. Your cousin might have confiscated everything, but for Marco."

The Khakhan nodded again to me, only briefly, before he swung back to my father and uncle. "Kaidu took nothing from you, uu?"

"Nothing, Sire. At your command, we will have servants bring in and display for you the wealth of gold and jewels and finery—"

"Vakh!" the Khakhan interrupted. "Never mind the trinkets. What of the maps, uu? Besides the wretched priests, you promised to bring maps. Did you make them, uu? Did Kaidu filch them from you, uu? I would gladly have had him steal everything else but those!"

I was understandably bewildered by the several and rapid changes of topic under discussion. The Khakhan was not chastising us, but interrogating us, and on a matter until now unsuspected by me. I might have been sufficiently astonished to hear a man say *vakh* to a gift of trinkets that would purchase any duchy in Europe. But I was more astonished to learn that my father and uncle had all this time been engaged on a project more secret and important than just the procurement of missionaries.

"The maps are safe, Sire," said my father. "It never occurred to Kaidu to think of any such things. And Mafìo and I believe we have compiled the best maps yet done of the western and central regions of this continent— especially those regions held by the Ilkhan Kaidu."

"Good . . . good . . . ," murmured Kubilai. "The maps drawn by the Han are unsurpassable, but they confine themselves to the Han lands. Those maps we captured from them in earlier years much aided the Mongol conquest of Kithai, and they will be of equal use as we march south against the Sung. But the Han have always ignored everything beyond their own borders as unworthy of consideration. If you have done your work well, then for the first time I have maps of the entire Silk Road into the farther reaches of my empire."

Beaming with satisfaction, he looked about him and caught sight of me. Perhaps he took my vapid gawking for a look of stricken conscience, for he beamed even more broadly and spoke directly to me. "I have already promised, young Polo, never to use the maps in any Mongol campaign against the territory or the holdings of the Dogato of Venice."

Then, turning again to my father and uncle, he said, "I will later arrange a private audience for us to sit together and examine the maps. In the meantime, a separate chamber and staff of servants have been appointed for each of you, conveniently close to my own in the main palace residence." He added, rather as an afterthought, "Your nephew may reside in either suite, as you choose."

(It is a curious thing, but for all Kubilai's acuity in every other area of human knowledge and experience, he never, through all the years I knew him, bothered to remember of which elder Polo I was the son and of which the nephew.)

"For tonight," he went on, "I have ordered a banquet of welcome, at which you will meet two other visitors newly come from the West, and we will all together discuss the vexing question of my insubordinate cousin Kaidu. Now Lin-ngan waits outside to escort you to your new quarters."

We all began a ko-tou, and again—as he always would do—he bade us rise before we had prostrated ourselves very deeply, and he said, "Until tonight, friends Polo," and we took our leave.

2

As I say, that was my first realization that my father and uncle, in their assiduous making of maps, had been working at least partly for the Khan Kubilai—and this is the first time I have ever publicly revealed that fact. I did not mention it in the earlier chronicle of my travels and theirs,

because at that time my father was still alive, and I hesitated to impute any suspicion that he might have served
the Mongol Horde in ways inimical to our Christian West.
However, as all men know, the Mongols never again have
invaded or threatened the West. Our foremost enemies for
many years have continued to be the Muslim Saracens,
and the Mongols have frequently been our friendly allies
against them.

Meanwhile, as my father and uncle all along intended,
Venice and the rest of Europe have profited from increased
trade with the East, a trade much facilitated by the copies
of all our maps of the Silk Road which we Polos brought
home from there. So I no longer see any need to maintain
the slightly preposterous fiction that Nicolò and Mafìo
Polo crossed and recrossed the whole extent of Asia simply
to herd a flock of priests with them. And not in that other
book, or ever, have I tried to keep secret the fact that I,
Marco Polo, also became an agent and journeyer and observer and mapmaker for the Khan Kubilai. But I will
here tell the beginning of my becoming so well regarded by
the Khakhan that he entrusted me with such missions.

It was at that night's welcoming banquet that I first attracted his notice. But it could have happened—and almost
did—that Kubilai's first attention to me might have been a
command that I deliver myself to the Fondler, with my
neck in my sphincter.

The banquet was laid in the largest hall of the main palace building, a hall which, one of the table servants
boasted to me, would accommodate six thousand diners at
a single seating. The high ceiling was held up on pillars
that seemed made of solid gold, twisted and convoluted, inset with gems and jade. The walls were paneled alternately in rich carved woods and fine embossed leathers,
and hung with Persian qali and Han scroll paintings and
Mongol trophies of the hunt. Those included the mounted
heads of snarling lions and spotted pards and great-horned
artak ("Marco's sheep") and large bearlike creatures
called da-maoxiong, the mounted heads of which were
startlingly snow-white except for black ears and black
masks about the eyes.

The trophies were probably of the Khakhan's own
hunts, for he was famous for his love of the chase, and
spent every spare day in forest or field. Even here in the

banquet hall, his affection for that manliest of sports was evident, for the guests seated closest to him were his dearest hunting partners. On either arm of his thronelike chair was perched a hooded hunting falcon, and to each of the chair's two front legs was tethered a hunting cat called a chita. The chita resembles a spotted pard, but is much smaller in size and proportionately much longer in the legs. It is different from all other cats in that it cannot climb a tree, and is even more different in that it will willingly chase and pull down game at its master's bidding. Here, however, the chitas and the falcons sat quietly, now and then politely accepting tidbits which Kubilai fed to them with his own fingers.

There were not six thousand persons present on that particular night, so the hall was partitioned by screens of black and gold and red lacquer, to make a more intimate enclosure for rather fewer people. Still, there must have been close on two hundred of us, plus as many servants and a constantly changing crew of musicians and entertainers. That many people breathing and sweating, and the savory steams from the hot foods served, should have made even that huge hall rather warm on that late-summer night. But, although we were screened about and all the outer doors were shut, the hall had a cool breeze mysteriously blowing through it. Not until some while later did I learn by what ingeniously simple means that coolness was effected. But there were other mysteries in that dining hall which made me goggle and thrill and wonder, and for them I never did manage to find adequate explanation.

For example, in the middle of all the many tables stood a tall artificial tree, crafted of silver, its multiple limbs and branches and twigs hung with beaten-silver leaves that fluttered gently in the hall's artificial breeze. Around the tree's silver-barked trunk were coiled four golden serpents. Their tails were twined among the upper branches and their heads snaked downward to poise, open-mouthed, above four immense porcelain vases. The vases were molded in the shape of fantastic lions with their heads thrown back and their mouths also wide. There were some other artificial creatures in the room; on several tables, including the one at which we guest Polos sat, was a life-sized peacock made of gold, its tail feathers finely articulated and colored by inlaid enamels. Now, the mystery about those objects was this. When the Khan Kubilai called for drink—and only when *he* called aloud, not when anyone else did—those several animals of precious metals did wondrous things. I will tell what they did, though I scarcely expect to be believed.

"Kumis!" Kubilai would bellow, and one of the golden serpents coiled about the silver tree would suddenly gush from its mouth a flow of pearly liquid into the mouth of the lion vase set below. A servant would bring the vase to the Khakhan's table and pour the beverage into his jewel-encrusted goblet and the goblets of other guests. They would sip and verify that it was indeed the mare's-milk kumis, and they would all clap their hands in applause of that marvel, and immediately another marvelous thing would occur. The golden peacock on the table—and every golden peacock in the room—would likewise applaud, raising and beating its golden wings, erecting and fanning out its splendid tail.

"Arkhi!" the Khakhan would shout next, and the second serpent on the tree would disgorge its measure into the second lion vase, and a servant would bring the drink and we all would find it to be that finer and tastier grade of kumis called arkhi. And we would applaud and so would the peacocks. And those animated creatures, the liquor-spouting serpents and the exuberant birds, they worked, mind you, without any human agency. I several times went close to observe them, both while they were performing and while they were at rest, and I could find no wires or strings or levers that might have been manipulated from a distance.

"Mao-tai!" the Khakhan would shout next, and the whole activity would be repeated, from serpent spout to lion vase to peacock fanning. The liquor dispensed by the third serpent, mao-tai, was new to me: a yellowish, slightly syrupy beverage of a tingling flavor. The Mongol diner at my elbow cautioned me to beware of its potency, which he demonstrated. He took a tiny porcelain cup of the liquor and applied to it the flame of one of the table candles. The mao-tai caught fire with a sizzling blue flame and burned like naft oil for a good five minutes before it was consumed. I understand that mao-tai is a Han concoction somehow expressed from common millet, but it is an uncommon beverage—as fiery a fuel to the belly and the brain as it is to any open flame.

"Pu-tao!" was the fourth command the Khakhan shouted to the serpent tree; the word pu-tao means grape wine. But to the consternation of all us guests, *nothing happened.* The fourth serpent simply hung there, sullenly dry, and we sat gaping, almost fearful, wondering what had gone wrong. The Khakhan, though, sat grinning with secret glee, enjoying the air of suspense, until he demonstrated the last and most magical magic of the apparatus. Not until he shouted "Pu-tao!" and then added a shout of either "hong!" or "bai!" would the fourth serpent begin to gush, and according to Kubilai's command it would dispense red (hong) or white (bai) wine, at which we guests erupted in a storm of cheers and applause, and the golden peacocks beat their wings and fanned their tails so wildly that they shed flakes of golden feathers.

The banquet guests that night, except for the visitors being welcomed, comprised the highest lords and ministers and courtiers of the Khanate, plus some women whom I took to be their wives. The lords were a mixture of nationalities and complexions: Arabs and Persians as well as Mongols and Han. But of course the women present were the non-Muslim Mongol and Han wives; if the Arabs and Persians had wives, they were not permitted to dine in mixed company. All the men were finely garbed in brocaded silks, some wearing robes, as did the Khakhan and other Mongols and the native Han, some wearing their silks in the form of Persian pai-jamah and tulband, and others wearing their silks as Arab aba and kaffiyah.

But the women were even more gorgeously arrayed. The Han ladies all had powdered their already ivory faces to the whiteness of snow, and wore their blue-black hair in voluminous piles and swirls atop their heads, pinned up there by long jeweled implements they called hair-spoons. The Mongol ladies were of slightly darker complexion, a sort of fawn color, and I was much interested to see that these women, unlike their plains-dwelling nomad sisters, were not coarsened to leather by sun and wind, nor were they bulkily muscular of body. Their coiffures were even more complex than that of the Han women. Their hair, ruddy-black instead of blue-black, was braided onto a framework to make it swoop in a wide crescent at either side of the head, rather like sheep horns, and those crescents were festooned with dangling brilliants. Also, though they wore the same simple, flowing gowns as the Han women, the Mongol ladies added to the shoulders of them some curious high fillets of padded silk that stood up like fins.

At the Khakhan's table with him sat members of his immediate family. Five or six of his twelve legitimate sons were ranged at his right. On his left sat his first and chief wife, the Khatun Jamui, then his aged mother, the Dowager Khatun Sorghaktani, then his three other wives. (Kubilai had also a considerable and constantly varying consort of concubines, all younger than his wives. The current contingent sat at a separate table. By his concubines, Kubilai had another twenty-five sons, and God knows how many legitimate and bastard daughters besides, from all his women.)

The whole dining area was divided so that the male guests occupied the tables to Kubilai's right and the females those to his left. Closest to the Khakhan's table, within easy speaking distance, was the table appointed for us Polos, and with us was seated a Mongol dignitary to converse with us, interpret for us when necessary, explain to us the unfamiliar dishes and drinks served, and so on. He was a fairly young man—exactly ten years older than myself, it turned out—who introduced himself as Chingkim, saying he held the office of Wang of Khanbalik, which was to say the Chief City Officer or Magistrate. That office being equivalent to a European city's mayor —or podestà, in the Venetian term—I gathered that we Polos were entitled to only a minor functionary as our table companion.

The Khakhan more formally introduced us to others of his lords and ministers seated at nearby tables. I will not attempt to list them all, for they included so many persons of so many different degrees of authority, and so many bore titles which I had never heard in any other court, or ever even heard of—the Master of the Black-Ink Arts (nothing but the Court Poet), the Master of the Mastiffs, Hawks and Chitas (the Khakhan's Chief Huntsman), the Master of the Boneless Colors (nothing but the Court Artist), the Chief of Secretaries and Scribes, the Archivist of Marvels and Wonders, the Recorder of Things Strange.

But I *will* mention by name some lords who seemed to me curiously out of place in a supposedly Mongol court—for example, Lin-ngan, whom we already knew, was one of the supposedly conquered Han, but held the fairly important post of Court Mathematician.

The young man Chingkim appeared to hold the grandest title assigned by Kubilai to any of his fellow Mongols, and Chingkim claimed to be only a mere city Wang. By contrast, the Khakhan's Chief Minister, whose office was called by the Han title of Jing-siang, was neither a conqueror Mongol nor a subject Han. He was an Arab named Achmad-az-Fenaket, and he himself preferred to be called by the Arab title signifying his office, which is Wali. By whatever honorific he was addressed—Jing-siang or Chief Minister or Wali—Achmad was the second most powerful man in the entire Mongol hierarchy, subordinate only to the Khakhan himself, for he also held the office of Vice-Regent, meaning that he literally ruled the empire whenever Kubilai was out hunting or making war or otherwise occupied, and Achmad also held the office of Finance Minister, meaning that at all times he controlled the purse strings of the empire.

It seemed equally odd to me that the Mongol Empire's Minister of War—war being the activity in which the Mongols most excelled and exulted—was *not* a Mongol but a Han gentleman named Chao Meng-fu. The Court Astronomer was a Persian named Jamal-ud-Din, a native of far-off Isfahan. The Court Physician was a Byzantine, a native of even farther-off Constantinople, the Hakim Gansui. The palace staff included other persons, not present at that banquet, of even more surprising alien origins, and I would eventually come to know them all.

The Khakhan had promised that we Polos would that night meet "two other visitors newly come from the West," and they were present, seated at a table within speaking distance of his table and ours. They were not Westerners, but Han, and I recognized them as the two men I had seen dismounting from mules in the palace courtyard on the evening of our arrival, and I still had the feeling that I had seen them somewhere else even before that.

The tables at which we all sat were surfaced with a pinkish-lavender inlay of what looked to me like precious stones. And so they were, said our tablemate Chingkim:

"Amethyst," he told me. "We Mongols have learned much from the Han. And the Han physicians have concluded that tables made of purple amethyst prevent drunkenness in those who sit drinking at them."

I thought that interesting, but I should also have been interested to see how much drunker the company might have got without the countering influence of the amethyst. Kubilai was not alone in bellowing for kumis and arkhi and mao-tai and pu-tao, and ingesting quantities of all those beverages. Even of the resident Arabs and Persians, the only one who stayed Muslimly sedate and sober all night was the Wali Achmad. And the guzzling was not confined to the male guests; the female Mongols put away their share, too, and gradually got quite raucous and bawdy. The Han females kept to wine only, and only infrequent sips of it, and maintained their ladylike propriety.

But the company did not get drunk immediately, or all at once. The banquet began at what is in Kithai known as the Hour of the Cock, and the first guests did not stagger from the hall or slide insensible under the amethyst tables until well into the Hour of the Tiger, which is to say that the feasting and talking and laughing and entertainment lasted from early evening until just before dawn the next morning, and the general inebriation was not too evident until the tenth or eleventh hour of that twelve-hour festa.

"Onyx," said Chingkim to me, and he pointed at the open area of the floor around the drink-pouring serpent tree, where at the moment two monstrously stout and sweatily naked Turki wrestlers were trying to dismember each other for our amusement. "The Han physicians have concluded that the black onyx stone imparts strength to those in contact with it. So the wrestling floor is paved with onyx to enliven the combatants."

After the two Turki had crippled each other to the company's satisfaction, we were regaled by a troupe of Uzbek girl singers, wearing gold-embroidered gowns of ruby red and emerald green and sapphire blue. The girls had rather pretty but exceptionally flat faces, as if their features were only painted on the fronts of their heads. They screeched for us some incomprehensible and interminable Uzbek ballads, in voices like ungreased wheels on a runaway wagon. Then some Samoyed musicians performed pieces of similar cacophony on an assortment of instruments—hand drums and finger cymbals and pipes resembling our fagotto and dulzaina.

Then there came Han jugglers who were far more entertaining, since they performed in silence as well as with incredible dexterity. It was astounding to see the tricks they could do with swords and rope loops and blazing torches, and how many such objects they could keep flying or spinning or suspended in the air at one time. But I really thought I could no longer trust my eyes when the jugglers began tossing into the air and to one another wine cups *full of wine,* and never spilling a drop! In the intervals between those performances, there wandered about the hall a tulhulos, which is a Mongol minstrel, sawing on a sort of three-stringed viella and dolefully wailing chronicles of battles and victories and heroes past.

Meanwhile, we all ate. And how we ate! We ate from paper-thin porcelain plates and bowls and platters, some softly colored in brown and cream colors, others blue with plum-color mottlings. I did not know then but later was told that those porcelains, called Chi-zho and Jen ware, were Han works of art, worthy of being treasured in collections, and not even the emperors of the Han would have dreamed of employing them for mere tableware. But, just as Kubilai had appropriated those art objects for his guests' convenience, so had he acquired for his palace kitchens the foremost cooks of all Kithai, and those, more than the Chi-zho and Jen porcelain, were loudly appreciated by us guests. As we were served with each new course of the meal, and sampled it, the whole room would breathe "Hui!" and "Hao!" in approval, and the cook responsible for that particular dish would emerge from the kitchens and smile and ko-tou, and we would applaud him by clicking together our nimble tongs, making a cricket crepitation. I might remark that we guests were supplied with eating tongs of intricately carved ivory, but those used by Kubilai—so I was told by Chingkim—were made from the forearm bones of a gibbon ape, because such tongs will turn black if they touch poisoned food.

Our tablemate also explained each dish that came to our table, because almost every one was of Han origin and had a Han name that was most intriguing but gave no hint of the dish's content, and I could not always determine what it was I was eating and applauding. Of course, at the start

of the feasting, when the first dish was announced as Milk
and Roses, I had no trouble seeing that those were simply
white grapes and pink grapes. (A meal in the Han style
goes contrary to ours; it begins with fruits and nuts and
ends with a soup.) But when I was presented with a dish
called Snow Babies, Chingkim had to explain that it was
made of bean curd and the cooked flesh of frogs' legs. And
the dish called Red-Beaked Green Parrot with Gold-
Trimmed Jade was a sort of multicolored custard containing the boiled and pulverized leaves of a Persian plant
called aspanakh, creamed mushrooms and the petals of
various flowers.

When the servants set before me One-Hundred-Year
Eggs, I nearly declined them, for they were only hens' and
ducks' eggs, hard-boiled, but the whites of them were a
ghastly green and the yolks were black, and they *smelled* a
hundred years old. However, Chingkim assured me that
they were really only pickled, and only for sixty days, so I
ate them and found them tasty. There were stranger
things—the meat of bear paws, and fish lips, and a broth
made of the saliva with which a certain bird glues its nest
together, and pigeons' feet in jelly, and a blob of substance
called go-ba, which is a fungus that grows on ricestalks—
but I valiantly partook of them all. There were also more
recognizable foods—the miàn pasta in numerous shapes
and sauces, dumplings stuffed and steamed, the familiar
aubergine in an unfamiliar fish gravy.

The banquet, like the banqueters and the banquet hall,
gave ample evidence that the Mongols had climbed a fair
way from barbarism toward civilization, and had done it
mainly by adopting so much of the Han people's culture,
from their foods to their costumes to their bathing habits
to their architecture. But the banquet's main culinary
treat—the piatanza di prima portata—Chingkim said was
a dish long ago devised by the Mongols, and only recently
but happily adopted by the Han. They called it Windblown
Duck, and Chingkim told me the complicated process of its
preparation.

A duck, he said, came from egg to kitchen in exactly
forty-eight days, then required forty-eight hours for the
proper cooking. Its brief lifetime included three weeks of
being force-fed (in the way that the Strasbourgeois of the
Lorraine stuff their geese). The well-fatted fowl was killed

and plucked and cleaned, and its body cavity was blown full of air and distended, and it was hung outdoors in a south wind. "Only a south wind will do," said Chingkim. Then it was glazed by being smoked over a fire in which camphor burned. Then it was roasted over an ordinary fire, meanwhile being basted with wine and garlic and bead molasses and a fermented-bean sauce. Then it was cut up and served in bite-sized pieces—the flakes of crisp black skin being the most prized part—with lightly cooked onion greens and water chestnuts and a transparent miàn vermicelli, and if there was anything to make the Han people less resentful of their Mongol conquerors, in my opinion it must be Windblown Duck.

After a confection of sugared lotus petals and a clear soup made from hami melons, the very last dish was placed upon each table: a huge tureen of plain boiled rice. This was purely symbolic, and no one partook of it. Rice is the staple of the diet of the Han people—in truth, in the southern Han realms, rice is almost the whole of the people's diet—and it therefore merits a place of honor on every table, even a rich man's table. But a rich man's guests will refrain from eating it, for to do so would insult the host, implying that all the foregoing delicacies had been insufficient.

Then, while the servants cleared the tables for the serious business of drinking, Kubilai and my father and uncle and some others began to converse. (As I have told, Mongol men do not customarily talk during a meal, and the other men in the hall had also observed that custom. It had, however, not at all deterred the Mongol women, who had cackled and shrieked all through the dinner.) Kubilai said to my father and uncle:

"These men, Tang and Fu"—he indicated the two Han I had already noticed—"came from the West about the same time that you did. They are spies of mine, clever and adept and unobtrusive. When I got word that a Han wagon train was going into the lands of my cousin Kaidu, to bring back Han cadavers for burial, I had Tang and Fu join that Karwan." Aha, I thought, so that explained my having seen them before, but I made no comment. Kubilai turned to them. "Tell us then, honorable spies, what secrets you ferreted out from Sin-kiang Province."

Tang spoke, and as if he were reciting from a written

list, though he used no such thing: "The Ilkhan Kaidu is orlok of a bok comprising an entire tuk, of which he can instantly put six tomans into the field."

The Khakhan did not look much impressed, but he translated that for my father and uncle: "My cousin commands a camp containing one hundred thousand horse warriors, of whom sixty thousand stand always ready for battle."

I wondered why the Khan Kubilai had had to employ professional spies to get such information by stealth, when I had learned as much simply by sharing a meal in a yurta.

Fu spoke in his turn: "Each warrior goes into battle with one lance, one mace, his shield, at least one sword and dagger, one bow and sixty arrows for it. Thirty arrows are light, with narrow heads, for long-range use. Thirty are heavy, with broad heads, for use at close quarters."

I knew that much, too, and more: that some of the arrowheads would scream and whistle furiously as they flew.

Tang took a turn again: "To be independent of the bok supplies, each warrior also carries one small earthenware pot for cooking, a small folding tent and two leather bottles. One is full of kumis, the other of grut, and on those he can subsist for a long time without weakening."

Fu added: "If he haply procures a piece of meat, he need not even pause to cook it, but tucks it between his saddle and his mount. As he rides, the pounding and the heat and the sweat cure the meat and make it edible."

Tang again: "If a warrior has no other nutriment, he will nourish himself and quench his thirst by drinking the blood of the first enemy he slays. He will also use that body's fat to grease his tack and weapons and armor."

Kubilai compressed his lips and fingered his mustache, in evident impatience, but the two Han said no more. With a trace of exasperation he muttered, "Numbers and details are all very well. But you have told me little that I have not known since I first straddled my own horse at the age of four. What of the mood and temper of the Ilkhan and his troops, uu?"

"No need to inquire privily into that, Sire," said Tang. "All men know that all Mongols are forever ready and eager to fight."

"To fight, yes, but to fight *whom,* uu?" the Khakhan persisted.

"At present, Sire," said Fu, "the Ilkhan uses his forces only for putting down bandits in his own Sin-kiang Province, and for petty skirmishes against the Tazhiks to secure his western borders."

"Hui!" said Kubilai, in a sort of pounce. "But is he doing those things merely to keep his fighting men occupied, uu? Or is he honing their skill and spirit for more ambitious undertakings, uu? Perhaps a rebellious thrust at *my* western borders, uu? Tell me that!"

Tang and Fu could only make respectful noises and shrugs to excuse their ignorance. "Sire, who can examine the inside of an enemy's head? Even the best spy can but observe the observable. The facts we brought we have gleaned with much perseverance, and much care that they be accurate, and at much hazard of our being discovered, which would have meant our being tied spread-eagle among four horses, and they whipped toward the four horizons."

Kubilai gave them a look of some disdain, and turned to my father and uncle. "You at least came face to face with my cousin, friends Polo. What did you make of him, uu?"

Uncle Mafìo said thoughtfully, "Certain it is that Kaidu is greedy for more than he has. And he is patently a man of bellicose temper."

"He is, after all, of the Khakhan's own family lineage," said my father. "It is an ancient truth: that a she-wolf does not drop lambs."

"Those things, too, I know very well," growled Kubilai. "Is there *no one* who has perceived more than the flagrantly obvious, uu?"

He had not put that "uu?" directly to me, but the question emboldened me to speak. Granted, I could more gracefully have imparted what I wanted to tell him. But I was still being scornful of what I took to have been his pose of cruel caprice when he made sure we heard his harsh sentences in the Cheng—hence I was still under the misapprehension that the Khan Kubilai was, in fondo, only an ordinary man. Perhaps also I had already imbibed rather too freely of the drinks dispensed by the serpent tree. Anyway, I spoke, and spoke somewhat more loudly than I need have done:

"The Ilkhan Kaidu called you decadent and effete and

degenerate, Sire. He said that you have become no better
than a Kalmuk."

Every person present heard me. Every person present
must have known what a squalid thing a Kalmuk is. An
instant and vast and appalled hush fell upon the whole
banquet hall. Every man stopped talking, and even the
strident Mongol women to suffocate in mid-gabble. My father and uncle covered their faces with their hands, and
the Wang Chingkim stared at me in utter horror, and the
Khakhan's sons and wives all gasped, and Tang and Fu
put trembling hands to their mouths, as if they had untimely laughed or belched, and all the other varicolored
faces within my view went uniformly pale.

Only the face of the Khan Kubilai did not go ashen. It
went maroon and murderous, and it began to contort as he
started framing words of condemnation and command.
Had he ever got those words out, I know now, he never
would have retracted them, and nothing would have miti-
gated my gross offense or moderated my condign sentence,
and the guards would have hauled me off to the Fondler,
and the manner of my execution must have become a legend in Kithai forevermore. But Kubilai's face kept on
working, as he evidently discarded one set of words as too
mild, and substituted another and another more terribly
damnatory, and that gave me time to finish what I wished
to say:

"However, when it thunders, Sire, the Ilkhan Kaidu invokes your name for protection against the wrath of
Heaven. He does it silently, under his breath, but I have
read your name upon his lips, Sire, and his own warriors
confided the same to me. If you doubt it, Sire, you could ask
the two of Kaidu's personal guardsmen that he sent as our
escort, the warriors Ussu and Donduk . . ."

My voice trailed off into the dreadful hush that still prevailed. I could hear droplets of kumis or pu-tao or some
other of the liquids dripping, plink, plunk, from a serpent
spout into a lion vase beneath. In that breathless, monumental quiet, Kubilai kept his black eyes impaling me, but
his face slowly ceased its contortions and became still as
stone, and the violent color slowly ebbed from it, and at
last he said, only in a murmur, but again all present
heard:

"Kaidu invokes my name when he is affrighted. By the

great god Tengri, that single observation is worth more to
me than six tomans of my best and fiercest and most loyal
horsemen.''

3

I awoke the next day, in the afternoon, in a bed in my father's chambers, with a head that I almost wished *had*
been lopped off by the Fondler. The last thing that I clearly
remembered of the banquet was the Khakhan's roaring to
the Wang Chingkim, "See to this young Polo! Appoint him
separate quarters of his own! And servants of twenty-two
karats!'' That had sounded fine, but to be given immobile
metal servants, even of nearly pure gold, did not make
much sense, so I assumed that Kubilai had been as drunk
as was I at the time, and Chingkim, and everybody else.

However, after my father's two women servants had
helped him and me to get up and get bathed and get
dressed, and had brought us each a potion to clear the
head—a spicy and aromatic drink, but so heavily laced
with mao-tai that I could not force it down—Chingkim
came calling, and father's servants fell down in ko-tou to
him. The Wang, looking as if he felt much the way I did,
gently booted the two prostrate bodies out of his way, and
told me he had come, as ordered, to conduct me to the new
suite prepared for my occupancy.

As we went there—no far distance along the same hall
that my father's and uncle's quarters opened onto—I
thanked Chingkim for the courtesy and, seeking to be polite even to a minor functionary assigned to serve me, I
added, "I do not know why the Khakhan should have ordered you to see to my comfort. After all, you are the Wang
of the city, and an official of some small importance.
Surely the palace guests should be a steward's responsibility, and this palace has as many stewards as a Buddhist
has fleas.''

He gave a laugh, only a small one, not to jar his own
head, and said, "I do not object to being given a trivial duty
now and then. My father believes that a man can only

learn to command others by learning himself to obey the least command."

"Your father seems to lean as heavily on wise proverbs as mine does," I said companionably. "Who is your father, Chingkim?"

"The man who gave me the order. The Khakhan Kubilai."

"Oh?" I said, as he bowed me through the doorway of my new quarters. "One of the bastards, are you?" I said offhandedly, as I might have spoken to the son of a Doge or a Pope, nobly born, but on the wrong side of the blanket. I was looking with appreciation at the doorway, for it was not rectangular in the Western style or peaked to an arch in the Muslim fashion. It and the others between my various rooms were called variously Moon Gate and Lute Gate and Vase Gate, because their openings were contoured in the outlines of those objects. "This is a sumptuous apartment."

Chingkim was regarding me with somewhat the same appraisal I was giving to the suite's luxurious appointments. He said quietly, "Marco Polo, you do have your own peculiar way of speaking to your elders."

"Oh, you are not that much older than I, Chingkim. How nice, these windows open onto a garden." Truly I was being very dense, but my head, as I have said, was not at its best. Also, at the banquet, Chingkim had not sat at the head table with Kubilai's legitimate sons. That recollection made me think of something. "I saw none of the Khakhan's concubines who looked old enough to have a son your age, Chingkim. Which of last night's women was your mother?"

"The one who sat nearest the Khakhan. Her name is Jamui."

I paid little attention, being occupied in the admiration of my bed-chamber. The bed was most lovelily springy, and it had a Western style pillow for me. Also—apparently in case I should invite a court lady to bed—it had one of the Han-style pillows, a sort of shallow pedestal of porcelain, itself molded in the form of a reclining woman, to prop up a lady's neck without disarranging her coiffure.

Chingkim went on chatting idly, "Those of Kubilai's sons who sat with him last night are Wangs of provinces and ortoks of armies, things like that."

For summoning my servants, there was a brass gong as big around as a Kashgar wagon wheel. But it was fashioned like a fish with a great round head, mostly a vast mouth, and only a stumpy brass body, for resonance, behind its wide opening.

"I was appointed Wang of Khanbalik," Chingkim prattled on, "because Kubilai likes to keep me near him. And he sat me at your table to do honor to your father and uncle."

I was examining a most marvelous lamp in my main room. It had two cylindrical paper shades, one inside the other, both fitted with paper blades inside their circumference, so that somehow the heat of the lamp flame made the shades slowly turn in opposite directions. They were painted with various lines and spots, and were translucent, so that their movement and the light within made the paints intermittently resolve themselves into a recognizable picture—and the picture *moved.* I later saw other such lamps and lanterns displaying different scenes, but this one of mine showed, over and over, a mule kicking up its heels and catching a little man in his backside and sending him flying. I was entranced.

"I am not Kubilai's eldest son, but I am the only son born to him by his premier wife, the Khatun Jamui. That makes me Crown Prince of the Khanate and Heir Apparent to my father's throne and title."

By that time, I was down on my knees, puzzling over the composition of the strange, flat, pale carpet on the floor. After close scrutiny, I determined that it was made of long strips of thin-peeled ivory, woven together, and I had never before seen or heard of any such wondrous artisanry as *woven ivory.* Since I was already kneeling—when Chingkim's words at last penetrated into my dismally dimmed mind—it was easy for me to slide prostrate and make kotou at the feet of the next Khan of All Khans of the Mongol Empire, whom I had a moment ago addressed as Bastard.

"Your Royal Highness . . . ," I began to apologize, speaking to the woven ivory on which my aching and sweating forehead was pressed.

"Oh, get up," the Crown Prince said affably. "Let us continue to be Marco and Chingkim. Time enough for titles when my father dies, and I trust that will not be for many years yet. Get up and greet your new servants. Biliktu and

Buyantu. Good Mongol maidens, whom I selected for you personally."

The girls made ko-tou four times to Chingkim and then four times to us both and then four times to me alone. I mumbled, "I expected to get statues."

"Statues?" echoed Chingkim. "Ah, yes. Twenty-two karat, these maidens. That grading system is of my father's devising. If you will command for me a goblet of head-clearing potion, we can sit down and I will explain about the karats."

I gave the command, and ordered cha for myself, and the two girls bowed their way backwards out of the room. From their names, and from what little I had glimpsed of them, Buyantu and Biliktu were sisters. They were about my own age, and far prettier than the other Mongol females I had seen so far—certainly much prettier than the middle-aged women who had been assigned to my father and uncle. When they came back with our drinks, and Chingkim and I sat down on facing benches, and the maids brought fans to fan us, I could see that they were twins, identical in comeliness and wearing identical costumes. I would have to direct them to dress differently, I thought, so I could tell them apart. And when they were undressed? That thought, too, came naturally to my mind, but I dismissed it, to listen to the Prince, who, after taking a long draft from his goblet, had begun to talk again.

"My father, as you know, has four wedded wives. Each in her turn receives him in her own separate yurtu, but—"

"Yurtu!" I interrupted.

He laughed. "So it is called, though no Mongol plainsman would recognize it. In the old nomad days, you see, a Mongol lord kept his wives dispersed about his territory, each in her own yurtu, so that wherever he rode he never had to endure a wifeless night. Now, of course, each wife's so-called yurtu is a splendid palace here in these grounds—and a populous place, more like a bok than a yurtu. Four wives, four palaces. And my mother's alone has a permanent staff of more than three hundred. Ladies-in-waiting and attendants and physicians and servants and hairdressers and slaves and wardrobe mistresses and astrologers . . . But I started out to tell you about the karats."

He broke off to touch a hand tenderly to his head, and swigged again from his goblet before going on:

"I think my father is now of an age that a mere four women in rotation would suffice him, even well-worn wives who are also getting on in years. But it is an ancient custom for all his subject lands—as far away as Poland and India Aryana—to send him each year the finest of their newly nubile maidens. He cannot possibly take them all as concubines, or even as servants, but neither can he disappoint his subjects by refusing their gifts outright. So he now has those annual crops of girls weeded down at least to a manageable number."

Chingkim emptied his goblet and handed it, without looking, over his shoulder, where Biliktu-or-Buyantu took it and scurried off.

"Each year," he resumed, "as the maidens are delivered to the various Ilkhans and Wangs in the various lands and provinces, those men examine the girls and assay them like so much gold bullion. Depending on the quality of a maiden's facial features and bodily proportions and complexion and hair and voice and grace of gait and so on, she is rated at fourteen karats—or sixteen or eighteen, as the case may be, and so on up. Only those above sixteen karats are sent on here to Khanbalik, and only those assayed at the fineness of pure unalloyed gold, twenty-four karats, have any hope of getting near the great Khakhan."

Though Chingkim could not have heard my maid's silent approach, he put up his hand and she arrived just in time to place the refilled goblet in his grasp. He appeared not at all surprised to receive it—as if he had naturally assumed it would be there—and he gulped from it and went on:

"Even those comparatively few maidens of twenty-four karats must first live for a while with older women here in the palace. The old women inspect them even more closely, especially their behavior in the nighttime. Do the girls snore in their sleep, or toss restlessly in the bed? Are their eyes bright and their breath sweet when they awaken in the morning? Then, on the old women's recommendations, my father will take a few of the girls as his concubines for the next year, others to be his maidservants. The rest of them he apportions out, according to their karat grade, to his lords and ministers and court favorites, according to their rank. Congratulate yourself, Marco, that you suddenly rank high enough to merit these twenty-two-karat virgins."

He paused, and laughed again. "I do not quite know *why* you do—unless it is your propensity for reviling your betters as Kalmuks and bastards. I hope all the other courtiers do not start imitating your style of address, and expect to emulate your rise to favor."

I cleared my throat and said, "You mentioned that the girls come from all lands. Had you any particular reason for selecting Mongols for me?"

"Again, my father's instructions. You already speak our tongue very well, but he desires that you achieve impeccable fluency. And it is a known fact that pillow talk is the best and quickest way to learn a language. Why do you ask? Would you have preferred some other breed of women?"

"No, no," I said hastily. "The Mongol is one breed of woman I have not yet had an opportunity to—er—assay. I look forward to the experience. I am honored, Chingkim."

He shrugged. "They are twenty-two karat. Near perfect." He sipped again at his drink, then leaned toward me to say seriously, speaking now in Farsi, that the maids might not eavesdrop, "There are many lords here, Marco, and older ones, and very high-ranking ones, who have never yet received better than a sixteen-karat regard from the Khan Kubilai. I suggest you keep that in mind. Any palace community is an anthill teeming with intrigues and plots and conspiracies, even at the level of page boys and kitchen scullions. It will rankle many in this court, that a young man like you is *not* consigned to that grubant level of pages and scullions. You are a newcomer and a Ferenghi, which would make you suspect enough, but abruptly and incomprehensibly you have been exalted. Overnight, you have become an interloper, a target for envy and spite. Believe me, Marco. No one else would give you this friendly warning, but I do, because I am the only one who can. Second only to my father, I am the one man in the entire Khanate who need not be fearful and jealous of his position. Everyone else must be—and so must see you as a threat. Be always on your guard."

"I believe you, Chingkim, and I thank you. Can you suggest any way I might make myself less of a target?"

"A Mongol horseman takes care never to ride on the sky-line of the hills, but always a little way below the crest."

I sat and considered that advice. Just then, there came a scratching noise from the hall door, and one of the maids glided away to answer it. I could not quite determine how I might stay off the skyline while resident inside a palace, unless perhaps I went about in a permanent posture of ko-tou. The maid came back into the room.

"Master Marco, it is a caller who gives his name as Sind-bad, and urgently entreats audience."

"What?" I said, preoccupied with skylines. "I am acquainted with no person named Sindbad."

Chingkim looked at me and raised his eyebrows, as if to say, "Already come the enemies?"

Then I shook my head and got it to working again, and said, "Oh, of course I know the man. Bid him come in."

He did, and rushed straight to me, looking distraught, wringing his hands, his eyes and central orifice wildly dilated. Without ko-tou or salaam, he bleated in Farsi, "By the seven voyages of my namesake, Master Marco, but this is a terrible place!"

I held up a hand to stop his saying something as indiscreet as I had several times done lately, and turned to say to Chingkim in the same language, "Allow me, Royal Highness, to introduce my slave Nostril."

"Nostril?" Chingkim murmured wonderingly.

Taking my hint, Nostril made a perfect ko-tou to the Prince and then to me, and said meekly, "Master Marco, I would beg a boon."

"You may speak in the Prince's presence. He is a friend. But why are you going about under an assumed name?"

"I have been seeking you everywhere, master. I used all my names, a different one to every person I asked. I thought it prudent, since I go in fear for my life."

"Why? What have you done?"

"Nothing, master! I swear it! I have been so well behaved for so long that Hell itches with impatience. I am spotless as a new-dropped lamb. But so were Ussu and Donduk. Master, I beg that you rescue me from that sty called a barrack. Let me come and lodge in your quarters. I ask not even a pallet. I will lay me down across your threshold like a watchdog. For the sake of all the times I saved your life, Master Marco, now save mine!"

"What? I do not recall your ever saving my life."

Chingkim looked amused and Nostril looked befuddled.

"Did I not? Some earlier master, perhaps. Well, if I have not, it was only for lack of opportunity. However, if and when some such dread opportunity occurs, it is best that I be near at hand and—"

I interrupted, "What about Ussu and Donduk?"

"That is what has terrified me, master. The frightful fate of Ussu and Donduk. They did nothing wrong, did they? Only escorted us from Kashgar to here, did they not, and performed capably in that duty?" He did not wait for a reply, but babbled on. "This morning a squad of guards came and manacled Donduk and dragged him away. Ussu and I, certain that some terrible mistake had been made, inquired around the barracks, and were told that Donduk was being *questioned.* After a while of worrying, we inquired again, and were told that Donduk had not satisfactorily answered the questions, so he was at that moment being *buried.*"

"Amoredèi!" I cried. "He is dead?"

"One hopes so, master; otherwise an even more terrible mistake has been made. Then, master, after a while the guards came again and manacled Ussu and dragged *him* away. After another while of wringing my hands, I inquired again about the two of them, and I was rudely told to inquire no more about matters of *torture.* Well, Donduk had been taken and slain and buried, and Ussu had been taken, and who else was there to torture but *me?* So I fled the barrack to come looking for you and—"

"Hush," I said. I turned to look a query at Chingkim.

He said, "My father is anxious to know all he can learn about his eternally restive cousin Kaidu. It was you who mentioned to him last night that your escorts were men of Kaidu's personal guard. No doubt my father assumes them to be well informed about their master—about any possible insurrection Kaidu may be planning." He paused and looked down into his goblet and said, "It is the Fondler who does the questioning."

"The Fondler?" Nostril murmured wonderingly.

I pondered, which hurt my head, and after a moment said to Chingkim, "It would be obtrusive of me to interfere in Mongol affairs that involve Mongols only. But I do feel in a measure responsible. . . ."

Chingkim drained his cup and stood. "Let us go and see the Fondler."

I would much rather have stayed in my new quarters all day, and nursed my head, and got acquainted with the twins Buyantu and Biliktu, but I went, and made Nostril come with us.

We went a long way, through enclosed passages and open areas and more passages, and then down some stairs that led underground, and then another long way through subterranean workshops full of busy artisans, and through storage cellars and lumber rooms and wine cellars. When Chingkim was leading us through a series of torch-lit but unpeopled chambers, their rock walls damp with slime and mottled with fungus, he paused to say in an undertone to Nostril, though surely meaning the advice for me, too:

"Do not again use the word torture, slave. The Fondler is a sensitive man. He resents and recoils from such rough terms. Even when a matter of importance necessitates his plucking out a person's eyeballs and putting hot coals in the sockets, it is never torture. Call it questioning, call it caressing, call it tickling—call it anything but torture—lest someday it is required that you be fondled by the Fondler and he remembers your disrespect of his profession."

Nostril only gulped loudly, but I said, "I understand. In Christian dungeons the practice is formally known as the Asking of the Question Extraordinaire."

Chingkim finally led us into a room that, except for its torch light and beslimed rock walls, might have been a counting room in a prosperous mercantile establishment. It was full of counting desks at which stood clerks busy with ledgers and documents and abachi and the petty routine of any well-run institution. This might be a human abattoir, but it was an orderly abattoir.

"The Fondler and all his staff are Han," Chingkim said to me aside. "They are so much better at these things than we."

Evidently even the Crown Prince did not demand entry straightaway into the Fondler's domain. We all waited until one of the Han clerks, the tall and austerely expressionless chief of those clerks, deigned to approach us. He and the Prince spoke for a time in the Han language, then Chingkim translated to me:

"The man called Donduk was first questioned, and with

propriety, but declined to betray anything he knew of his
master Kaidu. So then he was questioned extraordinarily,
as you put it, to the limits of the Fondler's ingenuity. But
he remained obdurate and so—as is my father's standing
order in such cases—he was relinquished to the Death of a
Thousand. Then the man Ussu was brought in. He also has
resisted both the questioning and the questioning extraordinary, and will also be accorded the Death of a Thousand.
They deserve it, of course, being traitors to their ultimate
ruler, my father. But"—he said this with some pride—
"they are loyal to their Ilkhan, and they are stubborn and
they are brave. They are true Mongols."

I said, "Pray, what is the Death of a Thousand? A thousand what?"

Chingkim said, again in an undertone, "Marco, call it
the death of a thousand caresses, a thousand cruelties, a
thousand endearments, what matter? Given a thousand of
anything, a man will die. The name only signifies a death
long drawn out."

He was plainly urging that I not pursue the matter, but I
did. I said, "I never held any affection for Donduk. Ussu,
though, was a more congenial companion on the long trail.
I should like to know how his long trail ends."

Chingkim made a face, but he turned to speak again to
the chief clerk. The man looked surprised and doubtful,
but he went out of the room by an iron-studded door.

"Only my father or I could even contemplate doing
this," muttered Chingkim. "And even I must convey to the
Fondler most fulsome compliments and abject apology for
interrupting him when he is actually engaged in his
work."

I expected the chief clerk to come back bringing a monstrous, shaggy brute of a man, broad of shoulder, brawny
of arm, beetling of brow, black-garbed like the Meatmaker
of Venice or all in Hellfire-red like the executioner of the
Baghdad Daiwan. But if the chief clerk had looked the picture of a clerk, the man who returned with him was the
very essence of clerkness. He was gray-haired and pale and
frail, fussy and fidgety of manner, prissily dressed in
mauve silks. He tripped across the room with small, precise steps, and he looked at us, despite his diminutive Han
nose, very much de haut en bas. He was a man born to be a

clerk. Surely, I thought, he cannot be other than that. But he spoke in the Mongol tongue, and said:

"I am Ping, the Fondler. What wish you of me?" His voice was tight, with the barely controlled and not at all concealed indignation that is the natural speech of a clerk interrupted in his clerking.

"I am Chingkim, the Crown Prince. I should like you, Master Ping, to explain to this honored guest of mine the manner of giving the Death of a Thousand."

The creature sniffed clerkishly. "I am not accustomed to requests of that indelicate nature, and I do not grant them. Also, the only honored guests here are my own."

Chingkim perhaps stood in awe of the Fondler's title of office, but he himself was entitled Prince. More than that, he was a Mongol being affronted by a mere Han. He drew himself up tall and rigid, and snarled:

"You are a public servant and we are the public! You are a civil servant and you will be civil! I am your Prince and you have arrogantly neglected to make ko-tou! Do so at once!"

The Fondler Ping flinched back as if we had pelted him with some of his own hot coals, and obediently fell down and did the ko-tou. All the other clerks in the chamber peered awestricken over their counting desks at what must have been a first-ever occurrence. Chingkim smoldered down at the prostrate man for some moments before bidding him to rise. When Ping did, he was suddenly all conciliation and solicitude, as is the way of clerks when someone has the temerity to bark at them. He fawned on Chingkim and expressed himself willing, nay, avid to fulfill the Prince's every least whim.

Chingkim said grumpily, "Just tell the Lord Marco here how the Death of a Thousand is administered."

"With pleasure," said the Fondler. He turned on me the same benign smile he had bestowed on Chingkim, and spoke in the same unctuous voice, but his eyes on me were snake cold and malevolent.

"Lord Marco," he began. (Actually he said Lahd Mahko, in the Han manner, but I eventually got so used to not hearing r's when a Han spoke that I will henceforth forbear from remarking on the fact.)

"Lord Marco, it is named the Death of a Thousand because it requires one thousand small pieces of silk paper,

folded and tossed haphazard in a basket. Each paper bears
a word or two, no more than three, signifying some part of
the human body. Navel or right elbow or upper lip or left
middle toe or whatever. Of course, there are not one thousand parts to the human body—at any rate, not one thousand capable of feeling sensation, like a fingertip, say, or
being caused cessation of function, like a kidney. To be precise, there are, by the traditional Fondler's Count, only
three hundred and thirty-six such parts. So the inscribed
papers are almost all in triplicate. That is to say, three
hundred and thirty-two parts of the body and thrice written on separate papers, making a total of nine hundred
and ninety-six. Are you following this, Lord Marco?''

"Yes, Master Ping."

"Then you will have noted that there are four parts of
the body not inscribed thrice on the papers. Those four are
written only once apiece, on the four papers remaining of
the thousand. I will later explain why—if you have not
guessed by then. Very well, we have one thousand inscribed and folded little papers. Every time a man or
woman is sentenced to the Death of a Thousand, before I
commence my attentions to the Subject, I have my assistants newly mix and toss and tumble those papers in the
basket. I do that mainly to reduce the likelihood of repetition in the Fondling, which might be unnecessarily distressing to the Subject or boring to me."

He really was a clerk at heart, I thought, with his finicking numbers and his calling the victim the Subject and his
lofty condescension to my interest in the matter. But I was
not fool enough to say so. Instead, I remarked respectfully:

"Excuse me, Master Ping. But all of this—this writing
and folding and tossing of papers—what has this to do with
death?"

"Death? It has to do with *dying!*" he said sharply, as if I
had strayed into irrelevance. Flicking a sly glance sideways at Prince Chingkim, he said, "Any crude barbarian
can kill a Subject. But artfully to lead and guide and
beckon and cajole a man or woman through the dying—ah,
for that, the Fondler!"

"I see," I said. "Please do go on."

"After having been purged and evacuated, to avert unseemly accidents, the Subject is securely but not uncomfortably tied erect between two posts, so that I can easily

do the Fondling at his or her front or back or side, as required. My work tray has three hundred and thirty-six compartments, each neatly labeled with the name of a bodily part, and in each reposes one or several instruments exquisitely designed to be used on that certain part. Depending on whether the part is of flesh or sinew or muscle or membrane or sac or gristle, the implements may be knives of certain shapes, or awls, probes, needles, tweezers, scrapers. The instruments are newly whetted and polished, and my assistants are ready—my Blotters of Fluids and Retrievers of Pieces. I commence by doing the traditional Fondler's Meditations. Thereby I attune myself not only to the Subject's fears, which are usually apparent, but also to his inmost apprehensions and deepest levels of response. The artful Fondler is the man who can very nearly feel the same sensations as his Subject. According to legend, the most perfect of all Fondlers was a long-ago *woman,* who could so closely attune herself that she would actually cry out and writhe and weep in unison with her Subject, and even plead with herself for mercy."

"Speaking of women—" said Nostril. All this time he had been standing, almost huddling for invisibility, behind me. But his ever lewd inquisitiveness must have overcome his timorousness. He spoke in Farsi to the Prince, "Women and men do differ, Prince Chingkim. You know . . . in their bodily parts . . . here and there. How do the Master Fondler's labels and implements reconcile those differences?"

The Fondler took a step backward and said, *"Who . . . is . . . this?"* with dainty revulsion, as he might have done if he had stepped on a street turd and it had had the effrontery to protest aloud.

"Forgive the slave's impertinence, Master Ping," Chingkim said smoothly. "But the question had occurred to me, too." He repeated it in Mongol.

The executioner sniffed clerkishly again. "The differences between male and female, as regards the Fondling, are merely superficial. If the folded paper reads 'red jewel,' that means the frontmost genital organ, of which there is a large one in the male, a tiny one in the female. If the paper reads 'jade gland,' left or right, it means the man's testicle or the woman's internal gonad. If it reads 'deep valley,' that literally means the woman's womb, but in the case of a man can be taken to mean his internal almond gland, the so-called third testicle."

Involuntarily, Nostril made an "ooh!" noise of pain. The Fondler glared at him.

"Now, *may* I proceed? After my Meditations, the proceeding goes thus. I select a paper from the basket, at random, and unfold it, and it tells me the part of the Subject destined for the first Fondling. Suppose it says left little finger. Do I simply step up to the Subject, as a butcher would do, and saw off his left little finger? No. Or what would I do if the identical paper came up again later? So the first time I may merely drive a needle deep under that finger's nail. The second time perhaps slice the finger to the bone all along its length. Only if it came up a third time would I lop the finger off entirely. Usually, of course, the second paper I select will direct me to a different part of the Subject—another extremity, or the nose, or the jade gland perhaps. However, given the triplication of the papers and the randomness of choice, it can occasionally happen that the same part will be called for twice in succession, but that does not occur too boringly often. And in all my career there has been just one single occasion when three papers in a row all named the exact same part of the Subject's body. Most unusual, that. Memorable. I later asked the Mathematician Lin-ngan to calculate for me the rarity of that having happened. As I remember, he said something like one chance in three million. Years ago, that was. Her left nipple, it was . . ."

There he seemed to drift off into a blissful contemplation of that time past. Then, after a moment, he came abruptly back to us.

"Perhaps you have begun to perceive the expertness required in the Fondling. One does not simply run back and forth, snatching up papers and then slicing bits off the Subject. No, I proceed only leisurely—very leisurely—back and forth, for the Subject must have ample time to appreciate each individual pain. And they must vary in nature—this time an incision, next a piercing, then a rasping, a burning, a mashing, and so on. Also, the wounds must vary in keenness, so that the Subject experiences not just an overall agony, but a multitude of separate pains that he can differentiate and *locate.* Here, an upper molar slowly wrenched out and a nail driven where it had been, up into the frontal sinus. There, his elbow joint cracking and crumbling in an ingenious slow vise of my own invention. Yonder, a red-hot metal probe inserted down his red jewel's inner canal—or delicately and repeatedly applied to the tender little bulb at the opening of *her* red jewel. And in between, perhaps, the skin flayed from the chest and peeled loose and hanging down like an apron."

I swallowed and asked, "How long does this go on, Master Ping?"

He gave a fastidious small shrug. "Until the Subject perishes. It is, after all, called the *Death* of a Thousand. But no one has ever died of dying, if you take my meaning. Therein lies my greatest art—the prolongation of that dying, and the ever increasing excrucation of it. To put it another way, no one has ever died of sheer pain. Even I am sometimes astonished at how much pain can be borne, and for how long. Also, I was a physician before I became the Fondler, so I never inadvertently inflict a mortal injury, and I know how to prevent a Subject's untimely death from blood loss or shock to his constitution. My assistant Blotters are adept at stanching blood flow and, if I am required to puncture a troublesome organ like the bladder, early on in the Fondling, my Retrievers are competent at replacing any plugs I have to take out."

"To put it another way, then," I said, mimicking his own words, "how long until the Subject perishes of those attentions?"

"It depends mainly on chance. On which of the folded papers, and in which order, chance puts into my hand. Do you believe in some god or gods, Lord Marco? Then presumably the gods regulate the papers' chance according to the magnitude of the Subject's crime and the severity of punishment it merits. Chance, or the gods, can guide my hand at any time to one of those four papers I earlier mentioned."

He raised his thin eyebrows at me. I nodded and said:

"I think I have guessed. There must be four vital parts of the body where a wound would cause quick death instead of slow dying."

He exclaimed, "The indigo dye is bluer than the indigo plant! Which is to say: the pupil exceeds the master." He smiled thinly at me. "An apt student, Lord Marco. You yourself would make a good—" I expected him to say Fondler, of course. I would not wish to be a Fondler, good or

not. I was perversely gratified when he said, "—a good
Subject, because all your apprehensions and perceptions
would be heightened by your intimate knowledge of the
Fondling. Yes, there are four spots—the heart, naturally,
and also one place in the spinal column and two places in
the brain—where an inserted blade or point causes death
quite instantaneously and, as far as one can tell, quite
painlessly. That is why they are written on only one paper
apiece, for if and when one of those papers comes to my
hand, the Fondling is finished. I always instruct the Subject to pray that it comes soon. He or she always does pray,
and eventually out loud, and sometimes very loudly indeed. The Subject's fond entertainment of that hope—
really a rather meager hope: four chances out of the
thousand—seems to add a certain extra refinement to his
or her agonies."

"Excuse me, Master Ping," Chingkim put in. "But you
still have not said how long the Fondling lasts."

"Again, it depends, my Prince. Aside from the incalculable factors of gods and chance, the duration depends on me.
If I am not overpressed by other Subjects waiting their
turn, if I can proceed at leisure, I may take an hour between picking up one paper and the next. If I put in a respectable working day of, say, ten hours, and if chance
dictates that we must go through almost every one of the
thousand folded papers, then the Death of a Thousand can
last for very near a hundred days."

"Dio me varda!" I cried. "But they tell me that Donduk
is already dead. And you only got him this morning."

"That Mongol, yes. He went deplorably quickly. His constitution had been rather impaired by the preliminary
questioning. But no need to commiserate with me, though
I thank you, Lord Marco. I am not unduly chagrined. I
have the other Mongol already secured for Fondling." He
sniffed once more. "Indeed, if you seek reason for commiseration, do so because you interrupted my Meditations."

I turned to Chingkim and, speaking Farsi for privacy,
demanded of him, "Does your father really decree these—
these hideous tortures? To be performed by this—this simpering enjoyer of other people's torments?"

Nostril, at my side, began to make meaningful and urgent plucks at my sleeve. The Fondler was at my other

side, so I did not see, as Nostril did, the man's glower of loathing, boring into me like one of his ghastly probes.

Chingkim manfully tried to subdue his own anger at me. Through clenched teeth he said, "Elder Brother," in the formal style of address, though he was the elder of us two. "Elder Brother Marco, the Death of a Thousand is prescribed only for a few of the most serious crimes. And of all capital crimes, treason leads the list."

I was hastily revising my estimate of his father. If Kubilai could decree such an unspeakable end for two of his fellow Mongols—two good warriors whose only crime had been loyalty to the Khakhan's own underchief Kaidu—then obviously I was wrong when I took his behavior in the Cheng to have been mere posturing to impress us visitors. Evidently Kubilai did not mean for the sentences he handed down to be cautionary or exemplary to others. He did not care one whit whether anyone else ever took note of them or not. (I might never have known the gruesome fate of Ussu and Donduk, so *this* was certainly not being done to impress our party.) The Khakhan simply exercised his absolute power absolutely. To criticize or question or deride his motives was suicidal—happily, I had done so only in the privacy of my head—and even to commend his actions would be needless and futile and ignored. Kubilai would do what he would do. Well, for me at least, this episode had been an exemplary one. From now on, as long as I was in the realms of the Khan of All Khans, I would walk lightly and speak softly.

But just this once, before I subsided into docility, I would make one attempt to change one thing.

"I told you, Chingkim," I said to him, "Donduk was no friend of mine, and he is gone in any case. But Ussu—I liked him, and it was my incautious words that put him down here, and he still lives. Can nothing be done to moderate his punishment?"

"A traitor must die the Death of a Thousand," Chingkim said stonily. But then he relented enough to say. "There is only one possible amelioration."

"Ah, you know of it, of course, my Prince," said the Fondler, with a smirk. To my surprise and horror, he spoke in perfect Farsi. "And you know the manner of arranging the amelioration. Well, my chief clerk handles that sort of transaction. If you will excuse me, Prince Chingkim, Lord Marco . . ."

He minced away across the room again, motioning for his chief clerk to attend upon us, and went out through the iron-studded door.

"What will be done?" I asked Chingkim.

He growled, "A bribe that is paid now and then, in these cases. Though never before by me," he added disgustedly. "Usually it is done by the Subject's family. They may bankrupt themselves and mortgage their whole future lives to scrape together the bribe. Master Ping must be one of the richest officials in Khanbalik. I hope my father never hears of this folly of mine; he would laugh me to scorn. And you, Marco, I suggest that you do not ask this sort of favor ever again."

The chief clerk sauntered over to us and raised his eyebrows in inquiry. Chingkim dug into a purse at his waist, and said in the roundabout Han way:

"For the Subject Ussu, I would pay the balance weight for the scales, to make the four papers ascend." He took out some gold coins and slipped them into the clerk's discreetly cupped hand.

I asked, "What does that mean, Chingkim?"

"It means that the four papers naming vital parts will be moved to the top of the basket, where the Fondler's hand is likely to pick them up soonest. Now come away."

"But how—?"

"It is all that *can* be done!" he gritted at me. "Now come, Marco!" Nostril was tugging at me, too, but I persisted. "How can we be sure it will be done? Can we trust the Fondler to do all that work—all those folded papers to be unfolded and read first—and all alike—"

"No, my lord," said the chief clerk, unbending for the first time, almost kindly, and speaking in Mongol for my benefit. "All the others of the thousand papers are colored red, which is the Han color signifying good fortune. Only those four papers are purple, which is the Han color of mourning. The Fondler always knows where those four papers lurk."

4

DURING the next several days, I was left on my own. I got
unpacked and settled into my private quarters—with the
help of Nostril, for I let the slave move in and lay his pallet
in one of my more commodious closets—and I began to get
acquainted with the twins Biliktu and Buyantu, and I began to learn my way around that central palace building
and the rest of the edifices and gardens and courtyards
that constituted the palace city-within-a-city. But I will
speak later of how I spent my private time, because my
working time also soon began.

One day a palace steward came to bid me attend upon
the Khan Kubilai and the Wang Chingkim. The Khakhan's suite was not far from my own, and I went there with
celerity, but not with much alacrity, for I assumed that he
had learned of our visit to the dungeons and was going to
castigate me and Chingkim for our having meddled in the
Fondler's business. However, when I got there, and was
bowed through a succession of luxurious chambers by a
succession of attendants and secretaries and armed guards
and beautiful women, and arrived at last in the Khakhan's
innermost sitting room, and started my ko-tou, and was
bidden to take a seat, and was offered my choice of beverages from a maid's tray laden with decanters, and took a
goblet of rice wine, the Khakhan began the interview amiably enough, inquiring:

"How go your language lessons, young Polo?"

I tried not to blush, and murmured, "I have acquired numerous new words, Sire, but not of the kind I could speak
in your august presence."

Chingkim said drily, "I did not think there were any
words, Marco, that you would hesitate to speak in any
place."

Kubilai laughed. "I had intended to converse politely for
a while in the Han manner, rambling only indirectly to the
subject at hand. But my rude Mongol son comes straight to
the point."

"I have already made a vow to myself, Sire," I said,
"that I will henceforth be careful of my too ready tongue
and too abrupt opinions."

He considered that. "Well, yes, you might be more re-

spectfully circumspect in your choice of words before you
blurt them out. But I shall want your opinions. It is for
those that I would have have you become fluent and precise in our language. Marco, look yonder. Do you know
what that thing is?"

He indicated an object in the center of the room. It was a
giant bronze urn, standing some eight feet high and about
half that in diameter. It was richly engraved, and on the
outside of it clung eight lithe and elegant bronze dragons,
their tails curled at the top rim of the urn, their heads
downward near its base. Each one held in its toothed jaws
an immense and perfect pearl. There were eight bronze
toads squatting around the urn's pedestal, one under each
dragon, its mouth gaping as if eager to snatch the pearl
above.

"It is an impressive work of art, Sire," I said, "but I have
no idea of its function."

"That is an earthquake engine."

"Sire?"

"This land of Kithai is now and again shaken by earth
tremors. Whenever one occurs, that engine informs me of
it. The thing was designed and cast by my clever Court
Goldsmith, and only he fully understands the workings of
it. But somehow an earthquake, even if it is so far away
from Khabalik that none of us here can feel it, makes the
jaws of one of the dragons to open, and he drops his pearl
into the maw of the toad beneath. Tremors of other sorts
have no effect. I have stamped and jumped and danced all
about that urn—and I am no butterfly—but it ignores me."

I saw in my mind the majestic Great Khan of All Khans
bouncing about the chamber like an inquisitive boy, his
rich robes billowing and his beard wagging and his hel-
met-crown askew, and probably all his ministers goggling.
But I remembered my vow, and I did not smile.

He said, "According to which pearl drops, I know the direction where the earth shook. I cannot know how distant
it was, or how devastating, but I can dispatch a troop at the
gallop in that direction, and eventually they will bring me
word of the damage and casualties incurred."

"A miraculous contrivance, Sire."

"I could wish that my human informants were as succinct and reliable in reporting the occurrences in my domains. You heard those Han spies of mine, that night at

the banquet, rattling off numbers and items and tabulations, and telling me nothing."

"The Han are infatuated with numbers," said Chingkim. "The five constant virtues. The five great relationships. The thirty positions of the sex act, and the six ways of penetration and the nine modes of movement. They even regulate their politeness. I understand they have three hundred rules of ceremony and three *thousand* rules of behavior."

"Meanwhile, Marco," said Kubilai, "my other informants—my Muslim and even Mongol officials—they tend to leave out of their reports any fact they think I might find inconvenient or distressing. I have a large realm to administer, but I cannot personally be everywhere at once. As a wise Han counselor once said: you can conquer on horseback, but to rule you must get down from the horse. So I depend heavily on reports from afar, and they too often contain everything but the necessary."

"Like those spies," Chingkim put in. "Send them to kitchen to see about tonight's dinner soup, and they would report its quantity and density and ingredients and coloration and aroma and the volume of steam it throws off. They would report everything except whether it tastes good or not."

Kubilai nodded. "What struck me at the banquet, Marco —and my son agrees—is that you appear to have a talent for discerning the taste of things. After those spies had talked interminably, you said only a few words. True, they were not very tactful words, but they told me the taste of the soup brewing in Sin-kiang. I should like to verify that seeming talent of yours, in order to make further use of it."

I said, "You wish me to be a spy, Sire?"

"No. A spy must blend into the locality, and a Ferenghi could hardly do that anywhere in my domains. Besides, I would never ask a decent man to take up the trade of sneak and tattler. No, I have other missions in mind. But to undertake them you must first learn many things besides fluency of language. They will not be easy things. They will demand much time and effort."

He was looking keenly at me, as if to see whether I flinched from the prospect of hard work, so I made bold to say:

"The Khakhan does me great honor if he asks only

drudgery of me. So much greater the honor, Sire, if the drudgery is a preparation for some task of significance."

"Be not too eager to accede. Your uncles, I hear, are planning some trading enterprises. That should be easier work, and profitable, and probably more safe and secure than what I may require of you. So I give you permission to stay in association with your uncles, if you prefer."

"Thank you, Sire. But if I valued only safety and security I would not have left home."

"Ash, yes. It is truly said: He who would climb high must leave much behind."

Chingkim added, "It is also said: For a man of fortitude there are nowhere any walls, only avenues."

I decided I would ask my father if it was here in Kithai that he had got crammed so full of proverbs that he continually overflowed.

"Let me say this, then, young Polo," Kubilai went on. "I would not ask you to puzzle out for me how that earthquake engine performs its function—and that would be a difficult task enough—but I will ask of you something even harder. I wish you to learn as much as you can about the workings of my court and my government, which are infinitely more intricate than the insides of that mysterious urn."

"I am at your command, Sire."

"Come here to this window." He led the way to it. Like those in my quarters, it was not of transparent glass, but of the shimmery, only translucent Muscovy glass, set in a much curlicued frame. He unlatched it, swung it open and said, "Look there."

We were looking down onto a considerable extent of the palace grounds which I had not yet visited, for this part was still under construction, only an expanse of yellow earth littered with piles of wall stones and paving stones and barrows and tools and gangs of sweating slaves and—

"Amoredèi!" I exclaimed. "What are those gigantic beasts? Why do their horns grow so oddly?"

"Foolish Ferenghi, those are not horns, those are the tusks from which come ivory. That animal, in the southern tropics where it comes from, is called a gajah. There is no Mongol word for it."

Chingkim supplied the Farsi word, "Fil," and I knew that one.

"Elephants!" I breathed, marveling. "Of course! I have seen a drawing of one, but the drawing cannot have been very good."

"Never mind the gajah," said Kubilai. "Do you see what they are piling up?"

"It looks like a great mountain of kara blocks, Sire."

"It is. The Court Architect is building for me an extensive park out there, and I instructed him to put a hill in it. I have also instructed him to plant much grass on it. Have you seen the grass in my other courtyards?"

"Yes, Sire."

"You remarked nothing distinctive about it?"

"I fear not, Sire. It looked just like the same grass we have traveled through, for countless thousands of li."

"That is its distinction—that it is not an ornamental garden growth. It is the simple, ordinary, sweet grass of the great plains where I was born and grew up."

"I am sorry, Sire, but if I am supposed to draw some lesson from this . . ."

"My cousin the Ilkhan Kaidu told you that I had degenerated to something less than a Mongol. In a sense, he was right."

"Sire!"

"In a sense. I did get down from my horse to do the ruling of these domains. In doing so, I have found admirable many things of the cultured Han, and I have embraced them. I try to be more mannerly than uncouth, more diplomatic than demanding, more of an ordained emperor than an occupying warlord. In all those ways, I have changed from being a Mongol of Kaidu's kind. But I do not forget or repudiate my origins, my warrior days, my Mongol blood. That hill says it all."

"I regret, Sire," I said, "that the example still eludes my understanding."

He said to his son, "Explain it, Chingkim."

"You see, Marco, the hill will be a pleasure park, with terraces and walks and willowed waterfalls and comely pavilions cunningly set here and there. The whole thing will be an ornament to the palace grounds. In that, it is very Han, and reflects our admiration of Han art. But it will be more. The Architect could have mounded it of the local yellow earth, but my Royal Father commanded kara. The burnable rock will probably never be needed, but just in

case this palace should ever come under siege, we will
have there an unlimited supply of fuel. That is a warrior's
thinking. And the whole hill, roundabout the buildings
and streams and flower beds, will be greened over by
plains grass. A living reminder to us of our Mongol heritage."

"Ah!" I said. "Now it all is clear."

"The Han have a concise proverb," said Kubilai. "Bai
wen buru yi jian. To hear tell a hundred times is not as
good as once seeing. You have seen. So now let me speak of
another aspect of rulership."

We returned to our seats. In response to some inaudible
summons, the maidservant glided in and refilled our goblets.

The Khakhan resumed, "There are times when I, too—
like you, Marco Polo—can taste the attitudes of other people. You have expressed your willingness to join my
retinue, but I wonder if I taste in you a lingering trace of
your disapprobation."

"Sire?" I said, quite jolted by his bluntness. "Who am I,
Sire, to disapprove of the Khan of All Khans? Why, even
for me to approve would be presumptuous."

He said, "I was informed of your visit to the Fondler's
cavern." I must have cast an involuntary glance, for he
went on, "I am aware that Chingkim was with you, but it
was not he who told. I gather that you were dismayed by
my treatment of Kaidu's two men."

"I might have hoped, Sire, that their treatment had
been a little less extreme."

"You do not tame a wolf by pulling one of his teeth."

"They had been my companions, Sire, and they did nothing lupine during that time."

"On arrival here, they were hospitably quartered with
my own palace guards. A Mongol trooper is not ordinarily
garrulous, but those two asked a great many and very
searching questions of their barrackmates. My men answered only evasively, so those two would not have taken
much intelligence home with them, anyway. You knew
that I had sent spies into Kaidu's lands. Did you think him
incapable of doing the same?"

"I did not know—" I gasped. "I did not think—"

"As ruler of a far-spread empire, I must rule over a considerable diversity of peoples, and try to bear in mind their

peculiarities. The Han are patient and devious, the Persians are couched lions and all other Muslims are rabid sheep, the Armeniyans are blustering grovelers, and so on. I may not always deal with all of them as I ought. But the Mongols I understand very well. There I must rule with an iron hand, for in them I rule an iron people."

"Yes, Sire," I said weakly.

"Have you reservations about my treatment of any others?"

"Well," I said, for it seemed he already knew, "I thought—that day in the Cheng—you dismissed those starving Ho-nan farmers rather brusquely."

Just as brusquely now, he said, "I do not help those in trouble who snivel for help. I prefer to reward those who survive the trouble. Any man who must be *kept* alive is generally not worth the keeping. When people are stricken with either a sudden calamity or a long siege of misfortune, the best and most worthwhile will survive. The remainder are dispensable."

"But were they asking for a favor, Sire, or only a fair chance?"

"In my experience, when a runt piglet squeals for a fair chance at the teat, he really means a head start. Think about it."

I thought about it. My thoughts took me a long way back in time—to when I was a child, and was trying to help the survival of the boat children. The pinched, pretty face of little Doris came to my memory.

I said, "Sire, when you speak of feckless, sniveling men and women, no one could disagree. But starving children?"

"If they are the offspring of the dispensable, they too are dispensable. Realize this, Marco Polo. Children are the most easily and cheaply renewed resource in the world. Cut down a tree for timber; it takes nearly a lifetime to replace. Dig kara from the ground for burning; it is gone forever. But if a child is lost in a famine or flood, what is required for its replacement? A man and a woman and less than a year's time. If the man and woman are the strong and capable who have defied the disaster, the better the replacement child is likely to be. Have you ever killed a man, Marco Polo?"

I blinked and said, "Yes, Sire, I have."

"Good. A man better deserves the space he occupies on this earth if he has cleared that space for his occupancy. There is only *so much* space on this earth, only so much game to hunt and grass for pasturage and kara to burn and wood to build with. Before we Mongols took Kithai, there were one hundred million people living here, the Han and their related races. Now there are only half that many, according to my Han counselors, who are anxious for their countrymen to multiply again. If I will relax some of my strictures, they say, the population will soon again be what it was. They assure me that a single mou of land is sufficient to feed and support an entire Han family. To which I retort: would that family not feed better if it had two mou of land? Or three, or five? The family would be better nourished, healthier, probably happier. The sad fact is that the fifty or so million who perished in the years of conquest were mostly the best of the Han—the soldiers, the young and strong and vital. Should I now let them be replaced with mere indiscriminate *spawning?* No, I will not. I think the former rulers here liked to count heads only, and boast that they ruled great swarming numbers. I had rather boast that I rule a populace of quality, not quantity."

"You would be envied by many other rulers, Sire," I murmured.

"As to my manner of ruling them, let my say this. I am again unlike Kaidu in that I can recognize some limitations in us Mongols, and some superiorities in other nationalities. We Mongols excel in action, in ambition, in the dreaming of bold dreams and the making of grand plans—and in military affairs, most certainly. So for my ministers of overall administration I have mostly Mongols. But the Han know their own country and countrymen best, so I have recruited many Han for my ministries dealing with Kithai's internal management. The Han are also incredibly adept in matters mathematical."

"Like the regulation of the thirty sexual postures," said Chingkim, with a laugh.

"However," Kubilai went on, "the Han would naturally cheat me if I put them in charge of revenues. So for those offices I have Muslim Arabs and Persians, who are almost the equal of the Han when it comes to finances. I have let the Muslims establish what they call an Ortaq, a net of

Muslim agents dispersed over all Kithai to supervise its
trade and commerce. They are very good at exploiting the
material resources of this land the talents of its natives. So
I let the Muslims do the squeezing and I take a specified
share of the Ortaq's profits. That is much easier for me
than to levy a multitude of separate taxes on separate
products and transactions. Vakh, I have enough trouble
collecting the simple land and property taxes due me from
the Han."

I asked, "Do not the natives chafe at having outlanders
supervising them?"

Chingkim said, "They have always had outlanders over
them, Marco. The Han emperors long ago devised an admirable system. Every magistrate and tax collector, every
provincial official of every sort, was always sent to serve
somewhere other than his birthplace, to ensure that in his
duties and dealings and gouges he would not favor his relatives. Also, he was never let to serve more than three years
in any post before being moved on somewhere else. That
was to ensure his not making close friends and cronies
whom he might favor. So in any province, town or village,
the natives always had outsiders governing. Probably they
find our Muslim minions only a trifle more foreign."

I said, "Besides Arabs and Persians, I have seen men of
other nationalities around the palace."

"Yes," said the Khakhan. "For lesser officers of the
court—the Winemaster, the Firemaster, the Goldsmith
and such—I simply install the men who perform those
functions most ably, whether they be Han, Muslims, Ferenghi, Jews, whatever."

"It all sounds most sensible and efficient, Sire."

"You are to ascertain whether that is so. You are to do it
by exploring the chambers and halls and counting rooms
from which the Khanate is administered. I have instructed
Chingkim to introduce you to every official and courtier of
every degree, and he will instruct them to speak freely to
you of their offices and duties. You will be paid a liberal
stipend, and I will set an hour each week when you will report to me. Thus I will judge how well you are learning
and, more important, how well you are perceiving the *taste*
of things."

"I will do my best, Sire," I said, and Chingkim and I

made the perfunctory ko-tou, we were permitted, and we
left the room.

I had already determined that, with my first report to
the Khakhan after my very first week of employment, I
would make sure to astonish him—and I did. When I called
upon him the next time, a week or so later, I said:

"I will show you, Sire, how the earthquake engine
works. You see—here—suspended down the throat of the
vase is this heavy pendulum. It is daintily hung, but it
does not move, no matter how much jumping or banging
goes on in this room. Only if the whole great urn trembles,
which is to say the whole ponderous weight of this palace
building, then does that trembling make the pendulum
seem to move. In reality, it hangs steady and still, and its
apparent slight displacement is caused by the imperceptible quiver of its container. Thus, when a remote earthquake sends the least tremor through the earth and the
palace and the floor and the vase, that tremor leans the
pendulum's pressure against one of these delicate linkages—you see, there are eight—and thereby loosens the
hinged jaw of one of the dragons sufficiently that it lets go
of its pearl."

"I see. Yes. Very clever, my Court Goldsmith. And you,
too, Marco Polo. You apprehended that the haughty Khakhan would never demean himself to confess ignorance to a
mere smith and plead for an explanation. So you did it in
my stead. Your taste perception is still very good."

5

BUT those gratifying words came later. On the day Chingkim and I left his Royal Father's presence, the Prince said
cheerfully to me, "Well? Which high or lowly courtier
would you like to interrogate first?" And when I requested
audience with the Court Goldsmith, he said, "Curious
choice, but very well. That gentleman is often in his noisy
forge, which is no place for talking. I will see that he
awaits us in his quieter studio workshop. I will call for you
in an hour."

So I went then to the suite of my own father, to tell him

of my new situation. I found him sitting and being fanned
by one of his women servants. He waved toward an inner
room and said, "Your Uncle Mafìo is in yonder, closeted
with some Han physicians we knew when we were here before. Having them appraise his physical condition."

I sat down to share the being fanned, and I told him all
that had transpired during my interview with the Khan
Kubilai, and asked if I had his parental permission to turn
courtier instead of trader for a while.

"By all means," he said warmly. "And I congratulate
you on having won the Khakhan's esteem. Your new situation, far from depriving me and your uncle of your active
partnership, should redound to our good. A very apt illustration of the old proverb: chi fa per sè fa per tre."

I echoed, "Do for myself and I will do for all three? Then
you and Uncle Mafìo plan to stay in Kithai for a time?"

"Indeed, yes. We are traveling traders, but we have been
traveling for long enough; now we are eager to start trading. We have already applied to the Finance Minister Achmad for the necessary licenses and franchises to deal with
the Muslims' Ortaq. In that and other matters, Mafìo and
I may benefit from having you now as a friend at court.
Surely you did not think, Marco, that we came all this way
to turn right around."

"I thought your prime concern was to take back to Venice the maps of the Silk Road and start to spur the East–
West trade in general."

"Ah, well, as to that, we believe our Compagnia Polo
ought to enjoy first advantage of the Silk Road before we
throw it open to competition. Also, we ought to set a good
example, to fire enthusiasm in the West. So we will stay
here while we earn an estimable fortune, and send it home
as it accumulates. With those riches, your Marègna Fiordelisa can dazzle the stay-at-homes and whet their appetite. Then, when we finally do go home, we will freely
proffer our maps and experience and advice to all our
confratelli in Venice and Constantinople."

"A fair plan, Father. But is it not likely to take a long
time—to work up to a fortune from a very meager beginning? You and Uncle Mafìo have no trading capital except
our cods of musk and whatever zafràn still remains."

"The most fortunate of all merchants in the legends of
Venice, the Jew Nascimbene, set forth with nothing to his

name but a cat he picked up from the street. The fable tells
that he landed in a kingdom overrun with mice, and by
hiring out his cat he founded his fortune."

"There may be plenty of mice here in Kithai, Father, but
there are also plenty of cats. Not least among the cats, I
think, are the Muslims of the Ortaq. From what I have
heard, they may be voracious."

"Thank you, Marco. As the saying goes, a man warned is
already armed. But we are not starting quite so small as
did Nascimbene. In addition to our musk, Mafio and I have
also the investment we left on deposit here during our
earlier visit."

"Oh? I did not know."

"Quite literally on deposit—planted in the ground. You
see, we brought crocus culms on that journey, too. Kubilai
kindly granted us a tract of farmland in the province of Ho-
pei, where the climate is benign, and a number of Han
slaves and overseers, whom we instructed in the methods
of cultivation. According to report, we have now a quite extensive crocus plantation and already a fair stock of zafràn
pressed into bricks or dried into hay. That commodity
being still a novelty throughout the East, and we having a
monopoly—well!"

I said admiringly, "I should have known better than to
worry about your prospects. God help the Muslim cats if
they try to pounce upon Venetian mice."

He smiled and oozed another proverb, "It is better to be
envied than consoled."

"Bruto scherzo!" came a bellow from the inner room, and
our colloquy was interrupted. We heard several raised
voices, loudest among them Uncle Mafìo's, and other
noises, from which it seemed that furniture and things
were being thrown about and smashed, to the accompaniment of my uncle's shouted curses in Venetian, Farsi,
Mongol and perhaps some other languages. "Scarabazze!
Badbu qassab! Karakurt!"

As if they had been flung, three elderly Han gentlemen
flew out through the curtains of the room's Vase Gate.
Without a nod to me or my father, they continued their
rapid progress across the room, running for dear life, and
on out of the suite. After their swift passage, Uncle Mafìo
burst out through the curtains, still erupting scandalous
profanity. His eyes were glaring, his beard bristling like

quills, and his clothes were disarranged where evidently the physicians had been examining him.

"Mafìo!" my father said in alarm. "What in the world has happened?"

Alternately shaking his fist and stabbing the vulgar gesture of the figa in the direction of the already departed doctors, my uncle continued roaring epithets of description and suggestion. "Fottuti! Pedarat namard! Che ghe vegna la giandussa! Kalmuk, vakh!"

My father and I took hold of the agitated man and gently eased him down to a seat, saying, "Mafìo!" and "Uncle!" and "Ste tranquilo!" and "What in God's name has happened?"

He snarled, "I do not wish to speak of it!"

"Not speak?" my father said mildly. "You have already waked echoes as far as Xan-du."

"Merda!" my uncle grunted, and sulkily began rearranging his clothes.

I said, "I will see if I can catch the doctors and ask them."

"Oh, never mind!" growled Uncle Mafìo. "I might as well tell." He did, and interspersed the explanation with exclamations. "You recall the malady with which I was afflicted? Dona Lugia!"

"Yes, of course," said my father. "But I believe it was called the kala-azar."

"And you remember the Hakim Mimdad's prescription of stibium, which would save my life but cost my balls? Which it did, sangue de Bacco!"

"Of course," said my father again. "What is it, Mafìo? Did the physicians find that you have taken a turn for the worse?"

"Worse, Nico? What could be *worse?* No! The damned scataroni have just informed me, in honeyed words, that I never had to take the damned stibium at all! They say they could have cured the kala-azar simply by having me eat mildew!"

"Mildew?"

"Well, some kind of green mold that grows in empty old millet bins. That treatment would have restored me to health, they say, with no ugly side effect. I need never have shriveled my pendenti! Is it not nice to hear this *now?* Mildew! Porco Dio!"

"No, it cannot be very pleasant to hear."

"Need the the damned scataroni have told me at all? Now that it is too late? Mona Merda!"

"It was not very tactful of them."

"The damned saptuèli simply wanted me to know that they are superior to the backwoods charlatan who castrated me! Aborto de natura!"

"There is an old saying, Mafìo. This world is like a pair of shoes that—"

"Bruto barabào! *Shut up, Nico!*"

Looking pained, my father withdrew into the other room. I could hear him picking up and straightening things in there. Uncle Mafìo sat and simmered and fizzed like a kettle on slow boil. But finally he looked up, caught my eye, and said more calmly:

"I am sorry, Marco, for the display of temper. I know I said once that I would regard my predicament with resignation. But now to learn that the predicament was unnecessary . . ." He ground his teeth. "I hope I may rot if I can decide which is worse, being a eunuch or knowing I need not have been."

"Well . . ."

"If you tell me a proverb, I will break your neck."

So I sat silent for a while, wondering how best to express my sympathy and at the same time suggest that his diminishment might not be totally deplorable. Here among the manly Mongols, his formerly perverse tendencies would not be so tolerantly accepted as they had been, for example, in the Muslim countries. If he were still subject to the urge to fondle some man or boy, he might well find himself being caressed by the Fondler. But how was I to say so? Prepared to dodge a blow of his still-knotted fist, I cleared my throat and tried:

"It seems to me, Uncle Mafìo, that almost every time I have strayed into serious trouble or embarrassment, it was my candelòto that lit the way. I would not, on that account, willingly forfeit the candelòto and the pleasures it more often affords me. But I think, if I were deprived of it, I could more easily be a good man."

"You think that, do you?" he said sourly.

"Well, of all the priests and monks I have known, the most admirable were those who took seriously their vow of celibacy. I believe it was because they had closed their senses to the distractions of the flesh that they could concentrate on being good."

"O merda o beretta rossa. You believe that, do you?"

"Yes. Look at San Agostino. In his youth he prayed, 'Lord, make me chaste, but not just yet.' He knew very well where evil lay lurking. So he was anything *but* a saint, until finally he did renounce the temptations of—"

"Chiava el santo!" raged Uncle Mafìo, the most terrible thing he had yet uttered.

After a moment, when no thunderbolt had sizzled down at us, he said in a more temperate but still grim voice:

"Marco, I will tell you what I believe. I believe that your beliefs, if not puling hypocrisy, are exactly backward. There is no difficulty in being good. Every man and woman of mankind is as evil as he or she is capable of being and dares to be. It is the less capable, more timorous persons who are called good, and then only by default. The least capable, most fainthearted of all are called saints, and then usually first by themselves. It is easier to proclaim, 'Look at me, I am a saint, for I have fastidiously withdrawn from striving with bolder men and women!' than to say honestly, 'I am incapable of prevailing in this wicked world and I fear even to try.' Remember that, Marco, and be bold."

I sat and tried to think of an adequate riposte that would not sound simply sanctimonious. But, seeing that he had subsided into muttering to himself again, I rose and quietly took my leave.

Poor Uncle Mafìo. He seemed to be arguing, first, that his abnormal nature had been no infirmity, but a superiority merely unrecognized in a mediocre world and, second, that he might have made the purblind world acknowledge that superiority, if only he had not been untimely cheated of it. Well, I have known many people, unable to hide some gross deficiency or imperfection, try instead to flaunt it as a blessing. I have known the parents of a deformed or witless child to drop its baptismal name and call it "Christian," in the pathetic pretense that the Lord predestined it for Heaven and so deliberately made it ill-equipped for life. I could be sorry for cripples, but I would never believe that giving a blemish a noble name made it either an ornament or a noble blemish.

I went to my own chambers, and found the Wang Ching-

kim already waiting, and he and I went together to the distant palace building where was the studio of the Court
Goldsmith.

"Marco Polo—the Master Pierre Boucher," said Chingkim, introducing us, and the Goldsmith smiled cordially
and said, "Bon jour, Messire Paule," and I do not recall
what I said, for I was much surprised. The young man, no
older than myself, was the first real Ferenghi I had met
since leaving home—I mean to say, a genuine Frank, a
Frenchman.

"Actually, I was born in Karakoren, the old Mongol capital," he told me, speaking an amalgam of Mongol and
half-forgotten French, as he showed me about the workshop. "My parents were Parisians, but my father Guillaume was Court Goldsmith to King Bela of Hungary, so
he and my mother were taken prisoner by the Mongols
when the Ilkhan Batu conquered Bela's city of Buda. They
were brought captive to the Khakhan Kuyuk at
Karakoren. But when the Khakhan recognized my father's talent, alors, he entitled him Maître Guillaume and
raised him to the court, and he and my mother lived happily in these lands for all the rest of their lives. So have I,
having been born here, during the reign of the Khakhan
Mangu."

"If you are so well regarded, Pierre," I said, "and a freeman, could you not resign from the court and go back to the
West?"

"Ah, oui. But I doubt that I could live as well there as
here, for my talent is somewhat inferior to my late father's. I am competent enough in the arts of gold and silver
work and the cutting of gemstones and the fabrication of
jewelry, mais voilà tout. It was my father who made most
of the ingenious contrivances you will see around the palace here. When I am not making jewelry, my chief responsibility is to keep those engines in good repair. So the
Khakhan Kubilai, like his predecessor, favors me with
privilege and largesse, and I am comfortably situated, and
I am about to marry an estimable Mongol lady of the court,
and I am quite content to abide."

At my request, Pierre explained the workings of the
earthquake engine in the Khakhan's chambers—which, as
I have told, enabled me later to impress Kubilai. However,
Pierre refused, with good humor but with firmness, to sat-

isfy my curiosity about the banquet hall's drink-dispensing serpent tree and animated gold peacocks.

"Like the earthquake urn, they were invented by my father, but they are considerably more complex. If you will forgive my obstinacy, Marco—and Prince Chingkim"—he made a little French bow to each of us—"I will keep secret the workings of the banquet engines. I like being the Court Goldsmith, and there are many other artisans who would like to take my place. Since I am only an outlander, vous savez, I must guard what advantage I possess. As long as there are at least a few contrivances which only I can keep in operation, I am safe against usurpers."

The Prince smiled understandingly and said, "Of course, Master Boucher."

So did I, and then I added, "Speaking of the banquet hall, I wondered at another thing there. Though the hall was crowded, the air never got stale, but stayed cool and fresh. Is that done by some other apparatus of yours, Pierre?"

"Non," he said. "That is a very simple affair, devised long ago by the Han, and presently in the charge of the Palace Engineer."

"Come, Marco," said Chingkim. "We can pay him a visit. His workshop is very near."

So we said au revoir to the Court Goldsmith, and went on our way, and I was next introduced to one Master Wei. He spoke only Han, so Chingkim repeated my query about the banquet hall's ventilation, and translated to me the Engineer's explanation.

"A very simple affair," he said also. "It is well-known that cool air from below will always displace warm air above. There are cellars beneath all the palace buildings, and passages connecting them. Under each building is a cellar room used only as a repository for ice. We are continuously supplied with ice blocks cut by slaves in the ever cold northern mountains, wrapped in straw and brought here by swift-traveling trains. At any time, by the judicious opening of doors and passages here and there, I can make breezes waft the ice stores' coolness wherever it is wanted, or shut it off when it is not."

Without my asking, Master Wei went on to boast of some other devices under his control.

"By the agency of a waterwheel of Han design, some of

the water from the gardens' decorative streams is diverted
and forced into tanks under the peaks of all the palace
buildings' roofs. From each tank the water can be loosed,
at my direction, to flow through pipes over the ice rooms or
over the kitchen ovens. Then, when it has been cooled or
warmed, I can command it to make artificial weather."

"Artificial weather?" I said, marveling.

"In every garden are pavilions in which the lords and
ladies take their leisure. If a day is very warm, and some
lord or lady wishes the refreshment of a rain, without getting rained on—or if some poet merely wishes to meditate
in a mood of melancholy—I have only to twist a wheel.
From the roof eaves of the pavilion a curtain of rain will
fall gently all around the outside. Also in the garden pavilions, there are seats that appear to be of solid stone, but
they are hollow. By directing cool water through them in
summer, or warm water in spring or fall, I make the seats
more comfortable to the august rumps that repose on
them. When the new Kara Hill is completed, I shall install
in the pavilions there some even more pleasurable devices.
The piped waters will move linkages to wave cooling fans,
and will bubble through jug flutes to play a warbling soft
music."

And they did. I know they did, for in after years I passed
many a dreamy afternoon with Hui-sheng in those pavilions, and I translated the murmurous music for her into
gentle touches and soft caresses . . . . But that was in after
years.

I have so far mentioned only a very few of the novelties
and marvels I encountered in Kithai and in Khanbalik
and within the confines of the Khakhan's palace—perhaps
insufficiently to illustrate how different Kithai was from
any other place I had known. But different it was; I should
like to emphasize that difference. Be it remembered that
the Khan Kubilai owned an empire comprising all sorts of
peoples and communities and terrains and climates. He
could have made his residence in the Mongols' earlier, far-
northern capital of Karakoren, or in the Mongols' original,
very-far-north homeland of Sibir, or he could have chosen
to locate his habitation anywhere else on the continent.
But of all his lands he deemed Kithai the most appealing,
and so did I, and so it was.

I had been seeing exotic countries and cities all the long

way from Acre, but their differences were mainly in the
foreground of them. By that I mean: whenever I entered a
new city, my eye naturally lighted first on the things closest. They would be people of strange complexions and comportment, wearing strange costumes, and behind them
would be buildings of unfamiliar architecture. But at
ground level would always be street dogs and cats, no different from those anywhere else, and overhead would be
the trash-picker birds—pigeons or gulls or kites or whatever—as in any other city in the world. And around the
outskirts of the city would stretch humdrum hills or mountains or plains. The countryside and its wildlife might
sometimes, at first, be striking—like the mighty snowclad
crags of the high Pai-Mir and the magnificent "Marco's
sheep"—but after long journeying, one finds repetition and
familiarity even in most landscapes and their fauna and
flora.

By contrast, almost anywhere in Kithai, not only was
the foreground of interest to an observer, but so also was
the least glimpse of things going on at the corner of one's
eye, and the sounds at the edge of one's hearing, and the
smells wafting from all sides. On a walk through the
streets of Khanbalik, I might fix my gaze anywhere, from
the swooping, curly-eaved rooflines to the multifarious
faces and garments of the passersby, and still be conscious
that much else worth notice was awaiting my glance.

If I dropped my gaze to street level, I would see cats and
dogs, but I would not mistake them for the scavengers of
Suvediye or Balkh or anywhere else. Most of the Kithai
cats were small and handsomely colored, all-over dun except for brown ears and paws and tail, or silvery-gray with
extremities almost indigo-blue, and the cats' tails were
oddly short and even more oddly kinked at the very tip,
like hooks for hanging them up with. Some of the dogs running about resembled tiny lions, bushy-maned, with
pushed-in muzzles and bulging eyes. Another breed looked
like no thing ever seen before on this earth, except maybe
an ambulatory tree stump, if there ever was such a thing.
Indeed, that kind of dog was called shu-pei, meaning
"loose-barked," for its skin was so voluminously too large
for it that none of the dog's features was perceptible, nor
even its shape; it was only a grotesque, waddling heap of
wrinkles.

Yes another breed of dog I saw employed in a way I almost hesitate to tell, for I would probably not believe anyone else telling of it. That dog was large, of a reddish and bristly pelt, and was called xiang-gou. Every one wore a harness like a pony, and walked with great care and dignity, because its harness had an upstanding handle, by which the dog led a man or woman. The person holding to the handle was blind—not a beggar, but a man or woman going forth on business or to the market or just for a stroll. It is true. The xiang-gou, meaning "leader-dog," was bred and trained to lead a blind master about his own premises, without a stumble or collision, and just as confidently through teeming crowds and clashing cart traffic.

Besides the sights, there were the sounds and smells, which sometimes proceeded from the same source. On every corner was a stall or handcart selling hot cooked foods for the outdoor workers or busy passersby who had to eat on the run. So the smell of fish or meat morsels frying came to one's nose simultaneously with the sizzle coming to one's ears. Or the faint garlicky smell of miàn boiling was accompanied by the slurping of its eaters shoveling the pasta from bowl to mouth with nimble tongs. Khanbalik being the Khan's own city, it was continuously patrolled by street cleaners wielding brooms and buckets. So it was generally free of noxious odors like that of human excrement—more so than any other Kithai city, and ineffably more so than cities elsewhere in the East. The basic odor of Khanbalik was a mingled smell of spices and frying oil. To that, as I walked by different shops and market stalls, were variously added the smells of jasmine, cha, brazier smoke, sandalwood, fruits, incense, occasionally the fragrance of a passing lady's perfumed hand-fan.

Most of the street noises went on incessantly, day and night: the chatter and jabber and singsong of the constantly talking street people, the rumble and clatter of wagon and cart wheels—and as often the jingly music of them, for many carters strung little bells to slide along the spokes of their wheels—the thud of horse and yak hoofs, the lighter patter of asses' hoofs, the shuffle of camels' big pads, the rustle of the straw sandals worn by the ceaselessly scampering porters. That continuous blend of noise was frequently punctuated by the wail of a fish vendor, or the howl of a fruit vendor, or the *thwock-thwock* of a poul-

try vendor pounding on his hollow wooden duck, or the
reverberating *boom-boom-boom* that was one of the city
drum towers sounding the alarm of a fire somewhere. Only
now and again would the street noise diminish to a respectful hush—when a troop of palace guards came trotting through, one of the men playing a fanfare by beating
on a sort of lyre of brass rods, the others swinging quarter-
staffs to clear the way for the noble lord coming behind
them on horseback or being carried in a palanquin.

Sometimes, above the street noise—literally above it—
could be heard a thin melodious fluting in the air. The first
few times, I was puzzled by it. But then I realized that at
least one in every flock of the city's common pigeons had
been banded with a little whistle that sang as it flew. Also,
among the more ordinary pigeons was a very fluffy sort I
have never seen anywhere else. In its flight it would suddenly pause in midair and somehow, like a tightrope
tumbler but without a tightrope, it would topple end for
end, merrily making a perfect somersault in the air, and
then fly on as sedately as if it had done nothing wonderful.

And if I lifted my gaze even higher above the city roofs,
on any breezy autumn day I would see flocks of feng-zheng
flying. These were not birds, though some were shaped and
painted like birds; others were made to resemble immense
butterflies or small dragons. The fenz-zheng was a construction of light sticks and very thin paper, and to it a
string from a reel was tied. A man would run with the
feng-zheng and let the breeze take it, and then, by subtle
twitches at his end of the string, he could make it ascend
and fly and swoop and curvet in the sky. (Myself, I never
could master the art of it.) The height of its ascent was limited only by the amount of string on the flyer's reel, and
sometimes one would go up almost out of sight. Men liked
to engage in freng-zheng battles. They would glue on their
string an abrasive grit of powdered porcelain or Muscovy
glass and then let their feng-zheng fly, and try to guide
them so that one's string would saw and cut another's, and
make that contraption come tumbling down from the sky.
The flyers and other men would make heavy wagers on the
battle's outcome. But women and children liked to fly the
feng-zheng just for enjoyment.

In the nighttimes, I did not have to make any special effort to observe the peculiar things that happened in the Ki-

thai sky—for my head would be jerked up, volente o nolente, by the noises of those things. I mean the violent booms and bangs and sputters of the artificial lightnings and thunders, the so-called fiery trees and sparkling flowers. As in so many other Eastern countries, in Kithai too every day seemed to mark some folk holiday or anniversary requiring celebration. But only in Kithai did the festivities go on into the night, so there would be reason to send those curious fires flying skyward to burst into brighter fires and then into corpuscles of multicolored fire drifting down to the ground. I regarded the displays with admiration and awe, which was not lessened when later I discovered how those marvels were effected.

Outside the cities, Kithai's variegated landscape also differed from those of other countries. I have already described a few of Kithai's distinctive terrains, and will speak of others in their turn. But let me here say this. While I lived in Khanbalik I could, whenever I wished to spend a day in the country, command a horse from the palace stables and in just a morning's ride go to look at something to be seen in no other landscape on this earth. It may be a relic of total uselessness and vainglory, but the Great Wall, that monster serpent petrified in the act of wriggling from horizon to horizon, is still a fantastic feast for the eyes.

I do not mean to give the impression that everything in Kithai, or even within the Khan's capital city, was all beautiful, easy, rich and sweet. I would not have wished things so, for an unrelieved niceness can be as tiresome as the monotonously grand landscape of the Pai-Mir. Kubilai could have located his capital in a city of more temperate climate, for instance—there were places to the south that enjoyed perpetual springtime, and some much farther south that basked in perpetual summer. But the people who lived in such places, I found when I visited them, also were boringly bland. The climate of Khanbalik was very like that of Venice: springtime rains, winter snows and a sometimes oppressive summer heat. While its inhabitants did not have to contend with the mildewing dampness of Venice, their houses and clothes and furnishings were pervaded by the yellow dust forever being blown from the western deserts.

Like the seasons and the weathers, Khanbalik was ever

changing and various and invigorating, never cloying. For
one reason, besides such splendors and happy novelties as
I have cited, there were dark and not so happy aspects as
well. Beneath the Khan's magnificent palace crouched the
dungeons of the Fondler. The gorgeous robes of nobles and
courtiers sometimes cloaked men of mean ambitions and
base designs. Even my own two pretty maidservants
evinced some not so pretty turns of temperament. And outside the palace, in the streets and markets, not everybody
in those throngs was a prosperous merchant or an opulent
purchaser. There were poor people, too, and wretched ones.
I remember seeing a market stall that sold meat to the
poor, and someone translated its signboard for me: "Forest
shrimp, household deer, brushwood eels"—then told me
those were only high-flown Han names. The meats for sale
were really grasshoppers and rats and the tripes of snakes.

6

FOR many months, my workdays consisted of talking to
and asking respectful questions of one after another of the
many lords-ministers and administrators and accountants
and courtiers responsible for the smooth functioning of the
entire Mongol Khanate and this land of Kithai and this
city of Khanbalik and this palace court. Chingkim introduced me to most of them, but he had his own work to do as
Wang of Khanbalik, so he then left it to me and them to arrange our meetings at our mutual convenience. Some of
the men, including lords of high position, were most hospitable to my interest and forthcoming in their explications
of their offices. Others, including some mere palace stewards of laughably low degree, regarded me as a prying busy-
body and would talk only grudgingly. But all, by their
Khakhan's command, had to receive me. So I did not neglect to visit any of them, and did not let even the
unfriendly ones put me off with scanty or evasive inter-
views. I must admit, though that I found some of the men's
work more interesting than others', and so spent more
time with some than with others.

My colloquy with the Court Mathematician was particularly brief. I have never had much of a head for arithmetic, as my old teacher Fra Varisto could have attested. Although Master Lin-ngan was friendly—having been the first courtier I had met on arrival in Khanbalik—and was proud of his duties and eager to explain them, I fear that my lackluster responses rather dampened his enthusiasm. We did not get any further, in fact, than his showing me a nan-zhen, a Kithai-style instrument for marine navigation.

"Ah, yes," I said. "The north-pointing needle. Venetian ships' captains have them, too. It is called a bussola."

"We call it the south-riding carriage, and I submit that it cannot be compared to your crude Western versions. You in the West are still dependent on a circle divided into only three hundred and sixty degrees. That is but a clumsy approximation of the truth, arrived at by some of your primitive forebears, who could not count the days of the year any better than that. The true span of the solar year was known to us Han three thousand years ago. You will notice that our circle is divided into the accurate number of three hundred and sixty-five and one-quarter degrees."

I looked, and it was so. After contemplating the circle for some moments, I ventured to say, "A perfect count, certainly. A perfect division of the circle, undoubtedly. But what good is it?"

He stared at me, aghast. "What *good* is it?"

"Our outmoded Western circle is at least easily divisible into fourths. How could a man using this one ever mark off a right angle?"

His serenity somewhat ruffled, he said, "Marco Polo, honored guest, do you not realize what genius is represented here? What patient observation and refined calculation? And how sublimely superior to the slapdash mathematics of the West?"

"Oh, I freely concede that. I merely remark on the impracticality of it. Why, this would drive a land-surveyor mad. It would make hash of all our maps. And a builder could never erect a house with true corners or square rooms."

His serenity totally flown, he snapped in exasperation, "You Westerners are concerned only with amassing knowledge. You have no concern at all for acquiring wisdom. I speak to you of pure mathematics and you speak to me of carpenters!"

Humbly I said, "I am ignorant of philosophies, Master Lin-ngan, but I have known a few carpenters. This circle of Kithai, they would laugh at."

"*Laugh?!*" he cried, in a strangled voice.

For someone usually so wise and remote and dispassionate, he worked himself into quite a decent fury. Being not entirely unwise myself, I made my adieux and respectfully backed out of his chambers. Well, it was just one more of my encounters with Han ingenuity that made me dubious of their renown for ingenuity.

But in a somewhat similar interview, at the palace Observatory of the Astronomers, I managed better to hold my own, with self-assurance and aplomb. The Observatory was an unroofed upper terrace of the palace, cluttered with immense and complex instruments: armillary spheres and sundials and astrolabes and alidades, all beautifully made of marble and brass. The Court Astronomer, Jamal-ud-Din, was a Persian, by reason of the fact that all those instruments, he told me, had been invented and designed ages ago in his native land, so he knew best how to operate them. He was chief of half a dozen Under Astronomers, and they were all Han, because, said Master Jamal, the Han had been keeping scrupulous records of astronomical observations longer than any other people. Jamal-ud-Din and I conversed in Farsi, and he interpreted the comments made by his colleagues.

I began by admitting frankly, "My lords, the only education I ever had in astronomy was the Bible's account of how the Prophet Joshua, in order to prolong a battle for an extra day, made the sun to stand still in its course across the sky."

Jamal gave me a look, but repeated my words to the six elderly Han gentlemen. They seemed to get extremely excited, or confounded, and chattered among themselves, and then put a question to me, saying politely:

"Stopped the sun, did he, this Joshua? Most interesting. When did this occur?"

"Oh, a long, long time ago," I said. "When the Israelites strove against the Amorrhites. Several books before Christ was born and the calendar began."

"This is most interesting," they repeated, after some

more consultation among themselves. "Our astronomical
records, the Shu-king, go back more than three thousand
five hundred and seventy years, and they contain no least
mention of the occurrence. One would imagine that a cos-
mic event of that nature would have occasioned some comment even from the man in the street, let alone the
astronomers of the time. Would it have been longer ago
than that, do you suppose?"

The solemn old men were clearly trying to dissemble
their consternation at my knowing more of historical astronomy than they did, so I graciously changed the subject.

"Though I lack formal education in your profession, my
lords, I do possess some curiosity, and have frequently myself observed the sky, and therefrom have conceived some
theories of my own."

"Indeed?" said Master Jamal, and, after consulting the
others, "We would be honored to hear them."

So, with due modesty but with no paltering equivoca-
tion, I told them one of the conclusions I had come to: that
the sun and the moon are closer to the earth in their orbits
at morning and evening than at other hours.

"It is easy to see, my lords," I said. "Merely observe the
sun at its rise or setting. Or better, observe the full moon
rising, since it can be looked at without paining the eyes.
As it ascends from the other side of the earth, it is immense. But as it rises it dwindles, until at its zenith it is
only a fraction of its earlier size. I have remarked that phenomenon many times, watching the moon rise from beyond the Venetian lagoon. Obviously that heavenly body
is getting farther from the earth as it proceeds in its orbit.
The only other explanation for its diminishment would be
that it *shrinks* as it goes, and that would be too foolish to
credit."

"Foolish, truly," muttered Jamal-ud-Din. He and the
Under Astronomers soberly shook their heads, seeming
much impressed, and there was more muttering. Finally
one of the sages must have determined to test the extent of
my astronomical knowledge, for he put another question,
by way of Jamal:

"What is your opinion, Marco Polo, of sun spots?"

"Ah," I said, pleased to be able to answer promptly. "A
most damaging disfigurement, those. Terrible things."

"Say you so? We have been divided, among ourselves, as

to whether, in the universal scheme of things, they mean good or evil."

"Well, I do not know that I would say *evil.* But ugly, yes, most certainly. For a long time, I mistakenly believed that all Mongol women were ugly, until I saw the ones here at the palace."

The gentlemen looked blank, and blinked at me, and Master Jamal said uncertainly, "What has that to do with the topic?"

I said, "I realized that it was only the *nomad* Mongol women, those who spend all their lives out of doors, who are sun-spotted and blotched and tanned like leather. These more civilized Mongol ladies of the court, by contrast, are—"

"No, no, no," said Jamal-ud-Din. "We are speaking of the spots *on the sun.*"

"What? Spots on the sun?"

"Verily. The desert dust ever blowing herabouts is usually a pestilence, but it has at least one good property. At times it veils the sun sufficiently that we can gaze directly at it. We have seen—severally and independently, and often enough to be in no doubt—that the sun occasionally is marred by dark spots and speckles on its otherwise luminous face."

I smiled and said, "I see," and then began laughing as expected. "You make a jest. I am amused, Master Jamal. But I do think, in all humanity, that you and I should not laugh at the expense of these hapless Han."

He looked even more blank and confounded than before, and he said, "What are we talking about *now?*"

"You make fun of their eyesight. Sun spots, indeed! Poor fellows, it is not their fault that they are constructed so. Having to peer all their lives from between those constricted eyelids. No wonder they have spots before their eyes! Nevertheless, a good jest, Master Jamal." And, bowing in the Persian fashion, still laughing, I took my departure.

The palace's Master Gardener and Master Potter were Han gentlemen, each supervising whole legions of young Han apprentices. So when I called on them I was again treated to a typically Han spectacle—of ingenuity being lavished on the inconsequential. In the West, such occupations are relegated to menials who do not care how dirty their hands get, not to men of intellect who can be better employed. But the Palace Gardener and Palace Potter seemed proud to be putting their wit and devotion and inventiveness at the service of garden manure and potter's clay. They seemed no less proud to be training a new generation of youngsters for a similar lifetime of mean and mucky manual labor.

The Palace Gardener's workshop was a vast hothouse built entirely of panes of Muscovy glass. At its several long tables his numerous apprentices sat hunched over boxes full of what looked like the culms of crocus flowers, doing something to them with very tiny knives.

"Those are bulbs of the celestial lily, being readied for planting." said the Master Gardener. (When later I saw them in bloom, I recognized the flower as what we in the West call the narcissus.) He held up one of the dry bulbs and pointed and said, "By making two very precise, minute incisions in the bulb, it will grow in the shape we deem most attractive for this flower. Two stems will spring from the bulb, sideways and apart. But then, as the stems leaf out, they will curve inward again. So the lovely flowers, when they bloom, will bend toward each other like arms about to embrace. To the beauty of the flower we add grace of line."

"A remarkable art," I murmured, refraining from saying that I considered it also a negligible one to occupy so many people.

The Palace Potter's workshop, equally vast, was in the cellars underground and was lighted by lamps. His shop did not make crude table pottery, but the finest porcelain works of art. He showed me his bins of various clays and the mixing vessels and wheels and kilns and jars of colors and glazes which, he assured me, were "of most secret composition." Then he took me to a table where some dozen of his apprentices were working. They each had a finished porcelain bud vase, elegant little things of bulbous body and high narrow neck, but still of raw clay color. The apprentices were painting them preparatory to their firing.

"Why are all the boys' brushes broken?" I asked, for each young man was wielding a fine-haired brush that had a definite kink in its long handle.

"They are not broken," said the Master Potter. "The brushes are specially angled. These apprentices are paint-

ing the designs of flowers, birds, reeds, whatever—purely
by feel and instinct and art—onto the *inside* of the vases.
When the article is finished, its decoration will be invisible
except when it is set before a light, and then the paper-thin
white porcelain will allow the colorful picture to be delicately, mistily, subtly seen."

He led me to another table and said, "These are the newest and youngest apprentices, just learning their art."

"What art?" I said. "They are playing with eggshells."

"Yes. Porcelain objects of great value sometimes unfortunately get broken. These lads are learning to repair
them. But naturally they do not practice on valuable articles. I take blown eggs and shatter their shells and give to
each boy the commingled shards of two eggs. He must pick
out and separate the fragments to reconstruct the two.
That he does, putting each shell back together with those
tiny brass rivets you see there. Not until an apprentice can
rebuild an entire egg, so artfully that it appears never to
have been broken, is he trusted to work on actual porcelain
objects."

Nowhere else in the world had I seen so many instances
of capable men devoting their lives to such minikin pursuits, and high intelligence dedicated to trivial ends, and
stupendous skill and labor expended on paltry endeavors.
And I do not mean just among the court craftsmen. I saw
much the same sort of thing even among the lofty ministers at the uppermost levels of the Khanate's administration.

The Minister of History, for example, was a Han gentleman who looked ever so scholarly, and was fluent in many
languages, and seemed to have memorized all of Western
history as well as the Eastern. But his employment
consisted only in being very busy at doing nothing worthwhile. When I asked what he was engaged upon at the moment, he got up from his big writing desk, opened a door of
his chamber and showed me a much bigger chamber beyond. It was full of small writing desks very close together,
and bent over each one was a scribe hard at work, almost
hidden behind the books and rolled scrolls and sheaves of
documents piled at his place.

Speaking perfect Farsi, the Minister of History said,
"The Khakhan Kubilai decreed four years ago that his
reign will commence a Yuàn Dynasty comprising all sub-

sequent reigns of his successors. The title he chose, Yuàn,
means 'the greatest' or 'the principal.' Which is to say, it
must eclipse the lately extinguished Chin Dynasty, and
the Xia before that, and every other dynasty dating back
to the beginning of civilization in these lands. So I am
compiling, and my assistants are writing, a glowing history to assure that future generations will recognize the
supremacy of the Yuàn Dynasty."

"A deal of writing is being done, certainly," I said, looking at all the bowed heads and twitching ink brushes. "But
how much can there be to write, if the Yuàn Dynasty is
only four years old?"

"Oh, the recording of current events is nothing," he said
dismissively. "The difficult part is rewriting all the history that has gone before."

"What? But how? History is history, Minister. History is
what has happened."

"Not so, Marco Polo. History is what is remembered of
what has happened."

"I see no difference," I said. "If, say, a devastating flood
of the Yellow River occurred in such and such a year,
whether or not anyone made written record of the event, it
is likely that the flood will be remembered and so will the
date."

"Ah, but not all the attendant circumstances. Suppose
the then-emperor came promptly to the aid of the flood victims, and rescued them and fetched them to safe ground,
and gave them new land and helped them again to prosperity. If those beneficent circumstances were to stay in the
archives as part of the history of that reign, then this Yuàn
Dynasty might, by comparison, appear deficient in benevolence. So we change the history just slightly, to record that
earlier emperor as having been callous to his people's suffering."

"And the Yuàn seems kind by comparison? But suppose
Kubilai and his successors prove to be *truly* callous in such
calamities?"

"Then we must rewrite again, and make the earlier rulers *more* hard-hearted. I trust you perceive now the importance of my work, and the diligence and creativeness
required. It is no job for a lazy man, or a stupid one. History is not just a daily setting down of events, like keeping

a ship's log. History is a fluid process, and the work of a
historian is never done."

I said, "Historical events may be variously rendered,
but current ones? For instance, in the Year of Our Lord
one thousand two hundred seventy-five, Marco Polo arrived in Khanbalik. What more could be said of such a trifle?"

"If it is indeed a trifle," said the Minister, smiling,
"then it need not be mentioned in history at all. But it
could prove later to be significant. So I make a note of even
such a trifle, and wait to see if it should be inscribed in the
archives as an occasion to be treasured or regretted."

He went back to his writing besk, opened a large leather
folder and riffled through the papers inside it. He picked
out one and read from it:

"At the hour of Xu in the sixth day of the seventh moon,
in the Year of the Boar, the year three thousand nine hundred seventy-three of the Han calendar, the year four of
Yuàn, there returned from the Western city of Wei-ni-si to
the City of the Khan the two foreigners, Po-lo Ni-klo and
Po-lo Mah-fyo, bringing with them a third and younger
Po-lo Mah-ko. It remains to be seen whether this young
man will make Khanbalik better for his presence"—he
threw me a mischievous side glance, and I could tell that
he was no longer reading from the paper—"or whether he
will be merely a nuisance, inflicting himself upon busy officials and interrupting them in their pressing duties."

"I will go away," I said, laughing. "Just one last question, Minister. If you can write a whole new history, cannot someone else rewrite yours?"

"Of course," he said. "And someone will." He looked
surprised that I had even asked. "When the late Chin Dynasty was new, its first Minister of History rewrote everything that had gone before. And Chin historians continued
so to write, to make the Chin period appear the Golden
Age of all time. But dynasties come and go; the Chin lasted
only a hundred and nineteen years. It could well happen
that the Yuàn Dynasty and all I accomplish here"—he
waved an arm to indicate his chamber and the other full of
scribes—"may not outlast my own lifetime."

So I went away, resisting the temptation to suggest to
the Minister that instead of exerting his scholarship and
erudition, he might better employ his muscles, helping to

pile up the kara blocks for the new hill being built in the palace gardens. That hill would less likely be dismantled by future generations than would the pile of falsehoods he was building in the capital archives.

The conclusion I was coming to—that a great many men were engaged in doing very little of moment—I did not immediately confide to the Khakhan during my audience that week. But he himself began talking of a matter rather similar. It seemed that he had recently had a count made of the various and numerous holy men currently habitant in Kithai, and was disgruntled by it.

"Priests," he growled. "Lamas, monks, Nestorians, malangs, imams, missionaries. All looking to accrete a congregation on which they can batten. I would not mind so much if they only preached sermons and then held out their begging bowls. But as soon as they do accumulate a few believers, they command ᴄhe deluded wretches to despise and detest everyone who prefers some other faith. Of all the religions being propagated, only the Buddhists are tolerant of every other. I do not wish either to impose or oppose any religion, but I am seriously considering an edict against the *preachers*. My ukaz would command that what time the preachers now spend on petty ritual and ranting and prayer and evangelism and meditation be spent instead with a fly whisk, swatting flies. What do you think, Marco Polo? They would do incalculably more than they are doing now to make this world a better place."

"I think, Sire, the preachers are chiefly concerned with the next world."

"Well? Making this one better should earn them high credit in the next one. Kithai is overrun with pestiferous flies and with self-proclaimed holy men. I cannot abolish the flies by ukaz. But would you not agree that it would be good use of the holy men to kill the flies?"

"I have lately reflected, yes, Sire, that a large proportion of men are misemployed."

"*Most* men are misemployed, Marco," he said emphatically, "and do no manly work. To my mind, only warriors, laborers, explorers, craftsmen, artists, cooks and physicians are worth esteem. They do things or they discover things or they make things or they preserve things. All other men are scavengers and parasites dependent on the doers and the makers. Government functionaries, counselors, tradesmen, astrologers, money changers, factors, scribes, priests, clerks, they perform activity and call it action. They do nothing but move things about—and usually nothing weightier than bits of paper—or they exist only to proffer commentary or advice or criticism to the doers and the makers of things."

He paused and frowned, and then almost spat. "Vakh! What am I, since I got down from my horse? I lift no lance any longer, only a yin seal to stamp approval or disapproval. In honesty, I must include myself among the busy men who do nothing. Vakh!"

In that, of course, he was dead wrong.

I was no expert on monarchs, but I had long ago, from my reading in *The Book of Alexander,* taken that great conqueror as my ideal of what a sovereign should be. And I had by now met quite a number of real, living, ruling rulers, and I had formed some opinions of them: Edward, now King of England, who had seemed to me only a good soldier dutifully playing at princedom; and the miserable Armeniyan governor Hampig; and the Persian Shah Zaman, a henpecked zerbino of a husband inhabiting royal robes; and the Ilkhan Kaidu, not even pretending to be other than a barbarian warlord. Only this most recently met ruler, the Khakhan Kubilai, came anywhere near my imagined ideal.

He was not beautiful, as Alexander is portrayed in the *Book*'s illuminations, and not as young. The Khakhan was near twice the age Alexander had been when he died; but, by the same token, he held an empire some three times the size of that won by Alexander. And in other respects Kubilai came close to resembling my classical ideal. Though I early learned awe and dread of his tyrant power and his penchant for sudden, sweeping, unqualified, irrevocable judgments and decisions (his every published decree concluded thus: "The Khakhan has spoken; tremble, all men, and obey!"), it must be granted that such limitless power and the impetuous exercise of it are, after all, attributes to be expected of an absolute monarch. Alexander exhibited them, too.

In after years, some have called me "a posturing liar," refusing to believe that mere Marco Polo could ever have been more than remotely acquainted with the most powerful man in the world. Others have called me "a slavish syc-

ophant," contemning me as an apologist for a brutal dicta-
tor.

I can understand why it is hard to believe that the high
and mighty Khan of All Khans should have lent a moment
of his attention to a lowly outsider like me, let alone his affection and trust. But the fact is that the Khakhan stood so
high above *all* other men that, in his eyes, lords and nobles
and commoners and maybe even slaves seemed of the same
level and of indistinguishable characteristics. It was no
more remarkable that he should deign to notice me than
that he should give regard to his closest ministers. Also,
considering the humble and distant origin of the Mongols,
Kubilai was as much an outsider as I was in the exotic pur-
lieus of Kithai.

As for my alleged sycophancy, it is true that I never personally suffered from any of his whims and caprices. It is
true that he became fond of me, and entrusted me with responsibilities, and made me a close confidant. But it is not
on that account that I still defend and praise the Khakhan.
It was because of my closeness to him that I could see, better than some, that he wielded his vast authority as wisely
as he knew how. Even when he did so despotically, it was
always as a means to an end he thought right, not just expedient. Contrary to that philosophy expressed by my Uncle Mafio, Kubilai was as evil as he had to be and as good
as he could be.

The Khakhan had layers and circles and envelopes of
ministers and advisers and other officers about him, but he
never let them wall him off from his realm, his subjects or
his scrupulous attention to the details of government. As I
had seen him do in the Cheng, Kubilai might delegate to
others some minor matters, even the preliminary aspects
of some major matters, but in everything of importance he
always had the last word. I might liken him and his court
to the fleets of vessels I first saw on the Yellow River. The
Khakhan was the chuan, the biggest ship on the water,
steered by a single firm rudder gripped by a single firm
hand. The ministers in attendance on him were the san-
pan scows that did the ferrying of cargoes to and from the
master chuan vessel, and ran the lesser errands in
shallower waters. Just one there was among the ministers—the Arab Achmad, Chief Minister, Vice-Regent and
Finance Minister—who could be likened to the lopsided

hu-pan skiff, cunningly designed to skirt curves, forever
turning end for end, while always staying in safe water
close to shore. But of Achmad, that man as warped as the
hu-pan boat, I will tell in due time.

Kubilai, like the fabled Prete Zuàne, had to rule over a
conglomeration of diverse nations and disparate peoples,
many of them hostile to each other. Like Alexander, Kubilai sought to meld them by discerning the most admirable
ideas and achievements and qualities in all those varied
cultures, and disseminating them broadcast for the good of
all his different peoples. Of course, Kubilai was not saintly
like Prete Zuàne, nor even a Christian, nor even a devotee
of the classical gods, like Alexander. As long as I knew
him, Kubilai recognized no deity except the Mongol war
god Tengri and some minor Mongol idols like the household god Nagatai. He was *interested* in other religions, and
at one time or another studied many of them, in hope of
finding the One Best, which could be another benefit to his
subjects and another unifying force among them. My father and uncle and others repeatedly urged Christianity
upon him, and the swarms of Nestorian missionaries
never ceased preaching at him their heretic brand of
Christianity, and other men championed the oppressive
religion of Islam, the godless and idolatrous Buddhism,
the several religions peculiar to the Han, even the nauseous Hinduism of India.

But the Khakhan never could be persuaded that Christianity is the one True Faith, and never found any other he
favored. He said once—and I do not remember whether at
the time he was amused or exasperated or disgusted—
"What difference what god? God is only an excuse for the
godly."

He may ultimately have become what a theologian
would call a skeptic Pyrrhonist, but even his disbeliefs he
did not force upon anyone. He remained always liberal and
tolerant in that respect, and let every man believe in and
worship what he would. Admittedly, Kubilai's lack of any
religion at all left him without any guidance of dogma and
doctrine, free to regard even the basic virtues and vices as
narrowly or liberally as he saw fit. So his notions of charity, mercy, brotherly love and other such things were often
at dismaying variance with those of men of ingrained or-
thodoxy. I myself, though no paragon of Christian princi-

ple, often disagreed with his precepts or was aghast at his
applications of them. Even so, nothing that Kubilai ever
did—however much I may have deplored it at the time—
ever diminished my admiration of him, or my loyalty to
him, or my conviction that the Khan Kubilai was the supreme sovereign of our time.

7

I N subsequent days and weeks and months, I was granted
audience with every one of the Khakhan's ministers and
counselors and courtiers of whose offices I have earlier spoken in these pages, and with numerous others besides, of
mentioned—the three Ministers of Farming, Fishing and
Herding, the Chief of Digging the Great Canal, the Minister of Roads and Rivers, the Minister of Ships and Seas,
the Court Shamàn, the Minister of Lesser Races—and ever
so many others.

From every audience I came away knowing new things
of interest or usefulness or edification, but I will not here
recount them all. From one of the meetings I came away
embarrassed, and so did the minister concerned. He was a
Mongol lord named Amursama, and he was Minister of
Roads and Rivers, and the embarrassment arose most unexpectedly, while he was discoursing on a really prosaic
matter: the post service he was putting into effect all
across Kithai.

"On every road, minor as well as major, at intervals of
seventy-five li, I am building a comfortable barrack, and
the nearest communities are responsible for keeping it
supplied with good horses and men to ride them. When a
message or a parcel must be swiftly conveyed in either direction, a rider can take it at a stretch-out gallop from one
post to the next. There he flings it to a new rider, ready
saddled and waiting, who rides to the next post, and so on.
Between dawn and dawn, a succession of riders can transport a light load as far as an ordinary karwan train could
take it in twenty days. And, because bandits will hesitate
to attack a known emissary of the Khanate, the deliveries
arrive safely and reliably."

I was later to know that that was true, when my father and Uncle Mafìo began to prosper in their trading ventures. They would usually convert their proceeds into precious gems that made a small, light packet. Utilizing the Minister Amursama's horse post, they would send the packets from Kithai all the way to Constantinople, where my Uncle Marco would deposit them in the coffers of the Compagnia Polo.

The Minister went on, "Also, because occasionally something unusual or important may occur in the regions between the horse posts—a flood, an uprising, some marvel worth reporting—I am establishing, every ten li or so, a lesser station for foot runners. So, from anywhere in the realm, there is a run of less than an hour to the next station, and the runners continue by relays until one gets to the nearest horse post, whence the news can be conveyed farther and more quickly. I am just now getting the system organized throughout Kithai, but eventually I will have it operating across the entire Khanate, to bring news or important burdens even from the farthermost border of Poland. Already I have the service so efficient that a white-flag porpoise caught in Tung-ting Lake, more than two thousand li south of here, can be cut up and packed in saddlebags of ice and hurried here to the Khakhan's kitchen while it is still fresh."

"A fish?" I respectfully inquired. "Is that an important burden?"

"That fish lives only in one place, in that Tung-ting Lake, and is not easily caught, so it is reserved for the Khakhan. It is a great table delicacy in spite of its great ugliness. The white-flag porpoise is as big as a woman, has a head like a duck, with a snout like a duck's beak, and its slanted eyes are sadly blind. But it is a fish only by enchantment."

I blinked and said, "Uu?"

"Yes, each is a royal descendant of a long-ago princess, who was changed by enchantment into a porpoise after she drowned herself in that lake, because . . . because of a . . . a tragic love affair . . . ."

I was surprised that a typically brisk and brusque Mongol should begin stammering like a schoolboy. I looked up at him, and saw that his formerly brown face had flushed red. He avoided my eye and clumsily fumbled to turn our

conversation to something else. Then I remembered who
he was, so I—probably also reddening in sympathy—made
some excuse to terminate the interview, and I withdrew. I
had totally forgotten, you see, that that Minister Amursama was the lord who, after his lady was taken in adultery, had been ordered to strangle her with her own
sphincter. Actually, a great many of the palace residents
were curious to know the grisly details of Amursama's
compliance with that order, but were shy of bringing up
the matter in his presence. However, they said, he himself
seemed somehow always to be stumbling onto reminders
of the subject, and then getting tongue-tied and uncomfortable, and making everybody around him just as uncomfortable.

Well, I could understand that. But I could not understand why another minister, likewise discoursing on a prosaic subject, should have seemed equally distraught and
evasive. He was Pao Nei-ho and he was the Minister of
Lesser Races. (As I have told, the Han people are everywhere in the majority, but in Kithai and in the southerly
lands which were then the Sung Empire, there are some
sixty other nationalities.) Minister Pao told me, at tedious
length, how it was his responsibility to ensure that all of
Kithai's minority peoples enjoyed the same rights as the
Han majority. It was one of the duller disquisitons I had so
far endured, but Minister Pao told it in Farsi—in his position, he had to be multilingual—and I could not see why
the telling of it made him so nervously falter and fidget
and sprinkle his speech with er and uh and ahem.

"Even the er conqueror Mongols are uh few compared to
us Han," he said. "The ahem lesser nationalities are fewer
still. In the er western regions, for example, the uh so-
called Uighur and the ahem Uzbek, Kirghiz, Kazhak and
er Tazhik. Here in the uh north we find also the ahem
Manchu, the Tungus, the Hezhe. And when the er Khan
Kubilai completes his uh conquest of the ahem Sung Empire, we will absorb all the other er nationalities down
there. The uh Naxi and the Miao, the Puyi, the Chuang.
Also ahem the obstreperous Yi people who populate the er
entire province of Yun-nan in the uh far southwest . . ."

He went on and on like that, and I might have dozed, except that my mind was busy sieving out the ers and uhs
and ahems. But even when I had done that, I found the

speech still a dry one. It seemed to contain nothing shameful or sinister that would require concealment in a lot of
vocal weeds. I did not know why Minister Pao should be
speaking so haltingly. Neither did I know why I was being
suspicious of that fractured oratory. But I was. He was saying *something* that I was not supposed to grasp. I was sure
of it. And, as it turned out, I was right.

When I finally got loose of him that day, I went to my
own rooms and to the closet which I let Nostril use for his
pallet chamber. He was sleeping at that moment, though it
was only midafternoon. I shook him and said:

"You have not enough work to do, slovenly slave, so I
have thought of a job for you."

In truth, the slave was lately having quite an indolent
life. My father and uncle, having no need for him, had relinquished his services entirely to me. But I was so well
served by the maids Buyantu and Biliktu that I employed
Nostril only for such things as buying me a wardrobe of
suitable Kithai-style clothing, and keeping it well stocked
and in good order, and occasionally to groom and saddle a
horse for me. Between times, Nostril did not do much
roaming about or mischief making. He seemed to have
subdued his former nasty habits and natural inquisitiveness. He spent most of his time in his closet, except when
he ventured as far as the palace kitchens to seek a meal,
or, when I invited him, to dine with me in my chambers. I
did not allow that often, for the girls were clearly repelled
by his appearance and uncomfortable in the role of Mongols waiting upon a mere slave.

Now he came awake, grumbling, "Bismillah, master,"
and yawning so that even his dreadful nose hole seemed to
gape wider.

I said sternly, "Here am I, busy all the day, while my
slave slumbers. I am supposed to be evaluating the Khakhan's courtiers by talking to them face to face, but you
could do even better behind their backs."

He mumbled, "I gather, master, that you wish me to
snoop about among their servants and attendants. But
how? I am an outlander and a newcomer, and my grasp of
the Mongol tongue is still imperfect."

"There are many outlanders among the domestic staff.
Prisoners taken from every land. The servants' talk belowstairs must be a Babel of languages. And I know very well

that your one nostril is adept at sniffing out gossip and scandal."

"I am honored that you ask me, master, but—"

"I am not asking. I am commanding. You are henceforth to spend all your spare time, of which you have an ample measure, mingling with the servants and your fellow slaves."

"Master, to be honest, I am fearful of wandering about these halls. I might blunder into the Fondler's precincts."

"Do not talk back or I will take you there myself. Hear me. Every evening from now on, you and I will sit down and you will repeat to me every least morsel of tattle and tale you have heard."

"About anything? Everything? Most of the talk is trivial."

"Everything. But right now I am interested to know all I can find out about the Minister of Lesser Races, the Han lord named Pao Nei-ho. Whenever you can subtly turn the conversation to that subject, do so. But *subtly.* Meanwhile, I shall want everything else you hear, as well. There is no foretelling what tidbit may be of value to me."

"Master Marco, I must make some respectful demur in advance. I am not so handsome now as I once was, when I could beguile even princesses to blurt their innermost—"

"Oh, that imbecilic old lie again! Nostril, you and all the world know that you have always been damnably ugly, and you never once so much as touched the hem of a princess's gown!"

Undeterred, he persisted, "On the other hand, you have at your command two pretty maids who could easily employ their comeliness for come-hitherness. They are far better fitted for wheedling secrets out of—"

"Nostril," I said patiently. "You will spy for me because I tell you to, and I need give no other reason. However, I will mention just this. It apparently has not occurred to you, but it has to me, that those two maids are very likely spying on *my* doings. Watching my every move and reporting it. Remember, it was the son of the Khakhan, on the orders of the Khakhan, who gave me the girls."

I always spoke of them as "the girls" when speaking to others, because to use both their names every time would have been unwieldy, and I did not speak of them as "the servants" because they were rather more than that to me, but I would not speak of them as "the concubines" because that seemed to me a slightly derogatory term. In private, however, I addressed them separately as Buyantu and Biliktu, for I had early learned to tell them apart. Although when dressed they were identical, I now knew their individualities of expression and gesture. Undressed, although still identical even to the dimples in their cheeks, the dimples at their elbows and those especially winsome dimples on either side of the base of their spines, the twins were more easily identifiable. Biliktu had a sprinkle of freckles on the underswell of her left breast, and Buyantu had a tiny scar on her upper right thigh from some child-hood mishap.

I had taken note of those things on our very first night together, and of some other things as well. The girls were both nicely shaped and, not being Muslims, were complete in all their private parts. In general, they were built like other mature females I had known, except that they were a trifle shorter in the leg and a trifle less indented at the waistline than, say, Venetian and Persian women are. But their one most intriguing difference from women of other races was the matter of their inguinal hair. They had the usual dark triangle in the usual place—the han-mao, they called it, their "little warmer"—but it was not a curly or bushy tuft. Through some quirk of nature, Mongol wom-en—at least those I have known—have an exceptionally smooth escutcheon; the hair lies as flat and neat there as on the pelt of a cat. When earlier lying with a woman, I had sometimes amused myself (and her) by twining and twiddling my fingers in her little warmer; with Buyantu or Biliktu, I stroked and petted it as I would a kitten (and made her purr like one).

On my first night in my private apartments, the twins had made it plain that they expected me to take one of them to bed with me. When they bathed me, they also stripped and bathed themselves, and most fastidiously washed my and their dan-tian, our "pink places," our pri-vate parts. When they had dusted me and themselves with fragrant powders, they slipped into dressing gowns of silk so sheer that their little warmers were still quite visible, and the girl I would come to recognize as Buyantu asked me, straight out:

"Will you be desiring children of us, Master Marco?"

Involuntarily I blurted, "Dio me varda, no!" She could not have understood the words, but evidently could not mistake the meaning, for she nodded and went on:

"We have procured fern seed, which is the best preventive of conception. Now, as you know, master, we are both of twenty-two-karat quality, and of course are virgins. So we have been speculating all afternoon as to which of us will have the honor of being first qing-du chu-kai—awakened to womanhood—by our handsome new master."

Well, I was pleased that they were not, like so many virgins, dreading the event. Indeed, they seemed to have been, in a sisterly way, contending for precedence, for Buyantu added, "As it happens, master, I am the elder of the two."

Biliktu laughed and told me, "By a matter of minutes only, according to our mother. But all our lives, Elder Sister has been claiming privilege on that account."

Buyantu shrugged and said, "One of us must have the first night, and the other wait for the second. If you would prefer not to make the choice yourself, master, we could draw straws."

I said airily, "Far be it from me to leave delight to chance. Or to discriminate between two such compelling attractions. You will both be first."

Buyantu said chidingly, "We are virgins, but we are not ignorant."

"We helped raise our two younger brothers," said Biliktu.

"So, while bathing you, we saw that you are normally equipped in your dan-tian," said Buyantu. "Bigger than boys in that respect, of course, but not *multiplied.*"

"Therefore," said Biliktu, "you can be in only one place at a time. How can you pretend that we both could be first?"

"The bed is beautifully commodious," I said. "We will all three lie together and—"

"That would be indecent!"

They both looked so shocked that I smiled. "Come, come. It is well-known that men sometimes disport themselves with more than one woman at a time."

"But—but those are concubines of long experience, long past modesty, and of no embarrassing relation. Master Marco, we are *sisters,* and this is our first jiao-gou, and we

will . . . that is to say, we cannot . . . in each other's presence . . ."

"I promise," I said, "you will find it no less sisterly than
bathing in each other's presence. Also, that you will soon
cease to fret about proprieties. Also, that you will both so
enjoy the jiao-gou that you will not notice which of you was
first. Or ever care."

They hesitated. Buyantu frowned prettily in contemplation. Biliktu meditatively bit her lower lip. Then they
looked shyly sideways at each other from the corners of
their eyes. When their glances met, they blushed—so extensively that their sheer gowns turned pink all down the
breast. Then they laughed, a little shakily, but they made
no further objection. Buyantu got from a drawer a phial of
fern seed, and she and Biliktu turned their backs on me
while each of them took a pinch of that fine, almost pow-
dery seed and, with a finger, inserted it deep inside themselves. Then they let me take them each by a hand and let
me lead them to the inviting bed, and let me go on leading
from there.

Harking back to my youthful experience in Venice, I put
to use the modes of music making I had learned from the
Lady Ilaria and then had refined by practicing on the little
maiden Doris. Thus I was able to make the initiation of
these virgins, too, an occasion for them to remember, not
just without wincing, but with genuine joy. At first, as I
turned or moved from Buyantu to Biliktu and back again,
they kept their eyes not on me but sideways on each other,
and were obviously trying not to make any visible or audible responses to my ministrations, lest the other consider
her immodest. But as I worked delicately with fingers and
lips and tongue and even my eyelashes, they eventually
closed their own eyes and ignored each other and gave
themselves up to their own feelings.

I might remark that that night's jiao-gou, my first such
activity in Kithai, was endowed with a special piquancy,
just because of the fanciful Han terms which were employed there for all parts of the human body. As I had already learned, the name "red jewel" can mean either the
male or female parts in general. But it is usually reserved
for the male's organ, while the female's is the "lotus" and
its lips are its "petals" and what I had formerly called the
lumaghèta or zambur is the "butterfly between the petals

of the lotus." The female posterior is her "calm moon" and
its dainty valley is the "rift in the moon." Her breasts are
her "flawless jade viands" and her nipples are her "small
stars."

So, by variously and adroitly touching, caressing, teasing, tasting, fondling, tickling, nibbling jade viands and
flowers and petals and moons and stars and butterflies, I
succeeded marvelously in making both the twins achieve
their first peak of jiao-gou simultaneously. Then, before
they could realize how much unabashed singing and
thrashing they had done on the way there, and perhaps get
mutually embarrassed, I did other things to urge them up
again to the peaks. They were quick learners and eager to
partake again of those heights, so I kept my mind off my
own urgent yearnings and devoted myself entirely to their
enjoyments. At times, one girl would be up among the
peaks by herself, and her sister would regard her—and my
ministrations to her—with a wondering and marveling
smile. Then it would be her turn, while the other watched
and approved. Not until both the girls were dazed and delighted with their new-discovered sensations, and well
moistened by their own secretions, did I play them both at
once to a veritable frenzy. While both were oblivious to
everything but their ecstasy, I penetrated first one, then
the other—easily and pleasurably for me and them, too—
and continued giving myself into one and the other, so that
even I do not remember in which order, or in which twin I
first made spruzzo.

After that first and musically perfect triad, I let the girls
rest and pant and perspire happily for a while, and smile
at me and each other, until, when they had regained their
breath, Biliktu and Buyantu were joking aloud and laughing at their earlier silliness about modesty and decorum.
So then, free of restraints, we did many other things, and
more leisurely, so that when one girl was not actively participating she could get a vicarious enjoyment by watching
and assisting the other two of us. But I did not neglect
either of them for very long. I had, after all, learned from
the Persian Princesses Moth and Shams how two females
could be throughly pleasured at once, and myself with
them. The doing of that was of course far nicer with these
Mongol twins, since neither of them had to remain invisible during the proceedings. Indeed, before the night was

over, they had shed all vestiges of prudery, and were quite ready for their innermost dan-tian to be seen by me or each other, and for their and my pink places to do or be done to, in every variation I and they could think of.

So our first night together was an unqualified success, and the precursor of many other such nights, during which we became ever more inventive and acrobatic. It surprised even me: how many more combinations can be made of three than of two. But we did not always frolic in a threesome. The twins, otherwise so identical, were dissimilar in one physiological respect: they got their jing-gi, their monthly affliction, in a tidy alternation. Hence, for a few days every two weeks or so, I enjoyed an ordinary coupling with just a single female, while the other slept apart and jealously sulked.

However, young and lusty as I was, I did have some physical limits, and I also had other occupations that required my strength and stamina and alertness. After a couple of months, I began to find rather debilitating what the twins called their xing-yu or "sweet desires"—and what I called their insatiable appetites. So I suggested to them that my participation was not *always* necessary, and I told them about the "hymn of the convent," as the Lady Ilaria had named it. At the notion of a woman's manipulating her own petals and stars and so on, Buyantu and Biliktu looked as shocked as they had on our first night of acquaintance. When I went on to tell them what the Princess Moth had once confided to me—how she relieved and gratified the neglected women of the Shah Zaman's anderun, the twins looked even more shocked, and Buyantu exclaimed:

"That would be indecent!"

I said mildly, "You complained about indecency once before, and I think I proved you mistaken."

"But—a woman doing to another woman! An act of gua-li! That *would* be indecent!"

"I daresay it would, if one of both of you were old or ugly. But you are both beautiful and desirable women. I see no reason why you could not find as much pleasure in each other as I find in you."

Again the girls looked askance at each other, and again that caused them to blush, and that made them giggle—a trifle naughtily, a trifle guiltily. Still, it took some persua-

sion on my part before they would lie down naked together, without me between them, and let me remain fully
clothed while I instructed and guided their movements.
They were tense and reticent to do to each other what they
let me do with no reticence whatever. But as I took them
through the nuns' hymn, note by note, so to speak—gently
moving Buyantu's fingertip to caress Biliktu here, gently
moving Biliktu's head so that her lips pressed Buyantu
there—I could see them get aroused in spite of themselves.
And after some time of play under my guidance, they began to forget about me. When their small stars twinkled
erect, the girls did not need me to show them how they
could employ those darling protrusions to good effect on
each other. When first Biliktu's lotus began to unfold its
petals, Buyantu needed no one to show her how to gather
its dew. And when both their butterflies were aroused and
fluttering, the girls twined together as naturally and passionately as if they had been born to be lovers instead of
sisters.

I must confess that, by this time, I had myself become
aroused, and had forgotten whatever debility I had earlier
felt, and so doffed my own garments and joined in the play.

That happened quite often, from then on. If I came to my
chambers weary from a day's work, and the twins were
itching with xing-yu, I would give them leave to begin on
their own, and they would do so with alacrity. I might go
on down the hall to Nostril's closet and sit with him for a
time, listening to his day's gleanings of gossip from the
servants' quarters. Then I would return to my bedroom,
and perhaps pour a goblet of arkhi, and sit down and take
my ease while I watched the girls frolicking together. After a while, my fatigue would abate and my normal urges
would come alive and I would ask the girls' permission to
join them. Sometimes they would mischievously make me
wait until they had fully enjoyed and exhausted their sisterly ardors. Only then would they let me onto the bed
with them, and sometimes they would mischievously pretend that I was unneeded, unwanted, an intruder—and
would mischievously pretend reluctance to open their pink
places to me.

After some more time, it began to happen that I would
come home to my chambers to find the twins already abed,
and doing vigorous jiao-gou in their fashion. They laugh-

ingly referred to their style of coupling as chuai-sho-ur, a
Han term which translates as "tucking the hands into opposite sleeves." (We Westerners would speak of "folding
our arms," but that gesture is done by Eastern folk *inside*
their capacious sleeves.) I thought the twins were clever to
adopt that term to describe the way two women make love.

When I joined them, it would often happen that Biliktu
would profess herself already quite emptied of joys and
juices—she was less robust than her sister, she said; perhaps from being a few minutes the younger—and she
would ask to be allowed just to sit by and admire while Buyantu and I cavorted. And on those occasions, Buyantu
would sometimes pretend that she found me and my equipment and my performance deficient in comparison to what
she had just been ejoying, and she would laugh derisively
and call me gan-ga, which means awkward. But I always
played along with the pretense, and pretended to be insulted by her pretended disdain, so she would laugh more
loudly and give herself to me with passionate abandon, to
show that she had only been jesting. And if I asked Biliktu,
after she had rested for a while, to come and join me and
her sister, she might sigh, but she would usually accede,
and she would give good account of herself.

So, for a long time, the twins and I enjoyed a cozy and
convivial ménage à trois. That they were almost certainly
spies for the Khakhan, and probably reporting to him
everything including our bedtime diversions, did not
worry me, because I had nothing to hide from him. I was
ever loyal to Kubilai, and faithful in his service, and doing
naught that could be reported as contrary to his best interests. My own small spying—Nostril's nosing about among
the palace servants—I was doing in the Khakhan's behalf,
so I took no great pains to conceal even that from the girls.

No, there was at that time only one thing that troubled
me about Buyantu and Biliktu. Even when we were all
three in the rapturous throes of jiao-gou, I could never
cease remembering that these girls, according to the prevailing system of grading females, were of *only* twenty-
two-karat quality. Some conventicle of old wives and
concubines and senior servants had discovered in them
some trace of base alloy. To me, the twins seemed excellent
specimens of womanhood, and indubitably they were nonpareil servants, in bed or out, and they did not snore or

have bad breath. What, then, did they lack that they fell
short of the twenty-four-karat perfection? And why was
that lack imperceptible to me? Any other man would
doubtless have rejoiced to be in my situation, and would
cheerfully have brushed aside any such finical reservations. But then as always my curiosity never would rest
until it was satisfied.

8

AFTER that uninformative interview in which the Minister of Lesser Races had been so reserved and uneasy, my
next, with the Minister of War, was refreshingly open and
candid. I would have expected a holder of such an important office to be quite the opposite, but then there were a
lot of anomalies about the Minister of War. As I have said,
he was unaccountably a Han and not a Mongol. Also, the
Minister Chao Mengfu looked to me exceedingly young to
have been given such high office.

"That is because the Mongols do not *need* a Minister of
War," he said cheerfully, bouncing a round ball of ivory in
one hand. "They make war as naturally as you or I would
make jiao-gou with a woman, and they are probably better
at doing war than jiao-gou."

"Probably," I said. "Minister Chao, I would be grateful
if you would tell me—"

"Please, Elder Brother," he said, raising the hand which
held the ivory ball. "Ask me nothing about war. I can tell
you absolutely nothing about war. If, however, you require
advice on the making of jiao-gou . . ."

I looked at him. It was the third time he had spoken that
slightly indelicate term. He looked placidly back at me,
squeezing and revolving the carved ivory ball in his right
hand. I said, "Forgive my persistence, Minister Chao, but
the Khakhan has enjoined me to make inquiry of every—"

"Oh, I do not *mind* telling you anything. I mean only
that I am totally ignorant of war. I am much better informed about jiao-gou."

That made the fourth mention. "Could I be mistaken?" I
asked. "Are you not the Minister of War?"

Still cheerfully, he said, "It is what we Han call passing
off a fish eye for a pearl. My title is an empty one, an honor
conferred for other functions I perform. As I said, the Mongols *need* no Minister of War. Have you yet called on the
Armorer of the Palace Guard?"

"No."

"Do so. You would enjoy the encounter. The Armorer is
a handsome woman. My wife, in fact: the Lady Chao
Ku-an. That is because the Mongols no more require an adviser on armaments that they require advice on making
war."

"Minister Chao, you have me quite confounded. You
were drawing at that table when I came in, drawing on a
scroll. I assumed you were making a map of battle plans,
or something of the sort."

He laughed and said, "Something of the sort. If you consider jiao-gou as a sort of battle. Do you not see me
palpating this ivory ball, Elder Brother Marco? That is to
keep my right hand and fingers supple. Do you not know
why?"

I suggested feebly, "To be deft in the caresses of jiao-
gou?"

That sent him into a real convulsion of laughter. I sat
and felt like a fool. When he recovered, he wiped his eyes
and said, "I am an artist. If you ever meet another, you
will find him also playing with one of these hand balls. I
am an artist, Elder Brother, a master of the boneless colors, a holder of the Golden Belt, the highest accolade bestowed upon artists. More to be desired than an empty
Mongol title."

"I still do not understand. There is already a Court Master of the Boneless Colors."

He smiled. "Yes, old Master Chien. He paints *pretty* pictures. Little flowers. And my dear wife is famous as the
Mistress of the Zhu-gan Cane. She can paint just the shadows of that graceful cane, and make you see it entire. But
I—" He stood tall, and thumped his chest with his ivory
ball, and said proudly, "I am the Master of the Feng-shui,
and feng-shui means 'the wind, the water'—which is to
say, I paint that which cannot be grasped. *That* is what
won me the Golden Belt from my artist peers and elders."

I said politely, "I should like to see some of your work."

"Unfortunately, I now have to paint the feng-shui on my

own time, if ever. The Khan Kubilai gave me my bellicose
title just so I could be installed here in the palace to paint
another sort of thing. My own fault. I was incautious
enough to reveal to him that other talent of mine."

I tried to return to the subject that had brought me.
"You have nothing to do with war, Master Chao? Not in
the least?"

"Well, the least possible, yes. That cursed Arab Achmad
would probably withhold my wages if I did not make some
pretense at fulfilling my titular office. Therefore, with my
unsupple left hand, so to speak, I keep records of the Mongols' battles and casualties and conquests. The orloks and
sardars tell me what to write, and I write it down. Noboby
ever looks at the records. I might as well be writing poetry.
Also, I set little flags and simulated yak tails on a great
map to keep visible account of what the Mongols have conquered, and what yet remains to be conquered."

Chao said all of that in a very bored voice, unlike the
happy fervor with which he had spoken of his feng-shui
painting. But then he cocked his head and said, "You also
spoke of maps. You are interested in maps?"

"I am, yes, Minister. I have assisted in the making of
some."

"None like this, I wager." He led me to another room,
where a vast table, nearly as big as the room, was covered
by a cloth, lumped and peaked by what it protected. He
said, "Behold!" and whisked off the cloth.

"Cazza beta!" I breathed. It was not just a map, it was a
work of art. "Did you make this, Minister Chao?"

"I wish I could say yes, but I cannot. The artist is unknown and long dead. This sculptured model of the Celestial Land is said to date back to the reign of the First
Emperor Chin, whenever that was. It was he who commanded the building of the wall called the Mouth, which
you can see there in miniature."

Indeed I could. I could see everything of Kithai, and the
lands around it as well. The map was, as Chao said, a
model, not a drawing on a sheet of paper. It appeared to
have been molded of gesso or terracotta, flat where the
earth was in fact flat, raised and convoluted and serrated
where the earth actually rose in hills and mountains—and
then the whole of it had been overlaid with precious metals
and stones and colored enamels. To one side lay a tur-

quoise Sea of Kithai, its curving shores and bays and inlets all carefully delineated, and into that sea ran the land's rivers, done in silver. All the mountains were gilded, the highest of them tipped with diamonds to represent snow, and the lakes were little pools of blue sapphires. The forests were done, almost to the individual *tree,* in green jade, and farmlands were a brighter green enamel, and the major cities were done, almost to the individual *house,* in white alabaster. Hither and yon ran the wavery line of the Great Wall—or Walls, as it is in places—done in rubies. The deserts were sparkling flats of powdered pearl. Across the whole great table-sized landscape were lines inlaid in gold, appearing squiggly where they undulated over mountains and highlands, but when I looked directly down on them, I could see that the lines were straight—up and down the model, back and forth, making an overlay of squares. The east–west lines were clearly the climatic parallels, and the north-south lines the longitudes, but from what meridian they measured their distances I could not discern.

"From the capital city," said Chao, having noticed my scrutiny. "In those times it was Xian." He pointed to the tiny alabaster city, far to the southwest of Khanbalik. "That is where this map was found, some years ago."

I noticed also the additions Chao had made to the map—little paper flags to represent the battle standards of orloks, and feathers to represent the yak tails of sardars—outlining what the Khan Kubilai and his Ilkhans and Wangs held of the lands represented.

"Not all of the map, then, is within the empire," I observed.

"Oh, it will be," said Chao, in the same bored voice with which he talked of his office. He began to point. "All of this, here, to the south of the River Yang-tze, is still the Empire of Sung, with its capital over here in the beautiful coast city of Hang-zho. But you can see how closely the Sung Empire is pressed about by our Mongol armies on its borders. Everything north of the Yang-tze is what used to be the Empire of Chin and is now Kithai. Over yonder, the entire west is held by the Ilkhan Kaidu. And the high country of To-Bhot, south of there, is ruled by the Wang Ukuruji, one of Kubilai's numerous sons. The only battles being waged at the moment are down here—in the south-

west—where the Orlok Bayan is campaigning in the province of Yun-nàn."

"I have heard of that place."

"A rich and fertile country, but inhabited by the obstreperous Yi people," Chao said indifferently. "When the Yi finally have the good sense to succumb to Bayan, and we
have Yun-nan, then, you see, we will have the remaining
Sung provinces so tightly encircled that they are bound to
surrender, too. The Khakhan has already picked out a new
name for those lands. They will be called Manzi. The Khan
Kubilai will then reign over everything you see on this
map, and more. From Sibir in the frozen north to the borders of the hot jungle lands of Champa in the south. From
the Sea of Kithai on the east to far, far beyond the western
extent of this map."

I said, "You seem to think that will not be enough to satisfy him."

"I know it will not. Only a year ago, he ordered the Mongols' first venture ever *eastward*. Yes, their first foray
upon the sea. He sent a fleet of chuan out across the Sea of
Kithai, to the islands called Jihpen-kwe, the Empire of the
Dwarfs. That tentative probe was repulsed by the dwarfs,
but Kubilai is certain to try again, and more energetically." The Minister stood for a moment, looking over the
immense and beautiful map model, then said, "What matter what more he takes? When Sung falls, he has all the
Celestial Land that once was Han."

He sounded so uncaring about it that I remarked, "You
can say it more emotionally, if you like, Minister. I would
understand. You are, after all, a Han."

"Emotion? Why?" He shrugged. "A centipede, even
when it dies, does not fall. Being likewise many-legged,
the Han have always endured and always will." He began
replacing the cloth cover on the table. "Or, if you prefer a
more vivid image, Elder Brother: like a woman in jiao-gou,
we simply envelop and absorb the impaling lance."

I said—and not critically, for I had become fond of the
young artist in just this short time—"Minister Chao, the
matter of jiao-gou seems rather to tincture all your
thoughts."

"Why not? I am a whore." He sounded cheerful again,
and led me back into his main room. "On the other hand, it
is said that, of all women, a whore most resents being

raped. Here, look at what I was painting when you ar-
rrived." He unrolled the silk scroll on the drawing board,
and again I breathed an exclamation:

"Porco Dio!"

I had never seen a picture like it. And I mean that in
more than one sense. Not in Venice, where there are many
works of art to be seen, nor in any of the countries I had
come through, in some of which also were many works of
art, had I ever seen a picture so exquisitely drawn and
tinted that it was veritable *life* captured in the round; so
lighted and shaded that it seemed my fingers could stroke
its rotundities and delve into its recesses; so sinuous in its
forms that they seemed to move before my eyes; yet at the
same time a picture—well, there it lay, easily to be seen—
done, like any other, *on a flat surface.*

"Observe the likenesses," said Master Chao, droning in
the manner of a San Marco docent showing the Basilica's
mosaic saints. "Only an artist capable of painting the impalpable feng-shui could so perfectly render, as well, substantial flesh and meat."

Indeed, the six persons depicted in Master Chao's painting were instantly and unmistakably recognizable. I had
seen every one of them in this very palace, alive and
breathing and moving about. Yet here they were on silk—
from the hairs of their head and the hues of their skin to
the intricate brocaded designs on their robes and the tiny
glints of light that gave animation to their eyes—all six
alive still, but frozen in their movement, and each person
magically reduced to the size of my hand.

"Observe the composition," said Master Chao, still good-
humoredly sounding humorless. "All the curves, the directions of movement, they beguile the eye to the main
subject and what he is doing."

And therein the picture was egregiously different from
any other I had ever seen. The main subject referred to by
Master Chao was his and my liege lord, the Khan of All
Khans—Kubilai, no doubt about it—though the picture's
only intimation of his regnancy was the gold morion helmet he wore, that being *all* he was wearing. And what he
was doing in the picture he was doing to a young lady who
was lying back on a couch with her brocade robes shamelessly caught up above her waist. I recognized the lady
(from her face, which was all I had ever before seen of her)

as one of Kubilai's current concubines. Two additional concubines, also considerably dishevelled in their garments and exposed in their persons, were pictured as assisting in the coupling, while the Khatun Jamui and one other of Kubilai's wives stood by, fully and modestly clothed, but looking not at all disapproving.

Master Chao, still playing the dullard docent, said, "This one is entitled 'The Mighty Stag Mounts the Third of His Yearning Does.' You will observe that he has already had two—you can see the pearly droplets of his jing-ye dribbling down their inner thighs—and there are two more yet to be enjoyed. Correctly, in the Han, this one's title would be 'Huang-se Gong-chu—' ''

"This one?" I gasped. "You have made other pictures like this?"

"Well, not identical to this. The last one was entitled 'Kubilai Is Mightiest of Mongols Because He Partakes of Yin to Augment His Yang.' It showed him on his knees before a very young, naked girl, his tongue lapping from her lotus the pearly droplets of her yin juices, while she—"

"*Porco Dio!*" I exclaimed again. "And you have not yet been dragged off to the Fondler?"

Mimicking my outcry, he said cheerfully, "Porco Dio, I hope not to be. Why do you suppose I continue in this artistic whoredom? As we Han say, it is my wineskin and my rice bag. It was to have such pictures that the Khakhan honored me with this ministry-in-name-only."

"He *wants* these made?"

"He must have whole galleries hung with my scrolls by now. I also do hand-fans. My wife paints on a fan a superb design of zhu-gan cane or peony flowers and, if the fan is unfolded in the usual direction, that is all you see. But if the fan is flirtatiously flicked open the other way, you glimpse an erotic bit of dalliance."

"So this—this sort of thing is really your main work for Kubilai."

"Not only for Kubilai, curse it. By his decree, I am as biddable as the banquet-hall jugglers. My talent is at the command of all my fellow ministers and courtiers. Even you, I would not be surprised. I must remember to inquire."

"Imagine . . . ," I marveled. "The Khanate's Minister of War . . . spending his time painting vile pictures . . ."

"Vile?" He pretended to recoil in horror. "Really, you wound me. Subject matter aside, they are, after all, from the supple hand of Chao Meng-fu, Golden Belt Master of Feng-shui."

"Oh, I do not denigrate the expertness of them. The artistry of this one is impeccable. Except—"

"If this one distresses you," he said, "you should see what I have to paint for that degenerate Arab, Achmad. But go on, Elder Brother. Except, what?"

"Except—no man, not even the great Khakhan, ever possessed a masculine red jewel like that one in the picture. You certainly made it vividly red enough—but the size and the veining of it! It looks like he is ramming a rough-barked log into her."

"Ah, that. Yes. Well. Of course he does not pose for these portrayals, but one must flatter one's patron. The only male model I employ is myself, in a looking glass, to get the anatomical articulations correct. However, I must confess that the virile member of any male Han—myself unhappily included—would hardly be worth a viewer's looking at. If it could be discerned at all in a picture of that size."

I started to say something condoling, but he raised his hand.

"Please! Do not offer. Go and show yours, if you must, to the Armorer of the Palace Guard. She might appreciate its contrast to her husband's. But I have already been shown one Westerner's gross organ, and that will suffice. I was nauseated to see that the Arab's unwholesome red jewel, even in repose, is bald-headed!"

"Muslims are circumcised; I am not," I said loftily. "And I was not about to volunteer. But you might sometime like to paint my twin maid-servants, who do some wondrous—" I paused there, and frowned, and inquired, "Master Chao, did you mean to say that the Minister Achmad *does* pose for the pictures you paint for him?"

"Yes," he said, making a face of disgust. "But I would never show to you or to anyone any of those, and I am certain Achmad will not. As soon as a painting is finished, he even sends away the other models employed—away to far corners of the empire—so they cannot make gossip or complaint hereabout. But this I will wager: however far they go, they never forget him. Or me. For my having seen what

happened, and having made permanent record of their
shame."

Chao's former cheerfulness had all dissipated, and he
seemed disinclined to talk further, so I took my leave. I
went to my chambers, thinking deeply—and not about
erotic paintings, much as that work had impressed me, nor
about the Chief Minister Achmad's secret diversions,
much as they had interested me. No, I went pondering on
two other things Chao had mentioned while he was speaking as Minister of War:

Yun-nan Province.

The Yi people.

The evasive Minister of Lesser Races, Pao Nei-ho, had
also touched briefly on those subjects. I wanted to know
more about them, and about him. But I did not learn anything further that day. Though Nostril was waiting for me,
returned from his latest foraging among the domestic
staff, he could not yet tell me anything concerning the
Minister Pao. We sat down together, and I bade Biliktu
bring us each a goblet of good putao white wine, and she
fanned us with a perfumed fan while we talked. Nostril,
pridefully showing off how much his grasp of Mongol had
lately improved, said in that language:

"Here is a juicy bit, Master Marco. When it was confided
to me that the Armorer of the Palace Guard is a most promiscuous voluptuary, it did not at first intrigue me. After
all, what soldier is not a fornicator? But that officer, it
transpires, is a young *woman*, a Han lady of some degree.
Her whorishness is evidently notorious, but is not punished, because her lord husband is such a poltroon that he
condones her indecent conduct."

I said, "Perhaps he has other worries that trouble him
more. Let us then, in compassion, you and I, not add our
voices to the general tattling. Not about that poor fellow,
anyway."

"As you command, master. But I have nothing to tell
about anyone else . . . except the servants and slaves
themselves, in whom you surely have no interest."

True, I had not. But I got the feeling that Nostril wanted
to say something more. I studied him speculatively, then
said:

"Nostril, you have been extraordinarily well behaved
for quite a while now. For you, that is. I recollect only one

recent misdemeanor—when I caught you peeping that
night at me and the girls—and I cannot recall any outright
felony in ever so long. There are other things different
about you lately. You are dressing as finely as all the other
palace servants and slaves. And you are letting your beard
grow. I always wondered how you managed to keep it forever looking like a scruffy two weeks' growth. But now it
looks a respectable beard, though much grayer than it
used to be, and your receding chin is no longer so noticeable. Why the turnout of whiskers? Are you hiding from
somebody?"

"Not exactly, master. As you say, slaves here at this resplendent palace are encouraged not to look like slaves.
And, as you say, I simply wished to appear more respectable. More like the handsome man I used to be." I sighed.
But he did not elaborate in his usual braggart way; he
added only, "I have recently espied someone in the slave
quarters. Someone I think I knew long ago. But I hesitate
to approach, until I can be sure."

I laughed heartily. "Hesitate? *You?* Reticent of being
thought forward? And to another slave? Why, even the
kitchen's trash-pile pigs do not hesitate to approach a
slave."

He winced slightly, but then drew himself up as tall as
he could.

"The pigs are not also slaves, Master Marco. And we
slaves were not always so. There used to be some social distinctions among some of us, when we were free. The one
dignity we can exercise now is to observe those bygone distinctions. If this slave is who I believe her to be, then she
was once a high-born lady. I was a freeman in those days,
but only a drover. I would ask, master, if you would do me
the favor of ascertaining who she is, before I make myself
known to her, that I may do so with the appropriate formality of address."

For a moment I almost felt ashamed of myself. I had
commanded compassion for the cuckold Master Chao, yet
laughed heartlessly at this poor wretch. Was I, like him, so
ready to make ko-tou to class distinctions? But in the next
moment I reminded myself that Nostril really *was* a
wretch, of repellent nature and, as long as I had known
him, doing none but revolting deeds.

I snapped, "Do not play the noble slave at me, Nostril.

You live a life far better than you deserve. However, if you merely wish me to corroborate someone's identity, I will. What do I ask, and of whom?"

"Could you just inquire, master, whether the Mongols have ever taken prisoners from a kingdom called Cappadocia in Anatolia? That will tell me what I wish to know."

"Anatolia. That is north of the route by which we came from the Levant into Persia. But my father and uncle must have traveled through it on their earlier journeys. I will ask them, and perhaps I will not need to ask anyone else."

"May Allah smile ever on you, kind master."

I left him to finish his wine, though Biliktu sniffed with disapproval of his continuing to loll in her presence. I went along the palace corridors to my father's chambers, and found my uncle also there, and said I had a question to ask of them. But first my father informed me that they were contending with some problems of their own.

"Obstacles," he said, "being thrown in the way of our mercantile ventures. The Muslims are proving less than eager to welcome us into their Ortaq. Delaying issuance of permits for us even to sell our accumulated stock of zafràn. Clearly they are reflecting some jealousy or spitefulness on the part of the Finance Minister Achmad."

"We have two options," muttered my uncle. "Bribe the damned Arab or put pressure on him. But how do you bribe a man who already has everything, or can easily get it? How do you influence a man who is the second most powerful in the realm?"

It occurred to me that if I told them what hints I had had of Achmand's private life, they might profitably wield a threat to expose him. But on second thought I did not mention it. My father would refuse to stoop to any such tactic, and would forbid my uncle to do so. Also, I suspected that my hearsay knowledge was a dangerous thing even for me to have acquired, and I would not hand on the risk of danger to them. I made only one mild suggestion:

"Can you perhaps employ, as they say, the devil that tempted Lucifer?"

"A woman?" grunted Uncle Mafìo. "I doubt it. There seems to be a deal of mystery about Achmad's tastes—whether he prefers women or men or children or ewes or what. In any case, he could take his pick from the whole empire, excepting only the Khakhan's prior choices."

"Well," said my father, "if he truly does have everything he could possibly want, there is an old proverb that
applies. Ask favors of the man with a full stomach. Let us
cease quibbling with the petty underlings of the Ortaq. Go
direct to Achmad and put our case before him. What can he
do?"

"From what little I know of him," growled Uncle Mafìo,
"that man would laugh at a leper."

My father shrugged. "He will tergiversate for a time,
but he will eventually concede. He knows we stand well
with Kubilai."

I said, "I would be happy to put in a word with the Khakhan when I call on him next."

"No, Marco, do not you fret about this. I would not wish
you to compromise your own standing on our account. Perhaps later, when you have been longer in the Khakhan's
confidence, and when perhaps we have real need of your
intercession. But with this situation, Mafìo and I will cope.
Now, you wished to ask a question?"

I said, "You first came here to Kithai and went home
again by way of Constantinople, so you must have gone
through the lands of Anatolia. Did you happen to traverse
a place there called Cappadocia?"

"Why, yes," said my father. "Cappadocia is a kingdom
of the Seljuk Turki people. We stopped briefly in its capital
city of Erzincan on our way back to Venice. Erzincan is
very nearly directly north of Suvediye—where you have
been, Marco—but a long way to the north of it."

"Were those Turki ever at war with the Mongols?"

"Not then," said Uncle Mafìo. "Not yet, as far as I know.
But there was some trouble there, which involved the
Mongols, because Cappadocia abuts on the Persian realm
of the Ilkhan Abagha. The trouble occurred while we were
passing through, as a matter of fact. That was what, Nico—
eight, nine years ago?"

"And what was it that happened then?" I asked.

My father said, "The Seljuk King Kilij had an overly
ambitious Chief Minister—"

"As Kubilai has the Wali Achmad," grumbled Uncle
Mafìo.

"And that Minister secretly connived with the Ilkhan
Abagha, promising to make the Cappadocians vassals of

the Mongols if Abagha would help him depose the King. And that is what happened."

"How did it come about?" I asked.

"The King and the whole royal family were assassinated, right there in his Erzincan palace," said my uncle. "The people knew it was the doing of the Chief Minister, but none dared denounce him, for fear that Abagha would take advantage of any internal dispute, to march his Mongols in and ransack the country."

"So," my father concluded the tale, "the Minister put his own infant son on the throne as King—with himself as ruling Regent, of course—and what few survived of the royal family, he handed over to Abagha for disposal as he wished."

"I see," I said. "And presumably they are now dispersed all over the Mongol Khanate. Would you know, Father, if there were any women among them?"

"Yes. The survivors may *all* have been female. The Chief Minister was a practical man. He probably slew every one of the King's male descendants, so there could be no legitimate claimant to the throne he had won for his own son. The females would not have mattered."

"The survivors were mostly cousins and such," said Uncle Mafìo. "But there was at least one of the King's daughters among them. She was said to be beautiful, and it was said that Abagha would have taken her for his concubine, except—he found some fault with her. I forget. Anyway, he simply gave her to the slave traders, with the others."

"You are right, Mafìo," said my father. "There was at least that one royal daughter. Mar-Janah was her name."

I thanked them and returned to my own suite. Nostril, in his sly way, had made capital of my generosity, and was still being wined and fanned by a scowling Biliktu. Exasperated, I said, "Here you sprawl like a lordly courtier, you sloth, while I run about on your errands."

He grinned drunkenly and in a slurred voice inquired, "With any success, master?"

"This slave you think you recognized. Could it have been a woman of the Seljuk Turki people?"

His grin evaporated. He bounded to his feet, spilling his wine and making Biliktu squeal in complaint. He stood almost trembling before me and waited for my next words.

"By any chance, could it be a certain Princess Mar-Janah?"

However much he had drunk, he was suddenly sober—and also stricken speechless, it seemed, for perhaps the first time in his life. He only stood and vibrated and stared at me, his eyes as wide as his nostril.

I said, "That speculation I got from my father and uncle." He made no comment, still standing transfixed, so I said sharply, "I take it that *is* the identity you wished confirmed?"

He whispered, so low that I barely heard, "I did not really know . . . whether I wished it to be so . . . or I dreaded that it was so . . ." Then, without ko-tou or salaam or even a murmur of thanks for my pains, he turned away and, very slowly, like an aged man, he shuffled off to his closet.

I dismissed the matter from my mind and I also went to bed—with only Buyantu, because Biliktu had been for some nights indisposed for that service.

9

I had been in residence at the palace for a long time before I had the opportunity to meet the courtier whose work most fascinated me: the Court Firemaster responsible for the so-called fiery trees and sparkling flowers. I was told that he was almost continuously traveling about the country, arranging those displays wherever and whenever this town or that had some festa to celebrate. But one winter day, Prince Chingkim came to tell me that the Firemaster Shi had returned to his palace quarters, to begin his preparations for Khanbalik's biggest annual celebration—the welcoming-in of the New Year, which was then imminent—and Chingkim took me to call on him. The Master Shi had an entire small house for his residence and workshop, and it was situated—for the sake of the palace's safety, said Chingkim—well apart from the other palace buildings, in fact on the far side of what was now the Kara Hill.

The Firemaster was bent over a littered work table when we entered, and from his garb I took him first to be

an Arab. But when he turned to greet us, I decided he had
to be a Jew, for I had seen those lineaments before. His
blackberry eyes looked haughtily but good-humoredly at
me down a long, hooked nose like a shimshir, and his hair
and beard were like a curly fungus, gray but showing still
a trace of red.

Chingkim said, speaking in Mongol, "Master Shi Ix-me,
I would have you meet a Palace guest."

"Marco Polo," said the Firemaster.

"Ah, you have heard of his visit."

"I have heard of him."

"Marco is much interested in your work, and my Royal
Father would have you tell him something of it."

"I will attempt to do so, Prince."

When Chingkim had gone, there was a brief silence, myself and the Firemaster eyeing each other. At last he said,
"Why are you interested in the fiery trees, Marco Polo?"

I said simply, "They are beautiful."

"The beauty of danger. That attracts you?"

"You know it always has," I said, and waited.

"But there is also danger in beauty. That does not repel
you?"

"Aha!" I crowed. "Now I suppose you are going to tell
me that your name is not really Mordecai!"

"I was not going to tell you anything. Except about my
work with the beautiful but dangerous fires. What would
you wish to know, Marco Polo?"

"How did you get a name like Shi Ix-me?"

"That has nothing to do with my work. However . . ."
He shrugged. "When the Jews first came here, they were
allotted seven Han surnames to apportion among them.
Shi is one of the seven, and was originally Yitzhak. In the
Ivrit, my full name is Shemuel ibn-Yitzhak."

I asked, "When did you come to Kithai?" expecting him
to say that he had arrived only shortly before me.

"I was born here, in the city of Kai-feng, where my forebears settled some hundreds of years ago."

"I do not believe it."

He snorted, as Mordecai had done so often at my comments. "Read the Old Testament of your Bible. Chapter
forty-nine of Isaiah, where the prophet foresees a regath-
ering of all the Jews. 'Behold, these shall come from afar,
and behold these from the north, and from the sea, and

these from the land of Sinim.' This land of Kithai is still in Ivrit called Sina. So there were Jews here in Isaiah's time, and that was more than one thousand eight hundred years ago."

"Why would Jews have come *here?*"

"Probably because they were unwelcome somewhere else," he said wryly. "Or perhaps they took the Han to be one of their own lost tribes, wandered away from Israel."

"Oh, come now, Master Shi. The Han are pork eaters, and always have been."

He shrugged again. "Nevertheless, they have things in common with the Jews. They slaughter their animals in a ceremonial manner almost kasher, except that they do not remove the terephah sinews. And they are even more than Jewishly strict in the customs of dress, never wearing garments mixed of animal and vegetable fibers."

Stubbornly I maintained, "The Han could never have been a lost tribe. There is no least physical resemblance between them and the Jews."

Master Shi laughed and said, "But there is now—between the Jews and the Han. Do not judge by my looks. It only happens that the Shi family never much intermarried here. Most others of the seven names did. So Kithai is full of Jews with ivory skins and squinty eyes. Only sometimes by their noses shall you know them. Or a man by his gid." He laughed again, then said more seriously, "Or you may know a Jew because, wherever he wanders, he still observes the religion of his fathers. He still turns toward Jerusalem to pray. Also, wherever he wanders, he still keeps the memory of old Jewish legends—"

"Like the Lamed-vav," I interrupted. "And the tzaddikim."

"—and, wherever he wanders, he continues to share with other Jews what things he remembers of the old, and what worthwhile new things he learns along his way."

"That is how you knew of me! One telling another. Ever since Mordecai escaped from the Vulcano—"

He gave no sign of having heard a single work I had interposed, but went right on. "Happily, the Mongols do not discriminate among us lesser races. So I, albeit a Jew, am the Court Firemaster to the Khan Kubilai, who respects my artistry and cares not at all that I bear one of the seven surnames."

"You must be very proud, Master Shi," I said. "I should like to hear how you came to take up this extraordinary profession, and how you became so successful in it. I have always thought of Jews as being money-lenders and pawn-brokers, not as artists or seekers of success."

He snorted again. "When did you ever hear of an inartistic money-lender? Or an unsuccessful pawnshop?"

I could give no answer to that, and he seemed to expect none, so I inquired, "How did you come to invent the fiery trees?"

"I did not. The secret of making them was discovered by a Han, and that was ages ago. My contribution has been to make that secret more easy of application."

"And what is the secret, Master Shi?"

"It is called huo-yao, the flaming powder." He motioned me to the work table and, from one of the many jars and phials thereon, he took a pinch of dark-gray powder. "Observe what happens when I place this very little bit of huo-yao on this porcelain plate, and touch it with fire—so." He picked up a stick of already smoldering incense and applied its spark end to the powder.

I started as, with a quick, angry, fizzing noise, the huo-yao burned away in a brief, intense flash, leaving a puff of the blue smoke whose acrid smell I had come to recognize.

"Essentially," said the Firemaster, "all that the powder does is to burn with the fiercest rapidity of any substance. But when it is confined in a fairly tight container, its burning bursts that confinement, making a loud noise and much light as it does so. Adding to the basic huo-yao other powders—metallic salts of one kind or another—makes it burn in different colors."

"But what makes it fly?" I asked. "And sometimes explode in sequacious bursts of those different colors?"

"For such an effect, the huo-yao is packed into a paper tube like this one, with a small opening at one end." He showed me such a tube, made of stiff paper. It looked like a large, hollow candle, with a hole where the wick would have been. "When touched with a spark at that hole, the powder burns and the intense flame spurting from that aperture at the nether end throws the whole tube forward—or upward, if it is pointed that way."

"I have seen it do so," I said. "But *why* should it do so?"

"Come, come, Polo," he chided me. "We have here one of

the first principles of natural philosophy. *Everything* flinches away from fire."

"Of course," I said. "Of course."

"This being the fiercest of fires, the container flinches away most energetically. So violently that it recoils to a great distance or a great altitude."

"And," I said, to show how well I understood, "having the fire in its own vitals, it perforce takes the fire with it."

"Exactly so. And takes with it more than the fire, in fact, for I have previously attached other tubes around the one that flies. When the first has consumed itself—and I can predetermine how long that will take—it ignites the other tubes. Depending on what sorts I have used, they either explode at that instant, scattering fire of one color or another, or they go flinging off on their own, to explode at another distance. By combining in one engine a number of flying tubes and explosive tubes, I can contrive a fiery tree that sprouts upward to any height, and then bursts into one of various patterns of the sparkling flowers in many different colors. Peach blossoms, poppy flowers, tiger lilies, whatever I choose to make bloom in the sky."

"Ingenious," I said. "Fantastic. But the main ingredient—the huo-yao—of what magical elements is it compounded?"

"It was indeed an ingenious man who first compounded them," the Firemaster concurred. "But the constituent elements are the simplest imaginable." From each of three other jars he took a pinch of powder and dropped them on the table; one powder was black, one yellow, one white. "Tan-hua, liu and tung-bian. Taste them and you should know them."

I licked a fingertip and picked up a few grains of the fine black powder and touched my tongue, then said, wondering, "Nothing but charcoal of wood." Of the yellow powder, I said, "Only common sulphur." Of the white powder, I said thoughtfully, "Hm. Salty, bitter, almost vinegary. But what . . . ?"

Master Shi grinned and said, "The crystallized urine of a virgin boy."

"Vakh," I grunted, and rubbed my sleeve across my mouth.

"Tung-bian, the autumn stone, so the Han call it," he said, wickedly enjoying my discomfiture. "The sorcerers and wizards and practitioners of al-kimia deem it a precious element. They employ it in medicines, love philters and the like. They take the urine of a boy no older than twelve, filter it through wood ash, then let it solidify into crystals. Rather difficult of procurement, you see, and in only trifling amounts. But it was specified in the original recipe for making the flaming powder: charcoal, sulphur and the autumn stone—and that recipe was handed unchanged down through the ages. Charcoal and sulphur have always been plentiful, but the third ingredient was not. So there simply *was* not much making of the flaming powder, until my lifetime."

"You found some way to procure maiden boys in quantity?"

He snorted, very Mordecai-like. "Sometimes there are benefits in coming from a humble family. When I first tasted the element, as you just did, I recognized it as another and much less exquisite substance. My father was a fish peddler, and to make the fillets of cheap fish look more delectably pink, he soaked them in a brine of the lowly salt called saltpeter. That is all the autumn stone is—saltpeter. I do not know why it should be present in boys' urine, and I do not care, for I have no need of boys to make it. Kithai is abundantly supplied with salt lakes, and they are abundantly rimmed with crusts containing saltpeter. So, these many centuries after the flaming powder was first compounded by some Han genius of al-kimia, I, merely the inquisitive son of the Jewish fish peddler Shi, am the first to make it in vast quantities, and to make the glorious displays of its fiery trees and sparkling flowers enjoyable by all men everywhere."

"Master Shi," I said diffidently. "In addition to my admiration of the beauty of those works, I have been struck by the thought of turning them to more useful account. The thought came to me when my own horse shied and bucked at first seeing a display of the fiery trees. Could not these engines of yours be used as weapons of war? To break up a cavalry charge, for example?"

He snorted yet again. "A good idea, yes, but you are more than sixty years late with it. In the year when I was born—let me see, that would have been by your Christian count the year one thousand two hundred fourteen—my native city of Kai-feng was the first besieged by the Mongols of the Khan Chinghiz. His horse troops were affrighted and dispersed by balls of fire which flew into their midst, trailing sprarks and whistling and banging. The Mongols were not stopped for long, needless to say, and they eventually took the city, but that valiant defense contrived by the Kai-feng Firemaster became legendary. And, as I told you, we Jews are great rememberers of legends. Thus it was that I grew up enthralled by the subject, and finally myself became a Firemaster. That employment of the flaming powder at Kai-feng was its first recorded use in warfare."

"Its first," I echoed. "Then it has been used since?"

"Our Khan Kubilai is not a warrior likely to ignore any promising tool of war," said Master Shi. "Even if I were not personally interested in trying new applications of my art, and I am, he has charged me with investigating every possible use of the huo-yao for war missiles. And I have had some partial successes."

I said, "I should be gratified to hear of them."

The Firemaster seemed hesitant to confide. He looked from under his fungoid eyebrows at me and said, "The Han have a story. Of the master archer Yi, all his life prevailing over every foe, until he taught all his skills to an eager pupil, and that man finally slew him."

"I do not seek to appropriate any of your ideas," I said. "And I will freely tell you any that might occur to me. They could be of some small worth."

"The danger of beauty," he mumbled. "Well, are you acquainted with the large, hairy nut called the India nut?"

Wondering what that had to do with anything, I said, "I have eaten its meat in certain confections served at table here."

"I have taken hollowed-out India nuts and packed them full of the huo-yao, and inserted wicks to supply the spark after a suitable interval. I have done the same with joints of the stout zhu-gan cane. Those objects can be thrown by a man or a simple catapult into an enemy's defenses and—when they work properly—they let loose their energy with such explosive force that a single nut or cane would well nigh wreck this whole house."

"Marvelous," I said.

"When they work. I have also used cylinders of large zhu-gan cane in another manner. By inserting one of my flying engines into a long empty cane before lighting its wick, a warrior can literally aim the missile like an arrow, and send it flying toward a target, more or less straightly."

"Ingenious," I said.

"When it works. I have also made missiles in which the huo-yao is compounded with naft oil, with kara dust, even with barnyard dung. When they are hurled into an enemy's defenses, they spread an almost inextinguishable fire, or a dense, stinking, choking smoke."

"Fantastic," I said.

"When they work. Unfortunately, there is one flaw in the huo-yao that renders it totally impractical for military use. Its three component elements, as you have seen, are finely ground powders. But each of those powders has a different inherent density, or weight. Therefore, no matter how tightly the huo-yao is packed into a container, the three elements gradually separate out from one another. The least movement or vibration of the container makes the heavier saltpeter discombine and sift down to the bottom, so the huo-yao becomes inert and impotent. Thus it is impossible to make and store any supply of any of my inventions. The mere movement of them into a storehouse, not to mention out of it, causes them to become absolutely useless."

"I see," I said, sharing his air of deep disappointment. "That is why you are perpetually on the road, Master Shi?"

"Yes. To arrange a fiery-tree display in any city, I must go there and make the things on the spot. I travel with a supply of paper tubes, wicks, barrels of each of the constituent powders, and it is no great chore to mix the huo-yao and charge my various engines. That is obviously what the Kai-feng Firemaster did, when my city was besieged. But can you imagine doing all that in wartime, *in the field*, in the midst of battle? Every company of warriors would have to have its own separate Firemaster, and he to have at hand all his supplies and equipment, and he would have to be inhumanly quick and proficient. No, Marco Polo, I fear that the huo-yao will forever be only a pretty toy. There seems no hope of its military application, except in the occasional case of a city under siege."

"A pity," I murmured. "But the only problem is the powder's tendency to separate?"

"That is the *only* problem," he said, with heavy irony, "just as the only impediment to a man's flying is that he has no wings."

"Only the separation . . . ," I said to myself, several times, then I snapped my fingers and exclaimed, "I have it!"

"Have you now?"

"Dust blows about, but mud does not, and hardened clods do not. Suppose you wetted the huo-yao into mud? Or baked it into a solid?"

"Imbecile," he said, but with some amusement. "Wet the powder and it does not burn at all. Put a baking fire to it and it may blow up in your face."

"Oh," I said, deflated.

"I told you, there is danger in this stuff of beauty."

"I am not over timid of danger, Master Shi," I said, still pondering the problem. "I know you are busy preparing for the New Year celebrations, so I would not obtrude my company upon you. But, while you are occupied, would you let me have some jars of the huo-yao, so that I could speculate on ways and means—"

"Bevakashà! This is nothing to play with!"

"I will be most careful, Master Shi. I will not ignite so much as a pinch of it. I will but study its properties and try to think of a solution to the problem of its sifting down—"

"Khakma! As if I and every other Firemaster have not devoted our lives to that, ever since the flaming powder was first compounded! And you, who never even saw the stuff before—you truly are suggesting that I play the master archer Yi!"

I said, with insinuation, "So might have spoken, once upon a time, the Firemaster of Kai-feng." There was a short silence, and I said, "The inquisitive son of a Jewish fish peddler might not have been trusted, either, to bring a new idea to the art."

There was another and longer silence. Then Master Shi sighed and said, evidently to his deity:

"Lord, I am committed. I hope You see that. This Marco Polo must once have done something right, and the proverb instructs us that one mitzva deserves another."

From under the work table, he picked up two tightly woven cane baskets and thrust them into my arms. "Here, estimable fool. In each, fifty liang measures of huo-yao. Do

as you will, and l'chaim to you. I hope the next I hear of
Marco Polo is not his thunderous departure from this
world."

I took the baskets back to my apartment, intending to
start my essay at al-kimia straight away. But I found Nostril again waiting for me, so I asked if he had brought any
information.

"Precious little, master. Only a salacious small item
about the Court Astrologer, if you are interested. It seems
he is a eunuch, and for fifty years he has kept his spare
parts pickled in a jar that stands beside his bed. He intends
to have them buried with him, so that he will go entire to
the afterworld."

"That is all?" I said, wanting to get to work.

"Elsewhere, all is preparation for the New Year. Every
courtyard is strewn with dry straw, so that any approaching evil kwei spirits will be frightened off by the crackling
noise when they tread on it. The Han women are all cooking the Eight-Ingredient Pudding, which is a holiday
treat, and the men are making the many lanterns to light
the festivities, and the children are making little paper
windmills. It is said that some families spend their entire
year's savings on this celebration. But not everybody is ex-
hilarated; a good many of the Han are committing suicide."

"Whatever for?"

"It is their custom that all outstanding debts be settled
at this season. The creditors are going about knocking on
doors, and many a desperate debtor is hanging himself—to
save his face, as the Han say—from the shame of not being
able to pay. Meanwhile, the Mongol folk, who do not care
much about face, are smearing molasses on the faces of
their kitchen gods."

"What?"

"They have the quaint belief that the idol they keep over
the kitchen hearth, the house god Nagatai, ascends to
Heaven at this time to report their year's behavior to the
great god Tengri. So they feed molasses to Nagatai in the
quaint belief that thus his lips are sealed, and he cannot
tattle anything detrimental."

"Quaint, yes," I said. Biliktu came into the room just
then and took the baskets from me. I motioned for her to
set them on a table. "Anything else, Nostril?"

He wrung his hands. "Only that I have fallen in love."

"Oh?" I said, immersed in my own thoughts. "With what?"

"Master, do not mock me. With a woman, what else?"

"What *else?* To my own knowledge, you have previously had congress with a Baghdad pony, with a young man of Kashan, with a Sindi baby of indeterminate sex—"

He wrung his hands some more. "Please, master, do not tell her."

"Tell whom?"

"The Princess Mar-Janah."

"Oh, yes. That one. So you have now fixed your regard on a princess, have you? Well, I give you credit for craving wide variety. And I will not tell her. Why should I tell her anything at all?"

"Because I would beg a boon, Master Marco. I would ask you to speak to her in my behalf. To tell her of my virtues and uprightness."

"Upright? Virtuous? You? Por Dio, I have never even been sure that you are human!"

"Please, master. You see, there are certain palace rules regarding the marriage of slaves to one another—"

"Marriage!" I gasped. "You are contemplating marriage?"

"It is true, as the Prophet declares, that women are all stones," he said meditatively. "But some are millstones hung about our neck, and some are gemstones hung about our heart."

"Nostril," I said, as kindly as I could be. "This woman may have come down in the world, but not—" I stopped myself. I could not say "as low down as you." I began again, "She may be now a slave, but she was once a princess, and you said you were only a drover then. Also, from what I have heard, she is handsome, or she once was."

"She is," he said, and added feebly, "So was I . . . once."

Exasperated anew by his persistence in that old fiction, I said, "Has she seen you lately? Look at yourself! There you stand, as graceless as a camel-bird, pot-bellied, pig-eyed, with your finger picking your one nose hole. Tell me truthfully, since you spied out her identity have you made yourself known to this Princess Mar-Janah? Did she recognize you? Did she flee in revulsion, or merely burst out laughing?"

"No," he said, hanging his head. "I have not introduced myself. I have only worshiped her from afar. I was hoping that you would first say some words to her . . . to prepare her . . . to make her desire to know me. . . ."

At which, it was I who burst out laughing. "It needed but this! I have never heard such effrontery. Asking me to pimp between one slave and another. What am I to tell her, Nostril?" I put on a wheedling voice, as if I were addressing the princess: "So far as I know, Your Highness, your adoring suitor does not at this moment suffer any shameful disease of his amative parts." Then I said sternly, "What could I possibly tell, without such lying as to imperil my immortal soul, that could possibly make any female—let alone a former princess—look favorably on such a creature as I know you to be?"

With preposterous dignity for such a creature, he said, "If the master would have the goodness to listen for just a little, I would tell some of the history of this affair."

"Tell, then, but make haste. I have things to do."

"It began twenty years ago in the Cappadocian capital city of Erzincan. True, she was a Turki princess, the daughter of King Kilij, and I was only a Sindi drover of horses in his employ. Neither he nor she knew it, probably, since I was only one of many stable servants they would have seen, whenever they called for a mount or a carriage. But I saw *her,* and then as now I worshiped her dumbly from afar. Nothing would ever have come of it, of course. Except that Allah caused both her and me to fall among Arab bandits—"

"Oh, Nostril, no!" I pleaded. "Not another account of your heroics. I have had my laugh for the day."

"I will not dwell on the abduction episode, master. Sufficient to say that the princess had cause to notice me, then, and she regarded me with melting eyes. But when we had escaped from the Arabs and returned to Erzincan, her father rewarded me with a higher position in his service, which sent me into the countryside at a considerable remove from the palace."

"That," I murmured, "I believe."

"And unhappily I once more fell among marauders. Kurdi slavetakers, this time. I was borne away, and I never saw Cappadocia or the princess again. I kept an ear open for every rumor and gossip from that part of the world, and I never heard of her marrying, so I still had some small cause for hopefulness. But then I heard of the wholesale slaughter of that Seljuk royal family, and I supposed she had died with the rest. Who knows, if I had been still at the palace when that occurred, what might not—?"

"Please, Nostril."

"Yes, master. Well, if Mar-Janah was dead, I cared no longer what became of me. I was a slave—the lowest form of life—so I would *be* the lowest form of life. I endured every kind of humiliation, and I did not care. I invited humiliation. I even began to humiliate myself. I wallowed in humiliation. I would be the worst thing in the world, because I had lost the best. I became a wretch degraded and contemptible. I did not care that it cost me my handsomeness and my self-respect and the respect of all other men. I would not even have cared if it had cost me my vital parts, but, for some reason, none of my many masters ever thought to make me a eunuch. So I was still a man, but, having no hope of love, I abandoned myself to lust. I took anyone or anything accessible to a slave—and not many but vile things are. Thus I was when you found me, Master Marco, and thus I continued to be."

"Until now," I said. "Let me finish for you, Nostril. Now that long lost love has reentered your life. Now you are going to *change.*"

He surprised me by saying, "No. No, master, too many men have too often said that. None but a fool would believe that, and my master is no fool. So I will say instead that I wish only to change *back.* Back to what I was before I became . . . this Nostril."

I looked long at him, and I considered long before I spoke.

"None but a wicked master would refuse a man the chance at that much, and I am not wicked. Indeed, I should be interested to see what it was that you once were." I was also a little interested to see the draggled sloven he had set his heart on. She had to be a pitiful drab, of course, after eight or nine years of slavery among the Mongols, whatever she had begun as. "Very well. You wish me to apprise this Mar-Janah that her onetime hero still exists. I will do that much. How do I do it?"

"I shall simply pass the word in the slave quarters that the Master Marco wishes to speak with her. And then, if you could find it in your compassionate generosity to say—"

"I will tell no lies for you, Nostril. I promise only to skirt the nastier truths, insofar as I can."

"It is all I could ask. May Allah ever bless—"

"Now I have other things to think about. Do not have her come here until after the New Year doings are done with."

When he had gone, I sat down to gaze at the huo-yao I had brought, and occasionally I dabbled my fingers in it, and now and again I shook one of the baskets, to see for myself how readily the white grains of saltpeter separated from among the black specks of charcoal and the yellow sulphur, and sank out of sight. That day—and for many days afterward, because other things took precedence—I did not do anything else with the flaming powder.

That night, when I went to bed, and only Buyantu joined me, I grumbled, "What is this indisposition Biliktu is suffering? I saw her only hours ago in these rooms, and she appeared perfectly healthy. But it must be more than a month now since she has slept in this bed with me or with us. Is she avoiding me? Have I somehow displeased her?"

Buyantu made only a teasing reply: "Do you miss her? Am I not enough for you? After all, my sister and I are identical. Hold me and see." She snuggled into my arms. "There. You cannot complain that you yearn for what you are this moment holding. But, if you like, I give you leave to pretend that I am Biliktu, and I challenge you to tell me in what respect I am not."

She was right. When, in the dark, I pretended that she was her sister, she very well could have been, and I could hardly claim that I was being deprived.

10

In Venice, we do not take much account of any new year's coming. It is merely the first day of March, on which we begin the next year's calendar, and it is no cause for celebration unless it chances to fall on the day of Carnevale. But in Kithai every New Year was regarded as portentous, and had to be fittingly welcomed. So it was the excuse for festivities that consumed an entire month, lapping over from the old year into the new one. Like our Christian movable holy days, the entire Kithai calendar depends on the moon, so its First Day of the First Moon can fall any time between mid-January and mid-February. The celebrations commenced on the seventh night of the old year's Twelfth Moon, when families sat down to partake of the traditional Eight-Ingredient Pudding, then exchanged gifts among themselves, their neighbors and friends and relatives.

From that time on, there seemed to be some kind of observance every day and night. On the twenty-third day of that Twelfth Moon, for example, everyone set up a clamor to wish "bon viazo" to their kitchen god Nagatai, as he ostensibly ascended to Heaven to make his report on the household of which he was overseer. Since he allegedly does not return to his place over the hearth until the eve of the New Year, the people all took advantage of his absence to indulge in libertine feasting and drinking and gambling and other things they would be afraid or ashamed to do under Nagatai's scrutiny.

The final day of the old year was the most frenetic of the whole season, that being the last day on which debts were to be collected and accounts settled. Every street leading to a pawnshop was clogged with people pledging, for a pitiful few tsien, their valuables, furniture, even the clothes they wore. Every other street was similarly crowded and turmoiled by the creditors dashing about in search of their debtors and the debtors dashing about in desperate search of some means either to pay them or avoid them. Everybody was chasing somebody, and himself was being chased by somebody else. There was much vociferation and loud abuse and blows exchanged and even, as Nostril had told me, the occasional self-immolation of a debtor no longer able to hold up his head—or his face, as the Han say.

As that last day of the old year turned into night and became the eve of the First Day of the First Moon, it turned also into a night-long display of Master Shi's fiery trees and sparkling flowers, in wondrous variety, accompanied by parades and street dances and tumultuous noise and the music of chimes and gongs and trumpets. When the New Year day dawned, the interminable festivities were tempered by their only token touch of a Lenten abstention,

that being the one day of the year when all were forbidden
to eat meat. And on the subsequent five days, no one was
allowed to throw away anything at all. Even for a scullion
to throw out the kitchen's waste water would risk throwing out the household's good fortune for the next year.
Apart from those two gestures of austerity, the celebrating
went on unceasingly, right through the fifteenth day of the
First Moon.

The common people put up new pictures of all their old
gods, ceremoniously pasting them over the tattered old
ones that had hung for the past year on their house doors
and walls. Every family that could afford it paid a scribe to
compose for them a "spring couplet," likewise to be pasted
up somewhere. The streets perpetually teemed with acrobats, masquers, stiltwalkers, storytellers, wrestlers, jugglers, hoop twirlers, fire eaters, astrologers and fortune-
tellers, purveyors of every sort of food and drink, even
"dancing lions"—each consisting of two extremely agile
men inside a costume of gilt plaster and red cloth, doing
some unbelievable and most unleonine contortions.

In their temples, the Han priests of every religion rather
unreligiously presided over public games of chance. These
were attended by multitudes of players—creditors squandering their new gains, I assumed, and debtors trying to
recoup their losses—and, most of them being drunk and
wagering heavily and playing ineptly, their contributions
no doubt supported all the temples and priests for the entire year to come. One game was merely the familiar
throwing of dice. Another, called ma-jiang, was played
with little bone tiles. Another game was played with stiff
paper cards called zhi-pai.

(I myself later got intrigued by the intricacies of the
zhi-pai and learned to play all the games—for there are
innumerable gambling pastimes possible with a pack of
seventy-eight cards divided into orders of hearts, bells,
leaves and acorns, and they subdivided into cards of points
and coats and emblems. But, since I brought back a pack of
the cards to Venice, and they have been so much admired
and copied and, now called tarocchi, are so well and widely
known, I need not expatiate on the zhi-pai.)

The weeks of celebration concluded with the Feast of
Lanterns, on the fifteenth day of the First Moon. In addition to everything else that was still going on in the streets

of Khanbalik, every family vied that night to see which
could flaunt the most marvelously made lantern. They paraded with their creations, of paper or silk or translucent
horn or Muscovy glass, in shapes of balls, cubes, fans, little
temples, all illuminated by candles or wick lamps inside.

Toward midnight occurred the romping through the
streets of a wonderful dragon. More than forty paces long,
it was constructed of silk stiffened with ribs of cane, the
ribs outlined in little stuck-on candles, and was carried by
some fifty men, of whom only their dancing feet were visible, shod with shoes made to look like great claws. The
head of the dragon was of plaster and wood, gilded and
enameled, with flaring gold-and-blue eyes, silver horns, a
green floss beard under its chin, a red velvet tongue lolling
from its fearsome mouth. The head alone was so big and
heavy that it required four men to carry, and to make it
lunge at the people in the streets and champ its jaws at
them. The whole dragon pranced and undulated and cur-
vetted most realistically as it wound up one street and
down another. And finally, when the last late reveler went
off to bed or fell drunkenly unconscious in the open, the
weary dragon also slithered back to its lair, and the New
Year had officially begun.

The city folk of Khanbalik had enjoyed a whole month of
freedom from their more usual occupations. But the work
of public servants, like the work of farmers, does not abate
just because the calendar declares a holiday. The palace
courtiers and government ministers, except for occasional
ventures outside to watch the people's enjoyments, went
right on working through the whole festive season. I continued making my calls upon one after another of them,
and every week having my audience with the Khan Kubilai, that he might judge the progress of my education. At
every visit, I tried either to impress or astonish him with
whatever new things I had learned. Sometimes, of course, I
had nothing to report but a trifle like, "Did you know, Sire,
that the eunuch Court Astrologer keeps his cast-off equipment preserved in a jar?"

To which he replied, with some asperity, "Yes. It is rumored that, in doing his predictions, the old fool consults
those pickles oftener than he does the stars."

But usually we talked of weightier matters. In one of our
meetings, sometime after that New Year season, and after

I had spent the foregoing week interviewing the eight Justices of the Cheng, I made so bold as to discuss with the Khakhan the laws and statutes by which his domain was regulated. The mode of that conversation was as interesting as its content, because we talked outdoors and in singular circumstances.

The Court Architect and his slaves and his elephants had, by then, finished piling up the Kara Hill, and had covered it with soft turf, and the Master Gardener and his men had planted its lawns and flowers and trees and shrubs. None of those things was yet flourishing , so the hill still was quite bald. But many of its architectural additions were already done, and they, being in the Han style, gave the hill color enough. The Khakhan and Prince Chingkim were that day inspecting the latest work completed, and they invited me to accompany them. The hill's newest adornment was a round pavilion about ten paces across, an edifice that was all curlicues: swooping roof and convoluted pillars and filigreed balustrades, not a single straight line about it. It was encircled by a tiled terrace, as wide across as the pavilion's diameter, and that was encircled by a solid wall about twice man-high, its entire inner and outer surface a mosaic of gems, enamels, gilt, tesserae of jade and porcelains.

The pavillion was sufficiently striking to the eye, but it had one feature apparent only to the ear. I do not know if the Court Architect had planned it so, or if it came about merely fortuitously. Two or more persons could stand anywhere within the encircling wall, at any distance apart, and, speaking even in a whisper, be able to hear each other perfectly well. The place later became known to all as the Echo Pavilion, but I believe the Khakhan, the Prince and I were the first to amuse ourselves with its peculair property. We conversed by standing at three points equidistant inside the wall, some eighty feet from each other, none of us able to see each other around the pavilion in the middle, but all speaking in normal tones, and we conversed as easily as if we had been seated about a table indoors.

I said, "The Justices of the Cheng read to me Kithai's current code of laws, Sire. I thought some of them severe. I remember one which commanded that, if a crime is committed, the magistrate of the prefecture must find and

punish the guilty party—or himself suffer the punishment
specified by law for that crime."

"What is so severe about that?" asked Kubilai's voice.
"It only ensures that no magistrate shirks his duty."

"But is it not likely, Sire, that an innocent person is
often punished, simply because *somebody* must be?"

"And so?" said Chingkim's voice. "The crime is re-
quited, and all people know that any crime always will be.
So the law tends to make all people shun all crime."

"But I have noticed," I said, "that the Han people, when
left to themselves, seem adequately to rely on their traditions of good manners to guide their behavior in all things,
from everyday matters to those of the greatest gravity.
Take common courtesy, for example. If a carter were to be
so rude as to ask directions of a passerby without politely
getting down from his wagon, he would at the least be told
a wrong direction, if not reviled for his bad behavior."

"Ah, but would that reform him?" asked Kubilai's voice.
"As a good whipping would do?"

"He need not be reformed, Sire, because he would never
do such an unmannerly thing in the first place. Take another example: simple honesty. If a man walking along the
road discovers an object someone has lost, he will not appropriate it, but stand guard over it. He will relinquish
that guard duty to the next comer, and he to the next. That
object will be sedulously kept safe until its loser comes
back looking for it."

"You are talking now of happenstance," said the Khakhan's voice. "You began with crimes and laws."

"Very well, Sire, consider an actual tort. If one man is
wronged by another, he does not run to a magistrate and
demand forced redress. Indeed, the Han have a proverb:
advising the dead to avoid damnation and the living to
avoid the law court. If a man of the Han disgraces himself,
he will take his own life in expiation, as I have seen often
happen during the past New Year. If another man does
him a grievous wrong, and *his* conscience does not soon resolve the matter, the *victim* will go and hang himself outside the guilty man's door. The disgrace thus conferred on
the transgressor is considered far worse than any revenge
that could have been inflicted."

Kubilai inquired drily, "Would you say that that fact

gives much satisfaction to the dead man? You call that redress?"

"I am told, Sire, that the malefactor can only remove the
taint of that shame by making restitution to the hanged
man's surviving family."

"So does he under the Khanate's code of law, Marco. But
if anybody has to get hanged, it is *he*. You may call that severity, but I see nothing unfair about it."

"Sire, I once remarked that you were rightly to be admired and envied—for the quality of your subjects in
general—by every other ruler in the world. But I wonder:
how are you regarded by the people themselves? Might you
not better secure their affection and fealty if you were not
quite so strict in your standards for them?"

"Define that," he said sharply. " 'Not quite so strict.' "

"Sire, regard my native Republic of Venice. It is patterned on the classical republics of Rome and Greece. In a
republic, the citizen has the liberty to be an individual, to
shape his own destiny. There are slaves in Venice, true,
and class levels. But in theory a stalwart man can rise
above his class. On his own, he can climb from poverty and
misery to prosperity and ease."

Chingkim's quiet voice said, "Does that happen often in
Venice?"

"Well," I said, "I remember one or two who took calculated advantage of their good looks, and thereby married
above their station."

"You call that being stalwart? Here it would be called
concubinage."

"It is only that offhand I cannot think of other instances
to cite. But—"

"In Rome or Greece," said Kubilai, "were there any
such instances? Your Western histories, do they record
any instances?"

"I honestly cannot say, Sire, not being a scholar of history."

Chingkim spoke again. "Do you believe it could happen,
Marco? That all men could and would make themselves
equal and free and rich, if only they were given the liberty
to do so?"

"Why not, my Prince? Some of our foremost philoso-
phers have believed it."

"A man will believe anything that does not cost him

anything," said Kubilai's voice. "That is another proverb
of the Han. Marco, I know what happens when people are
set free—and I did not get that knowledge from reading
history. I know because I have done that for people myself."

Some moments passed. Then Chingkim said in an amused
tone, "Marco is shocked to silence. But it is true, Marco. I
saw my Royal Father employ that tactic one time to conquer a province in the land of To-Bhot. The province resisted our frontal attacks, so the Khakhan simply made
announcement to the Bho people: 'You are free of your
former tyrant rulers and oppressors. And I, being a liberal
ruler, I give you license to take your rightful places in the
world as you deserve.' And do you know what happened?"

"I hope, my Prince, it made them happy."

Kubilai gave a laugh that resounded around the wall
like the noise of an iron cauldron being pounded with a
mallet. He said:

"What happens, Marco Polo, is this. Tell a poor man that
he has free permission to rob the rich he has envied for so
long. Does he sally forth and ransack the gilded mansion of
some lord? No, he seizes the pig owned by his peasant
neighbor. Tell a slave that he is set free at last and made
the equal of all other men. Perhaps his first display of
equality is to murder his former master, but the second
thing he does: he acquires a slave. Tell a troop of soldiers,
unwillingly impressed into military service, that they may
freely desert and go home. Do they, as they go, assassinate
the lofty generals who drafted them? No, they butcher the
man who was promoted from among them to be their troop
sergeant. Tell *all* the downtrodden that they have free permission to rise up against their most brutal oppressor. Do
they march in grand array against their tyrant Wang or
Ilkhan? No, they go in a mob and tear to pieces the village
moneylender."

There was another silence. I could think of no comment
to make. Finally Chingkim spoke again:

"The ruse worked there in To-Bhot, Marco. It threw the
whole province into chaos, and we took it quite easily, and
my brother Ukuruji is now Wang of To-Bhot. Of course,
nothing is changed for the Bho people, as regards class and
privilege and prosperity and liberty. Life goes on there as
before."

I still could think of no comment to make, for the Khakhan and the Prince were obviously not talking just of some
ignorant rustics in the backward land of To-Bhot. The
opinion they had of the common folk was of all common
folk everywhere, and it was no high opinion, but I had no
argument with which to controvert it. So we three moved
from our places around the Echo Pavilion and went back
inside the palace and drank mao-tai together and talked of
other things. And I did not again suggest any moderations
of the Mongol code of laws, and to this day the decrees proclaimed throughout the Khanate conclude as they did
then: "The Khakhan has spoken; tremble, all men, and
obey!"

Kubilai never made any comment on the order in which
I was calling upon his various ministers, though he might
have supposed that I should rightly have commenced with
his highest of all: that Chief Minister Achmad-az-Fenaket
of whom I have by now so often spoken. But I would have
been glad to omit the Arab entirely, especially after I
heard so many unpleasant things about him. In fact, I
never did seek audience with him, and it was Achmad who
impelled our meeting at last. He sent a servant to me with
a testy message, requiring me to appear before him and
collect my wages from his own hand, in his capacity as Finance Minister. I gathered that he had got annoyed by the
money's having accumulated untouched, and by my having let the New Year season go past without a settling of
account. Ever since my being taken into employment by
the Khakhan, I had not bothered to inquire by whom I was
to be paid, or even how much, for I had so far had no need of
a single bagatìn—or tsien, as the smallest unit of Kithai
currency was called. I was elegantly housed and fed and
supplied with everything, and could not imagine how I
would spend any money if I had any.

Before I obeyed Achmad's summons, I went to ask my father if the Compagnia Polo's enterprises were still being
thwarted, and, if so, whether he would like me to broach
the subject with the obstructive Arab. Failìng to find my
father in his suite, I went to my uncle's. He was reclining
on a couch, being shaved by one of his women servants.

"What is this, Uncle Mafìo?" I exclaimed. "Getting rid
of your journeyer's beard! Why?"

Through the lather he said, "We shall be dealing mainly

with Han merchants, and the Han despise hairiness as a
mark of the barbarian. Since all the Arabs of the Ortaq are
bearded, I thought Nico and I might enjoy some advantage
if one of us was clean-shaven. Also, to be frank, it troubled
my vanity that my older brother's beard is still its natural
color, while mine has gone as gray as Nostril's."

My uncle, I assumed, was also still keeping his crotch
hairless, so I remarked, somewhat waspishly, "Many of
the Han shave their heads as well. Are you going to do
that, too?"

"And many of them let their hair grow as long as a woman's," he said equably. "I may do that. Did you come in
here just to criticize my toilet?"

"No, but I think you have answered what I was going to
ask. When you say you will be dealing with merchants, I
gather it means that you and Father have resolved your
differences with the evil Arab Achmad."

"Yes, and quite pleasantly. He has conceded all the necessary permits. Do not speak of the Chief Minister in such
a tone, Marco. He turns out to be—not so bad, after all."

"I am pleased to hear it," I said, though not much
believing it. "I have to go and see him right now."

Uncle Màfio sat up from his recumbent position. "Did he
bid you stop to see me—for any reason?"

"No, no. I merely must collect from him some money
that I do not know what to do with."

"Ah," said my uncle, lying back again. "Give it to Nico
to invest in the Compagnia. You could not make any better
investment."

I said, after some hesitation, "I must remark, uncle, that
you seem in a much better humor now than when we last
spoke in private."

"E cussì? I am back in business again."

"I was not referring to—well, material things."

"Ah, my famous *condition*," he said wryly. "You would
prefer to see me drooped and draped in melancholy."

"I would not, uncle. I am delighted if you have in some
measure made peace with yourself."

"That is kind of you, nephew," he said in a more gentle
voice. "And in truth I have. I discovered that a man who
cannot any longer be given pleasure can yet find considerable pleasure in *giving* pleasure."

"Whatever that means, I am glad for you."

"You may not believe this," he said, almost shyly. "But, in a mood to experiment, I found I could even give pleasure to this one who is shaving me. Yes—do not look so startled—to a female. And in return she taught me some feminine arts of giving pleasure." He seemed suddenly embarrassed by his own air of embarrassment, and gave a loud laugh to blow it away. "I may have a whole new career ahead of me. Thank you for inquiring, Marco, but spare me my blushes. If Achmad is expecting you, you had best run along."

When I entered the sumptuously appointed sanctum of the Chief Minister, the Vice-Regent, the Finance Minister, he did not rise or salute me. Instead, unlike the Khan of All Khans, he obviously expected me to make ko-tou, and waited for me to do it, and when I stood up again he did not offer me a seat. The Wali Achmad looked like any other Arab—hawk-beak nose, stiff black beard, dark and grainy complexion—except that he was cleaner than most Arabs I had seen in Arab lands, he having adopted the Kithai custom of frequent bathing. Also, he had the coldest eyes I ever saw in an Arab or any other Easterner. Brown eyes are usually as warm as qahwah, but his looked more like chips of the Mukha agate stone. He wore Arab aba and kaffiyah, but not of flimsy cotton; of silks colored like a rainbow.

"Your wages, Folo," he said ungraciously, and shoved across his table no purse of money, but an untidy pile of slips of paper.

I picked them up and examined them. The slips were all alike: made of dark and durable mulberry paper, decorated on both sides with complex designs and a multitude of words both in Han characters and Mongol alphabet, done in black ink, over which a large and intricate seal mark had been added in red ink. I did not say thank you. I had taken an instant, instinctive dislike to the man, and was quite prepared to suspect chicanery. So I said:

"Excuse me, Wali Achmad, but am I being paid in pagherì?"

"I do not know," he said languidly. "What does the word mean?"

"Pagherì are papers promising to repay a loan, or to pay in the future some pledge made. They are a convenience of the commerce of Venice."

"Then I suppose you could call these pagherì, for they are also a convenience, being the legal tender of this realm. We took over the system from the Han, who call it 'flying money.' Each of those papers you hold is worth a liang of silver."

I pushed the little pile back across the table toward him. "If it please the Wali, then, I should prefer to take the silver."

"You have the equivalent," he snapped. "That much silver would make your purse drag the floor. It is the beauty of the flying money that large sums, even immense sums, can be exchanged or transported without weight or bulk. Or hidden away in your mattress, if you are a miser. Also, when you pay for a purchase, the merchant need not every time weigh the currency and verify its metal's purity."

"You mean," I said, unconvinced, "I could go into the market and buy a bowl of miàn to eat and the vendor would accept one of these pieces of paper in payment?"

"Bismillah! He would give you his whole market-stall for it. Probably his wife and children as well. I told you: each of those is worth a whole liang. A liang is one thousand tsien, and for *one* tsien you could buy twenty or thirty bowls of miàn. If you have need of small change—here." He took from a drawer several packets of smaller sized papers. "How do you want it? Notes of half a liang each? A hundred tsien? What?"

Marveling, I said, "The flying money is made in all denominations? And the common folk accept them like real money?"

"It *is* real money, unbeliever! Cannot you read? Those words on the paper attest its realness. They proclaim its face value, and appended are the signatures of all the Khakhan's numerous officers and bursars and clerks of the imperial treasury. My own name is among them. And over all is stamped in red ink a much bigger yin—the great seal of Kubilai himself. Those are guarantees that at any time the paper can be exchanged for its face amount in actual silver from the treasury stores. Thus the paper is as real as the silver it represents."

"But if," I persisted, "someday someone should wish to redeem one of these papers, and it were repudiated . . . ?"

Achmad said drily, "If the time ever comes when the

Khakhan's yin evokes disrespect, you will have many more urgent things to worry about than your wages. We all will."

Still examining the flying money, I mused aloud, "Nevertheless, I should think it would be less trouble for the treasury simply to issue the bits of silver. I mean, if there are sheaves of these little papers circulating throughout the realm, and if every official must write his name on every last one—"

"We do not write our names over and over again," said Achmad, beginning to sound very annoyed. "We write them only once, and from that signature the palace Master Yinmaker makes a yin, which is a backward-written work like an engraved seal, and can be inked and stamped on paper innumerable times. Surely even you uncivilized Venetians are familiar with seals."

"Yes, Wali Achmad."

"Very well. For the making of a piece of money, all the necessary separate yin for words and characters and letters are arranged and locked together into a form of the proper size. The form is repeatedly inked and the papers pressed onto it one by one. It is a process the Han call zi-shu-ju, which means something like 'the gathered writing.'"

I nodded. "Our Western monks will often cut a backward block of wood for the big initial letter of a manuscript, and impress several pages with it, for the several Friars Illuminators to color and elaborate in their individual styles, before proceeding to write the rest of the page by hand."

Achmad shook his head. "In the gathered writing the impression need not be limited to the initial letter, and no hand writing need be done at all. By the molding in terracotta of many identical yin of every character in the Han language—and now having yin of every letter of the Mongol alphabet—this zi-shu-ju can combine any number of yin into any number of words. Thus can be composed whole pages of writing, and those combined into whole books. Zi-shu-ju can produce them in great quantities, every copy alike, far more quickly and perfectly than any scribes can indite by hand. If provided with yin of the Arabic alphabet and of the Roman alphabet, the process could produce books in any known language, equally easily and abundantly and cheaply."

"Say you so?" I murmured. "Why, Wali, that is an invention more to be admired than the advantages of the flying money."

"You are right, Folo. I perceived that myself, the first time I saw one of the gathered-writing books. I thought of sending some of the Han experts westward to teach the doing of the zi-shu-ju in my native Arabia. But fortunately I learned in time that the zi-shu-ju forms are inked with brushes made of the bristles of swine. So it would be unthinkable to suggest the process to the nations of holy Islam."

"Yes, I can see that. Well, I thank you, Wali Achmad, both for the instruction and for the wages." I began to put the papers away in my belt purse.

"Allow me," he said casually, "to proffer one or two other bits of instruction. There are some places you *cannot* spend the flying money. The Fondler, for example, will take bribes only in solid gold. But I think you already knew that."

Taking care to make my face expressionless, I raised my eyes from my purse to his cold agate gaze. I wondered how much else he knew about my doings, and obligingly he told me:

"I would not dream of suggesting that you disobey the Khakhan. He did instruct you to make inquiries. But I will suggest that you confine your inquiries to the upper stories of the palace. Not down in Master Fing's dungeons. Not even in the servants' quarters."

So he knew that I had put an ear belowstairs. But did he know why? Did he know that I was interested in the Minister of Lesser Races, and, if he did, why should he care? Or did he fear that I might hear something damaging to Achmad the Chief Minister? I kept my face expressionless and waited.

"Cellar dungeons are unhealthy places," he went on, as indifferently as if he were warning me against rheumatic damp. "But tortures can happen aboveground as well, and far worse ones than anything the Fondler inflicts."

I had to correct him there. "I am sure there could be nothing worse than the Death of a Thousand. Perhaps, Wali Achmad, you are unacquainted with—"

"I am acquainted with it. But even the Fondler knows
how to inflict a death worse than that one. And I know several." He smiled—or his lips did; his stone eyes did not.
"You Christians think of Hell as the most terrible torture
there can be, and your Bible tells you that Hell consists of
pain. 'To be cast into the Hell of fire, where their worm
dieth not, and the fire is not extinguished.' So spoke your
gentle Jesus, at Capharnaum, to His disciples. Like your
Jesus, I warn you not to flirt with Hell, Marco Folo, and
not to pursue any temptations that might put you there.
But I will tell you something more about Hell than your
Christian Bible does. Hell is not necessarily an ever burning fire or a gnawing worm or a physical pain of any sort.
Hell is not necessarily even a place. Hell is whatever hurts
worst."

11

I went from the chambers of the Chief Minister directly to
my own, intending to tell Nostril to cease his spy activities—at least until I could give some serious cogitation to
the Wali's warnings and threats. But Nostril was not
there; another slave was. Biliktu and Buyantu met me in
the vestibule, their eyebrows haughtily aloft, to inform me
that a slave, a stranger, had come calling and had begged
leave to stay and wait my return. The twins, not being
owned by me or anybody, were always disdainful of their
inferiors, but they seemed even more than usually bothered by this one. Rather curious to see what had provoked
them, I went into my main room. A woman was seated on a
bench there. When I came in, she swept down to the floor
in a graceful ko-tou, and stayed kneeling until I bade her
rise. She stood up, and I looked at her, and I looked with
wide eyes.

The palace slaves, when their errands brought them
from their cellars or kitchens or stables up among their
betters, were always well dressed, to reflect credit on their
masters, so it was not the woman's fine garb that made me
stare. What struck me was that she wore it as if she *deserved* nothing but the best, and was used to it, and was

aware that no richest raiment would ever outshine her
own radiance.

She was not a girl; she must have been about the same
age as Nostril or my Uncle Mafìo. But her face was unlined, and the years had marked her beauty only with dignity. If any youthful brook-twinkle had gone from her
eyes, it had been replaced by forest-pool depth and placid-
ity. There were some threads of silver in her hair, but it
was mostly a warm, ruddy black, and not Kithai-straight,
but a tumble of curls. Her figure was erect and, as far as I
could make out through the brocade robes, still firm and
nicely shaped.

When I continued to greet her only with a gawk, she
said, in a velvet voice, "You are, I believe, the master of
the slave Ali Babar."

"Who?" I said stupidly. "Oh, him. Yes, Ali Babar belongs to me."

To cover my momentary confusion, I mumbled an excuse-
me, and went to peer into a jar to see how my flaming powder was doing. So this was the Turki Princess Mar-Janah!
A day or two ago, I had poured the huo-yao from one of the
two baskets into a sturdier jar. No wonder Nostril had
been enamored once before, and was now again. Then I
had poured some water into that portion of the powder. No
wonder Nostril was ready to promise an extravagant
change in himself, to win this woman. Despite the Firemaster's skepticism, I had wanted to see whether I could
make the powder more stable in the form of a thick mud.
Any man would make that extravagant promise, and probably *would* change, too, or die trying. But it seemed the
Firemaster had been right to scoff at my suggestion. How
in God's name had a buffoon like Nostril ever got even remotely acquainted with such a woman as this? The wet
powder was only a morose, dark-gray sludge, and showed
no sign of ever becoming anything else. A woman such as
this ought to laugh at a thing like Nostril—or jeer. The
powder might be stable in the form of muck, but it would
never ignite. Or retch violently. Vakh!

"Tell me if I have guessed right, Master Marco," said
Mar-Janah. She sounded amused, but was obviously trying to help me compose my scattered wits. "You asked me
here to regale me with praises of your slave Ali Babar."

I coughed a few times, and tried: "Nost—" I coughed

again and tried again: "Ali can boast of a good many virtues and talents and attainments."

That much I could say without a blush, and without speaking one word of falsehood, for if any true thing could be said about Nostril it was, by God, that he could boast.

Mar-Janah smiled slightly and said, "As I have it from our fellow slaves, they cannot decide which is greater: Ali Babar's monumental self-admiration or the windiness with which he expresses it. But all agree that those are traits to be commended in a man who has so abjectly failed at everything else."

I stared at her, and I think my mouth hung open. Then I said, "Wait a moment. You evidently know a great deal about Nost—about Ali. Yet you are not even supposed to know he is in residence here."

"I know more than that. I know that the other slaves are wrong in their mocking appraisal of him. When I first met Ali Babar, he was everything that he now only pretends he is."

"I do not believe it," I said flatly. Then I more courteously put a question, "Will you take cha with me?"

I clapped my hands and Buyantu appeared so promptly that I suspected she had been jealously lurking and listening just outside the curtained doorway. I ordered cha for the visitor and pu-tao for myself, and Buyantu went out again.

I turned back to Mar-Janah. "I would be interested to know more—about you and Ali Babar."

"We were young then," she said reminiscently. "The Arab bandits galloped out of the hills, down on my carriage, and they killed the coachman, but Ali was riding postilion, and they took him alive. They bore us away to their caves in the hills, and Ali was to be the messenger who would carry their ransom demand to my father. But I bade him refuse, and he did. At which, they laughed and they beat him most cruelly and they sealed him into a great jar of sesame oil. It would soften his obduracy, they said."

I nodded. "It is a thing the Arabs do. It softens more than obduracy."

"But Ali Babar did not soften. I did, or I pretended to. I feigned an infatuation for the bandit leader, though it was the staunch and loyal Ali with whom I had fallen in love.

My pretense won me some measure of freedom, and one
night I contrived to free Ali from the big jar, and to procure
for him a sword."

Buyantu returned, and Biliktu with her, each of them
carrying a drink. They gave Mar-Janah her cup, and me
my goblet, lingering to get a good look at the handsome
visitor, as if they feared that I was recruiting an unwelcome fourth for our ménage. I waved them out, and
prompted Mar-Janah to continue: "Well?"

"All went well. On Ali's instructions, I pretended further. I feigned submission to the chieftain's lust that
night, and, as planned, when I had him most vulnerable,
Ali Babar leapt through the bed curtains and slew him.
Then Ali bravely slashed our way through the other bandits, as they awakened and converged, and we got to the
horses. By Allah's mercy, we got safe away."

"This is all very hard to believe."

"The only disadvantage to our plan was that I had to
make my escape stark naked." She modestly turned her
face away from me. "But that made it sublimely easy for
me—when we lay down for the rest of the night in a
friendly forest glade—to reward Ali as he deserved."

"A better reward—or so I understand—than your father
the King gave him."

She sighed. "He promoted Ali to Chief Drover, and sent
him far away from the palace. A royal father prefers a
royal son-in-law. He never got one, though. Much to his
vexation, I spurned all later suitors, even after I heard
that Ali Babar had been taken away in slavery. My spinsterhood probably saved my life when, some years afterward, our royal house was overthrown."

"I know about that, yes."

"I was left my life, but not much else. Allah's ways are
sometimes inscrutable. When I was handed over to the Ilkhan Abagha, he thought he was getting a royal concubine.
He was outraged to find I was not a virgin, and he gave me
to his Mongol troops. They cared nothing about virginity
and were much amused to have a royal plaything. When
they had had their sport, the remains of me were sold in
the slave market. I have passed through many hands since
then."

"I am sorry. What can one say? It must have been terrible."

"Not so very." Like a spirited mare, she tossed her mane of dark curls. "I had learned how to pretend, you see. I pretended that every man was my handsome, brave Ali Babar. And now I hope Allah has brought me near to my own reward. If you had not summoned me to this meeting, Master Marco, I should have sought audience—to ask if you will assist our reunion. Will you tell Ali that I yearn to be his again, and that I hope we will be allowed to marry?"

I coughed some more, uncertain of how to proceed. "Ahem—Princess Mar-Janah . . ."

"Slave Mar-Janah," she corrected me. "There are even stricter marriage rules for slaves than for royalty."

"Mar-Janah, the man you remember so fondly—I assure you he remembers you the same way. But he believes you have not yet recognized him. Frankly, I am amazed that you could have done."

She smiled again. "You see him, then, as his fellows slaves do. From what they tell me, he has changed most markedly."

"From what they—? Then you *have* not seen him."

"Oh, of course I have. But I do not know what he looks like. I still see the champion who battled for me against the Arab abductors, twenty years ago, and made tender love to me that night. He is young, and as straight and slender as the written letter alif, and beautiful in a manly way. Much as you are, Master Marco."

"Thank you," I said, but faintly, for I was still bemused. Had she not even noticed the one outstanding unbeautifulness that had earned him the name of Nostril? I said, "Far be it from me to disillusion a lovely lady of her lovely imaginings, but—"

"Master Marco, no woman can ever be disillusioned about the man she truly loves." She set down her cup and came close to me and shyly put out a hand to touch my face. "I am near old enough to be your mother. May I tell you a motherly thing?"

"Please do."

"You too are handsome, and young, and someday soon a woman will truly love you. Whether Allah grants that you and she live together all your lives—or requires, as happened to Ali Babar and me, that you be not united until a long time after your first meeting—you will grow older, and so will she. I cannot predict whether you will grow fee-

ble and bent, or gross, or bald, or ugly, but it will not matter. This I can say with certainty: she will see you always
as you were when you met. To the very end of your days.
Or hers."

"Your Highness," I said, and with feeling, for if ever
anyone merited a lofty title, it was she. "God grant that I
find a woman of such loving heart and eye as you possess.
But, in conscience, I must remark that a man can change
in ways that cannot be seen."

"You feel you must inform me that Ali Babar has not remained a good man during all these years? Not a steadfast
or faithful or admirable or even a manly man? I know that
he has been a slave, and I know that slaves are expected to
be creatures less than human."

"Well, yes," I muttered. "He said something of the same
sort. He said he tried to become the worst thing in the
world, because he had lost the best."

She thought about that, and said pensively, "Whatever
he and I have been, he will more readily see the marks on
me than I on him."

It was my turn to correct her. "That is flagrantly untrue.
To say that you have survived beautifully would be to say
the least. When I first heard of Mar-Janah, I expected to
see a pitiable ruin, but I see a princess still."

She shook her head. "I was a maiden when Ali Babar
knew me, and I was entire. That is to say, although I was
born a Muslim, I was of royal blood and so had not been deprived of my bizir in infancy. I had then a body to be proud
of, and Ali exulted in it. But since then, I have been the toy
of half a Mongol army, and of as many men afterward, and
some men mistreat their toys." She looked away from me
once more, but went on: "You and I have spoken frankly; I
will continue to do so. My meme are ringed with the scars
of teethmarks. My bizir has been stretched to flaccidity.
My göbek is slack and loose-lipped. I have miscarried three
times and now can never conceive again."

I had to guess the meaning of the Turki words she had
used, but I could not mistake the sincerity with which she
concluded:

"If Ali Babar can love what is left of me, Master Marco,
do you think I cannot love what is left of him?"

"Your Highness," I said again, and again with feeling,
though my voice was a little choked, "I stand abashed and

ashamed—and enlightened. If Ali Babar can deserve a woman like you, he is more of a man than I ever suspected. And I should be less the man if I did not exert myself to see you wed to him. So that I may start immediately to make arrangements, tell me: what are the palace rules regarding slave marriages?"

"That the owners of both parties must give permission, and must concur in the matter of where the couple shall reside. That is all, but not every master is so lenient as you."

"Who is your master? I will send to ask audience with him."

Her voice faltered a bit. "My master, I am sorry to say, has little mastery in his household. You will have to address his wife."

"Singular household," I observed. "But that need not complicate matters. Who is she?"

"The Lady Chao Ku-an. She is one of the court artists, but by title she is the Armorer of the Palace Guard."

"Oh. Yes. I have heard of her."

"She is—" Mar-Janah paused, to choose carefully the description. "She is a strong-willed woman. The Lady Chao desires that her slaves be entirely hers, and commandable at all hours."

"I am not exactly weak-willed, myself," I said. "And I have promised that your twenty-year separation is to end here and now. As soon as the arrangements are made, I will see you and your champion reunited. Until then . . ."

"May Allah bless you, good master and friend Marco," she said, with a smile as bright as the tears in her eyes.

I called for Buyantu and Biliktu, and told them to see the visitor to the door. They accompanied her ungraciously, with frowning brows and curled lips, so, when they returned, I spoke to them severely.

"Your superiority of manner is less than mannerly, and it ill becomes you, my dears. I know you to be of only twenty-two-karat valuation. The lady you have so grudgingly attended is, in my estimation, of a perfect twenty-four. Now, Buyantu, you go and present my compliments to the Lady Chao Ku-an, and say that Marco Polo requests an appointment to call upon her."

When she left, and Biliktu flounced off to sulk in some other room, I went and took one more disappointed look at my jar full of huo-yao sludge. Clearly, those fifty liang of the flaming powder were now ruined beyond salvage. So I set the jar aside, picked up the remaining basket and contemplated the contents of that. After a while, I began very carefully to pick out from the mixture some grains of the saltpeter. When I had a dozen or so of the white specks, I lightly moistened the end of an ivory fan handle. I picked up the saltpeter with that, and idly held it in the flame of a nearby candle. The grains instantly melted into a glaze on the ivory. I gave that some thought. The Firemaster had been right about wetting the powder, and he had warned me not to try baking it. But suppose I set a pot of the huo-yao on a low fire, not very hot, so that its integral saltpeter *melted* and thereby held the whole together . . . ? My meditations were interrupted by the return of Buyantu, reporting that the Lady Chao would see me that very moment.

I went, and I introduced myself, "Marco Polo, my lady," and I made a proper ko-tou.

"My lord husband has spoken of you," she said, indicating that I should rise by giving me a playful nudge with a bare foot. Her hands were occupied in playing with an ivory ball, as her husband had done, for the suppling of the fingers.

As I stood, she went on, "I wondered when you would deign to call upon this lowly female courtier." Her voice was as musical as wind chimes, but seemed somehow just as devoid of any human agency in the making of that music. "Would you wish to discuss my titular office, or my real work? Or my pastimes in between?"

That last was said with a leer. Lady Chao evidently and correctly assumed that, like everyone else, I had heard of her gluttonous appetite for men. I will confess that I was briefly tempted to join her cupboard of morsels. She was about my own age and would have been fetchingly beautiful if she had not had her eyebrows plucked entirely off and her delicate features coated with a dead-white powder. I was, as always, curious to discover what was beneath the rich silk robes—in this case, especially, because I had not yet lain with a woman of the Han race. But I restrained my curiosity and said:

"None of those today, my lady, if you please. I come on a different—"

"Ah, a bashful one," she said, and changed her leer to a

simper. "Let us begin, then, by talking of *your* favorite pastimes."

"On some other occasion, perhaps, Lady Chao. I would speak today of your female slave named Mar-Janah."

"Aiya!" she exclaimed, which is the Han equivalent of "vakh!" She sat abruptly upright on her couch, and she frowned—and a frown is very unpleasant to look at when it is done without eyebrows—and she snapped, "You find that Turki wench more appealing than I am?"

"Why, no, my lady," I lied. "Having been nobly born in my native land, I would never—there or here—even consider admiring any but a woman of perfect pedigree, such as yourself." I tactfully did not point out that she was only nobility and Mar-Janah was royalty.

But she seemed mollified. "That is well said." She leaned voluptuously back again. "On the other hand, I have sometimes discovered that a grimy and sweaty soldier can be appealing. . . ."

She trailed off, as if inviting comment, but I did not care to be drawn into a contest of comparing our experiences of perversity. So I attempted to continue, "Regarding the slave—"

"The slave, the slave . . ." She sighed, and pouted, and petulantly tossed and caught the ivory ball. "For a moment there, you were well spoken, as a gallant should be when calling on a lady. But you prefer to talk of slaves."

I reminded myself that any business with a Han ought to be approached roundabout, only after long exchanges of trivialities. So I said gallantly, "I would much rather talk of my Lady Chao, and her surpassing beauty."

"That is better."

"I am a little surprised that, with such a choice model so conveniently at hand, the Master Chao has not made many paintings of her."

"He has," she said, and smirked.

"I regret that he showed me none."

"He would not if he could, and he cannot. They are in the possession of the various other lords who were portrayed in the same pictures. And those lords are not likely to show them to you, either."

I did not have to ponder on that remark to realize what it meant. I would defer making judgment on Master Chao— whether I felt sympathy for his predicament or disgust for

his pliant complicity in it—but I knew that I did not much
like his young lady, and I would be glad to quit her company. So I made no further attempt at small talk.

"I beg that my lady will forgive my persistence in the
subject of the slave, but I seek to right a wrong of long duration. I entreat the Lady Chao's permission for her slave
Mar-Janah to marry."

"Aiya!" she exclaimed again, and loudly. "That aging
slut is pregnant!"

"No, no."

Unhearing, she went on, while her nonexistent eyebrows writhed. "But that does not obligate you! No man
weds a slave just because he has impregnated her."

"I did not!"

"The embarrassment is slight, and easily disposed of. I
will call her in and kick her in the belly. Concern yourself
no further."

"My concern is not—"

"It is, however, a matter for speculation." Her little red
tongue came out and licked her little red lips. "The physicians all pronounced that woman barren. You must be exceptionally potent."

"Lady Chao, the woman is *not* pregnant and it is *not I*
who would marry her!"

"What?" For the first time, her face lost all expression.
"It is a man slave of my own who has been long enamored
of your Mar-Janah. I merely entreat your concurrence in
my permission for them to wed and live together."

She stared at me. Ever since I had come in, the young
lady had been assuming one expression after another—of
invitation, of coyness, of petulance—and now I saw why
she had kept her features so much in motion. That white
face, without some conscious contortion, was as empty as a
sheet of unwritten paper. I wondered: would the rest of her
body be as unexciting? Were Han women all blanks that
only sporadically assumed human semblance? I was almost grateful when she put on a look of annoyance and
said:

"That Turki woman is my dresser and applier of cosmetics. Not even my lord husband infringes on her time. I do
not see why I should share her with a husband on her
own."

"Then perhaps you would sell her outright? I can pay a sum that will purchase an excellent replacement."

"Are you now trying to insult me? Do you imply that I cannot afford to give away a slave, if I so choose?"

She bounded up from the couch and, her little bare feet twinkling, her robes and ribbons and tassels and perfumed powder swirling in her wake, she left the room. I stood and wondered if I had been summarily dismissed or if she had gone for a guardsman to take me in charge. The young woman was as exasperatingly changeable as her inconstant face. In just our brief conversation, she had managed to accuse me in quick succession of being bashful, presumptuous, salacious, meddlesome, gullible and finally offensive. I was not surprised that such a woman required an endless supply of lovers; she probably forgot each one in the moment that he slunk from her bed.

But she came tripping into the room again, unaccompanied, and flung at me a piece of paper. I snatched and caught it before it drifted to the floor. I could not read the Mongol writing on it, but she told me what it was, saying contemptuously:

"Title to the slave Mar-Janah. I give it to you. The Turki is yours to do with as you please." In its fickle way, her face went from contempt to a seductive smile. "And so am I. Do what you will—to render me proper thanks."

I might have had to, and I could probably have nerved myself to do it, if she had commanded it earlier. But she had incautiously given me the paper now, before setting a price on it. So I folded it into my purse, and bowed, and said with all the floweriness I could muster:

"Your humble supplicant does indeed most fervently thank the gracious Lady Chao Ku-an. And, I am sure, so will the lowly slaves likewise honor and bless your name, as soon as I inform them of your bountiful goodness, which I shall this minute go and do. Until we meet again, then, noble lady—"

"What?" she screeched, like a wind chime being blown to pieces. "You would simply turn and walk away?"

I was inclined to say no, that I would run if it were not undignified. However, having told her I was well born, I maintained my courteous manner and bowed repeatedly as I backed toward the door, murmuring things like "most benevolent" and "undying gratitude."

Her paper face was now a palimpsest written over with disbelief, shock and outrage, all at once. She was holding the ivory ball as if about to throw it at me. "Many men have regretted my sending them away," she said menacingly, through clenched teeth. "You will be the first to regret having gone away unbidden."

I had bowed my way out into the corridor by then, but I heard her shriek a few words as I turned to flee for my own chambers.

"And I promise! That you will! Regret it!"

I have to say that it was not any sudden access of rectitude that made me run from the Lady Chao's proffered embrace, nor any concern I felt for her husband's sensibilities, nor any fear of compromising consequences that might ensue. It seemed likelier that consequences would ensue from my *not* having ravished her. No, it was none of those things, and it was not even the general repugnance she inspired in me. To be perfectly honest, I had been mainly repelled by her feet. I must explain about that, because many other Han women had the same sort of feet.

They were called "lotus points," and the incredibly tiny shoes for them were called "lotus cups." Not until later did I learn that the Lady Chao—apart from her other immodesties which I easily recognized—had been lascivious beyond the bounds of harlotry just in letting me see her feet bare of their lotus cups. The lotus points of a woman were deemed by the Han her most intimate parts, to be kept more carefully covered than even the pink parts between her legs.

It seems that, many years ago, there lived a Han court dancer who could dance on her toes, and that posture—her seeming to be balanced on points—excited every man who saw her dance. So other women, ever since, had enviously been trying to emulate that fabled seductress. Her contemporary sister dancers must have tried various ways to diminish their already woman-sized feet, and not too successfully, for the women of later days went further. By the time I came to Khanbalik, there were many Han women who had had their feet compressed by their mothers from their infancy, and had grown up thus crippled, and were carrying on the gruesome tradition by binding their own daughters' feet.

What a mother would do was take her girl-child's foot
and double it under, the toes as near to the heel as possible,
and tie it so, until it stayed that way, and then double it
even more tightly, and tie it so. By the time a girl reached
womanhood, she could wear lotus cups that were literally
no bigger than drinking cups. Naked, those feet looked
like the claws of a small bird just yanked from its grip on a
twig perch. A lotus-pointed woman had to walk with mincing, precarious steps, and only seldom walked at all, because that gait was regarded by the Han as other people
would regard a woman's most flagrantly provocative gesture. Just to say certain words—feet or toes or lotus points
or walking—in reference to a woman, or in the presence of
a decent woman, would cause as many gasps as shouting
"pota!" in a Venetian drawing room.

I grant that the lotus crippling of a Han woman constituted a less cruel multilation than the Muslim practice of
snipping off the butterfly from between the petals of her lotus higher up her body. Nevertheless, I winced at sight of
such feet, even when they were modestly shod, for the
lotus-cup shoes resembled the leather pods with which
some beggars cover the stumps of their amputations. My
detestation of the lotus points made me something of a curiosity among the Han. All the Han men with whom I became acquainted thought me odd—or maybe impotent, or
even depraved—when I averted my eyes from a lotus-
pointed woman. They frankly confessed that they got
aroused by the glimpse of a woman's nether extremities,
as I might by a glimpse of her breast. They proudly
averred that their little virile organs actually came erect
whenever they heard an unmentionable word like "feet,"
or even when they let their minds imagine those unreveal-
able parts of a female person.

At any rate, the Lady Chao that afternoon had so dampened my natural ardors that, when Buyantu undressed me
at bedtime, and insinuated into the act some suggestive
fondling, I asked to be excused. So she and Biliktu lay
down together on my bed and merely sat drinking arkhi
and looking on, while the naked girls played with each
other and with a su-yang. That was a kind of mushroom
native to Kithai, shaped exactly like a man's organ, even
to having a reticulation of veins about it, but somewhat
smaller in length and girth. However, as Buyantu demon-

strated, when she gently slid it in and out of her sister a few times, and Biliktu's yin juices began to flow, the suyang somehow absorbed those juices and got bigger and firmer. When it had attained a quite prodigious size, the twins had themselves a joyous time, using that phallocrypt on each other in various and ingenious ways. It was a sight that should have been as rousing to me as feet to a Han man, but I only smiled on them tolerantly and, when they had exhausted each other, I lay down between their warm, moist bodies and went to sleep.

12

THE twins, fatigued, were still sleeping when I eased out from between them the next morning. Nostril had not been anywhere in evidence the night before, and was not in his closet when I went to look for him. So, being temporarily without any servants at all, I stirred up the embers of the brazier in my main room and brewed myself a pot of cha with which to break my fast. While I sipped at it, I bethought myself of trying the experiment I had been contemplating the previous day. I put just enough charcoal on the brazier to keep it burning, but at a very low flame. Then I rummaged about my chambers until I found a stoneware pot with a lid, and I poured into that my remaining fifty-liang measure of flaming powder, lidded it securely and set it on the brazier. At that moment, Nostril came in, looking rather rumpled and seedy, but pleased with himself.

"Master Marco," he said, "I have been up all night. Some of the menservants and horse herders started a gambling game of zhi-pai cards in the stable, and it is still going on. I watched the play for some hours until I grasped the rules of the game. Then I wagered some silver, and I won, too. But when I scooped in my winnings I was dismayed to see that I had won only this sheaf of dirty papers, so I quit in disgust at men who play only with worthless vouchers."

"You ass," I said. "Have you never seen flying money before? As well as I can tell, you are holding there the

equivalent of a month of my wages. You should have
stayed, as long as you were doing so well." He looked bewildered, so I said, "I will explain later. Meanwhile, I rejoice to see that one of us can squander his time in frivolity.
The slave plays the prodigal while his master labors and
scurries about on the slave's errands. I have had a visit
from your Princess Mar-Janah and—"

"Oh, master!" he exclaimed, and turned colors, as if he
had been an adolescent boy and I were twitting him on his
first mooncalf love.

"We will speak later of that also. I will just say that your
gambling earnings should serve you and her to set up
housekeeping together."

"Oh, master! Al-hamdo-lillah az iltifat-i-shoma!"

"Later, later. Right now, I must bid you to cease your
spying activities. I have heard intimations of displeasure,
from a lord whom I think we would be wise not to dis-
please."

"As you command, master. But it may be that I have already procured a trifle of information that may interest
you. That is why I stayed sleepless and absent from my
master's quarters all the night long, being not frivolous
but assiduous in my master's behalf." He put on a look of
self-sacrifice and self-righteousness. "Men get as talkative
as women when they play at cards. And these men, for
mutual comprehension, all talked in the Mongol tongue.
When one of them made a passing reference to the Minister Pao Nei-ho, I thought I ought to linger. Since I was instructed by my master to make no overt inquiries, I could
only listen. And my devoted patience kept me there all
night, never drowsing, never getting drunk, never even
departing to relieve my bladder, never—"

"No need to beat me over the head with hints, Nostril. I
accept that you were working while you played. Come to
the point."

"For what it is worth, master, the Minister of Lesser
Races is himself of a lesser race."

I blinked. "How say you?"

"He evidently passes here for a Han, but he is really of
the Yi people of Yun-nan Province."

"Who told you so? How reliable is this information?"

"As I said, the game was played in the stables. That is
because a stud of horses was yesterday brought in from the

south, and their drovers are at leisure until they are dispatched on another karwan. Several of them are natives of Yun-nan, and one of them said, offhand, that he had glimpsed the Minister Pao here at the palace. And later another said yes, he had recognized him also, as a former petty magistrate of some little Yun-nan prefecture. And later another said yes, but let us not give him away. If Pao has escaped from the backwoods and prospers by passing as a Han here in the great capital, let us let him go on enjoying his success. Thus they spoke, Master Marco, and not falsely but credibly, it seemed to me."

"Yes," I murmured. I was remembering: the Minister Pao had indeed spoken of "us Han" as if he belonged among that people, and of "the obstreperous Yi" as if he concurred in regarding that people as distasteful. Well, I mused, the Chief Minister Achmad may have warned me too late to cease my covert investigations. But, if he was to be angry because I had learned this much of a secret, I must risk making him angrier still.

The twins had waked, perhaps from hearing us talking, and Buyantu came into the main room, looking rather prettily tousled. To her I said, "Run straight to the chambers of the Khan Kubilai, and present to his attendants the compliments of Marco Polo, and inquire if an early appointment can be fixed for me to see the Khakhan on a matter of some urgency."

She started to go back into the bedroom to arrange her dress and hair more orderly, but I said, "Urgency, Buyantu, is urgency. Go as you are, and go quickly." To Nostril I said, "You go to your closet and catch up on your sleep. We will discuss our other concerns when I return."

If I return, I thought, as I went into my bedchamber to dress in my most formal court costume. For all I knew, the Khakhan might, like the Wali Achmad, disapprove of my having taken it upon myself to ferret out secrets, and might express his disapproval in some violent manner not at all to my liking.

Biliktu was just then making up the very disordered bed, and she grinned impishly at me when she found among the covers the su-yang phallocrypt, now as small and limp as any real organ would have been after the exercise it had enjoyed. Seeing it, I decided to take this opportunity for some similar exercise of my own, since there was

no knowing whether it might not be my last opportunity
for a while. So, being at that moment undressed, I took
gentle hold of Biliktu and began to undress her.

She seemed faintly startled. It had, after all, been a long
time since she and I had indulged. She struggled a little
and murmured, "I do not think I should, Master Marco."

"Come," I said heartily. "You cannot be still indisposed.
If you could employ that"—I nodded at the discarded su-
yang—"you can employ a real one."

And she did, with no further demur except an occasional
whimper, and a tendency to keep moving away from my
caresses and thrusts, as if to prevent my penetrating her
very deeply. I assumed that she was merely still weary, or
perhaps a little sore, from the preceding night, and her
maidenly show of reluctance did not prevent my enjoying
myself. Indeed, my enjoyment may have been keener than
it had been for some while past, from the realization that I
was inside Biliktu for a change, and not her twin.

I had finished, and most delightfully, but still had my
red jewel inside Biliktu, relishing the final few diminishing squeezes of her lotus-petal muscles, when a voice
said harshly, "The Khakhan will see you as soon as you
can get there."

It was Buyantu, standing over the bed, glowering fiercely at me and her sister. Biliktu gave another whimper that
was almost a whinny of fright, wriggled out of my embrace
and out of the bed. Buyantu spun on her heel and stamped
from the room. I also got up and got dressed, taking great
care with my appearance. Biliktu dressed at the same
time, but seemed to be dawdling, as if deliberately to make
sure that I was the first to confront Buyantu.

That one stood waiting in the main room, with her arms
folded tight inside her sleeves and a thundercloud expression on her face, like a schoolmistress waiting to chastise a
naughty pupil. She opened her mouth, but I raised a mas-
terly hand to stop her.

"I had not realized until now," I said. "You are displaying jealousy, Buyantu, and I think that is most selfish of
you. For months now, it is clear, you have been gradually
weaning me away from Biliktu. I ought to be flattered, I
suppose, that you want me all for yourself. But I really
must protest. Any such unsisterly jealousy could disturb
the peace our little domicile has heretofore enjoyed. We

will all continue to share, and share alike, and you must simply resign yourself to sharing with your sister my affection and attentions."

She stared at me as if I had uttered pure gibberish, and then she burst into a laughter that did not signify amusement.

"Jealous?" she cried. "Yes, I have grown jealous! And you will regret having taken that sordid advantage of my absence. You will regret that furtive quick frolic! But you think I am jealous of *you?* Why, you blind and strutting fool!"

I rocked with astonishment, never in my life having been so addressed by any servant. I thought she must have lost her senses. But in the next instant, I was even more severely shaken, for she raged on:

"You conceited goat of a Ferenghi! Jealous of you? It is *her* love I want! And for me alone!"

"You have it, Buyantu, and you know you have it!" cried Biliktu, hastening into the room and laying a hand on her sister's arm.

Buyantu shrugged the hand away. "That is not what I saw."

"I am sorry that you saw. And I am sorrier for having done it." She glanced hatefully at me, where I stood stunned. "He took me unaware. I did not know how to resist."

"You must learn to say no."

"I will. I have. I promise."

"We are twins. Nothing should ever come between us."

"Nothing ever will, dearest, not ever again."

"Remember, you are *my* little one."

"Oh, I am! I am! And you are mine!"

Then they were in each other's arms, and weeping lovers' tears down each other's necks. I stood shifting foolishly from one foot to the other, and finally cleared my throat and said:

"Well . . ."

Biliktu gave me a wet-eyed look of hurt and reproach.

"Well . . . uh . . . the Khakhan is waiting for me, girls."

Buyantu gave me a look brimming with massacre.

"When I come back, we will . . . that is, I will be glad to hear suggestions . . . that is, somehow to rearrange . . ." I gave it up, and said instead, "Please, my dears. Until I re-

turn, if you can leave off groping at each other, I have a
small chore for you. Do you see this pot on this brazier?"

They turned their heads to cast an indifferent regard on
it. The pot had got quite hot, so I used a corner of my robe
to lift its lid and look in. The contents emitted a thin, peevish sort of smoke, but showed no sign of having melted at
all. I set the lid securely on it again and said, "Keep up the
fire under it, girls, but keep it a very low fire."

They unwound from each other, and dutifully came to the
brazier, and Biliktu laid a few new chips of charcoal on
the embers.

"Thank you," I said. "It will require no other attendance
than that. Simply stay close by it and keep it at a sim-
mering heat. And when I return . . ."

But they had already dismissed me and were gazing
soulfully at each other, so I went on my way.

Kubilai received me in his earthquake-engine chamber,
and with no one else present, and he greeted me cordially
but not effusively. He knew that I had something to say,
and he was ready for me to say it at once. However, I did
not wish just to blurt out the information I had brought, so
I began circumspectly.

"Sire, I am desirous that I do not, in my ignorance, give
undue weight or impetuosity to my small services. I believe I bring news of some value, but I cannot properly
evaluate it without knowing more than the little I now
know of the Khakhan's disposition of his armies, and the
nature of their objectives."

Kubilai did not take affront at my presumption or tell
me to go and inform myself from his underlings.

"Like any conqueror, I must hold what I have won. Fifteen years ago, when I was chosen Khan of All Khans of
the Mongols, my own brother Arikbugha challenged my
accession, and I had to put him down. More recently, I
have several times had to stifle similar ambitions on the
part of my cousin Kaidu." He waved a dismissal of such
trifles. "The mayflies continually plot to topple the cedar.
Nuisances only, but they require my keeping portions of
my troops on all the borders of Kithai."

"May I ask, Sire, about those on the march, not in garrison?"

He gave me another summary, just as succinct. "If I am
to keep secure this Kithai I won from the Chin, I must also

have the southern lands of the Sung. I can best conquer
them by encirclement, taking first the province of Yun-
nan. So that is the only place where my armies are actively
campaigning right now, under my very capable Orlok
Bayan."

Not to impugn the capability of his Orlok Bayan, I chose
my next words with care.

"He has been engaged in that for some while now, I understand. Is it possible, Sire, that he is finding the conquest of Yun-nan more difficult than expected?"

Kubilai regarded me narrowly. "He is not about to be defeated, if that is what you mean. But neither is he having
an easy victory. His advance had to be made from the land
of To-Bhot, meaning that he had to come down into Yun-
nan through the steeps of the Hang-duan Mountains. Our
horse armies are better suited and more accustomed to
fighting on flat plains. The Yi people of Yun-nan know
every crevice of those mountains, and they fight in a shifty
and cunning way—never facing us in force, but sniping
from behind rocks and trees, then running to hide somewhere else. It is like trying to swat mosquitoes with a hod
of bricks. Yes, you could fairly say that Bayan is finding it
no easy conquest."

I said, "I have heard the Yi called obstreperous."

"Again, a fair enough description. From their safe con-
cealments, they shout taunts of defiance. They evidently
hold the delusion that they can resist long enough to make
us go away. They are wrong."

"But the longer they resist, the more men dead on both
sides, and the land itself made poorer and less worth the
taking."

"Again, true enough. Unfortunately."

"If they were disabused of their delusion of invincibility,
Sire, might not the conquest be easier? With fewer dead
and less ravagement of the province?"

"Yes. Do you know some way to dissolve that delusion?"

"I am not sure, Sire. Let me put it this way. Do you suppose the Yi are bolstered in their resistance by knowing
that they have a friend here at court?"

The Khakhan's gaze became that of a hunting chita. But
he did not roar like a chita, he said as softly as a dove,
"Marco Polo, let us not dance around the subject, like two
Han in the market. Tell me who it is."

"I have information, Sire, apparently reliable, that the Minister of Lesser Races, Pao Nei-ho, though posing as a Han, is really a Yi of Yun-nan."

Kubilai sat pensive, though the blaze in his eyes did not abate, and after a while he growled to himself, "Vakh! Who can tell the damnable slant-eyes apart? And they are all equally perfidious."

I thought I had better say, "That is the only information I have, Sire, and I accuse the Minister of Pao of nothing. I have no evidence that he has spied for the Yi, or even been in communication with them in any way."

"Sufficient is it that he misrepresented himself. You have done well, Marco Polo. I will call Pao in for questioning, and I may later have reason to speak to you again."

When I left the Khakhan's suite, I found a palace steward waiting for me in the corridor, with a message that the Chief Minister Achmad would have me call upon him that moment. I went to his chambers, not gleefully, thinking: How could he have heard already?

The Arab received me in a room decorated with a single massive piece of—I suppose it would be called a sculpture made by nature. It was a great rock, twice as tall as a man and four times as big around, a tremendous piece of solidified lava that looked like petrified flames, all gray twists and convolutions and holes and little tunnels. Somewhere in the base of it a bowl of incense smoldered, and the perfumed blue smoke rose and coiled through the sculpture's sinuosities and seeped out from some apertures and in through others, so that the whole thing seemed to writhe in a slow, ceaseless torment.

"You disobeyed and defied me," Achmad said immediately, with no greeting or other preliminary. "You kept listening until you heard something damaging to a high minister of this court."

I said, "It was a piece of news that came to me before I could withdraw the ear." I offered no further apology or extenuation, but boldly added, "I thought it had come *only* to me."

"What is spoken on the road is heard in the grass," he said indifferently. "An old Han proverb."

Still boldly, I said, "It requires a listener in the grass. All this time, I had assumed that my maidservants were reporting my doings to the Khan Kubilai or the Prince

Chingkim, and I accepted that as reasonable. But all this time they have been *your* spies, have they not?"

I do not know whether he would have bothered to lie and deny it, or would even have bothered to confirm the fact, for at that moment came a slight interruption. From an adjoining room, a woman started in through the curtained doorway, and then, perceiving that Achmad had company, abruptly swished back through them again. All I saw of her was that she was a strikingly large woman, and elegantly garbed. From her behavior, it was evident that she did not wish to be seen by me, so I supposed that she was somebody else's wife or concubine engaging in an illicit adventure. But I could not recall ever having seen such a tall and robust woman anywhere about the palace. I reflected that the painter, Master Chao, in speaking of the Arab's depraved tastes, had not said anything about the *objects* of his tastes. Did the Wali Achmad have a special liking for women who were larger than most men? I did not inquire, and he paid no attention to the interruption, but said:

"The steward found you at the Khakhan's chambers, so I take it that you have already imparted to him your information."

"Yes, Wali, I have. Kubilai is summoning the Minister Pao to interrogate him."

"A fruitless summons," said the Arab. "It seems that the Minister has made a hasty departure, destination unknown. Lest you be so brash as to accuse me of having connived in his flight, let me suggest that Fao probably recognized the same visitors from the southland who recognized him, and whose indiscreet gossip your ear overheard."

I said, and truthfully, "I am not brash to the extreme of being suicidal, Wali Achmad. I would accuse you of nothing. I will only mention that the Khakhan seemed gratified to have the information I brought him. So, if you deem that a disobedience to you, and punish me for it, I imagine Kubilai will wonder why."

"Impertinent piglet of a sow mother! Are you daring me to punish you, with a threat of the Khakhan's displeasure?"

I made no reply to that. His black agate eyes got even stonier, and he went on:

"Get this clear in your mind, Folo. My fortunes are de-

pendent on the Khanate of which I am Chief Minister and
Vice-Regent. I would be not only traitorous—I would be
imbecilic—if I did anything to undermine the Khanate. I
am as eager as Kubilai that we take Yun-nan, and then
the Sung Empire, and then all the rest of the world as well,
if we can do so and if Allah wills it so. I do not berate you
for having discovered, before I did, that the Khanate's interests may have been imperiled by that Yi impostor. But
get this also clear in your mind. *I am the Chief Minister.* I
will not tolerate disobedience or disloyalty or defiance
from my inferiors. Especially not from a younger man who
is an inexperienced outsider in these parts and a despicable Christian and a rank newcomer to this court and, for
all that, an impudent upstart of overweening ambition."

I started angrily to say, "I am no more an outsider here
than—" but he imperiously raised his hand.

"I will not utterly demolish you for this instance of disobedience, since it was not to my disservice. But I promise
that you will regret it, Folo, sufficiently that you will not
be inclined to repeat it. Earlier, I only *told* you what Hell
is. It seems you require a demonstration." Then, perhaps
reflecting that his lady visitor might be within hearing, he
lowered his voice. "In my own good time, I will provide
that demonstration. Go now. And go well away from me."

I went, but not too far, in case I should be wanted again
by the Khakhan. I went outdoors and through the palace
gardens and up the Kara Hill to the Echo Pavilion, to let
the clear breezes of the heights blow through my cluttered
mind. I strolled around the promenade within the mosaic
wall, mentally sorting among all the numerous things I
had recently been given or had taken upon myself to worry
about: Yun-nan and the Yi, Nostril and his lady lost and
found, the twins Buyantu and Biliktu, now revealed as
more than sisters to each other and less than faithful to
me. . . .

Then, as if I had not enough to concern me, I was suddenly given a new thing. A voice whispered in my ear, in
the Mongol tongue, "Do not turn. Do not move. Do not
look."

I froze where I was, expecting next to feel a stabbing
point or a slashing blade. But there came only the voice
again:

"Tremble, Ferenghi. Dread the coming of what you have

deserved. But not now, for the waiting and the dread and the not knowing are part of it."

By then, I had realized that the voice was not really at my ear. I turned and looked all about me, and I saw no one, and I said sharply, "What have I deserved? What do you want of me?"

"Only expect me," whispered the voice.

"Who? And when?"

The voice whispered just seven more words—seven short and simple words, but words freighted with a menace more chilling than the most fearsome threat—and it never spoke again afterward. It said only and flatly and finally:

"Expect me when you least expect me."

13

I waited for more, and, when I heard no more, I asked another question or two, and got no answer. So I ran around the terrace to my right, and got to the Moon Gate in the wall without having seen anyone, so I continued to run all the way around the Echo Pavilion, back to the Moon Gate again, and still had seen no one. There was only that one entranceway in the wall, so I stood in it and looked down the Kara Hill. There were several lords and ladies also taking the air that day, strolling about in ones and twos on lower levels of the hill. Any one of them could have been the person who had invisibly accosted me—could have run that far, then slowed to a walk. Or the whisperer could have run another way. The flagstone pathway from the Moon Gate descended only a short distance before forking in two, and one of the paths circled around behind the pavilion to descend the back slope of the hill. Or the whisperer could still be right inside the wall with me, and could easily keep the pavilion between us, no matter how speedily I ran or how stealthily I prowled around the promenade. It was useless to search, so I simply stood there in the entranceway and pondered.

The voice could have been that of either a man or a woman, and of any of several people who had lately had cause to wish me hurt. Just since this hour yesterday, I

had been told by three people that I would "regret" some
action of mine: the icy Achmad, the irate Buyantu and the
outraged Lady Chao. I could also assume that the fugitive
Minister Pao was not now any friend of mine, and might
still be within the palace confines. And, if I were to count
all the palace people whom I had alienated since coming
here, I would have to include Master Ping, the Fondler. All
of those persons spoke Mongol, as had the whisperer.

There were even other possibilities. The immense lady
lurking in Achmad's chambers might think that I had recognized her, and resent me for it. Or the Lady Chao could
have told her lord husband some lie about my visit to her,
and he might now be as angry at me as she was. I had repeated nasty gossip about the eunuch Court Astrologer,
and eunuchs were notoriously vindictive. For that matter,
I had once remarked to Kubilai that I thought most of his
ministers were misemployed, and that word could have got
back to them, and every single one of them might be mortally peeved at me.

I was casting my gaze back and forth over the curly-
eaved roofs of the many palace edifices, as if trying to see
through their yellow tiles to identify my accoster, when I
saw a vast cloud of smoke erupt abruptly from the main
building. The smoke was too much to have come from a
brazier or a kitchen hearth, and was too sudden to have
come from a room caught fire or anything of that sort. The
black cloud seemed to *boil* as it billowed, and it appeared to
have fragments of the building and the roof mixed into it.
A fraction of an instant later, the sound of it reached me—a
thunderclap so loud and slapping that it actually stirred
my hair and the loose folds of my robes. I saw the other few
persons on the hill also wince at the sound, and turn to
look, and then we were all running down the slope toward
the scene.

I did not have to get very close before I recognized that
the eruption had come from my own chambers. In fact, the
main room of my suite had burst its walls and roof, and
was now laid open to the sky and the view of the gathering
crowd, and what few of its contents had not disintegrated
outright were now burning. The black cloud of the initial
blast, still quite intact and still writhing in its slow boil,
was now drifting out over the city, but the lesser smoke
from the room's burning was yet dense enough to keep

most of the onlookers at a respectful distance. Only a number of palace servants were scuttling in and out of the smoke, carrying buckets of water and dashing them into the burning remains. One of them dropped his bucket when he saw me, and came running—tottering, rather—to meet me. He was so blackened by smoke and singed of garments that it was a moment before I recognized Nostril.

"Oh, master, come no closer! It is a frightful destruction!"

"What happened?" I asked, though I had already guessed.

"I do not know, master. I was asleep in my closet when all of a sudden—bismillah!—I found myself awake and floundering here on the grass of this garden court, my clothes all a-smolder, and shards of broken furniture falling all about me."

"The girls!" I said urgently. "What of the girls?"

"Mashallah, master, they are dead, and in a most horrible manner. If this was not the doing of a vengeful jinni, it was the attack of a fire-breathing dragon."

"I think not," I said miserably.

"Then it must have been a rukh, insanely tearing with its beak and talons, for the girls are not just dead—they no longer exist, not as separate girls. They are nothing but a spatter on the remaining walls. Bits of flesh and blobs of gore. Twins they were in life, and twinned they have gone into death. They will be inseparable forever, since no funeral practitioner could possibly sort out the fragments and say which were of whom."

"Bruto barabào," I breathed, appalled. "But it was not any rukh or jinni or dragon. Alas, it was *I* who did this."

"And to think, master, you once told me that you could never kill a woman."

"Unfeeling slave!" I cried. "I did not do it deliberately!"

"Ah, well, you are young yet. Meanwhile, let us be thankful that those two did not keep any pet dog or cat or ape, to be intermingled also with them in the afterlife."

I swallowed sickly. Whether this was my fault or God's doing, it was a terrible loss of two lovely young women. But I had to reflect that, in a very real sense, to me they had been lost already. One or both of them had been betraying me to the inimical Achmad, and I had entertained suspicion of Buyantu as the secret whisperer at the Echo

Pavilion. Whoever that was, though, it evidently had not been she. But just then I jumped, as another voice spoke in my ear:

"Lamentable mamzar, what have you done?"

I turned. It was the Court Firemaster, who no doubt had come at a run because he had known the distinctive noise of his own product.

"I was trying an experiment in al-kimia, Master Shi," I said, contrite. "The girls were instructed to keep the fire very low, but they must have—"

"I told you," he said through his teeth. "The flaming powder is not a thing to play with."

"No one can tell Marco Polo anything," said Prince Chingkim, who, as Wang of Kahnbalik, had come apparently to see what havoc had been visited upon his city. He added drily, "Marco Polo must be shown."

"I would rather not have been shown this," I mumbled.

"Then do not look, master," said Nostril. "For here come the Court Funeralmaster and his assistants, to gather the mortal remains."

The fire had been damped down, by now, to wisps of smoke and occasional little sizzles of steam. The spectators and the water-carrying servants all went away, for people naturally disliked to linger in the vicinity of the funeral preparers. I remained, out of respect for the departed, and so did Nostril, to keep me company, and so did Chingkim, in his capacity as Wang, to see that all was properly concluded, and so did the Master Shi, out of a professional desire to examine the wreckage and make notes for future reference in his work.

The purple-garbed Funeralmaster and his purple-garbed men, although they must have been accustomed to seeing death in many forms, clearly found this job distasteful. They took a look about, then went away, to return with some black leather containers and wooden spatulas and cloth mops. With those objects, and with expressions of revulsion, they went through my rooms and the garden area outside, scraping and swabbing and depositing the results in the containers. When finally they were done, we other four went in and examined the ruins, but only cursorily, for the smell was dreadful. It was a stink compounded of smoke, char, cooked meat and—though it is ungallant to say of the beautiful young departed—the stench of excrement, for I had given the girls no opportunity that morning to make their toilet.

"To have done all this damage," said the Firemaster, as we were glumly poking about in the main room, "the huo-yao must have been tightly confined at the moment it ignited."

"It was in a securely lidded stoneware pot, Master Shi," I said. "I would have thought no spark could have got near it."

"The pot itself only had to get hot enough," he said, with a glower at me. "And a stoneware pot? More explosive potential than an Indian nut or a heavy zhu-gan cane. And if the women were huddled over it at the time . . ."

I moved away from him, not wanting to hear any more about the poor girls. In a corner, to my surprise, I found one undestroyed thing in that destroyed room. It was only a porcelain vase, but it was entire, unbroken, except for some chips lost from its rim. When I looked into it, I saw why it had survived. It was the vase into which I had poured the first measure of huo-yao, and then poured in water. The powder had dried to a solid cake that nearly filled the vase, and so had made it impervious to damage.

"Look at this, Master Shi," I said, taking it to show to him. "The huo-yao can be a preservative as well as a destroyer."

"So you first tried wetting it," he said, looking into the vase. "I could have told you that it would dry solid and useless like that. As a matter of fact, I believe I *did* tell you. Ayn davàr, but the Prince is right. You cannot be told anything by anybody. . . ."

I had stopped listening, and went away from him again, for a dim recollection was stirring in my mind. I took the vase out into the garden, and pried up a stone from a whitewashed ring of them around a flower bed, and used it for a hammer to shatter the porcelain. When all the fragments fell away, I had a heavy, gray, vase-shaped lump of the solid-caked powder. I regarded it, and the dim memory came clearer in my mind. What I remembered was the making of that foodstuff the Mongols called grut. I remembered how the Mongol women of the plains would spread milk curd in the sun, and let that dry to a hard cake, then crumble it into pellets of grut, which would keep indefinitely without spoiling, until someone wished to make an emergency meal of it. I took up my stone again, and hammered on the lump of huo-yao until a few pellets, the size and appearance of mouse droppings, crumbled off from it. I regarded them, then went once again to the Firemaster and said diffidently:

"Master Shi, would you look at these and tell me if I am wrong—"

"Probably," he said, with a contemptuous snort. "They are mouse turds."

"They are pellets broken from that lump of huo-yao. It appears to me that these pellets hold in firm suspension the correct proportions of the three separate powders. And, being now dry, they should ignite just as if—"

"Yom mekhayeh!" he exclaimed huskily, in what I took to be the Ivrit language. Very, very slowly and tenderly, he picked the pellets from my palm, and held them in his, and bent to peer closely at them, and again huskily exclaimed, in what I recognized as Han, several other words like "hao-jia-huo," which is an expression of amazement, and "jiao-hao," which is an expression of delight, and "chan-juan," which is a term usually employed to praise a beautiful woman.

He suddenly began dashing about the ruined room, until he found a splinter of wood still smoldering. He blew that into a glow, and ran out into the garden. Chingkim and I followed him, the Prince saying, "What now?" and "Not again!" as the Firemaster touched the ember to the pellets and they went off with a bright flare and fizz, just as if they had been in their original finely powdered form.

"Yom mekhayeh!" Master Shi breathed once more, and then turned to me and, wide-eyed, murmured, "Bar mazel!" and then turned to Prince Chingkim and said in Han, "Mu bu jian jie."

"An old proverb," Chingkim told me. "The eye cannot see its own lashes. I gather that you have discovered something new about the flaming powder that is new even to the experienced Firemaster."

"It was just an idea that came to me," I said modestly.

Master Shi stood looking at me, still saucer-eyed, and shaking his head, and muttering words like "khakhem" and "khalutz." Then again he addressed Chingkim:

"My Prince, I do not know if you were contemplating a prosecution of this incautious Ferenghi for the damage and casualties he has caused. But the Mishna tells us that a thinking bastard, even, is more highly to be regarded than a high priest who preaches by rote. I suggest that this one has accomplished something worth more than any number of women servants and bits of palace."

"I do not know what the Mishna is, Master Shi," grumbled the Prince, "but I will convey your sentiments to my Royal Father." He turned to me. "I will convey you, too, Marco. He had already sent me looking for you when I heard the thunder of your—accomplishment. I am glad I do not have to carry you to him in a spoon. Come along."

"Marco," said the Khakhan without preamble, "I must send a messenger to the Orlok Bayan in Yun-nan, to apprise him of the latest developments here, and I think you have earned the honor of being that messenger. A missive is now being written for you to take to him. It explains about the Minister Pao and suggests some measures that Bayan may take, now that the Yi are deprived of their secret ally in our midst. Give Bayan my letter, then attend upon him until the war is won, and then you will have the honor of bringing me the word that Yun-nan at last is ours."

"You are sending me to war, Sire?" I said, not quite sure that I was eager to go. "I have had no experience of war."

"Then you should have. Every man should engage in at least one war in his lifetime—else how can he say that he has savored all the experiences which life offers a man?"

"I was not thinking of life, Sire, so much as death." And I laughed, but not with much merriment.

"Every man dies," Kubilai said, rather stiffly. "Some deaths are at least less ignominious than others. Would you prefer to die like a clerk, dwindling and wilting into the boneyard of a secured old age?"

"I am not afraid, Sire. But what if the war drags on for a long time? Or never *is* won?"

Even more stiffly, he said, "It is better to fight in a losing cause than to have to confess to your grandchildren that you never fought at all. Vakh!"

Prince Chingkim spoke up. "I can assure you, Royal Father, that this Marco Polo would never dodge any confrontation imaginable. He is, however, at the moment a trifle shaken by a recent calamity." He went on to tell Kubilai about the accidental—he stressed accidental—devastation of my ménage.

"Ah, so you are bereft of women servants and the services of women," the Khakhan said sympathetically. "Well, you will be traveling too rapidly on the road to Yunnan to have need of servants, and you will be too fatigued each night to yearn for anything more than sleep. When you get there, of course, you will do your share of the pillage and rape. Take slaves to serve you, take women to service you. Behave like a Mongol born."

"Yes, Sire," I said submissively.

He leaned back and sighed, as if he missed the good old days, and murmured in reminiscence:

"My esteemed grandfather Chinghiz, it is said, was born clutching a clot of blood in his tiny fist, from which the shamàn foretold for him a sanguinary career. He lived up to the prophecy. And I can still remember him telling us, his grandsons, 'Boys, a man can have no greater pleasure than to slay his enemies, and then, besmeared and reeking with their blood, to rape their chaste wives and virgin daughters. There is no more delightful sensation than to spurt your jing-ye into a woman or a girl-child who is weeping and struggling and loathing you and cursing you.' So spake Chinghiz Khan, the Immortal of Mongols."

"I will bear it in mind, Sire."

He sat forward again and said, "No doubt you have arrangements to make before your departure. But make them as expeditiously as possible. I have already sent advance riders to ready your route. If, on your way along it, you can sketch for me maps of that route—as you and your uncles did of the Silk Road—I shall be grateful and your reward will be handsome. Also, if in your travels you should catch up to the fugitive Minister Pao, I give you leave to slay him, and your reward for that would also be handsome. Now go and prepare for the journey. I will have fast horses and a trustworthy escort ready when you are."

Well, I thought, as I went to my chambers, this would at least put me out of reach of my own court adversaries—the Wali Achmad, the Lady Chao, the Fondler Ping, whoever else that whisperer might have been. Better to fall in open warfare than to someone sneaking up behind me.

The Court Architect was in my suite, making measurements and muttering to himself and snapping orders to a team of workmen, who were commencing the replacement of the vanished walls and roof. Happily, I had kept most of my personal possessions and valuables in my bedroom, which had been unravaged. Nostril was in there, burning incense to clear the air. I bade him lay out a traveling wardrobe for me and to make a light pack of other necessities. Then I gathered up all the journal notes I had written and accumulated since leaving Venice, and carried them to my father's chambers.

He looked a little surprised when I dropped the pile on a table beside him, for it was an unprepossessing mound of smudged and wrinkled and mildewed papers of all different sizes.

"I would be obliged, Father, if you would send these to Uncle Marco, the next time you entrust some shipment of goods to the Silk Road horse post, and ask him to send them on to Venice for safekeeping by Marègna Fiordelisa. The notes may be of interest to some future cosmographer, if he can decipher them and arrange them in order. I had intended to do that myself—someday—but I am bidden to a mission from which I may not return."

"Indeed? What mission?"

I told him, and with dramatic somberness, so I was taken aback when he said, "I envy you, doing something I have never done. You should appreciate the opportunity Kubilai is giving you. Da novèlo tuto xe belo. Not many white men have watched the Mongols make war—and lived to remember it."

"I only hope I do," I said. "But survival is not my sole consideration. There are other things I had rather be doing. And I am sure that there are more profitable things I could be doing."

"Now, now, Marco. To a good hunger there is no bad bread."

"Are you suggesting, Father, that I should *enjoy* wasting my time in a war?"

He said reprovingly, "It is true that you were trained for trade, and you come from a merchant lineage. But you must not look at everything with a tradesman's eye, always asking yourself, 'What is this good for? What is this worth?' Leave that grubby philosophy to the tradesmen who never step beyond their shop doors. You have ventured out to the farthest edge of the world. It would be a pity if you take home only profit, and not at least a little of poetry."

"That reminds me," I said. "I turned a profit yesterday. May I borrow one of your maidservants for an errand?"

I sent her to fetch from the slave quarters the Turki woman called Mar-Janah, formerly the possession of the Lady Chao Ku-an.

"Mar-Janah?" my father repeated, as the servant departed. "And a Turki . . . ?"

"Yes, you know of her," I said. "We have spoken of her before." And I told him the whole story, of which he had so long ago heard only a part of the beginning.

"What a wondrously intricate web!" he exclaimed. "And to have been at last unraveled! God does not always pay His debts just on Sundays." Then, as I had done on first seeing her, he widened his eyes when the lovely woman came smiling into the chamber, and I introduced him to her.

"My Mistress Chao did not seem pleased about it," she said shyly to me, "but she tells me that I am now your property, Master Marco."

"Only briefly," I said, taking the paper of title from my purse and holding it out to her. "You are your own property again, as you should be, and I will hear you call no one Master any more."

With a tremulous hand she accepted the paper, and with her other hand she brushed tears from her long eyelashes, and she seemed to have trouble finding words to speak.

"Now," I went on, "I doubt not that the Princess Mar-Janah of Cappadocia could take her pick of men from this court or any other. But if Your Highness still has her heart set on Nost—on Ali Babar, he awaits you in my chambers down the hall."

She started to kneel in ko-tou, but I caught her hands, raised her, turned her to the door, said, "Go to him," and she went.

My father approvingly followed her with his gaze, then

asked me, "You will not wish to take Nostril with you to Yun-nan?"

"No. He has waited twenty years or more for that woman. Let them be married as soon as can be. Will you tend to those arrangements, Father?"

"Yes. And I will give Nostril his own certificate of title as a wedding present. I mean Ali Babar. I suppose we ought to accustom ourselves to addressing him more respectfully, now that he will be a freeman and consort to a princess."

"Before he is entirely free, I had better go and make sure he has packed for me properly. So I will say goodbye now, Father, in case I do not see you or Uncle Mafìo before I leave."

"Goodbye, Marco, and let me take back what I said before. I was wrong. You may *never* make a proper tradesman. You just now gave away a valuable slave for no payment at all."

"But, Father, I got her free of payment."

"What better way to turn a clear profit? Yet you did not. You did not even set her free with fanfare and fine words and noble gesticulations, letting her kiss and slobber over your hands, while a numerous audience applauded your liberality and a palace scribe recorded the scene for posterity."

Mistaking the tenor of his words, I said in some exasperation, "To quote one of your own adages, Father: one minute you are lighting torches and the next you are counting candle wicks."

"It is poor business to give things away, and worse business to get not even praise for doing so. Clearly you know the value of nothing—except perhaps a human being or two. I despair of you as a tradesman. I have hope of you as a poet. Goodbye, Marco, my son, and come back safe."

I got to see Mar-Janah one more time. The next morning, she and Nostril-now-Ali came to wish me "salaam aleikum" before my departure, and to thank me again for having helped to bring them together. They had risen early, to make sure of catching me—and evidently had got up from a shared bed, for they were disheveled and sleepy-eyed. But they were also smiling and blithesome, and, when they tried to describe to me their rapturous reunion, they were quite rapturously and absurdly inarticulate.

He began, "It was almost as if—"

"No, it *was* as if—" said she.

"Yes, it was *indeed* as if—" he said. "All the twenty years since we last knew each other—it was as if they, well—"

"Come, come," I said, laughing at the foolish locutions. "Neither of you used to be such an inept teller of tales."

Mar-Janah laughed too, and finally said what was meant: "The twenty intervening years might never have been."

"She still thinks me handsome!" exclaimed Nostril. "And she is more beautiful than ever!"

"We are as giddy as two youngsters in first love," she said.

"I am happy for you," I said. Though they were both perhaps forty-five years old, and though I still could not help feeling that a love affair between persons nearly old enough to be my parents was a quaint and risible thing, I added, "I wish you joy forever, young lovèrs."

I went then to call on the Khakhan, to collect his letter for the Orlok Bayan—and found that he already had visitors: the Court Firemaster, whom I had seen only the day before, the Court Astronomer and the Court Goldsmith, whom I had not seen for quite some time. They all three looked curiously bloodshot, but their red eyes gleamed with something like excitement.

Kubilai said, "These gentlemen courtiers wish you to carry to Yun-nan something of theirs also."

"We have been up all night, Marco," said the Firemaster Shi. "Now that you have devised a way to make the flaming powder transportable, we are eager to see it employed in combat. I have spent the night wetting quantities of it and drying it into cakes and then pulverizing it into pellets."

"Et voilà, I have been making new containers for it," said the Goldsmith Boucher, displaying a shiny brass ball, about the size of his head. "Master Shi told us how you destroyed half the palace with just a stoneware pot."

"It was not half the palace," I protested. "It was only—"

"Qu'importe?" he said impatiently. "If a mere lidded pot could do that, we reckoned that an even stouter confinement of the powder should make it trebly powerful. We decided on brass."

"And I worked out, by comparison with the planetary orbs," said the Astronomer Jamal-ud-Din, "that a globular container would be best. It can be most accurately and farthest thrown by hand or by catapult, or can even be rolled among the enemy, and its shape—inshallah!—will most effectually disperse its destructive forces in all directions."

"So I made balls like this, in sections of two hemispheres," said Master Boucher. "Master Shi filled them with the powder pellets, and then I brazed them together. Nothing but their internal force will ever break them apart. But when it does—les diables sont déchaînés!"

"You and the Orlok Bayan," said Master Shi, "will be the first to put the huo-yao to practical use in field warfare. We made a dozen of the balls. Take them with you and let Bayan use them as he will, and they ought to work without fail."

"So it sounds," I said. "But how do the warriors ignite them?"

"You see this string like a wick sticking out? It was inserted before the halves were brazed together. It is actually of cotton twisted around a core of the huo-yao itself. Only touch a spark to it—a smoldering stick of incense will serve—and it will give a long count of ten before the spark reaches the charge inside."

"Then they cannot discharge accidentally? I am disinclined to devastate some innocent karwansarai before I even get there."

"No fear," said Master Shi. "Just please do not let any women play with them." He added drily, "It is not for nothing that my people's morning thanksgiving prayer contains the words 'Blessed art Thou, O Lord our God, Who hath not made me a woman.'"

"Is that a fact?" said the Master Jamal, sounding interested. "Our Quran says likewise, in the fourth sura: 'Men are superior to women on account of the qualities with which Allah has gifted the one above the other.'"

I decided the old men must be lightheaded from lack of

sleep, to be starting a discussion of the demerits of women, so I cut it short by saying, "I will gladly take the things, then, if the Khan Kubilai is in favor."

The Khakhan made a gesture of assent, and the three courtiers hurried off to load the dozen balls onto my train's pack horses. When they had gone, Kubilai said to me:

"Here is the letter to Bayan, sealed and chained for carrying safely about your neck, under your clothes. Here also is my yellow-paper letter of authority, as you have seen your uncles carry. But you should not often have to show it, for I am giving you also this more visible pai-tzu. You have only to wear it on your chest or hung on your saddle, and at sight of it anyone in this realm will do you kotou and accord you every hospitality and service."

The pai-tzu was a tablet or plaque, as broad as my hand and nearly as long as my forearm, made of ivory with an inset silver ring for hanging it by, and inlaid gold lettering, in the Mongol alphabet, instructing all men to welcome and obey me, under pain of the Khakhan's displeasure.

"Also," Kubilai went on, "since you may have to sign vouchers of expenses, or messages, or other documents, I had the Court Yinmaster engrave this personal yin for you."

It was a small block of smooth stone, a soft gray in color with blood-red veinings through it, about an inch square and a finger-length long, rounded at one end for comfortable holding in the hand. The squared-off front end of it was intricately incised, and Kubilai showed me how to stamp that end of an inked pad of cloth and then onto any paper that required my signature. I never would have recognized the imprint it made—as *being* my signature, I mean—but it looked nicely impressive, and I commented admiringly on the fineness of the work.

"It is a good yin, and it will last forever," said the Khakhan. "I had the Yinmaster Liu Shen-dao make it of the marble which the Han call chicken-blood stone. As to the fineness of the engraving, that Master Liu is so expert that he can inscribe an entire prayer on a single human hair."

And so I left Khanbalik for Yun-nan, carrying, besides my own pack and clothes and other necessities, the twelve brass balls of flaming powder, the sealed letter to the Orlok Bayan, my own letter of authority and the confirming pai-tzu plaque—and my very own personal yin, with which I could leave my name stamped, if I chose, all across Kithai. This is what my name looks like, in the Han characters, for I still have the little stone yin:

I was not sure, when I set out to war, how long I would last. But, as the Khan Kubilai said, my yin could last forever, and so might my name.

TO-BHOT

1

I_T was a long journey from Khanbalik to the Orlok Bayan's site of operations, nearly as many li as from Khanbalik to Kashgar, but my two escorts and I rode light and fast. We carried only essential traveling gear—no food or cookware or bedding—and the heaviest items, the powder-charged brass balls, were divided among our three extra horses. Those were also fleet steeds, not the usual trudging pack animals, so all six horses were capable of proceeding at the Mongol's war-march pace of canter and walk and canter. Whenever any horse began to show signs of wearying, we had only to pause at the nearest of the Road Minister's horse posts and demand six fresh ones.

I had not known what Kubilai had meant when he said that he had already sent advance riders to "ready the route." But I learned that that was an arrangement made whenever the Khakhan or any of his important emissaries made a long cross-country journey. Those riders went ahead to announce the journeyer's imminent approach, and every Wang of every province, every prefect of every prefecture, even the elders of every least village, were expected to prepare for the passing-through. So there were always comfortable beds waiting in the best possible accommodations, good cooks waiting to prepare the best available fare, even new wells dug if necessary to supply sweet water in arid regions. That is why we were enabled to carry only the lightest of packs. Every night, too, there were women supplied for our enjoyment, but, as Kubilai had also said, I was too fatigued and saddle sore to make

use of them. Instead, I spent each night's short interval between table and bed in scribbling down on paper what details and landmarks I had noticed during that day's travel.

We rode in a southwestering arc from Khanbalik, and I
cannot remember how many villages, towns and cities we
passed through or spent a night in, but only two of them
were of estimable size. One was Xian, which the War Minister Chao had pointed out to me on his great map and told
me had once been the capital city of the First Emperor of
these lands. Xian had dwindled considerably in the centuries since, and, though still a busy and prosperous crossroads city, possessed none of the finery of an imperial
capital. The other big city was Cheng-du—in what was
called the Red Basin country, because the earth there is
not yellow, as in most of the rest of Kithai. Cheng-du was
the capital city of the province called Si-chuan, and its
Wang inhabited a palace city-within-a-city almost as
grand as that of Khanbalik. The Wang Mangalai, another
of Kubilai's sons, would gladly have had me stay a long
time as his honored guest, and I was much tempted to rest
there for a least a while. But, mindful of my mission, I
made my excuses, and of course Mangalai accepted them,
and I spent only a single night in his company.

From Cheng-du, my escorts and turned directly west—
into the mountainous border country where the Kithai
province of Si-chuan and the Sung province of Yun-nan
and the land of To-Bhot all mingled together—and our pace
slowed as we began a long climb that soon became a steep
climb. The mountains were not so sky-reaching as, for instance, the Pai-Mir of High Tartary. These had much more
forest growth on them and no snow, and even in deep
winter, I was told, the snow never clung to them for long,
except on their very tops. But these mountains, if less high
than others I had seen, were much more vertical in their
general configuration. Except for the wooded slopes, they
were mostly monstrous slabs set on end, separated by narrow, deep, dark ravines. But at least they were solid mountains; we did not have to dodge any avalanches, and I did
not ever hear any of them booming roundabout. The country was called by its inhabitants the Land of the Four Rivers, those four streams being locally named the N'mai, the
Nu, the Lan-kang and the Jin-sha. But those waters, said
the natives, broadened and deepened as they flowed out of

the mountains, to become the four greatest rivers of that
part of the world, better known by their downstream
names of Irawadi, Sal-win, Me-kong and Yang-tze. The
first three of those, when they got beyond Yun-nan Province, ran southward or southeastward into the tropical
lands called Champa. The fourth would become that Yang-
tze of which I have earlier spoken—the Tremendous River—which runs eastward clear to the Sea of Kithai.

But I and my escorts were crossing those rivers far upstream of where they became only four—in the highlands
where the rivers began as a multitude of tributary
streams. There were so many that they did not all have
names, but none was contemptible on that account. Every
single stream was a rushing white water which, through
the ages, had worn its own individual channel through the
mountains, and every single channel was a slab-sided
gorge that might have been cleft by the downward slash of
some jinni's giant shimshir sword. The only way along and
across those precipitous gashes in the mountains was by
way of what the local people proudly called their Pillar
Road.

Calling it a road at all was a considerable exaggeration,
but it did stand on pillars—or, more accurately, corbels—
logs driven and wedged into cracks and crannies in the
cliffsides, and planks laid across them, and layers of earth
and straw piled on. It could better have been called the
Shelf Road. Or even better, the Blind Road, because I traveled most of it with my eyes shut, trusting in the sure-
footedess and imperturbability of my horse, and hoping it
was shod with the never-slip shoes made of the "Marco's
sheep" horn. To open my eyes and look up, down, ahead,
behind or sideways made me equally giddy. Glancing upward or downward gave much the same sight: two walls of
gray rock converging with distance to a narrow, bright,
green-edged crack—up there the sky between two fringes
of trees, down yonder the water that looked like a moss-
lined brook, but was really a rushing river between two
belts of forest. Ahead or behind was the vertiginous view of
the Pillar Road shelf that looked too fragile to bear its own
weight, never mind a horse and rider, or a train of them.
Looking to one side, I would see the cliff that brushed my
stirrup and seemed to threaten to give me a sudden shove.
Looking the other way, I would see the farther cliff, which

appeared to stand so close that I was tempted to reach out and touch it—and to lean was to risk toppling from my saddle and falling forever.

The only thing more dizzying than following the Pillar Road along the cliffsides was the crossing from one side of a gorge to the other, on what the mountain folk, without exaggeration, called the Limp Bridges. Those were made of planks and thick ropes of twisted cane strips, and they swayed worse when a man stepped out onto them, and they swayed even worse when he led his horse out behind him, and during those crossings I think even the horses shut their eyes.

Though Kubilai's advance riders had made sure that all the mountain inhabitants expected the arrival of me and my escorts, and we got the best hospitality those people could give us, it was not exactly of royal quality. Only occasionally did we come to a place in the mountains flat and habitable enough to support even a meager village of woodcutters' huts. More often we spent the night in a cliff niche where the road was built wide enough for travelers going in opposite directions to edge past each other. At those places there was a group of rough men stationed, waiting to receive us, having erected a yak-hair tent for us to sleep in, and having brought some meat or killed a mountain sheep or goat to cook for us over an open camp fire.

I well remember the first time we stopped in such a place, when the day was just darkening to dusk. The three mountain men awaiting us made salutations and ko-tou and—since we could not converse; they knew no Mongol, and spoke some tongue which was not even Han—they immediately set about making our evening meal. They built up a good fire, and spitted some cutlets of musk deer over it, and hung a pot of water to heat. I noticed that the men had made the fire of wooden branches—which must have required much labor of clambering up and down the steep ravine sides to collect—but also had a small pile of pieces of zhu-gan cane lying beside it. The dusk had deepened to full darkness by the time the food was ready, and, while two of the men served us, the other tossed one of those bits of cane onto the fire.

The deer meat was better than the usual mountain fare of mutton or goat, but the accompaniments were ghastly.

The meat was handed to me in a hunk, for me to hold while I tore at it with my teeth. The only implement provided me was a shallow wooden bowl, into which one of the servers poured hot green cha. But I had taken only a couple of sips before the other server politely took it from me, to add to it. He held a platter of yak butter, all stuck about with hairs and lint and road dust, and grooved by the fingers of those who had dug at it previously, and with his own black fingernails raked off a lump and dropped it into my cha to melt. The dirty yak butter would have been repellent enough, but then he opened a filthy cloth sack and poured into the cha bowl something that looked like sawdust.

"Tsampa," he said.

When I only peered at the mess with disgust and bewilderment, he demonstrated what was to be done with it. He stuck his grimy fingers into my bowl and worked the sawdust and butter together until it became a paste, then a doughy lump when it had absorbed all the cha in the bowl. Then, before I could move to prevent it, he pinched off a wad of that tepid, dirty dough and poked it into my mouth.

"Tsampa," he said again, and chewed and swallowed as if to show me how.

I could now taste—apart from the bitter green cha and the rancid, cheesy yak butter—that the apparent sawdust was really barley meal. But I do not know if I would voluntarily have swallowed the wad, except that I was abruptly startled into doing so. The camp fire gave a sudden, tremendous *bang!* and threw up a constellation of sparks into the darkness—and I gulped my tsampa and leaped to my feet, and so did my two escorts, while the noise echoed and reechoed from all the mountains around. Two things went through my mind in that instant. One was the dreadful thought that one of the charged brass balls had somehow fallen into the fire. The other was a recollection of words once heard: "Expect me when you least expect me."

But the mountain men were laughing at our surprise, and making gestures to calm us and explain what had happened. They held up one of the pieces of zhu-gan cane and pointed to the fire and jumped about and bared their teeth and growled. They made it clear enough. The mountains were full of tigers and wolves. To keep them off, it was their practice to toss into the camp fire every so often a joint of zhu-gan. The heat evidently made its inner juices

seethe until the steam burst the cane apart—quite like a
charge of the flaming powder—with that enormous noise. I
had no doubt that it would keep predators at bay; it had
made me swallow the awful stuff called tsampa.

Later on, I got so I could eat tsampa, never with enjoyment, but at least without violent repugnance. A man's
body requires other nourishment than meat and cha, and
barley was the only domestic vegetable grown in those
highlands. Tsampa was cheap and easily transportable
and sustaining, if nothing else, and could be made a trifle
more appetizing by the addition of sugar or salt or vinegar
or the fermented bean sauce. I never got as fond of it as
were the natives, who, after making the dough at mealtime, would tuck balls of the stuff inside their clothes and
wear the tsampa all night and next day, so it got salted by
their sweat, and they would pluck out a bit whenever they
felt like having a snack.

I also got better acquainted with the zhu-gan cane. In
Khanbalik, I had known it only as a graceful floral subject
for painters like the Lady Chao and the Master of the
Boneless Colors. But in these regions it was such a staple
of life that I believe the people could not have existed without it. The zhu-gan grew wild, everywhere in the lowlands,
from the Si-Chuan–Yun-nan border country southward
throughout the tropics of Champa—where it was variously
named in the various languages: banwu and mambu and
other names—and everywhere it was used for many more
purposes than frightening off tigers.

The zhu-gan would resemble any ordinary reed or cane,
at least when it is young and only as thick as a finger, except that at intervals it has—very like a finger—nodes or
knuckles along its length. Those mark little walls inside
the cane, which interrupt its tubular length into separate
compartments. For some uses—such as being thrown into
a fire to burst—a single joint-length of the cane is employed, the wall intact at either end. For other purposes,
the walls inside are punched through to make the can a
long tube. When the zhu-gan is no bigger around than a
finger, it is easily cut with a knife. As it grows—and a
single cane can get as tall and as big around as any tree—it
must be laboriously sawed, for then it is almost as rigid as
iron. But big or small, the zhu-gan is a beautiful plant, the
cane part of it a golden color, the nodes sprouting withes

with delicate green leaves at the ends; an immense clump
of zhu-gan, all gold and green and catching the sun in its
fronds, is a subject worthy of any painter.

In one of the few lowland places we crossed in that region, we came to a village built entirely of zhu-gan, and
furnished with it, and totally dependent on it. The village,
called Chieh-chieh, sat in a wide valley, through which ran
one of the innumerable rivers of that country, and the
whole valley bottom was thick with groves of the zhu-gan,
and Chieh-chieh looked as if it too had grown there. Its
houses were all made of the golden cane. Their walls were
composed of arm-thick stalks of it, stood up side by side
and lashed together; thicker lengths of zhu-gan were the
posts and columns that held up roofs of split-cane segments
laid over-and-underlapping like curved tiles. Inside each
house, the furniture of tables and couches and floor mats
was woven of slender strips peeled from the zhu-gan, as
also were things like boxes, bird cages and baskets.

Because the river was bordered by extensive marshes,
Chieh-chieh was situated several li distant from it, but the
river's water was brought all that way through a pipe
made of waist-thick canes joined end to end, and in the village square that water spilled into a trough made of half a
log-sized zhu-gan. From the trough, the village boys and
girls carried water to their cane-built homes in buckets
and pots and bottles, all of which were joints of zhu-gan of
various sizes. In the homes, the women used splinters of
the cane for pins and needles, and the unraveled fiber of it
for thread. The menfolk made from split lengths of the
cane both their hunting bows and the arrows for them, and
carried the arrows in a quiver that was only a big joint of
zhu-gan. They used tree-sized stalks of the cane as the
masts for their fishing boats and, with ropes braided of
zhu-gan fibers, hung from those masts sails of lattice-
worked zhu-gan strips. The village's headman probably
had little writing to do, but he did it with a pen made of
cane strip, split at one end, and wrote on paper made from
the pulp scraped from the soft interior walls of the cane,
and kept his written scrolls in a vase-sized joint of zhu-gan.

When my escorts and I dined that night in Chieh-chieh,
the meal was served in bowls that were halved joints of big
zhu-gan, and the nimble tongs were slender sticks of zhu-
gan, and the meal included—beside river fish fresh-caught

with a zhu-gan fiber net and broiled over a fire of burning zhu-gan scraps—the soft-boiled and succulent shoots of new-sprouted zhu-gan, and some of the same shoots pickled for a condiment, and some more of them candied for a sweet. None of us visitors was ill or injured, but, if we had been, we might have been doctored with tang-zhu, which is a liquid that fills the hollow joints of the zhu-gan when it has just come to maturity, and that tang-zhu has many medicinal uses.

I learned all those things about the zhu-gan from Chieh-chieh's elderly headman, one Wu. He was the only villager who spoke Mongol, and in consequence he and I sat up talking quite late, while my two escorts, one after the other, wearied of listening to us and went off to their allotted bedchambers. Old Wu and I were at last interrupted by a young woman coming into the cane-walled room where we sat on cane couches, to make what sounded like a whine of complaint.

"She wishes to know if you are never coming to bed," said Wu. "This is the prime female of Chieh-chieh, chosen from all the others to make your night here memorable, and she is eager to get on with it."

"Hospitable of her," I said, and regarded her with speculation.

The people in that Land of the Four Rivers, men and women alike, wore clothing that was lumpy and shapeless: a hat like a sort of pod for the head, robes and wraps and shawls layered from shoulders to feet, clumsy boots with upturned toes. The body garments were all patterned in broad stripes of two different colors, and everybody in a village wore the same two colors, and the colors of each village were different—so a "foreigner" from the next village down the road could be instantly recognized—and the colors were always dark and dingy ones (in Chieh-chieh they were brown and gray) so they would not show the ingrained dirt of them. In the mountain communities, that costume made the people blend into their background, which may have been useful for hunting or hiding. But in Chieh-chieh, against the background of bright gold and green, it made them obtrusively unsightly.

Since the men and women were indistinguishably garbed, indistinguishably hairless of face, flat of features, ruddy-brown of complexion, they had to show—even for

their own convenience, I would suppose—something to
mark their sex. So the stripes of a woman's garments went
up and down, the stripes of a man's from side to side. A real
foreigner like myself, not immediately perceiving that
subtle difference of costume, could only tell them apart
when they took off their pod hats. The men could then be
seen to have their heads shaven and a gold or silver ring in
the left ear. The women had their hair twisted into a multitude of thin, spiky braids—to be specific, exactly one hundred and eight braids, that being the number of books in
the Kandjur, the Buddhist scriptures, and these people
being all Buddhists.

Since my journey that day had not been a punishing one,
and since the prettiness of the cane-built village had relaxed and rested me, I was inclined to indulge my curiosity
as to what other evidences of femininity might lurk beneath this young woman's graceless garments. I noticed
that she was wearing an ornament: a neck chain from
which depended a fringe of jingling silver coins—and, assuming that they also numbered one hundred and eight, I
said to old Wu:

"When you call her the village's prime female, do you refer to her wealth or her piety?"

"Neither," he said. "The coins attest to her female
charms and desirability."

"Indeed?" I said, and stared at her. The neck chain was
attractive enough, but I could not see how it made *her* any
more so.

"In this land, our young women compete," he explained,
"as to which of them can lie with the most men—those of
their own village, or other villages, or casual passersby, or
the men of trains traveling through—and require of each
man a coin in token of the coupling. Clearly, the girl who
amasses the most coins has attracted and satisfied the
most men, and is preeminent among women."

"You mean marked an outcast, surely."

"I mean preeminent. When she finally is ready to marry
and settle down, she can take her pick of husbands. Every
eligible young man vies for her hand."

"Her hand no doubt being the least used-up part of her,"
I said, slightly scandalized. "In civilized lands, a man
marries a virgin whom he knows is his alone."

"That is all that *can* be known of a virgin," said old Wu,

with a disparaging sniff. "A man wedding a virgin risks getting a fish less warm than the one you ate at dinner. A man wedding any of our women gets credentials of her desirability and experience and talents. He also gets, not incidentally, a fair dowry of coins. And this young lady is most eager now to add your coin to her string, for she has never had one from a Ferenghi."

I was not averse to lying with nonvirgins, and it might have been instructive to lie with one who brought credentials to the encounter. But the young woman *was* most regrettably plain, and I did not much like being regarded as just one more of a string. So I mumbled some excuse about being on a pilgrimage, and bound by a vow of the Ferenghi religion. I gave her a coin anyway, as recompense for my spurning of her well-attested charms, and escaped to my bed. It was a bedstead woven of strips of zhu-gan and it was very comfortable, but it creaked all night, with just me alone in it, and must have waked the whole village if I had availed myself of Chieh-chieh's prime female. So I decided that the zhu-gan cane, for all its marvelous usefulness to mankind, was not ideal for every human purpose.

2

My escorts and I rode on, through the alternation of mountains, ravines and valleys, sometimes up on the stark heights of the Pillar Road, occasionally down in the bright zhu-gan lowlands. That terrain did not change noticeably, but we realized that we had reached the High Land of To-Bhot when the people we met began to greet us by uncovering their heads, scratching the right ear, rubbing the left hip, and sticking out their tongues at us. That absurd salute—signifying that the greeter intends to think, hear, do or speak no evil—was peculiar to the people called Drok and Bho. Actually, they were the same people, only the nomands were called Drok and the settled ones Bho. The herder-and-hunter Drok lived like the plains-dwelling Mongols, and might have been indistinguishable from them except for their style of tent, which was black instead of yellow and was not supported by an interior lattice, as

was the yurtu. A Drok tent had its walls pegged to the
ground and its top hung by long ropes which ran over high
poles propped some distance away, then down to ground
pegs farther off. That gave the tent the appearance of a
black karakurt spider, crouched among its skinny, high-
kneed legs.

The farmer-and-merchant Bho, though they had settled
in communities, lived even more uncomfortably than the
nomad Drok. They had tucked their villages and towns
into high cliff crannies, which required them to pile their
houses one atop another and another. That was contrary to
what I knew of the Buddhist religion, which holds that the
human head is the residence of the soul, so that a mother
will not even pat the head of her own child. Yet here were
the Bho living in such a manner that everybody dumped
his wastes and trash and excretions on his neighbor's plot
and rooftop, and often enough in his very hair. That custom of building as high up as possible, I learned, dated
from some long-ago time when the Bho worshiped a god
called Amnyi Machen, or "Old Man Great Peacock," who
was believed to live in the highest peaks, and everyone
tried to reside close to the god.

But now all the Bho were Buddhists, so on top of every
community was perched a lamasarai, called by its inhabitants the Pota-lá. (Lá meant mount, and Pota was the Bho
pronunciation of Buddha. And I will not make ribald word-
play on that fact, from the indecorous meaning of "pota" in
the Venetian tongue. No one has any need to *invent* deri-
sions of the Bho and their religion.) The Pota-lá being the
topmost and most populous building in every community,
the result was that the priests and monks—here called
lamas and trapas—excreted copiously on all their lay congregation downhill. I was to find that Buddhism, in its To-
Bhot form of Potaism, was dismally degraded by even
stranger lunacies.

A Bho town might look charming when we saw it from
afar—say, across the landscape of the huge blue-and-
yellow poppies unique to To-Bhot, and the "Pota's hair"
willow trees hung with yellow bloom, and the clear blue
sky speckled pink and black with rose finches and ravens.
Any cliffside town was a vertical jungle of cliff-colored
houses, distinguishable from the cliff because they oozed
smoke from their little windows—curiously shaped win-

dows, wider at the top than at the bottom—and that clutter
of houses was overtopped by the even more jumbled Pota-
lá, all turrets and gilded roofs and promenades and outside
staircases and varicolored pennants flapping in the breeze,
and dark-robed trapas pacing sedately about the terraces.
But when we got closer, what had appeared from a distance comely, serene, even holy of aspect, was revealed to
be ugly, torpid and squalid.

The quaint little windows of the town's residences were
set only in the upper stories, to be above the ghastly mess
and smell of the streets. The populace at first seemed to
consist only of wandering goats and fowl and skulking yellow mastiffs, and the steep, narrow, twisty alleys were
thick with droppings we assumed to be theirs. But then we
would begin to meet people, and wish we had been satisfied with the cleaner animals, because when the people
stuck out their tongues in greeting, we could see that their
tongues were the only un-dirt-caked things about them.
They wore robes as drab and grimy as had the people in the
lowlands; if males and females wore differing patterns of
the drabness and griminess, I could not discern them.
There were very few men, and a great many women, but I
could tell the sexes apart because the men took the trouble
to open their long robes when they urinated in the street;
the women simply squatted; they wore nothing under
their outer robes, or I hoped they did not. Sometimes a
larger than ordinary heap of dung in the street would stir
feebly, and I would see that it was a human being laid out
to die, usually a very old man or woman.

My Mongol escorts confided to me that the Bho, in
former times, disposed of their old folks by eating their
corpses—on the theory that the dead could wish no finer
resting place than the guts of their own get—and had dis-
continued that practice only after Potaism became the prevailing religion, because the Pota-Buddha had frowned on
the eating of meat. The only relic of the former custom was
that families now conserved the skulls of their dead and
made them into drinking bowls or little drums, so that the
departed could still partake of holiday feasts and music
making. Nowadays the Bho observed four other methods
of sepulture. They burned the dead on mountaintops, or
left them there for the birds, or they threw them into the
rivers and ponds from which they got their drinking water,

or they cut the corpses into pieces and fed them to dogs. The latter was the method most preferred, because that hastened the dissolution of the flesh, and until the old flesh was gone, its habitant soul was marooned in a sort of Purgatory between death here and rebirth elsewhere. The bodies of the poor were merely thrown to the packs of street curs, but the bodies of the rich were conveyed to special lamasarais which maintained kennels of sanctified mastiffs.

Those practices doubtless accounted for To-Bhot's teeming population of scavenger vultures and ravens and magpies and gos, but they also accounted for more humans' dying than necessary. The dogs were so many that they were exceedingly liable to the canine madness, and in their fits they bit people as well as each other. More of the Bho were slain by the canine infection than by all the vile diseases engendered by their own squalor. Often, the heap in the street would be not just feebly stirring, but writhing and contorting and howling like a dog, in the terrible death agonies of that madness.

Because I had no wish to be bitten, and because I was on my way to war, I procured a bow and arrows and began to improve my aim and my arm by shooting every stray dog that came within range. That earned me black looks from the religious and the lay Potaists alike, who would rather that people die for no reason than that people should kill for good reason. However, since I carried the Khakhan's plaque, no one dared to do more than scowl and mutter, and I became quite proficient with both the broad-head and narrow-head arrows, and I hope I effected some small improvement in that wretched land, but I doubt it. I doubt that anyone or anything could.

On our arrival in any Bho community, my escorts and I climbed as quickly as we could to the Pota-lá on top, where we honored visitors were always put up, it affording the best of local accommodations. That meant only that we did not get excreted on from above—though, if we had, it could not have made the rooms and the bedding and the food and the company much filthier. Before leaving Kithai, I had heard a Han gentleman quote a contemptuous saying of his people—that the three national products of To-Bhot were lamas, women and dogs—and now I believed him. It was apparent that the disproportionate number of women

in the town down the hill was owing to the fact that at
least a third of their men had taken holy orders and residence in some lamasarai. Having seen the Bho women, I
could not much fault the Bho men for having fled, but I did
think that they might have fled to some existence better
than a living embalmment.

Entering a Pota-lá courtyard, we were greeted first by
the creaking, fluttering and clattering of prayer mills,
prayer flags and prayer bones, then by the roars and snarls
of the savage yellow To-Bhot mastiffs, which in those
places were at least kept chained to the walls. Also along
those walls, in every least niche, there was incense or a ju-
niper sprig burning, but its perfume was insufficient to
mask the overall miasma of yak-dung fires, putrid yak butter and unwashed religiosity. After meeting the noise and
the stench, we met a number of monks and a few priests
plodding majestically toward us, each of them holding out
across his palms the khata, the pale blue silk scarf with
which (instead of his tongue) every upper-class Bho salutes
an equal or superior. They addressed me as Kungö, which
means "Highness," and I properly addressed each lama as
Kundün, "Presence," and each trapa as Rimpoche, "Treasured One"—though it nearly gagged me to utter such honorific lies. I could see nothing treasurable about any of
them. Their robes, which had first seemed to be of ecclesi-
astically sedate colors, could be seen up close to have been
originally bright red, and were dark only from years of accumulated dirt. Their faces, hands and shaved heads were
blotched with a brown plant-sap they daubed on their various skin diseases, and their chins and chops were shiny
with the yak butter that drenched everything they ate.

In the matter of foods at the lamasarais, we were most
often served Potaist vegetable meals, of course—tsampa,
boiled nettles, ferns—and a strange, stringy, slimy,
bright-pink stalk of some plant unknown to me. I suspect
that the holy men ate it only because it made one's urine
pink for days afterward, and that effluent trickle no doubt
awed the people downhill of the lamasarai. But the Bho
had a peculiar selectivity about the Potaist injunction
against eating meat. They would not slaughter domestic
fowl or cattle, but would allow the slaying of game pheas-
ants and antelope. So the lamas and trapas sometimes provided those venisons for us, as an excuse for them to enjoy

the meats as well. (I am not unjustly scoffing at their hypo-
crite austerities. One lama was introduced to me as "a
most holy of holy men" because he subsisted on "absolutely no nourishment except a few bowls of cha a day."
Out of skeptic curiosity, I kept a close eye on that lama,
and eventually caught him in the preparation of his mealtime bowl. It was not cha leaves he used in the steeping,
but cha-like shreds of dried meat.)

However un-Potaistly lavish our meals sometimes were,
they were never very elegant. We being honored guests,
we were always seated to dine in the Pota-la's "chanting
hall," so we had the mealtime entertainment of several
dozen trapas dolefully chanting while they thumped skull
drums and rattled prayer bones. Among the serving platters and eating bowls, the banquet table bore an array of
spittoons, and the holy men used them to the point of overflow. All about the dark hall stood statues of the Pota and
his numerous disciple godlings and the numerous adversary demons, and every one of them was visible even in the
gloom, because it gleamed with its slathering of yak butter. Where we Christians would light a candle to a saint, or
perhaps leave with him a taolèta, it was the Bho's practice
to smear their idols with yak butter, and the thick and ancient layers reeked of rancid decay. Whether the Pota and
the other images were gratified by that, I do not know, but
I can attest that the local vermin were. Even when the hall
was full of noisy diners and chanters, I could hear the
squeaks and snickers of mice and rats as they—plus cock-
roaches, centipedes and God knows what else—scurried
foraging up and down the statues. Most nauseating of all,
we and our dinner hosts always sat on what I at first took
to be a low dais built up above the floor level. It felt rather
spongy under me, so I furtively investigated to see what it
was made of—and discovered that we were seated atop
nothing but a mound of compacted food droppings, the detritus of decades or maybe centuries of the holy men's slovenly droolings and slobberings of their meals.

When their mouths were not masticating or otherwise
occupied, the holy men chanted almost continuously, in
concert at the top of their lungs, in solitude under their
breaths. One chant went like this: "Lha so so, khi ho ho,"
which meant more or less, "Come gods, begone demons!" A
shorter one went like this: "Lha gyelo," meaning "The

gods are victorious!" But the chant that was heard most
often and interminably and everywhere in To-Bhot went
like this: "Om mani pémé hum." The opening and closing
noises of it were always intoned in a drawn-out manner,
so: "O-o-o-om" and "Hu-u-u-um," and they constituted just
a sort of "amen." The other words meant, literally, "the
jewel in the lotus," in the same sense that those terms are
used in the Han lexicon of sex. In other words, the holy
men were chanting, "Amen, the male organ is inside the
female's! Amen!"

Now, one of the Han religions prevailing back in Kithai,
the one they call Tao, "the Way," has an unashamed connection with sex. In Taoism, the male essence is called
yang and the female's is yin, and everything else in the
universe—whether material, intangible, spiritual, whatever—is regarded as being either yang or yin, hence totally
discrete and opposite (as men and women are) or comple-
mentary and necessary to each other (as men and women
are). Thus active things are called yang, passive ones yin.
Heat and cold, the heavens and the earth, sun and moon,
light and darkness, fire and water, they are all respec-
tively yang and yin, or, as anyone can recognize, inextricably yang-yin. At the most basic level of human behavior,
when a man couples with a woman and absorbs her female
yin by means of his male yang, he is not in any sense
tinged with effeminacy, but becomes more of a *complete
man,* stronger, more alive, more aware, more worthwhile.
And just so, the woman becomes more of a woman by accepting his yang with her yin. From that elementary foundation, Tao proceeds up to metaphysical heights and
abstractions that I cannot pretend to grasp.

It may be that some Han Taoist, wandering into To-Bhot
long ago, when the natives still worshiped the Old Peacock, kindly tried to explain to them his amiable religion.
The Bho could hardly have misunderstood the universal
act of putting male organ into female—or jewel into lotus,
as the Han would have expressed it—or mani into pémé, in
their language. But such oafs would have been baffled by
the higher significances of yang and yin, so all they ever
retained of Tao was that preposterous chant of "Om mani
pémé hum." Still, not even the Bho could have built much
of a religion on a prayer that had no loftier meaning than
"Amen, stick it in her! Amen!" So, as they later and

gradually adopted Buddhism from India, they must have
adapted the chant to fit that religion. All they had to do
was construe the "jewel" as Buddha, or Pota, because
he is so often portrayed as sitting in meditation on a large
lotus blossom. So the chant came to mean something like
"Amen, Pota is in his place! Amen!" And then, no doubt,
some later lamas—in the way that self-appointed sages always complicate even the purest faith with their
unsolicited commentaries and interpretations—decided to
festoon the simple chant with more abstruse aspects. So
they decreed that the word mani (jewel, male genitals,
Pota) would henceforth signify The Means, and the word
pémé (lotus, female genitals, Pota's place) would henceforth refer to Nirvana. Thus the chant became a prayer be-
seeching The Means to achieve that Nirvana oblivion
which Potaists deem the highest end of life: "Amen, blot
me out! Amen!"

Certainly, Potaism no longer had any laudable connection with sexual relations between men and women, because at least one of every three Bho males, at puberty or
even younger, fled from the prospect of ever having to endure sex with any Bho female, and took the red robe of religion. So far as I could tell, that vow of celibacy was the only
qualification necessary for entrance into a Pota-lá and
eventual elevation through the ascending degrees of
monkhood and priesthood. The chabis, or novices, were
given nothing like a secular education or seminary instruction, and I encountered only three or four of the oldest
and highest-grade lamas who could even read and write
the "Om mani pémé hum," let alone the one hundred and
eight books of the Kandjur scriptures, let alone the two
hundred and twenty-five Tengyur books of commentary on
the Kandjur. In speaking of the holy men's celibacy, however, I should rightly have said celibacy in regard to females. Many of the lamas and trapas flagrantly flaunted
their amorousness toward each other, to leave no doubt
that they had forsworn sordid, ordinary, normal sex.

Potaism, however it developed, was a religion demanding only sheer quantity of devotion, not any quality of it.
By that I mean a seeker of oblivion simply had to repeat
"Om mani pémé hum" *enough times* during his life and he
expected that would take him to Nirvana when he died. He
did not even have to speak the words, or repeat them in

any way requiring his own volition. I have mentioned
prayer mills; they were everywhere in the lamasarais, and
in every house, and even to be found standing in empty
countryside. They were drumlike cylinders within which
were wound paper scrolls on which the mani chant was
written. A man had only to give the cylinder a spin with
his hand and those "repetitions" of the prayer counted to
his credit. Sometimes he rigged it like a waterwheel, so
that a stream or cascade kept it turning and praying constantly. Or he could hoist a flag inscribed with the prayer,
or a whole line of them—those were far more frequently to
be seen in To-Bhot than any lines of washing hung out—
and every flag the wind gave every flag was credited to
him. Or he could run his hand along a line of dangling
sheep shoulder blades, each bone inscribed with the mani,
strung like wind chimes, and they prayed for him as long
as they went on clattering.

I once came upon a trapa crouched beside a creek,
flinging into it and hauling out again a tile attached to a
string. He had been doing that, he said, all his adult life,
and would go on doing it until he died.

"Doing *what?*" I asked, thinking that perhaps, in some
idiotic Bho way, he was trying to emulate San Piero as a
fisher of souls. The monk showed me his tile; it was engraved with the mani prayer, in the fashion of a yin seal.
He explained that he was "imprinting" the prayer on the
running water, stamping it there over and over again, and
he was accruing piety with every invisible "impression."

Another time, in a Pota-lá courtyard, I saw two trapas
come to violent blows because one of them had given a
twirl to a prayer mill and then, glancing back as he walked
on, saw a brother monk stop the mill and spin it in the
other direction to pray for *him*.

Atop one of the major towns on our way was an especially large lamasarai, and there I made bold to seek audience of its venerable and filthy and sap-daubed Grand
Lama.

"Presence," I addressed the old abbot, "I seldom observe
anything going on in any Pota-lá that looks like ecclesiastical activity. Aside from twirling prayer mills or shaking
prayer bones, what exactly are your religious duties?"

In a voice like the rustle of far-off leaves, he said, "I sit in my cell, my son Highness, or sometimes in a remote cave, or on a lonely mountaintop, and I meditate."

"Meditate on what, Presence?"

"On my once having laid eyes on the Kian-gan Kundün."

"And what would that be?"

"The Sovereign Presence, the Holiest of Lamas, he who is an actual reincarnation of the Pota. He resides in Lha-Ssa, the City of the Gods, a long, long journey from here, where the people are building for him a Pota-lá worthy of his occupancy. They have been building on it for more than six hundred years now, but they expect to have it completed in only four or five hundred more. The Holiest will be pleased to grace it with his Sovereign Presence, for it will be a palace most magnificent when it is finally done."

"Are you saying, Presence, that this Kian-gan Kundün has been alive and waiting for six hundred years? And he will still be alive when the palace is finished?"

"Assuredly, so, my son Highness. Of course you, being ch'hipa—outside the belief—might not see him so. His corporeal integument dies from time to time, and then his lamas must cast about the land and find the infant boy into whom his soul has transmigrated. So the Sovereign Presence looks physically different, from lifetime to lifetime. But we nang-pa—we within the belief—we know him to be always the same Holiest of Lamas, and the Pota reincarnated."

It seemed to me somewhat unfair that the Pota, having created and prescribed Nirvana for his devotees, evidently never got to rest obliviously there himself, but had to keep on being fetched back to Lha-Ssa, a town doubtless as awful as any other in To-Bhot. But I refrained from remarking on that, and gently prompted the old abbot:

"So you made the far journey to Lha-Ssa, and you saw the Holiest of Lamas . . . ?"

"Yes, my son Highness, and that event has occupied my meditations and contemplations and devotions ever since. You may not believe this, but the Holiest actually opened his own rheumy old eyes and looked at *me.*" He put on a wrinkled smile of rapt reminiscence. "I think, if the Holiest had not been then so ancient and approaching his next transmigration, he might almost have summoned up his strength and *spoken* to me."

"You and he only looked at each other? And that has furnished you with meat for meditation ever since?"

"Ever since. Just that one bleared glance from the Holiest was the commencement of my wisdom. Forty-eight years ago, that was."

"For nearly half a century, Presence, you have done nothing but contemplate that single fleeting occurrence?"

"A man blessed with the beginning of wisdom is obligated to let it ripen without distraction. I have forgone all other interests and pursuits. I do not interrupt my meditation even to take meals." He arranged his wrinkles and blotches in a look of blissful martyrdom. "I subsist on only an occasional bowl of weak cha."

"I have heard of such wondrous abstentions, Presence. Meanwhile, I suppose you share with your underlamas the fruits of your meditations, for their instruction."

"Dear me, no, young Highness." His wrinkles rearranged into a startled and slightly offended look. "Wisdom cannot be taught, it must be learned. The learning to be done by others is up to them. Now, if you will excuse me for saying so, this brief audience with you has constituted the longest distraction of my meditative life. . . ."

So I made my obeisances and left him, and sought out a lama of fewer pustules and less exalted degree, and inquired what *he* did when he was not churning prayers out of a mill.

"I meditate, Highness," he said. "What else?"

"Meditate on what, Presence?"

"I fix my mental regard on the Grand Lama, for he once visited Lha-Ssa and looked uopn the visage of the Kiangan Kundün. From that, he acquired great holiness."

"And you hope to absorb some holiness from meditating on him?"

"Dear me, no. Holiness cannot be taken, only bestowed. I can, however, hope from that meditation to extract some small wisdom."

"And that wisdom you will impart to whom? To your junior lamas? To the trapas?"

"Really, Highness! One never casts one's regard downward, only upward! Where else is wisdom? Now, if you will excuse me. . . ."

So I went and found a trapa, recently accepted into monkhood after a long novitiate as a chabi, and asked what *he* contemplated while awaiting elevation to the priesthood.

"Why, the holiness of my elders and superiors, of course, Highness. They are the receptacles containing all the wisdom of all the ages."

"But, if they never teach you anything, Treasured One, whence comes that knowledge to you? You all claim to be eager to acquire it, but what is the source of it?"

"Knowledge?" he said, with lofty contempt. "Only worldly creatures like the Han fret about knowledge. *We* wish to acquire *wisdom.*"

Interesting, I thought. That same disdainful estimate had once been made of me—and by a Han. Nevertheless, I was not prepared to believe, then or now, that inertness and torpor represent the highest attainment humanity can aspire to. In my opinion, stillness is not always evidence of intelligence, and silence is not always evidence of a mind at work. Most vegetables are still and silent. In my opinion, meditation is not infallibly productive of profound ideas. I have seen vultures meditate on a full belly, and then do nothing more profound than regurgitate. In my opinion, inarticulate and obscure pronouncements are not always expressive of a wisdom so mystically sublime that only sages can comprehend it. The mouthings of the Potaist holy men were inarticulate and obscure, but so were the yappings of their lamasarai curs.

I went and found a chabi, the lowest form of life in a Pota-lá, and asked how *his* time was spent.

"My admission here was granted on condition that I apprentice as a cleaning orderly," he said. "But of course I pass most of my time meditating on my mantra."

"And what is that, boy?"

"A few syllables from the Kandjur of holy scripture, assigned to me for my contemplation. When I have meditated long enough upon the mantra—some years perhaps—and it has expanded my mind sufficiently, I may be considered fit to rise to the status of trapa, and then begin to contemplate larger bits of the Kandjur."

"Did it ever occur to you, boy, actually to spend your time in cleaning this sty, and studying ways to clean it better?"

He stared at me as if I had been rendered rabid by a dog bite. "Instead of my mantra, Highness? Whatever for?

Cleaning is the lowliest of occupations, and he who would
rise should look upward, not downward."

I snorted. "Your Grand Lama does nothing but squat
and contemplate the Holiest of Lamas, while his underlamas do nothing but squat and contemplate *him*. All the
trapas do nothing but squat and contemplate the lamas. I
would wager that the first apprentice who ever actually
learned cleanliness could overthrow the whole regime. Become the master of this Pota-lá, and then the Pope of Potaism, and eventually the Wang of all To-Bhot."

"You have been grievously mad-bit by a dog, Highness,"
he said, looking alarmed. "I will run and fetch one of our
physicians—the pulse-feeler or the urine-smeller—that he
may attend you in your affliction."

Well, so much for the holy men. The influence of Potaism on the lay population of To-Bhot was about equally
elevating. The men had learned to twirl any prayer mill
they encountered, and the women had learned to screw up
their hair into one hundred and eight braids, and both men
and women were careful always, when walking past any
holy edifice, to walk to the left of it and keep it always on
their right hand. I do not know exactly, why, except that
there was a saying, "Beware the demons on the left," and
there were to be found in the countryside a great many
stone walls and piled-up heaps of stone that had some in-
discernible religious significance, and the road always divided around them, so that a traveler from either direction
could keep the holiness on his right.

At every twilight, all the men, women and children of
every community would leave off their day's occupations,
if any, and squat in the town streets or on their own
rooftops, while they were led by the lamas and trapas of
the Pota-lá overhead, in chanting their evening appeal for
oblivion, "Om mani pémé hum," over and over again. I
might have been impressed by what was at least an example of popular solidarity and unabashed religiosity—in
contrast to Venice, say, where my sophisticated townsfolk
would blush to make even the sign of the cross in any gathering more public than a church service—but I simply
could not admire a people's devotion to a religion that did
no good for them, or anyone.

Presumably it prepared them for the oblivion of Nirvana, but it made them so phlegmatic in this life, and so

oblivious to this world, that I could not imagine how they
would recognize the other oblivion when they got there.
Most religions, I think, inspire their followers to an occasional activity and enterprise. Even the destestable Hindus sometimes bestir themselves, if only to butcher each
other. But the Potaists had not enough initiative to kill a
rabid dog, or even bother to step out of its way when it
lunged. As well as I could tell, the Bho evinced one sole ambition: to break out of their constitutional torpor only long
enough to advance into absolute and eternal coma.

Regard just one example of Bho apathy. In a land where
so many men had retreated into celibacy and there was a
consequent abundance of women, I would have expected to
find the normal men enjoying a paradise: taking their pick
of the females and taking as many as they wished. Not so.
It was the females who did the picking and collecting. The
women followed the custom I had earlier encountered: casually coupling before marriage with as many passersby as
possible, and extorting a memento coin from each, so that,
at marriageable age, the female laden with the most coins
was the most desirable wife-to-be. But she did not simply
take for husband the most eligible man in her community;
she took *several* of them. Instead of each man being the
Shah of a whole anderun of wives and concubines, every
marriageable woman possessed a whole anderun of men,
and the legions of her less comely sisters were doomed to
spinsterhood.

One might say, well, that at least showed some enterprise on the part of at least a few women. But it was a poor
showing, because what sort of eligible men could a woman
choose her consorts *from?*

All those males with enough ambition and energy to
walk uphill had done exactly that, and vanished into the
Pota-lá. Of the remainder, the only ones with any verifia-
ble manhood and livelihood were usually those committed
to the carrying-on of an established family farm or herd or
trade. So a woman who could take her pick of men did so,
not by marrying *into* one of those "best families," but by
marrying the *whole family*—anyway, the male members of
it. That made for some complex conjugalities. I met one
woman who was married to two brothers and to a son of
each of them, and had children by all. Another woman was
married to three brothers, while her daughter by one of

them was married to the two others of them, plus another man she had procured somewhere outside the house.

How anybody in those tangled and inbred unions ever knew whose children were whose, I have no notion, and I suspect that none of them cared to know. I have concluded that the Bho people's atrocious marital customs accounted for their general feeblemindedness, and also for their Potaist travesty of the Buddhist religion, and their continued sapless adherence to it, and their laughable belief that Potaism represented the accumulation of "all the wisdom of all the ages." I came to that conclusion when, much later, I talked about the Bho to some distinguished Han physicians. They told me that generations of close inbreeding— common to mountain communities, and inevitable in those fanatically faith-bound—must produce a people of physical lethargy and disminished brain. If that is true, and I am convinced it is, then Potaism represents To-Bhot's accumulation of all the imbecility of all the ages.

3

"Your Royal Father Kubilai prides himself on ruling peoples of quality," I said to the Wang Ukuruji. "Why did he ever trouble to conquer and annex this miserable land of To-Bhot?"

"For its gold," said Ukuruji, without great enthusiasm. "Gold dust can be panned from almost every river or creek bed in this country. We could get a lot more of it, of course , if I could make the wretched Bho dig and mine the sources of it. But they have been persuaded by their cursed lamas that gold nuggets and veins are the *roots* of the metal. Those must be left undisturbed, or they will not produce the gold dust, which is their *pollen.*" He laughed, and ruefully wagged his head. "Vakh!"

"One more evidence of the Bho intellect," I said. "The land may be worth something, but the people are not. Why did Kubilai condemn his own son to govern them?"

"Somebody has to," he said, with a resigned shrug. "The lamas would probably tell you that I must have committed

some vile crime in some former existence, to deserve being
made ruler of the Drok and the Bho. They might be right."

"Perhaps," I said, "your father will give you Yun-nan to
rule instead—or in addition to To-Bhot."

"That is what I devoutly hope," he said. "Which is why I
removed my court from the capital to this garrison town to
be close to the Yun-nan war zone, and await here the war's
outcome."

This garrison town, actually a trade-route market city
named Ba-Tang, was where my escorts and I had ended
our long journey from Khanbalik, and found the Wang
Ukuruji, alerted by our advance riders, awaiting our arrival. Ba-Tang was in To-Bhot, but was the largest city
conveniently close to the Yun-nan frontier of the Sung Empire. So this was where the Orlok Bayan had chosen to set
his headquarters, and from which he repeatedly led or sent
incursions southward against the Yi people. Ba-Tang had
not been evacuated of its Bho inhabitants, but they were
almost outnumbered by the Mongols occupying the city
and its outskirts and the valley roundabout—five tomans
of troops and their camp-follower women, the Orlok and
his numerous staff, the Wang and his courtiers.

"I am ready and eager to move on again at a moment's
notice," Ukuruji continued, "if ever Bayan succeeds in
taking Yun-nan, and if my father gives me leave to go
there. The Yi people will naturally be inimical to a Mongol
overlord at first, but I had rather go among raging enemies
than stay among the blighted Bho."

"You mentioned your capital, Wang. I assume you mean
the city of Lha-Ssa."

"No. Why?"

"I was told that there dwells the Holiest of Lamas, the
Sovereign Presence. I took it to be the chief city of the nation."

He laughed. "Yes, there is the Holiest of Lamas at Lha-
Ssa. There is another Holiest of Lamas at a place called
Dri-Kung, and another at Pak-Dup, and another at Tsal,
and others in other places. Vakh! You must understand
that there is not just a single noxious Potaism, but innumerable rival sects of it, no one to be any more admired or
abominated than another, and every one recognizing a different Holiest Lama at his head. For convenience, I recognize a Holiest Lama named Phags-pa, whose lamasarai is

at the city of Shigat-Se, so that is where I have located the
capital. Nominally at least, the venerable Phags-pa and I
are co-governors of the country, he of its spiritual aspects, I
of the temporal. He is a despicable old fraud, but no worse
than any of the other Holiest Lamas, I suspect."

"And Shigat-Se?" I asked. "Is it as fine a city as I have
heard Lha-Ssa to be?"

"Probably," he grunted. "Shigat-Se is a dunghill. And
so, no doubt, is Lha-Ssa."

"Well," I said, as cheerfully as I could, "you must be
grateful to be residing for a while in this more beautiful
place."

Ba-Tang was situated on the east bank of the river Jin-
sha, which was here a white-water stream tumbling down
the middle of a broad valley plain, but downstream in Yun-
nan it would collect other tributary waters and widen and
eventually become the mighty river Yang-tze. The Ba-
Tang valley, in this season of summer, was gold and green
and blue, with bright touches of other colors. The blue was
the high, windswept sky. The gold was the color of the
Bho's barley fields and zhu-gan groves and the countless
yellow yurtu tents of the Mongol bok. But beyond the cultivated and camped-on areas, the valley was the rich green
of forests—elms and junipers and pines—besprinkled
with the colors of wild roses, bluebells, anemones, colum-
bine, irises and, over all, morning glories of every hue
wreathing every tree and bush.

In such a setting, any town would have been as obtrusive as an ulcer on a beautiful face. But Ba-Tang, since it
had the whole valley to spread out in, had set its buildings
side by side, not atop each other, and not squashed close together, and the river disposed of most of its wastes, so it
was not quite so ugly and filthy as most Bho communities.
The inhabitants even dressed better than other Bho. At
any rate, the upper-class folk among them could be recognized by their garnet-colored robes and gowns, nicely
trimmed with fur of otter, pard or tiger, and an upper-class
woman's hundred-and-eight braids of hair were adorned
with kauri shells, bits of turquoise and even coral from
some far distant sea.

"Can it be that these Bho here are superior to those elsewhere in To-Bhot?" I asked hopefully. "They at least appear to have different customs. As I rode into the town, the

people were commencing their New Year celebration. Everywhere else, the year begins in midwinter."

"So it does here. And there is no such thing as a superior Bho, not anywhere in the world. Do not deceive yourself."

"I could not have been deceived about the festivities, Wang. A parade—with the dragons and the lanterns and all—it was clearly in honor of the New Year. Listen, you can hear the gongs and drums from here." He and I were seated, drinking from horns of arkhi, on a terrace of his temporary palace, some way upriver of Ba-Tang.

"Yes, I hear them. The poor sheep-wits." He shook his head in deprecation. "It is indeed a New Year festivity, but not to welcome a real new year. It seems there has been an outbreak of sickness in the town. Only the flux, which is a common summertime affliction of the bowels, but no Pota-ist can be convinced that anything ever happens normally. The local lamas, in their wisdom, decided that the flux was the doing of demons, and they decreed a New Year celebration, so the demons will think they were mistaken in the season, and will go away and take their summer sickness with them."

I said with a sigh, "You are right. To find a Bho with good sense would be as unlikely as finding a white crow."

"However, the lamas being furious with me, they may also have intended the celebration to drive the bowel de-mons upriver to here, and flush me out of this Pota-lá."

For his temporary palace, Ukuruji had commandeered the town's lamasarai, and had summarily evicted its en-tire population of lamas and trapas, and kept only the chabi novices to be servants to him and his courtiers. The holy men, he told me—jolted out of their stupor for once in their lives—had departed shaking their fists and invoking every curse the Pota could inflict. But the Wang and his court had now been for some months ensconced and com-fortable. He had allotted me a whole suite of rooms on my arrival and, because my Mongol escorts desired to join our advance riders and their other fellows in the Orlok's bok, had assigned me a retinue of chabis also.

Ukuruji went on, "Still, we ought to be thankful for the unseasonal New Year. Only on that holiday do the Bho clean their abodes or wash their garments or bathe them-selves. So this year the Bho of Ba-Tang have twice got clean."

"No wonder I took the town and the people to be out of the ordinary," I muttered. "Well, as you say, let us be thankful. And let me laud you, Wang Ukuruji, for being perhaps the first man ever to have taught something more useful than religion to these folk. You have certainly made them transform this Porta-lá. I have lodged in lamasarais all across To-Bhot, but to see a clean chanting hall—or to see it at all—is something of a revelation."

I looked from the terrace into that hall. No longer a gloomy cavern layered with stinking yak butter and ancient food droppings, it had been unshuttered to the sunlight, and the whole place scraped clean, and the encrusted images removed, and now it could be seen to have a floor of fine marble slabs. A chabi servant, at Ukuruji's command, had just spread candle grease on that floor and was now polishing it by shuffling about wearing sheep-fleece hats on his feet.

"Also," said the Wang, "as soon as the people washed themselves and their faces were discernible, I was able to cull out a few goodlooking females. Even I, a non-Bho, think them almost worthy of the many coins they wear. Shall I send two or three tonight for your selection?" When I did not immediately accept, he said, "Surely you would not prefer one of the gaping leather bags of the bok!" Then he thought to add, delicately, "There are, among the chabis, two or three pretty boys."

"Thank you, Wang," I said. "I prefer women, but I prefer to be a woman's first coin, so to speak, not her latest. Here in To-Bhot, that would mean coupling with a woman ugly and undesirable. So I shall decline, with thanks, and continue in chastity until perhaps I can get down south into Yun-nan, and hope the Yi women there are more to my taste."

"I have been hoping the same," he said. "Well, old Bayan is due to return any day from his latest foray down there. So you can present to him my Royal Father's missive, and I will be greatly gratified if it contains order for me to proceed southward with the armies. Until we convene, then, make yourself free of what comforts this place affords."

That most hospitable young Wang must have gone straightaway to see if he could find for me a female who had not yet conferred her favors, but would merit a coin for

them when she did. For, when I retired to my chambers at
bedtime, my chabis proudly ushered forth two small persons. They had smiling, un-sap-splotched faces and were
clad in clean, fur-trimmed, garnet-colored gowns. Like all
the Bho, these small persons wore no underclothes, as I
saw when the chabis whisked the gowns off them to show
me that they were females. The chabis also made gestures
and noises to acquaint me with the little girls' names—
Ryang and Odcho—and made further gestures to indicate
that they were to be my bedmates. I could not speak the
language of the chabis and the girls, but I managed, also
with gestures, to inquire their age. Odcho was ten years
old and Ryang was nine.

I could not help bursting into laughter, though it seemed
to bewilder the chabis and offend the girls. Clearly, to find
a passably good-looking virgin in To-Bhot, one had to rummage among the very children. I found that amusing, but
also slightly frustrating to my curiosity for pertinent details. Since females of that tender age are so formless and
so nearly devoid of sexual characteristics, Ryang and
Odcho gave no indication of how they would look or perform when they grew up. Thus I cannot claim that I ever
enjoyed a real Bho woman, or even examined one unclothed, and so am unable to report—as I have sedulously
tried to report of women of other races—what physical attributes or interesting bodily features or copulative eccen-
tricities may be noticed in the adult females of the Bho.

The only peculiarity I saw in the two girl children was
that each of them bore a discoloration, like a birthmark, on
her lower back just above the buttock cleft. It was a pur-
plish spot on the creamy skin, about the size of a saucer,
somewhat darker on the nine-year-old Ryang than on the
older girl. Since the children were not sisters, I wondered
at the coincidence, and one day asked Ukuruji if all Bho females had that blemish.

"All children, male as well as female," he said. "And not
just those of the Bho and Drok. The Han, the Yi, even Mongol infants are born with it. Your Ferenghi babies are
not?"

"I never saw any such thing, no. Nor among the Persians, the Armeniyans, the Semitic Arabs and Jews. . . ."

"Indeed? We Mongols call it the 'deer dapple,' because it
slowly fades and disappears—like the spots on a fawn—as a

child grows older. It is usually gone by the age of ten or
eleven. Another difference between us and you Westerners, eh? But a trifling one, I suppose.''

Some days later, the Orlok Bayan returned from his expedition, at the head of several thousand mounted warriors. The column looked travel-weary, but not much
decimated by combat, as it included only a few dozen
horses with empty saddles. When Bayan had changed into
clean clothes at his yurtu pavilion in the bok, he came to
the Pota-lá palace, accompanied by some of his sardars and
other officers, to pay his respects to the Wang and to meet
me. We three sat around a table on the terrace, and the
lesser officers sat at a distance apart, and all were attended by chabis dispensing horns and skulls of kumis and
arkhi and some native Bho beverage brewed from barley.

"The Yi did their usual cowardly evasions," Bayan
grumbled, by way of report on his foray. "Hide and snipe
and run away. I would chase the cursed runaways clear to
the jungles of Champa, but that is what they hope for—
that I will expose my flanks and outrun my supply lines.
Anyway, a rider brought me word that a message from my
Khakhan was on the way to here, so I broke off and turned
back. Let the misbegotten Yi think they repulsed us; I do
not care; I will savage them yet. I hope, Messenger Polo,
you bring some good advice from Kubilai on how to do
that.''

I handed over the letter, and the rest of us sat silent
while he broke its waxen yin seals and unfolded it and
read it. Bayan was a man of late middle age, sturdy and
swarthy and scarred and ferocious-looking as any other
Mongol warrior, but he also had the most fearsome teeth I
ever saw in a human mouth. I watched him champ them as
he perused the letter, and for a while I was more fascinated
by his mouth than by the words that came out of it.

After some time of watching closely, I made out that the
teeth were not his. That is to say, they were imitation
teeth, made of heavy porcelain. They had been constructed
for him—he told me later—after he lost all his real ones
when a Samoyed foeman hit him in the mouth with an iron
mace. I eventually saw other Mongols and Han wearing
artificial teeth—they were called kin-chi by the Han physicians who specialized in the making of them—but Bayan's
were the first I ever saw, and the worst, evidently having

been made for him by a physician not very fond of him.
They looked as ponderous and granitic as roadside mile-
stones, and they were held together and held in place by an
elaborate grid of garish, glittering goldwork. Bayan himself told me that they were painfully uncomfortable, so he
only wedged them between his gums when he had to call
upon some dignitary, or had to eat, or wished to seduce a
woman with his beauty. I did not say so, but it was my
opinion that his kin-chi must have revolted every dignitary he champed them at, and every servant who waited
upon him at table—and their effect upon a woman I did not
wish even to speculate on.

"Well, Bayan," Ukuruji was saying eagerly, "does my
Royal Father command that I am to follow you into Yun-
nan?"

"He does not say that you are not to," Bayan replied dip-
lomatically, and handed the document to the Wang for him
to read for himself. Then the Orlok turned to me. "Very
well. As Kubilai suggests, I will cause a proclamation to be
made, loud and within hearing of the Yi, that they no
longer have a secret friend in the Khanbalik court. Is that
supposed to make them surrender on the spot? It seems to
me that they would fight the harder, out of sheer peevishness."

I said, "I do not know, Orlok."

"And why does Kubilai suggest that I do the very thing I
have tried to avoid doing? Penetrate so far into Yun-nan
that my flanks and my rear are vulnerable?"

"I really do not know, Orlok. The Khakhan did not confide to me his ideas for either strategy or tactics."

"Humph. Well, you must know this much, Polo. He ap-
pends a postscript—something about you having brought
me some new weapon."

"Yes, Orlok. It is a device that might help prosecute a
war without too many soldiers being killed."

"Being killed is what soldiers are for," he said decisively. "What is this device?"

"A means by which to employ in combat the powder
called huo-yao."

He erupted, rather like the flaming powder himself,
"Vakh! That again?" He gnashed his ghastly teeth and
bellowed what I took to be a terrible profanity: "By the
smelly old saddle of the sweaty god Tengri! Every year or

so, another lunatic inventor proposes to replace cold steel with hot smoke. It has never worked yet!"

"This time it might, Orlok," I said. "It is a totally new kind of huo-yao." I beckoned to a hovering chabi and sent him running to my chambers to fetch one of the brass balls.

While we waited, Ukuruji finished reading the letter and said, "I think, Bayan, I perceive the intent in my Royal Father's tactical proposal. So far, your troops have failed to close with the Yi in a decisive battle, because they continually melt away before you into the mountain recesses. But if your columns were to proceed far enough—so that the Yi saw an opportunity of utterly surrounding you—why, then they would have to trickle down from their hideaways and collect in mass at your flanks and rear." The Orlok appeared both bored and exasperated by this explication but, out of respect for rank, he let him go on: "Thus, for the first time, you would have all the Yi foemen gathered and exposed, and distant from their bolt holes, and engageable in close combat. Well?"

"If my Wang will permit me," said the Orlok. "That is all very likely true. But my Wang has himself mentioned the egregious flaw in that argument. I *would* be utterly surrounded. If I may draw a parallel, I submit that the most practical way of extinguishing a fire is *not* to plump one's bare rump down on it."

"Hm," said Ukuruji. "Well . . . suppose you ventured only a portion of your troops, and held others in reserve . . . to swoop down when the Yi had collected behind the first columns . . . ?"

"Wang Ukuruji," the Orlok said patiently. "The Yi are shifty and elusive, but they are not stupid. They know how many men and horses I have at my disposal, and probably even how many women usable for warriors. They would not be drawn into such a trap unless they could see and count that I had committed my entire force. And then— who is in the trap?"

"Hm," Ukuruji murmured again, and subsided into a thoughtful silence.

The chabi returned, bringing the brass ball, and I explained to the Orlok all the incidents leading up to its contrivance, and how the Firemaster Shi had seen in it a new potential for military usefulness. When I had done, the

Orlok champed his teeth some more, and gave me much the same look with which he had received the Wang's tactical advice.

"Let me see if I understand you correctly, Polo," he said. "You have brought me twelve of these elegant baubles, right? Now, correct me if I am wrong. From your own experience, you can assure me that each of the twelve will effectually demolish *two* persons—*if* they are both unarmored, delicate, incautious and unsuspecting *women.*"

I mumbled, "Well, true, it happened that the two I spoke of were women, but—"

"Twelve balls. Each capable of killing two defenseless women. Meanwhile, down the farther valleys to the south, there are some fifty thousand staunch Yi *men*—warriors encased in leather armor stout enough to turn a blade. I cannot really expect them to huddle close when I roll a ball among them. Even if they did, let me think, fifty thousand minus, um, twenty-four . . . leaves, um. . . ."

I coughed and cleared my throat and said, "On my way hither, along the Pillar Road, I was struck by a notion for a different use of the balls than just to project them among the enemy. I perceived that the mountains hearabout are not much subject to landslides or rockslides—like the Pai-Mir, say—and these mountain people are evidently unwary of any such occurrences."

For a change, he did not munch his teeth at me, but regarded me narrowly. "You are right. These mountains are reliably solid. So?"

"So if the brass balls were to be securely tucked into tight crevices of the high peaks along both crests above a valley, and all ignited at the same and proper moment, they should set loose a mighty avalanche. It would thunder down from both sides and completely fill the valley and mash and bury every living thing in it. To a people who have for so long felt safe among these mountains, even sheltered and protected by them, it would be a cataclysm immense and unexpected and inescapable. The avalanche would come down upon them like God's boot heel. Of course, as the Wang has said, it would be necessary to arrange that all the foe be congregated in that one valley. . . ."

"Hui! That is it!" Ukuruji exclaimed. "First, Bayan, you have heralds make that proclamation proposed by my

Royal Father. Then, as if that had given you mandate for a
full-scale assault, you send your whole force into the
likeliest valley, the mountains alongside it having previously been seeded with the huo-yao balls. The Yi will think
you have taken leave of your senses, but they will take advantage of it. They will filter down from their hiding
places and collect and cluster and prepare to assault from
your sides and rear. And then—"

"Honorable Wang!" the Orlok bleated, almost pleadingly. "I should *have* to take leave of my senses! Not
enough that I commit my entire five tomans—half a
tuk—to be surrounded by the enemy. Now you wish me to
condemn my fifty thousand men as well to a devastating
avalanche! What good for us to wipe out the Yi warriors
and have all Yun-nan prostrate before us, if we have no
troops of our own left alive to take it and hold it?"

"Hm," said Ukuruji yet again. "Well, our troops would
at least be expecting the avalanche. . . ."

The Orlok refrained even from dignifying that with a
comment. Just then, one of the serving chabis came out of
the Pota-lá onto the terrace, bringing a leather flask of
arkhi to refill our drinking horns and skull cups. Bayan,
Ukuruji and I were sitting now with our eyes pensively
fixed on the tabletop, so my gaze was caught by the bright
garnet sleeves of that young Bho man dispensing the liquor. Then my eyes, idling on those movements of color,
caught the similarly idling gaze of Ukuruji, and I saw his
eyes quicken with light, and I think the garnet sleeves inspired in both of us the same outrageous idea at the same
instant, but I was glad to let him do the expressing of it. He
leaned urgently toward Bayan and said:

"Suppose we do not risk our own men to bait the trap.
Suppose we send the worthless and expendable Bho. . . ."

YUN-NAN

1

I⊤ had to be done either quickly or in a secrecy so strict that it would have been almost impossible to sustain. So it was done quickly.

The first thing done was the posting of pickets all around the Ba-Tang valley, alert day and night to stop any Yi scouts from sneaking into the area, or any already planted Yi spies from sneaking out with word of what we were up to.

I have seen animal flocks march willingly to a slaughter pen when led by a Judas goat, but the Bho required not even that much cajolery or duress. Ukuruji merely outlined our plan to the lamas he had evicted from the Potalá. Those selfish and heartless holy men were all too anxious to do anything that would get the Wang and his court out of their lamasarai and themselves back into it—and the Bho would do anything their holy men told them to do. So the lamas, evincing no fatherly concern for their Potaist followers, no feeling for their fellows, no loyalty to their own country or reluctance to aid their Mongol overlords, showing no qualms or scruples whatever, made proclamation to the people of Ba-Tang that they must obey every order the Mongol officers gave them, and go anywhere they might be sent—and the mindless Bho complied.

Bayan immediately had his warriors begin corralling every able-bodied Bho in the city and environs—men, women, boys and girls of sufficient size—and begin outfitting them with cast-off Mongol arms and armor, giving them the more worn horses for mounts, and forming them

693

into columns complete with pack animals and yurtu-
carrier wagons, Bayan's own orlok flag, the yak tails of his
sardars, other suitable pennants and guidons. Except for
the lamas and trapas and chabis, only the very oldest,
youngest and frailest Bho were spared to be left behind—
plus a few others. Ukuruji kindly excepted the several
culled-out women he had been keeping for the enjoyment
of himself and his courtiers, and I likewise sent Ryang and
Odcho safely to their homes, each with a necklace of coins
to help her further her career of bedding toward a prospect
of wedding.

Meanwhile, Bayan sent heralds under white flags of
truce riding southward to bellow over and over, in the Yi
language, something like this: "Your traitor spy in the
capital of Kithai has been exposed and overthrown! You
have no more hope of standing under siege! Therefore this
province of Yun-nan is declared annexed to the Khanate!
You are to throw down your arms and welcome the conquerors when they come! The Khan Kubilai has spoken!
Tremble, all men, and obey!" Of course, we did not expect
the Yi either to tremble or to obey. We merely trusted that
they would be enough bemused and distracted by those
heralds arrogantly riding through the valleys that they
would not notice the other men flitting furtively along the
mountaintops—engineers finding the best places to secrete
the brass balls, and then hiding near them, ready to fire
their wicks on a signal from me.

In case the Yi had any watchers of excellent eyesight
posted far beyond our pickets surrounding Ba-Tang, the
whole bok was struck and the yurtu tents collapsed, and
all that equipment and the wagons and animals not going
with the pretended invasion were hidden away. All the
thousands of real Mongol men and women moved into
the evacuated buildings of the city. But they did not don
the drab and dirty civilian clothing of the displaced Bho.
They—and I and Ukuruji and his courtiers as well—stayed
clad in battle dress and armor and accouterments, ready to
move out on the track of the doomed columns as soon as we
got word that the trap was sprung.

It was necessary to send some real Mongols along with
those decoy columns of mock Mongols, but Bayan only had
to call for volunteers and he got them. The men knew they
were volunteering to commit suicide, but these were war-

riors who had bested death so often that they firmly believed their long service under the Orlok had imbued them
with some power always to do so. Any few who survived
this latest perilous mission would simply rejoice in Bayan's having once again proved their indestructibility, and
the dead would not reproach him. So a band of the men
rode at the front of the simulated invasion army, playing
on musical instruments the Mongols' war anthems and
marching music (which the Bho, for all their willingness,
would not have known how to play), and, with that music,
setting the alternate canter-walk-canter pace for the thousands behind. At the tail end of that army had to ride another troop of real Mongols, to keep the columns from
straggling, and also to send couriers back to us when the
Yi—as we hoped—began to congregate for their assault.

The Bho knew very well that they were posing as Mongols, and their lamas had commanded them to do so with a
will—though I doubt that the lamas had told them it was
probably the last thing they would ever do—and they entered into the pretense most heartily. When they learned
that they would be led by a band of military musicians,
some of them asked Bayan and Ukuruji, "Lords, should
not we chant and sing, as real Mongols do on the march?
What should we chant? We know nothing but the 'om
mani pémé hum.' "

"Anything but that," said the Orlok. "Let me think. The
capital of Yun-nan is named Yun-nan-fu. I suppose you
could go clamoring, 'We march to seize Yun-nan-fu!' "

"Yun-nan-pu?" they said.

"No," said Ukuruji, laughing. "Forget about shouting
or chanting." He explained to Bayan, "The Bho are incapable of enunciating the sounds of v and f. Better have
them not voice anything at all, or the Yi may recognize
that deficiency." He paused, struck by a new idea. "One
other thing we might have them do, though. Tell the leaders always to lead the column to the right around any holy
structure, like a mani wall or a ch'horten stone pile, leaving that on their *left* hand."

The Bho made a feeble wail of protest at that—it would
be an insult to those monuments to the Pota—but their
lamas quickly stepped in and bade them obey, and even
took the pains to say a hypocritical prayer giving the peo-

ple special dispensation on this occasion to insult the almighty Pota.

The preparations took only a few days, while the heralds and the engineers went on ahead, and the columns moved out as soon as they were finally formed up, on a beautiful morning of bright sunshine. I must say that even that mock army made a magnificent sight and sound as it left Ba-Tang. Up front, the band of Mongol musicians led with an unearthly but blood-stirring martial music. The trumpeters sounded the great copper trumpets called karachala, which name could rightly translate as "the hellhorns." The drummers had tremendous copper and hide drums like kettles, one slung on either side of the saddle, and they did marvels of twirling and flailing their mallets and crossing and uncrossing their arms as they hammered the thunderous beat for the march. Cymbalists clashed immense brass platters that flashed a flare of sunlight with every stunning ring of sound. Bell players beat a sort of scampanio—metal tubes of various sizes arranged in a lyre-shaped frame. Between and among the louder, blaring noises could be heard the sweeter string music of lutes made with specially short necks for playing while riding.

The music moved on and gradually diminished as it blended into the sound of the thousands of hoofs clip-clopping along behind, and the heavy rumble of wagon wheels, and the creak and jingle of armor and harness. The Bho, for once in their lives, looked not pathetic or contemptible, but as proud and disciplined and determined as if they had actually been going out to war, and on their own account. The horsemen rode rigidly upright in their saddles and facing sternly forward, except to do a very respectable eyes-right when they passed the reviewing Orlok Bayan and his sardars. As the Wang Ukuruji remarked, the decoy men and women did indeed resemble genuine Mongol warriors. They had even been persuaded to ride using the long Mongol stirrups—which enable a hard-riding bowman to stand for better aim with his arrows—instead of the short, cramped, knees-up stirrups favored by the Bho and the Drok and the Han and the Yi.

When the last column's last rank and its rear guard of real Mongols had disappeared downriver, there was nothing for the remainder of us to do except wait and, while waiting, try to maintain, for the benefit of any putative

keen-eyed watchers from afar, the illusion that Ba-Tang
was an ordinary, nasty Bho city going about its ordinary,
nasty Bho business. In the daytimes, our people thronged
the market areas and, at twilights, gathered on rooftops as
if praying. Whether we ever really were spied upon, I do
not know. But if we were, our stratagem could not have
been discovered by the Yi down south, for it worked exactly as planned—up to a point, anyway.

About a week after the leavetaking, one of the rear-
guard Mongols came galloping to report that the decoy
army had got well within Yun-nan, and was still proceeding forward, and the Yi apparently had been fooled by the
imposture. Scouts, he said, had seen the scattered individual snipers in the mountains, and outpost groups of them,
beginning to collect together and to move downhill like
tributary streams converging to become a river. We
waited some more, and in another few days another rider
came galloping to report that the Yi were unmistakably
massing in force behind and on both rear quarters of our
mock army—that, in fact, he had had to ride most evasively to get around the gathering Yi and get out of Yun-
nan with that information for us.

So now the real army rode forth, and—though it moved
as discreetly as possible, with no marching music—that
must have been a *really* magnificent sight to see. The entire half a tuk surged out of the Ba-Tang valley like an ele-
mental force of nature on the move. The fifty thousand
troops were divided into tomans of ten thousand, each led
by a sardar, and those divided into the flag-captains' thousands, and those into the chiefs' hundreds—each riding in
broad ranks of ten in files of ten—and each hundred riding
far enough apart not to be suffocated by the dust kicked up
by those ahead. I say the departure must have made a
magnificent spectacle, because I did not get to see it go
past me. I rode out well ahead of it, in company with
Bayan, Ukuruji and a few senior officers. The Orlok, of
course, had to go first, and Ukuruji was in the forefront because he wished to be, and I was there because Bayan ordered me to be there. I had been provided with a special,
immense banner of brilliant yellow silk, and I was to un-
furl that at the proper moment to signal for the avalanche.
Any trooper could have done the signaling, but Bayan in-

sisted on regarding the brass balls as "mine," and their
employment as my responsibility.

So we cantered a good many li in advance of the tuk, following the river Jin-sha and the broad, trampled track beside it that was the spoor of the mock army. After only a
few days of hard riding and spartan camping, the Orlok
grunted, "Here we are crossing the border into Yun-nan
Province." A few days farther on, we were intercepted by a
Mongol sentry, one of that army's rear guard set to wait
for us, and he led us off the river route, taking us to one
side of the line of march and around a hill. At the far side
of that hill, in late afternoon, we came upon eight more of
the Mongol rear guard, where they had made a fireless
camp. The captain of the guard respectfully invited us to
dismount and share some of their cold rations of dried
meat and tsampa balls.

"But first, Orlok," he said, "you may wish to climb to
the top of this hill and look over. It will give you a view
down this valley of the Jin-sha, and I think you will recognize that you have come just in time."

The captain led the way, as Bayan, Ukuruji and I all
made the climb on foot. We did it rather slowly, being stiff
from our long ride. Toward the top, our guide motioned for
us to crouch and then to crawl, and at last we only cautiously poked our heads over the grass at the crest. We
could see that it was well we had been intercepted. Had we
followed the river and the tracks for a few hours more, we
should have rounded the other side of this hill and entered
the long but narrow valley opening before us, in which our
mock army was camped. The Bho, as instructed, were
behaving more like an occupying force than an invading
one. They had not erected any tents, but they had camped
this evening as nonchalantly as if they had been invited by
the Yi to Yun-nan and were welcome there—with innumerable camp fires and torches twinkling throughout the
twilit valley, and only a few guards negligently posted
around the camp perimeter, and much movement and
noise going on.

"We would have ridden right into the camp," said Ukuruji.

"No, Lord Wang, you would not," said our guide. "And I
respectfully suggest that you subdue your voice." Keeping
his own voice low, the captain explained, "All down the

other side of this hill are the Yi, lurking in force, and at the entrance to the valley, and on the farther slopes—in fact, everywhere between us and that camp, and beyond. You would have ridden right into their rear, and been seized. The foe are massed in a great horseshoe, around this end and both valley sides of the decoy camp. You cannot see the Yi because, like us, they have lighted no fires and they are concealed in every available cover."

Bayan asked, "They have done so every night the army has camped?"

"Yes, Lord Orlok, and each time increasing in their numbers. But I think tonight's camp will be the last that mock army will make. I might be wrong. But, as best I could count, today was the first day the foe have not added to their numbers. I think every fighting man in this area of Yun-nan is now congregated in this valley—a force of some fifty thousand, about equal to our own. And, if I were commanding the Yi, I should deem this rather narrow defile the perfect place to make a crushing assault on what appears to be a singularly unapprehensive invader. As I say, I might be wrong. But my warrior instinct tells me the Yi will attack at tomorrow's dawn."

"A good report, Captain Toba." I think Bayan knew by name every man of his half a tuk. "And I am inclined to share your intuition. What of the engineers? Have you any idea of their disposition?"

"Alas, no, Lord Orlok. Communication with them would be impossible without revealing them to the enemy. I have had to assume and trust that they have been keeping pace along the mountain crests, and each day newly placing and readying their secret weapons."

"Let us trust they did it this day, anyway," said Bayan. He lifted his head enough to make a slow scan of the mountains ringing the valley.

So did I. If the Orlok was going to persist in holding me responsible for the secret weapons, it was to my best interest that the things do what I hoped they would. If they did, some fifty thousand Bho were going to perish, and about that many Yi as well. It was a considerable responsibility, indeed, for a noncombatant and a Christian. But it would mean winning the war for my chosen side, and a victory would show that God was also on our side, and that would allay any Christian qualms about wholesale slaughter. If the brass balls did not perform as warranted, the Bho would die anyway, but the Yi would not. The war would have to go on, and that might cause me some Christian pangs of conscience—killing so many people, even if they were only Bho, to no purpose at all.

But what mainly concerned me, I must confess, was the satisfaction of my curiosity. I was interested to see if the flaming-powder balls *did* work, and how well. Certainly, I said to myself, I could see a dozen vantage points on the mountains where, if I had been doing the placing, I would have laid the charges. Those were outcrops of bare rock, like Crusader castles towering up from the forest growth, and showing clefts and checkerings where they had been split by time or weather, and where, if they were suddenly split farther asunder, the slabs ought to topple and fall and, in falling, take other chunks of their mountains with them. . . .

Bayan grunted a command, and we slithered down the hill the way we had come. At the bottom, he gave orders to the waiting men:

"The real army should be about forty or fifty li behind us, and also preparing to stop for the night. Six of you start riding toward it, this instant. One of you pull off to the trailside every ten li, and wait there, so your horses will be fresh tomorrow. The sixth rider should reach there before sunrise. Tell the sardars not to start marching again. Tell them to wait where they are, lest the dust of their march be visible from here, and spoil all our plans. If all goes as planned tomorrow, I will send Captain Toba riding next and riding hard, and you will rush the word on in relays to the tuk. The word will be for the sardars to bring the whole army on, at a stretch-out gallop, to do the mopping up of any remnants of the enemy that might be left alive in this valley. If things go wrong here, well . . . I will send Captain Toba with different orders to impart. Now go. Ride."

The six men left, leading their horses until they should be well out of hearing. Bayan turned to the rest of us.

"Let us eat a little and sleep a little. We must be watching from the hilltop before first light."

2

AND we were there: the Orlok Bayan and his accompanying officers, the Wang Ukuruji, myself, Captain Toba and the remaining two men of his troop. The others were each carrying a sword, a bow and a quiver of arrows, and Bayan—ready for combat, not parade—was toothless. I, since I had the unwieldy flag-lance to handle, had no other weapon but my belt knife. We lay in the grass and watched as the scene before us slowly became visible. The morning would have to be well advanced before the sun would show itself above the mountaintops, but its rise lightened the cloudless blue sky, and that light gradually reflected down into the black bowl of the valley, and it sucked a mist up off the river. At first, that was the only movement we could see, a milky luminescence drifting against the blackness. But then the valley assumed shape and color: misty blue at its mountain edges, dark green of forests, paler green of the grass and undergrowth in the clearings, silver glitter of the river as the obscuring mist evaporated. With shape and color came movement also: the horse herd began to stir and mill a little, and we could hear an occasional distant whicker and neigh. Then the women of the bok began to arise from their bedrolls and move about, blowing the banked camp fires into flame and setting water to heat for cha—we heard the distant clink of kettles—before waking the menfolk.

The Yi had often enough, by now, watched that camp awaken to know its routine. And they chose this moment for their assault: when there was light enough for them to see their objective clearly, but only the women were astir and the men still asleep. I do not know how the Yi signaled for the attack; I saw no banner waved and heard no trumpet blown. But the Yi warriors moved all in an instant and all together, with admirable precision. One moment, we watchers were looking down an empty hill slope at the bok in the valley; we might have been at the top of an empty amphitheater, looking down the unpeopled seat-shelves at a tableau on the distant stage. The next moment, our view was blocked by the slope's being no longer empty, as if all the amphitheater's shelves had magically and silently sprouted a vast audience in tier upon tier. Out of the grass

701

and weeds and bushes downhill of us, there sprang erect a
taller growth—leather-armored men, each with a bow already bent and an arrow already nocked to the string. So
abruptly did it happen that it seemed to me that some of
them had arisen from right before my face; I fancied I
could *smell* the half dozen nearest; and I think I was not
the only one of us lurkers who did not have to repress an
impulse to start up, too. But I only widened my eyes and
moved my head enough to gaze about, seeing all around
the valley amphitheater that suddenly visible and menacing audience, standing in thousands, in horseshoe rows
and tiers—man-sized where they were near me, doll-sized
farther away, insect-sized on the more distant valley
slopes—all those ranks quilled and fringed and fuzzed with
arrows aimed at a central point that was the stage-tableau
encampment.

That had all happened in near silence, and far more
quickly than it takes to tell. The next thing that happened—the first sound made by the Yi—was not a concerted, ululating battle cry, as a Mongol army would have
made. The sound was only the weird, whishing, slightly
whistling noise of all their arrows loosed at once, the thousands of them making all together a sort of fluttering roar,
like a wind soughing along the valley. Then the sound, as
it diminished away from us, was repeated, but fragmented
and doubled into an overlapping noise of whish-whish-
whish as the Yi, with great rapidity but no longer simulta-
neity, plucked from their quivers more arrows—while the
first were still in flight—and nocked them and loosed
them, meanwhile running full tilt toward the bok. The arrows went high against the sky and briefly darkened the
blue of it, even as they dwindled in size from discernible
sticks to twigs to slivers to toothpicks to whiskers, and
then arced lazily over to become a dim, shady haze that
drizzled down on the camp, looking no more dreadful than
a gray patter of early morning rain. We watchers, being
out behind and near to the archers, had seen and heard
that first movement of the assault. But its targets—the
standing women and horses and recumbent men in the
bok—would probably have noticed nothing until the thousands of arrows began showering down and among and
around and into them. No mere haze or fuzz at that extremity of their flight, the arrows were sharp-pointed and

heavy and moving fast from their long fall, and many must
have fallen upon flesh and struck to the bone.

And by then the ranks of the Yi nearest to the camp
were running into the outskirts of it, still making no warning outcry and heedless of their own fellows' arrows still
falling, their swords and lances already flashing and
stabbing and slashing. All the time, up where we were, we
watched the Yi warriors still new-sprouting from our hillside and all the mountainsides around, as if the valley
greenery was incessantly blooming over and over again
into dark flowers that were standing archers, then shed-
ding those and letting them run down toward the bok, then
blossoming with more of them. Now there was also noise,
louder than the wind-and-rain sound of the arrows—shouts
of alarm and outrage and fright and pain from the people
in the camp. When that noise began and surprise was no
longer enjoined, the Yi also began to bellow battle cries as
they ran and converged on their objective, now at last allowing themselves the yells that raise a warrior's courage
and ferocity and, he hopes, strike terror into his foe.

When all was clamor and confusion down in the valley,
Bayan said, "I think now is the time, Marco Polo. The Yi
are all running for the bok, and no more are springing up,
and I see none held in reserve outside the combat area."

"Now?" I said. "Are you sure, Orlok? I will be highly visible, standing here and waving a flag. It may give the Yi
reason for suspicion and pause. If they do not drop me with
an immediate arrow."

"No fear," he said. "No advancing warrior ever looks
back. Get up there."

So I clambered to my feet, expecting any moment to feel
a thumping puncture of my leather cuirass, and hurriedly
unfurled the silk from my lance. When nothing struck me
down, I gripped the lance in both hands, raised the banner
as high as I could, and began waving it from left to right
and back again, the yellow shining bright in the morning
light and the silk snapping briskly. I could not just wave it
once or twice and then again drop prone, on the assumption that it had been seen from afar. I had to stand there
until I *knew* that the distant engineers had seen the signal
and acted on it. I was mentally calculating:

How long will it take? They must be already looking this
way. Yes, they would have known where we had come

from, at the rear of the enemy. So, from their hiding
places, the engineers are peering in this direction. They
are scanning this end of the valley, alert for a moving dot
of yellow among all the ambient greenery. Now—hui!
alalà! evviva!—they see the distant, tiny, wagging banner.
Now they scramble back from their lookout positions to
wherever they earlier secreted the brass balls. That may
take them some moments. Allow a few moments for that.
Very well, now they pick up their smoldering incense
sticks and blow on them—*if* they had the good sense to
have them already alight and waiting. Perhaps they did
not! So now they must fumble with flint and steel and
tinder. . . .

Allow a few more moments for that. God, but the banner
was getting heavy. Very well, so *now* they have their
tinder glowing, and now they are wheedling into flame a
pile of dry leaves or something. Now they have each got a
twig or an incense stick afire, and now they are bearing
those over to the brass balls. Now they are touching the
fire to the wicks. Now the wicks are burning and sputtering and the engineers are leaping up and running hard
for a safe distance. . . .

I wished them good luck and much distance and safe
shelter, for I myself was feeling exceptionally exposed and
visible and vulnerable. I seemed to have been flaunting
my flag and my bravata and my person for an eternity already, and the Yi must be blind not to have spotted me.
Now—how long had the Firemaster said?—a slow count of
ten after the wicks were lit. I counted ten slow wags of my
big, rippling yellow banner. . . .

Nothing happened.

Caro Gèsu, what had gone wrong? Could it be that the
engineers had misunderstood? My arms were weary of the
waving, and I was sweating profusely, though the sun was
still behind the mountains and the morning was not yet
warm. Could it be that the engineers had waited to see my
signal before even *placing* the balls? Why had I entrusted
this enterprise—and now my very life—to a dozen thick-
headed Mongol rankers? Would I have to stand here,
waving more and more feebly, for another eternity or two,
while the engineers leisurely did what should have been
done already? And how long after that would it be before
they even began lackadaisically to rummage around in

their belt purses for flint and steel? And during all that
time, must I stand here flailing this extremely eye-invit-
ing yellow flag? Bayan might be convinced that no warrior
ever looked back *voluntarily,* but any of those Yi had only
to stumble and fall, or be knocked sprawling, so that his
head turned this way. He could hardly fail to see such an
uncommon battlefield sight as I presented. He would yell
to his companion warriors, and they would come pelting toward me, loosing arrows as they came. . . .

The green landscape was blurred by sweat running into
my eyes, but I saw a brief flicker of yellow at the corner of
my vision. Maledetto! I was letting the banner sag; I must
hold it higher. But then, where the flick of yellow had
been, there was now a puff of blue against the green. I
heard a chorus of "Hui!" from my fellows still prone in the
grass, and then they leapt up to stand beside me, cheering
"Hui!" again and again. I let the flag and its lance drop,
and I stood panting and sweating and watching the yellow
flashes and blue smokes of the huo-yao balls doing what
they had been intended to do.

The whole center of the valley, where now the Yi and the
Bho mock-Mongols were intimately commingled, was
clouded by the dust raised by their fierce confusion. But
the flashes and smokes were high above that dome of dust,
and not obscured by it. They were up where I would have
put them myself, twinkling and puffing from those crevices in the castle-like rock outcrops. They did not all ignite
at once, but flared by ones and twos, from one mountain
height and then another. I was pleased that the engineers
had placed them where I would have done, and I was
pleased when I counted twelve ignitions; every single ball
had performed as warranted—but I was dismayed by the
apparent puniness of them. Such tiny flashes of fire, and so
soon extinguished—and leaving only such insignificant
plumes of blue smoke. The sound of them came much later
and, though the noises were loud enough to be heard above
the clamor of shouting and scuffling down in the valley,
they were no such thunderous roar as I had heard when
my palace chamber was demolished. These noises of igni-
tion were only sharp slaps of sound—as might have been
produced by a Yi warrior yonder hitting the flat of his
sword on a horses's flank—one and two slapping sounds,

and then several together in a sustained crackle of slaps, and then the final few separate again.

And then nothing more happened, except that the furious but futile battle continued unabated down in the valley, where none of the combatants seemed to have noticed our byplay in the heights. The Orlok turned and gave me a lacerating look. I shrugged my eyebrows helplessly at him. But suddenly all the other men were murmuring "Hui!" in a wondering way, and they were all pointing, and most of them in different directions. Bayan and I looked first where one was pointing, and then where another was, and another. Over here, high up, the cleft gashed in a wall-like rock was perceptibly widening. Over there, high up, two great slabs of rock that had been side by side were gradually leaning apart. Over yonder, high up, a pinnacle of rock like a castle keep was toppling over, and breaking into separate rocks as it did so, and spraying those rocks apart, and doing all those things as slowly as if it had been under water.

If those mountains truly never had suffered an avalanche before, then *because* they never had, they may have been ready and poised for one. I think we could have accomplished our intentions with just three or four of the brass balls lodged on either side of the valley; we had put six on each side, and all had done their work. And, puny as was the commencement of the performance, the conclusion was spectacular. I can best describe it thus: consider the high rocks to have been a few exposed knobs of the backbones of the mountains, and consider our charges to have been hammer blows that broke the bones. As the mountains' spines crumbled, their earth cover began to peel away here and there, like a hide being skinned piecemeal off an animal. And as the hide wrinkled and folded, the forests began to shed and shred off it, as a camel's fur does in summertime, in unsightly tufts and patches.

As early as the breaking-away of the first rocks, we watchers could feel the hill under us tremble, though we were many li distant from the very nearest of those rockslides. The valley floor had to be quivering then, too, but the two armies conjoined in battle still took no notice; or, if they did, every man and woman no doubt believed it to be only his or her own personal quaking of fear and rage. I remember thinking: that must be the way we mortals

will ignore the first tremors of Armageddon, continuing to
pursue our trivial and pitiful and spiteful little strifes even
while God is loosing the unimaginable devastation that
will end the world and all.

But a goodly piece of the world was being devastated
right here. The falling rocks dislodged other rocks below
them and, rolling and sliding, they gouged up great
swathes and whole zonte of earth and then, rocks and
earth together, they scoured their various mountainsides
of their vegetation, the trees toppling and colliding and
heaping up and overlying and splintering, and then the
surface of each mountain and everything that grew upon it
or was contained within it—boulders, rocks, stones, clods,
loose earth, meadow-sized pieces of rumpled turf, trees,
bushes, flowers, probably even the forest creatures caught
unawares—all came *down,* down into the valley, in a dozen
or more separate avalanches, and the noise of them, until
now delayed by distance, finally began to batter our ears.
It wa a mutter that grew to a growl that grew to a roar that
grew to a thunder, but a thunder like I never heard
before—not even in the unstable heights of the Pai-Mir,
where the noises had often been loud, but never for longer
than a few minutes. This thunder here continued to grow
in volume and to create echoes and to collect and absorb
the echoes, and to bellow ever louder, as if it never would
reach its loudest. Now the hill on which we stood was quivering like a jelly—the noise alone might have been enough
to shake it—so that we could scarcely keep our feet, and all
the trees nearby us were rustling so they shed many of
their leaves, and birds were bursting up everywhere,
squawking and screeching, and the very air around us
seemed to quake.

The rumblings of the several avalanches would have
overwhelmed the noise of battle in the valley, but there
was no more of that shouting and war-crying and clinking
together of sword blades. The poor people had at least perceived what was happening, and so had the camp's herds of
horses, and the people and horses were scurrying hither
and thither. Being myself in a state of some agitation, I
could not too well discern what the people were doing indi-
vidually. I saw them rather as an indistinct mass—like the
blurred masses of landscape coming down the mountains
roundabout—the thousands of people and horses all run-

ning in a tremendous, untidy bunch. The way they were
moving, I might have thought the whole valley floor was
tilting back and forth and sloshing them from side to side
of it. Except for the numbers already struck down in combat, lying motionless or moving only feebly, the people and
horses seemed first, and all at the same time, to glimpse
the havoc hurtling toward them down the western slopes,
and they all ran in a body away from there, only to see the
other calamity coming down the eastern slopes, and all in
a body they surged back again to the middle of the valley
floor, all but a few who jumped into the river, as if they
were fleeing a forest fire and might find safety in the cool
water. Some two or three dozen individuals—I did make
out that much—were running straight down the valley's
middle, toward us, and probably others were scampering
up it in the other direction. But the avalanches were moving faster than any mere human could.

And down they came. Though the swooping blurs of
brown and green contained whole forests of full-sized trees
and countless boulders as big as houses, they looked, from
where we stood, like cascades of dirty, gritty, lumpy
tsampa porridge being poured down the sides of a giant tureen to puddle in its bottom, and the towering clouds of
dust they raised on the way looked like the steam rising
from that tsampa porridge. When the several separate
slides reached the lower skirts of their mountains, they co-
alesced on either side into a single stupendous avalanche
roaring into the valley—one from the east, one from the
west—to meet in the middle. Rasping across the flat valley
floor, they must have slowed their rush to some slight degree, but not so I could see it, and the front face of each cat-
aract was still as high as a three-story wall when they
came together. And when they did that, it made me remember once having seen two great mountain rams, in the
season of rut, gallop at each other and butt their huge
horned heads together with a shock that made my own
teeth shake.

I would have expected to hear a similarly teeth-rattling
crash when the two monster avalanches met head on, but
their thunder climaxed instead with a sort of cosmically
loud kissing noise. The Jin-sha River, on its way through
this valley, ran along its eastern edge. So the landslide
sluicing down from the east simply scooped up a consider-

able length of that river as it careered across it, and, as it continued on, must have churned that water into its forward content so that its front became a wall of sticky muck. When the two careening masses came together, then, it was with a loud, slapping, moist *slurp!*, suggesting that the avalanches were cemented there to be the valley's new and higher floor for all time to come. Also, at the instant of their collision, the sun bounded into view beyond the eastern mountains, but the sky was so thick with dust that its disk was discolored. The sun came up as suddenly and as brassy of hue and as blurred around the rim as if it had been a cymbal thrown up there to ring the finale to all the commotion in the valley. And, while the trailing rubble skirts of the slides continued to sweep down from the heights, the noise did indeed die down, not all at once, but with the kind of wobbling, clashing, diminishing clangor that a cymbal makes as its blur slows to stillness.

In the sudden hush—it was not a total silence, for many boulders were still thudding and bouncing down from the heights, and trees still crunching and skidding down, and patches of turf still skittering down, and unidentifiable other things still caroming about in the distance—the first words I heard were the Orlok's:

"Ride now, Captain Toba. Fetch our army."

The captain went back the way we had come. Bayan leisurely took out from a purse the great gleaming device of gold and porcelain that was his teeth, and forced it into his mouth, and gnashed it a few times to settle its jaws to his own. Looking now a proper Orlok, ready for his triumphal parade, he strode off down the hill in the direction we were facing. When he dimmed into the cloud of dust, the rest of us followed after him. I did not know why we were doing that, unless to gloat on the completeness of our unusual victory. But there was nothing to be seen of it, or of anything really, in that dense and stifling pall. When we had gone only as far as the bottom of the hill, I had lost sight of my companions, and only heard Bayan's muffled voice, off to my right somewhere, saying to somebody, "The troops will be disappointed when they get here. No battlefield loot to pick over."

The enormous cloud of dust thrown up by the avalanches had, by the time the two masses met, entirely obscured our view of the valley and its ultimate devastation. So I cannot say that I actually witnessed the annihilation of something like a hundred thousand people. Nor, in all the noise, did I hear their last hopeless screams or the snapping of their limbs. But they were now gone, together with all the horses, weapons, their personal belongings and other equipment. The valley had been resurfaced, and the people had been wiped out as if they had been no bigger or more worth keeping than the crawling ants and beetles that had inhabited the old ground.

I remembered the bleached bones and skulls I had seen lying about the Pai-Mir, the remains of animal herds and karwan trains that had encountered other avalanches. There would not be even that much trace left here. None of the Ba-Tang Bho we had excused from the march—little Odcho and Ryang, for instance—if they journeyed here to visit the place where their city's population was last seen, would ever find the skull of a father or brother to fashion into a sentimental keepsake like a drinking bowl or a festa drum. Maybe some Yi farmer tilling this valley in some far distant century would turn up with his digging stick a fragment of one of the less deeply buried corpses. But, until then. . . .

It occurred to me that, of all the men and women who had been so frantically running about, and those who had crouched pathetically in the river, and those who had been already lying wounded or unconscious or dead, only the insensible had been the fortunate few. The others had had to endure at least one terrible last moment of knowing that they were about to be stamped on like insects or, even worse, buried alive. Maybe some of them were *yet* alive, uncrushed, still conscious, trapped underground in dark, tight, contorted little graves and tunnels and pockets of air that would persist until the great weight of earth and rocks and rubble had finished shifting and settling in its new location.

It would take some while for the valley to accommodate itself to its changed topography. I could tell that because, even while I groped about and coughed and sneezed in the cloud of dry dust, I found that I was sloshing about in muddy water that had not been there before. The Jin-sha River was nuzzling and probing at the barrier that had so abruptly impeded its flow, and was having to spread out sideways beyond what had formerly been its banks. Evi-

dently, in my trudging about in the dimness, I had veered
over to the left, to the eastward. Not wanting to walk any
deeper into the gathering water, I turned right and, my
boots alternately sucking and slipping in the new mud,
went to rejoin the others. When a human shape loomed up
before me in the murk, I called to him in the Mongol language, and that was an almost fatal mistake.

I never had a chance to inquire how he had survived the
catastrophe—whether he was one of those who had gone
running the length of the valley instead of back and forth,
or whether he had simply and inexplicably been lifted up
by the avalanche instead of crushed beneath it. Maybe he
could not have told me, for maybe he did not know himself
how he had been spared. It seems that there were always
at least a few survivors of even the worst disaster—
perhaps there will even be a few after Armageddon—and
in this case we would discover that there were about four
score still alive of the hundred thousand. Half of those
were Yi, and about half of the Yi were quite undamaged
and ambulatory—and at least two of them were still armed
and brimming with a rage for immediate revenge—and I
had had the misfortune to meet one of those.

He may have believed himself to be the *only* Yi left
alive, and may have been startled to encounter another
human form in the dust cloud, but I gave him the advantage when I spoke in Mongol. I did not know what he was,
but he knew instantly that I was an enemy—one of the enemy that had just swept away his army and his companions in arms and probably close friends, even brothers of
his. With the instinctive action of an angered hornet, he
made a swipe at me with his sword. Had it not been for the
new mud in which we stood, I should have perished at that
moment. I could not have consciously dodged the sudden
blow, but my involuntary flinch made me slip in the mud,
and I fell down as the sword went *whish!* where I had been.

I still did not know who or what had attacked me—one
thing went through my mind: "Expect me when you least
expect me"—but there was no mistaking the attack. I
rolled away from his feet and grabbed for the only weapon
I carried, my belt knife, and tried to stand, but got only to
one knee before he lunged again. We were both still only
indistinct figures in the dust, and his footing was as slippery as mine, so his second swing also missed me. That

blow brought him close enough to me that I made a dart
with my knife point, but it fell short when I slid again in
the mud.

Let me say something about close combat. I had earlier,
in Khanbalik, seen the imposing map of the Minister of
War, with its little flags and yak tails marking the positions of armies. At other times, I have watched high officers plotting out battle tactics and following the progress
of them, using a tabletop and colored blocks of different
sizes. Such exercises make battle look neat and tidy and
perhaps, to a remote officer or an observer not involved,
even predictable in the outcome. Back home in Venice, I
had seen pictures and tapestries depicting famous Venetian victories on land and sea—over here Our fleet or cavalry, over yonder Theirs, the combatants always facing
each other squarely and loosing arrows or aiming lances
with precision and assuredness and even a calm look of
equanimity. A viewer of such pictures would take a battle
to be a thing as orderly and trim and methodical as a Game
of Squares, or Shahi, played on a flat board in a well-
lighted, comfortable room.

I doubt that any battle has ever been like that, and I
know that close combat cannot be. It is a flailing, messy,
desperate confusion, usually on wretched terrain and in
vile weather, one man against another, both of them having forgotten in their rage and terror everything they ever
were taught about how to fight. I suppose every man has
learned the rules of swordplay and knifeplay: do thus and
so to parry your opponent's offense, move like this to get
past his guard, execute these other feints to expose the
weak places in his defense and the gaps in his armor. Perhaps those rules apply when two masters stand toe to toe
in a gara di scherma, or when two duelists politely face off
in a pleasant meadow. It is quite different when you and
your opponent are grappling in a mud puddle with dense
cloud all about, when both of you are dirty and sweaty,
when your eyes are gritty and watering so you can barely
see.

I will not try to describe our struggle, blow by blow. I do
not remember the sequence. All I recall is that it was a
time of grunting, panting, squirming, thrashing desperation—a very long time, it seemed—with me trying to get
close enough to him to stab with my knife, and he trying to

keep enough distance to swing his sword. We were both
body-armored in leather, but differently, so that we each
had an advantage over the other. My cuirass was of supple
hides, allowing me freedom to move and dodge. His was of
cuirbouilli so stiff that it stood out around him like a barrel; it hampered his agility, but made an effective barrier
against my short, wide-bladed knife. When at last, more by
chance than skill, I struck at his chest and the blade went
in, I realized that it had penetrated the cuirass, and was
stuck there, but could only lightly have pricked his rib
cage. So in that moment he had me at his mercy, my knife
wedged in his leather, I clinging to its handle, while he
was free to wield his sword.

He took that moment to laugh derisively, triumphantly
before he struck, and that was *his* mistake. My knife was
the one I had long ago been given by a Roman girl whose
name meant Blade. I squeezed its haft in the proper way,
and I felt the wide blades jar apart, and I knew the inner,
slim, third blade had leapt out from between them, for my
foe bulged his eyes in unbelieving surprise. He gave a
snarling gasp and his mouth stayed open, and his back-
flung hand let drop his sword, and he belched blood all
over me, and he toppled away from me and fell. I yanked
my knife loose of him and wiped it clean and closed it up
again, and I stood up, thinking: now I have slain two men
in my lifetime. Not to mention the twin women in Khanbalik. Do I also take credit for the whole victory here, and
count my lifetime kill as one hundred thousand and four?
The Khan Kubilai ought to be proud of me, having cleared
such ample room for myself on the overcrowded earth.

3

MY companions, I saw when I located and rejoined them,
had also encountered a vengeful enemy in the fog, but had
not fared so well as I. They were grouped around two figures stretched on the ground, and Bayan whirled with his
sword in his hand as I approached.

"Ah, Polo," he said, relaxing as he recognized me,
though I must have been bloody all over. "Looks as if you

met one, too—and dispatched him. Good man. This one was insanely fierce." He pointed his blade at one of the supine figures, a Yi warrior, much hacked about and obviously dead. "It took three of us to slay him, and not before he had got one of us." He indicated the other figure.

I exclaimed, "A tragedy! Ukuruji has been hurt!" The young Wang was lying with his face screwed up in pain, and his own two hands clutched around his neck. I cried, "He seems to be strangling!" and bent to loosen his hands and examine the injury to his throat. But when I raised the clenched hands, his head came along in their grasp. It had been completely severed from his body. I grunted and recoiled, then stood looking sadly down at him, and murmured, "How terrible. Ukuruji was a good fellow."

"He was a Mongol," said one of the officers. "Next to killing, dying is what Mongols do best. It is nothing to weep over."

"No," I agreed. "He was eager to help win Yun-nan, and he did."

"He will not govern it, unfortunately," said the Orlok. "But his last sight was of our total victory. That is no bad moment to die."

I asked, "You regard Yun-nan as ours, then?"

"Oh, there will be other contested valleys. And cities and towns to take. We have not annihilated every last one of the foe. But the Yi will be demoralized by this crushing defeat, and will be putting up only token resistance. Yes, I can safely say that Yun-nan is ours. That means we will next be battering at the back door of the Sung, and the whole empire must fall very soon. That is the word you will take back to Kubilai."

"I wish I were taking him the good news unalloyed with bad. It cost him a son."

One of the officers said, "Kubilai has many other sons. He may even adopt you, Ferenghi, after what you did for him here. Behold, the dust is settling. You can see what you accomplished with your ingenious brass engines."

We all turned from contemplating Ukuruji's body, and looked down the valley. The dust was finally sifting out of the air and laying itself like a soft, gentle, age-yellowed shroud on the tormented and tumbled landscape. The

mountain slopes on both sides, which earlier in the morning had been thickly forested, now had trees and greenery
only fringing the edges of their open wounds—great
gouged-out gullies and gorges of raw brown earth and new-
broken rock. There was just enough foliage left on the
mountains that they looked like matronly women who had
been stripped and violated, and now were clutching to
themselves the vestiges of their finery. Down in the valley,
some few living people were picking their way through the
last shreds of dust fog, across the jumble of rubble and
rocks and tree limbs and upended tree roots. They had apparently espied us, gathered at this clear end of the valley,
and decided this was the place to regroup.

They kept plodding and hobbling up to us during the
rest of that day, singly and in little groups. Most of them,
as I have said, were Bho and Yi survivors of the devastation—with no idea how they had lived through it—some injured or crippled, but some entirely unscathed. Most of the
Yi, even the unhurt ones, had lost all will to fight, and approached us with the resignation of prisoners of war. Some
of them might have come running and frothing and swinging steel, as two of them already had done, but they came
in custody of Mongol warriors who had disarmed them on
the way. The Mongols were the volunteers who had accompanied the mock army as musicians and rear guards. Since
they had been at the leading and trailing ends of the
march, hence at the farther ends of the camp, and had had
foreknowledge of our plans, they had had the best chance
to run out of the way of the avalanches. Though they were
only a score of two in number, those men were loud with
congratulations on the success of our stratagem, and with
self-congratulation on their own escape from it.

Even more to be congratulated—and I made sure to give
each of them a comradely embrace—were the Mongol engineers. They were the last survivors to join us, for they had
to come all the way down the ravaged mountain slopes.
They arrived looking justifiably proud of what they had
done, but looking also rather stunned, some of them because they had been standing close to the concussion when
their engines ignited, but some because of the sheer awesomeness of what had then occurred. But I told every one

of them, and sincerely, "I could not have done the positioning better myself!" and took his name, to praise him personally to the Khakhan. I must remark, though, that I collected only eleven names. Twelve men had gone up into the mountains, and twelve balls had done what they were supposed to do, but we never learned what happened to the man who did not return.

It was the middle of the night when Captain Toba returned, in company with the leading columns of the authentic Mongol army, but I was still awake at that hour and glad to see them. Some of the blood with which I was caked was my own, and some of it was still flowing, for I had not emerged entirely undamaged from my private contest with the Yi. That warrior had given me some cuts on the hands and forearms, which I had hardly noticed at the time, but by now were quite painful. The first thing the army troops did was to erect a small yurtu for a hospital tent, and Bayan made sure that I was the first casualty attended by the shamàn physician-priest-sorcerers.

They cleaned my cuts and anointed them with vegetable salves and bandaged them, which would have sufficed me. But then they had to engage in some sorcery to divine whether I might have sustained internal injuries not visible. The chief shamàn set upright before me a knotted bunch of dried herbs that he called the chutgur, or "demon of fevers," and read aloud to it from a book of incantations, while all the lesser physicians made an infernal noise with little bells and drums and sheep's-horn trumpets. Then the head shamàn tossed a sheep's shoulder bone onto the brazier burning in the middle of the tent and, when it had charred black, raked it out and peered at it to read the cracks the heat had produced. He finally adjudged me to be internally intact, which I could have told him with a lot less fuss, and let me leave the hospital. The next casualty brought in was the Wang Ukuruji, to be sewn back together and made presentable for his funeral the next day.

Outside the yurtu, the darkness of the night had been considerably abolished by the light of many tremendous camp fires. Around them, the troops were doing their stamping, leaping, pounding victory dances, and yelling "Ha!" and "Hui!" and liberally sloshing all onlookers with arkhi and kumis from the cups they held while they danced. They were all rapidly getting quite drunk.

I found Bayan and a couple of the just-arrived sardars, still fairly sober, waiting to present me with a gift. On the army's march south from Ba-Tang, they told me, its advance scouts had routinely swept every town and village and isolated building, to rout out any suspicious persons who might be Yi soldiers passing as civilians to get behind the Mongol lines as spies or agents of random destruction. And, in a rundown karwansarai on a back road, they had found a man who could not give a satisfactory account of himself. They produced him for me, with the air of giving me a great prize, but he looked no such thing. He was just another dirty, smelly Bho trapa with his head shaven and his face clotted with that medicinal brown plant-sap.

"No, a Bho he is not," said one of the sardars. "A question was put to him which contained the name of the city Yun-nan-fu, in such a way that he had to repeat the name in his reply. And he said *fu,* not Yun-nan-pu. Further, he claims his own name to be Gom-bo, but he was carrying in his loincloth this signature yin."

The sardar handed the stone seal to me, and I duly examined it, but it could equally well have said Gom-bo or Marco Polo, as far as I could tell. I asked what it did say.

"Pao," said the sardar. "Pao Nei-ho."

"Ah, the Minister of Lesser Races." Now that I knew who he was, I could recognize him despite the disguise. "I remember once before, Minister Pao, you had trouble speaking out plain and clear."

He only shrugged and did not speak at all.

I said to the sardar, "The Khan Kubilai commanded that, if this man was found, I was to slay him. Will you have someone see to that for me? I have already done enough killing for one day. I will keep this yin to show to the Khakhan as evidence that his order was obeyed." The sardar saluted, and began to lead the prisoner away. "One moment," I said, and again addressed Pao. "Speaking of speaking—did you ever have occasion to whisper words, 'Expect me when you least expect me'?"

He denied it, as he probably would have done in any case, but this expression of genuine surprise and baffle-

ment convinced me that he had not been the whisperer in
the Echo Pavilion. Very well, one after another, I was diminishing my list of suspects: the servant girl Buyantu,
now this Minister Pao. . . .

But the next day I found that Pao was still alive. The
whole bok woke late, and most of its people with aching
heads, but all of them immediately set to preparing for
Ukuruji's sepulture. Only the shamàns seemed to be taking no part in the preparations, now that they had readied
the funeral's centerpiece. They sat apart, in a group, with
the condemned Minister Pao among them, and they appeared to be solicitously feeding him his breakfast meal. I
went in search of the Orlok Bayan, and asked in annoyance why Pao had not been slain.

"He is being slain," said Bayan. "And in a particularly
nasty way. He will be dead by the time the tomb is dug."

Still somewhat testily, I inquired, "What is so nasty
about letting him *eat* himself to death?"

"The shamàns are not feeding him, Polo. They are
spooning quicksilver into him."

"Quicksilver?"

"It kills with cruelly agonizing cramps, but it is also a
most efficacious embalming agent. When he is dead, he
will keep. And he will retain the color and freshness of life.
Go look at the Wang's corpse, which the shamàns also
filled with quicksilver. Ukuruji looks as healthy and rosy
as any bouncing babe, and will look so throughout eternity."

"If you say so, Orlok. But why accord the same funerary
rites to the treacherous Pao?"

"A Wang must go to his grave attended by servants for
the afterlife. We will also be killing and entombing with
him all the Yi who emerged from this disaster yesterday—
and a couple of Bho women survivors, too, for his afterlife
enjoyment. They may get handsomer in the afterlife; one
never knows. But we are giving special attention to Pao.
What better servant could Ukuruji take into death than a
former Minister of the Khanate?"

When the shamàns adjudged the hour to be auspicious, the troops did a lot of marching about the cata-
falque on which Ukuruji lay, some afoot and others on

horseback, with commendable dash and precision, and with much martial music and doleful chanting, and the shamàns lit many fires making colored smokes, and wailed their foolish incantations. Those performances were all recognizably funerary of aspect, but some other details of the ceremony had to be explained to me. The troops had dug for Ukuruji a cave in the ground, right at the edge of the avalanche rubble. Bayan told me the position was chosen so it would be unnoticeable to any potential grave robbers.

"We will eventually erect a properly grandoise monument over it. But while we are still occupied with the war, some Yi might sneak back into this valley. If they cannot find the Wang's resting place, they cannot loot his belongings or mutilate his corpse or desecrate the tomb by making water and excrement in it."

Ukuruji's body was reverentially laid in the grave, and about it were laid the fresher cadavers of the newly slaughtered Yi prisoners and the two unfortunate Bho females, and close beside Ukuruji was laid the body of the Minister of Lesser Races. Pao had so contorted himself in his death agonies that the proceedings had to be briefly delayed while the shamàns broke numerous of his bones to straighten him out decently. Then the burial detail of troops set up a wooden rack between the bodies and the cave entrance, and began to affix to it some bows and arrows. Bayan explained that for me:

"It is an invention of Kubilai's Court Goldsmith Boucher. We military men do not always scorn inventors. Regard—the arrows are strung so they aim at the entrance, and the bows are hard bent, and that rack holds them so, but on a sensitive arrangement of levers. If grave robbers ever should find the place and dig into it, their opening the tomb will trip those levers, and they will be met by a killing barrage of arrows."

The gravediggers closed the entrance with earth and rocks so deliberately untidy that the tomb was indistinguishable from the nearby rubble, at which I inquired:

"If you take such pains to make the tomb undiscoverable, how will *you* find it when the time comes to build the monument?"

Bayan merely glanced to one side, and I looked over there. Some troopers had brought one of their herd mares on a lead rein, closely accompanied by her nursling foal. Some of the men held to the lead rein while the others dragged the little infant horse away from its mother and over to the grave site. The mare began to plunge and whinny and rear, and did so even more frantically when the men holding the foal raised a battle-ax and brained it. The mare was led kicking and neighing away, while the buriers scraped earth over the new body, and Bayan said:

"There. When we come this way again, even if it is two or three or five years hence, we have only to let the same mare loose and she will lead us to this spot." He paused, and champed his great teeth thoughtfully, and said, "Now, Polo, although you deserve much credit for the victory here, you did it so thoroughly that there is no plunder for you to share in, and I think that deplorable. However, if you care to continue riding with us, we shall next assail the city of Yun-nan-fu, and I promise that you will be among the high officers who are let to take first choice of the loot. Yun-nan-fu is a large city, and respectably rich, I am told, and the Yi women are not at all repulsive. What say you?"

"It is a generous offer, Orlok, and a tempting one, and I am honored by your kind regard. But I think I had best resist the temptation, and hurry back to tell the Khakhan all the news, good and bad, of what has occurred here. By your leave, I shall depart tomorrow, when you march on southward."

"I thought as much. I took you to be a dutiful man. So I have already dictated to a yeoman scribe a letter for you to carry to Kubilai. It is properly sealed for his eyes only, but I make no secret of its highly praising you and suggesting that you deserve more praise than only mine. I will go now to detach two advance riders to leave immediately and start making ready your route for you. And when you depart tomorrow, I will provide two escorts and the best horses."

So that was all I got to see of Yun-nan, and that was my only experience of war on land, and I took no plunder, and I had no chance to form any opinion of Yi women. But those who had observed my brief military career—the survivors of it, anyway—seemed to agree that I had acquitted myself well. And I had ridden with the Mongol Horde, which was something to tell my grandchildren, if I ever had any. So I turned again for Khanbalik, feeling quite the seasoned old campaigner.

XAN-DU

1

It was again a long ride, and again my escorts and I rode hard. But, when we were yet some two hundred li southwest of Khanbalik, we found our advance riders waiting at a crossroads to intercept us. They had already been to Khanbalik, and had ridden back along the route to inform us that the Khan Kubilai was not presently in residence there. He was out enjoying the hunting season, meaning that he was staying at his country palace of Xan-du, to which the riders would lead us instead. Waiting with them was another man, and he was so richly attired, in Arab-style garments, that at first I mistook him for some gray-bearded Muslim courtier unknown to me. He waited for the riders to give me their message, and then addressed me exuberantly:

"Former Master Marco! It is I!"

"Nostril!" I exclaimed, surprised that I was glad to see him. "I mean Ali Babar. It is good to see you! But what do you out here, so far from city comforts?"

"I came to meet you, former master. When these men brought word of your imminent return, I joined them. I have been given a missive to deliver to you, and it seemed a good excuse to take a holiday from toil and care. Also, I thought you might have some use for the services of your former slave."

"That was thoughtful of you. But come, we will make holiday together."

The Mongols led the way, the two advance riders and my two escorts, and Ali and I rode side by side behind them.

We turned more northerly than we had been traveling, because Xan-du is up in the Dama-qing Mountains, a considerable distance directly north of Khanbalik. Ali groped about under his embroidered aba and brought out a paper, folded and sealed, with my name written on the outside in Roman letters and also in the Arabic and Mongol letters and in the Han character.

"Someone wanted to make sure I got it," I muttered. "From whom did it come?"

"I know not, former master."

"We are equally freemen now, Ali. You may call me Marco."

"As you will, Marco. The lady who gave me that paper was heavily veiled, and she accosted me in private and in the nighttime. Since she spoke no word, neither did I, taking her probably to be—ahem—some secret friend of yours, and maybe the wife of some other. I am far more discreet and less inquisitive than perhaps I used to be."

"You have the same perfervid imagination, however. I was conducting no such intrigue at court. But thank you, anyway." I tucked the paper away to read that night. "But now, what of you, old companion? How fine you do look!"

"Yes," he said, preening. "My good wife Mar-Janah insists that I dress and comport myself now like the affluent proprietor and employer I have become."

"Indeed? Proprietor of what? Employer of whom?"

"Do you remember, Marco, the city called Kashan in Persia?"

"Ah, yes. The city of beautiful boys. But surely Mar-Janah has not let you open a male brothel!"

He sighed and looked pained. "Kashan is also famous for its distinctive kashi tiles, you may recall."

"I do. I remember that my father took an interest in the process of their manufacture."

"Just so. He thought there might be a market here in Kithai for such a product. And he was right. He and your Uncle Mafìo put up the capital for the establishment of a workshop, and helped teach the art of kashi-making to a number of artificers, and put the whole enterprise in the charge of Mar-Janah and myself. She designs the patterns for the kashi and supervises the workshop, and I do the peddling of the product. We have done very well, if I may say so. The kashi tiles are much in demand as an adorn-

ment for rich men's houses. Even after paying the share of
the profits owed to your father and uncle, Mar-Janah and I
have become eminently affluent. We are all still learning
our trade—she and I and our artificers—but earning while
we do so. Prospering to such an extent that I could well afford to take some time off to do this bit of journeying with
you."

He chattered on for the rest of the day, telling me every
last detail of the business of making and selling tiles—not
all of which I found compellingly interesting—and occasionally imparting other news of Khanbalik. He and the
beautiful Mar-Janah were blissfully happy. He had not
seen my father in some time, the elder Polo being also
out traveling on some mercantile venture, but he had
glimpsed my uncle about the city, now and then of late.
The beautiful Mar-Janah was more beautiful than ever.
The Wali Achmad was holding the Vice-Regency and the
reins of government in the Khan's absence. The beautiful
Mar-Janah was still as loving of Ali Babar as he of her.
Many courtiers had accompanied Kubilai to Xan-du for
the autumn hunting, including several of my acquaintances: the Wang Chingkim, the Firemaster Shi and the
Goldsmith Boucher. The beautiful Mar-Janah agreed with
Ali that the time they had so far spent in wedlock had
been, though coming late in life, the best time of both their
lives, and worth having waited all their lives to attain. . . .

We put up that night at a comfortable Han karwansarai
in the shadow of the Great Wall, and when I had bathed
and dined, I sat down in my room to open the missive Ali
had brought me. It did not take me long to read it—though
I had to spell it out letter by letter, being still not very accomplished at the Mongol alphabet—for it consisted of only
a single line, translating as: "Expect me when you least
expect me." The words had lost none of their chill, but I
was getting rather more weary of their refrain than apprehensive of their threat. I went to Ali's room and demanded:

"The woman who gave you this for me. Surely you would
have recognized her, even veiled, if she had been the Lady
Chao Ku-an. . . ."

"Yes, and she was not. Which reminds me: the Lady
Chao is dead. I only heard of it myself a day or two ago,
from a courier riding the horsepost route. It happened

since I left Khanbalik. An unfortunate accident. According to the courier, it is believed that the lady must have been chasing from her chambers some lover who had displeased her, and in running after him—you know she had the lotus feet—she tripped on the staircase and fell headlong."

"I regret to hear it," I said, though I really did not. One more off my list of suspect whisperers. "But about the letter, Ali. Was the lady who brought it perhaps a very *large* lady?" I was remembering the extraordinary female I had briefly seen in the chambers of the Vice-Regent Achmad.

Ali thought about it, and said, "She may have been taller than I am, but most people are. No, I would not say she was notably large."

"You said she did not speak. It suggests that you would have known her by her voice, does it not?"

He shrugged. "How do I answer that? Since she did not, I did not. Does the letter contain bad news, Marco, or some other cause for despondency?"

"I could better decide that if I knew where it came from."

"All I can tell you is that your advance riders arrived in the city on a day some days ago, heralding your imminent return, and—"

"Wait. Did they announce anything else?"

"Not really. When people asked how went the war in Yun-nan the two would say nothing—except that *you* were bringing the official word—but their swaggering implied that the word would be of some Mongol victory. Anyway, it was in the night of that day that the veiled lady came to me with that missive for you. So, with Mar-Janah's blessing, when the two men left again the next morning to ride back to you, I rode with them."

He could add nothing more, and I truly could not think of any females who might be nursing a grudge against me, what with the Lady Chao and the twins Buyantu and Biliktu all dead. If the veiled woman had been someone else's agent, I had no idea whose. So I said no more about the matter, and tore up the vexing letter, and we continued on our journey, reaching Xan-du without anything dreadful happening to us, of either unexpected or expectable nature.

Xan-du was just one of four or five subsidiary palaces

that the Khakhan maintained in places outside Khanbalik, but it was the most sumptuous of those. In the Da-ma-
qing Mountains, he had had an extensive hunting park
laid out, and stocked with all manner of game, and staffed
with expert huntsmen and gamekeepers and beaters, who
lived there the year around, in villages on the park's outskirts. In the center of the park stood a marble palace of
goodly size, containing the usual halls for gathering and
dining and entertaining and holding court, plus ample
quarters for any number of the royal family and their
courtiers and guests, and for all the numerous servants
and slaves they would require, and for all the musicians
and mountebanks brought along to enliven the nighttime
hours. Every room, down to the smallest bedchamber, was
decorated with wall paintings done by the Master Chao
and other court artists, depicting scenes of the chase and
the course and the hunt, and all marvelously done. Outside the main palace building were grand stables for the
mounts and the pack animals—elephants as well as horses
and mules—and mews for the Khan's hawks and falcons,
and kennels for his dogs and chita cats, and all those buildings were as finely built and adorned and as spotlessly
clean as the palace itself.

The Khakhan had also at Xan-du a sort of portable palace. It was like a tremendous yurtu pavilion, only so *very*
tremendous that it could not have been constructed of
cloth or felt. It was mostly made of the zhu-gan cane and
palm leaves, and was supported on wooden columns carved
and painted and gilded to seem dragons, and was held together by an ingenious webbing of silk ropes. Although of
great size, it could be taken apart and carried about and
put up again as easily as a yurtu. So it was continually
being moved about the Xan-du parkland and the surrounding countryside—a train of elephants was reserved for the
task of transporting its components—to wherever the
Khakhan and his company chose to hunt on any day.

Every time Kubilai went out to hunt, he did it in consummate style. He and his guests would depart from the
marble palace in a numerous and colorful and glittering
train. Sometimes the Khan rode on one of his "dragon
steeds"—the milk-white horses specially bred for him in
Persia—and sometimes in the little house called a hauda,
rocking atop an elephant's high shoulders, and at other

times in a lavishly ornamented, two-wheeled chariot, drawn by either horses or elephants. When he went on horseback, he always carried one of the sleek chita cats draped elegantly across the horse's withers in front of his saddle, and would loose it whenever some small animal started up in his path. The chita could run down anything that moves, and would always dutifully fetch its catch back to the train, but, since a chita always mangled its prey considerably, a huntsman would toss that game into a separate bag and later mince it for feed for the birds in the palace mews. When Kubilai rode out in a hauda or his chariot, he always had two or more of his milk-white gerfalcons perched on its rim and would start them at sight of small game running or flying.

Behind the Khakhan's chariot or steed or elephant would come the train of his company, all lords and ladies and distinguished guests mounted only a little less royally than the Khan himself, and all—depending on the game to be sought that day—carrying hooded hawks on their gauntleted wrists, or accompanied by servants carrying their lances or bows or leading on leash their chase dogs. Out ahead of the train, earlier in the day, would have gone the many beaters, to form up in three sides of a vast square and, at the proper time, to start flushing the game—stags or boars or otters or whatever—out the fourth side of the square, toward the approaching hunters.

Whenever Kubilai's train passed through or by one of the villages situated around his parkland, all the families of women and children living there would run outdoors to cry "Hail!" They also kept welcome fires always burning, in case the Khan should come that way, and would cast into the flames spices and incense to perfume the air as the Khakhan went by. At midday, the hunting party would repair to the zhu-gan palace, always set up at a convenient place, for food and drink and soft music and a brief nap before going afield again in the afternoon. And when the day's hunt was done, depending on how tired they all might be, or how far from the main palace, they would either return there or stop the night in the zhu-gan palace, for it had copious room and comfortable bedding.

I and Ali and our four Mongols reached Xan-du in the middle of a morning, and were told by a steward where to find the Khakhan's portable palace, and arrived there at midday, when the whole party was lolling over its meal. Several people recognized me and hailed me, including Kubilai. I introduced Ali Babar to him as "a citizen of Khanbalik, Sire, one of your rich merchant princes," and Kubilai received him cordially, not having noticed Ali in my company in the days when he had been the lowly slave Nostril. Then I started to say, "I bring from Yun-nan both good and bad news, Sire—" but he held up his hand to stop me.

"Nothing," he said firmly. "Nothing is important enough to interrupt a good hunt. Hold your news until we return to the Xan-du palace this evening. Now, are you hungry?" He clapped for a servant to bring food. "Are you fatigued? Would you rather precede us to the palace and rest while you wait, or would you take a lance with us? We have been starting some admirably big and vicious boar hogs."

"Why, thank you, Sire. I should like to join the hunt. But I have little experience with a lance. Can boar be killed with bow and arrow?"

"Anything can be killed with anything, including bare hands. And those you may have to use, to finish a boar." He turned and called, "Hui! Mahawat, make ready an elephant for Marco Polo!"

It was my first ride aboard an elephant, and it was most pleasant, infinitely more so than riding a camel, and very different from riding a horse. The hauda was made like a basket, woven zhu-gan strips, with a little bench on which I sat beside the elephant driver, who is properly called a mahawat. The hauda had high sides to protect us from flicking tree branches, and a roof canopy over us, but was open in the front, so the mahawat could direct the elephant by prodding it with a stick, and so I could let fly my arrows. At first I was a little dizzied by my great height above the ground, but I soon got used to that. And when the animal first stepped out on the march through the park, I did not immediately realize that it was walking rather faster than a horse or camel does. Also, when it came time to chase a fleeing boar, it took me a while to realize that the elephant, for all its immense bulk, was running as fast as a galloping horse.

The mahawat took great pride in his great charges, and bragged about them, and I found his bragging informative.

Only cow elephants, he told me, were used as working beasts. The bulls being not very amenable to training, only a few of those were kept in any domestic herd, as company for the cows. The elephants all wore bells, big chunky things carved of wood, that sounded with a hollow thunking noise instead of a jangle. The mahawat said that if I ever heard a clanging metal bell, I had better move in a hurry, because metal bells were hung only on elephants that had misbehaved and so could not any longer be trusted—in other words, those elephants most resembling people: usually a cow maddened, like any human mother, by the loss of a calf, or a bull gone grumpy and mean and irascible with age, like any old man.

An elephant, said the mahawat, was more intelligent than a dog, and more obedient than a horse, and more adept with its trunk and tusks than a monkey with its paws, and could be taught to do many things both useful and entertaining. In the timber forests, two elephants could work a saw between them to cut down a tree, then pick up and stack the giant logs or drag them to a log road, with the attendance of only a single human logger to select the trees to be cut. As a beast of burden, the elephant was incomparable to any others—being able to carry as much of a load as three strong oxen, and carry it for a distance of thirty to forty li in an ordinary working day, or more than fifty li in an emergency. The elephant was not at all shy of water, as a camel is, for it is a good swimmer, and a camel cannot swim at all.

I do not know if an elephant could have negotiated a precarious trail like the Pillar Road, but than animal carried us swiftly and surely across a variety of Da-ma-qing terrain. Since my elephant was just one in a line of them, the Khan's and several others ahead of me, my mahawat did not have to do much directing. But when he wished the elephant to turn, he merely had to touch one or the other of the door-sized ears. When we were traveling among trees, the animal would, unbidden, use its trunk to move aside any impeding limbs, and the more whippy branches it would even break off to ensure that they did not swipe back at us riders. It went sometimes between trees that looked too close together to allow passage, and did that so sinuously and smoothly as not to scrape the belts that held our hauda on its shoulders. When we came to the wet clay bank of a small stream, the elephant, almost as playfully as a child, put its four tree-trunk feet close together and *slid* down the slope to the water's edge. At that place, the river was laid with stepping-stones for crossing. Before venturing out onto them, the elephant first gently tested its weight on one, and sounded with its trunk the depth of the water roundabout. Then, seeming satisfied, it stepped out onto the stones and from one to the next, never hesitating, but treading as delicately and precisely as a fat man who has drunk a drop too much.

If the elephant has one unlovely trait, it is one that is common to all creatures, but is amplified to a prodigious degree by the animal's size. That is to say that the elephant I rode frequently had appallingly broke wind. Other animals do that—camels, horses, even human beings, God knows—but no other animal in God's Creation can do it so thunderously and odoriferously as an elephant, which produces a noxious miasma almost as visible as it is audible. With heroic effort, I pretended not to notice those lapses of manners. But I did make some small complaint of another trait: the elephant several times coiled its trunk back over its head and *sneezed* in my face—so windily as to rock me on my seat, and so wetly that I was soon damp all over. When I voiced my vexation at the sneezing, the mahawat said loftily:

"Elephants do not sneeze. The cow is just blowing your aroma away from her."

"Gèsu," I muttered. *"My* aroma is bothering *her?"*

"It is only that you are a stranger, and she is unaccustomed to you. When she gets to know you, she will put up with your smell and will moderate her behavior."

"I rejoice to hear it."

So we rollicked along, rhythmically swaying in the high hauda, and the mahawat told me other things. Down in the jungles of Champa, he said, where the elephants came from, there were such things as white elephants.

"Not *really* white, of course, like the Khakhan's snow-white horses and hawks. But a paler gray than ordinary. And because they are rare, like albinos among humans, they are held to be sacred. They are often employed for revenge against an enemy."

"Sacred," I repeated, "but instruments of revenge? I do not understand."

He explained. When a white elephant was caught, it was always presented to the local king, because only a king could afford to keep one. Being sacred, the elephant could never be put to labor, but had to be pampered with a fine stable and dedicated attendants and a princely diet, and its only function was to march in religious processions, when it had to be festooned with gold-threaded blankets and jeweled chains and baubles and such. That was a burdensome expense even for a king. However, said the mahawat, suppose a king got displeased with some one of his lords, or feared his rivalry, or simply took a dislike to him. . . .

"In the old days," he said, "a king would have sent him poisoned sweetmeats, so that the recipient would die when he ate them—or a beautiful slave girl poisoned in her pink places, so that the noble would die after he lay with her. But those stratagems are now too well-known. So the king nowadays simply sends the noble a white elephant. He cannot refuse a sacred gift. He can make no profit from it. But he has the ruinous expense of maintaining it in proper style, so he is soon bankrupted and broken—if he waits to be. Most commit suicide on first receiving the white elephant."

I refused to believe such a story, and accused the mahawat of inventing it. But then he told me something else unbelievable—that he could calculate for me the exact height of any elephant without even seeing it—and when at the close of the day we got down from ours, he demonstrated that ability, and even I could do it. So, being forced to believe him about that, I ceased scoffing at his white elephant story. Anyway, the measurement is done thus. You simply find an elephant's track and pick out the print of one of its forefeet and measure the circumference of that. Everyone knows that a perfectly proportioned woman has a waist exactly twice the circumference of her neck, and her neck twice that of her wrist. Just so, the elephant's height at the shoulder is exactly twice the circumference of its forefoot.

When he heard the beaters hooting and thrashing up ahead of us, I nocked an arrow to my bowstring. And when a spiny black shape shouldered its way through a thicket and snorted at us, and clashed its yellow tusks as if it would challenge those of my elephant, I let fly the arrow. I

hit the boar; I could hear the *thwock* and see the puff of
dust go up from the coarse-haired hide. I believe he would
have gone down on the instant if I had chosen one of the
heavy, broad-headed arrows. But I had expected it to be a
long shot, and it had been, so I had used one of the narrow-
headed, long-range arrows. It pierced the boar clean and
deep, but only made him turn and run.

Without waiting for the goad, my elephant ran after
him, following as closely on his jinks and curvettings as a
trained boar-hound, while I and the mahawat bounced
about in the jouncing hauda. It was impossible for me to
nock another arrow, let alone shoot it and hope to hit anything. But the wounded boar soon realized that it was
fleeing into the line of beaters. It skidded awkwardly to a
stop in a dry creek bed, and turned at bay, and lowered its
long head, its red eyes blinking angrily above and behind
the four upcurved tusks. My elephant also slid to a halt,
which must have made a humorous sight to see, if I had
been elsewhere looking on. But the mahawat and I were
pitched out of the hauda's open front to sprawl atop the elephant's great head, and would have gone on falling, if we
had not been clutching at each other and the beast's big
ears and the straps holding the hauda and anything else in
reach.

When the elephant again curled her trunk backward
over her head, I confusedly wished she had thought of
something better to do than sneeze—but it turned out that
she had. She curled the trunk around my waist and, as if I
had been no weightier than a dry leaf, lifted me off her
head, twirled me in midair and set me down on my feet—
between her and the enraged, pawing, snorting boar. I did
not know whether the elephant maliciously intended that
I, the new-smelling stranger, should suffer the brunt of the
boar's charge, or whether she was trained to do that in order to give a hunter a second shot at the quarry. But if she
thought she was being helpful, she was mistaken, for she
had put me down without my bow and arrows, still up in
the hauda. I could have turned to see whether the little
eyes among her wrinkles were bright with mischief or solemn with concern—elephants' eyes are as expressive as
women's—but I dared not turn my back to the wounded
boar.

From where I now stood, it looked bigger than a barnyard brood sow, and inexpressibly more savage. It stood with its black snout close to the ground, above it the four wicked tusks curling up and out, above them the blazing red eyes, the tufty ears twitching and, behind them, the powerful black shoulders hunching for a lunge. I threw my hand to my belt knife, yanked it out and in front of me, and flung myself headlong toward the boar in the same moment that it charged. Had I waited a breath longer, I should have moved too late. I fell atop the boar's long snout and high-humped back, but the beast did not jerk its tusks upward into my groin, for it died too quickly. My knife went through the hide and deep into flesh, and I squeezed its handle in the instant of thrust, so that I struck with all three blades at once. The boar's dying plunge carried me with it for some way, then its legs crumpled and we came down in a heap.

I scrambled up quickly, fearful that the animal might still have one last convulsion left in it. When it only lay still and bled, I plucked out my knife and then the arrow, and wiped them clean on the quill-like black hairs. Closing the trusty squeeze-knife and putting it back into its sheath, I mentally sent another thank-you into the far away and long ago. Then I turned and gave a not-so-thankful look at the elephant and the mahawat. He sat up there gawking with awe and perhaps some admiration. But the elephant only stood rocking gently from foot to foot, her eye regarding me with self-complacent feminine composure, as if to say, "There. You did it just as I expected you to," which no doubt was the offhand remark made by the liberated princess to San Zorzi after he slew her dragon captor.

2

BACK at the Xan-du palace, Kubilai took me walking with him in the gardens while we waited for the cooks to prepare a dinner of the boars—my own trophy and the several others brought in by other hunters of the party (who have speared theirs from the more usual and safer distances). The afternoon was waning into twilight as the Khakhan and I stood on an inverted bridge and looked out over an artificial lake of some size. That lake was fed by a small waterfall, and the bridge was built in front of it, not arching over it, but in the form of a letter U, with stairs going down from one bank and upward to the other, so that at the middle of the bridge one stood at the foaming foot of the little cascade.

I admired it for a time, then turned to look at the lake, while Kubilai perused the letter from the Orlok Bayan, which I had given him to read before the light was gone. It was a lovely and peaceful autumn evening. There were flaming sunset clouds high in the sky above the lake, and then a patch of clear ice-blue sky between them and the black serration of the farther lakeside's treetops, which looked as flat as if they had been cut from black paper and pasted there. The mirror-smooth lake reflected only the black trees and the clear blue of the lower sky, except where a few ornamental ducks were leisurely paddling across it. They rumpled the water behind them just enough that it reflected there the high sunset clouds, so each duck was trailing a long wedge of warm flame across the ice-blue surface.

"So Ukuruji is dead," sighed Kubilai, folding the paper. "But a great victory has been accomplished, and all of Yun-nan will soon capitulate." (Neither the Khan nor I could have known it at that moment, but the Yi had by then already laid down their arms, and another messenger was riding hard from Yun-nan-fu to bring the news.) "Bayan says that you can tell me the details, Marco. Did my son die well?"

I told him all the how and where and when of it—our employment of the Bho as an expendable mock army, the laudable efficacy of the brass balls, the dwindling of the battle into two final skirmishes, man against man, one of which I had survived, the other which Ukuruji had not, and I concluded with the capture and execution of the treacherous Pao Nei-ho. I had meant to show Kubilai the yin seal of the Minister Pao, but I realized as I spoke that I had left it in my saddlebags, which were now in my palace chamber, so I did not mention it, and of course the Khakhan demanded no such proof.

I added, perhaps a little wistfully, "I must apologize,

Sire, that I neglected to follow the noble precepts of your grandfather Chinghiz."

"Uu?"

"I left Yun-nan at once, Sire, to bring you the news. So I took no opportunity to ravish any chaste Yi wives or virgin Yi daughters."

He chuckled and said, "Ah, well. Too bad you had to forgo the handsome Yi women. But when we have taken the Sung Empire, perhaps you will have occasion to travel to the Fu-kien Province there. The females of the Min people of Fu-kien are so gloriously beautiful, it is said, that parents will not send a daughter out of the house even to fetch water or cut firewood, for fear that she will be abducted by slave hunters or the emperor's concubine collectors."

"I shall look forward to my first meeting with a Min girl, then."

"Meanwhile, it appears that your prowess in other aspects of warfare would have pleased the warrior Khan Chinghiz." He indicated the letter. "Bayan here gives you much of the credit for the Yun-nan victory. You evidently impressed him. He even makes the brash suggestion that I might console myself for the loss of Ukuruji by making you an honorary son of mine."

"I am flattered, Sire. But please to reflect that the Orlok wrote that while he was flushed with triumphal enthusiasm. I am sure he meant no disrespect."

"And I still have a sufficiency of sons," said the Khan, as if he were reminding himself, not me. "On the son Chingkim, of course, I long ago settled the mantle of heir apparent. Also—you would not yet have heard this, Marco—Chingkim's young wife Kukachin has recently been delivered of a son, my premier grandson, so the continued succession of our line is assured. They have named him Temur." He went on, as if he had forgotten my presence, "Ukuruji most earnestly desired to become Wang of Yun-nan. A pity he died. He would have been a capable viceroy for a newly conquered province. I think now . . . I will award that Wangdom to his half-brother Hukoji . . ." Then he turned abruptly to me again. "Bayan's suggestion that I insinuate a Ferenghi into the Mongol royal dynasty is unthinkable. However, I agree with him that such good blood as yours should not be ignored. It might profitably be infused into the lesser Mongol nobility. There is precedent, after all. My late brother, the Ilkhan Hulagu of Persia, during his conquest of that empire, was so impressed by the valor of the foemen of Hormuz that he put them to stud with all his camp-following females, and I believe that the get was worthwhile."

"Yes, I heard that bit of history, Sire, while I was in Persia."

"Well, then. You have no wife, I know that. Are you bound or vowed to any other woman or women at present?"

"Why . . . no, Sire," I said, suddenly apprehensive that he was thinking of marrying me off to some spinster Mongol lady or minor princess of his choosing. I was not yearning to be married, and certainly not to una gata nel saco.

"And if you neglected to take advantage of the Yi women, you must by now be aching for an outlet for your ardors."

"Well . . . yes, Sire. But I can myself seek—"

He waved me to silence and nodded decisively. "Very well. Shortly before I brought the court from Khanbalik, there arrived this year's accumulation of presentation maidens. I brought here to Xan-du some two score of them whom I have not yet covered. Among them are about a dozen choice Mongol girls. They may not be up to the Min standard of beauty, but they are all of twenty-four-karat quality, as you will see. I will send them to your chambers, one a night, first bidding them not to employ any fern seed, that they may readily be impregnated. You will do me and the Mongol Khanate the favor of servicing them."

"A dozen, Sire?" I said, with some incredulity.

"Surely you do not demur. The last command I gave you was that you go to war. A command to go to bed—with a succession of prime Mongol virgins—is rather more eagerly to be obeyed, is it not?"

"Oh, assuredly, Sire."

"Be it done, then. And I shall expect a good crop of healthy Mongol-Ferenghi hybrids. Now, Marco, let us wend our way back to the palace. Chingkim must be apprised of his half-brother's death so that, as Wang of Khanbalik, he can order his city draped in purple mourning. Meanwhile, the Firemaster and the Goldsmith are in a fever to hear exactly how you utilized their brass-ball invention. Come."

The dining hall of the Xan-du palace was an imposing chamber, hung with painted scrolls and stuffed animal-head trophies of the hunt, but dominated by a sculpture of fine green jade. It was a single, solid piece of jade that must have weighed five tons, and God knows what it was worth in gold or flying money. It was carved into the semblance of a mountain very like those I had helped destroy in Yun-nan—complete with cliffs and crags and forests of trees and winding steep paths like the Pillar Road, being toilsomely climbed by little carved peasants and porters and horse carts.

The boar meat made a tasty meal, and I ate it sitting at the high table with the Khan, the Prince Chingkim, the Goldsmith Boucher and the Firemaster Shi. I tendered Chingkim my condolences on his brother's demise and my congratulations on his son's birth. The other two courtiers alternated between plying me with intense questions about the successful working of the huo-yao balls and fulsomely praising me and each other for having invented a true invention, one that would be imitated throughout the world, and would endure down the ages, changing the whole face of war, and making forever famous the names Shi and Polo and Boucher.

"For shame!" I chided. "You said yourself, Master Shi, that the flaming powder was invented by some unknown Han."

"Peu de chose!" cried Boucher. "It was nothing but a toy until its full potential was realized by a wily Venetian, a renegade Jew and a brilliant young Frenchman!"

"Gan-bei!" cried old Shi. "L'chaim!" as he toasted us all with a goblet of mao-tai, and then downed it in a gulp. Boucher emulated him, but I took only a sip of mine. Let my fellow immortals get drunk; I would not, for I expected later to have need of my faculties.

Some Uighur musicians played during the meal—mercifully softly—and after it we were entertained by jugglers and funambulists and then a company performing a play which, for all its foreignness, I found familiar. A Han storyteller droned and yammered and bellowed the tale, and the conversations occurring in it, while his associates worked the strings of marionettes acting out the various roles. I could not understand a word, but found it perfectly comprehensible, because the Han characters—Aged Cuckold and Comic Physician and Sneering Villain and Bumbling Sage and Lovelorn Maiden and Valiant Hero and so on—were so recognizably similar to those of any Venetian puppet show: our fuddled Pantaleone and inept physician Dotòr Balanzòn and rascal Pulcinella and dim-witted lawyer Dotòr da Nulla and coquette Colombina and dashing Trovatore and so on. But Kubilai seemed not much to enjoy the show, grumbling to us near him, "Why use puppets to portray people? Why not have people portray people?" (And obediently, in after years, all the player companies did exactly that: dispensed with the narrator and the marionettes, and presented human players each speaking his or her own part in the story.)

Most of the court was still loudly making merry when I retired to my chambers. But evidently Kubilai had given his instructions some while earlier, for I had just got into bed and not yet blown out the bedside lamp when there was a scratching at my door and a young woman came in, bearing what looked like a small white chest.

"Sain bina, sain nai," I said politely, but she made no response, and when she came into the lamplight I saw that she was not a Mongol, but a Han or one of the related races.

She was obviously just a maid preparing for the entry of her lady, for now I discerned that the white object she carried was only an incense burner. I hoped that her lady would prove to be as comely and as exquisitely delicate as the servant. She set down the burner near my bed, a lidded porcelain box, shaped like a jewel chest and embossed with intricate raised designs. Then she took up my lamp, shyly smiling a silent request for permission and, when I nodded, used the lamp's flame to set smoldering a stick of incense, lifted the burner's lid and carefully placed the incense inside. I took note that it was the purple tsan-xi-jang, which is the very finest incense, compounded of aromatic herbs, musk and gold dust, to give a room not a heavy, spicy, closed-in smell, but the scent of summer fields. The servant girl sank down to sit meek and silent beside my bed, her eyes discreetly lowered, while the fragrant and calming perfume permeated my room. It did not calm me quite enough; I felt almost as nervous as if I had been

really a bridegroom. So I tried to make small talk with the
maid, but either she was well trained to imperturbability
or was totally ignorant of Mongol, for she never even
raised her eyes. Finally there was another scratching at
the door, and her lady came proudly in. I was pleased to see
that she *was* handsome—exceptionally so, for a Mongol—if
not so tiny and dainty and porcelain-lovely as her servant.

I said again in Mongol, "Good meeting, good woman,"
and this one murmured back, "Sain bina, sain urkek."

"Come! Do not call me brother," I said, with a shaky
laugh.

"It is the accepted salutation."

"Well, at least try not to think of me as a brother."

And she and I continued to make such small talk—very
small talk, indeed, quite inane—as the maid helped her
unpeel and get out of her considerable nuptial finery. I introduced myself, and she responded, in a sort of cascade of
words, that she was called Setsen, and she was of the Mongol tribe called Kerait, and she was a Nestorian Christian,
all the Kerait having been converted, in a bunch, by some
long-ago wandering Nestorian bishop, and she had never
set foot outside her nameless village in the far-northern
fur-trapping country of Tannu-Tuva until she was selected
for concubinage and transported to a trading town called
Urga, where, to her surprise and delight, the provincial
Wang had graded her at twenty-four karats and sent her
on south to Khanbalik. Also, she said, she had never before
laid eyes on a Ferenghi, and excuse her impudence, but
were my hair and beard really naturally pale of color or
had they simply gone gray with age? I told Setsen that I
was not a great deal older than she, and still far from senile, as she ought to have descried from my rising excitement while I watched her disrobe. I would offer further
evidence of my youthful vigor, I promised, as soon as the
maid-servant quitted the room. However, that girl, after
tucking her naked lady in beside me, sank down again beside the bed as if to stay there, and did not even put out the
light. So the subsequent conversation between me and
Setsen got worse than inane, it got ridiculous.

I said, "You may dismiss your servant."

She said, "The lon-gya is not a servant. She is a slave."

"Whatever. You may dismiss her."

"She is commanded to attend my qing-du chu-kai—my defloration."

"I undo the command."

"You cannot, Lord Marco. She is my attendant."

"I do not care, Setsen, if she is your Nestorian bishop. I would prefer that she attend elsewhere."

"I cannot send her away and neither can you. She is here by order of the Court Procurer and the Lady Matron of Concubines."

"I take precedence over matrons and procurers. I am here by order of the Khan of All Khans."

Setsen looked hurt. "I thought you were here because you wanted to be."

"Well, that, too," I said, instantly contrite. "But I did not expect to have an audience to cheer my endeavors."

"She will not cheer. She is a lon-gya. She will not say anything."

"Perdiziòn! I do not care if she sings an inno imeneo, only she must do it somewhere else!"

"What is that?"

"A wedding song. A hymeneal hymn. It celebrates the— well, the breaking of the—that is to say, the defloration."

"But that is exactly what she is here for, Lord Marco!"

"To *sing?*"

"No, no, as a witness. She will depart as soon as you—as soon as she sees the stain on the bedsheet. Then she goes to report to the Lady Matron that all is as it should be. You comprehend?"

"Protocol, yes. Vakh."

I glanced over at the girl, who seemed to be occupied in studying the white convolutions of the incense burner, and paying no least heed to our squabble. I was glad I was not a real bridegroom, or the circumstances would have stopped my living up to my earlier braggery. However, since I was only a sort of surrogate bridegroom and since neither the bride nor the bride's maid found the situation embarrassing, why should I find it inhibiting? So I proceeded to provide the evidence the slave was waiting to get, and Setsen amiably if inexpertly cooperated, and during those exertions, so far as I noticed, the slave paid no more attention than if we had been as inert as her incense burner. But, after some while, Setsen leaned out from the bed and shook the girl by the shoulder, and she got up and helped Setsen untangle the bedclothes, and they found the small red smear. The slave nodded and smiled brightly at us, bent and blew out the lamp and left the room and left us to any nonobligatory consummations we might care to make for ourselves.

Setsen left me at morning, and I joined the Khan and his courtiers for a day of hawking. Even Ali Babar came along, after I had assured him that falconry involved no such risks to the hunter as did the more strenuous veneries, like boar-sticking. We started much game that day, and the sport was good. Since the sharp-eyed falcons could see to wait on and stoop and strike well into the twilight, our whole company stayed out that night in the zhu-gan field palace. We returned to Xan-du the next day, with an abundance of game birds and hares for the kitchen pots, and that night, after a good dinner of venison, I received the second of Kubilai's contributions to the improvement of the Mongol race.

However, she also was preceded by a slave bringing the white porcelain incense burner and, when I saw that it was the *same* pretty slave girl, I tried to convey to her my discomfiture at her having to attend *two* of these nuptial nights. But she only smiled winningly, and either failed or refused to comprehend me. So, when the Mongol maiden finally arrived and introduced herself as Jehol, I said:

"Forgive my unmanly agitation, Jehol, but I find it more than a little disquieting that the same monitor must twice oversee my nighttime doings."

"Do not concern yourself with the lon-gya," said Jehol indifferently. "She is only a slave girl of the lowly Min people of the Fu-kien Province."

"Is she indeed?" I said, interested to hear that. "Of the Min, is she? Nevertheless, I do not care to have my successive performances compared—in their degree or prowess or stupration or efficacy or whatever other aspect."

Jehol only laughed and said, "She will make no comparisons, neither here nor in the concubine quarters. She cannot do any such thing."

By this time, with the slave girl's assistance, Jehol had undressed to an extent that took my mind off other matters. So I said, "Well, if you do not care, I suppose I need not," and the night proceeded as had the other one.

But, when came the night for the next Mongol maiden—

her name was Yesukai—and she was preceded by that same Min slave girl bearing that same incense burner, I once more raised objections. Yesukai only shrugged and said:

"When we were at the palace in Khanbalik, we had a numerous complement of servants and slaves. But when the Lady Matron brought us out here to Xan-du for the season, we came with only a few domestics, and this slave is the only lon-gya among them. If we girls must make do with her, you must get used to her."

"She may be admirably reticent about what goes on in this chamber," I grumbled. "But I have ceased to fret that she may indiscreetly talk. Now I fear that, after many more such nights as this, she will start *laughing.*"

"She cannot laugh," said Cheren, who was the next of the Mongol maidens to visit me. "No more than she can talk or hear. The slave is a lon-gya. You do not know the word? It means a deaf-mute."

"Is that a fact?" I murmured, regarding the slave with more compassion that I had done. "No wonder she has never answered when I railed at her. All this time, I thought lon-gya was her name."

"If she ever had a name, she cannot tell it," said Toghon, who was the next of the Mongol maidens. "In the concubine quarters, we call her Hui-sheng. But that is only our feminine malice, when we make sport of her."

"Hui-sheng," I repeated. "What malice in that? It is a most mellifluous name."

"It is a most unfitting name, for it means Echo," said Devlet, the next of the Mongol maidens. "But no matter. She neither hears it nor answers to it."

"A soundless Echo," I said, and smiled. "An unfitting name, perhaps, but a pleasing paradox. Hui-sheng. Hui-sheng. . . ."

To Ayuka, the seventh or eighth of the Mongol maidens, I said, "Tell me, does your Lady Matron deliberately seek deaf-mute slaves for the duty of overseeing the nuptial nights?"

"She does not seek them. She makes them so from childhood. Incapable either of eavesdropping or of gossiping. They cannot gasp in surprise or disapproval if they see strange sights in the bedchamber, or afterward prattle of

perverse things they have witnessed. If they do ever misbe-
have and must be beaten, they cannot scream."

"Bruto barabào! *Makes* them so? How?"

"Actually, the Lady Matron has a shamàn physician do
the silencing operation," said Merghus, who was the
eighth or ninth of the Mongol maidens. "He puts a red-hot
skewer down each ear and through the neck into the gullet. I cannot tell you exactly what is done, but look at Hui-
sheng—you can see the tiny scar on her throat."

I looked, and it was so. But I saw more than that when I
gazed upon Hui-sheng, for Kubilai had spoken truly when
he said that the girls of the Min were unsurpassably beautiful. At least this one was. Being a slave, she wore not the
blank white-powdered face of the other women native to
these lands, nor the elaborate stiff hairdos of her Mongol
mistresses. Her pale-peach skin was her own, and her hair
was but simply piled in soft billows on her head. Except for
the little crescent scar on her throat, she bore not a blemish, which was not true of the noble maidens she attended.
They, having grown up mostly outdoors, in rude living conditions, among horses and such, had many nicks and pocks
and abrasions marring even the more intimate areas of
their flesh.

Hui-sheng was at that moment seated in the most graceful and endearing posture a woman can ever unconscious-
ly assume. Quite unaware of anyone's regard, she was fixing a flower in her soft black hair. Her left hand held the
pink blossom above her left ear, and she had her right
hand arched over her head to assist in the arranging. That
particular placement of the head and hands and arms and
upper torso makes of any woman, clothed or naked, a poem
of curves and gentle angles—her face turned a little downward and to one side, her arms framing it in harmonious
composition, her neck line flowing smoothly to the bosom,
her breasts sweetly uplifted by the raised arms. In that
posture even an old woman looks young, a fat one looks
lithe, a gaunt one looks sleek, and a beautiful woman is
never more beautiful.

I remember also noticing that Hui-sheng had, in front of
each ear, a fluff of very fine black hair growing as far down
as her jaw line, and another feathery floss growing down
the back of her neck into her collar. They were winsome
details, and they made me wonder if a Min woman might

be exceptionally furry in more private places. The Mongol
maidens, I might mention, all had in their most private
places those peculiarly Mongol "little warmers" of
smooth, flat hair like small swatches of cat pelt. But, if I
have uncharacteristically said little else about their
charms, or about my nights of frolicking with them, it is
owing to no sudden access of modesty or reserve on my
part; it is only that I do not too well remember those girls. I
have even forgotten now whether I was visited by an even
dozen of them, or eleven, or thirteen, or some other number.

Oh, they were handsome, enjoyable, competent, satisfying, but they were that and no more. I recall them as just a
succession of fleeting incidents, a different one each night.
My consciousness was more impressed by the small, unobtrusive, silent Echo—and not simply for the reason that
she was present every night, but because she outshone all
the Mongol maidens together. Had she not been a distract-
ing influence, I probably would not have found them so forgettable. They were, after all, the pick of Mongol
womanhood, of twenty-four-karat quality, eminently well
suited to their function of bed partnership. But, even while
I enjoyed the sight of them being undressed by the lon-gya
slave, I could not help observing how unnecessarily over-
sized they seemed alongside the diminutive, dainty Hui-
sheng, and how coarse of complexion and physiognomy,
alongside her peach-blossom skin and exquisite features.
Even their breasts, which in other circumstances I would
have adored as beautifully voluptuous, I thought somehow
too aggressively mammalian, compared to the almost
childlike slimness and fragility of Hui-sheng's body.

In honesty, I will say that the Mongol maidens must
have found me not their ideal, either, and they must have
been less than overjoyed to be mating with me. They had
been recruited, and had survived a rigorous system of selection, to be bedded with the Khan of All Khans. He was
an old man, and perhaps also not the dream man of a
young woman, but he *was* the Khakhan. It must have been
a considerable disappointment for them to be allotted to a
foreigner instead—a Ferenghi, a nobody—and worse yet, to
be commanded not to take the fern-seed precaution before
lying with me. They were, presumably, of twenty-four-
karat fecundity, meaning that they had to expect impreg-

nation by me, and the consequent bearing not of noble
Mongol descendants of the Chinghiz line, but of half-breed
bastards, who were bound to be regarded askance by the
rest of the Kithai population, if not actively despised.

I had doubts of my own about the wisdom of Kubilai's
having set me and the concubines to this conjoining. It was
not that I felt myself either superior or inferior to them, for
I was aware that they and I and all other folk in the world
are of the same single human race. I had been taught that
from my earliest years, and I had in my travels seen ample
evidence of it. (Two small examples: all men everywhere,
except sometimes the holy and the hermit, are ever ready
to get drunk; all women everywhere, when they run, run
as if their knees are hobbled together.) Clearly, all people
are descendants of the same original Adam and Eve, but it
is just as clear that the progeny have diverged widely in
the generations since the expulsion from Eden.

Kubilai called me a Ferenghi, and he meant no offense
by it, but the word lumped me into a mistakenly undiffer-
entiated mass. I knew that we Venetians were quite distinct from the Slavs and Sicilians and all others of the
Western nationalities. While I could not perceive as much
variety among the numerous Mongol tribes, I knew that
every person took pride in his own, and regarded it as the
foremost breed of Mongols, even while asserting that all
Mongols were the foremost of mankind.

In my travels, I did not always conceive an affection for
every new people I met, but I did find them all of interest—
and the interest was in their differences. Different skin
colors, different customs, foods, speech, superstitions, entertainments, even interestingly different deficiencies and
ignorances and stupidities. Some while after this time at
Xan-du, I would visit the city of Hang-zho, and I would see
that it, like Venice, was a city all of canals. But in every
other respect, Hang-zho was not at all like Venice, and it
was the variances, not the similarities, that made the
place lovely in my eyes. So is Venice still lovely and dear to
me, but it would cease to be if it were not unique. In my
opinion, a world of cities and places and views all alike
would be the dullest world imaginable, and I feel much the
same way about the world's peoples. If all of them—white
and peach and brown and black and whatever other colors
exist—were stirred together into a bland tan, every other

of their jagged and craggy differences would flatten down
into featurelessness. You can walk confidently across a
tan sand desert because it is not fissured by any chasms,
but neither does it have any high peaks worth looking at. I
realized that my contribution to the blending of Ferenghi
and Mongol bloodlines would be negligible. Still I was reluctant that people so distinct should be blended at all—
by fiat, deliberately, not even by casual encounter—and
thereby made in any degree less various, and therefore
less interesting.

I was first attracted to Hui-sheng at least partly by her
differences from all other women I had so far known. To
see that Min slave girl among her Mongol mistresses was
like seeing a single spray of pink-ivory peach blossom in a
vase of shaggy, spiky, brass- and copper- and bronze-
colored chrysanthemums. However, she was beautiful not
only in comparison with those less so. Like a peach blossom, she was comely all by herself, and she would have
stood out even among a whole flowering peach orchard of
her comely sisters of the Min. There were reasons for that.
Hui-sheng lived in a perpetually silent world, so her eyes
were full of dreaming even when she was wide awake. Yet
her deprivation of speech and hearing was not a total
handicap, nor even very noticeable to others—I myself had
not realized, until I was told, that she was a deaf-mute—
for she had evolved a liveliness of facial expression and a
vocabulary of small gestures that communicated her
thoughts and feelings without a sound but without any
mistaking them. In time, I learned to read at a glance her
every infinitesimal movement of qahwah-colored eyes,
rose-wine lips, feathery brows, twinkling dimples, willow
hands and frond fingers. But that was later.

Inasmuch as I had become enthralled of Hui-sheng under the worst possible circumstances—while she was seeing me shamelessly cavort with her dozen or so Mongol
mistresses—I could hardly commence any courtship of her,
without risking her derisive repulsion, until some time
had passed and, I would hope, blurred her memory of those
circumstances. I determined that I would delay a decent
while before beginning any overtures, and in the meantime I would arrange to put some distance between her
and those concubines, while not distancing her from me.

To do those things, I needed the help of the Khakhan himself.

So, when I was sure there were no more Mongol maidens forthcoming, and when I knew Kubilai to be in a good mood—the messenger had recently arrived to tell him that Yun-nan was his and that Bayan was forging into the heartland of the Sung—I requested audience with him and was cordially received. I told him that I had accomplished my service to the maidens, and thanked him for giving me that opportunity to leave some trace of myself in the posterity of Kithai, and then said:

"I think, Sire, now that I have enjoyed this orgy of unrestrained pleasure, it might stand as the capstone to my bachelor career. That is to say, I believe I have attained to an age and maturity where I ought to cease the prodigal squandering of my ardors—the filly-chasing, as we call it in Venice, or the dipping of the ladle, as you say in these parts. I think it would be fitting for me now to contemplate a more settled conjugality, perhaps with an especially favored concubine, and I ask your permission, Sire—"

"Hui!" he exclaimed, with a smile of delight. "You were captivated by one of those twenty-four-karat damsels!"

"Oh, by all of them, Sire, it goes without saying. However, the one I would have for my keeping is the slave girl who attended them."

He sat back and grunted, with rather less delight, "Uu?"

"She is a girl of the Min, and—"

"Aha!" he cried, smiling broadly again. "Tell me no more. That captivation I can appreciate!"

"—and I would ask your leave, Sire, to purchase the slave's freedom, for she serves your Lady Matron of Concubines. Her name is Hui-sheng."

He waved a hand and said, "She will be deeded to you as soon as we get back to Khanbalik. Then she will be your servant or slave or consort, whatever you and she may choose. She is my gift to you in return for your help in acquiring Manzi for me."

"I thank you, Sire, most sincerely. And Hui-sheng will thank you, too. Are we returning soon to Khanbalik?"

"We will leave Xan-du tomorrow. Your companion Ali

Babar has already been informed. He is probably in your chambers packing for you at this moment."

"Is this an abrupt departure, Sire? Has something happened?"

He smiled more broadly than ever. "Did you not hear me mention the acquisition of Manzi? A messenger just rode up from the capital with the news."

I gasped, "Sung has fallen!"

"The Chief Minister Achmad sent the word. A company of Han heralds rode into Khanbalik to announce the imminent arrival of the Sung's Dowager Empress Xi-chi. She is coming herself to surrender that empire and the Imperial Yin and her own royal person. Achmad could receive her, of course, as my Vice-Regent, but I prefer to do that myself."

"Of course, Sire. It is an epochal occasion. The overthrow of the Sung and the creation of a whole new Manzi nation for the Khanate."

He sighed comfortably. "Anyway, the cold weather is upon us, and the hunting here will be less enjoyable. So I shall go and take an Empress trophy instead."

"I did not know that the Sung Empire was ruled by a woman."

"She is only Regent herself, mother to the Emperor who died a few years ago, and died young, leaving only infant sons. So the old Xi-chi was reigning until her first grandson should grow up and take the throne. Which now he will not. Go then, Marco, and make ready to ride. I return to Khanbalik to rule an expanded Khanate, and you to start putting down roots. May the gods give wisdom to us both."

I hurried to my chamber, and burst in shouting, "I have momentous news!"

Ali Babar was helpfully gathering up the traveling things I had brought with me to Xan-du, and the few things I had acquired while in residence—the tusks of my first-killed boar, for example, to keep as mementos—and was packing them into saddlebags.

"I have heard already," he said, with not much enthusiasm. "The Khanate is bigger and greater than ever."

"More amazing news than that! I have met the woman of my life!"

"Let me think if I can guess which. There has lately been quite a procession through this room of yours."

"You would never guess!" I said gleefully, and started to extol the charms of Hui-sheng. But then I checked myself, for Ali was not rejoicing with me. "You look unusually glum, old companion. Has something cast you down?"

He mumbled, "That rider from Khanbalik brought other news, not so inspiriting. . . ."

I looked more attentively at him. If he had had a chin under that gray beard, it would have been quivering. "What other news?"

"The messenger said that, when he was leaving the city, he was intercepted by one of my kashi artisans, who asked him to tell me that Mar-Janah has gone away."

"What? Your good wife Mar-Janah? Gone away? Gone where?"

"I have not the least idea. My shop man said that, some while back—it must be a month ago, by now, or more—two palace guards called at the kashi shop. Mar-Janah departed with them, and has not been seen or heard of since. The workers are consequently in some confusion and disarray. My man told the messenger no more than that."

"Palace guards? Then it must have been official business. I will run again to Kubilai and ask—"

"He professes to know nothing of the matter. I naturally went to inquire of him. That is when he told me to pack for us. And, since we are going back to Khanbalik immediately, I have made no great outcry. I suppose, when we get there, I will learn what has occurred. . . ."

"This is most strange," I murmured.

I said no more than that, though a recollection had come suddenly and unbidden into my mind—the message Ali had brought: "Expect me when you least expect me." I had not shown it to Ali or told him what it said. I had seen no need to burden him with my troubles—or what I then assumed were my troubles only—and I had torn up and thrown away the missive. Now I wished I had not. As I have said, Mongol writing was not easy for me to unravel. Could I perhaps have misread it? Could it, this time, have said something slightly different? "Expect me *where* you least expect me," perhaps? Had it been given to Ali Babar to deliver, not only to threaten and alarm me again, but also to get *him* out of the city while dirty deeds were being done?

Whoever in Khanbalik wished me evil must have been aware that—when I was absent from the city—I was vulnerable only vicariously, through the few persons I held dear there. A mere three persons, in fact. My father and uncle were two. But they were grown men, and strong, and anyone who harmed them would have to answer to an irate Khakhan. The third, however, was the good and beauteous and sweet Mar-Janah, who was only a weakling woman, and an insignificant former slave, and treasured by ñone but me and *my* former slave. With a pang, I remembered her saying, "I was left my life, but not much else . . ." and wistfully, "If Ali Babar can love what is left of me. . . ."

Had my unknown enemy, the lurking, sneaking whisperer, abducted that blameless woman for no reason but to hurt me? If so, the enemy was loathsomely vile, but clever in his choice of surrogate victim. I had helped to rescue the fallen Princess Mar-Janah from a life of abuse and degradation, and had helped her at last to safe and happy harbor—I remembered her saying, "The intervening twenty years might never have been"—and if I should now be the cause of her enduring yet another kind of misery, it would be a bitter hurt to me indeed.

Well, we would know when we got to Khanbalik. And I had a strong apprehension: if we were ever to find the vanished Mar-Janah, we should have first to find the veiled woman who had given Ali that missive for me. But, for the time being, I said nothing of that to him; he was already worried enough. I also ceased to exult over my newfound Hui-sheng, out of regard for his concern for his own darling, so long lost before and now lost again.

"Marco, could we not ride out ahead of this slow cortege?" he asked anxiously, when we and the whole Xan-du court had been on the road for two or three days. "You and I could be in Khanbalik much sooner if we could put spurs to our horses."

He was right, of course. The Khakhan traveled with much ceremony and no haste at all, holding the whole train to a stately slow march. It would not have been seemly for him to travel otherwise, especially when this was something in the nature of a triumphal procession. All his people in towns and villages along the way—having heard of the Sung war's successful conclusion—were eager to gather along the roadside and cheer and wave and throw flowers as he passed.

Kubilai rode in a majestic, thronelike, canopied carriage adorned with jewels and gilding, drawn by four immense elephants likewise much bedizened. Kubilai's carriage was followed by others carrying a number of his wives and many more of his other women, including those maidens he had lent to me, and servants and slaves and so forth. Variously before and behind and beside the carriage rode Prince Chingkim and all the other courtiers on horses gorgeously arrayed. Behind the carriages came wagons loaded with luggage and equipment and hunting arms and trophies of the season and traveling provender of wines and kumis and viands; one wagon was occupied by a band of musicians and their instruments, to play for us at our nighttime stops. A troop of Mongol warriors rode one day's journey ahead of us, to trumpet our approach to each community, so that its inhabitants could prepare to light their incense-fires and, if we arrived in twilight, to ignite the fiery trees and sparkling flowers (stores of which the Firemaster Shi had deposited with them on the outward march), and another troop of horsemen followed a day behind us, to retrieve any broken-wheeled wagons or lamed horses that had to fall out of the train. Also, the Khakhan, as usual in this season, had two or three brace of white gerfalcons riding on the sideboards of his carriage, and the whole procession would have to halt whenever we started some game that he wished to fly the falcons at.

"Yes, Ali, we could make better time on our own," I replied to his query. "But I think we ought not. For one reason, it would appear disrespectful of the Khakhan, and we may have need of his continued warm friendship. For another reason, if we stay with the train, anyone who has any news of Mar-Janah will have no trouble finding us to tell us."

That was quite true, though I did not confide to Ali all my reasoning in that regard. I had convinced myself that Mar-Janah had been abducted by my whisperer enemy. Since I knew not who that was, I saw no use in our riding furiously to the city just to cast about in desperation. It was more logical to assume that the whisperer would be keeping an eye out for me, and would the sooner see me if I

arrived in conspicuous pomp, and could the sooner deliver
his next message, or his ransom demand for Mar-Janah's
deliverance, nor just another taunting threat. It was our
best hope for making contact with him, or at least with his
veiled woman courier, and eventually with Mar-Janah.

My staying with the Khakhan's entourage also enabled
me to keep a protective watch over Hui-sheng, but that
had no influence on my decision not to hurry ahead. Hui-
sheng was still traveling in company with her Mongol mistresses, and had no knowledge of my interest in her or the
arrangements I had made for her future. I did pay her
some occasional little attentions, just so she would not forget me—helping her climb in or out of the concubines' carriage when we stopped at a karwansarai or some provincial
offical's country mansion, fetching her a dipper of water
from an inn-yard well, gathering a posy of a village's
thrown flowers and presenting it to her with a gallant
bow—trifles like that. I wished her to think well of me, but
I had now more reason than before not to force my suit
upon her.

I had earlier decided to wait a decent interval; now I *had*
to. It seemed to me that my whisperer enemy knew always
where I was and what I was doing. I dared not risk that enemy's learning that I had any special attachment to Hui-
sheng. If he was malicious enough to strike at me through
a dearly esteemed friend like Mar-Janah, God only knew
what he might do to someone he thought *really* dear to me.
It was hard for me to keep my gaze from lingering on her
and to resist doing little services for the reward of her dim-
pled smile. I would have had an easier time of it if Ali and I
had ridden on ahead, as he wanted to do. But, for his sake
and Mar-Janah's, I stayed with the train, trying not to
stay always near Hui-sheng.

KHANBALI KAGAIN

1

IN addition to the troop of horsemen staying a day ahead of us, there were other riders continually galloping off to Khanbalik or galloping up to us, ostensibly to keep the Khakhan informed of developments there. Ali Babar anxiously questioned each arriving courier, but none had any further word of his missing wife. In fact, the riders' only function was to keep track of the train of the Dowager Empress of the Sung, which was also approaching the city. That enabled Kubilai to set our rate of march so that our procession finally swept down the great central avenue of Khanbalik on the same day—at the same hour—that hers entered from the south.

The entire populace of the city, and probably of the whole province for hundreds of li around, was jammed along the sides of the avenue and clogging every fringe street and dangling from windows and clinging to roof eaves, to greet the triumphant Khakhan with roars of approval, with flapping banners and swirling pennants, with the booming and flaring overhead of the fiery trees and sparkling flowers, with a ceaseless and ear-thumping fanfare of trumpets and gongs and drums and bells. The people continued to carry on as the only slightly less splendiferous train of the Sung Empress came up the avenue and halted respectfully on meeting ours. The crowds muted their clamor a little when the Khakhan got chivalrously down from his throne-carriage and advanced to take the old Empress's hand. He gently helped her down from her carriage to the street, and enfolded her in a broth-

erly embrace of welcome, at which the people bellowed and
blared a really deafening uproar of noise and music.

After the Khan and the Empress had both got into his
throne-carriage, there was a period of confused milling, as
the contingents of the two trains churned about to coalesce
and march all together to the palace, where would begin
the many days required for the ceremonies of formal surrender: the conferences and discussions, the drafting and
inditing and signing of documents, the handing over to
Kubilai of Sung's great seal of state or Imperial Yin, the
public readings of proclamations, the balls and banquets
mingling celebration of victory and condolence of defeat.
(So condolent was Kubilai's chief wife, the Khatun Jamui,
that she settled a generous pension on the deposed Empress and granted that she and her two grandsons be let to
live out their lives in religious retirement, the old woman
in a Buddhist nunnery, the boys in a lamasarai.)

I held my horse back in the less congested rear of the procession as it moved toward the palace, and motioned for
Ali to do the same. When I had the opportunity, I reined
my mount alongside his and leaned close so he could hear
me over the ambient tumult without my having to shout:
"You see now why I wanted us to arrive with the Khakhan. Everybody in the city is congregated here today, including any who know where Mar-Janah is, and so now
they know we are here, too."

"It would seem so," he said. "But no one has plucked at
my stirrup to volunteer any word."

"I think I know where the word will be volunteered," I
said. "Stay with me as far as the palace courtyard and
then, when we dismount, let us seem to separate, for I am
sure we are being watched. Then this is what we will do."
And I gave him certain instructions.

The untidy procession went shouldering and elbowing
and nudging its way through the pressing onlookers and
well-wishers, so slowly that the day was ending when we
finally reached the palace, and Ali and I entered the stable
court as we had done on our very first arrival at Khanbalik, in a deepening twilight. The courtyard was a turmoil
of people and animals and noise and confusion; if anyone
was watching us, he could not have had a very clear view.
Nevertheless, when we got down from our horses and
handed them over to stable hands, we made a distinct

show of waving farewells and going off in opposite directions.

Walking as tall and visibly as I could, I went to a horse trough and splashed water on my dusty face. When I straightened up, I looked about and made faces expressive of distaste at the surrounding commotion. I started jostling through the mob toward the nearest palace portal, then stopped and made flagrant gestures of repugnance—not worth the effort—and plowed my way out of the crowd to where I was conspicuously alone and apart. Keeping my distance from everyone I met, I sauntered slowly across uncovered walks and through gardens and over streamlet bridges and along terraces until I came to the newer parkland on the other side of the palace. I stayed always in the open, out from under roofs or trees, so that anyone who wanted to could see me and follow me. On the farther side of the palace grounds, there were fewer people, but still there were people about—minor functionaries trotting here and there on court business, servants and slaves scurrying about at their chores—for the Khakhan's arrival naturally caused a beehive stir.

However, when I came to the Kara Hill and began idly to climb its path, as if I were only seeking to get away from the crush of people below, I really did. There was no one else in sight up there. So I strolled on uphill to the Echo Pavilion, and first walked around its entire outside perimeter, to give my putative pursuer a chance to dodge inside the wall. Finally, as if paying no least attention to where I was or what I was doing, I ambled through the Moon Gate in the wall and around the inside terrace. When I was at the farthest remove from the Moon Gate, the pavilion squarely between me and it, I leaned back against the ornamental wall and contemplated the stars coming out one by one in the plum-colored sky above the pavilion's dragon-ridge roof. I had moved only leisurely the whole way from the entry courtyard to here, but my heart was beating as if I had run hard, and I feared that its thumping must be audible all around the pavilion precincts. But I had not long to worry about that. The voice came, as it had come before: a whisper in the Mongol tongue, low and sibilant and unidentifiable even as to gender, but as clearly as if the whisperer were right at my side, whispering the words I expected:

"Expect me when you least expect me."

I immediately bellowed, *"Now, Nostril!"*—in my excitement forgetting his new name and estate.

So did he, for he bellowed back, *"I have him, Master Marco!"*

And then I heard the grunts and gasps of a scuffle, as clearly as if it were being fought right at my feet, though I had to run all the way around the pavilion before I found the two rolling and struggling together on the very jamb of the Moon Gate. One of them was Ali Babar. The other I could not recognize; he appeared to be just a shapeless welter of robes and scarves. But that one I seized and tore away from Ali and held while Ali got to his feet. Panting, he pointed and said, "Master—it is no man—it is the veiled woman."

I realized then that I was clutching a not very big or muscular body, but I did not lessen my grip. I held on, and the body writhed fiercely, while Ali reached out and yanked the veils off her.

"Well?" I snarled. "Who is the bitch?" All I could see was the back of her dark hair and, past that, Ali's face, which got very round of eye and dilated of nostril and astonished and almost comically frightened.

"Mashallah!" he gasped. "Master—it is the dead come alive! It is your onetime maidservant—Buyantu!"

At that exclamation of her name she ceased to struggle and stood slumped in sullen resignation. So I eased my tight grasp of her, and turned her around to scrutinize her in what remained of the twilight. She did not look as if she had ever been dead, but her face was much harder and tight-skinned and colder than I remembered it, and her dark hair had much silver in it, and her eyes were defiant slits. Ali was still regarding her with wary consternation, and my voice was not entirely steady when I said:

"Tell us everything, Buyantu. I am glad to see you still among the living, but by what miracle did you survive? Is it possible that Biliktu lives, too? *Somebody* died in that calamity in my chambers. And what do you here, whispering in the Echo Pavilion?"

"Please, Marco," said Ali, in an even more trembly voice. "First things first. Where is Mar-Janah?"

Buyantu snapped, "I will not talk to a lowly slave!"

"He is no longer a slave," I said. "He is a freeman who

has been bereft of his wife. She is a freewoman besides, so her abductor faces execution as a felon."

"I do not choose to believe a word you say. And I will not talk to a slave."

"Talk to me, then. You had best unburden yourself, Buyantu. I can promise no pardon for a felony but, if you tell us all—and if Mar-Janah is safely restored to us—the penalty may be something more lenient than execution."

"I spit on your pardon and leniency!" she said wildly. "The dead cannot be executed. I *did* die in that calamity!"

Ali's eyes and nostril widened again, and he took a step backward from her. I almost did, too, her words sounded so dreadfully sincere. But I stood my ground, and grasped her again and shook her and said menacingly, "Talk!"

Still stubborn, she said only, "I will not talk before a slave."

I could have wrung her until she did, but it might have taken all night. I turned to Ali and suggested:

"This may go more quickly if you absent yourself, and quickness may be vital." Either he saw the sense of that or he was not unwilling to leave the vicinity of one apparently come alive from the dead. Anyway, he nodded, so I told him, "Wait for me in my chambers. You can make sure for me that I do have those chambers again, and that they are habitable. I will come for you as soon as I know anything useful. Trust me."

When he had gone down the hill, out of hearing, I said again to Buyantu, "Talk. Is the woman Mar-Janah safe? Is she alive?"

"I do not know and I do not care. We dead care nothing. For the living *or* the dead."

"I have no time to hear your philosophies. Just tell me what happened."

She shrugged and said sullenly, "That day . . . " I did not have to inquire what day she meant. "On that day I first began to hate you, and I continued to hate you, and I hate you still. But on that day I also died. Dead bodies cool, and I suppose burning hatreds do, too. Anyway, I do not mind now, letting you know of my hatred and how I manifested it. That can make no difference now."

She paused, and I prodded, "I know you were spying on me for the Wali Achmad. Start with that."

"That day . . . you sent me to request audience for you

with the Khakhan. When I returned, I found you and my—
you and Biliktu in bed together. I was enraged, and I let
you see *some* of how enraged I was. You left me and Biliktu
to tend the brazier fire under a certain pot. You did not tell
us it was dangerous, and I did not suspect. Being still in a
rage and wishing you harm, I left Biliktu to watch the brazier, and I went to the Minister Achmad, who had long
been paying me to inform him of your doings."

Even though I had known about that, I must have made
a noise of displeasure, for she shrieked at me:

"Do not sniff! Do not pretend it is a practice beneath
your high principles. You used a spy, too. That slave yonder." She waved in the direction Ali had gone. "And you
paid him, too, by *pimping* for him! You paid him with the
female slave Mar-Janah."

"Never mind that. Go on."

She paused to recollect her thoughts. "I went to the Minister Achmad, for I had much to tell him. I had, that very
morning, overheard you and the slave talking of the Minister Pao, a Yi passing as a Han. It was that morning, too,
that you promised the slave he would wed that woman
Mar-Janah. I told those things to the Minister Achmad. I
told him that you were at that moment impeaching the
Minister Pao to the Khan Kubilai. The Minister Achmad
immediately wrote a message and sent it by a servant to
that Minister Pao."

"Aha," I muttered. "And Pao made a timely escape."

"Then the Minister Achmad sent another steward to
fetch you to him when you left the Khakhan. He bade me
wait, meanwhile, and I did. When you came, I was hiding
in his private quarters."

"And not alone," I interrupted. "There was someone
else in there that day. Who was she?"

"She?" echoed Buyantu, as if puzzled. Then she gave me
a calculating look from her slit eyes.

"The large woman. I know she was there, for she almost
came out into the room where the Arab and I were talking."

"Oh . . . yes . . . the large woman. That exceptionally
large woman. We did not speak. I assumed that person to
be merely some new fancy of the Minister Achmad. Perhaps you are aware that he has some eccentric fancies. If
that person had a woman's name, I did not ask it, and do

not know it. We merely sat in each other's company, looking sidelong at each other, until you departed again. Are you much interested in learning the identity of that large woman?"

"Perhaps not. Surely not *everyone* in Khanbalik was involved in these devious plots. Go on, Buyantu."

"As soon as you left his chambers, the Minister Achmad came for me again and took me to the window. He showed me—you were wandering up the Kara Hill—up here, to this Echo Pavilion. He told me to run after you, but unseen, and whisper the words you heard. I was pleased to make secret threats against you, even though I did not know what was threatened, for I hated you. *Hated you!*"

She choked on her rabid words, and stopped. I could not help feeling some compassion, so I said, "And a few minutes later, you had even more reason for hating me."

She nodded wretchedly, and swallowed, and got her voice working again. "I was returning to your chambers when they flew all apart, before my eyes, with that terrible noise and flame and smoke. Biliktu died then—and so did I, in everything but body. She had long been my sister, my twin, and we had long loved each other. I might have felt wrath enough if I had lost my twin sister. But it was *you* who made us more than sisters. You made us *lovers*. And then you destroyed my loved one. *You!*"

That last word burst out in a spray of spittle. I prudently said nothing, and again it took her a moment before she could go on.

"I would happily have killed you then. But too many things were happening, too many people about. And then you went suddenly away. I was left alone. I was as alone as a person can be. The only one I loved in the world was dead, and everyone else thought I was, too. I had no employment to occupy me, no one to answer to, no place I was expected to be. I felt quite thoroughly dead, myself. I still do."

She fell morosely silent again, so I prodded. "But the Arab found employment for you."

"He knew I had not been in the room with Biliktu. He was the only one who knew. No one else suspected my existence. He told me he might have use for such an invisible woman, but for a long time he did not. He paid me wages, and I lived alone in a room down in the city, and I sat and

looked at the walls of it." She sighed deeply. "How long
has it been?"

"Long," I said sympathetically. "It has been a long
time."

"Then one day he sent for me. He said you were on your
way back, and we must prepare a suitable surprise with
which to welcome you home. He wrote out two papers, and
had me heavily veil myself—even more of an invisible
woman—and I delivered them. One I gave to your slave to
give to you. If you have seen it, you know it was not signed.
The other paper he did sign, but not with his own yin, and
that one I delivered some while later to the Captain of the
Palace Guard. It was an order to arrest the woman Mar-
Janah and take her to the Fondler."

"Amoredèi!" I exclaimed in horror. "But . . . but . . . the
guardsmen do not arrest and the Fondler does not punish
just on someone's whim! What was Mar-Janah charged
with? What did the paper say? And how did the vile Wali
sign it, if not with is own name?"

While Buyantu had been telling of occurrences, her
voice had had some spirit in it, if only the spirit of a venomous snake taking satisfaction in malevolent accomplishment. But when I began demanding details, the spirit
went out of her, and her voice got leaden and lifeless.

She said, "When the Khan is away from the court, the
Minister Achmad is Vice-Regent. He has access to all the
yins of office. I suppose he can use whichever he pleases,
and sign it to any paper. He used the yin of the Armorer of
the Palace Guard, who was the Lady Chao Ku-an, who was
the former owner of the slave Mar-Janah. The order
charged that the slave was a runaway, passing as a freewoman of property. The guardsmen would not question
the written word of their own Armorer, and the Fondler
questions nobody but his victims."

I was still sputtering in appalled bewilderment. "But
. . . but . . . even the Lady Chao—she is no paragon of
virtue, but even she would refute an untrue charge illicitly
made in her name."

Buyantu said dully, "The Lady Chao died very shortly
thereafter."

"Oh. Yes. I had forgotten."

"She probably never knew of the misuse of her official

yin. In any case, she did not halt the proceedings, and now she never will."

"No. How very convenient for the Arab. Tell me, Buyantu. Did he ever confide to you why he was taking so much trouble, and involving so many people—or eliminating them—on my account?"

"He said only 'Hell is what hurts worst,' if that means anything to you. It does not to me. He said it again this evening, when he sent me again to follow you up here and whisper that threat once more."

I said between my teeth, "I think it is time I spread some of that Hell around." Then a chilling realization struck me, and I exclaimed, "Time! How much time? Buyantu—quick, tell me—what punishment would the Fondler inflict for Mar-Janah's alleged crime?"

She said, with indifference, "A slave posing as a free subject? I do not really know, but—"

"If it is not too severe, we still have hope," I breathed.

"—but the Minister Achmad said that such a crime is tantamount to treason against the state."

"Oh, dear God!" I groaned. "The penalty for treason is the Death of a Thousand! How—how long ago was Mar-Janah taken?"

"Let me think," she said languidly. "It was after your slave had gone to catch up to you and give you the unsigned message. So it has been . . . about two months . . . two and a half. . . ."

"Sixty days . . . seventy-five . . ." I tried to calculate, though my mind was in a ferment. "The Fondler once said he could stretch out that punishment, when he had the leisure and was in the mood, to near a hundred days. And a beautiful woman in his clutches ought to put him in a most leisurely mood. There might yet be time. I must run!"

"Wait!" said Buyantu, seizing my sleeve. Again there came a trace of life into her voice, though not very fittingly, for what she said was, "Do not go until you have slain me."

"I will not slay you, Buyantu."

"You must! I have been dead all this long time. Now kill me, so I can lie down at last."

"I will not."

"You would not be punished for it, since you could justify it. But you will not even be charged—for you are

slaying an invisible woman, nonexistent, already attested
dead. Come! You must feel the same rage that I felt when
you slew my love. I have been long working to your hurt,
and now I have helped to send your lady friend to the Fondler. You have every reason to slay me."

"I have more reason to let you live—and atone. You will
be my proof of Achmad's involvement in these filthy doings. There is no time now to explain. I must run. But I
need you, Buyantu. Will you just stay here until I return? I
will be as quick as I can."

She said wearily, "If I cannot lie in my grave, what matter where I am?"

"Only wait for me. Try to believe that you owe me that
much. Will you?"

She sighed and sank down, her back bowed against the
inner curve of the Moon Gate. "What matter? I will wait."

I went down the hill in long bounds, asking myself
whether I ought first accost the instigating Achmad or the
perpetrating Fondler. Better hasten first to the Fondler,
and hope I could stay his hand. But would he still be working at this late hour? As I scurried through the subterranean tunnels toward his cavern chambers, I groped in my
purse and tried to count my money by feel. Most of it was
paper, but there were some coins of good gold. The Fondler
might be wearying of his enjoyment by now, and be
cheaply bribable. As it turned out, he was still at his
labors, and was surprisingly amenable to my appeal—but
not from either boredom or avarice.

I had to do a lot of shouting and pounding of my fist on a
table and shaking of it at the austere and aloof chief of the
chambers clerks, but he finally unbent and went to interrupt his master at his work. The Fondler came mincing out
through the iron-studded door, fastidiously wiping his
hands on a silk cloth. Restraining my impulse to throttle
him then and there, I upended my purse on the table between us, and poured out all its contents, and said breathlessly, "Master Ping, you hold a Subject woman named
Mar-Janah. I have this moment learned that she was
unjustly condemned to you. Does she still live? Can I request a temporary cessation of due process?"

His eyes glittered as he studied me. "I have a warrant
for her execution," he said. "Do you bring a revoking warrant?"

"No, but I will get one."

"Ah. When you do, then. . . ."

"I ask only that the proceedings be suspended until I can do so. That is—if the woman still lives. Does she?"

"Of course she lives," he said haughtily. "I am not a butcher." He even laughed and shook his head, as if I had foolishly disparaged his professional skill.

"Then do me the honor, Master Ping, of accepting this token of my appreciation." I indicated the litter of money on the table. "Will that requite your kindness?"

He only grunted a noncommittal "Humpf," but began swiftly picking out the gold coins from the pile, without seeming to look at what he was doing. For the first time, I noticed his fingers had nails incredibly long and curved, like talons.

I said anxiously, "I understand that the woman was sentenced to the Death of a Thousand."

Contemptuously disregarding the paper money, he scooped the coins into his belt purse, and said, "No."

"No?" I echoed, hopefully.

"The warrant specified the Death Beyond a Thousand."

I was briefly stunned, and then afraid to ask for elucidation. I said, "Well, can that be suspended for a time? Until I can fetch a revocation order from the Khakhan?"

"It can," he said, rather too readily. "If you are certain that that is what you want. Mind you, Lord Marco—that is your name? I thought I remembered you. I am honest in my transactions, Lord Marco. I do not sell goods sight unseen. You had best come and take a look at what you are buying. I will refund your—token of appreciation—if you ask it."

He turned and tripped across the chamber to the iron-studded door, and held it open for me, and I followed him into the inner chamber, and—dear God—I wish I had not.

However, in my desperate urgency to rescue Mar-Janah, I had neglected to bear in mind certain things. She, simply in being a beautiful female Subject, would have inspired the Fondler to inflict his most infernal tortures, and to drag them out as cruelly long as possible. But more than that. The warrant would have told him that Mar-Janah was the spouse of one Ali Babar, and it would have been an easy matter for Master Ping to discover that Ali was the onetime slave who had visited these very chambers, to the

Fondler's extreme disgust. (He had said in revulsion, *"Who . . . is . . . this?"*) And Ping would have remembered that that slave was *my* slave, and that I had been an even more obnoxious visitor. (I had, not knowing that he understood Farsi, called him "this simpering enjoyer of other people's torments.") So he would have had every excuse for exerting himself to the utmost in his attentions to the condemned Subject, who was wife to the lowly slave of Marco Polo, who had once so brashly insulted him. And now he had the very same Marco Polo before him, abjectly suppliant and pleading and cringing. The Fondler was not just willing, but fiendishly eager and proud, to show me the handiwork he had wrought—and to let me realize that it had resulted, in no small part, from my own foolhardy impertinence.

In the stone-walled, torch-lighted, blood-warmed, gore-spattered, nauseously reeking inner chamber, Master Ping and I stood side by side and looked at the room's central object, red, and shiny and dripping and ever so slightly steaming. Or rather, I looked at it, and he looked sideways at me, gloating and waiting for my comment. I said nothing for a while. I could not have done, for I was repeatedly swallowing, determined not to let him hear me retch or see me vomit. So, probably to goad me, he began pedantically to explain the scene before us:

"You realize, I trust, that the Fondling has been going on for some time now. Observe the basket, and in it the comparatively few papers still unpicked from it and unfolded. Only those eighty-seven papers are left, because I had this day got to the nine hundred and thirteenth of them. You may believe it or not, but just that single paper has occupied my entire afternoon, and kept me working this late into the evening. That was because, when I unfolded it, it was the third directive to the Subject's 'red jewel,' which was somewhat hard to find in all that mess down there between the thigh stumps, and which of course had already received attention twice before. So it required all my skill and concentration to—"

I was able finally to interrupt him. I said harshly, "You told me this was Mar-Janah, and she was still living. This thing is not she, and it cannot conceivably be alive."

"Yes, it is, and yes, it is. Furthermore, she is capable of *staying* alive, too, with proper treatment and care—if anyone were unkind enough to want her to. Step closer, Lord Marco, and see for yourself."

I did. It was alive and it was Mar-Janah. At the top end of it, where must have been the head, there hung down, from what must have been the scalp, a single matted lock of hair not yet torn out by the roots, and it was long—a woman's hair—and it was still discernibly ruddy-black in color, and curly—Mar-Janah's hair. Also the thing made a noise. It could not have seen me, but it might dimly have heard my voice, through the remaining aperture where an ear had been, and perhaps even recognized my voice. The noise it made was only a faint bubbling blubber of sound, but it seemed feebly to say, "Marco?"

In a controlled and level voice—I would not have believed that I could manage that—I remarked to the Fondler, almost conversationally:

"Master Ping, you once described to me, in loving detail, the Death of a Thousand, which is what this seems to me to be. But you called this one by another name. What is the difference?"

"A trivial one. You could not be expected to notice. The Death of a Thousand, as you know, consists of the Subject's being gradually reduced—by the cutting off of bits, and slicings and probings and gougings and so on—a process prolonged by intervals of rest, during which the Subject is given sustaining food and drink. The Death Beyond a Thousand is much the same, differing only in that the Subject is given nothing but the bits of herself to eat. And to drink, only the—*what are you doing?*"

I had taken out my belt knife and plunged it into the glistening red pulp that I took to the remains of Mar-Janah's breast, and I gave the haft the extra squeeze to ensure that all three blades stabbed deep. I could only hope that the thing was more certainly dead than before, but it did seem to slump a little more limply, and it did not make any more utterances. In that moment, I remembered how I had protested to Mar-Janah's husband, a long time ago, that I could never knowingly kill a woman, and he had said casually, "You are young yet."

Master Ping was speechlessly grinding his teeth at me, and glaring at me with furious eyes. But I coolly reached out and took from him the silk cloth with which he had wiped his hands. I used it to clean my knife, and rudely tossed it back at him as I closed up the knife and returned it to my belt sheath.

He sneered hatefully and said, "An utter waste of the most refined finishing touches yet to come. And I was going to accord you the privilege of looking on. What a waste!" He replaced the sneer with a mocking smile. "Still, an understandable impulse, I daresay, for a layman and a barbarian. And you had, after all, paid for her."

"I have not done paying for her, Master Ping," I said, and shoved past him and went out.

2

I was anxious to get back to Buyantu, worried that she might have got restless by now, and I would gladly have put off telling Ali Babar the sad news. But I could not leave him wringing his hands in the Purgatory of not knowing, so I went to my old chambers, where he was waiting. In a pretense of cheerfulness, he made a sweeping gesture and said:

"All restored and refurnished and redecorated. But no one thought to assign you new servants, it seems. So I will stay tonight, in case you should need. . . ." His voice faltered. "Oh, Marco, you look stricken. Is it what I fear it is?"

"Alas, yes, old comrade. She is dead."

Tears started in his eyes, and he whispered, "Tanha . . . hamishè. . . ."

"I know no easier way to tell it. I am sorry. But she is free of captivity and free of pain." Let him, at least for now, think that she had had an easy death. "I will tell you, another time, the how and the why of it, for it was an assassination, and unnecessary. It was done only to hurt you and me, and you and I will avenge it. But tonight, Ali, do not question me and do not stay. You will wish to go and grieve by yourself, and I have many things to do—to set our vengeance in train."

I turned and went out abruptly, for if he had asked me anything I could not have lied to him. But just the telling of that much had made me more angry and determined

and bloodthirsty than before, so, instead of going directly
to the Echo Pavilion for Buyantu, I went first to the chambers of the Minister Achmad.

I was briefly impeded by his sentries and servants. They
protested that the Wali had endured a hectic day of making preparations for the Khakhan's return and the reception of the Dowager Empress, that he was much fatigued
and had gone already to bed, and that they dared not announce a visitor. But I snarled at them—"Do not announce
me! Admit me!"—so ferociously that they moved out of my
way, muttering fearfully, "On your head be it, then, Master Polo," and I slammed unannounced and ungentlemanly
through the door of the Arab's private apartments.

I was immediately reminded of Buyantu's words about
Achmad's "eccentric fancies" and similar words spoken by
the artist Master Chao long before. As I burst into the bedroom, I surprised a very large woman already there, and
she whisked out through another door. I got only a glimpse
of her, voluptuously gowned in filmy, flimsy, fluttering
robes the color of the flower called lilak. But I had to assume that she was the same tall and robust woman I had
seen in these chambers before. This particular one of Achmad's fancies, I thought, seemed to have lasted for some
while; but then I gave it no more thought. I confronted
the man who lay in the vast, lilak-sheeted bed, propped
against lilak-colored pillows. He regarded me calmly, his
black stone-chip eyes not flinching from the storm he must
have seen in my face.

"I trust you are comfortable," I said, through clenched
teeth. "Enjoy your swinishness. You will not for long."

"It is not mannerly to speak of swine to a Muslim, pork
eater. You are also addressing the Chief Minister of this
realm. Have a care how you do it."

"I am addressing a disgraced and deposed and dead
man."

"No, no," he said, with a smile that was not a pleasant
smile. "You may be Kubilai's current great favorite,
Folo—even invited to share his concubines, I hear—but he
will never let you lop off his good right hand."

I considered that remark, and said, "You know, I should
never have thought myself a very important personage in
Kithai—certainly not any rival to you, or any danger to
you—were it not that you have so plainly thought me so.

And now you mention the Mongol maidens I enjoyed. Are you resentful that *you* never have? Or that you never *could?* Was that the latest corrosive to eat at your good sense?"

"Haramzadè! *You* important? A rival? A danger? I have only to touch this bedside gong and my men will mince you in an instant. Tomorrow morning, I should have only to explain to Kubilai that you had spoken to me as you have just done. He would make no least fuss or comment, and your existence would be forgotten as readily as the ending of it."

"Why do you not do that, then? Why have you never done that? You said you would make me regret my having once flouted your express command—but why do so by attrition? Why have you only furtively and indolently made threats and menaces, while destroying instead the innocent folk around me?"

"It amused me to do so—Hell is what hurts worst—and I can do as I please."

"Can you? Until now, perhaps. Not any more."

"Oh, I think so. For my next amusement, I think I will make public some paintings the Master Chao did for me. The very name of Folo will be a laughingstock throughout the Khanate. Ridicule hurts worst of all." Before I could demand to know what he was talking about, he had gone on to another subject. "Are you really aware, Marco Folo, of who this Wali is that you presume to challenge? It was many years ago that I started serving as an adviser to the Princess Jamui of the Kungurat tribe of the Mongols. When the Khan Kubilai made her his first wife, and she therefore became the Khatun Jamui, I accompanied her to this court. I have served Kubilai and the Khanate ever since, in many capacities. Most recently, for many years, in this next-highest office of all. Do you really think you could topple an edifice of such firm foundation?"

Again I considered, and said, "It may surprise you, Wali, but I believe you. I believe that you have been dedicated in your service. I will probably never know why, at this late date, you have let an unworthy jealousy corrupt you into malversation."

"So say you. In all my career, I have done nothing wrong."

"Nothing wrong? Shall I enumerate? I do not think you

conspired to put the Yi named Pao in a ministerial office. I
do not think you even knew of his subversive presence. But
you most certainly connived in his escape when he was revealed. I call that treasonous. You have misused another
courtier's yin to your private purpose, and I call that mal-
feasance of office, if nothing worse. You have most foully
murdered the Lady Chao and the woman Mar-Janah—one
a noble, one a worthy subject of the Khan—all for no reason but to afflict me. You have done *nothing wrong?*"

"Wrong must be proven," he said, in a voice as stony as
his eyes. "Wrong is an abstract word of no independent existence. Wrong is, like evil, only a matter of other people's
judgment. If a man do a deed and none call it wrong, then
he did no wrong."

"You did, Arab. Many wrongs. And so they will be adjudged."

"Take murder now . . . ," he went on, as if I had not interrupted. "You have imputed to me murder. However, if
some woman named Mar-Janah *is* truly dead, and wrong-
fully, there is a reputable witness to her last hours. He can
testify that the Wali Achmad never once laid eyes on the
woman, let alone murderous hands. That witness can testify that the woman Mar-Janah died from a knife wound
administered by a certain Marco Folo." He turned on me a
gaze of arch and mocking good humor. "Why, Marco Folo,
how you do look! Is that a look of astonishment or guilt or
shame at being found out? Did you suppose I have been
tucked abed here all the night? I have been going about,
cleaning up after you. I was only just now able to lay my
weary self down to rest, and in you come, to annoy me yet
further."

But I was not discomfited by his sarcasm. I simply shook
my head and said, "I will freely confess the knife wound,
when we are on trial in the Hall of Justice."

"This will never get to the Cheng. I have just told you
that a wrong must be proven. But, before that, the wrong-
doer must be accused. Could you do such a reckless and
profitless thing? Would you really dare to lay charges
against the Chief Minister of the Khanate? The word of an
upstart Ferenghi against the reputation of the longest-
serving and highest-ranking courtier of the court?"

"It will not be only my word."

"There is no other to speak against me."

"There is the woman Buyantu, my former maidservant."

"Are you sure you wish to bring that up? Would it be wise? She also died by your doing. The whole court knows that, and so will every justice of the Cheng."

"You know different, damn you. She spoke to me this very evening, and told me everything. She waits for me now on the Kara Hill."

"There is no one on the Kara Hill."

"This once, you are mistaken," I said. "There is Buyantu." And I may even have smiled smugly at him.

"There is no one on the Kara Hill. Go and see. It is true that earlier this evening I sent a servant up there. I disremember her name, and now I cannot even recollect on what errand I sent her. But when she did not return after a time, I went to look for her. Most considerate of me, to do that personally, but Allah bids us be considerate of our underlings. Had I found her, it might have been she who told me you had gone running to visit the Fondler. However, I regret to report that I did not find her. Nor will you. Go and see."

"You murdering monster! Have you slain yet another—?"

"Had I found her," he went on implacably, "she might also have told me that you refused her exactly that consideration. But Allah bids us be more considerate than you heartless Christians. So—"

"Dio me varda!"

He dropped the mocking tone and snapped, "I begin to tire of this jousting. Let me say just one thing more. I foresee that it will raise some eyebrows, Folo, if you start claiming publicly to have heard disembodied voices in the Echo Pavilion, especially if you insist that you have heard the voice of a person known by all to be long defunct, and she a person slain in a misadventure of which you were the cause. The most charitable interpretation of your babblings will be that you are woefully demented by grief and guilt arising from that incident. Anything else you may babble—such as accusations against important and well-esteemed courtiers—will be similarly regarded."

I could not stand there and seethe at him, impotently.

"Mind you," he went on, "your pitiable affliction may redound to the public good, after all. In civilized Islam, we have institutions called Houses of Delusion, for the safe confinement of those persons possessed by the demon of insanity. I have long pressed Kubilai to establish the same hereabout, but he stubbornly maintains that no such demon infests these more wholesome regions. Your obviously troubled mind and troublesome behavior may convince him otherwise. In which event, I shall order the commencement of construction of Kithai's first House of Delusions, and I leave you to guess the identity of its first occupant."

"You—you—!" I might have lunged across the lilak bed at him, but he was stretching a hand toward the bedside gong.

"Now, I have told you to go and look and satisfy yourself that there is no one on the Kara Hill—no one anywhere to substantiate your demented imaginings. I suggest you go. There or somewhere. But go!"

What could I do but go? I went, miserably disheartened, and I plodded hopelessly up the Kara Hill to the Echo Pavilion once more, though knowing it would be as the Arab had said, barren of people, and it was. There was no least trace of Buyantu's ever having been there, or ever having been anything but dead. I came with dragging steps down the hill again, even more dejected and demolished, "with my bagpipes turned inside their sack," as the old Venetian phrase—and my father—would express it.

The sardonic thought of my father put me in mind of him and, having now no other destination, I trudged off to his chambers to pay a homecoming call. Maybe he would have some sage advice for me. But one of his maidservants answered to my scratch at the portal, and told me that her Master Polo was out of the city—still or again, I did not ask which. So I moped on farther along the corridor to Uncle Mafìo's suite. The maidservant there told me that yes, her Master Polo was in residence, but that he did not always spend the night in his chambers, and sometimes, not to disturb his servants unnecessarily, he came and went by a back door he had had cut in a rear wall of the suite.

"So I never know, at night, whether he is in his bedroom or not," she said, with a slightly sad smile. "And I would not intrude upon him."

I remembered that Uncle Mafìo had once claimed to have "given pleasure" to this servant woman, and I had been glad for him. Perhaps it had been only a brief foray

into normal sexuality, and he had since found it unsatis-
factory, and desisted, and that was why she looked a little
sad, and why she would not "intrude upon him."

"But you are his family, no intruder," she said, bowing
me in the door. "You may go and see for yourself."

I went through the rooms to his bedchamber, and it was
dark and the bed was unoccupied. He was not there. My
homecoming, I thought wryly, was not exactly being
greeted with open arms and shouts of joy, not by anybody.
In the lamplight spilling in from the main room, I began
feeling about for a piece of paper and something to write
with, to leave a note saying at least that I was back in residence. When I groped in the drawer of a cabinet, my fingernails snagged in some curiously filmy and flimsy cloth
goods. Wondering, I held them up in the half-light; they
seemed hardly garments sturdy enough for a man's wear.
So I went back to the main room and brought a lamp, and
held them up again. They were indisputably feminine
gowns, but of voluminous size. I thought: Dear God, is he
nowadays disporting himself with some female giant? Was
that why the maidservant seemed sad: because he had discarded her for something grotesque and perverse? Well, at
least it was female. . . .

But it was not. I lowered the robes to fold them away
again, and there stood Uncle Maflo, who had evidently
that moment come sidling in through his new back door.
He looked startled, embarrassed and angry, but that was
not what I noticed first. What I saw immediately was that
his beardless face was powdered blank white all over, even
over his eyebrows and lips, and his eyes were darkened
and lengthened with an application of al-kohl rimming the
eyelids and extending out from them, and a little puckered
rosebud mouth had been painted in the middle of where
his wide mouth should have been, and his hair was elaborately skewered by hair-spoons, and he was dressed all in
gossamer robes and wispy scarves and fluttering ribbons
the color of the flower called lilak.

"Gèsu . . ." I breathed, as my initial shock and horror
gave way to realization—or as much of realization as I
needed, and more than I wanted. Why had it not dawned
on me long ago? I had heard from enough people, God
knows, about the Wali Achmad's "eccentric tastes," and I
had long known of my uncle's desperate clutchings, like

those of a man adrift on an outgoing tide, at one crumbling anchorage after another. Just tonight, Buyantu had looked puzzled when I mentioned Achmad's "large woman," and then she had said evasively, "If that person had a woman's name. . . ." *She* had known, and she had probably decided, with female cunning, to save the knowledge for bargaining with, later on. The Arab had more forthrightly threatened, "I will make public some paintings . . ." and I should have remembered then the kind of pictures the Master Chao was forced to paint in private. "The very name of Polo will be a laughingstock. . . ."

"Gèsu, Uncle Mafìo . . ." I whispered, with pity, revulsion and disillusionment. He said nothing, but he had the good grace to look now ashamed instead of angry at being discovered. I slowly shook my head, and considered several things I might say, and at last said:

"You once preached to me, uncle, and most persuasively, on the profitable uses of evil. How it is only the boldly evil person who triumphs in this world. Have you followed your own preachings, Uncle Mafìo? Is this"—I gestured at his squalid disguise, his whole aspect of degradation—"is this the triumph it won for you?"

"Marco," he said defensively, and in a husky voice. "There are many kinds of love. Not all of them are nice. But no kind of love is to be despised."

"Love!" I said, making of it a dirty word.

"Lust, lechery . . . last resort . . . call it what you will," he said bleakly. "Achmad and I are of an age. And both of us, feeling much apart from other people . . . outcasts . . . uncommon. . . ."

"Aberrant, I would call it. And I would think you both of an age to subdue your more egregious urges."

"To retire to the chimney corner, you mean!" he flared, angry again. "To sit quiet there and decay, and gum our gruel and nurse our rheumatics. Do you think, because you are younger, that you have a monopoly on passion and longing? Do I look decrepit to you?"

"You look indecent!" I shouted back at him. He quailed and covered his horrible face with his hands. "At least the Arab does not parade his perversions in gossamer and ribbons. If he did, I should only laugh. When you do it, I weep."

He almost did, too. Anyway, he began sniffling pitifully.

He sank down on a bench and whimpered, "If you are fortunate enough to enjoy whole banquets of love, do not ridicule those of us who must make do with the leavings and droppings from the table."

"Love again, is it?" I said, with a scathing laugh. "Look, uncle, I grant that I am the last man qualified to lecture on bedroom morality and propriety. But have you no sense of discrimination? Surely you know how vile and wicked that man Achmad is, *outside* the bedroom."

"Oh, I know, I know." He flapped his hands like a woman in distress, and gave a sort of womanish squirm. It was ghastly to see. And it was ghastly to hear him gibber, like a woman agitated beyond coherence, "Achmad is not the best of men. Moody. Fearsome temper. Unpredictable. Not admirable in all his behavior, public or private. I have realized that, yes."

"And did nothing?"

"Can the wife of a drunkard stop him drinking? What could I do?"

"You could have ceased whatever it is that you *have* been doing."

"What? Loving? Can the wife of a drunkard cease loving him just because he is a drunkard?"

"She can refuse submission to his embrace. Or whatever you two—never mind. Please do not try to tell me. I do not want even to imagine it."

"Marco, be reasonable," he whined. "Would you give up a lover, a loving mistress, simply because others found her unlovable?"

"Per dio, I hope I would, uncle, if her unlovable characteristics included a penchant for cold-blooded murder."

He appeared not to hear that, or veered away from it. "All other considerations aside, nephew, Achmad is the Chief Minister, and the Finance Minister, hence he is head of the mercantile Ortaq, and on his permission has depended our success as traders here in Kithai."

"Was that permission contingent on your crawling like a worm? Demeaning and debasing yourself? Dressing up like the world's largest and least beautiful whore? Having to flit through back halls and back doors in that ridiculous garb? Uncle, I will not excuse depravity as *good business.*"

"No, no!" he said, squirming some more. "Oh, it was far

more than that to me! I swear it, though I can hardly expect you to understand."

"Sacro, I do not. If it were only the casual experiment in
curiosity, yes, I have done some such things myself. But I
know how long you have persisted in this folly. How could
you?"

"He wanted me to. And after a time, even degradation
becomes habitual."

"You never felt the least impulse to break the habit?"

"He would not let me."

"Not *let* you! Oh, uncle!"

"He is a . . . wicked man, perhaps . . . but a masterful
one."

"So were you, once. Caro Gèsu, how far you have fallen.
However, since you spoke of this as a business affair—tell
me, I must know—has my father been aware of this development? This entanglement?"

"No. Not this one. Not this time. No one knows, except
you. And I wish you would put it out of your mind."

"Be sure I will," I said acidly, "when I am dead. I trust
you know that Achmad is bent on my destruction. Have
you known it all this time?"

"No, I have not, Marco. That, too, I swear."

Then, in the manner of a woman—who, in any conversation, is always eager to turn it down some avenue where
she can run without check or hindrance or contradic-
tion—he began to prattle most fluently:

"I know it now, yes, because tonight when you came
there and I fled from the room, I put my ear to the door.
But only once before was I in his chambers when you and
he had words, and that time I took mannerly pains not to
overhear. He never otherwise disclosed to me the full extent of his animosity toward you, or the clandestine moves
he was making to harm you. Oh, I did know—I confess this
much—that he was no friend of yours. He often made disparaging remarks to me about 'that pestiferous nephew of
yours,' and sometimes facetious references to 'that *pretty*
nephew of yours,' and sometimes, when we were every
close, he would even say 'that provocative nephew of *ours.*'
And lately, after a messenger from Xan-du confided to him
that Kubilai had rewarded your war service by letting you
play stud to a string of Mongol mares, Achmad began
speaking of you as 'our wayward warrior nephew' and 'our

misguided voluptuary nephew.' And recently, in our most
intimate moments, when we were . . . when he was . . .
well, he would do it uncommonly hard and deep, as if to
hurt, and he would moan, 'Take *that*, nephew, and *that!*'
And at the surge, he would almost shriek, saying—"

He stopped, for I had clapped my hands over my ears.
Sounds can sicken, as well as sights. And I felt nearly as
nauseated as I had felt earlier, when I had to look upon the
flayed and limbless meat that had been Mar-Janah.

"But no," he said, when I would listen again, "I did not
know until tonight how much he really hates you. How he
has been impelled by that passion to do so many dreadful
things—and how he still seeks to discredit and destroy you.
Of course, I knew him to be a passionate man. . . ." And
the nausea rose in me again, as he once more lapsed into
broken sniveling. "But to threaten to use even *me* . . . the
paintings of us. . . ."

I barked harshly at him. "Well, then? It was some while
ago that you heard those threats. What have you been
doing since? Did you linger in his company—I devoutly
hope—to *kill* the son of a bitch shaqàl?"

"Kill my—kill the Chief Minister of the Khanate? Come,
come, Marco. You had as much opportunity as I, and more
reason, but you did not. Would you have your poor old uncle do the deed instead, and doom him to the fondling of the
Fondler?"

"Adrìo de vu! I have known you to kill before, and without such womanly compunction. In this instance, you
would have had at least more chance than I to escape
undetected. I presume Achmad has a back door for sneaking through, as you do."

"Whatever else he is, Marco, he is the Chief Minister of
this realm. Can you imagine the hue and cry? Can you believe that his slayer would go undiscovered? How long
would it have been before I was revealed, not only as his
murderer but—but—so much else revealed besides?"

"There. You almost said it. It is not the murder that you
shy from, nor the penalty for it. Well, neither do I fear killing or death. So this I promise you: I will get Achmad before he gets me. You can tell him so, next time you cuddle
together."

"Marco, I beg you—as I begged him—consider! He at
least told you the truth. There exists no single witness or

slightest evidence with which to impugn him, and his word will carry more weight than yours. If you contend with him, you are bound to lose."

"And if I do not, I lose. So the only matter still in doubt—and all you care about—is whether you lose your unnatural lover. Whoever is with him is against me. You and I are of a blood, Mafìo Polo, but if you can forget that, so can I."

"Marco, Marco. Let us discuss this like rational men."

"Men?" My voice cracked on the word, out of sheer fatigue and confusion and grief. I had been used to feeling, in the presence of my uncle, that I had grown up not at all from the boy I was when we first began our journeying together. Now suddenly, in the presence of this travesty of him, I felt much older than he was, and much the stronger of us two. But I was not sure that I was strong enough to endure this new conflict of feelings—in addition to all the other emotions that had been provoked in me this day—and I feared that I might myself break down into sobs and snivelings. To avert that, I raised my voice to a shout again. *"Men?* Here!" I seized up a shiny brass hand mirror from his bedside table. "Look at yourself, *man!"* I flung it into his silken and matronly lap. "I will converse no more with a painted drab. If you would speak again, let it be tomorrow—and come to me with a clean face. I am going to bed now. This has been the hardest day of all my life."

And indeed it had been, and it was not over yet. I tottered to my chambers like a hard-hunted and much-torn hare getting to its burrow just one jaw snap ahead of the hounds. The rooms were dark and empty, but I did not mistake them for any safe burrow. The Wali Achmad could very well know that I was alone and unattended—he might even have had the palace stewards arrange it so—and I decided to sit up all night, awake and full-dressed. I was too utterly tired to disrobe, in any case, but so very drowsy that I wondered how I could fend off sleep.

I had no sooner sunk down on a bench than I was jolted wide awake, to hunted-hare awareness, as my door silently swung open and a dim light shone in. My hand was already on my knife when I saw that it was only a maidservant, unarmed, no menace. Servants usually coughed politely or made some premonitory noise before entering a room, but this one had not because she could not. She was Hui-sheng, the silent Echo. The palace stewards might

have neglected to provide attendants for me, but the Khan
Kubilai never neglected or forgot anything. Even with all
his press of other concerns, he had remembered his latest
promise to me. Hui-sheng came in carrying a candle in one
hand and cradled in the other arm—perhaps she worried
that I would not recognize her without it—that white porcelain incense burner.

She set it down on a table and came across the room,
smiling, to me. The burner was already charged with that
finest quality tsan-xi-jang incense, and she brought with
her the fragrance of its smoke, the scent of clover fields
that have been warmed in the sun and then washed by a
gentle rain. I was immediately, blessedly refreshed and
heartened, and I would always thereafter associate Hui-
sheng and that aroma inseparably. Long years afterward,
the very thought of Hui-sheng reminds me of the incense,
or the actual smell of such a fragrant field reminds me of
her.

She took from her bodice a folded paper and handed it to
me, and held the candle so I could read. I had been so nicely
calmed and newly invigorated, by the sweet sight of her
and the sweet scent of clover, that I opened the paper without hesitation or apprehension. It bore a thicket of black-
inked Han characters, incomprehensible to me, but I
recognized the big seal of Kubilai stamped in red over
much of the writing. Hui-sheng raised an ivory small finger and pointed to another word or two, then tapped her
own breast. I understood that—her name was on the
paper—and I nodded. She pointed to another place on the
paper—I recognized the character; it was the same as on
my own personal yin—and she shyly tapped my chest. The
paper was the deed to ownership of the slave girl Hui-
sheng, and the Khan Kubilai had transferred that title to
Marco Polo. I nodded vigorously, and Hui-sheng smiled,
and I laughed aloud—the first joyful noise I had made in
ever so long—and I caught her to me in an embrace that
was not passionate or even amorous, but only glad. She let
me hug her small self, and she actually hugged back with
her free arm, for we were celebrating the event of our first
communication.

I sat down again and sat her beside me, and went on
holding her close like that—probably to her extreme dis-

comfort and bewilderment, but she never once wriggled in
complaint—all through that long night, and it seemed not
long at all.

3

I was eager to make my next communication to Hui-
sheng—actually to make a gift to her—which meant waiting for daylight when I could see what I was doing. But, by
the time the first light of dawn shone upon the translucent
windowpanes, she had fallen fast asleep in my arms. So I
simply sat still and held her, and took the opportunity to
look closely and admiringly and affectionately at her.

I knew that Hui-sheng was rather younger than I, but by
how many years I never would know, for she herself had no
idea of her exact age. Neither could I divine whether it was
owing to her youth or her race—or just her personal
perfection—but her face did not loosen and sag in sleep as I
had seen other women's faces do. Her cheeks, lips, jaw line,
all remained firm and composed. And her pale-peach complexion, seen close, was the clearest and most finely tex-
tured I ever saw, even on statues of polished marble. The
skin was so clear that, at her temples and just under either
ear, I could trace the faint-blue hint of delicate veins beneath, glowing through the skin the way the Master
Potter's paper-thin porcelain vases showed their inside-
painted designs when held to a light.

Another thing I realized while I had this chance to examine her features so closely. I had previously believed
that all the men and women of these nations had narrow,
slitlike eyes—*slant eyes,* Kubilai had once called them—
barren of eyelashes, expressionless and inscrutable. But
now I could see that it was only a matter of their having
just a tiny extra inner corner to their upper eyelids that
made the eyes look so, and then only from a distance. Up
close, I could see that Hui-sheng's eyes were most gorgeously equipped with perfect fans of perfectly fine, long,
gracefully curved black lashes.

And when the increasing daylight in the room finally
roused her and she opened her eyes, I could see that they

were, if anything, even larger and more brilliant than
those of most Western women. They were a rich, dark,
qahwah brown, but with tawny glints inside them, and the
whites around them were so pure-white that they had almost a blue sheen. Hui-sheng's eyes, when first opened,
were perceptibly brimming with leftover dreams—as anyone's are at waking—but as they took cognizance of the
real and daytime world, her eyes became lively and expressive of mood and thought and emotion. They were different from Western women's eyes only in that they were
not so readily readable; not inscrutable at all, merely requiring of a looker some attention and some *caring* to see
what message they held. What a Western woman's eyes
have to tell, they usually tell to anyone who will look.
What was in Hui-sheng's eyes was ever discernible only to
one—like me—who really wanted to know, and took the
trouble to gaze deep and see it.

By the time she woke, the morning was full upon us, and
it brought a scratching at my outer door. Hui-sheng of
course did not hear it, so I went to open the door—with
some caution, being still apprehensive of who might be
calling. But it was only a matched pair of Mongol maidservants. They made ko-tou and apologized for not having
been earlier in attendance, and explained that the palace's
Chief Steward had only belatedly realized that I was without servants. So now they had come to inquire what I
would eat to break my fast. I told them, and told them to
bring enough for two, and they did. Unlike my earlier servants, the twins, these maids seemed to have no objection
to serving a slave in addition to myself. Or maybe they
took Hui-sheng to be a visiting concubine, and possibly of
noble blood; she was pretty enough, and noble enough in
her bearing. Anyway, the maids served us both without demur, and hovered solicitously nearby while we dined.

When we were done, I made gestures to Hui-sheng (I did
this most awkwardly, with broad and unnecessary flourishes, but in time she and I would get so accomplished in
sign language, and so well attuned, that we could make
each other understand even complex and subtle communications, and with movements so slight that people around
us seldom noticed them, and marveled much that we could
"talk" in silence.) On this occasion, I wished to tell her to
go and bring to my chambers—if she wished to do so—all

her wardrobe and personal belongings. I clumsily ran my hands up and down my own costume, and pointed to her, and pointed to my closets, and so on. To a less perceptive person, it might have seemed that I was directing her to go and garb herself, as I was dressed at the time, in Persian-style male attire. But she smiled and nodded her understanding, and I sent the two maids with her to help carry her things.

While they were gone, I got out the paper Hui-sheng had brought me: the formal title to possession of her, relinquished by Kubilai to me. This was the gift I wanted to give her—namely, herself. I would sign the paper over to her, thereby manumitting her to the full status of freewoman, belonging to nobody, beholden to nobody. I had several reasons for wanting to do so, and to do it right away. For one, if I was likely soon to be condemned by the Arab to the cavern of the Fondler or the cell of a House of Delusion, I should have to flee or fight my way out, or fall in the fight—and so I wanted Hui-sheng to be in no way involved with me. But if I should live and keep my freedom and my courtier status, I hoped that eventually I would have possession of Hui-sheng in a different relation than master-and-slave. If it was to come about, it had to be of her own bestowing, and she could bestow herself only if she was at full liberty to do so.

I got from my bedroom the packs I had most recently carried and turned them out on the floor, looking for the little chicken-blood stone yin seal for affixing my signature firmly on the paper. When I found it, I also found the yellow-paper letter of authority and the large pai-tzu plaque Kubilai had given me to carry on my mission to Yun-nan. I probably ought to return those things to him, I thought. And that reminded me of something else I had brought for him: the paper on which I had scrawled the names of Bayan's engineers who had placed the brass balls, and whom I had promised to praise by name to the Khakhan. I found that, too, and it in turn made me recollect many other mementos I had picked up during even earlier journeying.

For all I knew, I might never have another chance to review my past, since I might not have any future to look forward to. So I went and rummaged among the older packs and saddlebags I had carried, and got out all those items and regarded them fondly. All my notes and partial maps I had given to my father to tend for me, but I had quite a few other things—dating clear back to the wood-and-string kamàl that a man named Arpad had given me in Suvediye to track our wanderings north and south . . . and a now rather rusty shimshir sword I had taken from the store of an old man named Beauty of Faith's Moon, and. . . .

There was another scratching at the door, and this time it was Mafìo. I was not overjoyed to see him, but at least he was dressed in man's clothes, so I let him come in. As if the change of raiment had restored some of his manhood, he spoke in the gruff voice of old, and even seemed emboldened to bluster. After giving me a perfunctory "Bondì," he began a harangue:

"I have lain awake all night, Neodo Marco, worrying over your situation—our several situations—and I came straight here without even taking time to break my fast, to tell you—"

"No!" I snapped. "I am long past being a little nephew boy, and you will do no telling to me. I also sat up all night, determining what I must do, though I have not yet determined exactly how I will do it. So, if you have any ideas, I shall be willing to hear them. But I will hear no telling of instructions or ultimatums."

He immediately pleaded, "Adasio, adasio," and raised his hands appeasingly, and let his shoulders slump as if he were enduring a lash. I was almost sorry to see him so quickly cowed by my strong rejoinder, so I said less harshly, "If you have not yet broken fast, yonder is a pot of cha still hot."

"Thank you," he said meekly, and sat down and poured a cup, and began again. "I came only to say, Marco—to suggest, that is—that you not embark on any drastic plan of action until I can talk again to the Wali Achmad."

Since I had in fact no plan of action, drastic or otherwise, I only shrugged and sat down on the floor to continue sorting through my keepsakes. He went on:

"As I tried to tell you last night, I have already petitioned Achmad to consider a truce between him and you. Mind you, I hold no brief for the atrocities he has committed. But, as I pointed out to him, in the doing of those things, he has bereft you of supporting witnesses, so he need not fear your crying calumny against him. At the

same time, as I also pointed out, he has sufficiently punished you for having angered him in the first place." Mafìo
sipped at his cup of cha, then leaned down to see what I
was doing. "Cazza beta! The relics of our journeys. I had
forgotten some of those things. Arpad's kamàl. And there,
a jar of the mumum shaving ointment. And that phial, is
that not a memento of the charlatan Hakim Mimdad? And
a pack of the zhi-pai playing cards. Olà, Marco, but you
and I and Nico were once a carefree threesome of journeyers, were we not?" He sat back again. "So my argument is this. If Achmad has no reason to pursue his
campaign against you, and you have no weapons against
him, then a declaration of truce between you—"

"Would mean," I said scornfully, "that nothing disrupts
your cozy affair with your masterful lover. Dolce far
niente. That is all you care about."

"That is not true. And if necessary, I am prepared to
prove my caring for—for all concerned. But even if you deplore that side result, there is much else to be said for a
truce. No one gets hurt and all are benefited."

"It does not much benefit the slain Mar-Janah and Buyantu and Lady Chao. Achmad slew them all, and all were
innocent of any harm or wrong to him, and Mar-Janah was
a friend of mine."

"What would benefit the dead?" he cried. "Nothing you
could do would bring them back alive!"

"I am still alive, and I must live with my conscience.
You just now mentioned us three carefree journeyers,
forgetting that for most of our journeys we were four. Nostril was one of us. And later, as Ali Babar, he was Mar-
Janah's devoted husband, and on my account he has lost
her. Your conscience may be infinitely pliable, but I will
not be able to look Ali in the eye again until I avenge Mar-
Janah."

"But how? Achmad is too powerful—"

"He is only a human being. He can die, too. I tell you
honestly that I do not know how I shall do it, but I swear to
you that I will kill the Wali Achmad-az-Fenaket."

"You would die for doing it."

"Then I die, as well."

"And what of me? What of Nicolò? What of the Compagnia—?"

"If you suggest *good business* to me again—" I began, but I strangled on it.

"Look, Marco. Do only what I asked a moment ago. Do not so rashly commit yourself until I have talked again with Achmad. I shall go immediately and plead with him. He may offer a palliative to your anger. Something you would accept. A new wife for Ali, perhaps."

"Gèsu," I said, with the deepest disgust that I had felt yet. "Go away, you creature. Go and crawl before him. Go and do whatever sordid things you do with him. Get him so delirious with love that he promises anything. . . ."

"I can do that!" he said eagerly. "You think you make only a cruel jest, but I can do that!"

"Enjoy the doing, then, for it will probably be the last time. I will see Achmad dead, and as soon as I can arrange it."

"You really mean that, I think."

"Yes! *How can I make you understand?* I care not what it costs me—or you—or the Compagnia or the Khanate or the Khan Kubilai himself. I shall seek only to shield my innocent father from the repercussions of my act, so I must do it before he returns. And I will. Achmad will die, and by my doing."

He must have been at last convinced, for he only said dully, "There is nothing I can say to dissuade you? Nothing I can do?"

I shrugged again. "If you are going to him now, you could kill him yourself."

"I love him."

"Kill him lovingly."

"I think I could not live, now, without him."

"Then die with him. Must I say it to you straight—to you who were my uncle and companion and trusted ally? I say it then: the friend of my enemy is as much my enemy!"

I did not even see him leave the room, because Hui-sheng and the two maids came back just then, and I was briefly occupied in showing them where to stow her little stock of clothes and belongings. Then, during another little while, I managed totally to forget the evil Achmad and my pitifully decayed Uncle Mafìo and all the other cares that weighed upon me and all the hazards that waited for me beyond this place and this moment—for I was happily engaged in giving to Hui-sheng the deed to herself.

I motioned for her to sit down at a table, which had on it the brushes and arm rest and ink block that the Han use for writing. I unfolded the title paper and laid it before her. I wetted the block to make ink, and brushed some of that onto the engraved surface of my yin, then pressed that firmly on a clear space on the paper, and showed her the mark. She looked at it and then at me, her lovely eyes striving to comprehend what I meant by those actions. I pointed to her, to the mark on the paper, to myself, then made dismissing gestures—the paper is no longer mine, *you* are no longer mine—and thrust the paper at her.

A great light came into her face. She imitated my gestures of dismissal, and looked questioningly at me, and I nodded definitely. She held the paper, still gazing at me, and made as if to tear it up—though she did not—and I nodded even more definitely, to assure her: that is correct, the slave deed no longer exists, you are a free woman. Tears came into her eyes, and she stood up and let go the paper and let it flutter to the floor, and gave me one last questioning look: there is no mistake? I made a wide, sweeping motion to indicate: the world is yours, you are free to go. There ensued one frozen moment, during which I held my breath, and we simply stood and regarded each other, and it seemed an interminably long moment. All she had to do was gather up her belongings and take her leave; I could not have prevented her. But then the frozen moment fractured. She made two gestures that I *hoped* I understood—putting one hand to her heart, the other to her lips, then extending both to me. I smiled uncertainly, and then I gave a happy laugh, for she threw her small self against me, and we were embracing as we had done the night before—not passionately or even amorously, but gladly.

I silently thanked and blessed the Khan Kubilai for having given me that yin seal. This was the first time I had ever used it, and behold, it had put this darling girl in my arms. It was truly amazing, I thought, what the simple impress of a mere carved stone on a piece of paper could accomplish. . . .

And then, abruptly, I let go of Hui-sheng and turned away from her and threw myself on the floor.

On the way down, I had a flashing glimpse of her startled little face, but there was no time to explain or apologize for my rudeness. I had been suddenly possessed of an idea—an outrageous and maybe even a lunatic idea, but a most enthralling one. It might have been Hui-sheng's own refreshing touch that had stimulated my wits to think of it. If it was, I would thank her later. Right now, sprawled on the floor, I ignored what must have been her great astonishment, and anxiously began pawing through the litter of oddments I had emptied from my packs. I found the pai-tzu plaque I had decided to return to Kubilai, and the list of engineers' names I wanted to give him, and—yes! there it was!—the yin seal engraved Pao Nei-ho, which I had taken from the Minister of Lesser Races just before his execution, and kept ever since. I seized upon it and gleefully regarded it and stood up clutching it, and I think I sang some song words and danced a few steps. I desisted when I realized that Hui-sheng and my two new servants were staring at me with wonder and dubiety.

One of the maids waved toward the door and said hesitantly, "Master Marco, a caller asking to see you."

I sobered immediately, for it was Ali Babar. I felt ashamed that he had found me capering, as if I were light of heart when he was bereaved and grieving. But it could have been worse; I should have felt more guilty if he had entered while I was embracing Hui-sheng. I strode to him and clasped his hand and drew him in, murmuring words of greeting and condolence and friendship. He looked terrible. His eyes were red from weeping, his great nose seemed to droop even more than usual, and he was wringing his hands, but that did not keep them from trembling.

"Marco," he said in a quaver. "I have just been to the Court Funeralmaster, seeking to look one last time at my dear Mar-Janah. But he says he has, among his store of the departed, not any such person!"

I should have anticipated that, and averted his going, and saved him the bewilderment of that announcement. I knew that executed felons did not go to the Funeralmaster; the Fondler disposed of them himself, without sacrament or ceremony. But I said nothing of that, only said soothingly, "Doubtless some confusion caused by the turmoil of the court's return from Xan-du."

"Confusion," mumbled Ali. "I am *much* confused."

"Leave everything to me, old friend. I will make all straight. I was just this moment about to do that. I am on my way to make various arrangements pertaining to this matter."

"But wait, Marco. You said you would tell me . . . all the how and the why of her dying. . . ."

"I will, Ali. As soon as I return from this errand. It is urgent, but it will not take long. Do you rest here, and let my ladies attend you." To the maids I said, "Prepare for him a hot bath. Rub him with balms. Fetch for him food and drink. Every kind of drink, and as much as he will take." I started out, but then thought of something else, and commanded most strictly, "Admit no one else to these chambers until I am back again."

I went, almost running, to call upon the Minister of War, the artist Master Chao, and by good fortune found him not occupied with either war or art so early in the day. I commenced by saying that I had heard of the accident which had taken his lady, and that I was sorry for it.

"Why?" he said languidly. "Were you among her stable of stallions?"

"No. I am merely observing the decencies."

"I must thank you. It is more than she ever did. But I imagine you did not come visiting for that only."

"No," I said again. "And if you prefer bluntness, so do I. Are you aware that the Lady Chao died by no accident? That it was so arranged by the Chief Minister Achmad?"

"I must thank him. It is more than he ever did for me before. Have you any notion why he took such an abrupt interest in tidying up the disarray of my small household?"

"He did not, Master Chao. It was purely in his own interest." I went on to tell of Achmad's use of the Lady Chao's official yin for the disposal of Mar-Janah, and the several preceding and subsequent events. I did not mention Mafìo Polo, but I did conclude by saying, "Achmad has threatened also to make public certain paintings done by you. I thought you might be averse to that."

"It would be embarrassing, yes," he murmured, still languidly, but his keen glance told me that he knew what paintings I referred to, and that they would be embarrassing to the Famiglia Polo as well. "I take it that you would like to interrupt the Jing-siang Achmad's suddenly headlong career of destruction."

"Yes, and I believe I know how. It occurred to me that if he could employ someone else's signature to covert purpose, so could I. And I also happen to be in possession of another courtier's yin."

I handed the stone to him, and I did not have to tell him whose it was, for he was able to read the name from it. "Pao Nei-ho. The former and impostor Minister of Lesser Races." He looked up at me and grinned. "Are you suggesting what I think you are?"

"The Minister Pao is dead. No one really knows why he had insinuated himself into this court, or whether he ever really used his office to the subversion of the Khanate. But if, all at once, a letter or a memorandum were found, bearing his signature, concerning some nefarious intention—say, a conspiracy somehow to defame the Khan and upraise the Chief Minister—well, Pao is not around to disown it, and Achmad might have a hard time refuting it."

Chao exclaimed delightedly, "By my ancestors, Polo, but you show certain ministerial talents yourself!"

"One talent I do not possess is an ability to write in the Han character. You do. There are others I could have applied to, but I took you to be no friend of the Arab Achmad."

"Well, if all you say is true, he did relieve me of one burden. But I still groan under his lading of others. You are right: I would happily join in deposing that son of a turtle. Except, you overlook one detail. You are proposing a *real* conspiracy. If it fails, you and I have an early appointment with the Fondler. If it succeeds—even worse—you and I are in each other's power forever after."

"Master Chao, I desire only vengeance against the Arab. If I can hurt him in the least degree, I care not if it costs me my head—tomorrow or some years hence. Simply by proposing this action, I have already put myself in your power. I can offer you no other surety of my bona fides."

"It is enough," he said with decision, and got up from his work table. "In any case, this is so wondrously grand a jest that I could not refuse. Come here." He led me into the next room, and whisked the cover off the tremendous map table. "Let us see. The Minister Pao was a Yi of Yun-nan, which was then under siege. . . ." We stood and looked at Yun-nan, which now was dotted with Bayan's flags. "Sup-

pose the Minister Pao was trying to aid his home province
. . . and the Minister Achmad was hoping to dethrone the
Khan Kubilai. . . . We need something to link those two
ambitions . . . some third component . . . I have it! Kaidu!"

"But the Ilkhan Kaidu rules way over yonder in the
northwest," I said dubiously, pointing to the Sin-kiang
Province. "Is he not rather remote to be involved in the
conspiracy?"

"Come, come, Polo," he chided me, but with high good
humor. "In this sin of perpetrating a lie, I am incurring
the wrath of my revered ancestors, and you are putting at
peril your immortal soul. Would you go to Hell for a
merely feeble and pusillanimous lie? Have you no artistry,
man? No sweeping scope of vision? Let us make it a *thundering* lie, and a sin to scandalize all the gods!"

"It should at least be a believable lie."

"Kubilai will believe anything of his barbarian cousin
Kaidu. He loathes the man. And he knows Kaidu to be
reckless and voracious enough to enter into any wildest
scheme."

"That is true enough."

"So there we have it. I shall concoct a missive in which
the Minister Pao privily discusses with the Jing-siang
Achmad their mutual and secret and culpable conspiracy
with the Ilkhan Kaidu. Those are the picture's main outlines. Leave the details of its composition to a master artist."

"Gladly," I said. "God knows you paint believable pictures."

"Now. How will you have come to be in possession of this
highly volatile document?"

"I was one of the last to see the Minister Pao alive. I
shall have discovered the paper while searching him. As I
really did find the yin."

"You never found the yin. Forget that altogether."

"Very well."

"You found on him only an old and much-creased paper.
I shall make it a letter which, here in Khanbalik, Pao
wrote to Achmand but had no chance to deliver, because he
was forced to flee. So he simply and foolishly carried it
with him. Yes. I shall rumple and dirty it a bit. How soon
do you want this?"

"I *should* have given it to the Khan back when I first arrived at Xan-du."

"Never mind. You had no way of recognizing its significance. You have just now found it while unpacking your travel gear. Give it to Kubilai, saying most ingenuously, 'Oh, by the way, Sire. . . .' The very offhandedness will lend verisimilitude. But the sooner the better. Let me get right at it."

He sat down to his work table again, and began busily to get out papers and brushes and ink blocks of red and black and other appurtenances of his art, saying meanwhile:

"You applied to the right man for your conspiracy, Polo, though I would wager much money that you do not even realize why. To you, no doubt, any two pages of Han characters look alike, so you are unaware that not every scribe can counterfeit another's writing. I must now try to remember Pao's hand, and practice until I can fluently imitate it. But that should not take me too long. Go now and leave me to it. I will have the paper in your hands as soon as I can."

As I moved toward the door, he added, in a voice combining cheer and rue, "Do you know something else? This may be the crowning effort of my whole career, the masterpiece of my entire life." And as I went out, he was saying, though still cheerfully enough, "Why could you not have conceived a work to which I could sign Chao Meng-fu? Curse you, Marco Polo."

4

"IF all goes well," I told Ali, "the Arab will be flung to the Fondler. And, if you like, I will petition permission for you to be present and *help* the Fondler put Achmad to the Death of a Thousand."

"I should like to help put him to death," mumbled Ali. "But help the hateful Fondler? You said it was he who did the actual ravagement of Mar-Janah."

"That is true, and God knows he is hateful in the extreme. But in this case he was acting at the Arab's bidding."

I had returned to my chambers to find, as I had hoped, that the maidservants had plied Ali Babar with enough liquor to numb him somewhat. So, although he variously had gasped with horror, wailed with grief and moaned with regret, as I told him all the circumstances attendant on Mar-Janah's demise, he had not indulged in the extravagant thrashing about and howling which most Muslims consider the only proper form of lamentation. Of course, I had not dwelt in detail on what last remnants I had found of Mar-Janah, or her last minutes of life.

"Yes," said Ali, after a long, pensive silence. "If you can arrange it, Marco, I *would* like to be present at the Arab's execution. Without Mar-Janah, I have not any other desires or anticipations to be realized. If only that wish is granted, it will suffice."

"I shall see to it—if all does go well. You might sit there and beseech Allah that all does go well."

Saying which, I got out of my own chair and knelt down on the floor again, to pick up and put away the litter of keepsakes. As I collected the various things—Arpad's kamàl, the pack of zhi-pai cards, and so on—I got the curious impression that something was gone from among them. I sat back and wondered, what could that be? I was not missing the Minister Pao's yin, for I had taken that away myself. But something was gone that had been there when I first emptied my packs. Suddenly I realized what it was.

"Ali," I said. "Did you perhaps pick up something from among this mess while I was absent?"

"No, nothing," he said, with an air of not even having noticed the litter on the floor, which in his stunned and preoccupied condition he probably had not.

I asked the two Mongol maids, and they denied having touched anything. I went and got Hui-sheng, who was in the bedroom putting her own few belongings carefully away in closets and drawers. I smiled at that; it indicated that she planned to stay, and for more than a brief while. I took her hand and drew her into the main room, and indicated the goods on the floor, and made questioning gestures. Evidently she comprehended, for she replied with a shake of her pretty head.

So only Mafìo could have taken it. What was missing

was the small clay phial at which he had exclaimed, "Is that not a memento of the charlatan Hakim Mimdad?"

It was. It was the love philter the Hakim had given me on the Roof of the World, the potent potion allegedly employed by the long-ago poet Majnun and his poetess Laila to enhance their making of love. Mafìo knew exactly what it was, and he knew it was unpredictably dangerous, for he had heard me berating Mimdad after my one horrible experience with the stuff, and he had seen me only warily accept from the Hakim a second little bottle to carry away with me. Now he had filched that phial. What could he want it for?

There came to me, with a jolt, some other words he had spoken this morning: "If necessary, I am prepared to prove my caring . . ." And when I jeered, "Go and get the Arab delirious with love!" he had said: "I can do that!"

Dio le varda! I must run and find him and stop him! God knows I had ample reason to be disillusioned and disgusted with Mafìo Polo, and not to care a bagatìn what became of him, but still . . . he was blood of my blood. And any self-pitying or self-glorifying act of self-sacrifice he might make now was futile and unnecessary, for I already had a trap in preparation for the damnable Arab Achmad. So I scrambled to my feet—causing Hui-sheng again to regard me with mild wonderment. But I got only as far as the door, for there stood the happily beaming Master Chao.

"It is accomplished," he said. "And so is your vengeance, the moment you show this to Kubilai."

He glanced past me and saw the others in the room, and tugged me by my sleeve out of their hearing down the corridor. He took out from some recess of his robes a folded, wrinkled, smudged paper that truly looked as if it had had a hard journey from Khanbalik to Yun-nan and back again. I opened it and gazed at what looked to me—as all Han documents looked to me—like a garden plot much tracked over by a flock of chickens.

"What does it say?"

"Everything necessary. Let us not take time for a translation. I hurried with it, and so must you. The Khan is right now on his way to the Hall of Justice, where he is about to declare the Cheng in session. Many matters of litigation have accumulated to await his judgment. He is conscientious about such things, even to the delaying of his

acceptance of Sung's surrender. But if you do not catch
him before the Cheng convenes, he will be occupied there,
and later in negotiations with the Sung Empress. It may
be days before you can get to him again, and in that time
Achmad could be busy to your detriment. Go quickly."

"The moment I do this," I said, "I am putting not just
Achmad's fate, but mine also, irrevocably in your hands,
Master Chao."

"And I mine, Polo, in yours. Go."

I went, after running into my rooms again to gather up
the other things I had for the Khakhan. And I did catch
him, just as he and the lesser justices and the Tongue were
taking their seats on the dais of the Cheng. He motioned
amiably for me to approach the dais, and, when I gave him
the items I had brought, he said, "There was no hurry
about returning these things, Marco."

"I had already kept them longer than I should have
done, Sire. Here is the ivory pai-tzu plaque, and your
yellow-paper letter of authority, and a paper the late Minister Pao was carrying at the time of his capture, and this
note of mine, which lists those engineers who so capably
positioned the huo-yao balls. Since I set down their names
in Roman letters, Sire, perhaps you would listen as I read
them. I hope I can pronounce them correctly, and that you
can comprehend them, for you may wish to reward those
men with some mark of—"

"Read, read," he said indulgently.

I did so, while he idly laid aside the plaque and the letter
he had given me to carry, and idly opened and glanced at
the paper the Master Chao had forged. When he saw that
it was written in Han, he idly handed it to the many-
tongued Tongue, and went on listening to me. I was struggling to comprehend my own not clearly legible list of
scrawls, reading aloud, "A man named Gegen, of the
Kurai tribe . . . a man named Jassak, of the Merkit tribe
. . . a man named Berdibeg, also of the Merkit—" when the
Tongue suddenly leapt to his feet and, for all his grasp of
many languages, gave a cry that was entirely inarticulate.

"Vakh!" exclaimed the Khakhan. "What ails you, man?"

"Sire!" the Tongue gasped excitedly. "This paper—a
matter of the utmost importance! It must take precedence
over all else! This paper—brought by that man yonder."

"Marco?" Kubilai turned back to me. "You said it was

taken from the late Minister Pao?" I said it was. He turned
again to the Tongue. "Well?"

"You might prefer, Sire—" said the Tongue, looking
pointedly at me, at the other justices and the guards. "You
might prefer to clear the hall before I divulge the contents."

"Divulge them," growled the Khan, "and then I will decide if the hall is to be cleared."

"As you command, Sire. Well, I can give you a word by
word translation at your leisure. But suffice it now to say
that this is a letter signed with the yin Pao Nei-ho. It
hints—it implies—no, it bluntly reveals—a treacherous
conspiracy between your cousin the Ilkhan Kaidu and—
and one of your most trusted ministers."

"Indeed?" said Kubilai frostily. "Then I think it best
that *no one* leave this hall. Go on, Tongue."

"In brief, Sire, it appears that the Minister Pao, whom
we all now know to have been a Yi impostor here, hoped to
avert the total devastation of his native Yun-nan. It appears that Pao had persuaded the Ilkhan Kaidu—or perhaps bribed him; money is mentioned—to march south and
fling his forces upon the rear of ours then invading Yun-
nan. It would have been an act of rebellion and civil war.
In that event, it was expected that you yourself, Sire,
would take the field. In your absence and the ensuing confusion, the—the Vice-Regent Achmad was to proclaim himself Khakhan—"

The assembled Cheng justices all cried "Vakh!" and
"Shame!" and "Aiya!" and other expressions of horror.

"—upon which," the Tongue resumed, "Yun-nan would
declare its surrender and fealty to the new Khakhan Achmad, in return for an easy peace. Next, it seems also to
have been agreed, the Yi would join with Kaidu in falling
upon the Sung, and help to conquer that empire. And after
all was done, Achmad and Kaidu would divide and rule the
Khanate between them."

There were more exclamations of "Vakh!" and "Aiya!"
Kubilai had yet made no comment, but his face was like
the black buran sandstorm rising over the desert. While
the Tongue waited for some command, the ministers began passing the letter around among them.

"Is it truly Pao's hand?" asked one.

"Yes," said another. "He always wrote in the grass stroke, not the formal upright character."

"And there, see?" said another. "To write money, he used the character for kauri-shell, which is currency among the Yi."

Another asked, "What of the signature?"

"It looks to be genuinely his."

"Send for the Yinmaster!"

"No one is to leave this room."

But Kubilai heard and nodded, and a guard went running out. In the meantime, the ministers kept up a muted hubbub of argument and expostulation, and I heard one say solemnly, "It is too outrageous to be believed."

"There is precedent," said another. "Remember, some years ago, our Khanate acquired the land of Cappadocia by a similar ruse. A likewise trusted Chief Minister of the Seljuk Turki enlised the covert aid of our Ilkhan Abagha of Persia to help him overthrow the rightful King Kilij. And, once the treachery was accomplished, the upstart allied Cappadocia to our Khanate."

"Yes," remarked another. "But happily there was a difference in those circumstances. Abagha conspired not for his own aggrandizement, but for the benefit of his Khakhan Kubilai and the whole Khanate."

"Here comes the Yinmaster."

Hurried along by the guardsman, old Master Yiu came shuffling into the Cheng. He was shown the paper, and had to squint at it only briefly before he pronounced:

"I cannot mistake my own work, my lords. That is indeed the yin I cut for the Minister of Lesser Races, Pao Nei-ho."

"There!" said several of them, and "It is all true!" and "It is beyond question now!" and they all looked to Kubilai. He inhaled a great breath of air, and slowly sighed it out, and then said in a doomful voice, "Guards!" Those men snapped to rigid attention, and thumped their lances on the floor in unison. "Go and demand the presence here of the Chief Minister Achmad-az-Fenaket." They thumped their lances again, and wheeled to march out, but Kubilai halted them for a moment and turned to me.

"Marco Polo, it seems that you have once again been of service to our Khanate—albeit inadvertently this time." The words were commendatory enough, but, from the ex-

pression on his face, one would have thought I had tracked
into the hall on my boots some dog dirt from the outdoors.
"You may see it through to the close, Marco. Go with the
guards and yourself utter to the Chief Minister the formal
command: 'Arise and come, dead man, for Kubilai the
Khan of All Khans would hear your last words.' "

So I went, as instructed. But the Khakhan had not ordered me to return to the Cheng in company with the
Arab, and, as it happened, I did not. I and my troop of
guards arrived at Achmad's chambers to find its outer
doors unguarded and wide open. We went inside, and
found his own sentries and all his servants gathered in attitudes of anxious listening and hand-wringing indecision
outside his closed bedroom door. When they saw our arrival, the servants raised a clamor of greeting, and
thanked Tengri and praised Allah that we had come, and
it was some time before we could quiet them down and get
a coherent account of what was going on.

The Wali Achmad, they said, had been in his bedchamber all day. That was not an uncommon occurrence, they
said, because he often took work with him at night and
continued, after awakening and breaking his fast, to deal
with it while lying comfortably abed. But this day, there
had begun to proceed from inside the bedroom some extraordinary noises and, after some understandable hesitation, a maidservant had pecked at the door to inquire if all
was well. She had been answered by a voice recognizably
the Wali's, but in an unnaturally high and nervous tone,
commanding, "Leave me be!" The unaccountable sounds
had then resumed and continued: giggles rising to wild
laughter, squeaks and sobs increasing to moans and
groans, laughter again, and so on. The listeners—by then
comprising Achmad's whole staff clustered against the
door—had been unable to decide whether the noises expressed pleasure or distress. In the course of what had now
been some hours, they had frequently called out to their
master and knocked on the door and tried to open it and
peer in. But the door was fastened tight shut, and they
were debating the propriety of breaking through it when
fortunately we arrived and saved them having to decide.

"Listen for yourselves," they said, and I and the corporal
of the guard pressed our ears to the panels.

After an interval, the corporal said wonderingly to me, "I never heard anything like it."

I had, but it had been a long time ago. In the anderun of the palace of Baghdad, I had once watched through a peephole as a young girl inmate seduced an ugly, hairy simiazza ape. The sounds I now heard through this door were much like the sounds I had heard then—the girl's murmured endearments and encouragements, the ape's puzzled gibbering, his grunts and her moans of consummation, all mingled with little yips and squeaks of pain, because the ape, in clumsily satisfying her, had also clumsily given her many small bites and scratches.

I said nothing of that to the corporal, saying only, "I suggest that you have you men clear all these servants away from here, away to their quarters. We must arrest the Minister Achmad, but we need not humiliate him before his staff. Get rid of his guards, too. We have enough of our own."

"We go in, then?" asked the corporal, as that was being done. "Even if he is indisposed?"

"We go in. Whatever is happening in there, the Khakhan wants that man and wants him now. Yes, force the door."

I had ordered the onlookers removed, not because I was concerned for Achmad's feelings, but for my own, since I expected to find my uncle conspicuously present in there. To my considerable relief, he was not, and the Arab was in no condition to care about humiliation.

He lay naked on the bed, his scrawny and sweaty brown body squirming in a welter of his own secretions. The bedclothes today were of pale-green silk, but much slimed and crusted with white and also with pink, for it appeared that, after many emissions, Achmad's later ones had been streaky with blood. He was still uttering the gibberish noises, though only in a muffled voice, for he had in his mouth one of those su-yang mushroom phallocrypts, moisture-bloated to such a bigness that it stretched his lips and cheeks. There was another pretend-organ protruding from his backside, but that was made of fine green jade. At his front, his own true organ was invisible inside something that looked like a Mongol warrior's wintertime fur hat, and with both hands he was frantically jerking it back and forth to fricate himself. His agate eyes were wide open, but

their stoniness looked blurred, as if by moss, and, whatever he was seeing, it was not us.

I gestured to the guards. A couple of them bent over the
Arab and began plucking the various devices off him and
out of him. When the su-yang was withdrawn from his
sucking mouth, his whimpered utterances got louder, but
were still only senseless noises. When the jade cylinder
was yanked out of him, he moaned lasciviously and his
body briefly convulsed. When the furry thing was taken off
him, he feebly continued moving his hands, though they
had not much left to play with down there, for he was
rubbed raw and bloody and small. The corporal of the
guard turned the hatlike object over and over, curiously
examining it, and I observed that it was hairy only in part,
but then I averted my eyes, as a quantity of white substance and stringy blood oozed out of it.

"By Tengri!" growled the corporal to himself. "Lips?"
Then he flung it down and said loathingly, "Do you know
what that *is?*"

"No," I said. "And I do not wish to know. Stand the creature on his feet. Throw cold water on him. Wipe him down.
Get some clothes on him."

As those things were done to him, Achmad seemed to re-
vive to some degree. At first he was utterly limp, and the
guards attending him had to hold him upright. But gradually, after much wobbling and teetering, he was able to
stand alone. And, after several drenchings with cold water, he began to make comprehensible words of his whimpers, though they were still disjointed.

"We were both dewy children . . .," he said, as if repeating some poetry that only he could hear. "We fitted well together. . . ."

"Oh, shut up," grunted the grizzled soldier who was
swabbing the sweat and scum off him.

"Then I grew up, but she stayed small . . . with only tiny
apertures . . . and she cried. . . ."

"Shut up," grunted the other leathery veteran who was
trying to get an aba onto him.

"Then she became a stag . . . and I a doe . . . and it was I
who cried. . . ."

The corporal snapped, "You have been told to be silent!"

"Let him talk and clear his head," I said indulgently.
"He will have need of it."

"Then we were butterflies . . . embracing inside a fragrant flower blossom. . . ." His rolling eyes momentarily steadied on me, and he said quite distinctly, "Folo!" But the eyes' stone hardness was still mossed over, and so were his other faculties, for he added only a mumble: "Make that name a laughingstock. . . ."

"You may try," I said indifferently. "I am commanded to speak to you thus: Go with these guards, dead man, for Kubilai the Khan of All Khans would hear your last words." I motioned one more time and said, "Take him away."

I had let Achmad continue babbling just to prevent the guards' noticing another sound I had heard in that room—a faint but persistent and musical sort of noise. As the guards left with their prisoner, I stayed behind to investigate the source of that sound. It did not come from anywhere in the room itself, nor from outside either of the room's two doors, but from behind some one of the walls. I listened closely and traced it to one particularly garish Persian qali hanging opposite the bed, and I swept that aside. The wall behind it looked solid, but I had only to lean on it and a section of the paneling swung inward like a door, giving on a dark stone passage, and I could make out now what the noise was. It was a strange sound to be hearing in a secret corridor in the Mongol palace of Khanbalik, for it was an old Venetian song being sung. And it was most exceedingly strange in these circumstances, for it was a simple song in praise of Virtue—something notably lacking in the Wali Achmad and his vicinity and everything to do with him. Mafìo Polo was singing, in a low quaver:

> La virtù te dà grazia anca se molto
> Vechio ti fussi e te dà nobil forme. . . .

I reached back into the bedroom for a lamp to light my way, and went into the darkness and swung the secret door shut behind me, trusting that the qali would fall and cover it. I found Mafìo sitting on the cold, damp stone floor, not far along the passage. He was again costumed in the ghastly "large woman" raiment—this time all in pale green—and he looked even more dazed and deranged than the Arab had done. But at least he was not smeared or caked with blood or any other body fluids. Evidently, whatever part he had played in the love-philter orgy, it had not been a very active one. He showed no recognition of me, but he made no resistance when I took him by the arm and stood him up and began walking him farther along the passage. He only went on singing quietly:

> La virtù te fa belo anca deforme,
> La virtù te fa vivo anca sepolto.

Though I had never been in that secret walkway before, I was well enough acquainted with the palace to have a general idea of where the passage's twists and turns were taking us. The whole way, Mafìo went on murmurously singing the virtues of Virtue. We passed numerous other closed doors in the wall, but I took us a considerable distance before choosing one door to open just a crack and peep out.

It gave on a small garden not far from the palace wing where we were quartered. I tried to hush Mafìo as I drew him outdoors, but to no avail. He was abiding in some other world, and would have taken no notice if I had dragged him through the garden's lotus pond. However, by good fortune, there was no one about, and I think no one at all saw us as I hurried him the rest of the way to his chambers. But there, since I did not know how to find *his* back door, I had to take him in through the usual one, and we were met there by the same woman servant who had admitted me the night before. I was somewhat surprised but much pleased when she evinced no shock or horror at seeing her master and onetime paramour so grotesquely attired. She only looked sad again, and pitying, as he crooned to her:

> La virtù è un cavedàl che sempre è rico,
> Che no patisse mai rùzene o tarlo. . . .

"Your master is taken ill," I told the woman, that being the only explanation I could think of—and it was true enough.

"I will attend him," she said, with calm compassion. "Do not worry."

* * *

. . . Che sempre cresse e no se pol robarlo,
E mai no rende el possessòr mendico.

I gladly left him in her care. And I might as well tell,
here, that it was in her tender and solicitous care that
Mafìo remained long afterward, for he never recovered his
reason.

It had already been quite an arduous day, and the one
before had been even worse, and I had passed a sleepless
night between. So I dragged myself to my own chambers,
to rest and myself enjoy some solicitude from my servants
and pretty Hui-sheng, while I kept Ali Babar company and
watched him drink himself unconscious of his own misery.

I never saw Achmad again. He was accused and tried
and judged and convicted and sentenced, all in that same
day, and I will tell of it just as quickly. I have no wish to
dwell on the subject, because it happened that, even in
winning my vengeance, I had to suffer one more loss.

In all the long time since then, I have felt no least remorse for having destroyed Achmad-az-Fenaket through
the agency of a forged letter, nor for its having implicated
him in a crime which was never committed. He was guilty
of enough other crimes and vices. Indeed, the false letter
might easily have failed in its purpose, but for the Arab's
truly perverted nature, which had led him to indulge in
the love philter with Mafìo. From that experiment in hal-
lucination, he emerged with his shrewd mind addled and
his sharp wits blunted and his serpent tongue knotted.
Perhaps he had been less severely impaired by the experience than had my uncle—the Arab at least briefly recognized me afterward, and Mafìo did not, ever again—and
perhaps Achmad would have recovered after a time, but he
did not get that time.

When he was dragged before the irate Khakhan that
day and confronted with the really flimsy evidence of his
"treason," he could readily have talked his way out of the
predicament. All he had to do was invoke the privilege of
office and request an adjournment of the Cheng until an
embassy could be sent to the Ilkhan Kaidu, the other of the
alleged triumvirate of conspirators. Kubilai and the justices could hardly have refused to wait and hear what word
Kaidu might send back. But Achmad never asked for that
or for anything else, according to those who were present.

He was unprepared to defend himself at all, they said, they
not being aware that he was *unable* to defend himself, incapable of it. They said he only gibbered and ranted and
twitched, giving the unmistakable impression of a culprit
felon deranged by his guilt and his having been apprehended and his dread of the penalty. Then and there, the
assembled justices of the Cheng found against him, and
the still outraged Kubilai did not overrule them. Achmad
was adjudged guilty of treason, and the punishment for
that was the Death of a Thousand.

The whole affair had blown up as suddenly as a summer
storm, but it constituted the most serious and spectacular
scandal in the memory of the oldest courtier. People talked
of nothing else, and were avid to hear or to recount any
least detail of news or rumor, and anyone who had a juicy
tidbit to impart was a center of a crowd. The greatest celebrity accrued to the Fondler, who had been given the most
illustrious Subject of his career, and Master Ping reveled
in that celebrity. Contrary to his usual dark secrecy, he
boasted openly that he was stocking his cavern dungeon
with provender to last for a hundred days, and that he was
dismissing all his assistants and clerks on holiday—even
his Blotters and Retrievers—so that he could give this distinguished Subject his undivided and *unshared* attention.

I went to call on Kubilai. By then, he had calmed somewhat and resigned himself to the defection and loss of his
Chief Minister, and he no longer looked at me the way ancient kings used to look at the bearers of ill tidings. I told
him, without going into unnecessary detail, that Achmad
had been responsible for the inexcusable murder of Ali
Babar's blameless wife. I asked, and got, the Khakhan's
permission for Ali to attend the execution of his wife's executioner. The Fondler Ping was aghast at this, of course,
but he could not countermand the permission, and he did
not even dare make any loud complaint, lest a closer look
be given to his own willing part in Mar-Janah's murder.

So, on the appointed day, I went with Ali to the underground cavern, and bade him be manfully stalwart as he
witnessed the piecemeal reduction of our mutual enemy.
Ali looked pale—he had never had stomach for bloodshed—
but he looked determined, even while he said his salaams
and farewells to me as solemnly as if he himself were going
to the Death of a Thousand. Then he and the Master Ping,

who was still grumbling at this unwelcome intrusion, went through the iron-studded door to where Achmad was already dangling and waiting, and closed the door behind them. I came away with only one regret at the time: that the Arab, from what I had heard, was still numb and be-mazed. If it was true, as Achmad had once told me, that Hell is what hurts worst, then I regretted that he might not feel the hurts as keenly as I would have wished.

Since the Fondler had given notice that this Fondling might occupy a full hundred days, everyone naturally ex-pected that it would. So not until the expiration of that time did his clerks and assistants return to congregate in the outer chamber and await their master's triumphant emergence. When several more days passed, they began to fidget, but dared not intrude. Not until I sent one of my maidservants, seeking word of Ali Babar, was the chief clerk emboldened to open the iron-studded door a crack. He was met by a charnel-house stench that sent him reeling backward. Nothing else came out of the inner room, and no one could even peek in without fainting dead away. The Palace Engineer had to be sent for and asked to direct his artificial breezes through the underground tunnels. When the chambers had been blown clean enough to be bearable, the Fondler's chief clerk ventured in and came out, looking stunned, to report what he had found.

There were three dead bodies, or the constituents and re-mains of three bodies. That of the ex-Wali Achmad was a mere shred, obviously having endured at least a Death of Nine Hundred and Ninety-nine. As well as could be ascer-tained, Ali Babar had watched that entire dissolution, had then seized and bound *the Fondler,* and proceeded to imi-tate, on his sacrosanct and inviolate person, the whole pro-cess of the Fondling. However, the chief clerk reported, it had not gone much beyond a Death of Perhaps One or Two Hundred. The supposition was that Ali had got too ill—from the miasma of Achmad's decay and all the other accu-mulated gore and carnage and excrement—to presevere to the end. He had left the only partially dismembered Mas-ter Ping hanging to die at his leisure, and had taken up one of the longer knives and plunged it into his own breast, and died himself.

So Ali Babar, Nostril, Sindbad, Ali-ad-Din, whom I had scorned and derided as a coward and an empty braggart all

the time I had known him, at the very last was impelled by
the one praiseworthy motive of his life—his love for Mar-
Janah—to do something eminently courageous and laudable. He took revenge on both of her slayers, the instigator
and the perpetrator, and then took his own life, so that
none other (meaning myself) could be blamed for the deed.

The palace population, and the city of Khanbalik, and
probably all of Kithai, if not the whole of the Mongol Empire, were still buzzing and twittering with the scandal of
Achmad's precipitous downfall. The new scandal from underground provided still more fodder for the gossips to
chew—and set Kubilai to regarding me again with stern
exasperation. But this latest news contained one revelation so macabre, so almost risible, that even the Khakhan
was bemused and distracted from any inclination to vin-
dictiveness. What happened was that, when the Fondler's
assistants collected and reassembled his cadaver for decent burial, they discovered that the man had all his life
had *lotus feet*, bound since infancy, warped and contorted
to dainty points, like those of a Han noblewoman. So the
resultant mood of everybody, including Kubilai, was not so
much glowering: "Now who should pay for *this* outrage?"—but speculative and almost amused, people asking
each other: "What awful kind of mother must the Master
Ping have had?"

My own mood, I have to say, was less frivolous. My vengeance had been accomplished, but at the cost of a longtime companion, and I was melancholy. That depression
was not alleviated when I went to Mafìo's chambers, as I
did every day or so, to regard what was left of *him*. That devoted woman servant kept him clean and nicely dressed (in
proper men's clothes), and she kept neatly trimmed the
gray beard that was growing in again. He appeared well-
fed and healthy enough, and he might have been taken for
the hearty and blustering Uncle Mafìo of old, except that
his eyes were vacant and he was again singing, in a sort of
cow-moo voice, his litany to Virtue:

> La virtù è un cavedàl che sempre è rico,
> Che no patisse mai rùzene o tarlo. . . .

I was contemplating him morosely and feeling very low
indeed when another visitor unexpectedly arrived, finally

come back from his latest trading karwan around the country. I had never—not even on his first arrival in Venice when I was a boy—been so glad to see my bland and gentle and dull and benign and colorless old father.

We fell into each other's arms and made the Venetian abrazzo, and then stood side by side while he looked sadly at his brother. He had, on the roads hither, heard in broad outline of all the events that had occurred during his journeying: the end of the Yun-nan war, my return to court, the surrender of Sung, the death of Achmad and the Master Ping, the suicide of his once-slave Nostril, the unfortunate indisposition of the Ferenghi Polo, his brother. Now I told him all the facts of those events which only I could tell. I omitted nothing but the most vile details and, when I had done, he looked again at Mafìo and shook his head, fondly, ruefully, regretfully, murmuring, "Tato, tato . . ." the diminutive and affectionate way of saying, "Brother, brother. . . ."

". . . Belo anca deforme," Mafio mooed, in seeming response. "Vivo anca sepolto. . . ."

Nicolò Polo mournfully shook his head again. But then he turned and clapped a comradely hand on my sagging shoulders, and squared his own, and perhaps for the very first time I was grateful to hear one of his stock encouragements:

"Ah, Marco, sto mondo xe fato tondo."

Which is to say that, whatever happens, good or bad, cause for rejoicing or lament, "the world will still be round."

MANZI

1

THE storm of scandal gradually abated. The Khan-balik court, like a ship that had been dangerously careened, gradually came upright again and steadied on its keel. As far as I know, Kubilai never tried to call his cousin Kaidu to account for his presumed part in the recent outrages. Kaidu being still far away in the west, and all danger of his involvement being now past, the Khakhan was content to leave him there, and instead devoted his energies to cleaning up the mess on his own doorstep. He sensibly began by dividing the late Achmad's three different offices among three different men. To his son Chingkim's duties as Wang of the city, he added the responsibility to serve as Vice-Regent during the Khakhan's absences. He promoted my old battlefield companion Bayan to the rank of Chief Minister, but, since Bayan preferred to stay in the field as an active orlok, that office too devolved onto Prince Chingkim. Kubilai might have desired another Arab to replace Achmad as Finance Minister—or a Persian or a Turki or a Byzantine—since he had such a high opinion of Muslims' financial abilities, and since that ministry had charge of the Muslim Ortaq of merchants and traders. However, the settling of the late Achmad's estate produced another revelation that soured the Khakhan on Muslims forever after. It was the rule in Kithai, as in Venice and elsewhere, that a traitor's belongings be confiscated by the state. And it was discovered that the Arab's estate consisted of a vast amount of wealth he had fraudulently appropriated and embezzled and extorted during his official career. (Some others of his belongings—including his hoard of paintings—never did come to light.)

The irrefutable evidence of Achmad's longtime duplicity so enraged Kubilai, all over again, that he appointed as Finance Minister the elderly Han scholar of my acquaintance, the Court Mathematician Lin-ngan. In his new detestation of Muslims, Kubilai went further, proclaiming new laws that severely abridged the freedom of Kithai's Muslims, and limited the extent of their mercantile activities, and forbade them to practice usury as heretofore, and diminished their exorbitant profits. He also made all Muslims publicly foreswear that part of their Holy Quran which permits them to dupe, cheat and kill all who are not of Islam. He even passed a law requiring Muslims to *eat pork,* if it were served to them by a host or innkeeper. I think that law was never much obeyed or stringently enforced. And I know that the other laws envenomed many already rich and powerful Muslims resident in Khanbalik. I know because I heard them muttering imprecations, not against Kubilai, but against us "infidel Polos" whom they held to blame for inciting him to the persecution of Muslims.

Ever since my return from Yun-nan to Khanbalik, I had been finding the city not a very hospitable or pleasant place. Now the Khakhan, occupied with so many other things, including the posting of a Wang and magistrates and prefects in the newly acquired Manzi, assigned me no work to do for him, and the Compagnia Polo likewise had no need of me. The appointment of our old acquaintance Lin-ngan as Finance Minister had caused no interference in my father's trading activities. If anything, the new suppression of Muslim business had meant an increase in his own, but he was capable of handling it all by himself. He was currently engaged in picking up the reins of what ventures Mafio had guided, and in training new overseers for the kashi works Ali Babar and Mar-Janah had headed. So I was at loose ends anyway, and it occurred to me that by leaving Khanbalik for a while I might allay some of the local unrest and grievances still smoldering. I went to the Khakhan and asked if he had any mission abroad that I could undertake for him. He studied on the matter and then said, with a trace of malicious amusement:

"Yes, I have, and I thank you for volunteering. Now that

Sung has become Manzi, it is a part of our Khanate, but it
is not yet subscribing any funds to our treasury. The late
Finance Minister would already have flung his Ortaq net
over that whole land, and would by now be seining rich
tribute out of it. Since he is not, and since you contributed
to the fact that he is not, I think it only right that you volunteer to take on the task in his place. You will go to the
Manzi capital of Hang-zho and inaugurate some system of
tax collection that will satisfy our imperial treasury and
not too seriously dissatisfy the Manzi population."

It was rather more of a mission than I had meant to volunteer for. I said, "Sire, I know nothing about taxation—"

"Then call it something else. The former Finance Minister called it a tariff on trade transactions. You can call it
impost or levy—or involuntary benevolence, if you like. I
will not ask you to bleed those newly annexed subjects of
every drop in their veins. But I shall expect a respectable
amount of tribute paid by every head of household in all
the provinces of Manzi."

"How many heads are there, Sire?" I was sorry I had
ever come calling on him. "How much would you deem a
respectable amount?"

He said drily, "I daresay you can count the heads yourself, when you get there. As to the amount, I will let you
know very promptly if it is not to my liking. Now do not
stand there gulping at me like a fish. You requested a mission. I have given you one. All the necessary documents of
appointment and authority will be ready by the time you
are ready to leave."

I set off for Manzi not much more enthusiastically than I
had set off for the war in Yun-nan. I could not know that I
was setting forth upon the happiest and most satisfying
years of my life. In Manzi, as in Yun-nan, I would successfully accomplish the mission set me, and again win the
plaudits of the Khan Kubilai, and become quite legitimately wealthy—in my own right, by my own doing, not
merely as a sharer in the Compagnia Polo—and I would be
entrusted with other missions, and would accomplish
them as well. But when I now say "I" it should be taken as
"I and Hui-sheng," for the silent Echo was now my traveling partner and my wise adviser and my steadfast
comrade, and without her beside me I could not have accomplished what I did in those years.

The Holy Bible tells us that the Lord God said, "It is not good for man to be alone: let Us make him a help like unto himself." Well, even Adam and Eve were not entirely like unto each other—a fact for which I, all these generations later, have never ceased thanking God—and Hui-sheng and I were physically different in many other ways. But more of a help no man could ever have asked, and many of our unlikenesses consisted, I must honestly say, in her being superior to me: in calm temperament, in tenderness of heart, in a wisdom that was something deeper than mere intelligence.

Even had she continued as a slave, doing nothing but serve me, or become my concubine, doing nothing but satisfy me, Hui-sheng would have been a valuable and welcome addition to my life, and an ornament to it, and a delight. She was beautiful to look at, and delicious to love, and a high-spirited joy to have around. Unbelievable as it may seem, her *conversation* was a pleasure to be enjoyed. As the Prince Chingkim had once remarked to me, pillow talk is the very best way to learn any language, and that was just as true for the language of signs and gestures, and no doubt our loving closeness on the pillow made our mutual learning quicker and our invented mutual language more fluent. When we got adept at that method of communication, I found that Hui-sheng's conversation was rich with meaning and good sense and nuances of real wittiness. All in all, Hui-sheng was far too bright and too talented to have been relegated to any of the underling positions where most women belong and are pleased to be and are best useful.

Hui-sheng's deprivation of sound had made all her other senses superlatively keen. She could see or feel or smell or *somehow* detect things that would have gone by me unnoticed, and she would direct my notice to them, so that I was perceiving more than I ever had before. For a very trivial example, she would sometimes dart from my side, when we were out walking, and run to what looked to me like a distant bank of nothing but weeds. She would kneel and pluck something unremarkably weed-looking, and bring it to show me that it was a flower not yet even budded, and she would keep that sprig and tend it until it bloomed and was beautiful.

Once, in the early days when we were still inventing our

language, we were idling away an afternoon in one of
those garden pavilions where the Palace Engineer had so
miraculously piped water to play jug flutes positioned under the eaves. I awkwardly managed to convey to Hui-
sheng how those things worked, though I assumed she had
not the least idea what music *was,* and I waved my hands
about in time to that murmurous warbling. She nodded
brightly, and I supposed she was pretending to comprehend, to please me. But then she caught one of my hands
and put it against one of the carved side columns, and held
it there, and signed for me to be very, *very* still. Perplexed
but fondly amused, I did so, and after a moment I realized,
with vast amazement, that I was feeling the very, *very*
faintest vibration—from the jug flute overhead, down
through the wood and so to my touch. My silent Echo had
shown me an echo in silence, indeed. She was capable of
appreciating and even enjoying the rhythms of that un-
hearable music—perhaps even better than I could, *hearing*
it—so delicate were her hands and her skin.

Those extraordinary faculties of hers were of incalculable value to me in my travels and my work and my dealings with others. That was especially true in Manzi, where
I was naturally regarded with distrust as an emissary of
the conquerors, and where I had to do business with resentful former overlords and grasping merchant chiefs and
reluctant hirelings. Just as Hui-sheng could discern a
flower invisible to others, so could she often discern a person's unvoiced thoughts and feelings and motives and intentions. She could reveal them to me, too—sometimes in
private, sometimes while that very person sat talking with
me—and on many occasions that gave me a notable advantage over other folk. But even more often, I had an advantage in merely being at my side. The men of Manzi,
nobles and commoners alike, were unused to women sitting in on masculine conferences. If mine had been an ordinary woman—plain, voluble, strident—they would have
disdained me as an uncouth barbarian or a henpecked ca-
pon. But Hui-sheng was such a charming and attractive
adornment to any gathering (and so blessedly silent) that
every man put on his most courtly manners, and spoke
most chivalrously, and postured and almost pranced for
her admiration, and many times—I know for a fact—
deferred to my demands or acceded to my instructions or

gave me the better of a bargain, just to earn Hui-sheng's look of approbation.

She was my fellow journeyer, and she adopted a costume that enabled her to ride a horse astride, and she rode always beside me. She was my capable companion, my trusted confidante and, in everything but title, my wife. I would have been ready at any time for us to have "broken the plate," as the Mongols called it (because their ceremony of wedding, performed by a shamàn-priest, culminated in the ceremonial smashing of a piece of fine porcelain). But Hui-sheng, again unlike the commonality of women, attached no importance to tradition or formality or superstition or ritual. She and I made what vows we wished to make, and made them in private, and that sufficed us both, and she was happy to forgo any public trumpeting and trumpery exhibition.

Kubilai advised me once, when the subject came up, "Marco, do not break the plate. So long as you have not yet taken a First Wife, you will find pliant and conciliatory every man with whom you have to deal, in matters of commerce or treaty negotiation or whatever. He will seek your good regard and will not obstruct your good fortune, because he will be nursing the secret hope of making his daughter or niece your First Wife and mother of your principle heir." That advice might well have made me hasten immediately to break a plate with Hui-sheng, for I scorned ever to order my life according to the dictates of "good business." But Hui-sheng pointed out, with some vigor, that as my wife she would *have* to observe some traditions—at least those enjoining wifely subordination—and so could not any longer ride joyously at my side, but, if she was allowed to go anywhere at all, would have to travel in a closed palanquin, and she could not any longer assist me in my working conferences with other men, and tradition would forbid her to—

"Enough, enough!" I said, laughing at her agitation. I caught and stopped her flickering fingers, and promised that *nothing* would make me marry her, *ever.*

So we remained lovers only, which may be the very best sort of marriage there could be. I did not treat her as a wife, an inferior, but accorded her—and insisted that all others accord her—full equality with myself. (That may not have been so liberal of me as it sounds, since I well rec-

ognized her many points of superiority, and so perhaps did
some cognitive others.) But I did treat her as a wife, a most
noble wife, in regaling her with gifts of jewelry and jade
and ivory, and the richest and most becoming garments for
her to wear, and, for her personal mount, a superb white
mare of the Khan's own "dragon horses." Only one husbandly rule did I lay down: she was never to mask her
beauty with cosmetics, in the Khanbalik fashion. She
complied, and so her peach-bloom complexion was never
slathered rice-white, her rose-wine lips were not discolored
or redrawn with garish paint, her feathery brows were not
plucked bald. That made her unfashionable, and so radiantly lovely that all other women cursed the fashion, and
their own slavishness to it. I did allow Hui-sheng to dress
her hair as she liked, since she never did it any way I did
not like, and I bought her jeweled combs and hair-spoons
for it.

Of jewels and gold and jade and such, she eventually
owned a trove that a Khatun might envy, but she always
treasured one thing most of all. So did I, really, though I
often pretended to consider it trash and urged her to throw
it away. It was a thing I had not given her, but one of the
pathetically few belongings she had brought when she
first came to me: that plain and inelegant white porcelain
incense burner. She lovingly bore it everywhere we journeyed and, in palace or karwansarai or yurtu or on open
camp ground, Hui-sheng made sure that the sweet scent of
warm clover after a gentle rain was the accompaniment of
all our nights.

All our nights . . .

We were lovers only, never wedded man and wife. Nevertheless, I will invoke the privacy of the marriage bed and
decline to relate the particulars of what she and I did
there. In recalling others of my intimate relationships, I
have spoken without reserve, but I prefer to keep some
things private to me and Hui-sheng.

I will make only some general observations on the subject of anatomy. That will not violate the privacy of Hui-
sheng, and would not cause her any blushes, for she often
maintained that she was physically no different from any
other female of the Min, and that those women were no different from the Han or any other race native to Kithai and
Manzi. I beg to differ with her. The Khan Kubilai himself

had once observed that the Min women were above all others in beauty, and Hui-sheng was outstanding even among the Min. But when she insisted, with modest and self-deprecatory gestures, that she was only ordinary of features and figure, I sensibly made no demur—for the most beautiful woman is the woman who does not realize she is.

And Hui-sheng was beautiful all over. That would adequately describe her, but I must go into some detail, to correct a few misapprehensions I myself had earlier entertained. I have mentioned the fine floss of hair that grew in front of her ears and at her nape, and I said then that I wondered if it implied an abundant hairiness in other places on her body. I could not have been more mistaken in that expectation. Hui-sheng was totally hairless on her legs and arms, under her arms, even on her artichoke. She was as clean and silkily smooth in that place as had been the child Doris of my youth. I did not mind that at all—an organ so accessible permits of various close attentions that a furred one does not—but I made mild inquiry. Was the hairlessness peculiar to her, or did she perhaps use a mumum to achieve it? She replied that no women of the Min (or the Han or the Yi or other such races) had hair on their bodies, or, if they did, had but the merest trace.

Her whole body was similarly childlike. Her hips were narrow and her buttocks small, just right for cupping in my hands. Her breasts were also small, but perfectly shaped and distinctly separate. I had long ago conceived a private belief that women with large nipples and considerable dark halo around them were far more sexually responsive than women with small and pale ones. Hui-sheng's nipples were minute by comparison with other women's, but not when regarded in proportion to her porcelain-cup breasts. They were neither dark nor pale, but bright, as pink as her lips. And they indicated no lack of responsiveness, because Hui-sheng's breasts, unlike those of larger women which are ticklish only at the extremity, were marvelously sensitive over their whole hemispheres. I had but to caress them anywhere, and their "small stars" pouted out as perkily as little tongues there. The same below. Perhaps because of the hairlessness, her lower belly and adjacent thighs were sensitive all over. Caress her anywhere there, and from her maidenly modest cleft would slowly emerge her pink and pretty "butterfly between the petals," the more appreciable and enticing for its not being concealed within any tuft.

I never knew, and refrained from ever asking, whether Hui-sheng had been a virgin when she first came to me. One reason that I never knew was that she was so *perpetually* virginal, which I will explain in a moment. Another reason was that—as she told me—women of those races *never* came to marriage with a maidenhead. They were accustomed to being bathed in infancy, and later bathing themselves, several times a day, and not only on the outside but—with dainty fluids made of flower juices—inside as well. Their fastidiousness went far beyond that of even the most civilized, refined, high-born Venetian ladies (at least until I later dictated that the custom be adopted by the women of my own Venetian family). One result of that scrupulous cleanliness was that a young girl's maidenhead got gradually, painlessly dilated and folded away to nonexistence. So she came to her nuptial bed with no fear of the first penetration, and no least twinge of hurt when it happened. And, in consequence, those races of Kithai and Manzi made no such fuss as other peoples do, about the sheet-stain certification of defloration.

While I am speaking of other peoples, let me remark that men of the Muslim countries treasure a certain belief. They believe that, when they die and go to the Heaven they call Djennet, they will disport themselves throughout eternity with whole anderuns of heavenly women called haura, who have, among their many other talents, the ability continually to renew their virginity. Buddhist men believe the same about the Devatas women they will enjoy in their heavenly Pure Land between lives. I do not know whether any such supernatural females exist in any afterlife, but I can testify that the Min women right here on earth possessed that wondrous quality of never getting slack and flaccid in their parts. Or at least Hui-sheng did.

Her opening was not just childishly small on the outside—the shyest and dearest dimple—but inside as well, most thrillingly tight and close-clasping. Yet it was mature, too, in that it was somehow delicately muscular all up along its inside length, so that it imparted not a constant squeeze but a repetitive rippling sensation from one end to the other. Aside from the other delicious effects pro-

duced by her smallness, my every entering of Hui-sheng
was like a first time. She was haura and Devatas: perpetually virginal.

Some of her anatomical uniqueness I recognized on our
very first night in bed together, and even before we coupled. I should also say of that first coupling that it occurred
not from my taking of Hui-sheng, but from her giving herself to me. I had resolutely kept my resolve not to urge or
press her, and instead had courted her with all the genteel
gallantries and flourishes of a trovatore minstrel demonstrating his affection for a lady high above his humble station. During that time, I ignored all other women and
every other sort of distraction, and spent every possible
moment with Hui-sheng or nearby, and she slept in my
chambers, but we slept always apart. What attraction or
attention of mine finally won her, I do not know, but I
know when it happened. It was the day she showed me, in
the jug-flute pavilion, how to feel music as well as hear it.
And that night, for the first time in my chambers, she
brought the incense burner and set it alight beside my bed,
and got into the bed with me, and—let me put it this way—
she allowed me again to feel music as well as hear it and
see it and taste it (and smell it, too, in that sweet incense
aroma of warm clover after gentle rain).

There was yet another smell and taste perceptible in my
making love to Hui-sheng. That first night, before we began, she inquired timidly whether I would desire children.
Yes, truly I would have, from one as precious as she—but,
because she *was* precious to me, I would not subject her to
the horrors of childbirth—so I said a definite no. She looked
a trifle downcast at that, but immediately took precautions against the eventuality. She went and got a very
small lemon, and peeled it to the white and cut it in half. I
expressed some disbelief that anything as simple and common as a lemon could do something as difficult as preventing conception. She smiled assurance and showed me
how it was employed. In fact, she gave me the piece of
lemon and let me do the applying. (In fact, she let me do
that every night we slept together, ever after.) She lay
back and spread her legs, baring the creased little peach-
hued purse down there, and I gently parted its cleft and
eased the bit of lemon inside. That was when I first realized how *very* small and virginally tight she was, a snug fit

even for my one finger, as it carefully, tremulously, worked the lemon up along the warm channel to the firm, smooth nub of her womb, where the lemon almost eagerly and lovingly cupped over it.

As I withdrew my hand, Hui-sheng smiled again—perhaps at the expression on my flushed face, or my breathlessness—and perhaps she mistook my excitement for concern, because she hastened to assure me that the lemon cap was a sure and certain preventive of accidents. She said it was provably superior to any other means, such as the Mongol women's fern seed, or the Bho women's insertion of a jagged nugget of rock salt, or the witless Hindu women's puffing of wood smoke inside themselves, or the Champa women's making their man clamp onto their organ a little hat of tortoise-shell. Most of those methods I had never heard of, and I cannot comment on the practicality of them. But I later had proof of the lemon's efficacy in that respect. And I also discovered, that same night, that it was a much more *pleasing* method than most, because it added a fresh, tart, bright scent and taste to Hui-sheng's already impeccably clean and fragrant parts and their emanations and essences. . . .

But there. I said I would not dwell on the particulars of our bedtime enjoyments.

2

WHEN we departed for Hang-zho, our karwan train consisted of four horses and ten or twelve asses. One horse was Hui-sheng's own high-stepping white mare; the other three, not quite so handsome, were for me and two armed Mongol escorts. The asses carried all our traveling packs, a Han scribe (to interpret and write for me), one of my Mongol maidservants (brought along to attend Hui-sheng), two nondescript male slaves to do the camping chores and any other hard labor.

I had another of Kubilai's gold-inscribed ivory plaques hanging at my saddle horn, but not until we were on the road did I open the documents of authority he had given me. They were of course written in Han, for the convenience of the Manzi officials to whom I would be showing them, so I ordered my scribe to tell me what they said. He reported, in tones of some awe, that I had been appointed an agent of the imperial treasury, and accorded the rank of Kuan, meaning that all the magistrates and prefects and other governing officers, everyone except the Wang overlord, would be required to obey me. The scribe added, as a point of information, "Master Polo—I mean Kuan Polo— you will be entitled to wear the coral button." He said it as if that would be the greatest honor of all, but it was not until later that I found out what that meant.

It was an easy, leisurely, pleasant and mostly level ride southward from Khanbalik through the province of Chih- li—the Great Plain of Kithai—which was one vast farm- land from horizon to horizon, except that it was crazily fenced into minuscule family holdings of just a mou or two apiece. Since no two adjoining farm families seemed to agree on the ideal crop for the land and the season, one plot would be of wheat, the next of millet, the next of clover or garden truck or something else. So that whole nation of greenery actually comprised a checkering and speckling of every different hue and tint and shade of green. After Chih-li came the province of Shan-dong, where the farms gave way to groves of mulberry trees, the leaves of which are sustenance for silkworms. It was from Shan-dong that came the heavy, nubbed, much-prized silk fabric also called shan-dong.

One thing I noticed on all the main roads in this south- ern region of Kithai: they were posted at intervals with in- formative signboards. I could not read the Han writing, but my scribe translated them for me. There would be a column erected at the roadside, with a board sticking out from it each way, and on one might be painted: "To the North to Gai-ri, nineteen li," and on the other: "To the South to Zhen-ning, twenty-eight li." So a traveler always knew where he was, and where he was going, and where (if he had forgotten) he had just come from. The signposts were especially informative at crossroads, where a whole thicket of them would list every city and town in every di- rection from there. I made a note of that very helpful Han contrivance, thinking it could well be recommended for adoption in all the rest of the Khanate—and, for that mat- ter, all over Europe—where there were no such things.

Most of the way southward through Kithai, we were
either riding close beside the Great Canal, or within sight
of it, and it teemed with water traffic, so, whenever we
were any distance from it, we had the odd view of boats and
ships apparently sailing seas of grain fields and navigat-
ing among orchard trees. That canal was inspired, or made
necessary, by the fact that the Huang or Yellow River had
so often changed its channel. Within recorded history, the
eastern length of the river had whipped back and forth
across the land like a snapped rope—though of course not
so rapidly. In one century or another, it had emptied into
the Sea of Kithai way up north of the Shan-dong Peninsula, just a couple of hundred li south of Khanbalik. Some
centuries later, its immense and serpentine length had
wriggled down the map to flow into the sea far *south* of the
Shan-dong Peninsula, fully a thousand li distant from its
earlier outlet. To envision that, try to imagine a river flowing through France and at one time spilling into the Bay of
Biscay at the English port of Bordeaux, then squirming
across that whole breadth of Europe to empty into the
Mediterranean at the Republic of Marseilles. And the Yellow River, at other times in history, had pushed out to the
Sea of Kithai at various shore points intermediate between those northernmost and southernmost reaches.

The river's inconstancy had left many lesser streams
and isolated lakes and ponds all across the lands where it
used to run. Some of the earlier ruling dynasties cunningly
took advantage of that, to dig a canal interconnecting and
incorporating the existent waters and make a navigable
waterway running roughly north and south, inland of the
sea. I believe it was, until recently, only a desultory and
fragmentary canal, connecting just two or three towns in
each stretch. But Kubilai, or rather his Chief of Digging
the Great Canal, with armies of conscript labor, had done
more trenching and dredging, and done it better. So the canal was now broad and deep and permanent, its banks
neatly beveled and faced with stone, with locks and hoist-
ing engines provided wherever it had to vault intervening
highlands. It enabled vessels of every size, from sanpan
scows to seagoing chuan ships, to sail or row or be towed all
the way from Khanbalik to the southern border of Kithai,
where the delta of the other great river, the Yang-tze,
fanned out into the Sea of Kithai. And now that Kubilai's

realm extended south of the Yang-tze, the Great Canal
was being pushed clear to Manzi's capital city of Hang-zho.
It was a modern-day accomplishment nearly as grand and
sightly and awesome as the ancient Great Wall—and far
more useful to mankind.

When our little karwan train was ferried across the
Yang-tze, the Tremendous River, it was like crossing a
dun-colored sea, so broad that we could barely distinguish
the darker dun line on the far side that was the shore of
Manzi. I had some difficulty in reminding myself that this
was the water I had been able to throw a stone across,
away to the west and upriver in Yun-nan and To-Bhot
where it was called the Jinsha.

Until now, we had been traversing a country inhabited
mostly by Han, but a country that had been for many years
under Mongol domination. Now here, in what had until
very recently been the Sung Empire, we were among Han
peoples whose ways of life had not yet been in the least impressed or overlaid by the more robust and vigorous Mongol society. To be sure, Mongol patrols roamed hither and
yon, to preserve order, and every community had a new
headman who, though usually a Han, had been imported
from Kithai and installed by the Mongols. But those had
not had time to make any changes in what the country had
been. Also, because Sung had surrendered to become
Manzi without any struggle, the land had not been fought
over or ravaged or blighted in any way. It was peaceful and
prosperous and pleasing to the eye. So, from the moment of
our landing on the Manzi shore, I began to take an even
keener interest in our surroundings, eager to see what the
Han were like in their natural state, so to speak.

The most noticeable aspect of them was their incredible
ingenuity. I had been inclined in the past to denigrate that
much-vaunted quality of theirs, having so often found
their inventions and discoveries to be as impractical as, for
instance, their circle divided into three hundred sixty-five
and a quarter segments. But I was more taken with the
cleverness of the Han in Manzi, and it was never better
demonstrated than by a prosperous landowner who took
me on a tour of his holdings, just outside the city of Su-zho.
I was accompanied by my scribe, who translated for me.

"A vast estate," said our host, waving at it expansively.
Perhaps it was, in a country where the average farmer

owned a miserable mou or two of land. But it would have
been accounted ridiculously tiny elsewhere—say, in the
Vèneto, where the properties are measured in sweeps of
zonte. All I could see here was a plot of ground just barely
big enough to contain the owner's one-room shack—his
"country house"; he had a substantial mansion in Su-zho—
and a cramped truck garden beside the shack, a single trel-
lis thickly grown with grapevine, some rickety pig sties, a
pond no bigger than the smallest in a Khanbalik palace
garden, and a sparse grove of trees which, from their
gnarled fistlike limbs, I took to be mere mulberries.

"Kan-kàn! Behold! My orchard, my piggery, my vine-
yard and my fishery!" he boasted, as if he were describing
an entire and fertile and thriving prefecture. "I harvest
silk and pork and zu-jin fish and grape wine, four staples of
gracious living."

That they were, I agreed, but remarked that there
seemed little room here to harvest any profitable quantity
of any of them, and that they struck me, besides, as a
strangely assorted quartet of crops.

"Why, they all support and increase one another," he
said, with some surprise. "So they do not require much
space to produce a bountiful harvest. You have seen my
abode in the city, Kuan Polo, so you know I am wealthy.
My wealth came all from this estate."

I could not gainsay him, so I asked politely if he would
explain his farming methods, for they must be masterful.
He began by telling me that in the skimpy garden plot he
grew radishes.

That sounded so trifling that I murmured, "You failed to
mention that staple of gracious living."

"No, no, not for the table, Kuan, nor for marketing. The
radishes are only for the grapes. If you bury your grapes
among a bin of radish roots, the grapes will stay fresh and
sweet and delicious for months, if necessary."

He continued. The radish tops, the greens, he fed to the
pigs in the sties. The sties were uphill of the mulberry
grove, and tiled channels were laid between, so the pigs' offal sluiced downhill to fertilize the trees. The trees' green
summer leaves nourished the silkworms, and, in autumn
when the leaves turned brown, they too were fodder for the
pigs. Meanwhile, the excreta of the silkworms was the favorite food of the zu-jin fish, and the fishes' excrement en-

riched the pond bottom, the silt of which was dredged up at intervals to nourish the grape arbor. And so—kan-kàn! ecco! behold!—in this miniature universe, every living thing was interdependent, and flourished by being so, and made him wealthy.

"Ingenious!" I exclaimed, and sincerely meant it.

The Han of Manzi were clever in other, less striking ways, too, and not just the upper classes, but the least of them. A Han farmer, when he judged the time of day by glancing at the altitude of the sun, was of course doing nothing that any Vèneto peasant could not. However, *indoors*, that farmer's wife at home in their hut could tell precisely when it was time to start making her man's evening meal—merely by glancing at the eyes of the family cat and judging how much its pupils had dilated in the waning light. The commonfolk were diligent, too, and thrify and unbelievably patient. No farmer ever bought a pitchfork, for example. He would find a tree limb terminating in three pliable twigs, tie those twigs parallel, wait years until they grew into sturdy branches, saw off the limb, and he would have a tool that would serve him and probably his grandsons as well.

I was much impressed by the ambition and perseverance of one farm boy I met. The majority of the Han country folk were illiterate and content to remain so, but this one lad had somehow learned to read, and was determined to rise above his poverty, and had borrowed books to study. Since he could not neglect his farm work—being the only stay of aged parents—he would tie a book to the horns of his ox and read while he led the beast about in tilling the field. And at night, because the household could not afford even a grease wick-lamp, he would read by the light of glowworms which he plucked from the farm furrows during the day.

I do not mean to assert that every Han in Manzi was the embodiment of virtues and talents and no less worthy attributes. I saw also some egregious evidences of fatuity and even lunacy. One night we came to a village where a religious festa of some sort was going on. There was music and song and dance and merry fires burning all about, and every so often the night was rent by the thunder and flash of the fiery trees and sparkling flowers. The center of all the celebration was a table set up in the village square. It

was piled with offerings to the gods: samples of the finest
local farm produce, flasks of pu-tao and mao-tai, slaughtered piglet and lamb carcasses, fine cooked viands, beautifully arranged vases of flowers. There was a gap among
all that bounty, where a hole was cut in the middle of the
table, and one villager after another would crawl under
the table, put his head up through the hole, pose that way
for a time, then remove himself to make way for another.
When I inquired in amazement what that was meant to
signify, my scribe asked about and then reported:

"The gods look down and see the sacrifices heaped up for
them. Among the offerings, the heads. So each villager
goes away confident that the gods, having seen him already dead, will take his name off their list of local mortals
to be afflicted with ills and sorrows and death."

I might have laughed. But it occurred to me that, however simple-mindedly those people were behaving, at least
they were being *ingeniously* simpleminded. After some
time in Manzi, and after admiring innumerable instances
of the Han's intelligence, and after deploring as many instances of witlessness, I eventually came to a conclusion.
The Han possessed prodigious intellect and industry and
imagination. They were mainly flawed in this respect:
they too often wasted their gifts in fanatic observance of
their religious beliefs, which were flagrantly fatuous. If
the Han had not been so preoccupied with their notions of
godliness, and so bent on seeking "wisdom instead of
knowledge" (as one of them had once expressed it to me), I
think those people, as a people, could have done great
things. If they had not forever lain worshipfully prostrate—a position which invited their being trodden on by
one oppressive dynasty after another—they might themselves by now be rulers of the whole world.

That farm boy I earlier spoke of, whose initiative and as-
siduity I found admirable, forfeited some of my regard as
we talked further and he told me, by way of my scribe:

"My passion for reading and my yearning for learning
might distress my aged parents. They might decry my ambition as an overwhelming arrogance, but—"

"Why on earth should they?"

"We follow the Precepts of Kong Fu-tze, and one of his
teachings was that a low-born person should not presume
above his ordained station in life. But I was about to say

that my parents do *not* object, for my reading affords me opportunity also to manifest my filial piety, and another of the Precepts is that parents be honored above all else. So, since each night I am so eager to get to my books and my glowworms, I am the first of us to retire. I can lie on my pallet and force myself to lie perfectly still while I read, so that all the mosquitoes in the house can freely suck my blood."

I blinked and said, "I do not understand."

"By the time my aged parents stretch their old bodies on their pallets, you see, the mosquitoes are gorged and sated, and do not molest them. Yes, my parents often boast of me to our neighbors, and I am held an example to all sons."

I said unbelievingly, "This is something marvelous. The old fools boast of you letting yourself be eaten alive, but not of your striving to better yourself?"

"Well, doing the one is being obedient to the Precepts, while the other. . . ."

I said, "Vakh!" and turned and went away from him. A parent too apathetic to swat his own mosquitoes seemed not much worth honoring, or humoring with attention—or preserving, for that matter. As a Christian, I believe in devotion to one's father and mother, but I think that not even the Commandment enjoins abject filiality to the exclusion of everything else. If that were so, no son would ever have time or opportunity to produce a son to honor *him*.

That Kong Fu-tze, or Kong-the-Master, of whom the boy had spoken, was a long-ago Han philosopher, the originator of one of the three chief religions of those people. The three faiths all were fragmented into numerous contradictory and antagonistic sects, and all three were much intermingled in popular observance, and they were interlarded with traces of ever so many lesser cults—worship of gods and goddesses, demons and demonesses, nature spirits, ancient superstitions—but in the main there were three: Buddhism, the Tao and the Precepts of Kong Fu-tze.

I have already mentioned Buddhism, holding out to man a salvation from the rigors of this world by means of continual rebirths ascending to the nothingness of Nirvana. I have also mentioned the Tao, the Way by which a man could hope to harmonize and live happily with all the good things of the world around him. The Precepts dealt less with the here or the hereafter than with all-that-has-gone-before. To put it simplistically, a practitioner of Buddhism looked to the empty void of the future. A follower of the Tao did his best to enjoy the teeming and eventful present. But a devotee of the Precepts was concerned mostly with the past, the old, the dead.

Kong Fu-tze preached respect for tradition, and tradition is what his Precepts became. He ordained that younger brothers must revere the older, and a wife revere her husband, and all revere the parents, and they the community elders, and so on. The result was that the greatest honor accrued not to the best, but to the oldest. A man who had heroically prevailed against fierce odds—to win some notable victory or attain to some notable eminence—was accounted less worthy than some human turnip who had merely sat inert and *existed* and survived to a venerable age. All the respect rightly owed to excellence was bestowed upon vegetable antiquity. I did not think that reasonable. I had known enough old fools—and not just in Manzi—to know that age does not, as a matter of inevitability, confer wisdom, dignity, authority or worth. Years do not do that by themselves; the years must have contained experience and learning and achievement and travail overcome; and most people's years do not.

Worse yet. If a living grandfather was to be venerated, well, *his* father and grandfather, though dead and gone, were even older—no xe vero?—and even more highly to be venerated. Or so the Precepts were interpreted by their devotees, and those Precepts had permeated the consciousness of all the Han, including those who professed faith in Buddhism or the Tao or the Mongols' Tengri or the Nestorian version of Christianity or some one of the lesser religions. There was a general attitude of "Who knows? It may not help, but it does no harm, to burn a bit of incense to the next fellow's deity, however absurd." Even the most nearly rational persons, those Han who had converted to Nestorian Christianity—who would never have made ko-tou to the next fellow's absurd fat idol, or a shamàn's divining bones, or a Taoist's advice-giving sticks, or whatever—saw no harm, and possible benefit, in making ko-tou to his own ancestors. A man may be poor in all material assets, but even the most impoverished wretch has whole nations of ancestors. Paying the requisite reverence to all of them kept every living person of the Han perpetually prone—if not in physical fact, certainly in his outlook on life.

The Han word mian-tzu meant literally "face," the face on the front of one's head. But, because the Han seldom let their faces show much surface expression of their feelings, the word had come to mean the feelings going on *behind* those faces. To insult a man or humiliate him or best him in a contest was to cause him to "lose face." And the vulnerability of his feeling-face persisted beyond the grave, into uttermost eternity. If a son dared not behave in any way to shame or sadden the feeling-faces of his elders, how much more reprehensible it would have been to hurt the disembodied feeling-faces of the dead. So all the Han ordered their lives as if they were being watched and scrutinized and judged by all their forebear generations. It might have been a worthwhile superstition, if it had spurred all men to attempt feats that their ancestors would applaud. But it did not. It made them only anxious to evade their ancestors' disapproval. A life entirely devoted to the avoidance of wrong seldom achieves anything exceptionally right—or anything at all.

Vakh.

3

THE city named Su-zho, through which we passed on our way south, was a lovely city, and we were almost loath to leave it. But when we reached our destination, Hang-zho, we found it an even more beautiful and gracious place. There is a rhyming adage which is known even to faraway Han who have never visited either of the cities:

> Shang ye Tian tang,
> Zhe ye Su, Hang!

Which could be translated thus:

> Heaven is far from me and you,
> But here for us are Hang and Su!

As I have said, Hang-zho was like Venice in one respect, being girt all about by water and riddled by waterways. It was both a riverside and a seaside city, but not a port city. It was situated on the north bank of a river called the Fu-chun, which here widened and shallowed and fanned out, eastward of the city, into many separate runnels across a vast, spreading, flat delta of sand and pebbles. That empty delta extended for some two hundred li, from Hang-zho to what was, most of the time, the distant edge of the Sea of Kithai. (I will shortly make plain what I mean by "most of the time.") Since no seaborne vessels could cross that immense sandy shoal, Hang-zho had no port facilities, except what docks were necessary to handle the comparatively few and small boats that plied the river inland from the city.

All the many main avenues of Hang-zho were canals running from the riverside into the city and through it and round about it. At places those canals broadened out into wide, serene, mirror-smooth lakes, and in those were islands that were public parks, all flowers and birds and pavilions and banners. The lesser streets of the city were neatly cobbled, and they were broad but tortuous and twisty, and they humped themselves over the canals on ornate, high-arched bridges, more of them than I could ever count. At every bend in every street or canal, one had a view of one of the city's many high and elaborate gates, or a tumultuous marketplace, or a palatial building or temple, as many as ten or twelve stories high, with the distinctive curly Han eaves projecting from every single story.

The Court Architect of Khanbalik had once told me that Han cities never had straight streets because the Han commonfolk foolishly believed that demons could travel only in straight lines, and foolishly believed that they were thwarting the demons by putting kinks in all their streets. But that was nonsense. In truth, the streets of any Han city—including both the paved and the watery ones of Hang-zho—were laid out in deliberate emulation of the Han style of writing. The city's marketplace—or each of the marketplaces, in a city like Hang-zho that had so many—was a straight-edged square, but all the surrounding streets would have bends and curves and sinuosities, gentle or abrupt, just as do the brush strokes of a written

Han word. My own personal yin signature could very well
be the street plan of some walled Han town.

Hang-zho was, as befits a capital city, very civilized and
refined, and it exhibited many touches of good taste. At intervals along every street were tall vases in which the
householders or shopkeepers put flowers for the delight of
the passersby. At this season they were all brimming with
glowing, dazzling chrysanthemums. That flower, incidentally, was the national symbol of Manzi, reproduced on all
official signboards and documents and such, revered because the exuberant florets of its blossom are so reminiscent of the sun and its sunbeams. Also at intervals along
the streets were posts bearing boxes labeled—so my scribe
told me—"Receptacle for the respectful deposit of sacred
paper." That meant, he told me, any piece of paper with
writing on it. Ordinary litter was simply swept up and removed, but the written word was held in such high regard
that all such papers were taken to a special temple and ritually burned.

But Hang-zho also was, as befits a prosperous trading
city, rather gaudily voluptuous in other respects. It seemed
that every last person on the streets, except for travel-
dusted new arrivals like us, was luxuriously garbed in
silks and velvets, and jingling with jewelry. Although ad-
mirers of Hang-zho called the city a Heaven on earth, people in other cities enviously called it "the Melting-Pot of
Money." I also saw on the streets, in full daylight, numbers of the sauntering young women-for-hire whom the
Han called "wild flowers." And there were many open-
fronted little wine shops and cha shops—with names like
the Pure Delight and the Fount of Refreshment and the
Garden of Djennet (that one patronized by Muslim residents and visitors)—some of which shops, said my scribe,
actually dispensed wine and cha, but all of which mainly
traded in wild flowers.

The names of Hang-zho's streets and landmarks, I suppose, ranked somewhere between the tasteful and the voluptuous. Many of them were nicely poetic: one park island
was called the Pavilion from Which the Herons Take
Flight at Dawn. Some names seemed to record some local
legends: one temple was the Holy House That Was Borne
Here Through the Sky. Some were tersely descriptive: a
canal known as Ink to Drink was not inky, but clear and

clean; it was lined with schoolhouses, and when a Han
spoke of drinking ink, he was referring to scholastic study.
Some names were more lavishly descriptive: the Lane of
Flowers Worked with Colorful Birds' Feathers was a short
street of shops where hats were made. And some names
were simply unwieldy: the main road going from the city
inland was labeled the Paved Avenue Which Winds a Long
Way Between Gigantic Trees, Among Streams Falling in
Cascades, and Upward at Last to an Ancient Buddhist
Temple on a Hilltop.

Hang-zho was again like Venice in not allowing large
animals into the center of the city. In Venice, a rider coming from Mestre on the mainland must tether his horse in
a campo on the northwest side of the island, and go by
gòndola the rest of the way. We, arriving at Hang-zho, left
our mounts and pack asses at a karwansarai on the outskirts, and went leisurely on foot—the better to examine
the place—through the streets and over the many bridges,
our slaves carrying our necessary luggage. When we came
to the Wang's immense palace, we even had to leave our
boots and shoes outside. The steward who met us at the
main portal advised us that that was the Han custom, and
gave us soft slippers to wear indoors.

The recently appointed Wang of Hang-zho was another
of Kubilai's sons, Agayachi, a little older than myself. He
had been informed by an advance rider of our approach,
and he greeted me most warmly, "Sain bina, sain urkek,"
and Hui-sheng too, addressing her respectfully as "sain
nai." When she and I had bathed and changed into presentable attire, and sat down with Agayachi to a welcoming banquet, he seated me on his right and Hui-sheng at
his left, not at a separate women's table. Few people had
given much notice to Hui-sheng in the days when she had
been a slave, because, although she had been then no less
comely, and had dressed as well as all court slaves were
made to do, she had cultivated the slave's demeanor of
unobtrusiveness. Now, as my consort, she dressed as
richly as any noblewoman, but it was her letting her radiant personality shine forth that made people notice her—
and approvingly, and admiringly.

The table fare of Manzi was opulent and delicious, but
somewhat different to what was popular in Kithai. The
Han, for some reason, did not care for milk and milk prod-

ucts, of which their neighbor Mongols and Bho were so
fond. So we had no butter or cheeses or kumis or arkhi, but
there were enough novelties to make up for the lack. When
the servants loaded my plate with something called Mao-
tai Chicken, I expected to get drunk from it, but it was not
spirituous, only delightfully delicate. The dining hall
steward told me that the chicken was not cooked in that
potent liquor, but killed with it. Giving a chicken a drink
of mao-tai, he said, made it as limp as it would make a
man, relaxing all its muscles, letting it die in bliss, so it
cooked most tenderly.

There was a tart and briny dish of cabbage, shredded
and fermented to softness, which I praised—and got myself
laughed at—my table companions informing me that it
was really a peasant food, and had first been concocted,
ages ago, as a cheap and easily portable provender for the
laborers who built the Great Wall. But another dish with a
genuinely peasant-sounding name, Beggar's Rice, was not
likely ever to have been available to many peasants. It got
the name, said the steward, because it had originated as a
mere tossing together of kitchen scraps and oddments.
However, at this palace table, it was like the most rich and
various risotto that ever was. The rice was but a matrix for
every kind of shellfish, and bits of pork and beef, and herbs
and bean sprouts and zhu-gan shoots and other vegetable
morsels, and the whole tinted yellow—with gardenia petals, not with zafràn; our Compagnia had not yet started
selling in Manzi.

There were crisp, crunchy Spring Rolls of egg batter
filled with steamed clover sprigs, and the little golden zu-
jin fish fried whole and eaten in one bite, and the miàn
pasta prepared in various ways, and sweet cubes of chilled
pea paste. The table also was laden with salvers of delicacies peculiar to the locality, and I took at least a taste of all
of them—tasting first and *then* inquiring their identity,
lest their names make me reluctant. They included ducks'
tongues in honey, cubes of snake and monkey meat in savory gravy, smoked sea slugs, pigeon eggs cooked with
what looked like a sort of silvery pasta, which was really
the tendons from the fins of sharks. For sweets, there were
big, fragrant quinces, and golden pears the size of rukh's
eggs, and the incomparable hami melons, and a soft-
frozen, fluffy confection made, said the steward, of "snow

bubbles and apricot blossoms." For drink there was am-
ber-colored kao-liang wine, and rose wine the exact color of
Hui-sheng's lips, and Manzi's most prized variety of cha,
which was called Precious Thunder Cha.

After we had concluded the meal with the soup, a clear
broth made from date plums, and after the soup cook had
emerged from the kitchen for us all to applaud him, we repaired to another hall to discuss my business here. We
were a group of a dozen or so, the Wang and his staff of
lesser ministers, all of whom were Han, but only a few of
them locals retained from the Sung administration; most
had come from Kithai and so could converse in Mongol. All
of them, including Agayachi, wore the floor-sweeping,
straight-lined but elegantly embroidered Han robes, with
ample sleeves for tucking the hands in and carrying things
in. The first order of business was the Wang's remarking
to me that I was at liberty to wear any costume I pleased—I
was then wearing, and had long been partial to, the Persian garb of neat tulband and blouse with tight sleeve
cuffs, and a cape for outdoors—but he suggested that, for
official meetings, I ought to replace the tulband with the
Han hat, as worn by himself and his ministers.

That was a shallow, cylindrical thing like a pillbox, with
a button on its top, and the button was the only indication
of rank among all those in the room. There were, I learned,
nine ranks of ministers, but all were dressed so finely and
looked so distinguished that only by the discreet insignia
of the buttons could they be told apart. Agayachi's hat button was a single ruby. It was big enough to have been
worth a fortune, and it betokened his being of the very
highest rank possible here, a Wang, but it was much less
conspicuous than, say, Kubilai's gleaming gold morion or
a Venetian Doge's scufieta. I was entitled to a hat with a
coral button, indicating the next-most rank, a Kuan, and
Agayachi had such a hat all ready to present to me. The
other ministers variously wore the buttons of descending
rank: sapphire, turquoise, crystal, white shell, and so on,
but it would be a while before I learned to sort them out at
a glance. I unwound my tulband and perched the pillbox
on my head, and all said I looked the very picture of a
Kuan, all but one aged Han gentleman, who grumbled:

"You ought to be more fat."

I asked why. Agayachi laughed and said:

"It is a Manzi belief that babies, dogs and government officials ought to be fat, or else they are assumed to be ill-tempered. But never mind, Marco. A fat official is assumed to be filching from the treasury and taking bribes. Any government official—fat, thin, ugly or handsome—is always an object of revilement."

But the same old man grumbled, "Also, Kuan Polo, you ought to dye your hair black."

Again I asked why, for his own hair was a dusty gray. He said:

"All Manzi loathes and fears the kwei—the evil demons —and all Manzi believes the kwei to have reddish fair hair, like yours."

The Wang laughed again. "It is we Mongols who are to blame for that. My great-grandfather Chinghiz had an orlok named Subatai. He did many depredations in this part of the world, so he was the Mongol general most hated by the Han, and he had reddish fair hair. I do not know what the kwei were supposed to look like in earlier times, but ever since Subatai's day, they have looked like *him.*"

Another man chuckled and said, "Keep your kwei hair and beard, Kuan Polo. Considering what you are here to do, it may *help* if you are feared and hated." He spoke Mongol well enough, but it was obviously a newly acquired language for him. "As the Wang has remarked, all government officials are reviled. You can imagine that, of all officials, tax collectors are the most detested. And I hope you can imagine how a *foreign* tax collector, collecting for a conqueror government, is going to be regarded. I propose that we spread the word that you really *are* a kwei demon."

I gave him a look of amusement. He was a plump, pleasant-faced Han of middle age, and he wore a wrought-gold button on his hat, identifying him as being of the seventh rank.

"The Magistrate Fung Wei-ni," Agayachi introduced him. "A native of Hang-zho, an eminent jurist and a man much esteemed by the people for his fairness and acumen. We are fortunate that he has consented to keep the same magistracy he held under the Sung. And I am personally pleased, Marco, that he has agreed to serve as your adjutant and adviser while you are attached to this court."

"I am also much pleased, Magistrate Fung," I said, as he and I both made the sedate, hands-together bow that

passes for a ko-tou between men of near equal rank. "I will
be grateful for any assistance. In undertaking this mission
of collecting taxes in Manzi, I am ignorant of two things
only. I know nothing whatever about Manzi. And I know
nothing whatever about tax collecting."

"Well!" grunted the grumbly gray-haired man, this
time grudgingly complimentary. "Well, frankness and a
lack of self-importance are at least refreshingly new qualities in a tax collector. I doubt, however, that they will help
you in your mission."

"No," said the Magistrate Fung. "No more than getting
fat or blacking your hair, Kuan Polo. I will be frank, also. I
see no way for you to extract taxes from Manzi for the Khanate, except by going yourself from door to door and demanding, or having a whole army of men to do it for you.
And even at starvation wages, an army would cost more
than you would collect."

"In any case," said Agayachi, "I have no army of men to
delegate to you. But I *have* provided—for you and your
lady—a fine house in a good quarter of the city, well staffed
with domestics. When you are ready, my stewards will
show you to the place."

I thanked him and then said to my new adjutant, "If I
cannot immediately start learning my job, perhaps I can
start learning of my surroundings. Would you accompany
us to our house, Magistrate Fung, and on the way show us
something of Hang-zho?"

"With pleasure," he said. "And I will show you first the
single most spectacular sight of our city. This is the phase
of the moon and—yes—the very hour is at hand for the appearance of the hai-xiao. Let us go at once."

There was no clock of sand or water in the room, and not
even a cat about, so I did not know how he could be so precise about the hour, or what the time had to do with seeing
a hai-xiao, or what a hai-xiao *was*. But Hui-sheng and I
made our good nights to the Wang and his staff, and we
and our little company of scribe and slaves left the palace
with the Magistrate Fung.

"We will take boat from here to your residence," he said.
"There is a royal barge waiting on the canal side of the palace. But first, let us walk up the promenade here, along
the riverside."

It was a fine night, balmy, softly lighted by a full moon,

so we had a good view. From the palace, we went along a
street that paralleled the river. It had a waist-high balustrade on that side, mainly constructed of some curiously
shaped stones. They were circular, each with a hole in its
center, and they were as big around as my encircled arms
and as thick as my waist. They were too small to have been
millstones, but too heavy to have been wheels. Whatever
they had once been used for, they had been retired to serve
here, set on the edge, rim to rim, and the spaces between
filled in with smaller stones, to make the balustrade a
solid wall and flat on top. I looked over, and saw that the
parapet fell away on the other side, a vertical wall of stone,
some two house-stories' distance to the river surface below.

I said, "I take it that the river rises considerably in flood
season."

"No," said Fung. "The city is built high above the water
on this side to allow for the hai-xiao. Fix your eyes yonder,
eastward, toward the ocean."

So he and I and Hui-sheng stood leaning against the parapet and gazed out toward the sea, across the flat, moonlit
plain of delta sand that stretched featurelessly to the black
horizon. Of course, there was no ocean to be seen; it was
some two hundred li away beyond that shoal. Or it usually
was. For now I began to hear, from that far distance, a
murmur of sound, like a Mongol army on horseback galloping toward us. Hui-sheng tugged at my sleeve, which surprised me, for she could not have heard anything. But she
indicated her other hand, which rested on the parapet, and
she gave me a querying look. Hui-sheng, I realized, was
again *feeling* the sound. However far away it was, I
thought, it must be a veritable thunder to be vibrating a
stone wall. I could only give her a shrug, no explanation.
Fung evidently expected whatever was coming, and without misgivings.

He pointed again, and I saw a line of bright silver suddenly split the darkness of the horizon. Before I could ask
what it was, it was close enough for me to make out: a line
of sea foam, brilliant in the moonlight, coming toward us
across the desert of sand, as rapidly as a line of charging,
silver-armored horsemen. Behind it was the whole weight
of the Sea of Kithai. As I have said, that shoal was fan-
shaped—a hundred li broad out where it met the ocean,

narrow here at the river mouth. So the inrushing sea came into the delta as a tumbling sheet of water and spume, but was rapidly constricted as it came, and compressed and piled up, and all its dark color was churned into white. The hai-xiao happened too quickly for me even to exclaim in astonishment. There, pounding toward us, was a wall of water as wide as the delta and as high as a house. But for its foamy glitter, it looked like the avalanche that had scoured across the Yun-nan valley, and rumbled very like it, too.

I glanced down at the river below us. Like a small animal emerging from its burrow and encountering a foam-muzzled rabid dog, it was flowing *backward*, recoiling, trying to vacate its invaded burrow mouth and retreat back toward the mountains it had come from. The next moment, that vast roaring wall of water surged by us, just below the level of the parapet, a welter and tumult of foam, and flecks of it spattered up upon us. I had been transfixed by the spectacle, but at least I had seen seawater before; I think Hui-sheng never had, so I turned to see if she was frightened. She was not. She was bright-eyed and smiling, and moon-glowing spindrift was in her hair like opals. To someone in a soundless world, I suppose, more than to the rest of us, it must be a delight to *see* splendid things, especially when they are so splendid as to be feelable. And even I had felt the stone balustrade beside us and the night all about us tremble under that impact. The rumbling, fizzing, sizzling sea continued to seethe past and upstream, the bright white of it getting streaked with black-green, and finally the black-green predominating, until it was all an unfoamed choppy sea occupying the whole river breadth beneath us.

When I could make myself heard, I said to Fung, "What in the name of all the gods *is* it?"

"Newcomers usually are impressed," he said, as if he had done it all himself. "It is the hai-xiao. The tidal bore."

"Tidal!" I exclaimed. "Impossible! Tides come and go with stately decorum."

"The hai-xiao is not always so dramatic," he conceded. "Only when the season and the moon and the time of day or night properly coincide. On those occasions, as you just saw, they bring the sea across those sands at the pace of a galloping horse—across two hundred li in no longer than it

takes a man to eat a leisurely meal. The river boatmen
learned, ages ago, to take advantage of it. They cast off
from here at just the right moment, and the hai-xiao takes
them upriver, hundreds of li, without their having to
stroke an oar."

I said politely, "Forgive my doubting you, Magistrate
Fung. But I come from a sea city myself, and I have seen
tides all my life. They move the sea perhaps an arm's-
reach up and down. This was a *mountain* of sea!"

He said politely, "Forgive my contradicting you, Kuan
Polo. But I must presume that your native city is on a
small sea."

I said loftily, "I never thought of it as small. But yes,
there are greater ones. Beyond the Pillars of Hercules is
the limitless Ocean Sea Atlantic."

"Ah. Well. So is this one a great sea. Beyond this coast
there are islands. Many of them. To the north of east, for
example, the islands called Jilpen-kwe, which compose the
Empire of the Dwarfs. But go east far enough, and the islands thin out, become sparse, are left behind. And *still*
goes on the Sea of Kithai. On and on."

"Like our Ocean Sea," I murmured. "No mariner has
ever crossed it, or known its end, or what lies there, or if it
has an end."

"Well, this one does," said Fung, very matter of fact.
"Or at least there is one record of its having been crossed.
Hang-zho now is separated from the ocean by that two-
hundred-li delta. But you see these stones?" He indicated
the rounds that constituted most of the balustrade. "They
are anchors for mighty seagoing vessels, and the counter-
weights for those vessels' boom ends. Or they were."

"Then Hang-zho was once a seaport?" I said. "And it
must have been a busy one. But a long time ago, or so I
judge from the extent that the delta has silted over."

"Yes. Nearly eight hundred years ago. There is in the
city archives a journal written by a certain Hui-chen, a
Buddhist trapa, and it is dated—by our count—in the year
three thousand one hundred, or thereabout. It tells how he
was aboard a seagoing chuan which had the misfortune to
be blown from this coast by the tai-feng—the great storm—
and kept on going eastward and at long last made landfall
somewhere yonder. By the trapa's estimate, a distance of
more than twenty-one thousand li to there. Nothing but

water all the way. And another twenty-one thousand li
back again. But he did come back from wherever he went,
for the journal exists."

"Hui! Twenty-one thousand li! Why, that is as far as
from here overland all the way back to Venice." A thought
came to me, and it was an excitingly beguiling one. "If
there is land that far from here to the eastward across this
sea, it must be my own continent of Europe! This continent
of Kithai and Manzi must be the far side of our own Ocean
Sea! Tell me, Magistrate, did the monk mention cities on
the other side? Lisboa? Bordeaux?"

"No cities, no. He called the land Fu-sang, which means
nothing more than the Place We Drifted To. The natives,
he said, resembled Mongols or Bho rather than Han, but
were even more barbaric, and spoke an uncouth tongue."

"It must have been Iberia . . . or Morocco. . .," I said
thoughtfully. "Both full of Muslim Moors even that long
ago, I think. Did the monk say anything else of the place?"

"Very little. The natives were hostile, so it was only
with hazard and difficulty that the mariners managed to
restock the chuan with food and water. They cast off in a
hurry, to come west again. The only other thing that seems
to have impressed Hui-chen was the vegetation. He described the trees of Fu-sang as being very odd. He said they
were not of wood and leafy branches, but of green flesh and
wicked thorns." Fung made a face of amused disbelief.
"That signifies little. I think all holy men tend to see flesh
and thorns everywhere."

"Hm. I do not know what kind of trees grow in Iberia or
Morocco," I muttered, unable to cease speculating. "But it
is awesome even to think that—just possibly—one could
sail from here to my homeland."

"Better not try it," Fung said offhandedly. "Not many
men since Hui-chen have encountered a tai-feng on the
open sea and lived to tell of it. That storm rages frequently, between here and the Jihpen-kwe islands. The
Khan Kubilai has twice now attempted to invade and conquer that empire, sending fleets of chuan full of warriors.
The first time, he sent too few, and the dwarfs repulsed
them. The last time, he sent hundreds of ships and nearly
an entire tuk of men. But the tai-feng came up and ravaged the fleet, and that invasion failed also. I hear that the
dwarfs, grateful to the storm, have named the tai-feng the

kamikaze, which in their uncouth language means Divine Wind."

"However," I said, still ruminating, "if the storm rages only *between* here and Jihpen-kwe, then—if Kubilai ever does take those islands—one might be able to sail safely eastward from *there.* . . .'"

But Kubilai never made another sortie against them, and never took those islands, and I never got to them, or any farther eastward. I was several times upon the Sea of Kithai, but never for long out of sight of the mainland. So I do not know whether that far-off Fu-sang was, as I suspected, the western shores of our known Europe, or if it was some new land, still undiscovered to this day. I am sorry for having failed, in that instance, to satisfy my curiosity. I should very much have liked to go there and see that place, and I never did.

4

HUI-SHENG and I and the Magistrate Fung and our servants stepped from the palace dock into an intricately carved teakwood san-pan, and sat under a stretched-silk canopy as ornate and curly-edged as any Han roof. A dozen oarsmen, naked to the waist and their bodies oiled so they gleamed in the moonlight, rowed us from there, along a winding canal route, to our new abode, and along the way Fung pointed out various things worth our notice.

He said, "That short street you see going off on our left is the Lane of Sweet Breezes and Stroking Airs. In other words, the lane of the fanmakers. Hang-zho's fans are prized throughout the land—this is where the folding fan was invented—some having as many as fifty sticks, and all being painted with the most exquisite pictures, often naughty ones. Nearly a hundred of our city's families have been engaged in the making of fans for generations, father to son to grandson."

And he said, "That building on our right is the biggest in the city. Only eight stories high, so it is not our tallest, but it extends from street to street in one direction, and canal to canal in the other. It is Hang-zho's permanent indoor marketplace, and I believe the only one in Manzi. In its hundred or more rooms are displayed for sale those wares too precious or too fragile to be outdoors in the weather of the open markets—fine furnishings, works of art, perishable goods, child slaves and the like."

And he said, "Here, where the canal has broadened out so expansively, this is called Xi Hu, the West Lake. You see the brightly lighted island in the middle? Even at this hour, there are barges and san-pans moored all around it. Some of the people may be visiting the temples on the island, but most are making merry. You hear the music? The inns there stay open all night long, dispensing food and drink and good cheer. Some of the inns are hospitable to all comers, others are for hire to wealthy families for their private celebrations and weddings and banquets."

And he said, "That street going off to our right, you will note, is hung all with lanterns of red silk over the doors, marking that as one of the streets of brothels. Hang-zho regulates its prostitutes most strictly, grading them into separate guilds, from grand courtesan down to riverboat drabs, and they are periodically examined to make sure they maintain good health and cleanliness."

I had so far been making only murmurs of acknowledgement and appreciation of Fung's remarks, but when he touched on the matter of prostitutes, I said:

"I noticed quite a number of them actually strolling the streets in daylight, something I never saw in any other city. Hang-zho seems quite tolerant of them."

"Ahem. Those abroad in daylight would have been the male prostitutes. A separate guild, but also regulated by statute. If you ever are solicited by a whore, and are inclined to use her, first examine her bracelets. If one among them is copper, she is not a female, however feminine her attire. That copper bracelet is dictated by the city—to prevent the male whores, poor wretches, from passing themselves off as what they are not."

Unpleasurably recollecting that I was the nephew of just such a wretch, I said, perhaps a little peevishly, "Hang-zho seems quite tolerant in many respects, and so do you."

He only said affably, "I am of the Tao. Each of us goes his own Way. A male lover of his own sex is, by choice, only what a eunuch is involuntarily. Both of them being a reproach to their ancestors, in not continuing their line, they require no additional rebuke from me. Now yonder, on our right, that high drum tower marks the center of the city, and is our tallest structure. It is manned day and night to drum the alarm of any fire. And Hang-zho does not depend on passersby and volunteers to quench any fires. There are one thousand men employed and paid to do nothing else but stand ready for that duty."

The barge eventually deposited us at the dock of our own house, just as if we had been in Venice, and the house was quite a palazzo. A sentry was posted on either side of the main portal, each man holding at attention a lance that had an ax blade as well as a point, and both the men were the biggest Han I had ever seen.

"Yes, good robust specimens," said Fung, when I admired them. "Each, I would say, easily sixteen hands tall."

"I think you are mistaken," I said. "I myself am seventeen handspans high, and they are half a head taller than I." I added jestingly, "If you are so inept at counting, I wonder if you are really suited to the arithmetical work of tax collecting."

"Oh, eminently so," he said, in an equally cheerful way, "for I know the Han methods of counting. A man's height is ordinarily reckoned to the top of his head, but a soldier's is measured only to his shoulders."

"Cazza beta! Why?"

"So they can be assigned in pairs to the carrying poles. Being foot soldiers, not horsemen, they are their own load bearers. But also it is taken for granted that a good and obedient soldier has no need for a mind, or a head to carry it in."

I shook my own head in admiring amazement, and apologized to the magistrate for having even mildly disparaged his knowledge. Then, when we had again exchanged our shoes for slippers, he accompanied me and Hui-sheng on a tour of the house. While servants in one room after another fell down in ko-tou to us, he pointed out this and that facility provided for our comfort and pleasure. The house even had its own garden, with a lotus pond in the middle and a flowering tree overhanging that. The gravel of the winding paths was not just raked smooth, but raked into graceful patterns. I was particularly taken by one ornament there: a carving of a large seated lion that guarded the doorway between house and garden. It was sculptured

from a single immense piece of stone, but done so cleverly
that the lion had a stone ball in its half-open mouth. The
ball could, with a finger, be rolled back and forth in there,
but could never be pried out from behind the lion's teeth.

I think I slightly impressed the Magistrate Fung with
my eye for artwork when, admiring the painted scrolls on
the walls of our bedroom, I remarked that those pictures of
landscapes were done differently here than by the artists
of Kithai. He gave me a sidewise look and said:

"You are right, Kuan. The northern artists think of all
mountains as resembling the rugged and craggy peaks of
their Tian Shan range. The artists here in Sung—Manzi, I
mean; excuse me—are better acquainted with the soft,
lush, rounded, woman's-breast mountains of our south."

He took his departure, declaring himself ready to be
with me again at the instant of my summons, whenever I
should feel like starting work. Then Hui-sheng and I
strolled about the new residence by ourselves, dismissing
one servant after another to their quarters, and getting acquainted with the place. We sat for a while in the moonlit
garden while, with gestures, I apprised Hui-sheng of what
details of the day's various events and comments she
might have failed to comprehend on her own. I concluded
by conveying the general impression I had got: that no one
seemed to hold very high hopes of my success as a tax gou-
ger. She nodded her understanding of each of my explications and, in the tactful way of a Han wife, made no
comment on my fitness for my work or my prospects in it.
She asked only one question:

"Will you be happy here, Marco?"

Feeling a truly hai-xiao surge of affection for her, I gestured back, "I *am* happy—here!" making it plain that I
meant "with you."

We allowed ourselves a holiday week or so to get settled
into our new surroundings, and I learned quickly to leave
all the multitudinous details of housekeeping to Hui-
sheng's supervision. As she had earlier done with the Mongol maid who came with us, she seemed easily to establish
some imperceptible mode of communication with the new
Han servants, and they leaped to obey her every whim,
and usually did so to perfection. I was not so good a master
as she was a mistress. For one thing, I could no more talk
in Han than she could. But also I had been long accus-

tomed to having Mongol servants, or servants trained by Mongols, and these of Manzi were different.

I could recite a whole catalogue of differences, but I will mention just two. One was that, owing to the Han reverence for antiquity, a servant could never be dismissed or retired on the mere ground of his or her getting old, useless, senile, even immobile. And, as servants got older, they got cranky and crafty and impudent, but they could not be discharged for that, either, or even beaten. One of ours was an ancient crone whose only duty was to make up our bedroom each morning after we arose. Whenever she smelled the scent of lemon on me or Hui-sheng or the bedclothes, she would cackle and whinny most abominably, and I would have to grit my teeth and bear it.

The other difference had to do with the weather, of all unlikely things. Mongols were indifferent to weather; they would go about their occupations in sunshine, rain, snow—probably in the chaos of a tai-feng, if they were ever to encounter one. And God knows, after all my journeying, I was as impervious to cold or heat or wet as any Mongol. But the Han of Manzi, for all their devotion to bathing at every opportunity, had a catlike aversion to rain. When it rained, *nothing* that involved going outdoors ever got done—and I do not mean just by servants; I mean by *anybody*.

Agayachi's ministers mostly resided in the same palace that he did, but those who lived elsewhere stayed at home when it rained. The marketplaces of the city, on rainy days, were vacant of both buyers and sellers. So was the vast indoor market, though it was under shelter, because people would have had to endure the rain to get there. Though I went about as I had always done, I had to do it on foot. There was not a palanquin to be found, nor even a canal boat. Though the boatmen spent all their lives on the water, most of the time soaked with water, they would not go out in the water that fell from the sky. Even the male prostitutes did not parade the streets.

Even my so-called adjutant, the Magistrate Fung, had the same eccentricity. He would not come across the city to my house on rainy days, and would not even make his appointed judicial sittings at the Cheng. "Why bother? No litigants would be there." He expressed sympathy at my annoyance over the many wasted wet days and evinced a mild amusement at his own and his countrymen's peculiarity, but he never tried to cure himself of it. Once, when I had not seen him during a whole week of rain, and railed at him indignantly, "How am I supposed to get anything done, when I have only a fair-weather adjutant?" he sat down, got out a paper and brushes and ink block, and wrote for me a Han character.

"That says 'an urgent action not yet taken,'" he informed me. "But see: it is composed of two elements. This one says 'stopped' and this one 'by rain.' Clearly, a trait enshrined in our writing must be ingrained in our souls."

But on clement days, anyway, we sat in my garden and had many long talks about my mission and about his own magistracy. I was interested to hear some of the local laws and customs, but, as he explained them, I gathered that in his judicial practice he relied more on his people's superstitions and his own arbitrary caprices.

"For example, I have my bell which can tell a thief from an honest man. Suppose something has been stolen, and I have a whole array of suspects. I bid each of them reach through a curtain and touch the hidden bell, which will ring at the guilty man's touch."

"And does it?" I asked skeptically.

"Of course not. But it is smeared with ink-powder. Afterward, I examine the men's hands. The man with clean hands is the thief, the one who feared to touch the bell."

I murmured, "Ingenious," a word I found myself often uttering here in Manzi.

"Oh, judgments are easy enough. It is the sentences and penalties that require ingenuity. Suppose I sentence that thief to wear the yoke in the jail yard. That is a heavy wooden collar, rather like the stone anchors, which gets locked around his neck, and he must sit in the jail yard while he wears it, to be jeered at by passersby. Suppose I judge that his crime merits his suffering that discomfort and humiliation for, say, two months. However, I know very well that he or his family will bribe the jailers, and they will only put him into the yoke at times when they know I will be passing in and out of the yard. Therefore, to make sure he is properly chastised, I sentence him to *six* months in the yoke."

"Do you," I said hesitantly, "do you employ a Fondler for the more felonious culprits?"

"Yes, indeed, and a very good one," he said cheerfully.
"My own son, in preparation for the study of law, is currently apprenticed to our Fondler. By way of teaching him
the trade, the Master has had young Fung beating a pudding for some weeks now."

"What?"

"There is a punishment called chou-da, which is to whip
a felon with a zhu-gan cane split at the end into a many-
thonged scourge. The object is to inflict the most terrible
pain and rupture all the internal organs without causing
visible mutilation. So, before he is permitted to wreak
chou-da on a human, young Fung must learn to pulverize a
pudding without breaking its surface."

"Gèsu. I mean interesting."

"Well, there are punishments more popular with the
crowds that come to look on—and some less so, of course.
They depend on the severity of the crime. Simple branding
on the face. A stay in the cage. The kneeling on sharp-
linked chains. The medicine that bestows instant old age.
Women especially like to watch that one inflicted on other
women. Another one popular with the women is to see an
adultress upended and poured full of boiling oil or molten
lead. And there are the punishments with self-descriptive
names: the Bridal Bed, the Affectionate Snake, the Monkey Sucking a Peach Dry. I must say modestly that I myself recently invented rather an interesting new one."

"What was that?"

"It was done to an arsonist who had burned down the
house of an enemy. He failed to get the enemy, who had
gone on a journey, but burned to death the wife and children. So I decreed a punishment to fit the crime. I directed
the Fondler to pack the man's nostrils and mouth with
huo-yao powder, and seal him tightly with wax. Then, before he could suffocate or strangle, the wicks were ignited
and his head was blown to pieces."

"While we are on the subject of meet punishments, Wei-
ni"—we were by this time informally using first names—
"what do you predict the Khakhan will inflict on you and
me, for indigence in office? We have not got very far with
our strategies for tax imposition. I do not believe Kubilai
will accept rainy weather as an excuse."

"Marco, why weary ourselves with the making of plans
that cannot be put into practice?" he said lazily. "And to-

day is not rainy. Let us just sit here and enjoy the sun and
the breeze and the tranquil sight of your lovely lady gathering flowers from the garden."

"Wei-ni, this is a rich city," I persisted. "The only
marketplace under roof I ever saw, and ten more market
squares outdoors. All of them teeming—except when it
rains, anyway. Pleasure pavilions on the lake islands.
Prosperous families of fanmakers. Thriving brothels. Not
a single one of them yet paying a single tsien to the new
government's treasury. And if Hang-zho is so wealthy,
what must the rest of Manzi be like? Are you asking me to
sit still and let *no one* in the nation *ever* pay a head tax or a
land tax or a trade tax or a—?"

"Marco, I can only tell you—as both I and the Wang have
told you repeatedly—every last tax record maintained by
the Sung regime disappeared *with* the Sung regime. Perhaps the old Empress ordered them destroyed, out of female malice. More likely her subjects invaded the halls of
records and the Cheng archives, the moment she left for
Kahnbalik to surrender her crown, and *they* destroyed the
records. It is understandable. It is expectable. It happens
in every newly conquered place, before the conquerors
march in, so that—"

"Yes, yes, I have accepted that as a fact. But I am not interested in knowing who paid how much to the late Sung's
tax officers! What do I care about a lot of old ledgers?"

"Because without them—look." He leaned forward and
held three fingers in front of my face. "You have three possible courses of action. Either you go yourself into every
single market stall, every inn on every island, every
whore's working cubicle—"

"Which is impossible."

"—or you have an army of men to do it for you."

"Which you have declared impractical."

"Yes. But, just for argument, say that you go to a market stall where a man is peddling mutton. You demand the
Khan's share of the value of that mutton. He says, 'But
Kuan, I am not the owner of this stall. Speak to the master
yonder.' You accost the other man and he says, 'I am master here, yes, but I only manage this stall for its owner,
who lives in retirement in Su-zho.' "

"I would refuse to believe either of them."

"But what do you do? Wring money from one? From

both? From whom you would get only a dribble. And perhaps overlook the real owner—perhaps the purveyor of all
the mutton in Manzi—who really is luxuriating beyond
your grasp in Su-zho. Also, do you go through the same
fuss at every market stall at every tax time?"

"Vakh! I would never get out of the one market!"

"But if you had the old ledgers, you would *know* who was
obligated and where to find him and how much he paid last
time around. So there is your third course of action, and
the only practical one: compile new records. Even before
you begin dunning, you must have a list of every going
business and shop and whorehouse and property and plot
of land. *And* the names of all their owners and proprietors
and heads of household. *And* an estimate of what their
holdings are worth and what their annual profits amount
to and—"

"Gramo mi! That alone would take my lifetime, Wei-ni.
And meanwhile I am collecting nothing!"

"Well, there you are." He sat indolently back again.
"Enjoy the day and the view of the eye-soothing Hui-
sheng. Salve your conscience with this consideration. The
Sung dynasty had existed here for three hundred and
twenty years before its recent fall. It had had that long to
collect and codify its records and make its taxation methods workable. You cannot expect to do the same thing overnight."

"No, I cannot. But the Khan Kubilai can expect just
that. What do I do?"

"Nothing, since anything you did do would be futile. Do
you hear that cuckoo in the tree yonder? 'Cu-cu . . . cu-
cu . . .' We Han like to think that the cuckoo is saying
'pu-ju ku-ei.' That means 'why not go home?' "

"Thank you, Wei-ni. I expect I will go home, someday.
All the way home. But I will not go, as we Venetians say,
with my bagpipes turned inside their sack."

There was some while of peaceful silence, except for the
cuckoo's reiterated advice. At last Fung resumed:

"Are you happy here in Hang-zho?"

"Exceptionally so."

"Then be happy. Try to regard your situation like this. It
may be a long and pleasant time before the Khakhan even
remembers he sent you here. When he does, you may still
evade his inquisition for a long and pleasant time. When

he finally does demand an accounting, he may accept your explanation of your delinquency. If he does not, then he may or may not put you to death. If he does, your worries are all over. If he does not, but only has you broken by the chou-da scourge, well, you can live out your life as a crippled beggar. The market stallkeepers will be kind and let you have a begging station in the market square—*because* you never harried and hounded them for taxes, do you see?"

I said rather sourly, "The Wang called you an eminent jurist, Wei-ni. Is that a sample of your jurisprudence?"

"No, Marco. That is Tao."

Some while later, after he had departed for his own dwelling, I said again, "What do I do?"

I said it again in the garden, but now it was the cool of the early evening, and the cuckoo had taken its own advice and gone home, too, and I was sitting with Hui-sheng after our dinner. I had related to her all that Fung and I had said about my predicament, and now appealed for her advice.

She sat pensive for a time, then signaled, "Wait," and got up and went to the house kitchen. She came back with a bag of dry beans and indicated that I was to sit with her on the ground among a bed of flowers. In a bare patch of earth there, she traced with her slim forefinger the figure of a square. Then she traced a line down the center of that and another across it, to divide the square into four smaller ones. Inside one of those she scratched a single little line, in the next two lines, in the next three, and in the last a sort of squiggle, then looked up at me. I recognized the marks as Han numerals, so I nodded and said, "Four little boxes, numbered one, two, three and four."

While I wondered what this had to do with my current and pressing and frustrating problems, Hui-sheng took out of the bag one bean, showed it to me and placed it on box number three. Then, without looking, she reached into the bag, took out a casual handful of beans and spread them beside the square. Very rapidly, she flicked out four beans from that spread, and four more, shoving them to one side, and kept on separating out four beans at a time from that spread. When they had all, by fours, been moved apart, there remained two beans over. She pointed to those two, pointed to the empty number-two box drawn on the

ground, snatched up the bean from the box numbered
three, added it to the ones she still had, grinned impishly
at me, and made a gesture signifying "too bad."

"I understand," I said. "I wagered on box number three,
but number two won, so I lost my bean. I am desolated."

She scooped all the beans back into the bag, took one
out, ostentatiously put it on a number for me again—this
time number four. She started to reach into the bag again,
but stopped, and motioned for me to do that. I understood:
the game was totally fair, the counting beans were
grabbed up at random. I took a considerable handful from
the bag and spread them beside her. She rapidly flicked
them aside again, four at a flick, and this time they happened to be divisible by four. There were none left to one
side at the finish.

"Aha," I said. "That means my number four wins. *What*
do I win?"

She held up four fingers, pointed to my wager, added to
it three beans more, and shoved them all toward me.

"If I lose, I lose my bean. If my numbered box is the
winner, I get my bean back fourfold." I made a face of toler-
ation. "It is a simple game, a childish game, no more complex than the old mariners' game of venturina. But if you
are suggesting that we play at it for a while—very well, my
dear, let us play. I assume you are trying to convey something more than boredom."

She gave me an ample stock of beans to wager with, and
indicated that I could risk as many as I liked, and on as
many boxes as I chose. So I piled ten beans in each of them,
all four boxes, to see what would happen. With an impatient look at me, and without even delving into her bag to
ascertain the winning number, she simply gave me forty
beans from it, then scooped up the forty on the ground. I realized that, by such a system of play, I could do no more
than stay even. So I began trying varieties of play—
leaving one box empty, piling different numbers of beans
on the other boxes, and so on. The game became a puzzle in
arithmetical terms. Sometimes I would win a whole handful of beans, and Hui-sheng would retain only a few. Sometimes the favor of chance went the other way: I would
heavily augment her supply and diminish my own.

I perceived that, if a man were seriously playing this
game, he could, by one lucky win, come out of it much

richer in beans—*if* he got up with his winnings, and went away, and could refuse the temptation to try again. But there was always the urge, especially when one was ahead, to try for more yet. I could also imagine, if one player were vying with three others, plus the banker with the bean bag, it could get absorbing, challenging, tantalizing. But, as well as I could gauge the probabilities, the banker would be getting richer all the time, and any winning player would be enriching himself mainly at the expense of the other three.

I gestured for Hui-sheng's attention. She raised her eyes from the playing ground, and I pointed to myself, to the game, to my money purse, indicating: "If a man were playing for money instead of beans, this could be an expensive sport."

She smiled and her eyes danced, and she nodded emphatically: "That is what I was trying to convey." And she swept an arm to indicate all of Hang-zho—or maybe all of Manzi—completing the sweep by pointing to the room in our house that I and my scribe used for our working quarters.

I stared at her eagerly glowing little face, then at the beans on the ground. "Are you suggesting this as a *substitute* for tax collecting?"

Emphatic nodding: "Yes." And a spreading of hands. "Why not?"

What a ridiculous idea, was my first thought, but then I reflected. I had seen Han men risking their money on the zhi-pai cards, on the ma-jiang tiles, even on the feng-zheng flying toys—and doing it avidly, feverishly, madly. Could they possibly be enticed into a madness for this simple-minded game? And with me—or rather, the imperial treasury—holding the bank?

"Ben trovato!" I muttered. "The Khakhan said it himself: involuntary benevolence!" I sprang up and raised Hui-sheng from the flower bed and embraced her enthusiastically. "You may have provided my succor and salvation. Tell me, did you learn this game as a child?"

Yes, she had. Some years ago—after a Mongol band of marauders torched her village and slew all the adults, and took her and the other children as slaves, and she was chosen to be raised as a lon-gya of concubines, and a shamàn did the cutting that made her and the whole world silent—the old woman who tended her convalescence had kindly taught her that game, because it was one that could be played without words spoken or heard. Hui-sheng thought she had been about six years old at the time.

I tightened my embrace of her.

5

WITHIN three years, I was accounted the richest man in Manzi. Of course, I really was not, because I scrupulously and punctiliously sent on all my profits to the imperial treasury in Khanbalik, by trustworthy Mongol carriers with heavily armed outriders. Over the years, they transported a fortune in paper money and coins, and, for all I know, they still are transporting more.

Hui-sheng and I between us decided on the name for the game—Hua Dou Yin-hang, which means roughly "Break the Bean Bank"—and it was a success from the very start. The Magistrate Fung, though at first incredulous, was soon enchanted with the idea, and convened a special session of his Cheng just to put the seal of legality on my venture and issue to me letters of patent and entitlement—all embossed with the Manzi chrysanthemum—so that no others could copy the idea and set up in competition to me. The Wang Agayachi, though at first dubious of the propriety of my venture—"Whoever heard of a *government* sponsoring a game of chance?"—soon was praising it, and me, and declaring that I had made Manzi the most lucrative of all the Khanate's acquired lands. To every accolade, I said modestly and truthfully, "It was not my doing, but that of my intelligent and talented lady. I am only the harvester. Hui-sheng is the gardener with the golden touch."

She and I commenced the venture with an investment so trivial and meager that it would have shamed a fishmonger outfitting a poor stall in the marketplace. Our equipment consisted of nothing but a table and a tablecloth. Hui-sheng procured a piece of brilliant vermillion red cloth—the Han color signifying good fortune—and embroidered on it in black the quartered square, and in gold the four numbers inside the boxes, and we spread that cloth over a stone table in our garden, and we sent all our servants out to cry along the streets and canals and the riverfront: "Come one, come all venturesome souls! Wager a tsien and win a liang! Come and Break the Bean Bank! Make your dreams come true and your ancestors raise their hands in wonderment! Quick fortune awaits at the establishment of Polo and Echo! Come one and all!"

They came. Perhaps some people came just to steal a close look at me, the demon-haired Ferenghi. Perhaps some came out of actual avarice to win an easy fortune, but most seemed merely curious to see what we were offering, and some simply idled in on their way to somewhere else. But they came. And, although some jested and jeered—"A game for children!"—all made at least one play at it. And, although they tossed their tsien or two onto the red cloth in front of Hui-sheng as if they were only humoring a pretty child, they waited to see if they had won or lost. And, although many then just laughed good-humoredly and left the garden, some got intrigued and stayed to play again. And again. And, because only four could play at once, there was some mild wrangling and pushing among them, and those who could not play stayed to watch enthralled. And by the end of the day, when we declared the game over, it was quite a crowd our servants ushered out of the garden. Some of the players went away with more money than they had brought, and went rejoicing that they had found "an unguarded money vault," and vowed to keep coming back and plundering it. And some went away rather lighter in the purse than when they had come, and they went berating themselves for having been bested by "such a juvenile sport," and vowed to come back for retaliation on the Bean Bank table.

So that night Hui-sheng embroidered another cloth, and our servants nearly ruptured themselves manhandling another stone table into the garden. And the next day, instead of just standing about to keep order while Hui-sheng played banker, I took the other table. I was not so swift at the play as she, and did not collect as much money. Most of the winners of the day before had come back again—and the losers, as well—and more people besides, who had heard of this unheard-of new establishment in Hang-zho.

Well, I need hardly go on. We never again had to send our servants out crying in public, "Come all!" The house of

Polo and Echo had overnight become a fixture, and a popular one. We taught the servants—the brighter ones—how
to act as bankers, so Hui-sheng and I could take a rest now
and then. It was not long before Hui-sheng had to make
more of the black-gold-and-red tablecloths, and we purchased all the stone tables in the stock of a neighbor
mason, and we set the servants at them as permanent
bankers. Curiously enough, our aged crone who always got
so gleeful at the smell of lemon turned out to be the best of
our apprentice bankers, as swift and accurate as Hui-
sheng herself.

I suppose I did not fully realize what a *grand* success we
had made of our venture until one day the sky drizzled
rain, and no one fled from the garden, and still more
patrons arrived, having come through the rain, and they
all went on playing all day, oblivious to the wet! No man of
the Han would previously have let himself get rained on,
even for the sake of visiting Hang-zho's most legendary
courtesan. When I realized that we had contrived a diversion more compelling than sex, I went out and about the
city and took hire of other disused gardens and empty
plots, and instructed our neighbor stonemason to start
chiseling more tables for us in a hurry.

Our patronage came from all levels of Hang-zho society
—rich nobles retired from the old regime, prosperous and
oily-looking merchants, harassed-looking tradesmen,
starved-looking porters and palanquin carriers, smelly
fishermen and sweaty boatmen—Han, Mongols, a scattering of Muslims, even some men I took to be native Jews.
The few fluttery and twittery players who looked at first to
be women turned out to be wearing copper bracelets. I do
not recall a genuine woman ever coming to our establishment, except to look on with supercilious amusement, as I
have seen the visitors do in a House of Delusion. The Han
women simply had no wagering instinct, but with the Han
men it was more of a passion than drinking to excess or
exercising their wee masculine organs.

The men of lower classes, who came desperately hoping
to improve their lot, wagered usually only the little center-
punched tsien coins that were the currency of the poor.
Men of the middle classes usually risked flying money, but
of small face-value (and often tattered paper). The already
rich men who came, thinking they could Break the Bean

Bank by heavy siege or long attrition, would thump down
large wads of the more valuable notes of flying money. But
a man, whether he wagered a single tsien or a heap of
liang, had the same chance of winning when the banker's
counting beans were flicked aside, four by four, to disclose
the winning box number. What exactly the chance of anyone's making a fortune *was*, I never even troubled to calculate. All I know is that about the same number of patrons
went home richer as went home poorer, but it was their
own money they had exchanged, and an appreciable portion of it had remained with our Bean Bank. My scribe and
I spent much of every night sorting the paper money into
sheaves of the same face-values, and threading the little
coins into strings of hundreds and skeins of thousands.

Eventually, of course, the business got too big and complex for me and Hui-sheng to be personally involved at all.
After we had established many Bean Banks all over Hang-
zho, we did the same in Su-zho, and then in other cities,
and within a few years there was not a single least village
in Manzi that did not have one in operation. We employed
only tested and trusted men and women to act as the bankers of them, and my Adjutant Fung, for his contribution,
put into every establishment a sworn officer of the law to
act as general overseer and auditor of accounts. I promoted
my scribe to be my manager of the entire wide-flung operation, and thereafter I had nothing to do with the business
except to keep tally of the receipts from all over the nation,
pay expenses out of that amount, and send on the considerable residue—the eminently considerable residue—to
Khanbalik.

I took nothing of the profits for myself. Here in Hang-
zho, as in Khanbalik, Hui-sheng and I had an elegant residence and plenty of servants and we dined from an opulent
table. All of that was provided to us by the Wang Agayachi—or rather, by his government, which, since it shared
in the imperial revenue, was largely supported by our
Bean Banks. For indulgence in any additional luxuries or
follies I might desire for myself and Hui-sheng, I had my
income from my father's Compagnia Polo, still thriving
and now sending zafràn and other commodities for trade
here in Manzi. So, from the Bean Bank's receipts, I regularly deducted only enough to pay the rentals and mainte-
nance of the banks' gardens and buildings, the wages of

the bankers and overseers and couriers, and the ludicrously small costs of equipment (nothing much beyond
tables and tablecloths and supplies of dried beans). What
went every month to the treasury was, as I have said, a fortune. And, as I have also said, it is probably still a continuing stream.

Kubilai had cautioned me not to bleed every drop from
the veins of his Manzi subjects. It might seem that I was
contravening his orders and doing precisely that. But I
was not. Most players ventured at our Bean Banks the
money they had already earned and hoarded and could afford to risk. If they lost it, they were impelled to work
harder and earn some more. Even those who injudiciously
impoverished themselves at our tables did not simply
slump into hopeless idleness and beggary, as they would
have done if they had lost their all to a tax collector. The
Bean Banks offered always a hope of recovering one's
losses—a tax collector never lets *anything* be retrieved—so
even the very bankrupts had reason to work their way up
again from nothing toward a prosperity that would enable
them to return to our tables. I am happy to say that our
system did not—as the old tax systems had done—force
anyone to the desperate expedient of borrowing at usuri-
ous terms and getting into the dire clutches of deep debt.
But I take no credit for that; it was thanks to the Khakhan's strictures against the Muslims; there simply were
no longer any usurers to borrow from. So in sum, as well as
I could see, our Bean Banks—far from bleeding Manzi—
gave it new drive and industry and productiveness. They
benefited all concerned, from the Khanate as a whole, to
the working population at large (not to forget the many
people who found steady employment *in* our banks), and so
on down to the poorest peasant in the farthest corner of
Manzi, to whom the lure of easy fortune gave at least an
aspiration.

Kubilai had threatened that he would let me know
promptly if he was dissatisfied with my performance as his
treasury's agent in Hang-zho. Of course, he never had reason to do any such thing. Quite to the contrary, he eventually sent the highest possible dignitary, the Crown Prince
and Vice-Regent Chingkim, to convey to me his heartiest
regards and congratulations on the exceptional job I was
doing.

"Anyway, that is what he told me to tell you," said Chingkim, in his usual lazily humorous way. "In truth, I think my Royal Father wanted me to spy about and see if you were actually leading bandits in plundering the whole countryside."

"No need to plunder," I said airily. "Why bother to rob what people are eager to bestow?"

"Yes, you have done well. The Finance Minister Lin-ngan tells me that this Manzi is pouring more wealth into the Khanate even than my cousin Abagha's Persia. Oh, speaking of family, Kukachin and the children also send their greetings to you and Hui-sheng. And so does your own estimable father Nicolò. He said to let you know that your uncle Mafìo's condition has improved enough that he has learned several new songs from his lady attendant."

Chingkim, instead of putting up at his half-brother Agayachi's palace, had done me and Hui-sheng the high honor of lodging with us during his visit. Since she and I had long ago delegated the management of our Bean Banks to our hirelings, we were now nobles of unlimited leisure, so we were able to devote all our time and attention to entertaining our royal guest. This day, the three of us, without any servants in attendance, were enjoying a merenda in the open country. Hui-sheng had with her own hands prepared a basket of food and drink, and we had got horses from the karwansarai where they kept them, and we had ridden out of Hang-zho along that Paved Avenue Which Winds a Long Way Between Gigantic Trees, Eccèt-era, and, well away from the city, we had spread a cloth and dined under those trees, while Chingkim told me of other things going on here and there in the world.

"We are now waging war in Champa," he said, as idly as a non-Mongol might remark, "We are building a lotus pond in our back garden."

"So I gathered," I said. "I have seen the troops moving overland, and transports of men and horses coming down the Great Canal. I take it that your Royal Father, balked of expanding eastward to Jihpen-kwe, has determined to expand southward instead."

"Actually it came about rather fortuitously," he said. "The Yi people of Yun-nan have accepted our sovereignty there. But there is a lesser race in Yun-nan, a people called the Shan. Unwilling to be ruled by us, they have been emigrating southward into Champa in great numbers. So my half-brother Hukoji, the Wang of Yun-nan, sent an embassy into Champa, to suggest to the King of Ava that he might obligingly turn those refugees around and send them back to us, where they belong. However, our ambassadors had not been warned that all persons, when calling on the King of Ava, are expected to remove their shoes, and they did not, and he was insulted, and he ordered his guards, 'Remove their feet instead!' So, of course, having our ambassadors mutilated *was* an insult to us, and ample incentive for the Khanate to declare war on Ava. Your old friend Bayan is on the march again."

"Ava?" I inquired. "Is that another name for Champa?"

"Not exactly. Champa refers to that whole tropical land, the country of jungles and elephants and tigers and heat and humidity. The people down there are of—who knows? —ten or twenty separate races, and almost every one has its own midget kingdom, and every kingdom has various names, depending on who is speaking of it. Ava, for example, is also known as Myama and Burma and Mien. The Shan people fleeing from our Yun-nan are seeking refuge in a kingdom that earlier Shan emigrants established in Champa a long time ago. It is variously known as Sayam and Muang Thai and Sukhothai. There are other kingdoms down there—Annam and Cham and Layas and Khmer and Kambuja—and maybe many more." Again offhandedly, he said, "While we are taking Ava, we may well take two or three of the others."

Like a proper merchant, I remarked, "It would save our paying the exorbitant prices they demand for their spices and woods and elephants and rubies."

"I had intended," said Chingkim, "to proceed southward from here and follow Bayan's route of march and have a look for myself at those tropical lands. But I really do not feel up to making such a rigorous journey. I shall simply rest here for a while with you and Hui-sheng, and then return to Kithai." He sighed and said, a little wistfully, "I am sorry not to be going there. My Royal Father is getting old, and it cannot be too long before I must succeed him as Khakhan. I should have liked to do a lot more traveling before I got permanently stabled in Khanbalik."

Such an air of lassitude and resignation was not usual to the Prince Chingkim, and now I took notice that he was in-

deed looking rather worn and weary. A little later, when
he and I walked a way into the wood to make water in private, I noticed something else, and commented lightly on
it:

"At some inn on the road hither, you must have dined on
that slimy red vegetable called dai-huang. You did not eat
it at our table, for I do not care for it."

"Neither do I," he said. "And neither have I taken a fall
from any horse lately, which might account for my pissing
pink like this. But I have been doing it for some time. The
Court Physician has been treating me for it—in the Han
manner, by sticking pins in my feet and burning little
heaps of moxa fluff up and down my spine. I keep telling
the idiot old Hakim Gansui that I do not piss through my
feet or—" He stopped and looked up into the trees. "Listen,
Marco. A cuckoo. Do you know what the Han believe the
cuckoo is saying?"

Chingkim did go home, as the cuckoo advised, but not
until he had spent a month or so enjoying our company and
the restful ambience of Hang-zho. I am glad he had that
month of simple pleasure, far from the cares of office and
state, for when he went home, he went to a much more distant home than Khanbalik. It was not long before the couriers came galloping to Hang-zho, on horses blanketed in
purple and white, to tell the Wang Agayachi to drape his
city in those Han and Mongol colors of mourning, for his
brother Chingkim had arrived home only to die.

As it happened, our city had no more than finished the
term of mourning for the Crown Prince, and started to
take down the crape bunting, than the couriers came
again, with orders to leave it hanging. Now it was in
mourning for the Ilkhan Abagha of Persia, who had died
also—and also not in battle, but of some illness. The loss of
a nephew was of course not so terrible a tragedy to Kubilai
as the loss of his son Chingkim, and it did not cause the
same widespread murmurs of speculation about future
succession. Abagha had left a full-grown son, Arghun, who
immediately assumed the Ilkhanate of Persia—and even
married one of his late father's Persian wives, to further
secure his claim to that throne. But Chingkim's son
Temur, the next heir apparent to the whole Mongol Empire, was still under-age. Kubilai was well along in years,
as Chingkim had remarked. The people worried that, if he

were soon to die, the Khanate might be much riven and
convulsed by claimants older than Temur, the many uncles and cousins and such, eager to oust him and make the
Khanate theirs.

But, for the time being, we suffered nothing worse than
grief from Chingkim's untimely demise. Kubilai did not
let his sorrow distract him from the affairs of state, and I
did not let mine interfere with my regular transmittal of
Manzi's tribute to the treasury. Kubilai continued to prosecute war against Ava, and even extended the Orlok Bayan's mission—as Chingkim had predicted—to seize, as
well, any of Ava's neighbor nations in Champa that might
be ripe for conquest.

It made me restless, to know that so much was happening in the world outside, while I simply lolled in luxury in
Hang-zho. My restlessness was irrational, of course. Look
at all I had. I was quite an esteemed personage in Hang-
zho. No one even looked askance at my kwei-colored hair
any more when I walked the streets. I had many friends,
and I was ever so comfortable, and I was blissfully content
with my loving and lovely consort. Hui-sheng and I might
have lived—as is said of the lovers at the concluding page
of a roman courtois—happily ever after, just as we were. I
possessed everything that any rational man could desire.
All those most precious things were mine then, at that
high moment, that skyline crest of my lifetime. Furthermore, I was no longer the reckless stripling I once had
been, with only tomorrows stretching out before me. There
were a lot of yesterdays behind me now. I was past thirty
years of age, and I found an occasional gray hair among
the demon-colored, and I might sensibly have been giving
thought to making the downhill slope of my life a soft and
easy glide.

Nevertheless, I was restless, and the restlessness inexo-
rably became dissatisfaction with myself. I had done well
in Manzi, yes, but was I to bask in the reflected glow of
that for the remainder of my days? Once the great thing
had been accomplished, it was no great thing merely to
perpetuate it. That required no more than my stamping
my yin signature on papers of receipt and dispatch, and
waving my couriers off to Khanbalik once a month. I was
no better than a roadside postmaster of the horse relay stations. I decided I had for too long now enjoyed too much of

having; I wanted something to *want.* I flinched at the vision of myself growing old in Hang-zho, like a vegetable Han patriarch, and having nothing to take pride in except my survival to old age.

"You will never get old, Marco," Hui-sheng told me when I broached the subject. She looked affectionately amused, but sincere, as she conveyed that pronouncement.

"Old or not," I said, "I think we have luxuriated in Hang-zho long enough. Let us move on."

She concurred: "Let us move on."

"Where would you like to go, my dearest?"

Simply: "Wherever you go."

6

So my next northbound courier took a message from me to the Khakhan, respectfully requesting that I be relieved of my long-since accomplished mission and my Kuan title and my coral hat button; that I be given permission to return to Khanbalik, where I could cast about for some new venture to occupy me. The courier returned with Kubilai's amiable acquiescence, and it took me and Hui-sheng not long to make ready to depart from Hang-zho. Our native servants and slaves all wept and agonized and fell about in frequent ko-tou, but we assuaged their bereavement by making gifts to them of many things we decided not to take with us. I made other parting gifts—and rich ones—to the Wang Agayachi and my Adjutant Fung Wei-ni and my manager-scribe and other worthies who had been our friends.

"The cuckoo calls," they all said sadly, one after another, as they toasted us with their wine goblets at the countless farewell banquets and balls given in our honor.

Our slaves packed into bales and crates our personal belongings and our wardrobes and our many Hang-zho acquisitions—furnishings, painted scrolls, porcelains, ivories, jades, jewelry and such—that we were taking with us. Taking also the Mongol maid we had brought from Khanbalik, and Hui-sheng's white mare (now somewhat silvery about the muzzle), we went aboard a sizable canal barge.

Only one of our possessions would Hui-sheng not let be
crated and stowed in the hold: she herself carried her
white porcelain incense burner.

During our residence, the Great Canal had been completed all the way to Hang-zho's riverside. But because we
had already covered the canal route before, following it on
our way south, we had decided to take a very different way
home. We stayed on the barge only as far as the port of
Zhen-jiang, where the Great Canal met the Yang-tze
River. There, for the first time (for either me or Hui-
sheng), we boarded a gigantic oceangoing chuan, and
sailed down the Tremendous River and out into the bound-
less Sea of Kithai and northward up the coast.

That chuan made the good ship *Doge Anafesto*, the
galeazza in which I had crossed the Mediterranean, seem
like a gòndola or a san-pan. The chuan—I cannot call it by
name, because it purposely had no name, so it could not be
cursed by rival shipowners, who might persuade the gods
to send it contrary winds or other misfortune—had *five
masts*, each like a tree. From them depended sails as big as
some towns' market squares, made of slats of the zhu-gan
cane, and employed as I have described elsewhere. The bigness of the chuan's duck-shaped hull was in proportion to
its sky-scraping upper works. On the deck and in the passenger quarters below were more than one hundred cabins, each comfortably adequate for six persons. That is to
say, the ship could carry more than six hundred passengers *in addition to* its crew, which totaled fully four hundred men, of several different races and languages. (There
were only a few passengers on this short trip. Besides Hui-
sheng, myself and the maid, there were some traveling
merchants, some minor government officials, and a number of other ships' captains, idle between voyages, aboard
for just a seaman's holiday.) In the chuan's holds was
loaded a variety of goods, seeming enough to stock a city.
But, simply for a measure of the hold's capacity, I would
say the ship could have carried two thousand Venetian
butts.

I have said "holds" advisedly, instead of hold, because
every chuan was ingeniously built with bulkheads dividing the hull's interior into numerous compartments, end
to end, and they were tarred watertight, so that if the
chuan should strike a reef or otherwise hole itself below

the waterline, only that one compartment would flood, while the others stayed dry and kept the ship afloat. However, it would have required a sharp and solid reef to hole that chuan. Its entire hull was triply planked, actually built three times over, one shell enveloping another. The Han captain, who spoke Mongol, took great pride in showing me how the innermost hull had its planking set vertically, from keel to deck, and the next was planked at an angle diagonal to that, and the outermost was laid in horizontal strakes, stem to stern.

"Solid as rock," he boasted, slamming his fist into a bulwark and producing a sound as of a rock hit with a mallet. "Good Champa teakwood, held with good iron spikes."

"We do not have teakwood in the West where I come from," I said, almost apologetically. "Our shipbuilders rely on oak. But we do use iron spikes."

"Foolish Ferenghi shipbuilders!" he roared, with a mighty laugh. "Have they not yet realized that oak wood exudes an acid which corrodes the iron? Teak, on the other hand, contains an essential oil which preserves iron!"

So I had once again been presented with an example of ingenious Eastern artistry that made my native West seem backward. Somewhat spitefully, I hoped for an example of Eastern simplemindedness to balance the scales, and I expected I would encounter one before the voyage was over—and I thought I had when one day, well out of sight of the safe shore, we sailed into a rather nasty thunderstorm. There was wind and rain and lightning, and the sea got choppy, and the ship's masts and yards got all laced with flickering blue Santermo's fire, and I heard the captain shouting to his crew, in various languages:

"Prepare the chuan for sacrifice!"

It seemed a shockingly unnecessary early surrender, when the chuan's ponderous bulk was barely rocking to the storm. I was only a "sweet-water seaman"—as real Venetian mariners derisively say—and such are supposed to be overly apprehensive of danger on the sea. But I saw no danger here that called for more than a simple shortening of sail. Certainly this was not the fierce storm that merited the dread name of tai-feng. However, I was seaman enough to know better than to volunteer advice to the captain, or to show any contempt of his apparently over-extreme agitation.

I am glad I did not. For, as I started glumly below to prepare my womenfolk to abandon ship, I met two seamen coming not fearfully but gaily up the companionway, carrying with care a ship made all of paper, a toy ship, a miniature replica of ours.

"The chuan for sacrifice," the captain told me, quite unperturbed, as he tossed it over the side. "It deceives the sea gods. When they see it dissolve in the water, they think they have sunk our real ship. So they let the storm abate instead of making it more troublesome."

It was just one more reminder to me that even when the Han did something simpleminded, they did it ingeniously. Whether or not the paper-ship sacrifice had any effect, the storm did soon abate, and a few days later we made landfall at Qin-huang-dao, which was the coast city nearest Khanbalik. From there we proceeded overland, with a small train of carts carrying our goods.

When we got to the palace, Hui-sheng and I naturally went first to make ko-tou to the Khakhan. At his royal chambers, I noticed that the elderly stewards and women servants formerly in attendance seemed to have been replaced by some half a dozen young page boys. They were all much of an age, and all handsome, and all had uncommonly light hair and eyes, rather like those tribesmen in India Aryana who had claimed to be descended from Alexander's soldiers. I vaguely wondered if Kubilai, in his old age, was developing a perverse affection for pretty boys, but then I gave it no further mind. The Khakhan greeted us most warmly, and he and I exchanged mutual condolences on the loss of his son and my friend, Chingkim. Then he said:

"I must congratulate you again, Marco, on the splendid success you made of your mission to Manzi. I believe you did not take a single tsien of the tribute for yourself during all those years? No, I thought not. It was my own fault. I neglected to tell you, before you left here, that a tax collector customarily gets no wage, but earns his keep by taking a twentieth part of what he collects. It makes him work more diligently. I have no complaint, however, upon the diligence of your own work. Therefore, if you will call upon the Minister Lin-ngan, you will find that he has, all this while, been putting aside your share, and it is a respectable amount."

"Respectable!" I gasped. "Why, Sire, it must amount to a fortune! I cannot accept it. I was not working for gain, but for my Lord Khakhan."

"All the more reason why you deserve it, then." I opened my mouth again, but he said sternly, "I will hear no dispute about it. However, if you would care to demonstrate your gratitude, you might take on one more charge."

"Anything, Sire!" I said, still gasping at the magnitude of the surprise.

"My son and your friend Chingkim wished most earnestly to see the jungles of Champa, and he never got there. I have messages for the Orlok Bayan, currently campaigning in the land of Ava. They are only routine communications, nothing urgent but they would give you reason to make the journey which Chingkim did not. And your going as surrogate for him might be a consolation to his spirit. Will you go?"

"Without hesitation or delay, Sire. Is there anything else I can do for you down there? Dragons I might slay? Captive princesses I could rescue?" I was only halfway being facetious. He had just made me a wealthy man.

He chuckled appreciatively, but a little sadly. "Bring me back some small memento. Something that a fond son might have brought home to his aged father."

I promised I would seek for something unique, something never before seen in Khanbalik, and Hui-sheng and I took our departure. We went next to greet my father, who embraced us both, and wept a little for joy, until I stopped his tears by telling him of the great beneficence just bestowed on me by the Khakhan.

"Mefè!" he exclaimed. "That is no hard bone to gnaw! I always thought of myself as a good businessman, but I swear, Marco, you could sell sunshine in August, as they say on the Rialto."

"It was all Hui-sheng's doing," I said, giving her an affectionate squeeze.

"Well . . . ," said my father thoughtfully. "This . . . on top of what the Compagnia has already sent home by way of the Silk Road . . . Marco, it may be time we started thinking of going home ourselves."

"What?" I said, startled. "Why, Father, you have always had another saying. To the right sort of man, the whole world is home. As long as we continue to prosper here—"

"Better an egg today than a chicken tomorrow."

"But our prospects all are still rosy. We are still in the Khakhan's high regard. The whole empire is at its richest, ripe for our exploitation. Uncle Mafìo is being well attended, and—"

"Mafìo is four years old again, so he cares not where he is. But I am touching sixty, and Kubilai is at least ten years older."

"You look nowhere near senility, Father. True, the Khakhan shows his age—and some despondency—but what of that?"

"Have you thought what our position would be if he should die suddenly? Just *because* he favors us, others resent us. Only furtively now, but they are likely to manifest that resentment when his protecting hand falls away. The very rabbits dance at the funeral of a lion. Also, there will be a resurgence of the Muslim factions he suppressed, and they love us not at all. I hardly need mention the likelihood of even worse troubles—upheavals from here to the Levant—if there should be a war of succession. But I am increasingly glad that I have all these years been sending our profits west to your Uncle Marco in Constantinople. I shall do the same with this new fortune of yours. However, anything else we shall have accrued at the moment of Kubilai's death is bound to be sequestered here."

"Can we really gnash our teeth if that happens, Father, considering all the wealth we have already taken out of Kithai and Manzi?"

He shook his head somberly. "What good our fortune waiting in the West, if we are marooned here? If we are dead here? Suppose, of all the claimants to the Khanate succession, it should be Kaidu who won!"

"Verily, we should be at hazard," I said. "But need we abandon ship right now, so to speak, when there is not yet any cloud in the sky?" With some amusement, I realized that, as usual in my father's presence, I was beginning to talk like him, in parables and metaphors.

"The hardest step is the one across the threshold," he said. "However, if your reluctance signifies a concern for your sweet lady here, I hope you do not think I am suggesting her abandonment. Sacro, no! Of course you will bring her with you. She may be a curiosity in Venice, for a little while, but she will be a beloved one. Da novèlo xe tuto belo. You would not be the first to come home with a foreign wife. I recall, there was a ship's captain, one of the Doria, who brought home a Turki wife when he retired from the sea. Tall as a campanile, she was. . . ."

"I take Hui-sheng everywhere," I said, and smiled at her. "I should be lost without her. I will be taking her on this journey to Champa. We will not even stop to unpack the household goods we brought from Manzi. And I have *always* intended to take her home to Venice. But, Father, you are not recommending, I trust, that we slip away this very day?"

"Oh, no. Only that we make plans. Be ready to go. Keep one eye on the frying pan and the other on the cat. It would take me some time, in any event, to close or dispose of the kashi works—to tidy up many other loose ends."

"There should be ample time. Kubilai looks old, but not moribund. If he has the vivacity, as I suspect, to be playing with boys, he is not apt to drop dead as suddenly as Chingkim did. Let me comply with this latest mission he has set me, and when I return . . ."

He said portentously, "No one, Marco, can foretell the day."

I almost snapped an exasperated reply. But it was impossible for me to feel exasperation at him, or share his morbidity, or work myself into a mood of apprehension. I was a new-made wealthy man, and a happy one, and about to go journeying into new country, and with my dearest companion at my side. I merely clapped an assuring hand on my father's shoulder and said, not with resignation but with genuine jollity, "Let come the day! Sto mondo xe fato tondo!"

CHAMPA

1

It was again the Orlok Bayan I was off to find, and this time he was much farther away, but this time I had no need to get to him in a hurry. So I again arranged that Hui-sheng and I travel with attendants and supplies—her Mongol maid, two slaves for any necessary camping chores, Mongol escorts for protection, and a string of pack animals. But I also laid out each day's march so that we traveled not arduously, and frequently got fresh mounts at the horse posts, and arrived each night at some decent karwansarai or some sizable town or even some provincial palace. In all, we had to cover about seven thousand li of every kind of terrain—plains, farmlands, mountains—but by doing it slowly and leisurely, we managed to sleep comfortably every night while we traversed more than five thousand of those long li. Going southwest from Khanbalik, we were, for much of the way, following the same course I had previously taken to Yun-nan, and so we stopped in many places I had stayed before—the cities of Xian and Cheng-du, for example—and only when we got beyond Cheng-du were we in territory I had not seen before.

From Cheng-du we did not, as I had had to do before, turn west into the highlands of To-Bhot. We continued southwest, directly into the province of Yun-nan, and to its capital, Yun-nan-fu, the last big city on our route, where we were royally received and entertained by the Wang Hukoji. I had one private reason for being eager to see Yun-nan-fu, but it was a reason I did not mention to Hui-sheng. When I had been last in these regions, I had finished my

part in the Yun-nan war and taken myself out of it before
Bayan besieged the capital city, not availing myself of his
invitation to be among the privileged first looters and
rapers. Having foregone that opportunity to "behave like
a Mongol born," I now looked about me with a special
interest—to see what I had missed—and I took notice that
the Yi women were indeed handsome, as reported. No
doubt I would have enjoyed disporting myself with Yun-
nan-fu's "chaste wives and virgin daughters," and no
doubt would have believed I was enjoying some of the most
comely women in the East. But I had since had the great
good fortune to discover Hui-sheng, so now the Yi women
looked to me distinctly inferior, and far less desirable than
she was, and I felt no deprivation at never having had any
of them.

From Yun-nan-fu onward, bearing ever southwest, we
were traveling what had been called, from ancient times,
the Tribute Road. It was so named, I learned, because the
several nations of Champa had, since earliest history, at
one time or another all been vassal states of the powerful
Han dynasties to the north—the Sung and its predeces-
sors—and that road had been tramped hard and smooth by
the traffic of elephant trains bearing to those masters
Champa's tribute of everything from rice to rubies, slave
girls to exotic apes.

From the last mountains of Yun-nan, the Tribute Road
brought us down into the nation of Ava at a river plain and
a place called Bhamo, which was only a chain of rather
primitively constructed forts. They were also apparently
ineffectual forts, for Bayan's invaders had easily overwhelmed their defending forces, and taken Bhamo and
gone on past. We were received by a captain commanding
the few Mongols left to garrison the place, and he informed
us that the war was already concluded, the King of Ava in
hiding somewhere, and Bayan now celebrating his victory
in the capital city of Pagan, a long way downriver. The
captain suggested that we could get there more comfortably and quickly by river barge, and gave us one, and Mongol crewmen for it, and a Mongol yeoman scribe named
Yissun, who knew the Mien language of the country.

So we left our other attendants there at Bhamo, and
Hui-sheng and her maid and I had a slow river voyage for
the last thousand li or more of our journey. That river was

the Irawadi, which had begun as a tumbling torrent called the N'mai, away up in the Land of the Four Rivers, high in To-Bhot. Down in this flatter country, the river was as broad as the Yang-tze, and flowed sedately southward in great swooping bends. It was full of so much silt, perhaps carried all the way down from To-Bhot, that its water was nearly viscous, like a thin glue, and unpleasantly tepid. It was a sickly tan color across its immense sunlit breadth, and brown in the deep shade on both extremes, where an almost unbroken forest of giant trees overhung the distant banks.

Even the enormous width and endless length of the Irawadi River must have looked, to the numberless birds flying overhead, like a mere insignificant gap meandering through the greenery that covered the land. Ava was almost entirely overgrown with what we would call jungle, and the jungle natives called the Dong Nat, or Forest of the Demons. The local nat, I gathered, were similar to the kwei of the north: demons of varying degrees of badness, from mischief to real evil, and usually invisible but capable of assuming any form, including the human. I privately imagined that the nat seldom put on corporeality, because in the dense tangle of that Dong jungle there was scarcely *room* for them to do so. Beyond the muddy riverbanks, there was no ground to be seen, only a welter of ferns and weeds and vines and flowering shrubs and thickets of zhu-gan cane. Out of that confusion towered the trees, rank on rank, shouldering and elbowing each other. At their tops, their crowns of leaves merged together high in the air to make a veritable thatch over the whole land, a thatch so thick that it was equally impervious to rainstorm and sunlight. It seemed permeable only by the creatures that lived up there, for the treetops continuously rustled and shook to the coming and going of gaudy birds and the leaps and swings of chattering monkeys.

Each evening, when our barge steered for the shore to make camp—unless we happened on a clearing with a cane-built Mien village in it—Yissun and the boatmen would have to get out first and, each wielding a broad, heavy blade called a dah, hack out a place sufficient for us to spread our bedrolls and lay our fire. I always had the impression that, on the next day, we would have got only around the next bend downstream before the rank, greedy, fervid jungle closed over the little dimple we had made in it. That was not an unlikely notion. Whenever we camped near a grove of zhu-gan cane, we could hear it crackling, even when there was not a breath of wind; that was the sound of it *growing*.

Yissun told me that sometimes the fast-growing, very hard cane would rub against a soft-wooded jungle tree, and the heat of friction would start a blaze and—damp and sticky though the vegetation always was—it could blaze up and burn for hundreds of li in all directions. Only those inhabitants and denizens able to reach the river would survive the terrible fire, and they would likely fall victim to the ghariyals which always converged on any scene of disaster. The ghariyal was a tremendous and horrible river serpent which I took to be related to the dragon family. It had a knobby body as big as a cask, eyes like upstanding saucers, dragon jaws and tail, but no wings. The ghariyals were everywhere along the riverbanks, usually lurking in the mud like logs with glaring eyeballs, but they never molested us. Evidently they subsisted mostly on the monkeys which, in their antics, frequently fell shrieking into the river.

We were not molested by any of the other jungle creatures, either, although Yissun and the Mien villagers along the way warned us that the Dong Nat was the habitat of worse things than the nat and the ghariyal. Fifty different kinds of venomous snakes, they said, and tigers and pards and wild dogs and boars and elephants, and the wild ox called the seladang. I remarked lightly that I should not care to meet a wild ox; the domestic kind I saw in the villages look vicious enough. It was as big as a yak, sort of blue-gray in color, with flat horns swooping in a crescent backward from its brow. Like the serpent ghariyal, it liked to lie wallowing in a mudhole, with only its snout and eyes above the surface, and when the huge beast lumbered loose from the mud, there was a noise like huo-yao exploding.

"That animal is only the karbau," Yissun said indifferently. "No more dangerous than a cow. The little children herd them. But a seladang stands higher at the shoulder than the top of your head, and even the tigers and elephants move out of its way when it walks through the jungle."

We could always tell from afar when we were approaching a riverside village, because it always had what looked like a cloud of rusty-black smoke hovering over it. That was actually a canopy of crows—called by the Mien "the feathered weeds"—raucously rejoicing over the village's rich litter of garbage. Besides the crows overhead and the swill underfoot, every village had also a span or two of the karbau draft oxen, and some scrawny black-feathered chickens running about, and a lot of those pigs with long bodies that sagged in the middle and dragged in the swill, and an incredible lot of naked children that very much resembled the pigs. Every village had also a span or two of tame cow elephants. That was because the jungle Mien's only trade and craft was the taking of timber and other tree products out of this wilderness, and the elephants did most of the work.

The jungle trees were not all ugly and useless, like the riverside draggles of mangrove, or pretty and useless, like the one called the peacock's tail, a solid mass of flame-colored flowers. Some gave edible fruits and nuts, and others were hung with pepper vines, and the one called chaulmugra gave a sap which is the only medicine known for leprosy. Others yielded good hardwood timber—the black abnus, the speckled kinam, the golden saka which, when the wood has seasoned to a rich, mottled brown, is known as teak. I might record that teakwood looks much more handsome in the form of a ship's decking and planking than it does in its natural state. The teak trees were tall and as straight as ledger lines, but dingy gray of bark, with only scraggly branches and sparse and untidy leaves.

I might also remark that the Mien people were no adornment to the landscape, either. They were ugly, squat and dumpy, most of the men being a good two handspan shorter than myself, and the women a hand or so shorter than that. Even in their daily toil, as I said, the men put most of the labor onto their elephants, and at all other times the men were idle slovens and the women limp slatterns. In Ava's tropical climate, they had no real need of clothes, but they could have contrived some costume more comely than they had done. Both sexes wore woven-fiber hats like large mushroom tops, but were otherwise bare from the waist up and the knees down, wearing a drab cloth wrapped around them like a skirt. The women, indif-

ferent to their flapping dugs, did add one article for modesty's sake. Each wore a sash with long ends, weighted with
beads and hanging front and rear, so that it dangled to
screen her private parts when she sat in a squat, which
was her customary position. Both sexes would put cloth
sleeves on their calves when they had to wade in the river,
as protection against the leeches. But they always went
barefoot, their feet having got so horny-hard that they
were proof against any irritant. As I recall, I saw just two
men in that whole region who owned shoes. They wore
them slung on a string around their neck, for preservation
of such rarities.

The men of the Mien were unlovely enough as they
stood, but they had devised a means of making themselves
even more so. They smirched their skin with colored pictures and patterns. I do not mean paint, but a coloring
pricked into and under the skin, and ineradicable ever after. It was done with a sharp sliver of zhu-gan and the soot
from burned sesame oil. The soot was black, but put under
the skin it showed as blue dots and lines. There were so-
called artists in that craft, who traveled from village to village, and were welcome everywhere, for a Mien man would
be considered effeminate if he were not decorated like a
qali carpet. The pricking was begun in boyhood and, with
time off for rest between the painful sessions, was continued until he was latticed with blue patterns from knees to
waist. Then, if he was really vain, and could afford the artist's further ministrations, a man would have other designs done, in some kind of red pigment, in among the
blue, and was considered handsome indeed.

That ugliness was reserved to the males, but they generously let the females share in another one: the unsightly
habit of constantly chewing. Indeed, I believe the jungle
Mien did their forestry work only so they could afford to
purchase another tree product—a chewable one—that they
could not grow, but had to import. It was the nut of a tree
called the areca, which was found only in seacoast regions.
The Mien bought those nuts, boiled them, sliced them and
let them dry black in the sun. Whenever they felt like having a treat—which was all the time—they would take a
slice of the areca nut, dab a little lime on it, roll it in a leaf
of a vine called the betel, pop that wad into the mouth and
chew it—or rather, chew a constant succession of wads—

the whole day long. It was to the Mien what the cud is to
cows: their only diversion, their only enjoyment, the only
activity they engaged in that was not absolutely necessary
to existence. A village full of Mien men, women and children was not pretty. It was not made prettier by the sight
of all of them champing their jaws up and down and about.

Even that was not the extremity of their deliberate self-
defilement. The chewing of a wad of areca and betel had
the further effect of making the chewer's saliva bright red.
Since a Mien child began chewing as soon as it was off the
teat, it grew up to have gums and lips as red as open sores,
and teeth as dark and corrugated as teak bark. Just as the
Mien accounted handsome a man who elaborated on his already awful body colors, they accounted beautiful a
woman who put a coat of lacquer on her already teak-bark
teeth and thereby colored them absolutely dead black. The
first time a Mien beauty gave me a smile all tar-black and
ulcer-red, I reeled backward in revulsion. When I recovered, I asked Yissun the motive for that ghastly disfigurement. He asked the woman, and relayed to me her
haughty response:

"Why, *white* teeth are for dogs and monkeys!"

Speaking of whiteness, I would have expected those people to show some surprise or even fright at my approach—
since I must have been the first white man ever seen in the
Ava nation. But they evinced no emotion whatever. I
might have been one of the less fearsome nat, and an inept
one, which had chosen to appear in a defectively colorless
human-body disguise. But neither did the Mien show any
resentment, fear or loathing of Yissun and our boatmen,
though they were all aware that the Mongols had recently
conquered their country. When I remarked on their lackadaisical attitude, they only shrugged and repeated—and
Yissun translated—what I took to be a Mien peasant proverb:

"When the karbau fight, it is the grass that gets trampled."

And when I inquired if they were not dismayed because
their king had fled into hiding, they only shrugged and repeated what they said was a traditional peasant prayer:
"Spare us the five evils," and then enumerated the five:
"Flood, fire, thieves, enemies and kings."

When I enquired of one village's headman, who seemed

a degree more intelligent than the village's karbau oxen, what he could tell me of the history of the Mien people, this is what Yissun relayed to me:

"Amè, U Polo! Our great people once had a splendid history and a glorious heritage. It was all written down in books, in our poetic Mien language. But there came a great famine, and the books were boiled and sauced and eaten, so now we remember nothing of our history and know nothing of writing."

He did not elucidate further, and neither can I, except to explain that "amè!" was the Mien's favorite exclamation and expletive and profanity (though it meant nothing but "mother") and "U Polo" was their way of addressing me respectfully. They entitled me "U" and Hui-sheng "Daw," which was their equivalent of saying Messere e Madona Polo. As for the story of the history books' having been "sauced and eaten," I can verify at least this much. The Mien did have a sauce that was their favorite food—they used it as often as they uttered "amè!"—and it was a stinking, revolting, absolutely nauseous liquid condiment which they expressed from *fermented fish*. The sauce was called nuoc-mam, and they slathered it on their rice, their pork and chicken, their vegetables, on everything they ate. Since nuoc-mam made everything taste ghastlily like itself, and since the Mien would eat any ghastlily thing if it had nuoc-mam poured on it, I did not for a moment disbelieve that they could have "sauced and eaten" all their historical archives.

We came one evening to a village where the inhabitants were, most unnaturally, *not* being phlegmatic and idle, but were leaping about in great excitement. They were all women and children, so I bade Yissun inquire what was happening and where all the men had gone to.

"They say the men have caught a badak-gajah—a unicorn—and should shortly be fetching it in."

Well, that news excited even me. As far away as Venice, unicorns were known by repute, and some people believed in their existence, and others regarded them as mythical creatures, but all thought fondly and admiringly of the *idea* of unicorns. In Kithai and Manzi, I had known many men—usually those well along in years—to ingest a medicine made of powdered "horn of unicorn," as an enhancer of virility. The medicine was scarce and only seldom avail-

able, and prodigiously costly, so that gave some evidence
that unicorns really existed, and were as rare as the legends said they were.

On the other hand, the legends told in Venice and Kithai
alike, and the pictures artists drew, depicted the unicorn
as a beautiful, graceful, horse- or deerlike animal with a
long, sharp, twisted, single golden horn springing from its
forehead. Somehow I had doubts that this Ava unicorn
could be the same. For one thing, it was hard to conceive of
such a dreamlike creature living in these nightmarish jungles, and letting itself be caught by the dullard Mien. For
another, that local name, badak-gajah, translated only as
"an animal as big as an elephant," which did not sound
right at all.

"Ask them, Yissun, if they take the unicorn by setting
out a virgin maiden to entice it to capture."

He asked, and I could see the blank looks with which
that query was received, and several of the women murmured "amè!" so I was not surprised when he reported
that no, they had never had opportunity to try that
method.

"Ah," I said. "The unicorns are that scarce, are they?"

"The virgins are that scarce."

"Well, let us see how they do take the creature. Can
someone show us where it is now?"

A little naked boy, running almost energetically ahead
of us, led me and Hui-sheng and Yissun there, to a mud flat
near the river. Unaccountably, a vast pile of rubbish was
burning furiously in the very middle of the mud, and all
the village men, exhibiting none of their usual torpor,
were actually dancing around the fire. There was no sign
of any unicorn, or any other animal, caught or not. Yissun
asked about and reported to me:

"The badak-gajah, like the karbau ox and the ghariyal
serpent, likes to sleep in the coolness of the mud. These
men, early this dawn, found one here asleep, only its horn
and nostrils visible above the surface. They took it in their
usual manner. Moving quietly, they piled over the spot
reeds and cane and dry grass, and set it afire. The beast
awoke, of course, but could not wallow loose of the mud before the fire began to crust it, and the smoke quickly rendered the unicorn unconscious."

I exclaimed, "What a dreadful way to treat an animal of

so many pretty legends! So then they made it captive, I suppose. Where is it?"

"Not captive. It is still under there. In the mud under the fire. Baking."

"What?" I cried. "They are *baking* the *unicorn?*"

"These people are Buddhists, and Buddhism forbids their hunting and killing any wild animal. But their religion cannot hold them to account if the animal simply suffocates and then cooks, all by itself. They can eat it without committing any sacrilege."

"Eat a unicorn? I cannot conceive of a worse sacrilege!"

However, when the sacrilege was finally concluded, and the middle of the mud flat had baked to pottery hardness, and the Mien chipped it apart and revealed the cooked animal, I saw that it was not a unicorn—anyway, not the unicorn of legend. The only thing it had in common with the stories and the pictures was its single horn. But that grew not from its forehead, it grew out of an ugly long snout. The rest of the animal was just as ugly and, though nowhere near as big as an elephant, at least as big as a karbau. It did not resemble a horse or a deer, or my image of a unicorn, or anything else I had ever seen. It had a leathery skin that was all in plates and folds, rather like cuirbouilli armor. Its feet were vaguely elephantine in shape, but its ears were only little tufts, and the long snout had an overhanging upper lip, but no trunk.

The whole animal had been cooked quite black by the mud baking, so I could not say what its original color was. But the single horn had never been golden. In fact, as I could see when the Mien carefully sawed it off the animal's casklike head, it was not really made of horn substance at all, nor of ivory, like a tusk. It seemed merely a compaction of long hairs all grown in a hard, heavy clump that rose to a blunt point. But the Mien assured me, with much exuberance at their good fortune, that this really was the source of the "horn of unicorn" virility enhancer, and they would receive much payment for it—by which I daresay they meant an ample exchange in areca nuts.

Their headman took possession of the precious horn, and the others began to skin off the heavy hide and cut up the carcass and bear the steaming portions back to the village. One of the men handed to me and Hui-sheng and Yissun each a piece of the meat—straight from the oven, so to

speak—and we all found it tasty, though somewhat string-
ily fibrous. We looked forward to sharing the Mien's evening meal, but we returned to the village to find that every
last morsel of the unicorn meat had been drenched in the
reeking nuoc-mam sauce. So we declined to join in, and instead that night ate some fish our boatmen had caught
from the river.

Although the Mien claimed to be Buddhists, the only remotely religious behavior we saw for a long time was their
fearful and fretful concern about the surrounding nat demons. The Mien addressed their children, whatever their
names, as "Worm" and "Pig," so the nat would deem them
beneath notice. Although there was plenty of oil locally
available—oil of fish and sesame and even naft oil seeping
from the jungle ground in places—the Mien would never
grease their elephants' harness or their cart and barrow
wheels. They said the squeaking kept the nat away. In one
village, where I saw that the women had to carry water
from a distant spring, I suggested building a conduit of
split zhu-gan cane to bring the water right into the village.
"Amè!" cried the villagers; that would bring the spring's
resident "water nat" too dangerously close to human habitation. The first time the Mien saw Hui-sheng light her incense burner in our camp at bedtime, they muttered
"amè!" and got Yissun to tell us that they never employed
incense or perfumes—as if we needed to be told that—for
fear sweet smells might attract the nat.

However, as our company got farther down the Irawadi,
into more populous country, we began to find in many villages a mud-brick temple. It was called a p'hra, and it was
circular, shaped like a large hand bell with its mouth on
the ground and its steeple-handle sticking up in the air,
and in each p'hra lived a Buddhist lama, here called a
pongyi. Each was shaven-headed, and yellow-robed, each
was disapproving of this world and his fellow Mien and life
in general, and was morosely impatient to get out of Ava
and on to Nirvana. But I met one who was at least convivial enough to converse with Yissun and me. That pongyi
proved to be so educated that he could even write, and he
showed me how the Mien writing was done. He could not
add anything to the tale I had heard—that the Mien's
earlier history had ended in their bellies—but he did know
that writing had been nonexistent in Ava until less than

two hundred years ago, when the nation's then King Kyansitha, all by himself, invented an alphabet.

"The good king was careful," he said, "not to make any of the letters angular in shape." He drew them for us with a finger in the dusty yard of his p'hra. "Our people have nothing to write on but leaves, and only sticks to scratch on them with, and angular characters might tear the leaves. So, you see, all the letters are rounded and easy-flowing."

"Cazza beta!" I blurted. "Even the *language* is lazy!"

Until now, I had been blaming the Mien people's lassitude and slovenliness on the Ava climate, which God knows was oppressive and enervating. But the friendly pongyi volunteered the real and astonishing and terrible truth about the Mien. They had taken that name, he said, when they first came to Champa and settled in this country that was now the Ava nation—and that had happened, he said, only about four hundred years ago.

"Who were they originally?" I asked. "Where did they come from?"

He said, "From To-Bhot."

Well, that explained the Mien! They were really nothing but a displaced overflow of To-Bhot's wretched Bho. And if the Bho could be lethargic of both intellect and energy, up in the bracing clean air of their native highlands, it was no wonder that, down here in the vigor-sapping hot low country, they should have degenerated even further—to where their only willful exertion was a bovine chewing and their most strenuous profanity was a milk-mild "mother!" and even their king's writing was limp.

In all charity, I have to say that not much ambition and vitality can be rightly expected of any people who live in a tropical climate and jungle conditions. It must take all their will just to exist at all. I myself was not usually a sluggard, but in Ava I felt always drained of strength and purpose, and even my usually pert and lively Hui-sheng got quite languid in her movements. I had known heat in other places, but never such a damp, heavy, dragging-down heat as I felt in Ava. I might as well have wrung a blanket in hot water, then flung it over my head so that I had both to wear it and try to breathe through it.

The cloacal climate would have been affliction enough, but it bred various other torments, chief among them the jungle vermin. During the daytimes, our barge went down-river in a thick accompanying cloud of mosquitoes. We could reach out and catch them by handfuls, and their massed buzzing was as loud as the snores of the ghariyal serpents on the mudbanks, and their biting was so contin-uous that it eventually and blessedly induced a sort of numb indifference. When any of our men stepped into the river shallows while beaching the barge at evening, he stepped out again with his legs and garments striped black and red, the black being long, slimy, clinging leeches that had fastened to him, right through the fabric of his clothes, sucking so avidly that they drooled streaks of his blood. Then, on land, we might be attacked either by enormous red ants or by darting oxflies, either insect's bite so painful that, we were told, they could drive even elephants to mad rampage. Nighttime brought little respite, because all the ground was infested with a breed of fleas so tiny they could hardly be seen and never be caught, but whose bite raised an enormous welt. Hui-sheng's incense smoke gave us some relief from the night-flying insects, and we did not care how many nat it might attract.

I do not know whether it was because of the heat, the hu-midity or the insects, or all those miseries, but many peo-ple in that jungle suffered from illnesses that seemed never to conclude either in death or recovery. (The people of Yun-nan referred to the whole of Champa as "the Valley of Fever.") Two of our sturdy Mongol boatmen fell to one of those maladies, or maybe several, and Yissun and I had to take over their chores. The men's gums bled almost as red as those of a Mien cud-chewer, and much of their hair fell out. Under their arms and between their legs the skin be-gan to rot, getting green and crumbly, like cheese going bad. Some kind of fungus attacked their fingers and toes, so that their fingernails and toenails got soft and moist and painful, and often bled.

Yissun and I asked a Mien village headman for advice from his own experience, and he told us to rub pepper into the men's sores. When I protested that that was bound to cause excruciating pain, he said, "Amè, of course, U Polo. But it will hurt the disease nat even worse, and the demon may depart."

Our Mongols bore that treatment stoically enough, but so did the nat, and the men stayed ill and prostrate all the

way downriver. At least they, and we other men, did not
contract another jungle affliction I heard about. Numerous
Mien men confided dolefully to us that they suffered from
it, and always would. They called it koro, and they described its very terrible effect: a sudden and dramatic and
irreversible shrinking of the virile organ, a retraction of it
into the body. I did not inquire for further details, but I
could not help wondering if the jungle koro was related to
the fly-borne kala-azar that had commenced my Uncle
Mafìo's pathetic dissolution.

For a time, Yissun and Hui-sheng and her Mongol maid
and I took turns tending our two sick men. From our experience and observation so far, we had got the impression
that the jungle's diseases troubled only the male sex, and
Yissun and I were not much inclined to worry about ourselves. But when the maidservant also started to show
signs of illness, I made Hui-sheng leave off her nursing,
and confine herself to the farthest end of the barge, and
sleep well apart from the rest of us at night. Meanwhile,
our best efforts did not improve the condition of the two
men. They were still ill and flaccid and gaunt when we finally reached Pagan, and they had to be carried ashore to
be put in the care of their army's shamàn-physicians. I do
not know what became of them after that, but at least they
survived to get that far. Hui-sheng's maid did not.

Her ailment had seemed identical to that of the men, but
she had been much more troubled and dismayed by it. I
suppose, being a female, she was naturally more frightened and embarrassed when she began to rot at her extremities and under her arms and between her legs.
However, she also began to complain, which the men had
not, of itching all over her body. Even *inside* it, she said,
which we took to be delirium. But Yissun and I gently undressed her and found, here and there, what looked like
grains of rice stuck to her skin. When we tried to pick them
off, we discovered that they were only the protruding
ends—heads or tails, we could not tell—of long, thin worms
that had burrowed deep into her flesh. We tugged, and
they came out reluctantly, and kept coming, span after
span, as we might have unspooled a web-thread from the
spinneret of a spider's body.

The poor woman wept and shrieked and weakly writhed
during most of the time we were doing that. Each worm

was no thicker than a string, but easily as long as my leg, greenish-white in color, slick to our touch, hard to grasp and resisting our pull, and there were many of them, and even the hardened Mongol Yissun and I could not help retching violently when we did that hand-over-hand hauling out of the worms and throwing them overboard. When we had done, the woman was no longer squirming, but lay still in death. Perhaps the worms had been coiled around organs inside her, and our pulling had disarranged those parts and thereby killed her. But I am disposed to believe that she died from the sheer horror of the experience. Anyway, to spare her any further miseries—because we had heard that the funeral practices of the Mien were barbaric—we rowed ashore at a deserted spot, and buried her deep, well out of reach of the ghariyals or any other jungle predators.

2

I was glad to see the Orlok Bayan again. I was even glad to see his teeth. Their garish glare of porcelain and gold was far more sightly than the snaggled and blackened teeth of the Mien I had been seeing all the way down the Irawadi. Bayan was somewhat older than my father, and he had lost some hair and added some girth since our campaign together, but he was still as leathery and supple as his own old armor. He was also, at the moment, slightly drunk.

"By Tengri, Marco, but *you* have put on great beauty since I saw you last!" He bawled that at me, but he was ogling Hui-sheng at my side. When I introduced her, she smiled a little nervously at him, for Bayan was on the throne of the King of Ava, in the throne room of the palace of Pagan, but he was not looking very kinglike. He was half-lying asprawl on the throne, guzzling from a jeweled cup, and his eyes were vividly bloodshot.

"Found the king's wine cellar," he said. "No kumis or arkhi, but something called choum-choum. Made of rice, they tell me, but I think it is really compounded of earthquake and avalanche. Hui, Marco! Remember our ava-

lanche? Here, have some." He snapped his fingers, and a
barefoot, bare-chested servant hurried to pour me a cup.

"What has become of the king, then?" I asked.

"Threw away his throne, his people's respect, his name
and his life," said Bayan, smacking his lips. "He was King
Narashinha-pati until he fled. Now his former subjects all
call him contemptuously Tayok-pyemin, which means the
King Who Ran Away. By comparison, they almost like
having us here. The king fled west as we approached, over
to Akyab, the port city on the Bay of Bangala. We thought
he would escape by ship, but he just stayed there. Eating
and calling for more and more food. He ate himself to
death. A singular way to go."

"That sounds like a Mien," I said disgustedly.

"Yes, it does. But he was not a Mien. The royal family
was of Bangali stock, originally from India. That is why we
thought he would escape to there. Anyway, Ava is now
ours, and I am acting Wang of Ava until Kubilai sends a
son or something to be my personal replacement. If you see
the Khakhan before I do, tell him to send somebody of
frosty blood who can endure this infernal climate. And tell
him to hurry. My sardars are now fighting over east, in
Muang Thai, and I want to join them."

Hui-sheng and I were given a grand suite in the palace,
together with some of the late royal family's exceptionally
obsequious servants. I asked Yissun to take one of our
many bedrooms and stay nearby as my interpreter. Hui-
sheng, being now bereft of a personal maid, chose a new
one from the staff given us, a girl of seventeen, of the race
sometimes called Shan and sometimes Thai. Her name
was Arùn, or Dawn, and she was almost as comely of face
as was her new mistress.

In our bathing chamber, which was as big and as well-
equipped as a Persian hammam, the maid helped Hui-
sheng and me, together, to bathe several times over, until
we felt clean of our encrustation of jungle, and then helped
us dress. For me, there was just a length of brocade silk to
be wrapped around me, skirt fashion. Hui-sheng's costume
was much the same, except that it wrapped high enough to
cover her breasts. Arùn, without shyness, opened and
rewrapped her own single garment several times, not to
show us that it was all she wore, but to show us how to
wrap ourselves so they would stay on. Nevertheless, I took

the opportunity to admire the girl's body, which was as fair as her name, and Hui-sheng made a face at me when she noticed, and I grinned and Arùn giggled. We were given no shoes or even slippers; everyone in the palace went barefoot, except the heavy-booted Bayan, and I later put on boots only when I went outdoors. Arùn did bring one other item of dress: earrings for both of us. But, since our ears were not bored for them, we could not wear them.

When Hui-sheng had, with Arùn's help, fetchingly arranged her hair and fixed flowers in it, we went downstairs again, to the palace's dining hall, where Bayan had commanded a welcoming feast for us. We were not much accustomed to eating at midday, which it then was, but I was looking forward to some decent food after our hard rations on the voyage, and I was a trifle dismayed to see what was set before us—black meat and purple rice.

"By Tengri," I growled to Bayan. "I knew the Mien blacked their teeth, but I never noticed that they also blacked the food to go between their teeth."

"Eat, Marco," he said complacently. "The meat is chicken, and the chickens of Ava have not only black plumage, but black skin, black flesh, black everything except their eggs. Never mind how the bird looks, it is cooked in the milk of the India nut, and is delicious. The rice is only rice, but in this land it grows in gaudy colors—indigo, yellow, bright red. Today we have purple. It is good. Eat. Drink." And with his own hand, he poured a brimming beaker of the rice liquor for Hui-sheng.

We did eat, and the meal was very good. In that country, even at the Pagan palace, there were no such things as nimble tongs or any other table implements. Eating was done with the fingers, which is how Bayan would have done it anyway. He sat taking alternately handfuls of the flamboyant food and great drafts of choum-choum—Hui-sheng and I only sipped at ours, for it was highly potent—while I told of our adventures on the Irawadi, and the considerable distaste I had developed for the inhabitants of Ava.

"In the river plain, you saw only the misbegotten Mien," said Bayan. "But you might think more kindly even of them, if you had come through the hill country, and seen the real aboriginal natives of these lands. The Padaung, for instance. Their females start in childhood to wear a brass ring around the neck, and add another above that, and another and another, until in womanhood they have a brass-ringed neck as long as a camel's. Or the Moi people. *Their* women bore holes in their earlobes and put increasingly large ornaments in the holes, until the lobes are distended to hoops that can hold a platter. I saw one Moi woman with earlobes she had to put her arms through, to keep them out of her way."

I assumed Bayan was only drunkenly babbling, but I listened respectfully. And I later realized, when I saw actual specimens of those barbarian tribes on the streets of Pagan itself, that he had been telling only sober truth.

"All those are country folk," he went on. "The city dwellers are a better mixture. Some visiting aborigines and Mien, a few Indian immigrants, but mostly the more civilized and cultured people called Myama. They have long been the nobility and upper classes of Ava, and they are far superior to all the others. The Myama have even had the good sense not to take their inferior neighbors as servants or slaves. They have always gone afield and got Shan for those purposes, the Shan—or Thai, if you prefer—being notably more handsome and cleanly and intelligent than any of the lesser local races."

"Yes, I have just now encountered one Thai," I said, and added, since Hui-sheng could not hear and object, "a Thai girl who is indeed a superb creature."

"It was on account of them that I came to Ava," said Bayan. I already knew that, but I did not interrupt. "They *are* worthy people. People worth keeping. And too many of them had been deserting our dominions, fleeing to the nation they call Muang Thai, Land of the Free. The Khanate wishes them to remain Shan, not turn Thai. That is, not go free, but remain subjects of the Khanate."

"I understand the Khanate's view," I said. "But if there really is a whole land full of such beautiful people, I should wish that it could go on existing."

"Oh, it can go on existing," said Bayan, "as long as it is ours. Let me but take the capital, a place called Chiang-Rai, and accept their king's surrender, and I will not lay waste the rest of the country. That way it will be a permanent source of the finest slaves, to serve and to adorn the rest of the Khanate. Hui! But enough of politics." He shoved aside his still-heaped plate and licked his lips most slaveringly and said, "Here comes our sweet to conclude our meal. The durian."

That was another dubious surprise. The sweet looked to be a melon with a spikily armored rind, but when the table steward cut it, I saw that it had large seeds inside, like chicken's eggs, and the odor that erupted from it nearly made me shove back from the table.

"Yes, yes," Bayan said testily. "Before you complain, I already know about the stink. But this is durian."

"Does the word mean carrion? That is what it smells like."

"It is the fruit of the durian tree. It has the most repellent smell of any fruit, and the most captivating taste. Ignore the stench and eat."

Hui-sheng and I looked at each other, and she looked as distressed as I probably did. But the male must show courage before his female. I took up a slice of the cream-colored fruit and, trying not to inhale, took a bite of it. Bayan was right again. The durian had a taste unlike anything I ever ate, before or since. I can taste it yet, but how do I describe it? Like a custard made with cream and butter, and flavored with almonds—but with that taste came hints of other flavors, most unexpected: wine and cheese and even shallots. It was not sweet and juicy, like a hami melon, nor a tart refreshment, like a sharbat, but it partook of those qualities and—providing one could persevere past the rank odor of it—the durian was a most delightful novelty.

"Many people get addicted to the eating of durian," said Bayan. He must have been one of them, for he was gorging on it, and talking with his mouth full. "They loathe the hideous climate of Champa, but they stay for the durian alone, because it grows nowhere except in this corner of the world." And again he was right. Both Hui-sheng and I would become ardent enthusiasts of the fruit. "And it is more than refreshing and delicious," he went on. "It incites and excites other appetites. There is a saying here in Ava: when the durian falls, the skirts go up." That was true, too, as Hui-sheng and I would later prove.

When we were all at last satiated with the fruit, Bayan leaned back and wiped his mouth on his sleeve and said, "So. It is good to have you here, Marco, especially when you come so handsomely accompanied." He reached out to pat Hui-sheng's hand. "But how long will you and she stay? What are your plans?"

"I have none at all," I said, "now that I have delivered the Khakhan's letters to you. Except that I did promise Kubilai I would bring him a memento from this new province of his. Something unique to this place."

"Hm," Bayan said reflectively. "Offhand, I can think of nothing better than a gift basket of durian, but they would spoil on the long road. Well, now. The day is getting on for evening, and that is the coolest time for walking. Take your good lady and your interpreter and stroll about Pagan. If anything strikes your fancy, it is yours."

I thanked him for the generous offer. As Hui-sheng and I got up to go, he added, "When it is dark, come back here to the palace. The Myama are great devotees of play-acting, and very good at it, and a troupe of them have been putting on a most beguiling play for me in the throne room each night. I do not understand a bit of it, of course, but I can assure you it is no trivial story. It is now in its eighth night, and the actors eagerly anticipate getting to the crucial scenes of it in just two or three nights more."

When Yissun joined us, he had with him the yellow-robed chief pongyi of the palace. That elderly gentleman kindly walked with us and, speaking through Yissun, explained many things that I might not otherwise have comprehended, and I was able to relay the explanations to Hui-sheng. The pongyi began by directing our attention to the exterior of the palace itself. That was an agglomeration of two- and three-storied buildings, almost equal in extent and splendor to the palace of Khanbalik. It was built somewhat in the Han style of architecture but, I might say, in a very refined essence of the Han style. All the buildings' walls and columns and lintels and such were, like those of the Han, much carved and sculptured and convoluted and filigreed, but in a manner more delicate. They reminded me of the reticella lace of Venice's Burano. And the dragon-ridge roof lines, instead of curving upward in a gentle swoop, soared more sharply and pointedly toward the sky.

The pongyi laid his hand on one finely finished outer wall and asked if we could tell what it was made of. I said, marveling, "It appears to have been worked from one vast piece of stone. A piece the size of a cliff."

"No." Yissun translated the explanation. "The wall is of brick, a multitude of separate bricks, but no one nowadays knows how it was done. It was made long ago, in the days of the Cham artisans, who had a secret process of somehow baking the bricks *after* they were laid in courses, to give this effect of one smooth and uninterrupted stone face."

Next he took us to an inner garden court, and asked if we could tell what it represented. It was square, as big as a market square, and bordered with flower banks and beds, but the whole interior of it was a lawn of well-kept grass. I should say a lawn or two of different varieties of grass, one pale green, one very dark, and the two seeded in alternate smaller squares, in a checkered effect. I could only venture, "It is for ornament. What else?"

"For a purpose of utility, U Polo," said the pongyi. "The King Who Ran Away was an avid player of the game called Min Tranj. Min is our word for king and Tranj means wár, and—"

"Of course!" I exclaimed. "The same as the War of the Shahi. So this is an immense outdoor playing board. Why, the king must have had playing pieces as large as himself."

"He did. He had subjects and slaves. For everyday games, he himself would represent one Min and a favorite courtier would be the opposing other. Slaves would be made to put on the masks and costumes of the various other pieces—the General on either side, and each side's two elephants, horsemen, and warriors and foot soldiers. Then the two Min would direct the play, and each piece that was lost was literally lost. Amè! Removed from the board and beheaded—yonder, among the flowers."

"Porco Dio," I murmured.

"However, if the Min—the real king, that is—got displeased with some courtier or some number of them, he would make *them* put on the costumes of the foot soldiers in the front ranks. It was, in a way, more merciful than simply ordering their decapitation, since they could have some hope of surviving the game and keeping their heads. But, sad to say, on those occasions the king would play most recklessly, and it was seldom—amè!—that the flower beds did not get well watered with blood."

We spent the rest of that afternoon wandering among Pagan's p'hra temples, those circular buildings like set-

down hand bells. I daresay a really devout explorer could
have spent his whole lifetime wandering among them,
without ever getting to see them all. The city might have
been the workshop of some Buddhist deity who was charged
with the making of those odd-shaped temples, for there
was a whole forest of their steeple-handles sticking up
from the river plain there, stretching some twenty-five li
up and down the Irawadi and extending six or seven li inland on both sides of the river. Our pongyi guide said
proudly that there were more than one thousand three
hundred of the p'hra, each crammed with images and each
surrounded by a score or more of lesser monuments, idol
statues and sculptured columns he called thupo.

"Evidence," he said, "of the great holiness of this city
and the piety of all its inhabitants, past and present, who
built these edifices. The rich people pay for their erection,
and the poor find gainful employment in doing so, and both
classes earn eternal merit. Which is why, here in Pagan,
one cannot move a hand or foot without touching some sacred thing."

But I could not help noticing that only about a third of
the buildings and monuments appeared in good repair,
and all the remainder were in various stages of decrepitude.
Indeed, as the brief tropical twilight came on, and temple
bells rang out across the plain, calling to Pagan's worship-
pers, the people filed into only the better-kept few p'hra,
while out of the many broken and crumbling ones came
long skeins of flittering bats, like plumes of black smoke
against the purpling sky. I remarked that the local piety
did not seem to extend to the preservation of holiness.

"Well, really, U Polo," the old pongyi said, with a touch
of asperity. "Our religion confers great merit on those who
build a holy monument, but little on those who merely repair one. So, even if a wealthy noble or merchant cared to
waste his merit on such an activity, the poor would be unwilling to do the work. Naturally, all would rather build
even a very small thupo than tend to the repair of even the
largest p'hra."

"I see," I said drily. "A religion of good business practices."

We wended our way back to the palace as the night came
swiftly down. We had done our wandering, as Bayan had
said, at the time of day that was cool by Ava standards.

Nevertheless, Hui-sheng and I felt again rather sweaty and dusty by the time we got back, and so decided to forgo Bayan's invitation to join him at the night's session of the interminable play that was being performed for him. Instead, we went directly to our own suite, and told the Thai maidservant Arùn to draw us another bath. When the immense teak tub was full of water, perfumed with miada grass and sweetened with gomuti sugar, we both stripped off our silks and got into it together.

The maid, while getting in hand her washcloths and brushes and unguents and little crock of palm-oil soap, pointed to me and smiled and said, "Kaublau," then smiled again and pointed to Hui-sheng and said, "Saongam." I later learned, by inquiry of others who spoke Thai, that she had called me "handsome" and Hui-sheng "radiantly beautiful." But right then, I could only raise my eyebrows, and so did Hui-sheng, for Arùn took off her own wrapping and prepared to get into the warm water with us. Seeing us exchange looks of some surprise and perplexity, the maid paused to do an elaborate pantomime of explanation. That might have been incomprehensible to most foreigners, but Hui-sheng and I, being ourselves adept at gesture language, managed to understand that the girl was apologizing for *not* having disrobed with us during our earlier bath. She conveyed that we then had been simply "too dirty" for her to attend us in the nude, as she was supposed to do. If we would forgive her for that earlier evasion of her due participation, she would now attend us in the proper manner. So saying, she slid down into the tub, with her bath equipment, and began to soap Hui-sheng's body.

We had both been often attended in the bath by servants of Hui-sheng's sex, and of course I had often been bathed by servants of my own sex, but this was our first experience of a servant bathing *with* us. Well, other countries, other customs, so we merely exchanged a look of amiable amusement. What harm in it? There was certainly nothing unpleasant about Arùn's participation—quite the contrary, to my mind, for she was a comely person, and I had no objection whatever to being in the company of two beautiful and naked females of different races. The girl Arùn was about the same size as the young woman Hui-sheng, and of very similarly childish figure—budlike breasts and

small neat buttocks and so on—differing mainly in that
her skin was more of a cream-yellow color, the color of durian flesh, and her "little stars" were fawn-colored instead
of rose-colored, and she had the merest feathering of body
hair, just along the line where the lips of her pink parts
joined.

Since Hui-sheng could not speak, and I could think of
nothing pertinent to say, we both were silent, and I simply
sat soaking in the perfumed water while, at the other side
of the tub, Arùn washed Hui-sheng, and chattered merrily
as she did so. I suppose she had not yet realized that Hui-
sheng was mute and deaf, for it became apparent that
Arùn was taking this opportunity to try teaching us a few
rudiments of her own language. She would touch Hui-
sheng here, then there, with a dab of soft suds, and pronounce the Thai words for those parts of the body, then
touch herself in the same places and repeat the words.

Hui-sheng's hand was a mu, and each finger a niumu,
and so were Arùn's. Hui-sheng's shapely leg was a khaa,
and her slim foot a tau, and each pearly toe a niutau, and
so were Arùn's. Hui-sheng only smiled tolerantly as the
girl touched her pom and kiu and jamo—her hair and eyebrows and nose—and she made a silent laugh of appreciation as Arùn touched her lips—baà—and then puckered
her own in a kissing way and said, "Jup." But Hui-sheng's
eyes widened a bit when the girl touched her breasts and
nipples with bubbly suds and identified them as nom and
kwanom. And then Hui-sheng blushed most beautifully,
because her little stars twinkled erect from the bubbles, as
if rejoicing in their new name of kwanom. Arùn laughed
aloud when she saw that, and companionably twiddled her
own kwanom until they matched Hui-sheng's in prominence.

Then she pointed out the difference between their bodies
which I had already noticed. She indicated that she had a
very scant trace of hair—this kind called moè—there
where Hui-sheng had none. However, she went on, they
did have one thing in common thereabouts, and she touched
first her own pink parts and then Hui-sheng's, in a lightly
fingering way, and said softly, "Hiì." Hui-sheng gave a
small jump that rippled the water in the tub, and turned a
wondering look on me, and then turned it on the girl, who
met it with a smile that was openly provocative and chal-

lenging. Arùn sloshed around to face me, as if asking for my approval of her impudence, and pointed to my corresponding organ and laughed and said, "Kwe."

I think Hui-sheng had earlier been only amused, not affronted, by Arùn's irrepressibly jaunty behavior. Perhaps at that latest and frankly fondling touch, she had seemed a little apprehensive of its portent. But now she joined the girl in pointing gleefully at me, and it was my turn to blush, for my kwe had got vigorously aroused by the foregoing events, and was most flagrantly in evidence. I started guiltily to cover it with a washcloth, but Arùn reached over, gently took hold of it with a soapy hand, saying "kwe" again, while with her other hand under the water, continuing to caress Hui-sheng's counterpart and saying again "hìì." Hui-sheng only went on silently laughing, not minding at all, seeming to have begun to take pleasure in the situation. Then Arùn briefly let go of both of us, said joyously, "Aukàn!" and clapped her hands together to show us what she was suggesting.

Hui-sheng and I had had no opportunity to enjoy each other during the voyage from Bhamo to Pagan, and not much inclination either, in the circumstances. We were more than ready to make up for that lost time, but we would never have dreamed of asking for assistance in doing so. We have never required any help before, and we did not now, but we let ourselves accept it—and revel in it. Perhaps it was simply because Arùn was so vivaciously *eager* to be of service. Or perhaps it was because we were in a new and exotic land, and amenable to the new experiences it offered. Or perhaps the durian and its alleged properties had something to do with it.

I have not before spoken, as I said I would not, of any of the activities private to Hui-sheng and myself, and I will not now. I will only remark that this night we did not exactly comport ourselves in the manner which, long ago, I and the Mongol twins had done. In this event, the extra girl's participation was mainly that of a very busy matchmaker and instructor and manipulator of our various parts, during which she showed us a number of things that were evidently accepted practice among her own people, but new to us. I remember thinking that it was no wonder her people were called Thai, meaning Free. However, either Hui-sheng or I, and usually both of us, always had some part of us otherwise unoccupied, with which to give Arùn pleasure, too, and she clearly found it pleasant, for she was frequently either crooning or exclaiming, "Aukàn! Aukàn!" and "Saongam!" and "Chan pom rak kun!" which means "I love you both!" and "Chakatì pasad!" which I will not tell the meaning of.

We did aukàn again and again, the three of us, on most of the nights Hui-sheng and I remained in the Pagan palace, and often during the days, too, when the weather was too hot for doing anything outdoors. But I best remember that first night—including every least Thai word Arùn taught me—not so much because of what we did, but because, a long while afterward, I had cause to remember one thing I failed to do that night.

3

SOME days later, Yissun came to tell me that he had just discovered the late King of Ava's royal stables, at a distance from the palace, and asked if I would like to visit them. Early the next morning, before the day got hot, he and I and Hui-sheng went there in palanquins borne by slaves. The stable steward and his workers were fond and proud of their kuda and gajah wards—the royal horses and elephants—and eager to show them off to us. Since Hui-sheng was well acquainted with horses, we only admired the fine kuda steeds as we passed through their sumptuous quarters, but spent more time at the gajah stable, for she had never before been very close to an elephant.

Evidently the great cow elephants had not been much exercised since the king had run away on one of their sisters, so the stable men were pleased and acquiescent when we inquired, through Yissun, if we might ride a gajah.

"Here," they said, as they brought out a towering one. "You may have the rare honor of riding a sacred *white* elephant."

It was splendidly attired in silk blanket and jeweled head cap and pearl-bedizened harness and a richly carved and gilded teak hauda, but, as I had long ago been told, the white elephant was not at all white. It did have some

vaguely human-flesh-colored patches on its wrinkled pale-
gray hide, but the steward and the mahawats told us that
"white" referred not even to that—"white" when spoken
of elephants meant only "special, distinctive, superior."
They pointed out some of the features of this one, which, to
elephant-men, marked it as well above the ordinary run of
elephants. Notice, they said, the pretty way her front legs
bowed outward, and how her crupper slanted low behind,
and how ponderous was the dewlap hanging from her
breast. But here, they said, taking us to view the animal's
tail, here was the unmistakable indication that it was worthy of being treated as a holy white elephant. This animal,
besides having the usual bristly tuft of hairs at the end of
her tail, had also a fringe of hair up both sides of that appendage.

To show off my experience and ease with these beasts, in
the way of any man posturing before his mate, I stood Hui-
sheng to one side and bade her watch. I borrowed from one
of the mahawats his ankus hook, and reached up with it
and tapped the elephant in the proper place on her trunk,
and she obediently bent it for a stirrup and lowered it for
me, and I stepped onto that and was hoisted up to the nape
of her neck. Down below, Hui-sheng danced and applauded
admiringly, like an excited little girl, and Yissun more sedately cheered, "Hui! Hui!" The steward and the mahawats looked approving of my management of the sacred
elephant, and gave waves of their hands to indicate that I
might take it away unsupervised. So I beckoned to Hui-
sheng, and had the elephant make a stirrup again, and
Hui-sheng, with only some pretty flutters of pretended
anxiety, was hoisted aboard with me. I helped her into the
hauda and turned the elephant by touching an ear with
the ankus, then tapped the go-ahead place on the shoulder.
And off we went for a swift-striding, pleasantly swaying
ride out beyond the innumerable riverside p'hra, along the
banyan-lined avenues beside the Irawadi, and some distance out of the city.

When the elephant began to make snuffling and whoof-
ing noises, I guessed that it was scenting ghariyals
basking in the river shallows, or perhaps a tiger lurking
among the serpentine tangles of banyan trees. I was disinclined to put a sacred white elephant to any risk, and besides the day was heating up, so I turned back for the

stables, and we covered the last several li at an
exhilarating full-out run. As I helped Hui-sheng down
from the hauda, I was loud in my thanks to the elephant-
men, and bade Yissun translate my words most fulsomely.
Hui-sheng thanked the men in silence, but with consummate grace, making to each of them the wai—the gesture
of palms together, brought to the face, the head given a
slight nod—which Arùn had taught her.

On the way back to the palace, Yissun and I discussed
the notion of my taking a white elephant back to Khanbalik, to be the unique gift I had promised to Khakhan. We
agreed that it was a memento distinctive of the Champa
lands, and rare even here. But then it occurred to me that
the task of getting an elephant across seven thousand li of
difficult terrain was best left to heroes like Hannibal of
Carthage, so I readily abandoned the notion after Yissun
remarked:

"Frankly, Elder Brother Marco, I would never be able to
tell a white elephant from any other, and I doubt that the
Khan Kubilai could, and he already has plenty of other elephants."

It was only midday, but Hui-sheng and I returned to our
suite and directed Arùn to draw us a bath, to get the smell
of elephant off us. (Actually, that is far from being an unpleasant smell; imagine the aroma of a good leather bag
stuffed with sweet hay.) The maid went with delighted
alacrity to fill the teak tub, and got undressed as we did.
But, when Hui-sheng and I were in the water, and Arùn
was perched on the rim of the tub, about to slide in between us, I stopped her there for a moment. I only wished
to make a small jest, for the three of us had got quite free
and easy in each other's presence by this time, and even
had begun to communicate with some facility. I gently
parted the girl's knees, and reached between her legs and
ran my fingertip lightly down the soft trace of hair that
fringed the closure of her pink parts, and called Hui-
sheng's attention to it, telling her: "Look—the tail of the
sacred white elephant!"

Hei-sheng dissolved into silent laughter, causing Arùn
to look rather worriedly down to see what might have gone
wrong with her body. But when, with rather more difficulty, I had translated the jest for her, Arùn too crowed
with appreciative laughter. It was probably the first time

in human history, and maybe the last, that a woman good-humoredly took as flattery her being compared to an elephant. In return, Arùn began calling me, instead of U Marco as heretofore, U Saathvan Gajah. That, I finally figured out, meant "U Sixty-Year-Old Elephant." But I took that good-humoredly, too, when she made me understand that it was the highest sort of compliment. Everywhere in Champa, she said, a bull elephant of sixty years was taken to represent the very peak of strength, virility and masculine powers.

A few nights later, Arùn brought some things to show us—"mata ling," she called them, which meant "love bells," and she also said, with a mischievous grin, "aukàn"—so I gathered that she was suggesting these things as an addition to our nighttime diversions. She held out a handful of the mata ling, which looked like tiny camel bells, each about the size of a hazelnut, made of a good gold alloy. Hui-sheng and I each took one and shook it, and some kind of pellet inside rang or rattled softly. However, the things had no openings that would enable their being fastened onto garments or camel harness or anything else, and we could not discern the purpose of them, so we merely regarded Arùn with bewilderment and waited for further explanation.

That took quite a while, with many repetitions and numerous bafflements to be resolved. But Arùn finally explained—mainly by several times uttering the word "kew" with various gestures—that the mata ling were designed for implantation under the skin of the masculine organ. When I grasped that much, I laughed at what I took to be a jest. But then I grasped that the girl was serious, and I made loud noises of appalled indignation and horror. Hui-sheng motioned for me to hush and be calm, and let Arùn go on explaining. She did—and I think, of all the curiosities I encountered on my journeys, the mata ling must have been the most curious.

They had been invented, said Arùn, by a long-ago Myama Queen of Ava, whose king-husband had been woefully inclined to prefer the company of small boys. The queen made mata ling of brass and—Arùn did not say how—secretly slit the skin of the king's kwe, put in a number of the little bells and sewed him up again. Thereafter, he had not been able to penetrate the small orifices of

small boys with his newly massive organ, and had had to
make do with the more hospitable hiì receptacle of his
queen. Somehow—again Arùn did not say how—the other
women of Ava heard of that, and persuaded their own men
to follow the royal precedent. At which, both the men and
women of Ava found that they were not only being fashionable, but also had infinitely increased their mutual pleasures, the men being prodigiously bigger of circumference
than before, and the vibration of the mata ling affording
an ineffably new sensation to both partners in the act of
aukàn.

The mata ling were still made in Ava, said Arùn, and
only in Ava, and only by certain old women who knew how
to do the implanting of them safely and painlessly and in
the most effective places on the kwe. Every man who could
afford one had at least one implanted, and those who could
afford more might eventually have a kwe worth more than
their money purse, and weighing more. She herself, said
Arùn, had formerly had a Myama master whose kwe was
like a knotted wooden club, even in repose, and when it
was aroused: "Amè!" She added that the love bells had
undergone some improvement over the centuries since the
queen invented them. For one thing, the Ava physicians
had decreed that they be made of incorruptible gold instead of brass, so they would not cause infection under the
delicate kwe skin. Also, the old women bellmakers had invented a whole new and exceedingly piquant capability for
the mata ling.

Arùn demonstrated for us. Some of the little things were
only bells or rattles, as we had perceived, their inside pellets vibrating only when they were shaken. Some others,
Arùn showed us, lay equally inert when she put them on a
table. But then she put one in each of our palms, and closed
our hands around them. Hui-sheng and I both started in
astonishment when, after a moment, the warmth of our
hands seemed to confer life on the little gold objects, as if
they had been eggs about to hatch, and they began quivering and twitching *all by themselves*.

That new and improved kind of mata ling, said Arùn,
contained some never-dying tiny creature or substance—
the old women never would reveal what it was—which ordinarily slept quietly in its little gold shell underneath a
man's kwe skin. But when his kwe was inserted in a wom-

an's hiì, the secret sleeper came awake and active and—
she solemnly asserted—the man and woman could lie together unmoving, totally still, and yet enjoy, through the
agency of that busy little love bell, all the sensations and
the mounting excitement and finally the bursting pleasure of consummation. In other words, they could perform
aukàn, and over and over again, without the least exertion
on their part.

When Arùn had concluded, quite out of breath from her
own exertions of explaining, I found her and Hui-sheng regarding me speculatively. I said loudly, "No!" I said it several times and in several different languages, including
that of emphatic gestures. The idea of utilizing the mata
ling in aukàn was an intriguing one, but I was not going to
sneak to some back door in some Pagan back alley and let
some hag sorceress meddle with my person, and I made
that as plain as I knew how.

Hui-sheng and Arùn pretended to look at me with disappointment and disdain, but really they were trying not to
laugh at the vehemence of my refusal. Next, they exchanged a glance, as if to say to each other, "Which of us
should speak?" and Arùn gave a slight nod, as if to say
that Hui-sheng could more easily communicate with me.
So Hui-sheng did, pointing out that the only function of the
mata ling was to be put inside the female hiì *with* the male
kwe, not necessarily as *part* of it. Would I care to try the
experience, she inquired with great delicacy (and no small
amusement), by doing only what we did normally, but allowing herself and Arùn to put the little love bells inside
themselves beforehand?

Well, of course I could have no objection to that, and before the night was out I had developed a great fondness
and enthusiasm for the mata ling, and so had Hui-sheng
and Arùn. But again I will draw the curtain of privacy
here. I will confide only that I found the love bells such a
worthwhile contrivance—and Hui-sheng and Arùn concurred in my opinion—that I naturally thought of making
those things the "unique gift" I would carry back to Kubilai. But I hesitated to decide definitely on that. One can
hardly approach the Khan of All Khans, the most puissant
sovereign in all the world, and he a dignified elderly gentleman besides, with the suggestion that he submit to an
"improvement" of his venerable organ. . . .

No, I really could not think of any way to present the gift of mata ling that would not cause instant affront, resentment and perhaps an outraged reprisal. However, the very next day, I was relieved to receive an alternative idea, a most appealing one, and I proceeded to act upon it straightaway. A thing unique is one of a kind, and therefore it is an impossibility for anything to be "more unique" than something else. But if the durian fruit was unique in its way, and so was a white elephant, and so were the mata ling love bells, then this new idea was unique among uniquities.

It was the aged palace pongyi who put the idea in my head. He and I and Hui-sheng and Yissun were again strolling about Pagan, while he expatiated on this and that sight we saw. On this day, he led us to the most substantial and holiest and highest regarded p'hra in all of Ava. It was not just one of those hand-bell-shaped affairs, but an enormous and beautiful and really magnificent temple, dazzlingly white, like an edifice built of foam, if it is possible to imagine a pile of foam as big as the Basilica of San Marco, and intricately carved and roofed with gold. It was called Ananda, a word meaning "Endless Bliss," which also had been the name of one of the Buddha's disciples during his lifetime. Indeed, said the pongyi as he showed us around the temple's interior, Ananda had been the Buddha's best-beloved disciple, as John was Jesus's.

"This was the reliquary of the Buddha's tooth," said the pongyi, as we passed a golden casket on an ivory stand. "And here is a statue of the dancing deity Nataraji. The sculpture was originally so perfectly made that *it* began dancing, and when a god dances the earth shudders. Our city was nearly shaken asunder, until the dancing image chipped off a finger in its cavorting, at which it quieted and became only a statue again. Therefore, to this day, all religious images are made with a single deliberate flaw. It will be so trivial that you may never see it, but it is there— just for safety's sake."

"Excuse me, Reverend Pongyi," I said. "But did you, in passing, say that the casket yonder held the Buddha's tooth?"

"It used to," he said sadly.

"A real tooth? Of the Buddha himself? A tooth preserved for seventeen centuries?"

"Yes," he said, and opened the casket to show us the velvet socket where it had lain. "A pilgrim pongyi from the island of Srihalam brought it here, some two hundred years ago, for the dedication of this Ananda temple. It was our most treasured relic."

Hui-sheng expressed surprise at the large size of the tooth's vacated resting place, and conveyed to me that the tooth must have been of a size to occupy the Buddha's whole head. I relayed that rather irreverent remark to Yissun and he to the pongyi.

"Amè, yes, a mighty tooth," said the old gentleman. "Why not? The Buddha was a mighty man. On that same island of Srihalam is still to be seen a footprint he made in a rock. From his foot size, the Buddha is calculated to have been nine forearms tall."

"Amè," I echoed. "That is forty hands. Thirteen feet and a half. The Buddha must have been of the race of Goliath."

"Ah, well, when he comes to earth again, in seven or eight thousand years, we expect him to be *eighty* forearms tall."

"His devotees should have no trouble recognizing him, as we might with Jesus," I said. "But what became of this sacred tooth?"

The pongyi sniffled slightly. "The King Who Ran Away purloined it as he went, and absconded with it. An execrable sacrilege. No one knows why he did it. He was presumed to be fleeing to India, and in India the Buddha is no longer worshiped."

"But the king got only as far as Akyab, and died there," I murmured. "So the tooth might still be among his effects."

The pongyi gave a shrug of hopeful resignation, and went on to show us some more of the Ananda's admirable treasures. But I had already conceived my idea and, as soon as I could politely do so, I terminated our tour for the day, and thanked the pongyi for his kind attentions, and hurried Hui-sheng and Yissun back to the palace, telling them of my idea as we went. At the palace, I asked an immediate audience with the Wang Bayan, and told him, too.

"If I can retrieve the tooth, *that* will be my gift to Kublai. Though the Buddha is not a god he reveres, still the tooth of a god ought to be a keepsake no other monarch has ever owned. Even in Christendom, though various relics

exist—bits of the True Cross, the Holy Nails, the Holy
Sudarium—nothing remains of the Corpus Christi except
some drops of the Holy Blood. The Khakhan should be
most pleased and proud to have the Buddha's very own
tooth."

"If you can retrieve it," said Bayan. "Me, I never even
got any of my *own* back, or I would not have to wear this
torture device in my mouth. How do you intend to go about
it?"

"With your permission, Wang Bayan, I shall proceed
from here to the seaport of Akyab, and examine the place
where the late king died, go through his belongings, interrogate any surviving family. It ought to be there somewhere. Meanwhile, I should like to leave Hui-sheng here,
under your protection. I know now that travel through
these lands is arduous, and I will not subject her to any
more of that until we are ready to return to Khanbalik.
She is well attended by her maid and our other servants, if
you will give her leave to stay in residence here. I should
like to ask the further favor of keeping Yissun with me as
my interpreter still. I need only him, and a horse for each
of us. I will ride light, that I may ride swiftly."

"You know you need not have asked, Marco, for you
carry the Khakhan's pai-tzu plaque, which is all the authority you need. But I thank you for the courtesy of asking, and of course you have my permission, and my
promise to see that no harm comes to your lady, and my
best wishes for your success in your quest." He concluded
with the traditional Mongol farewell: "A good horse to
you, and a wide plain, until we meet again."

4

My quest turned out to be not easily or quickly accomplished, although I enjoyed generally good fortune and ample assistance. To begin with, I was received at the squalid
seaside city of Akyab by the sardar Bayan had set in command of the Mongol occupation forces there, one Shaibani.
He received me cordially, almost eagerly, at the house he

had appropriated for his residency. It was the best house in Akyab, which is not to say much for it.

"Sain bina," he said. "It is good to greet you, Elder Brother Marco Polo. I see that you carry the Khakhan's pai-tzu."

"Sain bina, Sardar Shaibani. Yes, I come on a mission for our mutual Lord Kubilai."

Yissun led our horses around to the stable that occupied the rear half of the house. Shaibani and I went into the front half, and his aides set out a meal for us. While we ate, I told him that I was on the trail of Ava's late King Narashinha-pati, and why I was, and that I sought to examine the fugitive's remaining effects and to speak with any still-living members of his entourage.

"It shall be as you desire," said the Sardar. "Also, I am overjoyed to see you carrying the pai-tzu, for it gives you the authority to settle a vexatious dispute here in Akyab. It is a question that has caused much uproar, and divided the citizenry into opposing factions. They have been so embroiled in this local fuss that they scarcely paid any attention to our marching in. And until it is settled, I am balked of imposing any orderly administration. My men spend all their time breaking up street fights. So I am very glad you have arrived."

"Well," I said, a little mystified. "Whatever I can do, I will. But my business concerning the late king must come first."

"This does concern the late king," he said, and added in a growl, "May the worms gag on his cursed remains! The dispute is over those very effects and survivors you wish to get hold of—or what is left of them, anyway. May I explain?"

"I wish you would."

"This Akyab is a wretched and dismal city. You look to be a sensible man, so I assume you will leave here as soon as you can. I am assigned here, so I must stay, and I shall try to make it a useful addition to the Khanate. Now, wretchedness aside, this is a seaport, and in that it is like all seaport cities. Which is to say, it has two industries to justify its existence and support its citizens. One is the provision of port facilities—docks and chandlers and warehouses and such. The other industry, as in every port city, is the pandering to the appetites of ships' crews while they

lay over here. That means whorehouses, wineshops and
games of chance. But most of Akyab's trade is done with
India across the Bay of Bangala yonder, so most of the visiting mariners are miserable Hindus. They have no stomach for strong drink and they have not much vigor
between the legs, so they spend all their shore time at the
games of chance. For that reason, the whorehouses and
wineshops here are few and small and poor—and vakh! the
whores and the drinks are vile. But Akyab has several
halls of games, and they are the most thriving establishments of this city, and their proprietors are the leading citizens."

"This is all very interesting, Sardar, but I fail to—"

"Only allow me, Elder Brother. You will understand.
That King Who Ran Away—his cowardly action did not
make him much loved by his former subjects. Or by anyone. I am informed that he left Pagan with a substantial
train of elephants and pack animals and wives and children and courtiers and servants and slaves—and all the
treasure they all could carry. But every night, on the road,
that train dwindled. Under cover of darkness, his courtiers
stole away with much of the looted treasure. Servants departed, with whatever they could pilfer. Slaves ran away
to freedom. Even the king's wives—including even his
Queen First Wife—took their princeling children and vanished. Probably to change their names and hope to start a
new life unblemished."

"I almost feel sorry for the poor coward king."

"Meanwhile, just to buy an occasional meal and bed on
the road, the fugitive king had to pay heavily to village
headmen, innkeepers, everybody, all of them surly and inimical and eager to take advantage of him. I am told that
he arrived here in Akyab nearly impoverished and nearly
alone, with only one of his lesser and younger wives, a few
loyal old servants and a not very heavy purse. This city did
not receive him very hospitably, either. He managed to
find lodging for himself and his remaining goods and retinue at a waterfront inn. But, if he was to survive, he had to
go on farther, over the bay to India, which meant buying
passage for himself and his little company. Naturally, any
ship's captain demands a stiff price to transport any fugitive, but especially such a desperate one as he—a fleeing
king, with the conquering Mongols close behind him. I do

not know what price was asked, but it was more than he had."

I nodded. "So he tried to multiply what little he had. He resorted to the halls of games of chance."

"Yes. And, as is well known, misfortune likes to dog the already unfortunate. The king played at dice and, over a matter of some few days only, he lost every last thing he owned. Gold, jewels, wardrobe, belongings. Among them, I imagine, that sacred tooth you are chasing, Elder Brother. His losses were profligate and promiscuous. His crown, his old servants, the relic you speak of, his royal robes—there is no knowing which were won by residents of Akyab here, and which by mariners who have since sailed away."

"Vakh," I said glumly.

"At last the King of Ava was reduced to his own person, and the clothes in which he stood in that hall of games, and one wife waiting forlorn in their waterfront lodgings. And on that last desperate day of play, the king offered to wager *himself.* To become, if he lost, the slave of the winner. I do not know who accepted the wager, or how much wealth he staked against the winning of a king."

"But of course the king lost."

"Of course. All in the hall were already despising him, though he had enriched them no little, and now they despised him even more—they must have curled their lips— when the desolate man said, 'Hold. I have one last property besides myself. I have a beautiful Bangali wife. Without me, she will be destitute. She might as well chance having a master to care for her. I will stake my wife, the Lady Tofaa Devata, on one last throw of the dice.' The wager was taken, the dice were rolled, and he lost."

"Well, that was that," I said. "All gone. A misfortune for me, too. But where was there any cause for dispute?"

"Bear with me, Elder Brother. The king asked one last favor. He begged that, before he surrender himself into slavery, he be let to go and tell the sad news himself to his lady. Even wagering men are men of some compassion. They let him go, by himself, to the waterfront inn. And he was honorable enough to tell the Lady Tofaa bluntly what he had done, and he commanded her to present herself to her new master at the hall of games. She obediently set forth, and the king sat down to table, to have one last meal as a freeman. He gorged and guzzled, to the amazement of the innkeeper, and kept calling for more food, more drink. And finally he turned purple and toppled over in an apoplexy and died."

"So I had heard. But what, then? That was no ground for dispute. The man who won him still owned him, whatever his condition."

"Bear with me still. The Lady Tofaa, as ordered by her husband, presented herself at the hall. They say the winner's eyes lighted up when he saw what a choice slave he had won. She is a young woman, a fairly recent acquisition of the king's, neither a titled queen nor yet mother of any heirs, so she is hardly a valuable property just for her innate royalty. And this city's standards of beauty are not my own, but some men call her beautiful, and all call her cunning, and with that I must agree. For when Tofaa's new master reached to take her hand, she withheld it, long enough to speak to all in the hall. She spoke just one sentence, asked just one question: 'Before my husband wagered me, had he first wagered and lost his own self?' "

Shaibni finally fell silent. I waited a moment and then prodded, "Well?"

"Well, there you are. That was the start of the dispute. Since then, the question has echoed and reechoed all over this misbegotten city, and no two citizens can agree on the answer to it, and one magistrate argues with the next, and even brother has turned against brother, and they fight in the streets. I and my troops marched in not long after the events I have described, and all the litigants keep clamoring at me to settle the contention. I cannot, and frankly I am sick of it, and I am ready to put the whole foul city to the torch, if you cannot resolve it."

"What is to resolve, Sardar?" I said patiently. "You already *said* the king had wagered and lost his own person before he put his wife up at stake. So they both were fairly lost. And dead or alive, willing or unwilling, they belong to their winners."

"Do they? Or rather—since he already went to his funeral pyre—does *she*? That is what you must decide, but you must hear all the arguments. I took the lady into custody, pending resolution of the case. I have her in a room upstairs. I can fetch her down and also send for all the men who were gaming in the hall that day. If you will consent, Elder Brother, to be a one-man Cheng this once, it will at the same time give you your best opportunity for inquiring into the whereabouts of that tooth you seek."

"You are right. Very well, bring them on. And please send in my man Yissun to interpret for me."

The Lady Tofaa Devata, though her name meant Gift of the Gods, was not beautiful by my standards, either. She was about Hui-sheng's age, but she was ample enough to have made two of Hui-sheng. Shaibani had called her a Bangali, and evidently the King of Ava had imported her from that Indian state of Bangala, for she was typically Hindu: an oily brown skin that was almost black, and indeed *was* black in a semicircle under each of her eyes. I thought at first that she had misapplied her al-kohl eyelid-darkening cosmetic, but I was later to see that almost all Hindus, men as well as women, naturally had that unsightly discoloration of each eye pouch. The Lady Tofaa also had a red measle of paint on her forehead between her eyes, and a hole in one nostril where presumably she had worn a bauble before it was lost by her dicing husband. She wore a costume that appeared to be (and was, I discovered) a single length of cloth wound several times about her amplitude in such a way that her arms, one shoulder and a roll of unctuous dark-brown flesh around her waist were left bare. It was not a very seductive baring, and the cloth was a garish fabric of many blatant colors and metallic threads. The lady and her attire gave a general impression, besides, of being somewhat unwashed, but I gallantly attributed that to the hard times she had suffered lately. I might find her unappealing, but I would not prejudge her case on that account.

Anyway, the other claimants and witnesses and counselors in the Sardar's main room were considerably less prepossessing. They were of various races—Mien, Hindu, some Ava aborigines, maybe even some of the higher-class Myama—but hardly choice specimens of any. They were the usual assortment of layabouts that wait to prey on seamen in the waterfront alleys of any port city. Again I felt almost sorry for the pusillanimous King Who Ran Away, having pitched himself from a throne down among such base company as this. But neither would I prejudge this case because I found *all* the participants so unappealing.

I was acquainted with one rule of law in these regions: that a woman's testimony was to be far less regarded than a man's. So I motioned for the men first to have their say, and Yissun translated, as one ugly man stepped forward and deposed:

"My Lord Justice, the late king wagered his person, and I hazarded a stake he accepted, and the dice rolled in my favor. I won him, but he later cheated me of my winnings when—"

"Enough," I said. "We are concerned here only with the events in the hall of games. Let speak next the man who played next against the king."

An even uglier one stepped forth. "My Lord Justice, the king said he had one last property to offer, which was this woman here. I took that wager and the dice rolled in my favor. There has since been much foolish argument—"

"Never mind the since," I said. "Let us continue with the events in sequence. I believe, Lady Tofaa Devata, that next you presented yourself at the hall."

She took a heavy step forward, revealing that she was barefoot and dirty about the ankles, just like the nonroyal waterfront denizens in the room. When she began to speak, Yissun leaned over to me and muttered, "Marco, forgive me, but I do not speak any of the Indian languages."

"No matter," I said. "I understand this one." And I did, for she was speaking not any Indian tongue, but the Farsi of the trade routes.

She said, "I presented myself at the hall, yes—"

I said, "Let us observe protocol. You will address me as your Lord Justice."

She bridled in obvious rancor at being so bidden by a pale-skinned and untitled Ferenghi. But she contented herself with a regal sniff, and began again:

"I presented myself at the hall, Lord Justice, and I asked the players, 'Before my dear husband wagered me, had he first wagered and lost himself?' Because, if he had, you see, my lord, then he was already a slave himself, and by law slaves can own no property. Therefore I was not his to hazard in the play, and I am not bound to the winner, and—"

I stopped her again, but only to ask, "How is it that you speak Farsi, my lady?"

"I am of the nobility of Bangala, my lord," she said, standing very erect and looking as if I had sought to cast doubt on that. "I come from a noble merchant family of

Brahman shopkeepers. Of course, being a lady, I have never stooped to clerk's learning—of reading and writing. But I speak the trade tongue of Farsi, besides my native Bangali, and also most of the other major tongues of Greater India—Hindi, Tamil, Telugu. . . ."

"Thank you, Lady Tofaa. Let us now proceed."

After having spent so long in the far eastern parts of the Khanate, I had quite forgotten how prevalent in the rest of the world was the Trade Farsi. But clearly most of the men in the room, because they dealt always with the mariners of the sea trade, also knew the tongue. For several of them immediately spoke up, and in a vociferous clamor, but what they had to say, in effect, was this:

"The woman cavils and equivocates. It is a husband's legal right to venture any of his wives in a game of chance, just as it is his legal right to sell her or put her body out to hire or divorce her utterly."

And others, equally loudly, said in effect:

"No! The woman speaks true. The husband had forfeited himself, therefore all his husbandly rights. He was at that moment a slave himself, illegally venturing property he did not own."

I held up a magisterial hand and the room quieted, and I leaned my chin on my hand in a pose of thinking deeply. But I really was not doing any such thing. I did not pretend, even to myself, to be a Solomon of juridical wisdom, or a Draco or a Khan Kubilai of impulsive decision. But I had spent my boyhood reading about Alexander, and I well remembered how he opened the unopenable Gordian knot. However, I would at least pretend to ponder. While I did so, I said casually to the woman:

"Lady Tofaa, I have come here in search of something your late husband was carrying. The tooth of the Buddha that he took from the Ananda temple. Are you acquainted with it?"

"Yes, Lord Justice. He wagered that away, too, I am sorry to say. But I am pleased to say that he did it before he wagered me, plainly valuing *me* more than even that sacred relic."

"Plainly. Do you know who won the tooth?"

"Yes, my lord. The captain of a Chola pearl-fisher boat. He took it away rejoicing that it should bring good fortune to his divers. That boat sailed weeks ago."

"Do you have any idea where it sailed to?"

"Yes, Lord Justice. Pearls are fished in only two places. Around the island of Srihalam and along the Cholamandal coast of Greater India. Since the captain was of the Chola race, he undoubtedly returned to that coast of the mainland mandal, or region, inhabited by the Cholas."

The men in the room were muttering dourly at this seemingly irrelevant exchange, and the Sardar Shaibani sent me an imploring look. I ignored them and said to the woman:

"Then I must pursue the tooth to the Cholamandal. If you would be pleased to come with me as my interpreter, I will afterward assist you to make your way to your people's home in your native Bangala."

The men's muttering got mutinous at that. The Lady Tofaa did not like it, either. She flung her head back, so she could look down her nose at me, and she said frostily, "I would remind my *Lord* Justice that I am not of a station to accept menial employment. I am a noblewoman born, and the widow of a king, and—"

"And the slave of that ugly brute yonder," I said firmly, "if I should find in his favor in this proceeding."

She swallowed her pomposity—actually gulped aloud—and instantly went from arrogant to servile. "My Lord Justice is as masterful a man as my late dear husband. How could a mere fragile young woman resist such a dominant man? Of course, my lord, I will accompany you and work for you. *Slave* for you."

She was anything but fragile, and I was not complimented by being compared to the King Who Ran Away. But I turned to Yissun and said, "I have made my decision. Publish it to all here. This argument turns on the precedence of the late king's wagers. Therefore the whole matter is moot. From the moment King Narasinha-pati abdicated his throne in Pagan, he had surrendered all his rights and properties and holdings to the new ruler, the Wang Bayan. Whatever that late king spent or squandered or lost here in Akyab was and still is the rightful property of the Wang, who is here represented by the Sardar Shaibani."

When that was translated, everyone in the room, including Shaibani and Tofaa, gave a gasp, all of astonishment, but variously also of chagrin, relief and admiration. I went on:

"Each man in this room will be accompanied by a guard patrol back to his residence or business establishment, and all those plundered treasures will be retrieved. Any person of Akyab refusing to comply, or later found to be hoarding any such property, will be summarily executed. The emissary of the Khan of All Khans has spoken. Tremble, all men, and obey."

As the guards herded the men out, wailing and lamenting, the Lady Tofaa fell down flat on her face, totally prone before me, which is the abject Hindu equivalent of the more sedate salaam or ko-tou, and Shaibani regarded me with a sort of awe, saying:

"Elder Brother Marco Polo, you are a real Mongol. You put this one to shame—for not himself having thought of that master stroke."

"You can make up for it," I said genially. "Find me a trusty ship and crew that will take me and my new interpreter immediately across the Bay of Bangala." I turned to Yissun. "I will not drag you there, for you would be as speechless as I. So I relieve you from that duty, Yissun, and you may report back to Bayan or to your former commander at Bhamo. I shall be sorry not to have you with me, for you have been a staunch companion."

"It is I who should be sorry for you, Marco," he said, and pityingly shook his head. "To be on duty in Ava is dreadful enough fate. But *India . . . ?*"

INDIA

I

No sooner had our vessel cast off from the Akyab dock than Tofaa Devata said to me, very primly, "Marcowallah," and began to lay down rules for our good behavior while we traveled together.

Since I was no longer being a Lord Justice, I had given her leave to address me less formally, and she told me that the -wallah was a Hindu suffixion which denoted both respect and friendliness. I had not given her leave, as well, to preach at me. But I listened politely and even managed not to laugh.

"Marco-wallah, you must realize that it would be a grave sin for us to lie together, and exceedingly wicked in the sight of both men and gods. No, do not look so stricken. Let me explain, and you will be less heartbroken by your unrequited yearning. You see, your judicial decision resolved that dispute back yonder in Akyab, but without deciding on the merits of the opposing arguments, so those arguments must still be taken into account in our relationship. On the one hand, if my dear late husband was still my husband at his death, then I am still sati, unless and until I remarry, so you would be committing the very worst of sins when you lay with me. If, for example, over yonder in India, we were caught in the act of surata, you would be sentenced to do surata with a fire-filled, incandescent brass statue of a woman, until you scorched and shriveled horribly to death. And then, after death, you would have to abide in the underworld called Kala, and suffer its fires and torments, for as many years as there are

913

pores on my body. On the other hand, if I am now techni-
cally the slave of that Akyab creature who won me at dice,
then your lying with me, his slave woman, would make
you also legally his slave. In any event, I am of the Brahman jati—the highest of the four jati divisions of Hindu
humankind—and you are of no jati at all, and therefore inferior. So, when we lay together, we would be defying and
defiling the sacred jati order, and in punishment we would
be thrown to those dogs trained to each such heretics. Even
if you were gallantly willing to risk that frightful death by
raping me, I am still held to be an equal defiler and subject
to the same grisly punishment. If it is ever known in India
that you put your linga into my yoni, whether I actively
engulf it or only passively spread myself for it, we are both
in terrible disgrace and peril. Of course I am not a kanya, a
green and unripe and flavorless virgin. Since I am a widow
of some experience, not to say talent and ability and a capacious, warm, well-lubricated zankha, there would be no
physical evidence of our sin. And I daresay these barbarian sailors would take no notice of what we civilized persons might do in private. So it would probably never be
known in my homeland that you and I had reveled in ec-
static surata out here on the gentle ocean waters under the
caressing moon. But we must desist as soon as we touch
my native land, for all Hindus are most adept at scenting
the least whiff of scandal, and crying shame and jeering
nastily, and demanding bribes to keep silent about it, and
then gossiping and tattling anyway."

She had exhausted either her breath or the myriad aspects of the subject, so I said mildly, "Thank you for the
useful instruction, Tofaa, and set your mind at ease. I will
observe all the proprieties."

"Oh."

"Let me suggest just one thing."

"*Ah!*"

"Do not call the crewmen sailors. Call them seamen or
mariners."

"Ugh."

The Sardar Shaibani had gone to some trouble to find us
a good ship, not a flimsy Hindu-built coasting dinghi, but a
substantial lateen-rigged Arab qurqur merchant vessel
that could sail straight across the vast Bay of Bangala instead of having to skirt around its circumference. The crew

was composed entirely of some very black, wiry, extraordinarily tiny men of a race called Malayu, but the captain
was a genuine Arab, sea-wise and capable. He was taking
his ship to Hormuz, away west in Persia, but had agreed
(for a price) to take me and Tofaa as far as the Cholamandal. That was an open-sea, no-sight-of-land crossing of
some three thousand li, about half as far as my longest
voyage to date: the one from Venice to Acre. The captain
warned us, before departure, that the bay could be a boat-
eater. It was crossable only between the months of September to March—we were doing it in October—because only
in that season were the winds right and the weather not
murderously hot. However, during that season, when the
bay had got itself nicely provided with a copious meal of
many vessels bustling east and west across its surface, it
would frequently stir up a tai-feng storm and capsize and
sink and swallow them all.

But we encountered no storm and the weather stayed
fine, except at night, when a dense fog often obscured the
moon and stars, and wrapped us in wet gray wool. That did
not slow the qurqur, since the captain could steer by his
bussola needle, but it must have been miserably uncomfortable for the half-naked black crewmen who slept on the
deck, because the fog collected in the rigging and dripped
down a constant clammy dew. We two passengers, however, had a cabin apiece, and were snug enough, and we
were given food enough, though it was not viand dining,
and we were not attacked or robbed or molested by the
crew. The Muslim captain naturally despised Hindus
even more than Christians, and stayed aloof from our company, and he kept the seamen forever busy, so Tofaa and I
were left to our own diversions. That we had none—beyond
idly watching the flying fish skimming over the waves and
the porkfish frolicking among the waves—did not discourage Tofaa from prattling about what diversions we must
not succumb to.

"My strict but wise religion, Marco-wallah, holds that
there is more than one sinfulness involved in lying together. So it is not just the sweet surata that you must put
out of your mind, poor frustrated man. In addition to
surata—the actual physical consummation—there are
eight other aspects. The very least of them is as real and
culpable as the most passionate and heated and sweaty

and enjoyable embrace of surata. First there is smarana, which is *thinking* of doing surata. Then there is kirtana, which is speaking of doing it. Speaking to a confidant, I mean, as you might discuss with the captain your barely controllable desire for me. Then there is keli, which is flirting and dallying with the man or woman of one's affection. Then there is prekshana, which means peeping secretly at his or her kaksha—the unmentionable parts—as for example you frequently do when I am bathing over the bucket back yonder on the afterdeck. Then there is guyabhashana, which is conversing on the subject, as you and I are so riskily doing at this moment. Then there is samkalpa, which is *intending* to do surata. Then there is adyavasaya, which is resolving to do it. Then there is kriyanishpati, which is . . . well . . . doing it. Which we must not."

"Thank you for telling me these things, Tofaa. I shall manfully endeavor to restrain myself even from the wicked smarana."

"Oh."

She was right about my having frequently glimpsed her unmentionable kaksha, if that was what it was called, but I could hardly have avoided it. The wash bucket for us passengers was, as she had said, on the high afterdeck of the ship. All she had to do, for a measure of privacy while she sponged her nether parts, was to squat facing astern. But she seemed always to face the bow, and even the timorous Malayu crewmen would discover chores needing doing amidships, so they could peep upward when she opened the drapery of her sari garment and spread her thick thighs and mopped water up from the bucket to her wide-open and unclothed crotch. It bore a bush as black and thick as that on the black men's heads, so maybe it inspired lustful smarana in them, but not in me. Anyway, though repellent itself, that thicket at least concealed whatever was within it. All I knew of that was what Tofaa insisted on telling me.

"Just in case, Marco-wallah, you should fall enamored of some pretty nach dancing girl when we get to Chola, and should wish to make conversation with her as flirtatiously and naughtily as you do with me, I will tell you the words to say. Pay attention, then. Your organ is called the linga and hers is called the yoni. When that nach girl excites you to ravening desire, that is called vyadhi, and your linga then becomes sthanu, 'the standing stump.' If the girl reciprocates your passion, then her yoni opens its lips for you to enter her zankha. The word *zankha* means only 'shell,' but I hope your nach girl's is something better than a shell. My own zankha, for example, is more like a gullet, ever hungry, near to famishment, and salivating with anticipation. No, no, Marco-wallah, do not beseech me to let you feel with your trembling finger its eagerness to clasp and suck. No, no. We are civilized persons. It is good that we can stand close together like this, watching the sea and amiably conversing, with no compulsion to roll and thrash in surata on the deck, or in your cabin or mine. Yes, it is good that we can keep tight rein on our animal natures, even while discoursing so frankly and provocatively as we do, about your ardent linga and my yearning yoni."

"I like that," I said thoughtfully.

"You do?!"

"The words. Linga *sounds* sturdy and upright. Yoni *sounds* soft and moist. I must confess that we of the West do not give those things such nicely expressive names. I am something of a collector of languages, you see. Not in a scholarly way, only for my own use and edification. I like your teaching me all these new and exotic words."

"Oh. Only words."

However, I could not endure too many of hers at a time. So I went and sought out the reclusive Arab captain and asked him what he knew of the pearl fishers of the Cholamandal—whether we would be encountering them along the coast.

"Yes," he said, and snorted. "According to the Hindus' contemptible superstition, the oysters—the reptiles, as they call them—rise to the surface of the sea in April, when the rains begin to fall, and each reptile opens its shell and catches a raindrop. Then it settles to the sea bottom again, and there slowly hardens the raindrop into a pearl. That takes until October, so it is now that the divers are going down. You will arrive right when they are collecting the reptiles and the solidified raindrops."

"A curious superstition," I said. "Every educated person knows that pearls accrete around grains of sand. In fact, in Manzi, the Han may soon cease diving for the sea pearls, for they have recently learned to grow them in river mussels, by introducing into each mollusc a grain of sand."

"Try telling that to the Hindus," grunted the captain. "They have the *minds* of molluscs."

It was impossible, aboard a ship, to evade Tofaa for very long. The next time she found me idling at the rail, she leaned her considerable bulk to wedge me there while she continued my education in things Hindu.

"You should also learn, Marco-wallah, how to look with knowing eyes at the nach dancing girls, and compare their beauty, so that you fall enamored only of the most beautiful. You might best do that by comparing them in your mind with what you have seen of me, for I fulfill all the standards of beauty for a Hindu woman. As it is set down: the three and the five, five, five. Which is to say, in order of specification, that three things of a woman should be deep. Her voice, her understanding and her navel. Now, of course I am not so talkative as most—giddy girls who have not yet attained to dignity and reserve—but on the occasions when I do speak, I am sure you have taken note that my voice is not shrill, and that my utterances are full of deep feminine understanding. As for my navel . . ." She pushed down the waistband of her sari, and lifted up the billow of dark-brown flesh there. "Regard! You could hide your heart in that profound navel, could you not?" She plucked out some matted old fluff that had already hidden there, and went on:

"Then there are five things that should be fine and delicate: a woman's skin, her hair, her fingers, toes and joints. Surely you can find no fault with any of those attributes of mine. Then there are the five things that should be healthily bright pink: the woman's palms and soles and tongue and nails and the corners of her eyes." She went through quite an athletic performance: sticking out her tongue, flexing her talons, exhibiting her palms, tugging at the sooty pouches around her eyes to show me the red corner dots, and picking up each of her grimy feet to show me their leathery but rather cleaner undersides.

"Last, there are the five things that should be higharched: the woman's eyes, nose, ears, neck and breasts. You have seen and admired all of those except my bosom. Regard." She unwound the top part of her sari, and bared her pillowlike dark-brown breasts, and somewhere down the deck a Malayu uttered a sort of anguished whinny. "High-arched they are indeed, and set close together, like nestling hoopoe birds, no gap between. The ideal Hindu breasts. Slide a sheet of paper in that tight cleft and it will stay there. As for putting your linga there, well, do not even consider it, but imagine the sensation of that close, soft, warm envelopment of it. And behold the nipples, like thumbs, and their halos, like saucers, and all black as night against the golden fawn skin. When examining your nach girl, Marco-wallah, be sure to look closely at her teats, and give them a wet lick with your tongue, for many women try to deceive by darkening their with al-kohl. Not I. These exquisite paps are natural, given me by Vishnu the Preserver. It was not casually that my noble parents named me Gift of the Gods. I budded at the age of eight, and was a woman at ten, and a married woman at twelve. Ah, just see the nipples, how they expand and writhe and stand, even though touched only by your devouring gaze. Think how they must behave when actually touched and fondled. But no, no, Marco-wallah, do not dream of touching them."

"Very well."

Rather sulkily, she covered herself again, and the numerous Malayu who had congregated behind nearby deckhouses and things dispersed again about their business.

"I will not," Tofaa said stiffly, "enumerate the Hindu qualifications for beauty in the male, Marco-wallah, since you fall lamentably short of them. You are not even handsome. A handsome man's eyebrows meet above the bridge of his nose, and his nose is long and pendulous. My dear late husband's nose was as long as his royal pedigree. But as I say, I will not list your shortcomings. It would not be ladylike of me."

"By all means, Tofaa, be ladylike."

She may have been a beauty by Hindu standards—in truth, she was, as I later was often told by admiring Hindu men, openly envying me my companion—but I could think of no other people that would have judged her even passable, except possibly the Mien or the Bho. Despite Tofaa's daily and highly visible and well-attended ablutions, she somehow never got quite clean. There was always that measle on her forehead, of course, and always a gray scurf about her ankles and a darker gray curd between her toes.

But while I cannot say that the rest of her, from the measle down to the curd, was ever actually, in the Mien and Bho manner, encrusted, it *was* always just perceptibly dingy.

Back in Paga, Hui-sheng had gone always barefoot in the Ava fashion, and Arùn had done so all her life, and even after a day of padding about the dusty city streets, their feet had always been, even before bath time, kissably clean and sweet. I honestly could not understand how To-faa always managed to have such dirty feet, especially out here on the sea, where there was nothing to smirch them but fresh breezes and sparkling spindrift. It might have had something to do with the India-nut oil with which she coated all her exposed skin after each day's washing. Her late dear husband had left her with very little in the way of personal possessions: not much but a leather flask of the nut oil and a leather bag that contained a quantity of wood chips. As her employer, I had voluntarily bought her a new wardrobe of the sari fabrics and other necessities. But she had regarded the leather containers as necessities, too, and brought them along. I had known that the oil of India-nut was to keep herself glistening in that unattractively greasy way. But I had no notion of what the wood chips were for—until one day, when she did not emerge from her cabin at mealtime, I tapped on her door and she bade me come in.

Tofaa was squatting in her immodest bathing position, and facing me, but her thicket was hidden by a small ceramic pot she was pressing to her crotch. Before I could make my excuses and step back out of the cabin, she calmly lifted the pot away from herself. It was the sort of pot used for brewing cha, and the spout of it came sliding, slick with secretions, out from among the hair. That would have been surprising enough, but even more so was the fact that the spout was emitting blue smoke. Tofaa had evidently put into the pot some of those wood chips, and set them smoldering, and stuck the smoking spout up inside herself. I had seen women play with themselves before, and with a variety of playthings, but never with *smoke,* and I told her so.

"Decent women do not play with themselves," she said reprovingly. "That is what men are for. No, Marco-wallah, daintiness of the *inside* of one's person is more to be desired than any merely exterior *appearance* of being clean.

The application of nim-wood smoke is an age-old and cleanly practice of us fastidious Hindu women, and I do this for your sake, though little you appreciate it."

I frankly saw little there to appreciate: a plump, greasy, dark-brown female squatting on the cabin floor, with her legs shamelessly apart, and the entrapped blue smoke oozing lazily up through her dense bush. I could have remarked that *some* exterior daintiness might have improved her chances of attracting someone nearer to her interior, but I chivalrously refrained.

"Nim-wood smoke is a preventive of unexpected pregnancy," she went on. "It also makes the kaksha parts fragrant and tasty, should anyone happen to nuzzle or browse there. That is why I do this. Just in case you should sometime be overwhelmed by your brute passions, Marco-wallah, and seize me against my will, despite my pleas for mercy, and fling yourself upon me without giving me time to make ready, and force your rigid sthanu through my chaste but soft defenses, I take this precaution of administering the nim-wood smoke every day."

"Tofaa, I wish you would stop."

"You *want* me to?" Her eyes widened, and so must her yoni have done, for a voluminous puff of the blue smoke came suddenly up from there. "You *want* me to bear your children?"

"Gèsu. I want you to cease this everlasting preoccupation with matters below the waist. I engaged you to be my interpreter, and I am already shuddering for fear of what words you are likely to speak, ostensibly mine. But right now, Tofaa, our rice and goat meat are getting wet with salt spray. Come and put something in your other end."

I really believed, at that time, that in choosing a Hindu woman for my translator in India, I had unfortunately chosen a particularly unlovely and witless and pathetic specimen. How she had come to be the consort of a king was beyond my comprehension, but I sympathized more than ever with that wretched man, and thought I better understood now why he had thrown away a kingdom and his life. But I have here recounted a few of Tofaa's charmless attributes—only a few of them—and have repeated some of her fatuous garrulity—only some of it—by way of making her both visible and audible in all her awfulness. I do that because, on arriving in India, I discovered to my

horror that Tofaa was *not* an anomaly. She was an unexceptional and purely typical adult Hindu female. From a
crowd of Hindu women, whatever the assortment of
classes, or jati, I could hardly have picked out Tofaa. Worse
yet, I found the women to be immeasurably superior to the
Hindu men.

In my journeying I had got acquainted with numerous
other races and nations before visiting those of India. I had
concluded that the Mien droppings of the Bho of To-Bhot
had to be the lowest breed of mankind, and I had been mistaken. If the Mien represented humanity's ground level,
then the Hindus were its worm burrows. In some of those
countries I had earlier inhabited or visited, I could not help
seeing that some of the people despised and detested other
people—for their different language or their lesser refinement or their lower class in society or their peculiar ways
of life or their choice of religion. But in India I could not
help seeing that *everybody* despised and detested everybody else, and for all those reasons.

Let me be as fair as I can. Let me say that I was in some
small error from the start, in thinking of all Indians as
Hindus. Tofaa informed me that "Hindu" was only a variant of the name "Indian," and properly referred only to
those Indians who practised the Hindu religion of Sana-
tana Dharma, or Eternal Duty. Those preferred to be dignified by the name of "Brahmanists," after the chief god
(Brahma the Creator) of the three chief gods (the other two
being Vishnu the Preserver and Siva the Destroyer) of
their numberless multitude of gods. Other Hindus had
picked out some lesser god from that mob—Varuna, Krishna, Hanuman, whoever—and gave more devotion to that
one, and thereby rated themselves superior to the greater
ruck of Hindus. Many others of the population had adopted
the Muslim religion seeping in from the north and west. A
very few Indians still practiced Buddhism. That religion,
after originating in India and spreading afar, had almost
died out in its homeland, possibly because it enjoined
cleanliness. Still other Indians followed other religions or
sects or cults: Jain, Sikh, Yoga, Zarduchi. In all their
teeming diversity and jumble and overlap of faiths, however, the Indian people maintained one holy attribute in
common: the adherents of every religion despised and detested the adherents of every other.

The Indians did not much like, either, to be lumped all together as "Indians." They were a seething and still unmixed caldron of different races, or so they claimed. There were the Cholas, the Aryans, Sindi, Bhils, Bangali, Gonds . . . I do not know how many. The lighter brown Indians called themselves *white,* and claimed they were descended from fair-haired, pale-eyed ancestors who came from somewhere far to the north. If that was ever true, then there had since been so much intermingling that, over the centuries, the darker browns and blacks of the southern races had predominated—as mud does when poured into milk—and all the Indians were now but shades and tints of muddy brown. None was of any color worth boasting about, and the insignificant differences of hue served only as one more basis for their abhorring each other. The lighter brown ones could sneer at the darker brown, and they at the indisputably black.

Also, depending on their race, tribe, family lineage, place of original origin and place of current habitation, the Indians spoke *one hundred seventy-nine* different languages, hardly any two of them mutually comprehensible, and every one was deemed by its speakers the One True and Holy Tongue (though few of them ever bothered to learn to read and write it, if indeed it had a script or character or alphabet to be written in, which not many did), and the speakers of every True Tongue scorned and reviled those who spoke any False Tongue, which meant any of the one hundred and seventy-eight others.

Whatever their race, religion, tribe, or tongue, *all* the Indians spinelessly submitted to a social order imposed by the Brahmanists. That was the order of jati, which divided the people into four rigid classes and an overflow of discards. Jati having been first devised by some long-ago Brahman priests, their own descendants naturally constituted the highest class, called Brahman. Next were the descendants of long-ago warriors—*very* long ago, I surmised; I saw no man of the present day who could conceivably be imagined as a warrior—next, the descendants of long-ago merchants, and last the descendants of long-ago humble artisans. Those would have been the bottommost order, but there were also the discards, the paraiyar, or "untouchables," who could claim no jati at all. A man or woman born into any of the jati could not associate with anyone born into a higher, and of course would not with anyone of a lower. Marriages and alliances and business transactions were done only between matching jati, so the classes were eternally perpetuated, and a person could no more ascend to a higher one than he could ascend to the clouds. Meanwhile, the paraiyar dared not even let their defiling shadow fall on anyone of jati.

No person in India—except, I suppose, a Hindu of the Brahman class—was pleased with the jati he found himself born into. Every lower-jati person I met was anxious to tell me how his forebears had, in the long-ago, occupied a much nobler class, and had been undeservedly debased through the influence or trickery or sorcery of some enemy. Nevertheless, all preened in the fact that they were of higher order than *somebody* else, even if only the vile paraiyar. And any of the paraiyar could always point derisively to some still more miserable paraiyar to whom *he* was superior. What was most contemptible about the jati order was not that it existed, and had existed for ages, but that all the people caught in its toils—not just Hindus, but every single soul in India—willingly let it go on existing. Any other people, with the least scintilla of courage and sense and self-respect would long ago have abolished it, or died trying. The Hindus never had even tried, and I saw no sign that they ever would.

It is not impossible that even a people as degenerate as the Bho and Mien may have improved in the years since I was last among them, and made something halfway decent of themselves and their country. But, from what travelers' report I have had of India in these later years, nothing has changed there. To this day, if a Hindu ever feels bad about his being one of the dregs of humankind, he has only to look about for some other Hindu he feels better than, and he can feel good. And that satisfies him.

Since it would have been unwieldy for me to try to identify every person I met in India according to all his entitlements of race, religion, jati and language—one man might be simultaneously a Chola, a Jain, a Brahman and a Tamil-speaker—and since the whole population, in any event, was under the sway of the Hindu jati order, I continued to think indiscriminately of them all as Hindus, and to call them all Hindus, and I still do. If the fastidious Lady Tofaa considered that an improper or derogatory appella-

tion I did not and do not care. I could think of numerous epithets more fitting and a lot worse.

2

THE Cholamandal was the most dreary and uninviting
shore I ever sailed to. All along it, the sea and land merely
and indistinctly blended, in coastal flats that were nothing
but reedy, weedy, miasmal marshes created by a multitude of creeks and rivulets flowing sluggishly out from India's distant interior. The merging of land and water was
so gradual that vessels had to anchor three or four li out in
the bay, where there was keel room. We made landfall off a
village called Kuddalore, where we found a motley fleet of
fishing and pearl-fishing boats already riding at anchor,
with little dinghis ferrying their crewmen and cargoes
back and forth from the anchorage to the almost invisible
village far inland across the mud flats. Our captain adroitly maneuvered our qurqur among the fleet, while Tofaa
leaned over the rail and peered at the Hindus aboard the
other vessels and occasionally shouted queries at them.

"None of these," she finally reported to me, "is the
pearl-fisher boat that was at Akyab."

"Well," said the captain, also to me, "this Cholamandal
pearl coast is a good three hundred farsakhs from north to
south. Or, if you prefer, more than two thousand li. I hope
you are not going to suggest that I cruise up and down its
whole length."

"No," said Tofaa. "I think, Marco-wallah, we ought to go
inland to the nearest Chola capital, which is Kumbakonam.
Since all pearls are royal property, and go ultimately to
the Raja, he can probably easiest direct us to the fisher we
seek."

"Very well," I said, and to the captain, "If you will hail a
dinghi to take us ashore, we will leave you here, and we
thank you for the safe crossing. Salaam aleikum."

While a scrawny little black dinghi-man rowed us across
the brackish bay water, then poled us through the fetid
marshes toward the distant Kuddalore, I asked Tofaa,
"What is a Raja? A king, a Wang, what?"

"A king," she said. "Two or three hundred years ago reigned the best and fiercest and wisest king the Chola kingdom ever had, and his name was King Rajaraja the Great. So ever since, in tribute to him and in hope of emulating him, the rulers of Chola—and most other Indian nations, as well—have taken his name as their title of majesty."

Well, that was no uncommon sort of appropriation even in our Western world. Ceasar had originally been a Roman family name, but became a title of office, and in the form of Kaiser remains so for the rulers of the more recent Holy Roman Empire, and in the form of Czar is used by the petty rulers of the many trivial Slavic nations. But I was to discover that the Hindu monarchs were not satisfied just to appropriate the former Raja's name—that was not pretentious enough, all by itself—they had to elaborate and embroider upon it, to affect even more royalty and majesty.

Toffa went on, "This Chola kingdom was formerly immense and great and unified. But the last high Raja died some years back, and it has since fragmented into numerous mandals—the Chola, the Chera, the Pandya—and their lesser Rajas are all contending for possession of the whole of the land."

"They are welcome to it," I grumbled, as we stepped onto the dock at Kuddalore. We might have been stepping from the Irawadi River into a Mien village. I need not describe Kuddalore further.

On that dock a group of men were jabbering and gesticulating, as they stood around a large wet object lying on the boards. I took a look at it and saw that it was evidently some fisherman's catch. It was a dead fish, or at least it stunk like a fish, though I might better call it a sea creature, for it was bigger than I was, and like nothing I ever saw before. From midway down its body, it was definitely fishlike, terminating in a crescent fish tail. But it did not have fins or scales or gills. It was covered with a leathery skin, like that of a pork-fish, and the upper body was very curious. Instead of pork-fish flippers, it had stubby things like arms, ending in appendages like webbed paws. Even more remarkable, it had on its chest two immense but unmistakable *breasts*—very similar to Tofaa's—and its head was vaguely like that of an extremely ugly cow.

"What in God's name is it?" I asked. "If it were not so

appallingly hideous, I should almost believe it a mermaid."

"Only a fish," said Tofaa. "We call it the duyong."

"Then why all the fuss about a fish?"

"Some of the men are the crew of the boat that speared it and brought it in. The others are fishmongers who wish to buy portions of it to sell. The one well-dressed man is the village magistrate. He is demanding oaths and affidavits."

"Whatever for?"

"It happens every time one is caught. Before the duyong is allowed to be sold, the fishermen must swear that none of them did surata with the duyong on their way to shore."

"You mean . . . sexually coupled with it? With a *fish?*"

"They always do, though they always swear they did not." She shrugged and smiled indulgently. "You men."

There would be many later occasions and reasons for me to resent and lament my being included in the gender that also included male Hindus, but that was the first time. I walked in a wide circle around the duyong and the men, and proceeded on along Kuddalore's main street. All the plump women villagers wore the wrap-around sari which adequately covered most of the body dirt, except where the belly roll of flesh was exposed. The skinny men, having less to expose, exposed it, wearing nothing but a messily wound tulband and a loose, large, baggy diaper called a dhoti. The children wore nothing but the measle painted on the forehead.

"Is there a karwansarai?" I asked Tofaa. "Or whatever you call it, where we can take lodging while we make ready to journey on?"

"Dak bangla," she said. "Traveler's rest house. I will inquire."

She abruptly reached out and seized the arm of a passing man, and snapped a question at him. He did not, as a man of any other country would have done, take offense at being so brazenly accosted by a mere woman. Instead, he almost quailed, and spoke meekly in response. Tofaa said something that sounded very nearly accusing, and he replied even more feebly. The conversation went back and forth like that, she almost snarling, he finally almost whimpering. I regarded them with amazement, and at last Tofaa reported the result.

"There is no dak bangla in Kuddalore. So few strangers

ever come here, and fewer care to stay as long as a night. It is typical of the lowly Cholas. In my native Bangala, now, we would have been most hospitably received. However, the wretch offers us lodging in his own house."

"Well, that is hospitable enough, certainly," I said.

"He asks that we follow him there, and wait until he is inside for a few moments. Then we are to knock at the door and he will open it, and we are to request a bed and a meal, and he will rudely refuse us."

"I do not understand."

"It is usual. You will see."

She spoke again to the man, and he went off at an anxious trot. We followed, picking our way among the pigs and fowl and infants and excrement and other litter on the streets. Considering what the residents of Kuddalore had to live in—no house being any more substantial or elegant than a hut of the Ava jungle Mien—I was rather grateful that there was *not* a dak bangla for us, since anything maintained only for the occasional transient would have had to be a sty indeed. Our host's residence was not much more—built of mud bricks and plastered with cow dung—as we saw when we halted outside and he disappeared into the dark interior of it. After a brief wait, as commanded, Tofaa and I went up to the shack and she knocked on the rickety doorjamb. What happened thereafter I relate as Tofaa later translated it all to me.

The same man appeared in the doorway, and reared his head back to look down his nose at us. This time, Tofaa addressed him only in an obsequious mumble.

"What? Strangers?" he bawled, loudly enough to have been heard down at the bayside dock. "Pilgrim wayfarers? No, indeed, not here! I do not care, woman, if you *are* of Brahman jati! I do not give shelter to just any caller, and I do not allow my wife—"

He not only broke off in mid-bellow, he totally vanished, whisking sideways beyond the door opening, as a meaty brown-black arm thrust him aside. A meaty brown-black woman appeared in his place, and smiled out at us, and she said, syrup sweetly:

"Wayfarers, are you? And seeking a bed and a meal? Well, do come in. Pay no heed to this worm of a husband. In his speech, but in his speech alone, he plays the great lord. Come in, come in, do."

So Tofaa and I lugged our packs inside the house and were shown the bedchamber in which to stow them. The cow-dung-plastered room was entirely occupied by four beds, somewhat like the hindora bed I had encountered in other places, but not quite as good. A hindora was a pallet hung on ropes from a ceiling, but this kind, called a palang, was no more than a sort of slit cloth tube, like a sack opened lengthwise, roped at each end to the walls and swinging free in between. Two of the palangs held a swarm of naked brown-black children, but the woman swept them away as unceremoniously as she had done her husband, and made it plain that Tofaa and I would sleep there in the same room with her and him.

We went back to the other of the hut's two rooms, and the woman swept the children farther, outside onto the street, while she made a meal for us. When she handed us each a slab of wood, I recognized the food on it—or rather, I recognized that it was mostly the mucous kàri sauce I had, a long time ago, eaten in the Pai-Mir mountains. Kàri was the only native word I could remember from that long-ago journey in company with other men of the Chola race. As I remembered, those other brown-black men had shown at least a trifle more manly spirit than my present host. But then, they had had no Chola women with them.

This man and I, since we could not converse, simply squatted together and ate our unappetizing meal and occasionally nodded companionably to each other. I must have seemed as much a flattened and trampled zerbino as he was, both of us mute and mousily nibbling, while the two women chattered vociferously, trading comments—as Tofaa later informed me—on the general worthlessness of men.

"It is well said," remarked the woman of the house, "that a man is a man only when he is filled with angry passion, when he bears no vexation submissively. But is there anything more contemptibly pitiful"—she waved her food slab to indicate her husband—"than a weak man being angry?"

"It is well said," Tofaa volunteered, "that a small pond is easily filled, and the forepaws of a mouse, and likewise a man of no account is easily satisfied."

"I was first married to this one's brother," said the woman. "When I was widowed, when my husband's fellow

fishermen brought him home dead—crushed on the very
deck, they said, by a newly caught duyong flailing about—I
should have behaved like a proper sati, and thrown myself
on his funeral pyre. But I was still young, and childless, so
the village sadhu urged me to marry this brother of my
husband, and have children to carry on the family line.
Ah, well, I was still young."

"It is well said," Tofaa remarked, with a salacious giggle, "that a woman never grows old below the girdle."

"True, indeed!" said the woman, with a lubricous giggle.
"It is also well said: A fire cannot be laid with too many
logs, nor a woman with too many sthanu."

They both giggled lasciviously for a time. Then Tofaa
said, waving her food slab to indicate the children swarming on the doorstep, "At least he is fruitful."

"So is a rabbit," grunted the woman. "It is well said: A
man whose life and deeds are not outstanding above those
of his fellows, he does but add to the heap."

I finally got tired of seeming submissively to share my
host's cowed silence. In an attempt to make some communication with him, I indicated my still-heaped food slab
and made insincere lip-smackings, as if I had enjoyed the
slop, and then made gestures of asking what was the meat
under the kàri. He comprehended, and told me what it
was, and I realized that I did know one other word of the
native language:

"Duyong."

I got up and left the hut to inhale deeply of the evening
air. It reeked of smoke and fish and garbage and fish and
unwashed people and fish and pukey children, but it
helped some. I kept on walking the Kuddalore streets, both
of them, until well after dark, and returned to the hut to
find all the children asleep on the front-room floor, among
the detritus of our used food slabs, and the adults all
asleep, fully dressed, in their palangs. With some difficulty at first, I got into mine, and found it more comfortable than it had appeared, and fell asleep. But I was
awakened at some dark hour, by scuffling noises, and determined that the man had climbed into his wife's palang
and was noisily doing surata, though she kept snarling
and hissing something at him. Tofaa had waked and heard
it, too, and later told me what the wife had been saying:

"You are only brother to my late husband, remember,

even after all these years. As the sadhu commanded, you
are forbidden to enjoy yourself while performing your seed
function. No passion, do you hear? *Do not enjoy yourself!*

I had by now rather come to the opinion that I had at last
found the true homeland of the Amazons, and the source of
all the legends about them. One of the legends was that
they kept only some rather vestigial men about, to impreg-
nate them when it was necessary to make more Amazons.

The next day, our host kindly went out and inquired
among his neighbors and found one who was driving his ox
cart to the next village inland, and would take me and Tofaa along. We thanked our host and his wife for their hospitality, and I gave the man a bit of silver in payment for
our lodging, and his wife instantly snatched that for herself. Tofaa and I perched on the rear of the ox cart, and jostled a good deal as it lumbered off through the flat and
feculent marshland. To pass the time, I asked her what
that woman had meant when she spoke of sati.

"It is our old custom," said Tofaa. "Sati means a faithful
wife. When a man dies, if his widow is properly sati, she
will fling herself on the pyre consuming his body, and die
herself."

"I see," I said thoughtfully. Perhaps I had been wrong in
thinking of the Hindu women as all being overbearing
Amazons, of no uxorial qualities. "It is not entirely a grotesque idea. Almost winsome in a way. That a faithful wife
accompanies her dear husband to the afterworld, wanting
them to be together forever."

"Well, not exactly," said Tofaa. "It is well said: The
highest hope of a woman is to die *before* her husband. That
is because the plight of a widow is unthinkable. Her husband is probably worthless, but what does she do without
one? So many females are constantly ripening to the marriageable age of eleven or twelve, what chance does a used
and worn and not-young widow have of marrying again?
Left alone and undefended and unsupported in the world,
she is an object of uselessness, scorned and reviled. Our
word for widow means literally a dead-woman-waiting-to-
die. So, you see, she might as well jump in the fire and get
it over with."

That somewhat took the luster of lofty sentiment off the
practice, but I remarked that still it took some courage,
and was not devoid of a certain proud dignity.

"Well, actually," said Tofaa, "the custom originated because some wives *did* plan to remarry, and had their next husbands already picked out, and so poisoned their current ones. The practice of sati-sacrifice was mandated by the rulers and religious leaders, just to avert those frequent murders of husbands. It was made the law that, if a man died for whatever reason, and his wife was not demonstrably innocent of causing his death, she was to leap onto the pyre, and if she did not, the dead man's family were to throw her onto it. So it made wives think twice before poisoning their husbands, and even made them solicitous about *keeping* their men alive, when they fell ill or got old.

I decided I *had* been mistaken. This was not the homeland of the Amazons. It was the homeland of the Harpies.

That latest opinion was not shaken by what next transpired. We got to the village of Panruti well after sunset and found it also lacking any dak bangla, and Tofaa again snatched at a man in the street, and we went through the same performance as yesterday. He went home, we followed him, he loudly refused us entrance and was immediately overridden by a blustering female. The only difference in this case was that the henpecked husband was quite young and the hen was not.

When I thanked her for inviting us in, and Tofaa translated my thank-you, it came out something of a stammer. "We are grateful to you and your . . . uh . . . husband? . . . son?"

"He was my son," said the woman. "He is now my husband." I must have gaped, or blinked, for she went on to explain. "When his father died, he was our only child, and he would soon have been of an age to inherit this house and all its contents, and I would then have been a dead-woman-waiting-to-die. So I bribed the local sadhu to marry me to the boy—he being too young and ignorant to object—and thereby maintained my share in the property. Unhappily, he has not been much of a husband. So far, he has sired on me only these three: my daughters, his sisters." She indicated the slack-jawed and witless-looking brats sitting lumpishly about. "If they are all I have, their eventual husbands will inherit next. Unless I give the girls to be devadasi temple whores. Or perhaps, since they are woefully deficient in their mentality, I could donate them to the Holy Order of Crippled Mendicants. But they may be even too imbecile to make proper beggars. Anyway, I am naturally anxious, and naturally trying mightily every night, to produce another son, and to keep the family property in the direct family line." Briskly, she set before us some wood slabs of kàri-sauced food. "Therefore, if you do not mind, we will all eat in a hurry, so he and I can get to our palang."

And again that night I overheard the moist noises of surata going on in the same room, this time accompanied by urgent whispers, which Tofaa repeated to me the next morning—"Harder, son! You must strive harder!" I wondered whether the avaricious woman planned next to marry her grandson, but I did not really care, and I did not ask. Nor did I bother remarking to Tofaa that all she had told me during our voyage—regarding the Hindu religion's concern about sin, and strictures against it, and dire punishments for it—seemed to have had little elevating effect on Hindu morality in general.

Our destination, the capital city called Kumbakonam, was not impossibly far from where we had landed on the coast. But no Hindu peasant had any riding mounts to sell us, and not many men were willing to take us for hire to the next village or town down the road—or more likely, their wives would not let them—so Tofaa and I had to proceed by exasperatingly slow stages, whenever we could find a carter or a drover going our way. We rode jouncing in ox carts, and splayed across the sharp spine ridges of oxen, and dragged along on stone ledges, and straddling the rumps of pack asses, and once or twice riding real saddle horses, and many times we just set out walking, which usually meant we had to sleep in the roadside hedgerows. That was no intolerable hardship for me, except that on every one of those nights Tofaa gigglingly pretended I was bedding us down in the wilderness only to rape her, and when I did no such thing, she grumbled long into the night about the ungallant way I was treating a nobly born Lady Gift of the Gods.

The last outlying village on our way had a name that was bigger than its total population—Jayamkondacholapuram—and was otherwise remarkable only for something that happened, while we were there, to diminish its popu-

lace even further. Tofaa and I were again squatting in a
cow-dung hut and supping on some mystery substance disguised in kàri, when there arose a rumbling sound like distant thunder. Our host and hostess immediately sprang
erect and shrieked in unison, "Aswamheda!" and ran out
of the house, kicking aside several of their children littered about the floor.

"What is aswamheda?" I asked Tofaa.

"I have no idea. The word means only running away."

"Perhaps we ought to emulate our hosts and run away."

So she and I stepped over the children and went out into
the single village street. The rumbling was nearer now,
and I could tell that it was a herd of animals coming at a
gallop from somewhere to the south. All of the Jayamkon-
dacholapuramites were running away from the noise, in a
panicked and headlong mob, heedlessly trampling under
their feet the numerous very young and very old persons
who fell down. Some of the more spry villagers climbed up
trees or onto the thatched roofs of their dwellings.

I saw the first of the herd come galloping into the southern end of the street, and saw that they were horses. Now, I
know horses, and I know that, even among animals, they
are not the most intelligent of creatures, but I also know
that they have more sense than Hindus. Even a wild-eyed
and foam-flecked running herd of them will not step on a
fallen human being in its path. Every horse will leap over,
or swerve aside, or if necessary execute a tumbler's somersault, to avoid a fallen man or woman. So I simply threw
myself prone in the street and dragged Tofaa with me,
though she squealed in mortal terror. I held us both lying
still and, as I expected, the maddened herd diverged
around us and thundered past on our either side. The
horses also took care to avoid the inert bodies of aged and
infant Hindus already mashed by their own relatives and
friends and neighbors.

The last of the horses disappeared on up the road to the
northward, and the dust began to settle, and the villagers
began to clamber down from roofs and trees and to amble
back from whatever distances they had run to. They immediately commenced a concerted keening of grief and lament, as they peeled up their flattened dead, and they
shook their fists at the sky and squawled imprecations at

the Destroyer God Siva for having so unfeelingly taken so
many of the innocent and infirm.

Tofaa and I went back to our meal, and eventually our
host and hostess also returned, and counted their children.
They had not lost any, and had trodden on only a few, but
they were as sorrow-stricken and distraught as all the rest
of the village—she and he did not even, after we all went to
bed, perform surata for us that night—and they could not
tell us anything more about the aswamheda except that it
was a phenomenon which occurred about once a year, and
was the doing of the cruel Raja of Kumbakonam.

"You would be well advised, wayfarers, not to go to that
city," said the woman of the house. "Why not settle down
here in tranquil and civilized and neighborly Jayamkondacholapuram? There is ample room for you, now that Siva
has destroyed so many of our people. Why persist in going
to Kumbakonam, which is called the Black City?"

I said we had business there, and asked why it was so
called.

"Because black is the Raja of Kumbakonam, and black
his people, and black the dogs, and black the walls, and
black the waters, and black the gods, and black the hearts
of the people of Kumbakonam."

3

UNDETERRED by the warning, Tofaa and I went on southward, and eventually crossed a running sewer that was
dignified with the name of Kolerun River, and on the other
side of it was Kumbakonam.

The city was much larger than any community we had
yet come through, and it had filthier streets bordered with
deeper ditches full of stagnant urine, and a greater variety
of garbage rotting in the hot sun, and more lepers clicking
their warning sticks, and more carcasses of dead dogs and
beggars decaying in public view, and it was more rancid
with the odors of kàri and cooking grease and sweat and
unwashed feet. But the city really was no blacker of color
or layered no thicker with surface dirt then any lesser community we had seen, and the inhabitants were no darker of

skin and layered no thicker with accumulated grime. There were a great many more people, of course, than we had seen in one place before, and, like any city, Kumbakonam had attracted many eccentric types that had probably left their home villages in search of wider opportunity. For example, among the street crowds I saw quite a few individuals who wore gaudy feminine saris, but had on their heads the untidy tulbands usually worn by men.

"Those are the ardhanari," said Tofaa. "What would you call them? Androgynes. Hermaphrodites. As you can see, they have bosoms like women. But you cannot see, until you pay for the privilege, that they have the nether organs of both men and women."

"Well, well. I had always supposed them mythical beings. But I daresay, if they had to exist anywhere, it would be here."

"We being a very civilized people," said Tofaa, "we let the ardhanari parade freely about the streets, and openly ply their trade, and dress as elegantly as any women. The law requires only that they also wear the headdress of a man."

"Not to deceive the unwary."

"Exactly. A man who seeks an ordinary woman can hire a devanasi temple whore. But the ardhanari, although unsanctioned by any temple, are kept far more busy than the devanasi, since they can serve women as well as men. I am told they can even do both at once."

"And that other man, yonder?" I asked, pointing. "Is he also peddling his nether parts?"

If he was, he could have sold them by bulk weight. He was carrying them before him in a tremendous basket which he held by both hands. Although the parts were still attached to his body, his dhoti diaper could not have contained them. The basket was completely filled by his testicular sac, which was leathery and wrinkled and veined like an elephant's hide, and the testicles inside it must each have been twice the size of the man's head. Just to see the sight made my own parts hurt in sympathy and revulsion.

"Look below his dhoti," said Tofaa, "and you will see that he also has legs of elephant thickness and elephant skin. But do not feel sorry for him, Marco-wallah. He is only a paraiyar afflicted with the Shame of Santomè. Santomè is our name for the Christian saint you call Thomas."

The explanation was even more astounding than the sight of the pitiable man-elephant. I said unbelievingly, "What would this benighted land know of Saint Thomas?"

"He is buried somewhere near here, or so it is said. He was the first Christian missionary ever to visit India, but he was not well received, because he tried to minister to the vile paraiyar outcasts, which disgusted and offended the good jati folk. So they paid Santomè's own congregation of paraiyar converts to slay him, and—"

"His own congregation? And they did it?"

"The paraiyar will do anything for a copper coin. Dirty work is what they are for. However, Santomè must have been a powerfully holy man, albeit a heathen. The men who slew him, and their paraiyar descendants ever since, have been cursed with the Shame of Santomè."

We pressed on to the center of the city, where stood the Raja's palace. To get to it we had to cross a commodious market square, as crowded as all market squares, but on this day not with commerce. There was some kind of festa in progress, so Tofaa and I made our way across it leisurely, to let me see how the Hindus celebrated a joyous occasion. They seemed to be doing it more dutifully than joyously, I decided, for I could not see a happy or animated face anywhere. In fact, the faces, besides having a more than usually ornate measle painted on the forehead, were smeared with what looked like mud, but smelled worse.

"Dung of the sacred cattle," said Tofaa. "First they wash their faces in the cows' urine, then put the dung on their eyes, cheeks and breast."

I refrained from any comment except, "Why?"

"This festival is in honor of Krishna, the God of Many Mistresses and Lovers. When Krishna was only a lad, you see, he was a simple cowherd, and it was in the cowshed that he did his first seductions of the local milkmaids and his fellow cowherds' wives. So this festival, in addition to being a blithe celebration of high-spirited lovemaking, also has its aspect of solemnity in honoring Krishna's sacred cows. That music the musicians are playing, you hear it?"

"I hear it. I did not know it was music."

The players were grouped about a platform in the middle of the square, wringing noises from an assortment of devices—cane flutes, hand drums, wooden pipes, stringed things. In all that concert of strident screeching and twanging and squawking, the only perceptibly sweet notes came from a single instrument like a very long-necked lute with a gourd body, having three metal strings played with a plectrum on the musician's forefinger. The Hindu audience sweatily massed roundabout looked as morosely unmoved by the music and as barely enduring of it as I imagine I did.

"What the musicians are playing," said Tofaa, "is the kudakuttu, the pot-dance of Krishna, based on an ancient song the cowherds have always sung to their cows while milking them."

"Ah. Yes. If you had given me time, I should probably have guessed something like that."

"Here comes a lovely nach girl. Let us stay and watch her dance Krishna's pot-dance."

A brown-black and substantial female, lovely perhaps by the standards Tofaa had previously recited to me, and properly mammalian for the cow-worship occasion, got laboriously onto the platform, carrying a large clay pot—symbolic of Krishna's milking pot, I assumed—and began limbering up by doing various poses with it. She tried shifting it from one arm's crook to the other, and put it on top of her head a few times, and occasionally stamped a broad foot, evidently clearing the platform of ants.

Tofaa confided to me, "The worshipers of Krishna are the most lighthearted and blithesome of all the Hindu sects. Many condemn them for preferring gaiety to gravity and vivacity to meditation. But, as you see, they imitate the carefree Krishna, and they maintain that enjoyment of life gives bliss, and bliss gives serenity, and serenity gives wisdom, all together making for wholeness of soul. That is what the nach girl's pot-dance conveys."

"I should like to see that. When does she commence?"

"What do you mean? You *are* seeing that."

"I mean the dance."

"That *is* the dance."

We continued across the square—Tofaa seeming exasperated, but I not feeling much chastened—through the crowd of woebegone and nearly inanimate celebrations,

and to the palace gates. I was carrying Kubilai's ivory
plaque slung on my chest, and Tofaa explained to the two
gate guards what it represented. They were clad in not
very military-looking dhotis and holding their spears at lazily disparate angles, and they shrugged as if disinclined
either to bow us in or to take the trouble to keep us out. We
went through a dusty courtyard and into a palace which
was at least palatially built of stone, not the mud-and-
dung that constituted most of Kumbakonam.

We were received by a steward—perhaps of some rank,
since he wore a clean dhoti—and he did seem impressed by
my pai-tzu and Tofaa's explanation of it. He fell flat on his
face, and then scrabbled off like a crab, and Tofaa said we
should follow him. We did, and found ourselves in the
throne room. By way of describing the richness and magnificence of that hall, I will only say that the four legs of
the throne stood in tureens full of oil, to keep the local kaja
snakes from climbing up into the seat and to keep the local
white ants from gnawing and collapsing the whole thing.
The steward motioned for us to wait, and scuttled off
through another door.

"Why does that man go about on his belly?" I asked Tofaa.

"He is being respectful in the presence of his betters. We
too must do so, when the Raja joins us. Not fall down, but
make sure your head is never higher than his. I will nudge
you at the proper moment."

Half a dozen men came in just then, and stood in a line
and regarded us impassively. They were as nondescript in
person as any of the celebrants out in the square, but they
were gorgeously attired in gold-threaded dhotis, and even
fine jackets to cover their torsos, and almost neatly wound
tulbands. For the first time in India, I supposed I was
meeting some people of upper class, probably the Raja's
retinue of ministers, so I began a speech for Tofaa to translate, addressing them as "My lords," and starting to introduce myself.

"Hush," said Tofaa, tugging at my sleeve. "Those are
only the Raja's shouters and congratulators."

Before I could ask what that meant, there was a stir at
the door again, and the Raja stood ceremonially in at the
head of another group of courtiers. Instantly, the six shout-

ers and congratulators bellowed—and believe this or not, they bellowed in unison:

"All hail his Highness the Maharajadhiraj Raj Rajeshwar Narendra Karni Shriomani Sawai Jai Maharaja Sri Ganga Muazzam Singhji Jah Bahadur!"

I later had Tofaa repeat all that for me, slowly and precisely, so I could write it down—not just because the title was so marvelously grandiose, but also because it was so ludicrous a title for a small, black, elderly, bald, paunchy, oily Hindu.

It seemed for a moment to perplex even Tofaa. But she poked me with an elbow and she knelt—and, because she was no small woman, she discovered that even kneeling she was still a fraction taller than the little Raja, so she lowered herself still deeper, into an abject squat, and began falteringly, "Your Highness . . . Maharajadhiraj . . . Raj . . ."

"Your Highness is sufficient," he said expansively.

The shouters and congratulators roared, *"His Highness is the very Warden of the World!"*

He made a genial and modest gesture for them to be silent. They did not bellow again for a while, but neither were they ever entirely silent. Every time the little Raja did anything, they would comment on it, in a murmur, but somehow still in unison, things like: *"Behold, His Highness seats himself upon the throne of his dominion,"* and: *"Behold, how gracefully His Highness pats a hand upon his yawn . . ."*

"And *who,*" said the little Raja to Tofaa, "is *this?*" turning a very haughty look upon me, for I had not knelt or bent at all.

"Tell him," I said in Farsi, "that I am called Marco Polo the Insignificant and Unsung."

The little Raja's look of hauteur became displeasure, and he said, also in Farsi, "A fellow white man, eh? But a white-skinned one. If you are a Christian missionary, go away."

"His Highness bids the lowly Christian go away," murmured the shouters and congratulators.

I said, "I am a Christian, Your Highness, but—"

"Then go away, lest you suffer the fate of your long-ago predecessor Santomè. He had the outrageous nerve to come here preaching that we should worship a carpenter whose disciples were all fishermen. Disgusting. Carpenters and fishermen are of the lowest jati, if not downright paraiyar."

"His Highness is rightly and righteously disgusted."

"I am indeed on a mission, Your Highness, but not to preach." I decided to temporize for a while. "Mainly, I wished to see something of your great nation and"—it cost me an effort, but I lied—"and to admire it." I waved toward the windows, whence came the mournful music and the sullen muttering of the festival, so called.

"Ah, you have seen my people making merry!" the little Raja exclaimed, looking not so petulant. "Yes, one tries to keep the people happy and content. Did you enjoy the exhilarating Krishna frolic, Polo-wallah?"

I tried hard to think of something enjoyable about it. "I was much—much entertained by the music, Your Highness. One instrument in particular . . . a sort of long-necked lute . . ."

"Say you so?" he cried, seeming unaccountably pleased. *"His Highness is royally pleased."*

"That is an entirely new instrument!" he went on, excitedly. "It is called a sitar. It was invented by my very own Court Musicmaster!"

It appeared that I had, all fortuitously, melted any incipient frost between us. Tofaa gave me an admiring look as the little Raja bubbled enthusiastically, "You must meet the instrument's inventor, Polo-wallah. May I call you Marco-wallah? Yes, let us dine together, and I will bid the Musicmaster join us. It is a pleasure to welcome such a discerning guest, of such good taste. Shouters, command that the dining hall be prepared."

The six men trotted off down a corridor, bellowing the command, still in concert, and even trotting in step together. I discreetly gestured a suggestion to Tofaa, and she comprehended, and timidly asked the little Raja, "Your Highness, might we wash off some of our travel dust before we are honored by joining you at table?"

"Oh, yes. By all means. Forgive me, lovely lady, but your charms would distract any man from noticing any trivialities. Ah, Marco-wallah, again your good taste is evident. It is also evident that you have admired our country and our people, seeing that you have taken a lady wife from among them." I gasped. He added, archly, "But did

you have to take the most beauteous, and thereby so sorely
deprive us poor natives?" I tried to make an instant correc-
tion of that horrific misapprehension, but he went to
where the steward was still lying on his face, and kicked
the man and snarled, "Misbegotten wretch! Never to be
twice-born! Why did you not lead these eminent guests immediately to a state apartment and see them cared for? Do
so! Prepare for them the bridal suite! Assign them servants! Then see to the banquet and the entertainers!"

When I saw that the bridal suite had two separate beds,
I decided it would not be necessary to demand other quarters. And when a number of stout dark women dragged in
a tub and filled it, I found it not inconvenient for me and
Tofaa to have the same bathing chamber. I took the masculine prerogative of bathing first, then stayed to oversee Tofaa's ablutions and direct the women servants—causing
some incredulity among them at my insistent thorough-
ness—so that, for once, Tofaa got well washed. When we
put on the best clothes we carried and went downstairs to
the dining hall, even her bare feet were clean.

And I made certain, before indulging in any small table
talk, to inform the little Raja and all others present, "The
Lady Tofaa Devata is not my wife, Your Highness." That
sounded brusquely uncomplimentary of the lady, so, to
maintain his estimation of her importance, I added, "She
is one of the noble widows of the late King of Ava."

"Widow, eh?" grunted the little Raja, as if instantly losing all interest in her.

I continued, "The Lady Gift of the Gods most graciously
consented to accompany me on my journey through your
fair land, and to interpret for me the wit and wisdom of the
many fine people we have met along the way."

He grunted again, "Companion, eh? Well, to each his
custom. A sensible and tasteful Hindu, going on a journey,
takes not a female Hindu, but a Hindu boy, for his temper
is not so like a kaja snake's, and his hole not so like a
cow's."

To change the subject, I turned to the fourth at our table,
a man of my own age, bearded like me, and seeming more
tan than black of complexion behind the beard. "You
would be the inventive musician, I believe, Master . . ."

"Musicmaster Amir Khusru," said the little Raja proprietorially. "Master of melodies, and also dances, and

also poetry, being an accomplished composer of the licentious ghazal poems. A credit to my court."

"His Highness's court is blessed," crooned the shouters and congratulators, standing against the wall, *"and blessed most by the presence of His Highness"*—during which the Musicmaster only smiled self-deprecatingly.

"I never before saw a musical instrument with strings made of metal," I said, and Tofaa—now subdued to meekness—translated as I went on, "Indeed, I had never before thought of Hindus as inventors of anything so good and useful."

"You Westerners," the little Raja said peevishly, "are always looking to do good. We Hindus seek to *be* good. An infinitely superior attitude to life."

"Nevertheless," I said, "that new Hindu sitar is a doing of good. I congratulate Your Highness and your Master Khusru."

"Except that I am not a Hindu," the Musicmaster said in Farsi, with some amusement. "I am of Persian birth. The name I gave the sitar is from the Farsi, as you may have perceived. Si-tar: three-stringed. One string of steel wire and two of brass."

The little Raja looked still more peeved at my having learned that the sitar was no Hindu achievement. I wished to put him in a good mood again, but I was beginning to wonder if there was any subject that could be discussed without its blatantly or subtly denigrating the Hindus. In mild desperation, I turned to praising the food we had been served. It was some kind of venison, drowned as usual in the kàri sauce, but this kàri was at least colored a slightly yellow-gold and a little enhanced in its flavor, though only with turmeric, which is an inferior substitute for zafràn.

"Meat of the four-horned deer, this is," said the little Raja, when I complimented it. "A delicacy we reserve for only the most favored guests."

"I am honored," I said. "But I thought your Hindu religion forbade the hunting of wild game. Doubtless I was misinformed."

"No, no, you were rightly informed," said the little Raja. "But our religion also bids us be clever." He gave a broad wink. "So I ordered all the people of Kumbakonam to take holy water from the temples and go into the forests and sprinkle that holy water about, loudly declaring that all the forest animals were henceforth sacrifices to the gods. That makes our hunting of them quite permissible, you see—each killing being a tacit offering—and of course our hunters always give a haunch or something to the temple sadhus, so they will not inconveniently decide that we are misinterpreting any sacred text."

I sighed. It really was impossible to light on an innocuous subject. If it did not explicitly or implicitly denigrate the Hindus, it made them impugn themselves. But I tried again:

"Do Your Highness's hunters hunt on horseback? I ask because I wonder if some horses might have been lost from your royal stables. The Lady Tofaa and I encountered quite a herd running loose on the other side of the river."

"Ah, you met my aswamheda!" he cried, sounding now most jovial again. "The aswamheda is another cleverness of mine. A rival Raja, you see, holds that province beyond the Kolerun River. So every year, I have my drovers deliberately whip a horse herd over to there. If that Raja resents the trespass and keeps possession of the horses, then I have excuse for declaring war on him and invading and seizing his lands. However, if he rounds them up and returns them to me—which he has done every year so far—then it betokens his submission to me, and all the world knows I am his superior."

If this little Raja was the superior, I decided, as the meal concluded, then I was glad not to have encountered the other. Because this one marked the close of the banquet by leaning to one side, raising one little buttock and gustily, audibly, odoriferously passing wind.

"His Highness farts!" bellowed the shouters and congratulators, making me flinch even more than I had already done. *"The food was good, and the meal acceptable, and His Highness's digestion is still superb, and his bowels an example to us all!"*

I really had not much hope that this posturing monkey could be of any help in my current quest. However, as we sat on at the table, drinking tepid cha from elaborately jeweled but slightly misshapen cups, I recounted to the little Raja and the Master Khusru the events that had brought me hither, and the object of my pursuit, concluding, "I understand, Your Highness, that a pearl-fisher subject of yours was the man who acquired the Buddha's tooth, hoping that it would confer good fortune on his pearl fishing."

The little Raja, as I might have expected, responded by taking my story as a reflection on himself, on Hinduism and on Hindus in general.

"I am distressed," he muttered. "You imply, Marco-wallah, that some one of my subjects imputed supernatural power to that fragment of an alien god. Yes, I am distressed that you could believe that any Hindu had so little faith in his own stalwart religion, the religion of his fathers, the religion of his benevolent Raja."

I said placatively, "Doubtless the new possessor of the tooth has by now realized his error, and found the thing not at all magical, and repented his acquisition of it. He, being a good Hindu, would probably throw it in the sea, except that it cost him some time and perhaps some uncertainty in the winning of it. So, for a suitable exchange, he would probably be glad to give it up."

"Give it up he most certainly will!" snapped the little Raja. "I shall make proclamation that he come forward and surrender it—and surrender himself to the karavat!"

I did not know what a karavat was, but evidently Master Khusru did, for he remarked mildly, "That, Your Highness, is not likely to make anyone come hastening forward with the object."

"Please, Your Highness," I said. "Do not make demand or threat, but publish only a persuasive request and my offer of reward."

The little Raja grumbled for a while, but then said, "I am known as a Raja who always keeps his word. If I offer a reward, it will be paid." He eyed me sidewise. "You will pay it?"

"Assuredly, Your Highness, and most liberally."

"Very well. And then I will keep *my* word, which I have already spoken. The karavat." I did not know whether I should remonstrate on behalf of some unsuspecting pearl fisherman. But anyway, before I could, the little Raja summoned his steward and spoke rapidly to him. The man scuttled from the hall, and the Raja turned again to me. "The proclamation will immediately be cried throughout my realm: bring the heathen tooth and receive a munificent reward. It will bring the desired result, I promise you that, for all my people are honest and responsible and de-

vout Hindus. But it may take a while, because the pearl
fishers are constantly sailing back and forth between their
coastal villages and the reptile beds."

"I understand, Your Highness."

"You will be my guest—your female, too—until the relic
is retrieved."

"With gratitude, Your Highness."

"Then let us now cast off all dull business and sober
care," he said, dusting his little hands to demonstrate,
"and let mirth and joy reign in here as it does in the square
outside. Shouters, bring on the entertainers!"

This was the first entertainment: an aged and very
dirty, brown-black man, so ragged of dhoti that he was
quite indecent, shuffled woefully into the room and fell
prostrate before the little Raja. Master Khusru helpfully
murmured to me:

"What we call in Persia a darwish, a holy mendicant,
here called a naga. He will perform to earn his supper
crust and a few coppers."

The old beggar went to a cleared space in the room and
gave a hoarse call, and an equally ragged and filthy young
boy came in bearing a roll of what seemed to be cloth and
rope. When the two of them unrolled the bundle, it proved
to be one of the swing-style palang beds, its two ropes
terminating in little brass cups. The boy lay down in the
palang on the floor. The ancient naga knelt and slipped the
two brass cups onto his eyeballs, and pulled down his wrinkled black eyelids over them. Very slowly, he stood erect,
lifting the boy in the palang off the floor—not using his
hands or teeth or anything but his eyeballs—then swinging the boy from side to side until the little Raja felt moved
to applaud. Khusru and Tofaa and I politely did, too, and
we men threw the old beggar some coppers.

Next came into the dining hall a portly, squat, dark-
brown nach girl, who danced for us, about as listlessly as
the woman I had seen dancing at the Krishna festa. Her
only accompanying music was the jingling of a column of
gold bracelets which she wore from wrist to shoulder of
just one arm, and she wore nothing else at all. I was not
much enthralled—it might have been Tofaa stamping her
familiar soiled feet and undulating her familiar bushy
kaksha—but the little Raja giggled and snorted and slav-

ered throughout, and applauded wildly as the woman withdrew.

Then the tattered and filthy old mendicant returned. Rubbing his eyes, which had got bulged and reddened by his performance with the palang, he made a brief speech to the little Raja, who turned and told me:

"The naga says he is a Yogi, Marco-Wallah. The followers of the Yoga sect are accomplished in many strange and secret arts. You will see. If you truly harbor any belief, as I suspect you do, that we Hindus are backward or lacking in aptitude, then you are about to be convinced otherwise, for you will now witness a wonder that *only* a Hindu could show you." He called to the waiting beggar, "Which Yoga miracle will you show us, Oh Yogi? Will you be buried for a month underground and come up still alive? Will you make a rope stand erect and climb it and disappear into the heavens? Will you carve your boy assistant into pieces and then restore him whole? Will you at least levitate for us, Oh holy Yogi?"

The decrepit old man began to speak in a creaking small voice, but sounding earnest, as if making a momentous announcement, and doing much gesticulation. The little Raja and the Musicmaster leaned forward to listen intently, so now it was Tofaa who explained to me what was going on. She seemed pleased to do so, saying eagerly:

"It will be a wonder which you may wish to observe closely, Marco-wallah. The Yogi says he has discovered a revolutionary new way to do surata with a woman. Instead of his linga gushing out its juice at the climactic moment, as a man's customarily does, *his* gives a great inhaling suck *inward.* Thereby he ingests the life-force of the woman without expending any of his own. He says his discovery not only provides a fantastic new sensation, its continual practice could accrue to a man so much life-force that he might live forever. Would not you like to learn that ability, Marco-wallah?"

"Well," I said, "it sounds like an interestingly novel variation on the ordinary."

"Yes! Show us, Oh Yogi!" the little Raja called to him. "Show us this instant. Shouters, bring back the nach girl. She is already undressed and ready for use."

The six men went trotting out in lock step. But the Yogi held up a cautionary hand and declaimed some more.

"He says he dare not do it with a valuable dancing girl," Tofaa translated, "because any woman must wither to some degree when his linga does its sucking inside her. Instead, he requests a yoni with which he can demonstrate."

The six shouters trotted back in again, bringing the naked girl, but at another command from the little Raja they ran out once more.

I asked, "How can the Yogi be provided with a yoni without a woman attached?"

"A yoni stone," said Tofaa. "Around every temple you will see standing carved linga stone columns, which are representative of the god Siva, and also open-holed yoni stones, representative of his consort goddess Parvati."

The six men came back, one of them bringing a stone like a small wheel, with an oval opening cut through it, roughly resembling a woman's yoni, even having the kaksha hair carved around it.

The Yogi did a number of preparatory gesticulations, and spoke what sounded like solemn incantations, then parted his dhoti rags and unashamedly pulled out his linga, which was like a black-barked twig. With more incantations and gestures of demonstration—this is how it is done, gentlemen—he pushed his limp organ through the yoni hole in the stone. Then, holding the heavy stone against his crotch, he beckoned to the nach girl, who was also standing watching. He bade her take his linga in her fingers and bring it to arousal.

The girl did not recoil or complain, but she did not appear delighted with the idea. Nevertheless, she took hold of what protruded beyond the stone, and began working it, rather as if she were milking a cow. Her own udder bounced and all her bracelets jingled in rhythm to the motion. The old mendicant chanted down at the yoni and at the girl's hand yanking at him, and he narrowed his red eyes in intense concentration, and rivulets of sweat began to course down the dirt of his face. After some while, his linga grew enough to protrude farther past the stone, and we could even see its brown bulbous head creeping out a little beyond the nach girl's fricating fist. Finally the Yogi said something to her and she let go of him and stepped away.

Presumably the old beggar had stopped her just before she brought him to spruzzo. The stone was held to him now simply by the stiffness of his organ. He stared down at that peg and its constricting hoop, and so did the by now slightly breathless nach girl, and so did we at the table, and the shouters against the wall, and all the servants in the dining room. The Yogi's linga had attained a respectable size, considering the man's age and general scrawniness and beggarly debilitude. But it looked somehow strained and inflamed, bulging as it did from the narrow yoni of the stone it held firmly at his crotch.

The Yogi made several more gesticulations, but in a rather hurried and sketchy manner, and yammered a whole string of incantations, but in a rather strangled voice. Nothing happened that we could see. He glanced about at all of us, looking somewhat abashed, and glowered really hatefully at the nach girl, who was now humming indifferently and examining her fingernails, as if to say, "See? You should have used me." The Yogi yelled some more at his linga and borrowed yoni, as if cursing them, and made some more violent gestures, including shaking his fist. Still nothing happened, except that he sweated more copiously, and his tightly pinched organ was adding a distinct purple hue to its brown-black. The nach girl gave an audible snicker, and the Musicmaster an amused chuckle, and the little Raja began drumming his fingers on the tabletop.

"Well?" I said aside to Tofaa.

She whispered, "The Yogi appears to be having some difficulty."

Indeed he did. He was now dancing in place, more vigorously than the professional dancing girl had done, and his eyes were more redly extruded than they had been after the palang-swinging performance, and his vociferations were no longer incantory, but recognizable even to me as cries of pain. His ragged boy assistant came running, and tugged at the imprisoning stone, at which his master gave a frightful screech. The six shouters then also dashed forward to help, and there was a confusion of hands at that empurpled center of attention, until the agonized Yogi reeled wailing away from them and fell down, writhing and hammering his fists on the floor.

"Take him away!" the little Raja commanded, in a disgusted voice. "Take the old fraud to the kitchen. Try an application of grease."

The Yogi was carried from the room, not without some trouble, for he was contorting like a gaffed fish and trumpeting like a speared elephant. The entertainment appeared to be over. We four sat on at the table, in a mutually embarrassed silence, listening to the shrieks gradually diminishing down the corridors. I was the first to speak. I naturally did not remark on this having been one more affirmation of my opinion of Hindu foolishness and futility. Instead I said, by way of graciously excusing it:

"That happens all the time, Your Highness, to all the lower animals. Everyone has seen a dog and a bitch stuck together until the bitch's clasping yoni relaxes and the dog's swollen linga wilts."

"It may take some time for the Yogi," said Master Khusru, still with amusement. "The stone yoni will not relax and his linga's swelling therefore cannot go down."

"Bah!" exclaimed the little Raja, in furious exasperation. "I should have insisted that he levitate, not try something new. Let us go to bed." And he stamped out of the room, with no shouters present to congratulate himself and the world on the grace of his gait.

4

"I have your Buddha's tooth, Marco-wallah."

That was the very first thing the little Raja said to me when we first met the next day, and he said it about as cheerfully as he might have said, "I have a murderously *aching* tooth."

"Already, Your Highness? Why, that is wonderful. You said it might take some while to find."

"I thought it *would*," he said pettishly.

I understood his rancorous demeanor when he shoved at me a basket and I looked in. It was piled half full of teeth, most of them yellowed and mossy and carious, quite a few of them still bloody at the root, and some of them identifiably not even human—dogs' fangs and pigs' tushes.

"More than two hundred there," the little Raja said sourly. "And people are still arriving with more, from all

points of the horizon. Men, women, even holy naga mendicants, even one temple sadhu. Gr-r-r. You can present a
Buddha's tooth not only to your Raja Khakhan. You can
give one to every Buddhist of your acquaintance."

I tried not to laugh, for his anger was justified. He had
boasted of his people's honesty and of their devotion to
their Hindu faith, and here they came in flocks to confess
that they possessed a relic of the discredited Buddhist
religion—meaning they had to *lie* about it, besides.

Holding my face impassive, I inquired, "Am I expected
to pay a reward for every one of these?"

"No," he said, gritting his own teeth. "*I* am doing that.
The cursed reprobates come in the front door, hand their
counterfeit tooth to the steward, and are passed on out the
back door to where the Court Executioner is rewarding
them with fervent enthusiasm in the rear courtyard."

"Your Highness!" I exclaimed.

"Oh, I am not according them the karavat," he hastened
to assure me. "That is reserved for men who have done
crimes of some account. Also it takes a bit of time, and we
would never have done with this procession."

"Adrìo de mi. I can hear the wretches screaming from
here."

"No, you cannot," he growled. "They are being very
quietly dispatched with a wire loop whipped around the
throat and yanked. What you hear is that *other* fraud—
that degenerate old Yogi, still screeching in the kitchen.
No one has yet been able to get him loose from his clinging
rock yoni. We have tried greasing him with cooking fats,
softening him with sesame oil, shrinking him with boiling
water, wilting him by various natural means—surata by
the nach girl, buccal blandishment by his boy assistant—
nothing works. We may have to break the sacred yoni
stone, and what revenge the goddess Parvati will inflict, I
dare not think about."

"Well, I will not sympathize with the Yogi. But the tooth
bringers, Your Highness—it really is a trivial misdemeanor they have tried to commit, and in a trivially witless way. These teeth they have brought would not fool
even me, let alone a Buddhist."

"That is what is especially deplorable! My people's imbecility! That they would shame their Raja and insult
their religion, and with trickery so transparent. They are

incapable even of a decent crime. Dying is too good for them! They will only be reborn immediately in some lesser form—if there is any."

I frankly believed that any depletion of the Hindus could only improve the planet, but I did not want the little Raja later to realize how severely he had depopulated his realm, and be dismayed, and maybe hold me to blame for it. I said:

"Your Highness, as your guest I formally request that the surviving imbeciles be spared, and any newcomers turned away before they also can perjure themselves. This was, after all, the fault of an apparent omission in Your Highness's proclamation."

"Mine? An omission? Are you suggesting *I* am at fault? That a Brahman *and* a Maharajadhiraj Raj can *have* a fault?"

"I think it was only an understandable oversight. Since Your Highness is of course aware that the Buddha was a man nine forearms tall, and that any tooth of his must have been as big as a drinking cup, Your Highness no doubt assumed that all your people likewise knew that."

"Hm. You are right, Marco-wallah. I did take for granted that my subjects would remember that detail. Nine forearms, eh?"

"Perhaps an amended proclamation, Your Highness . . ."

"Hm. Yes. I will issue one. And I will mercifully pardon the dolts already here. A good Brahman kills no living thing, however lowly, unless it is necessary or expedient."

He called for his steward, and gave the instructions for the proclamation, and commanded also an end to the procession through the rear courtyard. When he returned to me, he was restored to quite good humor.

"There. It is done. A good Brahman host acquiesces in his guest's wishes. But enough of dull business and sober care! You are a guest, and you are not being entertained!"

"Oh, but I am, Your Highness. Constantly."

"Come! You shall admire my zenana."

I half expected him to fling open his dhoti diaper and expose something nasty, but he only reached up and took my arm and began walking me toward a far wing of the palace. As he escorted me through a succession of sumptuously furnished rooms, inhabited by females of various ages and various hues of brown, I realized that zenana must be the local word for an anderun—the apartments of

his wives and concubines. The women of mature age I
found no more attractive than I had Tofaa or the nach dancers, and they were mostly surrounded by swarms of children of all sizes. But some of the little Raja's consorts were
mere girls themselves, and not yet gross of flesh or
vulturine of eye or corvine of voice, and some were
delicately pretty in a dark-skinned way.

"I am frankly a bit surprised," I remarked to the little
Raja, "that Your Highness has so many wives. From
your evident aversion to the Lady Tofaa, I had rather
assumed . . ."

"Ah, well, if she had been your wife, as I first thought, I
should have plied you with concubines and nach girls to
distract you, while I seduced that lady to surata. But a
widow? What man wishes to couple with a cast-off husk—a
dead-woman-waiting-to-die—when there are so many still-
juicy wives of one's own and of others to be had, and also so
many newly-budding virgins?"

"Yes. I see. Your Highness is a manly man."

"Aha! You took me for a gand-mara, did you? A man-
lover and a woman-hater? For shame, Marco-wallah! I
grant you that, like any sensible man, for longtime companionship I prefer a quiet and mannerly and compliant
boy. But one has one's duties and obligations. A Raja is expected to maintain a teeming zenana, so I do. And I dutifully service them in regular rotation, even the youngest,
as soon as they have had their first flow."

"They are married to Your Highness *before* their first
menstruum?"

"Why, not just my wives, Marco-wallah. Every girl in India. The parents of any daughter are anxious to get her
married off before she is a woman, and before any mishap
to her virginity, which would make her unmarriageable.
For another reason, every time a daughter has her flow,
her parents are guilty of the hideous crime of letting die an
embryo that might prolong the family line. It is well said:
If a girl is unwed by the age of twelve, her ancestors in the
other world are mournfully drinking the blood she sheds
every month."

"Well said, yes."

"However, to return to the subject of my own wives.
They enjoy all the traditional wifely rights, but those do
not include any queenly rights, as in less civilized and

more debile monarchies. The women take no part in my
court or my rule. It is well said: What man would heed the
crowing of a hen? This one here, for instance, this is my
premier wife and my titular Maharani, but she never pre-
sumes to sit on a throne."

I bowed politely to the woman and said, "Your Highness." She only gave me the same look of dull detestation
she had given her Raja husband. Still trying to be polite, I
indicated the dark-brown swarm about her, and added,
"Your Highness has some handsome princes and princesses."

She still said nothing, but the little Raja growled, "They
are not princes and princesses. Do not give the woman
ideas."

I said, in some wonderment, "The royal line is not of pat-
rilineal primogeniture?"

"My dear Marco-wallah! How do I know if any of these
brats are mine?"

"Well, er . . . really . . .," I mumbled, embarrassed to
have broached the subject right in front of the woman and
her brood.

"Do not cringe, Marco-wallah. The Maharani knows I
am not insulting her specifically. I do not know if *any* of my
wives' offspring are of my begetting. I cannot know that.
You cannot know that, if you ever marry and have children. That is a fact of life."

He waved around at the various other wives whose
rooms we were strolling through, and repeated:

"That is a fact of life. No man can ever know, *for certain,*
that he is the father of his wife's child. Not even of a seemingly loving and faithful wife. Not even a wife so ugly a
paraiyar would shun her. Not even a wife so crippled she
cannot possibly stray. A woman can always find a way and
a lover and a dark place."

"But surely, Your Highness—the young little girls you
wed before they could possibly be fecundated—"

"Who knows, even then? I cannot always be on the spot
the instant they first flow. It is well said: If a woman sees
even her father or brother or son in secret, her yoni grows
moist."

"But you must bequeath your throne to *somebody,* Your
Highness. To whom, then, if not your presumed son or
daughter?"

"To the firstborn son of my sister, as all Rajas do. Every royal line in India descends sororially. You see, my sister is undisputably of my own blood. Even if our royal mother was promiscuously unfaithful to our royal father, and no matter if my sister and I were sired by different lovers, we did drop from the same womb."

"I understand. And then, no matter who sires her firstborn . . ."

"Well, of course, I hope it was I. I took my eldest sister for one of my early wives—fifth or sixth, I forget—and she has borne I think seven children, presumably mine. But the oldest boy, even if *not* my son, is still my nephew, and the royal bloodline remains intact and inviolate, and he will be the next Raja here."

We emerged from the zenana quite near to the part of the palace where the kitchen was, and we could still hear from in there moans and whimpers and sounds of thrashing about. The little Raja asked me if I could amuse myself for a while, since he had to attend to some royal duties.

"Go back to the zenana, if you like," he suggested. "Although I am careful to marry none but wives of my own white race, they keep producing children of disappointingly dark skin. A sprinkling of your seed, Marco-wallah, might lighten the strain."

Not to be discourteous, I murmured something about having taken a vow of continence, and said I would find something else to occupy me. I watched the little Raja strut away, and I quite pitied the man. He was a sovereign of sorts, holding the power of life and death over his people, and he was the tiny cock of a whole hen yard—and he was infinitely poorer and weaker and less contented than I, a mere journeyer with only one woman to love and cherish and keep for the rest of my life; but that one was Huisheng.

That reminded me: I could now dispense with my temporary cojourneyer. I went in search of Tofaa, who had been stertorously snoring when I left our chambers that morning. I found her on a palace terrace, gloomily watching the gloomy Krishna celebration still going on in the square below.

She immediately and accusingly said, "I smell the pachouli on you, Marco-wallah! You have been lying with per-

fumed women. Alas, and after such an admirably sinless
long time of behaving gentlemanly with me."

I ignored that, and said, "I came to tell you, Tofaa, that
you may resign your menial position of interpreter, whenever you wish, and—"

"I knew it! I was too demure and ladylike. Now you have
been beguiled by some shameless and forward palace
wench. Ah, you men."

I ignored that, too. "And as I promised, I will arrange for
your safe journey back to your homeland."

"You are eager to be rid of me. My genteel chastity is a
reproach to your goatishness."

"I was thinking of you, ungrateful woman. I have nothing to do now but wait here until the proper Buddha's
tooth is found and delivered. In the meantime, if I need
anything translated, both the Raja and the Musicmaster
are fluent in Farsi."

She sniffled noisily, and wiped her nose on her bare arm.
"I am in no hurry to go back to Bangala, Marco-wallah. I
would be only a widow there, too. In the meantime, the
Raja and the Master Khusru have occupations of their
own. They will not take time to lead you about and show
you the splendid sights of Kumbakonam, as I can do. I
have already inquired and sought them out, just for your
benefit."

So I did not compel her to leave. Instead, on that day and
during the days thereafter, I let her take me about and
show me the splendid sights of the city.

"Yonder, Marco-wallah, you see the holy man Kyavana.
He is the holiest inhabitant of Kumbakonam. It was many
years ago that he determined to stand still, like a tree
stump, to the greater glory of Brahma, and he is doing it
yet. That is he."

"I see three aged women, Tofaa, but no man. Where is
he?"

"There."

"There? That is only an enormous white-ant hill, with a
dog wetting on it."

"No, that is the holy man Kyavana. So still did he stand
that the white ants used him as framework for their clay
hill. It gets bigger every year. But that is he."

"Well . . . if he is in there, he is dead, surely?"

"Who knows? What does it matter? He stood just as immobile when he was alive. A most holy man. Pilgrims come from everywhere to admire him, and parents show their sons that example of high piety."

"This man did nothing but stand still. So very still that no one could tell if he was alive—or if now he may be dead. And that is called holy? That is an example to be admired? Emulated?"

"Do lower your voice, Marco-wallah, or Kyavana may manifest his great holy power at you, as he did at the three girls."

"What three girls? What did he do?"

"You see that shrine a little way beyond the anthill?"

"I see a mud shack, with those three old hags slumped in the doorway, scratching themselves."

"That is the shrine. Those are the girls. One is sixteen years old, the others seventeen, and—"

"Tofaa, the sun is very hot here. Perhaps we should go back to the palace so you can lie down."

"I am showing you the sights, Marco-wallah. When those girls were about eleven and twelve years old, they were as irreverent as you. They decided, for a frolic, to come here and open their garments and reveal their pubescent charms to the holy man Kyavana, and tempt at least one part of him out of immobility. You see what happened. They were instantly struck old and wrinkled and white-haired and haggard, as you see them now. The city built the shrine for them to live out their few remaining years in. The miracle has become famous all over India."

I laughed. "Is there any proof of this absurd story?"

"Indeed, yes. For a copper apiece, the girls will show you the very kaksha parts, once fresh and young, that were so suddenly made old and sour and stinking. See, they are already spreading their rags for you to—"

"Dio me varda!" I stopped laughing. "Here, throw them these coins and let us depart. I will take the miracle on faith."

"Now," said Tofaa, on another day, "here is a special sort of temple. A storytelling temple, You see the marvelously detailed carvings all over its exterior? They illustrate the many ways a man and a woman can do surata. Or a man and several women."

"Yes," I said. "Are you suggesting *this* is holy?"

"Very holy. When a girl is about to marry, it is assumed

—because she is still a child—that she does not yet know
how a marriage is consummated. So her parents bring her
here, and leave her with the wise and kindly sadhu. He
walks the girl about the outside of the temple, pointing to
this sculpture and that, and gently explaining to her, so
that, whatever her husband may do on the wedding night,
she will not be terrified. Here is the good sadhu now. Give
him some coppers, Marco-wallah, and he will take us
about, and I will repeat in Farsi what he tells us."

To my eye, the priest was just another black, dirty,
scrawny Hindu, in the usual dingy dhoti and tulband and
nothing else. I would hardly have asked road directions of
such a one. I would certainly never have entrusted a small
and apprehensive child bride to his attentions. She was
bound to be more repelled by him than by anything that
could happen on her wedding night.

But perhaps not. According to the temple sculptures,
some astonishing things could happen on her wedding
night. As the sadhu pointed out this and that, and snickered and leered and rubbed his hands together, I saw de-
pictions of acts that I had not known were possible until I
myself was well along in years and experience. The stone
men and women were conjoining in every conceivable position and combination and contortion, and in several ways
that—even at my present age—I would not have thought of
trying. Almost any one of those sculptured acts, if performed in a Christian land, even by a legitimately wedded
man and wife, would have required their going immediately afterward to a confessor. And if the performance
could be accurately described and related to that priest, *he*
would doubtless stagger away to seek shrift from a superior confessor.

I said, "I will accept, Tofaa, that a girl barely out of
childhood might be required to submit to the natural act of
surata with her new husband. But are you telling me that
she is required to be versed in all these wild variations?"

"Well, she makes a better wife, if she is. But in any case,
she should be prepared for whatever tastes her husband
might manifest. She is a child, yes, but he may be a mature
and lusty and experienced man. Or even a very old man,
who has long been surfeited by the natural act, and now requires novelty."

Having myself been all my life led about by my insatia-

ble curiosity, and led into some curious situations, I was
hardly one to point an accusing or ridiculing finger at the
private practices of any other person or people. So I merely
followed the smirking sadhu around the temple as he ges-
ticulated and jabbered, and I made no surprised or scandalized outcries as Tofaa explained, "This is the adharottara,
the upside-down act . . . this is the viparita surata, the perverse act. . . ." I was, in fact, regarding the sculptures
from a different point of view, and pondering on a different
aspect of them.

The carvings might well horrify a prudish spectator, but
even the most censorious could not deny that they were
fine art, beautifully and intricately done. The acts so explicitly portrayed were bawdy. God knows, even obscene,
but the men and women involved were all smiling happily,
and they were spirited and vivacious in their attitudes.
They were enjoying themselves. So the sculptures expressed both a superb craftsmanship and a wonderful
verve for life. They did not at all accord with the Hindus as
I knew them: inept in everything they did, and doing
everything with joyless sniveling, and doing very little.

As an example of their backwardness: in contrast to the
Han, whose historians had been minutely recording every
least event in their dominions for thousands of years, the
Hindus possessed not one written book recounting any of
their history. They had only some "sacred" collections of
unbelievable legends—unbelievable because, in them, all
the Hindu men were tiger-brave and resourceful, and all
the Hindu women angel-sweet and lovable. For another
example: the Hindu garments called sari and dhoti were
only swathings of fabric. That was because, although the
most primitive people elsewhere had long ago invented the
needle and the craft of sewing, the Hindus had not yet
learned to use a needle and had not any word for "tailor"
in any of their multitude of languages.

How, I asked myself, could a people ignorant even of
sewing have envisioned and crafted these delicate, artful
temple carvings? How could a people so slothful and furtive and woeful have portrayed here men and women joyous and nimble, inventive and adroit, lively and carefree?

They could not have done. I decided that these lands
must have been inhabited, ages before the Hindus came,
by some other and very different race, one with talent and

vivacity. God knows where that superior people had gone,
but they had left a few artifacts like this splendidly crafted
temple, and that was all. They had left no trace of themselves in the later-come, usurper Hindus. That was deplorable, but hardly surprising. Would any such people have
interbred with *Hindus?*

"Now here, Marco-wallah," Tofaa said instructively,
"this carven couple are entwined in what is called the kaja
posture, named for the hooded snake with which you are
acquainted."

It looked snaky enough, and it was a position new to me.
The man appeared to be sitting on the side of a bed. The
woman lay upon and against him, head down, her torso between the man's legs, her hands on the floor, her legs
about the man's waist, her buttocks held caressingly by
his hands, and presumably his linga inside her (upside-
down) yoni.

"A very useful position," the sadhu recited, Tofaa translating. "Say, for instance, if you wish to make surata with
a humpbacked woman. As you must know, you simply cannot put a humpbacked woman on a bed in the usual supine
position, or she teeters and rocks on her hump, most inconveniently, and—"

"Gèsu."

"You no doubt lust to try that kaja position, Marco-
wallah," said Tofaa. "But do not affront me by asking
me to do it with you. No, no. However, the sadhu says he
has, inside the temple, an exceedingly capable, exceedingly humpbacked devadasi woman who, for a trifle of
silver . . ."

"Thank you, Tofaa, and thank the sadhu for me. But I
will take this one, too, on faith."

5

"I have your Budda's tooth, Marco-walla!" said the little
Raja. "I rejoice in the happy conclusion of your quest!"

Some three months had gone by since his previous similar announcement, during which time no other teeth,
small or large, had been brought to the palace. I had con-

tained my impatience, assuming that a pearl fisher *was* an
elusive quarry. But I was glad to have the real thing at
last. I was by now very weary of India and of Hindus, and
the little Raja had also begun to make plain that he would
not weep loudly when I departed. He seemed not to be
tiring of my visit, exactly, but getting suspicious of it. Apparently his little mind had conceived the notion that I
might be using my tooth quest as a disguise for a real mission of spying out the local terrain in advance of a Mongol
invasion. Well, I knew that the Mongols would not have
had this dismal land even if it were freely donated to their
Khanate, but I was too polite to tell that to the little Raja. I
could better allay his suspicions by merely taking the
tooth and going, and I would.

"It is a magnificent tooth, indeed," I said, with un-
feigned awe. It was certainly no counterfeit. It was a yellowish molar, rather oblong from front to back, and the
grinder surface of it was bigger than my hand, and its
roots nearly as long as my forearm, and it weighed almost
as much as a stone of equal dimensions. I asked, "Was it
the pearl fisher who brought it? Is he here? I must give him
his reward."

"Ah, the pearl fisher," said the little Raja. "The steward
took the good man to the kitchen to give him a meal. If you
would care to let me have the reward, Marco-wallah, I will
see that he gets it." His eyes widened as I jingled half a
dozen gold coins into his hand. "Ach-chaa, so much?"

I smiled and said, "It is worth it to me, Your Highness"—not adding that I was beholden to the fisherman,
not only for the tooth, but also for my release from this
place.

"Overgenerous, but he shall have it," said the little
Raja. "And I will bid the steward find for you a nice box to
put the relic in."

"May I request also, Your Highness, a pair of horses for
me and my interpreter, that we may ride back to the coast
and seek sea transport from there?"

"You shall have them, first thing in the morning, and
likewise a stalwart pair of my palace guards for your escort."

I hurried off to start my packing for departure, and told
Tofaa to do the same, and she complied, though not very
cheerfully. We were still at it when the Musicmaster

stopped by our chambers to say his farewells. He and we
exchanged compliments and good wishes and salaam aleikum, and then his eye chanced to fall on the things laid
out on my bed to be packed, and he remarked:

"I see you are taking with you an elephant's tooth as a
memento of your stay."

"What?" I said. He was regarding the Buddha's tooth. I
laughed at his jest and said, "Come, come, Master Khusru.
You cannot fool me. An elephant's tusk is taller than I am,
and I could probably not lift one."

"A tusk, yes. But do you think an elephant chews its fodder with its tusks? For that, it has ample tiers of molars.
Like this one. You have never looked into an elephant's
mouth, I take it."

"No, I have not," I muttered, quietly gnashing my own
molars. I waited until he had made his last salaam and left
us, and then I burst out, "A cavàl donà no se ghe varda in
boca! Che le vegna la cagasangue!"

"What are you shouting, Marco-wallah?" asked Tofaa.

"May the bloody gripes take that cursed Raja!" I raged.
"The little wart was worried by my continued presence
here, and evidently he despaired of anybody ever coming
with another Buddha's tooth, real or false. So he provided
one himself. And took my reward for it! Come, Tofaa, let us
go and revile him to his face!"

We went downstairs and found the chief steward, and I
demanded audience with the little Raja, but the man said
apologetically:

"The Raja went out, borne in his palanquin, to ride
through the city and grant his subjects the privilege of observing him and admiring him and cheering at him. I was
just explaining that to this importunate caller who insists
he has come a far distance to see the Raja."

As Tofaa translated that, I glanced only impatiently at
the caller—just another Hindu man in a dhoti—but my eye
caught on an object he was carrying, and at the same moment Tofaa cried excitedly:

"It is he, Marco-wallah! It is the very pearl fisher whom
I remember from Akyab!"

And indeed the man was carrying a tooth. It was another immense one, and quite similar to my own latest acquisition, except that it was cupped in a mesh of gold
tracery, like a stone set in a jewel, and the whole had a

patina of unmistakable great age. Tofaa and the man jabbered together, then she turned to me again.

"It is truly he, Marco-wallah. The man who gamed with
my late dear husband in the Akyab hall. And this is the
relic he won with the dice that day."

"How many did he win?" I said, still skeptical. "He has
already delivered one."

Jabber, jabber, and Tofaa spoke to me once more. "He
knows nothing of any other. He has only this moment arrived, having trudged on foot all the way from the coast.
This tooth is the only tooth he has ever had, and he is sad
to part with it, for it much increased his crop of pearls in
the season past, but he is dutifully heeding his Raja's proclamation."

"What a happy coincidence," I said. "This seems to be a
day for teeth." I added, as I heard a commotion in the
courtyard outside. "And here the Raja returns now, just in
time to greet the one honest Hindu in his realm."

The little Raja strutted in, trailed by his fawning entourage of courtiers and congratulators and other toadies. He
halted in some surprise at seeing our group waiting in the
entry hall. Tofaa and the steward and the fisherman all
collapsed to lower themselves below the Raja's head level,
but, before any of them could speak, I addressed the little
Raja in Farsi, and said silkily:

"It appears, Your Highness, that the good pearl fisher
was so pleased with the reward for the first tooth—and the
meal to which you treated him—that he has brought another."

The little Raja looked startled and bewildered for a moment, but he quickly comprehended the situation, and realized that I had caught him out in his chicanery. He did
not act guilty or abashed, of course, but only indignant,
and flashed a look of pure venom at the innocent fisherman, and contributed another blatant lie:

"The greedy wretch is only trying to take advantage of
you, Marco-wallah."

"Perhaps he is, Your Highness," I said, continuing to
pretend that I was believing his farce. "But I will gratefully accept this new relic, as well. For now I can make this
one a gift to my Khakhan Kubilai, and leave the other as
my parting gift to Your Gracious Highness. Your Highness deserves it. There is only the question of the reward I

have already paid. Do I give the fisher an equal amount for
this new delivery?"

"No," the little Raja said coldly. "You have already paid
most generously. I shall persuade the man to be satisfied
with that. Believe me, I shall persuade him."

He snapped instructions to the steward to take the man
to the kitchen for a meal—*another* meal, he thought to
add—and went stamping furiously off to his quarters. Tofaa and I returned to our own to finish packing. I carefully
wrapped the new, gold-meshed tooth for safe carrying, but
left the other for whatever disposition the little Raja might
wish to make of it.

I never saw the man again. Perhaps he could not face
me, realizing that I was leaving Kumbakonam with my
never very high opinion of him lowered even further, now
knowing him to be not only a posturing travesty of a sovereign, but also a giver of false gifts, a cheater of his own people, an embezzler of another's rightful recompense and—
worse than all that—a man incapable ever of admitting
error or wrong or fault. Anyway, he did not say goodbye or
even get out of bed to see us off, when at dawn we took our
leave.

Tofaa and I, in the rear courtyard, were standing about
while our two assigned escorts saddled our horses and
strapped our packs on the cantles, when I saw two other
men emerge from a back door of the palace. In the early
half-light, I could not see who they were, but one of them
sat down on the ground while the other stood over him.
Our escorts paused in their work and muttered uneasily,
and Tofaa translated for me:

"Those are the Court Executioner and the condemned
prisoner. He must be guilty of some noteworthy crime, for
he is being accorded the karavat."

Curious, I went a little closer to them, but not close
enough to interfere. The karavat, I finally could see, was a
peculiar sort of sword blade. It had no handle, but was simply a crescent of sharp steel, like a new moon, each of its
points ending in a short chain, and each chain ending in a
sort of metal stirrup. The condemned prisoner—not in any
hurry, but not too reluctantly either—himself put the crescent blade at the back of his neck, with the chains draped
over his shoulders in front. Then he bent his knees and
drew up his feet to where he could put a foot in each of the

stirrups. Then, after the briefest moment to take a last deep breath, he leaned his neck back against the blade and kicked both feet out straight. The karavat very neatly, and by his own unaided action, sliced his head from his body.

I went closer yet and, while the executioner relieved the body of the karavat, I looked down at the head, which was still opening and shutting its eyes and mouth in a surprised kind of way. It was the pearl fisher who had brought the real Buddha's tooth, the only enterprising and honorable Hindu I had encountered in India. The little Raja had rewarded him, as he had said he would.

As we rode away, I reflected that I had at last seen something which the Hindus could be proud of calling their own. They had nothing else. They had long ago disowned their native-born Buddha and relinquished him to alien lands. The few splendors they could boastfully display to visitors had, in my opinion, been crafted by some different and vanished race. The Hindus' customs and morals and social order and personal habits had, in my opinion, been taught to them by the monkeys. Even their distinctive musical instrument, the sitar, was the contribution of a foreigner. If the karavat *was* the Hindus' own invention, then it had to be their only one, and I was willing to concede them that one—a lazy way of letting the condemned kill themselves—as the highest achievement of their race.

We could have ridden straight east from Kumbakonam to the Cholamandal coast, to seek the nearest village where the bay-crossing vessels put in. But Tofaa suggested, and I agreed, that we might best return the way we had come, to Kuddalore, since we knew from experience that considerable numbers of vessels called there. It was as well that we did, because, when we arrived and Tofaa began inquiring for a ship that we might engage, the local seamen told her there was already a ship there looking for *us*. That puzzled me, but only briefly, for the word of our presence quickly circulated about Kuddalore, and a man who was no Hindu came running and calling, "Sain bina!"

To my great surprise, it was Yissun, my former interpreter, whom I had last seen starting on his way from Akyab back through Ava toward Pagan. We pummeled each other and shouted salutations, but I cut them short to inquire, "What are you doing in this forsaken place?"

"The Wang Bayan sent me looking for you, Elder

Brother Marco. And, because Bayan said, 'Bring him *quickly*,' the Sardar Shaibani this time did not just engage a ship, but commandeered one, with all its crew, and put aboard Mongol warriors to urge the mariners on. We ascertained that you had made landfall here at Kuddalore, so this is where I came. But frankly, I was wondering where to look next. These stupid villagers told me you had gone inland only to the next village of Panrati, but that was many months ago, and I knew you must have gone farther than that. So it is a blessing that we have met by accident. Come, we will set sail for Ava at once."

"But why?" I asked. This worried me. Yissun's spate of words seemed intended to tell me everything but why. "What need has Bayan of me, and in such hurry? Is it war, insurrection, what?"

"I am sorry to say no, Marco, nothing natural and normal like that. It seems that your good woman Hui-sheng is in poor health. As best I can tell you—"

"Not now," I said instantly, feeling even on that hot day a cold wind blow. "Tell me on board. As you say, let us sail at once."

He had a dinghi and a Hindu boatman waiting at his service, and we went immediately out to the anchored ship, another good substantial qurqur, this one captained by a Persian and crewed by an assortment of races and colors. They were quite willing to hurry back across the bay, for the month was now March, and the winds would soon drop and the heat worsen and the drenching rains come. We took Tofaa with us, since her destination was Chittagong, and that chief port of Bangala was on the same eastern side of the bay as Akyab, and not far up that coast, so the ship could readily take her there after dropping me and Yissun.

When the qurqur had weighed anchor and was under way, Yissun and I and Tofaa stood at the stern rail—he and I thankfully watching India disappear behind us—and he told me about Hui-sheng.

"When your lady first discovered she was with child—"

"With child!" I said in consternation.

Yissun shrugged. "I repeat only what I have been told. I am told that she was both overjoyed at the fact and worried that you might disapprove."

"Dear God! She did not try to expel it, and hurt herself?"

"No, no. I think the Lady Hui-sheng would not do anything, Marco, without your approval. No, she did nothing, and I gather she did not even realize that anything might be wrong."

"Well, vakh, man! What *is* wrong?"

"When I left Pagan, nothing—nothing that anyone could see. The lady appeared to me to be in perfect health, and radiant with expectation, and more beautiful than ever before. There was nothing visibly amiss. What it is, I gather, is something that cannot be seen. Because, at the very beginning, when she first confided to her maidservant that she was pregnant, that servant—Arùn, you remember her—took it upon herself to approach the Wang Bayan and inform him that *she* had misgivings. Now remember, Marco, I am only telling you what Bayan told me the servant told him, and I am no shamàn or physician, and I am not much knowledgeable about the internal workings of women, and—"

"Do get to it, Yissun," I pleaded.

"The girl Arùn informed Bayan that, in her opinion, your Lady Hui-sheng is not physically well adapted for childbearing. Something about the shape of the bones of her pelvic cradle, whatever that is. You must excuse my mentioning intimate details of anatomy, Marco, but I am only reporting. And evidently the servant Arùn, being your lady's chamber attendant, is well acquainted with her pelvic cradle."

"So am I," I said. "And I never noticed anything wrong with it."

At that point, Tofaa spoke up, in her know-everything way, and inquired, "Marco-wallah, is your lady extremely obese?"

"Impudent woman! She is not at all obese!"

"I only asked. That is the most usual cause of difficulty. Well, then, tell me this. Is your lady's mount of love—you know, that little frontal cushion, where the hair grows—is it perhaps delightfully protrusive?"

I said coldly, "For your information, women of her race are not matted with sweaty hair there. However, now that you mention it, I would say yes—that frontal place on my lady is a trifle more prominent than I have seen on other women."

"Ah, well, there you are, then. A woman of that conformation is sublimely sweet and deep and enfolding in the act of surata—as no doubt you are well aware—but it can ill suit her for childbearing. It indicates that her pelvic bones are shaped in such a way that the opening of her pelvic cradle is heart-shaped instead of oval. Clearly, that distortion is what her maid servant recognized, and was worried by. But surely, Marco-wallah, your lady herself should have been aware. Her mother must have told her, or her nursemaid, at the time she became a woman and was sat down for her woman-to-woman counseling."

"No," I said, reflecting. "She could not have been told. Hui-sheng's mother died in her childhood, and she herself . . . well, thereafter she heard no counseling, she had no confidantes. But never mind that. What should she have been told?"

Tofaa said flatly, "Never to have children."

"Why? What does it mean, this pelvic conformation? Is she in great danger?"

"Not while she is pregnant, no. There would be no difficulty in carrying the baby through all nine months, if she is otherwise healthy. It should be an uneventful pregnancy, and a pregnant woman is always a happy woman. The problem comes at the time for delivery."

"And then?"

Tofaa looked away from me. "The hardest part is the extrusion of the infant's head. But its head is oval, and so is the normal pelvic opening. Whatever the labor and pain involved, it does get out. However, if that passage is constricted, as in the case of a heart-shaped pelvis . . ."

"Then?"

She said evasively, "Imagine that you are pouring grain from a sack that has a narrow neck, and a mouse has got into the grain, and it stops the neck. But the grain has to be emptied, so you press and wring and squeeze. Something must give."

"The mouse will burst. Or the neck will split asunder."

"Or the whole sack."

I moaned. "God, let it be the mouse!" Then I whirled on Yissun and demanded, "What is being done?"

"Everything possible, Elder Brother. The Wang Bayan well remembers that he promised you he would see to her safekeeping. All the physicians of the court of Ava are in attendance, but Bayan was not satisfied to trust in them.

He sent couriers galloping to Khanbalik to apprise the Khakhan of the situation. And the Khan Kubilai dispatched his own personal court physician, the Hakim Gansui. That aged man was himself nearly dead by the time he was hauled all the way south to Pagan, but he will wish he *were* dead if anything happens to the Lady Hui-sheng."

Well, I thought, after Yissun and Tofaa had gone away and left me to brood alone, I could hardly blame Bayan or Gansui or anyone else for whatever might happen. It was I who had put Hui-sheng in this peril. It had to have happened on that first night she and I and Arùn frolicked together, so excitedly that I had neglected what was my responsibility and my pleasure—the nightly emplacing of the preventive lemon cap. I tried to calculate when that had been. Right after our arrival in Pagan, so that was how long ago? Gèsu, at least eight months and perhaps nearly nine! Hui-sheng must by now be almost at term. No wonder Bayan was anxious for me to be found and brought back to her bedside.

He was no more anxious than I. If my darling Hui-sheng were in the least difficulty, I wanted to be beside her. Now she was in the worst possible trouble, and I was unforgivably far away. In consequence, this crossing of the Bay of Bangala seemed excruciatingly slower and longer than the first traverse, outward bound. The captain and crew did not find me a very agreeable passenger to be transporting on their ship, and my two fellow passengers did not find me a very agreeable companion. I snapped and snarled and fretted and paced the deck, and I cursed the mariners every time they did not have every single scrap of sail stretched to the mast top, and I cursed the uncaring immensity of the bay, and I cursed the weather every time the least cloud appeared in the sky, and I cursed the unfeeling way time was behaving—passing so slowly out here, but elsewhere hastening Hui-sheng toward the day of reckoning.

And mostly I cursed myself, because, if there was one man in the world who knew what he was inflicting on a woman when he made her pregnant, it was I. That time on the Roof of the World when, under the influence of the love philter, I briefly had *been* a woman in the throes of childbirth—whether it was fancy or reality, a drug-caused

delusion in my mind or a drug-caused transfiguration of
my body—I most definitely *had* experienced every ghastly
moment and hour and lifetime of the birthing process.
Learned it better than any man, better even than a male
physician could know it, however many births he had attended. I knew there was nothing pretty or dulcet or felicitous about it, as all the myths of sweet maternity would
have us believe. I knew it to be a filthy business, nauseous,
humiliating, terrible torture. I had seen a Fondler do vile
things to human Subjects, but even he could not do them
from the inside out. Childbirth was more terrible, and the
Subject could do nothing but scream and scream until the
torment ended in the final agonizing extrusion.

But poor Hui-sheng could not even scream.

And if the groping, raging, tearing thing inside her
could not *ever* get out . . . ?

I was to blame. I had neglected, on just one occasion, to
take the proper precaution. But actually I had been more
culpably neglectful than that. Ever after my own horrendous childbed experience, I had said, "I will never subject
any woman I love to such a fate." So, if I had rightly loved
Hui-sheng, I would never have lain with her and never
have put her even remotely at risk. It was hard to regret
all the lovely times she and I had engaged in the act of
love, but now I did regret them, for even with precautions
there was no certainty, and she had every time been in
danger. Now I swore to myself and God that if Hui-sheng
survived this peril, I would never lie with her again. I
loved her that much, and we would simply have to find
other ways of mutually demonstrating our love.

That bitter decision made, I tried to bury my apprehensions in happier recollections, but their very sweetness
made them bitter, too. I remembered the last time I had
seen her, when Yissun and I rode away from Pagan. Hui-
sheng could not have heard or responded to my calling as I
went, "Goodbye, my dear one." But she had heard, with
her heart. And she had spoken, too, with her eyes: "Come
back, my dear one." And I remembered how, bereft of ever
hearing music, she had so often felt it instead, and seen
it, and sensed it in other ways. She had even made
music, though unable to do it herself, for I had known
other people—even dour servants engaged in uncongenial
labor—often to hum or sing happily, just because Hui-

sheng was in the room. I remembered one occasion, one
summer day, when we had been caught outdoors in a sudden thundershower, and all the Mongols about us were
quaking uneasily and muttering their Khakhan's protecting name. But Hui-sheng had only smiled at the
displays of lightning, unafraid of the menacing noise it
made; to her, a storm was only another beautiful thing.
And I remembered how often, on our walks together, Hui-
sheng had run to pluck some flower my unimpaired but
duller senses had failed to perceive. Still, I was not totally
insensitive to beauty. Whenever she dashed away on one
of those forays, I had to smile at the awkward, knee-tied
way a woman runs, but it was a fond smile and, every time
she ran, my heart went tumbling after. . . .

After another eternity or two, the voyage was done. As
soon as we raised Akyab on the horizon, I had my packs
ready and said my farewells and thanks to the Lady Tofaa,
so that Yissun and I were able to leap from the deck to the
dock even before the ship's plank was down. With only a
wave to the Sardar Shaibani, we vaulted onto the horses
he had brought to the bayside, and we put the spurs to
them. Shaibani must also, as soon as our vessel was
sighted in the distance, have sent an advance court riding
hard for Pagan, because, as swiftly as Yissun and I covered
the four-hundred-li distance, the Pagan palace was expecting us. The Wang Bayan was not waiting to be the
first to greet us; no doubt he had decided he was too gruff
for such a delicate duty. He had posted instead the old Hakim Gansui and the little maidservant Arùn to receive us.
I got down from my mount, trembling, as much from inner
palpitation as from the muscular strain of the long gallop,
and Arùn came running to take my hands in hers, and
Gansui approached more sedately. They did not need to
speak. I saw from their faces—his grave, hers grieving—
that I had arrived too late.

"All that could have been done was done," said the hakim when, at his insistence, I had taken a bracing drink of
the fiery choum-choum. "I did not get here to Pagan until
well along in the lady's term, but I could yet have easily
and safely made her miscarry. She would not let me. Insofar as I could comprehend her, through the medium of this
servant girl, your Lady Hui-sheng insisted that that decision was not hers to make."

"You should have overruled her," I said huskily.

"The decision was not mine to make, either." He kindly refrained from saying that the decision should have been made by me, and I merely nodded.

He went on, "I had no recourse but to await the confinement. And in fact I was not without some hope. I am not one of the Han physicians, who do not even touch their female patients, but instead let them modestly point out on an ivory figurine the spots where they hurt. I insisted on making a full examination. You say you have only recently learned that your lady's pelvic cavity was constricted. I found that its oblique diameters were diminished by the sacral column's forward intrusion and the pubic extremity's being more pointed than rounded, giving the cavity a triradiate instead of oval shape. That is not usually any impediment to a woman—in her walking, riding, whatever—*until* she contemplates becoming a mother."

"She never knew," I said.

"I believe I managed to convey it to her, and to warn her of the possible consequences. But she was stubborn—or determined—or brave. And in truth I could not tell her that the birth was impossible, that it *must* be terminated. In my time, I have attended several African concubines, and of all races the black women have the most narrow pelvic passages, but they have children nonetheless. An infant's head is quite malleable and pliable, so I was not without hope that this one could effect its egress without too much trouble. Unfortunately, it could not."

He paused, to choose his next words carefully. "After some time of labor, it became evident that the fetus was inextricably impacted. And at that point, the decision *is* the physician's to make. I rendered the lady insensible with oil of teryak. The fetus was dissected and extracted. A full-term male infant of apparently normal development. But there already had been too much strain on the mother's internal organs and vessels, and bleeding was occurring in places where it is impossible to stanch. The Lady Huisheng never awoke from the teryak coma. It was an easy and painless death."

I wished he had stopped short of the last words. However compassionately intended, they were an outright lie. I have seen too many deaths to believe that any is ever "easy." And "painless," this one? I knew, better than he did, what "some time of labor" was like. Before he mercifully granted her oblivion, and minced the baby and plucked it out piecemeal, Hui-sheng had endured hours indistinguishable from Hell's own eternity. But I only said dully:

"You did what you could, Hakim Gansui. I am grateful. Can I see her now?"

"Friend Marco, she died four days ago. In this climate . . . Well, the ceremony was simple and dignified, not one of the local barbarities. A pyre at sunset, with the Wang Bayan and all the court as mourners . . ."

So I would not even see her one last time. It was hard, but perhaps it was best. I could remember her, not as a motionless and forever silent Echo, but as she once had been, alive and vibrant, as I last had seen her.

I went numbly through the formalities of greeting Bayan and hearing his rough condolences, and I told him I would depart again as soon as I was rested, to bear the Buddha relic to Kubilai. Then I went with Arùn to the chambers where Hui-sheng and I had last lived together, and where she had died. Arùn emptied closets and chests, to help me pack, though I selected only a few keepsakes to take with me. I told the girl she might have the clothes and other feminine things Hui-sheng no longer had any use for. But Arùn insisted on showing me every single item and asking my permission each time. I might have found that unnecessarily hurtful, but really the clothes and jewels and hair ornaments meant nothing to me without Hui-sheng the wearer of them.

I had determined that I would not weep—at least not until I reached some lonely place on the trail northward, where I could do so in seclusion. It required some exertion, I confess, not to let the tears flow, not to fling myself on the vacant bed we had shared, not to clutch her empty garments to me. But I said to myself, "I will bear this like a stolid Mongol—no, like a practical-minded merchant."

Yes, best to be like a merchant, for he is a man accustomed to the transitoriness of things. A merchant may deal in treasures, and he may rejoice when an exceptional treasure comes to hand, but he knows that he has it only for a while before it must go to other hands—or what is he a merchant for? He may be sorry to see that treasure go, but

if he is a proper merchant he will be the richer for having
possessed it even briefly. And I was, I was. Though she was
gone from me now, Hui-sheng had immeasurably enriched
my life, and left me with a store of memories beyond price,
and perhaps even made me a better man for having known
her. Yes, I had profited. That very practical way of regarding my bereavement made it easier for me to contain my
grief. I congratulated myself on my stony composure.

But then Arùn inquired, "Will you be taking this?" and
what she held was the white porcelain incense burner, and
the stone man broke.

HOME

1

M Y father greeted me with joy, and then with condolence when I told him why I had returned to Khanbalik without Hui-sheng. He started somberly to tell me that life was like a something or other, but I interrupted the homily.

"I see we are no longer the most recently arrived Westerners in Kithai," I said, for there was a stranger sitting with my father in his chambers. He was a white man, a little older than myself, and his garb, though travel-worn, identified him as a cleric of the Franciscan order.

"Yes," said my father, beaming. "At long last, a real Christian priest comes to Kithai. And a near countryman of ours, Marco, from the Campagna. This is Pare Zuàne—"

"Padre Giovanni," said the priest, pettishly correcting my father's Venetian pronunciation. "Of Montecorvino, near Salerno."

"Like us, some three years on the road," said my father. "And very nearly our same route."

"From Constantinople," said the priest. "Down into India, where I established a mission, then up through High Tartary."

"I am sure you will be welcome here, Pare Zuàne," I said politely. "If you have not yet been presented to the Khakhan, I am having audience with him shortly, and—"

"The Khan Kubilai has already most cordially received me."

"Perhaps," said my father, "if you asked, Marco, the

Pare Zuàne would consent to say a few words in memory of our dear departed Hui-sheng . . ."

I would not have asked him anyway, but the priest said stiffly, "I gather that the departed was not a Christian. And that the union was not according to the Sacrament."

So I rudely turned my back on him and rudely said, "Father, if these once remote and unknown and barbaric lands are now attracting civilized arrivisti like this one, the Khakhan should not feel too forlorn when we few pioneers take our departure. I am ready to leave whenever you are."

"I expected you would be," he said, nodding. "I have been converting all the holdings of the Compagnia into portable goods and currencies. Most has already gone westward by horse post along the Silk Road. And the rest is all packed. We need only to decide on our mode of travel and the route we shall take—and get the Khakhan's consent, of course."

So I went to get that. First I presented to Kubilai the Buddha relic I had brought, at which he expressed pleasure and some awe and many thanks. Then I presented a letter which Bayan had given me to carry, and I waited while he read it, and then I said:

"I also brought back with me, Sire, your personal physician, the Hakim Gansui, and I am eternally grateful for your having sent him to care for my late lady consort."

"Your *late* lady? Then Gansui could not have cared for her very effectively. I am desolated to hear it. He has always done well enough in treating my ever afflicting gout, and my more recent ills of old age, and I should be sorry to lose him. But ought he be executed for this lamentable dereliction?"

"Not at my behest, Sire. I am satisfied that he did what he could. And putting him to death would not bring back my lady or my unborn son."

"I commiserate, Marco. A lovely and beloved and loving lady is indeed irreplaceable. But sons?" He gave a casual wave, and I thought he was referring to his own considerable brood of progeny. But he made me start when he said, "You already have these half a dozen. And, I believe, three or four daughters besides."

For the first time, I realized who were the page boys that had replaced his former elderly stewards. I was speechless.

"Most handsome lads," he went on. "A great improvement in the sightliness of my throne room. Visitors can rest their gaze on those comely young men, instead of this aged hulk on the throne."

I looked around at the pages. The one or two within earshot, who had probably overheard that astonishing revelation—astonishing to me, anyway—gave me back timid and respectful smiles. Now I knew where they had got their lighter-than-Mongol complexions and hair and eyes, and I even fancied I could see a vague resemblance to myself. Still, they were strangers to me. They had not been conceived in love, and I would probably not recognize their mothers if we passed in a palace corridor. I set my jaw and said:

"My only son died in childbirth, Sire. The loss of him and his mother has left me sore of soul and heart. For that reason, I ask my Lord Khakhan's permission to make my report on this latest mission of mine, and then to request a favor."

He studied me for a time, and the age-eroded wrinkles and channels of his leather face seemed to deepen perceptibly, but he said only, "Report."

I did it briefly enough, since I had really had no mission except to observe. So I gave my impressions of what I had seen: that India was a country totally worthless of his acquisition or least attention; that the lands of Champa offered the same resources—elephants, spices, timber, slaves, precious gems—and much nearer at hand.

"Also, Ava is already yours, of course. However, I have one observation to make, Sire. Like Ava, the other nations of Champa may be susceptible to easy conquest, but I think the holding of them will be hard. Your Mongols are northern men, accustomed to breathing freely. In those tropical heats and damps, no Mongol garrison can endure for long without falling prey to fevers and diseases and the ambient indolence. I suggest, instead of actual occupation, Sire, that you simply install submissive natives as your Champa administrators and overseeing forces."

He nodded and again picked up the letter I had brought from Bayan. "The King Rama Khamhaeng of Muong Thai is already proposing just such an arrangement, as alternative to our demanding his unconditional surrender. He offers all the produce of his country's tin mines in continuing tribute. I think I shall accept those terms, and leave Muong Thai nominally an independent nation."

I was pleased to hear that, having conceived a real fondness for the Thai people. Let them have their Land of the Free.

Kubilai went on, "I thank you for your report, Marco. You have done well, as always. I should be an ungrateful lord were I to refuse any favor in my granting. Make your request, then."

He knew what I was going to ask. Nevertheless, I did not care to ask it baldly and abruptly: "Give me leave to leave you." So I began in the Han manner, with circumlocution.

"A long time ago, Sire, I had occasion to say, 'I could never slay a woman.' And when I said that, a slave of mine, a man wiser than I realized, said, 'You are young yet.' I could not then have believed it, but I have recently been the cause of the dying of the woman most dear to me in all the world. And I am no longer young. I am a man of middle age, well along in my fourth decade. That death has caused me much hurt and, like a wounded elephant, I should like to limp away to the seclusion of my home ground, there to recover from my wound or to languish of it. I ask your permission, Sire—and I hope your blessing— for the departure from your court of myself and my father and my uncle. If I am no longer young, they are already old, and their dying should also be done at home."

"And I am older yet," said Kubilai, with a sigh. "The scroll depicting my life has been wound much farther from the one hand to the other. And every turn of the scroll's rods reveals a picture with fewer friends standing about me. Someday, Marco, you will envy your lost lady. She died in the summer of her life, not having to see all that was flowery and green about her turn brown and dwindle and blow away like autumn leaves." He shivered as if he felt already the gusts of winter. "I shall be sorry to see my friends Polo depart, but I should be ill repaying your family's long service and companionship if I whined for its continuance. Have you yet made any travel arrangements?"

"Of course not, Sire. Not without your permission."

"You have it, certainly. But now I should like to ask a favor. One last mission for you, which you can perform on your way, and it will make easier your way."

"You have only to command it, Sire."

"I would ask if you and Nicolò and Mafìo could deliver a
certain valuable and delicate cargo to my grandnephew
Arghun in Persia. When Arghun succeeded to that Ilkhanate, he took a Persian wife as a politic gesture to his subjects. He doubtless has other wives, as well, but now he
wishes to have for his premier wife and Ilkhatun a woman
of pure Mongol blood and upbringing. So he sent envoys to
ask me to procure such a bride for him, and I have chosen a
lady named Kukachin."

"The widow of your son Chingkim, Sire?"

"No, no. She has the same name, but she is no relation,
and you have never met her. A young maiden straight
from the plains, from the tribe called Bayaut. I have provided for her an ample dowry and the usual rich bridal furnishings and a retinue of servants and maids, and she is
ready to journey to Persia to meet her pledged husband.
However, to send her overland would mean her having to
traverse the territories of the Ilkhan Kaidu. That das-
tardly cousin of mine is as unruly as ever, and you know
how inimical he always has been to his cousins who hold
the Ilkhanate of Persia. I would not put it past Kaidu to
capture the Lady Kukachin on her way and hold her—
either to demand a ransom payment from Arghun or just
to enjoy the spitefulness of the deed."

"You wish us to escort her through that unsafe territory?"

"No. I had rather she avoided it altogether. My notion is
to send her the whole way by sea. However, all my ships'
captains are of the Han, and vakh!—the Han mariners performed so disappointingly during our attempted invasions
of Jihpen-kwe that I hesitate to trust them with this mission. But you and your uncles are also of a seafaring people. You are familiar with the open sea and with the
handling of ships."

"True, Sire, but we have never actually *sailed* one."

"Oh, the Han can do that well enough. I should ask you
only to be in command. To keep a stern eye on the Han captains, so *they* do not run off with the lady, or sell her to pi-
rates. or lose her along the way. And you would keep an
eye on the course, so the captains do not sail the whole fleet
off the edge of the world."

"Yes, we could see to those things, Sire."

"You would again carry my pai-tzu, and have unques-

tioned and unlimited authority, both on the sea and at
every landfall you may have to make. It would mean comfortable traveling for you, from here to Persia, in good
shipboard accommodations, with good food and good servants all the way. Especially it would mean easy travel for
the invalid Mafìo, and attendants to care for him. You
would be met in Persia by a train sent to fetch the Lady
Kukachin, and you would be well and comfortably transported to wherever Arghun is currently making his capital. And surely he would see that you have good transport
from there onward. So, Marco, that is the mission. Would
you confer with your uncles and consider undertaking it?"

"Why, Sire, I am certain that I can speak now for all of
us. We would not only be honored to do it, and eager, we
are obligated to you for making the journey so easy for us."

And so, while the bridal fleet was being assembled and
provisioned, my father did the final clearing up of some
loose ends of our Compagnia's business, and I attended to
some loose ends of my own affairs. I dictated to Kubilai's
court scribes a letter to be enclosed with the next official
dispatch the Khakhan sent to the Wang Bayan in Ava. I
sent warm greetings and regards and farewells to my old
friend, and then suggested that, since the nation of Muong
Thai was to be left free and uninvaded, I would take it as a
personal favor if Bayan would see to it that the little Pagan maidservant Arùn was given her liberty and conveyed
safely to that land of her own people.

Then, from the last Kithai gains of the Compagnia Polo,
which my father had converted into portable goods for us
to carry home, I took my share—a parcel of fine rubies—
and carried it only as far as the chambers of the Finance
Minister Lin-ngan. He was the first Khanbalik courtier I
had met, and the first to whom I now said my goodbyes in
person. I gave him the parcel of gems and asked him to use
their value to make payment of a bequest to the Khakhan's page boys, as each of them reached manhood, so they
would have a start when they set out to seek their own fortunes.

Then I went about the palace, saying my farewells to
other people. Some of my calls were for duty's sake: on
such dignitaries as the Hakim Gansui and the Khatun
Jamui, Kubilai's aged premier wife. And some of my calls
were less formal, but still brief: on the Court Astronomer

and the Court Architect. And one call I made—on the Palace Engineer Wei—was just to thank him for having constructed that garden pavilion in which Hui-sheng had enjoyed the warbling water-piped music. And one call I made—on the Minister of History—was just to tell him:

"Now you can write in your archives another trifle. In the Year of the Dragon, by the Han count the year three thousand nine hundred ninety, the foreigner Po-lo Mah-ko finally left the City of the Khan to return to his native Wei-ni-si."

He smiled, remembering our one conversation so long ago, and said, "Do I record that Khanbalik was made better by his presence here?"

"That is for Khanbalik to say, Minister."

"No, that is for history to say. But here—see—" He took up a brush, wetted his ink block and wrote, on a paper already crowded with writing, a vertical line of characters. Among them I recognized the character that was on my yin seal. "There. The trifle is mentioned. Come back in a hundred years, Polo, or in a thousand, and see if this trifle is still remembered."

Others of my farewell visits were more warm and lingering. In fact, three of them—my calls on the Court Firemaster Shi Ix-me and the Court Goldsmith Pierre Boucher and especially my call on Chao Meng-fu, War Minister, Court Artist, once fellow conspirator—each lasted long into the night and concluded only when we were too drunk to drink more.

When word came that the ships were ready and waiting for us at the port of Quan-zho, my father and I led Uncle Mafìo to the Khakhan's chambers for our introduction to our lady charge. Kubilai first presented to us the three envoys who had come to procure her for the Ilkhan Arghun—their names were Uladai, Koja and Apushka—and then the Lady Kukachin, who was a girl of seventeen, as pretty as any Mongol female I had ever seen, dressed in finery designed to dazzle all Persia. But the young lady was not haughty and imperious, as might have been expected in a noblewoman on her way to become an Ilkhatun, heading an entourage of nearly six hundred, counting all her servants, maids, noble courtiers-to-be and escorting soldiers. As befitted a girl so suddenly promoted from a plains tribe—where probably her entire court had consisted of a horse herd—Kukachin was forthright and natural and pleasant of manner.

"Elder Brothers Polo," she said to us, "it is with the utmost trust and confidence that I put myself in the keeping of such renowned journeyers."

She and the leading nobles of her company and the three envoys from Persia and we three Polos and most of the Khanbalik court all sat down with Kubilai to a farewell banquet in the same vast chamber where we had enjoyed our welcoming banquet so long before. It was a sumptuous feast, and even Uncle Mafìo appeared to enjoy it—he being fed by his constant and faithful woman servant, who would remain with him as far as Persia—and the night was riotous with many and varied entertainments (Uncle Mafìo at one point rising to sing to the Khakhan a verse or two of his well-worn "Virtue" song) and everyone got exceedingly drunk on the liquors which the gold-and-silver serpent tree still dispensed on call. Before we got quite unconscious, my father and I and Kubilai made our mutual leavetakings, a process as lengthy and emotional and replete with embraces and fulsome toasts and speeches as a Venetian wedding.

But Kubilai also managed one private short colloquy with me. "Although I have known your uncles longer, Marco, I have known you best, and I shall be sorriest for your going. Hui, I remember, the first words you ever spoke to me were insulting." He laughed in recollection. "That was not wise of you, but it was brave of you, and it was right of you to speak so. Ever since then, I have relied much on your words, and I shall be the poorer for hearing no more of them. I will hope that you may come this way again. I will not be here to greet you. But you would be doing me a service still, if you befriended and served my grandson Temur with the same dedication and loyalty you have shown to me." He laid a heavy hand on my shoulder.

I said, "It will always be my proudest boast, Sire, and my only claim to having lived a useful life, that once, for a while, I served the Khan of All Khans."

"Who knows?" he said jovially. "The Khan Kubilai may be remembered only because he had for good adviser a man named Marco Polo." He gave my shoulder a companionable shake. "Vakh! Enough of sentiment. Let us drink and get drunk! And then"—he raised to me a jeweled beaker brimming with arkhi—"a good horse and a wide plain to you, good friend."

"Good friend," I dared to echo, raising my goblet, "a good horse and a wide plain to you."

And the next morning, with heavy heads and not entirely light hearts, we took our departure. Just getting that populous train out of Khanbalik was a tactical problem very nearly on the order of the Orlok Bayan's moving his tuk of warriors about in the Ba-Tang valley—and this was a herd consisting mostly of civilians not trained in military discipline. So, the first day, we did not get farther than the next village to the south, where we were received with cheers and thrown flowers and hosannahs and incense and bursts of the fiery trees. We did not make much better progress on the succeeding days, either, because of course every least village and town wanted to display its enthusiasm. Even after we got our company accustomed to forming up and moving out each morning, the train was so immense—my father and I and the three envoys, like most of the servants and all the escort troops, mounted on horses; the Lady Kukachin and her women and my Uncle Mafìo riding in horse-borne palanquins; a number of Khanbalik nobles riding elephant haudas; plus all the pack animals and drovers necessary for the luggage of six hundred persons—that we made a procession sometimes stretching the entire length of the road between the community where we had just spent the night and the next one we were bound for. Our final destination, the port of Quan-zho, was much farther south than I had ever been in Manzi—very far south of Hang-zho, my onetime city of residence—so the journey took an unconscionably long time. But it was an enjoyable journey because, for a change, the column was not of soldiers going to war, and we were welcome everywhere we arrived.

2

AT last we got to Quan-zho, and some of our escorting troops and nobles and the pack train turned back for Khanbalik, and the rest of us filed on board the great

chuan ships, and at the next tide we put out into the Sea of
Kithai. We made a water-borne procession even more imposing than our land parade had been, for Kubilai had provided an entire fleet: fourteen of the massive four-masted
vessels, each crewed by some two hundred mariners. We
had apportioned our company among them, my father and
uncle and I and the envoy Uladai aboard the one carrying
the Lady Kukachin and most of her women. The chuan
vessels were good and solid, of the triple-planked construction, and our cabins were luxuriously furnished, and I
think every one of us passengers had four or five servants
from the lady's entourage to wait upon us, in addition to
the sea stewards and cooks and cabin boys also seeing to
our comfort. The Khakhan had promised good accommodations and service and food, and I will give just one instance
to illustrate how the ships lived up to that promise. On
each of the fourteen vessels there was one seaman detailed
to a single job throughout the voyage: he kept forever
paddling and stirring the water in a deck tank the size of a
lotus pool, in which swam *freshwater* fish for our tables.

My father and I had little to do in the way of command or
supervision. The captains of the fourteen vessels had been
sufficiently impressed and awed, to see us white men
striding magisterially aboard with the Khakhan's pai-tzu
tablets slung on our chests, that they were commendably
sedulous and punctilious in all their responsibilities. As
for making sure that the fleet did not wander about, I
would from time to time stand conspicuously on deck at
night, eyeing the horizon through the Kamàl I had kept
ever since Suvediye. Though that little wooden frame told
me nothing except that we were bearing constantly south,
it always brought our ship's captain scurrying to assure
me that we were unswervingly keeping proper course.

The only complaint we passengers might have voiced
was about the slowness of our progress, but that was
caused by our captains' devotion to their duty and our comfort. The Khakhan had chosen the ponderous chuan vessels especially to ensure for the Lady Kukachin a safe and
smooth voyage, and the very stability of the big ships
made them exceedingly slow in the water, and the necessity for all fourteen to stay together imposed even more
slowness. Also, whenever the weather looked at all threatening, the captains would steer for a sheltered cove. So, in-

stead of making a straight southward run across the open
sea, the fleet followed the far longer westering arc of the
coastline. Also, though the ships were lavishly provisioned
with food and other supplies for fully two years' sailing,
they could not carry enough drinking water for more than
a month or so. To replenish those supplies, we had to put in
at intervals, and those were lengthier stops than the occasional shelterings. Just the heaving-to and anchoring of
such a numerous fleet of such leviathan ships occupied
most of a day. Then the rowing back and forth of barrels in
the ships' boats took another three or four days, and the
weighing of anchor and setting sail again took yet another
day. So every watering stop cost us about a week's progress. After leaving Quan-zho, I remember, we stopped for
water at a great island off Manzi, called Hainan, and at a
harbor village on the coast of Annam in Champa, called
Gai-dinh-thanh, and at an island as big as a continent,
called Kalimantan. In all, we were three months making
just the southward leg of our voyage down the coast of Asia
before we could turn westward in the direction of Persia.

"I have watched you, Elder Brother Marco," said the
Lady Kukachin, coming up to me on deck one night,
"standing here from time to time, manipulating a little
wooden device. Is that some Ferenghi instrument of navigation?"

I went and fetched it, and explained to her its function.

"It might be a device unknown to my pledged husband,"
she said. "And I might gain favor in his eyes if I introduced
him to it. Would you show me how to employ it?"

"With pleasure, my lady. You hold it at arm's length,
like this, toward the North Star—" I stopped, appalled.

"What is the matter?"

"The North Star has vanished!"

It was true. That star had, every night lately, been lower
toward the horizon. But I had not sought it for several
nights, and now I was aghast to see that it had sunk entirely out of view. The star which I had been able to see almost every night of my life, the steadfast beacon which
throughout history had guided all journeyers on land and
sea, had totally *gone from the sky.* That was frightening—to see the one constant, immutable, fixed thing in the
universe disappear. We might really have sailed over

some farthest edge of the world, and fallen into some unknown abyss.

I frankly confess that it made me uneasy. But, for the
sake of Kukachin's confidence in me, I tried to dissemble
my anxiety as I summoned the ship's captain to us. In as
steady a voice as possible, I inquired what had become of
the star, and how he could keep a course or know his position without that fixed point of reference.

"We are now below the bulge of the world's waist," he
said, "where the star is simply not visible. We must rely on
other references."

He sent a cabin boy running to the ship's bridge to bring
him back a chart, and he unrolled it for me and Kukachin.
It was not a depiction of the local coasts and landmarks,
but of the night sky: nothing but painted dots of different
sized indicating stars of different luminosities. The captain pointed upward, showing us the four brightest stars in
the sky—positioned as if marking the arms of a Christian
cross—and then pointed to their four dots on the paper. I
recognized that the chart was an accurate representation
of those unfamiliar skies, and the captain assured us that
it was sufficient for him to steer by.

"The chart appears as useful as your kamàl, Elder
Brother," Kukachin said to me, and then to the captain,
"Would you have a copy made for me—for my Royal Husband, I mean, in case he should ever wish to campaign
southward from Persia?"

The captain obligingly and immediately set a scribe to
doing that, and I voiced no more misgivings about the lost
North Star. However, I still felt a little uneasy in those
tropic seas, because even the sun behaved oddly there.

What I had always thought of as "sunset" might have
been better called "sunfall" there, for the sun did not ease
itself down from the sky each evening and gently settle beneath the sea—it made a sudden and precipitous *plunge*.
There was never a flamboyant sunset sky to admire, nor
any gradual twilight to soothe the way from day to night.
One moment we would be in bright daylight, and in little
more than an eye blink we would be in dark night. Also,
there was never any perceptible change in the length of
day and night. Everywhere from Venice to Khanbalik, I
had been accustomed to the long days and short nights of
summertime, and the opposite in wintertime. But, in all

the months we spent making our way through the tropics, I never could notice any seasonal lengthening of either day or night. And the captain verified that: he told me that the difference between the tropics' longest day of the year and the shortest was only three-quarters of an hour's trickle of sand in the glass.

Three months out from Quan-zho, then, we came to our farthest southern reach, in the archipelago of the Spice Islands, where we would alter course to the westward. But first, since our water needed replenishment again, we made landfall at one of the islands, called Jawa the Greater. From the moment we first saw it on the horizon until we reached it, a good half a day later, we passengers were already saying among ourselves that this must be a most felicitous place. The airs were warm and so laden with the heady aromas of spices that we were almost made giddy, and the island was a tapestry of rich greens and flower colors, and the sea all about was the soft, translucent, glowing color of milk-green jade. Unfortunately, our first impression of having found an island of Paradise did not endure.

Our fleet anchored in the mouth of a river called Jakarta, offshore of a port called Tanjung Priok, and my father and I went ashore with the water-barrel boats. We discovered the so-called seaport to be only a village of zhugan cane houses built on high stilts because all the land was quagmire. The community's grandest edifices were some long cane platforms, with palm-thatch roofs but no walls, piled with bags of spices—nuts and barks and pods and powders—waiting for the next passing trade ship. What we could see of the island beyond the village was only dense jungle growing out of more quagmire. The warehouses of spices did provide an aroma that overwhelmed the jungle's miasmic smell and the stench common to all tropical villages. But we learned that this island of Jawa the Greater was only by courtesy called one of the Spice Islands, for nothing more valuable than pepper grew here, and the better spices—nutmeg and clove and mace and sandal and so on—grew on more remote islands of the archipelago and were merely collected in this place because it was more convenient to the sea lanes.

We also soon discovered that Jawa had no Paradise climate, for we had no sooner got ashore than we were drenched by a thunderstorm. Rain falls on that island one day of every three, we were told, and usually in the form of a thunderstorm which, we did not have to be told, was a fair imitation of the end of the world. I trust that, after our eventual departure, Jawa enjoyed an uncommonly long spell of fine weather, because we had nothing but bad. That first storm simply continued, day and night, for weeks, the thunder and lightning taking a rest now and then, but the rain falling interminably, and we rode it out there at anchor in the river mouth.

Our captains had intended to go west from this place through the narrow passage called the Sunda Strait, which separates Jawa the Greater from the next westward island, Jawa the Lesser, also called Sumatera. They said that strait allowed the easiest run to India, but they also said the strait could only be negotiated in calm seas and unimpeded visibility. So our our fleet stayed in the Jakarta River mouth, where the downpour was so continuous and so heavy that Jawa was not even visible through it. But we knew the island was still there, because we were waked at every dawn by the howling and whistling of the gibbon apes in the jungle treetops. It was not really an uncomfortable place to be marooned—our boatmen brought from shore fresh pork and fowl and fruits and vegetables to augment our stores of smoked and salted foods, and we had a plenitude of spices to enhance our meals—but the waiting got extremely tiresome.

Whenever I got insupportably weary of seeing nothing but the harbor water jumping up to meet the rain, I would go ashore, but the view there was not much better. The Jawa people were quite comely of appearance—small and neatly proportioned and of golden skin, and the women as well as the men went bare to the waist—but the entire populace of Jawa, whatever religion it had originally espoused, had long ago been converted to Hinduism by the Indians who were the chief spice buyers. Inevitably, the Jawa people had adopted everything else that seems to go with the Hindu religion, meaning squalor and torpor and reprehensible personal habits. So I found the people no more appealing than any other Hindus, and Jawa no more appealing than India.

Some of the others of our company tried to alleviate their boredom in other ways, and came to grief by it. All

the Han crewmen of our fleet, like mariners of every race
and nationality, were mortally terrified of getting into
water. But the Jawa people were quite at home on it and in
it as well. A Jawa fisherman would skim about on even a
turbulent sea in a craft called a prau, so small and flimsy
that it would have been careened by the waves except that
it was balanced by a log carried at some distance alongside
on long cane spars. And even the Jawa women and children swam considerable distances from the shore through
quite fearsome surf. So a number of our Mongol male passengers, and a few venturesome females, all of them
inland-born and therefore incautious about large bodies of
water, decided to emulate the Jawa folk and frolic in that
warm sea.

Though the ambient air, full of the downpouring rain,
was almost as liquid as the sea, the Mongols stripped down
to a minimum of clothing and slid overboard to splash
about. As long as they held onto the many rope ladders
dangling overside, they were in no great danger. But many
got overdaring, and tried swimming at liberty, and of
every ten of them who vanished beyond the curtain of rain,
perhaps seven would reappear. We never knew what happened to the missing ones, but the attrition kept on. It did
not frighten others from venturing out, and we must have
lost at least twenty men and two women from Kukachin's
retinue.

We did know what happened to two of our casualties.
One man who had been swimming climbed back onto the
ship, cursing "Vakh!" to himself and shaking drops of
blood from one hand. As the ship's Han physician salved it
and bound it up, the man reported that he had rested his
hand on a rock, and a fish had been clinging to it, a fish
mottled with algae and looking just like the rock, and its
dorsal spines had stung him. He said that much, and then
screamed, "Vakh! Vakh! Vakhvakhvakh!" and went into
insane paroxysms, thrashing all about the deck, foaming
at the mouth, and when he finally slumped in a heap, we
found that he was dead.

A Jawa fisherman, who had just brought his catch to sell
to us, regarded that performance without emotion, and
then said—a Han crewman translating—"The man must
have touched a stonefish. It is the most venomous creature
in any sea. Touch it, you endure such terrible agony that

you go mad before you die. If that happens to anyone else, split a ripe durian and apply it to his wound. It is the only remedy."

I knew that the durian had many praiseworthy qualities—I had been voraciously eating of them ever since I discovered that they grew in profusion here—but I would never have suspected that the fruit had medicinal qualities. However, soon afterward, one of Kukachin's hairdressing women also went for a swim, and came back weeping from the pain of a spine-stung arm, and the physician tried the durian remedy. To everyone's pleased surprise, it worked. The girl suffered no more than a swollen and painful arm. The physician made a careful note for his collection of materia medica, saying in some amazement, "As nearly as I can judge, the durian pulp somehow *digests* the stonefish poison before it can take dire effect."

And we also saw what accounted for the loss of another two of our company. The rain had finally stopped, and the sun had come out, and our captains were all standing on their decks, scrutinizing the sky and waiting to see if the weather might continue fine, long enough for us to up anchor and be away, and they were muttering Han incantations to make it so. The jade-green Jawa Sea that day looked so pretty as almost to tempt *me* into it—a gentle chop, fish-scaled with glittering lunettes of light—and did tempt two other men, Koja and Apushka, two of the three envoys of the Ilkhan Arghun. They challenged each other to a water race to a distant reef, and plunged from the chuan's side and went flailing and splashing away, and we all gathered at the rail to cheer them on.

Then down from the sky swooped a number of albatrosses. The birds, I suppose, had been balked in their usual fishing by the long spell of rain, and were weary of scavenging our ships' garbage and wanted some fresh meat. They began making dives at the two swimmers, stabbing their long hooked beaks at whatever parts of the men showed above the water, which was their heads. Koja and Apushka stopped swimming, trying to fend off the clustering birds and stay above water at the same time. We could hear them shouting, then cursing, then screaming, and see the blood running down their faces. And, when the albatrosses had plucked the eyes out of both of them, the men in desperation sank under water. They tried to rise up for a gasp of air a time or two, but the birds were waiting. And finally the two men simply let themselves drown, in preference to being torn to pieces. But, of course, as soon as their bodies floated limply and soggily on the surface, the albatrosses settled on them and peeled and shredded them for all the rest of that day.

It was sad, that Apushka and Koja had come safely through the countless hazards of journeying overland from Persia to Kithai, and then the long sea way to here, to die so abruptly and in such an un-Mongol-like way. We were all, Kukachin especially, much grieved by the loss. We did not think to take it as a premonition of any future and perhaps more grievous loss—my father did not even murmur about "bad things always happening in threes"—though, as events turned out, we might well have seen an omen in it.

When the weather had kept bright and clear for two more days, our captains decided to trust that it would go on holding. The crews were set to their immense oar beams, and rowed our ponderous ships slowly out of the river mouth to the open sea, and the vast slatted sails were raised, and we again were taken by the wind, and turned westward toward home. But when we had rounded a high headland and turned southwest into a channel narrow enough that we could see another distant coast on our other side, a mast-top lookout on the leading ship called down. He did not cry one of the usual curt sea calls, like "Ship in sight!" or "Reefs ahead!"—no doubt because there *was* no accepted and abbreviated call for what he saw. He only shouted down, in a voice of wonderment, "Look how the sea boils!"

All of us on the decks went to look overside—and that is exactly what the Sunda Strait seemed to be doing: boiling and bubbling, like a pot of water set on a brazier to make cha. And then, right in the middle of the fleet, the sea heaved up in a hump, opened like a monster mouth and exhaled a great gust of steam. The plume kept spewing upwards for several minutes, and the steam drifted all among the ships. We passengers had been making exclamations of one kind or another, but when the cloud of steam enveloped us we began to cough and sputter, for it had the suffocating stench of rotten eggs. And when the steam had passed over us, we were all dusted with a fine yellow powder on our skin and clothes. I wiped the dust from my stinging eyes and licked it from my lips, and tasted the distinctive musty taste of sulphur.

The captains were shouting to their crews, and there was a deal of running about and shifting of sail spars, and all our ships turned about and fled the way they had come. When the boiling and belching patch of sea was safely behind us, our vessel's captain told me, apologetically:

"Farther along the strait lies the brooding black ring of sea mountains called the Pulau Krakatau. Those peaks are actually the tops of undersea volcanoes, and they have been known to erupt with devastating effect. Making waves as high as mountains, waves that scour the strait clean of every living thing, from end to end. Whether that boiling of the water yonder presaged an eruption I cannot know, but we cannot take the risk of sailing through."

So the fleet had to double back through the Jawa Sea and then turn northwestward up the Malacca Strait between Jawa the Lesser, or Sumatera, and the land of the Malayu. That was a reach of water three thousand li long and so broad I might have taken it for a sea, except that circumstances forced us to carom back and forth from one side of it to the other, so I knew well that there was extensive land on both verges of it, and got to know those lands rather better than I would have wished. What happened was that the weather turned foul again, and perniciously stayed so, harrying us constantly from the swampy western Sumatera side to the forested eastern Malayu side of the strait and back again, and making us take shelter in bays or coves on one shore or the other—and put in for water and fresh foods at wretched little cane villages too negligible to deserve names, though they all had names: Muntok and Singapura and Melaka and many others I have forgotten.

It took us fully five months to beat our way up the Malacca Strait. There was open sea at the northern end, where we might have turned due west, but our captains kept on northwestward, sailing us in prudent short lunges from one island to the next of a long string of islands called the Necuveram and Angamanam archipelago, using them in the manner of stepping-stones. Finally we came to the island that they said was the farthermost of the Angamanam, and there we anchored offshore and passed enough time to fill all our water tanks and take on all the fruits and vegetables we could wheedle out of the inhospitable natives.

Those were the smallest people I ever saw, and the ugliest. Men and women alike went about stark naked, but the sight of an Angamanam female would arouse no least lust even in a mariner long at sea. Men and women alike were squat and chunky of form, with enormous protruding underjaws, and skin blacker and glossier than any African's. I could easily have rested my chin atop the head of the tallest person among them—except that I would not have done any such thing, because their hair was their most repellent feature: merely random tufts of reddish fuzz. One would expect a people so grotesquely ugly to try to make up for it by cultivating a gracious nature, but the Angamanam folk were uniformly scowling and surly. That was because, a Han seamen told me, they were disappointed and irate that we had not wrecked a vessel or two of our fleet on the island's coral reefs, for the people's only occupation and only religion and only joy was the plundering of grounded ships and the slaughter of their crews and the ceremonial eating of them.

"Eating them? Why?" I asked. "Surely no inhabitants of a tropic isle, with all the provender of sea and jungle, can lack for food to eat."

"They do not eat the shipwrecked mariners for nourishment. They believe that the ingestion of an adventurous seafarer makes *them* as bold and venturesome as he was."

But we were too many and too well armed for the black dwarfs to make any assault on us. Our only problem was persuading them to part with their water and vegetables, for of course such people had no interest in gold or any other sort of monetary recompense. They did, however, like so many hopelessly ugly folk, have a high vanity. So, by doling out among them bits of trumpery cheap jewelry and ribbons and other fripperies with which they could adorn their unspeakable selves, we got what we required, and we sailed away.

From there, our fleet had an uneventful westward run across the Bay of Bangala, which is the only foreign sea that I have now traversed three times, and I will be gratified if I never have to do so again. This crossing was somewhat more to the southerly than my other two had been,

but the view was the same: an infinite expanse of azure
water with little white trapdoors of foam opening and closing here and there, as if mermaids were taking peeps at
the upper world, and herds of porkfish frisking about our
hulls, and so many flying-fish hurtling aboard that our
cooks, having long since depleted our tanks of Manzi freshwater fish, periodically collected them from the decks and
made us meals of them.

The Lady Kukachin humorously inquired, "If those
Angamanam people acquired courage by eating courageous people, will these meals make us able to fly like
flying-fish?"

"More likely make us smell like them," grumbled the
maid who attended her bathing chamber. She was disgruntled because, on this long run across the bay, the captains had commanded that we could bathe only in sea
water dipped up in buckets, not to waste the fresh. Salt
water gets one clean enough, but it leaves one cursedly
gritty and scratchy and uncomfortable afterward.

3

AT the western side of the great bay, we made landfall on
the island of Srihalam. That was not far south of the Cholamandal of India, where I had earlier made sojourn, and
the islanders were physically very similar to the Cholas
and, like the Cholas, the island's coastal residents were
mainly engaged in the trade of fishing for pearls. But there
the similarity ended.

The Srihalam islanders had adhered to the religion of
Buddha, hence were vastly superior to their mainland
Hindu cousins in morals and customs and vivacity and personal appeal. Their island was a lovely place, tranquil and
lush and of generally balmy weather. I have often noticed
that the most beautiful places are given a multiplicity of
names: witness the Garden of Eden, which is also variously called Paradise and Arcadia and Elysium and even
Djennet by the Muslims. Just so, Srihalam has been severally named by every people who ever admired it. The ancient Greeks and Romans called it Taprobane, meaning

Lotus Pond, and the early Moorish seafarers called it
Tenerism, or Isle of Delight, and nowadays Arab mariners
call it Serendib, which is only their faulty pronunciation of
the islanders' own name for the place, Srihalam. That
name, Place of Gems, is variously translated in other languages: Ilanare by the mainland Cholas, Lanka by other
Hindus, Bao Di-fang by our Han captains.

Though we had put into Srihalam of necessity, for water
and other supplies, our captains and crews and Lady Kukachin and her retinue and I and my father were not a bit
reluctant to tarry there for a while. My father even did
some trading—the name Place of Gems being descriptive
as well as poetic—and acquired some sapphires of a fineness we had never seen elsewhere, including some immense, deep-blue stones with starlike rays coruscating in
their depths. I did not engage in any business, but merely
wandered about to see the sights. Those included some ancient cities, deserted and abandoned to the jungle, but still
displaying a beauty of architecture and adornment that
made me wonder if these people of Srihalam could be the
remnants of the admirable race that had inhabited India
before the Hindus, and had built the temples which the
Hindus now pretended were their own.

Our ship's captain and I, glad to be stretching our legs
after so long on shipboard, spent a couple of days climbing
all the way to the shrine at the top of a mountain peak
where, as I had once been told by a pongyi in Ava, the Buddha had left his footprint. I should say that *Buddhists* call
it the imprint of the Buddha. Hindu pilgrams aver that it
is the print of their god Siva, and Muslim pilgrims insist
that it was made by Adam, and some Christian visitors
have surmised that it must have been done by San Tom-
maso or Prete Zuàne, and my Han companion gave it as
his opinion that it had been put there by Pan-ku, the Han
ancestor of all mankind. I am no Buddhist, but I am inclined to think that the oblong indentation in the rock
there—nearly as long and as broad as I am—must have
been done by the Buddha, because I have seen his tooth
and I *know* him to have been a giant, and I have never personally beheld any evidence pertaining to the other claimants.

To be honest, I was less interested in the footprint than
in a story told to us by the shrine's attendant bhikku (as a

pongyi was called in Srihalam). He said the island was rich in gems *because* the Buddha had spent time there, and had wept for the wickedness of the world, and each of his holy tears had congealed into a ruby, an emerald or a sapphire. But, said the bhikku, those gems could not just be picked up from the ground. They had all washed into valleys in the interior of the island, and those chasms were unapproachable because they teemed and squirmed with venomous snakes. So the islanders had had to contrive an ingenious method for harvesting the precious stones.

In the mountain crags about the valleys nested eagles which preyed on the serpents. So the islanders would sneak at night among those crags and throw cuts of raw meat down into the chasms, and when the meat hit the ground down there, some few gems would stick to it. Next day, the foraging eagles would pick up and eat the meat in preference to the snakes. Then, whenever an eagle was absent from its nest, a man could climb up there and finger through the bird's droppings and pick out the undigested rubies, sapphires and emeralds. I not only thought that an ingenious method of mining, I also thought it must be the origin of all the legends about the monster rukh bird, which allegedly snatches up and flies off with even bigger meats, includings persons and elephants. When I got back to our ship, I told my father he ought to treasure his newly acquired sapphires for more than their inherent value—for their having been got for him by the fabled rukh.

We might have stayed on longer yet in Srihalam, but one day the Lady Kukachin remarked, rather wistfully, "We have been journeying for a whole year now, and the captain tells me that we are only about two-thirds of the way to our destination."

I knew the lady well enough by this time to know that she was not being sordidly greedy for her entitlement as Ilkhatun of Persia. She merely was eager to meet her betrothed and marry him. She was, after all, a year older now and still a spinster.

So we called an end to our tarrying, and pushed off from the pleasant island. We sailed northward, close along the western coast of India, and made the best time possible, for none of us had any desire to visit or explore any part of that land. We put in to shore only when our water barrels absolutely had to be replenished—at a fair-sized port called

Quilon, and at a river-mouth port called Mangalore, where we had to anchor far offshore of the delta flats, and at a settlement scattered over seven pimples of land called the Bombay islets, and at a dismal fishing village called Kurrachi.

Kurrachi at least had good fresh water, and we made sure our tanks were topped full, because from that point we were sailing directly west again, and for some two thousand li—or I should say, now that I was back again where Persian measurements were used, about three hundred farsakhs—we were skirting the dry, dun-colored, baking, thirsty desert coast of the empty land called Baluchistan. The view of that sere coastline was only occasionally enlivened by two things peculiar to it. All year round, a south wind blows from the sea into Baluchistan, so wherever we saw a tree it was always grown in a contorted arc, bending inland, like an arm beckoning us to come ashore. The other peculiarity of that coast was its mud volcanoes: dumpy cone-shaped hills of dried mud, every so often spewing a gush of new, wet mud from the top, to slither down and slowly bake and await a new gush and a new layer. It was a most uninviting land.

But, following that drear shore, we did at last enter the Strait of Hormuz, and that led us to the city of that name, and once again I was in Persia. Hormuz was a very big and bustling city, so populous that some of its residential quarters were spilling from the mainland city center over to the islands offshore. It was also Persia's busiest port, a forest of masts and spars, a tumult of noise and a medley of smells, most of them not nice. The ships tied up or coming and going were, of course, mostly Arab qurqurs and falukahs and dhaos, the biggest of them looking like dinghis and praus alongside our massive vessels. No doubt an occasional trading chuan had been seen here before, but surely never such a fleet as we now brought into the harbor roads. As soon as a pilot boat had fussily led us to anchorage, we were surrounded by the skiffs and scows and barges of every kind of vendor, guide, pimp and waterfront beggar, all of them screeching solicitations. And what appeared to be the entire remainder of the population of Hormuz was collected along the dockside, gawking and jabbering excitedly. However, among that mob we could see nothing like what we had expected—a resplendent gathering of nobles to welcome their new Ilkhatun-to-be.

"Curious," muttered my father. "Surely the word of our coming raced ahead of us along the coast. And the Ilkhan Arghun must by now have been getting mightily impatient and eager."

So, while he turned to the daunting job of commanding the debarkation of all our company and our gear, I hailed a karaji fery skiff and, fending off the solicitors, was the first to go ashore. I accosted an intelligent-looking citizen and made inquiry. Then I immediately had myself rowed back to our ship, to tell my father and the envoy Uladai and the anxious-eyed Kukachin:

"You may wish to postpone the debarkation until we have held conference. I am sorry to be the one to bring this news, but the Ilkhan Arghun died of an illness, many months ago."

The Lady Kukachin burst into tears, as sincerely as if the man had been her long-wedded and much-loved husband, instead of just a name to her. As the lady's maids helped her away to her suite of cabins, and my father thoughtfully chewed on a corner of his beard, Uladai said, "Vakh! I will wager that Arghun died at the very moment my fellow envoys Koja and Apushka perished in Jawa. We should have suspected something dire."

"We could not have done much about it, if we had," said my father. "The question is: what do we do now about Kukachin?"

I said, "Well, there is no Arghun waiting for her. And they told me ashore that his son Ghazan is still under age to succeed to the Khanate."

"That is correct," said Uladai. "I suppose his Uncle Kaikhadu is ruling as Regent in the meantime."

"So they say. And either this Kaikhadu knew nothing of his late brother's having sent for a new wife, or he is not at all interested in exercising any levirate right to take her for himself. Anyway, he has sent no embassy to meet her and no transport for her."

"No matter," said Uladai. "She comes from his Lord Khakhan, so he is obliged to relieve you of her care and take her into his own. We shall take her to the capital at Maragheh. As for transportation, you carry the Khakhan's pai-tzu. We have only to command the Shah of Hormuz to supply us with everything we require."

And that is what we did. The local Shah received us not just dutifully but hospitably, and lodged us all in his palace—though we filled it nearly to bursting—while he assembled all his own camels and probably every other one within his domain, and loaded them with provisions and water bags, and marshaled camel-pullers for them, and also troops of his own to augment ours, and in a few days we were journeying overland, northwest toward Maragheh.

It was a traverse as long as the one my father and uncle and myself had previously made across Persia from west to east. But this time, going south to north, we had no very terrible terrain to cross, for our route took us well west of the Great Salt Desert, and we had good riding camels and copious supplies, and plenty of attendants to do every bit of work for us, and a formidable guard against any possible molesters. So it was a fairly comfortable trip, if not a very merry one. The Lady Kukachin did not wear any of the bridal finery she had brought, but every day wore brown, the Persian color of mourning, and on her pretty face wore a look that was partly apprehensive of what her fate might now be, and partly resigned to it. Since all the rest of us had got very fond of her, we worried with her, but did everything we could to make the journey easy and interesting for her.

Our route did take us through a number of places where I or my father or my uncle—or all of us together—had been before, so my father and I were constantly looking to see what changes, if any, had occurred in the years since then. Most of our stops along the way were only for a night's sleep, but when we got to Kashan, my father and I commanded an extra day's stay, so we could stroll about that city where we had rested before our plunge into the forbidding Dasht-e-Kavir. We led Uncle Mafìo walking with us, in a sort of meager hope that those scenes of long ago might jar him back to a semblance of what he had been long ago. But nothing in Kashan woke any glimmer in his dulled eyes, not even the "prezioni" boys and young men who were still the city's most visible asset.

We went to the house and stable where the kindly Widow Esther had given us lodging. The place was now in the possession of a man, a nephew who had inherited it years ago, he said, when that good lady died. He showed us where she was buried—not in any Jewish cemetery but, at her own deathbed insistence, in the herb garden behind her own abode. That was where I had watched her pounding scorpions with her slipper, while she exhorted me never to neglect any opportunity to "taste everything in this world."

My father respectfully crossed himself, and then went on along the street, leading Uncle Mafìo, to go and look again at Kashan's kashi-tile workshops, the which had inspired him to set up the same in Kithai, and from which our Compagnia had realized such handsome profits. But I stayed on with the widow's nephew for a while, looking pensively down at her herb-grown grave and saying (but not aloud):

"I followed your advice, Mirza Esther. I let no chance go by untaken. I never hesitated to follow where my curiosity beckoned. I willingly went where there was danger in beauty and beauty in danger. As you foretold, I had experiences in plenty. Many were enjoyable, some were instructive, a few I would rather have missed. But I had them, and I have them still in memory. If, as soon as tomorrow, I go to *my* grave, it will be no black and silent hole. I can paint the darkness with vivid colors, and fill it with music both martial and languorous, with the flicker of swords and the flutter of kisses, with flavors and excitements and sensations, with the fragrance of a field of clover that has been warmed in the sun and then washed by a gentle rain, the sweetest-scented thing God ever put on this earth. Yes, I can enliven eternity. Others may have to endure it; I can enjoy it. For that I thank you, Mirza Esther, and I would wish you shalom . . . but I think that you, too, would not be happy in an eternity of nothing but peace. . . ."

A black Kashan scorpion came scrabbling along the garden path, and I stepped on it for her. Then I turned to the nephew and said, "Your aunt once had a house maid named Sitarè . . ."

"Another of her deathbed dispositions. Every old woman is a matchmaker at heart. She found for Sitarè a husband, and had them married in this house before she died. Neb Efendi was a cobbler, a good craftsman and a good man, though a Muslim. He was also an immigrant Turkì, which made him not very popular hereabout. But it also made him not a pursuer of boys, and I trust he was a good husband to Sitarè."

"Was?"

"They moved away from here shortly afterward. He was a foreigner, and evidently folk prefer to have their shoes made and mended by their home folk, even if they are inept in their work. So Neb Efendi picked up his awls and his lasts and his new wife and departed—to his native Cappadocia, I believe. I hope they are happy there. It was a long time ago."

Well, I was a little disappointed not to get to see Sitarè again, but only a little. She would be a matron now, of about my own middle age, and to see her might be even more of a disappointment.

So we pushed on, and eventually arrived at Maragheh. The Regent Kaikhadu did receive us, not grudgingly but not with wild enthusiasm either. He was a typical, shaggy Mongol man at arms, who clearly would have been more comfortable astride a horse, hacking with a blade at some battlefield opponent, than he was on the throne to which his brother's death had shoved him.

"I truly did not know of Arghun's embassy to the Khakhan," he told us, "or you may be sure I would have had you escorted hither in great pomp and ceremony, for I am a devoted subject of the Khakhan. Indeed, it is because I have spent all my time afield, fighting the Khanate's campaigns, that I was unaware of Arghun's canvass for a new wife. Right this minute, I should properly be putting down a band of brigands that are rampaging over in Kurdistan. Anyway, I do not know quite what to do with this woman you have brought."

"She is a handsome one, Lord Kaikhadu," said the envoy Uladai. "And a good-natured one."

"Yes, yes. But I already have wives—Mongol, Persian, Circassian, even one frightful Armeniyan—in yurtus scattered from Hormuz to Azerbaizhan." He threw up his hands distractedly. "Well, I suppose I can inquire among my nobles. . . ."

"We will stay," my father said firmly, "until we see the Lady Kukachin settled according to her station."

But the lady took care of that herself, before we had been many days in residence at the Maragheh palace. My father and I were airing Uncle Mafìo in a rose garden one after-

noon when she came running up to us, smiling for the first
time since our arrival at Hormuz. She also had someone in
tow: a boy, very short and ugly and pimply, but in courtier's rich attire.

"Elder Brothers Polo," she said breathlessly. "You need
fret over me no longer. By good fortune, I have met a most
wonderful man, and we plan shortly to announce our betrothal."

"Why, that is stupendous news," said my father, but
cautiously. "I do hope, my dear, that he is of suitably high
birth and position and prospects. . . ."

"The highest!" she said happily. "Ghazan is the son of
the man I came here to wed. He will be Ilkhan himself in
two years."

"Mefè, you could not have done better! Lassar la strada
vechia per la nova. Is this his page? Can he fetch the good
fellow for us to meet?"

"But this is he. This is the Crown Prince Ghazan."

My father had to swallow before he could say, "Sain
bina, Your Royal Highness," and I bowed deeply to give
myself time to compose my face to sobriety.

"He is two years younger than myself," Kukachin chattered on, not giving the boy much chance to speak for himself. "But what is two years in a lifetime of happy
marriage? We will be wed as soon as he ascends to the Ilkhanate. In the meantime, you dear devoted Elder Brothers
can leave me in good conscience, knowing I am in good
hands, and go on about your own affairs. I shall miss you,
but I shall not be lonely or despondent any more."

We made the proper congratulations and good wishes,
and the boy grinned like an ape and mumbled acknowledgment, and Kukachin beamed as if she had just won an
unimaginably great trophy, and the two of them went off
hand in hand.

"Well," said my father with a shrug, "better the head of
a cat than the tail of a lion."

But Kukachin must have seen in the boy what we could
not. God knows he could never have been better than a
goblin for looks and physical stature—he was afterward
styled in all the Mongol chronicles "Ghazan the Ugly"—
but the fact that he did make history is proof that he was
more than he appeared to be. He and the lady were wed
when he replaced Kaikhadu as Ilkhan of Persia, and then

he went on to become the ablest Ilkhan and warrior of his generation, making many wars and winning many new lands for the Khanate. Unhappily, his loving Ilkhatun Kukachin did not live to share all his triumphs and celebrity, for she died in childbirth two years or so after their marriage.

4

So, having completed our last mission for the Khan Kubilai, my father and uncle and I pressed onward. We left at Maragheh the populous company we had so far been traveling with, but Kaikhadu generously gave us good horses and remounts and packhorses and ample provisions and an escort of a dozen mounted men of his own palace guard, to see us safely through all the Turki lands. However, as things turned out, we would have traveled more safely without that Mongol troop.

From the capital, we circled around the shores of a sea-sized lake named Urumia, which was also called the Sea of the Sunset. Then we climbed up and over the mountains which marked the northwestern frontier of Persia. One of the mountains in that range, said my father, was the biblical Mount Ararat, but it was too far off our route for me to go and climb it to see if any trace of the Ark was still there. Anyway, having recently scaled another mountain to see a footprint that might well have been Adam's, I was now inclined to think of Noah as rather a latecomer in history. On the other side of the mountains, we descended into the Turki lands at another sea-sized lake, this one named Van, but called the Sea Beyond the Sunset.

The country hereabout, and the nations composing it, and the borders thereof, were all in flux and had been for many years. What had formerly been part of the Byzantine Empire under Christian rulers was now the Seljuk Empire under rulers of the Turki race and Muslim religion. But these eastern parts of it were also known by older names, bestowed by peoples who had inhabited these lands since time before time, who had never conceded that they were not still the rightful owners of them, and who recognized

none of the vagaries of modern claimants and modern
boundary lines. Thus, at the point where we emerged from
Persia, we came down from the mountains into a country
which could equally well be named Turki, after the race of
its rulers, or the Seljuk Empire, as those Turki called it, or
Cappadocia, which was its name on older maps, or Kurdistan, for the Kurdi people who populated it.

The land was a green and pleasant one, the wildest parts
of it seeming hardly wild at all, but looking almost neatly
cultivated, with rolling hills of meadow grass tidily separated by clumps of forest, so that the whole countryside
was as trim as an artificial parkland. There was plenty of
good water, in sparkling streams as well as immense blue
lakes. The people here were all Kurdi, some of them farmers and villagers, but most of them nomad families following flocks of sheep or goats. They were as handsome a race
as I have seen in any Islamic land. They had very black
hair and eyes, but a complexion as fair as my own. The
men were large and solidly built, and wore great black
mustaches, and were famously fierce fighters. The Kurdi
women were not particularly delicate, either, but withal
were well formed and good-looking—and independent;
they scorned to wear the veil or live hidden in the pardah
imposed on most other women of Islam.

The Kurdi received us journeyers cordially enough—
nomads usually are hospitable to other seeming nomads—
but they cast unloving looks at our Mongol escorts. There
were reasons for that. Besides all the other complications
of national names and dominions and boundary lines, this
Seljuk Empire was also in enforced vassalage to the Ilkhanate of Persia. That situation dated from the time when a
traitorous Turki minister had foully murdered the King
Kilij—he who was the father of my one-time princèss
friend Mar-Janah—and usurped the throne by promising
to lay it under subjection to the then Ilkhan Abagha. So
this Seljuk Empire, though nominally ruled now by a King
Masud in the capital city of Erzincan, was really subordinate to Abagha's surviving son, the Regent Kaikhadu,
whose Maragheh court we had just come from and whose
palace guards were accompanying us. We journeyers were
welcome here; the warriors with us were not.

One might have supposed that the Kurdi—rebellious
throughout history against *every* non-Kurdi ruler ever im-

posed upon them—would have cared little whether Erzincan or Maragheh was the real ruling capital, because out here, a hundred farsakhs or more from either city, they were pretty much left unruled by anybody. But they seemed to regard the Mongols as a tyranny inflicted on top of the Turki tyranny they already chafed under, and the one to be even more hotly resented and hated. We learned how well the Kurdi could hate when, one afternoon, we stopped at an isolated hut to buy a sheep for our evening meal.

The evident proprietor of the hut was sitting in the doorway of it, holding his sheepskin robes around him as if he had a chill. My father and I and just one of our Mongols rode into the dooryard and politely dismounted, but the shepherd impolitely did not stand up. The Kurdi had a language of their own, but almost all of them spoke Turki as well, and so did our Mongol escorts, and in any case the Turki tongue was similar enough to the Mongol that I could usually understand any overheard conversation. Our Mongol asked the man if we might buy a sheep. The man, still seated, his eyes glumly on the ground, refused us.

"I think I ought not to trade with our oppressors."

The Mongol said, "No one is oppressing you. These Ferenghi wayfarers ask a favor of you, and will pay for it, and your Allah enjoins hospitality toward wayfarers."

The shepherd said, not in an argumentative way, but in seeming melancholy, "But the rest of you are Mongols, and you will also eat on the sheep."

"What of that? Once you sell the animal to the Ferenghi, what matter to you what becomes of it?"

The shepherd sniffled and said, almost tearfully, "I did a favor to a passing Turki not long since. Helped him change a broken shoe on his horse. And for that I have been chastised by the Chiti Ayakkabi. A small favor for a mere Turki. Estag farullah! What will the Chiti do to me if he hears I did a favor for a *Mongol?*"

"Come!" snapped our escort. "Will you sell us a sheep?"

"No, I cannot."

The Mongol sneered down at him. "You do not even stand like a man when you speak defiance. Very well, cowardly Kurdi, you refuse to sell. Then would you care to stand up and try to prevent my *taking* a sheep?"

"No, I cannot. But I warn you. The Chiti Ayakkabi will make you regret the robbery."

The Mongol laughed harshly and spat in the dust in front of the seated man, then remounted and rode to cut a fat ewe out of the flock grazing in the meadow beyond the hut. I remained there, curious, staring down at the slumped and defeated-looking shepherd. I knew that Chiti meant a brigand and, as best I knew, Ayakkabi meant a shoe. I wondered what kind of bandit would style himself "the Shoe Brigand" and would occupy himself in punishing his own fellow Kurdi for giving aid and comfort to their presumed oppressors.

I managed to inquire of the man, "What did this Chiti Ayakkabi do to chastise you?"

He did not speak a reply, but showed me, lifting the skirts of his sheepskins to reveal his feet. It was evident why he had not stood to greet us, and I got some idea of why the Kurdi bandit had such a strange name. Both of the shepherd's feet, otherwise bare, were clotted with dried blood and studded with nails—not nail heads but the upthrusting points of nails—where both his feet had been shod with iron horseshoes.

Two or three nights later, near a village called Tunceli, the Chiti Ayakkabi made us regret our robbery of the sheep. Tunceli was a village of the Kurdi, and it had only one karwansarai, and that very small and dilapidated. Since our company of fifteen riders and thirty-odd horses would have crowded it intolerably, we rode on through the village and made camp in a grassy glade beyond, convenient to a clear-flowing brook. We had eaten and rolled ourselves in our blankets and gone to sleep, leaving just one Mongol on guard, when the night erupted with bandits.

Our lone sentry had only time to bellow *"Chiti!"* before he was brained with a battle-ax. The rest of us thrashed free of our bedrolls, but the brigands were among us, with blades and cudgels, and all was a confused turbulence in the dim remaining firelight. My father and I had Uncle Mafìo to thank that we were not slain as abruptly as all our Mongol troop. Those warriors thought first to snatch for their weapons, so the bandits flew first at them. But my father and I both saw Mafìo standing by the fire, looking about him in numb bemusement, and we both at the same

moment threw ourselves toward him, and seized him and
dragged him to the ground, so he made not such a prominent target. The next moment, something clouted me
above the ear and, for me, the night went totally dark.

I woke, lying on the ground with my head cradled in a
soft lap, and as my vision cleared I looked up into a female
face illumined by the now built-up fire. It was not the
square, strong face of a Kurdi woman, and it was framed
by a tumble of hair that was not black, but dark-red. I labored to collect my wits, and said in Farsi, in a voice that
croaked:

"Am I dead, and are you a peri now?"

"You are not dead, Marco Efendi. I saw you just in time
to cry to the men to desist."

"You used to call me Mirza Marco, Sitarè."

"Marco Efendi means the same. I am more of a Kurdi
now than a Persian."

"What of my father? My uncle?"

"They are not even bruised. I am sorry you had to take a
blow. Can you sit up?"

I did, though the movement threatened to make my
head roll off my shoulders, and I saw my father sitting
with a group of the black-mustached bandits. They had
made gahwah, and he and they were drinking and chatting amiably together, with Uncle Mafìo sitting placidly
by. It would have looked quite a civilized scene, except that
others of the brigands were stacking the bodies of our dead
Mongols like cordwood off to one side of the glade. The
largest and most fiercely mustached of the newcomers,
seeing me stir, came over to me and Sitarè.

She said, "This is my husband, Neb Efendi, known also
as Chiti Ayakkabi."

He spoke Farsi as well as she did. "I apologize to you,
Marco Efendi. I would not knowingly have attacked the
man who made possible the treasure of my life."

I was still addled in my wits, and did not know what he
was talking about. But as I drank bitter black gahwah and
my head gradually cleared, he and Sitarè explained. He
was the Kashan cobbler whom the Almauna Esther had
introduced to her maidservant Sitarè. He had loved her at
first sight, but their marriage would of course have been
unthinkable had Sitarè not been a virgin, and Sitarè had
told him frankly that her being still intact was thanks to a

certain gentlemanly Mirza Marco's having declined to take advantage of her. I felt more than a little uncomfortable, listening to a rough and murderous bandit expressing his indebtedness for my not having preceded him in making "sikis," as he called it, with his bride. But also, if I was ever grateful for my onetime constraint, it was now.

"Qismet, we call it," he said. "Destiny, fate, chance. You were good to my Sitarè. Now I am being good to you."

It further transpired that Neb Efendi, having been balked of prospering as a cobbler in Kashan—where the people did not know the difference between a noble Kurdi and a vile Turki, but would have despised him in any event—had brought his wife back here to his native Kurdistan. But here he felt also estranged, a vassal to the Turki regime which was in turn vassal to the Mongol Ilkhanate. So he had given up his trade entirely, keeping only the name of it, and turned to insurrection as the Shoe Brigand.

"I have seen some of your cobblery," I told him. "It was—distinctive."

He said modestly, "Bosh," which is a Turki word meaning "you flatter me overmuch."

But Sitarè nodded proudly. "You mean the shepherd. It was he who set us on your trail to Tunceli here. Yes, Marco Efendi, my dear and valorous Neb is determined to rouse up all Kurdi against the oppressors, and to discourage any weaklings who truckle to them."

"I had rather divined that."

"Do you know, Marco Efendi," he said, thumping a fist loudly against his broad chest, "that we Kurdi are the oldest aristocracy in the world? Our tribal names go back to the days of Sumer. And all that time we have been fighting one tyranny after another. We battled the Hittites, the Assyrians, we helped Cyrus overthrow Babylon. We fought with Salah-ed-Din the Great against the first marauding Crusaders. Not forty years ago, unaided, we slaughtered twenty thousand Mongols at the battle of Arbil. But still we are not free and independent. So now it is my mission—first to throw off from Kurdistan the Mongol yoke and then the Turki."

"I wish you success, Chiti Ayakkabi."

"Well, my band and I are poor and ill-equipped. But your

Mongols' weapons and your good horses and the considerable treasure in their packs will help us immensely."

"You are going to rob us? You call that being good to us?"

"I could have been less good." He waved casually at the bloody heap of dead Mongols. "Be glad your qismet decreed otherwise."

"Speaking of qismet," Sitarè said brightly, to distract me, "tell me, Marco Efendi. What of my darling brother Aziz?"

We were in a precarious enough situation, I decided, that I would not hazard making it more so. Neither she nor her ferocious mate would be overjoyed to hear that her little brother had been dead for more than twenty years, that we had let him be slain by a robber band very like their own. Anyway, I was loath to sadden an old friend unnecessarily. So I lied, and lied loudly enough that my father could overhear, and not later contradict me.

"We carried Aziz to Mashhad, as you desired, Sitarè, and we guarded his chastity the whole way. There, he was fortunate enough to catch the admiring eye of a fine and prosperously fat merchant prince. We left them together, and they seemed more than fond of each other. As far as I know, they are still trading together, up and down the Silk Road between Mashhad and Balkh. Aziz would by now be a well-grown man, but I have no doubt he is still as beautiful as he was then. And as you are, Sitarè."

"Al-hamdo-lillah, I hope so," she sighed. "I saw much resemblance to Aziz in my own two sons, as they grew up. But my manly Neb, not being a Kashanite, would not let me insert the golulè in our boys, or show them how to use cosmetics, in preparation for their someday securing male lovers. So they have grown up to be most manly men themselves, and they sikismek only with women. Those are the boys, over yonder, Nami and Orhon, stripping the boots off those dead Mongols. Would you believe, Marco Efendi, that my sons are both older than *you* were when last I saw you? Ah, well, it is good to have news of dear Aziz after all these years, and to know that he made as glowing a success of his life as I have made of mine. We owe it all to you, Marco Efendi."

"Bosh," I said modestly.

I could have suggested that we might be owed our own

possessions, but I did not. And my father, when he too realized that we were to be plundered, merely sighed in resignation and said, "Well, when there is no banquet, at least
the candles are happy."

True, our lives had been spared. And of our portable valuables I had already dispensed with a third part before we
left Khanbalik, and anyway they represented only a trifle
compared to what our Compagnia had earlier sent home
from Kithai. And the brigands took only the things they
could easily spend, sell or trade, meaning that they left us
our clothes and personal belongings. So, while we could
hardly rejoice at being robbed at this late stage in our long
journeying—we especially regretted the loss of the magnificent star sapphires acquired in Srihalam—we neither of
us repined too much.

Neb Efendi and his band did allow us to ride our own
horses as far as the coast city of Trebizond, and even rode
that far with us as a protection against any further Kurdi
assault, and they courteously refrained from slaughtering
or shoeing anyone else along the way. When we dismounted at the outskirts of Trebizond, the Chiti Ayakkabi
gave us back a handful of our own coin, sufficient to pay for
our transport and sustenance the rest of the way to Constantinople. So we and they parted in a friendly enough
way, and the Shoe Brigand did not strike me dead when
Sitarè, as she had done twenty-some years before, kissed
me a voluptuous and lingering goodbye.

At Trebizond, on the shore of the Euxine or Kara or
Black Sea, we were still more than two hundred farsakhs
east of Constantinople, but we were glad to be standing
again on Christian ground for the first time since we had
left Acre in the Levant. My father and I decided against
the purchase of new horses, not out of dread of the overland journey, but out of concern that it might be too hard
on Uncle Mafìo, with none but us now to take care of him.
So, carrying what was left of our packs, we went to the Trebizond waterfront and, after some search, found a barge-
like gektirme fishing boat whose Christian Greek captain
—he was captain of a crew consisting of his four loutish
sons—would, with Christian goodness, sail us to Constantinople, and would feed us on the way and, with Christian
goodness, would charge us only all we had.

It was a tediously slow and miserable voyage, for the

gektirme was netting all the way, and netting only anchovies, so anchovies were what we were fed all the way, with pilaf of rice cooked in anchovy oil, and we lived in, slept in, breathed in the smell of anchovies all the way. Besides us and the Greeks, there was a mangy dog aboard, for no discernible reason, and I frequently wished we had not already paid over every coin we possessed, so that I could have bought the dog and offered him up to be cooked, just for a change from the anchovies. But just as well. The dog had been aboard for so long that I suppose he would have tasted no different.

After nearly two dismal months aboard our floating anchovy-cask, we finally made our way into the strait called Bosphorus, and along it to where it met the estuary called the Golden Horn, and there we raised the great city of Constantinople—but on a day of such dense fog that I could not see and appreciate the city's magnificence. The fog did permit me, however, to learn the reason for the gektirme's resident dog. One of the sons beat it regularly with a stick as we crept cautiously through the fog, so that the dog barked and snarled and cursed continuously. I could hear other invisible dogs similarly yowling all about us, and our captain at the steering oar kept his ear cocked to the noises, so I perceived that dog-beating—instead of bell-ringing, as in Venice—was the locally accepted fog warning device.

Our ungainly gektirme groped its way without collision across the Horn and under the walls of the city. Our captain told us he was heading for the Sirkeci dock allocated to fishing boats, but my father prevailed on him to take us instead to the Phanar quarter, which was the Venetian section of the city. And somehow, in that thick fog and after not having seen Constantinople for some thirty years, he managed to direct the captain there. Meanwhile, somewhere behind the fog, the sun was setting, and my father was in a fever of impatience, grumbling, "If we do not get there before dark, we must sleep another night on this wretched scow." We and the nightfall, about simultaneously, touched a wooden dock, and he and I said hasty farewells to the Greeks, helped Uncle Mafìo ashore, and my father led us at an old man's trot through the fog, through a gate in the high wall and then through a labyrinth of sinuous, cramped streets.

We came at last to one of many identical narrow-fronted buildings, this one with a shop at the street level, and my father gave a glad cry—"Nostra compagnia!"—at seeing still a light within. He flung the door open and ushered me and Mafìo inside. A white-bearded man was bent over an open ledger at a table piled with many ledgers, writing in the light of a candle at his elbow. He looked up and growled:

"Gèsu, spuzzolenti sardòni!"

They were the first Venetian words I had heard from anyone except Nicolò and Mafìo Polo in twenty-three years. And thus—as "stinking anchovies"—we were greeted by my Uncle Marco Polo.

But then, marveling, he recognized his brothers—"Xestu, Nico? Mafìo? *Tati!*"—and he bounded up most spryly from his chair, and the company clerks at counting tables roundabout looked on in wonder at our flurry of abrazzi and backslappings and handshakings and laughs and tears and exclamations.

"Sangue de Bacco!" he bellowed. "Che bon vento? But you have both gone gray, my Tati!"

"And you have gone white, Tato!" my father bellowed back.

"And what took you so long? Your last consignment brought your letter that you were on your way. But that was nearly three years ago!"

"Ah, Marco, do not ask! We have had the wind at our front the whole way."

"E cussì? But I expected you on jeweled elephants—I Re Magi, coming out of the East in a triumphal parade, with Nubian slaves beating drums. And here you creep in from a foggy night, smelling like the crotch of a Sirkeci whore!"

"From shallow waters, insignificant fish. We come penniless, marooned, derelict. We are castaways washed up on your doorstep. But we will talk of that later. Here, you have never yet met your namesake nephew."

"Neodo Marco! Arcistupendonazzìsimo!" So I got a hearty embrace too, and a benvegnùo, and my back pounded. "But our tonazzo Tato Mafìo, usually so loud. Why so silent?"

"He has been ill," said my father. "We will also talk of that. But come! For two months we have been eating nothing but anchovies, and—"

"And they have given you a powerful thirst! Say no more!" He turned to his clerks and bellowed for them to go home, and not to come in to work the next day. They all stood and gave us a rousing cheer—whether for our safe return or for their getting an unexpected holiday, I do not know—and we went out again into the fog.

Uncle Marco took us to his villa on the Marmara seaside, where we spent our first night, and the subsequent week or more, in swilling down good wines and rich viands—none of which was fish—and being bathed and scrubbed and rubbed in my uncle's private hammam—here called a humoun—and sleeping long hours in luxurious beds, and being waited on, hand and foot, by his numerous house servants. Meanwhile, Uncle Marco sent a special courier vessel hastening to Venice to apprise Dona Fiordelisa of our safe arrival here.

When I felt rested and well-fed enough, and looked and smelled presentable, I was introduced to Uncle Marco's son and daughter, Nicolò and Maroca. They were both about my own age, but Cousin Maroca was still a spinster, and kept giving me looks half speculative, half suggestive. I was not interested in responding; I was much more interested in sitting with my father and Uncle Marco as we bent our attention on the books of the Compagnia Polo. They quickly reassured us that we were anything but penniless. We were more than respectably wealthy.

Some of the shipments of goods and valuables my father had entrusted to the Mongol horse post had failed to make it the whole way along the Silk Road, but that was only to have been expected; what was more remarkable was that so many *had* got through to Constantinople. And here Uncle Marco had variously banked and invested and traded most shrewdly with those goods, and by his advice Dona Fiordelisa in Venice had been able to do the same. So by now our Compagnia Polo ranked with the mercantile houses of Spinola of Genoa and Carrara of Padua and Dandolo of Venice as a prima di tuto in the world of commerce. I was especially pleased that, among the consignments which had arrived intact, were those which had contained all the maps my father and Uncle Mafìo and I had made, and all the notes I had jotted down in all those years. Since the Shoe Brigand at Tunceli had not relieved me of my journal notes scribbled since leaving Khanbalik, I now possessed at least a fragmentary record of every one of my journeys.

We stayed on at the villa until spring, so I had time to get well acquainted with Constantinople. And that made for an easy transition between our long sojourn in the East and our return to the West, for Constantinople itself was a blend of both those ends of the earth. It was Eastern of architecture and bazàr markets and variegated races and complexions and costumes and languages and such. But its guazzabuglio of nationalities included some twenty thousand Venetians, about a tenth as many as in Venice itself, and the city had many other similarities to Venice—including its being overrun with cats. Most of the Venetians resided and did business in the Phanar quarter of the city allotted to them, and across the Golden Horn, in the so-called New City, about an equal number of Genoans occupied the Galata quarter.

The exigencies of commerce necessitated daily transactions between Venetians and Genoans. Nothing would ever stop them doing business. But they did their mutual dealings very coolly, at arm's length, so to speak, and were not mingling sociably or friendlily, because back home—as so often before—their native republics were again at war. I mention that because I was later to have some minor involvement in it. But I will not describe all the aspects of Constantinople, or dwell on our stay there, for it was really only a recuperative and resting place in our journey, and our hearts were already in Venice, and we were eager to follow them there.

So it was that, on a blue and gold May morning, twenty-four years after we had left La Città Serenissima, our galeazza tied up at the dock of our company warehouse, and my father and Uncle Mafìo and I walked down the plank and stepped again upon the cobblestones of the Riva Ca' de Dio, in the Year of Our Lord one thousand two hundred ninety-five, or, as it would have been counted in Kithai, the Year of the Ram, three thousand nine hundred ninety-three.

THE story of the Prodigal Son notwithstanding, I maintain that there is nothing like coming home *successful* to make the homecoming warm and tumultuous and welcoming. Of course, Dona Fiordelisa would have welcomed us happily, however we had arrived. But if we had slunk into Venice the way we had done at Constantinople, I wager we would have been contemptuously received by our merchant confratelli and the citizenry at large, and they would have cared nothing for the greater fact that we had made such journeys and seen such things as none other of them had ever done. However, since we *did* come home rich and well-dressed and walking tall, we were greeted like champions, like victors, like heroes.

For weeks after our arrival, there came so many people calling at the Ca' Polo that we hardly had time of our own to get reacquainted with Dona Lisa and other relatives and friends and neighbors, or to catch up on family news, or to learn the names of all our new servants and slaves and company workers. The old maggiordomo Attilio had died during our absence, and the old chief clerk Isidoro Priuli—and also our aged parish priest, Pare Nunziata—while other house servants, slaves and working men had departed our employ or been dismissed or been freed or been sold, and we had to meet and get to know their successors.

The converging crowds of visitors included some whom we knew from years past, but many others were total strangers. Some came just to fawn on us newly rich arrichisti and seek some advantage from us, the men bringing schemes and projects and soliciting our investment, the women bringing nubile daughters to present for my delectation. Others came with the obvious and venal hope of prying from us information and maps and advice that would enable them to emulate us. Some few came to say sincere congratulations on our safe return, many came to ask inane questions like, "How does it feel to be back?"

To me, at least, it felt good. It was good to walk about the dear old city and glory in the perpetually changing, lapping, liquid mirror light of Venice, so different from the infernal blaze of deserts and the harsh glare of mountain heights and the abrupt white sun and black shade of Eastern bazàrs. It was good to stroll through the piazza and hear all about me the softly inflected cantilena speech of Venice, so different from the rapid jabber of Eastern throngs. It was good to see that Venice was much as I had remembered it. The piazza campanile had been built somewhat taller, some few old buildings had been torn down and new ones put in their places, the interior of San Marco had been adorned with many new mosaics. But nothing was jarringly changed, and that was good.

And still the callers kept coming to the Ca' Polo. Some of them were agreeable to receive, some were nuisances, some were crass annoyances, and one of them, a fellow merchant, came to cast a pall on our homecoming. He told us, "Word has just arrived from the East, by way of my factor in Cyprus. The Great Khan is dead." When we pressed for details, we determined that the Khakhan must have died about the time we were making our way through Kurdistan. Well, it was saddening news, but not unexpected: he had been then seventy-eight years old, and simply had succumbed to the ravages of time. Some while later, we got further news: that his death had not precipitated any wars of succession; his grandson Temur had without opposition been elevated to the throne.

There had been changes of sovereignty here in the West, too, while we had been away. That Doge Tiepolo who banished me from Venice had died, and the scufieta was now worn by a Piero Gradenigo. Also long dead was His Holiness Pope Gregory X, whom we had known in Acre as the Archdeacon Visconti, and there had been a number of other Popes of Rome since then. Also, that city of Acre had fallen to the Saracens, so the Kingdom of Jerusalem was no more, and the whole of the Levant was now held by the Muslims—and appears likely to be theirs forever. Since I had been in Acre to witness briefly that eighth Crusade being desultorily directed by Edward of England, I think I can say that, among all the other things I saw during my journeyings, I saw the very last of the Crusades.

Now my father and stepmother—possibly impelled to the idea by the visitors thronging our Ca' Polo, or perhaps thinking we ought to start living up to our new prosperity, or perhaps deciding that we could now at last afford to live like the Ene Aca nobility we Polos always had been—

began talking of building a new and grander Casa Polo. So to the streams of visitors were now added architects and stonemasons and other aspiring artisans, all eagerly bringing with them sketches and proposals and suggestions that would have had us building something to rival the Doge's palazzo. That reminded me of something, and I reminded my father:

"We have not yet made our courtesy call upon the Doge Gradenigo. I realize that the moment we give official notice of our being in residence in Venice again, we subject ourselves to inquisition by the Dogana tax collectors. They will no doubt find some trinket among all our imports over the years on which Zio Marco failed to pay some trifling duty, and they will insist on wringing every possible bagatìn out of us. Nevertheless, we cannot postpone forever the paying of our respects to our Doge."

So we made formal request for a formal audience, and on the appointed day we took Zio Mafìo with us, and when, as custom dictates, we made gifts to the Doge, we presented some in Mafìo's name as well as ours. I have forgotten what he and my father presented, but I gave to Gradenigo one of the gold and ivory pai-tzu plaques we had carried as emissaries of the Khan of All Khans, and also the three-bladed squeeze knife which had served me so well so often in the East. I showed the Doge how cleverly it worked, and he played with it for a while, and asked me to tell him about the occasions of my employment of the knife, and I did, in brief.

Then he put some polite questions to my father, relevant mainly to East-West trade affairs, and Venice's prospects for an increase of that traffic. Then he expressed his delight that we—and through us, Venice—had prospered so richly by our sojourn abroad. Then, as expected, he said he hoped we would satisfy the Dogana that the proper share of all our successful enterprises had been duly paid into the coffers of the Republic. We said, as expected, that we looked forward to the tax collectors' scrutiny of our Compagnia's unfaultable books of account. Then we stood up, expecting to be dismissed. But the Doge raised one of his heavily beringed hands and said:

"Just one thing more, Messeri. Perhaps it has escaped your recollection, Messer Marco—I know you have had

many other things on your mind—but there is the minor
matter of your banishment from Venice."

I stared at him, dumbfounded, Surely he was not going
to resurrect that old charge against a now most respectable and esteemed (and heavily tax-paying) citizen. With
an air of offended hauteur I said, "I assumed, So Serenità,
that the statute of enforcement had expired with the Doge
Tiepolo."

"Oh, of course I am not *obliged* to respect the judgments
made and sentences imposed by my predecessor. But I too
like to keep my books unfaultable. And there *is* that little
blot upon the pages of the archives of the Signori della
Notte."

I smiled, thinking I understood now, and said, "Perhaps
a suitable fine would pay for the blot's erasure."

"I was thinking rather of an expiation in accordance
with the old Roman lege de tagiòn."

I was again dumbfounded. "An eye for an eye? Surely
the books show that I was never guilty of the killing of that
citizen."

"No, no, of course you were not. Nevertheless, that sad
affair involved a passage at arms. I thought you might
atone by engaging in another. Say, in our current war with
our old enemy Genoa."

"So Serenità, war is a game for young men. I am forty
years old, which is somewhat over-age for wielding a
sword, and—"

Snick! He squeezed the knife and made its inner blade
dart forth.

"By your own account, you wielded this one not too
many years since. Messer Marco, I am not suggesting that
you lead a frontal assault on Genoa. Only that you make a
token appearance of military service. And I am not being
despotic or spiteful or capricious. I am thinking of the future of Venice and the house of Polo. That house has now
been raised among the foremost of our city. After your father, you will be the head of it, and your sons after you. If,
as seems likely, the house of Polo keeps its commanding
position through the generations, I believe the family
arms should be totally senza macchia. Wipe off the blot
now, lest it embarrass and trouble all your posterity. It is
easily accomplished. I have only to write against that

page: 'Marco Polo, Ene Aca, loyally served the Republic in her war against Genoa.' "

My father nodded his agreement and contributed, "What is well closed is well kept."

"If I must," I said with a sigh. I had thought my war service was all behind me. However, I must confess, I thought it perhaps *would* look fine in the family history: that Marco Polo in his lifetime fought both with the Golden Horde and with the War Fleet of Venice. "What would you have me do, So Serenità?"

"Serve only as a gentleman at arms. Say, in supernumerary command of a supply ship. Make one sally with the fleet, out to sea and back to port, and then you retire—with new distinction and with old honor preserved."

Well, that is how, when a squadra of the Venetian fleet sailed out some months later under Almirante Dandolo, I came to be aboard the galeazza *Doge Particiaco*, which was actually only the victualler vessel to the squadra. I bore the courtesy rank of Sopracomito, meaning that I had approximately the same function I had had on the chuan that carried the Lady Kukachin—to look commanding and warlike and knowledgeable, and to stay out of the way of the Comito, the real master of the vessel, and the mariners who took his orders.

I do not aver that I could have done any better if I *had* been in command—of the galeazza or of the whole squadra —but I could hardly have done any worse. We sailed down the Adriatic and, near the island of Kurcola off the Dalmatia coast, we encountered a squadra of Genoan ships, flying the ensign of their great Almiranet Doria, and he demonstrated to us why he was called great. Our squadra, we could see from a distance, outnumbered the Genoans, so our Almirante Dandolo commanded that we surge forward in immediate attack. And Doria let our ships close with and disable some nine or ten of his, a deliberate sacrifice, just so our squadra would be enticed inextricably in amongst his own. And then, out of nowhere—or rather, out from behind the island of Peljesac, where they had been concealed—came ten or fifteen *more* fleet Genoan warships, The two-day battle cost many slain or wounded on both sides, but the victory was Doria's, for by sunset of the second day, the Genoans had taken our entire squadra

and some seven thousand Venetian seamen prize of war,
and I was one of them.

The *Doge Particiaco,* like all the other Venetian galleys,
was sailed—still by its prize crew, but under command of a
captor Genoan Comito—around the foot of Italy and up
through the Tyrrhenian and Ligurian seas to Genoa. From
the water, that looked no bad city in which to be interned:
its palazzi like layered cakes of alternate black and white
marble stacked up the slopes from the harbor. But when
we were marched ashore, we found Genoa to be sadly inferior to Venice: all cramped streets and alleys and meager
little piazze, and very dirty, not having canals to flush
away its effluents.

I do not know where the ordinary seamen and rowers
and archers and balestrieri and such were imprisoned,
but, if traditon was observed, they no doubt sat out the war
in misery and deprivation and squalor. The officers and
gentlmen at arms like myself were considerably better
treated, and put only under house arrest in the abandoned
and run-down palazzo of some defunct religious order, in
the Piazza of the Five Lanterns. The building was very
little furnished, and very cold and dank—I have suffered
worsening twinges of backache in chill weather ever
since—but our jailers were courteous and they fed us adequately, and we were allowed to give money to the visiting
Prisoners' Friends of the Brotherhood of Justice, to buy for
us any extra comforts and refinements we might wish. All
in all, it was a more tolerable confinement than I had once
endured in the Vulcano prison of my own native Venice.
However, our captors told us that they were breaking with
tradition in one respect. They would not allow the ran-
soming of prisoners by their families back home. They said
they had learned that it was no profit to profit from ransom payments, only to have to face the same officers again,
a little while later, across some other contested piece of
water. So we would stay in internment until this war was
concluded.

Well, I had not lost my life by going to war, but it appeared that I was going to lose a substantial piece of it. I
had carelessly squandered months and years before, making my way across interminable barren deserts or mountain snowfields, but at least I had been in the healthy open
air during those journeys, and perhaps had learned some-

thing along the way. There was not much to be learned while languishing in prison. I had no Mordecai Cartafilo for cellmate this time.

As well as I could ascertain, all my fellow prisoners were either dilettanti like myself—noblemen who had been only desultorily whiling away their military service obligation—or professional men of war. The dilettanti were devoid of conversation except whines and yearnings to get back to their feste and ballrooms and dancing partners. The officers at least had some war stories to tell. But each such story gets very like every other story after a telling or two, and the rest of their conversation had all to do with rank and promotions and seniority of service, and how unappreciated by their superiors they were. I gather that every military man in Christendom is undeservedly ranked at least two stripes below the grade he ought to have.

So, if I could learn nothing here in prison, perhaps I could instruct, or at least amuse. When the dull conversations threatened to get absolutely stultifying, I might venture a remark like:

"Speaking of stripes, Messeri, there is in the lands of Champa a beast called the tiger, which has stripes all over it. And curiously enough, no two tigers are striped exactly the same. The natives of Champa can recognize one tiger from another by the distinctive striping of its face. They call the beast Lord Tiger, and they say that by drinking a decoction made from the eyeballs of a dead one, you can always see My Lord Tiger before he sees you. Then, by the striping of his face, you can tell if he is a known man-eater or a harmless hunter of only lesser animals."

Or, when one of our jailers brought us our tin supper dishes and the meal was as unsavory as usual, and we greeted him with our usual taunts, and he complained that we were a troublesome bunch, that he wished he had volunteered for duty elsewhere, I might suggest to him:

"Be glad, Genovese, you are not on duty in India. When the servants brought me dinner there, they had to enter the dining room crawling on their bellies and pushing the trays of food before them."

At first, my unsolicited contributions to the barrack conversations were sometimes received with strange and wondering looks, as when, for instance, two foppish gentlemen

might be discussing, in high-flown language, the comparative virtues and charms of their lady loves back home, and
I might venture:

"Have you yet determined, Messeri, whether your
maidens are winter or summer women?" I would be regarded blankly, so I would explain: "The men of the Han
say that a woman whose intimate aperture is situated unusually near the front of her artichoke is most suitable for
cold winter nights, because you and she must closely inter-
twine to effect penetration. But a woman whose orifice is
situated farther back between her legs is better for summertime. She can sit on your lap in a cool and breezy outdoor pavilion, while you enter her from the rear."

The two elegant gentlemen might then reel away in horror, but less dandified sorts would come congregating to
hear more such revelations. And it was not long before,
every time I opened my mouth, I would have more listeners than any expounder of ballroom manners or sea-war lo-
gistics, and they would listen raptly. Not only did my
fellow Venetians cluster about me when I spun my tales,
but also the Genoan warders and guards, and the visiting
Brothers of Justice, and also Pisan and Corsican and
Paduan prisoners taken by the Genoans in other wars and
battles. And one day I was approached by one who said:

"Messer Marco, I am Luigi Rustichello, late of Pisa . . ."

And you introduced yourself as a scrivener, a fableor, a
romancier, and you asked my permission to write down my
stories in a book. So we sat down together and I told my
tales to you, and, through the agency of the Brotherhood of
Justice, I was enabled to send a request to Venice, and my
father dispatched to Genoa my collection of notes and
scraps and journals, which added to my recollection many
things that I myself had forgotten. Thus our year of confinement passed not wearisomely but busily and produc-
tively. And when the war was finally over, and a new
peace signed between Venice and Genoa, and we prisoners
were released to go home, I could say that the year had not
been a wasted time, as I had feared. Indeed, it may have
been the most fruitful year of my entire life, in that I accomplished one thing that has lasted, and gives promise of
lasting longer than I shall. I mean our book, Luigi, the *Description of the World.* Certainly, in the score or so of years
that now have passed since we said goodbye outside that

Genoa palazzo, I have accomplished nothing that gave me comparable satisfaction.

So here we are, Luigi. I have once more recounted my life from childhood to the end of my journeying. I have told again many of the tales you heard that long time ago, and many of those in more detail, and I have retold some others which you and I decided not to put into the earlier book, and I think many other stories besides, which I never did confide to you before. Now I give you leave to take any or all of my adventures, and ascribe them to the fictional hero of your latest work in progress, and make of them what you will.

There is not much more to tell of myself, and probably none of it would you find of any application to your new work, so I will tell it briefly.

6

I got back to Venice to find that my father and Marègna Lisa were well along in the building of our luxurious new Casa Polo—or rather, the making new of an old palazzo they had bought. It was on the Corte Sabionera, in a much more fashionable confino than our previous residence. It was also nearer to the Rialto, where, now that I was the recognized head of the Compagnia Polo, I was expected by tradition to mingle and converse with my fellow merchants twice a day, each morning just before noon and each evening at the close of the working day. That was and still is a pleasant custom, and I have often picked up the odd bit of useful information that might not have come to me in the ordinary course of business. I did not at all mind being respectfully addressed there as Messere, and respectfully listened to when I gave my sage opinion on this or that question of statutes or tariffs or whatever. I also did not *too much* mind being now head of the Compagnia Polo, though I had arrived at that eminence rather by default.

My father never did actually resign in my favor. He merely, from this time on, paid less and less attention to the company and more to other interests. For a while, he gave all his energies to supervision of the building and fur-

nishing and decoration of the new Ca' Polo. On several occasions during its construction, he pointed out to me that
this new palazzo was ample enough for many more people
than we were preparing to put into it.

"Remember what the Doge said, Marco," he reminded
me. "If there is to be a Compagnia Polo and a house of Polo
after you, there must be sons."

"Father, you of all people must know how I feel on that
subject. I should not mind paternity, but maternity has
cost me more than I can ever count."

"Nonsense!" my stepmother put in sternly, but then she
softened. "I do not mean to deprecate what you lost, Marco,
but I must protest. When you told that tragic story, you
were telling of a frail foreign woman. Venetian women are
born and bred to breed. They enjoy being 'pregnant to the
ears,' as the vulgar describe it, and they keenly feel the
lack when they are not. Find yourself a good, wide-hipped
Venetian wife, and leave the rest to her."

"Or," said my practical father, "find yourself a wife you
can love sufficiently to want to have children with, but one
you can love lightly enough that her loss would not be insupportable."

When the Ca' Polo was finished and we had moved in,
my father turned his attention to a project even more novel
and extraordinary. He founded what I might call a School
for Merchant Adventurers. In actuality, it never had a
name and it was not any academy of formal study. My father simply offered his experience and advice and access to
our map collection, to any who might care to seek their fortune on the Silk Road. It was mostly young men who applied to him for schooling, but a few were as old as myself.
For a stipulated percentage of the profit from a student's
putative first successful trading expedition—to Baghdad,
Balkh, anywhere else in the East, even all the way to
Khanbalik—Nicolò Polo would impart to the apprentice
adventurer all the useful information at his command, let
the apprentice copy the route from our own maps, teach
the apprentice some necessary phrases of Trade Farsi,
even give the apprentice the names he remembered of native merchants, camel-pullers, guides, drovers and such,
all along the route. He guaranteed nothing—since, after
all, much of his knowledge had to be out of date by now.
But neither did the apprentice journeyers have to pay him

anything for their schooling, until and unless they profited from it. As I recall, many novices did set out in the direction Maistro Polo had twice gone, and some came safely back from as far away as Persia, and one or two of them came back prosperous, and paid their dues. But I think my father would have continued in that whimsical occupation even if it had never paid him a bagatìn, for in a sense it kept him still journeying afar—and even into his last years.

However, the consequence was that I, who had been a vagabond as carefree and wandersome and willful as any wind, now found my once wide horizons narrowed down to daily attendance at the company counting house and warehouse, with twice-a-day intervals of conviviality and gossip on the Rialto. It was my obligation; somebody had to keep up the Compagnia Polo; my father had in effect retired from it, and Zio Mafìo was still and forever a housebound invalid. In Constantinople, my eldest uncle also gradually edged out of the business (and died, I think of boredom, not long after). So there my cousin Nicolò and here myself found ourselves inheriting the full responsibility of our separate branches of the company. Cuzìn Nico actually seemed to enjoy being a merchant prince. And I? Well, it was honest and useful and not onerous work I was doing, and I had not yet got bored with the humdrum sameness of it day after day, and I had more or less resigned myself to this being *all* of my life. But then two new things happened.

The first was your sending me, Luigi, my copy of your just-completed *Description of the World*. I immediately gave over every spare moment to reading our book and savoring it and, as I finished each sheet, giving it to a copyist to make additional manuscripts. I found it in all ways admirable, with only a few errors, which were no doubt to be blamed on my pace of narration while you set down the words, and my neglect to read over your original draft with a critical eye.

The errors consisted only in an occasional misdating of this or that event, an occasional adventure set down out of sequence, an occasional one of the difficult Eastern place-names misheard or misspelled—your writing Saianfu, for example, where it should have been Yun-nan-fu, and Yang-zho for Hang-zho (which would have put me and my

Manzi tax-collector career in a quite different city and distant from the one where I actually served). However, I never earlier bothered to point out those minor errors to you, and I hope my doing so now does not distress you. They could mean nothing to anyone but me—who else in this Western world would know there *is* any difference between Yang-zho and Hang-zho?—and I did not even trouble to have my scribe correct them while making his copies.

I made formal presentation of one of the copies to the Doge Gradenigo, and he must immediately have circulated it among his Council of nobles, and they to all their families and even servants. I presented another copy to the priest of our new parish of San Zuàne Grisostomo, and he must have circulated it among all his clergy and congregation, because in no time I was famous again. With even more avidity than they had shown when I first came home from Kithai, people began seeking to scrape my acquaintance, accosting me at public functions, pointing at me in the street, on the Rialto, from passing gòndole. And your own copies, Luigi, must have proliferated and scattered like dandelion seeds, for merchants and travelers visiting Venice from abroad said they came as much for a look at me as to see the San Marco Basilica and other notable sights of the city. If I received them, many told me they had read the *Description of the World* in their home country, already translated into their native language.

As I have said, Luigi, it did us little good to omit from that narrative many things we thought too marvelous to be believed. Some of the enthusiasts seeking to meet me were seeking to meet what they properly considered a Far Journeyer, but a great many wished to meet a man they mistakenly considered Un Grand Romancier, author of an imaginative and entertaining fiction, and others clearly wished only to ogle a Prodigious Liar, as they might have flocked to watch the frusta of some eminent criminal at the piazzetta pillars. It seemed that the more I protested—"I told nothing but the truth!"—the less I was believed, and the more humorously (but fondly) I was regarded. I could hardly complain of being the cynosure of all eyes, and all those eyes warmly admiring, but I should have preferred that they admired me as something other than a fable-maker.

I earlier said that our family's new Ca' Polo was situated in the Corte Sabionera. It was, yes, and of course it still *is*, physically, and I suppose even the latest street map of Venice gives the official name of that little square as Ships-Ballast Court. But no resident of the city called it that any more. It was known to everybody as the Corte del Milione—*in my honor*—for I was now known as Marco Milione, man of the million lies and fictions and exaggerations. I had become both famous and notorious.

In time, I learned to live with my new and peculiar reputation, and even to disregard the troops of urchins who sometimes followed me on my walks from the Corte to the Compagnia or the Rialto. They would brandish stick swords and prance in a sort of gallop gait, and spank their own behinds while they did so, and shout things like "Come hither, great princes!" and "The orda will get you!" Such constant attention was a nuisance, and enabled even strangers to recognize me and greet me at times when I might have preferred anonymity. But it was partly on account of my being now conspicuous that another new thing occurred.

I forget where I was walking that day, but, on the street, I came face to face with the little girl Doris who had been my childhood playmate and had in those days so much adored me. I was astonished. By rights, Doris should have been nearly as old as I was—in her early forties—and probably, she being of the lower class, already a gray and wrinkled and worn-out drudge of a maràntega. But here she was, grown only to young womanhood—in her middle twenties, no more—and decently attired, not in the shapeless black of old street women, and just as golden blonde and fresh-faced and pretty as she had been when I last saw her. I was more than astonished, I was thunderstruck. I so far forgot my manners as to blurt her name, right there on the street, but at least I thought to address her respectfully:

"Damìna Doris Tagiabue!"

She might have bridled at my effrontery and swept her skirts aside and stalked on past me. But she saw my trailing retinue of urchins playing Mongols, and she had to suppress a smile, and she said amiably enough:

"You are Messer Marco of the—I mean—"

"Marco of the Millions. You can say it, Doris. Everyone

does. And you used to call me worse things. Marcolfo and such."

"Messere, I fear you have mistaken me. I assume you must once have known my mother, whose maiden name was Doris Tagiabue."

"Your mother!" For a moment I forgot that Doris must by now be a matron, if not a crone. Perhaps because this girl was so like my memory of her, I remembered only the unformed and untamed little zuzzurrullona I had known. "But she was just a child!"

"Children grow up, Messere," she said, and added mischievously, "Even yours will," and she indicated my half-dozen miniature Mongols.

"Those are not mine. *Beat the retreat, men!*" I shouted at them, and with much rearing and wheeling of their imaginary steeds they retired to a distance.

"I was but jesting, Messere," said the so-familiar stranger, smiling openly now, and even more resembling the merry sprite of my recollection. "Among the things well-known in Venice is that the Messer Marco Polo is still a bachelor. My mother, however, grew up and married. I am her daughter and my name is Donata."

"A pretty name for a pretty young lady: the given one, the gift." I bowed as if we had been formally introduced. "Dona Donata, I would be grateful if you would tell me where your mother lives now. I should like to see her again. We were once—close friends."

"Almèi, Messere. Then I regret to tell you that she died of an influenza di febbre some years ago."

"Gramo mi! I lament to hear it. She was a dear person. My condolences, Dona Donata."

"Damìna, Messere," she corrected me. "My mother was the Dona Doris Loredano. I am, like you, unmarried."

I started to say something outrageously daring—and hesitated—and then said it:

"Somehow I cannot condole on your being unmarried." She looked faintly surprised at my boldness, but not scandalized, so I went on, "Damìna Donata Loredano, if I sent acceptable sensàli to your father, do you think he might be persuaded to let me call at your family residence? We could talk of your late mother . . . of old times. . . ."

She cocked her head and regarded me for a moment.

Then she said forthrightly, without archness, as her
mother might have done:

"The famous and esteemed Messer Marco Polo surely is
welcome everywhere. If your sensàli will apply to the
Maistro Lorenzo Loredano at his place of business in the
Merceria . . ."

Sensàli can mean business brokers or marriage brokers,
and it was the latter kind I sent, in the person of my staid
and starched stepmother, together with a formidable maid
or two of hers. Marègna Lisa returned from that mission to
report that the Maistro Loredano had acceded most hospitably to my request for permission to pay a series of calls.
She added, with a noticeable elevation of her eyebrows:

"He is an artisan of leather goods. Evidently an honest
and respectable and hardworking currier. But, Marco,
only a currier. Morel di mezo. You could be paying calls on
the daughters of the sangue blo. The Dandolo family, the
Balbi, the Candiani . . ."

"Dona Lisa, I once had a Nena Zulià who likewise complained of my tastes. Even in my youth I was contrary,
preferring a savory morel to one with a noble name."

However, I did not swoop upon the Loredano household
and abduct Donata. I paid court to her as properly and ritually and for as long a time as if she had been of the very
bluest blood. Her father, who gave the impression of having been assembled from some of his own tanned hides, received me cordially and made no comment on the fact that
I was nearly as old as he. After all, one of the accepted
ways for a daughter of the "middle mushroom" class to
sprout higher in the world was for her to make an advanta-
geous May-December marriage, usually to a widower with
numerous children. On that scale, I was really no older
than November, and I came unencumbered with any step-
brood. So the Maistro Lorenzo merely mumbled some of
the phrases traditionally spoken by an unmoneyed father
to a wealthy suitor, to dispel any suspicion that he was voluntarily surrendering his daughter to the diritto di signoria:

"I must make known my reluctance, Messere. A daughter should not aspire to higher station than life gave her.
To the natural burden of her low birth she risks adding a
heavier servitude."

"It is I who aspire, Messere," I assured him. "I can only

hope that your daughter will favor my aspirations, and I promise that she would never have cause to regret having done so."

I would bring flowers, or some small gift, and Donata and I would sit together, always with an accompagnatrice —one of Fiordelisa's iron-corseted maids—sitting nearby to make sure we behaved with rigid respectability. But that did not prevent Donata's speaking to me as freely and frankly as Doris had been wont to do.

"If you knew my mother in her youth, Messer Marco, then you know that she began life as a poor orphan. Literally of the low popolàzo. So I shall put on no false airs and graces in her behalf. When she married a prospering currier, owner of his own workshop, she did marry above her class. But no one would ever have known it, if she had not chosen to make no secret of it. There was never anything coarse or vulgar about her during all the rest of her life. She made a good wife to my father and a good mother to me."

"I would have made wager on it," I said.

"I think she was a credit to her higher station in life. I tell you this, Messer Marco, so that if you—if you should have any doubts about my own qualifications for moving higher yet . . ."

"Darling Donata, I have had no least doubt at all. Even when your mother and I were children together, I could see the promise in her. But I will not say 'like mother, like daughter.' Because, even if I had never known her, I should quickly have recognized your own promise. Shall I, like a mooning and courting trovatore, sing your qualities? Beauty, intelligence, good humor—"

"Please do not omit honesty," she interrupted. "For I would have you know everything there is to know. My mother never whispered any hint of this to me, and I should certainly never breathe it in my good father's hearing, but—but there are things a child gets to know, or at least suspect, without being told. Mind you, Messer Marco, I admire my mother for having made a good marriage. But I might be less admiring of the way she must have done it, and so might you. I have an unshakable suspicion that her marriage to my father was impelled by their having—how do I say?—their having *anticipated the event* to some degree. I fear that a comparison of the date written on their

consenso di matrimonio and that written on my own atta
di nascita might prove embarrassing."

I smiled at young Donata's thinking she might shock
someone as inured and impervious to shock as I was. And I
smiled more broadly at her innocent simplicity. She must
be quite unaware, I thought, that a great many marriages
among the lower classes never were solemnized by *any* document or ceremony or sacrament. If Doris had indeed, by
the oldest of feminine ruses, exalted herself from the
popolàzo to the morel di mezo, it did not lessen my regard
for her—or for this pretty product of her ruse. And if that
was the only impediment Donata could fear as a possible
interference to our marriage, it was a trifling one. I made
two promises at that moment. One was only to myself, and
unspoken: I took oath that never during our married lifetime would I reveal any of the secrets of my past or the
skeletons in my own cupboard. The other promise I made
aloud, after smoothing away my smile and assuming a
very solemn face:

"I swear, dearest Donata, that I shall never hold it
against you—that you were prematurely born. There is no
disgrace in that."

"Ah, you older men are so commendably tolerant of human frailty." I may have winced at that, for she added,
"You are a good man, Messer Marco."

"And your mother was a good woman. Do not think ill of
her for having been a determined woman, as well. She
knew how to get her own way." I remembered, somewhat
guiltily, one instance of that. The recollection made me
say, "I take it that she never mentioned having been acquainted with me."

"Not that I recall. Should she have?"

"No, no. I was nobody worth mentioning in those days.
But I should confess—" I stopped, for I had just sworn not
to confess anything that had happened in my past life. And
I could hardly confess that Doris Tagiabue had come to
Lorenzo Loredano no virgin as a consequence of her having
first practiced her wiles on me. So I merely repeated:

"Your mother knew how to get her own way. If I had not
had to leave Venice, it could very well have happened that
she would have married *me* when we were a little older."

Donata pouted prettily. "What an ungallant thing to

say, even if it is true. Now you make me seem like a second choice."

"And now you make *me* seem like someone browsing in a market. I did not choose you by volition, dear girl. I had no part in it. When I first saw you, I said to myself, 'She must have been put on this earth for me.' And when you spoke your name, I *knew* it. I knew that I had been given a gift."

And that pleased her, and made things right again.

On another occasion during our courtship, when we sat together, I put to her this question: "What of children when we are married, Donata?"

She blinked at me in perplexity, as if I had asked whether she intended to go on breathing after we were married. So I went on:

"A married couple are of course expected to have children. It is the natural thing. It is expected by their families, the Church, the Lord God, the community. But despite those expectations, there must be some people who do not wish to conform."

"I am not among them," she said, like a response to a catechism.

"And there are some who simply cannot."

After a moment of silence, she said, "Are you intimating, Marco—?" She had by this time eased into addressing me informally. Now she said, choosing her words with delicacy, "Are you intimating, Marco, that perhaps you were, um, during your journeying, um, injured in some way?"

"No, no, no. I am whole and healthy, and competent to be a father. As far as I know, I mean. I was rather referring to those unfortunate women who are, for one reason or another, barren."

She looked away from me, and blushed as she said, "I cannot protest 'no, no, no,' for I have no way of knowing. But I think, if you were to count the barren women you have heard of, you would find that they are mostly pale and fragile and vaporish noblewomen. I come of good, solid, redblooded peasant stock and, like any Christian woman, I *hope* to be the mother of multitudes. I pray to the good Lord that I will. But if He in His wisdom should somehow choose to make me barren, I would try with fortitude to bear the affliction. However, I have confidence in the Lord's goodness."

"It is not always of the good Lord's doing," I said. "In the East there are known various ways to prevent conception—"

Donata gasped and crossed herself. "Never say such a thing! Do not even speak of such a dreadful sin! Why, what would the good Pare Nardo say, if he even dreamed you had imagined such things? Oh, Marco, do assure me that you put no mention *in your book* of anything so criminal and sordid and un-Christian. I have not read the book, but I have heard some people call it scandalous. Was that the scandal they spoke of?"

"I really do not remember," I said placatively. "I think that was one of the things I left out. I merely wished to tell you that such things are possible, in case—"

"Not in Christendom! It is unspeakable! Unthinkable!"

"Yes, yes, my dear. Forgive me."

"Only if you promise me," she said firmly. "Promise me you will forget that and *all other* vile practices you may have witnessed in the East. That our good Christian marriage will never be tainted by anything un-Christian you learned or saw or even heard of in those pagan lands."

"Well, not everything pagan is vile. . . ."

"Promise me!"

"But, Donata, suppose I should have another opportunity or occasion to go eastward, and wished to take you with me. You would be the first Western woman, to my knowledge, ever to—"

"No. I will never go, Marco," she said flatly, and her blush had gone now. Her face was very white and her lips set. "I should not wish you to go. There. I have said it. You are a wealthy man, Marco, with no need to increase your wealth. You are famous for your journeying already, with no need to increase that fame or to journey ever again. You have responsibilities, and will shortly have me for another, and I hope we will both have others. You are no longer—you are no longer the boy you were when you set out before. I should not have wished to marry that boy, Marco, not then or now. I want a mature and sober and dependable man, and I want him at home. I took you to be that man. If you are not, if you still harbor a restless and reckless boy inside you, I think you had better confess it now. We will have to put on a good face for our families and friends and all the gossips of Venice, when we announce the dissolution of our betrothal."

"You are indeed very like your mother." I sighed. "But you are young. In time to come, you might even *desire* to journey—"

"Not outside Christendom," she said, still in that flat voice. "Promise me."

"Very well. I shall never take you outside Chris—"

"Nor will you go."

"Now that, Donata, I could not swear in good faith. My very business may require at least a return visit to Constantinople on occasion, and all around that city are un-Christian lands. My foot might slip, and—"

"This much, then. Promise me you will not go away until our children, if God gives us children, are grown to a responsible age. You have told me how your own father left his son to run wild among the street folk."

I laughed. "Donata, *they* were not all vile, either. One of them was your mother."

"My mother raised me to be better than my mother. My own children are not to be abandoned. Promise me."

"I promise," I said. I did not pause then to calculate that, if our marriage produced a son in the ordinary interval, I would be something like sixty-five years old before he had reached his majority. I was only thinking that Donata, still young herself, might have many changes of mind during our life together. "I promise, Donata. As long as there are children at home, and unless you decree otherwise, so will I be at home."

And in the first year of the new century, in the year one thousand three hundred and one, we were married.

All was done with punctilious observance of the proprieties. When our period of courtship was deemed suitably long enough, Donata's father and mine and a notary convened at the Church of San Zuàne Grisostomo for the ceremony of impalmatura, and they severally perused and signed and affirmed the marriage contract, just as if I had been some shy and awkward and adolescent bridegroom—when in fact it was I who had seen to the drawing up of the contract, with the counsel of my Compagnia attorneys-at-law. At the conclusion of the impalmatura, I put the betrothal ring on Donata's finger. On subsequent Sundays, Pare Nardo proclaimed from the pulpit the bandi, and

posted them on the church door, and no one came forward
to dispute the proposed marriage. Then Dona Lisa engaged a friar-scribe with an excellent hand to write the
partecipazioni di nozze, and sent them, each with the traditional gift parcel of confèti almonds, by liveried messenger
to all the invited guests. They included everyone of any
consequence in Venice, for, although there were sumptu-
ary laws limiting the extravagance of most families' public ceremonies, the Doge Gradenigo graciously granted us
exemption. And, when the day came, it was a celebration
on the scale of a citywide festa—after the nuptial mass, the
banquet and feasting, the music and song and dancing, the
drinking and brindisi and tipsy guests falling into the
Corte canal, the confèti and coriàndoli thrown. When all
that required the participation of Donata and myself was
over, her bridal maids gave her the donora: setting in her
arms for a moment a borrowed baby and tucking in her
shoe a gold sequin coin, symbols of her being evermore
blessed with fecundity and richness—and then we left the
still uproarious festa and betook ourselves inside the Ca'
Polo, deserted of all but servants, the family to stay with
friends during our luna di miele.

And in our bedchamber, in private, in Donata I discovered Doris all over again, for her body was the same milk-
white, adorned with the same two small shell-pink points.
Except that Donata was a grown woman and fully developed in womanhood, with a golden floss to prove it, she was
the image of her mother, even to the identical appurte-
nance that I had once likened to the morsel called ladylips.
Much else of the night was a repetition of a stolen afternoon long years ago. As I had taught then, so I taught now,
beginning with the turning of Donata's shell-pink points
to a blushing and eager coral-pink. But here I will again
draw the curtain of connubial privacy, though a little
belatedly, for I have already told it all—the events of this
night being very nearly the same as on that long-ago afternoon. And this time, too, it delighted us both. At risk of
sounding disloyal to olden time, I might even say that this
occasion was more delicious than the earlier, because this
time we were not sinning.

7

WHEN Donata came to her confinement, I was there at home, in the house, close at hand, partly in compliance with my promise to her and our then-unarrived family, partly in memory of another time when I had so unforgivably been absent. They would not let me into Donata's chamber for the event, of course, and I had no desire to be there. But I had done everything possible to prepare for the event, including the engagement of the sage physician Piero Abano, whom I paid lavishly to bequeath all his other patients to another mèdego and do nothing but attend Donata throughout her pregnancy. He early inculcated what he called his Six-Element Regimen: proper diet and drink, properly alternating periods of motion and rest, sleep and waking, evacuation and retention, fresh air during the day and close air at night, and "assuagement of the passions of the mind." Whether that regimen was the more to be credited, or Donata's "good peasant stock," there was no childbed difficulty. Dotòr Abano and his two midwives and my stepmother came, in a bunch, to tell me that Donata's labor had been easy and the birth like the squirting of an orange pip. They had to shake me awake to tell me, for I had again been reliving my own onetime experience of such travail and, to ameliorate it, had drunk three or four bottles of Barolo and succumbed into blessed oblivion.

"I am sorry she is not a boy," murmured Donata, when they let me into the chamber to view our daughter for the first time. "I should have known. The carrying and the labor were too easy. Next time I shall pay heed to what the old women say: Labor a little longer, and give birth to a male child."

"Hush, hush," I said. "Now I am the happy recipient of two gifts."

We named her Fantina.

Although Donata was from our earliest acquaintance wary of having me introduce any "un-Christian ideas" into our household, I was able to convince her of the worthiness of *some* alien customs. I do not mean any of the things I taught her in bed. Donata was a virgin when we wed, so she had no way of distinguishing the practices Venetian or exotic, universal or especial. But I also taught her, for instance, what I knew of the way the Han women kept themselves clean inside and out. I very delicately imparted that information to her, early in our marriage, and she saw the merit in that un-Christian bathing habit, and adopted it. After Fantina's birth I insisted that she be likewise frequently bathed on the outside and, when she was older, on the inside as well. Donata briefly balked, saying:

"Bathed, yes. But the inner irrigation? That is all very well for a woman already married, but it would efface Fantina's maidenhead. She would never have proof of her virginity."

I said, "In my opinion, purity is best detected in the wine, not in the waxen seal on the flask. Teach Fantina to keep her body clean and sweet, and I believe her morals are likely to remain so, as well. Any future husband will recognize that quality in her, and require no mere physical token of it."

So Donata complied, and instructed Fantina's nurse to bathe her frequently and thoroughly, and so instructed every subsequent nena we had in the house. Some were at first amazed and critical, but they gradually came to approve, and I think spread the word among their servant circles that an un-Christian cleanliness was not, as commonly believed, debilitating, for in time the Venetians of both sexes and all ages got noticeably cleaner than in the olden days. By introducing just that one custom of the Han, I may have done much to improve the entire city of Venice—from the skin out, so to speak.

Our second child was born almost exactly a year later, and also without difficulty, but not in the same place. The Doge Gradenigo had summoned me one day and asked if I would accept a consular post abroad, the one in Bruges. It was an honor to be invited to that civic duty, and I had by then trained up a good staff of assistants who could look after the Compagnia Polo during my absence, and in Bruges I could accomplish many things to the company's advantage. But I did not say yes on the spot. Although the post

...od Christian Flanders, I thought I ought to confer
...st with Donata.

She agreed with me that she should at least once in her
lifetime see *something* outside her native Venice, so I accepted the posting. Donata was already big with child
when we sailed, but we took our sage Venetian physician
along and, the voyage being made on a heavy, rock-solid
Flemish cog, it caused no distress to either her or our infant Fantina, but Dotòr Abano was seasick all the way.
Happily, he was well recovered by the time Donata came
to term, and again it was an easy birth, and again Donata
complained only that it had been *too* easy, for it produced
another daughter.

"Hush, hush," I said. "In the lands of Champa a man
and woman do not even get married until after they have
produced two children. So, in effect, we are just getting
started."

We named that one Bellela.

Venice maintained a permanent consulate in Bruges—
and favored its more distinguished Ene Aca citizens with
the opportunity to serve there in rotation—because twice a
year a numerous fleet of Venetian galleys sailed from
Bruges's harbor suburb of Sluys, laden with the produce of
all northern Europe. So Donata and I and Fantina—and
shortly little Bellela—spent a most enjoyable year or so in
the fine consular residence on the Place de la Bourse, a
house luxuriously furnished with every convenience, including a permanent staff of servants. I was not overbur-
dened with work, not having much to do except look over
the shipping manifests of the bi-yearly fleet, and decide
whether this time it would sail direct to Venice, or
whether it had hold room for other goods, in which case I
might route some or all of the ships by way of London or
Southampton across the Channel, or by way of Ibiza or
Majorca in the Mediterranean, to pick up some of the produce of those places.

Most of that consular year Donata and I spent being royally entertained by other consular delegations and by
Flemish merchant families, at balls and banquets and
local feste like the Procession of the Holy Blood. Many of
our hosts had read the *Description of the World*, in one language or another, and all had heard about it, and all spoke
the Sabir trade tongue, so I was much questioned on this or

that of the book's contents, and encouraged to elaborate on this and that aspect of it. An evening's entertainment would often go on late into the night, because the company would keep me talking, and Donata would sit and smile proprietorially. While there were ladies present, I would confine myself to innocuous subjects.

"Our fleet was today loading your good North Sea herring, my lords merchants. They are excellent fish, but I myself prefer to dine on fresh, as we did tonight, not salted or smoked or pickled fish. I suggest you consider marketing them fresh. Yes, yes, I know; fresh fish do not travel. But I *have* seen them do so in the north of Kithai, and your climate here is very similar. You might speculate on adopting the method used there, or some variant of it. In the north of Kithai, the summer is only three months long, so the fishermen plunder the lakes and rivers with all their energy, taking far more fish than they can sell in the same time. They toss the surplus fish into a shallow reservoir of water and keep them alive there until wintertime. Then they break the ice on the reservoir and take the fish out singly, at which exposure to the winter air the fish freeze solid. They are packed like kindling logs, in bundles on pack asses, and are sent thus to the cities, where the rich folk pay exorbitant prices for such delicacies. And when the fish are thawed and cooked, they taste as fresh as any caught in the summertime."

Such remarks would often inspire two or three of the more ambitious merchants present to call for a servant to carry an urgent message to their place of business: I suppose something on the order of "Let us try this man's preposterous notion." But the merchants themselves would not leave the gathering because, when the ladies had betaken themselves elsewhere to chat of feminine things, I would regale the men with more piquant tales.

"My personal traveling physician, the Dotòr Abano, pronounces himself dubious of this, Messeri, but I brought back from Kithai a prescription for long life, and I will share it with you. The men of the Han who profess the religion called Tao have a firm belief that the exhalations of all things contain particles so tiny they are invisible, but have a potent effect nonetheless. For example, the rose particles we call the fragrance of a rose make us feel benign when we inhale them. The meat particles given off as scent by a good roast of meat make our mouths water. Just so, the Taoists profess that the breath passing through the lungs of a young girl gets charged with particles of her young, fresh body and then, when she exhales, imbue the ambient air with vigorous and invigorating qualities. Thus the prescription: if you would live a long time, surround yourself with vivacious young maidens. Stay as close to them as you can. Inhale their sweet exhalations. They will enhance your blood and humors and other juices. They will strengthen your health and lengthen your life. It goes without saying that, if you should meanwhile find other employment for the delicious young virgins . . ."

Raucous laughter, loud and prolonged, and one old Fleming pounded a bony hand on his spiky knee and cried, "Damn your personal physician, Mynheer Polo! I think it a damned fine prescription! I would resort to the young girls in an instant, damn me if I would not, except that my damned old wife would think of some objection to make."

Louder laughter, over which I called to him, "Not if you go about it cunningly, Messere. The prescription for elderly women is, of course, young boys."

Louder laughter yet, and boisterous jests shouted, and the handing around of pitchers of the strong Flemish ale, and often, when Donata and I departed the company, I was glad I had a consular palanquin to ride home in.

Having less to do in the daytime, and Donata being then usually occupied as a mother to our daughters, I applied myself to what I believed would be a project beneficial to trade in general and Venice in particular. I decided to institute here in the West something I had found eminently useful in the East. I established a horse post in imitation of that devised so long ago by the Khan Kubilai's Minister of Roads and Rivers. It took some time and labor and argument to accomplish, since in these lands I had no absolute authority, as I would have had anywhere in the Khanate. I had to overcome a good deal of government torpor, timidity and opposition. And those difficulties were multiplied by the number of governments involved: Flanders, Lorraine, Swabia and so on—every suspicious, narrow-minded duchy and principality between Bruges and Venice. But I was determined and stubborn, and I did it. When I had that post-chain of riders and relay stations established, I could send to Venice the cargo manifests of the fleet as soon as it sailed from Sluys. The post would convey the papers those seven hundred miles in seven days, or one-quarter of the best time the fleet could make, so that recipient merchants in Venice often had every item of the cargo sold at a profit before it even reached them.

When it came time for me and my family to quit Bruges, I was much tempted to try posting *us* home the same swift way. But two of the family consisted of infant children, and Donata was pregnant again, so the idea was impractical. We came home as we had gone, by ship, and arrived in good time for our third daughter, Morata, to be born in Venice.

The Ca' Polo was still a place of pilgrimage for visitors wishing to meet and converse with Messer Marco Milione. During my stay in Flanders, my father had been receiving them. But he and Dona Lisa were wearying of that obligation, both of them being now very old and failing in health, and they were glad to have me assume the duty again.

There came to see me, during the years, besides mere gapers and gawkers, some distinguished and intelligent men. I remember a poet, Francesco da Barberino, who (like you, Luigi) wished to know some things about Kithai for a chanson de geste he was writing. And I remember the cartographer Marino Sanudo, who came asking to incorporate some of our maps into a great Map of the World he was compiling. And there came several friars-historians, Jacopo d'Acqui and Francesco Pipino and one from France, Jean d'Ypres, who were severally writing Chronicles of the World. And there came the painter Giotto di Bondone, already famous for his O and his chapel frescoes, who wished to know something of the illustrative arts as practiced by the Han, and seemed impressed by what I could tell him and show him, and went away saying he was going to try some of those exotic effects in his own paintings.

There came also, during the years, from my many correspondents in countries East and West, news of people and places I had known. I heard of the death of Edward, King of England, whom I had known as a Crusader prince in Acre. I heard that the priest Zuàne of Montecorvino, whom I had known just long enough to detest, had been appointed by the Church its first Archbishop of Khanbalik, and had been sent a number of under-priests to minister to the mis-

sions he was establishing in Kithai and Manzi. I heard of
the many successful wars waged by the once insignificant
boy Ghazan. Among his several triumphs, he swallowed
the Seljuk Empire wholly into his Ilkhanate of Persia, and
I wondered what became of the Kurdi Shoe Brigand and
my old friend Sitarè, but I never heard. I learned of other
expansions of the Mongol Khanate—in the south it took
Jawa, both the Greater and the Lesser, and in the west
moved into Tazhikistan—but, as I had advised Kubilai not
to do, none of his successors ever bothered to invade India.

Things happened closer to home, too, not all of them joyous things. In fairly close succession, my father and then
my Zio Mafìo and then my Marègna Fiordelisa died. Their
funerals were of such splendid pomp and thronged attendance and citywide mourning as almost to overshadow the
obsequies for the Doge Gradenigo, who died shortly afterward. About the same time, we here in Venice were set
aghast when the Frenchman who had become Pope Clement V summarily removed the Apostolic See from Rome to
Avignon in his native France, so that His Holiness might
remain near to his mistress, who, being the wife of the
Count of Périgord, could not conveniently visit him in the
Eternal City. We might have looked tolerantly on that as a
temporary aberrancy, typical of a Frenchman, except that,
three years ago, Clement was succeeded by another
Frenchman, and John XXII seems satisfied that the papal
palace remain in Avignon. My correspondents have not
kept me well informed of what the rest of Christendom
thinks of this sacrilege, but, to judge from the tempest it
has raised here in Venice—including some not at all frivolous suggestions that we Venetian Christians contemplate
shifting our allegiance to the Greek Church—I must surmise that poor San Piero is raging in his Roman catacomb.

The Doge succeeding Gradenigo was only briefly in office before he too died. The current Doge Zuàne Soranzo is
a younger man and should be with us for a while. He has
also been a man of innovations. He instituted an annual
race of gòndole and batèli on the Grand Canal, and called
it the Regata, because prizes were awarded to the winners.
In each of the four years since, the Regata has got more
lively and colorful and popular—being now a day-long
festa, with races for boats of one oar, of two oars, even
boats rowed by women, and the prizes have got ever richer

and more sought after—until the Regata has become as much of a yearly spectacle as the Wedding of the Sea.

Another thing the Doge Soranzo did was to ask me to assume civic office again, as one of the Proveditori of the Arsenàl, and I still continue in that post. It is purely a ceremonial duty, like being supracomito of a warship, but I do go out to that end of the island once in a while, to pretend that I really am supervising the shipyard. I enjoy being out there in the eternal aroma of boiling pitch, watching a galley begin life at one corner of the yard as just a single keel timber—then take shape as it moves along the ways, from one team of workers to the next, getting ribs and planking and, still slowly moving all the time, goes on through the sheds where workers on both sides stock its hull and holds with every necessity, from cordage and spare sails to armaments and staple provisions, while its decking and upper works are still being finished by other arsenaloti—until it floats out into the Arsenàl basin, a complete new vessel ready for auction to some buyer, ready to dip oars or hoist sail and go a-journeying. It is a poignant sight to one who will journey no more.

I shall not be going away again, not anywhere, and in many respects I might almost never have been away. I am still esteemed in Venice, but as a fixture now, not a novelty, and children do not prance bhind me in the streets any more. An occasional visitor from some foreign country, where the *Description of the World* has just made its first appearance, still comes seeking to meet me, but my fellow Venetians have tired of hearing my reminiscences and they do not thank me for my contributions of ideas I picked up in far places.

Not long ago, at the Arsenàl, the Master Shipwright got quite red in the face when I told, at some length, how the Han mariners somehow guide their massive chuan vessels more deftly—with only a single, centered steering oar—than do the helmsmen of our smaller galeazze with their double oars, one on each side. The Master Shipwright listened patiently while I discoursed, but he went away grumbling audibly about "dilettanti disrespectful of tradition." Only a month or so afterward, though, I saw a new galley come down the ways, not with the usual lateen sail but square-rigged in the manner of a Flemish cog, and with only a single, centered, stern-mounted steering oar. I was not invited aboard for that ship's trial voyage, but it must have handled well, for the Arsenàl has since been turning out more and more of the same design.

Also not long ago, when I was honored with an invitation to dine at the palazzo of the Doge Soranzo, the dinner was accompanied by muted music from a band of players in the gallery overlooking the chamber. At a lull in the conversation, I remarked to the table at large:

"Once upon a time, in the palace of Pagan, in the nation of Ava, in the lands of Champa, we were entertained at dinner by a troupe of musicians who were all blind men. I inquired of a steward if blind men in that country found easiest employment as musicians. The steward told me, 'No, U Polo. If a child shows a talent for music, he is deliberately blinded by his parents, so that his hearing will sharpen and he will concentrate his attention only on perfecting his music, so that someday he may be accorded a place as a palace musician.' "

There was a general silence. Then the Dogaressa said crisply, "I do not think that a fit story for the dining table, Messer Marco." And I have not been invited there since.

When a young man named Marco Bragadino, who has lately been making the cascamorto at my eldest daughter Fantina, lavishing on her languishing looks and heartfelt sighs, finally took his courage in both hands and came to me to inquire if he might commence formal calls of courtship, I tried to put him at ease by saying jovially:

"That reminds me, young Bragadino, of an occurrence in Khanbalik once upon a time. There was hauled into the Cheng—into the court of justice—a man accused of beating his wife. The Tongue of the Cheng asked the man if he had good reason for this behavior, and the wretch said yes, he was beating his wife for her having suffocated their baby daughter immediately after its birth. The wife was asked if she had anything to say, and she cried, 'It was only a daughter, my lords. There is no crime in disposing of excess daughters. Anyway, that happened fifteen years ago.' The Tongue then asked the man, 'Man, why in the world are you beating your wife for that *now?*' And the man said, 'My lords, fifteen years ago it did not matter. But recently a plague of some female disease has killed off almost all the other young maidens in our district. Brides are now at a premium, and the few available are fetching princess prices!' "

After a while, young Bragadino cleared his throat and asked, "Er, is that all, Messere?"

"That is all," I said. "I do not remember how the Cheng ruled in that case."

When young Bragadino had departed, looking confused and shaking his head, my wife and Fantina stormed into the room and began berating me. They had evidently both been listening behind the door.

"Papà, what have you done? Gramo mi, you have repulsed my best hope of marriage! I shall be a lonely and despised zitella all my life! I shall die with the jewel! What have you done?"

"Marcolfo vechio!" said Donata, in the memorable style of her own mother. "We have no scarcity of daughters in this house! You can ill afford to turn away any of their suitors!" She spared Fantina none of her frankness, either. "It is not as if they were sensational beauties, much sought after!" Fantina gave a despairing wail and flung herself out of the room. "Can you not curb your everlasting old reminiscences and your wandering old wits?"

"You are right, my dear," I said contritely. "I know better. One of these days I shall *do* better."

She *was* right, too. I concede that. In the matter of children, Donata had reposed her confidence in her Lord's goodness, but, after giving us three daughters, evidently her good Lord despaired of ever providing a son and heir to the Venetian house of Polo. That I had no male issue did not crushingly disappoint me or blight my life. It is not very Christian of me to say so, I know, but I do not believe that when my own life is over I shall be taking much interest in the affairs of this world, or wringing the pale hands of my soul because I left no Marcolino Polo in charge of all the warehouse goods and zafràn plantations I could not take with me. I did not confess this recusancy of mine to old Pare Nardo before he died (and that clement old man would probably have given me small penance for it)—and I shall not confess it to the grim-lipped young Pare Gasparo (who would be righteously severe)—but I am inclined to believe that if there is a Heaven I have not much hope of it; if there is a Hell, I daresay I will have other things to worry about than how my progeny are faring on the Rialto.

I may be less than a model Christian, but neither am I like those Eastern fathers whom I have heard say such things as: "No, I have no children. Only three daughters." I have never been prejudiced against daughters. Of course, I might have hoped for daughters with better looks and brighter wits. I am perhaps overparticular in that regard, having myself been blessed with the knowing of so many extraordinarily beautiful and intelligent women in my younger days. But Donata was one of those, in *her* younger days. If she could not replicate herself in her daughters, the fault must be mine.

The little Raja of the Hindus once harangued me about no man's ever knowing with surety who is the father of any of his children, but I have never had the least cause for anxiety. I have only to look at any one of them—Fantina, Bellela or Morata—they all look too exactly like me for there to be any doubt. Now, I hasten to asseverate that Marco Polo has all his life been no bad-looking man. But I should not wish to be a nubile young maiden and look like Marco Polo. If I was, and did, I should hope at least to have a bright intelligence by way of compensation. Unfortunately, my daughters have been scanted in that respect, as well. I do not mean to say that they are drooling imbeciles; they are no worse than unperceptive and lackluster and charmless.

But they are of my making. Should the potter despise the only pots he will ever produce? And they are good girls, with good hearts, or so I am repeatedly and consolingly told by my acquaintances who possess comely daughters. All I can say, from my own knowledge, is that my girls are cleanly of person and smell good. No, I can also say that they are fortunate in having a Papà who can dower them with the attractions of affluence.

Young Bragadino was not so repulsed by my dithering that day as to stay away forever, and the next time he called I confined my disquisition to topics like bequests and prospects and inheritances. He and Fantina are now formally betrothed, and Bragadino the Elder and I will shortly be convening with a notary for the impalmatura. My second daughter, Bellela, is being sedulously courted by a young man named Zanino Grioni. Morata will have someone, too, in due time. I have no doubt that all three girls will be grateful to be known no longer as the Damìne

Milione, and I have no overwhelming regrets that the Compagnia and the fortune and the house of Polo will henceforth percolate down through the generations as the Compagnie and houses of Bragadino, Grioni, Eccètera. If the precepts of the Han are true, this may cause consternation among my ancestors, from Nicolò all the way back to the Dalmatian Pavlo, but it causes not much to me.

8

If I had any real lament to make about our lack of sons, it would be a lament for what that did to Donata. She was only about thirty-two years old when Morata was born, but the birth of a third daughter clearly convinced her that she was incapable of male issue. And, as if to avert any hazard of producing yet another daughter, Donata thereafter began to discourage our further indulgence in conjugal relations. She never, by word or gesture, *refused* my amorous overtures, but she began to dress and look and comport herself in a manner calculated to diminish her appeal for me and dampen my ardor for her.

At thirty-two she began to let her face lose its radiance and her hair its luster and her eyes their lively sparkle, and she started dressing in the black bombazine and shawls of an old woman. At thirty-two! I was then fifty years old, but I was still straight and slim and strong, and I wore the rich garb to which my station entitled me and my taste for color inclined me. My hair and beard were still more life-colored than gray, and my blood was still unthinned, and I still had all my lusty appetites for life and pleasure, and my eyes still kindled when I glimpsed a lovely lady. But I have to say that they glazed when I looked at Donata.

Her posturing as an old woman *made* her an old woman. She is younger today than I was when Morata was born. But over these ensuing fifteen years, she has put on all the unsightly lineaments and contours of a woman many years older—the sagging facial features, the stringed and corded throat and that old-woman's hump at the back of the neck, and those tendons that operate the fingers are

visible through the spotted skin of her hands, and her elbows have become like old coins, and the meat of her upper
arms hangs loose and wobbly, and when she raises her
skirt to hobble and lurch from the Corte landing down the
steps to one of our boats, I can see that her ankles lop over
her shoes. What has become of the milk-white and shell-
pink and golden-flossed body, I do not know; I have not
seen it in a long time.

During these years, I repeat, she never denied me any of
my conjugal rights, but she always moped afterward, until
the moon came round again and relieved her of the fear
that she might again be pregnant. After a while, of course,
that became nothing to fear, and anyway by then I was not
giving her any cause to fear it. By then, too, I was occasionally spending an afternoon or a whole night away from
home, but she never even required from me a mendacious
excuse, let alone castigated me for my pecatazzi. Well, I
could not complain of her forbearance; there are many husbands who would be glad to have themselves such a lenient and unshrewish wife. And if today, at the age of
forty-seven, Donata is woefully and prematurely ancient, I
have caught up to her. I am now in my sixty-fifth year, so
there is nothing premature or extraordinary in my looking
as old as she does, and I no longer spend nights away from
home. Even if I wished to wander, I do not get many allur-
ing invitations to do so, and I should regretfully have to decline them if I did.

A German company has recently opened a branch manu-
factory here in Venice, producing a newly perfected sort of
looking glass, and they sell every one they make, and no
fashionable Venetian household, including ours, can be
without one or two of those. I admire the lucent mirrors
and the undistorted reflections they provide, but I consider
them also a mixed blessing. I should prefer to believe that
what I see when I look into a glass *is* blamable on imperfection and distortion, rather than have to concede that I am
seeing what I really look like. The now totally gray beard
and the thinning gray hair, the wrinkles and liverish skin
splotches, the dispirited pouches under eyes that are now
bleared and dimmed . . .

"No need to have dim eyes, friend Marco," said Dotòr
Abano, who has been our family physician all these years,
and who is as old as I am. "Those ingenious Germans have

created another marvel of glass. They call this device the Brille—occhiale, if you prefer. The two glass pieces in it do wonders for the eyesight. Merely hold the thing up before your face and look at this page of writing. Is it not clearer to read? Now look at yourself in the mirror."

I did, and murmured, "Once, in a harsh wintertime, at a place called Urumqi, I saw some savage-looking men come out of the frozen Gobi, and they frightened me to terror, for they all had great gleaming *eyes of copper.* When they got nearer, I saw that they were each wearing a device rather like this. A sort of dòmino mask made of thin copper and pierced with many pinholes. A man could not see very well through the thing, but they said it protected them from going blind in the snow glare."

"Yes, yes," Abano said impatiently. "You have told me more than once about the men with the copper eyes. But what do you think of the occhiale? Cannot you see more vividly?"

"Yes," I said, but not very enthusiastically, for what I was seeing was myself in the mirror. "I am noticing something I never noticed before. You are a mèdego, Abano. Is there a medical reason to account for my losing the hair from the top of my head but simultaneously growing bristles on *the point of my nose?*"

Still impatiently, he said, "The recondite medical term for that is 'old age.' Well, what of the occhiale? I can order a device made especially for you. Plain or ornate, made for holding in the hand or strapping around the head, gem-inlaid wood or tooled leather—"

"Thank you, old friend, but I think not," I said, laying down the mirror and giving him back the apparatus. "I have seen much in my lifetime. It might be a mercy now not to see all the signs of decay."

Just today, I realized that this is the twentieth day of the month of September. My birthday. I am no longer in my sixty-fifth year. I have this day tottered across the invisible but all too distinct line into my sixty-sixth. The realization bowed me down for a moment, but I raised myself to my fullest height—ignoring the twinge in my lower back—and squared my shoulders. Determined not to wallow in a maudlin mood of self-pity, thinking to cheer myself up, I ambled into the kitchen and leaned on the chopping block

while our cook bustled about at her work, and I said conversationally:

"Nastàsia, I will tell you an improving and edifying tale.
About this time every year, in the Kithai and Manzi lands,
the Han people celebrate what they call the Moon Cake
Festa. It is a warm and loving family holiday, nothing
grandiose. The families simply gather affectionately together and enjoy the eating of Moon Cakes. Those are
small, round pastries, heavy with richness and very tasty.
I will tell you how they are made, and perhaps you would
oblige me by making some, and the Dona and the Damìne
and I could pretend we are celebrating in the Han manner.
You take nuts and dates and cinnamon and—"

And almost immediately I was out of the kitchen and ca-
reering about the house in search of Donata. I found her in
her dressing chamber, doing needlework, and I bellowed:

"I have just been expelled from my own kitchen by my
own cook!"

Donata, not looking up, said with mild reproof, "Have
you been bothering Nata again?"

"Bothering her, indeed! Is she employed to serve us or is
she not? The woman had the effrontery to complain that
she is tired of hearing of the sumptuous viands I used to enjoy abroad, and she will hear not another word about them!
Che braga! Is that any way for a domestic to speak to her
own master?"

Donata clucked sympathetically. I stumped about the
room for a bit, peevishly kicking things that got in my
way. Then I resumed, and tragically:

"Our domestics, the Dogaressa, even my fellows on the
Rialto, they all seem disinclined nowadays to *learn* anything. They wish only to stagnate, and not to be stirred or
leavened out of their stagnation. Mind you, Donata, I do
not much care about outsiders, but *my own daughters!* My
own daughters heave sighs and drum their fingers and
look out the window when I try to relate some improving
and edifying tale from which they might derive great benefit. Are you by any chance encouraging this disrespect for
the patriarch of the family? I think it is reprehensible. I begin to feel like that prophet of whom Jesus spoke—the one
who was *not* without honor, save in his own country and in
his own house."

Donata sat smiling through my tirade, and imperturbably plying her needle, and when I was out of breath she said, "The girls are young. Young folk often find us older folk tiresome."

I roved about the room some more, until my wheezing abated. Then I said, "Old. Yes. Behold us dismal old folk. At least I can claim that I got old in the ordinary way, through the accumulation of years. But you did not have to, Donata."

"Everybody gets old," she said placidly.

"You are just about exactly the same age now, Donata, as I was on our wedding day. Was I old then?"

"You were in your prime of life. Stalwart and handsome. But women age differently than men do."

"Not if they do not wish to. You only desired to hasten past the childbearing years. And you need not have done. I told you long ago that I knew simple things that would prevent—"

"Things not fit to be mentioned by a Christian tongue, or heard by Christian ears. I do not wish to hear them now, any more than I did then."

"If you had listened then," I said accusingly, "you would not now be an Autumn Fan."

"A what?" she said, looking up at me for the first time.

"It is a very descriptive term the Han have. An Autumn Fan means a woman past her years of appeal and attractiveness. You see, in the autumn the air is cool and there is no *necessity* for a fan. It becomes an object without use or purpose or reason for existence. Just so, a woman who has ceased to be womanly, as you deliberately did, solely to avoid having more children—"

"All these years," she interrupted, but in a very soft voice. "All these years, have you thought that was why?"

I stopped, with my mouth still open. She laid down her needlework on her black bombazine lap, and folded her yellowed hands atop it, and fixed me with the faded eyes that had once been bright blue, and said:

"I ceased being a woman when I could no longer deceive myself. When I wearied of pretending to myself that you loved me."

I blinked in bewilderment and disbelief, and had to grope for my voice. "Donata, was I ever anything but tender and caring? Did I fail you in any way? Was I ever less than a good husband?"

"There. Even now you do not speak the word."

"I thought it was implicit. I am sorry. Very well, then. I did love you."

"There was something or someone you loved more, and always have. At our closest, Marco, we were never close. I could look into your face and see only distance, far distance. Was it farness of miles or of years? Was it another woman? God forgive me for believing this, but . . . was it not my mother?"

"Donata, she and I were *children.*"

"Children who are parted forget each other when they are grown. But you mistook me for her when we first met. On our wedding night, I was still wondering if I might not be just a substitute. I was a virgin, yes, and innocent. All I knew to expect was what I had been told by older confidantes, and you made it much better than what I had expected it to be. Nevertheless, I was not oblivious and obtuse, as one of our empty-headed daughters might be. In our cleaving together, Marco, there seemed to be . . . something . . . not quite right. That first time and every time afterward."

Justifiably affronted, I said stiffly, "You never made complaint."

"No," she said, looking pensive. "And that was part of the seeming wrongness: that I *did* enjoy it—always—and somehow felt I should not. I cannot explain it to you, any more than I could explain it to myself. All I ever could think was: it must be that I am enjoying what should rightly have been my mother's."

"How ridiculous. Whatever in your mother I was fond of, I have found also in you. And more. You have been much more to me, Donata—and much more dear to me—than she ever was."

Donata moved her hand across her face, as if brushing away a cobweb that had fallen there. "If it was not she, if it was not some other woman, then it must have been the sheer distance that I felt always between us."

"Come, my dear! I have scarcely been out of your sight since our wedding day, and never out of your reach."

"Not in your physical person, no. But yes, in the parts of you I could not see or reach. You have been ever in love with distance. You never really came home at all. It was unfair of you, to ask a woman to vie for your love with a rival she never could best. The distance. The far horizons."

"You exacted a promise about those far horizons. I made the promise. I kept to it."

"Yes. In your physical person, you kept to it. You never went away again. But did you ever once talk or think of anything but journeying?"

"Gèsu! Who is being unfair now, Donata? For nearly twenty years I have been as passive and compliant as that zerbino by the door yonder. I gave you possession of me, and the saying of where I should be and what I should do. Are you now complaining that I gave you no authority over my memory, my thoughts, my sleeping or waking dreams?"

"No, I am not complaining."

"That does not exactly answer the question I asked."

"You have left a few unanswered yourself, Marco, but I shall not pursue them." She finally took her mourning eyes off me, and picked up her needlework again. "After all, what are we arguing about? None of it matters anymore."

Again I was stopped with my mouth open and words unsaid—words unsaid by both of us, I imagine. I took another ruminative turn or two about the room.

"You are right," I said at last, and sighed. "We are old. We are past passion. Past striving and past strife. Past the beauties of danger and the dangers of beauty. Whatever we did right, whatever we did wrong, none of it matters any more."

She sighed also, and bent again to her sewing. I stood for a while in thought, watching her across the room. She sat in a shaft of September afternoon sunlight, where she could see best to work. The sun did not much enliven her sober attire, and her face was downcast, but the light did play in her hair. There was a time when that sunshine would have made her tresses gleam as golden bright as summer grain. Now her bowed head had more the sweetly melancholy glow of grain in the sheaf, a quiet, drowsy dun color, rimed with the first frost of autumn.

"September," I mused, not realizing that I said it aloud.

"What?"

"Nothing, my dear." I crossed the room to her and bent and, not amorously but only in a fond fatherly sort of way, kissed the top of her dear head. "What are you working on?"

"Parechio. Trifles of apparel for the wedding, for the luna di miele. No harm in getting started on them well ahead of time."

"Fantina is a fortunate girl, to have such a thoughtful mother."

Donata looked up and gave me a wan, shy smile. "You know, Marco . . . I was just thinking. That promise you made—it has been well kept, but it is near its expiration. I mean—Fantina about to be married and gone, Bellela betrothed, Morata nearly full grown. If you did still yearn to begone somewhere . . ."

"You are right again. I had not been counting, but I *am* very nearly at liberty again, am I not?"

"I freely give you leave. But I would miss you. Whatever I said before, I would miss you dreadfully. Still, I keep my promises, too."

"You do, yes. And now you mention it, I might just give the matter some thought. After Fantina's wedding, I could go abroad for—oh, no more than a short journey, to be back in time for Bellela's wedding. Maybe go only as far as Constantinople, see old Cuzìn Nico. Yes, I might do that. As soon as my back is better, anyway."

"Your back is ailing you again? Oh, my dear."

"Niente, niente. A twinge now and then, no more. Nothing to fret about. Why, my dear girl, one time in Persia, and again in Kurdistan, I had to get on a horse—no, the first time it was a camel—and ride despite having had my head near broken by the cudgels of brigands. I may have told you of those occurrences, and the—"

"Yes."

"Yes. Well. I do thank you for the suggestion, Donata. Journeying again. I will indeed give it some thought."

I went into the next room, which was my working chamber for when I brought home work to do, and she must have heard me rummaging about, for she called through the door:

"If you are looking for any of your maps, Marco, I think you have them all stored at the Compagnia fondaco."

"No, no. Merely getting some paper and a quill. I thought I would finish this latest letter to Rustichello."

"Why do you not do it in the garden? It is a tranquil and pleasant afternoon. You should be outside enjoying it. There will not be many more such days before winter."

As I started downstairs, she said, "The young men are coming to dinner tonight. Zanino and Marco. That is why Nata was so busy in the kitchen, and probably why she spoke rudely to you. Since we will be having guests, can we make a small pact? Not to bring any of our quarreling to the table?"

"No more quarreling, Donata, not tonight or ever. I am heartily sorry for whatever cause for quarrel I ever gave. As you say, let us tranquilly enjoy the remaining days. All that went before—none of it matters any more."

So I brought my writing materials out here to the little canalside courtyard we call our garden. It is planted now with chrysanthemums, the flower of Manzi, from seeds I brought from there, and the gold and fire and bronze colors make a gallant show in the mellow September sun. The occasional gòndola going by on the canal steers close here, so its occupants can admire my exotic blossoms, for most of the other gardens and window boxes in Venice contain summer flowers that have gone brown and limp and sad by this time of year. I sat myself down on this bench—slowly and carefully, not to rouse the twinge in my lower back—and I wrote down the conversation just concluded, and now for some time I have only sat here, thinking.

There is a word, *asolare,* that was first minted here in Venice but has now, I believe, been appropriated into every language of the Italian peninsula. It is a good and useful word, *asolare*—it means to sit in the sun and do absolutely nothing—all that in one word. I would not have thought it could ever in my whole life apply to me. For most of my life, God knows, it did not. But now, as I think back—over those busy years, the ceaseless journeying, the eventful miles and li and farsakhs, the friends and enemies and loved ones who journeyed too for a while and then were lost along the way—of all those things, I remember now a rule my father taught me long ago, when I first strode out as a journeyer. He said, "If ever you are lost in a wilderness, Marco, go always downhill. Always downhill, and eventually you will come to water, and where there is water there will also be provender and shelter and companionship. It may be a long way, but go always downhill and you will come at last to some place safe and warm and secure."

I have come a long, long way, and here is the foot of the hill at last, and here am I: an old man sunning himself in the last beams of an afternoon late in a waning month of the season of the falling leaf.

Once, when I rode with the Mongol army, I noticed a war horse galloping along in one of the columns, neatly keeping gait and place with the troops, handsomely caparisoned in leather body armor, with sword and lance in scabbard—but the horse's saddle was empty. The Orlok Bayan told me, "That was the steed of a good warrior named Jangar. It bore him into many battles in which he fought bravely, and into his last battle, in which he perished. Jangar's horse will continue to ride with us, fully armed, as long as its heart calls it to battle."

The Mongols knew well that even a horse would prefer to fall in combat, or run until its heart failed, than be retired to lush pasture and uselessness and the idle waiting, waiting, waiting.

I think back on everything I have chronicled here, and everything that was written in the earlier book, and I wonder if I might not have put it all into just seven small words: "I went away and I came back." But no, that would not be quite true. It is never the same man who comes home, whether he be returning from a humdrum day's labor at his counting house, or returning after many years in the far places, the long ways, the blue distances, in lands where magic is no mystery but an everyday occurrence, in cities fit to have poems made about them:

> Heaven is far from me and you,
> But here for us are Hang and Su!

For a while when I came home—before I was relegated to a commonplace, and ignored—I was derided as a liar and a braggart and a fabelor. But those who derided me were wrong. I came back with not nearly so many lies as I took with me when I went away. I departed Venice shining-eyed with expectation of finding those Cockaigne-dream lands described by the earlier Crusaders and the biographers of Alexander and all the other mythmakers—expecting unicorns and dragons and the legendary king-saint Prete Zuàne and fantastic wizards and mystical religions of enviable wisdom. I found them, too, and if I came back to tell that not all of them were what legend has made us believe, was not the truth about them just as wonderful?

Sentimental people speak of heartbreak, but those people are wrong, too. No heart ever really breaks. I know it well. When my heart leans eastward, as it does so often, it bends most poignantly, but it does not break.

Up there in Donata's chamber, I let her believe that she was pleasantly surprising me with the news that my long bondage to Home was finally over. I pretended I had not for years been thinking, "Shall I go now?" and each time deciding, "No, not now"—deferring to my responsibilities, to my promise to stay, to my aging wife and my three unexceptional daughters—every time saying to myself, "I will wait for a more propitious occasion to take my leave." Up there in Donata's chamber, I pretended also to receive her news gladly, that now I *could* go. And, just to appear properly grateful for her having volunteered that news, I pretended also that yes, I *might* now go again a-journeying. I know I will not. I was deceiving her when I implied that, but it was only a small deception of her, and I meant it kindly, and she will not be displeased when she realizes that I was deceiving her. But I cannot deceive myself. I waited too long, I am now too old, the time has come too late.

Old Bayan was still a fighting man at about the age I am now. And, at about this same age, my father and even my sleepwalking uncle made the long and rigorous return journey from Khanbalik to Venice. Old as I am, I am no more derelict than they were. Perhaps even my backache would benefit from being jolted by a long saddle ride. I do not believe it to be physical debility that dissuades me now from journeying again. Rather, I have the melancholy suspicion that I have seen all the best and worst and most interesting there *was* to see, and wherever I might go now would prove a disappointment by comparison.

Of course, if I could have the least hope that on some street in some city in Kithai or Manzi, I might astonishingly meet again a beautiful woman—as here in Venice I met Donata—who would remind me irresistibly of yet another beautiful woman long gone . . . Ah, for that chance I would journey, on hands and knees if necessary, to the ends of the earth. But that is an impossibility. And however much a new-met woman might resemble my remembered one, it would not be she.

So I go no more. *Io me asolo.* I sit in the last sunlight, here on the last slope of my life's long hill, and I do absolutely nothing . . . except remember, for I have much to remember. As I long ago remarked at someone else's graveside, I possess a treasure trove of memories with which to enliven eternity. I can enjoy those mementos through all the dying afternoons like this one, and then through the endless dead night underground.

But I also said once, maybe more than once, that I should like to live forever. And a lovely lady once told me that I would never get old. Well, thanks to you, Luigi, both those marvelous things may come to pass. Whether the fictional and disguised Marco Polo of your new work will be well received, I cannot predict, but the earlier book which you and I compiled together seems to have made its place secure in the libraries of many countries, and appears likely long to endure. In those pages I was not old, and in them I will go on living as long as the pages are read. I am grateful to you for that, Luigi.

Now the sun is setting, and the golden light fades, and the flowers of Manzi begin to fold their petals, and the blue mist rises from the canal, as blue as reminiscence, and now I would go to an old man's sleep, a young man's dreams. I bid you farewell, Rustichello of Pisa, and I subscribe myself

MARCO POLO OF VENICE
AND THE WORLD, HIS YIN:

set down this 20th day of September in the Year of Our Lord 1319, by the Han count 4017, the Year of the Ram.

AFTERWORD

*There are in existence today only a very few
relics of the journeyer Marco Polo. But one
thing he brought back from his journeys is in
the Céramique Chinoise collection of the Louvre.
It is a small incense burner of white porcelain.*

AZTEC

The National Bestseller by
GARY JENNINGS

"A blockbuster historical novel....From the start of this epic, the reader is caught up in the sweep and grandeur, the richness and humanity of this fictive unfolding of life in Mexico before the Spanish conquest....Anyone who lusts for adventure, or that book you can't put down, will glory in AZTEC!"
The Los Angeles Times

"A dazzling and hypnotic historical novel....AZTEC has everything that makes a story appealing...both ecstasy and appalling tragedy...sex...violence... and the story is filled with revenge....Mr. Jennings is an absolutely marvelous yarnspinner....
A book to get lost in!"
The New York Times

"Sumptuously detailed....AZTEC falls into the same genre of historical novel as SHOGUN."
Chicago Tribune

"Unforgettable images....Jennings is a master at graphic description."
Chicago Sun Times

An **AVON** Paperback   55889/$4.95